THE MODERN LIBRARY
of the World's Best Books

>>

101 YEARS' ENTERTAINMENT

>>>>>>>>>>>>>>>>>>>>>>>>>>>>>>>>

The publishers will be pleased to send, upon request, an illustrated folder setting forth the purpose and scope of THE MODERN LIBRARY, *and listing each volume in the series. Every reader will find titles he has been looking for, handsomely printed, in unabridged editions, and at an unusually low price.*

>>>>>>>>>>>>>>>>>>>>>>>>>>>>>>>>

101 YEARS'
Entertainment

THE GREAT DETECTIVE STORIES

1841–1941

>>

Edited by

ELLERY QUEEN

>>

THE MODERN LIBRARY
NEW YORK

THE MODERN LIBRARY

IS PUBLISHED BY

RANDOM HOUSE, INC.

BENNETT A. CERF · DONALD S. KLOPFER · ROBERT K. HAAS

Manufactured in the United States of America
By H. Wolff

INTRODUCTION

Those of you who find no charm in facts and figures, names and dates and footnotes, commentaries and asides, have the editors' permission to skip over this Introduction and proceed without delay to the fifty tales we have selected to commemorate the first 101 Years' Entertainment.

I. *Prenatal Note*

THE FIRST violent crime of literature was a murder, complete with victim, criminal, motive, and — inferentially — weapon; for although Chapter 4 of *Genesis* merely remarks: "Cain rose up against Abel his brother, and slew him," we may assume the instrument to have been a forked-stick plow, or a primitive hoe, since it came to pass "when they were in the field," and Cain, as everyone knows, was "a tiller of the ground."

This historic fratricide nevertheless cannot be said to have initiated the literature of detection for the profound reason that the case lacked the essential element — a detective. And while the bloody corpse of history swarms with homicides and inferior crimes, and literature has fattened on the pleasant details, the simple fact is that the detective story had to wait upon the detective, and the detective — as we know him today — did not make his début on the human scene until A.D. 1829, when Sir Robert Peel created the first official police force in London. After all, literature follows man like a dog, and in this connection man has lagged badly.

A round dozen years after the first bobby, the young editor of a Philadelphia magazine, *Graham's,* while pondering the problems of circulation, wrote a new kind of tale and inserted it — we may suppose with the twin-barreled anxiety of author and editor — into one of his issues. Mark well the date — April, 1841 — for upon this date the first detective story the world had ever known was thrust before its astonished nose.

Many editors since have found that Edgar Allan Poe, in this as in peculiarly literary matters, was a gentleman of prescience. For detective stories have saved many a bashful journal from oblivion, and to say that they have given joy and surcease to multitudinous millions for three long generations would be merely to repeat a point grown dull with repetition.

II. *The First Hundred Years*

Modern readers tend to think of "detective stories" as novels, and admittedly the novels are numberless. But the original, the "legitimate," form was the short story. The detective novel is a short story inflated by characterization and description and romantic nonsense, too often for purposes of padding, and adds only one innovation to the short-story form: the byplot, or red herring, which when badly used serves only to irritate when it is meant to confuse. Poe published the world's first detective short story in 1841, but what is generally considered the world's first detective novel — Gaboriau's *L'Affaire Lerouge* — did not appear in *Le Pays* until 1866, twenty-five years after *The Murders in the Rue Morgue*.

Notwithstanding the pristine purity of the short form, there has been a deplorable tendency among many prominent authors of detective fiction to avoid it. Whether this is because in the 20th Century the publication of detective short stories has proved commercially unprofitable — especially in more recent years — or for some less worthy reason, the fact remains that no short story exists which involves Detectives Charlie Chan (Earl Derr Biggers), Nero Wolfe (Rex Stout), Nick Charles (Dashiell Hammett), Perry Mason (Erle Stanley Gardner), or Philo Vance (S. S. Van Dine).* And so, unhappily, they will not be found in this book.

* We suspect the existence of one Philo Vance short story, a parody by Van Dine supposedly caricaturing his own creation. But we have been unable to confirm this suspicion. Certainly the story has never been published and, if it exists at all, is in the possession of the Willard Huntington Wright estate. The group of pieces Van Dine did some years ago for *Cosmopolitan* magazine involving the character of Vance

For that matter there are other, equally important, detectives of fiction whose short-story exploits are so few as to escape all but the keenest-eyed enthusiast. John Rhode's Dr. Priestley appears in only two short stories, *The Elusive Bullet* and *The Vanishing Diamond*. A. E. W. Mason's Hanaud appears in only one, *The Affair at the Semiramis Hotel;* Anthony Berkeley's Roger Sheringham in a mere two, *The Avenging Chance* (included in this volume) and *White Butterfly;* John Dickson Carr's Dr. Fell in three, *The Wrong Problem, The Proverbial Murder,* and *The Locked Room;* Anthony Abbot's Thatcher Colt in two, *About the Disappearance of Agatha King* and *About the Perfect Crime of Mr. Digberry;* David Frome's Mr. Pinkerton in one, *Policeman's Cape;* and Freeman Wills Crofts's Inspector French in five, *East Wind, The Match, The Hunt Ball, Mr. Pemberton's Commission,* and *The Vertical Line.*

But if the aforementioned worthies have been remiss, certainly others have not; and this book is dedicated to those others. The stories in *101 Years' Entertainment* are not necessarily "the best"; perfection is a matter of individual judgment, and it would be presumptuous of us to attempt to canonize for posterity our betters.

But we *can* paint a whole picture of what the First Hundred Years have brought forth by reprinting stories old, derivative, not so old, recent, and new; representative stories; interesting stories; unusual stories; the classic greats as well as tales which to the average reader — indeed, to many an expert — are unknown. For we have kept an eye cocked for that four-leaf clover which is the object of all who browse in the green pastures of literary research — the "discovery," the story overlooked by other anthologists. Of such we have been fortunate to detect a surprising number; and they are here, in this book, for your delight. Most readers know *The Purloined Letter* of Poe, *The Absent-Minded Coterie* of Robert Barr, and *The Cyprian Bees* of Anthony Wynne; but how many know Inspector Barraclough and *The Pink Edge,* or that fascinating female Gwynn Leith in *The Mackenzie Case* of Viola Brothers Shore, or *The Two Bottles of Relish,* by Lord Dunsany, in which an astounding deduction is made by a gentleman named Linley — a deduction which, if it were the only one he ever made (as hap-

were not short stories but "monologues" in which Vance related the facts of certain *outré* real-life cases from abroad.

pens to be the case), would give him automatic citizenship in the Eternal City of the élite?

For the rest, we give you joy of that hero of your boyhood, Nick Carter; that most durable of Sherlockian imitators, Arthur Morrison's Martin Hewitt; scholarly Dr. Thorndyke of R. Austin Freeman; that humble little genius of the cloth, Father Brown, invented by the master of paradox, Gilbert K. Chesterton; Melville Davisson Post's stalwart, religious, early-American Uncle Abner; Ernest Bramah's blind sleuth, Max Carrados; Agatha Christie's conceited and delightful exponent of the little gray cells, M. Hercule Poirot; H. C. Bailey's mourning, moaning, indefatigable Mr. Fortune; Dorothy L. Sayers's dilettante Lord Peter Wimsey; and E. C. Bentley's Philip Trent of *Trent's Last Case* renown.

Nor will you take less joy in these less advertised but no less brilliant lights: M. P. Shiel's Prince Zaleski; Samuel Hopkins Adams's Average Jones; Ronald A. Knox's Miles Bredon; Margery Allingham's Albert Campion; Dashiell Hammett's Sam Spade; Pulitzer Prizewinner T. S. Stribling's Professor Poggioli; Carter Dickson's Colonel March — among many many others known and unknown to the connoisseur of the detective short story.

III. *Sources and Classifications*

What have the First Hundred Years of the detective-crime short story produced? Let us examine the record.

The two principal sources of the detective-crime short story for student and lay reader are: periodicals and books. On the number of such tales published in magazines and newspapers since 1841, no statistics are available; but certainly their total must run into astronomical figures. All slick-paper popular magazines at one time or another publish detective-crime stories; and among the so-called "pulps" of America and England there have been hundreds of parti-colored publications dedicated vigorously to this brand of fiction. See your nearest kiosk.

As a rule, the best magazine stories eventually achieve book publication. This natural winnowing process has been a boon to enthusiasts, who may read in one volume the grist of scores of scattered and heterogeneous periodicals. Of course, not all the worthy stories find a home between hard covers; magazines do yield nuggets of gold if only one digs hard and deep enough. We unearthed Dashiell Hammett's *A Man Called Spade* in *American* magazine, Miss Shore's *The Mackenzie Case* in a long-deceased magazine named *Mystery League,* T. S. Stribling's *The Resurrection of Chin Lee* in that admirable pulp, *Adventure,* Octavus Roy Cohen's *The Mystery of the Missing Wash* in *Saturday Evening Post,* and Pearl S. Buck's *Ransom* in *Cosmopolitan.* None of these excellent stories has ever been reprinted in a book. But these are exceptions. The point to bear in mind is that, for convenience and quality, books remain the chief source of the detective-crime short story.

The volumes in which such tales have been collected may be divided into six groups: (a) The short stories of "pure" detection; (b) books containing tales of mixed types; (c) books of crook short stories; (d) parodies and pastiches of Sherlock Holmes; (e) pseudo-real life tales; and (f) anthologies.

IV. *The Short Story of "Pure" Detection*

Considering the virulence of the literary bug and its affinity for all manner of hosts, the first century since Poe has produced a remarkably small number of books of detective short stories. One reason for this we have already mentioned: even detective-story writers must live, and such books do not sell. It is interesting in this connection to note the extremes of desperation to which some authors (or their publishers) have resorted to keep from their innocent patrons, in whom this prejudice against volumes of short stories generally persists, the fact that a given book *is* in truth a book of short stories. The favorite device is to disguise the book as a novel. This feat of publishing magic is achieved by editorial and typographic legerdemain — dividing the book into "chapters" instead of candidly separate stories, and assigning consecutive chapter numbers and chapter titles to the stories — usually two or more "chapters" per story. An unsuspecting glance, and the purchaser is deceived. His subsequent howl, after the transaction, dies as he begins bitterly to read, and he finishes the book grumbling, but mollified. At least, this is the theory. Such business psychology no doubt dictated the interior format of Robert Barr's *The Triumphs of Eugène Valmont*

(1906), Jacques Futrelle's *The Thinking Machine on the Case* (1908), Baroness Orczy's *The Old Man in the Corner* (1909), T. W. Hanshew's *Cleek, the Man of the Forty Faces* (1910), Melville Davisson Post's *The Nameless Thing* (1912), and Herbert Jenkins's *Malcolm Sage, Detective* (1921).*

If the number of books of detective short stories of all types is surprisingly small, the number of those of the "pure" detection type is amazingly so. Only 347 known titles of this type exist, breaking down into three classifications: (1) 305 about male detectives, like Sherlock Holmes, Father Brown, Mr. Fortune; (2) 35 about female detectives — from C. L. Pirkis's Loveday Brooke (1894), George R. Sims's Dorcas Dene (1897), and McDonnell Bodkin's Dora Myrl (1900) to the more modern Mme. Storey (1926) of Hulbert Footner, Mignon Eberhart's Susan Dare (1934), and the Coles' Mrs. Warrender (1939); and (3) 7 about boy detectives. Five of these last concern the adventures in detection of young P. J. Davenant written by Lord Frederic Hamilton; the other two are *The Adventures of Detective Barney* by Harvey O'Higgins and *Bang! Bang!* by George Ade, about Eddie Parks, the Newsboy Detective.

Of the 347 volumes of stories of "pure" detection, 56 are the work of only 5 authors! These fertile scriveners are Dick Donovan (believe it or not, once an immensely popular writer — his real name was Joyce Emmerson Muddock); Gilbert K. Chesterton, who created not only Father Brown but also Horne Fisher, Mr. Pond, and Gabriel Gale; Arthur B. Reeve, creator of Craig Kennedy and Constance Dunlap; Agatha Christie; and H. C. Bailey. This leaves a mere 291 books of "pure" detective short stories written by all the rest of mankind since 1841! And many of these 291 volumes are so scarce today as to be virtually unobtainable — such rarities as Headon Hill's *Zambra the Detective* (1894); David Christie Murray's *The Investigations of John Pym* (1895); H. Frankish's *Dr. Cunliffe, Investigator* (1902); Duncan Dallas's *Paul Richards, De-*

---

* By some curious irony, first editions of these books are very scarce; a first of the Hanshew book is actually rare. As for the Post book, the celebrated bookseller Alfred Goldsmith for years was convinced the book did not exist; and Charles Honce hunted ten years before he found a copy. The only four copies known to the editors are owned by Honce, Norbert Lederer, E. T. (Ned) Guymon Jr., and themselves. (P.S. Since this footnote was first written, a few more copies have appeared.)

tective (1908); Victor Whitechurch's *Thrilling Stories of the Railway* (1912), about Thorpe Hazell, detective; Cecil Henry Bullivant's *Garnett Bell, Detective* (*circa* 1918); Scott Campbell's paperbacks about Detective Felix Boyd; and numerous others.

V. *The Books of "Mixed Types"*

To add to the labors of the research worker, many books exist whose stories are not exclusively devoted to the adventures of a single detective. In such collections of stories a tale of "pure" detection may be smothered under a haystack of straight mystery stories, or stories of crime-*sans*-detection. Such a heterogeneous volume is Anna Katharine Green's *Masterpieces of Mystery* (1913) — surely the publisher's title, which he regretted, for six years later it was reissued under the new title *Room Number 3.* J. S. Fletcher is the author of many such: *The Secret of the Barbican, The Malachite Jar*, etc. Prolific as he was, Fletcher produced only two volumes of stories of "pure" detection: *The Adventures of Archer Dawe, Sleuth-Hound* (1909) and *Paul Campenhaye: Specialist in Criminology* (1918). The books of William LeQueux often concern a single central character (as *In Secret*, 1920; *Bleke the Butler*, 1923; and others) but the tales are nonetheless of the mixed type — some detection, some mystery, some crime, and some out-and-out adventure.*

There are 350 titles in this "mixed-type" group. It should be noted that this figure does not include all of E. Phillips Oppenheim's books of short stories, which alone number 38. Most of these are not properly books of detection or crime, being of the adventure–spy–international-intrigue school. Oddly enough, for all his literary virility Oppenheim has fathered few books of "pure" detection: such works as *The Hon. Algernon Knox, Detective* (1920); *Nicholas Goade, Detective* (1927); and *Slane's Long Shots* (1930) are almost lost in the crowd. But these few Oppenheim books of "pure" detection and "mixed types" are included in their proper groups.

Even more exasperating to the bibliophilous Nimrod (and, by

---

* The sole exception is LeQueux's *Mysteries of a Great City* (1919) which are the reminiscences of M. Raoul Becq, *ex-sous-chef* of the Sûreté Générale of Paris, consistently tales of "pure" detection.

the identical token, upon discovery more satisfying) is the occasional publication of a volume of short stories by an author distinguished in a field of writing other than detection-crime. Here the ardent explorer may be pardoned if his foot slips, for who would associate W. W. Jacobs with detective tales, or Aldous Huxley, or Ben Hecht, or W. Somerset Maugham? Yet these literary respectables are merely a few who have composed stories of detection-crime. Jacobs has at least two in his *The Lady of the Barge* (1902). Huxley has one, the unforgettable *The Gioconda Smile,* from *Mortal Coils* (1922). Ben Hecht succumbed to the virus in his book, *The Champion from Far Away* (1931); he is also the author of a detective story, *The Mystery of the Fabulous Laundryman,* included with three other murder stories in *Actor's Blood* (1936). And W. Somerset Maugham has a story called *Footprints in the Jungle,* in *Ah King* (1933), which any self-respecting hunter must include in his bag; see also his fascinating book, *Ashenden.*

Other celebrities of letters who have strayed from their customary habitat into the enchanted land are Owen Johnson in his volume, *Murder in Any Degree* (1913), one story in which, *One Hundred in the Dark,* is especially notable; May Sinclair, whose *Uncanny Stories* (1923) are brilliant accomplishments; and Stacy Aumonier in *Miss Bracegirdle and Others* (1923), which contains at least one superb tale, *Miss Bracegirdle Does Her Duty.*

Some of Wilbur Daniel Steele's short stories flirt dangerously with the genre: note particularly *Blue Murder* and that strange, strange tale, *The Body of the Crime.* St. John Ervine's *The Brown Sandwich* is an unblushing detective story. And James Hilton wrote one detective novel, *Murder at School* (1931), under the pseudonym of Glen Trevor, which was published as *Was It Murder?* in America (1933).

From the obscure dossier of authors not usually linked with mystery and crime writings, we have reprinted in this book tales by these other illustrious culprits: Irvin S. Cobb, Thomas Burke, F. Tennyson Jesse, Hugh Walpole and Pearl S. Buck. There are one or two further surprises. Mary Roberts Rinehart has written many mystery stories; but who would dream of Tish as a sleuth? Yet the ineffable Tish is here in all her blithesome glory! As is Florian Slappey, that dark harlequin of Birmingham, in a comic-detective story by Octavus Roy Cohen (whose fat, gold-toothpick–wielding Jim Hanvey might have done a more workmanlike detecting job than Florian, but surely would not have executed it with such rapierlike *élan*.)

VI. *The Crooks*

The names Raffles and Arsène Lupin are so universally familiar that one would think the bound literature of crooks-in-short-stories to be a vast continent for exploration. Curiously enough, there are to the editors' knowledge a mere 100 different book titles — in one hundred years! These sing the roguish escapades of E. W. Hornung's Raffles; Maurice Leblanc's Arsène Lupin; and Leslie Charteris's Simon Templar, alias the Saint (most of which, however, are novellas) — to mention the best-known. They also include certain lesser luminaries who nevertheless have shed a scoundrelly fame: Frederick Irving Anderson's The Infallible Godahl; Bruce Graeme's Blackshirt (is it possible the Infallible Benito owes all to Mr. Graeme?); Frank Heller's Mr. Philip Collin; Harry Stephen Keeler's DeLancey, King of Thieves; and Frank L. Packard's Jimmie Dale. And you, O student, might do worse than to investigate the assorted sculduggeries of this obscure trio: Barry Pain's Constantine Dix (1905), A. C. Fox-Davies's Sir John Kynnersley (1908), and Edgar Wallace's Anthony Newton . . . What — have we neglected Grant Allen's Colonel Clay? Inexcusable omission! For surely you recall — if you are old enough — that engaging rapscallion. The Colonel beat Raffles to it by two years!

But come. Surely the ladies have amassed sufficient loot to merit inclusion in books of short stories? They have, and their small number is no reflection on their burglarious daring. These lovely creatures of sin include: Mrs. Raffles (1905), who stalks through the book of short stories of that name by John Kendrick Bangs, and who never tackled a "job" for less than millions; of course, this is parody typically Bangsian. Then there is Frederick Irving Anderson's *The Notorious Sophie Lang* (1925) who lives in that single volume of stories and, more recently, has been resurrected in motion pictures. And finally Edgar Wallace's *Four Square Jane* (1929), one of whose adventures — quite worthy of Lupin himself, we assure you! — will be found in this book.

VII. *Parodies and Pastiches of Holmes*

A parody is a burlesque imitating some serious work; a pastiche is usually a serious imitation in the exact manner of the original author. Only the illustrious call forth such passionate homage; and in the literature of detection who is more illustrious, as a character and a catholic institution, than Sherlock Holmes?

The parodies of Holmes far exceed the pastiches, which are rare. John Kendrick Bangs did lusty work in Sherlockian parody. Stories of this type may be found in these Bangs volumes: *The Pursuit of the Houseboat* (1897), *The Dreamers: a Club* (1899), *The Enchanted Typewriter* (1899), and *Potted Fiction* (1908). In 1903 Bangs wrote a series of Holmes parodies for newspapers which he called *The Posthumous Memoirs of Shylock Homes,* never assembled between boards; and in 1906, trifling with genetics, he created Raffles Holmes, the "son" of Sherlock Holmes and the "grandson" of A. J. Raffles, whose merry exploits were assembled under the title *R. Holmes & Co.*

Robert Barr wrote about Sherlaw Kombs in his story, *The Great Pegram Mystery* (from the book *The Face and the Mask,* 1895) — Barr, you will recall, was the creator of Eugène Valmont who, alas, has been parodied by no one. Bret Harte came up with Hemlock Jones in *The Stolen Cigar Case* (from *Condensed Novels, 2nd Series,* 1902). Maurice Leblanc, Gallically testing the commercial possibilities of a marriage of immovable detection and irresistible thievery, composed *Holmlock Shears Arrives Too Late,* which comes from the volume *The Exploits of Arsène Lupin* (1907), in which Lupin and Holmes clashed and — this was courteous of Leblanc — wound up in a pretty stalemate. In some pirated American editions the pirates, apparently none too sanguine about the intelligence of their prospective customers, changed the parody-name Holmlock Shears to the more recognizable Herlock Sholmes. Stephen Leacock, refusing to tamper with the master's Doyle-given name and calling him simply The Great Detective, parodied Holmes in *Maddened by Mystery: or, The Defective Detective,* which you will find in Mr. Leacock's *Nonsense Novels*. O. Henry labored to conceive Shamrock Jolnes — an appealing abortion! — in the tales *The Rival Sleuths* and *The Adventures of Shamrock Jolnes*, to be found in the otherwise respectable *Sixes and Sevens*. But for sheer stupendous imagination we have always bowed in admiration before the appellative genius of R. C. Lehmann, who gave us *The Adventures of Picklock Holes*.

The pastiche, whose intent is serious, and the fashioning of which requires immense knowledge, discrimination, and courage, is necessarily a rare literary form. The best pastiche of Sherlock Holmes is Vincent Starrett's *The Unique Hamlet* (1920). William O. Fuller's *A Night with Sherlock Holmes* (1929) also merits your respectful attention. Both were privately printed and, in first edition, are aggravatingly scarce.

VIII. *Pseudo-Real Life Stories*

Between 1856 and 1890 detective-crime literature suffered an epidemic of "realism." People became interested in crimes that actually happened and detectives who existed in the unusual three-dimensional form; so a gout of books gushed forth from the presses, professing to be the memoirs of this police officer or that, many of which were fiction concocted by professional writers; and fact and fiction were so jumbled that today it is difficult to differentiate one from the other. It is hardly necessary to add that most of these "diaries," "reminiscences," "memoirs," and "revelations" of supposedly real-life policemen were purest balderdash, and consequently few of them survive; in their original paperback state they are rare.

The survivors include the work of "Waters" (William Russell) — *Recollections of a Detective Police-Officer* (1856 and 1859); Charles Martel's (Thomas Delf) *The Detective's Note-Book* (1860); Lieut.-Col. H. R. Addison's *Diary of a Judge* (1860); James M'Levy's *Curiosities of Crime in Edinburgh* (1861); M. Canler's *Autobiography of a French Detective* (1863); Andrew Forrester Jr.'s *The Revelations of a Private Detective* (1863); James M'Govan's *Brought to Bay* (1878); William Henderson's *Clues, Or Leaves from a Chief Constable's Note Book* (1889); Inspector Maurice Moser's *Stories from Scotland Yard* (1890, in collaboration with Charles F. Rideal).

The editors know of 40 different titles in this group, although at the present writing, and after continuous bloodhound trailing, possess copies of only 20.*

You are not to confuse the abovementioned group with Allan Pinkerton's legitimate memoirs in *Thirty Years a Detective* and Arthur Train's (creator of Mr. Tutt) in *True Stories of Crime,* among many others, including the famous Major Arthur Griffiths's *Mysteries of Police and Crime.* These are the true constellations, and do not come within our orbit, which is thick with the planetary bodies of fiction.

IX. *Anthologies*

It goes without saying that where joy is truly precious, it begs to be communicated; and so it is not wonderful that detective-story anthologies should spring up and multiply like unregimented rabbits. The number of anthologies is relatively high — 125 known volumes, and half a dozen more in preparation (being edited by Anthony Boucher, Lee Wright, Howard Haycraft, ourselves, and others).

The earliest legitimate anthology was published by Chapman & Hall in London in 1895. It was called *The Long Arm & Other Detective Stories;* Mary E. Wilkins (Freeman) contributed *The Long Arm* and George Ira Brett (later known as Oswald Crawfurd), Roy Tellet, and Professor Brander Matthews contributed the *Others.* This pioneer work was followed (*circa* 1897) by the paperback *Diprose's Annuals,* which technically are anthologies because they contain some mystery-crime short stories by a variety of authors. The first American anthology did not appear until 1906: Vol. I (called *Detective Stories*) in the 3-volume set entitled *Great Short Stories,* edited by William Patten. Perhaps the first specialized

---

* Exclusive of "pseudo-real life" books, the Ellery Queen library of detective-crime short story volumes is at this writing 90% complete. But for research purposes connected with the present anthology we had access to most of the volumes missing from the Queen collection, thanks chiefly to E. T. (Ned) Guymon Jr. of San Diego, California, who possesses the largest library of mystery fiction (in total number of volumes) in the world.

anthology was *Twenty-Five Tales of the Railway* (Newnes, *circa* 1912), stories of crime, adventure, and detectives, but all on railway themes. A great many of the 125 known anthologies were published in England only; because of existing conditions they are nearly impossible to procure.

It is not remarkable that detective-story writers themselves should be prominent among the anthologists. For one thing, the writer in this field who has made his mark is generally infected with a pride of profession which erupts, like measles, in little pustulary desires to build a better anthology — "a truly *definitive* job, you know!" — than anyone living or dead. For another, it is the only certain method of immortalizing one of one's own stories. At any rate, we have had numerous professional anthologists (this is *our* second eruption!), among them Carolyn Wells, S. S. Van Dine, Vincent Starrett, Dorothy L. Sayers, Ronald A. Knox (with H. Harrington), Dashiell Hammett (more strictly a supernatural anthology), E. C. Bentley, E. Phillips Oppenheim, Raymond Postgate, and John Rhode.

The value of the anthology to both student and lay reader is threefold: (*a*) It often contains short stories which never saw book publication and are taken directly from periodicals and original manuscripts. (*b*) It keeps alive the best work of the older authors, whose books have been long out of print and would not therefore be available to present-day readers. (It can be said with exact truth that characters like The Old Man in the Corner and Eugène Valmont owe their continued existence wholly to anthologists). And (*c*) it memorializes the best stories of modern authors.

X. *Apology and Good Wishes*

So there are the statistics of the First Hundred Years of the detective-crime short story. In this book we have tried to range over as wide a terrain of places, authors, subjects, famous characters, and "discoveries" as possible in commemoration of the centennial event; but of course space limitations have forced us to be cruelly selective, and there are many excellent detectives and samples of their investigations which have had to be omitted. Perhaps a short auxiliary list of authors and titles would, to some degree, make up for these enforced omissions. We especially commend to your attention (if you can find the books!) the following:

Edwin Balmer and William MacHarg's *The Achievements of Luther Trant* (1910); Trant was the first detective to employ the then-newfangled science of psychology as a method of crime-detection — including the first use in fiction of the "lie-detector," although Craig Kennedy (of Arthur B. Reeve) ran Trant a close second as a scientific psychologist. Francis Lynde's *Scientific Sprague* (1912). Hesketh Prichard's *November Joe* (1913), the only backwoods detective on record, a sort of detecting Leatherstocking. Octavus Roy Cohen's *Jim Hanvey, Detective* (1923). Basil Thomson's *Mr. Pepper, Investigator* (1925), a *rara avis* indeed: the comic detective. Edgar Wallace's *The Orator* (1928), about Chief Inspector O. Rater, a little-known Wallace character and yet, next to Mr. J. G. Reeder, Wallace's best sleuth. Nicholas Olde's *The Incredible Adventures of Rowland Hern* (1928). Harvey O'Higgins's *Detective Duff Unravels It* (1929), literature's first approach to a psychoanalytical detective. Percival Wilde's *Rogues in Clover* (1929), about Bill Parmelee, who specializes in card and gambling mysteries. Henry Wade's *Policeman's Lot* (1933), about Inspector Poole, very Scotland Yard. Kenneth Livingston's *The Dodd Cases* (1934), about Cedric Dodd, a physician-detective. And C. Daly King's *The Curious Mr. Tarrant* (1935), a collection of 8 stories and one of the most imaginative books of detective short stories to appear in the last decade.

And now to the business at hand, which is to dip your nose into half a hundred tales in which you will find: murder, robbery, suicide, kidnaping, extortion, and assorted rogueries; poisons, dirks, bludgeons, revolvers, hunting rifles, strangling cords, axes, and even murder by starvation; old wills, ladders in the night, bloodstains, Greek inscriptions, thermos bottles, ancient coins, handcuffs, mysterious codes, fingerprints by the barrel, clocks, old masters, sealing wax, precious gems, a brassie. . . .

So here's to crime — and the Second Hundred Years!

ELLERY QUEEN

CONTENTS

THE GREAT DETECTIVES

THE GREAT CRIME STORIES

THE DETECTIVE STORY TO END DETECTIVE STORIES

ACKNOWLEDGMENTS

For their tireless advice and significant suggestions; for their lavish expenditure of time, and stamps, and stationery, and wrapping paper; in a few cases, where the editors' own library was uncooperative, for the use of their precious books; and in other cases for their enthusiastic assistance as booksellers far beyond the call of commerce, the editors make grateful acknowledgment to the following: —

Vincent Starrett; E. T. (Ned) Guymon Jr.; Howard Haycraft; Ira Friedman; David Randall; Ben Abramson; Charles Honce; P. M. Stone; Dr. A. S. W. Rosenbach; the O'Malley brothers of O'Malley's Book Store (N. Y.); Alfred Goldsmith (N. Y.); Alexander Norman Hall (Newton Center, Mass.); Henry Giersberg of Putnam's Book Store (N. Y.); Biblo & Tannen (N. Y.); P. Stammer (N. Y.); Carlton Pyetell (Mt. Vernon, N. Y.); Thoms & Eron (N. Y.); Argosy Book Stores (N. Y.); Charterock (Roseland, N. J.); the Messrs. Epstein and Wepplo of The Pickwick Book Shop (Hollywood, Calif.); W. & G. Foyle, Ltd. (London); and Bertram Rota (London).

And to these authors' representatives, publishers, and authors for their unhesitating assistance in clearing permission rights to reprint various stories contained in this book: —

Frederick Irving Anderson, for "Blind Man's Buff" from *The Adventures of the Infallible Godahl* (copyright, 1914).

The Bobbs-Merrill Company, for "Faith, Hope and Charity" from *Faith, Hope and Charity* by Irvin S. Cobb (copyright, 1934, used by special permission of the publishers, The Bobbs-Merrill Company).

Brandt & Brandt (especially to Miss Bernice Baumgarten), for "Arsène Lupin in Prison" from *The Exploits of Arsène Lupin* by Maurice Leblanc (copyright, 1907, by Alexander Teixeira de Mattos); for "The Red Silk Scarf" from *The Confessions of Arsène Lupin* by Maurice Leblanc (copyright, 1913, by Alexander Teixeira de Mattos); for "The Man Who Spoke Latin" from *Average Jones* by Samuel Hopkins Adams (copyright, 1911, 1939, by The Bobbs-Merrill

Company); for "The Most Dangerous Game" from *Variety* by Richard Connell (copyright, 1924, by Richard Connell, published by Minton, Balch & Company); for "Introducing Susan Dare" from *The Cases of Susan Dare* by Mignon G. Eberhart (copyright, 1934, by Mignon G. Eberhart, published by Doubleday, Doran & Company); for "The Stolen Romney" from *Four Square Jane* by Edgar Wallace (reprinted by permission, published by the Readers' Library, Inc.).

George T. Bye (especially to Jasper Spock), for "The Doomdorf Mystery" from *Uncle Abner* by Melville Davisson Post (copyright, 1918).

Octavus Roy Cohen, for "The Mystery of the Missing Wash" (from the *Saturday Evening Post*).

Dodd, Mead & Company, for "The Secret Garden" from *The Innocence of Father Brown* by Gilbert K. Chesterton (copyright, 1911); for "The Puzzle Lock" from *The Puzzle Lock* by R. Austin Freeman; for "The Dublin Mystery" from *The Man in the Corner* by Baroness Orczy (copyright, 1909). All used by permission of Dodd, Mead & Company, Inc.

Doubleday, Doran & Company, Inc. (especially to Miss Pollard), for "The Border-Line Case" from *Mr. Campion: Criminologist* by Margery Allingham (copyright, 1936, by Doubleday, Doran & Company, Inc.); for "The Silver Mask" from *All Souls' Night* by Hugh Walpole (copyright, 1933, by Doubleday, Doran & Company, Inc.).

Farrar & Rinehart, for "The Treasure Hunt" from *The Book of Tish* by Mary Roberts Rinehart (copyright, 1926, reprinted by permission of Farrar & Rinehart, Inc., publishers).

Mrs. Jacques Futrelle, for "The Problem of Cell 13" from *The Thinking Machine* by Jacques Futrelle (copyright, 1905, 1933, by May Futrelle).

Leland Hayward, Inc. (especially to Miss Pindyck), for "The Long Dinner" from *Mr. Fortune Objects* by H. C. Bailey (copyright, 1934, 1935, by the author, and permission granted by Doubleday, Doran & Company, Inc.); for "A Man Called Spade" by Dashiell Hammett (from the *American Magazine*).

Little, Brown & Company, for "The Hands of Mr. Ottermole" from *A Tea-Shop in Limehouse* by Thomas Burke (copyright, 1931).

David Lloyd, for "Ransom" by Pearl S. Buck (copyright, 1938, by Pearl S. Buck, originally published in *Cosmopolitan*, October, 1938).

Harold Ober, for "A Chess Problem" from *The Big Four* by Agatha Christie (copyright, 1927); for "The Disappearance of Mrs. Leigh Gordon," originally titled "The Case of the Missing Lady," from *Partners in Crime* by Agatha Christie (copyright, 1929, by Agatha Christie); for "Philomel Cottage" from *The Listerdale Mystery* by Agatha Christie (copyright, 1934, by Agatha Christie).

Ben Ray Redman, for "The Perfect Crime" (from *Harper's Monthly Magazine*).

Paul R. Reynolds & Son, for "The Mackenzie Case" by Viola Brothers Shore (from *Mystery League Magazine*).

Charles Scribner's Sons, for "The Criminologists' Club" from *A Thief in the Night* by E. W. Hornung (copyright, 1905).

Vincent Starrett, for "The Eleventh Juror" from *Real Detective Tales and Mystery Stories,* Chicago.

Frederick A. Stokes Company, for "The Mad Tea Party" from *The Adventures of Ellery Queen* by Ellery Queen (copyright, 1933, 1934).

Street & Smith Publications, Inc., for "The Mystery of Mrs. Dickinson" from *The Detective's Pretty Neighbor and Other Stories* by Nicholas Carter.

T. S. Stribling, for "The Resurrection of Chin Lee" (from *Adventure*).

Ann Watkins, Inc. (especially to Miss Margot Johnson), for "The Owl at the Window," originally titled "In a Telephone Cabinet," from *Superintendent Wilson's Holiday* by G. D. H. and M. I. Cole (copyright, 1929); for "The Crime in Nobody's Room" from *The Department of Queer Complaints* by Carter Dickson (copyright, 1940); for "A Matter of Taste" from *Lord Peter Views the Body* by Dorothy L. Sayers (copyright, 1928); for "Suspicion" from *In the Teeth of the Evidence* by Dorothy L. Sayers (copyright, 1940); for "The Cyprian Bees" from *Sinners Go Secretly* by Anthony Wynne (copyright, 1927).

A. P. Watt & Son, for "The Sweet Shot" from *Trent Intervenes* by E. C. Bentley (copyright, 1938); for "The Clock" from *The Four Corners of the World* by A. E. W. Mason (copyright, 1917).

Willis Kingsley Wing for "Paris Adventure" by Leslie Charteris.

THE GREAT DETECTIVES

THE PURLOINED LETTER

by EDGAR ALLAN POE

With the appearance in Graham's Magazine, Philadelphia, 1841, of "The Murders in the Rue Morgue," C. AUGUSTE DUPIN was born and the first detective story burst upon the world. Only two other DUPIN stories followed — "The Mystery of Marie Rogêt" and "The Purloined Letter" — but in these three tales Poe laid down for the first time and for all time the keystone principles of the sturdy literary form which has grown and grown until today, a full century after, it has become, as Philip Guedalla says, "the normal recreation of noble minds." So DUPIN must be called the Adam — the Original Sin — of fictional detectives. The Eve? — we believe her to have been one Mrs. Paschal, who first appeared in print in the year 1861.

AT PARIS, just after dark one gusty evening in the autumn of 18—, I was enjoying the twofold luxury of meditation and a meerschaum, in company with my friend C. Auguste Dupin, in his little back library, or bookcloset, *au troisième*, No. 33 *Rue Dunôt, Faubourg-St.-Germain*. For one hour at least we had maintained a profound silence; while each, to any casual observer, might have seemed intently and exclusively occupied with the curling eddies of smoke that oppressed the atmosphere of the chamber. For myself, however, I was mentally discussing certain topics which had formed matter for conversation between us at an earlier period of the evening; I mean the affair of the Rue Morgue, and the mystery attending the murder of Marie Rogêt. I looked upon it, therefore, as something of a coincidence, when the door of our apartment was thrown open and admitted our old acquaintance, Monsieur G——, the Prefect of the Parisian police.

We gave him a hearty welcome; for there was nearly half as much of the entertaining as of the contemptible about the man, and we had not seen him for several years. We had been sitting in the dark, and Dupin now arose for the purpose of lighting a lamp, but sat down again, without doing so, upon G.'s saying that he had called to consult us, or rather to ask the opinion of my friend, about some official business which had occasioned a great deal of trouble.

"If it is any point requiring reflection," observed Dupin, as he forebore to enkindle the wick, "we shall examine it to better purpose in the dark."

"That is another of your odd notions," said the Prefect, who had the fashion of calling everything "odd" that was beyond his comprehension, and thus lived amid an absolute legion of "oddities."

"Very true," said Dupin, as he supplied his visitor with a pipe, and rolled toward him a comfortable chair.

"And what is the difficulty now?" I asked. "Nothing more in the assassination way, I hope."

"Oh, no; nothing of that nature. The fact is, the business is *very* simple indeed, and I make no doubt that we can manage it sufficiently well ourselves; but then I thought Dupin would like to hear the details of it, because it is so excessively *odd*."

"Simple and odd," said Dupin.

"Why, yes; and not exactly that either. The fact is, we have all been a good deal puzzled because the affair *is* so simple, and yet baffles us altogether."

"Perhaps it is the very simplicity of the thing which puts you at fault," said my friend.

"What nonsense you *do* talk!" replied the Prefect, laughing heartily.

"Perhaps the mystery is a little *too* plain," said Dupin.

"Oh, good heavens! who ever heard of such an idea?"

"A little *too* self-evident."

"Ha! ha! ha! — ha! ha! ha! — ho! ho! ho!" roared our visitor, profoundly amused, "oh, Dupin, you will be the death of me yet!"

"And what, after all, *is* the matter on hand?" I asked.

"Why, I will tell you," replied the Prefect, as he gave a long, steady, and contemplative puff, and settled himself in his chair. "I will tell you in a few words; but, before I begin, let me caution you that this is an affair demanding the greatest secrecy, and that I should most probably lose the position I now hold, were it known that I confided it to anyone."

"Proceed," said I.

"Or not," said Dupin.

"Well, then; I have received personal information, from a very high quarter, that a certain document of the last importance has been purloined from the royal apartments. The individual who purloined it is known; this beyond a doubt; he was seen to take it. It is known, also, that it still remains in his possession."

"How is this known?" asked Dupin.

"It is clearly inferred," replied the Prefect, "from the nature of the document, and from the non-appearance of certain results which would at once arise from its passing *out* of the robber's possession — that is to say, from his employing it as he must design in the end to employ it."

"Be a little more explicit," I said.

"Well, I may venture so far as to say that the paper gives its holder a certain power in a certain quarter where such power is immensely valuable." The Prefect was fond of the cant of diplomacy.

"Still I do not quite understand," said Dupin.

"No? Well; the disclosure of the document to a third person, who shall be nameless, would bring in question the honor of a personage of most exalted station; and this fact gives the holder of the document an ascendancy over the illustrious personage whose honor and peace are so jeopardized."

"But this ascendancy," I interposed, "would depend upon the robber's knowledge of the loser's knowledge of the robber. Who would dare — "

"The thief," said G., "is the Minister D——, who dares all things, those unbecoming as well as those becoming a man. The method of the theft was not less ingenious than bold. The document in question — a letter, to be frank — had been received by the personage robbed while alone in the royal boudoir. During its perusal she was suddenly interrupted by the entrance of the other exalted personage from whom especially it was her wish to conceal it. After a hurried and vain endeavor to thrust it in a drawer, she was forced to place it, open as it was, upon a table. The address, however, was uppermost, and, the contents thus unexposed, the letter escaped notice. At this juncture enters the Minister D——. His lynx eye immediately perceives the paper, recognizes the handwriting of the address, observes the confusion of the personage addressed, and fathoms her secret. After some business transactions, hurried through in his ordinary manner, he produces a letter somewhat similar to the one in question, opens it, pretends to read it, and then places it in close juxtaposition to the other. Again he converses, for some fifteen minutes, upon the public affairs. At length, in taking leave, he takes also from the table the letter to which he had no claim. Its rightful owner saw but, of course, dared not call attention to, the act, in the presence of the third personage who stood at her elbow. The minister decamped; leaving his own letter — one of no importance — upon the table."

"Here, then," said Dupin to me, "you have precisely what you demand to make the ascendancy complete — the robber's knowledge of the loser's knowledge of the robber."

"Yes," replied the Prefect; "and the power thus attained has, for some months past, been wielded, for political purposes, to a very dangerous extent. The personage robbed is more thoroughly convinced, every day, of the necessity of reclaiming her letter. But this, of course, cannot be done openly. In fine, driven to despair, she has committed the matter to me."

"Than whom," said Dupin, amid a perfect whirlwind of smoke. "no more sagacious agent could, I suppose, be desired, or even imagined."

"You flatter me," replied the Prefect; "but it is possible that some such opinion may have been entertained."

"It is clear," said I, "as you observe, that the letter is still in the possession of the minister; since it is this possession, and not any employment of the letter, which bestows the power. With the employment the power departs."

"True," said G.; "and upon this conviction I proceeded. My first care was to make thorough search of the minister's hotel; and here my chief embarrassment lay in the necessity of searching without his knowledge. Beyond all things, I have been warned of the danger which would result from giving him reason to suspect our design."

"But," said I, "you are quite *au fait* in these investigations. The Parisian police have done this thing often before."

"Oh yes; and for this reason I did not despair. The habits of the minister gave me, too, a great advantage. He is frequently absent from home all night. His servants are by no means numerous. They sleep at a distance from their master's apartment, and, being chiefly Neapolitans, are readily made drunk. I have keys, as you know, with which I can open any chamber or cabinet in Paris. For three months a night has not passed, during the greater part of which I have not been engaged, personally, in ransacking the D—— Hotel. My honor is interested, and, to mention a great secret, the reward is enormous. So I did not abandon the search until I had become fully satisfied that the thief is a more astute man than myself. I fancy that I have investigated every nook and corner of the premises in which it is possible that the paper can be concealed."

"But is it not possible," I suggested, "that although the letter may be in possession of the minister, as it unquestionably is, he may have concealed it elsewhere than upon his own premises?"

"This is barely possible," said Dupin. "The present peculiar condition of affairs at court, and especially of those intrigues in which D—— is known to be involved, would render the instant availability of the document — its susceptibility of being produced at a moment's notice — a point of nearly equal importance with its possession."

"Its susceptibility of being produced?" said I.

"That is to say, of being *destroyed*," said Dupin.

"True," I observed; "the paper is clearly then upon the premises. As for its being upon the person of the minister, we may consider that as out of the question."

"Entirely," said the Prefect. "He has been twice waylaid, as if by footpads, and his person rigidly searched under my own inspection."

"You might have spared yourself this trouble," said Dupin. "D——, I presume, is not altogether a fool, and, if not, must have anticipated these waylayings, as a matter of course."

"Not *altogether* a fool," said G., "but then he is a poet, which I take to be only one remove from a fool."

"True," said Dupin, after a long and thoughtful whiff from his meerschaum, "although I have been guilty of certain doggerel myself."

"Suppose you detail," said I, "the particulars of your search."

"Why, the fact is, we took our time, and we searched *everywhere*. I have had long experience in these affairs. I took the entire building, room by room, devoting the nights of a whole week to each. We examined, first, the furniture of each apartment. We opened every possible drawer; and I presume you know that, to a properly trained police agent, such a thing as a 'secret' drawer is impossible. Any man is a dolt who permits a 'secret' drawer to escape him in a search of this kind. The thing is *so* plain. There is a certain amount of bulk — of space — to be accounted for in every cabinet. Then we have accurate rules. The fiftieth part of a line could not escape us. After the cabinets we took the chairs. The cushions we probed with the fine long needles you have seen me employ. From the tables we removed the tops."

"Why so?"

"Sometimes the top of a table, or other similarly arranged piece of furniture, is removed by the person wishing to conceal an article; then the leg is excavated, the article deposited within the cavity, and the top replaced. The bottoms and tops of bedposts are employed in the same way."

"But could not the cavity be detected by sounding?" I asked.

"By no means, if, when the article is deposited, a sufficient wadding of cotton be placed around it. Besides, in our case, we were obliged to proceed without noise."

"But you could not have removed — you could not have taken to pieces *all* articles of furniture in which it would have been possible to make a deposit in the manner you mention. A letter may be compressed into a thin spiral roll, not differing much in shape or bulk from a large knitting needle, and in this form it might be inserted into the rung of a chair, for example. You did not take to pieces all the chairs?"

"Certainly not; but we did better — we examined the rungs of every chair in the hotel, and, indeed, the jointings of every description of furniture, by the aid of a most powerful microscope. Had there been any traces of recent disturbance we should not have failed to detect it instantly. A single grain of gimlet dust, for example, would have been as obvious as an apple. Any disorder in the gluing — any unusual gaping in the joints — would have sufficed to insure detection."

"I presume you looked to the mirrors, between the boards and the plates, and you probed the beds and the bedclothes, as well as the curtains and carpets."

"That of course; and when we had absolutely completed every particle of the furniture in this way, then we examined the house itself. We divided its entire surface into compartments, which we numbered, so that none might be missed; then we scrutinized each individual square inch throughout the premises, including the two houses immediately adjoining, with the microscope, as before."

"The two houses adjoining!" I exclaimed; "you must have had a great deal of trouble."

"We had; but the reward offered is prodigious."

"You include the *grounds* about the houses?"

"All the grounds are paved with brick. They gave us comparatively little trouble. We examined the moss between the bricks, and found it undisturbed."

"You looked among D——'s papers, of course, and into the books of the library?"

"Certainly; we opened every package and parcel; we not only opened every book, but we turned over every leaf in each volume, not contenting ourselves with a mere shake, according to the fashion of some of our police officers. We also measured the thickness of every book *cover,* with the most accurate admeasurement, and applied to each the most jealous scrutiny of the microscope. Had any of the bindings been recently meddled with, it would have been utterly impossible that the fact should have escaped observation. Some five or six volumes, just from the hands of the binder, we carefully probed, longitudinally, with the needles."

"You explored the floors beneath the carpets?"

"Beyond doubt. We removed every carpet, and examined the boards with the microscope."

"And the paper on the walls?"

"Yes."

"You looked into the cellars?"

"We did."

"Then," I said, "you have been making a miscalculation, and the letter is *not* upon the premises as you suppose."

"I fear you are right there," said the Prefect. "And now, Dupin, what would you advise me to do?"

"To make a thorough research of the premises."

"That is absolutely needless," replied G——. "I am not more sure that I breathe than I am that the letter is not at the hotel."

"I have no better advice to give you," said Dupin.

"You have, of course, an accurate description of the letter?"

"Oh, yes!"—And here the Prefect, producing a memorandum book, proceeded to read aloud a minute account of the internal, and especially of the external, appearance of the missing document. Soon after finishing the perusal of this description, he took his departure, more entirely depressed in spirits than I had ever known the good gentleman before.

In about a month afterward he paid us another visit, and found us occupied very nearly as before. He took a pipe and a chair and entered into some ordinary conversation. At length I said:

"Well, but G——, what of the purloined letter? I presume you have at last made up your mind that there is no such thing as over-reaching the Minister?"

"Confound him, say I—yes; I made the re-examination, however, as Dupin suggested—but it was all labor lost, as I knew it would be."

"How much was the reward offered, did you say?" asked Dupin.

"Why, a very great deal—a *very* liberal reward—I don't like to say how much, precisely; but one thing I *will* say, that I wouldn't mind giving my individual check for fifty thousand francs to any one who could obtain me that letter. The fact is, it is becoming of more and more importance every day; and the reward has been lately doubled. If it were trebled, however, I could do no more than I have done."

"Why, yes," said Dupin, drawlingly, between the whiffs of his meerschaum, "I really—think, G——, you have not exerted yourself—to the utmost in this matter. You might—do a little more, I think, eh?"

"How?—in what way?"

"Why — puff, puff — you might — puff, puff — employ counsel in the matter, eh? — puff, puff, puff. Do you remember the story they tell of Abernethy?"

"No; hang Abernethy!"

"To be sure! hang him and welcome. But, once upon a time, a certain rich miser conceived the design of sponging upon this Abernethy for a medical opinion. Getting up, for this purpose, an ordinary conversation in a private company, he insinuated his case to the physician, as that of an imaginary individual.

" 'We will suppose,' said the miser, 'that his symptoms are such and such; now, doctor, what would *you* have directed him to take?'

" 'Take!' said the Abernethy, 'why, take *advice,* to be sure.' "

"But," said the Prefect, a little discomposed, "*I* am *perfectly* willing to take advice, and to pay for it. I would *really* give fifty thousand francs to any one who would aid me in the matter."

"In that case," replied Dupin, opening a drawer, and producing a check book, "you may as well fill me up a check for the amount mentioned. When you have signed it, I will hand you the letter."

I was astounded. The Prefect appeared absolutely thunderstricken. For some minutes he remained speechless and motionless, looking incredulously at my friend with open mouth, and eyes that seemed starting from their sockets; then apparently recovering himself in some measure, he seized a pen, and after several pauses and vacant stares, finally filled up and signed a check for fifty thousand francs, and handed it across the table to Dupin. The latter examined it carefully and deposited it in his pocket book; then, unlocking an escritoire, took thence a letter and gave it to the Prefect. This functionary grasped it in a perfect agony of joy, opened it with a trembling hand, cast a rapid glance at its contents, and then, scrambling and struggling to the door rushed at length unceremoniously from the room and from the house, without having uttered a syllable since Dupin had requested him to fill up the check.

When he had gone, my friend entered into some explanations.

"The Parisian police," he said, "are exceedingly able in their way. They are persevering, ingenious, cunning, and thoroughly versed in the knowledge which their duties seem chiefly to demand. Thus, when G—— detailed to us his mode of searching the premises at the Hotel D——, I felt entire confidence in his having made a satisfactory investigation — so far as his labors extended."

"So far as his labors extended?" said I.

"Yes," said Dupin. "The measures adopted were not only the best of their kind, but carried out to absolute perfection. Had the letter been deposited within the range of their search, these fellows would, beyond a question, have found it."

I merely laughed — but he seemed quite serious in all that he said.

"The measures, then," he continued, "were good in their kind, and well executed; their defect lay in their being inapplicable to the case and to the man. A certain set of highly ingenious resources are, with the Prefect, a sort of Procrustean bed, to which he forcibly adapts his designs. But he perpetually errs by being too deep or too shallow for the matter in hand; and many a schoolboy is a better reasoner than he. I knew one about eight years of age, whose success at guessing in the game of 'even and odd' attracted universal admiration. This game is simple, and is played with marbles. One player holds in his hand a number of these toys, and demands of another whether that number is even or odd. If the guess is right, the guesser wins one; if wrong he loses one. The boy to whom I allude won all the marbles of the school. Of course he had some principle of guessing; and this lay in mere observation and admeasurement of the astuteness of his opponents. For example, an arrant simpleton is his opponent, and, holding up his closed hand, asks, 'Are they even or odd?' Our schoolboy replies, 'Odd,' and loses; but upon the second trial he wins, for he then says to himself: 'The simpleton had them even upon the first trial, and his amount of cunning is just sufficient to make him have them odd upon the second; I will therefore guess odd'; — he guesses odd, and wins. Now, with a simpleton a degree above the first, he would have reasoned thus: 'This fellow finds that in the first instance I guessed odd, and, in the second, he will propose to himself, upon the first impulse, a simple variation from even to odd, as did the first simpleton; but then a second thought will suggest that this is too simple a variation and finally he will decide upon putting it even as before. I will therefore guess even'; — he guesses even, and wins. Now this mode of reasoning in the schoolboy, whom his fellows termed 'lucky,'—what, in its last analysis, is it?"

"It is merely," I said, "an identification of the reasoner's intellect with that of his opponent."

"It is," said Dupin; "and, upon inquiring of the boy by what means he effected the *thorough* identification in which his success consisted, I received answer as follows: 'When I wish to find out how wise, or how stupid, or how good, or how wicked is anyone, or what are his thoughts at the moment, I fashion the expression of my face, as accurately as possible, in accordance with the expression of his, and then wait to see what thoughts or sentiments arise in my mind or heart, as if to match or correspond with the expression.' This response of the schoolboy lies at the bottom of all the spurious profundity which has been attributed to Rochefoucauld, to La Bougive, to Machiavelli, and to Campanella."

"And the identification," I said, "of the reasoner's intellect with that of his opponent, depends, if I understand you aright, upon the accuracy with which the opponent's intellect is admeasured."

"For its practical value it depends upon this," replied Dupin; "and the Prefect and his cohort fail so frequently, first, by default of this identification, and, secondly, by ill-admeasurement, or rather through non-admeasurement, of the intellect with which they are engaged. They consider only their *own* ideas of ingenuity; and, in searching for anything hidden, advert only to the modes in which *they* would have hidden it. They are right in this much—that their own ingenuity is a faithful representative of that of the *mass;* but when the cunning of the individual felon is diverse in character from their own, the felon foils them of course. This always happens when it is above their own, and very usually when it is below. They have no variation of principle in their investigations; at best, when urged by some unusual emergency—by some extraordinary reward— they extend or exaggerate their old modes of *practice,* without touching their principles. What, for example, in this case of D——, has been done to vary the principle of action? What is all this boring, and probing, and sounding, and scrutinizing with the microscope, and dividing the surface of the building into registered square inches—what is it all but an exaggeration of the *application* of the one principle or set of principles of search, which are based upon the one set of notions regarding human ingenuity, to which the Prefect, in the long routine of his duty, has been accustomed? Do you not see he has taken it for granted that *all* men proceed to conceal a letter, not exactly in a gimlet hole bored in a chair leg, but, at least, in *some* out-of-the-way hole or corner suggested by the same tenor of thought which would urge a man to secrete a letter in a gimlet hole bored in a chair leg? And do you not see, also, that such *recherchés* nooks for concealment are adapted only for ordinary occasions, and would be adopted only by ordinary intellects; for, in all cases of concealment, a disposal of the article concealed — a disposal of it in this *recherché* manner — is, in the very first instance, presumable and presumed; and thus its discovery depends, not at all upon the acumen, but altogether upon the mere care, patience, and determination of the seekers; and where the case is of importance — or, what amounts to the same thing in the policial eyes, when the reward is of magnitude — the qualities in question have *never* been known to fail. You will now understand what I meant in suggesting that, had the purloined letter been hidden anywhere within the limits of the Prefect's examination — in other words, had the principle of its concealment been comprehended within the principles of the Prefect — its discovery would have been a matter altogether beyond question. This functionary, however, has been thoroughly mystified; and the remote source of his defeat lies in the supposition that the minister is a fool, because he has acquired renown as a poet. All fools are poets; this the Prefect *feels;* and he is merely guilty of a *non distributio medii* in thence inferring that all poets are fools."

"But is this really the poet?" I asked. "There are two brothers, I know; and both have attained reputation in letters. The minister I believe has written learnedly on the differential calculus. He is a mathematician, and no poet."

"You are mistaken; I know him well; he is both. As poet *and* mathematician, he would reason well; as mere mathematician, he could not have reasoned at all, and thus would have been at the mercy of the Prefect."

"You surprise me," I said, "by these opinions, which have been contradicted by the voice of the world. You do not mean to set at naught the well-digested idea of centuries? The mathematical reason has long been regarded as *the* reason *par excellence*."

"*'Il y a à parier,'*" replied Dupin, quoting from Chamfort, "*'que toute idée publique, toute convention reçue, est une sottise, car elle a convenue au plus grand nombre.'* The mathematicians, I grant you, have done their best to promulgate the popular error to which you allude, and which is none the less an error for its promulgation as truth. With an art worthy a better cause, for example, they have insinuated the term 'analysis' into application to algebra. The French are the originators of this particular deception; but if a term is of any importance — if words derive any value from applicability — then 'analysis' conveys 'algebra' about as much as, in Latin, *'ambitus'* implies 'ambition,' *'religio'* 'religion,' or *'homines honesti'* a set of *honorable* men."

"You have a quarrel on hand, I see," said I, "with some of the algebraists of Paris; but proceed."

"I dispute the availability, and thus the value, of that reason which is cultivated in any especial form other than the abstractly logical. I dispute, in particular, the reason educed by mathematical study. The mathematics are the science of form and quantity; mathematical reasoning is merely logic applied to observation upon form and quantity. The great error lies in supposing that even the truths of what is called *pure* algebra are abstract or general truths. And this error is so egregious that I am confounded at the universality with which it has been received. Mathematical axioms are *not* axioms of general truth. What is true of *relation* — of form and quantity — is often grossly false in regard to morals, for example. In this latter science it is very usually *un*true that the aggregated parts are equal to the whole. In chemistry also the axiom fails. In the consideration of motive it fails; for two motives, each of a given value, have not, necessarily, a value when united equal to the sum of their values apart. There are numerous other mathematical truths which are only truths within the limits of *relation*. But the mathematician argues from his *finite truths,* through habit, as if they were of an absolutely general applicability — as the world indeed imagines them to be. Bryant, in his very learned *Mythology,* mentions an analogous source of error, when he says that 'although the pagan fables are not believed, yet we forget ourselves continually, and make inferences from them as existing realities.' With the algebraists, however, who are pagans themselves, the 'pagan fables' *are* believed, and the inferences are made, not so much through lapse of memory as through an unaccountable addling of the brains. In short, I never yet encountered the mere mathematician who could be trusted out of equal roots, or one who did not clandestinely hold it as a point of his faith that $x^2 + px$ was absolutely and unconditionally equal to q. Say to one of these gentlemen, by way of experiment, if you please, that you believe occasions may occur where $x^2 + px$ is *not* altogether equal to q, and, having made him understand what you mean, get out of his reach as speedily as convenient, for, beyond doubt, he will endeavor to knock you down.

"I mean to say," continued Dupin, while I merely laughed at his last observations, "that if the minister had been no more than a mathematician, the Prefect would have been under no necessity of giving me this check. I knew him, however, as both mathematician and poet, and my measures were adapted to his capacity, with reference to the circumstances by which he was surrounded. I knew him as a courtier, too, and as a bold *intrigant*. Such a man, I considered, could not fail to be aware of the ordinary policial modes of action. He could not have failed to anticipate — and events have proved that he did not fail to anticipate — the waylayings to which he was subjected. He must have foreseen, I reflected, the secret investigations of his premises. His frequent absences from home at night, which were hailed by the Prefect as certain aids to his success, I regarded only as *ruses,* to afford opportunity for thorough search to the police, and thus the sooner to impress them with the conviction to which G——, in fact, did finally arrive — the conviction that the letter was not upon the premises. I felt, also, that the whole train of thought, which I was at some pains in detailing to you just now, concerning the invariable principle of policial action in searches for articles concealed — I felt that this whole train of thought would necessarily pass through the mind of the minister. It would imperatively lead him to despise all the ordinary *nooks* of concealment. *He* could not, I reflected, be so weak as not to see that the most intricate and remote recess of his hotel would be as open as his commonest closets to the eyes, to the probes, to the gimlets, and to the microscopes of the Prefect. I saw, in fine, that he would be driven, as a matter of course, to *simplicity,* if not deliberately induced to it as a matter of choice. You will remember, perhaps, how desperately the Prefect laughed when I suggested, upon our first interview, that it was just possible this mystery troubled him so much on account of its being so *very* self-evident."

"Yes," said I, "I remember his merriment well. I really thought he would have fallen into convulsions."

"The material world," continued Dupin, "abounds with very strict analogies to the immaterial; and thus some color of truth has been given to the rhetorical dogma, that metaphor, or simile, may be made to strengthen an argument as well as to embellish a description. The principle of the *vis inertiae,* for example, seems to be identical in physics and metaphysics. It is not more true in the former, that a large body is with more difficulty set in motion than a smaller one, and that its subsequent *momentum* is commensurate with this difficulty, than it is, in the latter, that intellects of the vaster capacity, while more forcible, more constant, and more eventful in their movements than those of inferior grade, are yet the less readily moved, and more embarrassed, and full of hesitation in the first few steps of their progress. Again: have you ever noticed which of the street signs over the shop doors are the most attractive of attention?"

"I have never given the matter a thought," I said.

"There is a game of puzzles," he resumed, "which is played upon a map. One party playing requires another to find a given word — the name of town, river, state, or empire — any word, in short, upon the motley and perplexed surface of the chart. A novice in the game generally seeks to embarrass his opponents by giving them the most minutely lettered names; but the adept selects such words as stretch, in large characters, from one end of the chart to the other. These, like the over-largely lettered signs and placards of the street, escape observation by dint of being excessively obvious; and here the physical oversight is precisely analogous with the moral inapprehension by which the intellect suffers to pass unnoticed those considerations which are too obtrusively and too palpably self-evident. But this is a point, it appears, somewhat above or beneath the understanding of the

Prefect. He never once thought it probable, or possible, that the minister had deposited the letter immediately beneath the nose of the whole world, by way of best preventing any portion of that world from perceiving it.

"But the more I reflected upon the daring, dashing, and discriminating ingenuity of D——; upon the fact that the document must always have been *at hand,* if he intended to use it to good purpose; and upon the decisive evidence, obtained by the Prefect, that it was not hidden within the limits of that dignitary's ordinary search — the more satisfied I became that, to conceal this letter, the minister had resorted to the comprehensive and sagacious expedient of not attempting to conceal it at all.

"Full of these ideas, I prepared myself with a pair of green spectacles, and called one fine morning, quite by accident, at the ministerial hotel. I found D—— at home, yawning, lounging, and dawdling, as usual, and pretending to be in the last extremity of ennui. He is, perhaps, the most really energetic human being now alive — but that is only when nobody sees him.

"To be even with him, I complained of my weak eyes, and lamented the necessity of the spectacles, under cover of which I cautiously and thoroughly surveyed the whole apartment, while seemingly intent only upon the conversation of my host.

"I paid especial attention to a large writing table near which he sat, and upon which lay confusedly some miscellaneous letters and other papers, with one or two musical instruments and a few books. Here, however, after a long and very deliberate scrutiny, I saw nothing to excite particular suspicion.

"At length my eyes, in going the circuit of the room, fell upon a trumpery filigree card rack of pasteboard, that hung dangling by a dirty blue ribbon, from a little brass knob just beneath the middle of the mantelpiece. In this rack, which had three or four compartments, were five or six visiting cards and a solitary letter. This last was much soiled and crumpled. It was torn nearly in two, across the middle — as if a design, in the first instance, to tear it entirely up as worthless had been altered, or stayed, in the second. It had a large black seal, bearing the D—— cipher *very* conspicuously, and was addressed, in a diminutive female hand, to D—— the minister, himself. It was thrust carelessly, and even, as it seemed, contemptuously, into one of the uppermost divisions of the rack.

"No sooner had I glanced at this letter than I concluded it to be that of which I was in search. To be sure, it was, to all appearance, radically different from the one of which the Prefect had read us so minute a description. Here the seal was large and black, with the D—*— cipher; there it was small and red, with the ducal arms of the S—— family. Here, the address, to the minister, was diminutive and feminine; there, the superscription, to a certain royal personage, was markedly bold and decided; the size alone formed a point of correspondence. But, then, the *radicalness* of these differences, which was excessive; the dirt; the soilèd and torn condition of the paper, so inconsistent with the *true* methodical habits of D——, and so suggestive of a design to delude the beholder into an idea of the worthlessness of the document; — these things, together with the hyperobtrusive situation of this document, full in the view of every visitor, and thus exactly in accordance with the conclusions to which I had previously arrived; these things, I say, were strongly corroborative of suspicion, in one who came with the intention to suspect.

"I protracted my visit as long as possible, and, while I maintained a most animated discussion with the minister, upon a topic which I knew well had never failed to interest and excite him, I kept my attention really riveted upon the letter. In this examination, I committed to memory its external appearance and arrangement in the rack; and also fell, at length, upon a discovery which set at rest whatever trivial doubt I might have entertained. In scrutinizing the edges of the paper, I observed them to be more *chafed* than seemed necessary. They presented the *broken* appearance which is manifested when a stiff paper, having been once folded and pressed with a folder, is refolded in a reversed direction, in the same creases or edges which had formed the original fold. This discovery was sufficient. It was clear to me that the letter had been turned, as a glove, inside out, re-directed and re-sealed. I bade the minister good morning, and took my departure at once, leaving a gold snuffbox upon the table.

"The next morning I called for the snuffbox, when we resumed, quite eagerly, the conversation of the preceding day. While thus engaged, however, a loud report, as if of a pistol, was heard immediately beneath the windows of the hotel, and was succeeded by a series of fearful screams, and the shoutings of a terrified mob. D—— rushed to a casement, threw it open, and looked out. In the meantime I stepped to the card rack, took the letter, put it in my pocket, and replaced it by a facsimile, (so far as regards externals) which I had carefully prepared at my lodgings — imitating the D—— cipher, very readily, by means of a seal formed of bread.

"The disturbance in the street had been occasioned by the frantic behavior of a man with a musket. He had fired it among a crowd of women and children. It proved, however, to have been without ball, and the fellow was suffered to go his way as a lunatic or a drunkard. When he had gone, D—— came from the window, whither I had followed him immediately upon securing the object in view. Soon afterward I bade him farewell. The pretended lunatic was a man in my own pay."

"But what purpose had you," I asked, "in replacing the letter by a facsimile? Would it not have been better, at the first visit, to have seized it openly, and departed?"

"D——," replied Dupin, "is a desperate man, and a man of nerve. His hotel, too, is not without attendants devoted to his interests. Had I made the wild attempt you suggest, I might never have left the ministerial presence alive. The good people of Paris might have heard of me no more. But I had an object apart from these considerations. You know my political prepossessions. In this matter, I act as a partisan of the lady concerned. For eighteen months the minister has had her in his power. She has now him in hers — since, being unaware that the letter is not in his possession, he will proceed with his exactions as if it was. Thus will he inevitably commit himself, at once, to his political destruction. His downfall, too, will not be more precipitate than awkward. It is all very well to talk about the *facilis descensus Averni;* but in all kinds of climbing, as Catalani said of singing, it is far more easy to get up than to come down. In the present instance I have no sympathy — at least no pity — for him who descends. He is that *monstrum horrendum,* an unprincipled man of genius. I confess, however, that I should like very well to know the precise character of his thoughts, when, being defied by her whom the Prefect terms 'a certain personage,' he is reduced to opening the letter which I left for him in the card rack."

"How? Did you put anything particular in it?"

"Why — it did not seem altogether right to leave the interior blank — that would have been insulting. D——, at Vienna once, did me an evil turn, which I told him, quite good-humoredly, that I should remember. So, as I knew he would feel some curiosity in regard to the identity of the person who had outwitted him, I thought it a pity not to give him a clew. He is well-acquainted with my MS., and I just copied into the middle of the blank sheet the words: —

Un dessein si funeste,
S'il n' est digne d' Atrée, est digne de Thyeste.

They are to be found in Crébillon's *Atrée*."

THE MYSTERY OF MRS. DICKINSON
by *NICHOLAS CARTER*

How many years is it since you read a Nick Carter story, behind the barn, or under the blanket by flashlight? And did you know that Nick Carter wrote short stories? At any rate, your Editors take pleasure in presenting this Nick Carter tale, not merely as a curiosity of American letters, but also to disprove the false notion that all Nick Carters were "trash." "The Mystery of Mrs. Dickinson" might have been written last year by an author of considerably less slandered reputation!

A FAT old man, a lean old man, and a young man who was neither fat nor lean, were Nick Carter's three visitors.

The fat man was Mr. Ferris, the lean man was Mr. Steele, and the young man was Richard Steele, nephew of the preceding.

Mr. Ferris opened the conversation.

"Few words are enough for busy men," he said.

"You know me. You know Mr. Steele. We're Ferris & Steele, the jewelers. Young Mr. Steele is our cashier.

"You also know Mr. George Dickinson, do you not?"

"Dealer in bric-a-brac and curios?" said Nick. "Doesn't need to deal in anything. Has money enough for a dozen men. In business for the love of it."

"Exactly. And Mrs. Dickinson — do you know her?"

"I do not. I heard of his marriage. She is very much his junior, I believe."

"He's nearly sixty; she can't be over twenty-five. And she's a beautiful woman, sir, if ever I saw one — sparkling black eyes, olive skin, the pure Spanish type. More than that, she is a lady by birth and breeding. I flatter myself that I know a lady when I see one, and Mrs. Dickinson could not be mistaken by anybody. Well, sir, our case has to do with her, and a sad case it is. Would you believe that this lovely creature is a kleptomaniac — that she's been robbing us for several months?"

"Would I believe it?" repeated Nick. "It depends on the evidence."

"Oh, the evidence is conclusive. Mr. Steele and myself have seen her do it."

"Why did you permit yourself to be robbed in this way?"

"Perhaps we were wrong; perhaps we were injudicious," said Mr. Ferris; "but our intentions were good. Let me tell you the story.

"It began in June, only a few months after the lady's marriage. She came into our store one day and introduced herself to us. It was I to whom she made herself known. Her husband has traded with us for many years. When we secure anything especially good in his line we always let him know of it, and our dealings with him in the last ten years will run up into six figures.

"Of course, I was very glad to see Mrs. Dickinson; indeed, I had some curiosity to see her. I showed her around our establishment. She asked the price of various articles, but bought nothing. The next day, however, she returned and purchased — let me see; what was the amount, Richard?"

Young Mr. Steele produced a memorandum book and consulted it.

"The first check," he said, "was for eighteen hundred and fifty dollars."

"Then she paid you by check?" said Nick.

"Yes," responded Ferris; "she gave us her husband's check."

"Was the check all right?"

"Of course it was. This is no case of common fraud, Mr. Carter; it is kleptomania — an insane passion for stealing. Her purchases have always been made in the most businesslike way.

"On this first occasion, in fact, there appears to have been no theft. She visited the store twice and purchased goods, always with her husband's check, before we had cause to suspect that anything was wrong.

"Even then we were by no means sure. It is true that after she had gone we missed a solitaire worth about two thousand dollars, but we could not be certain that she had taken it. Indeed, I never thought of such a thing. On the contrary, I suspected another person, and had some investigation made, but with a negative result.

"A few weeks later, while that investigation was still in progress, Mrs. Dickinson called a fourth time. She made a purchase amounting to six hundred dollars, and she stole another solitaire worth two thousand eight hundred dollars — a large and fine stone.

"On this occasion I was on the watch, and though I did not see her take the jewel, I was morally certain that she did it. It was there when she began to examine a tray of jewels; it was not there when she started to leave.

"In view of this fact, and our previous loss, I ventured to do something about it. I had our regular detective speak to her as she was going out.

"He did it in the most delicate manner possible. He spoke of the absence of the stone as if it had been lost while she was looking at the contents of the tray, and he suggested that it might have fallen and been caught in the trimmings of her dress.

"She returned with him immediately to the counter where I was standing, and we had the most disagreeable scene that ever I went through."

Here the elder Mr. Steele emitted a hard and dry laugh.

"Very well, very well," said Ferris; "I admit it to a certain extent. I lost my head. She took it so calmly. Her affectation of innocence was so perfect. In short, I let her go.

"I begged her pardon for the annoyance, and laid the blame on our detective. The fact was that I couldn't give the order for her arrest and search."

"If she hadn't been quite so handsome," croaked the withered Mr. Steele, "I guess my partner would have done better."

"Why, what could I do?" responded Ferris, tartly. "To arrest her would mean to raise the deuce of a row with Dickinson, and lose his trade. And if there had been a mistake, think of the position we'd have been in.

"There'd have been a horrible scandal, and you doubtless know, Mr. Carter, that such scandals are mighty bad for our business. Every jewelry house in this city has allowed itself to be robbed more than once rather than venture upon the arrest of a prominent woman, with the certain consequence of scaring away a lot of others.

"The long and short of it is that she got away. And she didn't take any offense at me. On the contrary, she seemed to think that I had behaved very well, and she gave a smile — "

"Worth two thousand eight hundred dollars?" asked Nick.

"Not exactly; no, sir," said Ferris, getting red in the face. "But I was glad to get out of it that way. There was something in her manner which made me doubt the evidence of my own senses. When she had gone I hunted for that solitaire, like a fool, for more than an hour. Of course it was gone, and she had it.

"I had a long consultation with Mr. Steele — many of them, in fact. Of course, we knew that Dickinson was good for the amount, and that he would pay it, if we succeeded in proving our case to him beyond a doubt.

"I knew, also, that a woman who has that mania will not stop stealing. She can't. And it is a mania with her; I'm sure of it. I believe that she takes those things without really knowing what she's about, and that she forgets the theft the very next minute.

"That's the only way in which I can account for the complete innocence of her manner when questioned. She's forgotten about it. She imagines herself to be innocent.

"Well, I knew, as I've said, that she'd certainly go on stealing if that was her mania. So I formed a sort of plan with Mr. Steele which was that we should wait until she tried it again, and then have so many witnesses that there'd be no chance of error.

"We agreed not to arrest her on any account, nor to make any trouble for her, but simply to go to Mr. Dickinson and lay the case before him.

"That is what we propose to do now, for the thing has gone so far that we can't afford to wait.

"She was in the store yesterday afternoon. She got away with a necklace worth forty thousand dollars! By heavens! Mr. Carter, think of our standing there and allowing such a trick to be done right under our noses!"

"Why not?" said Nick. "By your own story it was only a sale."

"A sale?"

"Yes, you are perfectly certain that Mr. Dickinson will pay the amount. Now I'll venture a guess that you hope to figure up a consid-

erable profit when he has done so. For instance, wouldn't you have
sold that necklace for thirty thousand dollars, and the solitaires for
fifteen per cent off the price you've named to me?"

Both Ferris and Steele protested in chorus. They had no idea of
making a profit out of Mr. Dickinson's misfortune. The figures
named were the bare worth of the goods at net cost.

"Suppose that they're recovered," said Nick, "what will you do?
Will you take them back and say nothing?"

"Of course; of course," said Ferris. "They will be found in Mrs.
Dickinson's rooms, I've no doubt. But I don't believe Dickinson will
return them. I think he'll prefer to pay a fair price for them."

"Probably," said Nick. "But what do you want me to do about it?"

"Why, we wish you to act as our adviser — as the detective in the
case."

"The duty of a detective is to learn things that other people don't
know. Now, you gentlemen know everything."

The tinge of sarcasm in Nick's tone escaped his listeners.

"Yes, to be sure," said Steele, "we know everything, but we still
desire advice. What we want is that you should go with us to Dickinson's office today and talk with him."

"Wouldn't it be better, every way, if I quietly recovered the jewels
for you? Then you could guard against Mrs. Dickinson's depreda-
tions in the future, and there would be no scandal."

But Ferris & Steele wouldn't have it that way. They wanted an immediate interview with Mr. Dickinson.

"Now, let me tell you just what you do want," said Nick at last.
"You want the money. You're pressed for ready cash, and this is the
easiest way to get it."

Ferris and Steele looked at each other as if they had been witnesses
of a great feat of mind reading.

"Moreover," continued Nick, "you want me to be present in order
that you can lay the whole blame upon me, and save your business
relations with Mr. Dickinson if anything goes wrong."

Both men protested that they had no such idea. They merely
wished to have a man of good counsel present at the interview.

"Very well," said Nick; "though my opinion is unchanged I will
go with you. As for advice, that is out of the question. You are both
as obstinate — if you'll pardon my saying so — as two Mississippi

mules. Nothing that I can say will have any effect upon you. But the case interests me and I will go with you."

Mr. George Dickinson is a man of majestic presence. At sixty years of age he has the figure of a college athlete, big and strong.

His face, too, is youthful, and the only sign of his age is the whiteness of his abundant hair, which curls crisply around his broad forehead.

It was no wonder that Messrs. Ferris & Steele hesitated to open such a subject to such a man. The window was quite convenient, and it was thirty feet or more above the ground, for Mr. Dickinson has his wonderful curio store on the third floor of a Broadway building.

"What's the matter, gentlemen?" asked Dickinson, when they were all seated in his office. "Perhaps this is a friendly call. You don't seem anxious to proceed to business."

He laughed a frank, boyish laugh, as he looked at Ferris and Steele. A child could have read the desperate embarrassment on their faces.

Each waited for the other to begin, and both looked imploringly at Nick, but he clearly indicated his determination to be only a listener, and so, at last, Ferris began.

"It's a case in which we want your advice," said he. "There's a customer of ours for whom we feel the warmest friendship; but it happens most unfortunately that his wife — a young and beautiful woman, suffering as we believe under a terrible affliction — his wife, I repeat — has visited our store and has taken goods valued at nearly fifty thousand dollars. Now we desire to act in this affair in a friendly manner. Our deep sympathy with the gentleman in question — "

Dickinson interrupted him by raising his hand.

There was a small part of the office separated from the remainder by a partition which did not reach to the ceiling. From behind this partition came the sound of a typewriter.

Dickinson stepped to the door of this inclosure, and said:

"Miss Adams, will you step out into the other office for a few minutes?"

Then he returned and walked straight up to the senior partner of the jewelers' firm.

"Ferris, you infernal fat old rascal," he said, "have you the face to come here and tell me such a story as that about my wife?"

Ferris turned a pale sea-green, and if he thought at all during the minute's pause which ensued, it was probably upon his sins. He found no words in which to beg for his life.

Steele meanwhile was trembling with a faint, rustling sound, like the wind among dead leaves. His nephew rose hastily and walked to a water cooler in the corner, where he drank something like a quart of ice water.

What might have resulted is uncertain, but at that moment there was a light tap on the door.

Immediately it opened and a woman entered.

"Not now, Elsie," cried Dickinson hastily. "I am engaged at present. In a few minutes I shall be at liberty. Ned," he added to a young man who was also at the door, "will you get my wife a chair out there?"

Both Steele and Ferris leaped to their feet.

"Is that lady your wife?" gasped Ferris. "It's impossible!"

"Impossible?" cried Dickinson, in a voice like Gabriel's trumpet. "Do you think I don't know my own wife?"

"Why, what's the matter, George?" asked Mrs. Dickinson in an agitated voice, as she hastily stepped forward.

Her husband had his arm around her in a moment, and was facing her three accusers, who were speechless.

"It seems that I shall have to explain," said Nick. "Messrs. Ferris & Steele, jewelers, have been the victims of a notable swindle. A woman, representing herself to be Mrs. Dickinson, has called at their store several times, and presuming upon their knowledge of your financial and social standing, and upon their unwillingness to offend you, has stolen about thirty thousand dollars' worth — "

"Forty-five thousand!" gasped Steele.

"Thirty thousand dollars' worth of jewels," Nick continued, without noticing the interruption, "before their very eyes.

"They came here to lay the case before you, Mr. Dickinson, and I came from simple curiosity regarding the affair. I am not surprised to find that they have totally misunderstood the nature of the case."

Dickinson reflected a minute, and meanwhile recovered control.

"What led your stupidity to suppose," he said, "that the woman was my wife?"

"She presented checks drawn to your order, and signed by you," said Ferris; "and the signature was genuine. It only remains for us to learn to what other woman you have been in the habit of giving checks, and — "

Nick stepped hastily in front of Ferris, for otherwise there might have been manslaughter.

The jeweler's chagrin at the discovery of the way in which he had been duped had overcome his prudence, and he had grossly insulted Dickinson in the presence of his wife.

It required all the great detective's strength to stop Dickinson's rush, but he did it, and at last succeeded in bringing all present to their senses.

"Now that I know who you really are," said Dickinson to Nick, "I have confidence that we shall get a little light on this business. When you were introduced at first as Mr. Carter I did not think of the celebrated detective. As for you, Ferris and Steele, I accept your apology — for what it is worth."

"The root of this matter," said Nick, "is evidently in those checks. I think you must admit that they amounted to an identification. Although I do not think good judgment has been used by Ferris & Steele, I will say that the method employed at the start would have deceived any merchant.

"Now, since these checks went through the bank all right, and have caused no confusion in your accounts, I infer that they must have been drawn by you, and made to serve the purposes of this fraud by a clever trick.

"Young Mr. Steele has the dates and amounts of these checks. Let us compare them with the stubs in your checkbook. The checks were drawn on the Chemical Bank, I believe."

Without a word of objection Mr. Dickinson produced the book.

"Is this your private or your business account?" asked Nick.

"I keep but one."

Comparison of Richard Steele's memoranda with the stubs in the book was the work of only a moment. They tallied exactly.

"Now we will send for the used checks," said Nick.

They were obtained from the bank. Ferris and the two Steeles identified them, and Dickinson admitted the signatures.

The last-named had made no comment upon the matter since the moment when the first stub was found to tally with the memorandum.

Finally he said: "Of course you know what these checks are?"

"What do you mean?" asked Ferris.

"Why, these are the regular payments made by me to you for articles bought of you, and I hold your receipt in every case. How then, could the checks have been used as you allege?"

Mrs. Dickinson got in ahead of all the others who wished to speak at this point by begging her husband to explain.

"I don't understand business at all," she said, "and I'm so interested in this case."

"It's like this," responded her husband: "these men tell me that certain checks have been given them by a woman purporting to be you. The checks are found. I admit having drawn them.

"But, here's the point: the checks were drawn as payments by me to their firm. For instance, I bought a watch studded with diamonds at their store on July 18. The next day I sent a check for it. The bill was six hundred dollars.

"They sent back the bill receipted. The check was indorsed by them and put in their bank. And that settled that check. There was no way to get it out of the bank so that that woman could use it over again."

"Hold on," said Richard Steele, who for some time had been trying to get in a word; "I'll have to beg your pardon, Mr. Dickinson, and make a correction. You haven't paid your account by check since the middle of May."

"What?" cried Dickinson.

"I'm positive about that," said Richard, "for I noticed the change. Your account has been paid in cash every time."

"Can you prove that?" exclaimed Dickinson, very much astonished.

"Certainly."

"How were the payments made?"

"A boy brought the cash."

"I know that to be true in one instance," said Ferris. "I was present."

Dickinson rang a bell. A boy entered. He rang again, and another boy appeared.

"Was it either of these boys?" he asked.

Both Richard and Ferris replied promptly in the negative.

"I have had no other boys in my employ," said Dickinson as he dismissed them.

"The method of the fraud is now clear," said Nick. "The checks have been intercepted. How did you suppose they were sent?"

"By mail."

"Who attended to the mailing?"

"My typist, Miss Adams."

"Is she a dark woman, like a Spaniard, with flashing black eyes, and an olive skin?" cried Ferris, springing to his feet.

"Why, yes," stammered Dickinson; "she answers that description well enough. What of it?"

"What of it?" yelled Ferris. "Why, she's the woman, that's all. I see the game well enough!

"She formed the plan when you were married. She stole a check — only pretended to mail it, you see. Then she managed to raise the amount in cash, and paid our bill.

"With the check she bought jewelry, and sold it for enough to pay the next bill, and so on. It's plain as day. She must be arrested at once."

Dickinson, with a brow dark with anger, rang his bell.

One of the boys entered the room.

"Send Miss Adams here," said Dickinson.

"She's gone out, sir," replied the boy.

"How long ago?"

"Not half a minute."

"After her!" cried Ferris, rushing toward the door with extraordinary speed, considering his bulk.

The two Steeles followed. Nick, with Mr. and Mrs. Dickinson, brought up the rear of the procession, which was headed by the office boy, flying along in his eagerness to do a favor.

Ferris was close upon his heels.

Nick tried to stop this mad stampede, but the others were deaf to his cries.

They all ran down the stairs, too impatient to wait for an elevator.

"There she is!" cried the boy, when he reached the street.

He pointed to the retreating figure of the typist.

With a sort of growl, Ferris set his great bulk once more in motion. He even distanced the boy.

The others followed as they might.

Ferris caught up with the girl, and seized her roughly.

She turned upon him with a little scream.

Ferris struck his forehead with his fat and oily hand.

"Ten thousand devils!" he gasped, breathless with running. "This isn't the woman, either!"

A crowd had gathered instantly, as crowds do in New York. The unusual spectacle of this absurd chase was sufficient to account for the throng.

Miss Adams's position was certainly very embarrassing. Both Dickinson and Nick were heartily sorry for her, and the former was so enraged against Ferris that he could hardly restrain himself.

"Look here, my fat friend," he said in Ferris's ear, "don't you think that you've made us all sufficiently ridiculous? Suppose you take a back seat and allow Mr. Carter to handle the reins; that is, if he is still willing to have anything to do with you."

"I will take this case," said Nick calmly, "but only on the condition that you name. I must conduct it."

Neither Ferris nor the two Steeles had a word to say.

"Miss Adams," said Nick, "I hope you will forget this annoyance, and go to lunch with a good appetite. I suppose that is where you were going."

"Yes, sir; but I'd like to know — "

"When you come back, this matter shall be explained to you."

The detective lifted his hat, and the girl walked away.

"Now, Messrs. Ferris and Steele, if you will return to your store, I will meet you there at five o'clock this afternoon."

"But — " Ferris began.

"On no other condition will I conduct this affair."

Ferris looked at his partner and the latter nodded assent.

"There is one thing, however," said Richard Steele, "which, it seems to me, should not be overlooked. While Miss Adams was certainly not the woman who came to our store, she may be in the plot. She may have handed the checks to a confederate."

"Thank you," said Nick, "I will consider that possibility. Good day."

The three men took their departure.

Nick walked back to the curio store with the Dickinsons.

They plied him with questions, but he would give no definite answer.

"I am not prepared to speak about the case yet," he said. "I will take it up again this afternoon at the hour named, and if you are sufficiently interested to be at Ferris & Steele's at that time, you shall learn all that I then know."

It is needless to say that, at the hour named, the Dickinsons were present. In fact, they were ahead of time. Nick arrived on the second, as usual.

"Shall we come into the private office?" said Steele. "We can talk there without interruption."

They were then standing near the door, before the principal diamond counter.

"What I have to say can be said here," replied Nick. "In fact, it is not very much.

"The theory of the case has already been correctly stated. The checks were intercepted, and were given to the woman who played the part of Mrs. Dickinson.

"The boy who came with the cash was, of course, in the pay of the schemers. After obtaining the receipted bills, he mailed them to Mr. Dickinson in one of Ferris & Steele's envelopes and that is all there is to the game. The remaining details I must keep in reserve for a few minutes. As to the woman, you have given me an accurate description of her.

"From what you tell me, I judge that she must very closely resemble that person now entering the store."

He pointed to a beautiful and richly dressed woman, who was just coming in from the street.

She had flashing black eyes, an olive-tinted oval face, of the Spanish type.

"By the eternal heavens!" exclaimed Ferris, but in a guarded tone, for Nick's hand had been laid upon him. "It is the woman herself!"

"So I supposed," said the detective. "Let us see what she will do."

She came smilingly up to the counter, and greeted Ferris pleasantly.

She simply glanced at Mr. and Mrs. Dickinson. It was evident that she did not know them.

"Well, sir," she said to Ferris, "have you anything pretty to show me today?"

"I will show you the inside of a prison, you thief!" exclaimed Ferris.

The woman paled till her face was ghastly. By a supreme effort she recovered something like command of herself and demanded "the reason for this insult."

It was given her in a very few words, and she had the unhappiness of making the acquaintance of "her husband," Mr. George Dickinson.

She was got into the private office as quickly and as quietly as possible, and there an explanation was demanded of her.

She refused to speak.

"I will refer you to my lawyer," she said. "He will clear me of this infamous charge."

It was all a bluff, of course. The woman knew that she had no defense.

But she tried one shrewd trick. She denied that she had ever pretended to be Mrs. Dickinson, and declared that it was all a case of mistaken identity.

"Call in our spotter and Richard," said Steele. "They both know her."

The spotter came, but not Richard. It appeared that the young man had left the store.

"That is by my arrangement," said Nick. "I know where he has gone, and why. If you will come with me, Mr. Ferris, and Mr. Steele, we will join Richard, and clear up the remainder of the case."

The woman was put in charge of an officer, and Ferris and Steele accompanied Nick.

They took a carriage and were driven rapidly uptown.

Just above Madison Square they turned out of Broadway into one of the side streets leading eastward.

They stopped before a handsome apartment house, and all alighted.

A young man who was standing on the steps approached Nick, at a signal from the detective.

"Has Mr. Steele arrived?" asked Nick.

"Yes," replied the other. "He is inside."

"This is one of my assistants," said the detective. "He is familiarly known as Patsy. He came up here with Richard to assist in the investigation."

"I think you might have told me about this," muttered Steele.

They entered the house and ascended to the third floor.

Nick opened the door of a suite, and they entered.

They passed into a parlor, and then into a dressing room.

At the farther end, before a mirror, stood a man with white hair.

He was in the act of adjusting a great false beard, also perfectly white.

At the sound of their steps he turned, revealing the face of Richard Steele.

An exclamation of rage escaped him, and in an instant there was a revolver in his hand.

But Nick had him by the wrist, and the weapon was wrested from his grasp. Then Nick handcuffed him; after which proceeding the detective opened a handbag on the dressing table, and produced most of the missing jewels, including the piece said to be worth forty thousand dollars.

"Richard!" gasped his uncle. "How do you account for this?"

"Easily enough," said the young man, with a sneer on his white lips. "It results from my poverty and your wealth. I was of your own blood. You kept me poor. You gave me hard work and small pay. Well, this is the result of your investment. I am a thief; your name is disgraced. I have no more to say."

"These are the woman's rooms," said Nick. "You see that such a woman requires money, and there are, unfortunately, men who are weak enough to steal it, as the price of what is called love."

"But how did you track her?" exclaimed Ferris in amazement. "I'm all at sea, Mr. Carter."

"Why, it was easy enough. The crime was evidently an 'inside job.' The recklessness with which this last theft was made proved to me that the woman knew of your determination not to make an arrest.

"It was clearly the last desperate play in the game. So much being learned, it was only necessary to get at that little business of the checks.

"The result pointed directly to your cashier — to Richard. Nobody in Mr. Dickinson's employ, and nobody else in your employ, had the requisite information.

"Richard had it easily in his power to extract the checks from the letters. He was at liberty to open the firm's mail.

"It remained, then, to track the woman. I did it by means of the boy, who, you remember, appeared in the case as the messenger with the cash.

"I visited your store early this afternoon in disguise, and secured a description of the boy. It happened to answer very closely to a youth who was recently discharged from the employ of the district messenger company on suspicion of dishonesty.

"I learned that it was the same boy. He was employed in the nearest office to your store, and used to answer your call sometimes.

"That was how Richard came to know him.

"Well, I found the boy, and broke his nerve. He confessed to having acted as messenger between Richard and this woman, whose name is Fanny Legrand.

"I made him take a message to her in Richard's name, asking her to appear at the store at five o'clock, in the character of Mrs. Dickinson.

"She did so. Of course, when Richard saw what took place he had no other recourse than flight. I knew that he would come here in order to get the diamonds.

"My young man, Patsy, followed him, and here he is.

"And now, Mr. Steele, what shall we do with him?"

"Prosecute!" said the withered old man, compressing his lips. "I have no sympathy with thieves."

"Nor I, either," said Nick; "and that reminds me, Mr. Ferris, to ask you, again, what is the price of this diamond necklace?"

Ferris screwed up one side of his face, and then the other.

"Considering the circumstances," he said, "we'll let you have it for twenty-nine thousand dollars."

"A fair price," responded the detective; "but I don't want the necklace at that money. I prefer my regular fee in cash."

THE LENTON CROFT ROBBERIES

by ARTHUR MORRISON

The only contemporary imitator of Sherlock Holmes to sur-vive the fickle years is MARTIN HEWITT, *who was born in the Holmesian period. Of the twenty-five* HEWITT *tales (including six never published in the United States) "The Lenton Croft Robberies" and "The Case of the Dixon Torpedo" are the best.*

At the head of the first flight of a dingy staircase leading up from an ever-open portal in a street by the Strand stood a door, the dusty ground-glass upper panel of which carried in its centre the single word "Hewitt," while at its right-hand lower corner, in smaller letters, "Clerk's Office" appeared. On a morning when the clerks in the ground-floor offices had barely hung up their hats, a short, well-dressed young man, wearing spectacles, hastening to open the dusty door, ran into the arms of another man who suddenly issued from it.

"I beg pardon," the first said. "Is this Hewitt's Detective Agency Office?"

"Yes, I believe you will find it so," the other replied. He was a stoutish, clean-shaven man, of middle height, and of a cheerful, round countenance. "You'd better speak to the clerk."

In the little outer office the visitor was met by a sharp lad with inky fingers, who presented him with a pen and a printed slip. The printed slip having been filled with the visitor's name and present business, and conveyed through an inner door, the lad reappeared with an invitation to the private office. There, behind a writing table, sat the stoutish man himself, who had only just advised an appeal to the clerk.

"Good-morning, Mr. Lloyd — Mr. Vernon Lloyd," he said affably, looking again at the slip. "You'll excuse my care to start even with my visitors — I must, you know. You come from Sir James Norris, I see."

"Yes; I am his secretary. I have only to ask you to go straight to Lenton Croft at once, if you can, on very important business. Sir James would have wired, but had not your precise address. Can you go by the next train? Eleven-thirty is the first available from Paddington."

"Quite possibly. Do you know anything of the business?"

"It is a case of a robbery in the house, or rather, I fancy, of several robberies. Jewelry has been stolen from rooms occupied by visitors to the Croft. The first case occurred some months ago — nearly a year ago, in fact. Last night there was another. But I think you had better get the details on the spot. Sir James has told me to telegraph if you are coming, so that he may meet you himself at the station; and I must hurry, as his drive to the station will be rather a long one. Then I take it you will go, Mr. Hewitt? Twyford is the station."

"Yes, I shall come, and by the 11.30. Are you going by that train yourself?"

"No, I have several things to attend to now I am in town. Good-morning; I shall wire at once."

Mr. Martin Hewitt locked the drawer of his table and sent his clerk for a cab.

At Twyford Station Sir James Norris was waiting with a dogcart. Sir James was a tall, florid man of fifty or thereabout, known away from home as something of a county historian, and nearer his own parts as a great supporter of the hunt, and a gentleman much troubled with poachers. As soon as he and Hewitt had found one another the baronet hurried the detective into his dogcart. "We've something over seven miles to drive," he said, "and I can tell you all about this wretched business as we go. That is why I came for you myself, and alone."

Hewitt nodded.

"I have sent for you, as Lloyd probably told you, because of a robbery at my place last evening. It appears, as far as I can guess, to be one of three by the same hand, or by the same gang. Late yesterday afternoon ——— "

"Pardon me, Sir James," Hewitt interrupted, "but I think I must ask you to begin at the first robbery and tell me the whole tale in proper order. It makes things clearer, and sets them in their proper shape."

"Very well! Eleven months ago, or thereabout, I had rather a large party of visitors, and among them Colonel Heath and Mrs. Heath — the lady being a relative of my own late wife. Colonel Heath has not been long retired, you know — used to be political resident in an Indian native state. Mrs. Heath had rather a good stock of jewelry of one sort and another, about the most valuable piece being a bracelet set with a particularly fine pearl — quite an exceptional pearl, in fact — that had been one of a heap of presents from the maharajah of his state when Heath left India.

"It was a very noticeable bracelet, the gold setting being a mere feather-weight piece of native filigree work — almost too fragile to trust on the wrist — and the pearl being, as I have said, of a size and quality not often seen. Well, Heath and his wife arrived late one evening, and after lunch the following day, most of the men being off by themselves, — shooting, I think, — my daughter, my sister (who is very often down here), and Mrs. Heath took it into their heads to go walking — fern hunting, and so on. My sister was rather long dressing, and, while they waited, my daughter went into Mrs. Heath's room, where Mrs. Heath turned over all her treasures to show her, as women do, you know. When my sister was at last ready, they came straight away, leaving the things littering about the room rather than stay longer to pack them up. The bracelet, with other things, was on the dressing table then."

"One moment. As to the door?"

"They locked it. As they came away my daughter suggested turning the key, as we had one or two new servants about."

"And the window?"

"That they left open, as I was going to tell you. Well, they went on their walk and came back, with Lloyd (whom they had met somewhere) carrying their ferns for them. It was dusk and almost dinner time. Mrs. Heath went straight to her room, and — the bracelet was gone."

"Was the room disturbed?"

"Not a bit. Everything was precisely where it had been left, ex-

cept the bracelet. The door hadn't been tampered with, but of course
the window was open, as I have told you."

"You called the police, of course?"

"Yes, and had a man from Scotland Yard down in the morning.
He seemed a pretty smart fellow, and the first thing he noticed on
the dressing table, within an inch or two of where the bracelet had
been, was a match, which had been lit and thrown down. Now
nobody about the house had had occasion to use a match in that
room that day, and, if they had, certainly wouldn't have thrown it
on the cover of the dressing table. So that, presuming the thief to
have used that match, the robbery must have been committed when
the room was getting dark — immediately before Mrs. Heath returned, in fact. The thief had evidently struck the match, passed it
hurriedly over the various trinkets lying about, and taken the most
valuable."

"Nothing else was even moved?"

"Nothing at all. Then the thief must have escaped by the window, although it was not quite clear how. The walking party approached the house with a full view of the window, but saw nothing, although the robbery must have been actually taking place a
moment or two before they turned up.

"There was no water pipe within any practicable distance of the
window, but a ladder usually kept in the stable yard was found
lying along the edge of the lawn. The gardener explained, however, that he had put the ladder there after using it himself early
in the afternoon."

"Of course it might easily have been used again after that and
put back."

"Just what the Scotland Yard man said. He was pretty sharp,
too, on the gardener, but very soon decided that he knew nothing
of it. No stranger had been seen in the neighborhood, nor had
passed the lodge gates. Besides, as the detective said, it scarcely
seemed the work of a stranger. A stranger could scarcely have
known enough to go straight to the room where a lady — only
arrived the day before — had left a valuable jewel, and away again
without being seen. So all the people about the house were suspected in turn. The servants offered, in a body, to have their boxes
searched, and this was done; everything was turned over, from

the butler's to the new kitchen maid's. I don't know that I should have had this carried quite so far if I had been the loser myself, but it was my guest, and I was in such a horrible position. Well, there's little more to be said about that, unfortunately. Nothing came of it all, and the thing's as great a mystery now as ever. I believe the Scotland Yard man got as far as suspecting *me* before he gave it up altogether, but give it up he did in the end. I think that's all I know about the first robbery. Is it clear?"

"Oh, yes; I shall probably want to ask a few questions when I have seen the place, but they can wait. What next?"

"Well," Sir James pursued, "the next was a very trumpery affair, that I should have forgotten all about, probably, if it hadn't been for one circumstance. Even now I hardly think it could have been the work of the same hand. Four months or thereabout after Mrs. Heath's disaster — in February of this year, in fact — Mrs. Armitage, a young widow, who had been a schoolfellow of my daughter's, stayed with us for a week or so. The girls don't trouble about the London season, you know, and I have no town house, so they were glad to have their old friend here for a little in the dull time. Mrs. Armitage is a very active young lady, and was scarcely in the house half an hour before she arranged a drive in a pony cart with Eva — my daughter — to look up old people in the village that she used to know before she was married. So they set off in the afternoon, and made such a round of it that they were late for dinner. Mrs. Armitage had a small plain gold brooch — not at all valuable, you know; two or three pounds, I suppose — which she used to pin up a cloak or anything of that sort. Before she went out she stuck this in the pincushion on her dressing table, and left a ring — rather a good one, I believe — lying close by."

"This," asked Hewitt, "was not in the room that Mrs. Heath had occupied, I take it?"

"No; this was in another part of the building. Well, the brooch went — taken, evidently, by some one in a deuce of a hurry, for, when Mrs. Armitage got back to her room, there was the pincushion with a little tear in it, where the brooch had been simply snatched off. But the curious thing was that the ring — worth a dozen of the brooch — was left where it had been put. Mrs. Armitage didn't remember whether or not she had locked the door herself, although she found it locked when she returned; but my niece, who was indoors all the time, went and tried it once — because she remembered that a gas fitter was at work on the landing near by — and found it safely locked. The gas fitter, whom we didn't know at the time, but who since seems to be quite an honest fellow, was ready to swear that nobody but my niece had been to the door while he was in sight of it — which was almost all the time. As to the window, the sash line had broken that very morning, and Mrs. Armitage had propped open the bottom half about eight or ten inches with a brush; and, when she returned, that brush, sash, and all were exactly as she had left them. Now I scarcely need tell *you* what an awkward job it must have been for anybody to get noiselessly in at that unsupported window; and how unlikely he would have been to replace it, with the brush, exactly as he found it."

"Just so. I suppose the brooch was really gone? I mean, there was no chance of Mrs. Armitage having mislaid it?"

"Oh, none at all! There was a most careful search."

"Then, as to getting in at the window, would it have been easy?"

"Well, yes," Sir James replied; "yes, perhaps it would. It is a first-floor window, and it looks over the roof and skylight of the billiard room. I built the billiard room myself — built it out from a smoking room just at this corner. It would be easy enough to get at the window from the billiard room roof. But, then," he added, "that couldn't have been the way. Somebody or other was in the billiard room the whole time, and nobody could have got over the roof (which is nearly all skylight) without being seen and heard. I was there myself for an hour or two, taking a little practice."

"Well, was anything done?"

"Strict enquiry was made among the servants, of course, but nothing came of it. It was such a small matter that Mrs. Armitage wouldn't hear of my calling in the police or anything of that sort, although I felt pretty certain that there must be a dishonest servant about somewhere. A servant might take a plain brooch, you know, who would feel afraid of a valuable ring, the loss of which would be made a greater matter of."

"Well, yes, perhaps so, in the case of an inexperienced thief, who also would be likely to snatch up whatever she took in a

hurry. But I'm doubtful. What made you connect these two robberies together?"

"Nothing whatever — for some months. They seemed quite of a
different sort. But scarcely more than a month ago I met Mrs.
Armitage at Brighton, and we talked, among other things, of the
previous robbery — that of Mrs. Heath's bracelet. I described the
circumstances pretty minutely, and, when I mentioned the match
found on the table, she said: 'How strange! Why, *my* thief left a
match on the dressing table when he took my poor little brooch!'"

Hewitt nodded. "Yes," he said. "A spent match, of course?"

"Yes, of course, a spent match. She noticed it lying close by the
pincushion, but threw it away without mentioning the circumstance. Still, it seemed rather curious to me that a match should
be lit and dropped, in each case, on the dressing-table cover an inch
from where the article was taken. I mentioned it to Lloyd when I got
back, and he agreed that it seemed significant."

"Scarcely," said Hewitt, shaking his head. "Scarcely, so far, to
be called significant, although worth following up. Everybody uses
matches in the dark, you know."

"Well, at any rate, the coincidence appealed to me so far that it
struck me it might be worth while to describe the brooch to the
police in order that they could trace it if it had been pawned. They
had tried that, of course, over the bracelet without any result, but
I fancied the shot might be worth making, and might possibly lead
us on the track of the more serious robbery."

"Quite so. It was the right thing to do. Well?"

"Well, they found it. A woman had pawned it in London — at
a shop in Chelsea. But that was some time before, and the pawn-
broker had clean forgotten all about the woman's appearance. The
name and address she gave were false. So that was the end of that
business."

"Had any of your servants left you between the time the brooch
was lost and the date of the pawn ticket?"

"No."

"Were all your servants at home on the day the brooch was
pawned?"

"Oh, yes! I made that enquiry myself."

"Very good! What next?"

"Yesterday — and this is what made me send for you. My late wife's sister came here last Tuesday, and we gave her the room from which Mrs. Heath lost her bracelet. She had with her a very old-fashioned brooch, containing a miniature of her father, and set in front with three very fine brilliants and a few smaller stones. Here we are, though, at the Croft. I'll tell you the rest indoors."

Hewitt laid his hand on the baronet's arm. "Don't pull up, Sir James," he said. "Drive a little further. I should like to have a general idea of the whole case before we go in."

"Very good!" Sir James Norris straightened the horse's head again and went on. "Late yesterday afternoon, as my sister-in-law was changing her dress, she left her room for a moment to speak to my daughter in her room, almost adjoining. She was gone no more than three minutes, or five at most, but on her return the brooch, which had been left on the table, had gone. Now the window was shut fast, and had not been tampered with. Of course the door was open, but so was my daughter's, and anybody walking near must have been heard. But the strangest circumstance, and one that almost makes me wonder whether I have been awake to-day or not, was that there lay *a used match* on the very spot, as nearly as possible, where the brooch had been — and it was broad daylight!"

Hewitt rubbed his nose and looked thoughtfully before him. "Um — curious, certainly," he said. "Anything else?"

"Nothing more than you shall see for yourself. I have had the room locked and watched till you could examine it. My sister-in-law had heard of your name, and suggested that you should be called in; so, of course, I did exactly as she wanted. That she should have lost that brooch, of all things, in my house is most unfortunate; you see, there was some small difference about the thing between my late wife and her sister when their mother died and left it. It's almost worse than the Heaths' bracelet business, and altogether I'm not pleased with things, I can assure you. See what a position it is for me! Here are three ladies, in the space of one year, robbed one after another in this mysterious fashion in my house, and I can't find the thief! It's horrible! People will be afraid to come near the place. And I can do nothing!"

"Ah, well, we'll see. Perhaps we had better turn back now. By-the-bye, were you thinking of having any alterations or additions made to your house?"

"No. What makes you ask?"

"I think you might at least consider the question of painting and decorating, Sir James — or, say, putting up another coach house, or something. Because I should like to be (to the servants) the architect — or the builder, if you please — come to look round. You haven't told any of them about this business?"

"Not a word. Nobody knows but my relatives and Lloyd. I took every precaution myself, at once. As to your little disguise, be the architect by all means, and do as you please. If you can only find this thief and put an end to this horrible state of affairs, you'll do me the greatest service I've ever asked for — and as to your fee, I'll gladly make it whatever is usual, and three hundred in addition."

Martin Hewitt bowed. "You're very generous, Sir James, and you may be sure I'll do what I can. As a professional man, of course, a good fee always stimulates my interest, although this case of yours certainly seems interesting enough by itself."

"Most extraordinary! Don't you think so? Here are three persons, all ladies, all in my house, two even in the same room, each successively robbed of a piece of jewelry, each from a dressing table, and a used match left behind in every case. All in the most difficult — one would say impossible — circumstances for a thief, and yet there is no clue!"

"Well, we won't say that just yet, Sir James; we must see. And we must guard against any undue predisposition to consider the robberies in a lump. Here we are at the lodge gate again. Is that your gardener — the man who left the ladder by the lawn on the first occasion you spoke of?" Mr. Hewitt nodded in the direction of a man who was clipping a box border.

"Yes; will you ask him anything?"

"No, no; at any rate, not now. Remember the building alterations. I think, if there is no objection, I will look first at the room that the lady — Mrs. —— " Hewitt looked up enquiringly.

"My sister-in-law? Mrs. Cazenove. Oh, yes! you shall come to her room at once."

"Thank you. And I think Mrs. Cazenove had better be there."

They alighted, and a boy from the lodge led the horse and dog-cart away.

Mrs. Cazenove was a thin and faded, but quick and energetic, lady of middle age. She bent her head very slightly on learning Martin Hewitt's name, and said: "I must thank you, Mr. Hewitt, for your very prompt attention. I need scarcely say that any help you can afford in tracing the thief who has my property — whoever it may be — will make me most grateful. My room is quite ready for you to examine."

The room was on the second floor — the top floor at that part of the building. Some slight confusion of small articles of dress was observable in parts of the room.

"This, I take it," enquired Hewitt, "is exactly as it was at the time the brooch was missed?"

"Precisely," Mrs. Cazenove answered. "I have used another room, and put myself to some other inconveniences, to avoid any disturbance."

Hewitt stood before the dressing table. "Then this is the used match," he observed, "exactly where it was found?"

"Yes."

"Where was the brooch?"

"I should say almost on the very same spot. Certainly no more than a very few inches away."

Hewitt examined the match closely. "It is burned very little," he remarked. "It would appear to have gone out at once. Could you hear it struck?"

"I heard nothing whatever; absolutely nothing."

"If you will step into Miss Norris's room now for a moment," Hewitt suggested, "we will try an experiment. Tell me if you hear matches struck, and how many. Where is the match stand?"

The match stand proved to be empty, but matches were found in Miss Norris's room, and the test was made. Each striking could be heard distinctly, even with one of the doors pushed to.

"Both your own door and Miss Norris's were open, I understand; the window shut and fastened inside as it is now, and nothing but the brooch was disturbed?"

"Yes, that was so."

"Thank you, Mrs. Cazenove. I don't think I need trouble you any further just at present. I think, Sir James," Hewitt added, turning to the baronet, who was standing by the door — "I think we will see the other room and take a walk outside the house, if you please. I suppose, by-the-bye, that there is no getting at the matches left behind on the first and second occasions?"

"No," Sir James answered. "Certainly not here. The Scotland Yard man may have kept his."

The room that Mrs. Armitage had occupied presented no peculiar feature. A few feet below the window the roof of the billiard room was visible, consisting largely of skylight. Hewitt glanced casually about the walls, ascertained that the furniture and hangings had not been materially changed since the second robbery, and expressed his desire to see the windows from the outside. Before leaving the room, however, he wished to know the names of any persons who were known to have been about the house on the occasions of all three robberies.

"Just carry your mind back, Sir James," he said. "Begin with yourself, for instance. Where were you at these times?"

"When Mrs. Heath lost her bracelet, I was in Tagley Wood all the afternoon. When Mrs. Armitage was robbed, I believe I was somewhere about the place most of the time she was out. Yesterday I was down at the farm." Sir James's face broadened. "I don't know whether you call those suspicious movements," he added, and laughed.

"Not at all; I only asked you so that, remembering your own movements, you might the better recall those of the rest of the household. Was anybody, to your knowledge — *anybody,* mind — in the house on all three occasions?"

"Well, you know, it's quite impossible to answer for all the servants. You'll only get that by direct questioning — I can't possibly remember things of that sort. As to the family and visitors — why, you don't suspect any of them, do you?"

"I don't suspect a soul, Sir James," Hewitt answered, beaming genially, "not a soul. You see, I *can't* suspect people till I know something about where they were. It's quite possible there will be independent evidence enough as it is, but you must help me if you can. The visitors, now. Was there any visitor here each time — or even on the first and last occasions only?"

"No, not one. And my own sister, perhaps you will be pleased to know, was only there at the time of the first robbery."

"Just so! And your daughter, as I have gathered, was clearly absent from the spot each time — indeed, was in company with the party robbed. Your niece, now?"

"Why, hang it all, Mr. Hewitt, I can't talk of my niece as a suspected criminal! The poor girl's under my protection, and I really can't allow —— "

Hewitt raised his hand and shook his head deprecatingly.

"My dear sir, haven't I said that I don't suspect a soul? *Do* let me know how the people were distributed, as nearly as possible. Let me see. It was your niece, I think, who found that Mrs. Armitage's door was locked — this door, in fact — on the day she lost her brooch?"

"Yes, it was."

"Just so — at the time when Mrs. Armitage herself had forgotten whether she locked it or not. And yesterday — was she out then?"

"No, I think not. Indeed, she goes out very little — her health is usually bad. She was indoors, too, at the time of the Heath robbery, since you ask. But come, now, I don't like this. It's ridiculous to suppose that *she* knows anything of it."

"I don't suppose it, as I have said. I am only asking for information. That is all your resident family, I take it, and you know nothing of anybody else's movements — except, perhaps, Mr. Lloyd's?"

"Lloyd? Well, you know yourself that he was out with the ladies when the first robbery took place. As to the others, I don't remember. Yesterday he was probably in his room, writing. I think that acquits *him,* eh?" Sir James looked quizzically into the broad face of the affable detective, who smiled and replied:

"Oh, of course nobody can be in two places at once, else what would become of the *alibi* as an institution? But, as I have said, I am only setting my facts in order. Now, you see, we get down to the servants — unless some stranger is the party wanted. Shall we go outside now?"

Lenton Croft was a large, desultory sort of house, nowhere more than three floors high, and mostly only two. It had been added to bit by bit, till it zigzagged about its site, as Sir James Norris expressed it, "like a game of dominoes." Hewitt scrutinized its external features carefully as they strolled round, and stopped some little while before the windows of the two bedrooms he had just seen from the inside. Presently they approached the stables and coach house, where a groom was washing the wheels of the dog-cart.

"Do you mind my smoking?" Hewitt asked Sir James. "Perhaps you will take a cigar yourself — they are not so bad, I think. I will ask your man for a light."

Sir James felt for his own match box, but Hewitt had gone, and was lighting his cigar with a match from a box handed him by the groom. A smart little terrier was trotting about by the coach house, and Hewitt stooped to rub its head. Then he made some observation about the dog which enlisted the groom's interest, and was soon absorbed in a chat with the man. Sir James, waiting a little way off, tapped the stones rather impatiently with his foot, and presently moved away.

For full a quarter of an hour Hewitt chatted with the groom, and, when at last he came away and overtook Sir James, that gentleman was about re-entering the house.

"I beg your pardon, Sir James," Hewitt said, "for leaving you in that unceremonious fashion to talk to your groom, but a dog, Sir James, — a good dog, — will draw me anywhere."

"Oh!" replied Sir James shortly.

"There is one other thing," Hewitt went on, disregarding the other's curtness, "that I should like to know: There are two windows directly below that of the room occupied yesterday by Mrs. Cazenove — one on each floor. What rooms do they light?"

"That on the ground floor is the morning room; the other is Mr. Lloyd's — my secretary. A sort of study or sitting room."

"Now you will see at once, Sir James," Hewitt pursued, with an affable determination to win the baronet back to good humor — "you will see at once that, if a ladder had been used in Mrs. Heath's case, anybody looking from either of these rooms would have seen it."

"Of course! The Scotland Yard man questioned everybody as to that, but nobody seemed to have been in either of the rooms when the thing occurred; at any rate, nobody saw anything."

"Still, I think I should like to look out of those windows myself; it will, at least, give me an idea of what *was* in view and what was not, if anybody had been there."

Sir James Norris led the way to the morning room. As they

reached the door a young lady, carrying a book and walking very languidly, came out. Hewitt stepped aside to let her pass, and afterward said interrogatively: "Miss Norris, your daughter, Sir John?"

"No, my niece. Do you want to ask her anything? Dora, my dear," Sir James added, following her in the corridor, "this is Mr. Hewitt, who is investigating these wretched robberies for me. I think he would like to hear if you remember anything happening at any of the three times."

The lady bowed slightly, and said in a plaintive drawl: "I, uncle? Really, I don't remember anything; nothing at all."

"You found Mrs. Armitage's door locked, I believe," asked Hewitt, "when you tried it, on the afternoon when she lost her brooch?"

"Oh, yes; I believe it was locked. Yes, it was."

"Had the key been left in?"

"The key? Oh, no! I think not; no."

"Do you remember anything out of the common happening — anything whatever, no matter how trivial — on the day Mrs. Heath lost her bracelet?"

"No, really, I don't. I can't remember at all."

"Nor yesterday?"

"No, nothing. I don't remember anything."

"Thank you," said Hewitt hastily; "thank you. Now the morning room, Sir James."

In the morning room Hewitt stayed but a few seconds, doing little more than casually glance out of the windows. In the room above he took a little longer time. It was a comfortable room, but with rather effeminate indications about its contents. Little pieces of draped silkwork hung about the furniture, and Japanese silk fans decorated the mantelpiece. Near the window was a cage containing a gray parrot, and the writing table was decorated with two vases of flowers.

"Lloyd makes himself pretty comfortable, eh?" Sir James observed. "But it isn't likely anybody would be here while he was out, at the time that bracelet went."

"No," replied Hewitt meditatively. "No, I suppose not."

He stared thoughtfully out of the window, and then, still deep in thought, rattled at the wires of the cage with a quill toothpick and played a moment with the parrot. Then, looking up at the window again, he said: "That is Mr. Lloyd, isn't it, coming back in a fly?"

"Yes, I think so. Is there anything else you would care to see here?"

"No, thank you," Hewitt replied; "I don't think there is."

They went down to the smoking room, and Sir James went away to speak to his secretary. When he returned, Hewitt said quietly: "I think, Sir James — I *think* that I shall be able to give you your thief presently."

"What! Have you a clue? Who do you think? I began to believe you were hopelessly stumped."

"Well, yes. I have rather a good clue, although I can't tell you much about it just yet. But it is so good a clue that I should like to know now whether you are determined to prosecute when you have the criminal."

"Why, bless me, of course," Sir James replied with surprise. "It doesn't rest with me, you know — the property belongs to my friends. And even if *they* were disposed to let the thing slide, I shouldn't allow it — I couldn't, after they had been robbed in my house."

"Of course, of course! Then, if I can, I should like to send a message to Twyford by somebody perfectly trustworthy — not a servant. Could anybody go?"

"Well, there's Lloyd, although he's only just back from his journey. But, if it's important, he'll go."

"It is important. The fact is we must have a policeman or two here this evening, and I'd like Mr. Lloyd to fetch them without telling anybody else."

Sir James rang, and, in response to his message, Mr. Lloyd appeared. While Sir James gave his secretary his instructions, Hewitt strolled to the door of the smoking room, and intercepted the latter as he came out.

"I'm sorry to give you this trouble, Mr. Lloyd," he said, "but I must stay here myself for a little, and somebody who can be trusted must go. Will you just bring back a police constable with you? or rather two — two would be better. That is all that is wanted. You won't let the servants know, will you? Of course there will be a female searcher at the Twyford police station? Ah — of course. Well, you needn't bring her, you know. That sort of thing is done at the station." And, chatting thus confidentially, Martin Hewitt saw him off.

When Hewitt returned to the smoking room, Sir James said suddenly: "Why, bless my soul, Mr. Hewitt, we haven't fed you! I'm awfully sorry. We came in rather late for lunch, you know, and this business has bothered me so I clean forgot everything else. There's no dinner till seven, so you'd better let me give you something now. I'm really sorry. Come along."

"Thank you, Sir James," Hewitt replied; "I won't take much. A few biscuits, perhaps, or something of that sort. And, by-the-bye, if you don't mind, I rather think I should like to take it alone. The fact is I want to go over this case thoroughly by myself. Can you put me in a room?"

"Any room you like. Where will you go? The dining room's rather large, but there's my study, that's pretty snug, or —— "

"Perhaps I can go into Mr. Lloyd's room for half an hour or so; I don't think he'll mind, and it's pretty comfortable."

"Certainly, if you'd like. I'll tell them to send you whatever they've got."

"Thank you very much. Perhaps they'll also send me a lump of sugar and a walnut; it's — it's just a little fad of mine."

"A — what? A lump of sugar and a walnut?" Sir James stopped for a moment, with his hand on the bell rope. "Oh, certainly, if you'd like it; certainly," he added, and stared after this detective of curious tastes as he left the room.

When the vehicle bringing back the secretary and the policemen drew up on the drive, Martin Hewitt left the room on the first floor and proceeded down stairs. On the landing he met Sir James Norris and Mrs. Cazenove, who stared with astonishment on perceiving that the detective carried in his hand the parrot cage.

"I think our business is about brought to a head now," Hewitt remarked on the stairs. "Here are the police officers from Twyford." The men were standing in the hall with Mr. Lloyd, who, on catching sight of the cage in Hewitt's hand, paled suddenly.

"This is the person who will be charged, I think," Hewitt pursued, addressing the officers, and indicating Lloyd with his finger.

"What, Lloyd?" gasped Sir James, aghast. "No — not Lloyd — nonsense!"

"He doesn't seem to think it nonsense himself, does he?" Hewitt placidly observed. Lloyd had sunk on a chair, and, gray of face, was staring blindly at the man he had run against at the office door that morning. His lips moved in spasms, but there was no sound. The wilted flower fell from his buttonhole to the floor, but he did not move.

"This is his accomplice," Hewitt went on, placing the parrot and cage on the hall table, "though I doubt whether there will be any use in charging *him*. Eh, Polly?"

The parrot put his head aside and chuckled. "Hullo, Polly!" it quietly gurgled. "Come along!"

Sir James Norris was hopelessly bewildered. "Lloyd — Lloyd," he said, under his breath, "Lloyd — and that!"

"This was his little messenger, his useful Mercury," Hewitt explained, tapping the cage complacently; "in fact, the actual lifter. Hold him up!"

The last remark referred to the wretched Lloyd, who had fallen forward with something between a sob and a loud sigh. The policemen took him by the arms and propped him in his chair.

"System?" said Hewitt, with a shrug of the shoulders, an hour or two after in Sir James's study. "I can't say I have a system. I call it nothing but common sense and a sharp pair of eyes. Nobody using these could help taking the right road in this case. I began at the match, just as the Scotland Yard man did, but I had the advantage of taking a line through three cases. To begin with, it was plain that that match, being left there in daylight, in Mrs. Cazenove's room, could not have been used to light the table top, in the full glare of the window; therefore it had been used for some other purpose — *what* purpose I could not, at the moment, guess. Habitual thieves, you know, often have curious superstitions, and some will never take anything without leaving something behind — a pebble or a piece of coal, or something like that — in the premises they have been robbing. It seemed at first extremely likely that this was a case of that kind. The match had clearly been *brought in* - -because, when I asked for matches, there were none in the stand, not even an empty box, and the room had not been disturbed. Also the match probably had not been struck there, nothing having been heard, although, of course, a mistake in this matter was just possible. This match, then, it was fair to assume, had been lit somewhere else and blown out immediately — I remarked at the time that it was very little burned. Plainly it could not have been treated thus for nothing, and the only possible object would have been to prevent it igniting accidentally. Following on this, it became obvious that the match was used, for whatever purpose, not *as* a match, but merely as a convenient splinter of wood.

"So far so good. But on examining the match very closely I observed, as you can see for yourself, certain rather sharp indentations in the wood. They are very small, you see, and scarcely visible, except upon narrow inspection; but there they are, and their positions are regular. See — there are two on each side, each opposite the corresponding mark of the other pair. The match, in fact, would seem to have been gripped in some fairly sharp instrument, holding it at two points above and two below — an instrument, as it may at once strike you, not unlike the beak of a bird.

"Now here was an idea. What living creature but a bird could possibly have entered Mrs. Heath's window without a ladder — supposing no ladder to have been used — or could have got into Mrs. Armitage's window without lifting the sash higher than the eight or ten inches it was already open? Plainly, nothing. Further, it is significant that only *one* article was stolen at a time, although others were about. A human being could have carried any reasonable number, but a bird could only take one at a time. But why should a bird carry a match in its beak? Certainly it must have been trained to do that for a purpose, and a little consideration made that purpose pretty clear. A noisy, chattering bird would probably betray itself at once. Therefore it must be trained to keep quiet both while going for and coming away with its plunder. What readier or more probably effectual way than, while teaching it to carry without dropping, to teach it also to keep quiet while carrying? The one thing would practically cover the other.

"I thought at once, of course, of a jackdaw or a magpie — these birds' thievish reputations made the guess natural. But the marks on the match were much too wide apart to have been made by the beak of either. I conjectured, therefore, that it must be a raven. So that, when we arrived near the coach house, I seized the opportunity of a little chat with your groom on the subject of dogs and pets in general, and ascertained that there was no tame raven in the place. I also, incidentally, by getting a light from the coach house box of matches, ascertained that the match found was of the sort generally used about the establishment — the large, thick, red-topped English match. But I further found that Mr. Lloyd had a parrot which was a most intelligent pet, and had been trained into comparative quietness — for a parrot. Also, I learned that more than once the groom had met Mr. Lloyd carrying his parrot under his coat, it having, as its owner explained, learned the trick of opening its cage door and escaping.

"I said nothing, of course, to you of all this, because I had as yet nothing but a train of argument and no results. I got to Lloyd's room as soon as possible. My chief object in going there was achieved when I played with the parrot, and induced it to bite a quill toothpick.

"When you left me in the smoking room, I compared the quill and the match very carefully, and found that the marks corresponded exactly. After this I felt very little doubt indeed. The fact of Lloyd having met the ladies walking before dark on the day of the first robbery proved nothing, because, since it was clear that the match had *not* been used to procure a light, the robbery might as easily have taken place in daylight as not — must have so taken place, in fact, if my conjectures were right. That they were right I felt no doubt. There could be no other explanation.

"When Mrs. Heath left her window open and her door shut, anybody climbing upon the open sash of Lloyd's high window could have put the bird upon the sill above. The match placed in the bird's beak for the purpose I have indicated, and struck first, in case by accident it should ignite by rubbing against something and startle the bird — this match would, of course, be dropped just where the object to be removed was taken up; as you know, in every case the match was found almost upon the spot where the missing article had been left — scarcely a likely triple coincidence had the match been used by a human thief. This would have been done as soon after the ladies had left as possible, and there would then have been plenty of time for Lloyd to hurry out and meet them before dark — especially plenty of time to meet them *coming back*, as they must have been, since they were carrying their ferns. The match was an article well-chosen for its purpose, as being a not altogether unlikely thing to find on a dressing table, and, if noticed, likely to lead to the wrong conclusions adopted by the official detective.

"In Mrs. Armitage's case the taking of an inferior brooch and the leaving of a more valuable ring pointed clearly to the operator being a fool or unable to distinguish values, and certainly, from other indications, the thief seemed no fool. The door was locked, and the gas fitter, so to speak, on guard, and the window was only eight or ten inches open and propped with a brush. A human thief entering the window would have disturbed this arrangement, and would scarcely risk discovery by attempting to replace it, especially a thief in so great a hurry as to snatch the brooch up without unfastening the pin. The bird could pass through the opening as it was, and *would have* to tear the pincushion to pull the brooch off, probably holding the cushion down with its claw the while.

"Now in yesterday's case we had an alteration of conditions. The window was shut and fastened, but the door was open — but only left for a few minutes, during which time no sound was heard either of coming or going. Was it not possible, then, that the thief was *already* in the room, in hiding, while Mrs. Cazenove was there, and seized its first opportunity on her temporary absence? The room is full of draperies, hangings, and what-not, allowing of plenty of concealment for a bird, and a bird could leave the place noiselessly and quickly. That the whole scheme was strange mattered not at all. Robberies presenting such unaccountable features must have been effected by strange means of one sort or another. There was no improbability — consider how many hundreds of examples of infinitely higher degrees of bird training are exhibited in the London streets every week for coppers.

"So that, on the whole, I felt pretty sure of my ground. But before taking any definite steps I resolved to see if Polly could not be persuaded to exhibit his accomplishments to an indulgent stranger. For that purpose I contrived to send Lloyd away again and have a quiet hour alone with his bird. A piece of sugar, as everybody knows, is a good parrot bribe; but a walnut, split in half, is a better — especially if the bird be used to it; so I got you to furnish me with both. Polly was shy at first, but I generally get along very well with pets, and a little perseverance soon led to a complete private performance for my benefit. Polly would take the match, mute as wax, jump on the table, pick up the brightest thing he could see, in a great hurry, leave the match behind, and scuttle away round the room; but at first wouldn't give up the plunder to *me*. It was enough. I also took the liberty, as you know, of a general look round, and discovered that little collection of brummagem rings and trinkets that you have just seen — used in Polly's education, no doubt. When we sent Lloyd away, it struck me that he might as well be usefully employed as not, so I got him to fetch the police, deluding him a little, I fear, by talking about the servants and a female searcher. There will be no trouble about evidence; he'll confess: of that I'm sure. I know the sort of man. But I doubt if you'll get Mrs. Cazenove's brooch back. You see, he has been to London to-day, and by this time the swag is probably broken up."

Sir James listened to Hewitt's explanation with many expressions of assent and some of surprise. When it was over, he smoked a few whiffs and then said: "But Mrs. Armitage's brooch was pawned, and by a woman."

"Exactly. I expect our friend Lloyd was rather disgusted at his small luck — probably gave the brooch to some female connection in London, and she realized on it. Such persons don't always trouble to give a correct address."

The two smoked in silence for a few minutes, and then Hewitt continued: "I don't expect our friend has had an easy job altogether with that bird. His successes at most have only been three, and I suspect he had many failures and not a few anxious moments that we know nothing of. I should judge as much merely from what the groom told me of frequently meeting Lloyd with his parrot. But the plan was not a bad one — not at all. Even if the bird had been caught in the act, it would only have been 'That mischievous parrot!' you see. And his master would only have been looking for him."

THE S.S.

by M. P. SHIEL

Words to describe this story? "Remarkable"? Well, yes, it's
remarkable. Also fantastic, epic, literary, mystical, scientific,
and modern. As a concept, it will take your breath away. As
a fantasy, it can only be described as weirdly delightful. As a
detective story, it offers — after almost fifty years! — still the
most extraordinary motive for mass murder ever conceived.
And yet this is a tale you probably never heard of about a
character you won't recognize who nevertheless stands, grandly
alone, a gigantic sport in literature. Meet PRINCE ZALESKI, *who*
has appeared in only three stories.

To say that there are epidemics of suicide is to give expression to
what is now a mere commonplace of knowledge. And so far are
they from being of rare occurrence, that it has even been affirmed
that every sensational case of *felo de se* published in the newspapers
is sure to be followed by some others more obscure: their frequency,
indeed, is out of all proportion with the *extent* of each particular
outbreak. Sometimes, however, especially in villages and small town-
ships, the wildfire madness becomes an all-involving passion, emu-
lating in its fury the great plagues of history. At such times it is as
if the optic nerve of the mind throughout whole communities became distorted, till in the noseless and black-robed Reaper it discerned an angel of very loveliness.

It was during the ever-memorable outbreak of this obscure mal-
ady in the year 1875 that I ventured to break in on the calm of that
deep silence in which, as in a mantle, my friend Prince Zaleski had
wrapped himself. I wrote, in fact, to ask him what he thought of

the epidemic. His answer was in the laconic words addressed to the Master in the house of woe at Bethany:

"Come and see."

To this, however, he added in postscript: "But what epidemic?"

I had momentarily lost sight of the fact that Zaleski had so absolutely cut himself off from the world, that he was not in the least likely to know anything even of the appalling series of events to which I had referred. And yet it is no exaggeration to say that those events had thrown the greater part of Europe into a state of consternation, and even confusion. In London, Manchester, Paris, and Berlin, especially, the excitement was intense. On the Sunday preceding the writing of my note to Zaleski, I was present at a monster demonstration held in Hyde Park, in which the Government was held up on all hands to the popular derision and censure — for it will be remembered that to many minds the mysterious accompaniments of some of the deaths daily occurring conveyed a still darker significance than that implied in mere self-destruction, and seemed to point to a succession of purposeless and hideous murders. The demagogues, I must say, spoke with some wildness and incoherence. Many laid the blame at the door of the police, and urged that things would be different were *they* but placed under municipal, instead of under imperial, control. A thousand panaceas were invented, a thousand aimless censures passed. But the people listened with vacant ear. Never have I seen the populace so agitated, and yet so subdued, as with the sense of some impending doom. The glittering eye betrayed the excitement, the pallor of the cheek the doubt, the haunting *fear*. None felt himself quite safe; men recognised shuddering the grin of death in the air. As for myself, I confess to being pervaded with a nameless and numbing awe during all those weeks. And this feeling appeared to be general in the land. The journals had but one topic; the party organs threw politics to the winds. I heard that on the Stock Exchange, as in the Paris Bourse, business decreased to a minimum. In Parliament the work of law threshing practically ceased, and the time of Ministers was nightly spent in answering volumes of angry "Questions," and in facing motion after motion for the "adjournment" of the House.

It was in the midst of all this commotion that I received Prince Zaleski's brief "Come and see." I was flattered and pleased: flattered, because I suspected that to me alone, of all men, would such an invitation, coming from him, be addressed; and pleased, because many a time in the midst of the noisy city street and the garish, dusty world, had the thought of that vast mansion, that dim and silent chamber, flooded my mind with a drowsy sense of the romantic, till, from very excess of melancholy sweetness in the picture, I was fain to close my eyes. I avow that that lonesome room — gloomy in its lunar bath of soft perfumed light — shrouded in the sullen voluptuousness of plushy, narcotic-breathing draperies — pervaded by the mysterious spirit of its brooding occupant — grew more and more on my fantasy, till the remembrance had for me all the cool refreshment shed by a midsummer-night's dream in the dewy deeps of some Perrhœbian grove of cornel and lotos and ruby stars of the asphodel. It was, therefore, in all haste that I set out to share for a time in the solitude of my friend.

Zaleski's reception of me was most cordial; immediately on my entrance into his sanctum he broke into a perfect torrent of wild, enthusiastic words, telling me, with a kind of rapture, that he was just then laboriously engaged in co-ordinating to one of the calculi certain new properties he had discovered in the parabola, adding with infinite gusto his "firm" belief that the ancient Assyrians were acquainted with all our modern notions respecting the parabola itself, the projection of bodies in general, and of the heavenly bodies in particular; and must, moreover, from certain inferences of his own in connection with the Winged Circle, have been conversant with the fact that light is not an ether, but only the vibration of an ether. He then galloped on to suggest that I should at once take part with him in his investigations, and commented on the timeliness of my visit. I, on my part, was anxious for his opinion on other and far weightier matters than the concerns of the Assyrians, and intimated as much to him. But for two days he was firm in his tacit refusal to listen to my story; and, concluding that he was disinclined to undergo the agony of unrest with which he was always tormented by any mystery which momentarily baffled him, I was, of course, forced to hold my peace. On the third day, however, of his own accord he asked me to what epidemic I had referred. I then detailed to him some of the strange events which were agitating the mind of the outside world. From the very first he was interested:

later on that interest grew into a passion, a greedy soul-consuming quest after the truth, the intensity of which was such at last as to move me even to pity.

I may as well here restate the facts as I communicated them to Zaleski. The concatenation of incidents, it will be remembered, started with the extraordinary death of that eminent man of science, Professor Schleschinger, consulting laryngologist to the *Charité* Hospital in Berlin. The professor, a man of great age, was on the point of contracting his third marriage with the beautiful and accomplished daughter of the Herr Geheimrath Otto von Friedrich. The contemplated union, which was entirely one of those *mariages de convenance* so common in good society, sprang out of the professor's ardent desire to leave behind him a direct heir to his very considerable wealth. By his first two marriages, indeed, he had had large families, and was at this very time surrounded by quite an army of little grandchildren, from whom (all his direct descendants being dead) he might have been content to select his heir; but the old German prejudices in these matters are strong, and he still hoped to be represented on his decease by a son of his own. To this whim the charming Ottilie was marked by her parents as the victim. The wedding, however, had been postponed owing to a slight illness of the veteran scientist, and just as he was on the point of final recovery from it, death intervened to prevent altogether the execution of his design. Never did death of man create a profounder sensation; *never was death of man followed by consequences more terrible*. The *Residenz* of the scientist was a stately mansion near the University in the *Unter den Linden* boulevard, that is to say, in the most fashionable *Quartier* of Berlin. His bedroom from a considerable height looked out on a small back garden, and in this room he had been engaged in conversation with his colleague and medical attendant, Dr. Johann Hofmeier, to a late hour of the night. During all this time he seemed cheerful, and spoke quite lucidly on various topics. In particular, he exhibited to his colleague a curious strip of what looked like ancient papyrus, on which were traced certain grotesque and apparently meaningless figures. This, he said, he had found some days before on the bed of a poor woman in one of the horribly low quarters that surround Berlin, on whom he had had occasion to make a post-mortem examination. The woman had suffered from partial paralysis. She had a small young family, none of whom, however, could give any account of the slip, except one little girl, who declared that she had taken it "from her mother's mouth" after death. The slip was soiled, and had a fragrant smell, as though it had been smeared with honey. The professor added that all through his illness he had been employing himself by examining these figures. He was convinced, he said, that they contained some archæological significance; but, in any case, he ceased not to ask himself how came a slip of papyrus to be found in such a situation, — on the bed of a dead *Berlinerin* of the poorest class? The story of its being taken from the *mouth* of the woman was, of course, unbelievable. The whole incident seemed to puzzle, while it amused him; seemed to appeal to the instinct — so strong in him — to investigate, to probe. For days, he declared, he had been endeavouring, in vain, to make anything of the figures. Dr. Hofmeier, too, examined the slip, but inclined to believe that the figures — rude and uncouth as they were — were only such as might be drawn by any schoolboy in an idle moment. They consisted merely of a man and a woman seated on a bench, with what looked like an ornamental border running round them. After a pleasant evening's scientific gossip, Dr. Hofmeier, a little after midnight, took his departure from the bedside. An hour later the servants were roused from sleep by one deep, raucous cry proceeding from the professor's room. They hastened to his door; it was locked on the inside; all was still within. No answer coming to their calls, the door was broken in. They found their master lying calm and dead on his bed. A window of the room was open, but there was nothing to show that anyone had entered it. Dr. Hofmeier was sent for, and was soon on the scene. After examining the body, he failed to find anything to account for the sudden demise of his old friend and chief. One observation, however, had the effect of causing him to tingle with horror. On his entrance he had noticed, lying on the side of the bed, the piece of papyrus with which the professor had been toying in the earlier part of the day, and had removed it. But, as he was on the point of leaving the room, he happened to approach the corpse once more, and bending over it, noticed that the lips and teeth were slightly parted. Drawing open the now stiffened jaws, he found — to his amazement, to his stupefaction — that.

neatly folded beneath the dead tongue, lay just such another piece of papyrus as that which he had removed from the bed. He drew it out — it was clammy. He put it to his nose, — it exhaled the fragrance of honey. He opened it, — it was covered by figures. He compared them with the figures on the other slip, — they were just so similar as two draughtsmen hastily copying from a common model would make them. The doctor was unnerved: he hurried homeward, and immediately submitted the honey on the papyrus to a rigorous chemical analysis: he suspected poison — a subtle poison — as the means of a suicide, grotesquely, insanely accomplished. He found the fluid to be perfectly innocuous, — pure honey, and nothing more.

The next day Germany thrilled with the news that Professor Schleschinger had destroyed himself. For suicide, however, some of the papers substituted murder, though of neither was there an atom of actual proof. On the day following, three persons died by their own hands in Berlin, of whom two were young members of the medical profession; on the day following that, the number rose to nineteen, Hamburg, Dresden, and Aachen joining in the frenzied death dance; within three weeks from the night on which Professor Schleschinger met his unaccountable end, eight thousand persons in Germany, France, and Great Britain, died in that startlingly sudden and secret manner which we call "tragic," many of them obviously by their own hands, many, in what seemed the servility of a fatal imitativeness, with figured, honey-smeared slips of papyrus beneath their tongues. Even now — now, after years — I thrill intensely to recall the dread remembrance; but to live through it, to breathe daily the mawkish, miasmatic atmosphere, all vapid with the suffocating death — ah, it was terror too deep, nausea too foul, for mortal bearing. Novalis has somewhere hinted at the possibility (or the desirability) of a simultaneous suicide and voluntary return by the whole human family into the sweet bosom of our ancient Father — I half expected it was coming, had come, *then*. It was as if the old, good-easy, meek-eyed man of science, dying, had left his effectual curse on all the world, and had thereby converted civilisation into one omnivorous grave, one universal charnel house.

I spent several days in reading out to Zaleski accounts of particular deaths as they had occurred. He seemed never to tire of listening, lying back for the most part on the silver-cushioned couch, and wearing an inscrutable mask. Sometimes he rose and paced the carpet with noiseless footfall, his steps increasing to the swaying, uneven velocity of an animal in confinement as a passage here or there attracted him, and then subsiding into their slow regularity again. At any interruption in the reading, he would instantly turn to me with a certain impatience, and implore me to proceed; and when our stock of matter failed, he broke out into actual anger that I had not brought more with me. Henceforth the Negro, Ham, using my trap, daily took a double journey — one before sunrise, and one at dusk — to the nearest townlet, from which he would return loaded with newspapers. With unimaginable eagerness did both Zaleski and I seize, morning after morning, and evening after evening, on these budgets, to gloat for long hours over the ever-lengthening tale of death. As for him, sleep forsook him. He was a man of small reasonableness, scorning the limitations of human capacity; his palate brooked no meat when his brain was headlong in the chase; even the mild narcotics which were now his food and drink seemed to lose something of their power to mollify, to curb him. Often rising from slumber in what I took to be the dead of night — though of day or night there could be small certainty in that dim dwelling — I would peep into the domed chamber, and see him there under the livid-green light of the censer, the leaden smoke issuing from his lips, his eyes fixed unweariedly on a square piece of ebony which rested on the coffin of the mummy near him. On this ebony he had pasted side by side several woodcuts — snipped from the newspapers — of the figures traced on the pieces of papyrus found in the mouths of the dead. I could see, as time passed, that he was concentrating all his powers on these figures; for the details of the deaths themselves were all of a dreary sameness, offering few salient points for investigation. In those cases where the suicide had left behind him clear evidence of the means by which he had committed the act, there was nothing to investigate; the others — rich and poor alike, peer and peasant — trooped out by thousands on the far journey, without leaving the faintest footprint to mark the road by which they had gone.

This was perhaps the reason that, after a time, Zaleski discarded the newspapers, leaving their perusal to me, and turned his attention exclusively to the ebon tablet. Knowing as I full well did the daring and success of his past spiritual adventures, — the subtlety, the imagination, the imperial grip of his intellect, — I did not at all doubt that his choice was wise, and would in the end be justified. These woodcuts — now so notorious — were all exactly similar in design, though minutely differing here and there in drawing. The following is a facsimile of one of them taken by me at random: —

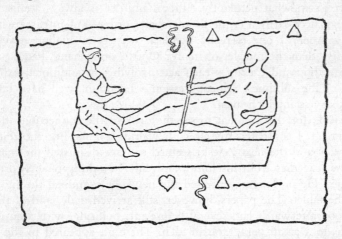

The time passed. It now began to be a grief to me to see the turgid pallor that gradually overspread the always ashen countenance of Zaleski; I grew to consider the ravaging life that glared and blazed in his sunken eye as too volcanic, demonic, to be canny: the mystery, I decided at last — if mystery there were — was too deep, too dark, for him. Hence perhaps it was that I now absented myself more and more from him in the adjoining room in which I slept. There one day I sat reading over the latest list of horrors, when I heard a loud cry from the vaulted chamber. I rushed to the door and beheld him standing, gazing with wild eyes at the ebon tablet held straight out in front of him.

"By heaven!" he cried, stamping savagely with his foot. "By heaven! Then I certainly *am* a fool! *It is the staff of Phœbus in the hand of Hermes!*"

I hastened to him. "Tell me," I said, "have you discovered any-thing?"

"It is possible."

"And has there really been foul play — murder — in any of these deaths?"

"Of that, at least, I was certain from the first."

"Great God!" I exclaimed, "could any son of man so convert himself into a fiend, a beast of the wilderness —— "

"You judge precisely in the manner of the multitude," he answered somewhat petulantly. "Illegal murder is always a mistake, but not necessarily a crime. Remember Corday. But in cases where the murder of one is really fiendish, why is it qualitatively less fiendish than the murder of many? On the other hand, had Brutus slain a thousand Cæsars — each act involving an additional exhibition of the sublimest self-suppression — he might well have taken rank as a saint in heaven."

Failing for the moment to see the drift or the connection of the argument, I contented myself with waiting events. For the rest of that day and the next Zaleski seemed to have dismissed the matter of the tragedies from his mind, and entered calmly on his former studies. He no longer consulted the news, or examined the figures on the tablet. The papers, however, still arrived daily, and of these he soon afterwards laid several before me, pointing, with a curious smile, to a small paragraph in each. These all appeared in the advertisement columns, were worded alike, and read as follows: —

"A true son of Lycurgus, *having news,* desires to know the *time* and *place* of the next meeting of his Phyle. Address Zaleski, at R—— Abbey, in the county of M——."

I gazed in mute alternation at the advertisement and at him. I may here stop to make mention of a very remarkable sensation which my association with him occasionally produced in me. I felt it with intense, with unpleasant, with irritating keenness at this moment. It was the sensation of being borne aloft — aloft — by a force external to myself — such a sensation as might possibly tingle through an earthworm when lifted into illimitable airy heights by the strongly daring pinions of an eagle.

"To that," he said, pointing to the paragraph, "we may, I think, shortly expect an answer. Let us only hope that when it comes it may be immediately intelligible."

We waited throughout the whole of that day and night, hiding our eagerness under the pretence of absorption in our books. If by chance I fell into an uneasy doze, I found him on waking ever watchful, and poring over the great tome before him. About the time, however, when, could we have seen it, the first grey of dawn must have been peeping over the land, his impatience again became painful to witness: he rose and paced the room, muttering occasionally to himself. This only ceased when, hours later, Ham entered the room with an envelope in his hand. Zaleski seized it — tore it open — ran his eye over the contents — and dashed it to the ground with an oath.

"Curse it!" he groaned. "Ah, curse it! unintelligible — every syllable of it!"

I picked up the missive and examined it. It was a slip of papyrus covered with the design now so hideously familiar, except only that the two central figures were wanting. At the bottom was written the date of the 15th of November — it was then the morning of the 12th — and the name "Morris." The whole, therefore, presented the following appearance:

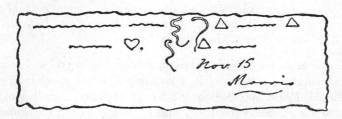

My eyes were now heavy with sleep, every sense half-drunken with the vapourlike atmosphere of the room, so that, having abandoned something of hope, I tottered willingly to my bed, and fell into a profound slumber, which lasted till what must have been the time of the gathering in of the shades of night. I then rose. Missing Zaleski, I sought through all the chambers for him. He was nowhere to be seen. The Negro informed me with an affectionate and anxious tremor in the voice that his master had left the rooms some hours before, but had said nothing to him. I ordered the man to descend and look into the sacristy of the small chapel wherein I had deposited my *calèche,* and in the field behind, where my horse should be. He returned with the news that both had disappeared.

Zaleski, I then concluded, had undoubtedly departed on a journey.

I was deeply touched by the demeanour of Ham as the hours went by. He wandered stealthily about the rooms like a lost being. It was like matter sighing after, weeping over, spirit. Prince Zaleski had never before withdrawn himself from the surveillance of this sturdy watchman, and his disappearance now was like a convulsion in their little cosmos. Ham implored me repeatedly, if I could, to throw some light on the meaning of this catastrophe. But I too was in the dark. The Titanic frame of the Ethiopian trembled with emotion as in broken, childish words he told me that he felt instinctively the approach of some great danger to the person of his master. So a day passed away, and then another. On the next he roused me from sleep to hand me a letter which, on opening, I found to be from Zaleski. It was hastily scribbled in pencil, dated "London, Nov. 14th," and ran thus: —

For my body — should I not return by Friday night — you will, no doubt, be good enough to make search. *Descend* the river, keeping constantly to the left; consult the papyrus; and stop at the *Descensus Æsopi*. Seek diligently, and you will find. For the rest, you know my fancy for cremation: take me, if you will, to the crematorium of *Père-Lachaise*. My whole fortune I decree to Ham, the Lybian.

Ham was all for knowing the contents of this letter, but I refused to communicate a word of it. I was dazed, I was more than ever perplexed, I was appalled by the frenzy of Zaleski. Friday night! It was then Thursday morning. And I was expected to wait through the dreary interval uncertain, agonised, inactive! I was offended with my friend; his conduct bore the interpretation of mental distraction. The leaden hours passed all oppressively while I sought to appease the keenness of my unrest with the anodyne of drugged sleep. On the next morning, however, another letter — a rather massive one — reached me. The covering was directed in the writing of Zaleski, but on it he had scribbled the words: "This need not be opened unless I fail to reappear before Saturday." I therefore laid the packet aside unread.

I waited all through Friday, resolved that at six o'clock, if nothing happened, I should make some sort of effort. But from six I remained, with eyes strained towards the doorway, until ten. I was so utterly at a loss, my ingenuity was so entirely baffled by the situation, that I could devise no course of action which did not immediately appear absurd. But at midnight I sprang up — no longer would I endure the carking suspense. I seized a taper, and passed through the doorway. I had not proceeded far, however, when my light was extinguished. Then I remembered with a shudder that I should have to pass through the whole vast length of the building in order to gain an exit. It was an all but hopeless task in the profound darkness to thread my way through the labyrinth of halls and corridors, of tumble-down stairs, of bat-haunted vaults, of purposeless angles and involutions; but I proceeded with something of a blind obstinacy, groping my way with arms held out before me. In this manner I had wandered on for perhaps a quarter of an hour, when my fingers came into distinct momentary contact with what felt like cold and humid human flesh. I shrank back, unnerved as I already was, with a murmur of affright.

"Zaleski?" I whispered with bated breath.

Intently as I strained my ears, I could detect no reply. The hairs of my head, catching terror from my fancies, erected themselves.

Again I advanced, and again I became aware of the sensation of contact. With a quick movement I passed my hand upward and downward.

It was indeed he. He was half reclining, half standing against a wall of the chamber: that he was not dead, I at once knew by his uneasy breathing. Indeed, when, having chafed his hands for some time, I tried to rouse him, he quickly recovered himself, and muttered: "I fainted; I want sleep — only sleep." I bore him back to the lighted room, assisted by Ham in the latter part of the journey. Ham's ecstasies were infinite; he had hardly hoped to see his master's face again. His garments being wet and soiled, the Negro divested him of them, and dressed him in a tightly-fitting scarlet robe of Babylonish pattern, reaching to the feet, but leaving the lower neck and forearm bare, and girt round the stomach by a broad gold-orphreyed *ceinture*. With all the tenderness of a woman, the man stretched his master thus arrayed on the couch. Here he kept an Argus guard while Zaleski, in one deep unbroken slumber of a night and a day, reposed before him. When at last the sleeper woke, in his eye — full of divine instinct — flitted the wonted falchion flash of the whetted, two-edged intellect; the secret, austere, self-conscious smile of triumph curved his lip; not a trace of pain or fatigue remained. After a substantial meal on nuts, autumn fruits, and wine of Samos, he resumed his place on the couch; and I sat by his side to hear the story of his wandering. He said: —

"We have, Shiel, had before us a very remarkable series of murders, and a very remarkable series of suicides. Were they in any way connected? To this extent, I think — that the mysterious, the unparalleled nature of the murders gave rise to a morbid condition in the public mind, which in turn resulted in the epidemic of suicide. But though such an epidemic has its origin in the instinct of imitation so common in men, you must not suppose that the mental process is a *conscious* one. A person feels an impulse to go and do, and is not aware that at bottom it is only an impulse to go and do *likewise*. He would indeed repudiate such an assumption. Thus one man destroys himself, and another imitates him — but whereas the former uses a pistol, the latter uses a rope. It is rather absurd, therefore, to imagine that in any of those cases in which the slip of papyrus has been found in the mouth after death, the cause of death has been the slavish imitativeness of the suicidal mania, — for this, as I say, is never *slavish*. The papyrus then — quite apart from the unmistakable evidences of suicide invariably left by each self-destroyer — affords us definite and certain means by which we can distinguish the two classes of deaths; and we are thus able to divide the total number into two nearly equal halves.

"But you start — you are troubled — you never heard or read of murder such as this, the simultaneous murder of thousands over wide areas of the face of the globe; here you feel is something outside your experience, deeper than your profoundest imaginings. To the question 'by whom committed?' and 'with what motive?' your mind can conceive no possible answer. And yet the answer must be, 'by man, and for human motives,' — for the Angel of Death with flashing eye and flaming sword is himself long dead; and again we can say at once, by no *one* man, but by many, a cohort, an army of men; and again, by no *common* men, but by men hellish (or heavenly) in cunning, in resource, in strength and unity of purpose; men laughing to scorn the flimsy prophylactics of society, separated by an infinity of self-confidence and spiritual integrity from the ordinary easily crushed criminal of our days.

"This much at least I was able to discover from the first; and immediately I set myself to the detection of motive by a careful study of each case. This, too, in due time, became clear to me, — but to motive it may perhaps be more convenient to refer later on. What next engaged my attention was the figures on the papyrus, and devoutly did I hope that by their solution I might be able to arrive at some more exact knowledge of the mystery.

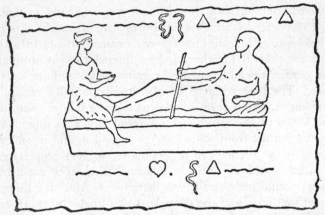

"The figures round the border first attracted me, and the mere *reading* of them gave me very little trouble. But I was convinced that behind their meaning thus read lay some deep esoteric signifi-cance; and this, almost to the last, I was utterly unable to fathom. You perceive that these border figures consist of waved lines of two different lengths, drawings of snakes, triangles looking like the Greek delta, and a heart-shaped object with a dot following it. These succeed one another in a certain definite order on all the slips. What, I asked myself, were these drawings meant to represent, — letters, numbers, things, or abstractions? This I was the more readily able to determine because I have often, in thinking over the shape of the Roman letter S, wondered whether it did not owe its convolute form to an attempt on the part of its inventor to make a picture of the serpent; S being the sibilant or hissing letter, and the serpent the hissing animal. This view, I fancy (though I am not sure), has

escaped the philologists, but of course you know that all letters were
originally *pictures of things,* and of what was S a picture, if not
of the serpent? I therefore assumed, by way of trial, that the snakes
in the diagram stood for a sibilant letter, that is, either C or S. And
thence, supposing this to be the case, I deduced: firstly, that all the
other figures stood for letters; and secondly, that they all appeared
in the form of pictures of the things of which those letters were
originally meant to be pictures. Thus the letter *m,* one of the four
'*liquid*' consonants, is, as we now write it, only a shortened form
of a waved line; and as a waved line it was originally written, and
was the character by which *a stream of running water* was represented in writing; indeed it only owes its name to the fact that when
the lips are pressed together, and *m* uttered by a continuous effort, a certain resemblance to the murmur of running water is
produced. The longer waved line in the diagram I therefore took
to represent *m;* and it at once followed that the shorter meant *n,* for
no two letters of the commoner European alphabets differ *only* in
length (as distinct from shape) except *m* and *n,* and *w* and *v;* indeed, just as the French call *w* 'double-ve,' so very properly might
m be called 'double-en.' But, in this case, the longer not being *w,*
the shorter could not be *v:* it was therefore *n.* And now there only
remained the heart and the triangle. I was unable to think of any
letter that could ever have been intended for the picture of a heart,
but the triangle I knew to be the letter A. This was originally written without the crossbar from prop to prop, and the two feet at the
bottom of the props were not separated as now, but joined; so that
the letter formed a true triangle. It was meant by the primitive man
to be a picture of his primitive house, this house being, of course,
hut-shaped, and consisting of a conical roof without walls. I had
thus, with the exception of the heart, disentangled the whole, which
then (leaving a space for the heart) read as follows: —

$$\text{mn} \begin{cases} \text{ss} \\ \text{anan . . . san.} \\ \text{cc} \end{cases}$$

But *c* before *a* being never a sibilant (except in some few so-called
'Romance' languages), but a guttural, it was for the moment discarded; also as no word begins with the letters *mn* — except *mne·*

monics and its fellows — I concluded that a vowel must be omitted between these letters, and thence that all vowels (except *a*) were omitted; again, as the double *s* can never come after *n* I saw that either a vowel was omitted between the two *s's,* or that the first word ended after the first *s.* Thus I got

m ns sanan . . . san,

or, supplying the now quite obvious vowels,

mens sana in . . . sano.

The heart I now knew represented the word *corpore,* the Latin word for *heart* being *cor,* and the dot — showing that the word as it stood was an abbreviation — conclusively proved every one of my deductions.

"So far all had gone flowingly. It was only when I came to consider the central figures that for many days I spent my strength in vain. You heard my exclamation of delight and astonishment when at last a ray of light pierced the gloom. At no time, indeed, was I wholly in the dark as to the *general* significance of these figures, for I saw at once their resemblance to the sepulchral reliefs of classical times. In case you are not minutely acquainted with the *technique* of these stones, I may as well show you one, which I myself removed from an old grave in Tarentum."

He took from a niche a small piece of close-grained marble, about a foot square, and laid it before me. On one side it was exquisitely sculptured in relief.

"This," he continued, "is a typical example of the Greek gravestone, and having seen one specimen you may be said to have seen almost all, for there is surprisingly little variety in the class. You will observe that the scene represents a man reclining on a couch; in his hand he holds a *patera,* or dish, filled with grapes and pomegranates, and beside him is a tripod bearing the viands from which he is banqueting. At his feet sits a woman — for the Greek lady never reclined at table. In addition to these two figures a horse's head, a dog, or a serpent may sometimes be seen; and these forms comprise the almost invariable pattern of all grave reliefs. Now, that this was the real model from which the figures on the papyrus were taken I could not doubt, when I considered the seemingly absurd fidelity with which in each murder the papyrus, smeared with honey, was placed under the tongue of the victim. I said to myself: it can only be that the assassins have bound themselves to the observance of a strict and narrow ritual from which no departure is under any circumstances permitted — perhaps for the sake of signalling the course of events to others at a distance. But what ritual? That question I was able to answer when I knew the answer to these others, — why *under the tongue,* and why *smeared with honey?* For no reason, except that the Greeks (not the Romans till very late in their history) always placed an *obolos,* or penny, beneath the tongue of the dead to pay his passage across the Stygian river of ghosts; for no reason, except that to these same Greeks honey was a sacred fluid, intimately associated in their minds with the mournful subject of Death; a fluid with which the bodies of the deceased were anointed, and sometimes — especially in Sparta and the Pelasgic South — embalmed; with which libations were poured to Hermes Psuchopompos, conductor of the dead to the regions of shade; with which offerings were made to all the chthonic deities, and the souls of the departed in general.

"The ritual then of the murderers was a *Greek* ritual, their cult a Greek cult — preferably, perhaps, a South Greek one, a Spartan one, for it was here that the highly conservative peoples of that region clung longest and fondliest to this semibarbarous worship. This then being so, I was made all the more certain of my conjecture that the central figures on the papyrus were drawn from a Greek model.

"Here, however, I came to a standstill. I was infinitely puzzled by the rod in the man's hand. In none of the Greek grave reliefs does any such thing as a rod make an appearance, except in one well-known example where the god Hermes — generally represented as carrying the *caduceus,* or staff, given him by Phœbus — appears leading a dead maiden to the land of night. But in every other example of which I am aware the sculpture represents a man *living,* not dead, banqueting *on earth,* not in Hades, by the side of his living companion. What then could be the significance of the staff in the hand of this living man? It was only after days of the hardest struggle, the cruelest suspense, that the thought flashed on me that the idea of Hermes leading away the dead female might, in this case, have been carried one step farther; that the male figure might be no living man, no man at all, but *Hermes himself* actually banqueting in Hades with the soul of his disembodied *protégée!* The thought filled me with a rapture I cannot describe, and you witnessed my excitement. But, at all events, I saw that this was a truly tremendous departure from Greek art and thought, to which in general the copyists seemed to cling so religiously. There must therefore be a reason, a strong reason, for vandalism such as this. And that, at any rate, it was no longer difficult to discover; for now I knew that the male figure was no mortal, but a god, a spirit, a DÆMON (in the Greek sense of the word); and the female figure I saw by the marked shortness of her drapery to be no Athenian, but a Spartan; no matron either, but a maiden, a lass, a LASSIE; and now I had forced on me lassie dæmon, *Lacedæmon.*

"This then was the badge, the so carefully buried badge, of this society of men. The only thing which still puzzled and confounded me at this stage was the startling circumstance that a *Greek* society should make use of a *Latin* motto. It was clear that either all my conclusions were totally wrong, or else the motto *mens sana in corpore sano* contained wrapped up in itself some acroamatic meaning which I found myself unable to penetrate, and which the authors had found no Greek motto capable of conveying. But at any rate, having found this much, my knowledge led me of itself one step farther; for I perceived that, widely extended as were their operations, the society was necessarily in the main an *English,* or at least an English-speaking one — for of this the word 'lassie' was plainly indicative: it was easy now to conjecture London, the monster-city in which all things lose themselves, as their headquarters; and at this point in my investigations I despatched to the papers the advertisement you have seen."

"But," I exclaimed, "even now I utterly fail to see by what mysterious processes of thought you arrived at the wording of the advertisement; even now it conveys no meaning to my mind."

"That," he replied, "will grow clear when we come to a right understanding of the baleful *motive* which inspired these men. I have already said that I was not long in discovering it. There was only one possible method of doing so — and that was, by all means, by any means, to find out some condition or other common to every one of the victims before death. It is true that I was unable to do this in some few cases, but where I failed, I was convinced that my failure was due to the insufficiency of the evidence at my disposal, rather than to the actual absence of the condition. Now, let us take almost any two cases you will, and seek for this common condition: let us take, for example, the first two that attracted the attention of the world — the poor woman of the slums of Berlin, and the celebrated man of science. Separated by as wide an interval as they are, we shall yet find, if we look closely, in each case the same pathetic tokens of the still uneliminated *striæ* of our poor humanity. The woman is not an old woman, for she has a 'small young' family, which, had she lived, might have been increased: notwithstanding which, she has suffered from hemiplegia, 'partial paralysis.' The professor, too, has had not one, but two, large families, and an 'army of grandchildren': but note well the startling, the hideous, fact that *every one of his children is dead!* The crude grave has gaped before the cock to suck in *every one* of those shrunk forms, so indigent of vital impulse, so pauper of civism, lust, so draughty, so vague, so lean — but not before they have had time to dower with the ah and wo of their infirmity a whole wretched 'army of grandchildren.' And yet this man of wisdom is on the point, in his old age, of marrying once again, of producing for the good of his race still more of this poor human stuff. You see the lurid significance, the point of resemblance, — you see it? And, O heaven, is it not too sad? For me, I tell you, the whole business has a tragic pitifulness too deep for words. But this brings me to the discussion of a large matter.

"What *precisely* was it that ruined the old nations — that brought, say Rome, to her knees at last? Centralisation, you say, top-heavy imperialism, dilettante pessimism, the love of luxury. At bottom, believe me, it was not one of these high-sounding things — it was simply War; the sum total of the battles of centuries. But let me explain myself: this is a novel view to you, and you are perhaps unable to conceive how or why war was so fatal to the old world, because you see how little harmful it is to the new. If you collected a few millions of modern Englishmen and slew them all simultaneously, what, think you, would be the effect from the point of view of the State? The effect, I conceive, would be insignificant, if your millions were taken promiscuously (as in the modern army), not if they were *picked* men — in *that* case the loss (or gain) would be excessive, and permanent for all time. Now, the war hosts of the ancient commonwealths — not dependent on the mechanical contrivances of the modern army — were necessarily composed of the very best men: the strong-boned, the heart-stout, the sound in wind and limb. Under these conditions the State shuddered through all her frame, thrilled adown every filament, at the death of a single one of her sons in the field. As only the feeble, the aged, bided at home, their number after each battle became larger *in proportion to the whole* than before. Thus the nation, more and more, with ever-increasing rapidity, declined in bodily, and of course spiritual, quality, until the *end* was reached, and Nature swallowed up the weaklings whole; and thus war was to the ancient a genuine and remorselessly fatal scourge.

"And now let me apply these facts to the Europe of our own time. We no longer have world-serious war — but in its place we have a scourge, the effect of which on the modern state is *precisely the same* as the effect of war on the ancient, only, — in the end, — far more destructive, far more subtle, sure, horrible, disgusting. The name of this pestilence is Medical Science. For just as the ancient State was wounded to the heart through the death of her healthy sons in the field, just so slowly, just so silently, is the modern receiving deadly hurt by the botching and tinkering of her unhealthy children. The net result is in each case the same — the altered ratio of the total amount of reproductive health to the total amount of reproductive disease. They recklessly spent their best; we sedulously conserve our worst; and as they pined and died of anæmia, so we, unless we repent, must perish in a paroxysm of black-blood apoplexy.

"Do you know that at this moment your hospitals are crammed with beings in human likeness suffering from a thousand obscure and subtly ineradicable ills, all of whom, if left alone, would die almost at once, but ninety in the hundred of whom will, as it is, be sent forth 'cured,' like missionaries of hell, and the horrent shapes of Night and Acheron, to mingle in the pure river of humanity the poison-taint of their protean vileness? Do you know that in your schools one quarter of the children are already purblind? Have you gauged the importance of your tremendous consumption of quack catholicons, of the fortunes derived from their sale, of the

spread of modern nervous disorders, of toothless youth and thrice
loathsome age among the helot classes? Do you know that in the
course of my late journey to London, I walked from Piccadilly
Circus to Hyde Park Corner, during which time I observed some
five hundred people, of whom twenty-seven only were perfectly
healthy, well-formed men, and eighteen healthy, beautiful women?
Less death, more disease — that is the sad, the unnatural record;
children especially — so sensitive to the physician's art — living on
by hundreds of thousands, bearing within them the germs of wide-
spreading sorrow, who in former times would have died. Nothing
is so sure as that to the unit it is a cruelty; nothing so certain as that
to humanity it is a wrong.

"Is it indeed part of man's strange destiny through the deeps of
Time that he one day bow his back to the duty of pruning himself
as a garden, so that he run not to a waste wilderness? Shall the
physician, the *accoucheur,* of the time to come be expected, and
commanded, to don the ephod and breastplate, anoint his head with
the oil of gladness, and add to the function of healer the function
of Sacrificial Priest? These, you say, are wild, dark questions. Wild
enough, dark enough. We know how Sparta — the 'man-taming
Sparta' Simonides calls her — answered them. Here was the complete subordination of all unit life to the well-being of the Whole.
The child, immediately on his entry into the world, fell under the
control of the State: it was not left to the judgment of his parents,
as elsewhere, whether he should be brought up or not, but a
commission of the Phyle in which he was born decided the question.
If he was weakly, if he had any bodily unsightliness, he was exposed
on a place called Taygetus, and so perished. It was a consequence of
this that never did the sun in his course light on man half so godly
stalwart, on woman half so houri-lovely, as in stern and stout old
Sparta. Death, like all mortal, they must bear; disease, once and
for all, they were resolved to have done with. The word which they
used to express the idea 'ugly' meant also 'hateful,' 'vile,' 'disgraceful' — and I need hardly point out to you the significance of that
fact alone; for they considered — and rightly — that there is no sort
of natural reason why every denizen of earth should not be perfectly
hale, integral, sane, beautiful — if only very moderate pains be taken
to procure this divine result. At any rate, from these remarks, you

will now very likely be able to arrive at some understanding of the wording of the advertisements which I sent to the papers."

Zaleski, having delivered himself of this singular tirade, paused; replaced the sepulchral relief in its niche; drew a drapery of silver cloth over his bare feet and the hem of his antique garment of Babylon; and then continued:

"After some time the answer to the advertisement at length arrived; but what was my disgust to find that it was perfectly unintelligible to me. I had asked for a date and an address: the reply came giving a date, and an address, too — but an address wrapped up in cypher, which, of course, I, as a supposed member of the society, was expected to be able to read. At any rate, I now knew the significance of the incongruous circumstance that the Latin proverb *mens sana etc.* should be adopted as the motto of a Greek society; the significance lay in this, that the motto *contained an address* — the address of their meeting place, or at least, of their chief meeting place. I was now confronted with the task of solving — and of solving quickly, without the loss of an hour — this enigma; and I confess that it was only by the most violent and extraordinary concentration of what I may call the dissecting faculty, that I was able to do so in good time. And yet there was no special difficulty in the matter. For looking at the motto as it stood in cypher, the first thing I perceived was that, in order to read the secret, the heart-shaped figure must be left out of consideration, if there was any *consistency* in the system of cyphers at all, for it belonged to a class of symbols quite distinct from that of all the others, not being, like them, a picture-letter. Omitting this, therefore, and taking all the other vowels and consonants whether actually represented in the device or not, I now got the proverb in the form *mens sana in . . . pore sano.* I wrote this down, and what instantly struck me was the immense, the altogether unusual, number of *liquids* in the motto — six in all, amounting to no less than one third of the total number of letters! Putting these all together you get *mnnnnr,* and you can see that the very appearance of the *m's* and *n's* (especially when *written*) running into one another, of itself suggests a stream of water. Having previously arrived at the conclusion of London as the meeting place, I could not now fail to go on to the inference of the *Thames;* there, or near there, would I find those whom I sought. The letters *mnnnnr,* then. meant the Thames: what did the still remaining letters mean? I now took these remaining letters, placing them side by side: I got *aaa, sss, ee, oo, p* and *i.* Juxtaposing these nearly in the order indicated by the frequency of their occurrence, and their place in the Roman alphabet, you at once and inevitably get the word *Æsopi.* And now I was fairly startled by this symmetrical proof of the exactness of my own deductions in other respects, but, above all, far above all, by the occurrence of that word *Æsopi.* For who was Æsopus? He was a slave who was freed for his wise and witful sallies: he is therefore typical of the liberty of the wise — their moral manumission from temporary and narrow law; he was also a close friend of Crœsus: he is typical, then, of the union of wisdom with wealth — true wisdom with real wealth; lastly, and above all, he was thrown by the Delphians from a rock on account of his wit: he is typical, therefore, of death — the shedding of blood — as a result of wisdom, this thought being an elaboration of Solomon's great maxim, 'in much wisdom is much sorrow.' But how accurately all this fitted in with what would naturally be the doctrines of the men on whose track I was! I could no longer doubt the justness of my reasonings, and immediately, while you slept, I set off for London.

"Of my haps in London I need not give you a very particular account. The meeting was to be held on the 15th, and by the morning of the 13th I had reached a place called Wargrave, on the Thames. There I hired a light canoe, and thence proceeded down the river in a somewhat zigzag manner, narrowly examining the banks on either side, and keeping a sharp outlook for some board, or sign, or house, that would seem to betoken any sort of connection with the word *Æsopi.* In this way I passed a fruitless day, and having reached the shipping region, made fast my craft, and in a spirit of *diablerie* spent the night in a common lodging house, in the company of the most remarkable human beings, characterised by an odour of alcohol, and a certain obtrusive *bonne camaraderie* which the prevailing fear of death could not altogether repress. By dawn of the 14th I was on my journey again — on, and ever on. Eagerly I longed for a sight of the word I sought: but I had misjudged the men against whose cunning I had measured my own. I should have remembered more consistently that they were no ordinary men. As I was destined to find, there lay a deeper, more cabalistic meaning in the motto than any I had been able to dream of. I had proceeded on my pilgrimage down the river a long way past Greenwich, and had now reached a desolate and level reach of land stretching away on either hand. Paddling my boat from the right to the left bank, I came to a spot where a little arm of the river ran up some few yards into the land. The place wore a specially dreary and deserted aspect: the land was flat, and covered with low shrubs. I rowed into this arm of shallow water and rested on my oar, wearily bethinking myself what was next to be done. Looking round, however, I saw to my surprise that at the end of this arm there was a short narrow pathway — a winding road — leading from the river bank. I stood up in the boat and followed its course with my eyes. It was met by another road also winding among the bushes, but in a slightly different direction. At the end of this was a little, low, high-roofed, round house, without doors or windows. And then — and then — tingling now with a thousand raptures — I beheld a pool of water near this structure, and then another low house, a counterpart of the first — and then, still leading on in the same direction, another pool — and then a great rock, heart-shaped — and then another winding road — and then another pool of water. All was a model — *exact to the minutest particular* — of the device on the papyrus! The first long-waved line was the river itself; the three short-waved lines were the arm of the river and the two pools; the three snakes were the three winding roads; the

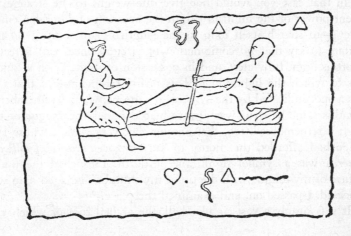

two triangles representing the letter A were the two high-roofed round houses; the heart was the rock! I sprang, now thoroughly excited, from the boat, and ran in headlong haste to the end of the last lake. Here there was a rather thick and high growth of bushes, but peering among them, my eye at once caught a white oblong board supported on a stake: on this, in black letters, was marked the words Descensus Æsopi. It was necessary, therefore, to go *down:* the meeting place was subterranean. It was without difficulty that I discovered a small opening in the ground, half hidden by the underwood; from the orifice I found that a series of wooden steps led directly downwards, and I at once boldly descended. No sooner, however, had I touched the bottom than I was confronted by an ancient man in Hellenic apparel, armed with the Greek *ziphos* and *peltè.* His eyes, accustomed to the gloom, pierced me long with an earnest scrutiny.

"'You are a Spartan?' he asked at length.

"'Yes,' I answered promptly.

"'Then, how is it you do not know that I am stone deaf?'

"I shrugged, indicating that for the moment I had forgotten the fact.

"'You *are* a Spartan?' he repeated.

"I nodded with emphasis.

"'Then, how is it you omit to make the sign?'

"Now, you must not suppose that at this point I was nonplussed, for in that case you would not give due weight to the strange inherent power of the mind to rise to the occasion of a sudden emergency — to stretch itself long to the length of an event; I do not hesitate to say that *no* combination of circumstances can defeat a vigorous brain fully alert, and in possession of itself. With a quickness to which the lightning flash is tardy, I remembered that this was a spot indicated by the symbols on the papyrus; I remembered that this same papyrus was always placed under the *tongue* of the dead; I remembered, too, that among that very nation whose language had afforded the motto, to 'turn up the *thumb*' (*pollicem vertere*) was a symbol significant of death. I touched the under surface of my tongue with the tip of my thumb. The aged man was appeased. I passed on, and examined the place.

"It was simply a vast circular hall, the arched roof of which was

supported on colonnades of what I took to be pillars of porphyry.
Down the middle and round the sides ran tables of the same material; the walls were clothed in hangings of sable velvet, on which,
in infinite reproduction, was embroidered in cypher the motto of
the society. The chairs were cushioned in the same stuff. Near the
centre of the circle stood a huge statue of what really seemed to me
to be pure beaten gold. On the great ebon base was inscribed the word
ΛΥΚΥΡΓΟΣ. From the roof swung by brazen chains a single misty
lamp.

"Having seen this much I reascended to the land of light, and
being fully resolved on attending the meeting on the next day or
night, and not knowing what my fate might then be, I wrote to
inform you of the means by which my body might be traced.

"But on the next day a new thought occurred to me: I reasoned
thus: 'these men are not common assassins; they wage a too rash
warfare against diseased life, but not against life in general. In all
probability they have a quite immoderate, quite morbid reverence
for the sanctity of healthy life. They will not therefore take mine,
unless they suppose me to be the only living outsider who has a
knowledge of their secret, and therefore think it absolutely necessary for the carrying out of their beneficent designs that my life
should be sacrificed. I will therefore prevent such a motive from
occurring to them by communicating to another their whole secret,
and — if the necessity should arise — *letting them know* that I have
done so, without telling them who that other is. Thus my life will
be assured.' I therefore wrote to you on that day a full account of
all I had discovered, giving you to understand, however, on the
envelope, that you need not examine the contents for some little
time.

"I waited in the subterranean vault during the greater part of the
next day; but not till midnight did the confederates gather. What
happened at that meeting I shall not disclose, even to you. All was
sacred — solemn — full of awe. Of the choral hymns there sung, the
hierophantic ritual, liturgies, pæans, the gorgeous symbolisms — of
the wealth there represented, the culture, art, self-sacrifice — of the
mingling of all the tongues of Europe — I shall not speak; nor shall
I repeat names which you would at once recognise as familiar to
you — though I may, perhaps, mention that the 'Morris' whose

name appears on the papyrus sent to me is a well-known *littérateur* of that name. But this in confidence, for some years at least.

"Let me, however, hurry to a conclusion. My turn came to speak. I rose undaunted, and calmly disclosed myself; during the moment of hush, of wide-eyed paralysis that ensued, I declared that fully as I coincided with their views in general, I found myself unable to regard their methods with approval — these I could not but consider too rash, too harsh, too premature. My voice was suddenly drowned by one universal, earth-shaking roar of rage and contempt, during which I was surrounded on all sides, seized, pinioned, and dashed on the central table. All this time, in the hope and love of life, I passionately shouted that I was not the only living being who shared in their secret. But my voice was drowned, and drowned again, in the whirling tumult. None heard me. A powerful and little-known anæsthetic — the means by which all their murders have been accomplished — was now produced. A cloth, saturated with the fluid, was placed on my mouth and nostrils. I was stifled. Sense failed. The incubus of the universe blackened down upon my brain. How I tugged at the mandrakes of speech! was a locked pugilist with language! In the depth of my extremity the half thought, I remember, floated, like a mist, through my fading consciousness, that now perhaps — now — there was silence around me; that *now*, could my palsied lips find dialect, I should be heard, and understood. My whole soul rose focussed to the effort — my body jerked itself upwards. At that moment I knew my spirit truly great, genuinely sublime. For I *did* utter something — my dead and shuddering tongue *did* babble forth some coherency. Then I fell back, and all was once more the ancient Dark. On the next day when I woke, I was lying on my back in my little boat, placed there by God knows whose hands. At all events, one thing was clear — I *had* uttered something — I was saved. With what of strength remained to me I reached the place where I had left your *calèche,* and started on my homeward way. The necessity to sleep was strong upon me, for the fumes of the anæsthetic still clung about my brain; hence, after my long journey, I fainted on my passage through the house, and in this condition you found me.

"Such then is the history of my thinkings and doings in connec-

tion with this ill-advised confraternity: and now that their cabala is
known to others — to how many others *they* cannot guess — I think
it is not unlikely that we shall hear little more of the Society of
Sparta."

THE DUBLIN MYSTERY

by BARONESS ORCZY

The original Armchair Detective, the nameless OLD MAN *sits in a London tea shop and solves mysteries without ever visiting the scene of a crime, or examining evidence, or questioning suspects — without, in fact, ever rising from his corner table. There are thirty-seven* OLD MAN *short stories, of which twelve have never been published in America.*

I ALWAYS thought that the history of that forged will was about as interesting as any I had read," said the man in the corner that day. He had been silent for some time, and was meditatively sorting and looking through a packet of small photographs in his pocket book. Polly guessed that some of these would presently be placed before her for inspection — and she had not long to wait.

"That is old Brooks," he said, pointing to one of the photographs, "Millionaire Brooks, as he was called, and these are his two sons, Percival and Murray. It was a curious case, wasn't it? Personally I don't wonder that the police were completely at sea. If a member of that highly estimable force happened to be as clever as the clever author of that forged will, we should have very few undetected crimes in this country."

"That is why I always try to persuade you to give our poor ignorant police the benefit of your great insight and wisdom," said Polly, with a smile.

"I know," he said blandly, "you have been most kind in that way, but I am only an amateur. Crime interests me only when it resembles a clever game of chess, with many intricate moves which all tend to one solution, the checkmating of the antagonist — the detective forces of the country. Now, confess that, in the Dublin mystery, the clever police there were absolutely checkmated."

"Absolutely."

"Just as the public was. There were actually two crimes committed in one city which have completely baffled detection: the murder of Patrick Wethered the lawyer, and the forged will of Millionaire Brooks. There are not many millionaires in Ireland; no wonder old Brooks was a notability in his way, since his business — bacon curing, I believe it was — is said to be worth over £2,000,000 of solid money.

"His younger son, Murray, was a refined, highly educated man, and was, moreover, the apple of his father's eye, as he was the spoilt darling of Dublin society; good-looking, a splendid dancer, and a perfect rider, he was the acknowledged 'catch' of the matrimonial market of Ireland, and many a very aristocratic house was opened hospitably to the favorite son of the millionaire.

"Of course, Percival Brooks, the eldest son, would inherit the bulk of the old man's property and also probably the larger share in the business; he, too, was good-looking, more so than his brother; he, too, rode, danced, and talked well, but it was many years ago that mammas with marriageable daughters had given up all hopes of Percival Brooks as a probable son-in-law. That young man's infatuation for Maisie Fortescue, a lady of undoubted charm but very doubtful antecedents, who had astonished the London and Dublin music halls with her extravagant dances, was too well known and too old-established to encourage any hopes in other quarters.

"Whether Percival Brooks would ever marry Maisie Fortescue was thought to be very doubtful. Old Brooks had the full disposal of all his wealth, and it would have fared ill with Percival if he introduced an undesirable wife into the magnificent Fitzwilliam Place establishment.

"That is how matters stood," continued the man in the corner, "when Dublin society one morning learnt, with deep regret and dismay, that old Brooks had died very suddenly at his residence after only a few hours' illness. At first it was generally understood that he had had an apoplectic stroke; anyway, he had been at business hale and hearty as ever the day before his death, which occurred late on the evening of February 1st.

"It was the morning papers of February 2nd which told the sad news to their readers, and it was those selfsame papers which on that eventful morning contained another even more startling piece of news, that proved the prelude to a series of sensations such as tranquil, placid Dublin had not experienced for many years. This was, that on that very afternoon which saw the death of Dublin's greatest millionaire, Mr. Patrick Wethered, his solicitor, was murdered in Phoenix Park at five o'clock in the afternoon while actually walking to his own house from his visit to his client in Fitzwilliam Place.

"Patrick Wethered was as well known as the proverbial town pump; his mysterious and tragic death filled all Dublin with dismay. The lawyer, who was a man sixty years of age, had been struck on the back of the head by a heavy stick, garrotted, and subsequently robbed, for neither money, watch, or pocket book were found upon his person, whilst the police soon gathered from Patrick Wethered's household that he had left home at two o'clock that afternoon, carrying both watch and pocket book, and undoubtedly money as well.

"An inquest was held, and a verdict of willful murder was found against some person or persons unknown.

"But Dublin had not exhausted its stock of sensations yet. Millionaire Brooks had been buried with due pomp and magnificence, and his will had been proved (his business and personalty being estimated at £2,500,000) by Percival Gordon Brooks, his eldest son and sole executor. The younger son, Murray, who had devoted the best years of his life to being a friend and companion to his father, while Percival ran after ballet dancers and music hall stars — Murray, who had avowedly been the apple of his father's eye in consequence — was left with a miserly pittance of £300 a year, and no share whatever in the gigantic business of Brooks & Sons, bacon curers, of Dublin.

"Something had evidently happened within the precincts of the Brooks's town mansion, which the public and Dublin society tried in vain to fathom. Elderly mammas and blushing *débutantes* were already thinking of the best means whereby next season they might more easily show the cold shoulder to young Murray Brooks, who had so suddenly become a hopeless 'detrimental' in the marriage market, when all these sensations terminated in one gigantic, overwhelming bit of scandal, which for the next three months furnished food for gossip in every drawing-room in Dublin.

"Mr. Murray Brooks, namely, had entered a claim for probate of a will, made by his father in 1891, declaring that the later will, made the very day of his father's death and proved by his brother as sole executor, was null and void, that will being a forgery.

"The facts that transpired in connection with this extraordinary case were sufficiently mysterious to puzzle everybody. As I told you before, all Mr. Brooks's friends never quite grasped the idea that the old man should so completely have cut off his favorite son with the proverbial shilling.

"You see, Percival had always been a thorn in the old man's flesh. Horse racing, gambling, theaters, and music halls were, in the old pork butcher's eyes, so many deadly sins which his son committed every day of his life, and all the Fitzwilliam Place household could testify to the many and bitter quarrels which had arisen between father and son over the latter's gambling or racing debts. Many people asserted that Brooks would sooner have left his money to charitable institutions than seen it squandered upon the brightest stars that adorned the music hall stage.

"The case came up for hearing early in the autumn. In the meanwhile Percival Brooks had given up his race-course associates, settled down in the Fitzwilliam Place mansion, and conducted his father's business, without a manager, but with all the energy and forethought which he had previously devoted to more unworthy causes.

"Murray had elected not to stay on in the old house; no doubt associations were of too painful and recent a nature; he was boarding with the family of a Mr. Wilson Hibbert, who was the late Patrick Wethered's, the murdered lawyer's, partner. They were quiet, homely people, who lived in a very pokey little house in Kilkenny Street, and poor Murray must, in spite of his grief, have felt very bitterly the change from his luxurious quarters in his father's mansion to his present tiny room and homely meals.

"Percival Brooks, who was now drawing an income of over a hundred thousand a year, was very severely criticized for adhering so strictly to the letter of his father's will, and only paying his brother that paltry £300 a year, which was very literally but the crumbs off his own magnificent dinner table.

"The issue of that contested will case was therefore awaited with eager interest. In the meanwhile the police, who had at first seemed fairly loquacious on the subject of the murder of Mr. Patrick Wethered, suddenly became strangely reticent, and by their very reticence aroused a certain amount of uneasiness in the public mind, until one day the *Irish Times* published the following extraordinary, enigmatic paragraph:

We hear, on authority which cannot be questioned, that certain extraordinary developments are expected in connection with the brutal murder of our distinguished townsman Mr. Wethered; the police, in fact, are vainly trying to keep it secret that they hold a clew which is as important as it is sensational, and that they only await the impending issue of a well-known litigation in the probate court to effect an arrest.

"The Dublin public flocked to the court to hear the arguments in the great will case. There were Percival Brooks and Murray his brother, the two litigants, both good-looking and well-dressed, and both striving, by keeping up a running conversation with their lawyers, to appear unconcerned and confident of the issue. With Percival Brooks was Henry Oranmore, the eminent Irish K.C., whilst Walter Hibbert, a rising young barrister, the son of Wilson Hibbert, appeared for Murray.

"The will of which the latter claimed probate was one dated 1891, and had been made by Mr. Brooks during a severe illness which threatened to end his days. This will had been deposited in the hands of Messrs. Wethered and Hibbert, solicitors to the deceased, and by it Mr. Brooks left his personalty equally divided between his two sons, but had left his business entirely to his youngest son, with a charge of £2000 a year upon it, payable to Percival. You see that Murray Brooks therefore had a very deep interest in that second will being found null and void.

"Old Mr. Hibbert had very ably instructed his son, and Walter Hibbert's opening speech was exceedingly clever. He would show, he said, on behalf of his client, that the will dated February 1st, 1908, could never have been made by the late Mr. Brooks, as it was absolutely contrary to his avowed intentions, and that if the late Mr. Brooks did on the day in question make any fresh will at all, it certainly was *not* the one proved by Mr. Percival Brooks, for that was absolutely a forgery from beginning to end. Mr. Walter Hibbert proposed to call several witnesses in support of both these points.

"On the other hand, Mr. Henry Oranmore, K.C., very ably and courteously replied that he too had several witnesses to prove that Mr. Brooks certainly did make a will on the day in question, and that, whatever his intentions may have been in the past, he must have modified them on the day of his death, for the will proved by Mr. Percival Brooks was found after his death under his pillow, duly signed and witnessed and in every way legal.

"Then the battle began in sober earnest. There were a great many witnesses to be called on both sides, their evidence being of more or less importance — chiefly less. But the interest centered round the prosaic figure of John O'Neill, the butler of Fitzwilliam Place, who had been in Mr. Brooks's family for thirty years.

" 'I was clearing away my breakfast things,' said John, 'when I heard the master's voice in the study close by. Oh, my, he was that angry! I could hear the words "disgrace," and "villain," and "liar" and "ballet dancer," and one or two other ugly words as applied to some female lady, which I would not like to repeat. At first I did not take much notice, as I was quite used to hearing my poor dear master having words with Mr. Percival. So I went downstairs carrying my breakfast things; but I had just started cleaning my silver when the study bell goes ringing violently, and I hear Mr. Percival's voice shouting in the hall: "John! quick! Send for Dr. Mulligan at once. Your master is not well! Send one of the men, and you come up and help me to get Mr. Brooks to bed."

" 'I sent one of the grooms for the doctor,' continued John, who seemed still affected at the recollection of his poor master, to whom he had evidently been very much attached, 'and I went up to see Mr. Brooks. I found him lying on the study floor, his head supported in Mr. Percival's arms. "My father has fallen in a faint," said the young master; "help me to get him up to his room before Dr. Mulligan comes." '

" 'Mr. Percival looked very white and upset, which was only nat- ural; and when we had got my poor master to bed, I asked if I should not go and break the news to Mr. Murray, who had gone to business an hour ago. However, before Mr. Percival had time to give me an order the doctor came. I thought I had seen death plainly writ in my master's face, and when I showed the doctor out an hour later, and he told me that he would be back directly, I knew that the end was near.

" 'Mr. Brooks rang for me a minute or two later. He told me to send at once for Mr. Wethered, or else for Mr. Hibbert, if Mr. Wethered could not come. "I haven't many hours to live, John," he says to me — "my heart is broke, the doctor says my heart is broke. A man shouldn't marry and have children, John, for they will sooner or later break his heart." I was so upset I couldn't speak; but I sent round at once for Mr. Wethered, who came himself just about three o'clock that afternoon.

" 'After he had been with my master about an hour I was called in, and Mr. Wethered said to me that Mr. Brooks wished me and one other of us servants to witness that he had signed a paper which was on a table by his bedside. I called Pat Mooney, the head foot- man, and before us both Mr. Brooks put his name at the bottom of that paper. Then Mr. Wethered give me the pen and told me to write my name as a witness, and that Pat Mooney was to do the same. After that we were both told that we could go.'

"The old butler went on to explain that he was present in his late master's room on the following day when the undertakers, who had come to lay the dead man out, found a paper underneath his pillow. John O'Neill, who recognized the paper as the one to which he had appended his signature the day before, took it to Mr. Per- cival, and gave it into his hands.

"In answer to Mr. Walter Hibbert, John asserted positively that he took the paper from the undertaker's hand and went straight with it to Mr. Percival's room.

" 'He was alone,' said John; 'I gave him the paper. He just glanced at it, and I thought he looked rather astonished, but he said nothing, and I at once left the room.'   ⊅

" 'When you say that you recognized the paper as the one which you had seen your master sign the day before, how did you actually recognize that it was the same paper?' asked Mr. Hibbert amidst breathless interest on the part of the spectators.

" 'It looked exactly the same paper to me, sir,' replied John, somewhat vaguely.

" 'Did you look at the contents, then?'

" 'No, sir; certainly not.'

" 'Had you done so the day before?'

" 'No, sir, only at my master's signature.'

" 'Then you only thought by the *outside* look of the paper that it was the same?'

" 'It looked the same thing, sir,' persisted John obstinately.

"You see," continued the man in the corner, leaning eagerly forward across the narrow marble table, "the contention of Murray Brooks's adviser was that Mr. Brooks, having made a will and hidden it — for some reason or other under his pillow — that will had fallen, through the means related by John O'Neill, into the hands of Mr. Percival Brooks, who had destroyed it and substituted a forged one in its place, which adjudged the whole of Mr. Brooks's millions to himself. It was a terrible and daring accusation directed against a gentleman who, in spite of his many wild oats sowed in early youth, was a prominent and important figure in Irish high life.

"But John O'Neill had not finished his evidence, and Mr. Walter Hibbert had a bit of sensation still up his sleeve. He had, namely, produced a paper, the will proved by Mr. Percival Brooks, and had asked John O'Neill if once again he recognized the paper.

" 'Certainly, sir,' said John unhesitatingly, 'that is the one the undertaker found under my poor dead master's pillow, and which I took to Mr. Percival's room immediately.'

"Then the paper was unfolded and placed before the witness.

" 'Now, Mr. O'Neill, will you tell me if that is your signature?'

"John looked at it for a moment; then he said: 'Excuse me, sir,' and produced a pair of spectacles which he carefully adjusted before he again examined the paper. Then he thoughtfully shook his head.

" 'It don't look much like my writing, sir,' he said at last. 'That is to say,' he added, by way of elucidating the matter, 'it does look like my writing, but then I don't think it is.'

"The learned counsel," continued the old man in the corner, "went on arguing, speechifying, cross-examining for nearly a week, until they arrived at the one conclusion which was inevitable from the very first, namely, that the will *was* a forgery — a gross, clumsy, idiotic forgery, since both John O'Neill and Pat Mooney, the two witnesses, absolutely repudiated the signatures as their own. The only successful bit of calligraphy the forger had done was the signature of old Mr. Brooks.

"It was a very curious fact, and one which had undoubtedly aided the forger in accomplishing his work quickly, that Mr. Wethered the lawyer, having, no doubt, realized that Mr. Brooks had not many moments in life to spare, had not drawn up the usual engrossed, magnificent document dear to the lawyer heart, but had used for his client's will one of those regular printed forms which can be purchased at any stationer's.

"Mr. Percival Brooks, of course, flatly denied the serious allegation brought against him. He admitted that the butler had brought him the document the morning after his father's death, and that he certainly, on glancing at it, had been very much astonished to see that that document was his father's will. Against that he declared that its contents did not astonish him in the slightest degree, that he himself knew of the testator's intentions, but that he certainly thought his father had entrusted the will to the care of Mr. Wethered, who did all his business for him.

" 'I only very cursorily glanced at the signature,' he concluded, speaking in a perfectly calm, clear voice; 'you must understand that the thought of forgery was very far from my mind, and that my father's signature is exceedingly well imitated, if, indeed, it is not his own, which I am not at all prepared to believe. As for the two witnesses' signatures, I don't think I had ever seen them before. I took the document to Messrs. Barkston and Maud, who had often done business for me before, and they assured me that the will was in perfect form and order.'

"Asked why he had not entrusted the will to his father's solicitors, he replied:

" 'For the very simple reason that exactly half an hour before the will was placed in my hands, I had read that Mr. Patrick Wethered had been murdered the night before. Mr. Hibbert, the junior partner, was not personally known to me.'

"After that, for form's sake, a good deal of expert evidence was heard on the subject of the dead man's signature. But that was quite unanimous, and merely went to corroborate what had already been established beyond a doubt, namely, that the will dated February 1st, 1908, was a forgery, and probate of the will dated 1891 was therefore granted to Mr. Murray Brooks, the sole executor mentioned therein.

"Two days later the police applied for a warrant for the arrest of Mr. Percival Brooks on a charge of forgery.

"The Crown prosecuted, and Mr. Brooks had again the support of Mr. Oranmore, the eminent K.C. Perfectly calm, like a man conscious of his own innocence and unable to grasp the idea that justice does sometimes miscarry, Mr. Brooks, the son of the millionaire, himself still the possessor of a very large fortune under the former will, stood up in the dock on that memorable day in October, 1908, which still no doubt lives in the memory of his many friends.

"All the evidence with regard to Mr. Brooks's last moments and the forged will was gone through over again. That will, it was the contention of the Crown, had been forged so entirely in favor of the accused, cutting out everyone else, that obviously no one but the beneficiary under that false will would have had any motive in forging it.

"Very pale, and with a frown between his deep-set, handsome Irish eyes, Percival Brooks listened to this large volume of evidence piled up against him by the Crown.

"At times he held brief consultations with Mr. Oranmore, who seemed as cool as a cucumber. Have you ever seen Oranmore in court? He is a character worthy of Dickens. His pronounced brogue, his fat, podgy, clean-shaven face, his not always immaculately clean large hands, have often delighted the caricaturist. As it very soon transpired during that memorable magisterial inquiry, he relied for a verdict in favor of his client upon two main points, and he had concentrated all his skill upon making these two points as telling as he possibly could.

"The first point was the question of time. John O'Neill, cross-examined by Oranmore, stated without hesitation that he had given the will to Mr. Percival at eleven o'clock in the morning. And now

the eminent K.C. brought forward and placed in the witness box
the very lawyers into whose hands the accused had then immediately placed the will. Now, Mr. Barkston, a very well-known solicitor of King Street, declared positively that Mr. Percival Brooks
was in his office at a quarter before twelve; two of his clerks testified to the same time exactly, and it was *impossible,* contended Mr.
Oranmore, that within three-quarters of an hour Mr. Brooks could
have gone to a stationer's, bought a will form, copied Mr. Wethered's writing, his father's signature, and that of John O'Neill and
Pat Mooney.

"Such a thing might have been planned, arranged, practiced, and
ultimately, after a great deal of trouble, successfully carried out, but
human intelligence could not grasp the other as a possibility.

"Still the judge wavered. The eminent K.C. had shaken but not
shattered his belief in the prisoner's guilt. But there was one point
more, and this Oranmore, with the skill of a dramatist, had reserved for the fall of the curtain.

"He noted every sign in the judge's face, he guessed that his client
was not yet absolutely safe, then only did he produce his last two
witnesses.

"One of them was Mary Sullivan, one of the housemaids in the
Fitzwilliam mansion. She had been sent up by the cook at a quarter past four o'clock on the afternoon of February 1st with some
hot water, which the nurse had ordered, for the master's room.
Just as she was about to knock at the door Mr. Wethered was
coming out of the room. Mary stopped with the tray in her hand,
and at the door Mr. Wethered turned and said quite loudly: 'Now,
don't fret, don't be anxious; do try and be calm. Your will is safe
in my pocket, nothing can change it or alter one word of it but
yourself.'

"It was, of course, a very ticklish point in law whether the housemaid's evidence could be accepted. You see, she was quoting the
words of a man since dead, spoken to another man also dead. There
is no doubt that had there been very strong evidence on the other
side against Percival Brooks, Mary Sullivan's would have counted
for nothing; but, as I told you before, the judge's belief in the prisoner's guilt was already very seriously shaken, and now the final

blow aimed at it by Mr. Oranmore shattered his last lingering doubts.

"Dr. Mulligan, namely, had been placed by Mr. Oranmore into the witness box. He was a medical man of unimpeachable authority, in fact, absolutely at the head of his profession in Dublin. What he said practically corroborated Mary Sullivan's testimony. He had gone in to see Mr. Brooks at half-past four, and understood from him that his lawyer had just left him.

"Mr. Brooks certainly, though terribly weak, was calm and more composed. He was dying from a sudden heart attack, and Dr. Mulligan foresaw the almost immediate end. But he was still conscious and managed to murmur feebly: 'I feel much easier in my mind now, doctor — I have made my will — Wethered has been — he's got it in his pocket — it is safe there — safe from that —' But the words died on his lips, and after that he spoke but little. He saw his two sons before he died, but hardly knew them or even looked at them.

"You see," concluded the man in the corner, "you see that the prosecution was bound to collapse. Oranmore did not give it a leg to stand on. The will was forged, it is true, forged in the favor of Percival Brooks and of no one else, forged for him and for his benefit. Whether he knew and connived at the forgery was never proved or, as far as I know, even hinted, but it was impossible to go against all the evidence, which pointed that, as far as the act itself was concerned, he at least was innocent. You see, Dr. Mulligan's evidence was not to be shaken. Mary Sullivan's was equally strong.

"There were two witnesses swearing positively that old Brooks's will was in Mr. Wethered's keeping when that gentleman left the Fitzwilliam mansion at a quarter past four. At five o'clock in the afternoon the lawyer was found dead in Phoenix Park. Between a quarter past four and eight o'clock in the evening Percival Brooks never left the house — that was subsequently proved by Oranmore up to the hilt and beyond a doubt. Since the will found under old Brooks's pillow was a forged will, where then was the will he did make, and which Wethered carried away with him in his pocket?"

"Stolen, of course," said Polly, "by those who murdered and

robbed him; it may have been of no value to them, but they naturally would destroy it, lest it might prove a clew against them."

"Then you think it was mere coincidence?" he asked excitedly.
"What?"

"That Wethered was murdered and robbed at the very moment
that he carried the will in his pocket, whilst another was being
forged in its place?"

"It certainly would be very curious, if it *were* a coincidence," she
said musingly.

"Very," he repeated with biting sarcasm, whilst nervously his
bony fingers played with the inevitable bit of string. "Very curious
indeed. Just think of the whole thing. There was the old man with
all his wealth, and two sons, one to whom he is devoted, and the
other with whom he does nothing but quarrel. One day there is
another of these quarrels, but more violent, more terrible than any
that have previously occurred, with the result that the father, heartbroken by it all, has an attack of apoplexy and practically dies of a
broken heart. After that he alters his will, and subsequently a will
is proved which turns out to be a forgery.

"Now everybody — police, press, and public alike — at once jump
to the conclusion that, as Percival Brooks benefits by that forged
will, Percival Brooks must be the forger."

"Seek for him whom the crime benefits, is your own axiom,"
argued the girl.

"I beg your pardon?"

"Percival Brooks benefited to the tune of £2,000,000."

"I beg your pardon. He did nothing of the sort. He was left with
less than half the share that his younger brother inherited."

"Now, yes; but that was a former will and — "

"And that forged will was so clumsily executed, the signature so
carelessly imitated, that the forgery was bound to come to light.
Did *that* never strike you?"

"Yes, but — "

"There is no but," he interrupted. "It was all as clear as daylight
to me from the very first. The quarrel with the old man, which
broke his heart, was not with his eldest son, with whom he was
used to quarreling, but with the second son whom he idolized, in

whom he believed. Don't you remember how John O'Neill heard the words 'liar' and 'deceit'? Percival Brooks had never deceived his father. His sins were all on the surface. Murray had led a quiet life, had pandered to his father, and fawned upon him, until, like most hypocrites, he at last got found out. Who knows what ugly gambling debt or debt of honor, suddenly revealed to old Brooks, was the cause of that last and deadly quarrel?

"You remember that it was Percival who remained beside his father and carried him up to his room. Where was Murray throughout that long and painful day, when his father lay dying — he, the idolized son, the apple of the old man's eye? You never hear his name mentioned as being present there all that day. But he knew that he had offended his father mortally, and that his father meant to cut him off with a shilling. He knew that Mr. Wethered had been sent for, that Wethered left the house soon after four o'clock.

"And here the cleverness of the man comes in. Having lain in wait for Wethered and knocked him on the back of the head with a stick, he could not very well make that will disappear altogether. There remained the faint chance of some other witnesses knowing that Mr. Brooks had made a fresh will, Mr. Wethered's partner, his clerk, or one of the confidential servants in the house. Therefore *a* will must be discovered after the old man's death.

"Now, Murray Brooks was not an expert forger; it takes years of training to become that. A forged will executed by himself would be sure to be found out — yes, that's it, sure to be found out. The forgery will be palpable — let it be palpable, and then it will be found out, branded as such, and the original will of 1891, so favorable to the young blackguard's interests, would be held as valid. Was it devilry or merely additional caution which prompted Murray to pen that forged will so glaringly in Percival's favor? It is impossible to say.

"Anyhow, it was the cleverest touch in that marvelously devised crime. To plan that evil deed was great, to execute it was easy enough. He had several hours' leisure in which to do it. Then at night it was simplicity itself to slip the document under the dead man's pillow. Sacrilege causes no shudder to such natures as Murray Brooks's. The rest of the drama you know already — "

"But Percival Brooks?"

"The jury returned a verdict of 'Not guilty.' There was no evidence against him."

"But the money? Surely the scoundrel does not have the enjoyment of it still?"

"No; he enjoyed it for a time, but he died about three months ago, and forgot to take the precaution of making a will, so his brother Percival has got the business after all. If you ever go to Dublin, I should order some of Brooks's bacon if I were you. It is very good."

THE PROBLEM OF CELL 13

by JACQUES FUTRELLE

The classic adventure of PROFESSOR A. S. F. X. VAN DUSEN, *otherwise* THE THINKING MACHINE. *Who knows what more epic and delightful adventures in logic this light-heartedly irritable little genius might not have had if Jacques Futrelle had survived the "Titanic" disaster?*

PRACTICALLY all those letters remaining in the alphabet after Augustus S. F. X. Van Dusen was named were afterward acquired by that gentleman in the course of a brilliant scientific career, and, being honorably acquired, were tacked on to the other end. His name, therefore, taken with all that belonged to it, was a wonderfully imposing structure. He was a Ph.D., an LL.D., an F.R.S., an M.D., and an M.D.S. He was also some other things — just what he himself couldn't say — through recognition of his ability by various foreign educational and scientific institutions.

In appearance he was no less striking than in nomenclature. He was slender with the droop of the student in his thin shoulders and the pallor of a close, sedentary life on his clean-shaven face. His eyes wore a perpetual, forbidding squint — the squint of a man who studies little things — and when they could be seen at all through his thick spectacles, were mere slits of watery blue. But above his eyes was his most striking feature. This was a tall, broad brow, almost abnormal in height and width, crowned by a heavy shock of bushy, yellow hair. All these things conspired to give him a peculiar, almost grotesque, personality.

Professor Van Dusen was remotely German. For generations his ancestors had been noted in the sciences; he was the logical result, the master mind. First and above all he was a logician. At least thirty-five years of the half century or so of his existence had been devoted exclusively to proving that two and two always equal four, except in unusual cases, where they equal three or five, as the case may be. He stood broadly on the general proposition that all things that start must go somewhere, and was able to bring the concentrated mental force of his forefathers to bear on a given problem. Incidentally it may be remarked that Professor Van Dusen wore a No. 8 hat.

The world at large had heard vaguely of Professor Van Dusen as The Thinking Machine. It was a newspaper catch-phrase applied to him at the time of a remarkable exhibition at chess; he had demonstrated then that a stranger to the game might, by the force of inevitable logic, defeat a champion who had devoted a lifetime to its study. The Thinking Machine! Perhaps that more nearly described him than all his honorary initials, for he spent week after week, month after month, in the seclusion of his small laboratory from which had gone forth thoughts that staggered scientific associates and deeply stirred the world at large.

It was only occasionally that The Thinking Machine had visitors, and these were usually men who, themselves high in the sciences, dropped in to argue a point and perhaps convince themselves. Two of these men, Dr. Charles Ransome and Alfred Fielding, called one evening to discuss some theory which is not of consequence here.

"Such a thing is impossible," declared Dr. Ransome emphatically, in the course of the conversation.

"Nothing is impossible," declared The Thinking Machine with equal emphasis. He always spoke petulantly. "The mind is master of all things. When science fully recognizes that fact a great advance will have been made."

"How about the airship?" asked Dr. Ransome.

"That's not impossible at all," asserted The Thinking Machine. "It will be invented some time. I'd do it myself, but I'm busy."

Dr. Ransome laughed tolerantly.

"I've heard you say such things before," he said. "But they mean nothing. Mind may be master of matter, but it hasn't yet found a way to apply itself. There are some things that can't be *thought* out of existence, or rather which would not yield to any amount of thinking."

"What, for instance?" demanded The Thinking Machine.

Dr. Ransome was thoughtful for a moment as he smoked.

"Well, say prison walls," he replied. "No man can *think* himself out of a cell. If he could, there would be no prisoners."

"A man can so apply his brain and ingenuity that he can leave a cell, which is the same thing," snapped The Thinking Machine.

Dr. Ransome was slightly amused.

"Let's suppose a case," he said, after a moment. "Take a cell where prisoners under sentence of death are confined — men who are desperate and, maddened by fear, would take any chance to escape — suppose you were locked in such a cell. Could you escape?"

"Certainly," declared The Thinking Machine.

"Of course," said Mr. Fielding, who entered the conversation for the first time, "you might wreck the cell with an explosive — but inside, a prisoner, you couldn't have that."

"There would be nothing of that kind," said The Thinking Machine. "You might treat me precisely as you treated prisoners under sentence of death, and I would leave the cell."

"Not unless you entered it with tools prepared to get out," said Dr. Ransome.

The Thinking Machine was visibly annoyed and his blue eyes snapped.

"Lock me in any cell in any prison anywhere at any time, wearing only what is necessary, and I'll escape in a week," he declared, sharply.

Dr. Ransome sat up straight in the chair, interested. Mr. Fielding lighted a new cigar.

"You mean you could actually *think* yourself out?" asked Dr. Ransome.

"I would get out," was the response.

"Are you serious?"

"Certainly I am serious."

Dr. Ransome and Mr. Fielding were silent for a long time.

"Would you be willing to try it?" asked Mr. Fielding, finally.

"Certainly," said Professor Van Dusen, and there was a trace of irony in his voice. "I have done more asinine things than that to convince other men of less important truths."

The tone was offensive and there was an undercurrent strongly resembling anger on both sides. Of course it was an absurd thing, but Professor Van Dusen reiterated his willingness to undertake the escape and it was decided upon.

"To begin now," added Dr. Ransome.

"I'd prefer that it begin to-morrow," said The Thinking Machine, "because —— "

"No, now," said Mr. Fielding, flatly. "You are arrested, figuratively, of course, without any warning locked in a cell with no chance to communicate with friends, and left there with identically the same care and attention that would be given to a man under sentence of death. Are you willing?"

"All right, now, then," said The Thinking Machine, and he arose.

"Say, the death cell, in Chisholm Prison."

"The death cell in Chisholm Prison."

"And what will you wear?"

"As little as possible," said The Thinking Machine. "Shoes, stockings, trousers and a shirt."

"You will permit yourself to be searched, of course?"

"I am to be treated precisely as all prisoners are treated," said The Thinking Machine. "No more attention and no less."

There were some preliminaries to be arranged in the matter of obtaining permission for the test, but all three were influential men and everything was done satisfactorily by telephone, albeit the prison commissioners, to whom the experiment was explained on purely scientific grounds, were sadly bewildered. Professor Van Dusen would be the most distinguished prisoner they had ever entertained.

When The Thinking Machine had donned those things which he was to wear during his incarceration he called the little old woman who was his housekeeper, cook and maidservant all in one.

"Martha," he said, "it is now twenty-seven minutes past nine o'clock. I am going away. One week from to-night, at half past nine, these gentlemen and one, possibly two, others will take supper with me here. Remember Dr. Ransome is very fond of artichokes."

The three men were driven to Chisholm Prison, where the

warden was awaiting them, having been informed of the matter by telephone. He understood merely that the eminent Professor Van Dusen was to be his prisoner, if he could keep him, for one week; that he had committed no crime, but that he was to be treated as all other prisoners were treated.

"Search him," instructed Dr. Ransome.

The Thinking Machine was searched. Nothing was found on him; the pockets of the trousers were empty; the white, stiff-bosomed shirt had no pocket. The shoes and stockings were removed, examined, then replaced. As he watched all these preliminaries, and noted the pitiful, childlike physical weakness of the man — the colorless face, and the thin, white hands — Dr. Ransome almost regretted his part in the affair.

"Are you sure you want to do this?" he asked.

"Would you be convinced if I did not?" inquired The Thinking Machine in turn.

"No."

"All right. I'll do it."

What sympathy Dr. Ransome had was dissipated by the tone. It nettled him, and he resolved to see the experiment to the end; it would be a stinging reproof to egotism.

"It will be impossible for him to communicate with anyone outside?" he asked.

"Absolutely impossible," replied the warden. "He will not be permitted writing materials of any sort."

"And your jailers, would they deliver a message from him?"

"Not one word, directly or indirectly," said the warden. "You may rest assured of that. They will report anything he might say or turn over to me, anything he might give them."

"That seems entirely satisfactory," said Mr. Fielding, who was frankly interested in the problem.

"Of course, in the event he fails," said Dr. Ransome, "and asks for his liberty, you understand you are to set him free?"

"I understand," replied the warden.

The Thinking Machine stood listening, but had nothing to say until this was all ended, then:

"I should like to make three small requests. You may grant them or not, as you wish."

"No special favors, now," warned Mr. Fielding.

"I am asking none," was the stiff response. "I should like to have some tooth powder — buy it yourself to see that it is tooth powder — and I should like to have one five-dollar and two ten-dollar bills."

Dr. Ransome, Mr. Fielding and the warden exchanged astonished glances. They were not surprised at the request for tooth powder, but were at the request for money.

"Is there any man with whom our friend would come in contact that he could bribe with twenty-five dollars?"

"Not for twenty-five hundred dollars," was the positive reply.

"Well, let him have them," said Mr. Fielding. "I think they are harmless enough."

"And what is the third request?" asked Dr. Ransome.

"I should like to have my shoes polished."

Again the astonished glances were exchanged. This last request was the height of absurdity, so they agreed to it. These things all being attended to, The Thinking Machine was led back into the prison from which he had undertaken to escape.

"Here is Cell 13," said the warden, stopping three doors down the steel corridor. "This is where we keep condemned murderers. No one can leave it without my permission; and no one in it can communicate with the outside. I'll stake my reputation on that. It's only three doors back of my office and I can readily hear any unusual noise."

"Will this cell do, gentlemen?" asked The Thinking Machine. There was a touch of irony in his voice.

"Admirably," was the reply.

The heavy steel door was thrown open, there was a great scurrying and scampering of tiny feet, and The Thinking Machine passed into the gloom of the cell. Then the door was closed and double locked by the warden.

"What is that noise in there?" asked Dr. Ransome, through the bars.

"Rats — dozens of them," replied The Thinking Machine, tersely.

The three men, with final good nights, were turning away when The Thinking Machine called:

"What time is it exactly, Warden?"

"Eleven seventeen," replied the warden.

"Thanks. I will join you gentlemen in your office at half past eight o'clock one week from to-night," said The Thinking Machine.

"And if you do not?"

"There is no 'if' about it."

Chisholm Prison was a great, spreading structure of granite, four stories in all, which stood in the center of acres of open space. It was surrounded by a wall of solid masonry eighteen feet high, and so smoothly finished inside and out as to offer no foothold to a climber, no matter how expert. Atop of this fence, as a further precaution, was a five-foot fence of steel rods, each terminating in a keen point. This fence in itself marked an absolute deadline between freedom and imprisonment, for, even if a man escaped from his cell, it would seem impossible for him to pass the wall.

The yard, which on all sides of the prison building was twenty-five feet wide, that being the distance from the building to the wall, was by day an exercise ground for those prisoners to whom was granted the boon of occasional semi-liberty. But that was not for those in Cell 13. At all times of the day there were armed guards in the yard, four of them, one patrolling each side of the prison building.

By night the yard was almost as brilliantly lighted as by day. On each of the four sides was a great arc light which rose above the prison wall and gave to the guards a clear sight. The lights, too, brightly illuminated the spiked top of the wall. The wires which fed the arc lights ran up the side of the prison building on insulators and from the top story led out to the poles supporting the arc lights.

All these things were seen and comprehended by The Thinking Machine, who was only enabled to see out his closely barred cell window by standing on his bed. This was on the morning following his incarceration. He gathered, too, that the river lay over there beyond the wall somewhere, because he heard faintly the pulsation of a motor boat and high up in the air saw a river bird. From that same direction came the shouts of boys at play and the occasional crack of a batted ball. He knew then that between the prison wall and the river was an open space, a playground.

Chisholm Prison was regarded as absolutely safe. No man had

ever escaped from it. The Thinking Machine, from his perch on the bed, seeing what he saw, could readily understand why. The walls of the cell, though built he judged twenty years before, were perfectly solid, and the window bars of new iron had not a shadow of rust on them. The window itself, even with the bars out, would be a difficult mode of egress because it was small.

Yet, seeing these things, The Thinking Machine was not discouraged. Instead, he thoughtfully squinted at the great arc light — there was bright sunlight now — and traced with his eyes the wire which led from it to the building. That electric wire, he reasoned, must come down the side of the building not a great distance from his cell. That might be worth knowing.

Cell 13 was on the same floor with the offices of the prison — that is, not in the basement, nor yet upstairs. There were only four steps up to the office floor, therefore the level of the floor must be only three or four feet above the ground. He couldn't see the ground directly beneath his window, but he could see it further out toward the wall. It would be an easy drop from the window. Well and good.

Then The Thinking Machine fell to remembering how he had come to the cell. First, there was the outside guard's booth, a part of the wall. There were two heavily barred gates there, both of steel. At this gate was one man always on guard. He admitted persons to the prison after much clanking of keys and locks, and let them out when ordered to do so. The warden's office was in the prison building, and in order to reach that official from the prison yard one had to pass a gate of solid steel with only a peephole in it. Then coming from that inner office to Cell 13, where he was now, one must pass a heavy wooden door and two steel doors into the corridors of the prison; and always there was the double-locked door of Cell 13 to reckon with.

There were then, The Thinking Machine recalled, seven doors to be overcome before one could pass from Cell 13 into the outer world, a free man. But against this was the fact that he was rarely interrupted. A jailer appeared at his cell door at six in the morning with a breakfast of prison fare; he would come again at noon, and again at six in the afternoon. At nine o'clock at night would come the inspection tour. That would be all.

"It's admirably arranged, this prison system," was the mental tribute paid by The Thinking Machine. "I'll have to study it a little when I get out. I had no idea there was such great care exercised in the prisons."

There was nothing, positively nothing, in his cell, except his iron bed, so firmly put together that no man could tear it to pieces save with sledges or a file. He had neither of these. There was not even a chair, or a small table, or a bit of tin or crockery. Nothing! The jailer stood by when he ate, then took away the wooden spoon and bowl which he had used.

One by one these things sank into the brain of The Thinking Machine. When the last possibility had been considered he began an examination of his cell. From the roof, down the walls on all sides, he examined the stones and the cement between them. He stamped over the floor carefully time after time, but it was cement, perfectly solid. After the examination he sat on the edge of the iron bed and was lost in thought for a long time. For Professor Augustus S. F. X. Van Dusen, The Thinking Machine, had something to think about.

He was disturbed by a rat, which ran across his foot, then scampered away into a dark corner of the cell, frightened at its own daring. After a while The Thinking Machine, squinting steadily into the darkness of the corner where the rat had gone, was able to make out in the gloom many little beady eyes staring at him. He counted six pair, and there were perhaps others; he didn't see very well.

Then The Thinking Machine, from his seat on the bed, noticed for the first time the bottom of his cell door. There was an opening there of two inches between the steel bar and the floor. Still looking steadily at this opening, The Thinking Machine backed suddenly into the corner where he had seen the beady eyes. There was a great scampering of tiny feet, several squeaks of frightened rodents, and then silence.

None of the rats had gone out the door, yet there were none in the cell. Therefore there must be another way out of the cell, however small. The Thinking Machine, on hands and knees, started a search for this spot, feeling in the darkness with his long, slender fingers.

At last his search was rewarded. He came upon a small opening in the floor, level with the cement. It was perfectly round and some-what larger than a silver dollar. This was the way the rats had gone. He put his fingers deep into the opening; it seemed to be a disused drainage pipe and was dry and dusty.

Having satisfied himself on this point, he sat on the bed again for an hour, then made another inspection of his surroundings through the small cell window. One of the outside guards stood directly opposite, beside the wall, and happened to be looking at the window of Cell 13 when the head of The Thinking Machine appeared. But the scientist didn't notice the guard.

Noon came and the jailer appeared with the prison dinner of re-pulsively plain food. At home The Thinking Machine merely ate to live; here he took what was offered without comment. Occasionally he spoke to the jailer who stood outside the door watching him.

"Any improvements made here in the last few years?" he asked.

"Nothing particularly," replied the jailer. "New wall was built four years ago."

"Anything done to the prison proper?"

"Painted the woodwork outside, and I believe about seven years ago a new system of plumbing was put in."

"Ah!" said the prisoner. "How far is the river over there?"

"About three hundred feet. The boys have a baseball ground be-tween the wall and the river."

The Thinking Machine had nothing further to say just then, but when the jailer was ready to go he asked for some water.

"I get very thirsty here," he explained. "Would it be possible for you to leave a little water in a bowl for me?"

"I'll ask the warden," replied the jailer, and he went away.

Half an hour later he returned with water in a small earthen bowl.

"The warden says you may keep this bowl," he informed the prisoner. "But you must show it to me when I ask for it. If it is broken, it will be the last."

"Thank you," said The Thinking Machine. "I shan't break it."

The jailer went on about his duties. For just the fraction of a second it seemed that The Thinking Machine wanted to ask a question, but he didn't.

Two hours later this same jailer, in passing the door of Cell No.

13, heard a noise inside and stopped. The Thinking Machine was down on his hands and knees in a corner of the cell, and from that same corner came several frightened squeaks. The jailer looked on interestedly.

"Ah, I've got you," he heard the prisoner say.

"Got what?" he asked, sharply.

"One of these rats," was the reply. "See?" And between the scientist's long fingers the jailer saw a small gray rat struggling. The prisoner brought it over to the light and looked at it closely.

"It's a water rat," he said.

"Ain't you got anything better to do than to catch rats?" asked the jailer.

"It's disgraceful that they should be here at all," was the irritated reply. "Take this one away and kill it. There are dozens more where it came from."

The jailer took the wriggling, squirmy rodent and flung it down on the floor violently. It gave one squeak and lay still. Later he reported the incident to the warden, who only smiled.

Still later that afternoon the outside armed guard on the Cell 13 side of the prison looked up again at the window and saw the prisoner looking out. He saw a hand raised to the barred window and then something white fluttered to the ground, directly under the window of Cell 13. It was a little roll of linen, evidently of white shirting material, and tied around it was a five-dollar bill. The guard looked up at the window again, but the face had disappeared.

With a grim smile he took the little linen roll and the five-dollar bill to the warden's office. There together they deciphered something which was written on it with a queer sort of ink, frequently blurred. On the outside was this:

"Finder of this please deliver to Dr. Charles Ransome."

"Ah," said the warden, with a chuckle. "Plan of escape number one has gone wrong." Then, as an afterthought: "But why did he address it to Dr. Ransome?"

"And where did he get the pen and ink to write with?" asked the guard.

The warden looked at the guard and the guard looked at the warden. There was no apparent solution of that mystery. The warden studied the writing carefully, then shook his head.

"Well, let's see what he was going to say to Dr. Ransome," he said at length, still puzzled, and he unrolled the inner piece of linen.

"Well, if that — what — what do you think of that?" he asked, dazed.

The guard took the bit of linen and read this: —

"Epa cseot d'net niiy awe htto n'si sih. T."

*   *   *

The warden spent an hour wondering what sort of a cipher it was, and half an hour wondering why his prisoner should attempt to communicate with Dr. Ransome, who was the cause of his being there. After this the warden devoted some thought to the question of where the prisoner got writing materials, and what sort of writing materials he had. With the idea of illuminating this point, he examined the linen again. It was a torn part of a white shirt and had ragged edges.

Now it was possible to account for the linen, but what the prisoner had used to write with was another matter. The warden knew it would have been impossible for him to have either pen or pencil, and, besides, neither pen nor pencil had been used in this writing. What, then? The warden decided to investigate personally. The Thinking Machine was his prisoner; he had orders to hold his prisoners; if this one sought to escape by sending cipher messages to persons outside, he would stop it, as he would have stopped it in the case of any other prisoner.

The warden went back to Cell 13 and found The Thinking Machine on his hands and knees on the floor, engaged in nothing more alarming than catching rats. The prisoner heard the warden's step and turned to him quickly.

"It's disgraceful," he snapped, "these rats. There are scores of them."

"Other men have been able to stand them," said the warden. "Here is another shirt for you — let me have the one you have on."

"Why?" demanded The Thinking Machine, quickly. His tone was hardly natural, his manner suggested actual perturbation.

"You have attempted to communicate with Dr. Ransome," said the warden severely. "As my prisoner, it is my duty to put a stop to it."

The Thinking Machine was silent for a moment.

"All right," he said, finally. "Do your duty."

The warden smiled grimly. The prisoner arose from the floor and removed the white shirt, putting on instead a striped convict shirt the warden had brought. The warden took the white shirt eagerly, and then and there compared the pieces of linen on which was written the cipher with certain torn places in the shirt. The Thinking Machine looked on curiously.

"The guard brought *you* those, then?" he asked.

"He certainly did," replied the warden triumphantly. "And that ends your first attempt to escape."

The Thinking Machine watched the warden as he, by comparison, established to his own satisfaction that only two pieces of linen had been torn from the white shirt.

"What did you write this with?" demanded the warden.

"I should think it a part of your duty to find out," said The Thinking Machine, irritably.

The warden started to say some harsh things, then restrained himself and made a minute search of the cell and of the prisoner instead. He found absolutely nothing; not even a match or tooth-pick which might have been used for a pen. The same mystery surrounded the fluid with which the cipher had been written. Although the warden left Cell 13 visibly annoyed, he took the torn shirt in triumph.

"Well, writing notes on a shirt won't get him out, that's certain," he told himself with some complacency. He put the linen scraps into his desk to await developments. "If that man escapes from that cell I'll — hang it — I'll resign."

On the third day of his incarceration The Thinking Machine openly attempted to bribe his way out. The jailer had brought his dinner and was leaning against the barred door, waiting, when The Thinking Machine began the conversation.

"The drainage pipes of the prison lead to the river, don't they?" he asked.

"Yes," said the jailer.

"I suppose they are very small."

"Too small to crawl through, if that's what you're thinking about," was the grinning response.

There was silence until The Thinking Machine finished his meal. Then:

"You know I'm not a criminal, don't you?"

"Yes."

"And that I've a perfect right to be freed if I demand it?"

"Yes."

"Well, I came here believing that I could make my escape," said the prisoner, and his squint eyes studied the face of the jailer. "Would you consider a financial reward for aiding me to escape?"

The jailer, who happened to be an honest man, looked at the slender, weak figure of the prisoner, at the large head with its mass of yellow hair, and was almost sorry.

"I guess prisons like these were not built for the likes of you to get out of," he said, at last.

"But would you consider a proposition to help me get out?" the prisoner insisted, almost beseechingly.

"No," said the jailer, shortly.

"Five hundred dollars," urged The Thinking Machine. "I am not a criminal."

"No," said the jailer.

"A thousand?"

"No," again said the jailer, and he started away hurriedly to escape further temptation. Then he turned back. "If you should give me ten thousand dollars I couldn't get you out. You'd have to pass through seven doors, and I only have the keys to two."

Then he told the warden all about it.

"Plan number two fails," said the warden, smiling grimly. "First a cipher, then bribery."

When the jailer was on his way to Cell 13 at six o'clock, again bearing food to The Thinking Machine, he paused, startled by the unmistakable scrape, scrape of steel against steel. It stopped at the sound of his steps, then craftily the jailer, who was beyond the prisoner's range of vision, resumed his tramping, the sound being apparently that of a man going away from Cell 13. As a matter of fact he was in the same spot.

After a moment there came again the steady scrape, scrape, and the jailer crept cautiously on tiptoes to the door and peered between the bars. The Thinking Machine was standing on the iron bed working at the bars of the little window. He was using a file, judging from the backward and forward swing of his arms.

Cautiously the jailer crept back to the office, summoned the warden in person, and they returned to Cell 13 on tiptoes. The steady scrape was still audible. The warden listened to satisfy himself and then suddenly appeared at the door.

"Well?" he demanded, and there was a smile on his face.

The Thinking Machine glanced back from his perch on the bed and leaped suddenly to the floor, making frantic efforts to hide something. The warden went in, with hand extended.

"Give it up," he said.

"No," said the prisoner, sharply.

"Come, give it up," urged the warden. "I don't want to have to search you again."

"No," repeated the prisoner.

"What was it — a file?" asked the warden.

The Thinking Machine was silent and stood squinting at the warden with something very nearly approaching disappointment on his face — nearly, but not quite. The warden was almost sympathetic.

"Plan number three fails, eh?" he asked, good-naturedly. "Too bad, isn't it?"

The prisoner didn't say.

"Search him," instructed the warden.

The jailer searched the prisoner carefully. At last, artfully concealed in the waistband of the trousers, he found a piece of steel about two inches long, with one side curved like a half moon.

"Ah," said the warden, as he received it from the jailer. "From your shoe heel," and he smiled pleasantly.

The jailer continued his search and on the other side of the trousers waistband found another piece of steel identical with the first. The edges showed where they had been worn against the bars of the window.

"You couldn't saw a way through those bars with these," said the warden.

"I could have," said The Thinking Machine firmly.

"In six months, perhaps," said the warden, good-naturedly.

The warden shook his head slowly as he gazed into the slightly flushed face of his prisoner.

"Ready to give it up?" he asked.

"I haven't started yet," was the prompt reply.

Then came another exhaustive search of the cell. Carefully the two men went over it, finally turning out the bed and searching that. Nothing. The warden in person climbed upon the bed and examined the bars of the window where the prisoner had been sawing. When he looked he was amused.

"Just made it a little bright by hard rubbing," he said to the prisoner, who stood looking on with a somewhat crestfallen air. The warden grasped the iron bars in his strong hands and tried to shake them. They were immovable, set firmly in the solid granite. He examined each in turn and found them all satisfactory. Finally he climbed down from the bed.

"Give it up, Professor," he advised.

The Thinking Machine shook his head and the warden and jailer passed on again. As they disappeared down the corridor The Thinking Machine sat on the edge of the bed with his head in his hands.

"He's crazy to try to get out of that cell," commented the jailer.

"Of course he can't get out," said the warden. "But he's clever. I would like to know what he wrote that cipher with."

It was four o'clock next morning when an awful, heart-racking shriek of terror resounded through the great prison. It came from a cell, somewhere about the center, and its tone told a tale of horror, agony, terrible fear. The warden heard and with three of his men rushed into the long corridor leading to Cell 13.

As they ran there came again that awful cry. It died away in a sort of wail. The white faces of prisoners appeared at cell doors upstairs and down, staring out wonderingly, frightened.

"It's that fool in Cell 13," grumbled the warden.

He stopped and stared in as one of the jailers flashed a lantern. "That fool in Cell 13" lay comfortably on his cot, flat on his back with his mouth open, snoring. Even as they looked there came again the piercing cry, from somewhere above. The warden's face blanched a little as he started up the stairs. There on the top floor he found a man in Cell 43, directly above Cell 13, but two floors higher, cowering in a corner of his cell.

"What's the matter?" demanded the warden.

"Thank God you've come," exclaimed the prisoner, and he cast himself against the bars of his cell.

"What is it?" demanded the warden again.

He threw open the door and went in. The prisoner dropped on his knees and clasped the warden about the body. His face was white with terror, his eyes were widely distended, and he was shuddering. His hands, icy cold, clutched at the warden's.

"Take me out of this cell, please take me out," he pleaded.

"What's the matter with you, anyhow?" insisted the warden, impatiently.

"I heard something — something," said the prisoner, and his eyes roved nervously around the cell.

"What did you hear?"

"I — I can't tell you," stammered the prisoner. Then, in a sudden burst of terror: "Take me out of this cell — put me anywhere — but take me out of here."

The warden and the three jailers exchanged glances.

"Who is this fellow? What's he accused of?" asked the warden.

"Joseph Ballard," said one of the jailers. "He's accused of throwing acid in a woman's face. She died from it."

"But they can't prove it," gasped the prisoner. "They can't prove it. Please put me in some other cell."

He was still clinging to the warden, and that official threw his arms off roughly. Then for a time he stood looking at the cowering wretch, who seemed possessed of all the wild, unreasoning terror of a child.

"Look here, Ballard," said the warden, finally, "if you heard anything, I want to know what it was. Now tell me."

"I can't, I can't," was the reply. He was sobbing.

"Where did it come from?"

"I don't know. Everywhere — nowhere. I just heard it."

"What was it — a voice?"

"Please don't make me answer," pleaded the prisoner.

"You must answer," said the warden, sharply.

"It was a voice — but — but it wasn't human," was the sobbing reply.

"Voice, but not human?" repeated the warden, puzzled.

"It sounded muffled and — and far away — and ghostly," explained the man.

"Did it come from inside or outside the prison?"

"It didn't seem to come from anywhere — it was just here, here, everywhere. I heard it. I heard it."

For an hour the warden tried to get the story, but Ballard had become suddenly obstinate and would say nothing — only pleaded to be placed in another cell, or to have one of the jailers remain near him until daylight. These requests were gruffly refused.

"And see here," said the warden, in conclusion, "if there's any more of this screaming I'll put you in the padded cell."

Then the warden went his way, a sadly puzzled man. Ballard sat at his cell door until daylight, his face, drawn and white with terror, pressed against the bars, and looked out into the prison with wide, staring eyes.

That day, the fourth since the incarceration of The Thinking Machine, was enlivened considerably by the volunteer prisoner, who spent most of his time at the little window of his cell. He began proceedings by throwing another piece of linen down to the guard, who picked it up dutifully and took it to the warden. On it was written:

"Only three days more."

The warden was in no way surprised at what he read; he understood that The Thinking Machine meant only three days more of his imprisonment, and he regarded the note as a boast. But how was the thing written? Where had The Thinking Machine found this new piece of linen? Where? How? He carefully examined the linen. It was white, of fine texture, shirting material. He took the shirt which he had taken and carefully fitted the two original pieces of the linen to the torn places. This third piece was entirely superfluous; it didn't fit anywhere, and yet it was unmistakably the same goods.

"And where — where does he get anything to write with?" demanded the warden of the world at large.

Still later on the fourth day The Thinking Machine, through the window of his cell, spoke to the armed guard outside.

"What day of the month is it?" he asked.

"The fifteenth," was the answer.

The Thinking Machine made a mental astronomical calculation and satisfied himself that the moon would not rise until after nine o'clock that night. Then he asked another question:

"Who attends to those arc lights?"

"Man from the company."

"You have no electricians in the building?"

"No."

"I should think you could save money if you had your own man."

"None of my business," replied the guard.

The guard noticed The Thinking Machine at the cell window frequently during that day, but always the face seemed listless and there was a certain wistfulness in the squint eyes behind the glasses. After a while he accepted the presence of the leonine head as a matter of course. He had seen other prisoners do the same thing; it was the longing for the outside world.

That afternoon, just before the day guard was relieved, the head appeared at the window again, and The Thinking Machine's hand held something out between the bars. It fluttered to the ground and the guard picked it up. It was a five-dollar bill.

"That's for you," called the prisoner.

As usual, the guard took it to the warden. That gentleman looked at it suspiciously; he looked at everything that came from Cell 13 with suspicion.

"He said it was for me," explained the guard.

"It's a sort of a tip, I suppose," said the warden. "I see no particular reason why you shouldn't accept —— "

Suddenly he stopped. He had remembered that The Thinking Machine had gone into Cell 13 with one five-dollar bill and two ten-dollar bills; twenty-five dollars in all. Now a five-dollar bill had been tied around the first pieces of linen that came from the cell. The warden still had it, and to convince himself he took it out and looked at it. It was five dollars; yet here was another five dollars, and The Thinking Machine had only had ten-dollar bills.

"Perhaps somebody changed one of the bills for him," he thought at last, with a sigh of relief.

But then and there he made up his mind. He would search Cell 13 as a cell was never before searched in this world. When a man could write at will, and change money, and do other wholly inexplicable things, there was something radically wrong with his prison. He planned to enter the cell at night — three o'clock would be an excellent time. The Thinking Machine must do all the weird things he did sometime. Night seemed the most reasonable.

Thus it happened that the warden stealthily descended upon Cell

13 that night at three o'clock. He paused at the door and listened. There was no sound save the steady, regular breathing of the prisoner. The keys unfastened the double locks with scarcely a clank, and the warden entered, locking the door behind him. Suddenly he flashed his dark lantern in the face of the recumbent figure.

If the warden had planned to startle The Thinking Machine he was mistaken, for that individual merely opened his eyes quietly, reached for his glasses and inquired, in a most matter-of-fact tone:

"Who is it?"

It would be useless to describe the search that the warden made. It was minute. Not one inch of the cell or the bed was overlooked. He found the round hole in the floor, and with a flash of inspiration thrust his thick fingers into it. After a moment of fumbling there he drew up something and looked at it in the light of his lantern.

"Ugh!" he exclaimed.

The thing he had taken out was a rat — a dead rat. His inspiration fled as a mist before the sun. But he continued the search. The Thinking Machine, without a word, arose and kicked the rat out of the cell into the corridor.

The warden climbed on the bed and tried the steel bars in the tiny window. They were perfectly rigid; every bar of the door was the same.

Then the warden searched the prisoner's clothing, beginning at the shoes. Nothing hidden in them! Then the trousers waistband. Still nothing! Then the pockets of the trousers. From one side he drew out some paper money and examined it.

"Five one-dollar bills," he gasped.

"That's right," said the prisoner.

"But the — you had two tens and a five — what the — how do you do it?"

"That's my business," said The Thinking Machine.

"Did any of my men change this money for you — on your word of honor?"

The Thinking Machine paused just a fraction of a second.

"No," he said.

"Well, do you make it?" asked the warden. He was prepared to believe anything.

"That's my business," again said the prisoner.

The warden glared at the eminent scientist fiercely. He felt — he knew — that this man was making a fool of him, yet he didn't know how. If he were a real prisoner he would get the truth — but, then, perhaps, those inexplicable things which had happened would not have been brought before him so sharply. Neither of the men spoke for a long time, then suddenly the warden turned fiercely and left the cell, slamming the door behind him. He didn't dare to speak, then.

He glanced at the clock. It was ten minutes to four. He had hardly settled himself in bed when again came that heart-breaking shriek through the prison. With a few muttered words, which, while not elegant, were highly expressive, he relighted his lantern and rushed through the prison again to the cell on the upper floor.

Again Ballard was crushing himself against the steel door, shrieking, shrieking at the top of his voice. He stopped only when the warden flashed his lamp in the cell.

"Take me out, take me out," he screamed. "I did it, I did it, I killed her. Take it away."

"Take what away?" asked the warden.

"I threw the acid in her face — I did it — I confess. Take me out of here."

Ballard's condition was pitiable; it was only an act of mercy to let him out into the corridor. There he crouched in a corner, like an animal at bay, and clasped his hands to his ears. It took half an hour to calm him sufficiently for him to speak. Then he told incoherently what had happened. On the night before at four o'clock he had heard a voice — a sepulchral voice, muffled and wailing in tone.

"What did it say?" asked the warden, curiously.

"Acid — acid — acid!" gasped the prisoner. "It accused me. Acid! I threw the acid, and the woman died. Oh!" It was a long, shuddering wail of terror.

"Acid?" echoed the warden, puzzled. The case was beyond him.

"Acid. That's all I heard — that one word, repeated several times. There were other things, too, but I didn't hear them."

"That was last night, eh?" asked the warden. "What happened to-night — what frightened you just now?"

"It was the same thing," gasped the prisoner. "Acid — acid — acid!" He covered his face with his hands and sat shivering. "It was acid I used on her, but I didn't mean to kill her. I just heard the words. It was something accusing me — accusing me." He mumbled, and was silent.

"Did you hear anything else?"

"Yes — but I couldn't understand — only a little bit — just a word or two."

"Well, what was it?"

"I heard 'acid' three times, then I heard a long, moaning sound, then — then — I heard 'No. 8 hat.' I heard that twice."

"No. 8 hat," repeated the warden. "What the devil — No. 8 hat? Accusing voices of conscience have never talked about No. 8 hats, so far as I ever heard."

"He's insane," said one of the jailers, with an air of finality.

"I believe you," said the warden. "He must be. He probably heard something and got frightened. He's trembling now. No. 8 hat! What the —— "

When the fifth day of The Thinking Machine's imprisonment rolled around the warden was wearing a hunted look. He was anxious for the end of the thing. He could not help but feel that his distinguished prisoner had been amusing himself. And if this were so, The Thinking Machine had lost none of his sense of humor. For on this fifth day he flung down another linen note to the outside guard, bearing the words: "Only two days more." Also he flung down half a dollar.

Now the warden knew — he *knew* — that the man in Cell 13 didn't have any half dollars — he *couldn't* have any half dollars, no more than he could have pen and ink and linen, and yet he did have them. It was a condition, not a theory; that is one reason why the warden was wearing a hunted look.

That ghastly, uncanny thing, too, about "Acid" and "No. 8 hat" clung to him tenaciously. They didn't mean anything, of course, merely the ravings of an insane murderer who had been driven by fear to confess his crime, still there were so many things that "didn't mean anything" happening in the prison now since The Thinking Machine was there.

On the sixth day the warden received a postal stating that Dr. Ransome and Mr. Fielding would be at Chisholm Prison on the following evening, Thursday, and in the event Professor Van Dusen had not yet escaped — and they presumed he had not because they had not heard from him — they would meet him there.

"In the event he had not yet escaped!" The warden smiled grimly. Escaped!

The Thinking Machine enlivened this day for the warden with three notes. They were on the usual linen and bore generally on the appointment at half past eight o'clock Thursday night, which appointment the scientist had made at the time of his imprisonment.

On the afternoon of the seventh day the warden passed Cell 13 and glanced in. The Thinking Machine was lying on the iron bed, apparently sleeping lightly. The cell appeared precisely as it always did from a casual glance. The warden would swear that no man was going to leave it between that hour — it was then four o'clock — and half past eight o'clock that evening.

On his way back past the cell the warden heard the steady breathing again, and coming close to the door looked in. He wouldn't have done so if The Thinking Machine had been looking, but now — well, it was different.

A ray of light came through the high window and fell on the face of the sleeping man. It occurred to the warden for the first time that his prisoner appeared haggard and weary. Just then The Thinking Machine stirred slightly and the warden hurried on up the corridor guiltily. That evening after six o'clock he saw the jailer.

"Everything all right in Cell 13?" he asked.

"Yes, sir," replied the jailer. "He didn't eat much, though."

It was with a feeling of having done his duty that the warden received Dr. Ransome and Mr. Fielding shortly after seven o'clock. He intended to show them the linen notes and lay before them the full story of his woes, which was a long one. But before this came to pass the guard from the river side of the prison yard entered the office.

"The arc light in my side of the yard won't light," he informed the warden.

"Confound it, that man's a hoodoo," thundered the official. "Everything has happened since he's been here."

The guard went back to his post in the darkness, and the warden phoned to the electric light company.

"This is Chisholm Prison," he said through the phone. "Send three or four men down here quick, to fix an arc light."

The reply was evidently satisfactory, for the warden hung up the receiver and passed out into the yard. While Dr. Ransome and Mr. Fielding sat waiting the guard at the outer gate came in with a special delivery letter. Dr. Ransome happened to notice the address, and, when the guard went out, looked at the letter more closely.

"By George!" he exclaimed.

"What is it?" asked Mr. Fielding.

Silently the doctor offered the letter. Mr. Fielding examined it closely.

"Coincidence," he said. "It must be."

It was nearly eight o'clock when the warden returned to his office. The electricians had arrived in a wagon, and were now at work. The warden pressed the buzz-button communicating with the man at the outer gate in the wall.

"How many electricians came in?" he asked, over the short phone. "Four? Three workmen in jumpers and overalls and the manager? Frock coat and silk hat? All right. Be certain that only four go out. That's all."

He turned to Dr. Ransome and Mr. Fielding.

"We have to be careful here — particularly," and there was broad sarcasm in his tone, "since we have scientists locked up."

The warden picked up the special delivery letter carelessly, and then began to open it.

"When I read this I want to tell you gentlemen something about how —— Great Cæsar!" he ended, suddenly, as he glanced at the letter. He sat with mouth open, motionless, from astonishment.

"What is it?" asked Mr. Fielding.

"A special delivery letter from Cell 13," gasped the warden. "An invitation to supper."

"What?" and the two others arose, unanimously.

The warden sat dazed, staring at the letter for a moment, then called sharply to a guard outside in the corridor.

"Run down to Cell 13 and see if that man's in there."

The guard went as directed, while Dr. Ransome and Mr. Fielding examined the letter.

"It's Van Dusen's handwriting; there's no question of that," said Dr. Ransome. "I've seen too much of it."

Just then the buzz on the telephone from the outer gate sounded, and the warden, in a semi-trance, picked up the receiver.

"Hello! Two reporters, eh? Let 'em come in." He turned suddenly to the doctor and Mr. Fielding. "Why, the man *can't* be out. He must be in his cell."

Just at that moment the guard returned.

"He's still in his cell, sir," he reported. "I saw him. He's lying down."

"There, I told you so," said the warden, and he breathed freely again. "But how did he mail that letter?"

There was a rap on the steel door which led from the jail yard into the warden's office.

"It's the reporters," said the warden. "Let them in," he instructed the guard; then to the two other gentlemen: "Don't say anything about this before them, because I'd never hear the last of it."

The door opened, and the two men from the front gate entered.

"Good-evening, gentlemen," said one. That was Hutchinson Hatch; the warden knew him well.

"Well?" demanded the other, irritably. "I'm here."

That was The Thinking Machine.

He squinted belligerently at the warden, who sat with mouth agape. For the moment that official had nothing to say. Dr. Ransome and Mr. Fielding were amazed, but they didn't know what the warden knew. They were only amazed; he was paralyzed. Hutchinson Hatch, the reporter, took in the scene with greedy eyes.

"How — how — how did you do it?" gasped the warden, finally.

"Come back to the cell," said The Thinking Machine, in the irritated voice which his scientific associates knew so well.

The warden, still in a condition bordering on trance, led the way.

"Flash your light in there," directed The Thinking Machine.

The warden did so. There was nothing unusual in the appearance of the cell, and there — there on the bed lay the figure of The Thinking Machine. Certainly! There was the yellow hair! Again the warden looked at the man beside him and wondered at the strangeness of his own dreams.

With trembling hands he unlocked the cell door and The Thinking Machine passed inside.

"See here," he said.

He kicked at the steel bars in the bottom of the cell door and three of them were pushed out of place. A fourth broke off and rolled away in the corridor.

"And here, too," directed the erstwhile prisoner as he stood on the bed to reach the small window. He swept his hand across the opening and every bar came out.

"What's this in bed?" demanded the warden, who was slowly recovering.

"A wig," was the reply. "Turn down the cover."

The warden did so. Beneath it lay a large coil of strong rope, thirty feet or more, a dagger, three files, ten feet of electric wire, a thin, powerful pair of steel pliers, a small tack hammer with its handle, and—and a derringer pistol.

"How did you do it?" demanded the warden.

"You gentlemen have an engagement to supper with me at half past nine o'clock," said The Thinking Machine. "Come on, or we shall be late."

"But how did you do it?" insisted the warden.

"Don't ever think you can hold any man who can use his brain," said The Thinking Machine. "Come on; we shall be late."

It was an impatient supper party in the rooms of Professor Van Dusen and a somewhat silent one. The guests were Dr. Ransome, Alfred Fielding, the warden, and Hutchinson Hatch, reporter. The meal was served to the minute, in accordance with Professor Van Dusen's instructions of one week before; Dr. Ransome found the artichokes delicious. At last the supper was finished and The Thinking Machine turned full on Dr. Ransome and squinted at him fiercely.

"Do you believe it now?" he demanded.

"I do," replied Dr. Ransome.

"Do you admit that it was a fair test?"

"I do."

With the others, particularly the warden, he was waiting anxiously for the explanation.

"Suppose you tell us how —— " began Mr. Fielding.

"Yes, tell us how," said the warden.

The Thinking Machine readjusted his glasses, took a couple of preparatory squints at his audience, and began the story. He told it from the beginning logically; and no man ever talked to more interested listeners.

"My agreement was," he began, "to go into a cell, carrying nothing except what was necessary to wear, and to leave that cell within a week. I had never seen Chisholm Prison. When I went into the cell I asked for tooth powder, two ten- and one five-dollar bills, and also to have my shoes blacked. Even if these requests had been refused it would not have mattered seriously. But you agreed to them.

"I knew there would be nothing in the cell which you thought I might use to advantage. So when the warden locked the door on me I was apparently helpless, unless I could turn three seemingly innocent things to use. They were things which would have been permitted any prisoner under sentence of death, were they not, warden?"

"Tooth powder and polished shoes, yes, but not money," replied the warden.

"Anything is dangerous in the hands of a man who knows how to use it," went on The Thinking Machine. "I did nothing that first night but sleep and chase rats." He glared at the warden. "When the matter was broached I knew I could do nothing that night, so suggested next day. You gentlemen thought I wanted time to arrange an escape with outside assistance, but this was not true. I knew I could communicate with whom I pleased, when I pleased."

The warden stared at him a moment, then went on smoking solemnly.

"I was aroused next morning at six o'clock by the jailer with my breakfast," continued the scientist. "He told me dinner was at twelve and supper at six. Between these times, I gathered, I would be pretty much to myself. So immediately after breakfast I examined my outside surroundings from my cell window. One look told me it would be useless to try to scale the wall, even should I decide to leave my cell by the window, for my purpose was to leave not only the cell, but the prison. Of course, I could have gone over the wall, but it would have taken me longer to lay my plans that way. Therefore, for the moment, I dismissed all idea of that.

"From this first observation I knew the river was on that side of the prison, and that there was also a playground there. Subsequently these surmises were verified by a keeper. I knew then one important thing — that anyone might approach the prison wall from that side if necessary without attracting any particular attention. That was well to remember. I remembered it.

"But the outside thing which most attracted my attention was the feed wire to the arc light which ran within a few feet — probably three or four — of my cell window. I knew that would be valuable in the event I found it necessary to cut off that arc light."

"Oh, you shut it off to-night, then?" asked the warden.

"Having learned all I could from that window," resumed The Thinking Machine, without heeding the interruption, "I considered the idea of escaping through the prison proper. I recalled just how I had come into the cell, which I knew would be the only way. Seven doors lay between me and the outside. So, also for the time being, I gave up the idea of escaping that way. And I couldn't go through the solid granite walls of the cell."

The Thinking Machine paused for a moment and Dr. Ransome lighted a new cigar. For several minutes there was silence, then the scientific jailbreaker went on:

"While I was thinking about these things a rat ran across my foot. It suggested a new line of thought. There were at least half a dozen rats in the cell — I could see their beady eyes. Yet I had noticed none come under the cell door. I frightened them purposely and watched the cell door to see if they went out that way. They did not, but they were gone. Obviously they went another way. Another way meant another opening.

"I searched for this opening and found it. It was an old drain pipe, long unused and partly choked with dirt and dust. But this was the way the rats had come. They came from somewhere. Where? Drain pipes usually lead outside prison grounds. This one probably led to the river, or near it. The rats must therefore come from that direction. If they came a part of the way, I reasoned that they came all the way, because it was extremely unlikely that a solid iron or lead pipe would have any hole in it except at the exit.

"When the jailer came with my luncheon he told me two important things, although he didn't know it. One was that a new system of plumbing had been put in the prison seven years before; another that the river was only three hundred feet away. Then I knew positively that the pipe was a part of an old system; I knew, too, that it slanted generally toward the river. But did the pipe end in the water or on land?

"This was the next question to be decided. I decided it by catching several of the rats in the cell. My jailer was surprised to see me engaged in this work. I examined at least a dozen of them. They were perfectly dry; they had come through the pipe, and, most important of all, they were *not house rats, but field rats*. The other end of the pipe was on land, then, outside the prison walls. So far, so good.

"Then, I knew that if I worked freely from this point I must attract the warden's attention in another direction. You see, by telling the warden that I had come there to escape you made the test more severe, because I had to trick him by false scents."

The warden looked up with a sad expression in his eyes.

"The first thing was to make him think I was trying to communicate with you, Dr. Ransome. So I wrote a note on a piece of linen I tore from my shirt, addressed it to Dr. Ransome, tied a five-dollar bill around it and threw it out the window. I knew the guard would take it to the warden, but I rather hoped the warden would send it as addressed. Have you that first linen note, warden?"

The warden produced the cipher.

"What the deuce does it mean, anyhow?" he asked.

"Read it backward, beginning with the 'T' signature and disregard the division into words," instructed The Thinking Machine.

The warden did so.

"*T-h-i-s,* this," he spelled, studied it a moment, then read it off, grinning:

"This is not the way I intend to escape."

"Well, now what do you think o' that?" he demanded, still grinning.

"I knew that would attract your attention, just as it did," said

The Thinking Machine, "and if you really found out what it was it would be a sort of gentle rebuke."

"What did you write it with?" asked Dr. Ransome, after he had examined the linen and passed it to Mr. Fielding.

"This," said the erstwhile prisoner, and he extended his foot. On it was the shoe he had worn in prison, though the polish was gone — scraped off clean. "The shoe blacking, moistened with water, was my ink; the metal tip of the shoe lace made a fairly good pen."

The warden looked up and suddenly burst into a laugh, half of relief, half of amusement.

"You're a wonder," he said, admiringly. "Go on."

"That precipitated a search of my cell by the warden, as I had intended," continued The Thinking Machine. "I was anxious to get the warden into the habit of searching my cell, so that finally, constantly finding nothing, he would get disgusted and quit. This at last happened, practically."

The warden blushed.

"He then took my white shirt away and gave me a prison shirt. He was satisfied that those two pieces of the shirt were all that was missing. But while he was searching my cell I had another piece of that same shirt, about nine inches square, rolled into a small ball in my mouth."

"Nine inches of that shirt?" demanded the warden. "Where did it come from?"

"The bosoms of all stiff white shirts are of triple thickness," was the explanation. "I tore out the inside thickness, leaving the bosom only two thicknesses. I knew you wouldn't see it. So much for that."

There was a little pause, and the warden looked from one to another of the men with a sheepish grin.

"Having disposed of the warden for the time being by giving him something else to think about, I took my first serious step toward freedom," said Professor Van Dusen. "I knew, within reason, that the pipe led somewhere to the playground outside; I knew a great many boys played there; I knew that rats came into my cell from out there. Could I communicate with some one outside with these things at hand?

"First was necessary, I saw, a long and fairly reliable thread, so — but here," he pulled up his trousers legs and showed that the tops of both stockings, of fine, strong lisle, were gone. "I unraveled those — after I got them started it wasn't difficult — and I had easily a quarter of a mile of thread that I could depend on.

"Then on half of my remaining linen I wrote, laboriously enough I assure you, a letter explaining my situation to this gentleman here," and he indicated Hutchinson Hatch. "I knew he would assist me — for the value of the newspaper story. I tied firmly to this linen letter a ten-dollar bill — there is no surer way of attracting the eye of anyone — and wrote on the linen: 'Finder of this deliver to Hutchinson Hatch, *Daily American,* who will give another ten dollars for the information.'

"The next thing was to get this note outside on that playground where a boy might find it. There were two ways, but I chose the best. I took one of the rats — I became adept in catching them — tied the linen and money firmly to one leg, fastened my lisle thread to another, and turned him loose in the drain pipe. I reasoned that the natural fright of the rodent would make him run until he was outside the pipe and then out on earth he would probably stop to gnaw off the linen and money.

"From the moment the rat disappeared into that dusty pipe I became anxious. I was taking so many chances. The rat might gnaw the string, of which I held one end; other rats might gnaw it; the rat might run out of the pipe and leave the linen and money where they would never be found; a thousand other things might have happened. So began some nervous hours, but the fact that the rat ran on until only a few feet of the string remained in my cell made me think he was outside the pipe. I had carefully instructed Mr. Hatch what to do in case the note reached him. The question was: Would it reach him?

"This done, I could only wait and make other plans in case this one failed. I openly attempted to bribe my jailer, and learned from him that he held the keys to only two of seven doors between me and freedom. Then I did something else to make the warden nervous. I took the steel supports out of the heels of my shoes and made a pretense of sawing the bars of my cell window. The warden raised a pretty row about that. He developed, too, the habit of shaking the bars of my cell window to see if they were solid. They were — then."

Again the warden grinned. He had ceased being astonished.

"With this one plan I had done all I could and could only wait to see what happened," the scientist went on. "I couldn't know whether my note had been delivered or even found, or whether the mouse had gnawed it up. And I didn't dare to draw back through the pipe that one slender thread which connected me with the outside.

"When I went to bed that night I didn't sleep, for fear there would come the slight signal twitch at the thread which was to tell me that Mr. Hatch had received the note. At half past three o'clock, I judge, I felt this twitch, and no prisoner actually under sentence of death ever welcomed a thing more heartily."

The Thinking Machine stopped and turned to the reporter.

"You'd better explain just what you did," he said.

"The linen note was brought to me by a small boy who had been playing baseball," said Mr. Hatch. "I immediately saw a big story in it, so I gave the boy another ten dollars, and got several spools of silk, some twine, and a roll of light, pliable wire. The professor's note suggested that I have the finder of the note show me just where it was picked up, and told me to make my search from there, beginning at two o'clock in the morning. If I found the other end of the thread I was to twitch it gently three times, then a fourth.

"I began the search with a small-bulb electric light. It was an hour and twenty minutes before I found the end of the drain pipe, half hidden in weeds. The pipe was very large there, say twelve inches across. Then I found the end of the lisle thread, twitched it as directed and immediately I got an answering twitch.

"Then I fastened the silk to this and Professor Van Dusen began to pull it into his cell. I nearly had heart disease for fear the string would break. To the end of the silk I fastened the twine, and when that had been pulled in I tied on the wire. Then that was drawn into the pipe and we had a substantial line, which rats couldn't gnaw, from the mouth of the drain into the cell."

The Thinking Machine raised his hand and Hatch stopped.

"All this was done in absolute silence," said the scientist. "But when the wire reached my hand I could have shouted. Then we tried another experiment, which Mr. Hatch was prepared for. I tested the pipe as a speaking tube. Neither of us could hear very clearly, but I dared not speak loud for fear of attracting attention in the prison. At last I made him understand what I wanted immediately. He seemed to have great difficulty in understanding when I asked for nitric acid, and I repeated the word 'acid' several times.

"Then I heard a shriek from a cell above me. I knew instantly that someone had overheard, and when I heard you coming, Mr. Warden, I feigned sleep. If you had entered my cell at that moment that whole plan of escape would have ended there. But you passed on. That was the nearest I ever came to being caught.

"Having established this improvised trolley it is easy to see how I got things in the cell and made them disappear at will. I merely dropped them back into the pipe. You, Mr. Warden, could not have reached the connecting wire with your fingers; they are too large. My fingers, you see, are longer and more slender. In addition I guarded the top of that pipe with a rat — you remember how."

"I remember," said the warden, with a grimace.

"I thought that if anyone were tempted to investigate that hole the rat would dampen his ardor. Mr. Hatch could not send me anything useful through the pipe until next night, although he did send me change for ten dollars as a test, so I proceeded with other parts of my plan. Then I evolved the method of escape which I finally employed.

"In order to carry this out successfully it was necessary for the guard in the yard to get accustomed to seeing me at the cell window. I arranged this by dropping linen notes to him, boastful in tone, to make the warden believe, if possible, one of his assistants was communicating with the outside for me. I would stand at my window for hours gazing out, so the guard could see, and occasionally I spoke to him. In that way I learned that the prison had no electricians of its own, but was dependent upon the lighting company if anything should go wrong.

"That cleared the way to freedom perfectly. Early in the evening of the last day of my imprisonment, when it was dark, I planned to cut the feed wire which was only a few feet from my window, reaching it with an acid-tipped wire I had. That would make that side of the prison perfectly dark while the electricians were searching for the break. That would also bring Mr. Hatch into the prison yard.

"There was only one more thing to do before I actually began the work of setting myself free. This was to arrange final details with Mr. Hatch through our speaking tube. I did this within half an hour after the warden left my cell on the fourth night of my imprisonment. Mr. Hatch again had serious difficulty in understanding me, and I repeated the word 'acid' to him several times, and later on the words: 'No. 8 hat' — that's my size — and these were the things which made a prisoner upstairs confess to murder, so one of the jailers told me next day. This prisoner heard our voices, confused of course, through the pipe, which also went to his cell. The cell directly over me was not occupied, hence no one else heard.

"Of course the actual work of cutting the steel bars out of the window and door was comparatively easy with nitric acid, which I got through the pipe in tin bottles, but it took time. Hour after hour on the fifth and sixth and seventh days the guard below was looking at me as I worked on the bars of the window with the acid on a piece of wire. I used the tooth powder to prevent the acid spreading. I looked away abstractedly as I worked and each minute the acid cut deeper into the metal. I noticed that the jailers always tried the door by shaking the upper part, never the lower bars, therefore I cut the lower bars, leaving them hanging in place by thin strips of metal. But that was a bit of dare-deviltry. I could not have gone that way so easily."

The Thinking Machine sat silent for several minutes.

"I think that makes everything clear," he went on. "Whatever points I have not explained were merely to confuse the warden and jailers. These things in my bed I brought in to please Mr. Hatch, who wanted to improve the story. Of course, the wig was necessary in my plan. The special delivery letter I wrote and directed in my cell with Mr. Hatch's fountain pen, then sent it out to him and he mailed it. That's all, I think."

"But your actually leaving the prison grounds and then coming in through the outer gate to my office?" asked the warden.

"Perfectly simple," said the scientist. "I cut the electric light wire with acid, as I said, when the current was off. Therefore when the current was turned on the arc didn't light. I knew it would take some time to find out what was the matter and make repairs. When the guard went to report to you the yard was dark. I crept out the window — it was a tight fit, too — replaced the bars by standing on a narrow ledge and remained in a shadow until the force of electricians arrived. Mr. Hatch was one of them.

"When I saw him I spoke and he handed me a cap, a jumper and overalls, which I put on within ten feet of you, Mr. Warden, while you were in the yard. Later Mr. Hatch called me, presumably as a workman, and together we went out the gate to get something out of the wagon. The gate guard let us pass out readily as two workmen who had just passed in. We changed our clothing and reappeared, asking to see you. We saw you. That's all."

There was silence for several minutes. Dr. Ransome was first to speak.

"Wonderful!" he exclaimed. "Perfectly amazing."

"How did Mr. Hatch happen to come with the electricians?" asked Mr. Fielding.

"His father is manager of the company," replied The Thinking Machine.

"But what if there had been no Mr. Hatch outside to help?"

"Every prisoner has one friend outside who would help him escape if he could."

"Suppose — just suppose — there had been no old plumbing system there?" asked the warden, curiously.

"There were two other ways out," said The Thinking Machine, enigmatically.

Ten minutes later the telephone bell rang. It was a request for the warden.

"Light all right, eh?" the warden asked, through the phone. "Good. Wire cut beside Cell 13? Yes, I know. One electrician too many? What's that? Two came out?"

The warden turned to the others with a puzzled expression.

"He only let in four electricians, he has let out two and says there are three left."

"I was the odd one," said The Thinking Machine.

"Oh," said the warden. "I see." Then through the phone: "Let the fifth man go. He's all right."

THE ABSENT–MINDED COTERIE

by ROBERT BARR

The literary forefather of Hercule Poirot, EUGÈNE VALMONT
lives in eight short stories. But if "The Absent-Minded Coterie"
were the only VALMONT *story, he would still be an immortal.*

I WELL remember the November day when I first heard of the
Summertrees case, because there hung over London a fog so thick
that two or three times I lost my way, and no cab was to be had
at any price. The few cabmen then in the streets were leading their
animals slowly along, making for their stables. It was one of those
depressing London days which filled me with ennui and a yearn-
ing for my own clear city of Paris, where, if we are ever visited by
a slight mist, it is at least clean, white vapor, and not this horrible
London mixture saturated with suffocating carbon. The fog was
too thick for any passer to read the contents bills of the newspapers
plastered on the pavement, and as there were probably no races
that day the newsboys were shouting what they considered the
next most important event — the election of an American President.
I bought a paper and thrust it into my pocket. It was late when I
reached my flat, and, after dining there, which was an unusual thing
for me to do, I put on my slippers, took an easy-chair before the
fire, and began to read my evening journal. I was distressed to learn
that the eloquent Mr. Bryan had been defeated. I knew little about
the silver question, but the man's oratorical powers had appealed
to me, and my sympathy was aroused because he owned many
silver mines, and yet the price of the metal was so low that apparently he could not make a living through the operation of them.
But, of course, the cry that he was a plutocrat, and a reputed mil-

lionaire over and over again, was bound to defeat him in a democracy where the average voter is exceedingly poor and not comfortably well-to-do, as is the case with our peasants in France. I always took great interest in the affairs of the huge republic to the West, having been at some pains to inform myself accurately regarding its politics; and although, as my readers know, I seldom quote anything complimentary that is said of me, nevertheless, an American client of mine once admitted that he never knew the true inwardness — I think that was the phrase he used — of American politics until he heard me discourse upon them. But then, he added, he had been a very busy man all his life.

I had allowed my paper to slip to the floor, for in very truth the fog was penetrating even into my flat, and it was becoming difficult to read, notwithstanding the electric light. My man came in, and announced that Mr. Spenser Hale wished to see me, and, indeed, any night, but especially when there is rain or fog outside, I am more pleased to talk with a friend than to read a newspaper.

"*Mon Dieu,* my dear Monsieur Hale, it is a brave man you are to venture out in such a fog as is abroad tonight."

"Ah, Monsieur Valmont," said Hale with pride, "you cannot raise a fog like this in Paris!"

"No. There you are supreme," I admitted, rising and saluting my visitor, then offering him a chair.

"I see you are reading the latest news," he said, indicating my newspaper. "I am very glad that man Bryan is defeated. Now we shall have better times."

I waved my hand as I took my chair again. I will discuss many things with Spenser Hale, but not American politics; he does not understand them. It is a common defect of the English to suffer complete ignorance regarding the internal affairs of other countries.

"It is surely an important thing that brought you out on such a night as this. The fog must be very thick in Scotland Yard."

This delicate shaft of fancy completely missed him, and he answered stolidly:

"It's thick all over London, and, indeed, throughout most of England."

"Yes, it is," I agreed, but he did not see that either.

Still, a moment later, he made a remark which, if it had come from some people I know, might have indicated a glimmer of comprehension.

"You are a very, very clever man, Monsieur Valmont, so all I need say is that the question which brought me here is the same as that on which the American election was fought. Now, to a countryman, I should be compelled to give further explanation, but to you, monsieur, that will not be necessary."

There are times when I dislike the crafty smile and partial closing of the eyes which always distinguishes Spenser Hale when he places on the table a problem which he expects will baffle me. If I said he never did baffle me, I would be wrong, of course, for sometimes the utter simplicity of the puzzles which trouble him leads me into an intricate involution entirely unnecessary in the circumstances.

I pressed my finger tips together, and gazed for a few moments at the ceiling. Hale had lit his black pipe, and my silent servant placed at his elbow the whisky and soda, then tiptoed out of the room. As the door closed my eyes came from the ceiling to the level of Hale's expansive countenance.

"Have they eluded you?" I asked quietly.

"Who?"

"The coiners."

Hale's pipe dropped from his jaw, but he managed to catch it before it reached the floor. Then he took a gulp from the tumbler.

"That was just a lucky shot," he said.

"*Parfaitement,*" I replied carelessly.

"Now, own up, Valmont, wasn't it?"

I shrugged my shoulders. A man cannot contradict a guest in his own house.

"Oh, stow that!" cried Hale impolitely. He is a trifle prone to strong and even slangy expressions when puzzled. "Tell me how you guessed it."

"It is very simple, *mon ami.* The question on which the American election was fought is the price of silver, which is so low that it has ruined Mr. Bryan, and threatens to ruin all the farmers of the West who possess silver mines on their farms. Silver troubled America, *ergo* silver troubles Scotland Yard.

"Very well; the natural inference is that some one has stolen bars of silver. But such a theft happened three months ago, when the metal was being unloaded from a German steamer at Southampton, and my dear friend Spenser Hale ran down the thieves very cleverly as they were trying to dissolve the marks off the bars with acid. Now crimes do not run in series, like the numbers in roulette at Monte Carlo. The thieves are men of brains. They say to themselves, 'What chance is there successfully to steal bars of silver while Mr. Hale is at Scotland Yard?' Eh, my good friend?"

"Really, Valmont," said Hale, taking another sip, "sometimes you almost persuade me that you have reasoning powers."

"Thanks, comrade. Then it is not a *theft* of silver we have now to deal with. But the American election was fought on the *price* of silver. If silver had been high in cost, there would have been no silver question. So the crime that is bothering you arises through the low price of silver, and this suggests that it must be a case of illicit coinage, for there the low price of the metal comes in. You have, perhaps, found a more subtle illegitimate act going forward than heretofore. Some one is making your shillings and your half crowns from real silver, instead of from baser metal, and yet there is a large profit which has not hitherto been possible through the high price of silver. With the old conditions you were familiar, but this new element sets at naught all your previous formulas. That is how I reasoned the matter out."

"Well, Valmont, you have hit it, I'll say that for you; you have hit it. There is a gang of expert coiners who are putting out real silver money, and making a clear shilling on the half crown. We can find no trace of the coiners, but we know the man who is shoving the stuff."

"That ought to be sufficient," I suggested.

"Yes, it should, but it hasn't proved so up to date. Now I came tonight to see if you would do one of your French tricks for us, right on the quiet."

"What French trick, Monsieur Spenser Hale?" I inquired with some asperity, forgetting for the moment that the man invariably became impolite when he grew excited.

"No offense intended," said this blundering officer, who really is a good-natured fellow, but always puts his foot in it, and then apologizes. "I want some one to go through a man's house without a search warrant, spot the evidence, let me know, and then we'll rush the place before he has time to hide his tracks."

"Who is this man, and where does he live?"

"His name is Ralph Summertrees, and he lives in a very natty little *bijou* residence, as the advertisements call it, situated in no less a fashionable street than Park Lane."

"I see. What has aroused your suspicions against him?"

"Well, you know, that's an expensive district to live in; it takes a bit of money to do the trick. This Summertrees has no ostensible business, yet every Friday he goes to the United Capital Bank in Piccadilly, and deposits a bag of swag, usually all silver coin."

"Yes; and this money?"

"This money, so far as we can learn, contains a good many of these new pieces which never saw the British Mint."

"It's not all the new coinage, then?"

"Oh, no, he's a bit too artful for that! You see, a man can go round London, his pockets filled with new-coined five-shilling pieces, buy this, that, and the other, and come home with his change in legitimate coins of the realm — half crowns, florins, shillings, sixpences, and all that."

"I see. Then why don't you nab him one day when his pockets are stuffed with illegitimate five-shilling pieces?"

"That could be done, of course, and I've thought of it, but, you see, we want to land the whole gang. Once we arrested him, without knowing where the money came from, the real coiners would take flight."

"How do you know he is not the real coiner himself?"

Now poor Hale is as easy to read as a book. He hesitated before answering this question, and looked confused as a culprit caught in some dishonest act.

"You need not be afraid to tell me," I said soothingly, after a pause. "You have had one of your men in Mr. Summertrees' house, and so learned that he is not the coiner. But your man has not succeeded in getting you evidence to incriminate other people."

"You've about hit it again, Monsieur Valmont. One of my men has been Summertrees' butler for two weeks, but, as you say, he has found no evidence."

"Is he still butler?"

"Yes."

"Now tell me how far you have got. You know that Summertrees deposits a bag of coin every Friday in the Piccadilly Bank, and I suppose the bank has allowed you to examine one or two of the bags."

"Yes, sir, they have, but, you see, banks are very difficult to treat with. They don't like detectives bothering round, and while they do not stand out against the law, still they never answer any more questions than they're asked, and Mr. Summertrees has been a good customer at the United Capital for many years."

"Haven't you found out where the money comes from?"

"Yes, we have; it is brought there night after night by a man who looks like a respectable city clerk, and he puts it into a large safe, of which he holds the key, this safe being on the ground floor, in the dining room."

"Haven't you followed the clerk?"

"Yes. He sleeps in the Park Lane house every night and goes up in the morning to an old curiosity shop in Tottenham Court Road, where he stays all day, returning with his bag of money in the evening."

"Why don't you arrest and question him?"

"Well, Monsieur Valmont, there is just the same objection to his arrest as to that of Summertrees himself. We could easily arrest both, but we have not the slightest evidence against either of them, and then, although we put the go-betweens in clink, the worst criminals of the lot would escape."

"Nothing suspicious about the old curiosity shop?"

"No. It appears to be perfectly regular."

"This game has been going on under your noses for how long?"

"For about six weeks."

"Is Summertrees a married man?"

"No."

"Are there any women servants in the house?"

"No, except that three charwomen come in every morning to do up the rooms."

"Of what is his household comprised?"

"There is the butler, then the valet, and last the French cook."

"Ah," cried I, "the French cook! This case interests me. So Summertrees has succeeded in completely disconcerting your man. Has he prevented him going from top to bottom of the house?"

"Oh, no! He has rather assisted him than otherwise. On one occasion he went to the safe, took out the money, had Podgers — that's my chap's name — help him to count it, and then actually sent Podgers to the bank with the bag of coin."

"And Podgers has been all over the place?"

"Yes."

"Saw no signs of a coining establishment?"

"No. It is absolutely impossible that any coining can be done there. Besides, as I tell you, that respectable clerk brings him the money."

"I suppose you want me to take Podgers's position?"

"Well, Monsieur Valmont, to tell you the truth, I would rather you didn't. Podgers has done everything a man can do, but I thought if you got into the house, Podgers assisting, you might go through it night after night at your leisure."

"I see. That's just a little dangerous in England. I think I should prefer to assure myself the legitimate standing of being amiable Podgers's successor. You say that Summertrees has no business?"

"Well, sir, not what you might call a business. He is by way of being an author, but I don't count that any business."

"Oh, an author, is he? When does he do his writing?"

"He locks himself up most of the day in his study."

"Does he come out for lunch?"

"No; he lights a little spirit lamp inside, Podgers tells me, and makes himself a cup of coffee, which he takes with a sandwich or two."

"That's rather frugal fare for Park Lane."

"Yes, Monsieur Valmont, it is, but he makes it up in the evening, when he has a long dinner, with all them foreign kickshaws you people like, done by his French cook."

"Sensible man! Well, Hale, I see I shall look forward with pleasure to making the acquaintance of Mr. Summertrees. Is there any restriction on the going and coming of your man Podgers?"

"None in the least. He can get away either night or day."

"Very good, friend Hale; bring him here tomorrow, as soon as our author locks himself up in his study, or rather, I should say, as soon as the respectable clerk leaves for Tottenham Court Road, which I should guess, as you put it, is about half an hour after his master turns the key of the room in which he writes."

"You are quite right in that guess, Valmont. How did you hit it?"

"Merely a surmise, Hale. There is a good deal of oddity about that Park Lane house, so it doesn't surprise me in the least that the master gets to work earlier in the morning than the man. I have also a suspicion that Ralph Summertrees knows perfectly well what the estimable Podgers is there for."

"What makes you think that?"

"I can give no reason except that my opinion of the acuteness of Summertrees has been gradually rising all the while you were speaking, and at the same time my estimate of Podgers's craft has been as steadily declining. However, bring the man here tomorrow, that I may ask him a few questions."

Next day, about eleven o'clock, the ponderous Podgers, hat in hand, followed his chief into my room. His broad, impassive, immobile, smooth face gave him rather more the air of a genuine butler than I had expected, and this appearance, of course, was enhanced by his livery. His replies to my questions were those of a well-trained servant who will not say too much unless it is made worth his while. All in all, Podgers exceeded my expectations, and really my friend Hale had some justification for regarding him, as he evidently did, a triumph in his line.

"Sit down, Mr. Hale, and you, Podgers."

The man disregarded my invitation, standing like a statue until his chief made a motion; then he dropped into a chair. The English are great on discipline.

"Now, Mr. Hale, I must first congratulate you on the make-up of Podgers. It is excellent. You depend less on artificial assistance than we do in France, and in that I think you are right."

"Oh, we know a bit over here, Monsieur Valmont!" said Hale, with pardonable pride.

"Now then, Podgers, I want to ask you about this clerk. What time does he arrive in the evening?"

"At prompt six, sir."

"Does he ring, or let himself in with a latchkey?"

"With a latchkey, sir."

"How does he carry the money?"

"In a little locked leather satchel, sir, flung over his shoulder."

"Does he go direct to the dining room?"

"Yes, sir."

"Have you seen him unlock the safe, and put in the money?"

"Yes, sir."

"Does the safe unlock with a word or a key?"

"With the key, sir. It's one of the old-fashioned kind."

"Then the clerk unlocks his leather money bag?"

"Yes, sir."

"That's three keys used within as many minutes. Are they separate or in a bunch?"

"In a bunch, sir."

"Did you ever see your master with this bunch of keys?"

"No, sir."

"You saw him open the safe once, I am told?"

"Yes, sir."

"Did he use a separate key, or one of a bunch?"

Podgers slowly scratched his head, then said:

"I don't just remember, sir."

"Ah, Podgers, you are neglecting the big things in that house! Sure you can't remember?"

"No, sir."

"Once the money is in the safe locked up, what does the clerk do?"

"Goes to his room, sir."

"Where is this room?"

"On the third floor, sir."

"Where do you sleep?"

"On the fourth floor with the rest of the servants, sir."

"Where does the master sleep?"

"On the second floor, adjoining his study."

"The house consists of four stories and a basement, does it?"

"Yes, sir."

"I have somehow arrived at the suspicion that it is a very narrow house. Is that true?"

"Yes, sir."

"Does the clerk ever dine with your master?"

"No, sir. The clerk don't eat in the house at all, sir."

"Does he go away before breakfast?"

"No, sir."

"No one takes breakfast to his room?"

"No, sir."

"What time does he leave the house?"

"At ten o'clock, sir."

"When is breakfast served?"

"At nine o'clock, sir."

"At what hour does your master retire to his study?"

"At half past nine, sir."

"Locks the door on the inside?"

"Yes, sir."

"Never rings for anything during the day?"

"Not that I know of, sir."

"What sort of a man is he?"

Here Podgers was on familiar ground, and he rattled off a description minute in every particular.

"What I meant was, Podgers, is he silent, or talkative, or does he get angry? Does he seem furtive, suspicious, anxious, terrorized, calm, excitable, or what?"

"Well, sir, he is by way of being very quiet, never has much to say for hisself; never saw him angry or excited."

"Now, Podgers, you've been at Park Lane for a fortnight or more. You are a sharp, alert, observant man. What happens there that strikes you as unusual?"

"Well, I can't exactly say, sir," replied Podgers, looking rather helplessly from his chief to myself, and back again.

"Your professional duties have often compelled you to enact the part of butler before, otherwise you wouldn't do it so well. Isn't that the case?"

Podgers did not reply, but glanced at his chief. This was evidently a question pertaining to the service, which a subordinate was not allowed to answer. However, Hale said at once:

"Certainly. Podgers has been in dozens of places."

"Well, Podgers, just call to mind some of the other households where you have been employed, and tell me any particulars in which Mr. Summertrees's establishment differs from them."

Podgers pondered a long time.

"Well, sir, he do stick to writing pretty close."

"Ah, that's his profession, you see, Podgers. Hard at it from half past nine till toward seven, I imagine?"

"Yes, sir."

"Anything else, Podgers? No matter how trivial."

"Well, sir, he's fond of reading, too; leastways, he's fond of newspapers."

"When does he read?"

"I never seen him read 'em, sir; indeed, so far as I can tell, I never knew the papers to be opened, but he takes them all in, sir."

"What, all the morning papers?"

"Yes, sir, and all the evening papers, too."

"Where are the morning papers placed?"

"On the table in his study, sir."

"And the evening papers?"

"Well, sir, when the evening papers come, the study is locked. They are put on a side table in the dining room, and he takes them upstairs with him to his study."

"This has happened every day since you've been there?"

"Yes, sir."

"You reported that very striking fact to your chief, of course?"

"No, sir, I don't think I did," said Podgers, confused.

"You should have done so. Mr. Hale would have known how to make the most of a point so vital."

"Oh, come now, Valmont," interrupted Hale, "you're chaffing us! Plenty of people take in all the papers!"

"I think not. Even clubs and hotels subscribe to the leading journals only. You said *all,* I think, Podgers?"

"Well, *nearly* all, sir."

"But which is it? There's a vast difference."

"He takes a good many, sir."

"How many?"

"I don't just know, sir."

"That's easily found out, Valmont," cried Hale, with some impatience, "if you think it really important."

"I think it so important that I'm going back with Podgers myself. You can take me into the house, I suppose, when you return?"

"Oh, yes, sir!"

"Coming back to these newspapers for a moment, Podgers. What is done with them?"

"They are sold to the ragman, sir, once a week."

"Who takes them from the study?"

"I do, sir."

"Do they appear to have been read very carefully?"

"Well, no, sir; leastways, some of them seem never to have been opened, or else folded up very carefully again."

"Did you notice that extracts have been clipped from any of them?"

"No, sir."

"Does Mr. Summertrees keep a scrapbook?"

"Not that I know of, sir."

"Oh, the case is perfectly plain!" said I, leaning back in my chair, and regarding the puzzled Hale with that cherubic expression of self-satisfaction which I know is so annoying to him.

"*What's* perfectly plain?" he demanded, more gruffly perhaps than etiquette would have sanctioned.

"Summertrees is no coiner, nor is he linked with any band of coiners."

"What is he, then?"

"Ah, that opens another avenue of inquiry! For all I know to the contrary, he may be the most honest of men. On the surface it would appear that he is a reasonably industrious tradesman in Tottenham Court Road, who is anxious that there should be no visible connection between a plebeian employment and so aristocratic a residence as that in Park Lane."

At this point Spenser Hale gave expression to one of those rare flashes of reason which are always an astonishment to his friends.

"That is nonsense, Monsieur Valmont," he said; "the man who is ashamed of the connection between his business and his house is one who is trying to get into society, or else the women of his family are trying it, as is usually the case. Now Summertrees has no family. He himself goes nowhere, gives no entertainments, and accepts no invitations. He belongs to no club; therefore, to say that he is ashamed of his connection with the Tottenham Court Road shop is absurd. He is concealing the connection for some other reason that will bear looking into."

"My dear Hale, the Goddess of Wisdom herself could not have made a more sensible series of remarks. Now, *mon ami,* do you want my assistance, or have you enough to go on with?"

"Enough to go on with? We have nothing more than we had when I called on you last night."

"Last night, my dear Hale, you supposed this man was in league with coiners. Today you know he is not."

"I know you *say* he is not."

I shrugged my shoulders, and raised my eyebrows, smiling at him.

"It is the same thing, Monsieur Hale."

"Well, of all the conceited—" and the good Hale could get no farther.

"If you wish my assistance, it is yours."

"Very good. Not to put too fine a point upon it, I do."

"In that case, my dear Podgers, you will return to the residence of our friend Summertrees, and get together for me in a bundle all of yesterday's morning and evening papers that were delivered to the house. Can you do that, or are they mixed up in a heap in the coal cellar?"

"I can do it, sir. I have instructions to place each day's papers in a pile by itself in case they should be wanted again. There is always one week's supply in the cellar, and we sell the papers of the week before to the ragman."

"Excellent. Well, take the risk of abstracting one day's journals, and have them ready for me. I will call upon you at half past three o'clock exactly, and then I want you to take me upstairs to the clerk's bedroom in the third story, which I suppose is not locked during the daytime?"

"No, sir, it is not."

With this the patient Podgers took his departure. Spenser Hale rose when his assistant left.

"Anything further I can do?" he asked.

"Yes; give me the address of the shop in Tottenham Court Road. Do you happen to have about you one of those new five-shilling pieces which you believe to be illegally coined?"

He opened his pocket book, took out the bit of white metal, and handed it to me.

"I'm going to pass this off before evening," I said, putting it in my pocket, "and I hope none of your men will arrest me."

"That's all right," laughed Hale as he took his leave.

At half past three Podgers was waiting for me, and opened the front door as I came up the steps, thus saving me the necessity of ringing. The house seemed strangely quiet. The French cook was evidently down in the basement, and we had probably all the upper part to ourselves, unless Summertrees was in his study, which I doubted. Podgers led me directly upstairs to the clerk's room on the third floor, walking on tiptoe, with an elephantine air of silence and secrecy combined, which struck me as unnecessary.

"I will make an examination of this room," I said. "Kindly wait for me down by the door of the study."

The bedroom proved to be of respectable size when one considers the smallness of the house. The bed was all nicely made up, and there were two chairs in the room, but the usual washstand and swing mirror were not visible. However, seeing a curtain at the farther end of the room, I drew it aside, and found, as I expected, a fixed lavatory in an alcove of perhaps four feet deep by five in width. As the room was about fifteen feet wide, this left two thirds of the space unaccounted for. A moment later I opened a door which exhibited a closet filled with clothes hanging on hooks. This left a space of five feet between the clothes closet and the lavatory. I thought at first that the entrance to the secret stairway must have issued from the lavatory, but examining the boards closely, although they sounded hollow to the knuckles, they were quite evidently plain match boarding, and not a concealed door. The entrance to the stairway, therefore, must issue from the clothes closet. The right-hand wall proved similar to the match boarding of the lavatory, so far as the casual eye or touch was concerned, but I saw at once it was a door. The latch turned out to be somewhat ingeniously operated by one of the hooks which held a pair of old trousers. I found that the hook, if pressed upward, allowed the door to swing outward, over the stairhead. Descending to the second floor, a similar latch let me into a similar clothes closet in the room beneath. The two rooms were identical in size, one directly above the other, the only difference being that the lower-room door gave into the study, instead of into the hall, as was the case with the upper chamber.

The study was extremely neat, either not much used, or the abode of a very methodical man. There was nothing on the table except a pile of that morning's papers. I walked to the farther end, turned the key in the lock, and came out upon the astonished Podgers.

"Well, I'm blowed!" exclaimed he.

"Quite so," I rejoined; "you've been tiptoeing past an empty room for the last two weeks. Now, if you'll come with me, Podgers, I'll show you how the trick is done."

When he entered the study I locked the door once more, and led the assumed butler, still tiptoeing through force of habit, up the stair into the top bedroom, and so out again, leaving everything exactly as we found it. We went down the main stair to the front hall, and there Podgers had my parcel of papers all neatly wrapped up. This bundle I carried to my flat, gave one of my assistants some instructions, and left him at work on the papers.

I took a cab to the foot of Tottenham Court Road, and walked up that street till I came to J. Simpson's old curiosity shop. After gazing at the well-filled windows for some time, I stepped inside, having selected a little iron crucifix displayed behind the pane; the work of some ancient craftsman.

I knew at once from Podgers's description that I was waited upon by the veritable respectable clerk who brought the bag of money each night to Park Lane, and who, I was certain, was no other than Ralph Summertrees himself.

There was nothing in his manner differing from that of any other quiet salesman. The price of the crucifix proved to be seven-and-six, and I threw down a sovereign to pay for it.

"Do you mind the change being all in silver, sir?" he asked, and I answered without any eagerness, although the question aroused a suspicion that had begun to be allayed:

"Not in the least."

He gave me half a crown, three two-shilling pieces, and four separate shillings, all coins being well-worn silver of the realm, the undoubted inartistic product of the reputable British Mint. This seemed to dispose of the theory that he was palming off illegitimate money. He asked me if I were interested in any particular branch of antiquity, and I replied that my curiosity was merely general, and exceedingly amateurish, whereupon he invited me to look around. This I proceeded to do, while he resumed the addressing and stamping of some wrapped-up pamphlets which I surmised to be copies of his catalogue.

He made no attempt either to watch me or to press his wares upon me. I selected at random a little inkstand, and asked its price. It was two shillings, he said, whereupon I produced my fraudulent five-shilling piece. He took it, gave me the change without comment, and the last doubt about his connection with coiners flickered from my mind.

At this moment a young man came in who, I saw at once, was not a customer. He walked briskly to the farther end of the shop, and disappeared behind a partition which had one pane of glass in it that gave an outlook toward the front door.

"Excuse me a moment," said the shopkeeper, and he followed the young man into the private office.

As I examined the curious heterogeneous collection of things for sale, I heard the clink of coins being poured out on the lid of a desk or an uncovered table, and the murmur of voices floated out to me. I was now near the entrance of the shop, and by a sleight-of-hand trick, keeping the corner of my eye on the glass pane of the private office, I removed the key of the front door without a sound, and took an impression of it in wax, returning the key to its place unobserved. At this moment another young man came in, and walked straight past me into the private office. I heard him say:

"Oh, I beg pardon, Mr. Simpson! How are you, Rogers?"

"Hello, Macpherson," saluted Rogers, who then came out, bidding good night to Mr. Simpson, and departed, whistling, down the street, but not before he had repeated his phrase to another young man entering, to whom he gave the name of Tyrrel.

I noted these three names in my mind. Two others came in together, but I was compelled to content myself with memorizing their features, for I did not learn their names. These men were evidently collectors, for I heard the rattle of money in every case; yet here was a small shop, doing apparently very little business, for I had been within it for more than half an hour, and yet remained the only customer. If credit were given, one collector would certainly have been sufficient, yet five had come in, and had poured their contributions into the pile Summertrees was to take home with him that night.

I determined to secure one of the pamphlets which the man had been addressing. They were piled on a shelf behind the counter, but I had no difficulty in reaching across and taking the one on top, which I slipped into my pocket. When the fifth young man went down the street Summertrees himself emerged, and this time he carried in his hand the well-filled locked leather satchel, with the straps dangling. It was now approaching half past five, and I saw he was eager to close up and get away.

"Anything else you fancy, sir?" he asked me.

"No, or, rather, yes and no. You have a very interesting collection here, but it's getting so dark I can hardly see."

"I close at half past five, sir."

"Ah! in that case," I said, consulting my watch, "I shall be pleased to call some other time."

"Thank you, sir," replied Summertrees quietly, and with that I took my leave.

From the corner of an alley on the other side of the street I saw him put up the shutters with his own hands, then he emerged with overcoat on, and the money satchel slung across his shoulder. He locked the door, tested it with his knuckles, and walked down the street, carrying under one arm the pamphlets he had been addressing. I followed him at some distance, saw him drop the pamphlets into the box at the first post office he passed, and walk rapidly toward his house in Park Lane.

When I returned to my flat and called in my assistant, he said:

"After putting to one side the regular advertisements of pills, soap, and what not, here is the only one common to all the newspapers, morning and evening alike. The advertisements are not identical, sir, but they have two points of similarity, or perhaps I should say three. They all profess to furnish a cure for absent-mindedness; they all ask that the applicant's chief hobby shall be stated, and they all bear the same address: Dr. Willoughby, in Tottenham Court Road."

"Thank you," said I, as he placed the scissored advertisements before me.

THE ABSENT—MINDED COTERIE

I read several of the announcements. They were all small, and perhaps that is why I had never noticed one of them in the newspapers, for certainly they were odd enough. Some asked for lists of absent-minded men, with the hobbies of each, and for these lists, prizes of from one shilling to six were offered. In other clippings Dr. Willoughby professed to be able to cure absent-mindedness. There were no fees and no treatment, but a pamphlet would be sent, which, if it did not benefit the receiver, could do no harm. The Doctor was unable to meet patients personally, nor could he enter into correspondence with them. The address was the same as that of the old curiosity shop in Tottenham Court Road. At this juncture I pulled the pamphlet from my pocket, and saw it was entitled, "Christian Science and Absent-Mindedness," by Dr. Stamford Willoughby, and at the end of the article was the statement contained in the advertisements, that Dr. Willoughby would neither see patients nor hold any correspondence with them.

I drew a sheet of paper toward me, wrote to Dr. Willoughby, alleging that I was a very absent-minded man, and would be glad of his pamphlet, adding that my special hobby was the collecting of first editions. I then signed myself, "Alport Webster, Imperial Flats, London, W."

I may here explain that it is often necessary for me to see people under some other name than the well-known appellation of Eugène Valmont. There are two doors to my flat, and on one of these is painted, "Eugène Valmont"; on the other there is a receptacle, into which can be slipped a sliding panel bearing any *nom de guerre* I choose. The same device is arranged on the ground floor, where the names of all the occupants of the building appear on the right-hand wall.

I sealed, addressed, and stamped my letter, then told my man to put out the name of Alport Webster, and if I did not happen to be in when any one called upon that mythical person, he was to make an appointment for me.

It was nearly six o'clock next afternoon when the card of Angus Macpherson was brought in to Mr. Alport Webster. I recognized the young man at once as the second who had entered the little shop, carrying his tribute to Mr. Simpson the day before. He held

three volumes under his arm, and spoke in such a pleasant, insinu-
ating sort of way, that I knew at once he was an adept in his profession of canvasser.

"Will you be seated, Mr. Macpherson? In what can I serve you?"

He placed the three volumes, backs upward, on my table.

"Are you interested at all in first editions, Mr. Webster?"

"It is the one thing I am interested in," I replied; "but unfortunately they often run into a lot of money."

"That is true," said Macpherson sympathetically, "and I have here
three books, one of which is an exemplification of what you say. This
one costs a hundred pounds. The last copy that was sold by auction
in London brought a hundred and twenty-three pounds. This next
one is forty pounds, and the third ten pounds. At these prices I am
certain you could not duplicate three such treasures in any bookshop
in Britain."

I examined them critically, and saw at once that what he said was
true. He was still standing on the opposite side of the table.

"Please take a chair, Mr. Macpherson. Do you mean to say you
go round London with a hundred and fifty pounds' worth of goods
under your arm in this careless way?"

The young man laughed.

"I run very little risk, Mr. Webster. I don't suppose anyone I
meet imagines for a moment there is more under my arm than
perhaps a trio of volumes I have picked up in the fourpenny box to
take home with me."

I lingered over the volume for which he asked a hundred pounds,
then said, looking across at him:

"How came you to be possessed of this book, for instance?"

He turned upon me a fine, open countenance, and answered without hesitation in the frankest possible manner:

"I am not in actual possession of it, Mr. Webster. I am by way
of being a connoisseur in rare and valuable books myself, although,
of course, I have little money with which to indulge in the collection of them. I am acquainted, however, with the lovers of desirable
books in different quarters of London. These three volumes, for
instance, are from the library of a private gentleman in the West
End. I have sold many books to him, and he knows I am trustworthy. He wishes to dispose of them at something under their real

value, and has kindly allowed me to conduct the negotiations. I make it my business to find out those who are interested in rare books, and by such trading I add considerably to my income."

"How, for instance, did you learn that I was a bibliophile?"

Mr. Macpherson laughed genially.

"Well, Mr. Webster, I must confess that I chanced it. I do that very often. I take a flat like this, and send in my card to the name on the door. If I am invited in, I ask the occupant the question I asked you just now: 'Are you interested in rare editions?' If he says no, I simply beg pardon and retire. If he says yes, then I show my wares."

"I see," said I, nodding. What a glib young liar he was, with that innocent face of his, and yet my next question brought forth the truth.

"As this is the first time you have called upon me, Mr. Macpherson, you have no objection to my making some further inquiry, I suppose. Would you mind telling me the name of the owner of these books in the West End?"

"His name is Mr. Ralph Summertrees, of Park Lane."

"Of Park Lane? Ah, indeed!"

"I shall be glad to leave the books with you, Mr. Webster, and if you care to make an appointment with Mr. Summertrees, I am sure he will not object to say a word in my favor."

"Oh, I do not in the least doubt it, and should not think of troubling the gentleman."

"I was going to tell you," went on the young man, "that I have a friend, a capitalist, who, in a way, is my supporter; for, as I said, I have little money of my own. I find it is often inconvenient for people to pay down any considerable sum. When, however, I strike a bargain, my capitalist buys the books, and I make an arrangement with my customer to pay a certain amount each week, and so even a large purchase is not felt, as I make the installments small enough to suit my client."

"You are employed during the day, I take it?"

"Yes, I am a clerk in the City."

Again we were in the blissful realms of fiction!

"Suppose I take this book at ten pounds, what installments should I have to pay each week?"

"Oh, what you like, sir. Would five shillings be too much?"

"I think not."

"Very well, sir; if you pay me five shillings now, I will leave the book with you, and shall have pleasure in calling this day week for the next installment."

I put my hand into my pocket, and drew out two half crowns, which I passed over to him.

"Do I need to sign any form or undertaking to pay the rest?"

The young man laughed cordially.

"Oh, no, sir, there is no formality necessary. You see, sir, this is largely a labor of love with me, although I don't deny I have my eye on the future. I am getting together what I hope will be a very valuable connection with gentlemen like yourself who are fond of books, and I trust some day that I may be able to resign my place with the insurance company and set up a choice little business of my own, where my knowledge of values in literature will prove useful."

And then, after making a note in a little book he took from his pocket, he bade me a most graceful good-by and departed, leaving me cogitating over what it all meant.

Next morning two articles were handed to me. The first came by post and was a pamphlet on "Christian Science and Absent-Mindedness," exactly similar to the one I had taken away from the old curiosity shop; the second was a small key made from my wax impression that would fit the front door of the same shop — a key fashioned by an excellent anarchist friend of mine in an obscure street near Holborn.

That night at ten o'clock I was inside the old curiosity shop, with a small storage battery in my pocket, and a little electric glowlamp at my buttonhole, a most useful instrument for either burglar or detective.

I had expected to find the books of the establishment in a safe, which, if it was similar to the one in Park Lane, I was prepared to open with the false keys in my possession, or to take an impression of the keyhole and trust to my anarchist friend for the rest. But to my amazement I discovered all the papers pertaining to the concern in a desk which was not even locked. The books, three in number, were the ordinary daybook, journal, and ledger referring to the shop; bookkeeping of the older fashion; but in a portfolio lay half a dozen foolscap sheets, headed, "Mr. Rogers's List," "Mr. Macpherson's," "Mr. Tyrrel's," the names I had already learned, and three others. These lists contained in the first column, names; in the second column, addresses; in the third, sums of money; and then in the small, square places following were amounts ranging from two-and-sixpence to a pound. At the bottom of Mr. Macpherson's list was the name Alport Webster, Imperial Flats, £10; then in the small, square place, five shillings. These six sheets, each headed by a canvasser's name, were evidently the record of current collections, and the innocence of the whole thing was so apparent that, if it were not for my fixed rule never to believe that I am at the bottom of any case until I have come on something suspicious, I would have gone out empty-handed as I came in.

The six sheets were loose in a thin portfolio, but standing on a shelf above the desk were a number of fat volumes, one of which I took down, and saw that it contained similar lists running back several years. I noticed on Mr. Macpherson's current list the name of Lord Semptam, an eccentric old nobleman whom I knew slightly. Then turning to the list immediately before the current one the name was still there; I traced it back through list after list until I found the first entry, which was no less than three years previous, and there Lord Semptam was down for a piece of furniture costing fifty pounds, and on that account he had paid a pound a week for more than three years, totaling a hundred and seventy pounds at the least, and instantly the glorious simplicity of the scheme dawned upon me, and I became so interested in the swindle that I lit the gas, fearing my little lamp would be exhausted before my investigation ended, for it promised to be a long one.

In several instances the intended victim proved shrewder than old Simpson had counted upon, and the word "Settled" had been written on the line carrying the name when the exact number of installments was paid. But as these shrewd persons dropped out, others took their places, and Simpson's dependence on their absent-mindedness seemed to be justified in nine cases out of ten. His collectors were collecting long after the debt had been paid. In Lord Semptam's case, the payment had evidently become chronic, and the old man was giving away his pound a week to the suave Macpherson two years after his debt had been liquidated.

From the big volume I detached the loose leaf, dated 1893, which recorded Lord Semptam's purchase of a carved table for fifty pounds, and on which he had been paying a pound a week from that time to the date of which I am writing, which was November, 1896. This single document, taken from the file of three years previous, was not likely to be missed, as would have been the case if I had selected a current sheet. I nevertheless made a copy of the names and addresses of Macpherson's present clients; then, carefully placing everything exactly as I had found it, I extinguished the gas, and went out of the shop, locking the door behind me. With the 1893 sheet in my pocket I resolved to prepare a pleasant little surprise for my suave friend Macpherson when he called to get his next installment of five shillings.

Late as was the hour when I reached Trafalgar Square, I could not deprive myself of the felicity of calling on Mr. Spenser Hale, who I knew was then on duty. He never appeared at his best during office hours, because officialism stiffened his stalwart frame. Mentally he was impressed with the importance of his position, and added to this he was not then allowed to smoke his big black pipe and terrible tobacco. He received me with the curtness I had been taught to expect when I inflicted myself upon him at his office. He greeted me abruptly with:

"I say, Valmont, how long do you expect to be on this job?"

"What job?" I asked mildly.

"Oh, you know what I mean: the Summertrees affair?"

"Oh, *that!*" I exclaimed, with surprise. "The Summertrees case is already completed, of course. If I had known you were in a hurry, I should have finished up everything yesterday, but as you and Podgers, and I don't know how many more, have been at it sixteen or seventeen days, if not longer, I thought I might venture to take as many hours, as I am working entirely alone. You said nothing about haste, you know."

"Oh, come now, Valmont, that's a bit thick. Do you mean to say you have already got evidence against the man?"

"Evidence absolute and complete."

"Then who are the coiners?"

"My most estimable friend, how often have I told you not to jump at conclusions? I informed you when you first spoke to me about the matter that Summertrees was neither a coiner nor a confederate of coiners. I secured evidence sufficient to convict him of quite another offense, which is probably unique in the annals of crime. I have penetrated the mystery of the shop, and discovered the reason for all those suspicious actions which quite properly set you on his trail. Now I wish you to come to my flat next Wednesday night at a quarter to six, prepared to make an arrest."

"I must know whom I am to arrest, and on what counts."

"Quite so, *mon ami* Hale; I did not say you were to make an arrest, but merely warned you to be prepared. If you have time now to listen to the disclosures, I am quite at your service. I promise you there are some original features in the case. If, however, the present moment is inopportune, drop in on me at your convenience, previously telephoning so that you may know whether I am there or not, and thus your valuable time will not be expended purposelessly."

With this I presented to him my most courteous bow, and although his mystified expression hinted a suspicion that he thought I was chaffing him, as he would call it, official dignity dissolved somewhat, and he intimated his desire to hear all about it then and there. I had succeeded in arousing my friend Hale's curiosity. He listened to the evidence with perplexed brow, and at last ejaculated he would be blessed.

"This young man," I said, in conclusion, "will call upon me at six on Wednesday afternoon, to receive his second five shillings. I propose that you, in your uniform, shall be seated there with me to receive him, and I am anxious to study Mr. Macpherson's countenance when he realizes he has walked in to confront a policeman. If you will then allow me to cross-examine him for a few moments, not after the manner of Scotland Yard, with a warning lest he incriminate himself, but in the free and easy fashion we adopt in Paris, I shall afterwards turn the case over to you to be dealt with at your discretion."

"You have a wonderful flow of language, Monsieur Valmont," was the officer's tribute to me. "I shall be on hand at a quarter to six on Wednesday."

"Meanwhile," said I, "kindly say nothing of this to any one. We must arrange a complete surprise for Macpherson. That is essential. Please make no move in the matter at all until Wednesday night."

Spenser Hale, much impressed, nodded acquiescence, and I took a polite leave of him.

The question of lighting is an important one in a room such as mine, and electricity offers a good deal of scope to the ingenious. Of this fact I have taken full advantage. I can manipulate the lighting of my room so that any particular spot is bathed in brilliancy, while the rest of the space remains in comparative gloom, and I arranged the lamps so that the full force of their rays impinged against the door that Wednesday evening, while I sat on one side of the table in semidarkness and Hale sat on the other, with a light beating down on him from above which gave him the odd, sculptured look of a living statue of Justice, stern and triumphant. Any one entering the room would first be dazzled by the light, and next would see the gigantic form of Hale in the full uniform of his order.

When Angus Macpherson was shown into this room, he was quite visibly taken aback, and paused abruptly on the threshold, his gaze riveted on the huge policeman. I think his first purpose was to turn and run, but the door closed behind him, and he doubtless heard, as we all did, the sound of the bolt being thrust in its place, thus locking him in.

"I — I beg your pardon," he stammered, "I expected to meet Mr. Webster."

As he said this, I pressed the button under my table, and was instantly enshrouded with light. A sickly smile overspread the countenance of Macpherson as he caught sight of me, and he made a very creditable attempt to carry off the situation with nonchalance.

"Oh, there you are, Mr. Webster; I did not notice you at first."

It was a tense moment. I spoke slowly and impressively.

"Sir, perhaps you are not unacquainted with the name of Eugène Valmont."

He replied brazenly:

"I am sorry to say, sir, I never heard of the gentleman before."

At this came a most inopportune "Haw-haw" from that blockhead Spenser Hale, completely spoiling the dramatic situation I had elaborated with such thought and care. It is little wonder the English possess no drama, for they show scant appreciation of the sensationai moments in life; they are not quickly alive to the lights and shadows of events.

"Haw-haw," brayed Spenser Hale, and at once reduced the emotional atmosphere to a fog of commonplace. However, what is a man to do? He must handle the tools with which it pleases Providence to provide him. I ignored Hale's untimely laughter.

"Sit down, sir," I said to Macpherson, and he obeyed.

"You have called on Lord Semptam this week," I continued sternly.

"Yes, sir."

"And collected a pound from him?"

"Yes, sir."

"In October, 1893, you sold Lord Semptam a carved antique table for fifty pounds?"

"Quite right, sir."

"When you were here last week you gave me Ralph Summertrees as the name of a gentleman living in Park Lane. You knew at the time that this man was your employer?"

Macpherson was now looking fixedly at me, and on this occasion made no reply. I went on calmly:

"You also knew that Summertrees, of Park Lane, was identical with Simpson, of Tottenham Court Road?"

"Well, sir," said Macpherson, "I don't exactly see what you're driving at, but it's quite usual for a man to carry on a business under an assumed name. There is nothing illegal about that."

"We will come to the illegality in a moment, Mr. Macpherson. You and Rogers and Tyrrel and three others are confederates of this man Simpson."

"We are in his employ; yes, sir, but no more confederates than clerks usually are."

"I think, Mr. Macpherson, I have said enough to show you that the game is what you call up. You are now in the presence of Mr. Spenser Hale, from Scotland Yard, who is waiting to hear your confession."

Here the stupid Hale broke in with his:

"And remember, sir, that anything you say will be — "

"Excuse me, Mr. Hale," I interrupted hastily, "I shall turn over the case to you in a very few moments, but I ask you to remember our compact, and to leave it for the present entirely in my hands. Now, Mr. Macpherson, I want your confession, and I want it at once."

"Confession? Confederates?" protested Macpherson, with admirably simulated surprise. "I must say you use extraordinary terms, Mr. — Mr. — What did you say the name was?"

"Haw-haw," roared Hale. "His name is Monsieur Valmont."

"I implore you, Mr. Hale, to leave this man to me for a very few moments. Now, Macpherson, what have you to say in your defense?"

"Where nothing criminal has been alleged, Monsieur Valmont, I see no necessity for defense. If you wish me to admit that somehow you have acquired a number of details regarding our business, I am perfectly willing to do so, and to subscribe to their accuracy. If you will be good enough to let me know of what you complain, I shall endeavor to make the point clear to you, if I can. There has evidently been some misapprehension, but for the life of me, without further explanation, I am as much in a fog as I was on my way coming here, for it is getting a little thick outside."

Macpherson certainly was conducting himself with great discretion, and presented, quite unconsciously, a much more diplomatic figure than my friend Spenser Hale, sitting stiffly opposite me. His tone was one of mild expostulation, mitigated by the intimation that all misunderstanding speedily would be cleared away. To outward view he offered a perfect picture of innocence, neither protesting too much nor too little. I had, however, another surprise in store for him, a trump card, as it were, and I played it down on the table.

"There!" I cried with vim, "have you ever seen that sheet before?"

He glanced at it without offering to take it in his hand.

"Oh, yes," he said, "that has been abstracted from our file. It is what I call my visiting list."

"Come, come, sir," I cried sternly, "you refuse to confess, but I warn you we know all about it. You never heard of Dr. Willoughby, I suppose."

"Yes, he is the author of the silly pamphlet on Christian Science."

"You are in the right, Mr. Macpherson; on Christian Science and Absent-Mindedness."

"Possibly. I haven't read it for a long while."

"Have you ever met this learned doctor, Mr. Macpherson?"

"Oh, yes. Dr. Willoughby is the pen name of Mr. Summertrees. He believes in Christian Science and that sort of thing, and writes about it."

"Ah, really. We are getting your confession bit by bit, Mr. Macpherson. I think it would be better to be quite frank with us."

"I was just going to make the same suggestion to you, Monsieur Valmont. If you will tell me in a few words exactly what is your charge against either Mr. Summertrees or myself, I will know then what to say."

"We charge you, sir, with obtaining money under false pretenses, which is a crime that has landed more than one distinguished financier in prison."

Spenser Hale shook his fat forefinger at me, and said:

"Tut, tut, Valmont; we mustn't threaten, we mustn't threaten, you know"; but I went on without heeding him.

"Take, for instance, Lord Semptam. You sold him a table for fifty pounds, on the installment plan. He was to pay a pound a week, and in less than a year the debt was liquidated. But he is an absent-minded man, as all your clients are. That is why you came to me. I had answered the bogus Willoughby's advertisement. And so you kept on collecting and collecting for something more than three years. Now do you understand the charge?"

Mr. Macpherson's head, during this accusation, was held slightly inclined to one side. At first his face was clouded by the most clever imitation of anxious concentration of mind I had ever seen, and this was gradually cleared away by the dawn of awakening perception. When I had finished, an ingratiating smile hovered about his lips.

"Really, you know," he said, "that is rather a capital scheme. The absent-minded league, as one might call them. Most ingenious. Summertrees, if he had any sense of humor, which he hasn't, would be rather taken by the idea that his innocent fad for Christian Science had led him to be suspected of obtaining money under false pretenses. But, really, there are no pretensions about the matter at all. As I understand it, I simply call and receive the money through the forgetfulness of the persons on my list, but where I think you would have both Summertrees and myself, if there was anything in your audacious theory, would be an indictment for conspiracy. Still, I quite see how the mistake arises. You have jumped to the conclusion that we sold nothing to Lord Semptam except that carved table three years ago. I have pleasure in pointing out to you that his lordship is a frequent customer of ours, and has had many things from us at one time or another. Sometimes he is in our debt; sometimes we are in his. We keep a sort of running contract with him by which he pays us a pound a week. He and several other customers deal on the same plan, and in return, for an income that we can count upon, they get the first offer of anything in which they are supposed to be interested. As I have told you, we call these sheets in the office our visiting lists, but to make the visiting lists complete you need what we term our encyclopedia. We call it that because it is in so many volumes; a volume for each year, running back I don't know how long. You will notice little figures here from time to time above the amount stated on this visiting list. These figures refer to the page of the encyclopedia for the current year, and on that page is noted the new sale and the amount of it, as it might be set down, say, in a ledger."

"That is a very entertaining explanation, Mr. Macpherson. I suppose this encyclopedia, as you call it, is in the shop at Tottenham Court Road?"

"Oh, no, sir. Each volume of the encyclopedia is self-locking. These books contain the real secret of our business, and they are kept in the safe at Mr. Summertrees's house in Park Lane. Take Lord Semptam's account, for instance. You will find, in faint figures under a certain date, 102. If you turn to page 102 of the encyclopedia for that year, you will then see a list of what Lord Semptam has bought, and the prices he was charged for them. It is really a very simple matter. If you will allow me to use your telephone for a moment, I will ask Mr. Summertrees, who has not yet begun dinner, to bring with him here the volume for 1893, and within a quarter of an hour you will be perfectly satisfied that everything is quite legitimate."

I confess that the young man's naturalness and confidence staggered me, the more so as I saw by the sarcastic smile on Hale's lips that he did not believe a single word spoken. A portable telephone stood on the table, and as Macpherson finished his explanation, he reached over and drew it toward him. Then Spenser Hale interfered.

"Excuse *me*," he said, "I'll do the telephoning. What is the call number of Mr. Summertrees?"

"One forty Hyde Park."

Hale at once called up Central, and presently was answered from Park Lane. We heard him say:

"Is this the residence of Mr. Summertrees? Oh, is that you, Podgers? Is Mr. Summertrees in? Very well. This is Hale. I am in Valmont's flat — Imperial Flats — you know. Yes, where you went with me the other day. Very well, go to Mr. Summertrees, and say to him that Mr. Macpherson wants the encyclopedia for 1893. Do you get that? Yes, encyclopedia. Oh, don't understand what it is. Mr. Macpherson. No, don't mention my name at all. Just say Mr. Macpherson wants the encyclopedia for the year 1893, and that you are to bring it. Yes, you may tell him that Mr. Macpherson is at Imperial Flats, but don't mention my name at all. Exactly. As soon as he gives you the book, get into a cab, and come here as quickly as possible with it. If Summertrees doesn't want to let the book go, then tell him to come with you. If he won't do that, place him under arrest, and bring both him and the book here. All right. Be as quick as you can; we're waiting."

Macpherson made no protest against Hale's use of the telephone; he merely sat back in his chair with a resigned expression on his face which, if painted on canvas, might have been entitled, "The Falsely Accused." When Hale rang off, Macpherson said:

"Of course you know your business best, but if your man arrests Summertrees, he will make you the laughingstock of London. There is such a thing as unjustifiable arrest, as well as getting money under false pretenses, and Mr. Summertrees is not the man to forgive an insult. And then, if you will allow me to say so, the more I think over your absent-minded theory the more absolutely grotesque it seems, and if the case ever gets into the newspapers, I am sure, Mr. Hale, you'll experience an uncomfortable half hour with your chiefs at Scotland Yard."

"I'll take the risk of that, thank you," said Hale stubbornly.

"Am I to consider myself under arrest?" inquired the young man.

"No, sir."

"Then, if you will pardon me, I shall withdraw. Mr. Summertrees will show you everything you wish to see in his books, and can explain his business much more capably than I, because he knows more about it; therefore, gentlemen, I bid you good night."

"No, you don't. Not just yet awhile," exclaimed Hale, rising to his feet simultaneously with the young man.

"Then I *am* under arrest," protested Macpherson.

"You're not going to leave this room until Podgers brings that book."

"Oh, very well," and he sat down again.

And now, as talking is dry work, I set out something to drink, a box of cigars, and a box of cigarettes. Hale mixed his favorite brew, but Macpherson, shunning the wine of his country, contented himself with a glass of plain mineral water, and lit a cigarette. Then he awoke my high regard by saying pleasantly, as if nothing had happened:

"While we are waiting, Monsieur Valmont, may I remind you that you owe me five shillings?"

I laughed, took the coin from my pocket, and paid him, whereupon he thanked me.

"Are you connected with Scotland Yard, Monsieur Valmont?" asked Macpherson, with the air of a man trying to make conversation to bridge over a tedious interval; but before I could reply Hale blurted out:

"Not likely!"

"You have no official standing as a detective, then, Monsieur Valmont?"

"None whatever," I replied quickly, thus getting in my oar ahead of Hale.

"That is a loss to our country," pursued this admirable young man, with evident sincerity.

I began to see I could make a good deal of so clever a fellow if he came under my tuition.

"The blunders of our police," he went on, "are something deplorable. If they would but take lessons in strategy, say, from France, their unpleasant duties would be so much more acceptably performed, with much less discomfort to their victims."

"France," snorted Hale in derision, "why, they call a **man** guilty there until he's proven innocent."

"Yes, Mr. Hale, and the same seems to be the case in Imperial Flats. You have quite made up your mind that Mr. Summertrees is guilty, and will not be content until he proves his innocence. I venture to predict that you will hear from him before long in a manner that may astonish you."

Hale grunted and looked at his watch. The minutes passed very slowly as we sat there smoking and at last even I began to get uneasy. Macpherson, seeing our anxiety, said that when he came in the fog was almost as thick as it had been the week before, and that there might be some difficulty in getting a cab. Just as he was speaking the door was unlocked from the outside, and Podgers entered, bearing a thick volume in his hand. This he gave to his superior, who turned over its pages in amazement, and then looked at the back, crying:

"*Encyclopedia of Sport, 1893!* What sort of a joke is this, Mr. Macpherson?"

There was a pained look on Mr. Macpherson's face as he reached forward and took the book. He said with a sigh:

"If you had allowed me to telephone, Mr. Hale, I should have made it perfectly plain to Summertrees what was wanted. I might have known this mistake was liable to occur. There is an increasing demand for out-of-date books of sport, and no doubt Mr. Summertrees thought this was what I meant. There is nothing for it but to send your man back to Park Lane and tell Mr. Summertrees that what we want is the locked volume of accounts for 1893, which we call the encyclopedia. Allow me to write an order that will bring it. Oh, I'll show you what I have written before your man takes it," he said, as Hale stood ready to look over his shoulder.

On my note paper he dashed off a request such as he had outlined, and handed it to Hale, who read it and gave it to Podgers.

"Take that to Summertrees, and get back as quickly as possible. Have you a cab at the door?"

"Yes, sir."

"Is it foggy outside?"

"Not so much, sir, as it was an hour ago. No difficulty about the traffic now, sir."

"Very well, get back as soon as you can."

Podgers saluted, and left with the book under his arm. Again the door was locked, and again we sat smoking in silence until the stillness was broken by the tinkle of the telephone. Hale put the receiver to his ear.

"Yes, this is the Imperial Flats. Yes. Valmont. Oh, yes; Macpherson is here. What? Out of what? Can't hear you. Out of print. What, the encyclopedia's out of print? Who is that speaking? Dr. Willoughby; thanks."

Macpherson rose as if he would go to the telephone, but instead (and he acted so quietly that I did not notice what he was doing until the thing was done) he picked up the sheet which he called his visiting list, and walking quite without haste, held it in the glowing coals of the fireplace until it disappeared in a flash of flame up the chimney. I sprang to my feet indignant, but too late to make even a motion toward saving the sheet. Macpherson regarded us both with that self-depreciatory smile which had several times lighted up his face.

"How dared you burn that sheet?" I demanded.

"Because, Monsieur Valmont, it did not belong to you; because you do not belong to Scotland Yard; because you stole it; because you had no right to it; and because you have no official standing in this country. If it had been in Mr. Hale's possession I should not have dared, as you put it, to destroy the sheet, but as this sheet was abstracted from my master's premises by you, an entirely unauthorized person, whom he would have been justified in shooting dead if he had found you housebreaking, and you had resisted him on his discovery, I took the liberty of destroying the document. I have always held that these sheets should not have been kept, for, as has been the case, if they fell under the scrutiny of so intelligent a person as Eugène Valmont, improper inferences might have been drawn. Mr. Summertrees, however, persisted in keeping them, but made this concession, that if I ever telegraphed him or telephoned him the word 'Encyclopedia,' he would at once burn these records, and he, on his part, was to telegraph or telephone to me 'The encyclopedia is out of print,' whereupon I would know that he had succeeded.

"Now, gentlemen, open this door, which will save me the trouble of forcing it. Either put me formally under arrest, or cease to restrict my liberty. I am very much obliged to Mr. Hale for telephoning, and I have made no protest to so gallant a host as Monsieur

Valmont is, because of the locked door. However, the farce is now terminated. The proceedings I have sat through were entirely illegal, and if you will pardon me, Mr. Hale, they have been a little too French to go down here in old England, or to make a report in the newspapers that would be quite satisfactory to your chiefs. I demand either my formal arrest or the unlocking of that door."

In silence I pressed a button, and my man threw open the door. Macpherson walked to the threshold, paused, and looked back at Spenser Hale, who sat there silent as a sphinx.

"Good evening, Mr. Hale."

There being no reply, he turned to me with the same ingratiating smile:

"Good evening, Monsieur Eugène Valmont," he said, "I shall give myself the pleasure of calling next Wednesday at six for my five shillings."

THE RED SILK SCARF

by MAURICE LEBLANC

Sometimes the great ARSÈNE *is a thief, sometimes he is a detective. But here is the only short story in which he is both thief and detective — in fact, the only short story to exploit such a fascinating dualism in the whole catalogue of detective fiction. Eagle-eyed disputants please correspond.*

O N LEAVING his house one morning at his usual early hour for going to the Law Courts, Chief Inspector Ganimard noticed the curious behavior of an individual who was walking along the Rue Pergolèse in front of him. Shabbily dressed and wearing a straw hat, though the day was the first of December, the man stooped at every thirty or forty yards to fasten his bootlace, or pick up his stick, or for some other reason. And, each time, he took a little piece of orange peel from his pocket and laid it stealthily on the curb of the pavement. It was probably a mere display of eccentricity, a childish amusement to which no one else would have paid attention; but Ganimard was one of those shrewd observers who are indifferent to nothing that strikes their eyes and who are never satisfied until they know the secret cause of things. He therefore began to follow the man.

Now, at the moment when the fellow was turning to the right, into the Avenue de la Grande-Armée, the inspector caught him exchanging signals with a boy of twelve or thirteen, who was walking along the houses on the left-hand side. Twenty yards farther, the man stooped and turned up the bottom of his trousers legs. A bit of orange peel marked the place. At the same moment, the boy stopped and, with a piece of chalk, drew a white cross, surrounded by a circle, on the wall of the house next to him.

The two continued on their way. A minute later, a fresh halt. The strange individual picked up a pin and dropped a piece of orange peel; and the boy at once made a second cross on the wall and again drew a white circle round it.

"By Jove!" thought the chief inspector, with a grunt of satisfaction. "This is rather promising. . . . What on earth can those two merchants be plotting?"

The two "merchants" went down the Avenue Friedland and the Rue du Faubourg-Saint-Honoré, but nothing occurred that was worthy of special mention. The double performance was repeated at almost regular intervals and, so to speak, mechanically. Nevertheless, it was obvious, on the one hand, that the man with the orange peel did not do his part of the business until after he had picked out with a glance the house that was to be marked and, on the other hand, that the boy did not mark that particular house until after he had observed his companion's signal. It was certain, therefore, that there was an agreement between the two; and the proceedings presented no small interest in the chief inspector's eyes.

At the Place Beauveau the man hesitated. Then, apparently making up his mind, he twice turned up and twice turned down the bottom of his trousers legs. Hereupon, the boy sat down on the curb, opposite the sentry who was mounting guard outside the Ministry of the Interior, and marked the flagstone with two little crosses contained within two circles. The same ceremony was gone through a little farther on, when they reached the Elysée. Only, on the pavement where the President's sentry was marching up and down, there were three signs instead of two.

"Hang it all!" muttered Ganimard, pale with excitement and thinking, in spite of himself, of his inveterate enemy, Lupin, whose name came to his mind whenever a mysterious circumstance presented itself. "Hang it all, what does it mean?"

He was nearly collaring and questioning the two "merchants." But he was too clever to commit so gross a blunder. The man with the orange peel had now lit a cigarette; and the boy, also placing a cigarette end between his lips, had gone up to him, apparently with the object of asking for a light.

They exchanged a few words. Quick as thought, the boy handed his companion an object which looked — at least, so the inspector believed — like a revolver. They both bent over this object; and the man, standing with his face to the wall, put his hand six times in his pocket and made a movement as though he were loading a weapon.

As soon as this was done, they walked briskly to the Rue de Surène; and the inspector, who followed them as closely as he was able to do without attracting their attention, saw them enter the gateway of an old house of which all the shutters were closed, with the exception of those on the third or top floor.

He hurried in after them. At the end of the carriage entrance he saw a large courtyard, with a house painter's sign at the back and a staircase on the left.

He went up the stairs and, as soon as he reached the first floor, ran still faster, because he heard, right up at the top, a din as of a free fight.

When he came to the last landing he found the door open. He entered, listened for a second, caught the sound of a struggle, rushed to the room from which the sound appeared to proceed and remained standing on the threshold, very much out of breath and greatly surprised to see the man of the orange peel and the boy banging the floor with chairs.

At that moment a third person walked out of an adjoining room. It was a young man of twenty-eight or thirty, wearing a pair of short whiskers in addition to his moustache, spectacles, and a smoking jacket with an astrakhan collar and looking like a foreigner, a Russian.

"Good morning, Ganimard," he said. And turning to the two companions, "Thank you, my friends, and all my congratulations on the successful result. Here's the reward I promised you."

He gave them a hundred-franc note, pushed them outside and shut both doors.

"I am sorry, old chap," he said to Ganimard. "I wanted to talk to you . . . wanted to talk to you badly."

He offered him his hand and, seeing that the inspector remained flabbergasted and that his face was still distorted with anger, he exclaimed:

"Why, you don't seem to understand! . . . And yet it's clear enough. . . . I wanted to see you particularly. . . . So what could I do?" And, pretending to reply to an objection, "No, no, old chap," he continued. "You're quite wrong. If I had written or telephoned, you would not have come . . . or else you would have come with a regiment. Now I wanted to see you all alone; and I thought the best thing was to send those two decent fellows to meet you, with orders to scatter bits of orange peel and draw crosses and circles, in short, to mark out your road to this place. . . . Why, you look quite bewildered! What is it? Perhaps you don't recognize me? Lupin. . . . Arsène Lupin. . . . Ransack your memory. . . . Doesn't the name remind you of anything?"

"You dirty scoundrel!" Ganimard snarled between his teeth.

Lupin seemed greatly distressed and, in an affectionate voice:

"Are you vexed? Yes, I can see it in your eyes. . . . The Dugrival business, I suppose. I ought to have waited for you to come and take me in charge? . . . There now, the thought never occurred to me! I promise you, next time. . . ."

"You scum of the earth!" growled Ganimard.

"And I thinking I was giving you a treat! Upon my word, I did. I said to myself, 'That dear old Ganimard! We haven't met for an age. He'll simply rush at me when he sees me!'"

Ganimard, who had not yet stirred a limb, seemed to be waking from his stupor. He looked around him, looked at Lupin, visibly asked himself whether he would not do well to rush at him in reality and then, controlling himself, took hold of a chair and settled himself in it, as though he had suddenly made up his mind to listen to his enemy:

"Speak," he said. "And don't waste my time with any nonsense. I'm in a hurry."

"That's it," said Lupin, "let's talk. You can't imagine a quieter place than this. It's an old manor house, which once stood in the open country, and it belongs to the Duc de Rochelaure. The duke, who has never lived in it, lets this floor to me and the outhouses to a painter and decorator. I always keep up a few establishments of this kind: it's a sound, practical plan. Here, in spite of my looking like a Russian nobleman, I am M. Daubreuil, an ex-cabinet-minister. . . . You understand, I had to select a rather overstocked profession, so as not to attract attention. . . ."

"Do you think I care a hang about all this?" said Ganimard, interrupting him.

"Quite right, I'm wasting words and you're in a hurry. Forgive me. I shan't be long now. . . . Five minutes, that's all. . . . I'll start at once. . . . Have a cigar? No? Very well, no more will I."

He sat down also, drummed his fingers on the table, while thinking, and began in this fashion:

"On the 17th of October, 1599, on a warm and sunny autumn day . . . Do you follow me? . . . But, now that I come to think of it, is it really necessary to go back to the reign of Henry IV, and tell you all about the building of the Pont-Neuf? No, I don't suppose you are very well up in French history; and I should only end by muddling you. Suffice it, then, for you to know that, last night, at one o'clock in the morning, a boatman passing under the last arch of the Pont-Neuf aforesaid, along the left bank of the river, heard something drop into the front part of his barge. The thing had been flung from the bridge and its evident destination was the bottom of the Seine. The bargee's dog rushed forward, barking, and, when the man reached the end of his craft, he saw the animal worrying a piece of newspaper that had served to wrap up a number of objects. He took from the dog such of the contents as had not fallen into the water, went to his cabin and examined them carefully. The result struck him as interesting; and, as the man is connected with one of my friends, he sent to let me know. This morning I was waked up and placed in possession of the facts and of the objects which the man had collected. Here they are."

He pointed to them, spread out on a table. There were, first of all, the torn pieces of a newspaper. Next came a large cut-glass inkstand, with a long piece of string fastened to the lid. There was a bit of broken glass and a sort of flexible cardboard, reduced to shreds. Lastly, there was a piece of bright scarlet silk, ending in a tassel of the same material and color.

"You see our exhibits, friend of my youth," said Lupin. "No doubt, the problem would be more easily solved if we had the other objects which went overboard owing to the stupidity of the dog. But it seems to me, all the same, that we ought to be able to manage, with a little reflection and intelligence. And those are just your great qualities. How does the business strike you?"

Ganimard did not move a muscle. He was willing to stand Lupin's chaff, but his dignity commanded him not to speak a single word in answer nor even to give a nod or shake of the head that might have been taken to express approval or criticism.

"I see that we are entirely of one mind," continued Lupin, without appearing to remark the chief inspector's silence. "And I can sum up the matter briefly, as told us by these exhibits. Yesterday evening, between nine and twelve o'clock, a showily dressed young woman was wounded with a knife and then caught round the throat and choked to death by a well-dressed gentleman, wearing a single eyeglass and interested in racing, with whom the aforesaid showily dressed young lady had been eating three meringues and a coffee éclair."

Lupin lit a cigarette and, taking Ganimard by the sleeve:

"Aha, that's up against you, Chief Inspector! You thought that, in the domain of police deductions, such feats as those were prohibited to outsiders! Wrong, sir! Lupin juggles with inferences and deductions for all the world like a detective in a novel. My proofs are dazzling and absolutely simple."

And, pointing to the objects one by one, as he demonstrated his statement, he resumed:

"I said, after nine o'clock yesterday evening. This scrap of newspaper bears yesterday's date, with the words, 'Evening edition.' Also, you will see here, pasted to the paper, a bit of one of those yellow wrappers in which the subscribers' copies are sent out. These copies are always delivered by the nine-o'clock post. Therefore, it was after nine o'clock. I said, a well-dressed man. Please observe that this tiny piece of glass has the round hole of a single eyeglass at one of the edges and that the single eyeglass is an essentially aristocratic article of wear. This well-dressed man walked into a pastry cook's shop. Here is the very thin cardboard, shaped like a box, and still showing a little of the cream of the meringues and éclairs which were packed in it in the usual way. Having got his parcel, the gentleman with the eyeglass joined a young person whose eccentricity in the matter of dress is pretty clearly indicated by this bright-red silk scarf. Having joined her, for some reason as yet unknown he first stabbed her with a knife and then strangled her with the help of this same scarf. Take your magnifying glass, Chief Inspector, and you will see, on the silk, stains of a darker red which are, here, the marks of a knife wiped on the scarf and, there, the marks of a hand, covered with blood, clutching the material. Having committed the murder, his next business is to leave no trace behind him. So he takes from his pocket, first, the newspaper to which he subscribes — a racing-paper, as you will see by glancing at the contents of this scrap; and you will have no difficulty in discovering the title — and, secondly, a cord, which, on inspection, turns out to be a length of whipcord. These two details prove — do they not? — that our man is interested in racing and that he himself rides. Next, he picks up the fragments of his eyeglass, the cord of which has been broken in the struggle. He takes a pair of scissors — observe the hacking of the scissors — and cuts off the stained part of the scarf, leaving the other end, no doubt, in his victim's clenched hands. He makes a ball of the confectioner's cardboard box. He also puts in certain things that would have betrayed him, such as the knife, which must have slipped into the Seine. He wraps everything in the newspaper, ties it with the cord and fastens this cut-glass inkstand to it, as a make-weight. Then he makes himself scarce. A little later, the parcel falls into the waterman's barge. And there you are. Oof, it's hot work! . . . What do you say to the story?"

He looked at Ganimard to see what impression his speech had produced on the inspector. Ganimard did not depart from his attitude of silence.

Lupin began to laugh:

"As a matter of fact, you're annoyed and surprised. But you're suspicious as well: 'Why should that confounded Lupin hand the business over to me,' say you, 'instead of keeping it for himself, hunting down the murderer and rifling his pockets, if there was a robbery?' The question is quite logical, of course. But — there is a 'but' — I have no time, you see. I am full up with work at the present moment: a burglary in London, another at Lausanne, an exchange of children at Marseilles, to say nothing of having to save a young girl who is at this moment shadowed by death. That's always the way: it never rains but it pours. So I said to myself, 'Suppose I handed the business over to my dear old Ganimard? Now that it is half-solved for him, he is quite capable of succeeding. And what a service I shall be doing him! How magnificently he will be able to distinguish himself!' No sooner said than done. At eight o'clock in the morning, I sent the joker with the orange peel to meet you. You swallowed the bait; and you were here by nine, all on edge and eager for the fray."

Lupin rose from his chair. He went over to the inspector and, with his eyes in Ganimard's, said:

"That's all. You now know the whole story. Presently, you will know the victim: some ballet dancer, probably, some singer at a music hall. On the other hand, the chances are that the criminal lives near the Pont-Neuf, most likely on the left bank. Lastly, here are all the exhibits. I make you a present of them. Set to work. I shall only keep this end of the scarf. If ever you want to piece the scarf together, bring me the other end, the one which the police will find round the victim's neck. Bring it me in four weeks from now to the day, that is to say, on the 29th of December, at ten o'clock in the morning. You can be sure of finding me here. And don't be afraid: this is all perfectly serious, friend of my youth; I swear it is. No humbug, honor bright. You can go straight ahead. Oh, by the way, when you arrest the fellow with the eyeglass, be a bit careful: he is left-handed! Good-by, old dear, and good luck to you!"

Lupin spun round on his heel, went to the door, opened it and disappeared before Ganimard had even thought of taking a decision. The inspector rushed after him, but at once found that the handle of the door, by some trick of mechanism which he did not know, refused to turn. It took him ten minutes to unscrew the lock and ten minutes more to unscrew the lock of the hall door. By the time that he had scrambled down the three flights of stairs, Ganimard had given up all hope of catching Arsène Lupin.

Besides, he was not thinking of it. Lupin inspired him with a queer, complex feeling, made up of fear, hatred, involuntary admiration and also the vague instinct that he, Ganimard, in spite of all his efforts, in spite of the persistency of his endeavors, would never get the better of this particular adversary. He pursued him from a sense of duty and pride, but with the continual dread of being taken in by that formidable hoaxer and scouted and fooled in the face of a public that was always only too willing to laugh at the chief inspector's mishaps.

This business of the red scarf, in particular, struck him as most suspicious. It was interesting, certainly, in more ways than one, but so very improbable! And Lupin's explanation, apparently so logical, would never stand the test of a severe examination!

"No," said Ganimard, "this is all swank: a parcel of suppositions and guesswork based upon nothing at all. I'm not to be caught with chaff."

When he reached the headquarters of police, at 36 Quai des Orfèvres, he had quite made up his mind to treat the incident as though it had never happened.

He went up to the Criminal Investigation Department. Here, one of his fellow inspectors said:

"Seen the chief?"

"No."

"He was asking for you just now."

"Oh, was he?"

"Yes, you had better go after him."

"Where?"

"To the Rue de Berne . . . there was a murder there last night."

"Oh! Who's the victim?"

"I don't know exactly . . . a music hall singer, I believe."

Ganimard simply muttered: —

"By Jove!"

Twenty minutes later he stepped out of the underground railway station and made for the Rue de Berne.

The victim, who was known in the theatrical world by her stage name of Jenny Saphir, occupied a small flat on the second floor of one of the houses. A policeman took the chief inspector upstairs and showed him the way, through two sitting rooms, to a bedroom, where he found the magistrates in charge of the inquiry, together with the divisional surgeon and M. Dudouis, the head of the detective service.

Ganimard started at the first glance which he gave into the room. He saw, lying on a sofa, the corpse of a young woman whose hands clutched a strip of red silk! One of the shoulders, which appeared above the low-cut bodice, bore the marks of two wounds surrounded with clotted blood. The distorted and almost blackened features still bore an expression of frenzied terror.

The divisional surgeon, who had just finished his examination, said:

"My first conclusions are very clear. The victim was twice stabbed with a dagger and afterward strangled. The immediate cause of death was asphyxia."

"By Jove!" thought Ganimard again, remembering Lupin's words and the picture which he had drawn of the crime.

The examining magistrate objected:

"But the neck shows no discoloration."

"She may have been strangled with a napkin or a handkerchief," said the doctor.

"Most probably," said the chief detective, "with this silk scarf, which the victim was wearing and a piece of which remains, as though she had clung to it with her two hands to protect herself."

"But why does only that piece remain?" asked the magistrate. "What has become of the other?"

"The other may have been stained with blood and carried off by the murderer. You can plainly distinguish the hurried slashing of the scissors."

"By Jove!" said Ganimard, between his teeth, for the third time. "That brute of a Lupin saw everything without seeing a thing!"

"And what about the motive of the murder?" asked the magistrate. "The locks have been forced, the cupboards turned upside down. Have you anything to tell me, M. Dudouis?"

The chief of the detective service replied:

"I can at least suggest a supposition, derived from the statements made by the servant. The victim, who enjoyed a greater reputation on account of her looks than through her talent as a singer, went to Russia, two years ago, and brought back with her a magnificent sapphire, which she appears to have received from some person of importance at the court. Since then, she went by the name of Jenny Saphir and seems generally to have been very proud of that present, although, for prudence's sake, she never wore it. I daresay that we shall not be far out if we presume the theft of the sapphire to have been the cause of the crime."

"But did the maid know where the stone was?"

"No, nobody did. And the disorder of the room would tend to prove that the murderer did not know either."

"We will question the maid," said the examining magistrate.

M. Dudouis took the chief inspector aside and said:

"You're looking very old-fashioned, Ganimard. What's the matter? Do you suspect anything?"

"Nothing at all, chief."

"That's a pity. We could do with a bit of showy work in the department. This is one of a number of crimes, all of the same class, of which we have failed to discover the perpetrator. This time we want the criminal . . . and quickly!"

"A difficult job, chief."

"It's got to be done. Listen to me, Ganimard. According to what the maid says, Jenny Saphir led a very regular life. For a month past she was in the habit of frequently receiving visits, on her return from the music hall, that is to say, at about half past ten, from a man who would stay until midnight or so. 'He's a society man,' Jenny Saphir used to say, 'and he wants to marry me.' This society man took every precaution to avoid being seen, such as turning up his coat collar and lowering the brim of his hat when he passed the porter's box. And Jenny Saphir always made a point of sending away her maid, even before he came. This is the man whom we have to find."

"Has he left no traces?"

"None at all. It is obvious that we have to deal with a very clever scoundrel, who prepared his crime beforehand and committed it with every possible chance of escaping unpunished. His arrest would be a great feather in our cap. I rely on you, Ganimard."

"Ah, you rely on me, chief?" replied the inspector. "Well, we shall see . . . we shall see. . . . I don't say no. . . . Only . . ."

He seemed in a very nervous condition, and his agitation struck M. Dudouis.

"Only," continued Ganimard, "only I swear . . . do you hear, chief? I swear . . ."

"What do you swear?"

"Nothing. . . . We shall see, chief . . . we shall see. . . ."

Ganimard did not finish his sentence until he was outside, alone. And he finished it aloud, stamping his foot, in a tone of the most violent anger:

"Only, I swear to Heaven that the arrest shall be effected by my own means, without my employing a single one of the clues with which that villain has supplied me. Ah, no! Ah, no! . . ."

Railing against Lupin, furious at being mixed up in this business and resolved, nevertheless, to get to the bottom of it, he wandered aimlessly about the streets. His brain was seething with irritation; and he tried to adjust his ideas a little and to discover, among the chaotic facts, some trifling detail, unperceived by all, unsuspected by Lupin himself, that might lead him to success.

He lunched hurriedly at a bar, resumed his stroll and suddenly stopped, petrified, astounded and confused. He was walking under the gateway of the very house in the Rue de Surène to which Lupin had enticed him a few hours earlier! A force stronger than his own will was drawing him there once more. The solution of the problem lay there. There and there alone were all the elements of the truth. Do and say what he would, Lupin's assertions were so precise, his calculations so accurate, that, worried to the innermost recesses of his being by so prodigious a display of perspicacity, he could not do other than take up the work at the point where his enemy had left it.

Abandoning all further resistance, he climbed the three flights of stairs. The door of the flat was open. No one had touched the exhibits. He put them in his pocket and walked away.

From that moment, he reasoned and acted, so to speak, mechanically, under the influence of the master whom he could not choose but obey.

Admitting that the unknown person whom he was seeking lived in the neighborhood of the Pont-Neuf, it became necessary to discover, somewhere between that bridge and the Rue de Berne, the first-class confectioner's shop, open in the evenings, at which the cakes were bought. This did not take long to find. A pastry cook near the Gare Saint-Lazare showed him some little cardboard boxes, identical in material and shape with the one in Ganimard's possession. Moreover, one of the shopgirls remembered having served, on the previous evening, a gentleman whose face was almost concealed in the collar of his fur coat, but whose eyeglass she had happened to notice.

"That's one clue checked," thought the inspector. "Our man wears an eyeglass."

He next collected the pieces of the racing paper and showed them to a news vender, who easily recognized the *Turf Illustré.* Ganimard at once went to the offices of the *Turf* and asked to see the list of subscribers. Going through the list, he jotted down the names and addresses of all those who lived anywhere near the Pont-Neuf and principally — because Lupin had said so — those on the left bank of the river.

He then went back to the Criminal Investigation Department, took half a dozen men and packed them off with the necessary instructions.

At seven o'clock in the evening, the last of these men returned and brought good news with him. A certain M. Prévailles, a subscriber to the *Turf,* occupied an entresol flat on the Quai des Augustins. On the previous evening, he left his place, wearing a fur coat, took his letters and his paper, the *Turf Illustré,* from the porter's wife, walked away and returned home at midnight. This M. Prévailles wore a single eyeglass. He was a regular race-goer and himself owned several hacks which he either rode himself or jobbed out.

The inquiry had taken so short a time and the results obtained were so exactly in accordance with Lupin's predictions that Ganimard felt quite overcome on hearing the detective's report. Once more he was measuring the prodigious extent of the resources at Lupin's disposal. Never in the course of his life — and Ganimard was already well-advanced in years — had he come across such perspicacity, such a quick and far-seeing mind.

He went in search of M. Dudouis.

"Everything's ready, chief. Have you a warrant?"

"Eh?"

"I said, everything is ready for the arrest, chief."

"You know the name of Jenny Saphir's murderer?"

"Yes."

"But how? Explain yourself."

Ganimard had a sort of scruple of conscience, blushed a little and nevertheless replied:

"An accident, chief. The murderer threw everything that was likely to compromise him into the Seine. Part of the parcel was picked up and handed to me.

"By whom?"

"A boatman who refused to give his name, for fear of getting into trouble. But I had all the clues I wanted. It was not so difficult as I expected."

And the inspector described how he had gone to work.

"And you call that an accident!" cried M. Dudouis. "And you say that it was not difficult! Why, it's one of your finest performances! Finish it yourself, Ganimard, and be prudent."

Ganimard was eager to get the business done. He went to the Quai des Augustins with his men and distributed them around the house. He questioned the portress, who said that her tenant took his meals out of doors, but made a point of looking in after dinner.

A little before nine o'clock, in fact, leaning out of her window, she warned Ganimard, who at once gave a low whistle. A gentleman in a tall hat and a fur coat was coming along the pavement beside the Seine. He crossed the road and walked up to the house.

Ganimard stepped forward:

"M. Prévailles, I believe?"

"Yes, but who are you?"

"I have a commission to . . ."

He had not time to finish his sentence. At the sight of the men appearing out of the shadow, Prévailles quickly retreated to the wall and faced his adversaries, with his back to the door of a shop on the ground floor, the shutters of which were closed.

"Stand back!" he cried. "I don't know you!"

His right hand brandished a heavy stick, while his left was slipped behind him and seemed to be trying to open the door.

Ganimard had an impression that the man might escape through this way and through some secret outlet:

"None of this nonsense," he said, moving closer to him. "You're caught. . . . You had better come quietly."

But, just as he was laying hold of Prévailles's stick, Ganimard remembered the warning which Lupin gave him: Prévailles was left-handed; and it was his revolver for which he was feeling behind his back.

The inspector ducked his head. He had noticed the man's sudden movement. Two reports rang out. No one was hit.

A second later, Prévailles received a blow under the chin from the butt end of a revolver, which brought him down where he stood. He was entered at the Dépôt soon after nine o'clock.

Ganimard enjoyed a great reputation even at that time. But this capture, so quickly effected, by such very simple means, and at once made public by the police, won him a sudden celebrity. Prévailles was forthwith saddled with all the murders that had remained unpunished; and the newspapers vied with one another in extolling Ganimard's prowess.

The case was conducted briskly at the start. It was first of all ascertained that Prévailles, whose real name was Thomas Derocq, had already been in trouble. Moreover, the search instituted in his rooms, while not supplying any fresh proofs, at least led to the discovery of a ball of whipcord similar to the cord used for doing up the parcel and also to the discovery of daggers which would have produced a wound similar to the wounds on the victim.

But, on the eighth day, everything was changed. Until then Prévailles had refused to reply to the questions put to him; but now, assisted by his counsel, he pleaded a circumstantial alibi and maintained that he was at the Folies-Bergère on the night of the murder.

As a matter of fact, the pockets of his dinner jacket contained the counterfoil of a stall ticket and a program of the performance, both bearing the date of that evening.

"An alibi prepared in advance," objected the examining magistrate.

"Prove it," said Prévailles.

The prisoner was confronted with the witnesses for the prosecution. The young lady from the confectioner's "thought she knew" the gentleman with the eyeglass. The hall porter in the Rue de Berne "thought he knew" the gentleman who used to come to see Jenny Saphir. But nobody dared to make a more definite statement.

The examination, therefore, led to nothing of a precise character, provided no solid basis whereon to found a serious accusation.

The judge sent for Ganimard and told him of his difficulty.

"I can't possibly persist, at this rate. There is no evidence to support the charge."

"But surely you are convinced in your own mind, monsieur *le juge d'instruction!* Prévailles would never have resisted his arrest unless he was guilty."

"He says that he thought he was being assaulted. He also says that he never set eyes on Jenny Saphir; and, as a matter of fact, we can find no one to contradict his assertion. Then again, admitting that the sapphire has been stolen, we have not been able to find it at his flat."

"Nor anywhere else," suggested Ganimard.

"Quite true, but that is no evidence against him. I'll tell you what we shall want, M. Ganimard, and that very soon: the other end of this red scarf."

"The other end?"

"Yes, for it is obvious that, if the murderer took it away with him, the reason was that the stuff is stained with the marks of the blood on his fingers."

Ganimard made no reply. For several days he had felt that the whole business was tending to this conclusion. There was no other proof possible. Given the silk scarf — and in no other circumstances — Prévailles's guilt was certain. Now Ganimard's position required that Prévailles's guilt should be established. He was responsible for the arrest, it had cast a glamour around him, he had been praised to the skies as the most formidable adversary of criminals; and he would look absolutely ridiculous if Prévailles were released.

Unfortunately, the one and only indispensable proof was in Lupin's pocket. How was he to get hold of it?

Ganimard cast about, exhausted himself with fresh investigations, went over the inquiry from start to finish, spent sleepless nights in turning over the mystery of the Rue de Berne, studied the records of Prévailles's life, sent ten men hunting after the invisible sapphire. Everything was useless.

On the 28th of December, the examining magistrate stopped him in one of the passages of the Law Courts:

"Well, M. Ganimard, any news?"

"No, monsieur *le juge d'instruction*."

"Then I shall dismiss the case."

"Wait one day longer."

"What's the use? We want the other end of the scarf; have you got it?"

"I shall have it to-morrow."

"To-morrow!"

"Yes, but please lend me the piece in your possession."

"What if I do?"

"If you do, I promise to let you have the whole scarf complete."

"Very well, that's understood."

Ganimard followed the examining magistrate to his room and came out with the piece of silk:

"Hang it all!" he growled. "Yes, I will go and fetch the proof and I shall have it too . . . always presuming that Master Lupin has the courage to keep the appointment."

In point of fact, he did not doubt for a moment that Master Lupin would have this courage, and that was just what exasperated him. Why had Lupin insisted on this meeting? What was his object, in the circumstances?

Anxious, furious and full of hatred, he resolved to take every precaution necessary not only to prevent his falling into a trap himself, but to make his enemy fall into one, now that the opportunity offered. And, on the next day, which was the 29th of December, the date fixed by Lupin, after spending the night in studying the old manor house in the Rue de Surène and convincing himself that there was no other outlet than the front door, he warned his men that he was going on a dangerous expedition and arrived with them on the field of battle.

He posted them in a café and gave them formal instructions: if he showed himself at one of the third-floor windows, or if he failed to return within an hour, the detectives were to enter the house and arrest any one who tried to leave it.

The chief inspector made sure that his revolver was in working order and that he could take it from his pocket easily. Then he went upstairs.

He was surprised to find things as he had left them, the doors

open and the locks broken. After ascertaining that the windows of
the principal room looked out on the street, he visited the three
other rooms that made up the flat. There was no one there.

"Master Lupin was afraid," he muttered, not without a certain
satisfaction.

"Don't be silly," said a voice behind him.

Turning round, he saw an old workman, wearing a house-
painter's long smock, standing in the doorway.

"You needn't bother your head," said the man. "It's I, Lupin.
I have been working in the painter's shop since early morning.
This is when we knock off for breakfast. So I came upstairs."

He looked at Ganimard with a quizzing smile and cried:

" 'Pon my word, this is a gorgeous moment I owe you, old chap!
I wouldn't sell it for ten years of your life; and yet you know how
I love you! What do you think of it, artist? Wasn't it well thought
out and well foreseen? Foreseen from alpha to omega? Did I understand the business? Did I penetrate the mystery of the scarf?
I'm not saying that there were no holes in my argument, no links
missing in the chain . . . But what a masterpiece of intelligence!
Ganimard, what a reconstruction of events! What an intuition of
everything that had taken place and of everything that was going
to take place, from the discovery of the crime to your arrival here
in search of a proof! What really marvellous divination! Have you
the scarf?"

"Yes, half of it. Have you the other?"

"Here it is. Let's compare."

They spread the two pieces of silk on the table. The cuts made
by the scissors corresponded exactly. Moreover, the colors were
identical.

"But I presume," said Lupin, "that this was not the only thing
you came for. What you are interested in seeing is the marks of the
blood. Come with me, Ganimard: it's rather dark in here."

They moved into the next room, which, though it overlooked the
courtyard, was lighter; and Lupin held his piece of silk against
the window-pane:

"Look," he said, making room for Ganimard.

The inspector gave a start of delight. The marks of the five
fingers and the print of the palm were distinctly visible. The evi-

dence was undeniable. The murderer had seized the stuff in his blood-stained hand, in the same hand that had stabbed Jenny Saphir, and tied the scarf round her neck.

"And it is the print of a left hand," observed Lupin. "Hence my warning, which had nothing miraculous about it, you see. For, though I admit, friend of my youth, that you may look upon me as a superior intelligence, I won't have you treat me as a wizard."

Ganimard had quickly pocketed the piece of silk. Lupin nodded his head in approval:

"Quite right, old boy, it's for you. I'm so glad you're glad! And, you see, there was no trap about all this . . . only the wish to oblige . . . a service between friends, between pals. . . . And also, I confess, a little curiosity. . . . Yes, I wanted to examine this other piece of silk, the one the police had. . . . Don't be afraid: I'll give it back to you. . . . Just a second. . . ."

Lupin, with a careless movement, played with the tassel at the end of this half of the scarf, while Ganimard listened to him in spite of himself:

"How ingenious these little bits of women's work are! Did you notice one detail in the maid's evidence? Jenny Saphir was very handy with her needle and used to make all her own hats and frocks. It is obvious that she made this scarf herself. . . . Besides, I noticed that from the first. I am naturally curious, as I have already told you, and I made a thorough examination of the piece of silk which you have just put in your pocket. Inside the tassel, I found a little sacred medal, which the poor girl had stitched into it to bring her luck. Touching, isn't it, Ganimard? A little medal of Our Lady of Good Succor."

The inspector felt greatly puzzled and did not take his eyes off the other. And Lupin continued:

"Then I said to myself, 'How interesting it would be to explore the other half of the scarf, the one which the police will find round the victim's neck!' For this other half, which I hold in my hands at last, is finished off in the same way . . . so I shall be able to see if it has a hiding place too and what's inside it. . . . But look, my friend, isn't it cleverly made? And so simple! All you have to do is to take a skein of red cord and braid it round a wooden cup, leaving a little recess, a little empty space in the middle, very small,

of course, but large enough to hold a medal of a saint . . . or anything. . . . A precious stone, for instance. . . . Such as a sap
phire. . . ."

At that moment he finished pushing back the silk cord and, from
the hollow of a cup he took between his thumb and forefinger
a wonderful blue stone, perfect in respect of size and purity.

"Ha! What did I tell you, friend of my youth?"

He raised his head. The inspector had turned livid and was
staring wild-eyed, as though fascinated by the stone that sparkled
before him. He at last realized the whole plot:

"You dirty scoundrel!" he muttered, repeating the insults which
he had used at the first interview. "You scum of the earth!"

The two men were standing one against the other.

"Give me back that," said the inspector.

Lupin held out the piece of silk.

"And the sapphire," said Ganimard, in a peremptory tone.

"Don't be silly."

"Give it back, or . . ."

"Or what, you idiot!" cried Lupin. "Look here, do you think I
put you on to this soft thing for nothing?"

"Give it back!"

"You haven't noticed what I've been about, that's plain! What!
For four weeks I've kept you on the move like a deer; and you
want to . . . ! Come, Ganimard, old chap, pull yourself together!
. . . Don't you see that you've been playing the good dog for four
weeks on end? . . . Fetch it, Rover! . . . There's a nice blue pebble over there, which master can't get at. Hunt it, Ganimard, fetch
it . . . bring it to master. . . . Ah, he's his master's own good
little dog! . . . Sit up! Beg! . . . Does'ms want a bit of sugar,
then? . . ."

Ganimard, containing the anger that seethed within him, thought
only of one thing, summoning his detectives. And, as the room in
which he now was looked out on the courtyard, he tried gradually
to work his way round to the communicating door. He would
then run to the window and break one of the panes.

"All the same," continued Lupin, "what a pack of dunderheads
you and the rest must be! You've had the silk all this time and
not one of you ever thought of feeling it, not one of you ever asked

himself the reason why the poor girl hung on to her scarf. Not one of you! You just acted at haphazard, without reflecting, without foreseeing anything. . . ."

The inspector had attained his object. Taking advantage of a second when Lupin had turned away from him, he suddenly wheeled round and grasped the door handle. But an oath escaped him: the handle did not budge.

Lupin burst into a fit of laughing:

"Not even that! You did not even foresee that! You lay a trap for me and you won't admit that I may perhaps smell the thing out beforehand. . . . And you allow yourself to be brought into this room without asking whether I am not bringing you here for a particular reason and without remembering that the locks are fitted with a special mechanism. Come now, speaking frankly, what do you think of it yourself?"

"What do I think of it?" roared Ganimard, beside himself with rage.

He had drawn his revolver and was pointing it straight at Lupin's face.

"Hands up!" he cried. "That's what I think of it!"

Lupin placed himself in front of him and shrugged his shoulders:

"Sold again!" he said.

"Hands up, I say, once more!"

"And sold again, say I. Your deadly weapon won't go off."

"What?"

"Old Catherine, your housekeeper, is in my service. She damped the charges this morning while you were having your breakfast coffee."

Ganimard made a furious gesture, pocketed the revolver and rushed at Lupin.

"Well?" said Lupin, stopping him short with a well-aimed kick on the shin.

Their clothes were almost touching. They exchanged defiant glances, the glances of two adversaries who mean to come to blows. Nevertheless, there was no fight. The recollection of the earlier struggles made any present struggle useless. And Ganimard, who remembered all his past failures, his vain attacks, Lupin's crushing reprisals, did not lift a limb. There was nothing to be done. He felt it. Lupin had forces at his command against which any individual force simply broke to pieces. So what was the good?

"I agree," said Lupin, in a friendly voice, as though answering Ganimard's unspoken thought, "you would do better to let things be as they are. Besides, friend of my youth, think of all that this incident has brought you: fame, the certainty of quick promotion and, thanks to that, the prospect of a happy and comfortable old age! Surely, you don't want the discovery of the sapphire and the head of poor Arsène Lupin in addition! It wouldn't be fair. To say nothing of the fact that poor Arsène Lupin saved your life. . . . Yes, sir! Who warned you, at this very spot, that Prévailles was left-handed? . . . And is this the way you thank me? It's not pretty of you, Ganimard. Upon my word, you make me blush for you!"

While chattering, Lupin had gone through the same performance as Ganimard and was now near the door. Ganimard saw that his foe was about to escape him. Forgetting all prudence, he tried to block his way and received a tremendous butt in the stomach, which sent him rolling to the opposite wall.

Lupin dexterously touched a spring, turned the handle, opened the door and slipped away, roaring with laughter as he went.

Twenty minutes later, when Ganimard at last succeeded in joining his men, one of them said to him:—

"A house painter left the house, as his mates were coming back from breakfast, and put a letter in my hand. 'Give that to your governor,' he said. 'Which governor?' I asked; but he was gone. I suppose it's meant for you."

"Let's have it."

Ganimard opened the letter. It was hurriedly scribbled in pencil and contained these words:—

This is to warn you, friend of my youth, against excessive credulity. When a fellow tells you that the cartridges in your revolver are damp, however great your confidence in that fellow may be, even though his name be Arsène Lupin, never allow yourself to be taken in. Fire first; and, if the fellow hops the twig, you will have acquired the proof (1) that the cartridges are not damp; and (2) that old Catherine is the most honest and respectable of housekeepers.

One of these days, I hope to have the pleasure of making her acquaintance.

Meanwhile, friend of my youth, believe me always affectionately and sincerely yours,

ARSÈNE LUPIN

THE PUZZLE LOCK

by R. AUSTIN FREEMAN

*We don't happen to dote on deductions from the left tibia of
the rare Patagonian weegee bird, so here is the great man's
most untypical case — in which he wrestles powerfully with a
chronogram. Two of the forty* THORNDYKE *short stories have
never appeared in America.*

I DO not remember what was the occasion of my dining with
Thorndyke at Giamborini's on the particular evening that is now
in my mind. Doubtless, some piece of work completed had seemed
to justify the modest festival. At any rate, there we were, seated
at a somewhat retired table, selected by Thorndyke, with our backs
to the large window through which the late June sunlight streamed.
We had made our preliminary arrangements, including a bottle
of Barsac, and were inspecting dubiously a collection of semi-edible
hors d'œuvres, when a man entered and took possession of a table
just in front of ours, which had apparently been reserved for him,
since he walked directly to it and drew away the single chair that
had been set aslant against it.

I watched with amused interest his methodical procedure, for he
was clearly a man who took his dinner seriously. A regular customer, too, I judged by the waiter's manner and the reserved table
with its single chair. But the man himself interested me. He was
out of the common and there was a suggestion of character, with
perhaps a spice of oddity, in his appearance. He appeared to be
about sixty years of age, small and spare, with a much-wrinkled,
mobile and rather whimsical face, surmounted by a crop of white,
upstanding hair. From his waistcoat pocket protruded the ends of
a fountain pen, a pencil and a miniature electric torch such as

surgeons use; a silver-mounted Coddington lens hung from his watch guard and the middle finger of his left hand bore the largest seal ring that I have ever seen.

"Well," said Thorndyke, who had been following my glance, "what do you make of him?"

"I don't quite know," I replied. "The Coddington suggests a naturalist or a scientist of some kind, but that blatant ring doesn't. Perhaps he is an antiquary or a numismatist or even a philatelist. He deals with small objects of some kind."

At this moment a man who had just entered strode up to our friend's table and held out his hand, which the other shook, with no great enthusiasm, as I thought. Then the newcomer fetched a chair, and setting it by the table, seated himself and picked up the menu card, while the other observed him with a shade of disapproval. I judged that he would rather have dined alone, and that the personality of the new arrival — a flashy, bustling, obtrusive type of man — did not commend him.

From this couple my eye was attracted to a tall man who had halted near the door and stood looking about the room as if seeking some one. Suddenly he spied an empty, single table, and, bearing down on it, seated himself and began anxiously to study the menu under the supervision of a waiter. I glanced at him with slight disfavour. One makes allowances for the exuberance of youth, but when a middle-aged man presents the combination of heavily greased hair parted in the middle, a waxed moustache of a suspiciously intense black, a pointed imperial and a single eyeglass, evidently ornamental in function, one views him with less tolerance. However, his get-up was not my concern, whereas my dinner was, and I had given this my undivided attention for some minutes when I heard Thorndyke emit a soft chuckle.

"Not bad," he remarked, setting down his glass.

"Not at all," I agreed, "for a restaurant wine."

"I was not alluding to the wine," said he, "but to our friend Badger."

"The Inspector!" I exclaimed. "He isn't here, is he? I don't see him."

"I am glad to hear you say that, Jervis," said he. "It is a better effort than I thought. Still, he might manage his properties a little better. That is the second time his eyeglass has been in the soup."

Following the direction of his glance, I observed the man with the waxed moustache furtively wiping his eyeglass; and the temporary absence of the monocular grimace enabled me to note a resemblance to the familiar features of the detective officer.

"If you say that is Badger, I suppose it is," said I. "He is certainly a little like our friend. But I shouldn't have recognized him."

"I don't know that I should," said Thorndyke, "but for the little unconscious tricks of movement. You know the habit he has of stroking the back of his head and of opening his mouth and scratching the side of his chin. I saw him do it just now. He had forgotten his imperial until he touched it, and then the sudden arrest of movement was very striking. It doesn't do to forget a false beard."

"I wonder what his game is," said I. "The disguise suggests that he is on the lookout for somebody who might know him; but apparently that somebody has not turned up yet. At any rate, he doesn't seem to be watching anybody in particular."

"No," said Thorndyke. "But there is somebody whom he seems rather to avoid watching. Those two men at the table in front of ours are in his direct line of vision, but he hasn't looked at them once since he sat down, though I noticed that he gave them one quick glance before he selected his table. I wonder if he has observed us. Probably not, as we have the strong light of the window behind us and his attention is otherwise occupied."

I looked at the two men and from them to the detective, and I judged that my friend was right. On the inspector's table was a good-sized fern in an ornamental pot, and this he had moved so that it was directly between him and the two strangers, to whom he must have been practically invisible; and now I could see that he did, in fact, steal an occasional glance at them over the edge of the menu card. Moreover, as their meal drew to an end, he hastily finished his own and beckoned to the waiter to bring his bill.

"We may as well wait and see them off," said Thorndyke, who had already settled our account. "Badger always interests me. He is so ingenious and he has such shockingly bad luck."

We had not long to wait. The two men rose from the table and walked slowly to the door, where they paused to light their cigars before going out. Then Badger rose, with his back towards them and his eyes on the mirror opposite; and as they went out, he snatched up his hat and stick and followed. Thorndyke looked at me inquiringly.

"Do we indulge in the pleasures of the chase?" he asked, and as I replied in the affirmative, we, too, made our way out and started in the wake of the inspector.

As we followed Badger at a discreet distance, we caught an occasional glimpse of the quarry ahead, whose proceedings evidently caused the inspector some embarrassment, for they had a way of stopping suddenly to elaborate some point that they were discussing, whereby it became necessary for the detective to drop farther in the rear than was quite safe, in view of the rather crowded state of the pavement. On one of these occasions, when the older man was apparently delivering himself of some excruciating joke, they both turned suddenly and looked back, the joker pointing to some object on the opposite side of the road. Several people turned to see what was being pointed at, and, of course, the inspector had to turn, too, to avoid being recognized. At this moment the two men popped into an entry, and when the inspector once more turned they were gone.

As soon as he missed them, Badger started forward almost at a run, and presently halted at the large entry of the Celestial Bank Chambers, into which he peered eagerly. Then, apparently sighting his quarry, he darted in, and we quickened our pace and followed. Halfway down the long hall we saw him standing at the door of a lift, frantically pressing the call-button.

"Poor Badger!" chuckled Thorndyke, as we walked past him unobserved. "His usual luck! He will hardly run them to earth now in this enormous building. We may as well go through to the Blenheim Street entrance."

We pursued our way along the winding corridor and were close to the entrance when I noticed two men coming down the staircase that led to the hall.

"By Jingo! Here they are!" I exclaimed. "Shall we run back and give Badger the tip?"

Thorndyke hesitated. But it was too late. A taxi had just driven up and was discharging its fare. The younger man, catching the driver's eye, ran out and seized the door handle; and when his companion had entered the cab, he gave an address to the driver, and, stepping in quickly, slammed the door. As the cab moved off, Thorndyke pulled out his notebook and pencil and jotted down the number of the vehicle. Then we turned and retraced our steps; but when we reached the lift door, the inspector had disappeared. Presumably, like the incomparable Tom Bowling, he had gone aloft.

"We must give it up, Jervis," said Thorndyke. "I will send him — anonymously — the number of the cab, and that is all we can do. But I am sorry for Badger."

With this we dismissed the incident from our minds — at least, I did; assuming that I had seen the last of the two strangers. Little did I suspect how soon and under what strange and tragic circumstances I should meet with them again!

It was about a week later that we received a visit from our old friend, Superintendent Miller of the Criminal Investigation Department. The passing years had put us on a footing of mutual trust and esteem, and the capable, straightforward detective officer was always a welcome visitor.

"I've just dropped in," said Miller, cutting off the end of the inevitable cigar, "to tell you about a rather queer case that we've got in hand. I know you are always interested in queer cases."

Thorndyke smiled blandly. He had heard that kind of preamble before, and he knew, as did I, that when Miller became communicative we could safely infer that the Millerian bark was in shoal water.

"It is a case," the superintendent continued, "of a very special brand of crook. Actually there is a gang, but it is the managing director that we have particularly got our eye on."

"Is he a regular 'habitual,' then?" asked Thorndyke.

"Well," replied Miller, "as to that, I can't positively say. The fact is that we haven't actually seen the man to be sure of him."

"I see," said Thorndyke, with a grim smile. "You mean to say that you have got your eye on the place where he isn't."

"At the present moment," Miller admitted, "that is the literal fact. We have lost sight of the man we suspected, but we hope to pick him up again presently. We want him badly, and his pals too. It is probably quite a small gang, but they are mighty fly; a lot too smart to be at large. And they'll take some catching, for there is some one running the concern with a good deal more brains than crooks usually have."

"What is their lay?" I asked.

"Burglary," he replied. "Jewels and plate, but principally jewels; and the special feature of their work is that the swag disappears completely every time. None of the stuff has ever been traced. That is what drew our attention to them. After each robbery we made a round of all the fences, but there was not a sign. The stuff seemed to have vanished into smoke. Now that is very awkward. If you never see the men and you can't trace the stuff, where are you? You've got nothing to go on."

"But you seem to have got a clue of some kind," I said.

"Yes. There isn't a lot in it; but it seemed worth following up. One of our men happened to travel down to Colchester with a certain man, and when he came back two days later, he noticed this same man on the platform at Colchester and saw him get out at Liverpool Street. In the interval there had been a jewel robbery at Colchester. Then there was a robbery at Southampton, and our man went at once to Waterloo and saw all the trains in. On the second day, behold! the Colchester sportsman turns up at the barrier, so our man, who had a special taxi waiting, managed to track him home and afterwards got some particulars about him. He is a chap named Shemmonds; belongs to a firm of outside brokers. But nobody seems to know much about him and he doesn't put in much time at the office.

"Well, then, Badger took him over and shadowed him for a day or two, but just as things were looking interesting, he slipped off the hook. Badger followed him to a restaurant, and, through the glass door, saw him go up to an elderly man at a table and shake hands with him. Then he took a chair at the table himself, so Badger popped in and took a seat near them where he could keep them in view. They went out together and Badger followed them, but he lost them in the Celestial Bank Chambers. They went up in the lift just before he could get to the door and that was the last he saw of them. But we have ascertained that they left the building in a taxi and that the taxi set them down at Great Turnstile."

"It was rather smart of you to trace the cab," Thorndyke remarked.

"You've got to keep your eyes skinned in our line of business," said Miller. "But now we come to the real twister. From the time those two men went down Great Turnstile, nobody has set eyes on either of them. They seem to have vanished into thin air."

"You found out who the other man was, then?" said I.

"Yes. The restaurant manager knew him; an old chap named Luttrell. And we knew him, too, because he has a thumping burglary insurance, and when he goes out of town he notifies his company. They make arrangements with us to have the premises watched."

"What is Luttrell?" I asked.

"Well, he is a bit of a mug, I should say, at least that's his character in the trade. Goes in for being a dealer in jewels and antiques, but he'll buy anything — furniture, pictures, plate, any blooming thing. Does it for a hobby, the regular dealers say. Likes the sport of bidding at the sales. But the knock-out men hate him; never know what he's going to do. Must have private means, for though he doesn't often drop money, he can't make much. He's no salesman. It is the buying that he seems to like. But he is a regular character, full of cranks and oddities. His rooms in Thavies Inn look like the British Museum gone mad. He has got electric alarms from all the doors up to his bedroom and the strong room in his office is fitted with a puzzle lock instead of keys."

"That doesn't seem very safe," I remarked.

"It is," said Miller. "This one has fifteen alphabets. One of our men has calculated that it has about forty million changes. No one is going to work that out, and there are no keys to get lost. But it is that strong room that is worrying us, as well as the old joker himself. The Lord knows how much valuable stuff there is in it. What we are afraid of is that Shemmonds may have made away with the old chap and be lying low, waiting to swoop down on that strong room."

"But you said that Luttrell goes away sometimes," said I.

"Yes; but then he always notifies his insurance company, and he seals up his strong room with a tape round the door handle and a great seal on the doorpost. This time he hasn't notified the company and the door isn't sealed. There's a seal on the doorpost — left from last time, I expect — but only the cut ends of tape. I got the caretaker to let me see the place this morning; and, by the way, Doctor, I have taken a leaf out of your book. I always carry a bit of squeezing wax in my pocket now and a little box of French chalk. Very handy they are, too. As I had 'em with me this morning, I took a squeeze of the seal. May want it presently for identification."

He brought out of his pocket a small tin box from which he carefully extracted an object wrapped in tissue paper. When the paper had been tenderly removed there was revealed a lump of moulding wax, one side of which was flattened and bore a sunk design.

"It's quite a good squeeze," said Miller, handing it to Thorndyke. "I dusted the seal with French chalk so that the wax shouldn't stick to it."

My colleague examined the "squeeze" through his lens, and passing it and the lens to me, asked:

"Has this been photographed, Miller?"

"No," was the reply, "but it ought to be before it gets damaged."

"It ought, certainly," said Thorndyke, "if you value it. Shall I get Polton to do it now?"

The superintendent accepted the offer gratefully and Thorndyke accordingly took the squeeze up to the laboratory, where he left it for our assistant to deal with. When he returned, Miller remarked:

"It is a baffling case, this. Now that Shemmonds has dropped out of sight, there is nothing to go on and nothing to do but wait for something else to happen; another burglary or an attempt on the strong room."

"Is it clear that the strong room has not been opened?" asked Thorndyke.

"No, it isn't," replied Miller. "That's part of the trouble. Luttrell has disappeared and he may be dead. If he is, Shemmonds will probably have been through his pockets. Of course there is no strong room key. That is one of the advantages of a puzzle lock. But it is quite possible that Luttrell may have kept a note of the combination and carried it about him. It would have been risky to trust entirely to memory. And he would have had the keys of the office about him. Any one who had those could have slipped in during business hours without much difficulty. Luttrell's premises are empty, but there are people in and out all day going to the other offices. Our man can't follow them all in. I suppose you can't make any suggestion, Doctor?"

"I am afraid I can't," answered Thorndyke. "The case is so very much in the air. There is nothing against Shemmonds but bare suspicion. He has disappeared only in the sense that you have lost sight of him, and the same is true of Luttrell — though there is an abnormal element in his case. Still, you could hardly get a search warrant on the facts that are known at present."

"No," Miller agreed, "they certainly would not authorize us to break open the strong room, and nothing short of that would be much use."

Here Polton made his appearance with the wax squeeze in a neat little box such as jewellers use.

"I've got two enlarged negatives," said he; "nice clear ones. How many prints shall I make for Mr. Miller?"

"Oh, one will do, Mr. Polton," said the superintendent. "If I want any more I'll ask you." He took up the little box, and, slipping it in his pocket, rose to depart. "I'll let you know, Doctor, how the case goes on, and perhaps you wouldn't mind turning it over a bit in the interval. Something might occur to you."

Thorndyke promised to think over the case, and when we had seen the superintendent launched down the stairs, we followed Polton up to the laboratory, where we each picked up one of the negatives and examined it against the light. I had already identified the seal by its shape — a *vesica piscis* or boat-shape — with the one that I had seen on Mr. Luttrell's finger. Now, in the photograph, enlarged three diameters, I could clearly make out the details. The design was distinctive and curious rather than elegant. The two triangular spaces at the ends were occupied respectively by a *memento mori* and a winged hourglass and the central portion was filled by a long inscription in Roman capitals, of which I could at first make nothing.

"Do you suppose this is some kind of cryptogram?" I asked.

"No," Thorndyke replied. "I imagine the words were run together merely to economize space. This is what I make of it."

He held the negative in his left hand, and with his right wrote down in pencil on a slip of paper the following four lines of doggerel verse:

> Eheu alas how fast the dam fugaces
> Labuntur anni especially in the cases
> Of poor old blokes like you and me Posthumus
> Who only wait for vermes to consume us.

"Well," I exclaimed, "it is a choice specimen; one of old Luttrell's merry conceited jests, I take it. But the joke was hardly worth the labour of engraving on a seal."

"It is certainly a rather mild jest," Thorndyke admitted. "But there may be something more in it than meets the eye."

He looked at the inscription reflectively and appeared to read it through once or twice. Then he replaced the negative in the drying rack, and, picking up the paper, slipped it into his pocket book.

"I don't quite see," said I, "why Miller brought this case to us or what he wants you to think over. In fact, I don't see that there is a case at all."

"It is a very shadowy case," Thorndyke admitted. "Miller had done a good deal of guessing, and so has Badger; and it may easily turn out that they have found a mare's nest. Nevertheless there is something to think about."

"As, for instance —— ?"

"Well, Jervis, you saw the men; you saw how they behaved; you have heard Miller's story and you have seen Mr. Luttrell's seal. Put all those data together and you have the material for some very interesting speculation, to say the least. You might even carry it beyond speculation."

I did not pursue the subject, for I knew that when Thorndyke used the word "speculation," nothing would induce him to commit himself to an opinion. But later, bearing in mind the attention that he seemed to bestow on Mr. Luttrell's schoolboy verses, I got a print from the negative and studied the foolish inscription exhaustively. But if it had any hidden meaning — and I could imagine no reason for supposing that it had — that meaning remained hidden; and the only conclusion at which I could arrive was that a man of Luttrell's age might have known better than to write such nonsense.

The superintendent did not leave the matter long in suspense. Three days later he paid us another visit and half-apologetically re-opened the subject.

"I am ashamed to come badgering you like this," he said, "but I can't get this case out of my head. I've a feeling that we ought to get a move of some kind on. And, by the way — though that is nothing to do with it — I've copied out the stuff on that seal and I can't make any sense of it. What the deuce are fugaces? I sup-pose 'vermes' are worms, though I don't see why he spelt it that way."

"The verses," said Thorndyke, "are apparently a travesty of a Latin poem; one of the odes of Horace which begins:

> 'Eheu! fugaces, Postume, Postume,
> Labuntur anni,'

which means, in effect, 'Alas! Postume, the flying years slip by.'"

"Well," said Miller, "any fool knows that — any middle-aged fool, at any rate. No need to put it into Latin. However, it's of no consequence. To return to this case; I've got an authority to look over Luttrell's premises — not to pull anything about, you know, just to look round. I called in on my way here to let the caretaker know that I should be coming in later. I thought that perhaps you might like to come with me. I wish you would, Doctor. You've got such a knack of spotting things that other people overlook."

He looked wistfully at Thorndyke, and as the latter was con-sidering the proposal, he added:

"The caretaker mentioned a rather odd circumstance. It seems that he keeps an eye on the electric metres in the building and that he has noticed a leakage of current in Mr. Luttrell's. It is only a small leak; about thirty watts an hour. But he can't account for it in any way. He has been right through the premises to see if any lamp has been left on in any of the rooms. But all the switches are off everywhere, and it can't be a short circuit. Funny, isn't it?"

It was certainly odd, but there seemed to me nothing in it to account for the expression of suddenly awakened interest that I detected in Thorndyke's face. However, it evidently had some special significance for him, for he asked almost eagerly:

"When are you making your inspection?"

"I am going there now," replied Miller, and he added coaxingly: "Couldn't you manage to run round with me?"

Thorndyke stood up. "Very well," said he. "Let us go together. You may as well come, too, Jervis, if you can spare an hour."

I agreed readily, for my colleague's hardly disguised interest in the inspection suggested a definite problem in his mind; and we at once issued forth and made our way by Mitre Court and Fetter Lane to the abode of the missing dealer, an old-fashioned house near the end of Thavies Inn.

"I've been over the premises once," said Miller, as the caretaker appeared with the keys, "and I think we had better begin the regular inspection with the offices. We can examine the stores and living rooms afterwards."

We accordingly entered the outer office, and as this was little more than a waiting room, we passed through into the private office, which had the appearance of having been used also as a sitting room or study. It was furnished with an easy-chair, a range of book shelves and a handsome bureau bookcase, while in the end wall was the massive iron door of the strong room. On this, as the chief object of interest, we all bore down, and the superintendent expounded its peculiarities.

"It is quite a good idea," said he, "this letter lock. There's no keyhole — though a safe lock is pretty hopeless to pick even if there was a keyhole — and no keys to get lost. As to guessing what the 'open sesame' may be — well, just look at it. You could spend a lifetime on it and be no forrader."

The puzzle lock was contained in the solid iron doorpost, through a slot in which a row of fifteen A's seemed to grin defiance on the would-be safe robber. I put my finger on the milled edges of one or two of the letters and rotated the discs, noticing how easily and smoothly they turned.

"Well," said Miller, "it's no use fumbling with that. I'm just going to have a look through his ledger and see who his customers were. The bookcase is unlocked. I tried it last time. And we'd better leave this as we found it."

He put back the letters that I had moved, and turned away to explore the bookcase; and as the letter lock appeared to present nothing but an insoluble riddle, I followed him, leaving Thorndyke earnestly gazing at the meaningless row of letters.

The superintendent glanced back at him with an indulgent smile.

"The doctor is going to work out the combination," he chuckled. "Well, well. There are only forty million changes and he's a young man for his age."

With this encouraging comment, he opened the glass door of the bookcase, and reaching down the ledger, laid it on the desk-like slope of the bureau.

"It is a poor chance," said he, opening the ledger at the index, "but some of these people may be able to give us a hint where to look for Mr. Luttrell, and it is worth while to know what sort of business he did."

He ran his finger down the list of names and had just turned to the account of one of the customers when we were startled by a loud click from the direction of the strong room. We both turned sharply and beheld Thorndyke grasping the handle of the strong room door, and I saw with amazement that the door was now slightly ajar.

"God!" exclaimed Miller, shutting the ledger and starting forward, "he's got it open!" He strode over to the door, and directing an eager look at the indicator of the lock, burst into a laugh. "Well, I'm hanged!" he exclaimed. "Why, it was unlocked all the time! To think that none of us had the sense to tug the handle! But isn't it just like old Luttrell to have a fool's answer like that to the blessed puzzle!"

I looked at the indicator, not a little astonished to observe the row of fifteen A's, which apparently formed the key combination. It may have been a very amusing joke on Mr. Luttrell's part, but it did not look very secure. Thorndyke regarded us with an inscrutable glance and still grasped the handle, holding the door a bare half inch open.

"There is something pushing against the door," said he. "Shall I open it?"

"May as well have a look at the inside," replied Miller. Thereupon Thorndyke released the handle and quickly stepped aside. The door swung slowly open and the dead body of a man fell out into the room and rolled over on to its back.

"Mercy on us!" gasped Miller, springing back hastily and staring with horror and amazement at the grim apparition. "That is not Luttrell." Then, suddenly starting forward and stooping over the dead man, he exclaimed: "Why, it is Shemmonds. So that is where he disappeared to. I wonder what became of Luttrell."

"There is somebody else in the strong room," said Thorndyke; and now, peering in through the doorway, I perceived a dim light, which seemed to come from a hidden recess, and by which I could see a pair of feet projecting round the corner. In a moment Miller had sprung in, and I followed. The strong room was L-shaped in plan, the arm of the L formed by a narrow passage at right angles to the main room. At the end of this a single small electric bulb was burning, the light of which showed the body of an elderly man stretched on the floor of the passage. I recognized him instantly in spite of the dimness of the light and the disfigurement caused by a ragged wound on the forehead.

"We had better get him out of this," said Miller, speaking in a flurried tone, partly due to the shock of the horrible discovery and partly to the accompanying physical unpleasantness, "and then we will have a look round. This wasn't just a mere robbery. We are going to find things out."

With my help he lifted Luttrell's corpse and together we carried it out, laying it on the floor of the room at the farther end, to which we also dragged the body of Shemmonds.

"There is no mystery as to how it happened," I said, after a brief inspection of the two corpses. "Shemmonds evidently shot the old man from behind with the pistol close to the back of the head. The hair is all scorched round the wound of entry and the bullet came out at the forehead."

"Yes," agreed Miller, "that is all clear enough. But the mystery is why on earth Shemmonds didn't let himself out. He must have known that the door was unlocked. Yet instead of turning the handle, he must have stood there like a fool, battering at the door with his fists. Just look at his hands."

"The further mystery," said Thorndyke, who, all this time, had been making a minute examination of the lock both from without and within, "is how the door came to be shut. That is quite a curious problem."

"Quite," agreed Miller. "But it will keep. And there is a still more curious problem inside there. There is nearly all the swag from that Colchester robbery. Looks as if Luttrell was in it."

Half-reluctantly he re-entered the strong room and Thorndyke and I followed. Near the angle of the passage he stooped to pick up an automatic pistol and a small, leather-bound book, which he opened and looked into by the light of the lamp. At the first glance he uttered an exclamation and shut the book with a snap.

"Do you know what this is?" he asked, holding it out to us. "It is the nominal roll, address book and journal of the gang. We've got them in the hollow of our hand; and it is dawning upon me that old Luttrell was the managing director whom I have been looking for so long. Just run your eyes along those shelves. That's loot; every bit of it. I can identify the articles from the lists that I made out."

He stood looking gloatingly along the shelves with their burden of jewellery, plate and other valuables. Then his eye lighted on a drawer in the end wall just under the lamp; an iron drawer with a disproportionately large handle and bearing a very legible label inscribed "unmounted stones."

"We'll have a look at his stock of unmounted gems," said Miller; and with that he bore down on the drawer, and seizing the handle, gave a vigorous pull. "Funny," said he. "It isn't locked, but something seems to be holding it back."

He planted his foot on the wall and took a fresh purchase on the handle.

"Wait a moment, Miller," said Thorndyke; but even as he spoke, the superintendent gave a mighty heave; the drawer came out a full two feet; there was a loud click, and a moment later the strong room door slammed.

"Good God!" exclaimed Miller, letting go the drawer, which immediately slid in with another click. "What was that?"

"That was the door shutting," replied Thorndyke. "Quite a clever arrangement; like the mechanism of a repeater watch. Pulling out the drawer wound up and released a spring that shut the door. Very ingenious."

"But," gasped Miller, turning an ashen face to my colleague, "we're shut in!"

"You are forgetting," said I — a little nervously, I must admit — "that the lock is as we left it."

The superintendent laughed, somewhat hysterically. "What a fool I am!" said he. "As bad as Shemmonds. Still we may as well —— " Here he started along the passage and I heard him groping his way to the door, and later heard the handle turn. Suddenly the deep silence of the tomb-like chamber was rent by a yell of terror.

"The door won't move! It's locked fast!"

On this I rushed along the passage with a sickening fear at my heart. And even as I ran, there rose before my eyes the horrible vision of the corpse with the battered hands that had fallen out when we opened the door of this awful trap. He had been caught as we were caught. How soon might it not be that some stranger would be looking in on our corpses.

In the dim twilight by the door I found Miller clutching the handle and shaking it like a madman. His self-possession was completely shattered. Nor was my own condition much better. I flung my whole weight on the door in the faint hope that the lock was not really closed, but the massive iron structure was as immovable as a stone wall. I was, nevertheless, gathering myself up for a second charge when I heard Thorndyke's voice close behind me.

"That is no use, Jervis. The door is locked."

As he spoke, there suddenly appeared a bright circle of light from the little electric lamp that he always carried in his pocket. Within the circle, and now clearly visible, was a second indicator of the puzzle lock on the inside of the doorpost.

"But it seems to be unlocked still," Miller said. "There is the same AAAAAA that it showed when we came in."

It was perfectly true. The slot of the letter lock still showed the range of fifteen A's, just as it had when the door was open. Could it be that the lock was a dummy and that there was some other means of opening the door? I was about to put this question to Thorndyke when he put the lamp into my hand, and, gently pushing me aside, stepped up to the indicator.

"Keep the light steady, Jervis," said he, and forthwith he began to manipulate the milled edges of the letter discs, beginning, as I noticed, at the right, or reverse end, of the slot and working backwards. I watched him with feverish interest and curiosity, as also did Miller, looking to see some word of fifteen letters develop in the slot. Instead of which, I saw, to my amazement and bewilderment, my colleague's finger transforming the row of A's into a succession of M's, which, however, were presently followed by an L and some X's. When the row was completed it looked like some remote, antediluvian date set down in Roman numerals.

"Try the handle now, Miller," said Thorndyke.

The superintendent needed no second bidding. Snatching at the handle, he turned it and bore heavily on the door. Almost instantly a thin line of light appeared at the edge; there was a sharp click, and the door swung right open. We fell out immediately — at least the superintendent and I did — thankful to find ourselves outside and alive. But, as we emerged, we both became aware of a man, white-faced and horror-stricken of aspect, stooping over the two corpses at the other end of the room. Our appearance was so sudden and unexpected — for the massive solidity of the safe door had rendered our movements inaudible outside — that, for a moment or two, he stood immovable, staring at us, wild-eyed and open-mouthed. Then, suddenly, he sprang up erect, and, darting to the door, opened it and rushed out with Miller close on his heels.

He did not get very far. Following the superintendent, I saw the fugitive wriggling in the embrace of a tall man on the pavement, who, with Miller's assistance, soon had a pair of handcuffs snapped on the man's wrists and then departed with his captive in search of a cab.

"That's one of 'em, I expect," said Miller, as we returned to the office; then, as his glance fell on the open strong room door, he mopped his face with his handkerchief. "That door gives me the creeps to look at it," said he. "Lord! what a shake-up that was! I've never had such a scare in my life. When I heard that door shut and I remembered how that poor devil, Shemmonds, came tumbling out — phoo!" He wiped his brow again, and, walking towards the strong room door, asked: "By the way, what was the magic word after all?" He stepped up to the indicator, and, after a quick glance, looked round at me in surprise. "Why!" he exclaimed, "blow me if it isn't AAAA still! But the Doctor altered it, didn't he?"

At this moment Thorndyke appeared from the strong room, where he had apparently been conducting some explorations, and to him the superintendent turned for an explanation.

"It is an ingenious device," said he; "in fact, the whole strong room is a monument of ingenuity, somewhat misapplied, but perfectly effective, as Mr. Shemmonds' corpse testifies. The key combination is a number expressed in Roman numerals, but the lock has a flyback mechanism which acts as soon as the door begins to open. That was how Shemmonds was caught. He, no doubt purposely, avoided watching Luttrell set the lock — or else Luttrell didn't let him — but as he went in with his intended victim, he looked at the indicator and saw the row of A's, which he naturally assumed to be the key combination. Then, when he tried to let himself out, of course, the lock wouldn't open."

"It is rather odd that he didn't try some other combinations," said I.

"He probably did," replied Thorndyke; "but when they failed he would naturally come back to the A's, which he had seen when the door was open. This is how it works."

He shut the door, and then, closely watched by the superintendent and me, turned the milled rims of the letter discs until the indicator showed a row of numerals thus: MMMMMMMCCCLXXXV. Grasping the handle, he turned it and gave a gentle pull, when the door began to open. But the instant it started from its bed, there was a loud click and all the letters of the indicator flew back to A.

"Well, I'm jiggered!" exclaimed Miller. "It must have been an awful suck-in for that poor blighter, Shemmonds. Took me in, too. I saw those A's and the door open, and I thought I knew all about it. But what beats me, Doctor, is how you managed to work it out. I can't see what you had to go on. Would it be allowable to ask how it was done?"

"Certainly," replied Thorndyke; "but we had better defer the explanation. You have got those two bodies to dispose of and some other matters, and we must get back to our chambers. I will write down the key combination, in case you want it, and then you must come and see us and let us know what luck you have had."

He wrote the numerals on a slip of paper, and when he had handed it to the superintendent, we took our leave.

"I find myself," said I, as we walked home, "in much the same position as Miller. I don't see what you had to go on. It is clear to me that you not only worked out the lock combination — from the seal inscription, as I assume — but that you identified Luttrell as the director of the gang. I don't, in the least, understand how you did it."

"And yet, Jervis," said he, "it was an essentially simple case. If you review it and cast up the items of evidence, you will see that we really had all the facts. The problem was merely to coördinate them and extract their significance. Take first the character of Luttrell. We saw the man in company with another, evidently a fairly intimate acquaintance. They were being shadowed by a detective, and it is pretty clear that they detected the sleuth, for they shook him off quite neatly. Later, we learn from Miller that one of these men is suspected to be a member of a firm of swell burglars and that the other is a well-to-do, rather eccentric and very miscellaneous dealer, who has a strong room fitted with a puzzle lock. I am astonished that the usually acute Miller did not notice how well Luttrell fitted the part of the managing director whom he was looking for. Here was a dealer who bought and sold all sorts of queer but valuable things, who must have had unlimited facilities for getting rid of stones, bullion and silver, and who used a puzzle lock. Now, who uses a puzzle lock? No one, certainly, who can conveniently use a key. But to the manager of a gang of thieves it would be a valuable safeguard, for he might at any moment be robbed of his keys, and perhaps made away with. But he could not be robbed of the secret password, and his possession of it would be a security against murder. So you see that the simple probabilities pointed to Luttrell as the head of the gang.

"And now consider the problem of the lock. First, we saw that Luttrell wore on his left hand a huge, cumbrous seal ring, that he carried a Coddington lens on his watch guard, and a small electric lamp in his pocket. That told us very little. But when Miller told us about the lock and showed us the squeeze of the seal, and when we saw that the seal bore a long inscription in minute lettering, a connection began to appear. As Miller justly observed, no man — and especially no elderly man — would trust the key combination exclusively to his memory. He would carry about him some record to which he could refer in case his memory failed him. But that record would hardly be one that anybody could read, or the secrecy and safety of the lock would be gone. It would probably be some kind of cryptogram; and when we saw this inscription and considered it in conjunction with the lens and the lamp, it seemed highly probable that the key combination was contained in the inscription; and that probability was further increased when we saw the nonsensical doggerel of which the inscription was made up. The suggestion was that the verses had been made for some purpose independent of their sense. Accordingly I gave the inscription very careful consideration.

"Now we learned from Miller that the puzzle lock had fifteen letters. The key might be one long word, such as 'superlativeness,' a number of short words, or some chemical or other formula. Or it was possible that it might be of the nature of a chronogram. I have never heard of chronograms being used for secret records or messages, but it has often occurred to me that they would be extremely suitable. And this was an exceptionally suitable case."

"Chronogram," said I. "Isn't that something connected with medals?"

"They have often been used on medals," he replied. "In effect, a chronogram is an inscription some of the letters of which form a date connected with the subject of the inscription. Usually the date letters are written or cut larger than the others for convenience in reading, but, of course, this is not essential. The principle of a chronogram is this. The letters of the Roman alphabet are of two kinds: those that are simply letters and nothing else, and those that are numerals as well as letters. The numeral letters are M = a thousand, D = five hundred, C = one hundred, L = fifty, X = ten, V = five, and I = one. Now, in deciphering a chronogram, you pick out all the numeral letters and add them up without regard to their order. The total gives you the date.

"Well, as I said, it occurred to me that this might be of the nature of a chronogram; but as the lock had letters and not figures, the number, if there was one, would have to be expressed in Roman numerals, and it would have to form a number of fifteen numeral letters. As it was thus quite easy to put my hypothesis to the test, I proceeded to treat the inscription as a chronogram and decipher it;

and behold! it yielded a number of fifteen letters, which, of course, was as near certainty as was possible, short of actual experiment."

"Let us see how you did the decipherment," I said, as we entered our chambers and shut the door. I procured a large notebook and pencil, and, laying them on the table, drew up two chairs.

"Now," said I, "fire away."

"Very well," he said. "We will begin by writing the inscription in proper chronogram form with the numeral letters double size and treating the U's as V's and the W's as double V's according to the rules."

Here he wrote out the inscription in Roman capitals thus:—

eheV aLas hoVV fast the DaM fVgaCes
LabVntVr annI espeCIaLLy In the Cases
of poor oLD bLokes LIke yoV anD Me posthVMVs
VVho onLy VVaIt for VerMes to ConsVMe Vs

"Now," said he, "let us make a column of each line and add them up, thus:—

1		2		3		4	
V	= 5	L	= 50	L	= 50	VV	= 10
L	= 50	V	= 5	D	= 500	L	= 50
VV	= 10	V	= 5	L	= 50	VV	= 10
D	= 500	I	= 1	L	= 50	I	= 1
M	= 1000	C	= 100	I	= 1	V	= 5
V	= 5	I	= 1	V	= 5	M	= 1000
C	= 100	L	= 50	D	= 500	C	= 100
		L	= 50	M	= 1000	V	= 5
		I	= 1	V	= 5	M	= 1000
		C	= 100	M	= 1000	V	= 5
				V	= 5		
1670		**363**		**3166**		**2186**	

"Now," he continued, "we take the four totals and add them together, thus:—

$$\begin{array}{r} 1670 \\ 363 \\ 3166 \\ 2186 \\ \hline 7385 \end{array}$$

and we get the grand total of seven thousand three hundred and eighty-five, and this, expressed in Roman numerals, is MMMMMM-MCCCLXXXV. Here, then, is a number consisting of fifteen letters, the exact number of spaces in the indicator of the puzzle lock; and I repeat that this striking coincidence, added to, or rather multiplied into, the other probabilities, made it practically certain that this was the key combination. It remained only to test it by actual experiment."

"By the way," said I, "I noticed that you perked up rather suddenly when Miller mentioned the electric metre."

"Naturally," he replied. "It seemed that there must be a small lamp switched on somewhere in the building, and the only place that had not been examined was the strong room. But if there was a lamp alight there, some one had been in the strong room. And, as the only person who was known to be able to get in was missing, it seemed probable that he was in there still. But if he was, he was pretty certainly dead; and there was quite a considerable probability that some one else was in there with him, since his companion was missing, too, and both had disappeared at the same time. But I must confess that that spring drawer was beyond my expectations, though I suspected it as soon as I saw Miller pulling at it. Luttrell was an ingenious old rascal; he almost deserved a better fate. However, I expect his death will have delivered the gang into the hands of the police."

Events fell out as Thorndyke surmised. Mr. Luttrell's little journal, in conjunction with the confession of the spy who had been captured on the premises, enabled the police to swoop down on the disconcerted gang before any breath of suspicion had reached them; with the result that they are now secured in strong rooms of another kind whereof the doors are fitted with appliances as effective as, though less ingenious than, Mr. Luttrell's puzzle lock.

THE SECRET GARDEN

by GILBERT K. CHESTERTON

E. M. Wrong thought Dr. Thorndyke "the greatest detective now in business." We think FATHER BROWN *is. Practically nobody agrees with us, but this is our story and we'll stick to it.*

ARISTIDE VALENTIN, CHIEF OF THE PARIS POLICE, was late for his dinner, and some of his guests began to arrive before him. These were, however, reassured by his confidential servant, Ivan, the old man with a scar, and a face almost as grey as his moustaches, who always sat at a table in the entrance hall — a hall hung with weapons. Valentin's house was perhaps as peculiar and celebrated as its master. It was an old house, with high walls and tall poplars almost overhanging the Seine; but the oddity — and perhaps the police value — of its architecture was this: that there was no ultimate exit at all except through this front door, which was guarded by Ivan and the armoury. The garden was large and elaborate, and there were many exits from the house into the garden. But there was no exit from the garden into the world outside; all round it ran a tall, smooth, unscalable wall with special spikes at the top; no bad garden, perhaps, for a man to reflect in whom some hundred criminals had sworn to kill.

As Ivan explained to the guests, their host had telephoned that he was detained for ten minutes. He was, in truth, making some last arrangements about executions and such ugly things; and though these duties were rootedly repulsive to him, he always performed them with precision. Ruthless in the pursuit of criminals, he was very mild about their punishment. Since he had been supreme over French — and largely over European — political methods, his great influence had been honourably used for the mitigation of sentences and the purification of prisons. He was one of the great humanitarian French freethinkers; and the only thing wrong with them is that they make mercy even colder than justice.

When Valentin arrived he was already dressed in black clothes and the red rosette — an elegant figure, his dark beard already streaked with grey. He went straight through his house to his study, which opened on the grounds behind. The garden door of it was open, and after he had carefully locked his box in its official place, he stood for a few seconds at the open door looking out upon the garden. A sharp moon was fighting with the flying rags and tatters of a storm, and Valentin regarded it with a wistfulness unusual in such scientific natures as his. Perhaps such scientific natures have some psychic prevision of the most tremendous problem of their lives. From any such occult mood, at least, he quickly recovered, for he knew he was late, and that his guests had already begun to arrive. A glance at his drawing-room when he entered it was enough to make certain that his principal guest was not there, at any rate. He saw all the other pillars of the little party; he saw Lord Galloway, the English Ambassador — a choleric old man with a russet face like an apple, wearing the blue ribbon of the Garter. He saw Lady Galloway, slim and threadlike, with silver hair and a face sensitive and superior. He saw her daughter, Lady Margaret Graham, a pale and pretty girl with an elfish face and copper-coloured hair. He saw the Duchess of Mont St.-Michel, black-eyed and opulent, and with her her two daughters, black-eyed and opulent also. He saw Dr. Simon, a typical French scientist, with glasses, a pointed brown beard, and a forehead barred with those parallel wrinkles which are the penalty of superciliousness, since they come through constantly elevating the eyebrows. He saw Father Brown, of Cobhole, in Essex, whom he had recently met in England. He saw — perhaps with more interest than any of these — a tall man in uniform, who had bowed to the Galloways without receiving any very hearty acknowledgment, and who now advanced alone to pay his respects to his host. This was Commandant O'Brien, of the French Foreign Legion. He was a slim yet somewhat swaggering figure, clean-shaven, dark-haired, and blue-eyed, and, as seemed natural in an officer of that famous regiment of victorious failures and successful suicides, he had an air at once dashing and melancholy. He was by birth an Irish gentleman, and in boyhood had known the Galloways — especially Margaret Graham. He had left his country after some crash of debts, and now expressed his complete freedom from British etiquette by swinging about in uniform, sabre and spurs. When he bowed to the Ambassador's family, Lord and Lady Galloway bent stiffly, and Lady Margaret looked away.

But for whatever old causes such people might be interested in each other, their distinguished host was not specially interested in them. No one of them at least was in his eyes the guest of the evening. Valentin was expecting, for special reasons, a man of worldwide fame, whose friendship he had secured during some of his great detective tours and triumphs in the United States. He was expecting Julius K. Brayne, that multi-millionaire whose colossal and even crushing endowments of small religions have occasioned so much easy sport and easier solemnity for the American and English papers. Nobody could quite make out whether Mr. Brayne was an atheist or a Mormon or a Christian Scientist; but he was ready to pour money into any intellectual vessel, so long as it was an untried vessel. One of his hobbies was to wait for the American Shakespeare — a hobby more patient than angling. He admired Walt Whitman, but thought that Luke P. Tanner, of Paris, Pa., was more "progressive" than Whitman any day. He liked anything that he thought "progressive." He thought Valentin "progressive," thereby doing him a grave injustice.

The solid appearance of Julius K. Brayne in the room was as decisive as a dinner bell. He had this great quality, which very few of us can claim, that his presence was as big as his absence. He was a huge fellow, as fat as he was tall, clad in complete evening black, without so much relief as a watchchain or a ring. His hair was white and well brushed back like a German's; his face was red, fierce and cherubic, with one dark tuft under the lower lip that threw up that otherwise infantile visage with an effect theatrical and even Mephistophelean. Not long, however, did that *salon* merely stare at the celebrated American; his lateness had already become a domestic problem, and he was sent with all speed into the dining-room with Lady Galloway on his arm.

Except on one point the Galloways were genial and casual enough

So long as Lady Margaret did not take the arm of that adventurer O'Brien, her father was quite satisfied; and she had not done so, she had decorously gone in with Dr. Simon. Nevertheless, old Lord Galloway was restless and almost rude. He was diplomatic enough during dinner, but when, over the cigars, three of the younger men — Simon the doctor, Brown the priest, and the detrimental O'Brien, the exile in a foreign uniform — all melted away to mix with the ladies or smoke in the conservatory, then the English diplomatist grew very undiplomatic indeed. He was stung every sixty seconds with the thought that the scamp O'Brien might be signalling to Margaret somehow; he did not attempt to imagine how. He was left over the coffee with Brayne, the hoary Yankee who believed in all religions, and Valentin, the grizzled Frenchman who believed in none. They could argue with each other, but neither could appeal to him. After a time this "progressive" logomachy had reached a crisis of tedium; Lord Galloway got up also and sought the drawing-room. He lost his way in long passages for some six or eight minutes: till he heard the high-pitched, didactic voice of the doctor, and then the dull voice of the priest, followed by general laughter. They also, he thought with a curse, were probably arguing about "science and religion." But the instant he opened the *salon* door he saw only one thing — he saw what was not there. He saw that Commandant O'Brien was absent, and that Lady Margaret was absent too.

Rising impatiently from the drawing-room, as he had from the dining-room, he stamped along the passage once more. His notion of protecting his daughter from the Irish-Algerian ne'er-do-weel had become something central and even mad in his mind. As he went towards the back of the house, where was Valentin's study, he was surprised to meet his daughter, who swept past with a white, scornful face, which was a second enigma. If she had been with O'Brien, where was O'Brien? If she had not been with O'Brien, where had she been? With a sort of senile and passionate suspicion he groped his way to the dark back parts of the mansion, and eventually found a servants' entrance that opened on to the garden. The moon with her scimitar had now ripped up and rolled away all the storm wrack. The argent light lit up all four corners of the garden. A tall figure in blue was striding across the lawn towards the study door; a glint of moonlit silver on his facings picked him out as Commandant O'Brien.

He vanished through the French windows into the house, leaving Lord Galloway in an indescribable temper, at once virulent and vague. The blue-and-silver garden, like a scene in a theatre, seemed to taunt him with all that tyrannic tenderness against which his worldly authority was at war. The length and grace of the Irishman's stride enraged him as if he were a rival instead of a father; the moonlight maddened him. He was trapped as if by magic into a garden of troubadours, a Watteau fairyland; and, willing to shake off such amorous imbecilities by speech, he stepped briskly after his enemy. As he did so he tripped over some tree or stone in the grass; looked down at it first with irritation and then a second time with curiosity. The next instant the moon and the tall poplars looked at an unusual sight — an elderly English diplomatist running hard and crying or bellowing as he ran.

His hoarse shouts brought a pale face to the study door, the beaming glasses and worried brow of Dr. Simon, who heard the nobleman's first clear words. Lord Galloway was crying: "A corpse in the grass — a blood-stained corpse." O'Brien at least had gone utterly out of his mind.

"We must tell Valentin at once," said the doctor, when the other had brokenly described all that he had dared to examine. "It is fortunate that he is here"; and even as he spoke the great detective entered the study, attracted by the cry. It was almost amusing to note his typical transformation; he had come with the common concern of a host and a gentleman, fearing that some guest or servant was ill. When he was told the gory fact, he turned with all his gravity instantly bright and businesslike; for this, however abrupt and awful, was his business.

"Strange, gentlemen," he said as they hurried out into the garden, "that I should have hunted mysteries all over the earth, and now one comes and settles in my own back yard. But where is the place?" They crossed the lawn less easily, as a slight mist had begun to rise from the river; but under the guidance of the shaken Galloway they found the body sunken in deep grass — the body of a very tall and broad-shouldered man. He lay face downwards, so they could only see that his big shoulders were clad in black cloth, and that his big head was bald, except for a wisp or two of brown hair that clung to his skull like wet seaweed. A scarlet serpent of blood crawled from under his fallen face.

"At least," said Simon, with a deep and singular intonation, "he is none of our party."

"Examine him, Doctor," cried Valentin rather sharply. "He may not be dead."

The doctor bent down. "He is not quite cold, but I am afraid he is dead enough," he answered. "Just help me to lift him up."

They lifted him carefully an inch from the ground, and all doubts as to his being really dead were settled at once and frightfully. The head fell away. It had been entirely sundered from the body; whoever had cut his throat had managed to sever the neck as well. Even Valentin was slightly shocked. "He must have been as strong as a gorilla," he muttered.

Not without a shiver, though he was used to anatomical abortions, Dr. Simon lifted the head. It was slightly slashed about the neck and jaw, but the face was substantially unhurt. It was a ponderous, yellow face, at once sunken and swollen, with a hawk-like nose and heavy lids — the face of a wicked Roman emperor, with, perhaps, a distant touch of a Chinese emperor. All present seemed to look at it with the coldest eye of ignorance. Nothing else could be noted about the man except that, as they had lifted his body, they had seen underneath it the white gleam of a shirt front defaced with a red gleam of blood. As Dr. Simon said, the man had never been of their party. But he might very well have been trying to join it, for he had come dressed for such an occasion.

Valentin went down on his hands and knees and examined with his closest professional attention the grass and ground for some twenty yards round the body, in which he was assisted less skilfully by the doctor, and quite vaguely by the English lord. Nothing rewarded their grovellings except a few twigs, snapped or chopped into very small lengths, which Valentin lifted for an instant's examination and then tossed away.

"Twigs," he said gravely; "twigs, and a total stranger with his head cut off; that is all there is on this lawn."

There was an almost creepy stillness, and then the unnerved Galloway called out sharply:

"Who's that? Who's that over there by the garden wall?"

A small figure with a foolishly large head drew waveringly near them in the moonlit haze; looked for an instant like a goblin, but turned out to be the harmless little priest whom they had left in the drawing-room.

"I say," he said meekly, "there are no gates to this garden, do you know?"

Valentin's black brows had come together somewhat crossly, as they did on principle at the sight of the cassock. But he was far too just a man to deny the relevance of the remark. "You are right," he said. "Before we find out how he came to be killed, we may have to find out how he came to be here. Now listen to me, gentlemen. If it can be done without prejudice to my position and duty, we shall all agree that certain distinguished names might well be kept out of this. There are ladies, gentlemen, and there is a foreign ambassador. If we must mark it down as a crime, then it must be followed up as a crime. But till then I can use my own discretion. I am the head of the police; I am so public that I can afford to be private. Please Heaven, I will clear every one of my own guests before I call in my men to look for anybody else. Gentlemen, upon your honour, you will none of you leave the house till to-morrow at noon; there are bedrooms for all. Simon, I think you know where to find my man, Ivan, in the front hall; he is a confidential man. Tell him to leave another servant on guard and come to me at once. Lord Galloway, you are certainly the best person to tell the ladies what has happened, and prevent a panic. They also must stay. Father Brown and I will remain with the body."

When this spirit of the captain spoke in Valentin he was obeyed like a bugle. Dr. Simon went through to the armoury and routed out Ivan, the public detective's private detective. Galloway went to the drawing-room and told the terrible news tactfully enough, so that by the time the company assembled there the ladies were already startled and already soothed. Meanwhile the good priest and the good atheist stood at the head and foot of the dead man motionless in the moonlight, like symbolic statues of their two philosophies of death.

Ivan, the confidential man with the scar and the moustaches, came out of the house like a cannon ball, and came racing across the lawn to Valentin like a dog to his master. His livid face was quite lively with the glow of this domestic detective story, and it was with almost unpleasant eagerness that he asked his master's permission to examine the remains.

"Yes; look, if you like, Ivan," said Valentin, "but don't be long. We must go in and thrash this out in the house."

Ivan lifted the head, and then almost let it drop.

"Why," he gasped, "it's — no, it isn't; it can't be. Do you know this man, sir?"

"No," said Valentin indifferently; "we had better go inside."

Between them they carried the corpse to a sofa in the study, and then all made their way to the drawing-room.

The detective sat down at a desk quietly, and even with hesitation; but his eye was the iron eye of a judge at assize. He made a few rapid notes upon paper in front of him, and then said shortly: "Is everybody here?"

"Not Mr. Brayne," said the Duchess of Mont St.-Michel, looking round.

"No," said Lord Galloway in a hoarse, harsh voice. "And not Mr. Neil O'Brien, I fancy. I saw that gentleman walking in the garden when the corpse was still warm."

"Ivan," said the detective, "go and fetch Commandant O'Brien and Mr. Brayne. Mr. Brayne, I know, is finishing a cigar in the dining-room; Commandant O'Brien, I think, is walking up and down the conservatory. I am not sure."

The faithful attendant flashed from the room, and before anyone could stir or speak Valentin went on with the same soldierly swiftness of exposition.

"Everyone here knows that a dead man has been found in the garden, his head cut clean from his body. Dr. Simon, you have examined it. Do you think that to cut a man's throat like that would need great force? Or, perhaps, only a very sharp knife?"

"I should say that it could not be done with a knife at all," said the pale doctor.

"Have you any thought," resumed Valentin, "of a tool with which it could be done?"

"Speaking within modern probabilities, I really haven't," said the doctor, arching his painful brows. "It's not easy to hack a neck through even clumsily, and this was a very clean cut. It could be done with a battle-axe or an old headsman's axe, or an old two-handed sword."

"But, good heavens!" cried the Duchess, almost in hysterics, "there aren't any two-handed swords and battle-axes round here."

Valentin was still busy with the paper in front of him. "Tell me," he said, still writing rapidly, "could it have been done with a long French cavalry sabre?"

A low knocking came at the door, which, for some unreasonable reason, curdled everyone's blood like the knocking in "Macbeth." Amid that frozen silence Dr. Simon managed to say: "A sabre — yes, I suppose it could."

"Thank you," said Valentin. "Come in, Ivan."

The confidential Ivan opened the door and ushered in Commandant Neil O'Brien, whom he had found at last pacing the garden again.

The Irish officer stood up disordered and defiant on the threshold. "What do you want with me?" he cried.

"Please sit down," said Valentin in pleasant, level tones. "Why, you aren't wearing your sword. Where is it?"

"I left it on the library table," said O'Brien, his brogue deepening in his disturbed mood. "It was a nuisance, it was getting —— "

"Ivan," said Valentin, "please go and get the Commandant's sword from the library." Then, as the servant vanished, "Lord Galloway says he saw you leaving the garden just before he found the corpse. What were you doing in the garden?"

The Commandant flung himself recklessly into a chair. "Oh," he cried in pure Irish, "admirin' the moon. Communing with Nature, me bhoy."

A heavy silence sank and endured, and at the end of it came again that trivial and terrible knocking. Ivan reappeared, carrying an empty steel scabbard. "This is all I can find," he said.

"Put it on the table," said Valentin, without looking up.

There was an inhuman silence in the room, like that sea of inhuman silence round the dock of the condemned murderer. The Duchess's weak exclamations had long ago died away. Lord Galloway's swollen hatred was satisfied and even sobered. The voice that came was quite unexpected.

"I think I can tell you," cried Lady Margaret, in that clear, quivering voice with which a courageous woman speaks publicly. "I can tell you what Mr. O'Brien was doing in the garden, since he is bound to silence. He was asking me to marry him. I refused; I said in my family circumstances I could give him nothing but my respect. He was a little angry at that; he did not seem to think much of my respect. I wonder," she added, with rather a wan smile, "if he will care at all for it now. For I offer it him now. I will swear anywhere that he never did a thing like this."

Lord Galloway had edged up to his daughter, and was intimidating her in what he imagined to be an undertone. "Hold your tongue, Maggie," he said in a thunderous whisper. "Why should you shield the fellow? Where's his sword? Where's his confounded cavalry —— "

He stopped because of the singular stare with which his daughter was regarding him, a look that was indeed a lurid magnet for the whole group.

"You old fool!" she said, in a low voice without pretence of piety, "what do you suppose you are trying to prove? I tell you this man was innocent while with me. But if he wasn't innocent, he was still with me. If he murdered a man in the garden, who was it who must have seen — who must at least have known? Do you hate Neil so much as to put your own daughter —— "

Lady Galloway screamed. Everyone else sat tingling at the touch of those satanic tragedies that have been between lovers before now. They saw the proud, white face of the Scotch aristocrat and her lover, the Irish adventurer, like old portraits in a dark house. The long silence was full of formless historical memories of murdered husbands and poisonous paramours.

In the centre of this morbid silence an innocent voice said: "Was it a very long cigar?"

The change of thought was so sharp that they had to look round to see who had spoken.

"I mean," said little Father Brown, from the corner of the room, "I mean that cigar Mr. Brayne is finishing. It seems nearly as long as a walking stick."

Despite the irrelevance there was assent as well as irritation in Valentin's face as he lifted his head.

"Quite right," he remarked sharply. "Ivan, go and see about Mr. Brayne again, and bring him here at once."

The instant the factotum had closed the door, Valentin addressed the girl with an entirely new earnestness.

"Lady Margaret," he said, "we all feel, I am sure, both gratitude and admiration for your act in rising above your lower dignity and explaining the Commandant's conduct. But there is a hiatus still. Lord Galloway, I understand, met you passing from the study to the drawing-room, and it was only some minutes afterwards that he found the garden and the Commandant still walking there."

"You have to remember," replied Margaret, with a faint irony in her voice, "that I had just refused him, so we should scarcely have come back arm in arm. He is a gentleman, anyhow; and he loitered behind — and so got charged with murder."

"In those few moments," said Valentin gravely, "he might really —— "

The knock came again, and Ivan put in his scarred face.

"Beg pardon, sir," he said, "but Mr. Brayne has left the house."

"Left!" cried Valentin, and rose for the first time to his feet.

"Gone. Scooted. Evaporated," replied Ivan, in humorous French. "His hat and coat are gone, too, and I'll tell you something to cap it all. I ran outside the house to find any traces of him, and I found one, and a big trace, too."

"What do you mean?" asked Valentin.

"I'll show you," said his servant, and reappeared with a flashing naked cavalry sabre, streaked with blood about the point and edge. Everyone in the room eyed it as if it were a thunderbolt; but the experienced Ivan went on quite quietly:

"I found this," he said, "flung among the bushes fifty yards up the road to Paris. In other words, I found it just where your respectable Mr. Brayne threw it when he ran away."

There was again a silence, but of a new sort. Valentin took the sabre, examined it, reflected with unaffected concentration of thought, and then turned a respectful face to O'Brien. "Commandant," he said, "we trust you will always produce this weapon if it is wanted for police examination. Meanwhile," he added, slapping the steel back in the ringing scabbard, "let me return you your sword."

At the military symbolism of the action the audience could hardly refrain from applause.

For Neil O'Brien, indeed, that gesture was the turning point of existence. By the time he was wandering in the mysterious garden again in the colours of the morning the tragic futility of his ordinary mien had fallen from him; he was a man with many reasons for happiness. Lord Galloway was a gentleman, and had offered him an apology. Lady Margaret was something better than a lady, a woman at least, and had perhaps given him something better than an apology, as they drifted among the old flower beds before breakfast. The whole company was more light-hearted and humane, for though the riddle of the death remained, the load of suspicion was lifted off them all, and sent flying off to Paris with the strange millionaire — a man they hardly knew. The devil was cast out of the house — he had cast himself out.

Still, the riddle remained; and when O'Brien threw himself on a garden seat beside Dr. Simon, that keenly scientific person at once resumed it. He did not get much talk out of O'Brien, whose thoughts were on pleasanter things.

"I can't say it interests me much," said the Irishman frankly, "especially as it seems pretty plain now. Apparently Brayne hated this stranger for some reason; lured him into the garden, and killed him with my sword. Then he fled to the city, tossing the sword away as he went. By the way, Ivan tells me the dead man had a Yankee dollar in his pocket. So he was a countryman of Brayne's, and that seems to clinch it. I don't see any difficulties about the business."

"There are five colossal difficulties," said the doctor quietly; "like high walls within walls. Don't mistake me. I don't doubt that Brayne did it; his flight, I fancy, proves that. But as to how he did it. First difficulty: Why should a man kill another man with a great hulking sabre, when he can almost kill him with a pocket knife and put it back in his pocket? Second difficulty: Why was there no noise or outcry? Does a man commonly see another come up waving a scimitar and offer no remarks? Third difficulty: A servant watched the front door all the evening; and a rat cannot get into Valentin's garden anywhere. How did the dead man get into the garden? Fourth difficulty: Given the same conditions, how did Brayne get out of the garden?"

"And the fifth?" said Neil, with eyes fixed on the English priest who was coming slowly up the path.

"Is a trifle, I suppose," said the doctor, "but I think an odd one. When I first saw how the head had been slashed, I supposed the assassin had struck more than once. But on examination I found many cuts across the truncated section; in other words, they were struck *after* the head was off. Did Brayne hate his foe so fiendishly that he stood sabring his body in the moonlight?"

"Horrible!" said O'Brien, and shuddered.

The little priest, Brown, had arrived while they were talking, and had waited, with characteristic shyness, till they had finished. Then he said awkwardly:

"I say, I'm sorry to interrupt. But I was sent to tell you the news!"

"News?" repeated Simon, and stared at him rather painfully through his glasses.

"Yes, I'm sorry," said Father Brown mildly. "There's been another murder, you know."

Both men on the seat sprang up, leaving it rocking.

"And, what's stranger still," continued the priest, with his dull eye on the rhododendrons, "it's the same disgusting sort; it's another beheading. They found the second head actually bleeding into the river, a few yards along Brayne's road to Paris; so they suppose that he —— "

"Great Heaven!" cried O'Brien. "Is Brayne a monomaniac?"

"There are American vendettas," said the priest impassively. Then he added: "They want you to come to the library and see it."

Commandant O'Brien followed the others towards the inquest, feeling decidedly sick. As a soldier, he loathed all this secretive carnage; where were these extravagant amputations going to stop? First one head was hacked off, and then another; in this case (he told himself bitterly) it was not true that two heads were better than one. As he crossed the study he almost staggered at a shocking coincidence. Upon Valentin's table lay the coloured picture of yet a third bleeding head; and it was the head of Valentin himself. A second glance showed him it was only a Nationalist paper, called *The Guillotine,* which every week showed one of its political opponents with rolling eyes and writhing features just after execution; for Valentin was an anti-clerical of some note. But O'Brien was an

Irishman, with a kind of chastity even in his sins; and his gorge
rose against that great brutality of the intellect which belongs only
to France. He felt Paris as a whole, from the grotesques on the
Gothic churches to the gross caricatures in the newspapers. He
remembered the gigantic jests of the Revolution. He saw the whole
city as one ugly energy, from the sanguinary sketch lying on Valentin's table up to where, above a mountain and forest of gargoyles,
the great devil grins on Notre Dame.

The library was long, low, and dark; what light entered it shot
from under low blinds and had still some of the ruddy tinge of
morning. Valentin and his servant Ivan were waiting for them at
the upper end of a long, slightly sloping desk, on which lay the
mortal remains, looking enormous in the twilight. The big black
figure and yellow face of the man found in the garden confronted
them essentially unchanged. The second head, which had been
fished from among the river reeds that morning, lay streaming and
dripping beside it; Valentin's men were still seeking to recover the
rest of this second corpse, which was supposed to be afloat. Father
Brown, who did not seem to share O'Brien's sensibilities in the least,
went up to the second head and examined it with his blinking care.
It was little more than a mop of wet white hair, fringed with silver
fire in the red and level morning light; the face, which seemed of an
ugly, empurpled and perhaps criminal type, had been much battered against trees or stones as it tossed in the water.

"Good morning, Commandant O'Brien," said Valentin, with
quiet cordiality. "You have heard of Brayne's last experiment in
butchery, I suppose."

Father Brown was still bending over the head with white hair,
and he said, without looking up:

"I suppose it is quite certain that Brayne cut off this head, too."

"Well, it seems common sense," said Valentin, with his hands in
his pockets. "Killed in the same way as the other. Found within
a few yards of the other. And sliced by the same weapon which we
know he carried away."

"Yes, yes; I know," replied Father Brown submissively. "Yet, you
know, I doubt whether Brayne could have cut off this head."

"Why not?" inquired Dr. Simon, with a rational stare.

"Well, Doctor," said the priest, looking up blinking, "can a man
cut off his own head? I don't know."

O'Brien felt an insane universe crashing about his ears; but the doctor sprang forward with impetuous practicality and pushed back the wet white hair.

"Oh, there's no doubt it's Brayne," said the priest quietly. "He had exactly that chip in the left ear."

The detective, who had been regarding the priest with steady and glittering eyes, opened his clenched mouth and said sharply: "You seem to know a lot about him, Father Brown."

"I do," said the little man simply. "I've been about with him for some weeks. He was thinking of joining our church."

The star of the fanatic sprang into Valentin's eyes; he strode towards the priest with clenched hands. "And, perhaps," he cried, with a blasting sneer, "perhaps he was also thinking of leaving all his money to your church."

"Perhaps he was," said Brown stolidly; "it is possible."

"In that case," cried Valentin, with a dreadful smile, "you may indeed know a great deal about him. About his life and about his —— "

Commandant O'Brien laid a hand on Valentin's arm. "Drop that slanderous rubbish, Valentin," he said, "or there may be more swords yet."

But Valentin (under the steady, humble gaze of the priest) had already recovered himself. "Well," he said shortly, "people's private opinions can wait. You gentlemen are still bound by your promise to stay; you must enforce it on yourselves — and on each other. Ivan here will tell you anything more you want to know; I must get to business and write to the authorities. We can't keep this quiet any longer. I shall be writing in my study if there is any more news."

"Is there any more news, Ivan?" asked Dr. Simon, as the chief of police strode out of the room.

"Only one more thing, I think, sir," said Ivan, wrinkling up his grey old face, "but that's important, too, in its way. There's that old buffer you found on the lawn," and he pointed without pretence of reverence at the big black body with the yellow head. "We've found out who he is, anyhow."

"Indeed!" cried the astonished doctor, "and who is he?"

"His name was Arnold Becker," said the under-detective, "though he went by many aliases. He was a wandering sort of scamp, and

238 THE SECRET GARDEN

is known to have been in America; so that was where Brayne got his knife into him. We didn't have much to do with him ourselves, for he worked mostly in Germany. We've communicated, of course, with the German police. But, oddly enough, there was a twin brother of his, named Louis Becker, whom we had a great deal to do with. In fact, we found it necessary to guillotine him only yesterday. Well, it's a rum thing, gentlemen, but when I saw that fellow flat on the lawn I had the greatest jump of my life. If I hadn't seen Louis Becker guillotined with my own eyes, I'd have sworn it was Louis Becker lying there in the grass. Then, of course, I remembered his twin brother in Germany, and following up the clue —— "

The explanatory Ivan stopped, for the excellent reason that nobody was listening to him. The Commandant and the doctor were both staring at Father Brown, who had sprung stiffly to his feet, and was holding his temples tight like a man in sudden and violent pain.

"Stop, stop, stop!" he cried; "stop talking a minute, for I see half. Will God give me strength? Will my brain make the one jump and see all? Heaven help me! I used to be fairly good at thinking. I could paraphrase any page in Aquinas once. Will my head split — or will it see? I see half — I only see half."

He buried his head in his hands, and stood in a sort of rigid torture of thought or prayer, while the other three could only go on staring at this last prodigy of their wild twelve hours.

When Father Brown's hands fell they showed a face quite fresh and serious, like a child's. He heaved a huge sigh, and said: "Let us get this said and done with as quickly as possible. Look here, this will be the quickest way to convince you all of the truth." He turned to the doctor. "Dr. Simon," he said, "you have a strong headpiece, and I heard you this morning asking the five hardest questions about this business. Well, if you will ask them again, I will answer them."

Simon's pince-nez dropped from his nose in his doubt and wonder, but he answered at once. "Well, the first question, you know, is why a man should kill another with a clumsy sabre at all when a man can kill with a bodkin?"

"A man cannot behead with a bodkin," said Brown calmly, "and for *this* murder beheading was absolutely necessary."

"Why?" asked O'Brien, with interest.

"And the next question?" asked Father Brown.

"Well, why didn't the man cry out or anything?" asked the doctor; "sabres in gardens are certainly unusual."

"Twigs," said the priest gloomily, and turned to the window which looked on the scene of death. "No one saw the point of the twigs. Why should they lie on that lawn (look at it) so far from any tree? They were not snapped off; they were chopped off. The murderer occupied his enemy with some tricks with the sabre, showing how he could cut a branch in mid-air, or whatnot. Then, while his enemy bent down to see the result, a silent slash, and the head fell."

"Well," said the doctor slowly, "that seems plausible enough. But my next two questions will stump anyone."

The priest still stood looking critically out of the window and waited.

"You know how all the garden was sealed up like an air-tight chamber," went on the doctor. "Well, how did the strange man get into the garden?"

Without turning round, the little priest answered: "There never was any strange man in the garden."

There was a silence, and then a sudden cackle of almost childish laughter relieved the strain. The absurdity of Brown's remark moved Ivan to open taunts.

"Oh!" he cried; "then we didn't lug a great fat corpse on to a sofa last night? He hadn't got into the garden, I suppose?"

"Got into the garden?" repeated Brown reflectively. "No, not entirely."

"Hang it all," cried Simon, "a man gets into a garden, or he doesn't."

"Not necessarily," said the priest, with a faint smile. "What is the next question, Doctor?"

"I fancy you're ill," exclaimed Dr. Simon sharply; "but I'll ask the next question if you like. How did Brayne get out of the garden?"

"He didn't get out of the garden," said the priest, still looking out of the window.

"Didn't get out of the garden?" exploded Simon.

"Not completely," said Father Brown.

Simon shook his fists in a frenzy of French logic. "A man gets out of a garden, or he doesn't," he cried.

"Not always," said Father Brown.

Dr. Simon sprang to his feet impatiently. "I have no time to spare on such senseless talk," he cried angrily. "If you can't understand a man being on one side of a wall or the other, I won't trouble you further."

"Doctor," said the cleric very gently, "we have always got on very pleasantly together. If only for the sake of old friendship, stop and tell me your fifth question."

The impatient Simon sank into a chair by the door and said briefly: "The head and shoulders were cut about in a queer way. It seemed to be done after death."

"Yes," said the motionless priest, "it was done so as to make you assume exactly the one simple falsehood that you did assume. It was done to make you take for granted that the head belonged to the body."

The borderland of the brain, where all the monsters are made, moved horribly in the Gaelic O'Brien. He felt the chaotic presence of all the horse-men and fish-women that man's unnatural fancy has begotten. A voice older than his first fathers seemed saying in his ear: "Keep out of the monstrous garden where grows the tree with double fruit. Avoid the evil garden where died the man with two heads." Yet, while these shameful symbolic shapes passed across the ancient mirror of his Irish soul, his Frenchified intellect was quite alert, and was watching the odd priest as closely and incredulously as all the rest.

Father Brown had turned round at last, and stood against the window with his face in dense shadow; but even in that shadow they could see it was pale as ashes. Nevertheless, he spoke quite sensibly, as if there were no Gaelic souls on earth.

"Gentlemen," he said, "you did not find the strange body of Becker in the garden. You did not find any strange body in the garden. In face of Dr. Simon's rationalism, I still affirm that Becker was only partly present. Look here!" (pointing to the black bulk of the mysterious corpse) "you never saw that man in your lives Did you ever see this man?"

He rapidly rolled away the bald, yellow head of the unknown, and put in its place the white-maned head beside it. And there, complete, unified, unmistakable, lay Julius K. Brayne.

"The murderer," went on Brown quietly, "hacked off his enemy's head and flung the sword far over the wall. But he was too clever to fling the sword only. He flung the *head* over the wall also. Then he had only to clap on another head to the corpse, and (as he insisted on a private inquest) you all imagined a totally new man."

"Clap on another head!" said O'Brien staring. "What other head? Heads don't grow on garden bushes, do they?"

"No," said Father Brown huskily, and looking at his boots; "there is only one place where they grow. They grow in the basket of the guillotine, beside which the chief of police, Aristide Valentin, was standing not an hour before the murder. Oh, my friends, hear me a minute more before you tear me in pieces. Valentin is an honest man, if being mad for an arguable cause is honesty. But did you never see in that cold, grey eye of his that he is mad? He would do anything, *anything,* to break what he calls the superstition of the Cross. He has fought for it and starved for it, and now he has murdered for it. Brayne's crazy millions had hitherto been scattered among so many sects that they did little to alter the balance of things. But Valentin heard a whisper that Brayne, like so many scatter-brained sceptics, was drifting to us; and that was quite a different thing. Brayne would pour supplies into the impoverished and pugnacious Church of France; he would support six Nationalist newspapers like *The Guillotine.* The battle was already balanced on a point, and the fanatic took flame at the risk. He resolved to destroy the millionaire, and he did it as one would expect the greatest of detectives to commit his only crime. He abstracted the severed head of Becker on some criminological excuse, and took it home in his official box. He had that last argument with Brayne, that Lord Galloway did not hear the end of; that failing, he led him out into the sealed garden, talked about swordsmanship, used twigs and a sabre for illustration, and —— "

Ivan of the Scar sprang up. "You lunatic," he yelled; "you'll go to my master now, if I take you by —— "

"Why, I was going there," said Brown heavily; "I must ask him to confess, and all that."

Driving the unhappy Brown before them like a hostage or sacrifice, they rushed together into the sudden stillness of Valentin's
study.

The great detective sat at his desk apparently too occupied to hear
their turbulent entrance. They paused a moment, and then something in the look of that upright and elegant back made the doctor
run forward suddenly. A touch and a glance showed him that there
was a small box of pills at Valentin's elbow, and that Valentin was
dead in his chair; and on the blind face of the suicide was more
than the pride of Cato.

THE MAN WHO SPOKE LATIN

by SAMUEL HOPKINS ADAMS

Don't ask us why, but the idea of a man who speaks only Latin popping up in the City of Baltimore, Maryland, U. S. A. makes the inclusion of this AVERAGE JONES *story a personal pleasure.* AVERAGE JONES *stories available: ten. We wish there were more.*

MEMENTOS of Average Jones's exploits in his chosen field hang on the walls of his quiet sanctum. Here the favored visitor may see the two red-ink dots on a dated sheet of paper, framed in with the card of a chemist and an advertised sale of lepidoptera, which drove a famous millionaire out of the country. Near by are displayed the exploitation of a lure for black bass, strangely perforated (a man's reason hung on those pin pricks), and a scrawled legend which seems to spell "Mercy" (two men's lives were sacrificed to that); while below them, set in somber black, is the funeral notice of a dog worth a million dollars; facing the call for a trombone player which made a mayor, and the mathematical formula which saved a governor. But nowhere does the observer find any record of one of the Ad-Visor's most curious cases, running back two thousand years; for its owner keeps it in his desk drawer, whence the present chronicler exhumed it, by accident, one day. Average Jones has always insisted that he scored a failure on this, because, through no possible fault of his own, he was unable to restore a document of the highest historical and literary importance. Of that, let the impartial reader judge.

It was while Average Jones was awaiting the break of that deadlock of events which, starting from the flat dweller with the poisoned face, finally worked out the strange fate of Telfik Bey, that he sat, one morning, breakfasting late. The cool and breezy inner portico of the Cosmic Club, where the small tables overlook a gracious fountain shimmering with the dart and poise of goldfish, was deserted save for himself, a summer-engagement star actor, a specialist in carbohydrates, and a famous adjuster of labor troubles; the four men being fairly typical of the club's catholicity of membership. Contrary to his impeccant habit, Average Jones bore the somewhat frazzled aspect of a man who has been up all night. Further indication of this inhered in the wide yawn, of which he was in mid-enjoyment, when a hand on his shoulder cut short his ecstasy.

"Sorry to interrupt so valuable an exercise," said a languid voice. "But — " and the voice stopped.

"Hello, Bert," returned the Ad-Visor, looking up at the faultlessly clad slenderness of his occasional coadjutor, Robert Bertram. "Sit down and keep me awake till the human snail who's hypothetically ministering to my wants can get me some coffee."

"What particular phase of intellectual debauchery have you been up to now?" inquired Bertram, lounging into the chair opposite.

"Trying to forget my troubles by chasing up a promising lead which failed to pan out. 'Wanted: a Tin Nose,' sounds pretty good, eh?"

"It is music to my untutored ear," answered Bertram.

"But it turned out to be merely the error of the imbecile, or perhaps facetious, printer, who sets up the *Trumpeter's* personal column. It should have read, 'Wanted — a Tea Rose.'"

"Even that seems far from commonplace."

"Only a code summons for a meeting of the Rosicrucians. I suppose you know that the order has been revived here in America."

"Not the true Rosicrucians, surely!" said Bertram.

"They pretend to be. A stupid lot, who make child's play of it," said Average Jones impatiently. "Never mind them. I'd rather know what's on your mind. You made an observation, when you came in, rather more interesting than your usual output of table talk. You said 'but' and nothing further. The conjunction 'but,' in polite grammar, ordinarily has a comet-like tail to it."

"Apropos of polite grammar, do you speak Latin?" asked Bertram carelessly.

"Not enough to be gossipy in it."

"Then you wouldn't care to give a job to a man who can't speak anything else?"

"On that qualification alone?"

"No-o, not entirely. He is a good military engineer, I believe."

"So that's the other end of the 'but,' is it?" said Average Jones. "Go on. Elaborate."

Bertram laid before his friend a printed clipping in clear, large type, saying: "When I read this, I couldn't resist the notion that somehow or other it was in your line; pursuit of the adventure of life, and all that. Let's see what you make of it."

Average Jones straightened in his chair.

"Latin!" he said. "And an ad, by the look of it. Can our blind friend, J. Alden Honeywell, have taken to the public prints?"

"Hardly, I think. This is from the *Classical Weekly,* a Baltimore publication of small and select patronage."

"Hm. Looks ra-a-a-ather alluring," commented Average Jones with a prolonged drawl. "Better than the Rosicrucian fakery, anyhow."

He bent over the clipping, studying these words: —

L. Livius M. F. Prænestinus, quodlibet in negotium non inhonestum qui victum meream locare velim. Litteratus sum; scriptum facere bene scio. Stipendia multa emeritus, scientiarum belli, præsertim muniendi, sum peritus. Hac de re pro me spondebit M. Agrippa. Latine tantum scio. Siquis me velit convenire, quovis die mane adesto in publicis hortis urbis Baltimorianæ ad signum apri.

"Can you make it out?" asked Bertram.

"Hm-m-m. Well — the general sense. Livius seems to yearn in modern print for any honest employment, but especially scrapping of the ancient variety or secretarying. Apply to Agrippa for references. Since he describes his conversation as being confined to Latin, I take it he won't find many jobs reaching out eagerly for him. Anybody who wants him can find him in the Park of the Wild Boar in Baltimore. That's about what I make of it. Now, what's his little lay, I wonder."

"Some lay of Ancient Rome, anyhow," suggested Bertram. "Association with Agrippa would put him back in the first century,

B. C., wouldn't it? Besides, my informant tells me that Mr. Livius, who seems to have been an all-around sort of person, helped organize fire brigades for Crassus, and was one of the circle of minor poets who wrote rhapsodies to the fair but frail Clodia's eyebrows, ear lobes and insteps."

"Your informant? The man's actually been seen, then?"

"Oh, yes. He's on view as per advertisement, I understand."

Average Jones rose and stretched his well-knit frame. "Baltimore will be hotter than the Pláce-as-Isn't," he said plaintively. "Martyrdom by fire! However, I'm off by the five-o'clock train. I'll let you know if anything special comes of it, Bert."

Barye's splendid bronze boar couches, semi-shaded, in the center of Monument Park, Baltimore's social hilltop. There Average Jones lounged and strolled through the longest hour of a glaring July morning. People came and went; people of all degrees and descriptions, none of whom suggested in any particular the first century, B. C. One individual only maintained any permanency of situation. He was a gaunt, powerful, freckled man of thirty who sprawled on a settee and regarded Average Jones with obvious and amused interest. In time this annoyed the Ad-Visor, who stopped short, facing the settee.

"He's gone," said the freckled man.

"Meaning Livius the Roman?" asked Average Jones.

"Exactly. Lucius Livius, son of Marcus Prænestinus."

"Are you the representative of this rather peculiar person, may I ask?"

"It would be a dull world, except for peculiar persons," observed the man on the settee philosophically. "I've seen very many peculiar persons lately by the simple process of coming here day after day. No, I'm not Mr. Livius's representative. I'm only a town-bound and interested observer of his."

"There you've got the better of me," said Average Jones. "I was rather anxious to see him myself."

The other looked speculatively at the trim, keen-faced young man. "Yet you do not look like a Latin scholar," he observed; "if you'll pardon the comment."

"Nor do you," retorted Jones; "if the apology is returnable."

"I suppose not," owned the other with a sigh. "I've often thought that my classical capacity would gain more recognition if I didn't have a skin like Bob Fitzsimmons and hands like Ty Cobb. Nevertheless, I'm in and of the department of Latin of Johns Hopkins University. Name, Warren. Sit down."

"Thanks," said the other. "Name, Jones. Profession, advertising advisor. Object, curiosity."

"A. V. R. E. Jones; better known as Average Jones, I believe?"

"*Experto crede!* Being dog Latin for 'You seem to know all about it.'" The newcomer eyed his *vis-à-vis*. "Perhaps you — er — know Mr. Robert Bertram," he drawled.

"*Oculus* — the eye — *tauri* — of the bull. Bull's-eye!" said the freckled one, with a grin. "I'd heard of your exploits through Bertram, and thought probably you'd follow the bait contained in my letter to him."

"Nothing wrong with your nerve system, is there?" inquired Average Jones with mock anxiety. "Now that I'm here, where is L. Livius And-so-forth?"

"Elegantly but uncomfortably housed with Colonel Ridgway Graeme in his ancestral barrack on Carteret Street."

"Is this Colonel Graeme a friend of yours?"

"Friend and foe, tried and true. We meet twice a week, usually at his house, to squabble over his method of Latin pronunciation and his construction of the ablative case. He's got a theory of the ablative absolute," said Warren with a scowl, "fit to fetch Tacitus howling from the shades."

"A scholar, then?"

"A very fine and finished scholar, though a faddist of the rankest type. Speaks Latin as readily as he does English."

"Old?"

"Over seventy."

"Rich?"

"Not in money. Taxes on his big place keep him pinched; that and his passion for buying all kinds of old and rare books. He's got, perhaps, an income of five thousand, clear, of which about three thousand goes in book auctions."

"Any family?"

"No. Lives with two ancient colored servants who look after him."

"How did our friend from B. C. connect up with him?"

"Oh, he ran to the old colonel like a chick to its hen. You see, there aren't so very many Latinists in town during the hot weather. Perhaps eighteen or twenty in all came from about here and from Washington to see the prodigy in 'the Park of the Boar,' after the advertisement appeared. He wouldn't have anything to do with any of us. Pretended he didn't understand our kind of Latin. I offered him a place, myself, at a wage of more *denarii* than I could well afford. I wanted a chance to study him. Then came the colonel and fairly grabbed him. So I sent for you — in my artless professional way."

"Why such enthusiasm on the part of Colonel Graeme?"

"Simple enough. Livius spoke Latin with an accent which bore out the old boy's contention. I believe they also agreed on the ablative absolute."

"Yes — er — naturally," drawled Average Jones. "Does our early Roman speak pretty ready Latin?"

"He's fairly fluent. Sometimes he stumbles a little on his constructions, and he's apt to be — well — monkish — rather than classical —when in full course."

"Doesn't wear the *toga virilis,* I suppose."

"Oh, no. Plain American clothes. It's only his inner man that's Roman, of course. He met with a bump on the head — this is his story, and he's got the scar to show for it — and when he came to, he'd lost ground a couple of thousand years and returned to his former existence. No English. No memory of who or what he'd been. No money. No connection whatsoever with the living world."

"Humph! Wonder if he's been a student of Kipling. You remember 'The Greatest Story in the World'; the reincarnated galley slave? Now as to Colonel Graeme; has he ever published?"

"Yes. Two small pamphlets, issued by the Classicist Press, which publishes the *Classical Weekly.*"

"Supporting his fads, I suppose."

"Right. He devoted one pamphlet to each."

Average Jones contemplated with absorbed attention an ant which was making a laborious spiral ascent of his cane. Not until it had gained a vantage point on the bone handle did he speak again.

"See here, Professor Warren: I'm a passionate devotee of the Latin tongue. I have my deep and dark suspicions of our present modes of pronunciation, all three of 'em. As for the ablative absolute, its reconstruction and regeneration have been the inspiring principle of my studious manhood. Humbly I have sat at the feet of Learning, enshrined in the Ridgway Graeme pamphlets. I must meet Colonel Graeme — after reading the pamphlets. I hope they're not long."

Warren frowned. "Colonel Graeme is a gentleman and my friend, Mr. Jones," he said with emphasis. "I won't have him made a butt."

"He shan't be, by me," said Average Jones quietly. "Has it perhaps struck you, as his friend, that — er — a close daily association with the psychic remnant of a Roman citizen might conceivably be nonconducive to his best interest?"

"Yes, it has. I see your point. You want to approach him on his weak side. But, have you Latin enough to sustain the part? He's shrewd as a weasel in all matters of scholarship, though a child whom anyone could fool in practical affairs."

"No; I haven't," admitted Average Jones. "Therefore, I'm a mute. A shock in early childhood paralyzed my centers of speech. I talk to you by sign language, and you interpret."

"But I hardly know the deaf-mute alphabet."

"Nor I. But I'll waggle my fingers like lightning if he says anything to me requiring an answer, and you'll give the proper reply. Does Colonel Graeme implicitly credit the Romanism of his guest?"

"He does, because he wants to. To have an educated man of the classic period of the Latin tongue, a friend of Cæsar, an auditor of Cicero and a contemporary of Virgil, Horace, and Ovid come back and speak in the accent he's contended for, makes a powerful support for his theories. He's at work on a supplementary thesis already."

"What do the other Latin men who've seen Livius think of the metempsychosis claim?"

"They don't know. Livius explained his remote antecedents only after he had got Colonel Graeme's private ear. The colonel has kept it quiet. 'Don't want a rabble of psychologists and soul pokers worrying him to death,' he says."

"Making it pretty plain sailing for the Roman. Well, arrange to take me there as soon as possible."

At the Graeme house, Average Jones was received with simple courtesy by a thin rosy-cheeked old gentleman with a dagger-like imperial and a dreamy eye, who, on Warren's introduction, made him free of the unkempt old place's hospitality. They conversed for a time, Average Jones maintaining his end with nods and gestures, and (ostensibly) through the digital mediumship of his sponsor. Presently Warren said to the host:

"And where is your visitor from the past?"

"Prowling among my books," answered the old gentleman.

"Are we not going to see him?"

The colonel looked a little embarrassed. "The fact is, Professor Warren, Livius has taken rather an aversion to you."

"I'm sorry. How so?"

A twinkle of malice shone in the old scholar's eye. "He says your Latin accent frets his nerves," he explained.

"In that case," said Warren, obeying a quick signal from his accomplice, "I'll stroll in the garden, while you present Mr. Jones to Livius."

Colonel Graeme led the way to a lofty wing, once used as a drawing-room, but now the repository for thousands of books, which not only filled the shelves but were heaped up in every corner.

"I must apologize for this confusion, sir," said the host. "No one is permitted to arrange my books but myself. And my efforts, I fear, serve only to make confusion more confounded. There are four other rooms even more chaotic than this."

At the sound of his voice a man who had been seated behind a tumulus of volumes rose and stood. Average Jones looked at him keenly. He was perhaps forty-five years of age, thin and sinewy, with a close-shaven face, pale blue eyes, and a narrow forehead running high into a mop of grizzled locks. Diagonally across the front part of the scalp a scar could be dimly perceived through the hair. Average Jones glanced at the stranger's hands, to gain, if possible, some hint of his former employment. With his faculty of swift observation, he noticed that the long, slender fingers were not only mottled with dust, but also scuffed, and, in places, scarified, as if their owner had been hurriedly handling a great number of books.

Colonel Graeme presented the newcomer in formal Latin. He bowed. The scarred man made a curious gesture of the hand, addressing Average Jones in an accent which, even to the young man's long-unaccustomed ears, sounded strange and strained.

"*Di illi linguam astrinxere; mutus est,*" said Colonel Graeme, indicating the younger man, and added a sentence in sonorous metrical Greek.

Average Jones recalled the Æschylean line. "Well, though 'a great ox hath stepped on my tongue,' it hasn't trodden out my eyes, praises be!" said he to himself as he caught the uneasy glance of the Roman.

By way of allaying suspicion, he scribbled upon a sheet of paper a few complimentary Latin sentences, in which Warren had sedulously coached him for the occasion, and withdrew to the front room, where he was presently joined by the Johns Hopkins man. Fortunately, the colonel gave them a few moments together.

"Arrange for me to come here daily to study in the library," whispered Jones to the Latin professor.

The other nodded.

"Now, sit tight," added Jones.

He stepped, soft-footed, on the thick old rug, across to the library door and threw it open. Just inside stood Livius, an expression of startled anger on his thin face. Quickly recovering himself, he explained, in his ready Latin, that he was about to enter and speak to his patron.

"Shows a remarkable interest in possible conversation," whispered Jones, on his withdrawal, "for a man who understands no English. Also does me the honor to suspect me. He must have been a wily chap — in the Consulship of Plancus."

Before leaving, Average Jones had received from Colonel Graeme a general invitation to spend as much time as he chose, studying among the books. The old man-servant, Saul, had orders to admit him at any hour. He returned to his hotel to write a courteous note of acknowledgment.

Many hours has Average Jones spent more tediously than those passed in the cool seclusion of Colonel Ridgway Graeme's treasure house of print. He burrowed among quaint accumulations of forgotten classics. He dipped with astonishment into the savage and ultra-Rabelaisian satire of Von Hutten's *Epistolæ Obscurorum Virorum,* which set early sixteenth century Europe aroar with laughter at the discomfited monks; and he cleansed himself from that tainted atmosphere in the fresh air and free English of a splendid Audubon "first" — and all the time he was conscious that the Roman watched, watched, watched. More than once Livius offered aid, seeking to apprise himself of the supposed mute's line of investigation; but the other smilingly fended him off. At the end of four days, Average Jones had satisfied himself that if Livius were seeking anything in particular, he had an indefinite task before him, for the colonel's bound treasures were in indescribable confusion. Apparently he had bought from far and near, without definite theme or purpose. As he bought he read, and having read, cast aside; and where a volume fell, there it had license to lie. No cataloguer had ever sought to restore order to that bibliographic riot. To seek any given book meant a blind voyage, without compass or chart, throughout the mingled centuries.

Often Colonel Graeme spent hours in one or the other of the huge bookrooms talking with his strange *protégé* and making co-pious notes. Usually the old gentleman questioned and the other answered. But one morning the attitude seemed, to the listening Ad-Visor, to be reversed. Livius, in the far corner of the room, was speaking in a low tone. To judge from the older man's impatient manner, the Roman was interrupting his host's current of queries with interrogations of his own. Average Jones made a mental note, and, in conference with Warren that evening, asked him to ascer-tain from Colonel Graeme whether Livius's inquiries had indicated a specific interest in any particular line of reading.

On the following day, however, an event of more immediate im-port occupied his mind. He had spent the morning in the upstairs library, at the unevadable suggestion of Colonel Graeme, while the colonel and his Roman collogued below. Coming down about noon, Average Jones entered the colonel's small study just in time to see Livius, who was alone in the room, turn away sharply from the desk. His elbow was held close to his ribs in a peculiar manner. He was concealing something under his coat. With a pretense of clumsiness, Average Jones stumbled against him in passing. Livius drew away, his high forehead working with suspicion. The Ad-Visor's expres-sion of blank apology, eked out with a bow and a grimace, belied the busy-working mind within. For, in the moment's contact, he had heard the crisp rustle of paper from beneath the ill-fitting coat.

What paper had the man from B. C. taken furtively from his benefactor's table? It must be large; otherwise he could have readily thrust it into his pocket. No sooner was Livius out of the room than Average Jones scanned the desk. His face lighted with a sudden smile. Colonel Graeme never read a newspaper; boasted, in fact, that he wouldn't have one about the place. But, as Average Jones distinctly recalled, he had, himself, that very morning brought in a copy of the *Globe* and dropped it into the scrap-basket near the writing table. It was gone. Livius had taken it.

"If he's got the newspaper-reading habit," said Average Jones to himself, "I'll set a trap for him. But Warren must furnish the bait."

He went to look up his aide. The conference between them was long and exhaustive, covering the main points of the case from the beginning.

"Did you find out from Colonel Graeme," inquired Average Jones, "whether Livius affected any particular brand of literature?"

"Yes. He seems to be specializing on late seventeenth century British classicism. Apparently he considers that the flower of British scholarship of that time wrote a very inferior kind of dog Latin."

"Late seventeenth century Latinity," commented Average Jones. "That — er — gives us a fair start. Now as to the body servant."

"Old Saul? I questioned him about strange callers. He said he remembered only two, besides an occasional peddler or agent. They were looking for work."

"What kind of work?"

"Inside the house. One wanted to catalogue the library."

"What did he look like?"

"Saul says he wore glasses and a worse tall hat than the colonel's and had a full beard."

"And the other?"

"Bookbinder and repairer. Wanted to fix up Colonel Graeme's collection. Youngish, smartly dressed, with a small waxed moustache."

"And our Livius is clean-shaven," murmured Average Jones. "How long apart did they call?"

"About two weeks. The second applicant came on the day of the last snowfall. I looked that up. It was March 27."

"Do you know, Warren," observed Average Jones, "I sometimes think that part of your talents, at least, are wasted in a chair of Latin."

"Certainly, there is more excitement in this hide-and-seek game, as you play it, than in the pursuits of a musty pedant," admitted the other, crackling his large knuckles. "But when are we going to spring upon friend Livius and strip him of his fake toga?"

"That's the easiest part of it. I've already caught him filling a fountain pen as if he'd been brought up on them, and humming the spinning chorus from *The Flying Dutchman;* not to mention the lifting of my newspaper."

"*Nemo mortalium omnibus horis sapit,*" murmured Warren.

"No. As you say, no fellow can be on the job *all* the time. But our problem is not to catch Livius, but to find out what it is he's been after for the last three months."

"Three months? You're assuming that it was he who applied for work in the library."

"Certainly. And when he failed at that he set about a very carefully developed scheme to get at Colonel Graeme's books anyway. By inquiries he found out the old gentleman's fad and proceeded to get in training for it. You don't know, perhaps, that I have a corps of assistants who clip, catalogue and file all unusual advertisements. Here is one which they turned up for me on my order to send me any queer educational advertisements: 'Wanted — Daily lessons in Latin speech from competent Spanish scholar. Write, Box 347, *Banner* office.' That is from the New York *Banner* of April third, shortly after the strange caller's second abortive attempt to get into the Graeme library."

"I suppose our Livius figured out that Colonel Graeme's theory of accent was about what a Spaniard would have. But he couldn't have learned all his Latin in four months."

"He didn't. He was a scholar already; an accomplished one, who went wrong through drink and became a crook, specializing in rare books and prints. His name is Enderby; you'll find it in the Harvard catalogue. He's supposed to be dead. My assistant traced him through his Spanish-Latin teacher, a priest."

"But even allowing for his scholarship, he must have put in a deal of work perfecting himself in readiness of speech and accent."

"So he did. Therefore the prize must be big. A man of Enderby's caliber doesn't concoct a scheme of such ingenuity, and go into bondage with it, for nothing. Do you belong to the Cosmic Club?"

The assistant professor stared. "No," he said.

"I'd like to put you up there. One advantage of membership is that its roster includes experts in every known line of erudition, from scarabs to skiing. For example, I am now going to telegraph for aid from old Millington, who seldom misses a book auction and is a human bibliography of the wanderings of all rare volumes. I'm going to find out from him what British publication of the late seventeenth century in Latin is very valuable; also what volumes of that time have changed hands in the last six months."

"Colonel Graeme went to a big book auction in New York early in March," volunteered Warren, "but he told me he didn't pick up anything of particular value."

"Then it's something he doesn't know about and Livius does. I'm going to take advantage of our Roman's rather un-B.-C.-like habit of reading the daily papers by trying him out with this advertisement."

Average Jones wrote rapidly and tossed the result to his coadjutor who read:

Lost — Old book printed in Latin. Buff leather binding, a little faded ("It's safe to be that," explained Average Jones). No great value except to owner. Return to Colonel Ridgway Graeme, 11 Carteret Street, and receive reward.

The advertisement made its appearance in big type on the front page of the Baltimore papers of the following day. That evening Average Jones met Warren, for dinner, with a puckered brow.

"Did Livius rise to the bait?" asked the scholar.

"Did he!" chuckled Average Jones. "He's been nervous as a cat all day and hardly has looked at the library. But what puzzles me is this." He exhibited a telegram from New York.

MILLINGTON SAYS POSITIVELY NO BOOK OF THAT TIME AND DESCRIPTION ANY GREAT VALUE. ENDERBY AT BARCLAY AUCTION IN MARCH AND MADE ROW OVER SOME BOOK WHICH HE MISSED BECAUSE IT WAS PUT UP OUT OF TURN IN CATALOGUE. BARCLAY AUCTIONEER THINKS IT WAS ONE OF PERCIVAL PRIVATELY BOUND BOOKS 1680–1703. AN ANONYMOUS BOOK OF PERCIVAL LIBRARY,

DE MERITIS LIBRORUM BRITANNORUM, WAS SOLD TO COLONEL GRAEME
FOR $47, A GOOD PRICE. WHEN DO I GET IN ON THIS?

(SIGNED) ROBERT BERTRAM

"I know that treatise," said Warren. "It isn't particularly rare."

Average Jones stared at the telegram in silence. Finally he drawled: "There are — er — books and — er — books — and — er — things in books. Wait here for me."

Three hours later he reappeared with collar wilted, but spirits elate, and abruptly announced:

"Warren, I'm a cobbler."

"A what?"

"A cobbler. Mend your boots, you know."

"Are you in earnest?"

"Certainly. Haven't you ever remarked that a serious-minded earnestness always goes with cobbling? Though I'm not really a practical cobbler, but a proprietary one. Our friend, Bertram, will dress and act the practical part. I've wired him and he's replied, collect, accepting the job. You and I will be in the background."

"Where?"

"No. 27 Jasmine Street. Not a very savory locality. Why is it, Warren, that the beauty of a city street is generally in inverse ratio to the poetic quality of its name? There I've hired the shop and stock of Mr. Hans Fichtel for two days, at the handsome rental of ten dollars per day. Mr. Fichtel purposes to take a keg of beer a-fishing. I think two days will be enough."

"For the keg?"

"For that noble Roman, Livius. He'll be reading the papers pretty keenly now. And in to-morrow's, he'll find this advertisement."

Average Jones read from a sheet of paper which he took from his pocket:

"FOUND — Old book in foreign language, probably Latin, marked 'Percival.' Owner may recover by giving satisfactory description of peculiar and obscure feature and refunding for advertisement. — FICHTEL, 27 Jasmine Street."

"What is the peculiar and obscure feature, Jones?" asked Warren.
"I don't know."

"How do you know there is any?"

"Must be something peculiar about the book or Enderby wouldn't put in four months of work on the chance of stealing it. And it must be obscure, otherwise the auctioneer would have spotted it."

"Sound enough!" approved the other. "What could it be? Some interpolated page?"

"Hardly. I've a treatise in my pocket on seventeenth century bookmaking, which I'm going to study to-night. Be ready for an early start, to meet Bertram."

That languid and elegant gentleman arrived by the first morning train. He protested mightily when he was led to the humble shoe shop. He protested more mightily when invited to don a leather apron and smudge his face appropriately to his trade. His protests, waxing vehement and eventually profane, as he barked his daintily kept fingers, in rehearsal for giving a correct representation of an honest artisan cobbling a boot, died away when Average Jones explained to him that on pretense of having found a rare book, he was to worm out of a cautious and probably suspicious criminal the nature of some unique and hidden feature of the volume.

"Trust me for diplomacy," said Bertram airily.

"I will because I've got to," retorted Average Jones. "Well, get to work. To you the outer shop: to Warren and me this rear room. And, remember, if you hear me whetting a knife, that means come at once."

Uncomfortably twisted into a supposedly professional posture, Bertram wrought with hammer and last, while putting off, with lame, blind and halting excuses, such as came to call for their promised footgear. By a triumph of tact he had just disposed of a rancid-tongued female who demanded her husband's boots, a satisfactory explanation, or the arbitrament of the lists, when the bell tinkled and the two watchers in the back room heard a nervous, cultivated voice say:

"Is Mr. Fichtel here?"

"That's me," said Bertram, landing an agonizing blow on his thumb-nail.

"You advertised that you had found an old book."

"Yes, sir. Somebody left it in the post office."

"Ah; that must have been when I went to mail some letters to

New York," said the other glibly. "From the advertised description, the book is without doubt mine. Now as to the reward — "

"Excuse me, but you wouldn't expect me to give it up without any identification, sir?"

"Certainly not. It was the *De Meritis Libror* — "

"I can't read Latin, sir."

"But you could make that much out," said the visitor with rising exasperation. "Come; if it's a matter of the reward — how much?"

"I wouldn't mind having a good reward; say ten dollars. But I want to be sure it's your book. There's something about it that you could easily tell me sir, for anyone could see it."

"A very observing shoemaker," commented the other with a slight sneer. "You mean the — the half-split cover?"

"Whish — swish; whish-swish," sounded from the rear room.

"Excuse me," said Bertram, who had not ceased from his pretended work. "I have to get a piece of leather."

He stepped into the back room where Average Jones, his face alight, held up a piece of paper upon which he had hurriedly scrawled:

"Mss. bound into cover. Get it out of him. Tell him you've a brother who is a Latin scholar."

Bertram nodded, caught up a strip of calfskin and returned.

"Yes, sir," he said, "the split cover and what's inside?"

The other started. "You didn't get it out?" he cried. "You didn't tear it!"

"No, sir. It's there safe enough. But some of it can be made out."

"You said you didn't read Latin."

"No, sir; but I have a brother that went through the Academy. He reads a little." This was thin ice, but Bertram went forward with assumed assurance. "He thinks the manuscript is quite rare. Oh, Fritz! Come in."

"Any letter of Bacon's is rare, of course," returned the other impatiently. "Therefore, I purpose offering you fifty dollars reward."

He looked up as Average Jones entered. The young man's sleeves were rolled up, his face was generously smudged, and a strip of cobbler's wax, beneath the upper lip, puffed and distorted the firm line of his mouth. Further, his head was louting low on his neck, so that the visitor got no view sufficient for recognition.

"Lord Bacon's letter — er — must be pretty rare, Mister," he drawled thickly. "But a letter — er — from Lord Bacon — er — about Shakespeare — *that* ought to be worth a lot of money."

Average Jones had taken his opening with his customary incisive shrewdness. The mention of Bacon had settled it, to his mind. Only one imaginable character of manuscript from the philosopher-scholar-politician could have value enough to tempt a thief of Enderby's caliber. Enderby's expression told that the shot was a true one. As for Bertram, he had dropped his shoemaker's knife and his shoemaker's rôle.

"Bacon on Shakespeare! Shades of the departed glory of Ignatius Donnelly!"

The visitor drew back. Warren's gaunt frame appeared in the doorway. Jones's head lifted.

"It ought to be as — er — unique," he drawled, "as an — er — Ancient Roman speaking perfect English."

Like a flash, the false Livius caught up the knife from the bench where the false cobbler had dropped it and swung toward Average Jones. At the same moment the ample hand of Professor Warren, bunched into a highly competent fist, flicked across and caught the assailant under the ear. Enderby, alias Livius, fell as if smitten by a cestus. As his arm touched the floor, Average Jones kicked unerringly at the wrist and the knife flew and tinkled in a far corner. Bertram, with a bound, landed on the fallen man's chest and pinned him.

"Did he get you, Average?" he cried.

"Not — er — this time. Pretty good — er — team work," drawled the Ad-Visor. "We've got our man for felonious assault, at least."

Enderby, panting under Bertram's solid knee, blinked and struggled.

"No use, Livius," said Average Jones. "Might as well quiet down and confess. Ease up a little on him, Bert. Take a look at that scar of his first though."

"Superficial cut treated with make-up paint; a clever job," pronounced Bertram after a quick examination.

"As I supposed," said Average Jones.

"Let me in on the deal," pleaded Livius. "That letter is worth ten thousand, twelve thousand, fifteen thousand dollars — anything you want to ask, if you find the right purchaser. And you can't manage it without me. Let me in."

"Thinks we're crooks, too?" remarked Average Jones. "Exactly what's in this wonderful letter?"

"It's from Bacon to the author of the book, who wrote about 1610. Bacon prophesies that Shakespeare, 'this vagabond and humble mummer,' would outshine and outlive in fame all the genius of his time. That's all I could make out by loosening the stitches."

"Well, that *is* worth anything one could demand," said Warren in a somewhat awed tone.

"Why didn't you get the letter when you were examining it at the auction room?" inquired Average Jones.

"Some fool of a binder had overlooked the double cover, and sewed it in. I noticed it at the auction, gummed the opening together while no one was watching, and had gone to get cash to buy the book; but the auctioneer put it up out of turn and old Graeme got it. Bring it to me and I'll show you the 'pursed' cover. Many of the Percival books were bound that way."

"We've never had it, nor seen it," replied Average Jones. "The advertisement was only a trap into which you stepped."

Enderby's jaw dropped. "Then it's still at the Graeme house," he cried, beating on the floor with his free hand. "Take me back there!"

"Oh, we'll take you," said Warren grimly.

Close-packed among them in a cab, they drove him back to Carteret Street. Colonel Ridgway Graeme was at home and greeted them courteously.

"You've found Livius," he said, with relief. "I had begun to fear for him."

"Colonel Graeme," began Average Jones, "you have —"

"What! Speech!" cried the old gentleman. "And you a mute! What does this mean?"

"Never mind him," broke in Enderby Livius. "There's something more important."

But the colonel had shrunk back. "English from you, Livius!" he cried, setting his hand to his brow.

"All will be explained in time, Colonel," Warren assured him. "Meanwhile, you have a document of the utmost importance and value. Do you remember buying one of the Percival volumes at the Barclay auction?"

The collector drew his brows down in an effort to remember.

"An octavo, in fairly good condition?" he asked.

"Yes, yes!" cried Enderby eagerly. "Where is it? What did you do with it?"

"It was in Latin — very false Latin." The four men leaned forward, breathless. "Oh, I remember. It slipped from my pocket and fell into the river as I was crossing the ferry to Jersey."

There was a dead, flat, stricken silence. Then Average Jones turned hollow eyes upon Warren.

"Professor," he said, with a rueful attempt at a smile, "what's the past participle, passive, plural, of the Latin verb, 'to sting'?"

THE DOOMDORF MYSTERY

by MELVILLE DAVISSON POST

Autobiographical commentary by Melville Davisson Post: "I was born like the sons of Atreus in the pasture land of horses. I was reared by a black woman who remembered her grandmother boiling a warrior's head in a pot. I was given a degree by a college of unbeautiful nonsense. I have eaten dinner with a god. And I have kissed a princess in a land where men grind their wheat in the sky." Now you can understand why UNCLE ABNER *is the most profoundly original American detective of fiction since Dupin.*

THE PIONEER was not the only man in the great mountains behind Virginia. Strange aliens drifted in after the colonial wars. All foreign armies are sprinkled with a cockle of adventurers that take root and remain. They were with Braddock and La Salle, and they rode north out of Mexico after her many empires went to pieces.

I think Doomdorf crossed the seas with Iturbide when that ill-starred adventurer returned to be shot against a wall; but there was no Southern blood in him. He came from some European race remote and barbaric. The evidences were all about him. He was a huge figure of a man, with a black spade beard, broad, thick hands, and square, flat fingers.

He had found a wedge of land between the Crown's grant to Daniel Davisson and a Washington survey. It was an uncovered triangle not worth the running of the lines; and so, no doubt, was left out, a sheer rock standing up out of the river for a base, and a peak of the mountain rising northward behind it for an apex.

Doomdorf squatted on the rock. He must have brought a belt of gold pieces when he took to his horse, for he hired old Robert Steuart's slaves and built a stone house on the rock, and he brought the furnishings overland from a frigate in the Chesapeake; and then in the handfuls of earth, wherever a root would hold, he planted the mountain behind his house with peach trees. The gold gave out; but the devil is fertile in resources. Doomdorf built a log still and turned the first fruits of the garden into a hell-brew. The idle and the vicious came with their stone jugs, and violence and riot flowed out.

The government of Virginia was remote and its arm short and feeble; but the men who held the lands west of the mountains against the savages under grants from George, and after that held them against George himself, were efficient and expeditious. They had long patience, but when that failed they went up from their fields and drove the thing before them out of the land, like a scourge of God.

There came a day, then, when my Uncle Abner and Squire Randolph rode through the gap of the mountains to have the thing out with Doomdorf. The work of this brew, which had the odors of Eden and the impulses of the devil in it, could be borne no longer. The drunken Negroes had shot old Duncan's cattle and burned his haystacks, and the land was on its feet.

They rode alone, but they were worth an army of little men. Randolph was vain and pompous and given over to extravagance of words, but he was a gentleman beneath it, and fear was an alien and a stranger to him. And Abner was the right hand of the land.

It was a day in early summer and the sun lay hot. They crossed through the broken spine of the mountains and trailed along the river in the shade of the great chestnut trees. The road was only a path and the horses went one before the other. It left the river when the rock began to rise and, making a detour through the grove of peach trees, reached the house on the mountain side. Randolph and Abner got down, unsaddled their horses and turned them out to graze, for their business with Doomdorf would not be over in an hour. Then they took a steep path that brought them out on the mountain side of the house.

A man sat on a big red-roan horse in the paved court before the door. He was a gaunt old man. He sat bareheaded, the palms of his hands resting on the pommel of his saddle, his chin sunk in his black stock, his face in retrospection, the wind moving gently his great shock of voluminous white hair. Under him the huge red horse stood with his legs spread out like a horse of stone.

There was no sound. The door to the house was closed; insects moved in the sun; a shadow crept out from the motionless figure, and swarms of yellow butterflies maneuvered like an army.

Abner and Randolph stopped. They knew the tragic figure — a circuit rider of the hills who preached the invective of Isaiah as though he were the mouthpiece of a militant and avenging over-lord; as though the government of Virginia were the awful theoc-racy of the Book of Kings. The horse was dripping with sweat and the man bore the dust and the evidences of a journey on him.

"Bronson," said Abner, "where is Doomdorf?"

The old man lifted his head and looked down at Abner over the pommel of the saddle.

" 'Surely,' " he said, " 'he covereth his feet in his summer chamber.' "

Abner went over and knocked on the closed door, and presently the white, frightened face of a woman looked out at him. She was a little, faded woman, with fair hair, a broad foreign face, but with the delicate evidences of gentle blood.

Abner repeated his question.

"Where is Doomdorf?"

"Oh, sir," she answered with a queer lisping accent, "he went to lie down in his south room after his midday meal, as his custom is; and I went to the orchard to gather any fruit that might be ripened." She hesitated and her voice lisped into a whisper: "He is not come out and I cannot wake him."

The two men followed her through the hall and up the stairway to the door.

"It is always bolted," she said, "when he goes to lie down." And she knocked feebly with the tips of her fingers.

There was no answer and Randolph rattled the doorknob.

"Come out, Doomdorf!" he called in his big, bellowing voice.

There was only silence and the echoes of the words among the rafters. Then Randolph set his shoulder to the door and burst it open.

They went in. The room was flooded with sun from the tall south windows. Doomdorf lay on a couch in a little offset of the room, a great scarlet patch on his bosom and a pool of scarlet on the floor.

The woman stood for a moment staring; then she cried out: "At last I have killed him!" And she ran like a frightened hare.

The two men closed the door and went over to the couch. Doomdorf had been shot to death. There was a great ragged hole in his waistcoat. They began to look about for the weapon with which the deed had been accomplished, and in a moment found it — a fowling piece lying in two dogwood forks against the wall. The gun had just been fired; there was a freshly exploded paper cap under the hammer.

There was little else in the room — a loom-woven rag carpet on the floor; wooden shutters flung back from the windows; a great oak table, and on it a big, round, glass water bottle, filled to its glass stopper with raw liquor from the still. The stuff was limpid and clear as spring water; and, but for its pungent odor, one would have taken it for God's brew instead of Doomdorf's. The sun lay on it and against the wall where hung the weapon that had ejected the dead man out of life.

"Abner," said Randolph, "this is murder! The woman took that gun down from the wall and shot Doomdorf while he slept."

Abner was standing by the table, his fingers round his chin.

"Randolph," he replied, "what brought Bronson here?"

"The same outrages that brought us," said Randolph. "The mad old circuit rider has been preaching a crusade against Doomdorf far and wide in the hills."

Abner answered, without taking his fingers from about his chin: "You think this woman killed Doomdorf? Well, let us go and ask Bronson who killed him."

They closed the door, leaving the dead man on his couch, and went down into the court.

The old circuit rider had put away his horse and got an ax. He had taken off his coat and pushed his shirtsleeves up over his long elbows. He was on his way to the still to destroy the barrels of liquor. He stopped when the two men came out, and Abner called to him.

"Bronson," he said, "who killed Doomdorf?"

"I killed him," replied the old man, and went on toward the still.

Randolph swore under his breath. "By the Almighty," he said, "everybody couldn't kill him!"

"Who can tell how many had a hand in it?" replied Abner.

"Two have confessed!" cried Randolph. "Was there perhaps a third? Did you kill him, Abner? And I too? Man, the thing is impossible!"

"The impossible," replied Abner, "looks here like the truth. Come with me, Randolph, and I will show you a thing more impossible than this."

They returned through the house and up the stairs to the room. Abner closed the door behind them.

"Look at this bolt," he said; "it is on the inside and not connected with the lock. How did the one who killed Doomdorf get into this room, since the door was bolted?"

"Through the windows," replied Randolph.

There were but two windows, facing the south, through which the sun entered. Abner led Randolph to them.

"Look!" he said. "The wall of the house is plumb with the sheer face of the rock. It is a hundred feet to the river and the rock is as smooth as a sheet of glass. But that is not all. Look at these window frames; they are cemented into their casement with dust and they are bound along their edges with cobwebs. These windows have not been opened. How did the assassin enter?"

"The answer is evident," said Randolph: "The one who killed Doomdorf hid in the room until he was asleep; then he shot him and went out."

"The explanation is excellent but for one thing," replied Abner: "How did the assassin bolt the door behind him on the inside of this room after he had gone out?"

Randolph flung out his arms with a hopeless gesture.

"Who knows?" he cried. "Maybe Doomdorf killed himself."

Abner laughed.

"And after firing a handful of shot into his heart he got up and put the gun back carefully into the forks against the wall!"

"Well," cried Randolph, "there is one open road out of this mystery. Bronson and this woman say they killed Doomdorf, and if they killed him they surely know how they did it. Let us go down and ask them."

"In the law court," replied Abner, "that procedure would be considered sound sense; but we are in God's court and things are managed there in a somewhat stranger way. Before we go let us find out, if we can, at what hour it was that Doomdorf died."

He went over and took a big silver watch out of the dead man's pocket. It was broken by a shot and the hands lay at one hour after noon. He stood for a moment fingering his chin.

"At one o'clock," he said. "Bronson, I think, was on the road to this place, and the woman was on the mountain among the peach trees."

Randolph threw back his shoulders.

"Why waste time in a speculation about it, Abner?" he said. "We know who did this thing. Let us go and get the story of it out of their own mouths. Doomdorf died by the hands of either Bronson or this woman."

"I could better believe it," replied Abner, "but for the running of a certain awful law."

"What law?" said Randolph. "Is it a statute of Virginia?"

"It is a statute," replied Abner, "of an authority somewhat higher. Mark the language of it: 'He that killeth with the sword must be killed with the sword.'"

He came over and took Randolph by the arm.

"Must! Randolph, did you mark particularly the word 'must'? It is a mandatory law. There is no room in it for the vicissitudes of chance or fortune. There is no way round that word. Thus, we reap what we sow and nothing else; thus, we receive what we give and nothing else. It is the weapon in our own hands that finally destroys us. You are looking at it now." And he turned him about so that the table and the weapon and the dead man were before him. "'He that killeth with the sword must be killed with the sword.' And now," he said, "let us go and try the method of the law courts. Your faith is in the wisdom of their ways."

They found the old circuit rider at work in the still, staving in Doomdorf's liquor casks, splitting the oak heads with his ax.

"Bronson," said Randolph, "how did you kill Doomdorf?"

The old man stopped and stood leaning on his ax.

"I killed him," replied the old man, "as Elijah killed the captains of Ahaziah and their fifties. But not by the hand of any man did

I pray the Lord God to destroy Doomdorf, but with fire from heaven to destroy him."

He stood up and extended his arms.

"His hands were full of blood," he said. "With his abomination from these groves of Baal he stirred up the people to contention, to strife and murder. The widow and the orphan cried to heaven against him. 'I will surely hear their cry,' is the promise written in the Book. The land was weary of him; and I prayed the Lord God to destroy him with fire from heaven, as he destroyed the Princes of Gomorrah in their palaces!"

Randolph made a gesture as of one who dismisses the impossible, but Abner's face took on a deep, strange look.

"With fire from heaven!" he repeated slowly to himself. Then he asked a question. "A little while ago," he said, "when we came, I asked you where Doomdorf was, and you answered me in the language of the third chapter of the Book of Judges. Why did you answer me like that, Bronson? — 'Surely he covereth his feet in his summer chamber.'"

"The woman told me that he had not come down from the room where he had gone up to sleep," replied the old man, "and that the door was locked. And then I knew that he was dead in his summer chamber like Eglon, King of Moab."

He extended his arm toward the south.

"I came here from the Great Valley," he said, "to cut down these groves of Baal and to empty out this abomination; but I did not know that the Lord had heard my prayer and visited His wrath on Doomdorf until I was come up into these mountains to his door. When the woman spoke I knew it." And he went away to his horse, leaving the ax among the ruined barrels.

Randolph interrupted.

"Come, Abner," he said; "this is wasted time. Bronson did not kill Doomdorf."

Abner answered slowly in his deep, level voice:

"Do you realize, Randolph, how Doomdorf died?"

"Not by fire from heaven, at any rate," said Randolph.

"Randolph," replied Abner, "are you sure?"

"Abner," cried Randolph, "you are pleased to jest, but I am in deadly earnest. A crime has been done here against the state. I am an officer of justice and I propose to discover the assassin if I can."

He walked away toward the house and Abner followed, his hands behind him and his great shoulders thrown loosely forward, with a grim smile about his mouth.

"It is no use to talk with the mad old preacher," Randolph went on. "Let him empty out the liquor and ride away. I won't issue a warrant against him. Prayer may be a handy implement to do a murder with, Abner, but it is not a deadly weapon under the statutes of Virginia. Doomdorf was dead when old Bronson got here with his Scriptural jargon. This woman killed Doomdorf. I shall put her to an inquisition."

"As you like," replied Abner. "Your faith remains in the methods of the law courts."

"Do you know of any better methods?" said Randolph.

"Perhaps," replied Abner, "when you have finished."

Night had entered the valley. The two men went into the house and set about preparing the corpse for burial. They got candles, and made a coffin, and put Doomdorf in it, and straightened out his limbs, and folded his arms across his shot-out heart. Then they set the coffin on benches in the hall.

They kindled a fire in the dining room and sat down before it, with the door open and the red firelight shining through on the dead man's narrow, everlasting house. The woman had put some cold meat, a golden cheese and a loaf on the table. They did not see her, but they heard her moving about the house; and finally, on the gravel court outside, her step and the whinny of a horse. Then she came in, dressed as for a journey. Randolph sprang up.

"Where are you going?" he said.

"To the sea and a ship," replied the woman. Then she indicated the hall with a gesture. "He is dead and I am free."

There was a sudden illumination in her face. Randolph took a step toward her. His voice was big and harsh.

"Who killed Doomdorf?" he cried.

"I killed him," replied the woman. "It was fair!"

"Fair!" echoed the justice. "What do you mean by that?"

The woman shrugged her shoulders and put out her hands with a foreign gesture.

"I remember an old, old man sitting against a sunny wall, and a little girl, and one who came and talked a long time with the old man, while the little girl plucked yellow flowers out of the grass and put them into her hair. Then finally the stranger gave the old man a gold chain and took the little girl away." She flung out her hands. "Oh, it was fair to kill him!" She looked up with a queer, pathetic smile.

"The old man will be gone by now," she said; "but I shall perhaps find the wall there, with the sun on it, and the yellow flowers in the grass. And now, may I go?"

It is a law of the story-teller's art that he does not tell a story. It is the listener who tells it. The story-teller does but provide him with the stimuli.

Randolph got up and walked about the floor. He was a justice of the peace in a day when that office was filled only by the landed gentry, after the English fashion; and the obligations of the law were strong on him. If he should take liberties with the letter of it, how could the weak and the evil be made to hold it in respect? Here was this woman before him a confessed assassin. Could he let her go?

Abner sat unmoving by the hearth, his elbow on the arm of his chair, his palm propping up his jaw, his face clouded in deep lines. Randolph was consumed with vanity and the weakness of ostentation, but he shouldered his duties for himself. Presently he stopped and looked at the woman, wan, faded like some prisoner of legend escaped out of fabled dungeons into the sun.

The firelight flickered past her to the box on the benches in the hall, and the vast, inscrutable justice of heaven entered and overcame him.

"Yes," he said. "Go! There is no jury in Virginia that would hold a woman for shooting a beast like that." And he thrust out his arm, with the fingers extended toward the dead man.

The woman made a little awkward curtsy.

"I thank you, sir." Then she hesitated and lisped, "But I have not shoot him."

"Not shoot him!" cried Randolph. "Why, the man's heart is riddled!"

"Yes, sir," she said simply, like a child. "I kill him, but have not shoot him."

Randolph took two long strides toward the woman.

"Not shoot him!" he repeated. "How then, in the name of heaven, did you kill Doomdorf?" And his big voice filled the empty places of the room.

"I will show you, sir," she said.

She turned and went away into the house. Presently she returned with something folded up in a linen towel. She put it on the table between the loaf of bread and the yellow cheese.

Randolph stood over the table, and the woman's deft fingers undid the towel from round its deadly contents; and presently the thing lay there uncovered.

It was a little crude model of a human figure done in wax with a needle thrust through the bosom.

Randolph stood up with a great intake of the breath.

"Magic! By the eternal!"

"Yes, sir," the woman explained, in her voice and manner of a child. "I have try to kill him many times — oh, very many times! — with witch words which I have remember; but always they fail. Then, at last, I make him in wax, and I put a needle through his heart; and I kill him very quickly."

It was as clear as daylight, even to Randolph, that the woman was innocent. Her little harmless magic was the pathetic effort of a child to kill a dragon. He hesitated a moment before he spoke, and then he decided like the gentleman he was. If it helped the child to believe that her enchanted straw had slain the monster — well, he would let her believe it.

"And now, sir, may I go?"

Randolph looked at the woman in a sort of wonder.

"Are you not afraid," he said, "of the night and the mountains, and the long road?"

"Oh no, sir," she replied simply. "The good God will be everywhere now."

It was an awful commentary on the dead man — that this strange half-child believed that all the evil in the world had gone out with him; that now that he was dead, the sunlight of heaven would fill every nook and corner.

It was not a faith that either of the two men wished to shatter, and they let her go. It would be daylight presently and the road through the mountains to the Chesapeake was open.

Randolph came back to the fireside after he had helped her into the saddle, and sat down. He tapped on the hearth for some time idly with the iron poker; and then finally he spoke.

"This is the strangest thing that ever happened," he said. "Here's a mad old preacher who thinks that he killed Doomdorf with fire from heaven, like Elijah the Tishbite; and here is a simple child of a woman who thinks she killed him with a piece of magic of the Middle Ages — each as innocent of his death as I am. And yet, by the eternal, the beast is dead!"

He drummed on the hearth with the poker, lifting it up and letting it drop through the hollow of his fingers.

"Somebody shot Doomdorf. But who? And how did he get into and out of that shut-up room? The assassin that killed Doomdorf must have gotten into the room to kill him. Now, how did he get in?" He spoke as to himself; but my uncle sitting across the hearth replied:

"Through the window."

"Through the window!" echoed Randolph. "Why, man, you yourself showed me that the window had not been opened, and the precipice below it a fly could hardly climb. Do you tell me now that the window was opened?"

"No," said Abner, "it was never opened."

Randolph got on his feet.

"Abner," he cried, "are you saying that the one who killed Doomdorf climbed the sheer wall and got in through a closed window, without disturbing the dust or the cobwebs on the window frame?"

My uncle looked Randolph in the face.

"The murderer of Doomdorf did even more," he said. "That assassin not only climbed the face of that precipice and got in through the closed window, but he shot Doomdorf to death and got out again through the closed window without leaving a single track or trace behind, and without disturbing a grain of dust or a thread of a cobweb."

Randolph swore a great oath.

"The thing is impossible!" he cried. "Men are not killed today in Virginia by black art or a curse of God."

"By black art, no," replied Abner; "but by the curse of God, yes. I think they are."

Randolph drove his clenched right hand into the palm of his left.

"By the eternal!" he cried. "I would like to see the assassin who could do a murder like this, whether he be an imp from the pit or an angel out of heaven."

"Very well," replied Abner, undisturbed. "When he comes back tomorrow I will show you the assassin who killed Doomdorf."

When day broke they dug a grave and buried the dead man against the mountain among his peach trees. It was noon when that work was ended. Abner threw down his spade and looked up at the sun.

"Randolph," he said, "let us go and lay an ambush for this assassin. He is on the way here."

And it was a strange ambush that he laid. When they were come again into the chamber where Doomdorf died he bolted the door; then he loaded the fowling piece and put it carefully back on its rack against the wall. After that he did another curious thing: He took the blood-stained coat, which they had stripped off the dead man when they had prepared his body for the earth, put a pillow in it and laid it on the couch precisely where Doomdorf had slept. And while he did these things Randolph stood in wonder and Abner talked:

"Look you, Randolph. . . . We will trick the murderer. . . . We will catch him in the act."

Then he went over and took the puzzled justice by the arm.

"Watch!" he said. "The assassin is coming along the wall!"

But Randolph heard nothing, saw nothing. Only the sun entered. Abner's hand tightened on his arm.

"It is here! Look!" And he pointed to the wall.

Randolph, following the extended finger, saw a tiny brilliant disk of light moving slowly up the wall toward the lock of the fowling piece. Abner's hand became a vise and his voice rang as over metal.

" 'He that killeth with the sword must be killed with the sword.' It is the water bottle, full of Doomdorf's liquor, focusing the sun.

. . . And look, Randolph, how Bronson's prayer was answered!"

The tiny disk of light traveled on the plate of the lock.

"It is fire from heaven!"

The words rang above the roar of the fowling piece, and Randolph saw the dead man's coat leap up on the couch, riddled by the shot. The gun, in its natural position on the rack, pointed to the couch standing at the end of the chamber, beyond the offset of the wall, and the focused sun had exploded the percussion cap.

Randolph made a great gesture, with his arm extended.

"It is a world," he said, "filled with the mysterious joinder of accident!"

"It is a world," replied Abner, "filled with the mysterious justice of God!"

THE SWEET SHOT

by E. C. BENTLEY

To all those who have ever brought a brassie down on a caddie's head: Here is TRENT, *of "Trent's Last Case" fame, indulging his cerebral talents on, of all places, a golf course. Sports mysteries are uncommon, which is why we've done four of them ourselves* (advt.).

No; I happened to be abroad at the time," Philip Trent said. "I wasn't in the way of seeing the English papers, so until I came here this week I never heard anything about your mystery."

Captain Royden, a small, spare, brown-faced man, was engaged in the delicate — and forbidden — task of taking his automatic telephone instrument to pieces. He now suspended his labours and reached for the tobacco jar. The large window of his office in the Kempshill clubhouse looked down upon the eighteenth green of that delectable golf course, and his eye roved over the whin-clad slopes beyond as he called on his recollection.

"Well, if you call it a mystery," he said as he filled a pipe. "Some people do, because they like mysteries, I suppose. For instance, Colin Hunt, the man you're staying with, calls it that. Others won't have it, and say there was a perfectly natural explanation. I could tell you as much as anybody could about it, I dare say."

"As being secretary here, you mean?"

"Not only that. I was one of the two people who were in at the death, so to speak — or next door to it," Captain Royden said. He limped to the mantelshelf and took down a silver box embossed on the lid with the crest and mottoes of the Corps of Royal Engineers. "Try one of these cigarettes, Mr. Trent. If you'd like to hear the yarn, I'll give it you. You have heard something about Arthur Freer, I suppose?"

"Hardly anything," Trent said. "I just gathered that he wasn't a very popular character."

"No," Captain Royden said with reserve. "Did they tell you he was my brother-in-law? No? Well, now, it happened about four months ago, on a Monday — let me see — yes, the second Monday in May. Freer had a habit of playing nine holes before breakfast. Barring Sundays — he was strict about Sunday — he did it most days, even in the beastliest weather, going round all alone usually, carrying his own clubs, studying every shot as if his life depended on it. That helped to make him the very good player he was. His handicap here was two, and at Undershaw he used to be scratch, I believe.

"At a quarter to eight he'd be on the first tee, and by nine he'd be back at his house — it's only a few minutes from here. That Monday morning he started off as usual —— "

"And at the usual time?"

"Just about. He had spent a few minutes in the clubhouse blowing up the steward about some trifle. And that was the last time he was seen alive by anybody — near enough to speak to, that is. No one else went off the first tee until a little after nine, when I started round with Browson — he's our local padre; I had been having breakfast with him at the Vicarage. He's got a game leg, like me, so we often play together when he can fit it in.

"We had holed out on the first green, and were walking on to the next tee, when Browson said, 'Great Scott! Look there. Something's happened.' He pointed down the fairway of the second hole; and there we could see a man lying sprawled on the turf, face down and motionless. Now there is this point about the second hole — the first half of it is in a dip in the land, just deep enough to be out of sight from any other point on the course, unless you're standing right above it — you'll see when you go round yourself. Well, on the tee, you *are* right above it; and we saw this man lying. We ran to the spot.

"It was Freer, as I had known it must be at that hour. He was dead, lying in a disjointed sort of way no live man could have lain in. His clothing was torn to ribbons, and it was singed too. So was his hair — he used to play bareheaded — and his face and hands. His bag of clubs was lying a few yards away, and the brassie, which he had just been using, was close by the body.

"There wasn't any wound showing, and I had seen far worse things often enough, but the padre was looking sickish, so I asked him to go back to the clubhouse and send for a doctor and the police while I mounted guard. They weren't long coming, and after they had done their job the body was taken away in an ambulance. Well, that's about all I can tell you at first hand, Mr. Trent. If you are staying with Hunt, you'll have heard about the inquest and all that, probably."

Trent shook his head. "No," he said. "Colin was just beginning to tell me, after breakfast this morning, about Freer having been killed on the course in some incomprehensible way, when a man came to see him about something. So, as I was going to apply for a fortnight's run of the course, I thought I would ask you about the affair."

"All right," Captain Royden said. "I can tell you about the inquest anyhow — had to be there to speak my own little piece, about finding the body. As for what had happened to Freer, the medical evidence was rather confusing. It was agreed that he had been killed by some tremendous shock, which had jolted his whole system to pieces and dislocated several joints, but had been not quite violent enough to cause any visible wound. Apart from that, there was a disagreement. Freer's own doctor, who saw the body first, declared he must have been struck by lightning. He said it was true there hadn't been a thunderstorm, but that there had been thunder about all that week-end, and that sometimes lightning did act in that way. But the police surgeon, Collins, said there would be no such displacement of the organs from a lightning stroke, even if it did ever happen that way in our climate, which he doubted. And he said that if it had been lightning, it would have struck the steel-headed clubs; but the clubs lay there in their bag quite undamaged. Collins thought there must have been some kind of explosion, though he couldn't suggest what kind."

Trent shook his head. "I don't suppose that impressed the court," he said. "All the same, it may have been all the honest opinion he could give." He smoked in silence a few moments, while Captain

Royden attended to the troubles of his telephone instrument with a camel-hair brush. "But surely," Trent said at length, "if there had been such an explosion as that, somebody would have heard the sound of it."

"Lots of people would have heard it," Captain Royden answered. "But there you are, you see — nobody notices the sound of explosions just about here. There's the quarry on the other side of the road there, and any time after seven a.m. there's liable to be a noise of blasting."

"A dull, sickening thud?"

"Jolly sickening," Captain Royden said, "for all of us living near by. And so that point wasn't raised. Well, Collins is a very sound man; but as you say, his evidence didn't really explain the thing, and the other fellow's did, whether it was right or wrong. Besides, the coroner and the jury had heard about a bolt from a clear sky, and the notion appealed to them. Anyhow, they brought it in death from misadventure."

"Which nobody could deny, as the song says," Trent remarked. "And was there no other evidence?"

"Yes; some. But Hunt can tell you about it as well as I can; he was there. I shall have to ask you to excuse me now," Captain Royden said. "I have an appointment in the town. The steward will sign you on for a fortnight, and probably get you a game too, if you want one to-day."

Colin Hunt and his wife, when Trent returned to their house for luncheon, were very willing to complete the tale. The verdict, they declared, was tripe. Dr. Collins knew his job, whereas Dr. Hoyle was an old footler, and Freer's death had never been reasonably explained.

As for the other evidence, it had, they agreed, been interesting, though it didn't help at all. Freer had been seen after he had played his tee shot at the second hole, when he was walking down to the bottom of the dip towards the spot where he met his death.

"But according to Royden," Trent said, "that was a place where he couldn't be seen, unless one was right above him."

"Well, this witness *was* right above him," Hunt rejoined. "About one thousand feet above him, so he said. He was an R.A.F. man, piloting a bomber from Bexford Camp, not far from here. He was up doing some sort of exercise, and passed over the course just at that time. He didn't know Freer, but he spotted a man walking down from the second tee, because he was the only living soul visible on the course. Gossett, the other man in the plane, is a temporary member here, and he did know Freer quite well — or as well as anybody cared to know him — but he never saw him. However, the pilot was quite clear that he saw a man just at the time in question, and they took his evidence so as to prove that Freer was absolutely alone just before his death. The only other person who saw Freer was another man who knew him well; used to be a caddy here, and then got a job at the quarry. He was at work on the hillside, and he watched Freer play the first hole and go on to the second — nobody with him, of course."

"Well, that was pretty well established then," Trent remarked. "He was about as alone as he could be, it seems. Yet something happened somehow."

Mrs. Hunt sniffed sceptically, and lighted a cigarette. "Yes, it did," she said. "However, I didn't worry much about it, for one. Edith — Mrs. Freer, that is: Royden's sister — must have had a terrible life of it with a man like that. Not that she ever said anything — she wouldn't. She is not that sort."

"She is a jolly good sort, anyhow," Hunt declared.

"Yes, she is; too good for most men. I can tell you," Mrs. Hunt added for the benefit of Trent, "if Colin ever took to cursing me and knocking me about, my well-known loyalty wouldn't stand the strain for very long."

"That's why I don't do it. It's the fear of exposure that makes me the perfect husband, Phil. She would tie a can to me before I knew what was happening. As for Edith, it's true she never said anything, but the change in her since it happened tells the story well enough. Since she's been living with her brother she has been looking far better and happier than she ever succeeded in doing while Freer was alive."

"She won't be living with him for very long, I dare say," Mrs. Hunt intimated darkly.

"No. I'd marry her myself if I had the chance," Hunt agreed cordially.

"Pooh! You wouldn't be in the first six," his wife said. "It will be Rennie, or Gossett, or possibly Sandy Butler — you'll see. But perhaps you've had enough of the local tittle-tattle, Phil. Did you fix up a game for this afternoon?"

"Yes; with the Jarman Professor of Chemistry in the University of Cambridge," Trent said. "He looked at me as if he thought a bath of vitriol would do me good, but he agreed to play me."

"You've got a tough job," Hunt observed. "I believe he is almost as old as he looks, but he is a devil at the short game, and he knows the course blindfold, which you don't. And he isn't so cantankerous as he pretends to be. By the way, he was the man who saw the finish of the last shot Freer ever played — a sweet shot if ever there was one. Get him to tell you."

"I shall try to," Trent said. "The steward told me about that, and that was why I asked the professor for a game."

Colin Hunt's prediction was fulfilled that afternoon. Professor Hyde, receiving five strokes, was one up at the seventeenth, and at the last hole sent down a four-foot putt to win the match. As they left the green he remarked, as if in answer to something Trent had that moment said, "Yes: I can tell you a curious circumstance about Freer's death."

Trent's eye brightened; for the professor had not said a dozen words during their game, and Trent's tentative allusion to the subject after the second hole had been met merely by an intimidating grunt.

"I saw the finish of the last shot he played," the old gentleman went on, "without seeing the man himself at all. A lovely brassie it was, too — though lucky. Rolled to within two feet of the pin."

Trent considered. "I see," he said, "what you mean. You were near the second green, and the ball came over the ridge and ran down to the hole."

"Just so," Professor Hyde said. "That's how you play it — if you can. You might have done it yourself to-day, if your second shot had been thirty yards longer. I've never done it; but Freer often did. After a really good drive, you play a long second, blind, over the ridge; and with a perfect shot, you may get the green. Well, my house is quite near that green. I was pottering about in the garden before breakfast, and just as I happened to be looking towards the green a ball came hopping down the slope and trickled right across to the hole. Of course, I knew whose it must be — Freer always came along about that time. If it had been anyone else, I'd have waited to see him get his three, and congratulate him. As it was, I went indoors, and didn't hear of his death until long afterwards."

"And you never saw him play the shot," Trent said thoughtfully. The professor turned a choleric blue eye on him. "How the deuce could I?" he said huffily. "I can't see through a mass of solid earth."

"I know, I know," Trent said. "I was only trying to follow your mental process. Without seeing him play the shot, you knew it was his second — you say he would have been putting for a three. And you said, too — didn't you? — that it was a brassie shot."

"Simply because, my young friend" — the Professor was severe — "I happened to know the man's game. I had played that nine holes with him before breakfast often, until one day he lost his temper more than usual, and made himself impossible. I knew he practically always carried the ridge with his second — I won't say he always got the green — and his brassie was the only club that would do it. It is conceivable, I admit," Professor Hyde added a little stiffly, "that some mishap took place, and that the shot in question was not actually Freer's second; but it did not occur to me to allow for that highly speculative contingency."

On the next day, after those playing a morning round were started on their perambulation, Trent indulged himself with an hour's practice, mainly on the unsurveyed stretch of the second hole. Afterwards he had a word with the caddy master; then visited the professional's shop, and won the regard of that expert by furnishing himself with a new mid-iron. Soon he brought up the subject of the last shot played by Arthur Freer. A dozen times that morning, he said, he had tried, after a satisfying drive, to reach the green with his second; but in vain. Fergus MacAdam shook his head. Not many, he said, could strike the ball with yon force. He could get there himself, whiles, but never for a certainty. Mr. Freer had the strength, and he kenned how to use it forbye.

What sort of clubs, Trent asked, had Freer preferred? "Lang

and heavy, like himsel'. Noo ye mention it," MacAdam said, "I hae them here. They were brocht here after the ahccident." He reached up to the top of a rack. "Ay, here they are. They shouldna be, of course; but naebody came to claim them, and it juist slippit ma mind."

Trent, extracting the brassie, looked thoughtfully at the heavy head with the strip of hard white material inlaid in the face. "It's a powerful weapon, sure enough," he remarked.

"Ay, for a man that could control it," MacAdam said. "I dinna care for yon ivorine face mysel'. Some fowk think it gies mair reseelience, ye ken; but there's naething in it."

"He didn't get it from you, then," Trent suggested, still closely examining the head.

"Ay, but he did. I had a lot down from Nelsons while the fashion for them was on. Ye'll find my name," MacAdam added, "stampit on the wood in the usual place, if yer een are seein' richt."

"Well, I don't — that's just it. The stamp is quite illegible."

"Tod! Let's see," the professional said, taking the club in hand. "Guid reason for its being illegible," he went on after a brief scrutiny. "It's been obleeterated — that's easy seen. Who ever saw sic a daft-like thing! The wood has juist been crushed some gait — in a vice, I wouldna wonder. Noo, why would onybody want to dae a thing like yon?"

"Unaccountable, isn't it?" Trent said. "Still, it doesn't matter, I suppose. And anyhow, we shall never know."

It was twelve days later that Trent, looking in at the open door of the secretary's office, saw Captain Royden happily engaged with the separated parts of some mechanism in which coils of wire appeared to be the leading motive.

"I see you're busy," Trent said.

"Come in! Come in!" Royden said heartily. "I can do this any time — another hour's work will finish it." He laid down a pair of sharp-nosed pliers. "The electricity people have just changed us over to A.C., and I've got to re-wind the motor of our vacuum cleaner. Beastly nuisance," he added, looking down affectionately at the bewildering jumble of disarticulated apparatus on his table.

"You bear your sorrow like a man," Trent remarked; and Royden laughed as he wiped his hands on a towel.

"Yes," he said, "I do love tinkering about with mechanical jobs, and if I do say it myself, I'd rather do a thing like this with my own hands than risk having it faultily done by a careless workman. Too many of them about. Why, about a year ago the company sent a man here to fit a new main fuse box, and he made a short circuit with his screw driver that knocked him right across the kitchen and might very well have killed him." He reached down his cigarette box and offered it to Trent, who helped himself; then looked down thoughtfully at the device on the lid.

"Thanks very much. When I saw this box before, I put you down for an R.E. man. *Ubique,* and *Quo fas et gloria ducunt.* Hm! I wonder why Engineers were given that motto in particular."

"Lord knows," the captain said. "In my experience, Sappers don't exactly go where right and glory lead. The dirtiest of all the jobs and precious little of the glory — that's what they get."

"Still, they have the consolation," Trent pointed out, "of feeling that they are at home in a scientific age, and that all the rest of the Army are amateurs compared with them. That's what one of them once told me, anyhow. Well now, Captain, I have to be off this evening. I've looked in just to say how much I've enjoyed myself here."

"Very glad you did," Captain Royden said. "You'll come again, I hope, now you know that the golf here is not so bad."

"I like it immensely. Also the members. And the secretary." Trent paused to light his cigarette. "I found the mystery rather interesting, too."

Captain Royden's eyebrows lifted slightly. "You mean about Freer's death? So you made up your mind it *was* a mystery."

"Why, yes," Trent said. "Because I made up my mind he had been killed by somebody, and probably killed intentionally. Then, when I had looked into the thing a little, I washed out the 'probably.'"

Captain Royden took up a penknife from his desk and began mechanically to sharpen a pencil. "So you don't agree with the coroner's jury?"

"No: as the verdict seems to have been meant to rule out murder or any sort of human agency, I don't. The lightning idea, which apparently satisfied them, or some of them, was not a very bright one, I thought. I was told what Dr. Collins had said against it at the inquest; and it seemed to me he had disposed of it completely when he said that Freer's clubs, most of them steel ones, were quite undamaged. A man carrying his clubs puts them down, when he plays a shot, a few feet away at most; yet Freer was supposed to have been electrocuted without any notice having been taken of them, so to speak."

"Hm! No, it doesn't seem likely. I don't know that that quite decides the point, though," the captain said. "Lightning plays funny tricks, you know. I've seen a small tree struck when it was sur-rounded by trees twice the size. All the same, I quite agree there didn't seem to be any sense in the lightning notion. It was thundery weather, but there wasn't any storm that morning in this neigh-bourhood."

"Just so. But when I considered what had been said about Freer's clubs, it suddenly occurred to me that nobody had said anything about *the* club, so far as my information about the inquest went. It seemed clear, from what you and the parson saw, that he had just played a shot with his brassie when he was struck down; it way lying near him, not in the bag. Besides, old Hyde actually saw the ball he had hit roll down the slope on to the green. Now, it's a good rule to study every little detail when you are on a problem of this kind. There weren't many left to study, of course, since the thing had happened four months before; but I knew Freer's clubs must be somewhere, and I thought of one or two places where they were likely to have been taken, in the circumstances, so I tried them. First, I reconnoitred the caddy-master's shed, asking if I could leave my bag there for a day or two; but I was told that the regular place to leave them was the pro.'s shop. So I went and had a chat with MacAdam, and sure enough it soon came out that Freer's bag was still in his rack. I had a look at the clubs, too."

"And did you notice anything peculiar about them?" Captain Royden asked.

"Just one little thing. But it was enough to set me thinking, and next day I drove up to London, where I paid a visit to Nelsons, the sporting outfitters. You know the firm, of course."

Captain Royden, carefully fining down the point of his pencil, nodded. "Everybody knows Nelsons."

"Yes; and MacAdam, I knew, had an account there for his stocks. I wanted to look over some clubs of a particular make — a

brassie, with a slip of ivorine let into the face, such as they had supplied to MacAdam. Freer had had one of them from him."

Again Royden nodded.

"I saw the man who shows clubs at Nelsons. We had a talk,
and then — you know how little things come out in the course of
conversation —— "

"Especially," put in the captain with a cheerful grin, "when the
conversation is being steered by an expert."

"You flatter me," Trent said. "Anyhow, it did transpire that a
club of that particular make had been bought some months before
by a customer whom the man was able to remember. Why he
remembered him was because, in the first place, he insisted on a
club of rather unusual length and weight — much too long and
heavy for himself to use, as he was neither a tall man nor of
powerful build. The salesman had suggested as much in a delicate
way; but the customer said no, he knew exactly what suited him,
and he bought the club and took it away with him."

"Rather an ass, I should say," Royden observed thoughtfully.

"I don't think he was an ass, really. He was capable of making
a mistake, though, like the rest of us. There were some other things,
by the way, that the salesman recalled about him. He had a slight
limp, and he was, or had been, an Army officer. The salesman
was an ex-Service man, and he couldn't be mistaken, he said, about
that."

Captain Royden had drawn a sheet of paper towards him, and
was slowly drawing little geometrical figures as he listened. "Go on,
Mr. Trent," he said quietly.

"Well, to come back to the subject of Freer's death. I think he
was killed by someone who knew Freer never played on Sunday,
so that his clubs would be — or ought to be, shall we say? — in his
locker all that day. All the following night, too, of course — in case
the job took a long time. And I think this man was in a position
to have access to the lockers in this clubhouse at any time he chose,
and to possess a master key to those lockers. I think he was a skilful
amateur craftsman. I think he had a good practical knowledge of
high explosives. There is a branch of the Army" — Trent paused a
moment and looked at the cigarette box on the table — "in which
that sort of knowledge is specially necessary, I believe."

Hastily, as if just reminded of the duty of hospitality, Royden lifted the lid of the box and pushed it towards Trent. "Do have another," he urged.

Trent did so with thanks. "They have to have it in the Royal Engineers," he went on, "because — so I'm told — demolition work is an important part of their job."

"Quite right," Captain Royden observed, delicately shading one side of a cube.

"*Ubique!*" Trent mused, staring at the box lid. "If you are 'everywhere,' I take it you can be in two places at the same time. You could kill a man in one place, and at the same time be having breakfast with a friend a mile away. Well, to return to our subject yet once more; you can see the kind of idea I was led to form about what happened to Freer. I believe that his brassie was taken from his locker on the Sunday before his death. I believe the ivorine face of it was taken off and a cavity hollowed out behind it; and in that cavity a charge of explosive was placed. Where it came from I don't know, for it isn't the sort of thing that is easy to come by, I imagine."

"Oh, there would be no difficulty about that," the captain remarked. "If this man you're speaking of knew all about H.E., as you say, he could have compounded the stuff himself from materials anybody can buy. For instance, he could easily make tetranitroaniline — that would be just the thing for him, I should say."

"I see. Then perhaps there would be a tiny detonator attached to the inner side of the ivorine face, so that a good smack with the brassie would set it off. Then the face would be fixed on again. It would be a delicate job, because the weight of the club-head would have to be exactly right. The feel and balance of the club would have to be just the same as before the operation."

"A delicate job, yes," the captain agreed. "But not an impossible one. There would be rather more to it than you say, as a matter of fact; the face would have to be shaved down thin, for instance. Still, it could be done."

"Well, I imagined it done. Now, this man I have in mind knew there was no work for a brassie at the short first hole, and that the first time it would come out of the bag was at the second hole, down at the bottom of the dip, where no one could see what happened. What certainly did happen was that Freer played a sweet shot, slap on to the green. What else happened at the same moment we don't know for certain, but we can make a reasonable guess. And then, of course, there's the question what happened to the club — or what was left of it; the handle, say. But it isn't a difficult question, I think, if we remember how the body was found."

"How do you mean?" Royden asked.

"I mean, by whom it was found. One of the two players who found it was too much upset to notice very much. He hurried back to the clubhouse; and the other was left alone with the body for, as I estimate it, at least fifteen minutes. When the police came on the scene, they found lying near the body a perfectly good brassie, an unusually long and heavy club, exactly like Freer's brassie in every respect — except one. The name stamped on the wood of the club head had been obliterated by crushing. That name, I think, was not F. MacAdam, but W. J. Nelson; and the club had been taken out of a bag that was not Freer's — a bag which had the remains, if any, of Freer's brassie at the bottom of it. And I believe that's all." Trent got to his feet and stretched his arms. "You can see what I meant when I said I found the mystery interesting."

For some moments Captain Royden gazed thoughtfully out of the window; then he met Trent's inquiring eye. "If there was such a fellow as you imagine," he said coolly, "he seems to have been careful enough — lucky enough too, if you like — to leave nothing at all of what you could call proof against him. And probably he had personal and private reasons for what he did. Suppose that somebody whom he was much attached to was in the power of a foul-tempered, bullying brute; and suppose he found that the bullying had gone to the length of physical violence; and suppose that the situation was hell by day and by night to this man of yours; and suppose there was no way on earth of putting an end to it except the way he took. Yes, Mr. Trent; suppose all that!"

"I will — I do!" Trent said. "That man — if he exists at all — must have been driven pretty hard, and what he did is no business of mine anyway. And now — still in the conditional mood — suppose I take myself off."

THE TRAGEDY AT BROOKBEND COTTAGE

by ERNEST BRAMAH

The celebrated blind detective, MAX CARRADOS, *has had a mere twenty-six short-story adventures. Nevertheless, thirteen have been reprinted in anthologies! Only Post's Uncle Abner shares this high-water percentage of anthological appearances (eighteen Uncle Abner stories, nine of them chosen).*

Max," SAID MR. CARLYLE, when Parkinson had closed the door behind him, "this is Lieutenant Hollyer, whom you consented to see."

"To hear," corrected Carrados, smiling straight into the healthy and rather embarrassed face of the stranger before him. "Mr. Hollyer knows of my disability?"

"Mr. Carlyle told me," said the young man, "but, as a matter of fact, I had heard of you before, Mr. Carrados, from one of our men. It was in connection with the foundering of the *Ivan Saratov*."

Carrados wagged his head in good-humoured resignation.

"And the owners were sworn to inviolable secrecy!" he exclaimed. "Well, it is inevitable, I suppose. Not another scuttling case, Mr. Hollyer?"

"No, mine is quite a private matter," replied the lieutenant. "My sister, Mrs. Creake — but Mr. Carlyle would tell you better than I can. He knows all about it."

"No, no; Carlyle is a professional. Let me have it in the rough, Mr. Hollyer. My ears are my eyes, you know."

"Very well, sir. I can tell you what there is to tell, right enough, but I feel that when all's said and done it must sound very little to another, although it seems important to me."

"We have occasionally found trifles of significance ourselves," said Carrados encouragingly. "Don't let that deter you."

This was the essence of Lieutenant Hollyer's narrative:

"I have a sister, Millicent, who is married to a man called Creake. She is about twenty-eight now and he is at least fifteen years older. Neither my mother (who has since died) nor I cared very much about Creake. We had nothing particular against him, except, perhaps, the moderate disparity of age, but none of us appeared to have anything in common. He was a dark, taciturn man, and his moody silence froze up conversation. As a result, of course, we didn't see much of each other."

"This, you must understand, was four or five years ago, Max," interposed Mr. Carlyle officiously.

Carrados maintained an uncompromising silence. Mr. Carlyle blew his nose and contrived to impart a hurt significance into the operation. Then Lieutenant Hollyer continued:

"Millicent married Creake after a very short engagement. It was a frightfully subdued wedding — more like a funeral to me. The man professed to have no relations and apparently he had scarcely any friends or business acquaintances. He was an agent for something or other and had an office off Holborn. I suppose he made a living out of it then, although we knew practically nothing of his private affairs, but I gather that it has been going down since, and I suspect that for the past few years they have been getting along almost entirely on Millicent's little income. You would like the particulars of that?"

"Please," assented Carrados.

"When our father died about seven years ago, he left three thousand pounds. It was invested in Canadian stock and brought in a little over a hundred a year. By his will my mother was to have the income of that for life and on her death it was to pass to Millicent, subject to the payment of a lump sum of five hundred pounds to me. But my father privately suggested to me that if I should have no particular use for the money at the time, he would propose my letting Millicent have the income of it until I did want it, as she would not be particularly well off. You see, Mr. Carrados, a great deal more had been spent on my education and advancement than on her; I had my pay, and, of course, I could look out for myself better than a girl could."

"Quite so," agreed Carrados.

"Therefore I did nothing about that," continued the lieutenant. "Three years ago I was over again but I did not see much of them. They were living in lodgings. That was the only time since the marriage that I have seen them until last week. In the meanwhile our mother had died and Millicent had been receiving her income. She wrote me several letters at the time. Otherwise we did not correspond much, but about a year ago she sent me their new address — Brookbend Cottage, Mulling Common — a house that they had taken. When I got two months' leave I invited myself there as a matter of course, fully expecting to stay most of my time with them, but I made an excuse to get away after a week. The place was dismal and unendurable, the whole life and atmosphere indescribably depressing." He looked round with an instinct of caution, leaned forward earnestly, and dropped his voice. "Mr. Carrados, it is my absolute conviction that Creake is only waiting for a favourable opportunity to murder Millicent."

"Go on," said Carrados quietly. "A week of the depressing surroundings of Brookbend Cottage would not alone convince you of that, Mr. Hollyer."

"I am not so sure," declared Hollyer doubtfully. "There was a feeling of suspicion and — before me — polite hatred that would have gone a good way towards it. All the same there *was* something more definite. Millicent told me this the day after I went there. There is no doubt that a few months ago Creake deliberately planned to poison her with some weed killer. She told me the circumstances in a rather distressed moment, but afterwards she refused to speak of it again — even weakly denied it — and, as a matter of fact, it was with the greatest difficulty that I could get her at any time to talk about her husband or his affairs. The gist of it was that she had the strongest suspicion that Creake doctored a bottle of stout which he expected she would drink for her supper when she was alone. The weed killer, properly labelled, but also in a beer bottle, was kept with other miscellaneous liquids in the same cupboard as the beer but on a high shelf. When he found that it had miscarried he poured away the mixture, washed out the bottle and put in the dregs from another. There is no doubt in my mind that if he had come back and found Millicent dead or dying he would have contrived it to appear that she had made a mistake in the dark and drunk some of the poison before she found out."

"Yes," assented Carrados. "The open way; the safe way."

"You must understand that they live in a very small style, Mr. Carrados, and Millicent is almost entirely in the man's power. The only servant they have is a woman who comes in for a few hours every day. The house is lonely and secluded. Creake is sometimes away for days and nights at a time, and Millicent, either through pride or indifference, seems to have dropped off all her old friends and to have made no others. He might poison her, bury the body in the garden, and be a thousand miles away before anyone began even to inquire about her. What am I to do, Mr. Carrados?"

"He is less likely to try poison than some other means now," pondered Carrados. "That having failed, his wife will always be on her guard. He may know, or at least suspect, that others know. No. . . . The common-sense precaution would be for your sister to leave the man, Mr. Hollyer. She will not?"

"No," admitted Hollyer, "she will not. I at once urged that." The young man struggled with some hesitation for a moment and then blurted out: "The fact is, Mr. Carrados, I don't understand Millicent. She is not the girl she was. She hates Creake and treats him with a silent contempt that eats into their lives like acid, and yet she is so jealous of him that she will let nothing short of death part them. It is a horrible life they lead. I stood it for a week and I must say, much as I dislike my brother-in-law, that he has something to put up with. If only he got into a passion like a man and killed her it wouldn't be altogether incomprehensible."

"That does not concern us," said Carrados. "In a game of this kind one has to take sides and we have taken ours. It remains for us to see that our side wins. You mentioned jealousy, Mr. Hollyer. Have you any idea whether Mrs. Creake has real ground for it?"

"I should have told you that," replied Lieutenant Hollyer. "I happened to strike up with a newspaper man whose office is in the same block as Creake's. When I mentioned the name he grinned.

'Creake,' he said, 'oh, he's the man with the romantic typist, isn't he?' 'Well, he's my brother-in-law,' I replied. 'What about the typist?' Then the chap shut up like a knife. 'No, no,' he said, 'I didn't know he was married. I don't want to get mixed up in anything of that sort. I only said that he had a typist. Well, what of that? So have we; so has everyone.' There was nothing more to be got out of him, but the remark and the grin meant — well, about as usual, Mr. Carrados."

Carrados turned to his friend.

"I suppose you know all about the typist by now, Louis?"

"We have had her under efficient observation, Max," replied Mr. Carlyle, with severe dignity.

"Is she unmarried?"

"Yes; so far as ordinary repute goes, she is."

"That is all that is essential for the moment. Mr. Hollyer opens up three excellent reasons why this man might wish to dispose of his wife. If we accept the suggestion of poisoning — though we have only a jealous woman's suspicion for it — we add to the wish the determination. Well, we will go forward on that. Have you got a photograph of Mr. Creake?"

The lieutenant took out his pocket book.

"Mr. Carlyle asked me for one. Here is the best I could get."

Carrados rang the bell.

"This, Parkinson," he said, when the man appeared, "is a photograph of a Mr. —— What first name, by the way?"

"Austin," put in Hollyer, who was following everything with a boyish mixture of excitement and subdued importance.

" — of a Mr. Austin Creake. I may require you to recognize him."

Parkinson glanced at the print and returned it to his master's hand.

"May I inquire if it is a recent photograph of the gentleman, sir?" he asked.

"About six years ago," said the lieutenant, taking in this new actor in the drama with frank curiosity. "But he is very little changed."

"Thank you, sir. I will endeavour to remember Mr. Creake, sir."

Lieutenant Hollyer stood up as Parkinson left the room. The interview seemed to be at an end.

"Oh, there's one other matter," he remarked. "I am afraid that I did rather an unfortunate thing while I was at Brookbend. It seemed to me that as all Millicent's money would probably pass into Creake's hands sooner or later I might as well have my five hundred pounds, if only to help her with afterwards. So I broached the subject and said that I should like to have it now as I had an opportunity for investing."

"And you think?"

"It may possibly influence Creake to act sooner than he otherwise might have done. He may have got possession of the principal even and find it very awkward to replace it."

"So much the better. If your sister is going to be murdered it may as well be done next week as next year so far as I am concerned. Excuse my brutality, Mr. Hollyer, but this is simply a case to me and I regard it strategically. Now Mr. Carlyle's organization can look after Mrs. Creake for a few weeks, but it cannot look after her for ever. By increasing the immediate risk we diminish the permanent risk."

"I see," agreed Hollyer. "I'm awfully uneasy but I'm entirely in your hands."

"Then we will give Mr. Creake every inducement and every opportunity to get to work. Where are you staying now?"

"Just now with some friends at St. Albans."

"That is too far." The inscrutable eyes retained their tranquil depth but a new quality of quickening interest in the voice made Mr. Carlyle forget the weight and burden of his ruffled dignity. "Give me a few minutes, please. The cigarettes are behind you, Mr. Hollyer." The blind man walked to the window and seemed to look out over the cypress-shaded lawn. The lieutenant lit a cigarette and Mr. Carlyle picked up *Punch*. Then Carrados turned round again.

"You are prepared to put your own arrangements aside?" he demanded of his visitor.

"Certainly."

"Very well. I want you to go down now — straight from here — to Brookbend Cottage. Tell your sister that your leave is unexpectedly cut short and that you sail to-morrow."

"The *Martian?*"

"No, no; the *Martian* doesn't sail. Look up the movements on your way there and pick out a boat that does. Say you are transferred. Add that you expect to be away only two or three months and that you really want the five hundred pounds by the time of your return. Don't stay in the house long, please."

"I understand, sir."

"St. Albans is too far. Make your excuse and get away from there to-day. Put up somewhere in town, where you will be in reach of the telephone. Let Mr. Carlyle and myself know where you are. Keep out of Creake's way. I don't want actually to tie you down to the house, but we may require your services. We will let you know at the first sign of anything doing and if there is nothing to be done we must release you."

"I don't mind that. Is there nothing more that I can do now?"

"Nothing. In going to Mr. Carlyle you have done the best thing possible; you have put your sister into the care of the shrewdest man in London." Whereat the object of this quite unexpected eulogy found himself becoming covered with modest confusion.

"Well, Max?" remarked Mr. Carlyle tentatively when they were alone.

"Well, Louis?"

"Of course it wasn't worth while rubbing it in before young Hollyer, but, as a matter of fact, every single man carries the life of any other man — only one, mind you — in his hands, do what you will."

"Provided he doesn't bungle," acquiesced Carrados.

"Quite so."

"And also that he is absolutely reckless of the consequences."

"Of course."

"Two rather large provisos. Creake is obviously susceptible to both. Have you seen him?"

"No. As I told you, I put a man on to report his habits in town. Then, two days ago, as the case seemed to promise some interest — for he certainly is deeply involved with the typist, Max, and the thing might take a sensational turn at any time — I went down to Mulling Common myself. Although the house is lonely it is on the electric tram route. You know the sort of market garden rurality that about a dozen miles out of London offers — alternate bricks and cabbages. It was easy enough to get to know about Creake locally. He mixes with no one there, goes into town at irregular times but generally every day, and is reputed to be devilish hard to get money out of. Finally I made the acquaintance of an old fellow who used to do a day's gardening at Brookbend occasionally. He has a cottage and a garden of his own with a greenhouse, and the business cost me the price of a pound of tomatoes."

"Was it — a profitable investment?"

"As tomatoes, yes; as information, no. The old fellow had the fatal disadvantage from our point of view of labouring under a grievance. A few weeks ago Creake told him that he would not require him again as he was going to do his own gardening in future."

"That is something, Louis."

"If only Creake was going to poison his wife with hyoscyamine and bury her, instead of blowing her up with a dynamite cartridge and claiming that it came in among the coal."

"True, true. Still —— "

"However, the chatty old soul had a simple explanation for everything that Creake did. Creake was mad. He had even seen him flying a kite in his garden where it was bound to get wrecked among the trees. A lad of ten would have known better, he declared. And certainly the kite did get wrecked, for I saw it hanging over the road myself. But that a sane man should spend his time 'playing with a toy' was beyond him."

"A good many men have been flying kites of various kinds lately," said Carrados. "Is he interested in aviation?"

"I dare say. He appears to have some knowledge of scientific subjects. Now what do you want me to do, Max?"

"Will you do it?"

"Implicitly — subject to the usual reservations."

"Keep your man on Creake in town and let me have his reports after you have seen them. Lunch with me here now. Phone up to your office that you are detained on unpleasant business and then give the deserving Parkinson an afternoon off by looking after me while we take a motor run round Mulling Common. If we have time we might go on to Brighton, feed at the 'Ship,' and come back in the cool."

"Amiable and thrice lucky mortal," sighed Mr. Carlyle, his glance wandering round the room.

But, as it happened, Brighton did not figure in that day's itinerary. It had been Carrados's intention merely to pass Brookbend Cottage on this occasion, relying on his highly developed faculties, aided by Mr. Carlyle's description, to inform him of the surroundings. A hundred yards before they reached the house he had given an order to his chauffeur to drop into the lowest speed and they were leisurely drawing past when a discovery by Mr. Carlyle modified their plans.

"By Jupiter!" that gentleman suddenly exclaimed, "there's a board up, Max. The place is to be let."

Carrados picked up the tube again. A couple of sentences passed and the car stopped by the roadside, a score of paces past the limit of the garden. Mr. Carlyle took out his notebook and wrote down the address of a firm of house agents.

"You might raise the bonnet and have a look at the engines, Harris," said Carrados. "We want to be occupied here for a few minutes."

"This is sudden; Hollyer knew nothing of their leaving," remarked Mr. Carlyle.

"Probably not for three months yet. All the same, Louis, we will go on to the agents and get a card to view whether we use it to-day or not."

A thick hedge, in its summer dress effectively screening the house beyond from public view, lay between the garden and the road. Above the hedge showed an occasional shrub; at the corner nearest to the car a chestnut flourished. The wooden gate, once white, which they had passed, was grimed and rickety. The road itself was still the unpretentious country lane that the advent of the electric car had found it. When Carrados had taken in these details there seemed little else to notice. He was on the point of giving Harris the order to go on when his ear caught a trivial sound.

"Someone is coming out of the house, Louis," he warned his friend. "It may be Hollyer, but he ought to have gone by this time."

"I don't hear anyone," replied the other, but as he spoke a door banged noisily and Mr. Carlyle slipped into another seat and ensconced himself behind a copy of the *Globe*.

"Creake himself," he whispered across the car, as a man appeared at the gate. "Hollyer was right; he is hardly changed. Waiting for a car, I suppose."

But a car very soon swung past them from the direction in which Mr. Creake was looking and it did not interest him. For a minute or two longer he continued to look expectantly along the road. Then he walked slowly up the drive back to the house.

"We will give him five or ten minutes," decided Carrados. "Harris is behaving very naturally."

Before even the shorter period had run out they were repaid. A telegraph boy cycled leisurely along the road, and, leaving his machine at the gate, went up to the cottage. Evidently there was no reply, for in less than a minute he was trundling past them back again. Round the bend an approaching tram clanged its bell noisily, and, quickened by the warning sound, Mr. Creake again appeared, this time with a small portmanteau in his hand. With a backward glance he hurried on towards the next stopping place, and, boarding the car as it slackened down, he was carried out of their knowledge.

"Very convenient of Mr. Creake," remarked Carrados, with quiet satisfaction. "We will now get the order and go over the house in his absence. It might be useful to have a look at the wire as well."

"It might, Max," acquiesced Mr. Carlyle a little dryly. "But if it is, as it probably is, in Creake's pocket, how do you propose to get it?"

"By going to the post office, Louis."

"Quite so. Have you ever tried to see a copy of a telegram addressed to someone else?"

"I don't think I have ever had occasion yet," admitted Carrados. "Have you?"

"In one or two cases I have perhaps been an accessory to the act. It is generally a matter either of extreme delicacy or considerable expenditure."

"Then for Hollyer's sake we will hope for the former here." And Mr. Carlyle smiled darkly and hinted that he was content to wait for a friendly revenge.

A little later, having left the car at the beginning of the straggling High Street, the two men called at the village post office. They had already visited the house agent and obtained an order to view Brookbend Cottage, declining with some difficulty the clerk's persistent offer to accompany them. The reason was soon forthcoming. "As a matter of fact," explained the young man, "the present tenant is under *our* notice to leave."

"Unsatisfactory, eh?" said Carrados encouragingly.

"He's a corker," admitted the clerk, responding to the friendly tone. "Fifteen months and not a doit of rent have we had. That's why I should have liked —— "

"We will make every allowance," replied Carrados.

The post office occupied one side of a stationer's shop. It was not without some inward trepidation that Mr. Carlyle found himself committed to the adventure. Carrados, on the other hand, was the personification of bland unconcern.

"You have just sent a telegram to Brookbend Cottage," he said to the young lady behind the brasswork lattice. "We think it may have come inaccurately and should like a repeat." He took out his purse. "What is the fee?"

The request was evidently not a common one. "Oh," said the girl uncertainly, "wait a minute, please." She turned to a pile of telegram duplicates behind the desk and ran a doubtful finger along the upper sheets. "I think this is all right. You want it repeated?"

"Please." Just a tinge of questioning surprise gave point to the courteous tone.

"It will be fourpence. If there is an error the amount will be refunded."

Carrados put down his coin and received his change.

"Will it take long?" he inquired carelessly, as he pulled on his glove.

"You will most likely get it within a quarter of an hour," she replied.

"Now you've done it," commented Mr. Carlyle, as they walked back to their car. "How do you propose to get that telegram, Max?"

"Ask for it," was the laconic explanation.

And, stripping the artifice of any elaboration, he simply asked for it and got it. The car, posted at a convenient bend in the road, gave him a warning note as the telegraph boy approached. Then Carrados took up a convincing attitude with his hand on the gate while Mr. Carlyle lent himself to the semblance of a departing friend. That was the inevitable impression when the boy rode up.

"Creake, Brookbend Cottage?" inquired Carrados, holding out his hand, and without a second thought the boy gave him the envelope and rode away on the assurance that there would be no reply.

"Some day, my friend," remarked Mr. Carlyle, looking nervously towards the unseen house, "your ingenuity will get you into a tight corner."

"Then my ingenuity must get me out again," was the retort. "Let us have our 'view' now. The telegram can wait."

An untidy workwoman took their order and left them standing at the door. Presently a lady whom they both knew to be Mrs. Creake appeared.

"You wish to see over the house?" she said, in a voice that was utterly devoid of any interest. Then, without waiting for a reply, she turned to the nearest door and threw it open.

"This is the drawing-room," she said, standing aside.

They walked into a sparsely furnished, damp-smelling room and made a pretence of looking round, while Mrs. Creake remained silent and aloof.

"The dining-room," she continued, crossing the narrow hall and opening another door.

Mr. Carlyle ventured a genial commonplace in the hope of inducing conversation. The result was not encouraging. Doubtless they would have gone through the house under the same frigid guidance had not Carrados been at fault in a way that Mr. Carlyle had never known him fail before. In crossing the hall he stumbled over a mat and almost fell.

"Pardon my clumsiness," he said to the lady. "I am, unfortunately, quite blind. But," he added, with a smile, to turn off the mishap, "even a blind man must have a house."

The man who had eyes was surprised to see a flood of colour rush into Mrs. Creake's face.

"Blind!" she exclaimed, "oh, I beg your pardon. Why did you not tell me? You might have fallen."

"I generally manage fairly well," he replied. "But, of course, in a strange house —— "

She put her hand on his arm very lightly.

"You must let me guide you, just a little," she said.

The house, without being large, was full of passages and inconvenient turnings. Carrados asked an occasional question and found Mrs. Creake quite amiable without effusion. Mr. Carlyle followed them from room to room in the hope, though scarcely the expectation, of learning something that might be useful.

"This is the last one. It is the largest bedroom," said their guide. Only two of the upper rooms were fully furnished and Mr. Carlyle at once saw, as Carrados knew without seeing, that this was the one which the Creakes occupied.

"A very pleasant outlook," declared Mr. Carlyle.

"Oh, I suppose so," admitted the lady vaguely. The room, in fact, looked over the leafy garden and the road beyond. It had a French window opening onto a small balcony, and to this, under the strange influence that always attracted him to light, Carrados walked.

"I expect that there is a certain amount of repair needed?" he said, after standing there a moment.

"I am afraid there would be," she confessed.

"I ask because there is a sheet of metal on the floor here," he continued. "Now that, in an old house, spells dry rot to the wary observer."

"My husband said that the rain, which comes in a little under the window, was rotting the boards there," she replied. "He put that down recently. I had not noticed anything myself."

It was the first time she had mentioned her husband; Mr. Carlyle pricked up his ears.

"Ah, that is a less serious matter," said Carrados. "May I step out onto the balcony?"

"Oh yes, if you like to." Then, as he appeared to be fumbling at the catch, "Let me open it for you."

But the window was already open, and Carrados, facing the various points of the compass, took in the bearings.

"A sunny, sheltered corner," he remarked. "An ideal spot for a deck chair and a book."

She shrugged her shoulders half contemptuously.

"I dare say," she replied, "but I never use it."

"Sometimes, surely," he persisted mildly. "It would be my favourite retreat. But then —— "

"I was going to say that I had never even been out on it, but that would not be quite true. It has two uses for me, both equally romantic; I occasionally shake a duster from it, and when my husband returns late without his latchkey he wakes me up and I come out here and drop him mine."

Further revelation of Mr. Creake's nocturnal habits was cut off, greatly to Mr. Carlyle's annoyance, by a cough of unmistakable significance from the foot of the stairs. They had heard a trade cart drive up to the gate, a knock at the door, and the heavy-footed woman tramp along the hall.

"Excuse me a minute, please," said Mrs. Creake.

"Louis," said Carrados, in a sharp whisper, the moment they were alone, "stand against the door."

With extreme plausibility Mr. Carlyle began to admire a picture so situated that while he was there it was impossible to open the door more than a few inches. From that position he observed his confederate go through the curious procedure of kneeling down on the bedroom floor and for a full minute pressing his ear to the sheet of metal that had already engaged his attention. Then he rose to his feet, nodded, dusted his trousers, and Mr. Carlyle moved to a less equivocal position.

"What a beautiful rose tree grows up your balcony," remarked Carrados, stepping into the room as Mrs. Creake returned. "I suppose you are very fond of gardening."

"I detest it," she replied.

"But this *Glorie,* so carefully trained —— ?"

"Is it?" she replied. "I think my husband was nailing it up recently." By some strange fatality Carrados's most aimless remarks seemed to involve the absent Mr. Creake. "Do you care to see the garden?"

The garden proved to be extensive and neglected. Behind the house was chiefly orchard. In front, some semblance of order had been kept up; here it was lawn and shrubbery, and the drive they had walked along. Two things interested Carrados: the soil at the foot of the balcony, which he declared on examination to be particularly suitable for roses, and the fine chestnut tree in the corner by the road.

As they walked back to the car Mr. Carlyle lamented that they had learned so little of Creake's movements.

"Perhaps the telegram will tell us something," suggested Carrados. "Read it, Louis."

Mr. Carlyle cut open the envelope, glanced at the enclosure, and in spite of his disappointment could not restrain a chuckle.

"My poor Max," he explained, "you have put yourself to an amount of ingenious trouble for nothing. Creake is evidently taking a few days' holiday and prudently availed himself of the Meteorological Office forecast before going. Listen: 'Immediate prospect for London warm and settled. Further outlook cooler but fine.' Well, well; I did get a pound of tomatoes for *my* fourpence."

"You certainly scored there, Louis," admitted Carrados, with humorous appreciation. "I wonder," he added speculatively, "whether it is Creake's peculiar taste usually to spend his week-end holiday in London."

"Eh?" exclaimed Mr. Carlyle, looking at the words again, "by gad, that's rum, Max. They go to Weston-super-Mare. Why on earth should he want to know about London?"

"I can make a guess, but before we are satisfied I must come here again. Take another look at that kite, Louis. Are there a few yards of string hanging loose from it?"

"Yes, there are."

"Rather thick string — unusually thick for the purpose?"

"Yes; but how do you know?"

As they drove home again Carrados explained, and Mr. Carlyle sat aghast, saying incredulously: "Good God, Max, is it possible?"

An hour later he was satisfied that it was possible. In reply to his inquiry someone in his office telephoned him the information that "they" had left Paddington by the four-thirty for Weston.

It was more than a week after his introduction to Carrados that Lieutenant Hollyer had a summons to present himself at The Turrets again. He found Mr. Carlyle already there and the two friends awaiting his arrival.

"I stayed in all day after hearing from you this morning, Mr. Carrados," he said, shaking hands. "When I got your second message I was all ready to walk straight out of the house. That's how I did it in the time. I hope everything is all right?"

"Excellent," replied Carrados. "You'd better have something before we start. We probably have a long and perhaps an exciting night before us."

"And certainly a wet one," assented the lieutenant. "It was thundering over Mulling way as I came along."

"That is why you are here," said his host. "We are waiting for a certain message before we start, and in the meantime you may as well understand what we expect to happen. As you saw, there is a thunderstorm coming on. The Meteorological Office morning forecast predicted it for the whole of London if the conditions remained. That was why I kept you in readiness. Within an hour it is now inevitable that we shall experience a deluge. Here and there damage will be done to trees and buildings; here and there a person will probably be struck and killed."

"Yes."

"It is Mr. Creake's intention that his wife should be among the victims."

"I don't exactly follow," said Hollyer, looking from one man to the other. "I quite admit that Creake would be immensely relieved if such a thing did happen, but the chance is surely an absurdly remote one."

"Yet unless we intervene it is precisely what a coroner's jury will decide has happened. Do you know whether your brother-in-law has any practical knowledge of electricity, Mr. Hollyer?"

"I cannot say. He was so reserved, and we really knew so little of him —— "

"Yet in 1896 an Austin Creake contributed an article on 'Alternating Currents' to the American *Scientific World*. That would argue a fairly intimate acquaintanceship."

"But do you mean that he is going to direct a flash of lightning?"

"Only into the minds of the doctor who conducts the post mortem, and the coroner. This storm, the opportunity for which he has been waiting for weeks, is merely the cloak to his act. The weapon which he has planned to use — scarcely less powerful than lightning but much more tractable — is the high voltage current of electricity that flows along the tram wire at his gate."

"Oh!" exclaimed Lieutenant Hollyer, as the sudden revelation struck him.

"Some time between eleven o'clock to-night — about the hour when your sister goes to bed — and one-thirty in the morning — the time up to which he can rely on the current — Creake will throw a stone up at the balcony window. Most of his preparation has long been made; it only remains for him to connect up a short length to the window handle and a longer one at the other end to tap the live wire. That done, he will wake his wife in the way I have said. The moment she moves the catch of the window — and he has care-fully filed its parts to ensure perfect contact — she will be electro-cuted as effectually as if she sat in the executioner's chair in Sing Sing prison."

"But what are we doing here!" exclaimed Hollyer, starting to his feet, pale and horrified. "It is past ten now and anything may happen."

"Quite natural, Mr. Hollyer," said Carrados reassuringly, "but you need have no anxiety. Creake is being watched, the house is being watched, and your sister is as safe as if she slept to-night in Windsor Castle. Be assured that whatever happens he will not be allowed to complete his scheme; but it is desirable to let him impli-cate himself to the fullest limit. Your brother-in-law, Mr. Hollyer, is a man with a peculiar capacity for taking pains."

"He is a damned cold-blooded scoundrel!" exclaimed the young officer fiercely. "When I think of Millicent five years ago —— "

"Well, for that matter, an enlightened nation has decided that electrocution is the most humane way of removing its superfluous citizens," suggested Carrados mildly. "He is certainly an ingenious-minded gentleman. It is his misfortune that in Mr. Carlyle he was fated to be opposed by an even subtler brain —— "

"No, no! Really, Max!" protested the embarrassed gentleman.

"Mr. Hollyer will be able to judge for himself when I tell him that it was Mr. Carlyle who first drew attention to the significance of the abandoned kite," insisted Carrados firmly. "Then, of course, its object became plain to me — as indeed to anyone. For ten min-utes, perhaps, a wire must be carried from the overhead line to the chestnut tree. Creake has everything in his favour, but it is just within possibility that the driver of an inopportune train might notice the appendage. What of that? Why, for more than a week he has seen a derelict kite with its yards of trailing string hanging in the tree. A very calculating mind, Mr. Hollyer. It would be interesting to know what line of action Mr. Creake has mapped out for himself afterwards. I expect he has half a dozen artistic little touches up his sleeve. Possibly he would merely singe his wife's hair, burn her feet with a red-hot poker, shiver the glass of the French window, and be content with that to let well alone. You see, lightning is so varied in its effects that whatever he did or did not do would be right. He is in the impregnable position of the body showing all the symptoms of death by lightning shock and nothing else but lightning to account for it — a dilated eye, heart contracted in systole, bloodless lungs shrunk to a third the normal weight, and all the rest of it. When he has removed a few outward traces of his work Creake might quite safely 'discover' his dead wife and rush off for the nearest doctor. Or he may have decided to arrange a convincing alibi, and creep away, leaving the discovery to another. We shall never know; he will make no confession."

"I wish it was well over," admitted Hollyer. "I'm not particularly jumpy, but this gives me a touch of the creeps."

"Three more hours at the worst, Lieutenant," said Carrados cheerfully. "Ah-ha, something is coming through now."

He went to the telephone and received a message from one quarter; then made another connection and talked for a few minutes with someone else.

"Everything working smoothly," he remarked between times over his shoulder. "Your sister has gone to bed, Mr. Hollyer."

Then he turned to the house telephone and distributed his orders.

"So we," he concluded, "must get up."

By the time they were ready a large closed motor car was waiting. The lieutenant thought he recognized Parkinson in the well-swathed form beside the driver, but there was no temptation to linger for a second on the steps. Already the stinging rain had lashed the drive into the semblance of a frothy estuary; all round the lightning jagged its course through the incessant tremulous glow of more distant lightning, while the thunder only ceased its muttering to turn at close quarters and crackle viciously.

"One of the few things I regret missing," remarked Carrados tranquilly; "but I hear a good deal of colour in it."

The car slushed its way down to the gate, lurched a little heavily across the dip into the road, and, steadying as it came upon the straight, began to hum contentedly along the deserted highway.

"We are not going direct?" suddenly inquired Hollyer, after they had travelled perhaps half a dozen miles. The night was bewildering enough but he had the sailor's gift for location.

"No; through Hunscott Green and then by a field path to the orchard at the back," replied Carrados. "Keep a sharp lookout for the man with the lantern about here, Harris," he called through the tube.

"Something flashing just ahead, sir," came the reply, and the car slowed down and stopped.

Carrados dropped the near window as a man in glistening waterproof stepped from the shelter of a lich gate and approached.

"Inspector Beedel, sir," said the stranger, looking into the car.

"Quite right, Inspector," said Carrados. "Get in."

"I have a man with me, sir."

"We can find room for him as well."

"We are very wet."

"So shall we all be soon."

The lieutenant changed his seat and the two burly forms took places side by side. In less than five minutes the car stopped again, this time in a grassy country lane.

"Now we have to face it," announced Carrados. "The inspector will show us the way."

The car slid round and disappeared into the night, while Beedel led the party to a stile in the hedge. A couple of fields brought them to the Brookbend boundary. There a figure stood out of the black foliage, exchanged a few words with their guide and piloted them along the shadows of the orchard to the back door of the house.

"You will find a broken pane near the catch of the scullery window," said the blind man.

"Right, sir," replied the inspector. "I have it. Now who goes through?"

"Mr. Hollyer will open the door for us. I'm afraid you must take off your boots and all wet things, Lieutenant. We cannot risk a single spot inside."

They waited until the back door opened, then each one divested himself in a similar manner and passed into the kitchen, where the remains of a fire still burned. The man from the orchard gathered together the discarded garments and disappeared again.

Carrados turned to the lieutenant.

"A rather delicate job for you now, Mr. Hollyer. I want you to go up to your sister, wake her, and get her into another room with as little fuss as possible. Tell her as much as you think fit and let her understand that her very life depends on absolute stillness when she is alone. Don't be unduly hurried, but not a glimmer of a light, please."

Ten minutes passed by the measure of the battered old alarum on the dresser shelf before the young man returned.

"I've had rather a time of it," he reported, with a nervous laugh, "but I think it will be all right now. She is in the spare room."

"Then we will take our places. You and Parkinson come with me to the bedroom. Inspector, you have your own arrangements. Mr. Carlyle will be with you."

They dispersed silently about the house. Hollyer glanced apprehensively at the door of the spare room as they passed it, but within was as quiet as the grave. Their room lay at the other end of the passage.

"You may as well take your place in the bed now, Hollyer," directed Carrados when they were inside and the door closed. "Keep well down among the clothes. Creake has to get up on the balcony, you know, and he will probably peep through the window, but he dare come no farther. Then when he begins to throw up stones slip on this dressing gown of your sister's. I'll tell you what to do after."

The next sixty minutes drew out into the longest hour that the lieutenant had ever known. Occasionally he heard a whisper pass between the two men who stood behind the window curtains, but he could see nothing. Then Carrados threw a guarded remark in his direction.

"He is in the garden now."

Something scraped slightly against the outer wall. But the night was full of wilder sounds, and in the house the furniture and the boards creaked and sprung between the yawling of the wind among the chimneys, the rattle of the thunder, and the pelting of the rain. It was a time to quicken the steadiest pulse, and when the crucial moment came, when a pebble suddenly rang against the pane with a sound that the tense waiting magnified into a shivering crash, Hollyer leapt from the bed on the instant.

"Easy, easy," warned Carrados feelingly. "We will wait for another knock." He passed something across. "Here is a rubber glove. I have cut the wire but you had better put it on. Stand just for a moment at the window, move the catch so that it can blow open a little, and drop immediately. Now."

Another stone had rattled against the glass. For Hollyer to go through his part was the work merely of seconds, and with a few touches Carrados spread the dressing gown to more effective disguise about the extended form. But an unforeseen and in the circumstances rather horrible interval followed, for Creake, in accordance with some detail of his never-revealed plan, continued to shower missile after missile against the panes until even the unimpressionable Parkinson shivered.

"The last act," whispered Carrados, a moment after the throwing had ceased. "He has gone round to the back. Keep as you are. We take cover now." He pressed behind the arras of an extemporized wardrobe, and the spirit of emptiness and desolation seemed once more to reign over the lonely house.

From half a dozen places of concealment ears were straining to catch the first guiding sound. He moved very stealthily, burdened, perhaps, by some strange scruple in the presence of the tragedy that he had not feared to contrive, paused for a moment at the bedroom door, then opened it very quietly, and in the fickle light read the consummation of his hopes.

"At last!" they heard the sharp whisper drawn from his relief. "At last!"

He took another step and two shadows seemed to fall upon him from behind, one on either side. With primitive instinct a cry of terror and surprise escaped him as he made a desperate movement to wrench himself free, and for a short second he almost succeeded in dragging one hand into a pocket. Then his wrists slowly came together and the handcuffs closed.

"I am Inspector Beedel," said the man on his right side. "You are charged with the attempted murder of your wife, Millicent Creake."

"You are mad," retorted the miserable creature, falling into a desperate calmness. "She has been struck by lightning."

"No, you blackguard, she hasn't," wrathfully exclaimed his brother-in-law, jumping up. "Would you like to see her?"

"I also have to warn you," continued the inspector impassively, "that anything you say may be used as evidence against you."

A startled cry from the farther end of the passage arrested their attention.

"Mr. Carrados," called Hollyer, "oh, come at once."

At the open door of the other bedroom stood the lieutenant, his eyes still turned towards something in the room beyond, a little empty bottle in his hand.

"Dead!" he exclaimed tragically, with a sob, "with this beside her. Dead just when she would have been free of the brute."

The blind man passed into the room, sniffed the air, and laid a gentle hand on the pulseless heart.

"Yes," he replied. "That, Hollyer, does not always appeal to the woman, strange to say."

Detective: INSPECTOR BARRACLOUGH

First Appearance: 1915

THE PINK EDGE

by FRANK FROEST AND GEORGE DILNOT

The only INSPECTOR BARRACLOUGH *story in existence, here brought to the American public for the first time. We say modestly: A Queen discovery.*

ROCKWARD'S hand was shaking, and his strong, heavy face was quivering as he finished. Yet he was held by common repute a man completely beyond human emotion — a man whose soul was wrapped in the collection of millions.

"If it is blackmail, why haven't they demanded money in the letter? I'd have paid anything — anything rather than the girl should run the risk. Here's three days gone since she vanished." He was working himself into a petulant anger, unusual for a man of his temperament. "If your people had taken it in hand at the first you might have done something. As it is, I've employed two confounded agencies, and we're not an inch nearer finding her."

"I'm sorry, Mr. Rockward," said Barraclough. "If we had known when you first reported it that your daughter had been abducted we might have handled it. You see," he went on soothingly, "more than ten thousand people are reported missing to the police every year. Very few of them have committed any criminal offence, and in the majority of cases there is some perfectly natural explanation of why they went away. There'd be no end of trouble if the department went chasing after each one. All that can be done is to circulate a description and have men keep their eyes open. But you can rely that now we have something to go upon in Miss Rockward's case she will turn up safe and well in the end."

The millionaire proffered his cigar case.

"Forgive me, Mr. Barraclough. I'm a little overstrained. I know you will do your utmost, and if you want money, call upon me — never mind for how much."

Detective-Inspector Barraclough did not often smoke half-crown Havanas, and he took one now with gratitude. He could understand the millionaire's feeling in the circumstances and make allowances. But in spite of his professional optimism — a detective, like a doctor, is bound to have a surface optimism in dealing with outsiders — it was with a perplexed mind that he made his way back to headquarters to lay the matter before his chief.

"It's a bit out of the ordinary run, sir," he said in the privacy of the superintendent's room. "Rockward's half off his head, and I don't wonder. Miss Elsie Rockward's a young girl — she'll be nineteen next June — and the old man would have spoilt her if he could. That's nothing to the point, though. As a matter of fact, she went out, according to the servants, at eleven o'clock on Monday morning — three days ago. She was believed to have been going to Regent Street. Anyhow, she's not been seen since. This morning Mr. Rockward had a letter. This is what it says." He produced from his pocket, and read: —

"Sir, — This is to inform you that your daughter is safe and well. She will be permitted to return to you unharmed in probably less than a week from to-day, provided you comply with a certain request which may be made to you, and which will cost you nothing. This is not blackmail. You will be wise to remain quiet and not approach the police.

"The letter is unsigned and in palpably disguised handwriting. It was posted at Winchmore Hill, and is postmarked midnight yesterday. That, of course, only means that the one place we're certain the writer will not be found is Winchmore Hill."

"There's more than one kind of blackmail," commented the chief. "In some City deals, for instance, if Rockward could be induced to throw his weight one way or the other it would tip the balance."

"Yes." Barraclough sucked in his lower lip. "Of course, I've not lost sight of that. I suppose I have a free hand."

"Entirely. Go ahead and good luck to you."

Barraclough went away to begin pulling the obvious wires necessary to an investigation. There was the already circulated description of Miss Rockward to be gone over, to see that nothing was omitted from the colour of her eyes to the texture of her stockings. Two photographs of the lady he sent down to have sufficient copies made to supply every divisional section of the Criminal Investigation Department, to say nothing of the more important provincial police forces.

In their little studio on the second storey the staff photographers were busy with the letter that had been sent to Rockward. One of the shirt-sleeved assistants came to tell Barraclough that all was ready. He followed the man up to a windowless room, at one end of which stood a square white screen. The photographer touched a switch and the screen alone remained illuminated. Then he inserted a slide in the magic lantern, and the letter, magnified enormously, leapt into being.

Very carefully Barraclough examined the enlargement, word by word and letter by letter. He had had the thing thrown on the screen, not because he had any definite idea as to what he was to look for, but on the general principle that it should be submitted to the minutest possible examination. At last he came to the final word and drew back.

"Thanks," he said. "It doesn't help much, but that isn't your fault. By the way, have you got the focus right? The edges of the letter seem to be in the shade."

The photographer switched on the light.

"That's not the focus, sir. That's on the letter itself. There's a kind of pinkish shade on the margin."

"Oh yes! I was forgetting," said Barraclough.

The tint around the margin of the letter had not escaped his notice, but it had not impressed him particularly. He went back to his own room and considered the original closely. There was a decided, uneven pink border, shading off irregularly into the cream colour of the paper itself. Moreover, the envelope showed the same peculiarity.

He called Cranley, the first-class detective-sergeant who was his invariable assistant in his investigations, and handed the sheet to him.

"Notepaper good — vellum, very best quality, I should say," commented Cranley. "It's an educated writing, though it's disguised. No fingerprints, sir? That's a pity. I imagine whoever wrote this is not an ordinary crook. Maybe one of Rockward's friends in the City."

"Oh, shut up!" said Barraclough irritably. "It may be the butler of one of Rockward's friends, or it may be the Lord Chancellor, but we don't know. You're a good chap, Cranley, but carrying deductions too far will bring you into trouble one day. An anchor tattooed on a man's hand doesn't prove that he is, or has been, a sailor, but it's a mark of identification."

All of which Cranley knew as well as Barraclough. Being a wise man, however, he recognised that he had laid himself open to rebuke, and apologised with a certain degree of humility.

"What we want," went on the inspector, "is something that'll save us guessing. I don't object to guessing when you can't do anything else, but if it's possible to *know*, I prefer that. Who's a good paper manufacturing firm?"

"I'll go and find out," said Cranley.

He went away, and in a little returned with a ponderous directory. He planked it on the table, and with a stubby forefinger turned over the leaves till he came to the trade section.

"There's Rogerfelt's in Upper Thames Street," he said. "They're about the biggest people in the trade."

"Right you are. I'll go along to see them. You'd better stay on tap here till I come back. I may want you."

When Inspector Barraclough emerged from behind the yellow-stained partition which shielded off the sanctum of one of the departmental managers of Rogerfelt's from the common herd, his face betrayed a supreme content. The most hardened campaigner does not seek discomfort. If he can sleep on a bed instead of the bare ground he does so. Equally so a detective does not enjoy being baffled. He prefers to see his way as clearly as possible. He does not climb a fence if he can open a gate.

Barraclough knew that his quest was still far from simple. Nevertheless, he had at last something to go upon, something definite to unravel. He made his way to a public telephone call office and called up Cranley.

"Yes, it's me, Barraclough. I want you to get through to the divisions. Find out if they know of any wrong 'un who's been ill lately, or who's had illness in the place where he's staying — it doesn't matter what for. I can't tell you over the wire. Get on to it as soon as you can, sonny. Get some one to help you if you can. Me? Oh yes, oh yes, I'll be about! I'll either drop in or ring up. I've got a lot of business to do."

He hung up the receiver and wended his way eastwards. It was a warm day, and by the time he had reached the Convent and Garter off the Commercial Road he was glad to turn into the gilded and plated saloon. He ordered a lime juice and soda, and leant against the bar with the air of a man to whom nothing mattered. All the while his eyes were quietly searching the groups of customers.

Presently he beckoned to a group of three, and they greeted him with deference. One would never have guessed from their joyous manner and their anxiety to pay for his drinks — which he would not permit — that they were each mentally checking off any secret exploit of theirs that might have excited the attention of a staff man from Scotland Yard.

Something of the same scene was enacted at Blackfriars, at Islington, Brixton, and half a dozen other districts of London. Barraclough was always genial, willing to buy drinks and talk over affairs. There was nothing of the stern, iron-handed, clumsy officer of police, beloved of the novelist, about him. Had he not strictly confined himself to non-intoxicating drinks it would have been a drunken man who reeled back to headquarters. As it was, disappointment and physical weariness were plain on his face when he dropped into his chair.

"If you offer me a drink, Cranley, I'll hit you," he said. "I'm full up to the lid with lime juice and ginger ale, and ten thousand other poisons. Who says we don't earn our pay?"

"Any luck, sir?" queried Cranley.

Barraclough shook his head.

"Not a ha'p'orth. How about you?"

His subordinate handed him a sheet of paper, which the inspector perused with wrinkled brows. Ultimately he crushed it up and, with a gesture of disgust, threw it into the waste paper basket.

"Not a bit of good," he declared. Then, as Cranley's puzzled gaze met his: "I meant some infectious disease — I ought to have made that clear. Ah, well!" He yawned wearily and drew out his watch. "Feel inclined to make a night of it, Cranley? It's eight o'clock. Let's have a bit of dinner and drop into the Alhambra and forget all about things for an hour."

At ten o'clock he and Cranley had commenced a fresh tour — this time of the supper rooms and restaurants of the West End. Cranley was puzzled — more puzzled than he would have cared to admit. He could have grasped it if they had been seeking some particular crook who could have given definite information. But apparently Barraclough was merely questing around in search of a scent. With the reticence which he sometimes displayed even to his most intimate colleagues, he would vouchsafe nothing beyond that he wanted to find a criminal who had recently been in some house where there was an infectious disease. For the life of him Cranley could not see how an infectious disease could be connected with the threatening letter that had been written to the millionaire.

But everything has an end. A string band was making an undercurrent of melody to the laughter and conversation of hundreds of men and women clustered in twos and threes about little tables under shaded lights, as they descended into the basement of one of the great supper rooms — where no one ever dreamt of taking supper.

"There's Big Billy sitting at the eighth table on your right," said Cranley.

"We'll go and have a talk with Billy," said Barraclough.

He picked his way along the tier of tables and dropped a hand heavily on the shoulder of the fat man who was seated with his back towards them.

Big Billy sprang to his feet with a start, and a liqueur glass tinkled in fragments on the carpet.

"Snakes!" he ejaculated. "Is it you, Mr. Barraclough? You shouldn't do that. You gave me the jumps."

"Sorry, Billy," said the detective penitently. "I'll be more careful another time." He sat down and indicated another chair for Cranley. "How's things? I haven't had a talk with you on business for a long time."

The twinkling little ferret eyes set in the heavy, broad face became a trifle apprehensive. Big Billy did not like the officer's tone.

"Business!" he said, with a laugh that ill concealed his nervousness. "I didn't know that you wanted to talk business with me or I'd have called on you before this."

Barraclough crossed his legs.

"Oh, it isn't exactly business, Billy. We spotted you just now, and we thought we'd like a talk over old times. I'm sure your lady friends will excuse us for ten minutes."

"Right you are. Run away for a little while, kids," said Billy.

"And now what'll you have?" said Barraclough.

"Absinthe will do me," said Billy. And as the detective gave the order: "Now, guv'nor, what's the lay?"

"Oh, nothing much, Billy." Barraclough lay idly back and began to toy with an empty glass. "Seen anything of Dongley Green lately?"

The fat man wrinkled his brows. "Dongley!" he repeated. "Why, Dongley went down at Nottingham for six years three months ago. Didn't you know that?"

"Come to think of it, so he did," said Barraclough. "It had slipped my mind. He always was unlucky, was Dongley. Do you remember that jewel business in Bond Street? You were on top then?"

The reminiscence was apparently not pleasing to Big Billy. He shot a malevolent glance at the detective. "He was a clumsy dog," he growled.

"Wasn't he in with Gwennie Lyne for a time?" queried Barraclough, with the air of one trying to keep up a languishing conversation.

Big Billy settled himself heavily.

"That old hag always seems to slide along, but any one who works with her seems to catch it," he growled. "There was Dongley. Now, poor old Brixton George is in for it. Kid Foster has been staying at her place down at Tooting, and he pretty well died of typhoid or measles or something. I'd like to wring her neck."

Cranley shot a significant glance at his superior, who seemed to be suppressing a yawn. Here was the information that Barraclough had been seeking, and yet it seemed to make little impression on him.

"Ah yes!" he said. "Brixton George! He was committed for trial a week or two back with one of the bank clerks. The Great Southern Bank forgery, wasn't it?"

"That was a neat job," broke in Billy. "Some one's split up a hundred and twenty-odd thousand, and all you get is George and the stool pigeon. That is, unless you've got some one in line." He looked cunningly across the table.

Barraclough smilingly shook his head.

"I'm not handling that case. Well, we won't keep you any longer from your friends. So long!"

He thrust his arm through Cranley's as they got outside, and hurried him with long, quick steps to Trafalgar Square, where they picked up a taxi. "The best piece of luck I've had to-day," insisted the inspector, more than once.

At Great Derby Street the cab halted, and Barraclough hurried into headquarters. When he returned ten minutes later he brought with him a third man, a sloping-shouldered individual with shrewd eyes and a light moustache.

"Three of us ought to be enough even for Gwennie," he said. "I've sent some one to drag Watford out of bed — he's looking after the Great Southern Bank case. But I doubt if we shall want him."

Cranley tugged at his moustache.

"I'm not quite clear what the point is yet, sir," he said.

Barraclough's eyes twinkled and he regarded the other whimsically.

"I'm too old a bird to show my hand until I'm dead sure," he smiled. "I'll tell you all about it sometime — when it's needful for you to know."

The car whizzed on and conversation languished. In half an hour it drew up panting at the corner of one of the neat, respectable streets of villas that fringe Tooting Common. Barraclough laughed as he got out, and cast a glance down the row of tiny front gardens arranged in geometrical designs of calceolarias and geraniums.

"Civil service clerks, small business men, and maiden ladies," he commented. "Wonder what some of the neighbours will say when they learn who Gwennie is. Come on, boys. You'd better wait, driver."

Not a soul did they meet as they sauntered down the dimly-lighted street, scrutinising the numbers on each side. At last Cranley lifted his hand in signal, and his companions joined him outside the gate at which he was standing.

"No. 107, sir," he said.

They advanced up the path and Barraclough plied knocker and bell. In a little a light was switched on at an upper window. They heard footsteps. Then a light sprang up in the hall and the door opened.

A skeleton of a man with deep-sunken eyes and a dressing gown hanging lankly about him stood peering out at them. "Well," he demanded curtly, "what is it?"

Cranley leant nonchalantly against the doorpost so that it was impossible to shut the door. Barraclough, dazzled somewhat by the sudden glare of electric light, wrinkled his brows at the interlocutor.

"That you, Velson?" he said, as he picked out the features of the man. "How's Gwennie?"

"I don't know you," retorted the other. "And my name's not Velson."

Barraclough stepped inside.

"No, very likely not," he admitted coolly. "Shall we cut all that out?"

A sudden blaze of wrath flamed in the dull, sunken eyes of the little man. He withdrew his right hand from beneath the folds of his dressing gown, and the blue barrel of a revolver showed in the electric light.

"No funny business!" he warned them. "You guys can't play it on me."

Cranley leapt swiftly. The revolver crackled noisily as he overbore the little man, and they fell a wriggling heap on the tiles. But Velson stood no chance. In rather less than sixty seconds he was disarmed, pulled to his feet, and handcuffed.

Barraclough picked up the revolver.

"I knew you were a gun man, Velson," he observed quietly, "but I didn't think you were a fool. You wouldn't have pulled out the weapon unless you were mighty frightened that something was going to happen."

"You go to blazes!" said the prisoner sulkily.

"All right." The inspector added the formal warning. "No need to tell you we're police officers. Anything you say may be used as evidence, you know. You look after him, Conder. Take him into the dining room. Cranley, you'd better stay at the door."

There were movements upstairs, the shuffling of footsteps, the sound of voices. Then the authoritative tone of a woman could be heard apparently ordering the frightened servants to bed.

As Barraclough reached the foot of the stairs the woman descended, dignified and self-possessed. She was somewhere about fifty years of age, not uncomely — indeed, at one time she must have been possessed of striking beauty. Her face showed no sign of perturbation. She smiled sweetly at Barraclough.

"Good morning, Gwennie!" he said urbanely. "It's a pity to wake you up. Suppose you know what we've come about."

The smile persisted.

"Good morning, Mr. Barraclough! I see it's gone one, so it is good morning!"

If Barraclough had hoped to surprise any admission out of her, he was disappointed.

"Is there any one else in the house?" he asked.

She shook her head.

"Only the two maidservants. But you won't take my word for it, I know. You'll search anyway."

"That's so. You're a sensible woman. Come on.'

He half led, half pulled her into the dining room, where Conder and the other prisoner were seated. She took a chair with composure.

"You've overdone it this time, Mr. Barraclough," she said. "What are you pulling us for?"

Barraclough shrugged his shoulders.

"You'll learn that a little later on," he said. In point of fact, he was still uncertain himself as to what the charge might be. "Meanwhile, if you will tell us where Miss Rockward is, it may save trouble."

She elevated her eyebrows.

"Miss Rockward! Who is she?"

The detective turned abruptly away.

"I'm going to search the house," he said.

He went through all the twelve rooms that composed the villa to make certain that Gwennie was speaking the truth when she said that there was no one else in the place but the maidservants.

From the two servants, all in a flutter by the unexpected raid, he

extracted little. Mrs. Frankton — which was the name by which
they knew Gwennie — had employed them for about six weeks —
that was since she had taken the house. They understood that she
was going to conduct it as a boarding house. There had been only
two boarders so far — Mr. Green (Barraclough understood that
Velson was meant) and a Mr. Shilworth. Mr. Shilworth was a
commercial traveller. He was now away on business — had been
away for four days.

Here was food for thought. Miss Rockward had been missing
for three days. Barraclough shot a question at the more intelligent
and less flustered of the two girls. Yes, Mr. Shilworth had been
away before — sometimes for one day, never more than two. He
was a middle-aged man with a scar on the right temple, had a
pointed beard, slightly auburn, and light hair, two-coloured.

Barraclough got them to point out the rooms which had been
occupied by Gwennie herself, by "Green," and by "Shilworth." It
was in the drawer of a writing table in the apartment of the commercial traveller that he came across what he wanted. He descended
to the dining room and addressed the two prisoners.

"See here, you two people. You know as well as I do that I've no
right to question you, but I may as well tell you that I'm not on
the bluff. I've got evidence that you were concerned in the abduction of Miss Rockward, and I know *why*. You can't do any good
by holding her up any longer. We're bound to find her — and Kid
Foster. Now, where is she?"

"You're a wise guy," sneered Velson.

"Shut up," ordered Gwennie imperatively, and the little man relapsed into scowling silence. She fixed an appraising gaze on Barraclough. "You're a gentleman, Mr. Barraclough," she said. "Will you
let up on us if we put you on the line?"

"I can't make bargains, I'm afraid," said Barraclough.

Gwennie placidly crossed her arms.

"Then you'll have to work out your own business," she observed.

Detective-Inspector Watford faced Detective-Inspector Barra-
clough as they sat in two of Gwennie's softly cushioned armchairs.
Gwennie and Velson were safely on their way by taxicab to King
Street Police Station, and a more minute search of the house than

Barraclough had been able to make was being systematically conducted by the three men Watford had brought with him.

The latter tapped the bowl of an empty pipe thoughtfully upon the heel of his boot.

"I wish I was sure you hadn't dragged me out of bed on a wild-goose chase," he observed. "It seems to me like a dead end. We can't prove that they had anything to do with the Great Southern Bank business, and that's my funeral. You may feel sure about the abduction, but you haven't got the lady. I'm not quite comfortable. I own it freely."

Barraclough stood up.

"Of all the infernal gratitude! Why, man, it's as clear as crystal! Here's this forgery committed. You suspect one of the bank clerks and keep young Elsleigh under observation. You find him colloquing with Brixton George, and, like a sensible man, you send 'em both down. They're both as tight as oysters, and there's a hundred thousand of the best stowed away somewhere that you can't lay your finger on."

"Well?" said Watford dryly.

"Well, it stands to reason that there's something behind it. They've briefed Luton, K.C., to defend them at the trial. Somebody's finding the money, and that somebody has got the hundred thousand stowed away in an old stocking. Now, you told me the other day that the defence intend to apply for an adjournment to the next sessions when the case comes up at the Old Bailey."

"Well?" repeated Watford.

"There'll be an application for bail," went on Barraclough. "The rest of the gang know Brixton George. They've got to get him out if they want him to save their own skins. He would talk too much if they deserted him. That's what Luton is for — to get bail — and then George could slip the country. Now the judge is bound to want a person of reputation as well as financial standing for bail — a man like Rockward, for instance."

His colleague moved till he was upright in his chair.

"I see your theory. Miss Rockward has been abducted to force Rockward to go bail for Brixton George."

"That's it. It's certain that Brixton George has been in close touch with Gwennie and Kid Foster. Add it all together, and you couldn't get a likelier gang than Gwennie, the Kid, Velson, and George for a job of this kind. And why did Velson draw a gun?"

A tap at the door and the entry of one of his men prevented Watford from answering. He took from him a couple of letters and three bank pass books, and looked them through. The creases smoothed out of his bronzed face.

"By the great horn spoon, you're right!" he cried. "Here's letters from the Kid. Why on earth Gwennie kept them I don't know. Where did you find them?"

"Stuffed between the mattress and the spring of her bed," replied the other.

"Listen to this," said Watford. He read: " 'You're a real wonder, Gwennie. After you had given the girl the dope in the tea room in Bond Street I got her away to Charing Cross as simply as A B C. She kept up her daze right across the water, though I got a bit of a shock at Boulogne when I thought she was coming round. However, it was a false alarm. We got here safe enough to your friend at Rue Vaillant 24.'

"Then there's the other letter: 'I went round to see the kid this morning. She's a little tartar, but I guess T. will teach her to be good. I am staying at the Bristol, and am feeling a heap better. Have you fixed up about Chelsea yet?' "

"The Bristol!" remarked Barraclough. "That's going some. I suspect the Kid will have worse lodgings before long. Will you go out and burn up the wires, or shall I?"

"I'll go," said Watford.

The unravelling of a skein, once the right end of a mystery is found, proceeds rapidly. It was ten o'clock in the morning when Barraclough and his assistants finished ransacking the house at Tooting. A bath and a shave effaced the traces of a sleepless night, and Barraclough made his way to Scotland Yard. He found Watford in his room with a packed bag in one corner.

"Paris?" he asked.

"Yes," replied his friend. "I'm off to fetch the Kid. The business is well weighed up now. Those bank books show that all the money has been paid into the account of Gwennie and her pals, and we shall have no difficulty in proving the case. The Brigade de Sûreté have nobbled Foster and found the girl. She was in a little house cooped up with an old hag named Templeton, who was with Gwennie in a ladies' bank swindling in the States some years ago. Rockward is going over with me. He asked to be remembered to you, and said that if the commissioner approved he would like to hand you over a cheque."

"That so?" said Barraclough wearily. "Good!"

Watford tapped him on the shoulder.

"See here, old man, I'm puzzling how you got on to this in the first place. You might tell."

Barraclough sighed, and dragged the note that had been sent to Rockward out of his pocket.

"See how that's edged with pink?" he said. "That's what got me on to it. Of course, that edging was bound to attract any one's attention. I didn't know whether it was important or not, so I took it to the people most likely to know — a firm of paper merchants. They told me that the paper — technically a cream-tinted vellum — was made of esparto grass, and that aniline sulphate solution would turn it pink. That didn't seem to help much. I asked if anything else would have done it. Then I got my tip. It seemed that sulphur fumes might have done the trick — they had heard of a case where it had happened when a room had been fumigated.

"I bit right on to that. A room would probably be fumigated after some infectious disease, and that was what I had to look for. I had gone right over London before I hit Big Billy and got the straight tip. That's all there was to it."

"Quite simple, my dear Barraclough," grinned Watford. "There's the guv'nor in his room waiting to pat you on the back." He looked at his watch. "Crikey! I'll have to run to catch that train. Good-bye."

"Good-bye," said Barraclough.

THE LONG DINNER

by H. C. BAILEY

H. C. Bailey has written more detective short stories about a single detective than any other author, living or dead. More than Doyle's Holmes stories, which number fifty-six; more than Chesterton's Father Brown stories, which number forty-eight. Not to keep you panting: MR. FORTUNE *appears in eighty-four short stories to date, all of them good, some of them great, and "The Long Dinner" — in our opinion — the very greatest.*

I DISLIKE you," said Mr. Fortune. "Some of the dirtiest linen I've seen." He gazed morosely at the Chief of the Criminal Investigation Department.

"Quite," Lomas agreed. "Dirty fellow. What about those stains?"

"Oh, my dear chap!" Mr. Fortune mourned. "Paint. All sorts of paint. Also food and drink and assorted filth. Why worry me? What did you expect? Human gore?"

"I had no expectations," said Lomas sweetly.

A certain intensity came into Mr. Fortune's blue eyes. "Yes. I hate you," he murmured. "Anything else you wanted to know?"

"A lot of things," Lomas said. "You're not useful, Reginald. I want to know what sort of fellow he was, and what's become of him."

"He was an artist of dark complexion. He painted both in oils and water colours. He lived a coarse and dissolute life, and had expensive tastes. What's become of him, I haven't the slightest idea. I should say he was on the way to the devil. What's it all about? Why this interest in the debauched artist?"

"Because the fellow's vanished," said Lomas. "He is a painter of sorts, as you say. Name — Derry Farquhar. He had a talent and a bit of a success years ago, and he's gone downhill ever since. Not altogether unknown to the police — money under false pretences and that sort of thing — but never any clear case. Ten days ago a woman turned up to give information that Mr. Derry Farquhar was missing. He had some money out of her — a matter of fifty pounds — three months ago. She don't complain of that. She was used to handing him donations — that kind of woman and that kind of man. What worries her is that, since this particular fifty pounds, he's faded out. And it is a queer case. He's lived these ten years in a rat-hole of a flat in Bloomsbury. He's not been seen there for months. That's unlike him. He's never been long away before. A regular London loafer. And his own money — he's got a little income from a trust — has piled up in the bank. August and September dividends untouched. That's absolutely unlike him. Besides that: one night about a fortnight ago — we can't fix the date — somebody was heard in the flat making a good deal of noise. When Bell went to have a look at things, he found the place in a devil of a mess, and a heap of foul linen. So we sent that to you."

"Hoping for proof of bloodshed," Reggie murmured. "Hopeful fellow. Shirts extremely foul, but affordin' no evidence of foul play. Blood is absent. Almost the only substance that is."

"So you don't believe there's anything in the case?"

"My dear chap! Oh, my dear chap." Reggie opened large, plaintive eyes. "Belief is a serious operation. I believe you haven't found anything. That's all. I should say you didn't look."

"Thank you," said Lomas acidly. "Bell raked it all over." He spoke into the telephone, and Superintendent Bell arrived with a fat folder.

"Mr. Fortune thinks you've missed something, Bell," Lomas smiled.

"If there was anything any use, I have," Bell said heavily. "I'll be glad to hear what it is. Here's some photographs of the place, sir. And an inventory."

"You might pick up a bargain, Reginald," said Lomas, while Reggie, with a decent solemnity, perused the inventory and contemplated the photographs.

"Four oil paintings, fifteen water colours. Unframed," he read, and lifted a gaze of innocent enquiry to Bell.

"I'd call 'em clever, myself," said Bell. "Not nice, you know, but very bright and showy. Nudes of ladies, and that sort of thing. I should have thought he could have made a tidy living out of them. But a picture dealer that's seen 'em priced 'em at half a dollar each. Slick rubbish, he called 'em. I'm no hand at art. Anyway — it don't tell us anything."

"I wouldn't say that. No," Reggie murmured. "Builds up the character of Mr. Farquhar for us. Person of no honour, even in his potboilin' art. However. Nothing else in the flat?"

"Some letters — mostly bills and duns. Nothing to show what he was up to. Nothing to work on."

Reggie turned over the correspondence quickly. "Yes. As you say." He stopped at a crumpled, stained card. "Where was this?"

"In a pocket of a dirty old sports coat," Bell said. "It's only a menu. I don't know why he kept it. Some faces drawn on the back. Perhaps he fancied 'em. No accounting for taste. Looks like drawing devils to me."

"Rather diabolical, yes," Reggie murmured. "Conventional devil. Mephistopheles in a flick." The faces were sketched, in pencil, with a few accomplished strokes, but had no distinction: the same face in variations of grin and scowl and leer: a face of black brows, moustache, and pointed beard. "Clever craftsman. Only clever." He turned the card to the menu written on the front. "My only aunt!" he moaned, and, in a hushed voice of awe, read out: —

"Dîner
Artichauts à l'Huile
Pommes de Terre à l'Huile
Porc frais froid aux Cornichons
Langouste Mayonnaise
Canard aux Navets
Omelette Rognons
Filet garni
Fromage à la Crème
Fruits, biscuits"

"Good Gad! Some dinner," Lomas chuckled.

"I don't say I get it all," Bell frowned. "But what's it come to? He did himself well sometime."

"Well!" Reggie groaned. "Oh, my dear chap! Artichokes in oil, cold pork, lobster, duck and turnips — and a kidney omelette and roast beef and trimmings."

"I've got to own it wants a stomach," said Bell gloomily. "What then?"

"Died of indigestion," said Lomas. "Or committed suicide in the pangs. Very natural. Very just. There you are, Bell. Mr. Fortune has solved the case."

"I was taking it seriously myself," Bell glowered at them.

"Oh, my Bell!" Reggie sighed. "So was I." He turned on Lomas. "Incurably flippant mind, your mind. This is the essential fact. Look for Mr. Farquhar in Brittany."

Bell breathed hard. "How do you get to that, sir?"

"No place but a Brittany inn ever served such a dinner."

Bell rubbed his chin. "I see. I don't know Brittany myself, I'm glad to say. I got to own I never met a dinner like it." He looked at Lomas. "That means putting it back on the French."

"Quite," Lomas smiled. "Brilliant thought, Reginald. Would you be surprised to hear that Paris is asking us to look for Mr. Derry Farquhar in England?"

"Well, well." Reggie surveyed him with patient contempt. "Another relevant fact which you didn't mention. Also indicatin' an association of your Mr. Farquhar with France."

"If you like," Lomas shrugged. "But the point is, they are sure he's here. Dubois is coming over to-day. I'm taking him to dine at the club. You'd better join us."

"Oh, no. No," Reggie said quickly. "Dubois will dine with me. You bring him along. Your club dinner would destroy his faith in the English intelligence. If any. And I like Dubois. Pleasant to discuss the case with a serious mind. Good-bye. Half past eight. . . ."

With a superior English smile, Lomas sat back and watched Reggie and Dubois consume that fantasia on pancakes, Crêpes Joan, which Reggie invented as an expression of the way of his wife with her husband. . . .

Dubois wiped his flowing moustaches. "My homage," he said reverently.

By way of a devilled biscuit, they came to another claret. Dubois looked and smelt and tasted, and his eyes returned thanks. "Try it with a medlar," Reggie purred.

"You are right. There is no fruit better with wine."

They engaged upon a ritual of ecstasy while Lomas gave himself a glass of port and lit a cigarette. At that, Reggie gave a reproachful stare. "My only aunt! Forgive him, Dubois. He's mere modern English."

"I pity profoundly," Dubois sighed. "A bleak life. This is a great wine, my friend. Of Pauillac, I think, eh? Of the last century?"

"Quite good, yes," Reggie purred. "Mouton Rothschild 1900."

Dubois's large face beamed. "Aha. Not so bad for poor old Dubois."

They proceeded to a duet on claret. . . .

Lomas became restive. "This unanimity is touching. Now you've embraced each other all over, we might come to business and see if you can keep it up."

Dubois turned to him with a gesture of deprecation. "Pardon, my friend. Have no fear. We agree always. But I will not delay you. The affair is, after all, very simple —— "

"Quite," Lomas smiled. "Tell Fortune. He has his own ideas about it."

"Aha." Dubois's eyebrows went up. "I shall be grateful. Well, I begin, then, with Max Weber. He is what you call a profiteer, but, after all, a good fellow. It is a year ago he married a pretty lady. She was by courtesy an actress, the beautiful Clotilde. One has nothing else against her. They live together very happily in an apartment of luxury. Two weeks ago, they find that some of her jewels, which she had in her bedroom, are gone. Not all that Weber had given her, the most valuable are at the bank, but diamonds worth five hundred thousand francs. Weber comes to the Sûreté and makes a complaint. What do we find? The servants, they have been with Weber many years, they are spoilt, they are careless; but dishonest — I think not. There is no sign of a burglary. But the day before the jewels were missed a man came to the Weber apartment who asked for Madame Weber and was told she was not at home. That was true in fact, but, also, Weber's man did not like his look. A *gouape* of the finest water — that is the description. What you call a blackguard, is it not? The man was shabby but showy; he resembled exactly a loafer in the Quartier Latin, an artist *décavé* — how do you say that?"

"On his uppers. Yes. Still more interesting. But not an identification, Dubois."

"Be patient still. You see — here is a type which might well have known *la belle* Clotilde before she was Madame Weber. Very well. This gentleman, when he was refused at the Weber door, he did not go far away. We have a *concierge* who saw him loitering till the afternoon at least. In the afternoon the Weber servants take their ease. The man went to a café — he admits it — one woman calls on a friend here, another there. What more easy than for the blackguard artist to enter, to take the jewel case, to hop it, as you say."

"We do. Yes."

"Well, then, I begin from a description of Monsieur the Blackguard. It is not so bad. A man who is plump and dark, with little dark whiskers, who has front teeth which stand out, who walks like a bird running, with short steps that go pit-pat. He speaks French well enough, but not like a Frenchman. He wears clothes of orange colour, cut very loose, and a soft black hat of wide brim. Then I find that a man like this got into the night train from the Gare St.-Lazare for Dieppe — that is, you see, to come back to England by the cheap way. Very well. We have worked in the Quartier Latin, we find that a man like this was seen a day or two in some of the cafés. They remember him well, because they knew him ten years ago, when he was a student. They are like that, these old folks of the Quartier — it pays. Then his name was Farquhar, Derek Farquhar, an Englishman." Dubois twirled his moustaches. "So you see, my friend, I dare to trouble Mr. Lomas to find me in England this Farquhar."

"Yes. Method quite sound," Reggie mumbled. "As a method."

"My poor Reginald," Lomas laughed. "What a mournful, reluctant confession! You've hurt him, Dubois. He was quite sure Mr. Farquhar was traversing the wilds of Brittany."

"Aha." Dubois put up his eyebrows, and made a gesture of respect to Reggie. "My dear friend, never I consult you but I find you see farther than I. Tell me then."

"Oh, no. No. Don't see it all," Reggie mumbled, and told him of the menu of the long dinner.

"Without doubt that dinner was served in Brittany," Dubois nodded. "I agree, it is probable he had been there not so long ago.

But what of that? He was a painter, he had studied in France, and Brittany is always full of painters."

"Yes. You're neglectin' part of the evidence. Faces on the back of the menu." He took out his pocket book, and sketched the black-browed, black-bearded countenance. "Like that."

"The devil," said Dubois.

"As you say. Devil of opera and fancy ball. The ordinary Mephistopheles. Associated by your Mr. Farquhar with Brittany."

"My dear Fortune!" Dubois's big face twisted into a quizzical smile. "You are very subtle. Me, I find this is to make too much of little things. After all, drawing devils, it is common sport — you find devils all over our comic papers — a devil and a pretty lady — and he drew pretty ladies often, you say, this Farquhar — and this is a very common devil."

"Yes, rational criticism," Reggie murmured, looking at him with dreamy eyes. "You're very rational, Dubois. However. Any association of the Webers with Brittany?"

"Oh, my friend!" Dubois smiled indulgently. "None at all. And when they go out of Paris, it is to Monte Carlo, to Aix, not to rough it in Brittany, you may be sure. No. You shall forgive me, but I find nothing in your menu to change my mind. I must look for my Farquhar here." He shook his head sadly at Reggie. "I am desolated that you do not agree." He turned to Lomas. "But this is the only way, *hein?*"

"Absolutely. There's no other line at all," said Lomas, with satisfaction. "Don't let Fortune worry you. He lives to see what isn't there. Wonderful imagination."

"My only aunt!" Reggie moaned. "Not me, no. No imagination at all. Only simple faith in facts. You people ignore 'em when they're not rational. Unscientific and superstitious. However. Let's pretend and see what we get. Go your own way."

"One does as one can," Dubois shrugged.

"Quite. Fortune is never content with the possible. We must work it out here. I've put things in train for you. We have a copy of Farquhar's photograph. That's been circulated with description, and there's a general warning out for him and the jewels. We're combing out all his friends and his usual haunts."

" 'So runs my dream, but what am I?' " Reggie murmured. " 'An infant cryin' in the night. An infant cryin' for the light —— ' Well, well. Are we down-hearted? Yes. A little Armagnac would be grateful and comfortin'." He turned the conversation imperatively to the qualities of that liqueur, and Dubois was quick with respectful responses. Lomas relapsed upon Olympian disdain and whisky and soda.

When he took Dubois away, "Fantastic fellow, Fortune, isn't he?" Lomas smiled. "Mind of the first order, but never content to use it."

"An artist, my friend," said Dubois. "A great artist. He feels life. We think about it."

"Damme, you don't believe he's right about this Brittany guess?"

"What do I know?" Dubois shrugged. "It means nothing. Therefore it is nothing for us. However, one must confess, he is disconcerting, your Mr. Fortune. He makes one always doubt."

This, when he heard of it, Reggie considered the greatest compliment which he ever had, except from his wife. He also thinks it deserved. . . .

Some days later he was engaged upon the production in his marionette theatre of the tragedy of *Don Juan,* lyrics by Lord Byron, prose and music by Mr. Fortune, when the telephone called him from a poignant passage on the rejection of his hero by hell.

"Yes, Fortune speaking. 'Between two worlds life hovers like a star.' Perhaps you didn't know that, Lomas. 'How little do we know that which we are.' Discovery of the late Lord Byron. I'm settin' it to music. Departmental ditty for the Criminal Investigation Department. I —— "

"Could you listen for a moment?" said Lomas sweetly. "You might be interested."

"Not likely, no. However. What's worryin' you?"

"Nothing, except sympathy for you, Reginald. I'm afraid you'll suffer. To break it gently, we've traced Farquhar. But not in Brittany, Reginald."

Reggie remained calm. "No. Of course not," he moaned. "You weren't trying. I don't want to hear what you've missed. Takes too long."

A sound of mockery came over the wire. "Are you ever wrong, Reginald? No. It's always the other fellow. But the awkward fact is, Farquhar hadn't gone to Brittany, he'd gone to Westshire. So

that was the only place we could find him. We have our limitations."

"You have. Yes. *C'est brutal, mais ça marche.* You're clumsy, but
you move — sometimes — like the early cars. What has he got to
say for himself?"

"I don't know. We haven't put our hands on him yet. We —
what?"

"Pardon me. It was only emotion. A sob of reverence. Oh, my
Lomas. You found the only place you could find him, so you
haven't found him. The perfect official. No results, but always the
superior person."

"Results quite satisfactory," Lomas snapped. "We had a clear
identification. He's been staying at Lyncombe. He's bolted again.
No doubt found we were on his track. But we shall get him. They're
combing out the district. Bell's gone down with Dubois."

"Splendid. Always shut the stable door when the horse has been
removed. I'll go too. I like watching that operation. Raises my confidence in the police force." . . .

As the moon rose over the sea, Reggie's car drove into Lyncombe.
It is a holiday town of some luxury. The affronts to nature of its
blocks of hotels and twisting roads of villas for the opulent retired
have not yet been able to spoil all the beauty of cliff and cove.

When Reggie saw it, the banal buildings and the headlands were
mingled in moonlight to make a dreamland, and the sea was a black
mystery with a glittering path on it.

He went to the newest hotel, he bathed well and dined badly,
and, as he sat smoking his consolatory pipe on a balcony where the
soft air smelt of chrysanthemums and the sea, Dubois came to him
with Bell.

"Aha." Dubois spoke. "You have not gone to Brittany then, my
friend?"

"No. No. Followin' the higher intelligence. I have a humble
mind. And where have you got to?"

"We have got to the tracks of Farquhar, there is no doubt of
that. What is remarkable, he had registered in his own name at the
hotel, and the people there they recognise his photograph — they
are sure of it. In fact, it is a face to be sure of, a rabbit face."

"The identification's all right," Bell grunted. "The devil of it is, he's gone again, Mr. Fortune. He went in a hurry too. Left all his traps behind, such as they were. The hotel people think he was just bilking them. He'd been a matter of ten days and not paid anything, and his baggage is worth about nothing — a battered old suitcase and some duds fit for the dustbin."

"Oh, Peter!" Reggie moaned. "No, Bell, no. I haven't got to look at his shirts again?"

"I'm not asking you, sir. There's no sort of reason to think there was anything done to him. He just went out and didn't come back. Three days ago. I don't see any light at all. What he was doing here beats me. You can say he was hiding with the swag he got in Paris. But then, why did he register in his own name? Say he was just a silly ass — you do get that kind of amateur thief. But what has he bolted for? He couldn't have had any suspicions we were on to him. We weren't, at the time he faded out."

"But, my friend, you go too fast," said Dubois. "From you, no, he could not have had any alarm. But there is the other end — Paris. It is very possible that a friend in Paris warned him the police were searching for him."

"All right," Bell grunted. "I give you that. Why would he make the hotel people notice him by bolting without paying his bill? Silly again. Sheer silly. He'd got a pot of money, if he did have the jewels, like you say. Going off without paying 'em, just sent them to inform the police quick."

"That is well argued. You have an insight, a power of mind, my friend." Dubois's voice was silky. "But what have we then? It is quite natural that Farquhar should disappear again, it is not natural that he should disappear like this. For me, I confess I do not find myself able to form an idea of Farquhar. That he is the type to rob such a woman as Clotilde, there is evidence enough — he had the knowledge, he had the opportunity. So far, there are a thousand cases like it. But that he should then retire to such a paradise of the bourgeois, that is not like his type at all."

"That's right," said Bell. "No sense in it anyway."

"No. As you say," Reggie murmured. "That struck me. Happy to agree with everybody. We don't know anything about anything."

"*Bigre!* You go a little strong," Dubois rumbled. "Come, there is at least a connection with Clotilde, and her jewels are gone. Be sure of that. Weber is an honest man — except in business. And what, now, is your hypothesis? You said look for him in Brittany. This at least is certain — he had not gone there. What the devil should he have to do with this so correct Lyncombe? As much as with our rough Brittany."

"Yes. Quite obscure. I haven't the slightest idea what he's been doing. However. Are we down-hearted? No. We're in touch with the fundamental problem now. Why does Mr. Farquhar deal with Brittany and Clotilde and Lyncombe? First method of solution clearly indicated. Find out what he did do in Lyncombe. That ought to be an easy one, Bell. He must have been noticed. He'd be conspicuous in this correct place. Good night."

The next day he sat upon the same balcony, spreading the first scone of his tea with clotted cream and blackberry jelly, when the two returned.

"What! Have you not moved since last night?" Dubois made a grimace at him.

"My dear chap! Just walked all along one of the bays. And back. Great big bay. Exercise demanded by impatient and fretful brain. Rest is better. Have a splitter. They're too heavy. But the cream is sound."

Dubois shuddered. "Brr! You are a wonderful animal. Me, I am only human. But Bell has news for you. Tell him, old fellow."

"It's like this," Bell explained. "About a week ago — that's three or four days before he disappeared, we can't fix the date nearer — Farquhar went to call at one of the big houses here. There's no doubt about that. It's rather like the Paris case. He was seen loafing round before and after — as you said, he's the sort of chap to get noticed. The house he went to belongs to an old gentleman — Mr. Lane Hudson. Lived here for years. Very rich, they say. Made his money in South Wales, and came here when he retired. Well, he's eighty or more; he's half paralysed — only gets about his house and grounds in a wheeled chair. I've seen him; I've had a talk with him. His mind's all right. He looks like a mummy, only a bit plumped out. Sort of yellow, leathery face that don't change or move. Sits in his chair looking at nothing, and talks soft and thick. He tells me he never heard of Farquhar: didn't so much as know Farquhar had been to his house: that's quite in order, it's his rule that the

servants tell anybody not known he's not well enough to see people, and I don't blame him. I wouldn't want strangers to come and
look at me if I was like he is. I gave him an idea of the sort of fellow Farquhar was, and watched him pretty close, but he didn't turn
a hair. He just said again he had no knowledge of any such person,
and I believe him. He wasn't interested. He told me the fellow had
no doubt come begging for money; he was much exposed to that
sort of thing — we ought to stop it — and good day Mr. Superintendent. Anyhow, it's certain Farquhar didn't see him. The old butler and the nurse bear that out, and they never heard of Farquhar
before. The butler saw him and turned him away — had a spot
of bother over it, but didn't worry. Like the old man, he says they
do have impudent beggars now and then. So here's another nice old
dead end."

"Yes. As you say. Rather weird, isn't it? The flamboyant debauched Farquhar knockin' at the door — to get to a paralysed old
rich man who never heard of him. I wonder. Curious selection of
people to call on by our Mr. Farquhar. A pretty lady of Paris who's
married money and settled down on it; a rich old Welshman who's
helpless on the edge of the grave. And neither of 'em sees Mr. Farquhar — accordin' to the evidence — neither will admit to knowin'
anything about him. Very odd. Yes." Reggie turned large, melancholy eyes on Dubois. "Takes your fancy, what? The blackguard
artist knockin', knockin', and, upstairs, a mummy of a man helpless
in his chair."

"Name of a name!" Dubois rumbled. "It is fantasy pure. One
sees such things in dreams. This has no more meaning."

"No. Not to us. But it happened. Therefore it had a cause. Mr.
Lane Hudson lives all alone, what — except for servants?"

"That's right, sir," Bell nodded. "He's been a widower this long
time. Only one child — daughter — and there's a grandson, quite a
kid. Daughter's been married twice — first to a chap called Tracy,
now to a Mr. Bernal — son by the first marriage, no other children."

"You have taken pains, Bell," Reggie smiled.

"Well, I got everything I could think of," said Bell, with gloomy
satisfaction. "Not knowing what I wanted. And there's nothing I
do want in what I've got. The Bernals come here fairly regular —
Mr. and Mrs. Bernal, not the child — they've been staying with the

old man just now. Usual autumn visit. They were there when Farquhar called, and after — didn't go away till last Wednesday; that's
before Farquhar disappeared, you see, the day before. Farquhar
didn't ask for the Bernals, and they didn't see him at all, the servants say. So there you are. The Bernals don't link up anyway. That
peters out, like everything else."

"Yes. Taken a lot of pains," Reggie murmured.

"What would you have?" Dubois shrugged. "To amass useless
knowledge — it is our only method; one is condemned to it. Ours
is a slow trade, my friend. We gather facts and facts and facts, and
so, if we are lucky, eliminate ninety-nine of the hundred and use,
at last, one."

"Yes. As you say," Reggie mumbled. "Where do the Bernals live,
Bell?"

"In France, sir," said Bell, and Reggie opened his eyes.

"Aha!" Dubois made a grimace, and pointed a broad finger at
him. "There, my friend. The one grand fact, is it not? In France!
And Brittany is in France! But alas, my dear Fortune, they do not
live in Brittany! Far from it. They live in the South, near Cannes;
they have lived there — what do I know? — since they were married, *hein?*" He turned to Bell.

"That's right," Bell grunted. "Lady set up house there with her
first husband. He had to live in the South of France — gassed in the
war."

"You see?" Dubois smiled. "It is still the useless knowledge. And
your vision of Brittany, my friend, it has no substance still."

"I wonder," Reggie mumbled, and sank deep in his chair. . . .

He is, even without hope, conscientious. That night he examined
another set of Farquhar's dirty linen, but neither in that nor the
rest of the worthless luggage found any information. Prodded by
him, Bell enquired of the Hudson household where the Bernals were
to be found, but could obtain only the address of their Cannes villa,
for they were reported to be going back by car. Dubois was persuaded to telegraph Cannes and received the reply that the Bernal
villa was shut up; monsieur and madame were away motoring, and
their boy at school — what school nobody knew.

"Then what?" Dubois summed up. "Nothing to do."

"Not to-night, no," Reggie yawned. "I'm going to bed."

"To dream of Brittany, *hein?*"

"I never dream," said Reggie, with indignation. . . .

But he was waked in the night. He rubbed his eyes and looked up to see Dubois's large face above him. "Oh, my hat," he moaned. "What is it? Why won't it wait?"

"Courage, my friend. They have found him. At least, they think so. Some fishermen, going out yesterday evening, they found a body on the rocks at what they call Granny's Cove. Come. The brave Bell wants you to see."

"Bless him," Reggie groaned, and rolled out of bed. "What is life that one should seek it? I ask you." And, slipping clothes on him, swiftly he crooned, " 'Three fishers went sailin' out into the west, out into the west, as the sun went down' — and incredibly caught the incredible Farquhar."

"You are right," Dubois nodded. "Nothing clear, nothing sure. The more it changes, the more it is the same, this accursed case. It has no shape; there is no reason in it."

"Structure not yet determined. No," Reggie mumbled, parting his hair, for he will always be neat. "We're not bein' very clever. Ought to be able to describe the whole thing from available evidence of its existence. Same like inferrin' the age of reptiles from a fossil or two — 'dragons of the prime, tearin' each other in the slime, were mellow music unto him.' Yes. The struggle for life of the reptiles might be mellow music compared to the diversions of Mr. Farquhar and friends. Progressive world, Dubois."

"Name of a dog!" Dubois exclaimed. "When you are philosophic, my stomach turns over. What is in your mind?"

"Feelin' of impotence. Very uncomfortable," Reggie moaned, and muffled himself to the chin and made haste out.

In the mortuary Bell introduced them to a body covered by a sheet. "Here you are, sir." He stepped aside. "The clothes seem to be Farquhar's clothes all right. Sort of orange tweed and green flannel trousers. But I don't know about the man."

Reggie drew back the sheet from what was left of a face.

"*Saprelotte!*" Dubois rumbled. "The fish have bitten."

"Well, I leave it to you," said Bell thickly. . . .

Under a sunlit breeze the sea was dancing bright, the mists flying inland from the valleys to the dim bank of the moor, when Reggie came out again.

He drove back to his hotel, and shaved and bathed and rang up the police station. Bell and Dubois arrived to find him in his room, eating with appetite grilled ham and buttered eggs.

"My envy; all my envy." Dubois pulled a face. "This is greatness. The English genius at the highest."

"Oh, no. No," Reggie protested. "Natural man. Well. The corpse is that of Mr. Farquhar as per invoice. Prominent teeth not impaired by activities of the lobsters. Some other contours still visible. The marmalade — thanks. Yes. Hair, colourin', size, and so forth agree. Mr. Farquhar's been in the sea three or four days. Correspondin' with date of disappearance. Cause of death, drowning. Severe contusions on head and body, inflicted before death. Possibly by blows, possibly by fall. Might have fallen from cliff; might have been dashed on rocks by sea. No certainty to be obtained. That's the medical evidence."

"You are talking!" Dubois exclaimed. "Flute! There we are again. Whatever arrives, it will mean nothing for us. Here is murder, suicide, accident — what you please."

"I wonder." Reggie began to peel an apple. "Anything in his pockets, Bell?"

"A lot of money, sir. Nothing else. The notes are all sodden, but it's a good wad, and some are fifties. Might be five or six hundred pounds. So he wasn't robbed."

"And then?" said Dubois. "It is not enough for all the jewels of Clotilde, but it is something in hand. Will you tell me what the devil he was doing at the door of this paralysed millionaire? It means nothing, none of it."

"No. Still amassin' useless knowledge, as you were sayin'." Reggie gazed at Dubois with dreamy eyes. "I should say that's what we came here for. Don't seem the right place, does it? However. As we are here, let's try and get a little more before departure. Usin' the local talent. Bell — your fishermen — have they got any idea where a fellow would tumble into the sea to be washed up into Granny's Cove?"

"Ah." Bell was pleased. "I have been asking about that, sir. Supposing he got in from the land, they think it would be somewhere round by Shag Nose. That's a bit o' cliff west o' the town. I'm having men search round and enquire. But the scent's pretty cold by now."

"Yes. As you say," Reggie sighed. His eyes grew large and melancholy. "Is it far?" he said, in a voice of fear.

"Matter of a mile or two."

"Oh, my Bell," Reggie groaned. He pushed back his chair. He rose stiffly. "Come on."

Shag Nose is a headland from which dark cliffs fall sheer. Below them stretches seaward a ridge of rocks, which stand bare some way out at low tide, and in the flood make a turmoil of eddies and broken water.

The top of the headland is a flat of springy turf, in which are many tufts of thrift and cushions of stunted gorse.

"Brr. It is bleak," Dubois complained. "Will you tell me why Farquhar should come here? He was not — how do you say? — a man for the great open spaces."

"Know the answer, don't you?" Reggie mumbled.

"Perfectly. He came to meet somebody in secret who desired to make an end of him. Very well. But who then? Not the paralysed one. Not the son-in-law either. It is in evidence that the son-in-law was gone before Farquhar disappeared."

"That's right. I verified that," Bell grunted. "Bernal and his wife left the night before."

"There we are again," Dubois shrugged. "Nothing means anything. For certain, it is not a perfect alibi. They went by car; they could come back and not be seen. But it is an alibi that will stand unless you have luck, which you have not yet, my dear Bell, God knows."

"Not an easy case. No," Reggie murmured. "However. Possibilities not yet examined. Lyncombe's on the coast. Had you noticed that? I wonder if any little boat from France came in while Farquhar was still alive."

Dubois laughed. Dubois clapped him on the shoulder. "Magnificent! How you are resolute, my friend. Always the great idea! A boat from Brittany, *hein*? That would solve everything. The good

Farquhar was so kind as to come here and meet it and be killed by the brave Bretons. And the paralysed millionaire, he was merely a diversion to pass the time."

"Yes. We are not amused," Reggie moaned. "You're in such a hurry. Bell — what's the local talent say about the tide? When was high water on the night Farquhar disappeared?"

"Not till the early morning, sir. Tide was going out from about three in the afternoon onwards."

"I see. At dusk and after, that reef o' rocks would be comin' out of the water. Assumin' he went over the cliff in the dark or twilight, he'd fall on the rocks."

"That's right. Of course he might bounce into the sea. But I've got a man or two down there searching the shore and the cliffside."

"Good man." Reggie smiled, and wandered away to the cliff edge.

"Yes. It is most correct," Dubois shrugged. "I should do it, I avow. But also I should expect nothing, nothing. After all, we are late. We arrive late at everything."

Reggie turned and stared at him. "I know. That's what I'm afraid of," he mumbled.

He wandered to and fro about the ground near the cliff edge, and found nothing which satisfied him, and at last lay down on his stomach where a jutting of the headland gave him a view of the cliffs on either side.

Two men scrambled about over the rocks below, scanning the cliff face, prying into every crevice they could reach . . . one of them vanished under an overhanging ledge, appeared again, working round it, was lost in a cleft . . . when he came out he had something in his hand.

"Name of a pipe!" Dubois rumbled. "Is it possible we have luck at last?"

"No." Reggie stood up. "Won't be luck, whatever it is. Reward of virtue. Bell's infinite capacity for takin' pains." . . .

A breathless policeman reached the top of the cliff, and held out a sodden book. "That's the only perishing thing there is down there, sir," he panted. "Not a trace of nothing else."

Bell gave it to Reggie. It was a sketchbook of the size to slide into a man's pocket. The first leaf bore, in a flamboyant scrawl, the name Derek Farquhar.

"Ah. That fixes it, then," said Bell. "He did go over this cliff, and his sketchbook came out of his pocket as he bounced on the ledges."

"Very well," Dubois shrugged. "We know now as much as we guessed. Which means nothing."

Reggie sat down and began to separate the book's wet pages.

Farquhar had drawn, in pencil, notes rather than sketches at first, scraps of face and figure and scene which took his unholy fancy, a drunken girl, a nasty stage dance, variations of impropriety. Then came some parades of men and women bathing, not less unpleasant, but more studied. "Aha! Here is something seen at least," said Dubois.

"Yes, I think so," Reggie murmured, and turned the page.

The next sketch showed children dancing — small boys and girls. Some touch of cruelty was in the drawing — they were made to look ungainly — but it had power; it gave them an intensity of frail life which was at once pathetic and grotesque. They danced round a giant statue — a block in which the shape of a woman was burlesqued, hideously fat and thin, with a flat, foolish face. There were no clothes on it, but rough lines which might be girdle and necklace.

"What the devil!" Dubois exclaimed. "This is an oddity. He discovers he had a talent, the animal."

Reggie did not answer. For a moment more he gazed at the children and the statue, and he shivered, then he turned the other pages of the book. There were some notes of faces, then several satires on the respectability of Lyncombe — the sea front, with nymphs in Bath chairs propelled by satyrs and satyrs propelled by nymphs. He turned back to the dancing children and the giant female statue, and stared at it, and his round face was pale. "Yes. Farquhar had talent," he said. "Played the devil with it all his life. And yet it works on the other side. What's the quickest way to Brittany? London and then Paris by air. Come on."

Dubois swore by a paper bag and caught him up. "What, then? How do you find your Brittany again in this?"

"The statue," Reggie snapped. "Sort of statue you see in Brittany. Nowhere else. He didn't invent that out of his dirty mind. He'd seen it. It meant something to him. I should say he'd seen the children too."

"You go beyond me," said Dubois. "Well, it is not the first time. A statue of Brittany, eh? You mean the old things they have among the standing stones and the menhirs and dolmens. A primitive goddess. The devil! I do not see our Farquhar interested in antiquities. But it is the more striking that he studied her. I give you that. And the children? I will swear he was not a lover of children."

"No. He wasn't. That came out in the drawing. Not a nice man. It pleased him to think of children dancin' round the barbarous female."

"I believe you," said Dubois. "The devil was in that drawing."

"Yes. Devilish feelin'. Yes. And yet it's going to help. Because the degenerate fellow had talent. Not wholly a bad world."

"Optimist. Be it so. But what can you make the drawing mean, then?"

"I haven't the slightest idea," Reggie mumbled. "Place of child life in the career of the late Farquhar very obscure. Only trace yet discovered, the Bernals have a child. No inference justified. I'm going to Brittany. I'm goin' to look for traces round that statue. And meanwhile — Bell has to find out if a French boat has been in to Lyncombe — you'd better set your people findin' the Bernals — with child. Have the Webers got a child?"

"Ah, no." Dubois laughed. "The beautiful Clotilde, she is not that type."

"Pity. However. You might let me have a look at the Webers as I go through Paris."

"With all my heart," said Dubois. "You understand, my friend, you command me. I see nothing, nothing at all, but I put myself in your hand." He made a grimace. "In fact there is nothing else to do. It is an affair for inspiration. I never had any."

"Nor me, no." Reggie was indignant. "My only aunt! Inspired! I am not! I believe in evidence. That's all. You experts are so superior." . . .

Next morning they sat in the *salon* of the Webers. It was overwhelming with the worst magnificence of the Second Empire — mirrors and gilding, marble and malachite and lapis lazuli. But the Webers, entering affectionately arm in arm, were only magnificent in their opulent proportions. Clotilde, a dark full-blown creature, had nothing more than powder on her face, no jewels but a string of pearls, and the exuberance of her shape was modified by a simple black dress. Weber's clumsy bulk was all in black too.

They welcomed Dubois with open arms; they talked together. What had he to tell them? They had heard that the cursed Farquhar had been discovered dead in England — it was staggering; had anything been found of the jewels?

Nothing, in effect, Dubois told them. Only, Farquhar had more money than such an animal ought to have. It was a pity.

Clotilde threw up her hands. Weber scolded.

Dubois regretted — but what to do? They must admit one had been quick, very quick, to trace Farquhar. They would certainly compliment his *confrère* from England — that produced perfunctory bows. What the English police asked — and they were right — it was could one learn anything of who had worked with Farquhar, why had he come to the apartment Weber?

The Webers were contemptuous. What use to ask such a question? One had not an acquaintance with thieves. As to why he came, why he picked out them to rob — a thief must go where there was something to steal — and they — well, one was known a little. Weber smirked at his wife, and she smiled at him.

"For sure. Everyone knows monsieur — and madame." Dubois bowed. "But I seek something more."

They stormed. It was not to be supposed they should know anything of such a down-at-heel.

"Oh, no. No," said Reggie quickly. "But in the world of business" — he looked at Weber — "in the world of the theatre" — he looked at Clotilde — "the fellow might have crossed your path, what?"

That was soothing. They agreed the thing was possible. How could one tell? They chattered of the detrimentals they remembered — to no purpose.

Under plaintive looks from Reggie, Dubois broke that off with a brusque departure. When they were outside — "Well, you have met them!" Dubois shrugged. "And if they are anything which is not ordinary I did not see it."

Reggie gazed at him with round reproachful eyes. "They were in mourning," he moaned. "You never told me that. Were they in mourning when you saw 'em before?"

"But yes," Dubois frowned. "Yes, certainly. What is the matter? Did you think they had put on mourning for the animal Farquhar?"

"My dear chap! Oh, my dear chap," Reggie sighed. "Find out why they are in mourning. Quietly, quite quietly. Good-bye. Meet you at the station." . . .

The night express to Nantes and Quimper drew out of Paris. They ate a grim and taciturn dinner. They went back to the sleeping car and shut themselves in Reggie's compartment. "Well, I have done my work," said Dubois. "The Webers are in mourning for their nephew. A child of ten, whom Weber would have made his heir — his sister's son."

"A child," Reggie murmured. "How did he die?"

"It was not in Brittany, my friend," Dubois grinned. "Besides it is not mysterious. He died at Fontainebleau, in August, of diphtheria. They had the best doctors of Paris. There you are again. It means nothing."

"I wonder," Reggie mumbled. "Any news of the Bernals?"

"It appears they have passed through Touraine. If it is they, there was no child with them. Have no fear, they are watched for. One does not disappear in France."

"You think not? Well, well. Remains the Bernal child. Not yet known to be dead. Of diphtheria or otherwise! I did a job o' work too. Talked to old Huet at the Institut. You know — the prehistoric man. He says Farquhar's goddess is the Woman of Sarn. Recognised her at once. She stands on about the last western hill in France. Weird sort o' place, Huet says. And he can't imagine why Farquhar thought of children dancin' round her. The people are taught she's of the devil."

"But you go on to see her?" Dubois made a grimace. "The fixed idea."

"No. Rational inference. Farquhar thought of her with children. And there's a child dead — and another child we can't find — belongin' to the people linked with Farquhar. I go on."

"To the land's end — to the end of the world — and beyond. For your faith in yourself. My dear Fortune, you are sublime. Well, I follow you. Poor old Dubois. Sancho Panza to your Don Quixote, *hein?*" . . .

They came out of the train to a morning of soft sunshine and mellow ocean air. The twin spires of Quimper rose bright among

their minarets, its sister rivers gleamed, and the wooded hill beyond glowed bronze. Dubois bustled away from breakfast to see
officials. "Don Quixote is a law to himself, but Sancho had better
be correct, my friend."

"Yes, rather," Reggie mumbled, from a mouth full of honey.
"Conciliate the authorities. Liable to want 'em."

"Always the optimist, my Quixote."

"No. No. Only careful. Don't tell 'em anything."

"Name of a name!" Dubois exploded. "That is necessary, that
warning. I have so much to tell!"

In an hour, they were driving away from Quimper, up over high
moorland of heather and gorse and down again to a golden bay
and a fishing village of many boats, then on westward, with
glimpses of sea on either hand. There was never a tree, only, about
the stone walls which divided the waves of bare land into a draught-
board of little fields, thick growth of bramble and gorse. Beyond
the next village, with its deep inlet of a harbour, the fields merged
into moor again, and here and there rose giant stones, in line, in
circle, and solitary.

"Brrr," Dubois rumbled. "Tombs or temples, what you please, it
was a gaunt religion which put them up here on this windy end
of the earth."

The car stopped, the driver turned in his seat and pointed, and
said he could drive no nearer, but that was the Woman of Sarn.
"She is lonely," Dubois shrugged. "There is no village near, my
lad?"

"There is Sarn." The driver pointed towards the southern sea.
"But it is nothing."

Reggie plodded away through the heather. "Well, this is hopeful,
is it not?" Dubois caught him up. "When we find her, what have
we found? An idol in the desert. But you will go on to the end,
my Quixote. Forward, then."

They came to the statue, and stood, for its crude head rose high
above theirs, looking up at it. "And we have found it, one must
avow," Dubois shrugged. "This is the lady Farquhar drew, devil
a doubt. But, *saperlipopette,* she is worse here than on paper. She
is real; she is a brute — all that there is of the beast in woman,
emerging from the shapeless earth."

"Inhuman and horrid human, yes," Reggie murmured. "Cruelty

of life. Yes. He knew about that, the fellow who made her, poor beggar. So did Farquhar."

"I believe it! But do you ask me to believe little children come and dance round this horror? Ah, no!"

"Oh, no. No. That never happened. Not in our time. Point of interest is, Farquhar thought it fittin' they should. Very interestin' point." Reggie gave another look at the statue, and walked on towards the highest point of the moor.

From that he could see the tiny village of Sarn, huddled in a cove, the line of dark cliff, a long rampart against the Atlantic. Below the cliff top he made out a white house, of some size, which seemed to stand alone.

His face had a dreamy placidity as he came back to Dubois. "Well, well. Not altogether desert," he murmured. "Something quite residential over there. Let's wander."

They struck southward towards the sea. As they approached the white house, they saw that it was of modern pattern — concrete, in simple proportions, with more window than wall. Its site was well chosen, in a little hollow beneath the highest of the cliff, sheltered yet high enough for a far prospect, taking all the southern sun.

"Of the new ugliness, eh?" said Dubois, whose taste is for elaboration in all things. "All the last fads. It should be a sanatorium, not a house."

"One of the possibilities, yes." Reggie went on fast.

They came close above the house. It stood in a large walled enclosure, within which was a trim garden, but most of the space was taken by a paved yard with a roofed platform like a bandstand in the middle. Reggie stood still and surveyed it. Not a creature was to be seen. The acreage of window blazed blank and curtainless.

"The band is not playing." Dubois made a grimace. "It is not the season."

Reggie did not answer. His eyes puckered to stare at a window within which the sun glinted on something of brass. He made a little inarticulate sound, and walked on, keeping above the house. But they saw no one, no sign of life, till they were close to the cliff edge.

Then a cove opened below them in a gleaming stretch of white shell sand, and on the sand children were playing: some of them at a happy-go-lucky game of rounders, some building castles, some tumbling over each other like puppies. On a rock sat, in placid guard over them, a man who had the black pointed beard, the heavy black brows, which Farquhar had sketched on his menu. But these Mephistophelean decorations did not display the leer and sneer of Farquhar's drawing. The owner watched the children with a grave and kindly attention which seemed to be interested in everyone. He called to them cheerily, and had gay answers. He laughed jovial satisfaction at their laughter.

Reggie took Dubois's arm and walked him away. "Ah, my poor friend!" Dubois rumbled chuckles. "There we are at last. We arrive. We have the brute goddess, we have the children, we have even the devil of our Farquhar. And behold! he is a genial paternal soul, and all the children love him. Oh, my poor friend!"

"Yes. Funny, isn't it?" Reggie snapped. "Dam' funny. Did you say the end? Then God forgive us. Which He wouldn't. He would not!"

Dubois gave him a queer look — something of derision, something of awe, and a good deal of doubt. "When you talk like that" — a shrug, a wave of the hands — "it is outside reason, is it not? An inspiration of faith."

"Faith that the world is reasonable. That's all," Reggie snarled. "Come on."

"And where?"

"Down to this village."

The huddled cottages of Sarn were already in sight. Then odours, a complex of stale fish and the filth of beast and man, could be smelt. Women clattered in sabots and laboured. Men lounged against the wall above the mess of the beach. A few small and ancient boats lay at anchor in the cove, and one of a larger size, and better condition, which had a motor engine.

They found a dirty *estaminet* and obtained from the landlord a bottle of nameless red wine. He said it was old, it was marvellous, but, being urged to share it, preferred a glass of the apple spirit, Calvados. "Marvellous, it is the word," Dubois grinned. "You are altogether right. Calvados for us also, my friend. It is more humane."

The landlord was slow of speech, and a pessimist. Even with several little glasses of Calvados inside him he would talk only of the hardness of life and the poverty of Sarn and the curse upon the modern sardine. Reggie agreed that life was dear and life was difficult, but, after all, they had still their good boats at Sarn — motor boats indeed. The landlord denied it with gloomy vehemence: motors — not one — only in the *Badebec,* and that was no fishing boat, that one. It was M. David's.

"Is it so?" Reggie yawned, and lit his pipe. He gazed dreamily down the village street to the hideous little church. From that — under a patched umbrella, to keep off the wind, which was high, or the sun, which was grown faint — came a fat and shabby *curé.* "Well, better luck, my friend," Reggie murmured, left Dubois to pay the bill, and wandered away.

He met the *curé* by the church gate. Was it permitted to visit that interesting church? Certainly, it was permitted, but monsieur would find nothing of interest — it was new; it was, alas! a poor place.

The *curé* was right — it was new; it was garish, it was mean. He showed it to Reggie with an affecting simplicity of diffident pride, and Reggie was attentive. Reggie praised the care with which it was kept. "You are kind, sir," the *curé* beamed. "You are just. In fact they are admirably pious, my poor people, but poor — poor."

"You will permit the stranger — " Reggie slipped a note into his hand.

"Ah, monsieur! You are generous. It will be rewarded, please God."

"It is nothing," said Reggie quickly. "Do not think of it." They passed out of the church. "I suppose this is almost the last place in France?"

"Sometimes I think we are forgotten," the *curé* agreed. "Yes, almost the last. Certainly we are all poor folk. There is only M. David, who is sometimes good to us."

"A visitor?" Reggie said.

"Ah, no. He lives here. The Maison des Iles, you know. No? It is a school for young children — a school of luxury. He is a good man, M. David. Sometimes he will take, for almost a nothing, chil-

dren who are weakly, and in a little while he has them as strong
as the best. I have seen miracles. To be sure it is the best air in
the world, here at Sarn. But he is a very good man. He calls his
school 'of the islands' because of the islands out there" — the *curé*
pointed to what looked like a reef of rocks. "My poor people call
them the islands of the blessed. It is not good religion, but they used
to think the souls of the innocent went there. Yes, the Maison des
Iles, his school is. But you should see it, sir. The children are
charming."

"If I had time —— " said Reggie, and said good-bye.

Dubois was at the gate. Dubois took his arm and marched him
off. "My friend, almost thou persuadest me —— " He spoke into
Reggie's ear. "Guess what I have found, will you? That motor
yacht, the yacht of M. David, she was away a week ten days ago.
And M. David on board. You see? It is possible she went over to
England. A guess, yes, a chance, but one must avow, it fits devilish
well, if one can make it fit. A connection with all your fantasy —
M. David over in England when Farquhar was drowned. Is it possible we arrive at last?"

"Yes, it could be. Guess what I've heard. M. David keeps school.
That wasn't a bandstand. Open-air classroom. M. David is a very
good man, and he uses his beautiful school to cure the children of
the poor. He does miracles. The old *curé* has seen 'em."

"The devil!" said Dubois. "That does not fit at all. But a priest
would see miracles. It is his trade."

"Oh, no. No. Not unless they happen," Reggie murmured.

"My friend, you believe more than any man I ever knew," Dubois rumbled. "Come, I must know more of this David. The sooner
we are back at Quimper the better."

"Yes. That is indicated. Quimper and telephone." He checked
a moment, and gazed anguish at Dubois. "Oh, my hat, how I hate
telephones."

Dubois has not that old-fashioned weakness. Dubois, it is beyond
doubt, enjoyed the last hours of that afternoon, shut into privacy
at the post office with its best telephone, stirring up London and
Paris and half France till sweat dripped from his big face and the
veins of his brow dilated into knotted cords.

When he came into Reggie's room at the hotel it was already past dinner time. Reggie lay on his bed, languid from a bath. "My dear old thing," he moaned sympathy. "What a battle! You must have lost pounds."

"So much the better," Dubois chuckled. "And also I have results. Listen. First. I praise the good Bell. He has it that a French boat —cutter rig with motor—was seen by fishermen in the bay off Lyncombe last week. They watched her, because they had suspicions she was poaching their lobsters and crabs, which they unaccountably believe is the habit of our honest French fishermen. She was lying in the bay the night of Tuesday—you see, the night that Farquhar disappeared. In the morning she was gone. They are not sure of the name, but they thought it was *Badboy*. That is near enough to *Badebec, hein?* In fact, myself, I do not understand the name *Badebec*."

"Lady in Rabelais," Reggie murmured. "Rather interestin'. Shows the breadth of M. David's taste."

"Aha. Very well. Here is a good deal for M. David to explain. Second, M. David himself. He is known; there is nothing against him. In fact he is like you, a man of science, a biologist, a doctor. He was brilliant as a student, which was about the same time that Farquhar studied art—and other things—in the Quartier Latin. David had no money. He served in hospitals for children; he set up his school here—a school for delicate children—four years ago. Its record is very good. He has medical inspection by a doctor from Quimper each month. But, third, Weber's nephew was at this school till July. He went home to Paris, they went out to Fontainebleau, and—piff!" Dubois snapped his fingers. "He is dead like that. There is no doubt it was diphtheria. Do you say fulminating diphtheria? Yes, that is it."

"I'd like a medical report," Reggie murmured.

"I have asked for it. However—the doctors are above suspicion, my friend. And now, fourth—the Bernals are found. They are at Dijon. They have been asked what has become of their dear little boy, and, they reply, he is at school in Brittany. At the school of M. David, Maison des Iles, Quimper."

"Yes. He would be. I see."

"Name of a name! I think you have always seen everything."

"Oh, no. No. Don't see it now," Reggie mumbled. "However. We're workin' it out. You've done wonderfully."

"Not so bad." Dubois smiled. "My genius is for action."

"Yes. Splendid. Yes. Mine isn't. I just went and had a look at the museum."

"My dear friend," Dubois condescended. "Why not? After all, the affair is now for me."

"Thanks, yes. Interestin' museum. Found a good man on the local legends there. Told me the Woman of Sarn used to have children sacrificed to her. That'll be what Farquhar had in his nice head. Though M. David is so good to children."

"Aha. It explains, and it does not explain," Dubois said. "In spite of you, M. David remains an enigma. Let poor old Dubois try. I have all these people under observation — the Webers, the Bernals — they cannot escape me now. And there are good men gone out to watch over M. David in his Maison des Iles. To-morrow we will go and talk to him, *hein?*"

"Pleasure," Reggie murmured. "You'd better go and have a bath now. You want it. And I want my dinner." . . .

When they drove out to Sarn in the morning a second car followed them. In a blaze of hot sunshine they started, but they had not gone far before a mist of rain spread in from the sea, and by the time they reached the Maison des Iles they seemed to be in the clouds.

"An omen, *hein?*" Dubois made a grimace. "At least it may be inconvenient — if he is alarmed; if he wishes to play tricks. We have no luck in this affair. But courage, my friend. Poor old Dubois, he is not without resource."

Their car entered the walled enclosure of the Maison des Iles, the second stopped outside. When Dubois sent in his card to M. David, they were shown to a pleasant waiting room, and had not long to wait.

David was dressed with a careless neatness. He was well-groomed and perfectly at ease. His full red lips smiled; his dark eyes quizzed them. "What a misery of a morning you have found, gentlemen. I apologise for my ocean. M. Dubois?" He made a bow.

"Of the Sûreté." Dubois bowed. "And M. Fortune, my distinguished *confrère* from England."

David was enchanted. And what could he do for them?

"We make some little enquiries. First, you have here a boy — Tracy, the son of Mme. Bernal. He is in good health?"

"Of the best." David lifted his black brows. "You will permit me to know why you ask."

"Because another boy who was here is dead. The little nephew of M. Weber. You remember him?"

"Very well. He was a charming child. I regret infinitely. But you are without doubt aware that he fell ill on the holidays. It was a tragedy for his family. But the cause is not here. We have had no illness, no infection at all. I recommend you to Dr. Lannion, at Quimper. He is our medical inspector."

"Yes. So I've heard," Reggie murmured. "Have you had other cases of children who went home for the holidays and died?"

"It is an atrocious question!" David cried.

"But you are not quite sure of the answer?" said Dubois.

"If that is an insinuation, I protest," David frowned. "I have nothing to conceal, sir. It is impossible, that must be clear, I should know what has become of every child who has left my school. But, I tell you frankly, I do not recall any death but that of the little nephew of Weber, poor child."

"Very well. Then you can have no objection that my assistant should examine your records," said Dubois. He opened the window, and whistled and lifted a hand.

"Not the least in the world. I am at your orders." David bowed. "Permit me, I will go and get out the books," and he went briskly.

"Now if we had luck he would try to run away," Dubois rumbled. "But do not expect it."

"I didn't," Reggie moaned.

And David did not run away. He came back and took them to his office, and there Dubois's man was set down to work at registers. "You wish to assist?" David asked.

"No, thanks. No," Reggie murmured. "I'd like to look at your school."

"An inspection!" David smiled. "I shall be delighted. I dare to hope for the approval of a man of science so eminent."

They inspected dormitories and dining room and kitchen, classrooms and workshop and laboratory. M. David was expansive and enthusiastic, yet modest. Either he was an accomplished actor, or he had a deep interest in school hygiene, and his arrangements were beyond suspicion. In the laboratory Reggie lingered. "It is elementary," David apologised. "But what would you have? Some general science, that is all they can do, my little ones: botany for the most part, as you see, a trifle of chemistry to amuse them."

"Yes. Quite sound. Yes. I'd like to see the other laboratory."

"What?" David stared. "There is only this."

"Oh, no. Another one with a big microscope," Reggie murmured. "North side of the house."

"Oh, la, la," David laughed. "You have paid some attention to my poor house. I am flattered. You mean my own den, where I play with marine biology still. Certainly you shall see it. But a little moment, I must get the key. You will understand. One must keep one's good microscope locked up. These imps, they play everywhere." He hurried out.

"*Bigre!* How the devil did you know there was another laboratory?" said Dubois.

"Saw the microscope yesterday," Reggie mumbled.

"Name of a dog! Is there anything you do not see?" Dubois complained. "Well, if we have any luck he has run away this time."

They waited some long while, and Dubois's face was flattened against the window to peer through the rain at the man on watch. But David had not run away, he came back at last, and apologised for some delay with a fool of a master, heaven give him patience! He took them briskly to the other laboratory, his den.

It was not pretentious. There were some shelves of bottles, and a bench with a sink, and a glass cupboard which stood open and empty. On the broad table in the window was a microscope of high power, and some odds and ends.

Reggie glanced at the bottles of chemicals and came to the microscope. "I play at what I worked at. That is middle age," David smiled. "Here is something a little interesting." He slipped a slide into the microscope and invited Reggie to look.

"Oh, yes. One of the diatoms. Pretty one," Reggie murmured, and was shown some more. "Thanks very much." A glance set Dubois in a hurry to go. David was affably disappointed. He had hoped they would lunch with him. The gentleman with the registers could hardly have finished his investigations. He desired an investigation the most complete.

"I will leave him here," Dubois snapped, and they got away. "Nothing, my friend?" Dubois muttered.

"No. That was the point," Reggie said. " 'When they got there the cupboard was bare.' "

As their car passed the gate, a man signalled to them out of the rain. They stopped just beyond sight of the house, and he joined them. "Bouvier has held someone," he panted. "A man with a sack." They got out of the car and Dubois waved him on.

Through the blinding rain clouds they came to the back of the house, and, on the way up to the cliffs, found Bouvier with his hand on the collar of a sullen, stupefied Breton. A sack lay on the ground at their feet.

"He says it is only rubbish," Bouvier said, "and he was taking it to throw into the sea, where they throw their waste. But I kept him."

"Good. Let us see." Dubois pulled the sack open. "The devil, it is nothing but broken glass!"

Reggie grasped the hand that was going to turn it over. "No, you mustn't do that," he said sharply. "Risky."

"Why? What then? It is broken glass and bits of jelly."

"Yes. As you say. Broken glass and bits of jelly. However." Over Reggie's wet face came a slow benign smile. "Just what we wanted. Contents of cupboard which was bare. I'll have to do some work on this. I'm going to the hospital. You'd better collect David — in the other car. Good-bye." . . .

Twenty-four hours later, he came into a grim room of a *gendarmerie* at Quimper. There Dubois and David sat with a table between them, and neither man was a pleasant sight. David's florid colour was gone, he had become untidy, he sagged in his chair, unable to hide fatigue and pain. Dubois also was dishevelled, and his eyes had sunk and grown small, but the big face wore a look of hungry cruelty. He turned to Reggie. "Aha. Here you are at last. And what do you tell M. David?"

"Well, we'll have a little demonstration." Reggie set down a box on the table and took from it a microscope. "Not such a fine instrument as yours, M. David, but it will do." He adjusted a slide.

"You showed me some beautiful marine diatoms in your laboratory. Let me show you this. Also from your laboratory. From the sackful of stuff you tried to throw into the sea."

David dragged himself up, and looked and stared at him, and dropped back in his chair.

"Oh, that's not all, no." Reggie changed the slide. "Try this one."

Again, and more wearily, David looked. He sat down again. His full lips curled back to show his teeth in a grin. "And then?" he said.

"What have you?" Dubois came to the microscope. "Little chains of dots, eh?" Reggie put back the first slide. "And rods with dots at the end."

"Not bad for a layman, is it, M. David?" Reggie murmured. "Streptococcus pyogenes, and the diphtheria bacillus. I've got some more —— "

"Indeed?" David sneered.

"Oh, yes. But these will do. Pyogenes was found in poor little Weber: accountin' for the virulence of the diphtheria. Very efficient and scientific murder."

"And the others?" Dubois thundered. "The other children who went home for their holidays and died. Two, three, four, is it, David?"

David laughed. "What does it matter? Yes, there are others who have gone to the isles of the blessed. But, also, there are many who have been made well and strong. I mock at you."

"You have cause, Herod," Dubois cried. "You have grown rich on the murder of children. But it is we who laugh last. We deliver you to justice now."

"Justice! Ah, yes, you believe that." David laughed again. "You are primitive, you are barbarous. Me, I am rational, I am a man of science. I sacrifice one life that a dozen may live well and happy. These who stand in the way of the rich, their deaths are paid for, and with the money I heal many. What, if life is valuable, is not this wisdom and justice? Let one die to save many — it is in all the religions, that. But no one believes his religions now. I — I believe in man. Well, I am before my time. But some day the world will be all Davids. With me it is finished."

"Not yet, name of God!" Dubois growled.

"Oh yes, my friend. I am sick to death already. I have made sure of that." He waved his hand at Reggie. "You will not save me — no, not even you, my clever *confrère*. Good night! Go chase the Weber and the Bernal and the rest. David, he is gone into the infinite." He fell back, a hand to his head.

Reggie went to him, and looked close and felt at him. "Better take him away," he pronounced. "Hospital, under observation."

Dubois gave the orders. . . . "Play acting, my friend," he shrugged.

"Oh, no. No. That kind of man. Logical and drastic. He's ill all right. There was the diplococcus of meningitis in his collection. Might be that." And it was. . . .

Ten days afterwards Dubois came to London with Reggie and gave Lomas a lecture on the case. "I am desolated that I cannot offer you anyone to hang, my friend. But what can one do? The wretched Farquhar — I have no doubt he was murdered between David and Bernal. But there is no evidence. And, after all, David, he is dead, and we have Bernal for conspiracy to murder his stepson. That will do. It was, in fact, a case profoundly simple, like all the great crimes. To make a trade of arranging the deaths of unwanted children, that is very old. The distinction of David was to organise it scientifically, that is all. The child who was an heir to fortune, with a greedy one waiting to succeed, that was the child for him. Weber's nephew stood in the way of the beautiful Clotilde to Weber's fortune. Mrs. Bernal's little boy was in the way of her second husband to the fortune of her father, the old millionaire. And the others! Well, here is a beautiful modern school for delicate children, nine out of ten of them thrive marvellously. But, for the tenth, there is David's bacteriological laboratory, and a killing disease to take home with him when he goes for his holidays. Always at home, they die; always a disease of infection they could pick up anywhere. *Bigre!* It was a work of genius. And it would have gone on forever but that this worthless Farquhar blunders into Brittany upon it, and begins to blackmail the beautiful Clotilde, the Bernal. Clotilde pays with her jewels, and has to pretend a robbery. Bernal will not pay — cannot, perhaps. Farquhar approaches the old grandfather, and Bernal calls in David, and the blackmailer is killed. The oldest story in the world. Rascals fall out,

justice comes in. There is your angel of justice." He bowed to
Reggie. "Dear master. You have shown me the way. Well, I am
content to serve. Does he serve badly, poor old Dubois?"

"Oh, no. No. Brilliant," Reggie murmured. "Queer case, though.
I believe David myself. He wanted to be a god. Make lives to his
desire. And he did. Cured more than he killed. Far more. Then this
fellow, who never wanted to be anything but a beast, blows in
and beats him. Queer world. And David might have been a kindly,
human fellow, if he hadn't had power. Dangerous stuff, science.
Lots of us not fit for it."

A CHESS PROBLEM

by AGATHA CHRISTIE

The magnificent M. POIROT *is at his undisputed best in Agatha Christie's novels, so that the problem of finding a short story worthy of* POIROT's *mercurial talents gave your editors many an insomniac night. Eureka! You will not recognize "A Chess Problem." It appears in no volume of Agatha Christie's short stories. In that sense, it's a new* POIROT *story — and a good one.*

POIROT and I often dined at a small restaurant in Soho. We were there one evening, when we observed a friend at an adjacent table. It was Inspector Japp, and as there was room at our table, he came and joined us. It was some time since either of us had seen him.

"Never do you drop in to see us nowadays," declared Poirot reproachfully. "Not since the affair of the Yellow Jasmine have we met, and that is nearly a month ago."

"I've been up north — that's why. Take any interest in chess, Moosior Poirot?" Japp asked.

"I have played it, yes."

"Did you see that curious business yesterday? Match between two players of world-wide reputation, and one died during the game?"

"I saw a mention of it. Dr. Savaronoff, the Russian champion, was one of the players, and the other, who succumbed to heart failure, was the brilliant young American, Gilmour Wilson."

"Quite right. Savaronoff beat Rubinstein and became Russian champion some years ago. Wilson is said to be a second Capablanca."

"A very curious occurrence," mused Poirot. "If I mistake not, you have a particular interest in the matter."

Japp gave a rather embarrassed laugh.

"You've hit it, Moosior Poirot. I'm puzzled. Wilson was sound as a bell — no trace of heart trouble. His death is quite inexplicable."

"You suspect Dr. Savaronoff of putting him out of the way?" I cried.

"Hardly that," said Japp dryly. "I don't think even a Russian would murder another man in order not to be beaten · at chess — and anyway, from all I can make out, the boot was likely to be on the other leg. The doctor is supposed to be very hot stuff — second to Lasker they say he is."

Poirot nodded thoughtfully.

"Then what exactly is your little idea?" he asked. "Why should Wilson be poisoned? For, I assume, of course, that it is poison you suspect."

"Naturally. Heart failure means your heart stops beating — that's all there is to that. That's what a doctor says officially at the moment, but privately he tips us the wink that he's not satisfied."

"When is the autopsy to take place?"

"To-night. Wilson's death was extraordinarily sudden. He seemed quite as usual and was actually moving one of the pieces when he suddenly fell forward — dead!"

"There are very few poisons would act in such a fashion," objected Poirot.

"I know. The autopsy will help us, I expect. But why should any one want Gilmour Wilson out of the way — that's what I'd like to know. Harmless unassuming young fellow. Just come over here from the States, and apparently hadn't an enemy in the world."

"It seems incredible," I mused.

"Not at all," said Poirot, smiling. "Japp has his theory, I can see."

"I have, Moosior Poirot. I don't believe the poison was meant for Wilson — it was meant for the other man."

"Savaronoff?"

"Yes. Savaronoff fell foul of the Bolsheviks at the outbreak of the Revolution. He was even reported killed. In reality he escaped, and for three years endured incredible hardships in the wilds of Siberia. His sufferings were so great that he is now a changed man. His friends and acquaintances declare they would hardly have recognised him. His hair is white, and his whole aspect that of a man terribly aged. He is a semi-invalid, and seldom goes out, living alone with a niece, Sonia Daviloff, and a Russian man-servant in a flat down Westminster way. It is possible that he still considers himself a marked man. Certainly he was very unwilling to agree to this chess contest. He refused several times point blank, and it was only when the newspapers took it up and began making a fuss about the 'unsportsmanlike refusal' that he gave in. Gilmour Wilson had gone on challenging him with real Yankee pertinacity, and in the end he got his way. Now I ask you, Moosior Poirot, why wasn't he willing? Because he didn't want attention drawn to him. Didn't want somebody or other to get on his track. That's my solu-tion — Gilmour Wilson got pipped by mistake."

"There is no one who has any private reason to gain by Savaro-noff's death?"

"Well, his niece, I suppose. He's recently come into an immense fortune. Left him by Madame Gospoja whose husband was a sugar profiteer under the old regime. They had an affair together once, I believe, and she refused steadfastly to credit the reports of his death."

"Where did the match take place?"

"In Savaronoff's own flat. He's an invalid, as I told you."

"Many people there to watch it?"

"At least a dozen — probably more."

Poirot made an expressive grimace.

"My poor Japp, your task is not an easy one."

"Once I know definitely that Wilson was poisoned, I can get on."

"Has it occurred to you that, in the meantime, supposing your assumption that Savaronoff was the intended victim to be correct, the murderer may try again?"

"Of course it has. Two men are watching Savaronoff's flat."

"That will be very useful if any one should call with a bomb under his arm," said Poirot dryly.

"You're getting interested, Moosior Poirot," said Japp, with a twinkle. "Care to come round to the mortuary and see Wilson's body before the doctors start on it? Who knows, his tie pin may be askew, and that may give you a valuable clue that will solve the mystery."

"My dear Japp, all through dinner my fingers have been itching to rearrange your own tie pin. You permit, yes? Ah! that is much more pleasing to the eye. Yes, by all means, let us go to the mortuary."

I could see that Poirot's attention was completely captivated by this new problem. It was so long since he had shown any interest over any outside case that I was quite rejoiced to see him back in his old form.

For my own part, I felt a deep pity as I looked down upon the motionless form and convulsed face of the hapless young American who had come by his death in such a strange way. Poirot examined the body attentively. There was no mark on it anywhere, except a small scar on the left hand.

"And the doctor says that's a burn, not a cut," explained Japp.

Poirot's attention shifted to the contents of the dead man's pockets which a constable spread out for our inspection. There was nothing much — a handkerchief, keys, notecase filled with notes, and some unimportant letters. But one object standing by itself filled Poirot with interest.

"A chessman!" he exclaimed. "A white bishop. Was that in his pocket?"

"No, clasped in his hand. We had quite a difficulty to get it out of his fingers. It must be returned to Dr. Savaronoff sometime. It's part of a very beautiful set of carved ivory chessmen."

"Permit me to return it to him. It will make an excuse for my going there."

"Aha!" cried Japp. "So you want to come in on this case."

"I admit it. So skilfully have you aroused my interest."

"That's fine. Got you away from your brooding. Captain Hastings is pleased, too, I can see."

"Quite right," I said, laughing.

Poirot turned back towards the body.

"No other little detail you can tell me about — him?" he asked.

"I don't think so."

"Not even — that he was left-handed?"

"You're a wizard, Moosior Poirot. How did you know that? He *was* left-handed. Not that it's anything to do with the case."

"Nothing whatever," agreed Poirot hastily, seeing that Japp was slightly ruffled. "My little joke — that was all. I like to play you the trick, you see."

We went out upon an amicable understanding.

The following morning saw us wending our way to Dr. Sa-varonoff's flat in Westminster.

"Sonia Daviloff," I mused. "It's a pretty name."

Poirot stopped, and threw me a look of despair.

"Always looking for romance! You are incorrigible."

The door of the flat was opened to us by a manservant with a peculiarly wooden face. It seemed impossible to believe that that impassive countenance could ever display emotion.

Poirot presented a card on which Japp had scribbled a few words of introduction, and we were shown into a low, long room furnished with rich hangings and curios. One or two wonderful ikons hung upon the walls, and exquisite Persian rugs lay upon the floor. A samovar stood upon a table.

I was examining one of the ikons which I judged to be of considerable value, and turned to see Poirot prone upon the floor. Beautiful as the rug was, it hardly seemed to me to necessitate such close attention.

"Is it such a very wonderful specimen?" I asked.

"Eh? Oh! the rug? But no, it was not the rug I was remarking. But it *is* a beautiful specimen, far too beautiful to have a large nail wantonly driven through the middle of it. No, Hastings," as I came forward, "the nail is not there now. But the hole remains."

A sudden sound behind us made me spin round, and Poirot spring nimbly to his feet. A girl was standing in the doorway. Her eyes, full upon us, were dark with suspicion. She was of medium height, with a beautiful, rather sullen face, dark-blue eyes, and very black hair which was cut short. Her voice, when she spoke, was rich and sonorous, and completely un-English.

"I fear my uncle will be unable to see you. He is a great invalid."

"That is a pity, but perhaps you will kindly help me instead. You are Mademoiselle Daviloff, are you not?"

"Yes, I am Sonia Daviloff. What is it you want to know?"

"I am making some inquiries about that sad affair the night before last — the death of M. Gilmour Wilson. What can you tell me about it?"

The girl's eyes opened wide.

"He died of heart failure — as he was playing chess."

"The police are not so sure that it was — heart failure, mademoiselle."

The girl gave a terrified gesture.

"It was true then," she cried. "Ivan was right."

"Who is Ivan, and why do you say he was right?"

"It was Ivan who opened the door to you — and he has already said to me that in his opinion Gilmour Wilson did not die a natural death — that he was poisoned by mistake."

"By mistake."

"Yes, the poison was meant for my uncle."

She had quite forgotten her first distrust now, and was speaking eagerly.

"Why do you say that, mademoiselle? Who should wish to poison Dr. Savaronoff?"

She shook her head.

"I do not know. I am all in the dark. And my uncle, he will not trust me. It is natural, perhaps. You see, he hardly knows me. He saw me as a child, and not since till I came to live with him here in London. But this much I do know, he is in fear of something. We have many secret societies in Russia, and one day I overheard something which made me think it was of just such a society he went in fear."

"Mademoiselle, your uncle is still in danger. I must save him. Now recount to me exactly the events of that fatal evening. Show me the chessboard, the table, how the two men sat — everything."

She went to the side of the room and brought out a small table. The top of it was exquisite, inlaid with squares of silver and black to represent a chessboard.

"This was sent to my uncle a few weeks ago as a present, with the request that he would use it in the next match he played. It was in the middle of the room — so."

Poirot examined the table with what seemed to me quite unnecessary attention. He was not conducting the inquiry at all as I would have done. Many of his questions seemed to me pointless, and upon really vital matters he seemed to have no questions to ask.

After a minute examination of the table and the exact position it had occupied, he asked to see the chessmen. Sonia Daviloff brought them to him in a box. He examined one or two of them in a perfunctory manner.

"An exquisite set," he murmured absent-mindedly.

Still not a question as to what refreshments there had been, or what people had been present.

I cleared my throat significantly.

"Don't you think, Poirot, that — "

He interrupted me peremptorily.

"Do not think, my friend. Leave all to me. Mademoiselle, is it quite impossible that I should see your uncle?"

A faint smile showed itself on her face.

"He will see you, yes. You understand, it is my part to interview all strangers first."

She disappeared. I heard a murmur of voices in the next room, and a minute later she came back and motioned us to pass into the adjoining room.

The man who lay there on a couch was an imposing figure. Tall, gaunt, with huge bushy eyebrows and white beard, and a face haggard as the result of starvation and hardships, Dr. Savaronoff was a distinct personality. I noted the peculiar formation of his head, its unusual height. A great chess player must have a great brain, I knew. I could easily understand Dr. Savaronoff being the second greatest player in the world.

Poirot bowed.

"*M. le Docteur,* may I speak to you alone?"

Savaronoff turned to his niece.

"Leave us, Sonia."

She disappeared obediently.

"Now, sir, what is it?"

"Dr. Savaronoff, you have recently come into an enormous fortune. If you should — die unexpectedly, who inherits it?"

"I have made a will leaving everything to my niece, Sonia Daviloff. You do not suggest — "

"I suggest nothing, but you have not seen your niece since she was a child. It would have been easy for any one to impersonate her."

Savaronoff seemed thunderstruck by the suggestion. Poirot went on easily.

"Enough as to that. I give you the word of warning, that is all. What I want you to do now is to describe to me the game of chess the other evening."

"How do you mean — describe it?"

"Well, I do not play the chess myself, but I understand that there are various regular ways of beginning — the gambit, do they not call it?"

Dr. Savaronoff smiled a little.

"Ah! I comprehend you now. Wilson opened Ruy Lopez — one of the soundest openings there is, and one frequently adopted in tournaments and matches."

"And how long had you been playing when the tragedy happened?"

"It must have been about the third or fourth move when Wilson suddenly fell forward over the table, stone dead."

Poirot rose to depart. He flung out his last question as though it was of absolutely no importance, but I knew better.

"Had he had anything to eat or drink?"

"A whisky and soda, I think."

"Thank you, Dr. Savaronoff. I will disturb you no longer."

Ivan was in the hall to show us out. Poirot lingered on the threshold.

"The flat below this, do you know who lives there?"

"Sir Charles Kingwell, a member of Parliament, sir. It has been let furnished lately, though."

"Thank you."

We went out into the bright winter sunlight.

"Well, really, Poirot," I burst out. "I don't think you've distinguished yourself this time. Surely your questions were very inadequate."

"You think so, Hastings?" Poirot looked at me appealingly. "I was *bouleversé*, yes. What would you have asked?"

I considered the question carefully, and then outlined my scheme to Poirot. He listened with what seemed to be close interest. My monologue lasted until we had nearly reached home.

"Very excellent, very searching, Hastings," said Poirot, as he inserted his key in the door and preceded me up the stairs. "But quite unnecessary."

"Unnecessary!" I cried, amazed. "If the man was poisoned —"

"Aha," cried Poirot, pouncing upon a note which lay on the table. "From Japp. Just as I thought." He flung it over to me. It was brief and to the point. No traces of poison had been found, and there was nothing to show how the man came by his death.

"You see," said Poirot, "our questions would have been quite unnecessary."

"You guessed this beforehand?"

" 'Forecast the probable result of the deal,' " quoted Poirot from a recent bridge problem on which I had spent much time. "*Mon ami,* when you do that successfully, you do not call it guessing."

"Don't let's split hairs," I said impatiently. "You foresaw this?"

"I did."

"Why?"

Poirot put his hand into his pocket and pulled out — a white bishop.

"Why," I cried, "you forgot to give it back to Dr. Savaronoff."

"You are in error, my friend. That bishop still reposes in my left-hand pocket. I took its fellow from the box of chessmen Mademoiselle Daviloff kindly permitted me to examine. The plural of one bishop is two bishops."

He sounded the final *s* with a great hiss. I was completely mystified.

"But why did you take it?"

"*Parbleu,* I wanted to see if they were exactly alike."

He stood them on the table side by side.

"Well, they are, of course," I said, "exactly alike."

Poirot looked at them with his head on one side.

"They seem so, I admit. But one should take no fact for granted until it is proved. Bring me, I pray you, my little scales."

With infinite care he weighed the two chessmen, then turned to me with a face alight with triumph.

"I was right. See you, I was right. Impossible to deceive Hercule Poirot!"

He rushed to the telephone — waited impatiently.

"Is that Japp? Ah! Japp, it is you. Hercule Poirot speaks. Watch the manservant, Ivan. On no account let him slip through your fingers. Yes, yes, it is as I say."

He dashed down the receiver and turned to me.

"You see it not, Hastings? I will explain. Wilson was not poisoned, he was electrocuted. A thin metal rod passes up the middle of one of those chessmen. The table was prepared beforehand and set upon a certain spot on the floor. When the bishop was placed upon one of the silver squares, the current passed through Wilson's body, killing him instantly. The only mark was the electric burn upon his hand — his left hand, because he was left-handed. The 'special table' was an extremely cunning piece of mechanism. The table I examined was a duplicate, perfectly innocent. It was substituted for the other immediately after the murder. The thing was worked from the flat below, which, if you remember, was let furnished. But one accomplice at least was in Savaronoff's flat. The girl is an agent of a Russian secret society, working to inherit Savaronoff's money."

"And Ivan?"

"I strongly suspect that Ivan is the girl's confederate."

"It's amazing," I said at last. "Everything fits in. Savaronoff had an inkling of the plot, and that's why he was so averse to playing the match."

Poirot looked at me without speaking. Then he turned abruptly away, and began pacing up and down.

"Have you a book on chess by any chance, *mon ami?*" he asked suddenly.

"I believe I have somewhere."

It took me some time to ferret it out, but I found it at last, and brought it to Poirot, who sank down in a chair and started reading it with the greatest attention.

In about a quarter of an hour the telephone rang. I answered it. It was Japp. Ivan had left the flat, carrying a large bundle. He had sprung into a waiting taxi, and the chase had begun. He was evidently trying to lose his pursuers. In the end he seemed to fancy that he had done so, and had then driven to a big empty house at Hampstead. The house was surrounded.

I recounted all this to Poirot. He merely stared at me as though he scarcely took in what I was saying. He held out the chess book.

"Listen to this, my friend. This is the Ruy Lopez opening. 1 P-K4, P-K4; 2 Kt-KB3, Kt-QB3; 3 B-Kt5. Then there comes a question as to Black's best third move. He has the choice of various defences. It was White's third move that killed Gilmour Wilson, 3B-Kt5. Only the third move — does that say nothing to you?"

I hadn't the least idea what he meant, and told him so.

"I suppose, Hastings, that while you were sitting in this chair, you heard the front door being opened and shut, what would you think?"

"I should think some one had gone out, I suppose."

"Yes — but there are always two ways of looking at things. Some one gone out — some one come *in* — two totally different things, Hastings. But if you assumed the wrong one, presently some little discrepancy would creep in and show you that you were on the wrong track."

"What does all this mean, Poirot?"

Poirot sprang to his feet with sudden energy.

"It means that I have been a triple imbecile. Quick, quick, to the flat in Westminster. We may yet be in time."

We tore off in a taxi. Poirot returned no answer to my excited questions. We raced up the stairs. Repeated rings and knocks brought no reply, but listening closely I could distinguish a hollow groan coming from within.

The hall porter proved to have a master key, and after a few difficulties he consented to use it.

Poirot went straight to the inner room. A whiff of chloroform met us. On the floor was Sonia Daviloff, gagged and bound, with a great wad of saturated cotton wool over her nose and mouth. Poirot tore it off and began to take measures to restore her. Presently a doctor arrived, and Poirot handed her over to his charge and drew aside with me. There was no sign of Dr. Savaronoff.

"What does it all mean?" I asked, bewildered.

"It means that before two equal deductions I chose the wrong one. You heard me say that it would be easy for any one to impersonate Sonia Daviloff because her uncle had not seen her for so many years?"

"Yes?"

"Well, precisely the opposite held good also. It was equally easy for any one to *impersonate the uncle!*"

"What?"

"Savaronoff *did* die at the outbreak of the Revolution. The man who pretended to have escaped with such terrible hardships, the man so changed 'that his own friends could hardly recognise him,' the man who successfully laid claim to an enormous fortune — is an impostor. He guessed I should get on the right track in the end, so he sent off the honest Ivan on a tortuous wild-goose chase, chloroformed the girl, and got out, having by now doubtless realised most of the securities left by Madame Gospoja."

"But — but who tried to kill him?"

"Nobody tried to kill *him*. Wilson was the intended victim all along."

"But why?"

"My friend, the real Savaronoff was the second greatest chess player in the world. In all probability his impersonator did not even know the rudiments of the game. Certainly he could not sustain the fiction of a match. He tried all he knew to avoid the contest. When that failed, Wilson's doom was sealed. At all costs he must be prevented from discovering that the great Savaronoff did not even know how to play chess. Wilson was fond of the Ruy Lopez opening, and was certain to use it. The false Savaronoff arranged for death to come with the third move, before any complications of defence set in."

"But, my dear Poirot," I persisted, "are we dealing with a lunatic? I quite follow your reasoning, and admit that you must be right, but to kill a man just to sustain his rôle! Surely there were simpler ways out of the difficulty than that! He could have said that his doctor forbade the strain of a match."

Poirot wrinkled his forehead.

"*Certainement,* Hastings," he said, "there were other ways, but none so convincing. Besides, you are assuming that to kill a man is a thing to avoid, are you not? Our impostor's mind, it does not act that way. I put myself in his place, a thing impossible for you. I picture his thoughts. He enjoys himself as the professor at that match. I doubt not he has visited the chess tourneys to study his part. He sits and frowns in thought; he gives the impression that he is thinking great plans, and all the time he laughs in himself. He is aware that two moves are all that he knows — and all that he *need know*. Again, it would appeal to his mind to foresee the events and to make Wilson his own executioner. . . . Oh, yes, Hastings, I begin to understand our friend and his psychology."

I shrugged.

"Well, I suppose you're right, but I can't understand any one running a risk he could so easily avoid."

"Risk!" Poirot snorted. "Where then lay the risk? Would Japp have solved the problem? No; if the false Savaronoff had not made one small mistake he would have run no risk."

"And his mistake?" I asked, although I suspected the answer.

"*Mon ami,* he overlooked the little gray cells of Hercule Poirot."

Poirot has his virtues. but modesty is not one of them.

Detective: SUPERINTENDENT WILSON
First Appearance: 1923

THE OWL AT THE WINDOW

by G. D. H. AND M. I. COLE

Everybody says this is the best SUPERINTENDENT WILSON *story. We included. Originally titled "In a Telephone Cabinet."*

THE DOWNSHIRE HILL MURDER (to give it its newspaper name) was discovered about half past nine on a Sunday morning of May, 1920, one of those lovely mornings with which our climate tries to pretend that it really knows how to make a summer. Superintendent Henry Wilson of New Scotland Yard was walking along Downshire Hill, Hampstead, in company with his friend Dr. Michael Prendergast. It was long before the sensational death of Radlett, the millionaire, which, as everyone will remember, covered England and America with placards, and drove Wilson, who had committed the unpardonable sin of detecting an ex-Home Secretary in shady courses, into the exile of private practice. He was still a C. I. D. man, liable at any moment to be called from bed and board to attend to public affairs, and it was not without some misgivings that he had obeyed the commands of his sister, with whom he was staying, to put himself for one day at least beyond reach of the telephone. However, it was a wonderful morning; and Michael Prendergast, one of his few intimate friends, who had spent the Saturday evening and night with him, had added his entreaties; and the result was that the two men, in flannels and tennis shirts, were now walking briskly down the road to the North London Station, where they intended to catch a train for Richmond.

"You'd almost think you were in the country here," Prendergast said appreciatively, noting the trees which filled the little front gardens and the young green of the Heath which closed the end of the road. "There was an owl hooting outside my window all night."

"They do come close to the houses here," Wilson replied, "but I never heard of one actually nesting in the wall of a house before."

"Nor I. Why?" For answer Wilson pointed to the ivy-clad wall of a little house about a hundred yards farther down, which was only just visible through a mass of lilac and young chestnut. "Something flew in and out of the ivy just there, between those boughs," he said.

Prendergast stared at him. "You have sharp eyes. I was looking at the lilac, and I didn't see anything. How do you know it was an owl, anyway, at this distance?"

"I don't," Wilson said. "It may not have been. I couldn't see it at all clearly. But it was too big for any other bird. Anyway, somebody else appears to have seen it too." They were now approaching the ivy-clad house, which, though hidden from view on the west, was quite open in front, and standing by its gate on the pavement was a man to whom it appeared to be an object of enormous interest. As the two friends passed, he looked up at them with a dubious air, which suggested that he was wondering whether to open a conversation; and Prendergast, who never could resist conversing with all and sundry, responded promptly to the suggestion.

"Have you seen the owl, too?" he asked.

"Owl!" said the man. "I ain't seen no owl. But I've seen a man go in there." He pointed to the house. "What's he want to go in for, that's what I want to know."

"Perhaps it's his house," Prendergast suggested.

"Ho!" said the man. "Then what's he want to go in by the window for, that's what I want to know. Banging on the door fit to wake the dead, he was. When he sees me, he says, 'Something wrong here,' he says. 'Can't get no answer,' and he outs with a knife and gets in at the window. And what's he want to bang for, if it's his house, and what's wrong in there, that's what I want to know." He spat suspiciously.

In a moment his question was answered in a sufficiently dramatic manner. There was a sound of feet within the house; the front door, which was only a matter of twenty yards from the gate, opened suddenly, and a little man, pale and frightened in appearance, looked out and yelled in a voice of surprising power to come from a person of his physique, "Murder!"

All three started; and indeed the cry had sounded as if it must reach Camden Town at least. On seeing their astonished faces the man at the door looked rather confused, and coming down to the gate, said in a considerably lower tone, "Will you fetch the police, please, gentlemen? Mr. Carluke's been murdered."

He then closed the gate, and made as if to return to the house; but Prendergast, with a nod from Wilson, followed him up the path. "Can I do anything?" he asked pleasantly. "I'm a doctor."

" 'Tisn't a doctor he wants, poor fellow," said the little man. "He's as cold as a fish. He must have died hours ago." He stopped with his hand on the hall door. "If you'll fetch the police, sir, I'll stay with him. I don't think the house ought to be left alone. And there's nobody there."

"That's all right." Wilson, who had stopped to speak to the man at the gate, now came up to them. "I am from Scotland Yard. Here's my card." He produced one from his cigarette case, and Michael looked on with amusement, wondering what use he had intended to make of his official dignity at Richmond. The little man took it gingerly, as if it had been a spider, and looked with obvious distaste at the owner's clothes. Quite clearly he thought that policemen ought to dress as policemen and not stroll about in flannel trousers.

"I've sent that man to the Rosslyn Hill station with a message," Wilson went on. "They'll be here in a few minutes. But, as you say, the place oughtn't to be left alone. So, if you'll show me where the body is, I can start making the preliminary investigations, and my friend here can see how he was murdered. You're certain he was, Mr. —— ?"

"Barton," said the little man, "Edward Barton. He was murdered all right, sir. Shot right through the head. His brains are all over the floor, poor fellow. This way, sir." He seemed a trifle hurt at the doubt thrown on his diagnosis.

"Well, well, we'll see," Wilson said soothingly. "Where is he?"

"Telephone cabinet," said Mr. Barton, pointing. "By the stairs on the right. That glass door. It's his foot that's holding it open. I haven't touched him. I just made sure he was dead, poor fellow."

*   *   *

It was not a pleasant sight which greeted them when Wilson pulled open the door of the little dark telephone cabinet; and it thoroughly justified Mr. Barton's confidence in his own verdict. On the floor, crumpled up, with one foot half across the sill of the door, lay what once must have been a hale man of between fifty and sixty years of age. His body had fallen in a heap, facing the telephone, and the fingers of both hands were curved as if he had died gripping something which he had subsequently dropped. But the cause of death was plain enough; for the whole front of his face and part of his head had been pierced in a number of places, and the blood and brains which had oozed out from the wounds had covered the floor. Michael Prendergast had been through the war, and thought himself used to death; but the sight of the old man lying shattered in that gloomy, musty shambles stirred emotions in him which he believed wholly conquered, and he had to struggle with a violent feeling of nausea before he dared step across the threshold.

"Go carefully, Michael," Wilson warned; and Prendergast noted with shame and annoyance that he seemed wholly unmoved by the sight. "Don't tread in more than you can help. We'll want all the clues we can get." He surveyed with displeasure some unmistakable footprints in the blood that covered the floor. "You've been in here, Mr. Barton?"

"Of course I have," said Mr. Barton in injured tones. "I went to see if I could do anything for him, naturally. When I found I couldn't, I looked round to see if there was a revolver or anything anywhere. In case he shot himself, you see — in case it was suicide."

"Turn on the light, will you?" came Prendergast's voice from where he was bending over the body. "I can't see anything in this coalhole."

"It's broken," said Mr. Barton. "I tried it when I came in." He was, however, obediently reaching his hand to the switch, a porcelain one of the old pattern, when Wilson forestalled him. With a handkerchief wrapped around his hand he turned the switch backwards and forwards several times, but without result.

"It's broken all right," he said. "Probably the bulb's gone. You must make shift with my torch, Michael. But be as quick as you can. It's pretty obvious that we can't do anything for this poor fellow now, except to find his murderer, and I want to get on with that as soon as possible." While Prendergast finished his examination he stood still in the doorway, staring at the little room as if memorizing its contents, at the telephone, which stood unperturbed on a rather high shelf at the far end, at a shelf above containing two or three old directories, and at a baize curtain which fell from the telephone shelf to the ground.

"What's behind that curtain, do you know?" he asked Barton.

"Boots — and some old rubbish, I think," the latter replied. "Mr. Carluke used to shove any stuff he didn't want there."

"You knew him quite well, then?"

"So-so," said Mr. Barton. "As well as anyone did, I daresay. He hadn't a great many friends; he was a bit of a queer old cuss, and didn't mind how much he was alone."

Prendergast straightened himself. "That's all I can do here," he said. "The poor chap's dead, of course — been dead about twelve hours, I should say, offhand. He can't have lived more than a few seconds after he was shot."

"Shot from close quarters?" Wilson asked.

"Very close. Not more than a few inches, I should say. And — he was shot by a blunderbuss."

"Blunderbuss!" exclaimed the other two.

"Blunderbuss or something with an enormous charge of soft-nosed slugs in it. Beastly little things. Here are two I picked off the floor, and there are some more in his head. There must have been dozens in the charge."

"Extraordinary!" said Mr. Barton, with a kind of irritable incredulity. "Why should anyone want to shoot poor Carluke with a blunderbuss?"

"That's what we have to find out," said Wilson. "Perhaps, as you know the house, Mr. Barton, you'd take us into a room where we can talk."

The little man led the way into a small room which was obviously a sort of study or morning room, and motioned Wilson and his companion to chairs. In broad daylight, Prendergast studied him with some interest, but found little to repay his scrutiny. He looked a very ordinary type of middle-class clerk or shopkeeper, about forty-five or fifty years old, with a bald crown fringed with greyish hair that had once been ginger, a ragged ginger moustache, and face and features of no particular shape. He appeared considerably upset and distressed by the position in which he found himself, rather more so than Prendergast would have expected, though, of course, it would have been very trying for any friend of the murdered man. For all his agitation, though, he answered Wilson's questions clearly enough.

"Can you tell me Mr. Carluke's full name, and how you came to be a friend of his?" Wilson began.

"Harold Carluke," Mr. Barton replied. "Only we weren't exactly friends, as I told you, more kind of acquaintances. We came together through working in the same place, and we used to play chess a bit and go for a walk together now and then and so on."

"What place was that?"

"Capital and Counties Bank. Hampstead branch. Mr. Carluke is the cashier, and I'm head counter clerk."

"Had he any relations, do you know? Was he married?"

No, he wasn't married, Mr. Barton said. And he didn't think he'd any relatives. He'd once or twice spoken of a nephew, rather a wild young fellow, who seemed to give him some trouble. But that was all. Mr. Carluke wasn't the man to talk about his family, nor the kind you could put questions to. Not the sort many knew anything about.

"How comes it," Wilson asked, "that he is apparently alone in the house? Didn't he keep any servants?"

Barton explained that he did not. Mr. Carluke, it would appear, was something of a fussy old maid, and did not like to see servants about the house. So he employed only a daily woman who came in after he had left for business in the morning to clean and leave his supper laid for him, and departed before he returned. On Sundays she did not come at all. "You never saw anyone in such a bait as he was," Mr. Barton added, "if he found her in the house any time after he'd come home."

"What if he were ill?" Michael Prendergast's profession suggested to him. But it appeared that the question had not arisen. Mr. Carluke's health was excellent; he had never been known to miss a day at the bank.

"This charwoman, she must have had a key?" Wilson asked.

"I suppose she must have. But she doesn't come in on a Sunday. Besides the door was bolted and chained when I got in."

"The front door, you mean?"

"Yes; but the back door was locked and bolted too."

"Oh!" Wilson took this in. "You had a look round, then, before giving the alarm?"

"Only the ground floor." Barton licked his lips and looked at him with a kind of frightened appeal. "I couldn't see anything I could do for *him*. So I thought I might just see — if there was anyone else about."

"And was there?"

Barton shook his head. "No. Not a sign. But I wasn't long at it. Then I opened the door."

"I see," said Wilson. "How did you get in yourself?"

"Through that window" — pointing. Wilson crossed and looked at the window, whose catch had plainly been forced back.

"Why did you break in?"

"Couldn't get any answer. I'd called to go for a walk with Mr. Carluke as we'd arranged. Then I knocked and rang and couldn't make anyone hear. And I was a good bit behind my time, too, so I got a bit anxious — I thought he might be ill, perhaps. So I got in."

"I see. When did you last see him?"

"Last night."

"What time?"

"About — about nine o'clock," said Mr. Barton, licking his lips again and looking considerably distressed. Prendergast gave a start of surprise; then, remembering that he was in effect representing the law, pulled himself together and tried to look as impassive as Wilson. No wonder the little man was showing signs of alarm. His own position was certainly dubious.

"Could you tell us what happened?" Wilson inquired. Mr. Barton could, and did, not without a good many nervous glances at Wilson's face. He had gone round at Mr. Carluke's invitation for high tea and a game of chess. He had had to leave about nine o'clock because he had promised to fetch his wife home from an evening party at some neighbours' in Hendon; but the two men had arranged to go for a country walk on the Sunday. Barton had then left, arranging to call at nine o'clock in the morning to fetch his friend, and Carluke had seen him out of the house and walked with him as far as the corner of Willow Road, where they had parted. Then Barton had gone on to fetch his wife; but they had stayed very much longer at the party than they had intended and had not got back to their home in Hendon until nearly one. As soon as he knew they were going to be late, he had tried to telephone Mr. Carluke to suggest a less early start in the morning; but though he had tried twice, once from his friend's house and once from his own when he returned, he had got no answer. "I supposed he was out," Barton said. "Though it was a bit odd, because he said he was going straight to bed when he left me. He liked to keep early hours. So I tried again; but there was still no answer, so I supposed he was asleep. So I came round this morning as early as I could, as he'd be waiting."

"I see," said Wilson again. "You didn't meet anyone as you left, did you? When you were with Mr. Carluke, I mean."

"Not *meet,* exactly," said Mr. Barton, looking very nervous. "There were a lot of people about — it was a fine evening — but we didn't meet anyone. But we stood outside the Dog and Duck, at the bottom there, a minute or two. The landlord was in the doorway — I saw him — and he might have noticed us. He knows Mr. Carluke quite well. Look here," he burst out suddenly. "I know what you're getting at, and I know what it looks like! If he went straight back and locked up when he left me I was the last to see him alive. But he *was* alive and perfectly all right when I left him — I'll swear he was!" He half rose in his seat, and sat down again, looking fearfully at the others.

"Quite, quite," said Wilson soothingly. "I'm not trying to cast any suspicion on you, Mr. Barton. But we must find out what happened, you know. Now, if you two will excuse me, I'll start having a look at the place. The police ought to be here in a minute or two, and then I want you, Mr. Barton, to go along with them to the station, if you will, and tell the officer in charge what you've just told me." He rose to his feet. "By the way, Michael, did you find any signs of a struggle on the body?"

"None whatever," Prendergast promptly replied. "I should say he was shot before he knew what was happening."

"That was my impression, too," Wilson nodded, and disappeared into the hall. Prendergast would have dearly liked to accompany him and see how a Scotland Yard man handled the scene of a murder (his association with Wilson having hitherto been entirely unprofessional); but he was distinctly in awe of his friend's official position, and felt sure that if he had been wanted he would have received an invitation. So he sat with what patience he could muster in the uncomfortable little study, while Mr. Barton, on the other side of the fireplace, huddled in his chair and uneasily bit his nails.

They had not long to wait, for in less than three minutes there was a sound as of heavy feet on the path, and a loud official knock rang through the house. Barton and Prendergast both sprang to their feet, but Wilson was before them; and as they went into the hall they heard him giving a rapid account of the circumstances to an awestruck sergeant.

"Constable Wren's got your bag, sir," the sergeant explained. "I sent him round to Fitzjohn's Avenue for it as soon as I got your note. Lord, sir!" By this time they had reached the door of the telephone cabinet. "Well, he stopped one then, and no mistake, poor chap!" the sergeant said. "What was it, sir? Looks almost like a charge of grapeshot."

"Dr. Prendergast says it was a blunderbuss," said Wilson. "But you'd best get him along to the station at once. Is the ambulance here? Good. Get your man in and tell the divisional surgeon to examine him as quickly as possible. They can take Mr. Barton along with them too, and get his statement down. Is Inspector Catling there?"

"Just coming, sir," the sergeant said. "We rang him up, and he'll be along by the time the men get back."

"Good. Then they might as well be getting on. You stay with me, and we'll go over the house. Put a constable to watch the door. I'm sorry, Michael" — he turned to Prendergast — "but I'm afraid poor Carluke has rather put a stop to our expedition. Will you go without me, or would you rather stay?"

"I'd rather stay, if I can be of any use," said Prendergast, as eager as a schoolboy; and Wilson smiled a little, and nodded. "I'd like you to go to the station with the constables if you will, Mr. Barton," he said to the morose little figure that hovered in the background, "and give your account to the inspector. But first there are one or two more things I want to know. Did Mr. Carluke ever have charge of money or valuables in his house, do you know? For the bank, I mean?"

"Not that I know of," Barton said. "But he wouldn't have told me if he had. He was as close as an oyster on bank business."

"Thank you. Now, this nephew that you spoke of. Do you know his name, or address, or anything about him?"

Barton thought. "Edgar Carluke, his name is. I think he's a ship's purser, and I *believe* he's ashore just now. But I don't know his address."

"He didn't stay here, then, when he was ashore."

"He did once," Barton said. "But they had a row about money, and he wasn't asked again. That's how I happen to know about the once, because I came to call in the middle of it."

"How do you mean — about money?"

"Oh, Edgar Carluke wanted some; and his uncle wouldn't let him have it. I don't know — I didn't hear any more than that. But perhaps Mr. Carluke would have something about him in his papers, if you want to know."

"Do you know where he kept his papers?"

"Upstairs, in a safe in his bedroom. It's the room above this."

"Thank you. What is the bank manager's name — the branch manager?"

"Mr. Warren. He lives in Belsize Park, but he's away."

"Thank you. By the way, we shall want a light in that telephone cabinet, and the bulb appears to be broken. Do you happen to know where Mr. Carluke kept his spares?"

"Yes, in a cupboard in the kitchen, left of the gas stove."

"Would you mind finding me one, as you know where they are? Medium strength, please." Wilson went to the door of the kitchen, and stood waiting while Mr. Barton groped in a cupboard and extracted an electric bulb.

"This do?" he said, unwrapping it. "It's a forty."

"Thank you." Wilson took it from him. "Now, Sergeant, call your men in and tell them to disturb things as little as possible in getting him out. Constable!" He called to the man standing on guard at the hall door. "Take Mr. Barton up to Inspector Catling at once and let him make his statement. Tell the inspector the sergeant and

I are going over the house and will let him know as soon as possible how things are going. And, Constable — " He drew the man aside a little, and the conversation dropped to a whisper. Meanwhile the ambulance men had come in and were taking out their melancholy burden. Prendergast, who shuddered afresh as the remains of Mr. Carluke came out of the telephone cabinet, could not but marvel at the cool calm with which the police officers did their business. When it was finished, Wilson dismissed the other constable, who strode firmly off, a dejected Mr. Barton following in his wake.

"This is a shocking affair, sir," the sergeant began as the door closed on them.

"Shocking," Wilson agreed, beginning to open the case which the constable had brought, and which appeared to contain principally a number of little bottles of various kinds. "Did you know this Mr. Carluke, Sergeant? Any idea why he should be murdered?"

"Not an earthly, sir," the sergeant said. "As quiet-spoken and nice an old gentleman as you could wish. Bit unsociable, they said, but nothing to matter. I shouldn't have said he'd an enemy in the world."

"So Mr. Barton seemed to think," said Wilson, extracting a thin pair of gloves and putting them on. "Well, we'd better get on. I've a feeling that we've no time to lose in this affair, if we want to catch the murderer. Will you go round the house, Sergeant, and look at the doors and windows and see if you can find how he got away? Michael, could you look in that cupboard and see if you can find me a sixty lamp? I think I won't use this one after all." He laid it on a shelf as he spoke; and the sergeant looked up suddenly as if he were going to speak, but apparently thought better of it. Prendergast found the required lamp without much difficulty, and was taking it into the telephone cabinet to replace the old one, when Wilson stopped him. "Let me do that," he said; and unscrewed the old lamp carefully from the top with his gloved hands. The sergeant gave a chuckle.

"Looking for finger prints, sir?" he said. "The murderer's not very likely to have held on to the lamp, is he? Especially as it was broken."

"Oh, you never know," said Wilson. "Come in, Michael, and tell me what you think of it. You needn't mind treading there now. I looked at the footprints carefully before the men came in. Tell me how you think the man died." As he spoke, he was dusting the broken lamp and a card which he held in his hands with powder from his little bottles.

Prendergast stared round the little cabinet, which measured about seven feet by three. "He was shot here," he said. "He couldn't have moved after he had been hit, and he couldn't have bled like that if he'd been carried from anywhere else."

"That's so. And where was he shot from? Where did his murderer stand?"

"There, at the far end of the cabinet. You can see by the direction of the slugs. There's one gone into the wall facing the telephone."

"And Carluke was standing — where?"

"Just by the telephone, I should think, from the way he fell. At the far end, anyway."

"Then where was the man who shot him standing? There doesn't appear to be any room for him. And do you suggest Carluke walked up to a blunderbuss and stood right in front of it?"

"It was dark. The light was broken."

"True, O Michael. But when it's on in the hall there is plenty light enough to see anyone inside the cabinet. I don't suppose Mr. Carluke kept his house in complete darkness. Try it yourself."

Prendergast went out into the hall to make the experiment, which resulted as Wilson had said. When he returned he found his friend blowing powder over the telephone. "He must have been behind the curtain," Prendergast said.

"Behind the curtain! My dear fellow, there isn't room! It's full of boots, and even if he'd removed the boots, the whole shelf is only a foot wide. A man couldn't get underneath it. You try. No, not this minute. Come and look at the telephone. This is rather interesting."

"Are those finger prints?" asked Prendergast, looking at the instrument, to which little bits of yellow powder were adhering. "They don't look to me like anything."

"No, they aren't. The telephone's been rubbed clean. That's rather interesting in itself. People's charwomen aren't usually so particular. But that wasn't what I meant. Look at the shelf just by it."

"There's a bloodstain on it," said Prendergast. "I suppose it's Carluke's. But why shouldn't there be?"

"Because," said Wilson, "that bloodstain was right *under* the telephone."

"What! Then he was actually telephoning when he was killed, and managed to put the telephone back! I shouldn't have thought he would have been able to."

"Neither should I," said Wilson. "What's more, I don't think he did."

"Then his murderer did. Jove, that was pretty cool. By the way, Harry, at that rate, couldn't you fix the time of his death, anyway? The telephone people keep records of calls, don't they? If you asked for the last call he had that would fix the time almost exactly."

"Perhaps," said Wilson. "*If* he was telephoning. But we don't know that he was, yet. And you haven't told me where the murderer stood."

"Well, damn it!" Prendergast cried after a pause, which Wilson utilized to powder the electric light switch. "If he wasn't behind the curtain, I don't know where he stood! Could he have been at the other end of the cabinet — no, that's impossible, the shots are all the wrong way. I suppose he must have sneaked in while Carluke was telephoning and come right up to him and shot him from just by his ear. But it seems an insane thing to do."

"It does," said Wilson. "Quite insane."

"Well, do *you* know where he stood? And why he used a blunderbuss? It seems an extraordinary sort of weapon. Why not a revolver? They're plentiful enough."

"I think I've an idea where he stood — or rather, where he *didn't* stand," Wilson replied, "though it's only an idea; and at present I haven't the ghost of a notion how to prove it. And I'm pretty sure I know why he used a blunderbuss. Think of the specific characteristics of blunderbusses, and you'll be able to answer that question for yourself. Hullo, what's this?" He was standing close by the telephone, peering at the shelf above it. "God be praised, the charwoman isn't as thorough as might have been gathered from the telephone. Look there." Prendergast stared at the shelf, which was fairly thick with an accumulation of London dust. At one end, the end to which Wilson was pointing, there was a round depression in the dust about six inches across. "Something round has stood there," he said; and felt he was being a little obvious.

"It has," said Wilson. "And it has only recently been taken down, and it hadn't been standing there long. The dust on the mark is practically as thick as that on the rest of the shelf — it's only been compressed. Now look around, Michael, and tell me what made that mark."

"The telephone," Prendergast said promptly. Indeed it was the only possible object in sight.

"So it would appear. But we'd better make sure," said Wilson, proceeding carefully to measure the diameter of both telephone and mark. "Now perhaps you can tell me why the late Mr. Carluke kept his telephone in so inconvenient a position? I can hardly reach it, and I should say I'm as tall as he was."

"Taller," said the man of science mechanically; and racked his brains to think why the telephone should have been removed to that distant shelf. To make room for the murderer, seemed the only possible answer; yet what could it possibly avail a murderer to have the telephone cleared out of the way? Prendergast's mind, as he told Wilson, could only conjure up the vision of a murderous gnome the size of a telephone, sitting on the shelf with a blunderbuss in his arms. He was rather surprised that Wilson smiled at him encouragingly.

"That's better," Wilson said. "You're beginning to use your brains."

"If the only result of using them is to produce hobgoblins," Prendergast grumbled, "I think they might as well be unused." At that moment he nearly jumped out of his skin, for the bell of the telephone shrilled suddenly through the silent house.

"Somebody ringing up Mr. Carluke?" he said, as Wilson lifted the receiver.

"No, it's the station," the latter said. "Yes, Inspector. Yes. Wilson speaking . . ." Prendergast wandered out into the hall, where the sergeant was just coming downstairs after a careful official search of the house.

"Well, whoever did that poor fellow in's got wings," he said. "There's nowhere for him to have got out at. Back door's locked and bolted; windows all fastened and the snibs as tight as anything with this weather. You couldn't possibly push any of them back from outside. There's one window open on the top floor, but no signs of anyone getting in or out. And the window's too small to climb through without leaving marks."

"What about the chimneys?" Prendergast suggested. "I suppose a murderer could climb up a chimney?"

"Not up a gas flue he couldn't, Doctor," said the sergeant. "It's gas all over the house, and the flues quite tightly fastened in. No, he flew, that's what he did. Unless he chopped himself up and put himself away in pieces. I've looked everywhere a man could possibly hide himself in this house, and there's no one there."

At this point the telephone bell tinkled to indicate the end of the conversation, and Wilson came out into the hall. "You've some very efficient men at your station, Sergeant," he said; and the sergeant blushed with pleasure. "They've checked Barton's statements already. His story's all right. The landlord of the Dog and Duck remembers him and Carluke passing the door last night, and actually watched Carluke back to his own house. Then they've got on to his hosts at Hendon, who say he arrived at nine thirty and didn't leave till nearly one, and his wife and son say he came straight home."

"Sounds all right," said the sergeant. "Unless he came back after one."

"That would make it nearly two when he got back," said Wilson. "Buses and tubes would have stopped running by then, and he hasn't got a car."

He looked at Prendergast with a question in his eyes.

"I don't think so," the latter answered. "I'm pretty sure he was dead long before midnight. Of course, one can't tell to an hour or so — but I'm pretty certain. Did you think Barton's alibi was wrong then?"

"No," said Wilson, "I didn't. But we had to check it."

"And in any case," said the sergeant, "if he did come back, how'd he get out again?" He explained to Wilson the difficulties. "What are we to do now, sir?"

"Search the house thoroughly," Wilson said. "And his papers. I've got his keys. I'll help you. Only we must be quick."

"Anything you're looking for particular, sir?"

"Oh, as for papers — anything bearing on the crime — or suggesting that anybody else has been at 'em. And for the rest — the weapon."

"Blunderbuss, sir?"

"That, or something like it. But it may have been taken to pieces. Look for anything that could conceivably be part of a blunderbuss. It ought to be somewhere in the house, I'm pretty certain, but I've no idea where."

"It's my belief, Doctor," the sergeant said admiringly, as they began their search, "that Mr. Wilson's got the whole thing solved already."

"Only half solved, Sergeant," said Wilson, turning a rather anxious face on him. "I haven't got the motive, and I haven't got the weapon. And if we don't find one of them quickly I'm afraid I shan't get the murderer either."

It was a long and depressing search that they conducted through the dead man's effects, while the minutes wore on, and Wilson's face got more and more tense. Prendergast felt that he had never till that morning known what a careful search really was. Wilson made them grope in every crevice, shake out every cushion and every piece of fabric; he felt along the seams of mattresses and chair seats; he made them turn out the dustbin and the sink and look under the traps; they even went into the little garden and searched the gravel path that encircled the house, and all its adjoining flower beds; but all in vain. There was no blunderbuss, nor any less unusual firearm, to be seen; there was not even anything that might have been part of a blunderbuss. At length, after more than two hours' searching, they came to the safe, which Wilson unlocked with the dead man's keys.

"Doesn't look as if there was much to be found here, sir," said the sergeant, looking at the neat bundles of documents.

"Well, we can but try," said Wilson, beginning to examine the first packet.

"You know," he said after a few minutes, "I'm inclined to think that somebody's been through these papers before us. They're just a little bit out of order — as if somebody had tried to put them back tidily who didn't really know what the order was. Like one's library after someone's been dusting it. But for the life of me I can't make out what the somebody was after. Whatever it was, if he took it away it's left no traces. What on earth could he have wanted? There's not much sign of the mysterious nephew, anyway. Mr. Carluke seems to have been in the habit of destroying his private papers."

"You didn't," Prendergast, having no answer to the last question, suggested, "you didn't think anything of my idea that the telephone people might be able to give you the time of his death? That would settle people's alibis, anyway."

"I know," said Wilson. "The difficulty is, that I'm pretty certain he wasn't telephoning when he died."

"But he was!" Prendergast cried. "You're forgetting his hands — his fingers, I mean. Don't you remember the way they were curved? I can just see them. They were exactly at the angle one uses to hold a telephone" — he illustrated with his own hands — "only a bit wider — as if it had been dragged out of them, and the rigor had fixed them in that position. I remember noticing at the time, and wondering what he could possibly have been holding. I thought it might have been the blunderbuss — but if it had been, of course, he'd be holding it still. But the telephone's much more likely." He stopped with a feeling of triumph, for Wilson had dropped the papers and was looking at him with real respect.

"By George, Michael, I believe you've got it!" he said. "I'd quite forgotten his hands, fool that I am. Sergeant, do you happen to know if the post office have lost a telephone lately?"

"A telephone? I'm afraid I don't, sir," the sergeant chuckled, while Prendergast gaped at this unexpected result of his suggestion. "The post office attend to their own lost property."

"Then ring them up and find out, as quick as you can," was the reply. "Hurry up, man, the whole thing may depend on it."

"Why ever should you think they've lost a telephone?" Prendergast asked.

"It's only a guess," Wilson answered. "But if it's right, it makes the thing pretty certain."

The sergeant was away a long time, while Wilson and Prendergast patiently searched through a quiet old gentleman's most uninteresting private papers. When he came back, he gazed at Wilson with an expression almost of reverence on his face.

"How *did* you know, sir?" he said. "They *have* lost one. There was one pinched out of an empty flat in Golders Green within the last week or two; but they can't say exactly when, and they've no idea who took it. How did you know?"

"Well, it was a fairly obvious conclusion, wasn't it?" said Wilson. "I wish it was as obvious where it had got to. Come, we *must* find this thing. It can't have left the house; there wasn't time. And there's nowhere he can have dropped it — Good Lord!" He sprang to his feet, and made for the door. "The owl!"

"What's the matter?" Prendergast said, following him breathlessly as he rushed down the stairs.

"What a fool! The owl, of course!" was all the answer he got. "No, wait a moment. I'll be back directly."

Prendergast and the sergeant stood at the hall door, gaping, while Wilson ran out into the road and about a hundred yards up the hill. There he stood for five seconds or so, staring up at the trees which all but screened the house from view; and then he returned at the same pace. "It's the bathroom window, I think," he said as he regained the house; and shot up the stairs, the other two following. Arrived at the bathroom he flung wide the window, which was the same that the sergeant had already found open, and leaned out as far as possible to the left, groping with his hand in the thick ivy that covered the wall. After two or three seconds' searching he gave an exclamation of triumph.

"Got it!" he said. "At least, I think so. Will you both please look carefully? I want to have a witness to this." He brought his hand back, with a fat envelope in it marked Capital and Counties Bank. This he handed to the sergeant. "The weapon, sir?" the latter said, puzzled. "There's more coming," said Wilson; and dived again into the ivy.

"This wants careful handling," he said as he returned for the second time. In his hand was what at first sight looked like an ordinary telephone receiver. But on looking closely, it was apparent that the mouthpiece and the top of the telephone had been removed, and in their place was a fat muzzle of metal. Prendergast came close to it and stared down the black mouth of the thing.

"My God, it's the blunderbuss!" he said.

"It seems to be," said Wilson, "though we'll have to take it to pieces to find out how it worked. But it seems quite clear what the murderer did. The inside of this instrument has been taken out to make room for the charge, and the hook for the earpiece is fastened to the trigger. A man going to answer a telephone ring in the dark — remember that broken light, Sergeant, which was probably broken by the murderer — would take hold of the earpiece and let the gun off. You see now the point of having a blunderbuss — and a blunderbuss, as Dr. Prendergast noticed, charged with a peculiarly nasty type of expanding slug, like soft-nosed bullets. You can't make quite certain where a man's head will be when he's answering the telephone, and the blunderbuss was pretty safe to hit him wherever he was. There are some finger prints on both the receiver and the earpiece" — he had been dusting it with powder as he spoke — "I'm pretty certain they are Carluke's, but we can compare them downstairs for certain. I took his prints on a card before he was taken away. *Now*, Michael, I think I can answer the question I asked you a while back — where did the murderer stand when he killed his victim? The answer is — at a private telephone in Hendon. Sergeant, will you send down to the station and tell them to detain Edward Barton on suspicion of being concerned in the murder of Harold Carluke? I think you'll find he's still there."

"Good God, sir," the sergeant said. "What a diabolical thing! Do you mean he fixed up this affair and then went off and left the poor old boy to be shot next time he went to the telephone?"

"And then rang him up to make sure he did go," said Wilson. "Twice, you remember, in case he should have been out the first time. The telephone people will be able to trace those abortive calls for us. But, of course, he was dead long before the second one was made."

"Good God!" said the sergeant again. "The cold-blooded devil! Why did he murder him, sir?" He spoke as though he regarded Wilson as an eye-witness of the whole thing.

"I don't know that, yet," said Wilson. "But I shouldn't be surprised if the envelope you have in your hand throws some light on it." He tore it open, and a small bundle of cheques drawn on the Capital and Counties Bank fell out. Drawing a lens from his pocket, he made a rapid examination of the signatures.

"Of course, I don't know the Hampstead clients of the Capital and Counties Bank," he said. "But I should say there's no doubt that some of these are forgeries. Look at the waviness of that line in the glass. That's no true signature." He handed cheque and glass to the sergeant, who nodded agreement. "I presume Friend Barton had either written them or helped to pass them through; and that Carluke had found it out. If we get into touch with the bank manager, we'll probably get the whole story. But you'd better go and make sure of your prisoner. I doubt whether Catling's finding it easy to detain him."

"You gave my eyesight better credit than it deserved. What I took for an owl was Barton's hand putting the papers away," said Wilson. "My only excuse is that I wasn't looking at the place at all. I only got a faint impression at the edge of the retina, and when I focused on it, it was gone. There is only one spot in the road from which that particular bit of ivy is visible at all — and that spot's not visible from the window. Barton must have thought himself quite unobserved. But I nearly lost the clue, all the same, through not following up my impression quickly enough."

"What I don't see," Prendergast said, "is why you were looking for a weapon at all — why you thought it hadn't been taken away." They were discussing the case again after Barton's execution. Faced with the forged cheques and the incriminating telephone, his nerve had gone and he had confessed everything — incidentally giving away the actual forgers of the cheques which he had paid over the counter. The bank manager on his return had supplied the information that investigations had been made on one of the forged cheques, which had been detected, and that the dead man had asked him for an interview on that very subject as soon as he came back. Hence the necessity for his murder. The rest of the crime was as Wilson had indicated — even to the stealing of the telephone from the empty flat in Golders Green and the careful breaking of the electric light bulb.

"Well," Wilson said, "I didn't see what else he could have done with it. He had only been in the house a few minutes, the man at the gate said — no time to take it anywhere else. Of course, he might have had it on him; but I didn't think he'd risk that, as he knew he would have to go to the police station. If I hadn't found it in the house, I was going to have him searched, as a last resort. But I didn't want to do that, because we should have had to let him go, after his complete alibi; and that would have given him plenty of time to find and destroy his weapon, or to leave the country."

"Then you knew all along he was guilty?" Prendergast asked. "How?"

"Well, I began to suspect him as soon as I'd had a look at the telephone cabinet. You see, it was so obvious, from the dimensions of the cabinet and the direction of the shots, that the murderer hadn't been in the cabinet at all. You saw that yourself, only you were convinced that he must have been. But there was no room for him to have been, and no signs of his departure. There were only Barton's footprints visible, and no one could have got out across the body and across that pool of blood without stepping in it. I tried myself. That suggested that the man was alone when he was killed, and that he was killed by some mechanical means or other; and the fact that the bulb — a practically new one, as I daresay you noticed — was broken, was suspiciously convenient for a trap. I got Barton to put his finger prints on another bulb for me so as to have a record of them, and later I discovered that the broken one bore prints of the same hand. Of course, that wasn't conclusive; but it was suggestive. The bulb's well out of Barton's reach; he wouldn't have been changing it in the ordinary course of events. That was his principal slip, by the way; he wiped everything else clean — the real telephone rather suspiciously so — but he forgot the bulb.

"Well, if the man was alone when he met his death, obviously his murderer could have a cast-iron alibi, so that any alibis could be left out of account in the preliminary investigations. Actually, it made Mr. Barton's own alibi a little suspicious — it almost suggested careful preparation. So when I'd got all I wanted out of him, I left you to look after him and went back to make a further study. Then I found, as I showed you, that there was blood *under* the telephone, showing that it had been put down after the crime. Carluke himself couldn't possibly have put it back, as you said; he must have fallen as soon as he was hit; and as additional evidence of that, I found, when I examined the telephone, that Carluke had apparently never touched it at all. That meant that somebody else must have put it back after his death, and cleaned it after moving. But, so far as we knew, only Mr. Barton had been in the cabinet after his death. So I tried a little more investigation of Mr. Barton's movements; and when I found, first, that the telephone had apparently stood for a few hours on an exceedingly inaccessible shelf very recently, and secondly, prints of somebody's bloodstained toe tips just below the place where it had stood, and a smudge on the shelf below which looked uncommonly like the mark of a knee resting there, I was pretty certain that it was he who had moved it — and moved it back again when he 'discovered' the corpse.

"But why? As you very pertinently said, to make room for the murderer. At this point, I must admit, I was criminally slow. I ought to have thought of the dummy telephone at once. But I was still looking for an ordinary blunderbuss — probably fixed to the upper shelf, and fired by some mechanical arrangement — when your lucky recollection of the corpse's hands gave me the clue. Then it was plain sailing; we had only to find the dummy."

"Why didn't he wait a little longer, and take the thing to pieces, instead of giving the alarm at once?" Prendergast wondered.

"Probably because he didn't dare delay for fear of exciting the suspicion of the man at the gate," Wilson said. "Of course he didn't expect to find us there too. He thought he would be able to send the man to the police station, and have a quiet twenty minutes to clear up. Our turning up was just a bit of bad luck for him. So was that tiny gap in the trees. Otherwise, except for the oversight in regard to the bulb, which might very easily never have been found, I think he showed remarkable intelligence. His acting of innocent apprehensiveness was very natural indeed, and his alibi, if I hadn't suspected him already, was just right, and not too circumstantial."

"Did you deduce the motive, too?" Prendergast inquired.

"Not really. I only noted that, as both men worked in a bank, there was one obvious possibility. But there might have been a hundred others. And you see, of course, the paramount necessity of haste. If we had stayed to look for the motive, we should never have got the man."

A MATTER OF TASTE

by DOROTHY L. SAYERS

LORD PETER *is* LORD PETER; *but in this story sometimes he is and sometimes he isn't. Chiefly we liked "A Matter of Taste" because it made us thirsty.*

"HALTE-LÀ! . . . *Attention!* . . . *F——e!*"

The young man in the grey suit pushed his way through the protesting porters and leapt nimbly for the footboard of the guard's van as the Paris-Evreux express steamed out of the Invalides. The guard, with an eye to a tip, fielded him adroitly from among the detaining hands.

"It is happy for monsieur that he is so agile," he remarked. "Monsieur is in a hurry?"

"Somewhat. Thank you. I can get through by the corridor?"

"But certainly. The *premières* are two coaches away, beyond the luggage van."

The young man rewarded his rescuer, and made his way forward, mopping his face. As he passed the piled-up luggage, something caught his eye, and he stopped to investigate. It was a suitcase, nearly new, of expensive-looking leather, labelled conspicuously: —

LORD PETER WIMSEY,
Hôtel Saumon d'Or,
Verneuil-sur-Eure

and bore witness to its itinerary thus: —

LONDON — PARIS
(Waterloo)   (Gare St.-Lazare)
via Southampton-Havre

PARIS—VERNEUIL
(Ch. de Fer de l'Ouest)

The young man whistled, and sat down on a trunk to think it out.

Somewhere there had been a leakage, and they were on his trail. Nor did they care who knew it. There were hundreds of people in London and Paris who would know the name of Wimsey, not counting the police of both countries. In addition to belonging to one of the oldest ducal families in England, Lord Peter had made himself conspicuous by his meddling with crime detection. A label like this was a gratuitous advertisement.

But the amazing thing was that the pursuers were not troubling to hide themselves from the pursued. That argued very great confidence. That he should have got into the guard's van was, of course, an accident, but, even so, he might have seen it on the platform, or anywhere.

An accident? It occurred to him — not for the first time, but definitely now, and without doubt — that it was indeed an accident for them that he was here. The series of maddening delays that had held him up between London and the Invalides presented itself to him with an air of pre-arrangement. The preposterous accusation, for instance, of the woman who had accosted him in Piccadilly, and the slow process of extricating himself at Marlborough Street. It was easy to hold a man up on some trumped-up charge till an important plan had matured. Then there was the lavatory door at Waterloo, which had so ludicrously locked itself upon him. Being athletic, he had climbed over the partition, to find the attendant mysteriously absent. And, in Paris, was it by chance that he had had a deaf taxi driver, who mistook the direction "Quai d'Orléans" for "Gare de Lyon," and drove a mile and a half in the wrong direction before the shouts of his fare attracted his attention? They were clever, the pursuers, and circumspect. They had accurate information; they would delay him, but without taking any overt step; they knew that, if only they could keep time on their side, they needed no other ally.

Did they know he was on the train? If not, he still kept the advantage, for they would travel in a false security, thinking him to be left, raging and helpless, in the Invalides. He decided to make a cautious reconnaissance.

The first step was to change his grey suit for another of inconspicuous navy-blue cloth, which he had in his small black bag. This he did in the privacy of the toilet, substituting for his grey soft hat a large travelling cap, which pulled well down over his eyes.

There was little difficulty in locating the man he was in search of. He found him seated in the inner corner of a first-class compartment, facing the engine, so that the watcher could approach unseen from behind. On the rack was a handsome dressing case, with the initials P. D. B. W. The young man was familiar with Wimsey's narrow, beaky face, flat yellow hair, and insolent dropped eyelids. He smiled a little grimly.

"He is confident," he thought, "and has regrettably made the mistake of underrating the enemy. Good! This is where I retire into a *seconde* and keep my eyes open. The next act of this melodrama will take place, I fancy, at Dreux."

It is a rule on the Chemin de Fer de l'Ouest that all Paris-Evreux trains, whether of Grande Vitesse or what Lord Peter Wimsey preferred to call Grande Paresse, shall halt for an interminable period at Dreux. The young man (now in navy-blue) watched his quarry safely into the refreshment room, and slipped unobtrusively out of the station. In a quarter of an hour he was back — this time in a heavy motoring coat, helmet, and goggles, at the wheel of a powerful hired Peugeot. Coming quietly onto the platform, he took up his station behind the wall of the *lampisterie,* whence he could keep an eye on the train and the buffet door. After fifteen minutes his patience was rewarded by the sight of his man again boarding the express, dressing case in hand. The porters slammed the doors, crying: "Next stop Verneuil!" The engine panted and groaned; the long train of grey-green carriages clanked slowly away. The motorist drew a breath of satisfaction, and, hurrying past the barrier, started up the car. He knew that he had a good eighty miles an hour under his bonnet, and there is no speed limit in France.

Mon Souci, the seat of that eccentric and eremitical genius the Comte de Rueil, is situated three kilometres from Verneuil. It is a sorrowful and decayed château, desolate at the termination of its neglected avenue of pines. The mournful state of a nobility without an allegiance surrounds it. The stone nymphs droop greenly over their dry and mouldering fountains. An occasional peasant creaks with a single waggonload of wood along the ill-forested glades. It has the atmosphere of sunset at all hours of the day. The woodwork is dry and gaping for lack of paint. Through the *jalousies* one sees the prim *salon,* with its beautiful and faded furniture. Even the last of its ill-dressed, ill-favoured women has withered away from Mon Souci, with her inbred, exaggerated features and her long white gloves. But at the rear of the château a chimney smokes incessantly. It is the furnace of the laboratory, the only living and modern thing among the old and dying; the only place tended and loved, petted and spoiled, heir to the long solicitude which counts of a more light-hearted day had given to stable and kennel, portrait gallery and ballroom. And below, in the cool cellar, lie, row upon row, the dusty bottles, each an enchanted glass coffin in which the Sleeping Beauty of the vine grows ever more ravishing in sleep.

As the Peugeot came to a standstill in the courtyard, the driver observed with considerable surprise that he was not the count's only visitor. An immense super-Renault, like a *merveilleuse* of the Directoire, all bonnet and no body, had been drawn so ostentatiously across the entrance as to embarrass the approach of any newcomer. Its glittering panels were embellished with a coat of arms, and the count's elderly servant was at that moment staggering beneath the weight of two large and elaborate suitcases, bearing in silver letters that could be read a mile away the legend: "LORD PETER WIMSEY."

The Peugeot driver gazed with astonishment at this display, and grinned sardonically. "Lord Peter seems rather ubiquitous in this country," he observed to himself. Then, taking pen and paper from his bag, he busied himself with a little letter writing. By the time that the suitcases had been carried in, and the Renault had purred its smooth way to the outbuildings, the document was complete and enclosed in an envelope addressed to the Comte de Rueil. "The hoist with his own petard touch," said the young man, and, stepping up to the door, presented the envelope to the manservant.

"I am the bearer of a letter of introduction to monsieur le comte," he said. "Will you have the obligingness to present it to him? My name is Bredon — Death Bredon."

The man bowed, and begged him to enter.

"If monsieur will have the goodness to seat himself in the hall for a few moments. Monsieur le comte is engaged with another gentleman, but I will lose no time in making monsieur's arrival known."

The young man sat down and waited. The windows of the hall looked out upon the entrance, and it was not long before the château's sleep was disturbed by the hooting of yet another motor horn. A station taxicab came noisily up the avenue. The man from the first-class carriage and the luggage labelled P. D. B. W. were deposited upon the doorstep. Lord Peter Wimsey dismissed the driver and rang the bell.

"Now," said Mr. Bredon, "the fun is going to begin." He effaced himself as far as possible in the shadow of a tall *armoire normande.*

"Good evening," said the newcomer to the manservant, in admirable French, "I am Lord Peter Wimsey. I arrive upon the invitation of Monsieur le comte de Rueil. Monsieur le comte is at liberty?"

"Milord Peter Wimsey? Pardon, monsieur, but I do not understand. Milord de Wimsey is already arrived and is with monsieur le comte at this moment."

"You surprise me," said the other, with complete imperturbability, "for certainly no one but myself has any right to that name. It seems as though some person more ingenious than honest has had the bright idea of impersonating me."

The servant was clearly at a loss.

"Perhaps," he suggested, "monsieur can show his *papiers d'identité.*"

"Although it is somewhat unusual to produce one's credentials on the doorstep when paying a private visit," replied his lordship, with unaltered good humour, "I have not the slightest objection. Here is my passport, here is a *permis de séjour* granted to me in Paris, here my visiting card, and here a quantity of correspondence addressed to me at the Hôtel Meurice, Paris, at my flat in Piccadilly, London, at the Marlborough Club, London, and at my brother's house at King's Denver. Is that sufficiently in order?"

The servant perused the documents carefully, appearing particularly impressed by the *permis de séjour*.

"It appears there is some mistake," he murmured dubiously; "if monsieur will follow me, I will acquaint monsieur le comte."

They disappeared through the folding doors at the back of the hall, and Bredon was left alone.

"Quite a little boom in Richmonds to-day," he observed, "each of us more unscrupulous than the last. The occasion obviously calls for a refined subtlety of method."

After what he judged to be a hectic ten minutes in the count's library, the servant reappeared, searching for him.

"Monsieur le comte's compliments, and would monsieur step this way?"

Bredon entered the room with a jaunty step. He had created for himself the mastery of this situation. The count, a thin, elderly man, his fingers deeply stained with chemicals, sat, with a perturbed expression, at his desk. In two armchairs sat the two Wimseys. Bredon noted that, while the Wimsey he had seen in the train (whom he mentally named Peter I) retained his unruffled smile, Peter II (he of the Renault) had the flushed and indignant air of an Englishman affronted. The two men were superficially alike — both fair, lean, and long-nosed, with the nondescript, inelastic face which predominates in any assembly of well-bred Anglo-Saxons.

"Mr. Bredon," said the count, "I am charmed to have the pleasure of making your acquaintance, and regret that I must at once call upon you for a service as singular as it is important. You have presented to me a letter of introduction from your cousin, Lord Peter Wimsey. Will you now be good enough to inform me which of these gentlemen he is?"

Bredon let his glance pass slowly from the one claimant to the other, meditating what answer would best serve his own ends. One, at any rate, of the men in this room was a formidable intellect, trained in the detection of imposture.

"Well?" said Peter II. "Are you going to acknowledge me, Bredon?"

Peter I extracted a cigarette from a silver case. "Your confederate does not seem very well up in his part," he remarked, with a quiet smile at Peter II.

"Monsieur le comte," said Bredon, "I regret extremely that I cannot assist you in the matter. My acquaintance with my cousin, like your own, has been made and maintained entirely through correspondence on a subject of common interest. My profession," he added, "has made me unpopular with my family."

There was a very slight sigh of relief somewhere. The false Wimsey — whichever he was — had gained a respite. Bredon smiled.

"An excellent move, Mr. Bredon," said Peter I, "but it will hardly explain —— Allow me." He took the letter from the count's hesitating hand. "It will hardly explain the fact that the ink of this letter of recommendation, dated three weeks ago, is even now scarcely dry — though I congratulate you on the very plausible imitation of my handwriting."

"If *you* can forge my handwriting," said Peter II, "so can this Mr. Bredon." He read the letter aloud over his double's shoulder.

" 'Monsieur le comte — I have the honour to present to you my friend and cousin, Mr. Death Bredon, who, I understand, is to be travelling in your part of France next month. He is very anxious to view your interesting library. Although a journalist by profession, he really knows something about books.' I am delighted to learn for the first time that I have such a cousin. An interviewer's trick, I fancy, monsieur le comte. Fleet Street appears well-informed about our family names. Possibly it is equally well-informed about the object of my visit to Mon Souci?"

"If," said Bredon boldly, "you refer to the acquisition of the de Rueil formula for poison gas for the British Government, I can answer for my own knowledge, though possibly the rest of Fleet Street is less completely enlightened." He weighed his words carefully now, warned by his slip. The sharp eyes and detective ability of Peter I alarmed him far more than the caustic tongue of Peter II.

The count uttered an exclamation of dismay.

"Gentlemen," he said, "one thing is obvious — that there has been somewhere a disastrous leakage of information. Which of you is the Lord Peter Wimsey to whom I should entrust the formula I do not know. Both of you are supplied with papers of identity; both appear completely instructed in this matter; both of your handwritings correspond with the letters I have previously received from Lord Peter, and both of you have offered me the sum agreed upon in Bank of

England notes. In addition, this third gentleman arrives endowed with an equal facility in handwritings, an introductory letter surrounded by most suspicious circumstances, and a degree of acquaintance with this whole matter which alarms me. I can see but one solution. All of you must remain here at the château while I send to England for some elucidation of this mystery. To the genuine Lord Peter I offer my apologies, and assure him that I will endeavour to make his stay as agreeable as possible. Will this satisfy you? It will? I am delighted to hear it. My servants will show you to your bedrooms, and dinner will be at half past seven."

"It is delightful to think," said Mr. Bredon, as he fingered his glass and passed it before his nostrils with the air of a connoisseur, "that whichever of these gentlemen has the right to the name which he assumes is assured to-night of a truly Olympian satisfaction." His impudence had returned to him, and he challenged the company with an air. "Your cellars, monsieur le comte, are as well-known among men endowed with a palate as your talents among men of science. No eloquence could say more."

The two Lord Peters murmured assent.

"I am the more pleased by your commendation," said the count, "that it suggests to me a little test which, with your kind coöperation, will, I think, assist us very much in determining which of you gentlemen is Lord Peter Wimsey and which his talented impersonator. Is it not matter of common notoriety that Lord Peter has a palate for wine almost unequalled in Europe?"

"You flatter me, monsieur le comte," said Peter II modestly.

"I wouldn't like to say unequalled," said Peter I, chiming in like a well-trained duet; "let's call it fair to middling. Less liable to misconstruction and all that."

"Your lordship does yourself an injustice," said Bredon, addressing both men with impartial deference. "The bet which you won from Mr. Frederick Arbuthnot at the Egotists' Club, when he challenged you to name the vintage years of seventeen wines blindfold, received its due prominence in the *Evening Wire*."

"I was in extra form that night," said Peter I.

"A fluke," laughed Peter II.

"The test I propose, gentlemen, is on similar lines," pursued the count, "though somewhat less strenuous. There are six courses ordered for dinner to-night. With each we will drink a different wine, which my butler shall bring in with the label concealed. You shall each in turn give me your opinion upon the vintage. By this means we shall perhaps arrive at something, since the most brilliant forger — of whom I gather I have at least two at my table to-night — can scarcely forge a palate for wine. If too hazardous a mixture of wines should produce a temporary incommodity in the morning, you will, I feel sure, suffer it gladly for this once in the cause of truth."

The two Wimseys bowed.

"In vino veritas," said Mr. Bredon, with a laugh. He at least was well seasoned and foresaw opportunities for himself.

"Accident, and my butler, having placed you at my right hand, monsieur," went on the count, addressing Peter I, "I will ask you to begin by pronouncing, as accurately as may be, upon the wine which you have just drunk."

"That is scarcely a searching ordeal," said the other, with a smile. "I can say definitely that it is a very pleasant and well-matured Chablis Moutonne; and, since ten years is an excellent age for a Chablis — a real Chablis — I should vote for 1916, which was perhaps the best of the war vintages in that district."

"Have you anything to add to that opinion, monsieur?" enquired the count, deferentially, of Peter II.

"I wouldn't like to be dogmatic to a year or so," said that gentleman critically, "but if I must commit myself, don't you know, I should say 1915 — decidedly 1915."

The count bowed, and turned to Bredon.

"Perhaps you, too, monsieur, would be interested to give an opinion," he suggested, with the exquisite courtesy always shown to the plain man in the society of experts.

"I'd rather not set a standard which I might not be able to live up to," replied Bredon, a little maliciously. "I know that it is 1915, for I happened to see the label."

Peter II looked a little disconcerted.

"We will arrange matters better in future," said the count. "Pardon me." He stepped apart for a few moments' conference with the butler, who presently advanced to remove the oysters and bring in the soup.

The next candidate for attention arrived swathed to the lip in damask.

"It is your turn to speak first, monsieur," said the count to Peter II. "Permit me to offer you an olive to cleanse the palate. No haste, I beg. Even for the most excellent political ends, good wine must not be used with disrespect."

The rebuke was not unnecessary, for, after a preliminary sip, Peter II had taken a deep draught of the heady white richness. Under Peter I's quizzical eye he wilted quite visibly.

"It is — it is Sauterne," he began, and stopped. Then, gathering encouragement from Bredon's smile, he said, with more aplomb, "Château Yquem, 1911 — ah! the queen of white wines, sir, as what's-his-name says." He drained his glass defiantly.

The count's face was a study as he slowly detached his fascinated gaze from Peter II to fix it on Peter I.

"If I had to be impersonated by somebody," murmured the latter gently, "it would have been more flattering to have had it undertaken by a person to whom all white wines were *not* alike. Well, now, sir, this admirable vintage is, of course, a Montrachet of — let me see" — he rolled the wine delicately upon his tongue — "of 1911. And a very attractive wine it is, though, with all due deference to yourself, monsieur le comte, I feel that it is perhaps slightly too sweet to occupy its present place in the menu. True, with this excellent *consommé marmite,* a sweetish wine is not altogether out of place, but, in my own humble opinion, it would have shown to better advantage with the *confitures.*"

"There, now," said Bredon innocently, "it just shows how one may be misled. Had not I had the advantage of Lord Peter's expert opinion — for certainly nobody who could mistake Montrachet for Sauterne has any claim to the name of Wimsey — I should have pronounced this to be, not the Montrachet-Aîné, but the Chevalier-Montrachet of the same year, which is a trifle sweeter. But no doubt, as your lordship says, drinking it with the soup has caused it to appear sweeter to me than it actually is."

The count looked sharply at him, but made no comment.

"Have another olive," said Peter I kindly. "You can't judge wine if your mind is on other flavours."

"Thanks frightfully," said Bredon. "And that reminds me —— "

He launched into a rather pointless story about olives, which lasted out the soup and bridged the interval to the entrance of an exquisitely cooked sole.

The count's eye followed the pale amber wine rather thoughtfully as it trilled into the glasses. Bredon raised his in the approved manner to his nostrils, and his face flushed a little. With the first sip he turned excitedly to his host.

"Good God, sir —— " he began.

The lifted hand cautioned him to silence.

Peter I sipped, inhaled, sipped again, and his brows clouded. Peter II had by this time apparently abandoned his pretensions. He drank thirstily, with a beaming smile and a lessening hold upon reality.

"*Eh bien,* monsieur?" enquired the count gently.

"This," said Peter I, "is certainly hock, and the noblest hock I have ever tasted, but I must admit that for the moment I cannot precisely place it."

"No?" said Bredon. His voice was like bean honey now, sweet and harsh together. "Nor the other gentleman? And yet I fancy I could place it within a couple of miles, though it is a wine I had hardly looked to find in a French cellar at this time. It is hock, as your lordship says, and at that it is Johannisberger. Not the plebeian cousin, but the *echter* Schloss Johannisberger from the castle vineyard itself. Your lordship must have missed it (to your great loss) during the war years. My father laid some down the year before he died, but it appears that the ducal cellars at Denver were less well-furnished."

"I must set about remedying the omission," said the remaining Peter, with determination.

The *poulet* was served to the accompaniment of an argument over the Lafitte, his lordship placing it at 1878, Bredon maintaining it to be a relic of the glorious 'seventy-fives, slightly over-matured, but both agreeing as to its great age and noble pedigree.

As to the Clos-Vougeot, on the other hand, there was complete agreement; after a tentative suggestion of 1915, it was pronounced finally by Peter I to belong to the equally admirable though slightly lighter 1911 crop. The *pré-salé* was removed amid general applause, and the dessert was brought in.

"Is it necessary," asked Peter I, with a slight smile in the direction of Peter II — now happily murmuring, "Damn good wine,
damn good dinner, damn good show" — "is it necessary to prolong
this farce any further?"

"Your lordship will not, surely, refuse to proceed with the discussion?" cried the count.

"The point is sufficiently made, I fancy."

"But no one will surely ever refuse to discuss wine," said Bredon,
"least of all your lordship, who is so great an authority."

"Not on this," said the other. "Frankly, it is a wine I do not care
about. It is sweet and coarse, qualities that would damn any wine
in the eyes — the mouth, rather — of a connoisseur. Did your excellent father have this laid down also, Mr. Bredon?"

Bredon shook his head.

"No," he said, "no. Genuine Imperial Tokay is beyond the opportunities of Grub Street, I fear. Though I agree with you that it is
horribly overrated — with all due deference to yourself, monsieur le
comte."

"In that case," said the count, "we will pass at once to the liqueur.
I admit that I had thought of puzzling these gentlemen with the
local product, but, since one competitor seems to have scratched, it
shall be brandy — the only fitting close to a good wine list."

In a slightly embarrassing silence the huge, round-bellied balloon
glasses were set upon the table, and the few precious drops poured
gently into each and set lightly swinging to release the bouquet.

"This," said Peter I, charmed again into amiability, "is, indeed, a
wonderful old French brandy. Half a century old, I suppose."

"Your lordship's praise lacks warmth," replied Bredon. "This is
the brandy — the brandy of brandies — the superb — the incomparable — the true Napoleon. It should be honoured like the emperor
it is."

He rose to his feet, his napkin in his hand.

"Sir," said the count, turning to him, "I have on my right a most
admirable judge of wine, but you are unique." He motioned to
Pierre, who solemnly brought forward the empty bottles, unswathed
now, from the humble Chablis to the stately Napoleon, with the
imperial seal blown in the glass. "Every time you have been correct
as to growth and year. There cannot be six men in the world with

such a palate as yours, and I thought that but one of them was an Englishman. Will you not favour us, this time, with your real name?"

"It doesn't matter what his name is," said Peter I. He rose. "Put up your hands, all of you. Count, the formula!"

Bredon's hands came up with a jerk, still clutching the napkin. The white folds spurted flame as his shot struck the other's revolver cleanly between trigger and barrel, exploding the charge, to the extreme detriment of the glass chandelier. Peter I stood shaking his paralysed hand and cursing.

Bredon kept him covered while he cocked a wary eye at Peter II, who, his rosy visions scattered by the report, seemed struggling back to aggressiveness.

"Since the entertainment appears to be taking a lively turn," observed Bredon, "perhaps you would be so good, Count, as to search these gentlemen for further firearms. Thank you. Now, why should we not all sit down again and pass the bottle round?"

"You — *you* are —— " growled Peter I.

"Oh, my name is Bredon all right," said the young man cheerfully. "I loathe aliases. Like another fellow's clothes, you know — never seem quite to fit. Peter Death Bredon Wimsey — a bit lengthy and all that, but handy when taken in instalments. I've got a passport and all those things, too, but I didn't offer them, as their reputation here seems a little blown upon, so to speak. As regards the formula, I think I'd better give you my personal cheque for it — all sorts of people seem able to go about flourishing Bank of England notes. Personally, I think all this secret diplomacy work is a mistake, but that's the War Office's pigeon. I suppose we all brought similar credentials. Yes, I thought so. Some bright person seems to have sold himself very successfully in two places at once. But you two must have been having a lively time, each thinking the other was me."

"My lord," said the count heavily, "these two men are, or were, Englishmen, I suppose. I do not care to know what Governments have purchased their treachery. But where they stand, I, alas! stand too. To our venal and corrupt Republic I, as a Royalist, acknowledge no allegiance. But it is in my heart that I have agreed to sell my country to England because of my poverty. Go back to your War

Office and say I will not give you the formula. If war should come between our countries — which may God avert! — I will be found on the side of France. That, my lord, is my last word."

Wimsey bowed.

"Sir," said he, "it appears that my mission has, after all, failed I am glad of it. This trafficking in destruction is a dirty kind of business after all. Let us shut the door upon these two, who are neither flesh nor fowl, and finish the brandy in the library."

THE CYPRIAN BEES

by ANTHONY WYNNE

"The Cyprian Bees" is DR. HAILEY's *triumph — principally because he knows what anaphylactic shock is. Do you?*

INSPECTOR BILES, of Scotland Yard, placed a small wooden box on the table in front of Dr. Hailey.

"There," he remarked in cheerful tones, "is a mystery which even you, my dear Doctor, will scarcely be able to solve."

Dr. Hailey bent his great head, and examined the box with minute care. It was merely a hollowed-out block of wood, to which a lid, also of wood, was attached at one point by a nail. The lid rotated on this nail. He put out his hand to open it, but Biles checked that intention immediately.

"Take care!" he exclaimed; "there are three live bees in that box." He added, "There were four of them originally, but one stung a colleague of mine, who was incautious enough to pull the lid open without first finding out what it covered."

He leaned back in his chair, and drew a long whiff of the excellent cigar with which Dr. Hailey had supplied him. He remained silent, while a heavy vehicle went lumbering down Harley Street. Then he said:

"Last night, one of my men found the box lying in the gutter in Piccadilly Circus, just opposite the Criterion Theatre. He thought it looked peculiar, and brought it down to the Yard. We have a bee-keeper of some distinction on the staff, and he declares that these insects are all workers, and that only a lunatic would carry them about in this fashion. Queens, it appears, are often transported in boxes."

Dr. Hailey raised his eyeglass and set it in his eye.

"So I have heard." He opened his snuffbox, and took a large pinch. "You know, of course, my dear Biles," he added, "what this particular box contained before the bees were put into it."

"No — I don't."

"Serum — either anti-diphtheria serum or one of the other varieties. Practically every manufacturer of these products uses this type of receptacle for them."

"H'm!" Biles leaned forward in his chair. "So that means that in all probability, the owner of the bees is a doctor. How very interesting!"

Dr. Hailey shook his head.

"It doesn't follow," he remarked. "The box was perhaps left in a patient's house after its contents had been used. The patient may have employed it for its present purpose."

Biles nodded. He appeared to hesitate a moment; then he said:

"The reason why I troubled you was that, last night, a woman was found dead at the wheel of a motor car — a closed coupé — in Leicester Square. She had been stung by a bee just before her death."

He spoke in quiet tones, but his voice nevertheless revealed the fact that the disclosure he was making had assumed great importance in his mind. He added:

"The body was examined by a doctor almost immediately. He observed the sting, which was in her forehead. The dead bee was recovered later, from the floor of the car."

As he spoke he took another box from his pocket and opened it. He held it out to the doctor.

"You will notice that there are rather unusual markings on the bee's body — these yellow rings. Our expert says that they indicate a special breed, the Cyprian, and that these insects are notoriously very ill-natured. The peculiar thing is that the bees in the wooden box are also Cyprian bees."

Dr. Hailey picked up a large magnifying glass which lay on the table beside him, and focused it on the body of the insect. His knowledge of bees was not extensive, but he recognised that this was not the ordinary brown English type. He set the glass down again, and leaned back in his chair.

"It is certainly very extraordinary," he declared. "Have you any theory?"

Biles shook his head. "None, beyond the supposition that the shock caused by the sting was probably the occasion for the woman's sudden collapse. She was seen to pull quickly to the side of the road, and stop the car, so she must have had a presentiment of what was coming. I suppose heart failure might be induced by a sting?"

"It is just possible." Dr. Hailey took more snuff. "Once, long ago," he said, "I had personal experience of a rather similar case — that of a beekeeper who was stung some years after he had given up his own apiary. He died in about five minutes. But that was a clear case of anaphylaxis."

"I don't understand."

Dr. Hailey thought a moment. "Anaphylaxis," he explained, "is the name given to one of the most amazing phenomena in the whole of medical science. If a human being receives an injection of serum or blood, or any extract or fluid from the animal body, a tremendous sensitiveness is apt to develop, afterwards, towards that particular substance. For example, an injection of the white of a duck's egg will, after the lapse of a week or so, render a man so intensely sensitive to this particular egg white that, if a further injection is given, instant death may result.

"Even if a duck's egg is eaten, there may be violent sickness and collapse, though hen's eggs will cause no ill effect. Queerly enough, however, if the injection is repeated within, say, a day of its first administration no trouble occurs. For the sensitiveness to develop, it is essential that time should elapse between the first injection and the second one. Once the sensitiveness has developed, it remains active for years. The beekeeper, whose death I happened to witness, had often been stung before: but he had not been stung for a very long time."

"Good God!" Biles's face wore an expression of new interest. "So it is possible that this may actually be a case of — *murder!*"

He pronounced the word in tones of awe. Dr. Hailey saw that already his instincts as a man hunter were quickening.

"It is just possible. But do not forget, my dear Biles, that the murderer using this method would require to give his victim a preliminary dose — by inoculation — of bee poison, because a single sting would scarcely be enough to produce the necessary degree of sensitiveness. That is to say, he would require to exercise an amount of force which would inevitably defeat his purpose — *unless he happened to be a doctor.*"

"Ah! the wooden serum box!" The detective's voice thrilled.

"Possibly. A doctor undoubtedly could inject bee poison, supposing he possessed it, instead of ordinary serum, or of an ordinary vaccine. It would hurt a good deal — but patients expect inoculation to hurt them."

Biles rose. "There is no test, is there," he asked, "by which it would be possible to detect the presence of this sensitiveness you speak of in a dead body?"

"None."

"So we can only proceed by means of circumstantial evidence." He drew a sharp breath. "The woman has been identified as the widow of an artist named Bardwell. She had a flat — a luxurious one — in Park Mansions, and seems to have been well off. But we have not been able to find any of her relations so far." He glanced at his watch. "I am going there now. I suppose I couldn't persuade you to accompany me?"

Dr. Hailey's rather listless eyes brightened. For answer he rose, towering above the detective in that act.

"My dear Biles, you know that you can always persuade me."

The flat in Park Mansions was rather more, and yet rather less, than luxurious. It bespoke prodigality, but it bespoke also restlessness of mind — as though its owner had felt insecure in her enjoyment of its comforts. The rooms were too full, and their contents were saved from vulgarity only by sheer carelessness of their bestowal. This woman seemed to have bought anything, and to have cared for nothing. Thus, in her dining-room, an exquisite Queen Anne sideboard was set cheek by jowl with a most horrible Victorian armchair made of imitation walnut. In the drawing-room there were flower glasses of the noblest period of Venetian craftsmanship, in which beauty was held captive in wonderful strands of gold, and beside these, shocking and obscene examples of "golden glass" ware from some third-rate Bohemian factory.

Dr. Hailey began to form a mental picture of the dead woman. He saw her, changeable, greedy, gaudy, yet with a certain instinctive charm — the kind of woman who, if she is young and beautiful, gobbles a man up. Women of that sort, his experience had shown him, were apt to drive their lovers to despair with their extravagances or their infidelities. Had the owner of the bees embarked on his terrible course in order to secure himself against the mortification of being supplanted by some more attractive rival? Or was he merely removing from his path a woman of whom he had grown tired? In any case, if the murder theory was correct, he must have stood in the relationship to the dead girl of doctor to patient, and he must have possessed an apiary of his own.

A young detective, whom Biles introduced as Tadcaster, had already made a careful examination of the flat. He had found nothing, not even a photograph. Nor had the owners of neighbouring flats been able to supply any useful information. Mrs. Bardwell, it appeared, had had men friends who had usually come to see her after dark. They had not, apparently, been in the habit of writing to her, or, if they had, she had destroyed all their letters. During the last few weeks, she seemed to have been without a servant.

"So you have found nothing?" Biles's tones were full of disappointment.

"Nothing, sir — unless, indeed, this is of any importance."

Tadcaster held out a crumpled piece of paper. It was a shop receipt, bearing the name of the *Times* Book Club, for a copy of *The Love Songs of Robert Browning*. There was no name on it.

Biles handed it to Dr. Hailey, who regarded it for a few moments in silence, and then asked:

"Where did you find this?"

"In the fireplace of the bedroom."

The doctor's eyes narrowed.

"It does not strike me," he said, "that such a collection of poems would be likely to interest the owner of this flat."

He folded the slip, and put it carefully into his pocket book. He added:

"On the other hand, Browning's love songs do appeal very strongly to some women." He fixed his eyeglass and regarded the young detective. "You have not found the book itself, have you?"

"No, sir. There are a few novels in the bedroom, but no poetry of any kind."

Dr. Hailey nodded. He asked to be shown the collection, and made a detailed examination of it. The novels were all of the lurid, sex type. It was as he had anticipated. He opened each of the books, and glanced at the flyleaves. They were all blank. He turned to Biles.

"I am ready to bet that Mrs. Bardwell did not pay that bill at the Book Club," he declared. "And I am ready to bet also that this book was not bought for her."

The detective shrugged his shoulders.

"Probably not," he said unconcernedly.

"Then, why should the receipt for it be lying in this room?"

"My dear Doctor, how should I know? I suppose, because the man who possessed it chose to throw it away here."

The doctor shook his head.

"Men do not buy collections of love songs for themselves, nor, for that matter, do women. They buy them — almost invariably — to give to people they are interested in. Everybody, I think, recognises that."

He broke off. A look of impatience came into Biles's face.

"Well?"

"Therefore, a man does not, as a rule, reveal to one woman the fact that he has made such a purchase on behalf of another. I mean, it is difficult to believe that any man on intimate terms with Mrs. Bardwell would have invited her jealousy by leaving such plain evidence of his interest in another woman lying about in her rooms. I assume, you see, that no man would give that poor lady this particular book."

Biles shrugged his shoulders. The point seemed to him immaterial. He glanced round the bedroom with troubled eyes.

"I wish," he declared, "that we had something to go on — something definite, leading towards some individual."

His words were addressed impartially to his subordinate and to Dr. Hailey. The former looked blank, but the doctor's expression was almost eager. He raised his eyeglass, and put it into his eye.

"My dear Biles," he said, "we have something definite to go on. I was about to suggest to you when you interrupted me that the receipt for the book probably fell from the pocket of the purchaser through a hole in that pocket. Just as the little box containing the additional bees, which he had not found it necessary to release, was destined to fall later, when the man, having assured himself that an insect of unimpaired vigour was loose and on the wing, descended in Piccadilly Circus from Mrs. Bardwell's car."

He paused. The detective had turned to him, interested once more. The thought crossed Dr. Hailey's mind that it was a pity Biles had not been gifted by Providence with an appreciation of human nature as keen as his grasp of material circumstances. He allowed his eyeglass to drop, in a manner which proclaimed that he had shot his bolt. He asked:

"You have not, perhaps, taken occasion to watch a man receiving a shop receipt for goods he has just bought and paid for? Believe me, a spectacle full of instruction in human nature. The receipt is handed, as a rule, by a girl, and the man, as a rule, pushes it into his nearest pocket, because he does not desire to be so rude or so untidy as to drop it on the floor. Shyness, politeness, and tidiness, my dear Biles, are all prominent elements in our racial character."

Again he broke off, this time to take a pinch of snuff. The two detectives watched that process with some impatience.

"A man with a hole in his coat pocket — a hole not very large, yet large enough to allow a piece of crumpled paper to work its way out as the wearer of the coat strode up and down the floor of the room — is not that a clue? A doctor, perhaps, with, deep in his soul, the desire for such women as Mrs. Bardwell — cheap, yet attractive women —— "

"I thought you expressed the opinion that he bought the love songs for some other woman!" Biles snapped.

"Exactly. Some other woman sufficiently like Mrs. Bardwell to attract him, though evidently possessed of a veneer of education to which Mrs. Bardwell could lay no claim." Dr. Hailey's large, kindly face grew thoughtful. "Has it not struck you," he asked, "that, though a man may not be faithful to any one woman, he is almost always faithful to a type? Again and again I have seen in first and second wives the same qualities of mind and appearance, both good and bad. Indeed, I would go so far as to say that our first loves and our last are kindred spirits, recognised and chosen by needs and desires which do not change, or change but little, throughout the course of life."

"Even so, my dear Hailey."

Biles's look of perplexity had deepened. The doctor, however, was too eager to be discouraged.

"If Mrs. Bardwell was, in fact, murdered," he continued, "the figure of her murderer is not, I think, very difficult to visualise: a doctor in early middle life — because the dead woman is at least thirty — with a practice in the country, but the tastes of a townsman; a trifle careless of his clothes, since he tolerates holes in his pockets, a sentimental egoist, since he buys Browning's love songs while plans of murder are turning over in his mind —— " He broke off, and thought a moment. "It is probable that Mrs. Bardwell was an expensive luxury. Such women, too, fight like tigers for the possession of the men they rely on. Yet, though she had undoubtedly obtained a great, perhaps a terrible, hold on him, she had failed to make him marry her."

He turned to Biles, and readjusted his eyeglass.

"Why do you suppose," he asked, "Mrs. Bardwell failed to make this doctor marry her?"

"I have no idea." The detective's tones were crisp, almost to the point of abruptness.

Dr. Hailey moved across the room to a writing table which stood near the window. He took a sheet of paper, and marked a small circle on it. Around this he drew a much larger circle. He returned to the detectives, who stood watching him.

"Here is London," he said, pointing to the small circle, "and here is the country round it up to a distance of forty miles — that is to say, up to a two-hour journey by motor car. As our doctor seems to make frequent visits to town, that is not, I think, too narrow a radius. Beyond about forty miles, London is no longer within easy reach."

He struck his pencil at two places through the circumference of the larger circle, marking off a segment.

"Here," he went on, "are the Surrey highlands, the area, within our district, where heather grows, and where, in consequence, almost everyone keeps bees."

He raised his head, and faced the two men, whose interest he seemed to have recaptured.

"It should not," he suggested, "be impossible to discover whether

or not, within this area, there is a doctor in practice who keeps
Cyprian bees, is constantly running up to London, wears an overcoat with a hole in one of the pockets, and lives apart from his
wife."

"Good heavens!" Biles drew his breath sharply. His instincts as a
man hunter had reasserted themselves. He glanced at the doctor
with an enthusiasm which lacked nothing of generosity. The younger
detective, however, retained his somewhat critical expression.

"Why should the doctor be living apart from his wife?" he asked.

"Because, had she not left him as soon as he tired of her, he would
probably have killed her long ago, and, in that case, he would almost
certainly have married Mrs. Bardwell during the first flush of his
devotion to her. I know these sensualists who are also puffed up
with literary vanity. Marriage possesses for them an almost incredible
attractiveness."

He glanced at his watch as he spoke. The recollection of a professional appointment had come suddenly to his memory.

"If you are to follow up the clue, my dear Biles," he remarked,
as he left the flat, "I hope you will let me know the result. *The
Medical Directory* should serve as a useful starting point."

Dr. Hailey was kept fully occupied during the next day, and was
unable, in consequence, to pursue the mystery of the Cyprian bees
any further. In the later afternoon, however, he rang up Inspector
Biles at Scotland Yard. A voice, the tones of which were sufficiently
dispirited, informed him that the whole of the home counties did
not contain a doctor answering the description with which he had
furnished the police.

"Mrs. Bardwell," Biles added, "kept a maid, who has been on
holiday. She returned last night, and has now told us that her mistress received very few men at her flat, and that a doctor was not
among the number. Of course, it is possible that a doctor may have
called during the last fortnight, in the girl's absence. But, in the
circumstances, I'm afraid we must look on the murder theory as
rather far-fetched. After all, the dead woman possessed a car, and
may have been in the country herself on the morning on which she
was stung. Bees often get trapped in cars."

Dr. Hailey hung up the receiver, and took a pinch of snuff. He
sat down in his big armchair, and closed his eyes that he might

pass, in fresh review, the various scraps of evidence he had collected. If the dead woman had not received the doctor at her house, then the idea that they were on intimate terms could scarcely be maintained. In that case, the whole of his deductions must be invalidated. He got up and walked down Harley Street to the *Times* Book Club. He showed the receipt which he had retained, and asked if he might see the assistant who had conducted the sale. This girl remembered the incident clearly. It had occurred about a week earlier. The man who had bought the volume of poems was accompanied by a young woman.

"Did you happen to notice," Dr. Hailey asked, "what his companion looked like?"

"I think she was very much 'made up.' She had fair hair; but I can't say that I noticed her carefully."

"And the man?"

The girl shrugged her shoulders. "I'm afraid I don't remember him clearly. A business man, perhaps." She thought a moment. "He was a good deal older than she was, I should say."

Dr. Hailey left the shop, and walked back towards Harley Street. On one point, at least, he had not been mistaken. The purchaser of the *Love Songs* was a man, and he had bought them for a woman who was not Mrs. Bardwell. Biles had mentioned that this lady had auburn hair. Why should the man have visited Mrs. Bardwell so soon after making this purchase? He sighed. After all, why not? Biles was quite right in thinking that no jury in the world would listen to evidence the only basis of which was character reading at second hand. He reached his door, and was about to let himself into the house when a cab drew up beside him. The young detective, Tadcaster, to whom Biles had introduced him at Park Mansions, got out.

"Can I see you a moment, Doctor?" he asked.

They entered the house together, Tadcaster produced a letter from his pocket, and handed it to Dr. Hailey. It was a prescription, written on Mrs. Bardwell's note paper, and signed only with initials, which were nearly indecipherable.

"I found it after you had gone," the young man explained. "It was dispensed, as you can see, by a local chemist. To-day I have seen him, and he says he has had other similar prescriptions to dispense.

But he has no idea who the writer is. Mrs. Bardwell had the medicine a few days ago."

Dr. Hailey read the prescription, which was a simple iron tonic. The signature was illegible. He shook his head.

"This does not carry us much further, I'm afraid," he declared.

"You can't tell from the initials who the doctor is."

"No."

"In that case, I think we shall have to throw our hands in." Tadcaster's voice expressed considerable disappointment. It was obvious that he had hoped to make reputation out of the solution of the mystery. "Your reasoning yesterday," he added, "impressed me very much, sir, if I may say so."

Dr. Hailey inclined his head, but his eyes were vacant. So a doctor had called on the dead woman recently — and also, apparently, made earlier visits — a doctor, too, whose prescriptions were unfamiliar to the local chemist. He turned to the young detective.

"I have just heard from Biles," he said, "that the maid has come back. Do you happen to know if she has any recollection of these professional visits?"

"I asked her that myself. She says that she knows nothing about them."

Again the far-away look came to the doctor's eyes. The fact that the prescriptions were written on Mrs. Bardwell's note paper showed that they had been given during an attendance at the flat. For what reason had the dead woman been at pains to hide her doctor's visits from her maid?

"Should I be troubling you very much," he said, "if I asked you to take me back to Park Mansions? I confess that I would like to ask that girl a few questions. A doctor can obtain information which is not likely to be imparted to any layman."

As they drove through the crowded streets, Dr. Hailey asked himself again the question which had caused him to embark on this fresh investigation. What reason had Mrs. Bardwell for hiding her need of medical attendance from her maid? Even supposing that her doctor was also her lover there seemed to be no sense in such a concealment. He opened his eyes and saw the stream of London's home-going population surging around the cab. Sweet-faced girls and splendid youths, mingled with women whose eyes told their story of disappointment, and men who wore pressing responsibility as an habitual expression. No wonder the police despaired of finding any one nameless human being in this vast tide of humanity, of hopes and fears, of desires and purposes!

The cab stopped. They entered the lift and came to the door of the flat. Tadcaster rang the bell. A moment later the door was opened by a young girl, who invited them to enter in tones which scarcely disguised the anxiety she apparently felt at the return of the police. She closed the door, and then led the way along the dim entrance corridor. She opened the door of the drawing-room.

As the light from the windows fell on her face, Dr. Hailey repressed an exclamation of amazement. He started, as though a new idea had sprung to his mind. A slight flush mounted to his cheeks. He raised his eyeglass and inserted it quickly in his eye.

"I have troubled you," he said to the girl, "because there are a few points about Mrs. Bardwell's health, before her fatal seizure, which I think you can help us to understand. I may say that I am a doctor, assisting the police."

"Oh, yes!"

The girl's voice was low. Her pretty, heavily powdered face seemed drawn with anxiety, and her eyes moved restlessly from one man to the other. She raised her hand in a gesture of uneasiness, and clasped her brow, seeming to press her golden curls into the white flesh.

"Perhaps it might be better if I spoke to you alone?"

Dr. Hailey's tones were very gentle. He looked at Tadcaster as he spoke, and the detective immediately got up and left the room. Then he turned to the girl.

"Your mistress," he asked, "discharged you from her employment a fortnight ago?"

The girl started violently, and all the blood seemed to ebb from her cheeks. Wild fear stared at him from her big, lustrous eyes.

"No!"

"My dear girl, if I may say so, you have everything to gain, nothing to lose, by telling the truth."

He spoke coldly, yet there was a reassuring note in his voice. He saw fear give place a little to that quality of weakness which he had expected to find in her character — the quality which had attracted Mrs. Bardwell's lover, and which explained, in some subtle fashion, the gift of the *Love Songs*. He repeated his question. The girl hung her head. She consented. He let his eyeglass fall.

"Because of your intimacy with a man she had been accustomed to look on as her own particular friend."

"Oh, no, no! It is not true!"

Again her eyes challenged him; she had thrown back her head, revealing the full roundness of her throat. The light gleamed among her curls. No wonder that this beauty had been able to dispossess her mistress!

"Listen to me." Dr. Hailey's face had grown stern. "You have denied that any doctor came to this flat — at least, so far as you know. As it happens, however, a number of prescriptions were dispensed for Mrs. Bardwell by the local chemist; so that, either she took great pains to hide from you the fact that she was calling in a doctor, or — you have not been speaking the truth."

"She did not tell me."

He raised his hand. "It will be easy," he said, "to get an answer to that question. If your mistress was really hiding her doctor's visits from you, she must have taken her prescriptions herself, personally, to the chemist. I shall find out from him later on whether or not that is so."

Again the girl's mood changed. She began to whimper, pressing a tiny lace handkerchief to her eyes in coquettish fashion.

Dr. Hailey drew a deep breath. He waited a moment before framing his next remark. Then he said:

"You realise, I suppose, that if a girl helps a man to commit a crime, she is as guilty as he is, in the eyes of the law."

"What do you mean?"

All her defences now were abandoned. She stood before him, abject in her terror, with staring eyes and trembling lips.

"That your presence here to-day proves you have had a share in this business. Why did you return to the flat?"

"Because — because —— "

"*Because he — the man you are shielding — wanted to find out what the police were doing in the place?*"

She tottered towards him, and laid her hands on his arm.

"Oh, God, I am so frightened," she whispered.

"You have reason — to be frightened."

He led her to a chair, but suddenly she seemed to get her strength anew. Her grasp on his arm tightened.

"I didn't want him to do it," she cried, in tones of anguish. "I swear that I didn't. And I swear that I have no idea, even yet, what he did do. We were going to be married — immediately."

"Married!" His voice seemed to underline the word.

"I swear that. It was honest and above-board, only he had her on his hands, and she had wasted so much of his money."

For the first time her voice rang true. She added:

"His wife cost a lot, too, though she was not living with him. She died a month ago."

They stood facing one another. In the silence of the room, the ticking of an ornate little clock on the mantel shelf was distinctly audible.

Dr. Hailey leaned forward.

"His name?" he asked.

"No, I shall not tell you."

She had recaptured her feeble courage. It gleamed from her eyes, for an instant transforming even her weakness. The vague knowledge that she loved this man in her paltry, immoral way, came to him. He was about to repeat his demand, when the door of the room opened. Tadcaster came in with a small, leather-bound volume in his hand.

The girl uttered a shrill cry and sprang towards him; but Dr. Hailey anticipated that move. He held her firmly.

"It is the collection of Browning's *Love Songs,*" the detective said. "I found it lying open in the next room. There is an inscription signed 'Michael Cornwall.'"

He held the book out for the doctor's inspection, but Dr. Hailey's face had grown as pale, almost, as that of the girl by his side.

He repeated the name — "Michael Cornwall" — almost like a man in a dream.

The place was hidden among its trees. Dr. Hailey walked up the avenue with slow steps. The thought of the mission which had brought him to this lovely Hampstead house lay — as it had lain through all the hours of the night — like death on his spirits. Michael Cornwall, the well-known Wimpole Street bacteriologist, and he had been boys together at Uppingham. They were still acquaintances.

He came to the front door, and was about to ring the bell when the man he was looking for appeared round the side of the house, accompanied by an old man and a girl.

"Hailey — well I'm dashed!"

Dr. Cornwall advanced with outstretched hand. His deep, rather sinister eyes welcomed his colleague with an enthusiasm which was entirely unaffected. He introduced: "My uncle, Colonel Cornwall, and my cousin, Miss Patsy Cornwall, whom you must congratulate on having just become engaged," in his quick staccato manner.

"We're just going round the garden," he explained, "and you must accompany us. And, after that, to luncheon. Whereupon, my dear Hailey, if you have — as I feel you have — great business to discuss with me, we shall discuss it."

His bantering tones accorded well with his appearance, which had changed but little in the years. He was the same astute, moody, inordinately vain fellow who had earned for himself, once upon a time, the nickname of "The Lynx."

They strolled across the lawn, and came to a brick wall of that rich russet hue which only time and the seasons can provide. Dr. Cornwall opened a door in the wall, and stood back for his companions to enter.

A sight of entrancing beauty greeted them, lines of fruit trees in full blossom, as though the snows of some Alpine sunset had been spread, in all their glowing tints, on this English garden. Dr. Hailey, however, had no eyes for this loveliness. His gaze was fixed on a row of white-painted beehives which gleamed in the sunlight under the distant wall. Patsy Cornwall exclaimed in sheer wonder. Then a new cry of delight escaped her, as she detected, in a large greenhouse which flanked the wall, a magnificent display of scarlet tulips. She took Dr. Hailey, in whose eyes the melancholy expression seemed to have deepened, to inspect these, while her father and cousin strolled on up the garden path. She stood with him in the narrow gangway of the greenhouse, and feasted ecstatic eyes on the wonderful blossoms.

"Don't they make you wish to gather them all and take them away somewhere where there are no flowers?"

She turned to him, but he had sprung away from her side.

A cry, shrill and terrible, pierced the lazy silence of the morning. She saw her father and cousin fleeing back, pursued by an immense swarm of winged insects, towards the garden gate.

Blindly, frantically, they sought to ward off the dreadful onslaught. The old man stumbled, and would have fallen, had not his nephew caught him in his arms. She had a momentary glimpse of his face; it was as though she had looked on the face of Death.

"*The bees!*"

The words broke from Dr. Hailey's lips as a moan of despair. He had come to the closed door of the greenhouse, and seemed to be about to open it; but at the same moment one of the infuriated insects in delirious flight struck the glass pane beside him. Then another — and another — and another. He came reeling back towards the girl.

"Lie down on the gangway!" he shouted, at the highest pitch of his voice. "There may be a broken pane somewhere."

She turned her horror-stricken eyes to him.

"My father — oh, God!"

"Lie down for your life!"

He stood beside her, watching, ready to strike if one of the bees succeeded in entering the greenhouse. Only once did he remove his straining eyes from this task. The sight which then greeted them wrought a fresh cry of horror from his lips.

The terrible swarm hung like a dust cloud in the air above the garden gate, rising and falling in swift undulations, which caused the light to flash and scintillate on a myriad gilded bodies and shining wings. A faint, shrill piping came to his ears across the silence. The door in the wall was open, and the garden now quite empty.

Biles leaned forward.

"Mrs. Bardwell's maid has confessed that she rang up Dr. Cornwall immediately before luncheon this morning," he said. "She tried to communicate with him before, but he had gone to the country, to a case, overnight. He got her warning that the police suspected him of being responsible for her mistress's death just after he had carried his second victim, his uncle, in a dying condition, from the garden."

The detective struck a match, and relit his cigar. Dr. Hailey sat watching him with sorrowful eyes.

"Ten minutes later, as you know," he went on, "Cornwall blew his brains out. He had the wit to see that the game was up. He had been badly stung, of course, but his long experience of the bees made this a less serious matter than it would have been in the case of an ordinary outsider. In any case, moreover, he had to accept that risk if his plan was to succeed."

Silence fell in the big consulting room. Then the doctor remarked: "Miss Cornwall has recently become engaged to be married?"

"Yes." Biles drew a long whiff. "That was the circumstance which made speed essential to her cousin's murderous plan. He was hopelessly in debt, as a result of Mrs. Bardwell's extravagance. Only his uncle's money, which is considerable, would have saved him. If Miss Cornwall married he must have lost all hope of obtaining it, and so of marrying the girl on whom he had set his fickle heart. I have ascertained that he insisted on inoculating both father and daughter against spring catarrh a month ago, and that the injections he gave them hurt them terribly. No doubt Mrs. Bardwell received a similar injection about the same time. Thus, for each of these three individuals, a single bee sting, on your showing, meant instant death."

Dr. Hailey inclined his head.

"The moment I saw the swarm, the truth flashed across my mind," he declared. "These Cyprian bees, as I have been at pains to find out, and as your bee-keeping friend told you, are exceedingly ill-natured. But no bees, unless they have been previously roused to frenzy, ever attack at sight people who have not even approached their hives. It was all too clear, even in that first terrible moment, that the swarm was part of a carefully prepared plan."

The detective rose, and held out his hand.

"But for you, my dear friend," he said, "Miss Cornwall must inevitably have shared her father's fate, and the most devilish murder of which I have ever so much as heard would, almost certainly, have gone unsuspected and unpunished."

SOLVED BY INSPECTION

by RONALD A. KNOX

Father Knox wrote one perfect detective short story, "Solved by Inspection," in which MILES BREDON *appeared; and then, logically, he stopped. This is the rarest form of literary restraint, and a great loss to the rest of us.*

MILES BREDON, the eminently indefatigable Enquiry Agent, was accustomed to describe himself as a perfect fool at his job. Here he was in agreement with his wife Angela; where he differed from her was in really regarding himself as a fool at his job. There she knew better; and so, fortunately for both of them, did the Indescribable — that vast Insurance Company which employed him to investigate the more questionable transactions of its clients, and saved itself about five thousand a year by doing so. On one occasion, however, Bredon did claim to have really solved a problem by inspection, without any previous knowledge to put him on the right track. Indeed, since he seldom read the cheaper kind of newspaper, it is probable that he had never heard of the eccentric millionaire, Herbert Jervison, until Herbert Jervison was found dead in his bed. He was only supplied with the facts of the situation as he travelled down in the train to Wiltshire with Dr. Simmonds, the expensive medical man whom the Indescribable valued almost as much as Bredon himself. It was a bright summer's morning, and the dewy fields, horizoned by lazy stretches of canal, would have been food enough for meditation if Simmonds had not been so confoundedly anxious to impart information.

"You must have heard of him," he was saying. "He was a newspaper boom long before he was a casualty. The Million and a Half

Mystic — that was the sort of thing they called him. Why is it that the grossly rich never have the least idea of how to spend money? This Jervison had pottered about in the East, and had got caught with all that esoteric bilge — talked about Mahatmas and Yogis and things till even the most sanguine of his poor relations wouldn't ask him to stay. So he settled down at Yewbury here with some Indian frauds he had picked up, and said he was the Brotherhood of Light. Had it printed on his note paper, which was dark green. Ate nuts and did automatic writing and made all sorts of psychic experiments, till the papers were all over him; that sort of stuff gets them where they live. And then, you see, he went and died."

"That's a kind of publicity we all achieve sooner or later. If they all did it later, our job with the Indescribable would be a soft one. Anyhow, why did they send for me? He probably choked on a Brazil nut or something. No question of murder or suicide or anything, is there?"

"That's just the odd part about it. He died suddenly, of starvation."

"I suppose you want me to say that's impossible. No medical man myself, I am astute enough to see that my leg is being pulled. Let's hear more about it. Did you ever see the fellow?"

"Not till he came in to be vetted for his insurance. I've been kicking myself over that; because, you see, I thought he was about the soundest life I'd ever struck. He was only fifty-three, and of course these people who go in for Oriental food fads do sometimes pull off a longevity record. In fact, he had the cheek to ask for a specially low premium, because he said he was in a fair way to discovering the secret of immortality — which, as he pointed out, would make his premium a permanent asset to the Company. And then he goes and kills himself by refusing his mash. Mark you, I'm not sure I wouldn't sooner starve than eat the sort of muck he ate; but then, he seemed to flourish on it."

"And there was really nothing wrong with him? What about his top-storey?"

"Well, he admitted to nerves, and I must say he showed up badly over some of the nerve tests. You know we take the nervy people up to the top of the Indescribable Building nowadays, to see whether it gives them the jim-jams. Well, this fellow was at the end of his tether; you couldn't get him to look over the edge for love or money. But if his relations had wanted him certified — and they'd every reason to — I couldn't have done it. Colney Hatch wasn't on the map; I'd swear to that, even at a Directors' Meeting."

"So he went off and died suddenly of starvation. Could you amplify that statement a bit?"

"Well, what really happened was that he shut himself up for ten days or so in the room he calls his laboratory. I haven't seen it, but it's an old gymnasium or racquet court, they tell me. There was nothing queer in that, because he was always shutting himself up to do his fool experiments; locked himself in and wasn't to be disturbed on any account. Probably thought his astral body was wandering about in Thibet. — But — this is the odd thing — he was fully victualled, so I hear, for a fortnight. And at the end of the ten days he was found dead in his bed. The local doctor, who had been out in the East and served a famine area, says it's the clearest case of starvation he's ever met."

"And the food?"

"The food was untouched. I say, this is Westbury, where the car's going to meet us. I didn't tell Dr. Mayhew I was bringing a friend; how exactly am I going to explain you?"

"Tell him I'm the representative of the Company. That always fetches them. Hullo, there's a black man on the platform."

"That'll be the chauffeur. . . . No thanks, no luggage. . . . Good-morning, are you from Yewbury? Dr. Simmonds, my name is; I think Dr. Mayhew expects me. Outside, is he? Good. Come along, Bredon."

Dr. Mayhew was a little round-faced man who seemed incapable of suspicion and radiated hospitality. You saw at once that he was the kind of country doctor who suffers from having too little company, and can scarcely be got to examine your symptoms because he is so anxious to exchange all the news first. He outdid Simmonds himself in his offhand way of referring to the tragedy.

"Awfully good of you fellows to come," he said. "Not that I'm anxious for a second opinion here. Nine cases out of ten, *you* know that well enough, one signs the death certificate on an off-chance; but there ain't any doubt about this poor devil. I've been in a famine area, you know, and seen the symptoms often enough to make you dream of it; not pleasant, are they? I expect Mr. — oh, yes, Bredon, to be sure — Mr. Bredon won't want to see the *corpus*. They've got it parked up at the Brotherhood House, ready to be disposed of when it's finished with; the — er — symptoms come on rather suddenly, you know, Mr. Bredon, in these cases. What about coming round to my house and having a spot of something on the way? Sure you won't? Oh, very well. Yes, they've got to bury him in some special way of their own, tuck him up with his feet towards Jericho, I expect, or something of that sort. Hope these beggars'll clear out after this," he added, lowering his voice for fear the driver should overhear him. "The neighbours don't like 'em, and that's a fact. They're not pukka Indians, you know; he picked them up in San Francisco or somewhere; lascars, I should call 'em."

"I don't know that you're likely to be rid of them, Doctor," explained Bredon. "I suppose you realise that they benefit heavily under Jervison's will. At least, his insurance policy is made out in favour of the Brotherhood, and I suppose there'll be a tidy piece of his own money coming to them as well."

"And your Company pays up, does it, Mr. Bredon?" said the little doctor. "Gad, I wonder if they'd let me into the Brotherhood. There are only four of them in it, and I could do with a few extra thousands."

"Well," explained Bredon, "that's what we're here about. If it's suicide, you see, they can't touch the money. Our policies don't cover suicide; it would be too much of a temptation."

"That so? Well then, you're on velvet. The thing can only be suicide, and unsound mind at that. There's Yewbury, up on the hill. Queer place; very rich man had it, name of Rosenbach, and fitted it all up like a palace, with a real racquet court; that's the roof of it you see there. Then he crashed, and the place was sold for next to nothing; taken on as a preparatory school, it was, by a young fellow called Enstone; I liked him, but he never could make the place pay properly, one way and another, so he sold out and went to the South Coast, and then Jervison took it on. Well, here we are. Would you like to wander about the grounds, Mr. Bredon, while we go in and look at the remains, or what?"

"I think I'd like to go into the room where he was found. Perhaps one of these natives would take me in; I'd like to have a chance of talking to one of them."

The arrangement was made without difficulty, though Bredon found his guide a source of embarrassment, almost of nervousness. The driver of the car had worn an ordinary dark suit, but this other representative of the community was dressed in flowing white robes, with a turban to match, and seemed covered all over with cabalistic emblems. He was tall and strongly built; his manner was at once impassive and continually alert; nothing seemed to disturb him, yet you felt that nothing escaped him. And when he spoke, he belied his whole appearance by talking English with a violently American intonation.

The racquet court stood at a considerable distance from the main block of buildings; perhaps five hundred yards away. The gallery which had once existed close to the door had been cleared away to make space when it had been turned into a gymnasium, and you entered directly into a huge oblong room, with something of a cathedral vastness in its effects of distance and of silence. The floor had been fitted with shiny red oilcloth, so that your footsteps were deadened, and the echoes of the place awoke only at the sound of your voice. The light came chiefly, and the ventilation entirely, from a well in the centre of the roof; the top of this was of fixed glass, and only the iron slats at the side were capable of letting in air. There were still memories of the gymnasium period; at four points in the ceiling were iron rings, which looked as if ropes had hung down from them by hooks, and there were lockers at one side which still seemed to demand the presence of juvenile boots. Little had been done since in the way of furnishing; the eccentric had evidently used the place when he wanted to be separated from his kind, with the thick walls shutting out the sounds of the countryside, the heavy locked doors preventing intrusion. Bredon could not help wondering if the owner had felt safer sleeping in here than under the same roof with his questionable *protégés*.

But two pieces of furniture there were, which attracted attention almost equally as symptoms of the recent tragedy. One was a bed, standing out in the very middle of the floor; a temporary arrangement, apparently, since it was a wheeled bed with iron railings, of the type common in hospitals, and the wheels had dragged lines across the linoleum, which still shone from their passage. The bed itself was absolutely bare; even the underblanket had been torn out from its position, and lay, with the other blankets and the sheets, on and around the bed in grotesque confusion. It had the air, Bredon felt, of a bed from which the occupant has been pulled out, rather than of one which the occupant has left, in whatever hurry or excitement, of his own free will. Beyond the bed, against the wall farthest from the entrance, stood a sideboard, plentifully laden with vegetarian food. There was a loaf of bread, made of some very coarse grain, a honeycomb in a glass dish, a box of dates, some biscuits which looked brittle as glue, even, in witness of Simmonds's accuracy, some nuts. It was not a room in which the ordinary man would have sat down cheerfully to a meal; but, what was more important, it was a room in which you could not possibly starve.

Bredon went to the sideboard first of all, and gave the exhibits a careful scrutiny. He felt the outside of the bread, and satisfied himself, from the hardness of the "fly walk," that it had remained for several days untasted. He tried some milk from a jug which stood there, and found it, as he had expected, thoroughly sour. "Did Mr. Jervison always have sour milk?" he asked of his guide, who was watching all his movements with grave interest. "No, sir," was the answer. "I took that milk in myself, the evening when we last saw the Prophet alive. It was sweet milk, fresh from the dairy. It has not been drunk, not one drop of it, till you tasted it, sir, just now." The box of dates, though it was opened, contained its full complement of fruit. The honey was thick, and furred over with dust. The plate on which the biscuits lay was not covered with crumbs, as it should have been if any of them had been broken. Altogether, it seemed a safe conclusion that the dead man had starved in sight of plenty.

"I want to ask some questions, if I may," said Bredon, turning to the native. "My Company wishes to satisfy itself whether Mr Jervison died by misadventure, or took his own life. You will not mind helping me?"

"I will tell you whatever you wish to know. I am sure you are a very just man."

"Look here, then — did Jervison often sleep here? And why did he want to sleep here that night — the night when you last saw him?"

"Never before; but that night he was trying a very special experiment; you do not understand these things here in the West. He was meaning to take a narcotic drug, one which he had prepared himself, which would set his soul free from his body. But because it is very dangerous to be disturbed from outside, while the soul is away from the body, he wanted to sleep here, where nobody could disturb him, and we wheeled that bed in from the house. All this you will find written in his diary; he was very careful to do that, because, he said, if any harm came to him from the experiment, he wished it to be known that it was no fault of ours. I will show you the diary myself."

"Oh, he was drugged, was he, that first night? You don't think he may have taken an overdose of the drug, and died from that?"

The Indian smiled ever so slightly, and shrugged his shoulders. "But the doctor has told us that he starved to death. Your friend is a doctor also; he will tell you the same. No, I will tell you what I think. The Prophet fasted very often, especially when he wished his soul to be free. And I think that when he woke up from his sleep he had had some revelation which made him want to go deeper into these mysteries; and therefore he fasted; only this time he fasted too long. He fasted perhaps till he fainted, and was too weak to reach his food, or to come out and find help. And we waited in the house, doing our own studies, while the Prophet was dying in here. It was fated that it should be so."

Bredon was less interested in the theological bearings of the question than in its legal aspect. Is a man who starves himself without meaning to kill himself a suicide? Anyhow, that was for the lawyers. "Thank you," he said, "I will wait for my friend here; don't let me keep you." The Indian bowed, and left him — with some reluctance, Bredon thought. But he was determined to search this room thoroughly; he did not like the look of things. The lock on the door — no, that did not seem to have been tampered with, unless there were a second key. The walls? You do not make secret doors in a racquet court. The windows? None, except those slats underneath the skylight, at the sides of the well; only just room for a man to put his hand in there, and that would be about forty feet up. Hang it all, the man had been alone for ten days; he had left the food untasted, and he had made no effort to get out. There was even a writing tablet with a pencil tied to it, not far from the bed; he had meant, Bredon supposed, to write down his revelations on it as he woke from sleep; yet the dust stood on the top sheet, and the dead man had left no message. Could it really be madness? Or was the Indian right in his guess? Or was it even possible . . . one heard of strange tricks these Eastern jugglers played; was it possible that these four adepts had managed to tamper with the inside of the room without entering it?

And then Bredon noticed something on the floor which interested him; and when Simmonds came back with the little doctor they found him on all fours beside the bed, and the face he turned towards them as they came in was a very grave one, yet with a light in the eyes that suggested the anticipation of a victory.

"What a time you've been!" he said reproachfully.

"There's been a good deal in the way of alarms and excursions," explained Simmonds. "Your friends the police have been round, and they've just taken off the whole Brotherhood in a suitably coloured Maria. Apparently they are known in Chicago. But I'm dashed if I see how they are going to fix anything on them over this business. The man starved to death. Don't talk to me about drugs, Bredon; there simply isn't any question of that."

"It's murder, though," said Bredon cheerfully. "Look here!" And he pointed to the shiny tracks drawn across the oilcloth by the movement of the bed's wheels. "You see those tracks? They don't lead right up to the place where the bed stands; they stop about two inches short of it. And that means murder, and a dashed ingenious kind of murder too. By rights, the police oughtn't to be able to fix it on them, as you say. But that's the bother about a murder which takes four men to do it; one of them is certain to break down under examination, and give the others away. I was wondering, Dr. Mayhew — when your friend Enstone left, did he take the fixtures away with him? The fixtures of this gymnasium, for example?"

"Sold the whole place, lock, stock and barrel. He needed all the money he could get, and the Brotherhood weren't particular. There's a sort of shed at the back, you know, where Enstone used to keep odds and ends, and I shouldn't be a bit surprised if you found the parallel bars and whatnot tidied away in there. Were you thinking of giving us a gymnastic display? Because I should suggest some lunch first."

"I just thought I'd like to look at them, that's all. And then, as you say, lunch." Dr. Mayhew's prophecy proved accurate. The shed at the back was plentifully littered with the appropriate *débris*. A vaulting horse stood there, mutely reproachful at having been so long turned out to grass; the parallel bars were still shiny from youthful hands; the horizontal ladder, folded in three, was dropped at an uneasy angle, and the floor was a network of ropes and rings. Bredon took up a rope at random and brought it out into the daylight. "You see," he said, passing his hands down it; "it's frayed all along. Boys don't fray ropes when they climb up them; they wear gym shoes. Besides, the fraying is quite fresh; looks only a day or two old. Yes, that's what they did; and I suppose we had better tell the police about it. The Company stands to lose, of course; but I don't see what is to be done with the policy now, unless they erect a mausoleum over the Brotherhood with it. There won't be any more Brotherhood now, Dr. Mayhew."

"You must excuse him," apologised Simmonds; "he is like this sometimes. I hate to say it, Bredon, but I haven't completely followed your train of thought. How did these fellows get at Jervison, when he was locked up in his gymnasium? You can't kill a man by starvation, unless you shut him up without any food, or hold him down so that he can't get at it."

"You're wrong there," objected Bredon. "There are all sorts of ways. You can poison the food, and tell him it is poisoned. Not that that happened here, because I've tasted some of the milk myself, and here I am. Besides, I think a starving man would always risk it when it came to the point. You can hypnotise the man, in theory, and persuade him that the food isn't there, or that it isn't food at all. But that's only in theory; you never hear of a crime like that being pulled off in real life. No, the Indians had their alibi all right, when poor Jervison died."

"You mean they starved him somewhere else, and brought his body in here afterwards?"

"Hardly that. You see, it would be very much simpler to starve your man in here, and bring the food in afterwards to look as if he'd starved himself deliberately. But to do either of those things you must have access to the building. Do you happen to know, Dr. Mayhew, who it was that first found the body? And what sort of difficulty they had in making their way into the gymnasium?"

"The door was locked, and the key fixed on the inside. We had to take the lock off. I was one of the party myself. The police, of course, had charge of things; but the Indians had called me in as well, the moment they got the idea that something was wrong."

"Really? Now, that's very instructive. It shows how criminals always overdo these things. You or I, if a friend locked himself up and didn't appear for ten days, would shout through the keyhole and then send for a locksmith. Whereas these gentlemen sent off at once for a doctor and the police, as if they knew that both would be wanted. That's the worst of thinking that you've covered your tracks."

"My dear Bredon, we're still taking your word for it that it *is* murder. If it is, I should say the murderers covered their tracks quite remarkably well. It looks to me the clearest possible case of lunacy and suicide."

"You're wrong there. Did you notice that there was a writing tablet and a pencil by the side of the bed? Now, what madman ever resisted the temptation to scrawl something on any odd piece of paper he came across? Especially if he thought he was being starved, or poisoned. That applies, too, if he were really making some fasting experiment; he would have left us a last message. And what did you make of the way the bedclothes were piled on and round the bed? Nobody, mad or sane, wants to get out of bed that way."

"Well, tell us all about it if you must. You may be mad or I may be mad, but I see no reason why either of us should starve, and we are keeping Dr. Mayhew from his lunch."

"Well, the outlines of the thing are simple. Jervison had picked up these rogues somewhere in America, and they were no more mystics than you or I are; they could talk the patter, that's all. They knew he was rich, and they stuck to him because they saw there was money to be made out of him. When they found he had made the Brotherhood his heirs, there remained nothing except to eliminate him; they went over the plan of the ground, and determined to make the fullest use of the weapons that lay ready to hand. Always a mistake to bring in weapons from outside; study your man's habits, and kill him along his own lines, so to speak. All they had to do was to encourage him in making these fool experiments, and to supply him with some ordinary kind of sleeping draught which pretended to have a magical effect; probably it was they who suggested his retiring to the gymnasium, where he could be quiet, and they who insisted on wheeling his bed out into the middle of the room, telling him that he ought to catch the noonday sun, or some nonsense of that kind. Whoever heard of a man wanting to have his bed out in the middle of the room? It's human nature to want it next to the wall, though why, I've no idea."

"And then?"

"They waited, that night, till the sleeping draught had taken its full effect; waited till it was early dawn, and they could see what was happening without being noticed by inquisitive neighbours. They tied ladders together, or more probably used that horizontal ladder, stretched out into a straight line, and climbed up onto the roof. All they took with them was ropes — the four ropes that used to hang from those hooks in the ceiling. They still had iron hooks on them; I dare say they tied handkerchiefs round the hooks, to prevent any noise. Through the skylight, they could look down on the sleeping man; between the iron slats they could let down the four ropes. The hooks acted as grapnels, and it did not take much fishing before they hooked the iron rails at the head and foot of the bed. Very quickly, very evenly, they pulled up the ropes; it was like a profane and ghastly parody of a scene you may remember in the Gospels. And still poor Jervison slept on, under the influence of his drug; dreaming, perhaps, that he was being levitated, and had at last got rid of the burden of the flesh. He nearly had.

"He slept on, and when he woke, he was hung up forty feet in the air, still in his bed. The bedclothes had been removed; it would not do to let him have the chance of climbing down. He hung there for over a week; and if his cries reached the outside world at all, they only reached the ears of four pitiless men, his murderers. Perhaps a braver man would have jumped for it, and preferred to end his life that way. But Jervison, you told me yourself, Simmonds, was a coward about heights; he couldn't jump."

"And if he had?"

"He would have been found dead, either from his fall or from its effects. And the Indians would have told us, gravely enough, that the Prophet must have been making an experiment in levitation, or something of that kind. As it was, all they had to do was to come back when all was safely over, to let down the ropes again, to throw his bedclothes in through the slats, falling where they would, and to take their ropes and ladder down again the way they had come. Only, as was natural, they did not bother to pay out the ropes quite evenly this time, and the bed came down in the wrong place, about two inches from where it had stood originally. So that it didn't fit in with the tracks across the oilcloth, and it was that, somehow, which gave me a notion of what had happened. The bed, evidently, had been lifted; and you do not lift a wheeled bed unless you have a special purpose to be served, as these devils had. Jervison was a fool, but I hate to think of the way he died, and I am going to do my best to see these four fellows hanged. If I had my way with them, I would spare them the drop."

THE AVENGING CHANCE

by ANTHONY BERKELEY

The founder, and First (and only) Freeman, of the Detection Club of London wrote only two short stories about ROGER SHER-INGHAM. *Berkeley himself sneers at one; but nobody sneers at the other, since from the writer's standpoint it is as nearly a perfectly plotted short story as has been written. Readers uninterested in the agonies of technique simply read — and enjoy.*

ROGER SHERINGHAM was inclined to think afterwards that the Poisoned Chocolates Case, as the papers called it, was perhaps the most perfectly planned murder he had ever encountered. The motive was so obvious, when you knew where to look for it — but you didn't know; the method was so significant when you had grasped its real essentials — but you didn't grasp them; the traces were so thinly covered, when you had realised what was covering them — but you didn't realise. But for a piece of the merest bad luck, which the murderer could not possibly have foreseen, the crime must have been added to the classical list of great mysteries.

This is the gist of the case, as Chief Inspector Moresby told it one evening to Roger in the latter's rooms in the Albany a week or so after it happened: —

On the past Friday morning, the fifteenth of November, at half past ten o'clock, in accordance with his invariable custom, Sir William Anstruther walked into his club in Piccadilly, the very exclusive Rainbow Club, and asked for his letters. The porter handed him three and a small parcel. Sir William walked over to the fireplace in the big lounge hall to open them.

A few minutes later another member entered the club, a Mr. Graham Beresford. There were a letter and a couple of circulars for him, and he also strolled over to the fireplace, nodding to Sir William, but not speaking to him. The two men only knew each other very slightly, and had probably never exchanged more than a dozen words in all.

Having glanced through his letters, Sir William opened the parcel and, after a moment, snorted with disgust. Beresford looked at him, and with a grunt Sir William thrust out a letter which had been enclosed in the parcel. Concealing a smile (Sir William's ways were a matter of some amusement to his fellow members), Beresford read the letter. It was from a big firm of chocolate manufacturers, Mason & Sons, and set forth that they were putting on the market a new brand of liqueur chocolates designed especially to appeal to men; would Sir William do them the honour of accepting the enclosed two-pound box and letting the firm have his candid opinion on them?

"Do they think I'm a blank chorus girl?" fumed Sir William. "Write 'em testimonials about their blank chocolates, indeed! Blank 'em! I'll complain to the blank committee. That sort of blank thing can't blank well be allowed here."

"Well, it's an ill wind so far as I'm concerned," Beresford soothed him. "It's reminded me of something. My wife and I had a box at the Imperial last night. I bet her a box of chocolates to a hundred cigarettes that she wouldn't spot the villain by the end of the second act. She won. I must remember to get them. Have you seen it — *The Creaking Skull?* Not a bad show."

Sir William had not seen it, and said so with force.

"Want a box of chocolates, did you say?" he added, more mildly. "Well, take this blank one. I don't want it."

For a moment Beresford demurred politely and then, most unfortunately for himself, accepted. The money so saved meant nothing to him for he was a wealthy man; but trouble was always worth saving.

By an extraordinarily lucky chance neither the outer wrapper of the box nor its covering letter were thrown into the fire, and this was the more fortunate in that both men had tossed the envelopes of their letters into the flames. Sir William did, indeed, make a bundle of the wrapper, letter and string, but he handed it over to Beresford, and the latter simply dropped it inside the fender. This bundle the porter subsequently extracted and, being a man of orderly habits, put it tidily away in the waste paper basket, whence it was retrieved later by the police.

Of the three unconscious protagonists in the impending tragedy, Sir William was without doubt the most remarkable. Still a year or two under fifty, he looked, with his flaming red face and thickset figure, a typical country squire of the old school, and both his manners and his language were in accordance with tradition. His habits, especially as regards women, were also in accordance with tradition — the tradition of the bold, bad baronet which he undoubtedly was.

In comparison with him, Beresford was rather an ordinary man, a tall, dark, not handsome fellow of two-and-thirty, quiet and reserved. His father had left him a rich man, but idleness did not appeal to him, and he had a finger in a good many business pies.

Money attracts money. Graham Beresford had inherited it, he made it, and, inevitably, he had married it, too. The daughter of a late shipowner in Liverpool, with not far off half a million in her own right. But the money was incidental, for he needed her and would have married her just as inevitably (said his friends) if she had not had a farthing. A tall, rather serious-minded, highly cultured girl, not so young that her character had not had time to form (she was twenty-five when Beresford married her, three years ago), she was the ideal wife for him. A bit of a Puritan perhaps in some ways, but Beresford, whose wild oats, though duly sown, had been a sparse crop, was ready enough to be a Puritan himself by that time if she was. To make no bones about it, the Beresfords succeeded in achieving that eighth wonder of the modern world, a happy marriage.

And into the middle of it there dropped with irretrievable tragedy, the box of chocolates.

Beresford gave them to her after lunch as they sat over their coffee, with some jesting remark about paying his honourable debts, and she opened the box at once. The top layer, she noticed, seemed to consist only of kirsch and maraschino. Beresford, who did not believe in spoiling good coffee, refused when she offered him the box, and his wife ate the first one alone. As she did so she exclaimed in surprise that the filling seemed exceedingly strong and positively burnt her mouth.

Beresford explained that they were samples of a new brand and then, made curious by what his wife had said, took one too. A burning taste, not intolerable but much too strong to be pleasant, followed the release of the liquid, and the almond flavouring seemed quite excessive.

"By Jove," he said, "they are strong. They must be filled with neat alcohol."

"Oh, they wouldn't do that, surely," said his wife, taking another. "But they are very strong. I think I rather like them, though."

Beresford ate another, and disliked it still more. "I don't," he said with decision. "They make my tongue feel quite numb. I shouldn't eat any more of them if I were you. I think there's something wrong with them."

"Well, they're only an experiment, I suppose," she said. "But they do burn. I'm not sure whether I like them or not."

A few minutes later Beresford went out to keep a business appointment in the City. He left her still trying to make up her mind whether she liked them, and still eating them to decide. Beresford remembered that scrap of conversation afterwards very vividly, because it was the last time he saw his wife alive.

That was roughly half past two. At a quarter to four Beresford arrived at his club from the City in a taxi, in a state of collapse. He was helped into the building by the driver and the porter, and both described him subsequently as pale to the point of ghastliness, with staring eyes and livid lips, and his skin damp and clammy. His mind seemed unaffected, however, and when they had got him up the steps he was able to walk, with the porter's help, into the lounge.

The porter, thoroughly alarmed, wanted to send for a doctor at once, but Beresford, who was the last man in the world to make a fuss, refused to let him, saying that it must be indigestion and he would be all right in a few minutes. To Sir William Anstruther, however, who was in the lounge at the time, he added after the porter had gone:

"Yes, and I believe it was those infernal chocolates you gave me, now I come to think of it. I thought there was something funny about them at the time. I'd better go and find out if my wife —— " He broke off abruptly. His body, which had been leaning back limply in his chair, suddenly heaved rigidly upright; his jaws locked together, the livid lips drawn back in a horrible grin, and his hands clenched on the arms of his chair. At the same time Sir William became aware of an unmistakable smell of bitter almonds.

Thoroughly alarmed, believing indeed that the man was dying under his eyes, Sir William raised a shout for the porter and a doctor. The other occupants of the lounge hurried up, and between them they got the convulsed body of the unconscious man into a more comfortable position. Before the doctor could arrive a telephone message was received at the club from an agitated butler asking if Mr. Beresford was there, and if so would he come home at once as Mrs. Beresford had been taken seriously ill. As a matter of fact she was already dead.

Beresford did not die. He had taken less of the poison than his wife, who after his departure must have eaten at least three more of the chocolates, so that its action was less rapid and the doctor had time to save him. As a matter of fact it turned out afterwards that he had not had a fatal dose. By about eight o'clock that night he was conscious; the next day he was practically convalescent.

As for the unfortunate Mrs. Beresford, the doctor had arrived too late to save her, and she passed away very rapidly in a deep coma.

The police had taken the matter in hand as soon as Mrs. Beresford's death was reported to them and the fact of poison established, and it was only a very short time before things had become narrowed down to the chocolates as the active agent.

Sir William was interrogated, the letter and wrapper were recovered from the waste paper basket, and, even before the sick man was out of danger, a detective inspector was asking for an interview with the managing director of Mason & Sons. Scotland Yard moves quickly.

It was the police theory at this stage, based on what Sir William and the two doctors had been able to tell them, that by an act of criminal carelessness on the part of one of Mason's employees, an excessive amount of oil of bitter almonds had been included in the filling mixture of the chocolates, for that was what the doctor had decided must be the poisoning ingredient. However, the managing director quashed this idea at once: oil of bitter almonds, he asserted, was never used by Mason's.

He had more interesting news still. Having read with undisguised astonishment the covering letter, he at once declared that it was a forgery. No such letter, no such samples had been sent out by the firm at all; a new variety of liqueur chocolates had never even been mooted. The fatal chocolates were their ordinary brand.

Unwrapping and examining one more closely, he called the Inspector's attention to a mark on the underside, which he suggested was the remains of a small hole drilled in the case, through which the liquid could have been extracted and the fatal filling inserted, the hole afterwards being stopped up with softened chocolate, a perfectly simple operation.

He examined it under a magnifying glass and the Inspector agreed. It was now clear to him that somebody had been trying deliberately to murder Sir William Anstruther.

Scotland Yard doubled its activities. The chocolates were sent for analysis, Sir William was interviewed again, and so was the now conscious Beresford. From the latter the doctor insisted that the news of his wife's death must be kept till the next day, as in his weakened condition the shock might be fatal, so that nothing very helpful was obtained from him.

Nor could Sir William throw any light on the mystery or produce a single person who might have any grounds for trying to kill him. He was living apart from his wife, who was the principal beneficiary in his will, but she was in the South of France, as the French police subsequently confirmed. His estate in Worcestershire, heavily mortgaged, was entailed and went to a nephew; but as the rent he got for it barely covered the interest on the mortgage, and the nephew was considerably better off than Sir William himself, there was no motive there. The police were at a dead end.

The analysis brought one or two interesting facts to light. Not oil of bitter almonds but nitrobenzine, a kindred substance, chiefly used in the manufacture of aniline dyes, was the somewhat surprising poison employed. Each chocolate in the upper layer contained exactly six minims of it, in a mixture of kirsch and maraschino. The chocolates in the other layers were harmless.

As to the other clues, they seemed equally useless. The sheet of Mason's note paper was identified by Merton's, the printers, as of their work, but there was nothing to show how it had got into the murderer's possession. All that could be said was that, the edges being distinctly yellowed, it must be an old piece. The machine on which the letter had been typed, of course, could not be traced. From the wrapper, a piece of ordinary brown paper with Sir William's address hand-printed on it in large capitals, there was nothing to be learnt at all beyond that the parcel had been posted at the office in Southampton Street between the hours of 8.30 and 9.30 on the previous evening.

Only one thing was quite clear. Whoever had coveted Sir William's life had no intention of paying for it with his or her own.

"And now you know as much as we do, Mr. Sheringham," concluded Chief Inspector Moresby; "and if you can say who sent those chocolates to Sir William, you'll know a good deal more."

Roger nodded thoughtfully.

"It's a brute of a case. I met a man only yesterday who was at school with Beresford. He didn't know him very well because Beresford was on the modern side and my friend was a classical bird, but they were in the same house. He says Beresford's absolutely knocked over by his wife's death. I wish you could find out who sent those chocolates, Moresby."

"So do I, Mr. Sheringham," said Moresby gloomily.

"It might have been anyone in the whole world," Roger mused. "What about feminine jealousy, for instance? Sir William's private life doesn't seem to be immaculate. I dare say there's a good deal of off with the old light-o'-love and on with the new."

"Why, that's just what I've been looking into, Mr. Sheringham, sir," retorted Chief Inspector Moresby reproachfully. "That was the first thing that came to me. Because if anything does stand out about this business it is that it's a woman's crime. Nobody but a woman would send poisoned chocolates to a man. Another man would send a poisoned sample of whisky, or something like that."

"That's a very sound point, Moresby," Roger meditated. "Very sound indeed. And Sir William couldn't help you?"

"Couldn't," said Moresby, not without a trace of resentment, "or wouldn't. I was inclined to believe at first that he might have his suspicions and was shielding some woman. But I don't think so now."

"Humph!" Roger did not seem quite so sure. "It's reminiscent, this case, isn't it? Didn't some lunatic once send poisoned chocolates to the Commissioner of Police himself? A good crime always gets imitated, as you know."

Moresby brightened.

"It's funny you should say that, Mr. Sheringham, because that's the very conclusion I've come to. I've tested every other theory, and so far as I know there's not a soul with an interest in Sir William's death, whether from motives of gain, revenge, or what you like, whom I haven't had to rule quite out of it. In fact, I've pretty well made up my mind that the person who sent those chocolates was some irresponsible lunatic of a woman, a social or religious fanatic who's probably never even seen him. And if that's the case," Moresby sighed, "a fat chance I have of ever laying hands on her."

"Unless Chance steps in, as it so often does," said Roger brightly, "and helps you. A tremendous lot of cases get solved by a stroke of sheer luck, don't they? *Chance the Avenger*. It would make an excellent film title. But there's a lot of truth in it. If I were superstitious, which I'm not, I should say it wasn't chance at all, but Providence avenging the victim."

"Well, Mr. Sheringham," said Moresby, who was not superstitious either, "to tell the truth, I don't mind what it is, so long as it lets me get my hands on the right person."

If Moresby had paid his visit to Roger Sheringham with any hope of tapping that gentleman's brains, he went away disappointed.

To tell the truth, Roger was inclined to agree with the Chief Inspector's conclusion, that the attempt on the life of Sir William Anstruther and the actual murder of the unfortunate Mrs. Beresford must be the work of some unknown criminal lunatic. For this reason, although he thought about it a good deal during the next few days, he made no attempt to take the case in hand. It was the sort of affair, necessitating endless inquiries that a private person would have neither the time nor the authority to carry out, which can be handled only by the official police. Roger's interest in it was purely academic.

It was hazard, a chance encounter nearly a week later, which translated this interest from the academic into the personal.

Roger was in Bond Street, about to go through the distressing ordeal of buying a new hat. Along the pavement he suddenly saw bearing down on him Mrs. Verreker-le-Flemming. Mrs. Verreker-le-Flemming was small, exquisite, rich, and a widow, and she sat at Roger's feet whenever he gave her the opportunity. But she talked. She talked, in fact, and talked, and talked. And Roger, who rather liked talking himself, could not bear it. He tried to dart across the road, but there was no opening in the traffic stream. He was cornered.

Mrs. Verreker-le-Flemming fastened on him gladly.

"Oh, Mr. Sheringham! *Just* the person I wanted to see. Mr. Sheringham, *do* tell me. In confidence. *Are* you taking up this dreadful business of poor Joan Beresford's death?"

Roger, the frozen and imbecile grin of civilised intercourse on his face, tried to get a word in; without result.

"I was horrified when I heard of it — simply horrified. You see, Joan and I were such *very* close friends. Quite intimate. And the awful thing, the truly *terrible* thing is that Joan brought the whole business on herself. Isn't that *appalling?*"

Roger no longer wanted to escape.

"What did you say?" he managed to insert incredulously.

"I suppose it's what they call tragic irony," Mrs. Verreker-le-Flemming chattered on. "Certainly it was tragic enough, and I've never heard anything so terribly ironical. You know about that bet she made with her husband, of course, so that he had to get her a box of chocolates, and if he hadn't Sir William would never have given him the poisoned ones and he'd have eaten them and died himself and good riddance? Well, Mr. Sheringham —— " Mrs. Verreker-le-Flemming lowered her voice to a conspirator's whisper and glanced about her in the approved manner. "I've never told anybody else this, but I'm telling you because I know you'll appreciate it. *Joan wasn't playing fair!*"

"How do you mean?" Roger asked, bewildered.

Mrs. Verreker-le-Flemming was artlessly pleased with her sensation.

"Why, she'd seen the play before. We went together, the very first week it was on. She *knew* who the villain was all the time."

"By Jove!" Roger was as impressed as Mrs. Verreker-le-Flemming could have wished. "Chance the Avenger! We're none of us immune from it."

"Poetic justice, you mean?" twittered Mrs. Verreker-le-Flemming, to whom these remarks had been somewhat obscure. "Yes, but Joan

Beresford of all people! That's the extraordinary thing. I should never have thought Joan *would* do a thing like that. She was such a *nice* girl. A little close with money, of course, considering how well-off they are, but that isn't anything. Of course it was only fun, and pulling her husband's leg, but I always used to think Joan was such a *serious girl,* Mr. Sheringham. I mean, ordinary people don't talk about honour, and truth, and playing the game, and all those things one takes for granted. But Joan did. She was always saying that this wasn't honourable, or that wouldn't be playing the game. Well, she paid herself for not playing the game, poor girl, didn't she? Still, it all goes to show the truth of the old saying, doesn't it?"

"What old saying?" said Roger, hypnotised by this flow.

"Why, that still waters run deep. Joan must have been deep, I'm afraid." Mrs. Verreker-le-Flemming sighed. It was evidently a social error to be deep. "I mean, she certainly took me in. She can't have been quite so honourable and truthful as she was always pretending, can she? And I can't help wondering whether a girl who'd deceive her husband in a little thing like that might not — oh, well, I don't want to say anything against poor Joan now she's dead, poor darling, but she can't have been *quite* such a plaster saint after all, can she? I mean," said Mrs. Verreker-le-Flemming, in hasty extenuation of these suggestions, "I do think psychology is so very interesting, don't you, Mr. Sheringham?"

"Sometimes, very," Roger agreed gravely. "But you mentioned Sir William Anstruther just now. Do you know him, too?"

"I used to," Mrs. Verreker-le-Flemming replied, without particular interest. "Horrible man! Always running after some woman or other. And when he's tired of her, just drops her — biff! — like that. At least," added Mrs. Verreker-le-Flemming somewhat hastily, "so I've heard."

"And what happens if she refuses to be dropped?"

"Oh dear, I'm sure I don't know. I suppose you've heard the latest." Mrs. Verreker-le-Flemming hurried on, perhaps a trifle more pink than the delicate aids to nature on her cheeks would have warranted.

"He's taken up with that Bryce woman now. You know, the wife of the oil man, or petrol, or whatever he made his money in. It began about three weeks ago. You'd have thought that dreadful business of being responsible, in a way, for poor Joan Beresford's death would have sobered him up a little, wouldn't you? But not a bit of it; he —— "

Roger was following another line of thought.

"What a pity you weren't at the Imperial with the Beresfords that evening. She'd never have made that bet if you had been." Roger looked extremely innocent. "You weren't, I suppose."

"I?" queried Mrs. Verreker-le-Flemming in surprise. "Good gracious, no. I was at the new revue at the Pavilion. Lady Gavelstoke had a box and asked me to join her party."

"Oh, yes. Good show, isn't it? I thought that sketch *The Sempiternal Triangle* very clever. Didn't you?"

"*The Sempiternal Triangle?*" wavered Mrs. Verreker-le-Flemming. "Yes, in the first half."

"Oh! Then I didn't see it. I got there disgracefully late, I'm afraid. But then," said Mrs. Verreker-le-Flemming with pathos, "I always do seem to be late for simply everything."

Roger kept the rest of the conversation resolutely upon theatres. But before he left her he had ascertained that she had photographs of both Mrs. Beresford and Sir William Anstruther, and had obtained permission to borrow them some time. As soon as she was out of view he hailed a taxi and gave Mrs. Verreker-le-Flemming's address. He thought it better to take advantage of her permission at a time when he would not have to pay for it a second time over.

The parlourmaid seemed to think there was nothing odd in his mission, and took him up to the drawing-room at once. A corner of the room was devoted to the silver-framed photographs of Mrs. Verreker-le-Flemming's friends, and there were many of them. Roger examined them with interest, and finally took away with him not two photographs but six, those of Sir William, Mrs. Beresford, Beresford, two strange males who appeared to belong to the Sir William period, and, lastly, a likeness of Mrs. Verreker-le-Flemming herself. Roger liked confusing his trail.

For the rest of the day he was very busy.

His activities would have no doubt seemed to Mrs. Verreker-le-Flemming not merely baffling but pointless. He paid a visit to a public library, for instance, and consulted a work of reference, after which he took a taxi and drove to the offices of the Anglo-Eastern Perfumery Company, where he inquired for a certain Mr. Joseph Lea Hardwick and seemed much put out on hearing that no such gentleman was known to the firm and was certainly not employed in any of their branches. Many questions had to be put about the firm and its branches before he consented to abandon the quest.

After that he drove to Messrs. Weall and Wilson, the well-known institution which protects the trade interests of individuals and advises its subscribers regarding investments. Here he entered his name as a subscriber, and explaining that he had a large sum of money to invest, filled in one of the special inquiry forms which are headed Strictly Confidential.

Then he went to the Rainbow Club, in Piccadilly.

Introducing himself to the porter without a blush as connected with Scotland Yard, he asked the man a number of questions, more or less trivial, concerning the tragedy.

"Sir William, I understand," he said finally, as if by the way, "did not dine here the evening before."

There it appeared that Roger was wrong. Sir William had dined in the club, as he did about three times a week.

"But I quite understood he wasn't here that evening," Roger said plaintively.

The porter was emphatic. He remembered quite well. So did a waiter, whom the porter summoned to corroborate him. Sir William had dined, rather late, and had not left the dining-room till about nine o'clock. He spent the evening there, too, the waiter knew, or at least some of it, for he himself had taken him a whisky and soda in the lounge not less than half an hour later.

Roger retired.

He retired to Merton's, in a taxi.

It seemed that he wanted some new note paper printed, of a very special kind, and to the young woman behind the counter he specified at great length and in wearisome detail exactly what he did want. The young woman handed him the books of specimen pieces and asked him to see if there was any style there which would suit him. Roger glanced through them, remarking garrulously to the young woman that he had been recommended to Merton's by a very dear friend, whose photograph he happened to have on him at that moment. Wasn't that a curious coincidence? The young woman agreed that it was.

"About a fortnight ago, I think, my friend was in here last," said Roger, producing the photograph. "Recognise this?"

The young woman took the photograph, without apparent interest.

"Oh, yes, I remember. About some note paper, too, wasn't it? So that's your friend. Well, it's a small world. Now this is a line we're selling a good deal of just now."

Roger went back to his rooms to dine. Afterwards, feeling restless, he wandered out of the Albany and turned up Piccadilly. He wandered round the Circus, thinking hard, and paused for a moment out of habit to inspect the photographs of the new revue hung outside the Pavilion. The next thing he realised was that he had got as far as Jermyn Street and was standing outside the Imperial Theatre. Glancing at the advertisements of *The Creaking Skull,* he saw that it began at half past eight. Glancing at his watch, he saw that the time was twenty-nine minutes past the hour. He had an evening to get through somehow. He went inside.

The next morning, very early for Roger, he called on Moresby at Scotland Yard.

"Moresby," he said without preamble, "I want you to do something for me. Can you find me a taximan who took a fare from Piccadilly Circus or its neighbourhood at about ten past nine on the evening before the Beresford crime to the Strand somewhere near the bottom of Southampton Street, and another who took a fare back between those points? I'm not sure about the first. Or one taxi might have been used for the double journey, but I doubt that. Anyhow, try to find out for me, will you?"

"What are you up to now, Mr. Sheringham?" Moresby asked suspiciously.

"Breaking down an interesting alibi," replied Roger serenely. "By the way, I know who sent those chocolates to Sir William. I'm just building up a nice structure of evidence for you. Ring up my rooms when you've got those taximen."

. He strolled out, leaving Moresby positively gaping after him.

The rest of the day he spent apparently trying to buy a second-hand typewriter. He was very particular that it should be a Hamilton

No. 4. When the shop people tried to induce him to consider other makes he refused to look at them, saying that he had had the Hamilton No. 4 so strongly recommended to him by a friend who had bought one about three weeks ago. Perhaps it was at this very shop? No? They hadn't sold a Hamilton No. 4 for the last three months? How odd.

But at one shop they had sold a Hamilton No. 4 within the last month, and that was odder still.

At half past four Roger got back to his rooms to await the telephone message from Moresby. At half past five it came.

"There are fourteen taxidrivers here, littering up my office," said Moresby offensively. "What do you want me to do with 'em?"

"Keep them till I come, Chief Inspector," returned Roger with dignity.

The interview with the fourteen was brief enough, however. To each man in turn Roger showed a photograph, holding it so that Moresby could not see it, and asked if he could recognise his fare. The ninth man did so, without hesitation.

At a nod from Roger, Moresby dismissed them, then sat at his table and tried to look official. Roger seated himself on the table, looking most unofficial, and swung his legs. As he did so, a photograph fell unnoticed out of his pocket and fluttered, face downwards, under the table. Moresby eyed it but did not pick it up.

"And now, Mr. Sheringham, sir," he said, "perhaps you'll tell me what you've been doing?"

"Certainly, Moresby," said Roger blandly. "Your work for you. I really have solved the thing, you know. Here's your evidence." He took from his notecase an old letter and handed it to the Chief Inspector. "Was that typed on the same machine as the forged letter from Mason's, or was it not?"

Moresby studied it for a moment, then drew the forged letter from a drawer of his table and compared the two minutely.

"Mr. Sheringham," he said soberly, "where did you get hold of this?"

"In a secondhand typewriter shop in St. Martin's Lane. The machine was sold to an unknown customer about a month ago. They identified the customer from that same photograph. As it happened, this machine had been used for a time in the office after it was repaired, to see that it was O.K., and I easily got hold of that specimen of its work."

"And where is the machine now?"

"Oh, at the bottom of the Thames, I expect," Roger smiled. "I tell you, this criminal takes no unnecessary chances. But that doesn't matter. There's your evidence."

"Humph! It's all right so far as it goes," conceded Moresby. "But what about Mason's paper?"

"That," said Roger calmly, "was extracted from Merton's book of sample note papers, as I'd guessed from the very yellowed edges might be the case. I can prove contact of the criminal with the book, and there is a gap which will certainly turn out to have been filled by that piece of paper."

"That's fine," Moresby said more heartily.

"As for the taximan, the criminal had an alibi. You've heard it broken down. Between ten past nine and twenty-five past, in fact during the time when the parcel must have been posted, the murderer took a hurried journey to that neighbourhood, going probably by bus or Underground, but returning, as I expected, by taxi, because time would be getting short."

"And the murderer, Mr. Sheringham?"

"The person whose photograph is in my pocket," Roger said unkindly. "By the way, do you remember what I was saying the other day about Chance the Avenger, my excellent film title? Well, it's worked again. By a chance meeting in Bond Street with a silly woman I was put, by the merest accident, in possession of a piece of information which showed me then and there who had sent those chocolates addressed to Sir William. There were other possibilities, of course, and I tested them, but then and there on the pavement I saw the whole thing, from first to last."

"Who was the murderer, then, Mr. Sheringham?" repeated Moresby.

"It was so beautifully planned," Roger went on dreamily. "We never grasped for one moment that we were making the fundamental mistake that the murderer all along intended us to make."

"And what was that?" asked Moresby.

"Why, that the plan had miscarried. That the wrong person had been killed. That was just the beauty of it. The plan had *not* miscarried. It had been brilliantly successful. The wrong person was *not* killed. Very much the right person was."

Moresby gasped.

"Why, how on earth do you make that out, sir?"

"Mrs. Beresford was the objective all the time. That's why the plot was so ingenious. Everything was anticipated. It was perfectly natural that Sir William should hand the chocolates over to Beresford. It was foreseen that we should look for the criminal among Sir William's associates and not the dead woman's. It was probably even foreseen that the crime would be considered the work of a woman!"

Moresby, unable to wait any longer, snatched up the photograph.

"Good heavens! But Mr. Sheringham, you don't mean to tell me that . . . Sir William himself!"

"He wanted to get rid of Mrs. Beresford," Roger continued. "He had liked her well enough at the beginning, no doubt, though it was her money he was after all the time.

"But the real trouble was that she was too close with her money. He wanted it, or some of it, pretty badly; and she wouldn't part. There's no doubt about the motive. I made a list of the firms he's interested in and got a report on them. They're all rocky, every one. He'd got through all his own money, and he had to get more.

"As for the nitrobenzine which puzzled us so much, that was simple enough. I looked it up and found that beside the uses you told me, it's used largely in perfumery. And he's got a perfumery business. The Anglo-Eastern Perfumery Company. That's how he'd know about it being poisonous, of course. But I shouldn't think he got his supply from there. He'd be cleverer than that. He probably made the stuff himself. Any schoolboy knows how to treat benzol with nitric acid to get nitrobenzine."

"But," stammered Moresby, "but Sir William . . . He was at Eton."

"Sir William?" said Roger sharply. "Who's talking about Sir William? I told you the photograph of the murderer was in my pocket." He whipped out the photograph in question and confronted the astounded Chief Inspector with it. "Beresford, man! Beresford's the murderer of his own wife.

"Beresford, who still had hankerings after a gay life," he went on more mildly, "didn't want his wife but did want her money. He contrived this plot, providing as he thought against every contingency that could possibly arise. He established a mild alibi, if suspicion ever should arise, by taking his wife to the Imperial, and slipped out of the theatre at the first interval. (I sat through the first act of the dreadful thing myself last night to see when the interval came.) Then he hurried down to the Strand, posted his parcel, and took a taxi back. He had ten minutes, but nobody would notice if he got back to the box a minute late.

"And the rest simply followed. He knew Sir William came to the club every morning at ten thirty, as regularly as clockwork; he knew that for a psychological certainty he could get the chocolates handed over to him if he hinted for them; he knew that the police would go chasing after all sorts of false trails starting from Sir William. And as for the wrapper and the forged letter, he carefully didn't destroy them because they were calculated not only to divert suspicion but actually to point away from him to some anonymous lunatic."

"Well, it's very smart of you, Mr. Sheringham," Moresby said, with a little sigh, but quite ungrudgingly. "Very smart indeed. What was it the lady told you that showed you the whole thing in a flash?"

"Why, it wasn't so much what she actually told me as what I heard between her words, so to speak. What she told me was that Mrs. Beresford knew the answer to that bet; what I deduced was that, being the sort of person she was, it was quite incredible that she should have made a bet to which she knew the answer. *Ergo,* she didn't. *Ergo,* there never was such a bet. *Ergo,* Beresford was lying. *Ergo,* Beresford wanted to get hold of those chocolates for some reason other than he stated. After all, we only had Beresford's word for the bet, hadn't we?

"Of course he wouldn't have left her that afternoon till he'd seen her take, or somehow made her take, at least six of the chocolates, more than a lethal dose. That's why the stuff was in those meticulous six-minim doses. And so that he could take a couple himself, of course. A clever stroke, that."

Moresby rose to his feet.

"Well, Mr. Sheringham, I'm much obliged to you, sir. And now I shall have to get busy myself." He scratched his head. "Chance the Avenger, eh? Well, I can tell you one pretty big thing Beresford left to Chance the Avenger, Mr Sheringham. Suppose Sir William hadn't handed over the chocolates after all? Supposing he'd kept 'em, to give to one of his own ladies?"

Roger positively snorted. He felt a personal pride in Beresford by this time.

"Really, Moresby! It wouldn't have had any serious results if Sir William had. Do give my man credit for being what he is. You don't imagine he sent the poisoned ones to Sir William, do you? Of course not! He'd send harmless ones, and exchange them for the others on his way home. Dash it all, he wouldn't go right out of his way to present opportunities to Chance.

"If," added Roger, "Chance really is the right word."

THE BORDER–LINE CASE

by MARGERY ALLINGHAM

The affair of the perspiring policeman — the shortest story in the book, and very nearly the best. Especially recommended reading for a cold night.

IT WAS SO HOT in London that night that we slept with the wide skylight in our city studio open and let the sootblacks fall in on us willingly, so long as they brought with them a single stirring breath to move the stifling air. Heat hung on the dark horizons and beneath our particular bowl of sky the city fidgeted, breathless and uncomfortable.

The early editions of the evening papers carried the story of the murder. I read it when they came along about three o'clock on the following afternoon. My mind took in the details lazily, for my eyelids were sticky and the printed words seemed remote and unrelated to reality.

It was a straightforward little incident, or so I thought it, and when I had read the guarded half-column I threw the paper over to Albert Campion, who had drifted in to lunch and stayed to sit quietly in a corner, blinking behind his spectacles, existing merely, in the sweltering day.

The newspapers called the murder "The Coal Court Shooting Case," and the facts were simple.

At one o'clock in the morning, when Vacation Street, N.E., had been a deserted lane of odoriferous heat, a policeman on the beat had seen a man stumble and fall to the pavement. The intense discomfort of the night being uppermost in his mind, he had not unnat-

urally diagnosed a case of ordinary collapse and, after loosening the
stranger's collar, had summoned the ambulance.

When the authorities arrived, however, the man was pronounced
to be dead and the body was taken to the mortuary, where it was
discovered that death had been due to a bullet wound neatly placed
between the shoulder blades. The bullet had made a small blue hole
and, after perforating the left lung, had furrowed the heart itself,
finally coming to rest in the bony structure of the chest.

Since this was so, and the fact that the police constable had heard
no untoward sound, it had been reasonable to believe that the shot
had been fired at some little distance from a gun with a silencer.

Mr. Campion was only politely interested. The afternoon certainly
was hot and the story as it then appeared was hardly original or exciting. He sat on the floor reading it patiently, his long thin legs
stretched out in front of him.

"Someone died at any rate," he remarked at last and added after
a pause: "poor chap! Out of the frying pan . . . Dear me, I suppose
it's the locality which predisposes one to think of that. Ever seen Vacation Street, Margery?"

I did not answer him. I was thinking how odd it was that a general
irritant like the heat should make the dozens of situations arising all
round one in the great city seem suddenly almost personal. I found I
was desperately sorry for the man who had been shot, whoever he was.

It was Stanislaus Oates who told us the real story behind the half-
column in the evening paper. He came in just after four looking for
Campion. He was a detective inspector in those days and had just
begun to develop the habit of chatting over his problems with the
pale young man in the horn-rimmed spectacles. Theirs was an odd
relationship. It was certainly not a case of the clever amateur and the
humble policeman: rather the irritable and pugnacious policeman
taking it out of the inoffensive, friendly representative of the general
public.

On this occasion Oates was rattled.

"It's a case right down your street," he said briefly to Campion as
he sat down. "Seems to be a miracle, for one thing."

He explained after a while, having salved his conscience by pointing out that he had no business to discuss the case and excusing himself most illogically on grounds of the heat.

"It's 'low-class' crime," he went on briskly. "Practically gang shooting. And probably quite uninteresting to all of you, who like romance in your crimes. However, it's got me right down on two counts: the first because the man who shot the fellow who died couldn't possibly have done so, and second because I was wrong about the girl. They're so true to type, these girls, that you can't even rely on the proverbial exception."

He sighed as if the discovery had really grieved him.

We heard the story of Josephine as we sat round in the paralysingly hot studio and, although I never saw the girl then or afterwards, I shall not forget the scene; the two of us listening, breathing rather heavily, while the inspector talked.

She had been Donovan's girl, so Oates said, and he painted a picture of her for us: slender and flat-chested, with black hair and eyes like a Russian madonna's in a transparent face. She wore blouses, he said, with lace on them and gold ornaments, little chains and crosses and frail brooches whose security was reinforced by gilt safety pins. She was only twenty, Oates said, and added enigmatically that he would have betted on her but that it served him right and showed him there was no fool like an old one.

He went on to talk about Donovan, who, it seemed, was thirty-five and had spent ten years of his life in jail. The inspector did not seem to think any the less of him for that. The fact seemed to put the man in a definite category in his mind and that was all.

"Robbery with violence and the R.O. boys," he said with a wave of his hand and smiled contentedly as though he had made everything clear. "She was sixteen when he found her and he's given her hell ever since."

While he still held our interest he mentioned Johnny Gilchick. Johnny Gilchick was the man who was dead.

Oates, who was never more sentimental than was strictly reasonable in the circumstances, let himself go about Josephine and Johnny Gilchick. It was love, he said — love, sudden, painful and ludicrous; and he admitted that he liked to see it.

"I had an aunt once who used to talk about the Real Thing," he explained, "and embarrassingly silly the old lady sounded, but after seeing those two youngsters meet and flame and go on until they were a single fiery entity — youngsters who were pretty ordinary tawdry material without it — I find myself sympathising with her if not condoning the phrase."

He hesitated and his smooth grey face cracked into a depreciating smile.

"Well, we were both wrong, anyway," he murmured, "my aunt and I. Josephine let her Johnny down just as you'd expect her to and after he got what was coming to him and was lying in the mortuary he was born to lie in she upped and perjured her immortal soul to swear his murderer an alibi. Not that her testimony is of much value as evidence. That's beside the point. The fact remains that she's certainly done her best. You may think me sentimental, but it depresses me. I thought that girl was genuine and my judgment was out."

Mr. Campion stirred.

"Could we have the details?" he asked politely. "We've only seen the evening paper. It wasn't very helpful."

Oates glared at him balefully.

"Frankly, the facts are exasperating," he said. "There's a little catch in them somewhere. It must be something so simple that I missed it altogether. That's really why I've come to look for you. I thought you might care to come along and take a glance at the place. What about it?"

There was no general movement. It was too hot to stir. Finally the inspector took up a piece of chalk and sketched a rough diagram on the bare boards of the model's throne.

"This is Vacation Street," he said, edging the chalk along a crack. "It's the best part of a mile long. Up this end, here by the chair, it's nearly all wholesale houses. This sand bin I'm sketching in now marks the boundary of two police divisions. We'll take that as the starting point. Well, here, ten yards to the left, is the entrance to Coal Court, which is a cul-de-sac composed of two blank backs of warehouse buildings and a café at the far end. The café is open all night. It serves the printers from the two big presses further down the road. That's its legitimate trade. But it is also a sort of unofficial headquarters for Donovan's mob. Josephine sits at the desk downstairs and keeps an eye on the door. God knows what hours she keeps. She always seems to be there."

He paused and there came into my mind a recollection of the

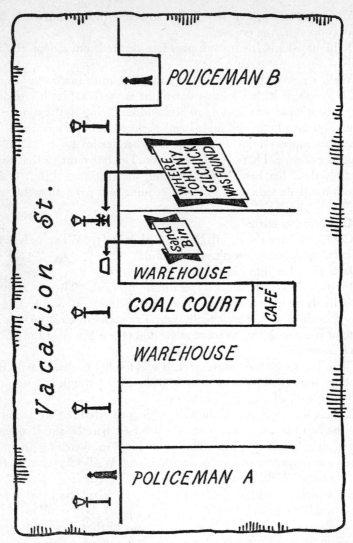

breathless night through which we had all passed, and I could imagine the girl sitting there in the stuffy shop with her thin chest and her great black eyes.

The inspector was still speaking.

"Now," he said, "there's an upstairs room in the café. It's on the second floor. That's where our friend Donovan spent most of his evening. I expect he had a good few friends with him and we shall locate them all in time."

He bent over the diagram.

"Johnny Gilchick died here," he said, drawing a circle about a foot beyond the square which indicated the sand bin. "Although the bobby was right down the road, he saw him pause under the lamppost, stagger and fall. He called the constable from the other division and they got the ambulance. All that is plain sailing. There's just one difficulty. Where was Donovan when he fired the shot? There were two policemen in the street at the time, remember. At the moment of the actual shooting one of them, the Never Street man, was making a round of a warehouse yard, but the other, the Phyllis Court chap, was there on the spot, not forty yards away, and it was he who actually saw Johnny Gilchick fall, although he heard no shot. Now I tell you, Campion, there's not an ounce of cover in the whole of that street. How did Donovan get out of the café, where did he stand to shoot Johnny neatly through the back, and how did he get back again without being seen? The side walls of the cul-de-sac are solid concrete backs of warehouses, there is no way round from the back of the café, nor could he possibly have gone over the roofs. The warehouses tower over the café like liners over a tug. Had he come out down the road one or other of the bobbies must have been certain to have seen him. How did he do it?"

"Perhaps Donovan didn't do it," I ventured and received a pitying glance for my temerity.

"That's the one fact," said the inspector heavily. "That's the only thing I do know. I know Donovan. He's one of the few English mob boys who carry guns. He served five years with the gangs in New York before Repeal and he has the misfortune to take his liquor in bouts. After each bout he has a period of black depression, during which he may do anything. Johnny Gilchick used to be one of Donovan's mob and when Johnny fell for the girl he turned in the gang, which was adding insult to injury where Donovan was concerned."

He paused and smiled.

"Donovan was bound to get Johnny in the end," he said. "It was never anything but a question of time. The whole mob expected it. The neighbourhood was waiting for it. Donovan had said openly that the next time Johnny dropped into the café would be his final appearance there. Johnny called last night, was ordered out of the place by the terrified girl, and finally walked out of the cul-de-sac. He turned the corner and strolled down the road. Then he was shot by Donovan. There's no way round it, Campion. The doctors say that death was as near instantaneous as may be. Johnny Gilchick could not have walked three paces with that bullet in his back. As for the gun, that was pretty obviously Donovan's too. We haven't actually picked it up yet, but we know he had one of the type we are after. It's a clear case, a straightforward case, if only we knew where Donovan stood when he fired the shot."

Mr. Campion looked up. His eyes were thoughtful behind his spectacles.

"The girl gave Donovan an alibi?" he enquired.

Oates shrugged his shoulders. "Rather," he said. "She was passionate about it. He was there the whole time, every minute of the time, never left the upper room once in the whole evening. I could kill her and she would not alter her story; she'd take her dying oath on it and so on and so on. It didn't mean anything either way. Still, I was sorry to see her doing it, with her boy friend barely cold. She was sucking up to the mob, of course; probably had excellent reasons for doing so. Yet, as I say, I was sorry to hear her volunteering the alibi before she was asked."

"Ah! She volunteered it, did she?" Campion was interested.

Oates nodded and his small grey eyes widened expressively.

"Forced it on us. Came roaring round to the police station with it. Threw it off her chest as if she were doing something fine. I'm not usually squeamish about that sort of thing but it gave me a distinct sense of distaste, I don't mind telling you. Frankly, I gave her a piece of my mind. Told her to go and look at the body, for one thing."

"Not kind of you," observed Mr. Campion mildly. "And what did she do?"

"Oh, blubbered herself sick, like the rest of 'em." Oates was still disgruntled. "Still, that's not of interest. What girls like Josephine do or don't do doesn't really matter. She was saving her own skin. If she hadn't been so enthusiastic about it I'd have forgiven her. It's Donovan who is important. Where was Donovan when he fired?"

The shrill chatter of the telephone answered him and he glanced at me apologetically.

"I'm afraid that's mine," he said. "You didn't mind, did you? I left the number with the sergeant."

He took off the receiver and as he bent his head to listen his face changed. We watched him with an interest it was far too hot to dissemble.

"Oh," he said flatly after a long pause. "Really? Well, it doesn't matter either way, does it? . . . Still, what did she do it for? . . . What? . . . I suppose so. . . . Yes? . . . Really?"

He seemed suddenly astounded as his informant at the other end of the wire evidently came out with a second piece of information more important than the first.

"You can't be certain . . . you are? . . . What?"

The faraway voice explained busily. We could hear its steady drone. Inspector Oates's exasperation grew.

"Oh all right, all right," he said at last. "I'm crackers . . . we're all crackers . . . have it your own damned way!"

With which vulgar outburst he rang off.

"Alibi sustained?" enquired Mr. Campion.

"Yes." The inspector grunted out the word. "A couple of printers who were in the downstairs room swear he did not go through the shop all the evening. They're sound fellows. Make good witnesses. Yet Donovan shot Johnny. I'm certain of it. He shot him clean through the concrete angle of a piano warehouse as far as I can see." He turned to Campion almost angrily. "Explain that, can you?"

Mr. Campion coughed. He seemed a little embarrassed.

"I say, you know," he ventured, "there are just two things that occur to me."

"Then out with them, son." The inspector lit a cigarette and wiped his face. "Out with them. I'm not proud."

Mr. Campion coughed. "Well, the — er — heat, for one thing, don't you know," he said with profound uneasiness. "The heat, and one of your concrete walls."

The inspector swore a little and apologised.

"If anyone could forget this heat he's welcome," he said. "What's the matter with the wall too?"

Mr. Campion bent over the diagram on the boards of the throne. He was very apologetic.

"Here is the angle of the warehouse," he said, "and here is the sand bin. Here to the left is the lamppost where Johnny Gilchick was found. Further on to the left is the P.C. from Never Street examining a courtyard and temporarily off the scene, while to the right, on the other side of the entrance to Coal Court, is another constable, P.C. someone-or-other, of Phyllis Court. One is apt to — er — think of the problem as though it were contained in four solid walls, two concrete walls, two policemen."

He hesitated and glanced timidly at the inspector.

"When is a policeman not a concrete wall, Oates? In — er — well, in just such heat . . . do you think, or don't you?"

Oates was staring at him, his eyes narrowed.

"Damn it!" he said explosively. "Damn it, Campion, I believe you're right. I knew it was something so simple that it was staring me in the face."

They stood together looking down at the diagram. Oates stooped to put a chalk cross at the entrance to the cul-de-sac.

"It was *that* lamppost," he said. "Give me that telephone. Wait till I get hold of that fellow."

While he was carrying on an excited conversation we demanded an explanation from Mr. Campion and he gave it to us at last, mild and apologetic as usual.

"Well, you see," he said, "there's the sand bin. The sand bin marks the boundary of two police divisions. Policeman A, very hot and tired, sees a man collapse from the heat under a lamppost on his own territory. The man is a little fellow and it occurs to Policeman A that it would be a simple matter to move him to the next lamppost on the other side of the sand bin, where he would automatically become the responsibility of Policeman B, who is even now approaching. Policeman A achieves the change and is bending over the prostrate figure when his colleague comes up. Since he knows nothing of the bullet wound, the entrance to the cul-de-sac, with its clear view to the café second-floor room, has no significance in his mind. Today, when its full importance must have dawned upon him, he evidently thinks it best to hold his tongue."

Oates came back from the phone triumphant.

"The first bobby went on leave this morning," he said. "He was an old hand. He must have spotted the chap was dead, took it for granted it was the heat, and didn't want to be held up here by the inquest. Funny I didn't see that in the beginning."

We were all silent for some moments.

"Then — the girl?" I began at last.

The inspector frowned and made a little grimace of regret.

"A pity about the girl," he said. "Of course it was probably an accident. Our man who saw it happen said he couldn't be sure."

I stared at him and he explained, albeit a little hurriedly.

"Didn't I tell you? When my sergeant phoned about the alibi he told me. As Josephine crossed the road after visiting the mortuary this morning she stepped under a bus. . . . Oh yes, instantly."

He shook his head. He seemed uncomfortable.

"She thought she was making a gesture when she came down to the station, don't you see? The mob must have told her to swear that no one had been in the upstairs room; that must have been their first story until they saw how the luck lay. So when she came beetling down to us she must have thought she was risking her life to give her Johnny's murderer away, while instead of that she was simply giving the fellow an alibi. . . . Funny the way things happen, isn't it?"

He glanced at Campion affectionately.

"It's because you don't get your mind cluttered up with the human element that you see these things so quickly," he said. "You see everything in terms of A and B. It makes all the difference."

Mr. Campion, the most gentle of men, made no comment at all.

THE TWO BOTTLES OF RELISH

by LORD DUNSANY

This is what happens when a celebrated littérateur stoops to conquer detective fiction. He creates a MR. LINLEY *and an unforgettable tale, and provides the Messrs. Queen with the opportunity to shout: "Discovery!" Friendly warning: Read this only when someone is in the house with you.*

SMITHERS is my name. I'm what you might call a small man and in a small way of business. I travel for Num-numo, a relish for meats and savouries — the world-famous relish I ought to say. It's really quite good, no deleterious acids in it, and does not affect the heart; so it is quite easy to push. I wouldn't have got the job if it weren't. But I hope some day to get something that's harder to push, as of course the harder they are to push, the better the pay. At present I can just make my way, with nothing at all over; but then I live in a very expensive flat. It happened like this, and that brings me to my story. And it isn't the story you'd expect from a small man like me, yet there's nobody else to tell it. Those that know anything of it besides me are all for hushing it up. Well, I was looking for a room to live in in London when first I got my job. It had to be in London, to be central; and I went to a block of buildings, very gloomy they looked, and saw the man that ran them and asked him for what I wanted. Flats they called them; just a bedroom and a sort of a cupboard. Well, he was showing a man round at the time who was a gent, in fact more than that, so he didn't take much notice of me — the man that ran all those flats didn't, I mean. So I just ran behind for a bit, seeing all sorts of rooms and waiting till I could be shown my class of thing. We came to a very nice flat, a sitting room, bedroom and bathroom, and a sort of little place that they called a hall. And that's how I came to know Linley. He was the bloke that was being shown round.

"Bit expensive," he said.

And the man that ran the flats turned away to the window and picked his teeth. It's funny how much you can show by a simple thing like. What he meant to say was that he'd hundreds of flats like that, and thousands of people looking for them, and he didn't care who had them or whether they all went on looking. There was no mistaking him, somehow. And yet he never said a word, only looked away out of the window and picked his teeth. And I ventured to speak to Mr. Linley then; and I said, "How about it, sir, if I paid half, and shared it? I wouldn't be in the way, and I'm out all day, and whatever you said would go, and really I wouldn't be no more in your way than a cat."

You may be surprised at my doing it; and you'll be much more surprised at him accepting it — at least, you would if you knew me, just a small man in a small way of business. And yet I could see at once that he was taking to me more than he was taking to the man at the window.

"But there's only one bedroom," he said.

"I could make up my bed easy in that little room there," I said.

"The Hall," said the man, looking round from the window, without taking his toothpick out.

"And I'd have the bed out of the way and hid in the cupboard by any hour you like," I said.

He looked thoughtful, and the other man looked out over London; and in the end, do you know, he accepted.

"Friend of yours?" said the flat man.

"Yes," answered Mr. Linley.

It was really very nice of him.

I'll tell you why I did it. Able to afford it? Of course not. But I heard him tell the flat man that he had just come down from Oxford and wanted to live for a few months in London. It turned out he wanted just to be comfortable and do nothing for a bit while he looked things over and chose a job, or probably just as long as he could afford it. Well, I said to myself, what's the Oxford manner worth in business, especially a business like mine? Why, simply everything you've got. If I picked up only a quarter of it from this

Mr. Linley I'd be able to double my sales, and that would soon mean I'd be given something a lot harder to push, with perhaps treble the pay. Worth it every time. And you can make a quarter of an education go twice as far again, if you're careful with it. I mean you don't have to quote the whole of the *Inferno* to show that you've read Milton; half a line may do it.

Well, about that story I have to tell. And you mightn't think that a little man like me could make you shudder. Well, I soon forgot about the Oxford manner when we settled down in our flat. I forgot it in the sheer wonder of the man himself. He had a mind like an acrobat's body, like a bird's body. It didn't want education. You didn't notice whether he was educated or not. Ideas were always leaping up in him, things you'd never have thought of. And not only that, but if any ideas were about, he'd sort of catch them. Time and again I've found him knowing just what I was going to say. Not thought reading, but what they call intuition. I used to try to learn a bit about chess, just to take my thoughts off Num-numo in the evening, when I'd done with it. But problems I never could do. Yet he'd come along and glance at my problem and say, "You probably move that piece first," and I'd say, "But where?" and he'd say, "Oh, one of those three squares." And I'd say, "But it will be taken on all of them." And the piece a queen all the time, mind you. And he'd say, "Yes, it's doing no good there: you're probably meant to lose it."

And, do you know, he'd be right.

You see, he'd been following out what the other man had been thinking. That's what he'd been doing.

Well, one day there was that ghastly murder at Unge. I don't know if you remember it. But Steeger had gone down to live with a girl in a bungalow on the North Downs, and that was the first we had heard of him.

The girl had £200, and he got every penny of it, and she utterly disappeared. And Scotland Yard couldn't find her.

Well, I'd happened to read that Steeger had bought two bottles of Num-numo; for the Otherthorpe police had found out everything about him, except what he did with the girl; and that of course attracted my attention, or I should have never thought again about the case or said a word of it to Linley. Num-numo was always on my mind, as I always spent every day pushing it, and that kept me from forgetting the other thing. And so one day I said to Linley, "I wonder with all that knack you have for seeing through a chess problem, and thinking of one thing and another, that you don't have a go at that Otherthorpe mystery. It's a problem as much as chess," I said.

"There's not the mystery in ten murders that there is in one game of chess," he answered.

"It's beaten Scotland Yard," I said.

"Has it?" he asked.

"Knocked them endwise," I said.

"It shouldn't have done that," he said. And almost immediately after he said, "What are the facts?"

We were both sitting at supper, and I told him the facts, as I had them straight from the papers. She was a pretty blonde, she was small, she was called Nancy Elth, she had £200, they lived at the bungalow for five days. After that he stayed there for another fortnight, but nobody ever saw her alive again. Steeger said she had gone to South America, but later said he had never said South America, but South Africa. None of her money remained in the bank where she had kept it, and Steeger was shown to have come by at least £150 just at that time. Then Steeger turned out to be a vegetarian, getting all his food from the greengrocer, and that made the constable in the village of Unge suspicious of him, for a vegetarian was something new to the constable. He watched Steeger after that, and it's well he did, for there was nothing that Scotland Yard asked him that he couldn't tell them about him, except of course the one thing. And he told the police at Otherthorpe five or six miles away, and they came and took a hand at it too. They were able to say for one thing that he never went outside the bungalow and its tidy garden ever since she disappeared. You see, the more they watched him the more suspicious they got, as you naturally do if you're watching a man; so that very soon they were watching every move he made, but if it hadn't been for his being a vegetarian they'd never have started to suspect him, and there wouldn't have been enough evidence even for Linley. Not that they found out anything much against him, except that £150 dropping in from nowhere, and it was Scotland Yard that found that, not the police of Otherthorpe. No, what the constable of Unge found out was about the larch trees, and that beat Scotland Yard utterly, and beat Linley up to the very last, and of course it beat me. There were ten larch trees in the bit of a garden, and he'd made some sort of an arrangement with the landlord, Steeger had, before he took the bungalow, by which he could do what he liked with the larch trees. And then from about the time that little Nancy Elth must have died he cut every one of them down. Three times a day he went at it for nearly a week, and when they were all down he cut them all up into logs no more than two foot long and laid them all in neat heaps. You never saw such work. And what for? To give an excuse for the axe was one theory. But the excuse was bigger than the axe; it took him a fortnight, hard work every day. And he could have killed a little thing like Nancy Elth without an axe, and cut her up too. Another theory was that he wanted firewood, to make away with the body. But he never used it. He left it all standing there in those neat stacks. It fairly beat everybody.

Well, those are the facts I told Linley. Oh yes, and he bought a big butcher's knife. Funny thing, they all do. And yet it isn't so funny after all; if you've got to cut a woman up, you've got to cut her up; and you can't do that without a knife. Then, there were some negative facts. He hadn't burned her. Only had a fire in the small stove now and then, and only used it for cooking. They got on to that pretty smartly, the Unge constable did, and the men that were lending him a hand from Otherthorpe. There were some little woody places lying round, shaws they call them in that part of the country, the country people do, and they could climb a tree handy and unobserved and get a sniff at the smoke in almost any direction it might be blowing. They did that now and then, and there was no smell of flesh burning, just ordinary cooking. Pretty smart of the Otherthorpe police that was, though of course it didn't help to hang Steeger. Then later on the Scotland Yard men went down and got another fact — negative, but narrowing things down all the while. And that was that the chalk under the bungalow and under the little garden had none of it been disturbed. And he'd never been outside it since Nancy disappeared. Oh yes, and he had a big file besides the knife. But there was no sign of any ground bones found on the file, or any blood on the knife. He'd washed them of course. I told all that to Linley.

Now I ought to warn you before I go any further. I am a small man myself and you probably don't expect anything horrible from me. But I ought to warn you this man was a murderer, or at any rate somebody was; the woman had been made away with, a nice pretty little girl too, and the man that had done that wasn't necessarily going to stop at things you might think he'd stop at. With the mind to do a thing like that, and with the long thin shadow of the rope to drive him further, you can't say what he'll stop at. Murder tales seem nice things sometimes for a lady to sit and read all by herself by the fire. But murder isn't a nice thing, and when a murderer's desperate and trying to hide his tracks he isn't even as nice as he was before. I'll ask you to bear that in mind. Well, I've warned you.

So I says to Linley, "And what do you make of it?"

"Drains?" said Linley.

"No," I says, "you're wrong there. Scotland Yard has been into that. And the Otherthorpe people before them. They've had a look in the drains, such as they are, a little thing running into a cesspool beyond the garden; and nothing has gone down it — nothing that oughtn't to have, I mean."

He made one or two other suggestions, but Scotland Yard had been before him in every case. That's really the crab of my story, if you'll excuse the expression. You want a man who sets out to be a detective to take his magnifying glass and go down to the spot; to go to the spot before everything; and then to measure the footmarks and pick up the clues and find the knife that the police have over-looked. But Linley never even went near the place, and he hadn't got a magnifying glass, not as I ever saw, and Scotland Yard were before him every time.

In fact they had more clues than anybody could make head or tail of. Every kind of clue to show that he'd murdered the poor little girl; every kind of clue to show that he hadn't disposed of the body; and yet the body wasn't there. It wasn't in South America either, and not much more likely in South Africa. And all the time, mind you, that enormous bunch of chopped larchwood, a clue that was staring everyone in the face and leading nowhere. No, we didn't seem to want any more clues, and Linley never went near the place. The trouble was to deal with the clues we'd got. I was completely mysti-fied; so was Scotland Yard; and Linley seemed to be getting no forwarder; and all the while the mystery was hanging on me. I mean if it were not for the trifle I'd chanced to remember, and if it were not for one chance word I said to Linley, that mystery would have gone the way of all the other mysteries that men have made nothing of, a darkness, a little patch of night in history.

Well, the fact was Linley didn't take much interest in it at first, but I was so absolutely sure that he could do it that I kept him to the idea. "You can do chess problems," I said.

"That's ten times harder," he said, sticking to his point.

"Then why don't you do this?" I said.

"Then go and take a look at the board for me," said Linley.

That was his way of talking. We'd been a fortnight together, and I knew it by now. He meant to go down to the bungalow at Unge. I know you'll say why didn't he go himself; but the plain truth of it is that if he'd been tearing about the countryside he'd never have been thinking, whereas sitting there in his chair by the fire in our flat there was no limit to the ground he could cover, if you follow my meaning. So down I went by train next day, and got out at Unge station. And there were the North Downs rising up before me, somehow like music.

"It's up there, isn't it?" I said to the porter.

"That's right," he said. "Up there by the lane; and mind to turn to your right when you get to the old yew tree, a very big tree, you can't mistake it, and then . . ." and he told me the way so that I couldn't go wrong. I found them all like that, very nice and helpful. You see, it was Unge's day at last. Everyone had heard of Unge now; you could have got a letter there any time just then without putting the county or post town; and this was what Unge had to show. I dare say if you tried to find Unge now . . . well, anyway, they were making hay while the sun shone.

Well, there the hill was, going up into sunlight, going up like a song. You don't want to hear about the spring, and all the may rioting, and the colour that came down over everything later on in the day, and all those birds; but I thought, "What a nice place to bring a girl to." And then when I thought that he'd killed her there, well I'm only a small man, as I said, but when I thought of her on that hill with all the birds singing, I said to myself, "Wouldn't it be odd if it turned out to be me after all that got that man killed, if he did murder her." So I soon found my way up to the bungalow and began prying about, looking over the hedge into the garden. And I didn't find much, and I found nothing at all that the police hadn't found already, but there were those heaps of larch logs staring me in the face and looking very queer.

I did a lot of thinking, leaning against the hedge, breathing the smell of the may, and looking over the top of it at the larch logs, and the neat little bungalow the other side of the garden. Lots of theories I thought of, till I came to the best thought of all; and that was that if I left the thinking to Linley, with his Oxford-and-Cambridge education, and only brought him the facts, as he had told me, I should be doing more good in my way than if I tried to do any big thinking. I forgot to tell you that I had gone to Scotland Yard in the morning. Well, there wasn't really much to tell. What they asked me was what I wanted. And, not having an answer exactly ready, I didn't find out very much from them. But it was quite different at Unge; everyone was most obliging; it was their day there, as I said. The constable let me go indoors, so long as I didn't touch anything, and he gave me a look at the garden from the inside. And I saw the stumps of the ten larch trees, and I noticed one thing that Linley said was very observant of me, not that it turned out to be any use, but anyway I was doing my best: I noticed that the stumps had been all chopped anyhow. And from that I thought that the man that did it didn't know much about chopping. The constable said that was a deduction. So then I said that the axe was blunt when he used it; and that certainly made the constable think, though he didn't actually say I was right this time. Did I tell you that Steeger never went outdoors, except to the little garden to chop wood, ever since Nancy disappeared? I think I did. Well, it was perfectly true. They'd watched him night and day, one or another of them, and the Unge constable told me that himself. That limited things a good deal. The only thing I didn't like about it was that I felt Linley ought to have found all that out instead of ordinary policemen, and I felt that he could have too. There'd have been romance in a story like that. And they'd never have done it if the news hadn't gone round that the man was a vegetarian and only dealt at the greengrocer's. Likely as not even that was only started out of pique by the butcher. It's queer what little things may trip a man up. Best to keep straight is my motto. But perhaps I'm straying a bit away from my story. I should like to do that for ever — forget that it ever was; but I can't.

Well, I picked up all sorts of information; clues I suppose I should call it in a story like this, though they none of them seemed to lead anywhere. For instance, I found out everything he ever bought at the village, I could even tell you the kind of salt he bought, quite plain with no phosphates in it, that they sometimes put in to make it tidy. And then he got ice from the fishmonger's, and plenty of vegetables, as I said, from the greengrocer, Mergin & Sons. And I had a bit of a talk over it all with the constable. Slugger he said his name was. I wondered why he hadn't come in and searched the place as soon as the girl was missing. "Well, you can't do that," he said. "And besides, we didn't suspect at once, not about the girl, that is. We only suspected there was something wrong about him on account of him being a vegetarian. He stayed a good fortnight after the last that was seen of her. And then we slipped in like a knife. But, you see, no one had been enquiring about her, there was no warrant out."

"And what did you find?" I asked Slugger, "when you went in?"

"Just a big file," he said, "and the knife and the axe that he must have got to chop her up with."

"But he got the axe to chop trees with," I said.

"Well, yes," he said, but rather grudgingly.

"And what did he chop them for?" I asked.

"Well, of course, my superiors has theories about that," he said, "that they mightn't tell to everybody."

You see, it was those logs that were beating them.

"But did he cut her up at all?" I asked.

"Well, he said that she was going to South America," he answered. Which was really very fair-minded of him.

I don't remember now much else that he told me. Steeger left the plates and dishes all washed up and very neat, he said.

Well, I brought all this back to Linley, going up by the train that started just about sunset. I'd like to tell you about the late spring evening, so calm over that grim bungalow, closing in with a glory all round it as though it were blessing it; but you'll want to hear of the murder. Well, I told Linley everything, though much of it didn't seem to me to be worth the telling. The trouble was that the moment I began to leave anything out, he'd know it, and make me drag it in. "You can't tell what may be vital," he'd say. "A tin tack swept away by a housemaid might hang a man."

All very well, but be consistent, even if you are educated at Eton and Harrow, and whenever I mentioned Num-numo, which after all was the beginning of the whole story, because he wouldn't have heard of it if it hadn't been for me, and my noticing that Steeger had bought two bottles of it, why then he said that things like that were trivial and we should keep to the main issues. I naturally talked a bit about Num-numo, because only that day I had pushed close on fifty bottles of it in Unge. A murder certainly stimulates people's minds, and Steeger's two bottles gave me an opportunity that only a fool could have failed to make something of. But of course all that was nothing at all to Linley.

You can't see a man's thoughts, and you can't look into his mind, so that all the most exciting things in the world can never be told of. But what I think happened all that evening with Linley, while I talked to him before supper, and all through supper, and sitting smoking afterwards in front of our fire, was that his thoughts were stuck at a barrier there was no getting over. And the barrier wasn't the difficulty of finding ways and means by which Steeger might have made away with the body, but the impossibility of finding why he chopped those masses of wood every day for a fortnight, and paid, as I'd just found out, £25 to his landlord to be allowed to do it. That's what was beating Linley. As for the ways by which Steeger might have hidden the body, it seemed to me that every way was blocked by the police. If you said he buried it, they said the chalk was undisturbed; if you said he carried it away, they said he never left the place; if you said he burned it, they said no smell of burning was ever noticed when the smoke blew low, and when it didn't they climbed trees after it. I'd taken to Linley wonderfully, and I didn't have to be educated to see there was something big in a mind like his, and I thought that he could have done it. When I saw the police getting in before him like that, and no way that I could see of getting past them, I felt real sorry.

Did anyone come to the house, he asked me once or twice. Did anyone take anything away from it? But we couldn't account for it that way. Then perhaps I made some suggestion that was no good, or perhaps I started talking of Num-numo again, and he interrupted me rather sharply.

"But what would you do, Smithers?" he said. "What would you do yourself?"

"If I'd murdered poor Nancy Elth?" I asked.

"Yes," he said.

"I can't ever imagine doing such a thing," I told him.

He sighed at that, as though it were something against me.

"I suppose I should never be a detective," I said. And he just shook his head.

Then he looked broodingly into the fire for what seemed an hour. And then he shook his head again. We both went to bed after that.

I shall remember the next day all my life. I was till evening, as usual, pushing Num-numo. And we sat down to supper about nine. You couldn't get things cooked at those flats, so of course we had it cold. And Linley began with a salad. I can see it now, every bit of it. Well, I was still a bit full of what I'd done in Unge, pushing Num-numo. Only a fool, I know, would have been unable to push it there; but still, I *had* pushed it; and about fifty bottles, forty-eight to be exact, are something in a small village, whatever the circumstances. So I was talking about it a bit; and then all of a sudden I realized that Num-numo was nothing to Linley, and I pulled myself up with a jerk. It was really very kind of him; do you know what he did? He must have known at once why I stopped talking, and he just stretched out a hand and said, "Would you give me a little of your Num-numo for my salad?"

I was so touched I nearly gave it him. But of course you don't take Num-numo with salad. Only for meats and savouries. That's on the bottle.

So I just said to him, "Only for meats and savouries." Though I don't know what savouries are. Never had any.

I never saw a man's face go like that before.

He seemed still for a whole minute. And nothing speaking about him but that expression. Like a man that's seen a ghost, one is tempted to write. But it wasn't really at all. I'll tell you what he looked like.

Like a man that's seen something that no one has ever looked at before, something he thought couldn't be.

And then he said in a voice that was all quite changed, more low and gentle and quiet it seemed, "No good for vegetables, eh?"

"Not a bit," I said.

And at that he gave a kind of sob in his throat. I hadn't thought he could feel things like that. Of course I didn't know what it was all about; but, whatever it was, I thought all that sort of thing would have been knocked out of him at Eton and Harrow, an educated man like that. There were no tears in his eyes, but he was feeling something horribly.

And then he began to speak with big spaces between his words, saying, "A man might make a mistake perhaps, and use Num-numo with vegetables."

"Not twice," I said. What else could I say?

And he repeated that after me as though I had told of the end of the world, and adding an awful emphasis to my words, till they seemed all clammy with some frightful significance, and shaking his head as he said it.

Then he was quite silent.

"What is it?" I asked.

"Smithers," he said.

"Yes," I said.

"Smithers," said he.

And I said, "Well?"

"Look here, Smithers," he said, "you must phone down to the grocer at Unge and find out from him this."

"Yes?" I said.

"Whether Steeger bought those two bottles, as I expect he did, on the same day, and not a few days apart. He couldn't have done that."

I waited to see if any more was coming, and then I ran out and did what I was told. It took me some time, being after nine o'clock, and only then with the help of the police. About six days apart they said; and so I came back and told Linley. He looked up at me so hopefully when I came in, but I saw that it was the wrong answer by his eyes.

You can't take things to heart like that without being ill, and when he didn't speak I said, "What you want is a good brandy, and go to bed early."

And he said, "No. I must see someone from Scotland Yard. Phone round to them. Say here at once."

But I said, "I can't get an inspector from Scotland Yard to call on us at this hour."

His eyes were all lit up. He was all there all right.

"Then tell them," he said, "they'll never find Nancy Elth. Tell one of them to come here, and I'll tell him why." And he added, I think only for me, "They must watch Steeger, till one day they get him over something else."

And, do you know, he came. Inspector Ulton; he came himself.

While we were waiting I tried to talk to Linley. Partly curiosity, I admit. But I didn't want to leave him to those thoughts of his, brooding away by the fire. I tried to ask him what it was all about. But he wouldn't tell me. "Murder is horrible," is all he would say. "And as a man covers his tracks up it only gets worse."

He wouldn't tell me. "There are tales," he said, "that one never wants to hear."

That's true enough. I wish I'd never heard this one. I never did actually. But I guessed it from Linley's last words to Inspector Ulton, the only ones that I overheard. And perhaps this is the point at which to stop reading my story, so that you don't guess it too; even if you think you want murder stories. For don't you rather want a murder story with a bit of a romantic twist, and not a story about real foul murder? Well, just as you like.

In came Inspector Ulton, and Linley shook hands in silence, and pointed the way to his bedroom; and they went in there and talked in low voices, and I never heard a word.

A fairly hearty-looking man was the inspector when they went into that room.

They walked through our sitting room in silence when they came out, and together they went into the hall, and there I heard the only words they said to each other. It was the inspector that first broke that silence.

"But why," he said, "did he cut down the trees?"

"Solely," said Linley, "in order to get an appetite."

A MAN CALLED SPADE

by DASHIELL HAMMETT

No definitive anthology of The First Hundred Years (division of the detective short story) could look itself in the eye unless it included a sample of the work of Dashiell Hammett, who gave the business its zippiest shot in the arm since Doyle. The American Magazine, which first published "A Man Called Spade," pronounced it more realistic than a photograph. And so it is — a story in dramatic word-pictures you will not forget.

SAMUEL SPADE put his telephone aside and looked at his watch. It was not quite four o'clock. He called, "Yoo-hoo!"

Effie Perine came in from the outer office. She was eating a piece of chocolate cake.

"Tell Sid Wise I won't be able to keep that date this afternoon," he said.

She put the last of the cake into her mouth and licked the tips of forefinger and thumb. "That's the third time this week."

When he smiled, the v's of his chin, mouth, and brows grew longer. "I know, but I've got to go out and save a life." He nodded at the telephone. "Somebody's scaring Max Bliss."

She laughed. "Probably somebody named John D. Conscience."

He looked up at her from the cigarette he had begun to make. "Know anything I ought to know about him?"

"Nothing you don't know. I was just thinking about the time he let his brother go to San Quentin."

Spade shrugged. "That's not the worst thing he's done." He lit his cigarette, stood up, and reached for his hat. "But he's all right now. All Samuel Spade clients are honest, God-fearing folk. If I'm not back at closing time just run along."

He went to a tall apartment building on Nob Hill, pressed a button set in the frame of a door marked *10K*. The door was opened immediately by a burly dark man in wrinkled dark clothes. He was nearly bald and carried a gray hat in one hand.

The burly man said, "Hello, Sam." He smiled, but his small eyes lost more of their shrewdness. "What are you doing here?"

Spade said, "Hello, Tom." His face was wooden, his voice expressionless. "Bliss in?"

"Is he!" Tom pulled down the corners of his thick-lipped mouth. "You don't have to worry about that."

Spade's brows came together. "Well?"

A man appeared in the vestibule behind Tom. He was smaller than either Spade or Tom, but compactly built. He had a ruddy, square face and a close-trimmed, grizzled mustache. His clothes were neat. He wore a black bowler perched on the back of his head.

Spade addressed this man over Tom's shoulder: "Hello, Dundy."

Dundy nodded briefly and came to the door. His blue eyes were hard and prying.

"What is it?" he asked Tom.

"B-l-i-s-s, M-a-x," Spade spelled patiently. "I want to see him. He wants to see me. Catch on?"

Tom laughed. Dundy did not. Tom said, "Only one of you gets your wish." Then he glanced sidewise at Dundy and abruptly stopped laughing. He seemed uncomfortable.

Spade scowled. "All right," he demanded irritably; "is he dead or has he killed somebody?"

Dundy thrust his square face up at Spade and seemed to push his words out with his lower lip. "What makes you think either?"

Spade said, "Oh, sure! I come calling on Mr. Bliss and I'm stopped at the door by a couple of men from the police Homicide Detail, and I'm supposed to think I'm just interrupting a game of rummy."

"Aw, stop it, Sam," Tom grumbled, looking at neither Spade nor Dundy. "He's dead."

"Killed?"

Tom wagged his head slowly up and down. He looked at Spade now. "What've you got on it?"

Spade replied in a deliberate monotone, "He called me up this afternoon — say at five minutes to four — I looked at my watch after he hung up and there was still a minute or so to go — and said somebody was after his scalp. He wanted me to come over. It seemed real enough to him — it was up in his neck all right." He made a small gesture with one hand. "Well, here I am."

"Didn't say who or how?" Dundy asked.

Spade shook his head. "No. Just somebody had offered to kill him and he believed them, and would I come over right away."

"Didn't he — ?" Dundy began quickly.

"He didn't say anything else," Spade said. "Don't you people tell me anything?"

Dundy said curtly, "Come in and take a look at him."

Tom said, "It's a sight."

They went across the vestibule and through a door into a green and rose living room.

A man near the door stopped sprinkling white powder on the end of a glass-covered small table to say, "Hello, Sam."

Spade nodded, said, "How are you, Phels?" and then nodded at the two men who stood talking by a window.

The dead man lay with his mouth open. Some of his clothes had been taken off. His throat was puffy and dark. The end of his tongue showing in a corner of his mouth was bluish, swollen. On his bare chest, over the heart, a five-pointed star had been outlined in black ink and in the center of it a T.

Spade looked down at the dead man and stood for a moment silently studying him. Then he asked, "He was found like that?"

"About," Tom said. "We moved him around a little." He jerked a thumb at the shirt, undershirt, vest, and coat lying on a table. "They were spread over the floor."

Spade rubbed his chin. His yellow-gray eyes were dreamy. "When?"

Tom said, "We got it at four twenty. His daughter gave it to us." He moved his head to indicate a closed door. "You'll see her."

"Know anything?"

"Heaven knows," Tom said wearily. "She's been kind of hard to get along with so far." He turned to Dundy. "Want to try her again now?"

Dundy nodded, then spoke to one of the men at the window. "Start sifting his papers, Mack. He's supposed to've been threatened."

Mack said, "Right." He pulled his hat down over his eyes and walked towards a green *secrétaire* in the far end of the room.

A man came in from the corridor, a heavy man of fifty with a deeply lined, grayish face under a broad-brimmed black hat. He said, "Hello, Sam," and then told Dundy, "He had company around half past two, stayed just about an hour. A big blond man in brown, maybe forty or forty-five. Didn't send his name up. I got it from the Filipino in the elevator that rode him both ways."

"Sure it was only an hour?" Dundy asked.

The gray-faced man shook his head. "But he's sure it wasn't more than half past three when he left. He says the afternoon papers came in then, and this man had ridden down with him before they came." He pushed his hat back to scratch his head, then pointed a thick finger at the design inked on the dead man's breast and asked somewhat plaintively, "What the deuce do you suppose that thing is?"

Nobody replied. Dundy asked, "Can the elevator boy identify him?"

"He says he could, but that ain't always the same thing. Says he never saw him before." He stopped looking at the dead man. "The girl's getting me a list of his phone calls. How you been, Sam?"

Spade said he had been all right. Then he said slowly, "His brother's big and blond and maybe forty or forty-five."

Dundy's blue eyes were hard and bright. "So what?" he asked.

"You remember the Graystone Loan swindle. They were both in it, but Max eased the load over on Theodore and it turned out to be one to fourteen years in San Quentin."

Dundy was slowly wagging his head up and down. "I remember now. Where is he?"

Spade shrugged and began to make a cigarette.

Dundy nudged Tom with an elbow. "Find out."

Tom said, "Sure, but if he was out of here at half past three and this fellow was still alive at five to four — "

"And he broke his leg so he couldn't duck back in," the gray-faced man said jovially.

"Find out," Dundy repeated.

Tom said, "Sure, sure," and went to the telephone.

Dundy addressed the gray-faced man: "Check up on the newspapers; see what time they were actually delivered this afternoon."

The gray-faced man nodded and left the room.

The man who had been searching the *secrétaire* said, "Uh-huh," and turned around holding an envelope in one hand, a sheet of paper in the other.

Dundy held out his hand. "Something?"

The man said, "Uh-huh," again and gave Dundy the sheet of paper. Spade was looking over Dundy's shoulder.

It was a small sheet of common white paper bearing a penciled message in neat, undistinguished handwriting:

When this reaches you I will be too close for you to escape — this time. We will balance our accounts — for good.

The signature was a five-pointed star enclosing a T, the design on the dead man's left breast.

Dundy held out his hand again and was given the envelope. Its stamp was French. The address was typewritten:

> MAX BLISS, ESQ.
> AMSTERDAM APARTMENTS
> SAN FRANCISCO, CALIF.
> U. S. A.

"Postmarked Paris," he said, "the second of the month." He counted swiftly on his fingers. "That would get it here today, all right." He folded the message slowly, put it in the envelope, put the envelope in his coat pocket. "Keep digging," he told the man who had found the message.

The man nodded and returned to the *secrétaire.*

Dundy looked at Spade. "What do you think of it?"

Spade's brown cigarette wagged up and down with his words. "I don't like it. I don't like any of it."

Tom put down the telephone. "He got out the fifteenth of last month," he said. "I got them trying to locate him."

Spade went to the telephone, called a number, and asked for Mr. Darrell. Then: "Hello, Harry, this is Sam Spade. . . . Fine. How's Lil? . . . Yes. . . . Listen, Harry, what does a five-pointed star with a capital T in the middle mean? . . . What? How do you spell it? . . . Yes, I see. . . . And if you found it on a body? . . . Neither do I. . . . Yes, and thanks. I'll tell you about it when I see you. . . . Yes, give me a ring. . . . Thanks. . . . 'By."

Dundy and Tom were watching him closely when he turned from the telephone. He said, "That's a fellow who knows things sometimes. He says it's a pentagram with a Greek tau — t-a-u — in the middle; a sign magicians used to use. Maybe Rosicrucians still do."

"What's a Rosicrucian?" Tom asked.

"It could be Theodore's first initial, too," Dundy said.

Spade moved his shoulders, said carelessly, "Yes, but if he wanted to autograph the job it'd been just as easy for him to sign his name."

He then went on more thoughtfully, "There are Rosicrucians at both San Jose and Point Loma. I don't go much for this, but maybe we ought to look them up."

Dundy nodded.

Spade looked at the dead man's clothes on the table. "Anything in his pockets?"

"Only what you'd expect to find," Dundy replied. "It's on the table there."

Spade went to the table and looked down at the little pile of watch and chain, keys, wallet, address book, money, gold pencil, handkerchief, and spectacle case beside the clothing. He did not touch them, but slowly picked up, one at a time, the dead man's shirt, undershirt, vest, and coat. A blue necktie lay on the table beneath them. He scowled irritably at it. "It hasn't been worn," he complained.

Dundy, Tom, and the coroner's deputy, who had stood silent all this while by the window — he was a small man with a slim, dark, intelligent face — came together to stare down at the unwrinkled blue silk.

Tom groaned miserably. Dundy cursed under his breath. Spade lifted the necktie to look at its back. The label was a London haberdasher's.

Spade said cheerfully, "Swell. San Francisco, Point Loma, San Jose, Paris, London."

Dundy glowered at him.

The gray-faced man came in. "The papers got here at three thirty, all right," he said. His eyes widened a little. "What's up?" As he crossed the room towards them he said, "I can't find anybody that saw Blondy sneak back in here again." He looked uncomprehendingly at the necktie until Tom growled, "It's brand-new"; then he whistled softly.

Dundy turned to Spade. "The deuce with all this," he said bitterly. "He's got a brother with reasons for not liking him. The brother just got out of stir. Somebody who looks like his brother left here at half past three. Twenty-five minutes later he phoned you he'd been threatened. Less than half an hour after that his daughter came in and found him dead — strangled." He poked a finger at the small, dark-faced man's chest. "Right?"

"Strangled," the dark-faced man said precisely, "by a man. The hands were large."

"O. K." Dundy turned to Spade again. "We find a threatening letter. Maybe that's what he was telling you about, maybe it was something his brother said to him. Don't let's guess. Let's stick to what we know. We know he — "

The man at the *secrétaire* turned around and said, "Got another one." His mien was somewhat smug.

The eyes with which the five men at the table looked at him were identically cold, unsympathetic.

He, nowise disturbed by their hostility, read aloud:

"Dear Bliss:
I am writing this to tell you for the last time that I want my money back, and I want it back by the first of the month, all of it. If I don't get it I am going to do something about it, and you ought to be able to guess what I mean. And don't think I am kidding.
                                Yours truly,
                                DANIEL TALBOT"

He grinned. "That's another T for you." He picked up an envelope. "Postmarked San Diego, the twenty-fifth of last month." He grinned again. "And that's another city for you."

Spade shook his head. "Point Loma's down that way," he said.

He went over with Dundy to look at the letter. It was written in blue ink on white stationery of good quality, as was the address on the envelope, in a cramped, angular handwriting that seemed to have nothing in common with that of the penciled letter.

Spade said ironically, "Now we're getting somewhere."

Dundy made an impatient gesture. "Let's stick to what we know," he growled.

"Sure," Spade agreed. "What is it?"

There was no reply.

Spade took tobacco and cigarette papers from his pocket. "Didn't somebody say something about talking to a daughter?" he asked.

"We'll talk to her." Dundy turned on his heel, then suddenly frowned at the dead man on the floor. He jerked a thumb at the small, dark-faced man. "Through with it?"

"I'm through."

Dundy addressed Tom curtly: "Get rid of it." He addressed the gray-faced man: "I want to see both elevator boys when I'm finished with the girl."

He went to the closed door Tom had pointed out to Spade and knocked on it.

A slightly harsh female voice within asked, "What is it?"

"Lieutenant Dundy. I want to talk to Miss Bliss."

There was a pause; then the voice said, "Come in."

Dundy opened the door and Spade followed him into a black, gray, and silver room, where a big-boned and ugly middle-aged woman in black dress and white apron sat beside a bed on which a girl lay.

The girl lay, elbow on pillow, cheek on hand, facing the big-boned, ugly woman. She was apparently about eighteen years old. She wore a gray suit. Her hair was blond and short, her face firm-featured and remarkably symmetrical. She did not look at the two men coming into the room.

Dundy spoke to the big-boned woman, while Spade was lighting his cigarette: "We want to ask you a couple of questions, too, Mrs. Hooper. You're Bliss's housekeeper, aren't you?"

The woman said, "I am." Her slightly harsh voice, the level gaze of her deep-set gray eyes, the stillness and size of her hands lying in her lap, all contributed to the impression she gave of resting strength.

"What do you know about this?"

"I don't know anything about it. I was let off this morning to go over to Oakland to my nephew's funeral, and when I got back you and the other gentlemen were here and — and this had happened."

Dundy nodded, asked, "What do you think about it?"

"I don't know what to think," she replied simply.

"Didn't you know he expected it to happen?"

Now the girl suddenly stopped watching Mrs. Hooper. She sat up in bed, turning wide, excited eyes on Dundy, and asked, "What do you mean?"

"I mean what I said. He'd been threatened. He called up Mr.

Spade" — he indicated Spade with a nod — "and told him so just a few minutes before he was killed."

"But who — ?" she began.

"That's what we're asking you," Dundy said. "Who had that much against him?"

She stared at him in astonishment. "Nobody would — "

This time Spade interrupted her, speaking with a softness that made his words seem less brutal than they were. "Somebody did." When she turned her stare on him he asked, "You don't know of any threats?"

She shook her head from side to side with emphasis.

He looked at Mrs. Hooper. "You?"

"No, sir," she said.

He returned his attention to the girl. "Do you know Daniel Talbot?"

"Why, yes," she said. "He was here for dinner last night."

"Who is he?"

"I don't know, except that he lives in San Diego, and he and Father had some sort of business together. I'd never met him before."

"What sort of terms were they on?"

She frowned a little, said slowly, "Friendly."

Dundy spoke: "What business was your father in?"

"He was a financier."

"You mean a promoter?"

"Yes, I suppose you could call it that."

"Where is Talbot staying, or has he gone back to San Diego?"

"I don't know."

"What does he look like?"

She frowned again, thoughtfully. "He's kind of large, with a red face and white hair and a white mustache."

"Old?"

"I guess he must be sixty; fifty-five at least."

Dundy looked at Spade, who put the stub of his cigarette in a tray on the dressing table and took up the questioning. "How long since you've seen your uncle?"

Her face flushed. "You mean Uncle Ted?"

He nodded.

"Not since," she began, and bit her lip. Then she said, "Of course, you know. Not since he first got out of prison."

"He came here?"

"Yes."

"To see your father?"

"Of course."

"What sort of terms were they on?"

She opened her eyes wide. "Neither of them is very demonstrative," she said, "but they are brothers, and Father was giving him money to set him up in business again."

"Then they were on good terms?"

"Yes," she replied in the tone of one answering an unnecessary question.

"Where does he live?"

"On Post Street," she said, and gave a number.

"And you haven't seen him since?"

"No. He was shy, you know, about having been in prison — " She finished the sentence with a gesture of one hand.

Spade addressed Mrs. Hooper: "You've seen him since?"

"No, sir."

He pursed his lips, asked slowly, "Either of you know he was here this afternoon?"

They said, "No," together.

"Where did — ?"

Someone knocked on the door.

Dundy said, "Come in."

Tom opened the door far enough to stick his head in. "His brother's here," he said.

The girl, leaning forward, called, "Oh, Uncle Ted!"

A big, blond man in brown appeared behind Tom. He was sunburned to an extent that made his teeth seem whiter, his clear eyes bluer, than they were.

He asked, "What's the matter, Miriam?"

"Father's dead," she said, and began to cry.

Dundy nodded at Tom, who stepped out of Theodore Bliss's way and let him come into the room.

A woman came in behind him, slowly, hesitantly. She was a tall woman in her late twenties, blond, not quite plump. Her features were generous, her face pleasant and intelligent. She wore a small brown hat and a mink coat.

Bliss put an arm around his niece, kissed her forehead, sat on the bed beside her. "There, there," he said awkwardly.

She saw the blond woman, stared through her tears at her for a moment, then said, "Oh, how do you do, Miss Barrow?"

The blond woman said, "I'm awfully sorry to — "

Bliss cleared his throat, and said, "She's Mrs. Bliss now. We were married this afternoon."

Dundy looked angrily at Spade. Spade, making a cigarette, seemed about to laugh.

Miriam Bliss, after a moment's surprised silence, said, "Oh, I do wish you all the happiness in the world." She turned to her uncle while his wife was murmuring "Thank you" and said, "And you too, Uncle Ted."

He patted her shoulder and squeezed her to him. He was looking questioningly at Spade and Dundy.

"Your brother died this afternoon," Dundy said. "He was murdered."

Mrs. Bliss caught her breath. Bliss's arm tightened around his niece with a little jerk, but there was not yet any change in his face. "Murdered?" he repeated uncomprehendingly.

"Yes." Dundy put his hands in his coat pockets. "You were here this afternoon."

Theodore Bliss paled a little under his sunburn, but said, "I was," steadily enough.

"How long?"

"About an hour. I got here about half past two and — " He turned to his wife. "It was almost half past three when I phoned you, wasn't it?"

She said, "Yes."

"Well, I left right after that."

"Did you have a date with him?" Dundy asked.

"No. I phoned his office" — he nodded at his wife — "and was told he'd left for home, so I came on up. I wanted to see him before Elise and I left, of course, and I wanted him to come to the wedding, but he couldn't. He said he was expecting somebody. We sat here and talked longer than I had intended, so I had to phone Elise to meet me at the Municipal Building."

After a thoughtful pause, Dundy asked, "What time?"

"That we met there?" Bliss looked inquiringly at his wife, who said, "It was just quarter to four." She laughed a little. "I got there first and I kept looking at my watch."

Bliss said very deliberately, "It was a few minutes after four that we were married. We had to wait for Judge Whitfield — about ten minutes, and it was a few more before we got started — to get through with the case he was hearing. You can check it up — Superior Court, Part Two, I think."

Spade whirled around and pointed at Tom. "Maybe you'd better check it up."

Tom said, "Oke," and went away from the door.

"If that's so, you're all right, Mr. Bliss," Dundy said, "but I have to ask these things. Now, did your brother say who he was expecting?"

"No."

"Did he say anything about having been threatened?"

"No. He never talked much about his affairs to anybody, not even to me. Had he been threatened?"

Dundy's lips tightened a little. "Were you and he on intimate terms?"

"Friendly, if that's what you mean."

"Are you sure?" Dundy asked. "Are you sure neither of you held any grudge against the other?"

Theodore Bliss took his arm free from around his niece. Increasing pallor made his sunburned face yellowish. He said, "Everybody here knows about my having been in San Quentin. You can speak out, if that's what you're getting at."

"It is," Dundy said, and then, after a pause, "Well?"

Bliss stood up. "Well, what?" he asked impatiently. "Did I hold a grudge against him for that? No. Why should I? We were both in it. He could get out; I couldn't. I was sure of being convicted whether he was or not. Having him sent over with me wasn't going to make it any better for me. We talked it over and decided I'd go it alone, leaving him outside to pull things together. And he did. If you look up his bank account you'll see he gave me a check for twenty-five thousand dollars two days after I was discharged from San Quentin, and the registrar of the National Steel Corporation can tell you a thousand shares of stock have been transferred from his name to mine since then."

He smiled apologetically and sat down on the bed again. "I'm sorry. I know you have to ask things."

Dundy ignored the apology. "Do you know Daniel Talbot?" he asked.

Bliss said, "No."

His wife said, "I do; that is, I've seen him. He was in the office yesterday."

Dundy looked her up and down carefully before asking, "What office?"

"I am — I was Mr. Bliss's secretary, and — "

"Max Bliss's?"

"Yes, and a Daniel Talbot came in to see him yesterday afternoon, if it's the same one."

"What happened?"

She looked at her husband, who said, "If you know anything, for heaven's sake tell them."

She said, "But nothing really happened. I thought they were angry with each other at first, but when they left together they were laughing and talking, and before they went Mr. Bliss rang for me and told me to have Trapper — he's the bookkeeper — make out a check to Mr. Talbot's order."

"Did he?"

"Oh, yes. I took it in to him. It was for seventy-five hundred and some dollars."

"What was it for?"

She shook her head. "I don't know."

"If you were Bliss's secretary," Dundy insisted, "you must have some idea of what his business with Talbot was."

"But I haven't," she said. "I'd never even heard of him before."

Dundy looked at Spade. Spade's face was wooden. Dundy glowered at him, then put a question to the man on the bed: "What kind of necktie was your brother wearing when you saw him last?"

Bliss blinked, then stared distantly past Dundy, and finally shut his eyes. When he opened them he said, "It was green with — I'd know it if I saw it. Why?"

Mrs. Bliss said, "Narrow diagonal stripes of different shades of green. That's the one he had on at the office this morning."

"Where does he keep his neckties?" Dundy asked the house-keeper.

She rose, saying, "In a closet in his bedroom. I'll show you."

Dundy and the newly married Blisses followed her out.

Spade put his hat on the dressing table and asked Miriam Bliss, "What time did you go out?" He sat on the foot of her bed.

"Today? About one o'clock. I had a luncheon engagement for one and I was a little late, and then I went shopping and then — " She broke off with a shudder.

"And then you came home at what time?" His voice was friendly, matter-of-fact.

"Some time after four, I guess."

"And what happened?"

"I f-found Father lying there and I phoned — I don't know whether I phoned downstairs or the police, and then I don't know what I did. I fainted or had hysterics or something, and the first thing I remember is coming to and finding those men here and Mrs. Hooper." She looked him full in the face now.

"You didn't phone a doctor?"

She lowered her eyes again. "No, I don't think so."

"Of course you wouldn't, if you knew he was dead," he said casually.

She was silent.

"You knew he was dead?" he asked.

She raised her eyes and looked blankly at him. "But he *was* dead," she said.

He smiled. "Of course; but what I'm getting at is, did you make sure before you phoned?"

She put a hand to her throat. "I don't remember what I did," she said earnestly. "I think I just knew he was dead."

He nodded understandingly. "And if you phoned the police it was because you knew he had been murdered."

She worked her hands together and looked at them and said, "I suppose so. It was awful. I don't know what I thought or did."

Spade leaned forward and made his voice low and persuasive. "I'm not a police detective, Miss Bliss. I was engaged by your father — a few minutes too late to save him. I am, in a way, working for you now, so if there is anything I can do — maybe something the police wouldn't — " He broke off as Dundy, followed by the Blisses and the housekeeper, returned to the room. "What luck?"

Dundy said, "The green tie's not there." His suspicious gaze darted from Spade to the girl. "Mrs. Hooper says the blue tie we found is one of half a dozen he just got from England."

Bliss asked, "What's the importance of the tie?"

Dundy scowled at him. "He was partly undressed when we found him. The tie with his clothes had never been worn."

"Couldn't he have been changing clothes when whoever killed him came, and was killed before he had finished dressing?"

Dundy's scowl deepened. "Yes, but what did he do with the green tie? Eat it?"

Spade said, "He wasn't changing clothes. If you'll look at the shirt collar you'll see he must've had it on when he was choked."

Tom came to the door. "Checks all right," he told Dundy. "The judge and a bailiff named Kittredge say they were there from about a quarter to four till five or ten minutes after. I told Kittredge to come over and take a look at them to make sure they're the same ones."

Dundy said, "Right," without turning his head and took the penciled threat signed with the T in a star from his pocket. He folded it so only the signature was visible. Then he asked, "Anybody know what this is?"

Miriam Bliss left the bed to join the others in looking at it. From it they looked at one another blankly.

"Anybody know anything about it?" Dundy asked.

Mrs. Hooper said, "It's like what was on poor Mr. Bliss's chest, but — " The others said, "No."

"Anybody ever seen anything like it before?"

They said they had not.

Dundy said, "All right. Wait here. Maybe I'll have something else to ask you after a while."

Spade said, "Just a minute. Mr. Bliss, how long have you known Mrs. Bliss?"

Bliss looked curiously at Spade. "Since I got out of prison," he replied somewhat cautiously. "Why?"

"Just since last month," Spade said as if to himself. "Meet her through your brother?"

"Of course — in his office. Why?"

"And at the Municipal Building this afternoon, were you together all the time?"

"Yes, certainly." Bliss spoke sharply. "What are you getting at?"

Spade smiled at him, a friendly smile. "I have to ask things," he said.

Bliss smiled too. "It's all right." His smile broadened. "As a matter of fact, I'm a liar. We weren't actually together all the time. I went out into the corridor to smoke a cigarette, but I assure you every time I looked through the glass of the door I could see her still sitting in the courtroom where I had left her."

Spade's smile was as light as Bliss's. Nevertheless, he asked, "And when you weren't looking through the glass you were in sight of the door? She couldn't've left the courtroom without your seeing her?"

Bliss's smile went away. "Of course she couldn't," he said, "and I wasn't out there more than five minutes."

Spade said, "Thanks," and followed Dundy into the living room, shutting the door behind him.

Dundy looked sidewise at Spade. "Anything to it?"

Spade shrugged.

Max Bliss's body had been removed. Besides the man at the *secrétaire* and the gray-faced man, two Filipino boys in plum-colored uniforms were in the room. They sat close together on the sofa.

Dundy said, "Mack, I want to find a green necktie. I want this house taken apart, this block taken apart, and the whole neighborhood taken apart till you find it. Get what men you need."

The man at the *secrétaire* rose, said "Right," pulled his hat down over his eyes, and went out.

Dundy scowled at the Filipinos. "Which of you saw the man in brown?"

The smaller stood up. "Me, sir."

Dundy opened the bedroom door and said, "Bliss."

Bliss came to the door.

The Filipino's face lighted up. "Yes, sir, him."

Dundy shut the door in Bliss's face. "Sit down."

The boy sat down hastily.

Dundy stared gloomily at the boys until they began to fidget. Then, "Who else did you bring up to this apartment this afternoon?"

They shook their heads in unison from side to side. "Nobody else, sir," the smaller one said. A desperately ingratiating smile stretched his mouth wide across his face.

Dundy took a threatening step towards them. "Nuts!" he snarled. "You brought up Miss Bliss."

The larger boy's head bobbed up and down. "Yes, sir. Yes, sir. I bring them up. I think you mean other people." He too tried a smile.

Dundy was glaring at him. "Never mind what you think I mean. Tell me what I ask. Now, what do you mean by 'them'?"

The boy's smile died under the glare. He looked at the floor between his feet and said, "Miss Bliss and the gentleman."

"What gentleman? The gentleman in there?" He jerked his head toward the door he had shut on Bliss.

"No, sir. Another gentleman, not an American gentleman." He had raised his head again and now brightness came back into his face. "I think he is Armenian."

"Why?"

"Because he not like us Americans, not talk like us."

Spade laughed; asked, "Ever seen an Armenian?"

"No, sir. That is why I think he — " He shut his mouth with a click as Dundy made a growling noise in his throat.

"What'd he look like?" Dundy asked.

The boy lifted his shoulders, spread his hands. "He tall, like this gentleman." He indicated Spade. "Got dark hair, dark mustache. Very" — he frowned earnestly — "very nice clothes. Very nice-looking man. Cane, gloves, spats, even, and — "

"Young?" Dundy asked.

The head went up and down again. "Young. Yes, sir."

"When did he leave?"

"Five minutes," the boy replied.

Dundy made a chewing motion with his jaws, then asked, "What time did they come in?"

The boy spread his hands, lifted his shoulders again. "Four o'clock — maybe ten minutes after."

"Did you bring anybody else up before we got here?"

The Filipinos shook their heads in unison once more.

Dundy spoke out the side of his mouth to Spade: "Get her."

Spade opened the bedroom door, bowed slightly, said, "Will you come out a moment, Miss Bliss?"

"What is it?" she asked warily.

"Just for a moment," he said, holding the door open. Then he suddenly added, "And you'd better come along, too, Mr. Bliss."

Miriam Bliss came slowly into the living room followed by her uncle, and Spade shut the door behind them. Miss Bliss's lower lip twitched a little when she saw the elevator boys. She looked apprehensively at Dundy.

He asked, "What's this fiddlededee about the man that came in with you?"

Her lower lip twitched again. "Wh-what?" She tried to put bewilderment on her face. Theodore Bliss hastily crossed the room, stood for a moment before her as if he intended to say something, and then, apparently changing his mind, took up a position behind her, his arms crossed over the back of a chair.

"The man who came in with you," Dundy said harshly, rapidly. "Who is he? Where is he? Why'd he leave? Why didn't you say anything about him?"

The girl put her hands over her face and began to cry. "He didn't have anything to do with it," she blubbered through her hands. "He didn't, and it would just make trouble for him."

"Nice boy," Dundy said. "So, to keep his name out of the newspapers, he runs off and leaves you alone with your murdered father."

She took her hands away from her face. "Oh, but he had to," she cried. "His wife is so jealous, and if she knew he had been with me again she'd certainly divorce him, and he hasn't a cent in the world of his own."

Dundy looked at Spade. Spade looked at the goggling Filipinos and jerked a thumb at the outer door. "Scram," he said. They went out quickly.

"And who is this gem?" Dundy asked the girl.

"But he didn't have any — "

"Who is he?"

Her shoulders drooped a little and she lowered her eyes. "His name is Boris Smekalov," she said wearily.

"Spell it."

She spelled it.

"Where does he live?"

"At the St. Mark Hotel."

"Does he do anything for a living except marry money?"

Anger came into her face as she raised it, but went away as quickly. "He doesn't do anything," she said.

Dundy wheeled to address the gray-faced man. "Get him."

The gray-faced man grunted and went out.

Dundy faced the girl again. "You and this Smekalov in love with each other?"

Her face became scornful. She looked at him with scornful eyes and said nothing.

He said, "Now your father's dead, will you have enough money for him to marry if his wife divorces him?"

She covered her face with her hands.

He said, "Now your father's dead, will — ?"

Spade, leaning far over, caught her as she fell. He lifted her easily and carried her into the bedroom. When he came back he shut the door behind him and leaned against it. "Whatever the rest of it was," he said, "the faint's a phony."

"Everything's a phony," Dundy growled.

Spade grinned mockingly. "There ought to be a law making criminals give themselves up."

Mr. Bliss smiled and sat down at his brother's desk by the window.

Dundy's voice was disagreeable. "You got nothing to worry about," he said to Spade. "Even your client's dead and can't complain. But if I don't come across I've got to stand for riding from the captain, the chief, the newspapers, and heaven knows who all."

"Stay with it," Spade said soothingly; "you'll catch a murderer sooner or later yet." His face became serious except for the lights in his yellow-gray eyes. "I don't want to run this job up any more alleys than we have to, but don't you think we ought to check up on the funeral the housekeeper said she went to? There's something funny about that woman."

After looking suspiciously at Spade for a moment, Dundy nodded, and said, "Tom'll do it."

Spade turned about and, shaking his finger at Tom, said, "It's a ten-to-one bet there wasn't any funeral. Check on it . . . don't miss a trick."

Then he opened the bedroom door and called Mrs. Hooper. "Sergeant Polhaus wants some information from you," he told her.

While Tom was writing down names and addresses that the woman gave him, Spade sat on the sofa and made and smoked a cigarette, and Dundy walked the floor slowly, scowling at the rug. With Spade's approval, Theodore Bliss rose and rejoined his wife in the bedroom.

Presently Tom put his notebook in his pocket, said, "Thank you," to the housekeeper, "Be seeing you," to Spade and Dundy, and left the apartment.

The housekeeper stood where he had left her, ugly, strong, serene, patient.

Spade twisted himself around on the sofa until he was looking into her deep-set, steady eyes. "Don't worry about that," he said, flirting a hand toward the door Tom had gone through. "Just routine." He pursed his lips, asked, "What do you honestly think of this thing, Mrs. Hooper?"

She replied calmly, in her strong, somewhat harsh voice, "I think it's the judgment of God."

Dundy stopped pacing the floor.

Spade said, "What?"

There was certainty and no excitement in her voice: "The wages of sin is death."

Dundy began to advance towards Mrs. Hooper in the manner of one stalking game. Spade waved him back with a hand which the sofa hid from the woman. His face and voice showed interest, but were now as composed as the woman's. "Sin?" he asked.

She said, " 'Whosoever shall offend one of these little ones that be- lieve in me, it were better for him that a millstone were hanged around his neck, and he were cast into the sea.'" She spoke, not as if quoting, but as if saying something she believed.

Dundy barked a question at her: "What little one?"

She turned her grave gray eyes on him, then looked past him at the bedroom door.

"Her," she said; "Miriam."

Dundy frowned at her. "His daughter?"

The woman said, "Yes, his own adopted daughter."

Angry blood mottled Dundy's square face. "What the heck is this?" he demanded. He shook his head as if to free it from some clinging thing. "She's not really his daughter?"

The woman's serenity was in no way disturbed by his anger. "No. His wife was an invalid most of her life. They didn't have any children."

Dundy moved his jaws as if chewing for a moment and when he spoke again his voice was cooler. "What did he do to her?"

"I don't know," she said, "but I truly believe that when the truth's found out you'll see that the money her father — I mean her real father — left her has been — "

Spade interrupted her, taking pains to speak very clearly, moving one hand in small circles with his words. "You mean you don't actually know he's been gypping her? You just suspect it?"

She put a hand over her heart. "I know it here," she replied calmly.

Dundy looked at Spade, Spade at Dundy, and Spade's eyes were shiny with not altogether pleasant merriment. Dundy cleared his throat and addressed the woman again. "And you think this" — he waved a hand at the floor where the dead man had lain — "was the judgment of God, huh?"

"I do."

He kept all but the barest trace of craftiness out of his eyes. "Then whoever did it was just acting as the hand of God?"

"It's not for me to say," she replied.

Red began to mottle his face again. "That'll be all right now," he said in a choking voice, but by the time she had reached the bedroom door his eyes became alert again and he called, "Wait a minute." And when they were facing each other: "Listen, do you happen to be a Rosicrucian?"

"I wish to be nothing but a Christian."

He growled, "All right, all right," and turned his back on her. She went into the bedroom and shut the door. He wiped his forehead with the palm of his right hand and complained wearily, "Great Scott, what a family!"

Spade shrugged. "Try investigating your own some time."

Dundy's face whitened. His lips, almost colorless, came back tight over his teeth. He balled his fists and lunged towards Spade. "What do you — ?" The pleasantly surprised look on Spade's face stopped him. He averted his eyes, wet his lips with the tip of his tongue, looked at Spade again and away, essayed an embarrassed smile, and mumbled, "You mean any family. Uh-huh, I guess so." He turned hastily towards the corridor door as the doorbell rang.

The amusement twitching Spade's face accentuated his likeness to a blond satan.

An amiable, drawling voice came in through the corridor door: "I'm Jim Kittredge, Superior Court. I was told to come over here."

Dundy's voice: "Yes, come in."

Kittredge was a roly-poly ruddy man in too-tight clothes with the shine of age on them. He nodded at Spade and said, "I remember you, Mr. Spade, from the Burke–Harris suit."

Spade said, "Sure," and stood up to shake hands with him.

Dundy had gone to the bedroom door to call Theodore Bliss and his wife. Kittredge looked at them, smiled at them amiably, said, "How do you do?" and turned to Dundy. "That's them, all right." He looked around as if for a place to spit, found none, and said, "It was just about ten minutes to four that the gentleman there came in the courtroom and asked me how long His Honor would be, and I told him about ten minutes, and they waited there; and right after court adjourned at four o'clock we married them."

Dundy said, "Thanks." He sent Kittredge away, the Blisses back to the bedroom, scowled with dissatisfaction at Spade, and said, "So what?"

Spade, sitting down again, replied, "So you couldn't get from here to the Municipal Building in less than fifteen minutes on a bet, so he couldn't've ducked back here while he was waiting for the judge, and he couldn't have hustled over here to do it after the wedding and before Miriam arrived."

The dissatisfaction in Dundy's face increased. He opened his mouth, but shut it in silence when the gray-faced man came in with a tall, slender, pale young man who fitted the description the Filipino had given of Miriam Bliss's companion.

The gray-faced man said, "Lieutenant Dundy, Mr. Spade, Mr. Boris — uh — Smekalov."

Dundy nodded curtly.

Smekalov began to speak immediately. His accent was not heavy enough to trouble his hearers much, though his r's sounded more like w's. "Lieutenant, I must beg of you that you keep this confidential. If it should get out it will ruin me, Lieutenant, ruin me completely and most unjustly. I am most innocent, sir, I assure you, in heart, spirit, and deed, not only innocent, but in no way whatever connected with any part of the whole horrible matter. There is no — "

"Wait a minute." Dundy prodded Smekalov's chest with a blunt finger. "Nobody's said anything about you being mixed up in anything — but it'd looked better if you'd stuck around."

The young man spread his arms, his palms forward, in an expansive gesture. "But what can I do? I have a wife who — " He shook his head violently. "It is impossible. I cannot do it."

The gray-faced man said to Spade in an inadequately subdued voice, "Goofy, these Russians."

Dundy screwed up his eyes at Smekalov and made his voice judicial. "You've probably," he said, "put yourself in a pretty tough spot."

Smekalov seemed about to cry. "But only put yourself in my place," he begged, "and you — "

"Wouldn't want to." Dundy seemed, in his callous way, sorry for the young man. "Murder's nothing to play with in this country."

"Murder! But I tell you, Lieutenant, I happen' to enter into this situation by the merest mischance only. I am not — "

"You mean you came in here with Miss Bliss by accident?"

The young man looked as if he would like to say "Yes." He said, "No," slowly, then went on with increasing rapidity: "But that was nothing, sir, nothing at all. We had been to lunch. I escorted her home and she said, 'Will you come in for a cocktail?' and I would. That is all, I give you my word." He held out his hands, palms up.

"Could it not have happened so to you?" He moved his hands in Spade's direction. "To you?"

Spade said, "A lot of things happen to me. Did Bliss know you were running around with his daughter?"

"He knew we were friends, yes."

"Did he know you had a wife?"

Smekalov said cautiously, "I do not think so."

Dundy said, "You know he didn't."

Smekalov moistened his lips and did not contradict the lieutenant.

Dundy asked, "What do you think he'd've done if he found out?"

"I do not know, sir."

Dundy stepped close to the young man and spoke through his teeth in a harsh, deliberate voice: "What *did* he do when he found out?"

The young man retreated a step, his face white and frightened.

The bedroom door opened and Miriam Bliss came into the room. "Why don't you leave him alone?" she asked indignantly. "I told you he had nothing to do with it. I told you he didn't know anything about it." She was beside Smekalov now and had one of his hands in hers. "You're simply making trouble for him without doing a bit of good. I'm awfully sorry, Boris, I tried to keep them from bothering you."

The young man mumbled unintelligibly.

"You tried, all right," Dundy agreed. He addressed Spade: "Could it've been like this, Sam? Bliss found out about the wife, knew they had the lunch date, came home early to meet them when they came in, threatened to tell the wife, and was choked to stop him." He looked sidewise at the girl. "Now, if you want to fake another faint, hop to it."

The young man screamed and flung himself at Dundy, clawing with both hands. Dundy grunted — "Uh!" — and struck him in the face with a heavy fist. The young man went backwards across the room until he collided with a chair. He and the chair went down on the floor together. Dundy said to the gray-faced man, "Take him down to the Hall — material witness."

The gray-faced man said, "Oke," picked up Smekalov's hat, and went over to help pick him up.

Theodore Bliss, his wife, and the housekeeper had come to the door Miriam Bliss had left open. Miriam Bliss was crying, stamping her foot, threatening Dundy: "I'll report you, you coward. You had no right to . . ." and so on. Nobody paid much attention to her; they watched the gray-faced man help Smekalov to his feet, take him away. Smekalov's nose and mouth were red smears.

Then Dundy said, "Hush," negligently to Miriam Bliss and took a slip of paper from his pocket. "I got a list of the calls from here today. Sing out when you recognize them."

He read a telephone number.

Mrs. Hooper said, "That is the butcher. I phoned him before I left this morning." She said the next number Dundy read was the grocer's.

He read another.

"That's the St. Mark," Miriam Bliss said. "I called up Boris." She identified two more numbers as those of friends she had called.

The sixth number, Bliss said, was his brother's office. "Probably my call to Elise to ask her to meet me."

Spade said, "Mine," to the seventh number, and Dundy said, "That last one's police emergency." He put the slip back in his pocket.

Spade said cheerfully, "And that gets us a lot of places."

The doorbell rang.

Dundy went to the door. He and another man could be heard talking in voices too low for their words to be recognized in the living room.

The telephone rang. Spade answered it. "Hello. . . . No, this is Spade. Wait a min — All right." He listened. "Right, I'll tell him. . . . I don't know. I'll have him call you. . . Right."

When he turned from the telephone Dundy was standing, hands behind him, in the vestibule doorway. Spade said, "O'Gar says your Russian went completely nuts on the way to the Hall. They had to shove him into a strait-jacket."

"He ought to been there long ago," Dundy growled. "Come here."

Spade followed Dundy into the vestibule. A uniformed policeman stood in the outer doorway.

Dundy brought his hands from behind him. In one was a necktie with narrow diagonal stripes in varying shades of green, in the other was a platinum scarfpin in the shape of a crescent set with small diamonds.

Spade bent over to look at three small, irregular spots on the tie. "Blood?"

"Or dirt," Dundy said. "He found them crumpled up in a newspaper in the rubbish can on the corner."

"Yes, sir," the uniformed man said proudly; "there I found them, all wadded up in — " He stopped because nobody was paying any attention to him.

"Blood's better," Spade was saying. "It gives a reason for taking the tie away. Let's go in and talk to people."

Dundy stuffed the tie in one pocket, thrust his hand holding the pin into another. "Right — and we'll call it blood."

They went into the living room. Dundy looked from Bliss to Bliss's wife, to Bliss's niece, to the housekeeper, as if he did not like any of them. He took his fist from his pocket, thrust it straight out in front of him, and opened it to show the crescent pin lying in his hand. "What's that?" he demanded.

Miriam Bliss was the first to speak. "Why, it's Father's pin," she said.

"So it is?" he said disagreeably. "And did he have it on today?"

"He always wore it." She turned to the others for confirmation.

Mrs. Bliss said, "Yes," while the others nodded.

"Where did you find it?" the girl asked.

Dundy was surveying them one by one again, as if he liked them less than ever. His face was red. "He always wore it," he said angrily, "but there wasn't one of you could say, 'Father always wore a pin. Where is it?' No, we got to wait till it turns up before we can get a word out of you about it."

Bliss said, "Be fair. How were we to know — ?"

"Never mind what you were to know," Dundy said. "It's coming round to the point where I'm going to do some talking about what I know." He took the green necktie from his pocket. "This is his tie?"

Mrs. Hooper said, "Yes, sir."

Dundy said, "Well, it's got blood on it, and it's not his blood, because he didn't have a scratch on him that we could see." He looked narrow-eyed from one to another of them. "Now, suppose you were trying to choke a man that wore a scarfpin, and he was wrestling with you, and — "

He broke off to look at Spade.

Spade had crossed to where Mrs. Hooper was standing. Her big hands were clasped in front of her. He took her right hand, turned it over, took the wadded handkerchief from her palm, and there was a two-inch-long fresh scratch in the flesh.

She had passively allowed him to examine her hand. Her mien lost none of its tranquillity now. She said nothing.

"Well?" he asked.

"I scratched it on Miss Miriam's pin fixing her on the bed when she fainted," the housekeeper said calmly.

Dundy's laugh was brief, bitter. "It'll hang you just the same," he said.

There was no change in the woman's face. "The Lord's will be done," she replied.

Spade made a peculiar noise in his throat as he dropped her hand. "Well, let's see how we stand." He grinned at Dundy. "You don't like that star-T, do you?"

Dundy said, "Not by a long shot."

"Neither do I," Spade said. "The Talbot threat was probably on the level, but that debt seems to have been squared. Now — wait a minute!" He went to the telephone and called his office. "The tie thing looked pretty funny, too, for a while," he said while he waited, "but I guess the blood takes care of that."

He spoke into the telephone: "Hello, Effie. Listen: Within half an hour or so of the time Bliss called me, did you get any call that maybe wasn't on the level? Anything that could have been a stall? . . . Yes, before . . . Think now."

He put his hand over the mouthpiece and said to Dundy, "There's a lot of deviltry going on in this world."

He spoke into the telephone again: "Yes? . . . Yes . . . Kruger? . . . Yes. Man or woman? . . . Thanks. . . . No, I'll be through in half an hour. Wait for me and I'll buy your dinner. 'By."

He turned away from the telephone. "About half an hour before Bliss phoned, a man called my office and asked for Mr. Kruger."

Dundy frowned. "So what?"

"Kruger wasn't there."

Dundy's frown deepened. "Who's Kruger?"

"I don't know," Spade said blandly. "I never heard of him." He took tobacco and cigarette papers from his pockets. "All right, Bliss, where's your scratch?"

Theodore Bliss said, "What?" while the others stared blankly at Spade.

"Your scratch," Spade repeated in a consciously patient tone. His attention was on the cigarette he was making. "The place where your brother's pin gouged you when you were choking him."

"Are you crazy?" Bliss demanded. "I was — "

"Uh-huh, you were being married when he was killed. You were not." Spade moistened the edge of his cigarette paper and smoothed it with his forefinger.

Mrs. Bliss spoke now, stammering a little: "But he — but Max Bliss called — "

"Who says Max Bliss called me?" Spade asked. "I don't know that. I wouldn't know his voice. All I know is a man called me and said he was Max Bliss. Anybody could say that."

"But the telephone records here show the call came from here," she protested.

He shook his head and smiled. "They show I had *a* call from here, and I did, but not that one. I told you somebody called up half an hour or so before the supposed Max Bliss call and asked for Mr. Kruger." He nodded at Theodore Bliss. "He was smart enough to get a call from this apartment to my office on the record before he left to meet you."

She stared from Spade to her husband with dumfounded blue eyes.

Her husband said lightly, "It's nonsense, my dear. You know — "

Spade did not let him finish that sentence. "You know he went out to smoke a cigarette in the corridor while waiting for the judge, and he knew there were telephone booths in the corridor. A minute would be all he needed." He lit his cigarette and returned his lighter to his pocket.

Bliss said, "Nonsense!" more sharply. "Why should I want to kill Max?" He smiled reassuringly into his wife's horrified eyes. "Don't let this disturb you, dear. Police methods are sometimes — "

"All right," Spade said, "let's look you over for scratches."

Bliss wheeled to face him more directly. "Damned if you will!" He put a hand behind him.

Spade, wooden-faced and dreamy-eyed, came forward.

Spade and Effie Perine sat at a small table in Julius's Castle on Telegraph Hill. Through the window beside them ferryboats could be seen carrying lights to and from the cities' lights on the other side of the bay.

". . . hadn't gone there to kill him, chances are," Spade was saying; "just to shake him down for some more money; but when the fight started, once he got his hands on his throat, I guess, his grudge was too hot in him for him to let go till Max was dead. Understand, I'm just putting together what the evidence says, and what we got out of his wife, and the not much that we got out of him."

Effie nodded. "She's a nice, loyal wife."

Spade drank coffee, shrugged. "What for? She knows now that he made his play for her only because she was Max's secretary. She knows that when he took out the marriage license a couple of weeks ago it was only to string her along so she'd get him the photostatic copies of the records that tied Max up with the Graystone Loan swindle. She knows — Well, she knows she wasn't just helping an injured innocent to clear his good name."

He took another sip of coffee. "So he calls on his brother this afternoon to hold San Quentin over his head for a price again, and there's a fight, and he kills him, and gets his wrist scratched by the pin while he's choking him. Blood on the tie, a scratch on his wrist — that won't do. He takes the tie off the corpse and hunts up another, because the absence of a tie will set the police to thinking. He gets a bad break there: Max's new ties are on the front of the rack, and he grabs the first one he comes to. All right. Now he's got to put it around the dead man's neck — or wait — he gets a better idea. Pull off some more clothes and puzzle the police. The tie'll be just as inconspicuous off as on, if the shirt's off too. Undressing him, he gets another idea. He'll give the police something else to worry about, so he draws a mystic sign he has seen somewhere on the dead man's chest."

Spade emptied his cup, set it down, and went on: "By now he's getting to be a regular master mind at bewildering the police. A threatening letter signed with the thing on Max's chest. The afternoon mail is on the desk. One envelope's as good as another so long as it's typewritten and has no return address, but the one from France adds a touch of the foreign, so out comes the original letter and in goes the threat. He's overdoing it now; see? He's giving us so much that's wrong that we can't help suspecting things that seem all right — the phone call, for instance.

"Well, he's ready for the phone calls now — his alibi. He picks my name out of the private detectives in the phone book and does the Mr. Kruger trick; but that's after he calls the blond Elise and tells her that not only have the obstacles to their marriage been removed, but he's had an offer to go in business in New York and has to leave right away, and will she meet him in fifteen minutes and get married? There's more than just an alibi to that. He wants to make sure *she* is dead sure he didn't kill Max, because she knows he doesn't like Max, and he doesn't want her to think he was just stringing her along to get the dope on Max, because she might be able to put two and two together and get something like the right answer.

"With that taken care of, he's ready to leave. He goes out quite openly, with only one thing to worry about now — the tie and pin in his pocket. He takes the pin along because he's not sure the police mightn't find traces of blood around the setting of the stones, no matter how carefully he wipes it. On his way out he picks up a newspaper — buys one from the newsboy he meets at the street door — wads tie and pin up in a piece of it, and drops it in the rubbish can at the corner. That seems all right. No reason for the police to look for the tie. No reason for the street cleaner who empties the can to investigate a crumpled piece of newspaper, and if something does go wrong — what the deuce! — the murderer dropped it there, but he, Theodore, can't be the murderer, because he's going to have an alibi.

"Then he jumps in his car and drives to the Municipal Building. He knows there are plenty of phones there and he can always say he's got to wash his hands, but it turns out he doesn't have to. While they're waiting for the judge to get through with a case he goes out to smoke a cigarette, and there you are — 'Mr. Spade, this is Max Bliss and I've been threatened.' "

Effie Perine nodded, then asked, "Why do you suppose he picked on a private detective instead of the police?"

"Playing safe. If the body had been found, meanwhile, the police might've heard of it and trace the call. A private detective wouldn't be likely to hear about it till he read it in the papers."

She laughed, then said, "And that was your luck."

"Luck? I don't know." He looked gloomily at the back of his left hand. "I hurt a knuckle stopping him and the job only lasted an afternoon. Chances are whoever's handling the estate'll raise hobs if I send them a bill for any decent amount of money." He raised a hand to attract the waiter's attention. "Oh, well, better luck next time. Want to catch a movie or have you got something else to do?"

THE RESURRECTION OF CHIN LEE

by T. S. STRIBLING

Psychologist POGGIOLI *is one of the rare birds among modern
detectives, so it was a thrill to unearth this story in Adventure
Magazine and pass it along to you.*

GALLOWAY, Superintendent of the Everglades Mill and Manufacturing Company, and Professor Henry Poggioli, his week-end
guest, were discussing at the breakfast table in the superintendent's
bungalow the rather didactic subject of recognition. The mill official
did not expect, it did not even occur to him, that an immediate personal relevance could arise from so detached a theme. He was
simply saying that he himself never could tell Negro babies or
Cubans or Chinamen apart.

Poggioli, the psychologist, was about to make some reply when
a tall, raw-boned white man came up the conk-lined walk and
halted just outside the screened breakfast room.

"Jim," he called to the mill official, "them last potatoes I got from
Tampa ain't fitten to feed hawgs on, much less mill han's. What
am I goin' to do about it?"

"Write to Farburger and Company and tell them about it."

"Yeh, and they'll think I'm tryin' to flim-flam 'em and next time
they'll want cash with their order."

"Just when did the Everglades Mill Company lose its reputation
for honesty?"

"These ain't mill potatoes. They're mine. I bought 'em for the
ships."

"Oh, I see. Well, that's different."

"So I figgered I'd send one hamper back by Chin Lee when he

goes up to buy supplies today, just to show 'em what rotten stuff they tried to put off on me. The freight won't be nothin'. Chin Lee can take one hamper along with him as personal baggage."

"M-m . . . Well, all right, do that. Good plan to show folks you're on the level when you happen to be — helps out at other times when you don't happen to be."

The superintendent opened his teeth but kept his lips closed with the expression of a man inwardly laughing at his own jest.

The man outside the screen wall was not amused.

"Then I'll tell Chin Lee to take a hamper with him."

He turned back down the garden path under the red flaming boughs of some poincianas.

The superintendent bestirred himself to make amends for a possible discourtesy.

"Wait a minute, Erb. I want to introduce you to Professor Poggioli. Professor Poggioli is one of the greatest criminal psychologists in America. He was attending a convention in Miami and I got him to come visit us over here in Everglades. Now I want you to spread yourself in the kitchen while he's here. Mr. Poggioli, this is Erb Skaggs, our cook."

The sun-tanned man peered at the guest through the wire.

"You say he's a criminal psychologist?"

"That's right."

"What's he done?"

Both gentlemen laughed. Galloway said —

"What he does is to find out what other folks do."

"Oh — you mean he's a detective?"

"In a way. He bears the same relation to an ordinary detective that the president of the Everglades Company bears to one of our lumberjacks."

"Gosh, he's a high priced man," said the cook soberly. "Who's he after down here?"

"Nobody at all. Just down for the week-end to eat and fish."

The rough-faced man pulled down his lips in a grimace meant to be humorous.

"Hope he uses jedgment in what he fishes after."

And with that he turned and walked back toward the mill kitchen.

"Good old Skaggs," remarked the superintendent half affectionately. "Always in hot water about a little ship chandlery business that he runs on the side, and he brings me his troubles."

Conversation paused for a moment and then the psychologist said:

"By the way, what were we talking about a moment ago? I had a question to ask."

"You mean just before Skaggs came in?"

"Yes."

"Well, now, lemme see — what *were* we talking about?"

For a moment or two the breakfasters sat trying to think back, but they came to nothing.

"I recall what I wanted to ask you," said Poggioli. "I wanted to know if you were especially fond of chop suey."

"Am I fond of chop suey?" Galloway smiled at the oddity of this question.

"Yes," Poggioli said, "but I can't remember why I wanted to ask it."

"That's funny. Why, no, I don't believe I ever tasted chop suey. I wonder why you wanted to ask that."

Poggioli shook his head with the air of a man giving up a problem, then ejaculated:

"Certainly I remember! What you said about not being able to tell Negro babies, Cubans and Chinese apart. I understand how you came to use Cubans and Negro babies, but I wondered where you had met enough Chinese to choose them for examples."

"Why, Chin Lee, our kitchen boy."

"Just Chin Lee? Don't you know other Chinese besides Chin Lee?"

"No, none at all," said the superintendent, rather amused at the psychologist's problem.

Poggioli puckered his brows.

"Why, that makes it more extraordinary than ever!"

"I don't see why."

"Because you seriously say you can't tell one Chinese from another, and here you never have known but just one Chinaman. You were serious, weren't you — you were not trying to be funny?"

Galloway broke out laughing.

"No, I wasn't trying to be funny. I meant what I said."

"Well, that's absolutely amazing. Have you any idea how you arrived at the generalization that all Chinese look alike when you have known only one?"

The superintendent became humorously thoughtful.

"Now, lemme see: Chin Lee — Chin Lee — What could there be about Chin Lee?" He pondered for some moments and finally nodded. "Yes, it must be that."

"Be what?"

"This may strike you as funny. I suppose it will. I never had thought of it myself before. The truth is I never have really known Chin Lee. I see him only now and then, and I don't remember how he looks from one time to the next. Of course I recognize his Chinese generalizations. I know he has a yellow face, slant eyes and wears his shirt outside his trousers; but the actual man himself — honestly, I can't recall his features at this moment."

Poggioli was astonished.

"How long have you known him?"

"He's worked here two or three years."

"That really is odd. I suppose it is a race obsession. You are so obsessed with Chin Lee's Chineseness, if I may coin a term, that your recognition stops there and doesn't reach the individual. It is probably based on our Anglo-Saxon superiority complex."

The superintendent laughed.

"I didn't know I felt that way until you asked me about it."

"Oh, well, a man is so accustomed to his own biases and slants that he never knows he has them."

Professor Poggioli sat considering the further queer fact that Galloway had decided all Chinese looked alike because the one Chinaman he did know never did quite resemble himself. A droller *non sequitur* he had never encountered.

He was smiling faintly when he saw a Negro man hurrying up the garden walk. The black man's expression caught the scientist's attention. His dark face was drawn and of a grayish cast. The whites of his eyes circled his black irises. He came to a halt some distance down the path and called in an unsteady tone —

"M-Mist' Jim, kin I see you a m-minute?"

"Now, Sam, why do you want to come bothering me when I've got company?"

The Negro made a desperate gesture.

"Mist' Jim, I jes' got to see you a minute."

The mill man gave a hopeless shrug and explained to Poggioli —

"Sam's the night watchman; somebody's probably been stealing lumber while he was asleep and now he's all cut up about it."

He opened the screen door, went as far down as the third poinciana, put a hand against its bole and asked in a bored tone —

"Well, what is it?"

The Negro's answer was in a voice too low for the psychologist to catch, but he nodded toward the mill and the docks with a terrified expression. Presently Galloway ejaculated:

"What! Chin Lee?"

Sam explained something more.

"How did it happen? Is he still there?"

Here the black man went into a long rigmarole, pointing at Poggioli on the porch. Galloway shook his head.

"No, no, I wouldn't bother Professor Poggioli with a little thing like this. Besides, he didn't come down here to work; he came down to rest up and fish."

This reference to himself induced the psychologist to call out —

"What is it he wants with me, Mr. Galloway?"

"Oh, he says he's heard about you," deprecated the superintendent, with an apologetic laugh.

"Is he uneasy because I am a criminologist?" inquired Poggioli, amused.

"Oh, no, Sam's all right. It's not about himself. He's begging me to have you take a look at Chin Lee."

"What's happened to Chin Lee?" inquired the psychologist with more interest.

"Why, he's lying over there on the lumber dock, Sam says, with a bullet hole in his head."

Poggioli arose quickly and came out into the garden.

"When did you find him, Sam?"

"J-jes' a li'l while ago."

"You were night watchman, I understand. You yourself didn't have any trouble with Chin Lee — catch him stealing lumber or anything like that?"

"Lawdy, no, suh; no!" cried the black man in a panic. "Theah you is, Mis' Jim, jes' whut I was tellin' you! He think 'cause I'se night watchman, I mus' 'a' shot Chin Lee. Why, I di'n' even know he was shot tull I walk up on him."

"You must have heard the shooting."

"N-no, suh — take mo'n a pistol to wake me up when I'se night watchin'."

The criminologist paused a moment, and then said —

"Let's walk over, Mr. Galloway, and see what we can find out."

The superintendent cleared his throat.

"Well — I suppose we ought to go and take a look around, Professor."

Poggioli was a little surprised at his host's attitude.

"You would naturally go, wouldn't you?"

"Oh, certainly, I'd have to go!"

"Well, you — don't mind my going with you?"

"Why, no-o — " Galloway cleared his throat again. "But if you don't object, Professor, may I say here that I hope your interest in this matter will be — uh — purely academic?"

Poggioli looked at his companion in amazement.

"Academic!"

"Y-yes — if you don't mind."

"What am I to understand by academic?"

Galloway blinked.

"Well, if you should find out who the murderer is, I — I hope you won't feel it necessary to — to make a great to-do about it."

"You mean not tell it — keep it quiet?"

"Well, baldly, I'd rather you would — keep it quiet."

Poggioli stood looking at his host for several moments.

"That is the most unusual request I have ever had made of me."

The superintendent moistened his lips.

"I suppose it is. But I have a good reason. These killings happen every now and then around the mill here. If the newspapers get wind of this one, they'll feature it because you're on the case. Then they'll get busy and dig up all the other killings and feature them, too. That will go all over the United States, and it will be damn rotten publicity for Everglades. It will prejudice investors against the place. So I do hope you'll keep quiet anything you find out. It's business with me."

The scientist listened in surprise to this odd reasoning.

"I had never thought of murder as adverse advertising."

"Well, if you had promoted as many boom towns as I have," said Galloway earnestly, "you'd know enough to hush up any little killing like this. Now if it were a big killing — like a banker or a preacher or a millionaire sportsman — I'd say go to it. A big murder trial would draw a lot of people to Everglades, and we'd sell 'em homes or business sites or something of the kind; but a dinky little killing like this — " Galloway shook his head. "It would do more harm than good."

Poggioli smiled dryly.

"Well, that's a Florida viewpoint. Come on, let's walk over for our private curiosities."

Here a discussion came up as to whether the three men should walk or ride to the lumber dock. The superintendent wanted to ride, because Everglades was laid out on the gigantic scale of a Florida boom town, and the houses in it which were actually built were so far apart that a neighborly call between any two residences was impossible without the aid of a motor car or a passing bus. The superintendent was about to send Sam for his automobile, but Poggioli said the walk would do them good, so the three set forth afoot.

After a long hike they reached the dock full of racks of lumber with the planks standing on end in order to season in the hot sun without warping. As they entered the vast lumber yard, Sam walked more and more slowly. Finally he stopped altogether and said the dead man was right around the next rack. It was clear that Sam did not mean to walk around the rack himself.

"When did you find him?" asked Poggioli.

" 'Bout a hour ago, suh."

"Did you move or touch the body?"

"No, I can tell you he didn't," interposed Galloway, walking on around the rack.

"Sam, do you know of anybody around here who had a grudge against Chin Lee?"

Just then he heard Galloway, from the other side, call out in annoyance —

"Sam, where in the hell is the thing?"

"Why, right theah befo' yo' eyes, Mist' Jim, layin' wid his face down an' a hole in his haid."

"Well, I don't see him."

" 'Fo' Gawd, I ain't gwi' have to come aroun' an' point out a daid Chinaman undah yo' nose, is I?"

"If I'm going to do anything about him, Sam, I've got to see him. I don't see what the hell you wanted to walk off and leave him like this for, anyway."

"Wh — whut you speck me to do wid him?"

"Well, there was the edge of the dock, wasn't it? Just what do you imagine the duties of a night watchman are?"

Poggioli came around the rack.

"Is it gone?"

Galloway drew a long breath of relief, got out and lighted a cigarette.

"It certainly is gone, and thank heaven that ends our problem. Got a match?"

Poggioli supplied a cigar lighter.

"I don't see how that ends the problem; it strikes me that it makes it more complicated."

"Oh, no — you don't know what problem I was talking about."

"Well, just what were you talking about?"

"Why, how to avoid an inquest and keep the mill from being held up half a day. You know every man jack in our plant would have to be questioned. Why, it would cost the company ten or twelve hundred dollars — just for a dead Chink." Galloway stood looking up and down the dock. "I imagine the man who killed him came back and rolled him in the water."

Poggioli looked more carefully at the planking.

"I suppose he was lying here on this stained place."

"Yes, suh, yes suh." The Negro nodded.

"Then he hasn't been rolled off the dock," said the psychologist.

"Why do you say that?" inquired Galloway antagonistically.

"Because there are no stains on the boards or trail in the dirt where he was dragged."

The mill official glanced about in his turn.

"There are no stains or trail in any other direction, either."

Poggioli stood pulling at his chin, looking up and down the dock's edge. After several moments he replied absently to Galloway:

"Yes, yes, so I had observed . . . How big a man was Chin Lee — about what did he weigh?"

Both white man and Negro began pondering this odd question.

"I figgahs 'bout a hun'erd an' fifty or sixty," hazarded Sam. "But I don' see whut diff'unce dat makes now, seein' as he's daid."

The professor continued musing over the situation.

"Did Chin Lee go with any women here in Everglades?" he inquired.

Here Galloway caught the drift.

"Oh, no, Chin Lee hasn't been seen with a woman since he came here . . . Would you say he had, Sam?"

"No, suh," corroborated Sam.

"Not being seen with a woman is not identical with never being with one," pointed out the psychologist. "Could you give me a list of the women here in Everglades, either white or colored, who are large and strong enough to lift a hundred and sixty pound man clear of the dock and carry him away without so much as a heel dragging?"

"Whut you gwi' do wid any sich list as dat?" asked Sam, thrusting out his head and dropping his mouth half an inch.

"I thought we might take such a list and just walk around among the more powerful women here in Everglades, and tell them that Chin Lee had been shot. We could watch how they take it."

"Just why do you think it was a woman who killed him in the first place?" inquired the mill official.

"Because whoever killed Chin Lee did it for a sentimental reason."

"How do you get that?"

"Because she didn't throw the body over the dock to the sharks. I can easily understand how in the excitement of homicide, any person, man or woman, could run away and forget to dispose of his or her victim; but here is the revelatory circumstance: This murderer escapes, but returns, not simply to destroy the evidence of her crime, but to pick it up and take it away with her.

"She could not endure the thought of her lover's body being thrown to the sharks or given over to any stranger who found it, or to the callousness of a coroner's jury. She even bound up the wound her own pistol shot had made. On this point I am undecided.

"Did she tie a piece of cloth around his head out of a useless tenderness, or was it merely to keep from leaving a trail of drops to

betray her direction? Of course, that has nothing to do with finding
the person, but it is an interesting point in criminal psychology."

Both men were amazed at such detailed deductions from the mere
fact that the body had been removed without leaving a trail. Still
both remained equally sure that Chin Lee had never gone with a
woman in Everglades.

Poggioli spread his hands.

"If what you say be true, this becomes one of the most puzzling
murders in my experience. If he were not spirited away from this
dock for a sentimental reason, I am forced to doubt that Chin Lee
was ever killed at all."

"Why couldn't he have been killed by crap shooters, or cock fight-
ers?" demanded Galloway impatiently. "He gambled heavily on
both sports."

"Because such a murderer would have tossed him over the dock
automatically. It would be the most natural reaction in the world.
You even reprimanded Sam for not doing it himself, and getting
rid of the whole unpleasantness at a stroke."

"M-m, yes, that is a fact, I did," admitted the superintendent.
"But, of course, I didn't exactly mean it."

"So my thoughts keep coming back to a woman," concluded the
psychologist. "Now, while you and Sam think up that list, suppose
we go to the dining hall and look through Chin Lee's things. We
might find a letter or a woman's picture — something to throw light
on who shot him."

The scientist's theory had a logical solidity which the superintendent was unable to shake, so he contented himself with saying rather
emptily that he didn't believe it was a woman, and the three set
out back for the kitchen.

The January sun was higher now and beat down with a sticky
heat. Galloway complained again that he had not brought his car.
Once, as the men trudged through the sunshine, Poggioli said —

"If there were any bloodhounds near here, this would be settled
in an hour or so."

"No, no," repeated Galloway. "The sheriff and his dogs would be
too much publicity — sorry."

The grub shack of the Everglades Mill and Manufacturing Company was a great wooden structure whose walls were made up

mainly of screened windows and doors. The only solid things about the place were a big electrical refrigerator run by current from the mill's dynamo, and the kitchen stove, which was an old ship's range that the New York manager of the company had bought at a marine auction in Brooklyn.

In the kitchen the two white men found Erb Skaggs directing two Negro helpers in picking chickens. They had twenty or thirty fryers piled in a tub for the noon meal. A tin pan held the livers and gizzards.

"I was just wonderin'," said Erb, meeting his visitors, "if Mr. Poggioli likes livers. Thought I'd fry him a chicken and stuff it full of livers."

Galloway nodded.

"There you are, Professor. When Erb decides to do you proud he does you proud . . . By the way, Erb, where does Chin Lee bunk around here?"

The cook changed his expression completely.

"Where does Chin Lee bunk?"

"Yes, I'm checking up on the men to see how they are billeted. I've got to send in a report."

The cook frowned and stood looking at the superintendent.

"Is that why Mr. Poggioli come down here?"

Galloway laughed shortly.

"No, it doesn't require the help of a psychologist to describe what a lot of mill hands' bunks look like."

"Well, my bunk's in that little screened off space yonder in the. corner of the kitchen. And you can tell the comp'ny when too many other things git in it with me, I take to a hammock that I got strung up outside."

"Yes, I know where yours is. Now where is Chin Lee's?"

"Mr. Galloway," cried the cook, "I be doggone if it ain't a shame for you to have to poke around lookin' at the dirty stinkin' bunks of these mill hands. Say so, an' I'll do it for you."

"No, just show me — "

"I'll go with you — I'll take you to it."

"We can get there all right if you'll just point it out."

The cook jiggled about, moved a skillet on the range, but finally complied.

"Well, Chin Lee bunks right yonder in that little shack yonder — " He followed them irresistibly for a few steps. "You didn't
want to see anything about Chin Lee hisse'f, did you — whether he
had any complaints to make or not?"

"I don't imagine he has any complaints to make," said Galloway.
Skaggs dropped behind.

"Well, n-o, I reckon not . . . That little shack, right there."

The shack in question was a trifle more than a large goods box. It
had in it three shelves. The bottom shelf was spread with a dirty
mill blanket, the middle one contained two bags.

"Now you want to look into those for a picture or a letter or something?" questioned Galloway.

"If you please."

"Sam, swing 'em down."

The black man lifted one gingerly to the dirty floor.

It was an ordinary pigskin bag, rather worn from travel. When
the valise was open, a variety of odds and ends lay spread before
them: Chinese shirts and trousers, a set of eight ivory chopsticks, a
Chinese print in a silk folder, a carved opium pipe and some tiny
porcelain teacups, without handles, nested together.

The psychologist squatted on his haunches in the chairless shack,
turning through the collection. Presently he opened a small ivory
box filled with tiny gold trinkets. He held it up to the superintendent.

"Know what these are, Mr. Galloway?"

The mill official picked one up.

"Look like gold gyves for a game rooster to me, but they are too
blunt."

The psychologist squatted, looking at them with a puzzled expression.

"They're too much for me."

"Don't you know what they are?"

"Oh, yes, they're fingernail guards. They protect the fingernails
so they'll grow long."

"What's the idea in that?"

"Why, it's a Chinese mark of high caste — it proves the owner
doesn't do any manual labor."

"Then what are you puzzled about?"

"Why a kitchen helper here in Everglades should own a set of gold nail protectors. What would a coolie want with nail guards?"

Galloway considered this proposition.

"Chin Lee might have brought them over as curios."

The psychologist shook his head slowly.

"If an American had brought them to this country, yes; a Chinaman, no. They are no more of a curio to a Chinese than a cigar clipper would be to you."

Galloway agreed to this.

"Then I would say at some time or other Chin Lee had been a man of leisure."

"Then what's he doing here in your kitchen, surrendering his caste?"

"Oh," cried Galloway, "that's nothing. What a man is in Florida is no sign at all of what he was where he came from. One of the biggest racetrack men in Miami was once an eminent Episcopal minister in Connecticut. And then, on the other hand, I know a Chicago gangster who is trying to reform our school system. He makes speeches about it and says the children of Florida ought to have the same chance to make good men and women as the children of Chicago."

"Well, at any rate," pondered Poggioli, "these nail guards give Chin Lee a background where one is likely to run across any sort of motive. Why was he in hiding? Was this a murder of revenge? If so, why should the man save the body? Was it the riddance of an heir to some large Chinese estate? In that instance the murderer might want to produce the body somewhere to prove his victim is dead."

"Oh, you're giving up the woman theory?"

"No, not at all; but if he has been a very wealthy man, it introduces other possibilities. Look here; I would really like to find the body. Suppose we have over the sheriff and his hounds." The psychologist glanced at his host interrogatively.

Galloway was tempted.

"Tell you what I'll do," he offered. "If you'll guarantee to me that Chin Lee was a millionaire and that somebody murdered him while he was at work in the company's kitchen, by George, I'll not only agree to the bloodhounds, but I'll telephone for the brightest newspaper reporters in Miami to fly over here and help you on the case. I'll do that if he's rich."

"Not if he has *been* rich?"

"No; he's got to be rich right now. There's no news value in the murder of a man who has been rich — at least not in Florida after the boom."

"But look at it this way," said Poggioli. "Suppose I showed you a spot on the ground bearing traces of petroleum; wouldn't you be willing to sink a well there, even if I couldn't absolutely guarantee that you would strike a gusher?"

The superintendent of the mill company shook his head.

"Not now. Five years ago, Mr. Poggioli, I'd have backed you to the limit if I had caught a whiff of oil, but since the boom I wouldn't put a nickel into a speculation of any kind unless it was guaranteed by the United States Treasury and insured by Lloyds."

The scientist shrugged.

"Well, all right. It's just that sort of psychology that is keeping this depression functioning, Galloway; but you fellows refuse to see it. I do wish I could find the body and examine it. It would be more revealing than these bags."

"I see that," agreed the superintendent, "and I'm really sorry I am not in a position to do anything about it."

This apology of the superintendent for not being able to assist in capturing the murderer of any cook's helper with a rating of less than AA1 in Bradstreet was interrupted by a shadow falling over the group.

The Negro Sam glanced about, gave a sort of grunt as if someone had struck him violently in the stomach, and abruptly scrambled up into the top bunk.

Galloway moved back from the valise and gave an odd kind of laugh.

"Well, I'll be damned — Chin Lee!" he exclaimed. "We thought you were dead. This damn fool, Sam, here — " He nodded angrily at the pop-eyed black man in the upper bunk.

"Me no dead," said Chin Lee. "Me fall, get hurt, wake up by me by, come back klitchen."

Galloway was outraged.

"Sam, you black ignoramus, you're a thunder of a night watchman! Run off and leave a wounded man lying on the dock!"

"He was daid!" cried Sam. "Yo' sho' was daid, Chin Lee, wid a great big hole in yo' haid!"

"Me pull out big fish," explained the cook's helper simply. "Foot slip, fall, hit head, by me by wake up again."

The head of the cook's boy was tied up with a great bandage.

"Well, Chin Lee," said Galloway, "sorry we mussed up your things."

"Allee lite," rattled the Chinese. "Me dead, somebody mus' open bag."

"That's true. Well, we're glad you're no deader than you are."

Chin Lee lifted a hand to his bandage.

"Big bump — feel allee lite now."

The Negro climbed down from his bunk and the visitors were about to go.

"Why did you come here, Chin Lee?" inquired Poggioli. "Skaggs send you down?"

"You say you look at my bunk. Me come say bunk good bunk."

"You heard us talking as we came through the kitchen?"

"Yes."

"What were you doing at that time?"

"Fix potato. Mis' Skaggs say fix potato go Tampa."

"I see. When do you go?"

"On 'leven."

The psychologist glanced at his watch.

"That isn't far off. We'd better go back and let you finish."

The four men moved out of the shack for the kitchen. In the big screened shed, the two Negro helpers were now pouring bread dough in an electric kneading machine.

"How do you fix the potatoes to go back to Tampa?" Poggioli inquired of the Chinese.

"Fill up hamper, put him in ice box till go," explained Chin Lee.

He led the way to the potato bin and resumed the simple business of filling a split basket with potatoes. The criminologist watched the work for a few moments, and a little later the white men set off for the superintendent's bungalow.

On the way back Galloway fell to bemeaning Sam for cowardice — too cowardly to walk up to a man on the dock and see whether he was dead or not.

"He sho was daid then, Mist' Jim; he ain't now, but he was then."

"Oh, you're not only a coward, you're an imbecile!"

"Don't be too hard on Sam," soothed the criminologist. "It seems to me there are some very odd things about Chin Lee's resuscitation."

"What's that?" inquired the superintendent sharply.

"Well, for instance — where did he get his head bound up?"

"In the kitchen, I suppose. Why?"

"Then why didn't he leave a trail of drops from the dock to the kitchen?"

"His head probably had stopped bleeding by that time."

"But if it were an arterial cut, wouldn't it have broken out again when he got up?"

"Well — it didn't do it."

"Apparently not," agreed the psychologist.

The two men entered the superintendent's garden and passed under the blue-green leaves and yellow melons of a papaya shrub.

"It's odd," went on the scientist, "after such a wound, he goes right back to work sorting out samples of spoiled potatoes and, apparently, he is going to Tampa on the eleven o'clock just as he had planned."

"I don't suppose he was hurt as badly as Sam thought."

"That's possible, too," admitted the psychologist. He walked on a space and then said, "There are two things about the way Chin Lee sorted out those potatoes that seemed very odd to me!"

"And just what were they?" inquired the superintendent, beginning to feel faintly ironic about his guest's finical logic.

"One thing was, his hands were perfectly steady."

"You mean if he had just been knocked out, he should have been shaky?"

"I think so; don't you?"

"Well, I don't know. He may have extraordinary recuperative powers."

"All right, I agree to that temporarily. Now how do you explain this final contradiction? Chin Lee picked up his sample potatoes and put them in the hamper in a very ordinary manner — in fact, just as you or I or Sam would have done it."

Galloway looked at his guest and then broke out laughing.

"Really, Professor, is that a matter for suspicion — filling a hamper with potatoes in an ordinary manner?"

"Certainly!" said the scientist tartly. "If a man has spent years and much care in growing long and delicate fingernails, don't you know he would have formed motor habits to protect those nails? He would have picked up the potatoes with fingers and thumbs held straight, and not bent at the knuckles in the usual manner."

The superintendent was a little bewildered at this.

"Look here, where is all this getting us, Mr. Poggioli?"

"Well, all these slight contradictions mean very little taken by themselves; but put together they amount to a great deal. However, I think they might be construed logically enough, if Sam's first diagnosis had been correct."

"Sam's first — what was Sam's first diagnosis?"

"That Chin Lee was dead."

Black Sam began to nod.

"Boss, now yo're shoutin' — you sho' is shoutin'."

Galloway smiled incredulously.

"Look here, what sort of a fellow are you anyway? When Sam came and told you Chin Lee was dead, you looked around the dock and decided if Chin Lee wasn't killed by a big strong woman, then he wasn't dead at all. Well, that was a good guess. You were right — Chin Lee turns up alive. But now, by George, you look at Chin Lee alive, sitting there picking up potatoes, and decide he must be dead. You are the hardest man to get to agree with anybody I ever saw. You won't even agree with yourself."

The psychologist disregarded this complaint, but after a moment asked gravely —

"Why is it so necessary to send a hamper of spoiled potatoes back to Tampa today?"

"It isn't necessary at all so far as the potatoes are concerned, but Chin Lee has to go anyway, so Erb might as well send the potatoes along."

"What does he have to go after?"

"For supplies for the *Mayaguez*. She is expected in tonight, and

Skaggs must deliver her a lot of green groceries and such-like stuff. As I told you, he's a ship's chandler in a small way."

The psychologist nodded with a sharpening of attention.

"When was the last Cuban boat in?" he inquired quickly.

"Why, I think the *Ponce* pulled out of here last night. Why?"

"Nothing, nothing; I was just curious . . . By the by, Mr. Galloway, I'm afraid I'm going to have to start home on the eleven o'clock train, if you don't mind my cutting my visit short a trifle."

The superintendent began the usual protest, then followed Poggioli up to his room and stood talking while his guest packed his personal belongings.

A few minutes later the two men got into the superintendent's car and set off.

When they came in sight of the station, Poggioli saw a solitary figure on the platform standing beside a large basket. Galloway saw him too.

"Yonder's Chin Lee with his potatoes — very faithful fellow."

A minute or two later they drove up to the station and entered the waiting room. At the office window, instead of purchasing transportation, Poggioli signaled the agent to him and asked *sotto voce* —

"That Chinaman on the platform — did he pay for his ticket in American gold?"

The agent looked at the criminologist and said that he had.

The investigator thanked him and turned to the outer platform. As the two men walked out, Galloway asked curiously —

"Why did you put such a question as that, Mr. Poggioli?"

"I wanted to see if your kitchen boy was just over from Cuba."

"Is he?"

"Yes."

"How does his paying for a ticket in gold show that?"

"Because a great deal of American gold is used in Cuba, while here in Everglades you pay off your men in bills."

"But Chin Lee hasn't been to Cuba. He must have had some gold of his own."

"Yes, but he wouldn't have spent it if he had had anything else. People don't spend gold when they can avoid it. No, he's just over from Cuba. He arrived on the *Ponce* last night and now he's on his way to New York."

Galloway stared at his companion, bewildered.

"Look here, what do you mean? Isn't that my Chin Lee standing there?"

"That is your present Chin Lee. You'll have another tonight when the *Ponce* comes in; but the Chin Lee you are thinking about is dead."

"Poggioli," said the superintendent in a shocked tone, "you're crazy!"

The criminologist said nothing more; the two men walked out on the platform and joined the kitchen boy. Poggioli placed a hand on the rim of the hamper.

"Boy," he asked in a casual tone, "why did you shoot Chin Lee?"

The yellow man looked at his questioner with an expressionless face.

"Me Chin Lee."

Poggioli nodded.

"I know you are now; you are one of a long line of Chin Lees, but why did you shoot the Chin Lee we had here yesterday? Why didn't you let him go on to New York, or Chicago, in his turn?"

The man with the bandaged head said blankly:

"No savvy. Me Chin Lee."

The scientist began throwing the decayed potatoes carelessly across the track. They were still cold from the ice.

"If you don't savvy now, you will in a minute or two." He began scooping out handfuls of the tubers. The Chinaman watched the performance for a few moments, then said casually —

"Me savvy."

"I thought you would. Now, why did you kill Chin Lee?"

"Him likee this," said the kitchen boy impassively. "Some China-man velly bad man — big general — fight Chinese government — velly bad — get run out of country. Try to come back, deserve die . . ." The Chinaman hesitated.

"That's all good and well," agreed the psychologist, "but why didn't you shove him off the dock when you had the chance? Why are you lugging him around in that hamper of spoiled potatoes?"

The Chinese lifted a brow as if he had no hope of making his questioner understand.

"After allee, Chin Lee Chinaman. Send him back to own country to sleep. No let him come to his fathers from land of barbarian."

The psychologist nodded.

"Simple enough. Odd, I didn't think of that myself."

Galloway interposed:

"What in the thunder is all this about? Chin Lee dead, and in that hamper?"

"Skaggs is smuggling Chinese into this country from Cuba, and one of them happened to be after the man just before him. That's all there is to it. And by the way, it also explains why you were never able to recognize one of your collective kitchen boys when you saw a sample of him before your eyes."

THE MAD TEA PARTY

by ELLERY QUEEN

---

*At this point, according to purple tradition, you should be
reading a whimsical statement by the Publisher to the effect
that under threat of corporeal violence he got the Editors to
include one of their own stories. We scorn this feeble subter-
fuge. Including "The Mad Tea Party" was strictly our own
idea.*

THE TALL young man in the dun raincoat thought that he had
never seen such a downpour. It gushed out of the black sky in a
roaring flood, gray-gleaming in the feeble yellow of the station
lamps. The red tails of the local from Jamaica had just been
drowned out in the west. It was very dark beyond the ragged blur
of light surrounding the little railroad station, and unquestionably
very wet. The tall young man shivered under the eaves of the platform roof and wondered what insanity had moved him to venture
into the Long Island hinterland in such wretched weather. And
where, damn it all, was Owen?

He had just miserably made up his mind to seek out a booth,
telephone his regrets, and take the next train back to the City, when
a lowslung coupé came splashing and snuffling out of the darkness,
squealed to a stop, and a man in chauffeur's livery leaped out and
dashed across the gravel for the protection of the eaves.

"Mr. Ellery Queen?" he panted, shaking out his cap. He was a
blond young man with a ruddy face and sun-squinted eyes.

"Yes," said Ellery with a sigh. Too late now.

"I'm Millan, Mr. Owen's chauffeur, sir," said the man. "Mr.

Owen's sorry he couldn't come down to meet you himself. Some guests — This way, Mr. Queen."

He picked up Ellery's bag and the two of them ran for the coupé. Ellery collapsed against the mohair in an indigo mood. Damn Owen and his invitations! Should have known better. Mere acquaintance, when it came to that. One of J. J.'s questionable friends. People were always pushing so. Put him up on exhibition, like a trained seal. Come, come, Rollo; here's a juicy little fish for you! . . . Got vicarious thrills out of listening to crime yarns. Made a man feel like a curiosity. Well, he'd be drawn and quartered if they got him to mention crime once! But then Owen had said Emmy Willowes would be there, and he'd always wanted to meet Emmy. Curious woman, Emmy, from all the reports. Daughter of some blueblood diplomat who had gone to the dogs — in this case, the stage. Stuffed shirts, her tribe, probably. Atavi! There were some people who still lived in mediæval . . . Hmm. Owen wanted him to see "the house." Just taken a month ago. Ducky, he'd said. "Ducky!" The big brute . . .

The coupé splashed along in the darkness, its headlights revealing only remorseless sheets of speckled water and occasionally a tree, a house, a hedge.

Millan cleared his throat. "Rotten weather, isn't it, sir. Worst this spring."

Ah, the conversational chauffeur! thought Ellery with an inward groan. "Pity the poor sailor on a night like this," he said piously.

"Ha, ha," said Millan. "Isn't it the truth, though. You're a little late, aren't you, sir? That was the eleven-fifty. Mr. Owen told me this morning you were expected tonight on the nine-twenty."

"Detained," murmured Ellery, wishing he were dead.

"A case, Mr. Queen?" asked Millan eagerly, rolling his squinty eyes.

Even he, O Lord. . . . "No, no. My father had his annual attack of elephantiasis. Poor Dad! We thought for a bad hour there that it was the end."

The chauffeur gaped. Then, looking puzzled, he returned his attention to the soggy pelted road. Ellery closed his eyes with a sigh of relief.

But Millan's was a persevering soul, for after a moment of silence he grinned — true, a trifle dubiously — and said: "Lots of excitement at Mr. Owen's tonight, sir. You see, Master Jonathan — "

"Ah," said Ellery, starting a little. Master Jonathan, eh? Ellery recalled him as a stringy, hot-eyed brat in the indeterminate years between seven and ten who possessed a perfectly fiendish ingenuity for making a nuisance of himself. Master Jonathan. . . . He shivered again, this time from apprehension. He had quite forgotten Master Jonathan.

"Yes, sir, Jonathan's having a birthday party tomorrow, sir — ninth, I think — and Mr. and Mrs. Owen've rigged up something special." Millan grinned again, mysteriously. "Something very special, sir. It's a secret, y'see. The kid — Master Jonathan doesn't know about it yet. Will he be surprised!"

"I doubt it, Millan," groaned Ellery, and lapsed into a dismal silence which not even the chauffeur's companionable blandishments were able to shatter.

Richard Owen's "ducky" house was a large rambling affair of gables and ells and colored stones and bright shutters, set at the terminal of a winding driveway flanked by soldierly trees. It blazed with light and the front door stood ajar.

"Here we are, Mr. Queen!" cried Millan cheerfully, jumping out and holding the door open. "It's only a hop to the porch; you won't get wet, sir."

Ellery descended and obediently hopped to the porch. Millan fished his bag out of the car and bounded up the steps. "Door open 'n' everything," he grinned. "Guess the help are all watchin' the show."

"Show?" gasped Ellery with a sick feeling at the pit of his stomach.

Millan pushed the door wide open. "Step in, step in, Mr. Queen. I'll go get Mr. Owen. . . . They're rehearsing, y'see. Couldn't do it while Jonathan was up, so they had to wait till he'd gone to bed. It's for tomorrow, y'see. And he was very suspicious; they had an awful time with him — "

"I can well believe that," mumbled Ellery. Damn Jonathan and all his tribe! He stood in a small foyer looking upon a wide brisk living room, warm and attractive. "So they're putting on a play.

Hmm. . . . Don't bother, Millan; I'll just wander in and wait until they've finished. Who am I to clog the wheels of Drama?"

"Yes, sir," said Millan with a vague disappointment; and he set down the bag and touched his cap and vanished in the darkness outside. The door closed with a click curiously final, shutting out both rain and night.

Ellery reluctantly divested himself of his drenched hat and raincoat, hung them dutifully in the foyer closet, kicked his bag into a corner, and sauntered into the living room to warm his chilled hands at the good fire. He stood before the flames soaking in heat, only half-conscious of the voices which floated through one of the two open doorways beyond the fireplace.

A woman's voice was saying in odd childish tones: "No, please go on! I won't interrupt you again. I dare say there may be *one*."

"Emmy," thought Ellery, becoming conscious very abruptly. "What's going on here?" He went to the first doorway and leaned against the jamb.

An astonishing sight. They were all — as far as he could determine — there. It was a large bookish room done in the modern manner. The farther side had been cleared and a home-made curtain, manufactured out of starchy sheets and a pulley, stretched across the room. The curtain was open, and in the cleared space there was a long table covered with a white cloth and with cups and saucers and things on it. In an armchair at the head of the table sat Emmy Willowes, whimsically girlish in a pinafore, her gold-brown hair streaming down her back, her slim legs sheathed in white stockings, and black pumps with low heels on her feet. Beside her sat an apparition, no less: a rabbity creature the size of a man, his huge ears stiffly up, an enormous bow tie at his furry neck, his mouth clacking open and shut as human sounds came from his throat. Beside the hare there was another apparition: a creature with an amiably rodent little face and slow sleepy movements. And beyond the little one, who looked unaccountably like a dormouse, sat the most remarkable of the quartet — a curious creature with shaggy eyebrows and features reminiscent of George Arliss's, at his throat a dotted bow tie, dressed Victorianwise in a quaint waistcoat, on his head an extraordinary tall cloth hat in the band of which was stuck a placard reading: "For This Style 10/6."

The audience was composed of two women: an old lady with pure white hair and the stubbornly sweet facial expression which more often than not conceals a chronic acerbity; and a very beautiful young woman with full breasts, red hair, and green eyes. Then Ellery noticed that two domestic heads were stuck in another doorway, gaping and giggling decorously.

"The mad tea party," thought Ellery, grinning. "I might have known, with Emmy in the house. Too good for that merciless brat!"

"They were learning to draw," said the little dormouse in a high-pitched voice, yawning and rubbing its eyes, "and they drew all manner of things — everything that begins with an M — "

"Why with an M?" demanded the woman-child.

"Why not?" snapped the hare, flapping his ears indignantly.

The dormouse began to doze and was instantly beset by the top-hatted gentleman, who pinched him so roundly that he awoke with a shriek and said: " — that begins with an M, such as mousetraps, and the moon, and memory, and muchness — you know you say things are 'much of a muchness' — did you ever see such a thing as a drawing of a muchness?"

"Really, now you ask me," said the girl, quite confused, "I don't think — "

"Then you shouldn't talk," said the Hatter tartly.

The girl rose in open disgust and began to walk away, her white legs twinkling. The dormouse fell asleep and the hare and the Hatter stood up and grasped the dormouse's little head and tried very earnestly to push it into the mouth of a monstrous teapot on the table.

And the little girl cried, stamping her right foot: "At any rate I'll never go *there* again. It's the stupidest tea party I was ever at in all my life!"

And she vanished behind the curtain; an instant later it swayed and came together as she operated the rope of the pulley.

"Superb," drawled Ellery, clapping his hands. "*Brava,* Alice. And a couple of *bravi* for the zoölogical characters, Messrs. Dormouse and March Hare, not to speak of my good friend the Mad Hatter."

The Mad Hatter goggled at him, tore off his hat, and came running across the room. His vulturine features under the make-up were both good-humored and crafty; he was a stoutish man in his prime, a faintly cynical and ruthless prime. "Queen! When on earth did you come? What held you up?"

"Family matter. Millan did the honors. Owen, that's your natural costume, I'll swear. I don't know what ever possessed you to go into Wall Street. You were born to be the Hatter."

"Think so?" chuckled Owen, pleased. "I guess I always did have a yen for the stage; that's why I backed Emmy Willowes's *Alice* show. Here, I want you to meet the gang. Mother," he said to the white-haired old lady, "may I present Mr. Ellery Queen. Laura's mother, Queen — Mrs. Mansfield." The old lady smiled a sweet, sweet smile; but Ellery noticed that her eyes were very sharp. "Mrs. Gardner," continued Owen, indicating the buxom young woman with the red hair and green eyes. "Believe it or not, she's the wife of that hairy Hare over there. Ho, ho, ho!"

There was something a little brutal in Owen's laughter. Ellery bowed to the beautiful woman and said quickly: "Gardner? You're not the wife of Paul Gardner, the architect?"

"Guilty," said the March Hare in a cavernous voice; and he removed his head and disclosed a lean face with twinkling eyes. "How are you, Queen? I haven't seen you since I testified for your father in that Schultz murder case in the Village."

They shook hands. "Surprise," said Ellery. "This *is* nice. Mrs. Gardner, you have a clever husband. He set the defense by their respective ears with his expert testimony in that case."

"Oh, I've always said Paul is a genius," smiled the red-haired woman. She had a queer husky voice. "But he won't believe me. He thinks I'm the only one in the world who doesn't appreciate him."

"Now, Carolyn," protested Gardner with a laugh; but the twinkle had gone out of his eyes and for some odd reason he glanced at Richard Owen.

"Of course you remember Laura," boomed Owen, taking Ellery forcibly by the arm. "That's the Dormouse. Charming little rat, isn't she?"

Mrs. Mansfield lost her sweet expression for a fleeting instant; very fleeting indeed. What the Dormouse thought about being publicly characterized as a rodent, however charming, by her husband was concealed by the furry little head; when she took it off she was smiling. She was a wan little woman with tired eyes and cheeks that had already begun to sag.

"And this," continued Owen with the pride of a stock raiser exhibiting a prize milch cow, "is the one and only Emmy. Emmy, meet Mr. Queen, that murder-smelling chap I've been telling you about. Miss Willowes."

"You see us, Mr. Queen," murmured the actress, "in character. I hope you aren't here on a professional visit? Because if you are, we'll get into mufti at once and let you go to work. I know *I've* a vicariously guilty conscience. If I were to be convicted of every mental murder I've committed, I'd need the nine lives of the Cheshire Cat. Those damn' critics — "

"The costume," said Ellery, not looking at her legs, "is most fetching. And I think I like you better as Alice." She made a charming Alice; she was curved in her slimness, half boy, half girl. "Whose idea was this, anyway?"

"I suppose you think we're fools or nuts," chuckled Owen. "Here, sit down, Queen. Maud!" he roared. "A cocktail for Mr. Queen. Bring some more fixin's." A frightened domestic head vanished. "We're having a dress rehearsal for Johnny's birthday party tomorrow; we've invited all the kids of the neighborhood. Emmy's brilliant idea; she brought the costumes down from the theatre. You know we closed Saturday night."

"I hadn't heard. I thought *Alice* was playing to S.R.O."

"So it was. But our lease at the Odeon ran out and we've our engagements on the road to keep. We open in Boston next Wednesday."

Slim-legged Maud set a pinkish liquid concoction before Ellery. He sipped slowly, succeeding in not making a face.

"Sorry to have to break this up," said Paul Gardner, beginning to take off his costume. "But Carolyn and I have a bad trip before us. And then tomorrow . . . The road must be an absolute washout."

"Pretty bad," said Ellery politely, setting down his three-quarters-full glass.

"I won't hear of it," said Laura Owen. Her pudgy little Dormouse's stomach gave her a peculiar appearance, tiny and fat and sexless. "Driving home in this storm! Carolyn, you and Paul must stay over."

"It's only four miles, Laura," murmured Mrs. Gardner.

"Nonsense, Carolyn! More like forty on a night like this," boomed Owen. His cheeks were curiously pale and damp under the make-up. "That's settled! We've got more room than we know what to do with. Paul saw to that when he designed this development."

"That's the insidious part of knowing architects socially," said Emmy Willowes with a grimace. She flung herself in a chair and tucked her long legs under her. "You can't fool 'em about the number of available guest rooms."

"Don't mind Emmy," grinned Owen. "She's the Peck's Bad Girl of show business: no manners at all. Well, well! This is great. How's about a drink, Paul?"

"No, thanks."

"You'll have one, won't you, Carolyn? Only good sport in the crowd." Ellery realized with embarrassment that his host was, under the jovial glaze of the exterior, drunk.

Mrs. Gardner raised her heavily-lidded green eyes to Owen's. "I'd love it, Dick." They stared with frank hunger at each other. Mrs. Owen suddenly smiled and turned her back, struggling with her cumbersome costume.

And, just as suddenly, Mrs. Mansfield rose and smiled her unconvincing sweet smile and said in her sugary voice to no one in particular: "*Will* you all excuse me? It's been a trying day, and I'm an old woman. . . . Laura, my darling." She went to her daughter and kissed the lined, averted forehead.

Everybody murmured something; including Ellery, who had a headache, a slow pinkish fire in his vitals, and a consuming wishfulness to be far, far away.

Mr. Ellery Queen came to with a start and a groan. He turned over in bed, feeling very poorly. He had dozed in fits since one o'clock, annoyed rather than soothed by the splash of the rain against the bedroom windows. And now he was miserably awake, attacked by an inexplicable insomnia. He sat up and reached for his wrist watch, which was ticking thunderously away on the night table beside his bed. By the radium hands he saw that it was five past two.

He lay back, tucking his palms behind his head, and stared into the half-darkness. The mattress was deep and downy, as one had a right to expect of the mattress of a plutocrat, but it did not rest his restless bones. The house was cosy, but it did not comfort him. His hostess was thoughtful, but uncomfortably woebegone. His host was a disturbing force, like the storm. His fellow guests; Master Jonathan snuffling away in his junior bed — Ellery was positive that Master Jonathan snuffled. . . .

At two-fifteen he gave up the battle and, rising, turned on the light and got into his dressing gown and slippers. That there was no book or magazine on or in the night table he had ascertained before retiring. Shocking hospitality! Sighing, he went to the door and opened it and peered out. A small night light glimmered at the landing down the hall. Everything was quiet.

And suddenly he was attacked by the strangest diffidence. He definitely did not want to leave the bedroom.

Analyzing the fugitive fear, and arriving nowhere, Ellery sternly reproached himself for an imaginative fool and stepped out into the hall. He was not habitually a creature of nerves, nor was he psychic; he laid the blame to lowered physical resistance due to fatigue, lack of sleep. This was a nice house with nice people in it. It was like a man, he thought, saying: "Nice doggie, nice doggie," to a particularly fearsome beast with slavering jaws. That woman with the sea-green eyes. Put to sea in a sea-green boat. Or was it pea-green. . . . "No room! No room!" . . . "There's *plenty* of room," said Alice indignantly. . . . And Mrs. Mansfield's smile did make you shiver.

Berating himself bitterly for the ferment his imagination was in, he went down the carpeted stairs to the living room.

It was pitch-dark and he did not know where the light switch was. He stumbled over a hassock and stubbed his toe and cursed silently. The library should be across from the stairs, next to the fireplace. He strained his eyes toward the fireplace, but the last embers had died. Stepping warily, he finally reached the fireplace wall. He groped about in the rain-splattered silence, searching for the library door. His hand met a cold knob, and he turned the knob rather noisily and swung the door open. His eyes were oriented to the darkness now and he had already begun to make out in the mistiest black haze the unrecognizable outlines of still objects.

The darkness from beyond the door however struck him like a

blow. It was darker darkness. . . . He was about to step across the sill when he stopped. It was the wrong room. Not the library at all. How he knew he could not say, but he was sure he had pushed open the door of the wrong room. Must have wandered orbitally to the right. Lost men in the dark forest. . . . He stared intently straight before him into the absolute, unrelieved blackness, sighed, and retreated. The door shut noisily again.

He groped along the wall to the left. A few feet. . . . There it was! The very next door. He paused to test his psychic faculties. No, all's well. Grinning, he pushed open the door, entered boldly, fumbled on the nearest wall for the switch, found it, pressed. The light flooded on to reveal, triumphantly, the library.

The curtain was closed, the room in disorder as he had last seen it before being conducted upstairs by his host.

He went to the built-in bookcases, scanned several shelves, hesitated between two volumes, finally selected *Huckleberry Finn* as blithe reading on a dour night, put out the light, and felt his way back across the living room to the stairway. Book tucked under his arm, he began to climb the stairs. There was a footfall from the landing above. He looked up. A man's dark form was silhouetted below the tiny landing light.

"Owen?" whispered a dubious male voice.

Ellery laughed. "It's Queen, Gardner. Can't you sleep, either?"

He heard the man sigh with relief. "Lord, no! I was just coming downstairs for something to read. Carolyn—my wife's asleep, I guess, in the room adjoining mine. How she can sleep—! There's something in the air tonight."

"Or else you drank too much," said Ellery cheerfully, mounting the stairs.

Gardner was in pajamas and dressing gown, his hair mussed. "Didn't drink at all to speak of. Must be this confounded rain. My nerves are all shot."

"Something in that. Hardy believed, anyway, in the Greek unities. . . . If you can't sleep, you might join me for a smoke in my room, Gardner."

"You're sure I won't be — "

"Keeping me up? Nonsense. The only reason I fished about downstairs for a book was to occupy my mind with something.

Talk's infinitely better than Huck Finn, though he does help at times. Come on."

They went to Ellery's room and Ellery produced cigarettes and they relaxed in chairs and chatted over tobacco about Inspector Queen, old books, and the price of green cheese until the early dawn began struggling to emerge from behind the fine gray wet bars of the rain outside. Then Gardner went yawning back to his room and Ellery fell into a heavy, uneasy slumber.

He was on the rack in a tall room of the Inquisition and his left arm was being torn out of his shoulder socket. The pain was almost pleasant. Then he awoke to find Millan's ruddy face in broad day-light above him, his blond hair tragically dishevelled. He was jerking at Ellery's arm for all he was worth.

"Mr. Queen!" he was crying. "Mr. Queen! For God's sake, wake up!"

Ellery sat up quickly, startled. "What's the matter, Millan?"

"Mr. Owen, sir. He's — he's gone!"

Ellery sprang out of bed. "What d'ye mean, man?"

"Disappeared, Mr. Queen. We — we can't find him. Just gone. Mrs. Owen is all — "

"You go downstairs, Millan," said Ellery calmly, stripping off his pajama coat, "and pour yourself a drink. Please tell Mrs. Owen not to do anything until I come down. And nobody's to leave or telephone. You understand?"

"Yes, sir," said Millan in a low voice, and blundered off.

Ellery dressed like a fireman, splashed his face, spat water, adjusted his necktie, and ran downstairs. He found Laura Owen in a crumpled négligé on the sofa, sobbing. Mrs. Mansfield was patting her daughter's shoulder. Master Jonathan Owen was scowling at his grandmother, Emmy Willowes silently smoked a cigarette, and the Gardners were pale and quiet by the gray-washed windows.

"Mr. Queen," said the actress quickly. "It's a drama, hot off the script. At least Laura Owen thinks so. Won't you assure her that it's all probably nothing?"

"I can't do that," smiled Ellery, "until I learn the facts. Owen's gone? How? When?"

"Oh, Mr. Queen," choked Mrs. Owen, raising a tear-stained face.

"I know something — something dreadful's happened. I had a feeling — You remember last night, after Richard showed you to your room?"

"Yes."

"Then he came back downstairs and said he had some work to do in his den for Monday, and told me to go to bed. Everybody else had gone upstairs. The servants, too. I warned him not to stay up too late and I went up to bed. I — I was exhausted, and I fell right asleep — "

"You occupy one bedroom, Mrs. Owen?"

"Yes. Twin beds. I fell asleep and didn't wake up until a half-hour ago. Then I saw — " She shuddered and began to sob again. Her mother looked helpless and angry. "His bed hadn't been slept in. His clothes — the ones he'd taken off when he got into the costume — were still where he had left them on the chair by his bed. I was shocked, and ran downstairs; but he was gone. . . ."

"Ah," said Ellery queerly. "Then, as far as you know, he's still in that Mad Hatter's rig? Have you looked over his wardrobe? Are any of his regular clothes missing?"

"No, no; they're all there. Oh, he's dead. I know he's dead."

"Laura, dear, please," said Mrs. Mansfield in a tight quavery voice.

"Oh, Mother, it's too horrible — "

"Here, here," said Ellery. "No hysterics. Was he worried about anything? Business, for instance?"

"No, I'm sure he wasn't. In fact, he said only yesterday things were picking up beautifully. And he isn't — isn't the type to worry, anyway."

"Then it probably isn't amnesia. He hasn't had a shock of some sort recently?"

"No, no."

"No possibility, despite the costume, that he went to his office?"

"No. He never goes down Saturdays."

Master Jonathan jammed his fists into the pockets of his Eton jacket and said bitterly: "I bet he's drunk again. Makin' Mamma cry. I hope he *never* comes back."

"Jonathan!" screamed Mrs. Mansfield. "You go up to your room this very minute, do you hear, you nasty boy? This minute!"

No one said anything; Mrs. Owen continued to sob; so Master Jonathan thrust out his lower lip, scowled at his grandmother with unashamed dislike, and stamped upstairs.

"Where," said Ellery with a frown, "was your husband when you last saw him, Mrs. Owen? In this room?"

"In his den," she said with difficulty. "He went in just as I went upstairs. I saw him go in. That door, there." She pointed to the door at the right of the library door. Ellery started; it was the door to the room he had almost blundered into during the night in his hunt for the library.

"Do you think —" began Carolyn Gardner in her husky voice, and stopped. Her lips were dry, and in the gray morning light her hair did not seem so red and her eyes did not seem so green. There was, in fact, a washed-out look about her, as if all the fierce vitality within her had been quenched by what had happened.

"Keep out of this, Carolyn," said Paul Gardner harshly. His eyes were red-rimmed from lack of sleep.

"Come, come," murmured Ellery, "we may be, as Miss Willowes has said, making a fuss over nothing at all. If you'll excuse me . . . I'll have a peep at the den."

He went into the den, closing the door behind him, and stood with his back squarely against the door. It was a small room, so narrow that it looked long by contrast; it was sparsely furnished and seemed a business-like place. There was a simple neatness about its desk, a modern severity about its furnishings that were reflections of the direct, brutal character of Richard Owen. The room was as trim as a pin; it was almost ludicrous to conceive of its having served as the scene of a crime.

Ellery gazed long and thoughtfully. Nothing out of place, so far as he could see; and nothing, at least perceptible to a stranger, added. Then his eyes wavered and fixed themselves upon what stood straight before him. That *was* odd. . . . Facing him as he leaned against the door there was a bold naked mirror set flush into the opposite wall and reaching from floor to ceiling — a startling feature of the room's decorations. Ellery's lean figure, and the door behind him, were perfectly reflected in the sparkling glass. And there, above . . . In the mirror he saw, above the reflection of the door against which he was leaning, the reflection of the face of a modern electric clock.

In the dingy grayness of the light there was a curious lambent quality about its dial. . . . He pushed away from the door and turned and stared up. It was a chromium-and-onyx clock, about a foot in diameter.

He opened the door and beckoned Millan, who had joined the silent group in the living room. "Have you a stepladder?"

Millan brought one. Ellery shut the door firmly, mounted the ladder, and examined the clock. Its electric outlet was behind, concealed from view. The plug was in the socket, as he saw at once. The clock was going; the time — he consulted his wrist watch — was reasonably accurate. But then he cupped his hands as best he could to shut out what light there was and stared hard and saw that the numerals and the hands, as he had suspected, were radium-painted. They glowed faintly.

He descended, opened the door, gave the ladder into Millan's keeping, and sauntered into the living room. They looked up at him trustfully.

"Well," said Emmy Willowes with a light shrug, "has the Master Mind discovered the all-important clue? Don't tell us that Dickie Owen is out playing golf at the Meadowbrook links in that Mad Hatter's get-up!"

"Well, Mr. Queen?" asked Mrs. Owen anxiously.

Ellery sank into an armchair and lighted a cigarette. "There's something curious in there. Mrs. Owen, did you get this house furnished?"

She was puzzled. "Furnished? Oh, no. We bought it, you know; brought all our own things."

"Then the electric clock above the door in the den is yours?"

"The clock?" They all stared at him. "Why, of course. What has that — "

"Hmm," said Ellery. "That clock has a disappearing quality, like the Cheshire Cat — since we may as well continue being Carrollish, Miss Willowes."

"But what can the clock possibly have to do with Richard's being gone?" asked Mrs. Mansfield with asperity.

Ellery shrugged. "*Je n'sais*. The point is that a little after two this morning, being unable to sleep, I ambled downstairs to look for a book. In the dark I blundered to the door of the den, mistaking it for the library door. I opened it and looked in. But I saw nothing, you see."

"But how could you, Mr. Queen?" said Mrs. Gardner in a small voice; her breasts heaved. "If it was dark — "

"That's the curious part of it," drawled Ellery. "I *should* have seen something *because* it was so dark, Mrs. Gardner."

"But — "

"The clock over the door."

"Did you go in?" murmured Emmy Willowes, frowning. "I can't say I understand. The clock's above the door, isn't it?"

"There is a mirror facing the door," explained Ellery absently, "and the fact that it was so dark makes my seeing nothing quite remarkable. Because that clock has luminous hands and numerals. Consequently I should have seen their reflected glow very clearly indeed in that pitch darkness. But I didn't, you see. I saw literally nothing at all."

They were silent, bewildered. Then Gardner muttered: "I still don't see — You mean something, somebody was standing in front of the mirror, obscuring the reflection of the clock?"

"Oh, no. The clock's above the door — a good seven feet or more from the floor. The mirror reaches to the ceiling. There isn't a piece of furniture in that room seven feet high, and certainly we may dismiss the possibility of an intruder seven feet or more tall. No, no, Gardner. It does seem as if the clock wasn't above the door at all when I looked in."

"Are you sure, young man," snapped Mrs. Mansfield, "that you know what you're talking about? I thought we were concerned with my son-in-law's absence. And how on earth could the clock not have been there?"

Ellery closed his eyes. "Fundamental. *It was moved from its position.* Wasn't above the door when I looked in. After I left, it was returned."

"But why on earth," murmured the actress, "should anyone want to move a mere clock from a wall, Mr. Queen? That's almost as nonsensical as some of the things in *Alice.*"

"That," said Ellery, "is the question I'm propounding to myself. Frankly I don't know." Then he opened his eyes. "By the way, has anyone seen the Mad Hatter's hat?"

Mrs. Owen shivered. "No, that — that's gone, too."

"You've looked for it?"

"Yes. Would you like to look yours — "

"No, no, I'll take your word for it, Mrs. Owen. Oh, yes. Your husband has no enemies?" He smiled. "That's the routine question, Miss Willowes. I'm afraid I can't offer you anything startling in the way of technique."

"Enemies? Oh, I'm sure not," quavered Mrs. Owen. "Richard was — is strong and — and sometimes rather curt and contemptuous, but I'm sure no one would hate him enough to — to kill him." She shivered again and drew the silk of her négligé closer about her plump shoulders.

"Don't say that, Laura," said Mrs. Mansfield sharply. "I do declare, you people are like children! It probably has the simplest explanation."

"Quite possible," said Ellery in a cheerful voice. "It's the depressing weather, I suppose. . . . There! I believe the rain's stopped." They dully looked out the windows. The rain had perversely ceased, and the sky was growing brighter. "Of course," continued Ellery, "there are certain possibilities. It's conceivable — I say conceivable, Mrs. Owen — that your husband has been . . . well, kidnaped. Now, now, don't look so frightened. It's a theory only. The fact that he has disappeared in the costume does seem to point to a very abrupt — and therefore possibly enforced — departure. You haven't found a note of some kind? Nothing in your letter box? The morning mail — "

"Kidnaped," whispered Mrs. Owen feebly.

"Kidnaped?" breathed Mrs. Gardner, and bit her lip. But there was a brightness in her eye, like the brightness of the sky outdoors.

"No note, no mail," snapped Mrs. Mansfield. "Personally, I think this is ridiculous. Laura, this is your house, but I think I have a duty. . . . You should do one of two things. Either take this seriously and telephone the *regular* police, or forget all about it. *I'm* inclined to believe Richard got befuddled — he *had* a lot to drink last night, dear — and wandered off drunk somewhere. He's probably sleeping it off in a field somewhere and won't come back with anything worse than pneumonia."

"Excellent suggestion," drawled Ellery. "All except for the sum-

moning of the *regular* police, Mrs. Mansfield. I assure you I possess
— er — *ex officio* qualifications. Let's not call the police and say we
did. If there's any explaining to do — afterward — I'll do it. Meanwhile, I suggest we try to forget all this unpleasantness and wait.
If Mr. Owen hasn't returned by nightfall, we can go into conference and decide what measures to take. Agreed?"

"Sounds reasonable," said Gardner disconsolately. "May I — " he
smiled and shrugged — "this *is* exciting! — telephone my office,
Queen?"

"Lord, yes."

Mrs. Owen shrieked suddenly, rising and tottering toward the
stairs. "Jonathan's birthday party! I forgot all about it! And all
those children invited — What *will* I say?"

"I suggest," said Ellery in a sad voice, "that Master Jonathan is
indisposed, Mrs. Owen. Harsh, but necessary. You might phone all
the potential spectators of the mad tea party and voice your regrets."
And Ellery rose and wandered into the library.

It was a depressing day for all the lightening skies and the crisp
sun. The morning wore on and nothing whatever happened. Mrs.
Mansfield firmly tucked her daughter into bed, made her swallow
a small dose of Luminal from a big bottle in the medicine chest, and
remained with her until she dropped off to exhausted sleep. Then
the old lady telephoned to all and sundry the collective Owen regrets over the unfortunate turn of events. Jonathan *would* have to
run a fever when . . . Master Jonathan, apprised later by his grandmother of the *débâcle,* sent up a healthy howl of anguish that caused
Ellery, poking about downstairs in the library, to feel prickles
slither up and down his spine. It took the combined labors of Mrs.
Mansfield, Millan, the maid, and the cook to pacify the Owen hope.
A five-dollar bill ultimately restored a rather strained *entente.* . . .
Emmy Willowes spent the day serenely reading. The Gardners list-
lessly played gin-rummy.

Luncheon was a dismal affair. No one spoke in more than mono-
syllables.

During the afternoon they wandered about, restless. Even the actress began to show signs of tension: she consumed innumerable cigarettes and cocktails and lapsed into almost sullen silence. No word

came; the telephone rang only once, and then it was merely the local confectioner protesting the cancellation of the ice cream order. Ellery spent most of the afternoon in mysterious activity in the library and den. What he was looking for remained his secret. At five o'clock he emerged from the den, rather gray of face. There was a deep crease between his brows. He went out onto the porch and leaned against a pillar, sunk in thought. The gravel was dry; the sun had quickly sopped up the rain. When he went back into the house it was already dusk and growing darker each moment with the swiftness of the country nightfall.

There was no one about; the house was quiet, its miserable occupants having retired to their rooms. Ellery sought a chair. He buried his face in his hands and thought for long minutes, completely still.

And then at last something happened to him and he went to the foot of the stairs and listened. No sound. He tiptoed back, reached for the telephone, and spent the next fifteen minutes in low-voiced, earnest conversation with someone in New York. When he had finished, he went upstairs to his room.

An hour later, while the others were downstairs gathering for dinner, he slipped down the rear stairway and out of the house unobserved even by the cook in the kitchen. He spent some time in the thick darkness of the grounds.

How it happened Ellery never knew. He felt its effects soon after dinner; and on retrospection he recalled that the others, too, had seemed drowsy at approximately the same time. It was a late dinner and a cold one, Owen's disappearance apparently having disrupted the culinary organization as well; so that it was not until a little after eight that the coffee — Ellery was certain later it had been the coffee — was served by the trim-legged maid. The drowsiness came on less than half an hour later. They were seated in the living room, chatting dully about nothing at all. Mrs. Owen, pale and silent, had gulped her coffee thirstily; had called for a second cup, in fact. Only Mrs. Mansfield had been belligerent. She had been definitely of a mind, it appeared, to telephone the police. She had great faith in the local constabulary of Long Island, particularly in one Chief Naughton, the local prefect; and she left no doubt in Ellery's mind of *his* incompetency. Gardner had been restless and a little rebellious; he had tinkered with the piano in the alcove. Emmy Willowes had drawn herself into a slant-eyed shell, no longer amused and very, very quiet. Mrs. Gardner had been nervous. Jonathan, packed off screaming to bed. . . .

It came over their senses like a blanket of snow. Just a pleasant sleepiness. The room was warm, too, and Ellery rather hazily felt perspiration on his forehead. He was half-gone before his dulled brain sounded a warning note. And then, trying in panic to rise, to use his muscles, he felt himself slipping, slipping into unconsciousness, his body as leaden and remote as Vega. His last conscious thought, as the room whirled dizzily before his eyes and he saw blearily the expressions of his companions, was that they had all been drugged. . . .

The dizziness seemed merely to have taken up where it had left off. Specks danced before his closed eyes and somebody was hammering petulantly at his temples. Then he opened his eyes and saw glittering sun fixed upon the floor at his feet. Good God, all night. . . .

He sat up groaning and feeling his head. The others were sprawled in various attitudes of labored-breathing coma about him — without exception. Someone — his aching brain took it in dully; it was Emmy Willowes — stirred and sighed. He got to his feet and stumbled toward a portable bar and poured himself a stiff, nasty drink of Scotch. Then, with his throat burning, he felt unaccountably better; and he went to the actress and pummeled her gently until she opened her eyes.

"What — when — "

"Drugged," croaked Ellery. "The crew of us. Try to revive these people, Miss Willowes, while I scout about a bit. And see if anyone's shamming."

He wove his way a little uncertainly, but with purpose, toward the rear of the house. Groping, he found the kitchen. And there were the trim-legged maid and Millan and the cook unconscious in chairs about the kitchen table over cold cups of coffee. He made his way back to the living room, nodded at Miss Willowes working over Gardner at the piano, and staggered upstairs. He discovered Master Jonathan's bedroom after a short search; the boy was still sleeping — a deep natural sleep punctuated by nasal snuffles. Lord, he *did* snuffle! Groaning, Ellery visited the lavatory adjoining the master bedroom. After a little while he went downstairs and into the den. He came out almost at once, haggard and wild-eyed. He took his hat from the foyer closet and hurried outdoors into the warm sunshine. He spent fifteen minutes poking about the grounds; the Owen house was shallowly surrounded by timber and seemed isolated as a Western ranch. . . . When he returned to the house, looking grim and disappointed, the others were all conscious, making mewing little sounds and holding their heads like scared children.

"Queen, for God's sake," began Gardner hoarsely.

"Whoever it was used that Luminal in the lavatory upstairs," said Ellery, flinging his hat away and wincing at a sudden pain in his head. "The stuff Mrs. Mansfield gave Mrs. Owen yesterday to make her sleep. Except that almost the whole of that large bottle was used. Swell sleeping draught! Make yourselves comfortable while I conduct a little investigation in the kitchen. I think it was the Java." But when he returned he was grimacing. "No luck. *Madame la Cuisinière,* it seems, had to visit the bathroom at one period; Millan was out in the garage looking at the cars; and the maid was off somewhere, doubtless primping. Result: our friend the Luminalist had an opportunity to pour most of the powder from the bottle into the coffeepot. Damn!"

"I *am* going to call the police!" cried Mrs. Mansfield hysterically, striving to rise. "We'll be murdered in our beds, next thing we know! Laura, I positively insist — "

"Please, please, Mrs. Mansfield," said Ellery wearily. "No heroics. And you would be of greater service if you went into the kitchen and checked the insurrection that's brewing there. The two females are on the verge of packing, I'll swear."

Mrs. Mansfield bit her lip and flounced off. They heard her no longer sweet voice raised in remonstrance a moment later.

"But, Queen," protested Gardner, "we can't go unprotected — "

"What I want to know in my infantile way," drawled Emmy Willowes from pale lips, "is who did it, and why. That bottle upstairs . . . It looks uncomfortably like one of us, doesn't it?"

Mrs. Gardner gave a little shriek. Mrs. Owen sank back into her chair.

"One of us?" whispered the red-haired woman.

Ellery smiled without humor. Then his smile faded and he cocked his head toward the foyer. "What was that?" he snapped.

They turned, terror-stricken, and looked. But there was nothing to see. Ellery strode toward the front door.

"What is it now, for heaven's sake?" faltered Mrs. Owen.

"I thought I heard a sound —" He flung the door open. The early morning sun streamed in. Then they saw him stoop and pick up something from the porch and rise and look swiftly about outside. But he shook his head and stepped back, closing the door.

"Package," he said with a frown. "I *thought* someone . . ."

They looked blankly at the brown-paper bundle in his hands. "Package?" asked Mrs. Owen. Her face lit up. "Oh, it may be from Richard!" And then the light went out, to be replaced by fearful pallor. "Oh, do you think — ?"

"It's addressed," said Ellery slowly, "to you, Mrs. Owen. No stamp, no postmark, written in pencil in disguised block letters. I think I'll take the liberty of opening this, Mrs. Owen." He broke the feeble twine and tore away the wrapping of the crude parcel. And then he frowned even more deeply. For the package contained only a pair of large men's shoes, worn at the heels and soles — sport Oxfords in tan and white.

Mrs. Owen rolled her eyes, her nostrils quivering with nausea. "Richard's!" she gasped. And she sank back, half-fainting.

"Indeed?" murmured Ellery. "How interesting. Not, of course, the shoes he wore Friday night. You're positive they're his, Mrs. Owen?"

"Oh, he *has* been kidnaped!" quavered Mrs. Mansfield from the rear doorway. "Isn't there a note, b-blood . . ."

"Nothing but the shoes. I doubt the kidnap theory now, Mrs. Mansfield. These weren't the shoes Owen wore Friday night. When did you see these last, Mrs. Owen?"

She moaned: "In his wardrobe closet upstairs only yesterday afternoon."

"There. You see?" said Ellery cheerfully. "Probably stolen from the closet while we were all unconscious last night. And now returned rather spectacularly. So far, you know, there's been no harm done. I'm afraid," he said with severity, "we're nursing a viper at our bosoms."

But they did not laugh. Miss Willowes said strangely: "Very odd. In fact, insane, Mr. Queen. I can't see the slightest purpose in it."

"Nor I, at the moment. Somebody's either playing a monstrous prank, or there's a devilishly clever and warped mentality behind all this." He retrieved his hat and made for the door.

"Wherever are you going?" gasped Mrs. Gardner.

"Oh, out for a thinking spell under God's blue canopy. But re-member," he added quietly, "that's a privilege reserved to detectives. No one is to set foot outside this house."

He returned an hour later without explanation.

At noon they found the second package. It was a squarish parcel wrapped in the same brown paper. Inside there was a cardboard carton, and in the carton, packed in crumpled tissue paper, there were two magnificent toy sailing boats such as children race on summer lakes. The package was addressed to Miss Willowes.

"This is getting dreadful," murmured Mrs. Gardner, her full lips trembling. "I'm all goose pimples."

"I'd feel better," muttered Miss Willowes, "if it was a bloody dag-ger, or something. Toy boats!" She stepped back and her eyes nar-rowed. "Now, look here, good people, I'm as much a sport as any-body, but a joke's a joke and I'm just a bit fed up on this particular one. Who's manœuvring these monkeyshines?"

"Joke," snarled Gardner. He was white as death. "It's the work of a madman, I tell you!"

"Now, now," murmured Ellery, staring at the green-and-cream boats. "We shan't get anywhere this way. Mrs. Owen, have you ever seen these before?"

Mrs. Owen, on the verge of collapse, mumbled: "Oh, my good dear God. Mr. Queen, I don't — Why, they're — they're Jona-than's!"

Ellery blinked. Then he went to the foot of the stairway and yelled: "Johnny! Come down here a minute."

Master Jonathan descended sluggishly, sulkily. "What you want?" he asked in a cold voice.

"Come here, son." Master Jonathan came with dragging feet. "When did you see these boats of yours last?"

"Boats!" shrieked Master Jonathan, springing into life. He

pounced on them and snatched them away, glaring at Ellery. "My boats! Never seen such a place. My boats! You stole 'em!"

"Come, come," said Ellery, flushing, "be a good little man. When did you see them last?"

"Yest'day! In my toy chest! My boats! Scan'lous," hissed Master Jonathan, and fled upstairs, hugging his boats to his scrawny breast.

"Stolen at the same time," said Ellery helplessly. "By thunder, Miss Willowes, I'm almost inclined to agree with you. By the way, who bought those boats for your son, Mrs. Owen?"

"H-his father."

"Damn," said Ellery for the second time that impious Sunday, and he sent them all on a search of the house to ascertain if anything else were missing. But no one could find that anything had been taken.

It was when they came down from upstairs that they found Ellery regarding a small white envelope with puzzlement.

"Now what?" demanded Gardner wildly.

"Stuck in the door," he said thoughtfully. "Hadn't noticed it before. This *is* a queer one."

It was a rich piece of stationery, sealed with blue wax on the back and bearing the same penciled scrawl, this time addressed to Mrs. Mansfield.

The old lady collapsed in the nearest chair, holding her hand to her heart. She was speechless with fear.

"Well," said Mrs. Gardner huskily, "open it."

Ellery tore open the envelope. His frown deepened. "Why," he muttered, "there's nothing at all inside!"

Gardner gnawed his fingers and turned away, mumbling. Mrs. Gardner shook her head like a dazed pugilist and stumbled toward the bar for the fifth time that day. Emmy Willowes's brow was dark as thunder.

"You know," said Mrs. Owen almost quietly, "that's Mother's stationery."

Ellery muttered: "Queerer and queerer. I *must* get this organized. . . . The shoes are a puzzler. The toy boats might be construed as a gift; yesterday was Jonathan's birthday; the boats are his — a distorted practical joke. . . ." He shook his head. "Doesn't wash. And this third — an envelope without a letter in it. That would seem to point to the envelope as the important thing. But the envelope's the property of Mrs. Mansfield. The only other thing — ah, the wax!" He scanned the blue blob on the back narrowly, but it bore no seal-insignia of any kind.

"That," said Mrs. Owen again in the quiet unnatural voice, "looks like our wax, too, Mr. Queen, from the library."

Ellery dashed away, followed by a troubled company. Mrs. Owen went to the library desk and opened the top drawer.

"Was it here?" asked Ellery quickly.

"Yes," she said, and then her voice quivered. "I used it only Friday when I wrote a letter. Oh, good . . ."

There was no stick of wax in the drawer.

And while they stared at the drawer, the front doorbell rang.

It was a market basket this time, lying innocently on the porch. In it, nestling crisp and green, were two large cabbages.

Ellery shouted for Gardner and Millan, and himself led the charge down the steps. They scattered, searching wildly through the brush and woods surrounding the house. But they found nothing. No sign of the bell ringer, no sign of the ghost who had cheerfully left a basket of cabbages at the door as his fourth odd gift. It was as if he were made of smoke and materialized only for the instant he needed to press his impalpable finger to the bell.

They found the women huddled in a corner of the living room, shivering and white-lipped. Mrs. Mansfield, shaking like an aspen, was at the telephone ringing for the local police. Ellery started to protest, shrugged, set his lips, and stooped over the basket.

There was a slip of paper tied by string to the handle of the basket. The same crude pencil scrawl. . . . "Mr. Paul Gardner."

"Looks," muttered Ellery, "as if you're elected, old fellow, this time."

Gardner stared as if he could not believe his eyes. "Cabbages!"

"Excuse me," said Ellery curtly. He went away. When he returned he was shrugging. "From the vegetable bin in the outside pantry, says Cook. She hadn't thought to look for missing *vegetables,* she told me with scorn."

Mrs. Mansfield was babbling excitedly over the telephone to a sorely puzzled officer of the law. When she hung up she was red as a newborn baby. "That will be *quite* enough of this crazy nonsense, Mr. Queen!" she snarled. And then she collapsed in a chair and laughed hysterically and shrieked: "Oh, I knew you were making the mistake of your life when you married that beast, Laura!" and laughed again like a madwoman.

The law arrived in fifteen minutes, accompanied by a howling siren and personified by a stocky, brick-faced man in chief's stripes and a gangling young policeman.

"I'm Naughton," he said shortly. "What the devil's goin' on here?"

Ellery said: "Ah, Chief Naughton. I'm Queen's son — Inspector Richard Queen of Centre Street. How d'ye do?"

"Oh!" said Naughton. He turned on Mrs. Mansfield sternly. "Why didn't you say Mr. Queen was here, Mrs. Mansfield? You ought to know — "

"Oh, I'm sick of the lot of you!" screamed the old lady. "Nonsense, nonsense, nonsense from the instant this week-end began! First that awful actress-woman there, in her short skirt and legs and things, and then this — this — "

Naughton rubbed his chin. "Come over here, Mr. Queen, where we can talk like human beings. What the deuce happened?"

Ellery with a sigh told him. As he spoke, the Chief's face grew redder and redder. "You mean you're serious about this business?" he rumbled at last. "It sounds plain crazy to me. Mr. Owen's gone off his nut and he's playing jokes on you people. Good God, you can't take this thing serious!"

"I'm afraid," murmured Ellery, "we must. . . . What's that? By heaven, if that's another manifestation of our playful ghost — !" And he dashed toward the door while Naughton gaped and pulled it open, to be struck by a wave of dusk. On the porch lay the fifth parcel, a tiny one this time.

The two officers darted out of the house, flashlights blinking and probing. Ellery picked up the packet with eager fingers. It was addressed in the now familiar scrawl to Mrs. Paul Gardner. Inside were two identically shaped objects: chessmen, kings. One was white and the other was black.

"Who plays chess here?" he drawled.

"Richard," shrieked Mrs. Owen. "Oh, my God, I'm going mad!"
Investigation proved that the two kings from Richard Owen's
chess-set were gone.

The local officers came back, rather pale, and panting. They had
found no one outside. Ellery was silently studying the two chessmen.

"Well?" said Naughton, drooping his shoulders.

"Well," said Ellery quietly. "I have the most brilliant notion,
Naughton. Come here a moment." He drew Naughton aside and
began to speak rapidly in a low voice. The others stood limply
about, twitching with nervousness. There was no longer any pretense of self-control. If this was a joke, it was a ghastly one indeed.
And Richard Owen looming in the background . . .

The Chief blinked and nodded. "You people," he said shortly,
turning to them, "get into that library there." They gaped. "I mean
it! The lot of you. This tomfoolery is going to stop right now."

"But, Naughton," gasped Mrs. Mansfield, "it couldn't be any of
us who sent those things. Mr. Queen will tell you we weren't out
of his sight today — "

"Do as I say, Mrs. Mansfield," snapped the officer.

They trooped, puzzled, into the library. The policeman rounded
up Millan, the cook, the maid, and went with them. Nobody said
anything; nobody looked at anyone else. Minutes passed; a half-
hour; an hour. There was the silence of the grave from beyond the
door to the living room. They strained their ears. . . .

At seven-thirty the door was jerked open and Ellery and the Chief
glowered in on them. "Everybody out," said Naughton shortly.
"Come on, step on it."

"Out?" whispered Mrs. Owen. "Where? Where is Richard?
What — "

The policeman herded them out. Ellery stepped to the door of the
den and pushed it open and switched on the light and stood aside.

"Will you please come in here and take seats," he said dryly; there
was a tense look on his face and he seemed exhausted.

Silently, slowly, they obeyed. The policeman dragged in extra
chairs from the living room. They sat down. Naughton drew the
shades. The policeman closed the door and set his back against it.

Ellery said tonelessly: "In a way this has been one of the most remarkable cases in my experience. It's been unorthodox from every angle. Utterly nonconforming. I think, Miss Willowes, the wish you expressed Friday night has come true. You're about to witness a slightly cock-eyed exercise in criminal ingenuity."

"Crim — " Mrs. Gardner's full lips quivered. "You mean — there's been a crime?"

"Quiet," said Naughton harshly.

"Yes," said Ellery in gentle tones, "there has been a crime. I might say — I'm sorry to say, Mrs. Owen — a major crime."

"Richard's d — "

"I'm sorry." There was a little silence. Mrs. Owen did not weep; she seemed dried out of tears. "Fantastic," said Ellery at last. "Look here." He sighed. "The crux of the problem was the clock. The Clock That Wasn't Where It Should Have Been, the clock with the invisible face. You remember I pointed out that, since I hadn't seen the reflection of the luminous hands in that mirror there, the clock must have been moved. That was a tenable theory. But it wasn't the *only* theory."

"Richard's dead," said Mrs. Owen, in a wondering voice.

"Mr. Gardner," continued Ellery quickly, "pointed out one possibility: that the clock may still have been over this door, but that something or someone may have been standing in front of the mirror. I told you why that was impossible. But," and he went suddenly to the tall mirror, "there was still another theory which accounted for the fact that I hadn't seen the luminous hands' reflection. And that was: that when I opened the door in the dark and peered in and saw nothing, the clock was still there but the *mirror* wasn't!"

Miss Willowes said with a curious dryness: "But how could that be, Mr. Queen? That — that's silly."

"Nothing is silly, dear lady, until it is proved so. I said to myself: How could it be that the mirror wasn't there at that instant? It's apparently a solid part of the wall, a built-in section in this modern room." Something glimmered in Miss Willowes's eyes. Mrs. Mansfield was staring straight before her, hands clasped tightly in her lap. Mrs. Owen was looking at Ellery with glazed eyes, blind and deaf. "Then," said Ellery with another sigh, "there was the very odd nature of the packages which have been descending upon us all day like manna from heaven. I said this was a fantastic affair. Of course it must have occurred to you that someone was trying desperately to call our attention to the secret of the crime."

"Call our at — " began Gardner, frowning.

"Precisely. Now, Mrs. Owen," murmured Ellery softly, "the first package was addressed to you. What did it contain?" She stared at him without expression. There was a dreadful silence. Mrs. Mansfield suddenly shook her, as if she had been a child. She started, smiled vaguely; Ellery repeated the question.

And she said, almost brightly: "A pair of Richard's sport Oxfords."

He winced. "In a word, *shoes*. Miss Willowes," and despite her nonchalance she stiffened a little, "you were the recipient of the second package. And what did that contain?"

"Jonathan's toy boats," she murmured.

"In a word, again — *ships*. Mrs. Mansfield, the third package was sent to you. It contained what, precisely?"

"Nothing." She tossed her head. "I still think this is the purest drivel. Can't you see you're driving my daughter — all of us — insane? Naughton, are you going to permit this farce to continue? If you know what's happened to Richard, for goodness' sake tell us!"

"Answer the question," said Naughton with a scowl.

"Well," she said defiantly, "a silly envelope, empty, and sealed with our own wax."

"And again in a word," drawled Ellery, "*sealing-wax*. Now, Gardner, to you fell the really whimsical fourth bequest. It was — ?"

"Cabbage," said Gardner with an uncertain grin.

"Cabba*ges,* my dear chap; there were two of them. And finally, Mrs. Gardner, you received what?"

"Two chessmen," she whispered.

"No, no. Not just two chessmen, Mrs. Gardner. Two *kings*." Ellery's gray eyes glittered. "In other words, in the order named we were bombarded with gifts . . ." he paused and looked at them, and continued softly, "*'of shoes and ships and sealing-wax, of cabbages and kings.'*"

There was the most extraordinary silence. Then Emmy Willowes gasped: "'The Walrus and the Carpenter.' *Alice's Adventures in Wonderland!*"

"I'm ashamed of you, Miss Willowes. Where precisely does Tweedledee's Walrus speech come in Carroll's duology?"

A great light broke over her eager features. "*Through the Looking Glass!*"

"*Through the Looking Glass,*" murmured Ellery in the crackling silence that followed. "And do you know what the subtitle of *Through the Looking Glass* is?"

She said in an awed voice: "*And What Alice Found There.*"

"A perfect recitation, Miss Willowes. We were instructed, then, to go through the looking glass and, by inference, find something on the other side connected with the disappearance of Richard Owen. Quaint idea, eh?" He leaned forward and said brusquely: "Let me revert to my original chain of reasoning. I said that a likely theory was that the mirror didn't reflect the luminous hands because the mirror wasn't there. But since the wall at any rate is solid, the mirror itself must be movable to have been shifted out of place. How was this possible? Yesterday I sought for two hours to find the secret of that mirror — or should I say . . . looking glass?" Their eyes went with horror to the tall mirror set in the wall, winking back at them in the glitter of the bulbs. "And when I discovered the secret, I looked *through the looking glass* and what do you suppose I — a clumsy Alice, indeed! — found there?"

No one replied.

Ellery went swiftly to the mirror, stood on tiptoe, touched something, and something happened to the whole glass. It moved forward as if on hinges. He hooked his fingers in the crack and pulled. The mirror, like a door, swung out and away, revealing a shallow closet-like cavity.

The women with one breath screamed and covered their eyes.

The stiff figure of the Mad Hatter, with Richard Owen's unmistakable features, glared out at them — a dead, horrible, baleful glare.

Paul Gardner stumbled to his feet, choking and jerking at his collar. His eyes bugged out of his head. "O-O-Owen," he gasped. "Owen. He *can't* be here. I b-b-buried him myself under the big rock behind the house in the woods. Oh, my God." And he smiled a dreadful smile and his eyes turned over and he collapsed in a faint on the floor.

Ellery sighed. "It's all right now, De Vere," and the Mad Hatter

moved and his features ceased to resemble Richard Owen's magi-
cally. "You may come out now. Admirable bit of statuary histrionics.
And it turned the trick, as I thought it would. There's your man,
Mr. Naughton. And if you'll question Mrs. Gardner, I believe
you'll find that she's been Owen's mistress for some time. Gardner
obviously found it out and killed him. Look out — there *she* goes,
too!"

"What I can't understand," murmured Emmy Willowes after a
long silence late that night, as she and Mr. Ellery Queen sat side
by side in the local bound for Jamaica and the express for Pennsylvania Station, "is — " She stopped helplessly. "I can't understand
so many things, Mr. Queen."

"It was simple enough," said Ellery wearily, staring out the window at the rushing dark countryside.

"But who is that man — that De Vere?"

"Oh, he! A Thespian acquaintance of mine temporarily 'at liberty.' He's an actor — does character bits. You wouldn't know him,
I suppose. You see, when my deductions had led me to the looking
glass and I examined it and finally discovered its secret and opened
it, I found Owen's body lying there in the Hatter costume — "

She shuddered. "Much too realistic drama to my taste. Why didn't
you announce your discovery at once?"

"And gain what? There wasn't a shred of evidence against the
murderer. I wanted time to think out a plan to make the murderer
give himself away. I left the body there — "

"You mean to sit there and say you knew Gardner did it all the
time?" she demanded, frankly skeptical.

He shrugged. "Of course. The Owens had lived in that house
barely a month. The spring on that compartment is remarkably well
concealed; it probably would never be discovered unless you knew
it existed and were looking for it. But I recalled that Owen himself
had remarked Friday night that Gardner had designed 'this development.' I had it then, naturally. Who more likely than the architect to know the secret of such a hidden closet? Why he designed
and had built a secret panel I don't know; I suppose it fitted into
some architectural whim of his. So it had to be Gardner, you see."
He gazed thoughtfully at the dusty ceiling of the car. "I recon-

structed the crime easily enough. After we retired Friday night Gardner came down to have it out with Owen about Mrs. Gardner —a lusty wench, if I ever saw one. They had words; Gardner killed him. It must have been an unpremeditated crime. His first impulse was to hide the body. He couldn't take it out Friday night in that awful rain without leaving traces on his night clothes. Then he remembered the panel behind the mirror. The body would be safe enough there, he felt, until he could remove it, when the rain stopped and the ground dried, to a permanent hiding place; dig a grave, or whatnot. . . . He was stowing the body away in the closet when I opened the door of the den; that was why I didn't see the reflection of the clock. Then, while I was in the library, he closed the mirror door and dodged upstairs. I came out quickly, though, and he decided to brazen it out; even pretended he thought I might be 'Owen' coming up.

"At any rate, Saturday night he drugged us all, took the body out, buried it, and came back and dosed himself with the drug to make his part as natural as possible. He didn't know I had found the body behind the mirror Saturday afternoon. When, Sunday morning, I found the body gone, I knew of course the reason for the drugging. Gardner by burying the body in a place unknown to anyone — without leaving, as far as he knew, even a clue to the fact that murder had been committed at all — was naturally doing away with the primary piece of evidence in any murder case . . . the *corpus delicti*. . . . Well, I found the opportunity to telephone De Vere and instruct him in what he had to do. He dug up the Hatter's costume somewhere, managed to get a photo of Owen from a theatrical office, came down here. . . . We put him in the closet while Naughton's man was detaining you people in the library. You see, I had to build up suspense, make Gardner give himself away, break down his moral resistance. He had to be forced to disclose where he had buried the body; and he was the only one who could tell us. It worked."

The actress regarded him sidewise out of her clever eyes. Ellery sighed moodily, glancing away from her slim legs outstretched to the opposite seat. "But the most puzzling thing of all," she said with a pretty frown. "Those perfectly fiendish and fantastic packages. Who sent them, for heaven's sake?"

Ellery did not reply for a long time. Then he said drowsily, barely audible above the clatter of the train: "You did, really."

"*I?*" She was so startled that her mouth flew open.

"Only in a manner of speaking," murmured Ellery, closing his eyes. "Your idea about running a mad tea party out of *Alice* for Master Jonathan's delectation — the whole pervading spirit of the Reverend Dodgson — started a chain of fantasy in my own brain, you see. Just opening the closet and saying that Owen's body had been there, or even getting De Vere to act as Owen, wasn't enough. I had to prepare Gardner's mind psychologically, fill him with puzzlement first, get him to realize after a while where the gifts with their implications were leading. . . . Had to torture him, I suppose. It's a weakness of mine. At any rate, it was an easy matter to telephone my father, the Inspector; and he sent Sergeant Velie down and I managed to smuggle all those things I'd filched from the house out into the woods behind and hand good Velie what I had. . . . He did the rest, packaging and all."

She sat up and measured him with a severe glance. "*Mr.* Queen! Is that cricket in the best detective circles?"

He grinned sleepily. "Drama, Miss Willowes. You ought to be able to understand that. Surround a murderer with things he doesn't understand, bewilder him, get him mentally punch-drunk, and then spring the knock-out blow, the crusher. . . . Oh, it was devilish clever of me, I admit."

She regarded him for so long and in such silence and with such supple twisting of her boyish figure that he stirred uncomfortably. "And what, if I may ask," he said lightly, "brings that positively lewd expression to your Peter Pannish face? You must be feeling — "

"As Alice would say," she said softly, leaning a little toward him, "curiouser and curiouser."

THE CRIME IN NOBODY'S ROOM

by CARTER DICKSON

The Great Detectives section of our collection begins with an American — Poe — and ends with an American — Dickson (who was born in Uniontown, Pennsylvania, although today he lives in England and writes about England). COLONEL MARCH's *début between covers of a book came in 1940, thus rounding out the First Hundred Years most agreeably.* MARCH *is a vital character, and a welcome newcomer to the charmed circle of The Great Detectives.*

Bands were playing and seven suns were shining; but this took place entirely in the head and heart of Mr. Ronald Denham. He beamed on the car-park attendant at the Regency Club, who assisted him into the taxi. He beamed on the taxidriver. He beamed on the night porter who helped him out at his flat in Sloane Street, and he felt an irresistible urge to hand banknotes to everyone in sight.

Now, Ronald Denham would have denied that he had taken too many drinks. It was true that he had attended an excellent bachelor party, to celebrate Jimmy Bellchester's wedding. But Denham would have maintained that he was upheld by spiritual things; and he had proved his exalted temperance by leaving the party at a time when many of the guests were still present.

As he had pointed out in a speech, it was only a month before his own wedding to Miss Anita Bruce. Anita, in fact, lived in the same block of flats and on the same floor as himself. This fact gave him great pleasure on the way home. Like most of us, Denham in this mood felt a strong urge to wake people up in the middle of the night and talk to them. He wondered whether he ought to wake up Anita. But in his reformed state he decided against it, and felt like a saint. He would not even wake up Tom Evans, who shared the flat with him — though that stern young business man usually worked so late at the office that Denham got in before he did.

At a few minutes short of midnight, then, Denham steered his way into the foyer of Medici Court. Pearson, the night porter, followed him to the automatic lift.

"Everything all right, sir?" inquired Pearson in a stage whisper. Denham assured him that it was, and that he was an excellent fellow.

"You — er — don't feel like singing, do you, sir?" asked Pearson with some anxiety.

"As a matter of fact," said Denham, who had not previously considered this, "I do. You are full of excellent ideas, Pearson. But let us sing nothing improper, Pearson. Let it be something of noble sentiment, like —— "

"Honestly, sir," urged Pearson, "if it was me, I wouldn't do it. *He's* upstairs, you know. We thought he was going to Manchester this afternoon, to stay a week, but he changed his mind. He's upstairs now."

This terrible hint referred to the autocrat of Medici Court, Cellini Court, Bourbon Court, and half a dozen other great hives. Sir Rufus Armingdale, high khan of builders, not only filled London with furnished flats which really were the last word in luxury at a low price: he showed his pride in his own merchandise by living in them.

"No special quarters for me," he was quoted as saying, with fist upraised for emphasis. "No castle in Surrey or barracks in Park Lane. Just an ordinary flat; and not the most expensive of 'em either. That's where I'm most comfortable, and that's where you'll find me."

Considering all the good things provided in Armingdale's Furnished Flats, even his autocratic laws were not much resented. Nor could anyone resent the fact that all the flats in a given building were furnished exactly alike, and that the furniture must be kept in the position Rufus Armingdale gave it. Medici Court was "Renaissance," as Bourbon Court was "Louis XV": a tower of rooms like luxurious cells, and only to be distinguished from each other by an ornament on a table or a picture on a wall.

But Sir Rufus's leases even discouraged pictures. Considering that he was something of an art collector himself, and had often been photographed in his own flat with his favourite Greuze or Corot, some annoyance was felt at this. Sir Rufus Armingdale did not care. You either leased one of his flats, or you didn't. He was that sort of man.

Otherwise, of course, Ronald Denham's adventure could not have happened. He returned from the bachelor party; he took Pearson's advice about the singing; he went up in the automatic lift to the second floor; and he walked into what the champagne told him was his own flat.

That he went to the second floor is certain. Pearson saw him put his finger on the proper button in the lift. But nothing else is certain, since the hall upstairs was dark. Pushing open a door — either his key fitted it or the door was open — Denham congratulated himself on getting home.

Also, he was a little giddy. He found himself in the small foyer, where lights were on. After a short interval he must have moved into the sitting room, for he found himself sitting back in an armchair and contemplating familiar surroundings through a haze. Lights were turned on here as well: yellow-shaded lamps, one with a pattern like a dragon on the shade.

Something began to trouble him. There was something odd, he thought, about those lamp shades. After some study, it occurred to him that he and Tom Evans hadn't any lamp shades like that. They did not own any bronze book ends either. As for the curtains . . .

Then a picture on the wall swam out of oblivion, and he stared at it. It was a small dull-coloured picture over the sideboard. And it penetrated into his mind at last that he had got into the wrong flat.

Everything now showed itself to him as wrong: it was as though a blur had come into focus.

"Here, I'm sorry!" he said aloud, and got up.

There was no reply. The heinousness of his offence partly steadied him. Where in the name of sanity was he? There were only three other flats on the second floor. One of these was Anita Bruce's. Of the others, one was occupied by a brisk young newspaper man named Conyers, and the other by the formidable Sir Rufus Armingdale.

Complete panic caught him. He felt that at any moment a wrathful occupant might descend on him, to call him a thief at worst or a snooper at best. Turning round to scramble for the door, he almost ran into another visitor in the wrong flat.

This visitor sat quietly in a tall chair near the door. He was a thin, oldish, well-dressed man, wearing thick-lensed spectacles, and his head was bent forward as though in meditation. He wore a soft hat and a thin oilskin waterproof coloured green: a jaunty and bilious-looking coat for such a quiet figure. The quiet light made it gleam.

"Please excuse —— " Denham began in a rush, and talked for some seconds before he realized that the man had not moved.

Denham stretched out his hand. The coat was one of those smooth, almost seamless American waterproofs, yellowish outside and green inside; and for some reason the man was now wearing it inside out. Denham was in the act of telling him this when the head lolled, the smooth oilskin gleamed again, and he saw that the man was dead.

Tom Evans, stepping out of the lift at a quarter past one, found the hall of the second floor in complete darkness. When he had turned on the lights from a switch beside the lift, he stopped short and swore.

Evans, lean and swarthy, with darkish eyebrows merging into a single line across his forehead, looked a little like a Norman baron in a romance. Some might have said a robber baron, for he carried a brief case and was a stern man of business despite his youth. But what he saw now made him momentarily forget his evening's work. The hall showed four doors, with their microscopic black numbers, set some distance apart. Near the door leading to Anita Bruce's flat, Ronald Denham sat hunched on an oak settle. There was a lump at the base of his skull, and he was breathing in a way Evans did not like.

It was five minutes more before Denham had been whacked and pounded into semi-consciousness; and to such a blinding headache that its pain helped to revive him. First he became aware of Tom's lean, hook-nosed face bending over him, and Tom's usual fluency at preaching.

"I don't mind you getting drunk," the voice came to him dimly. "In fact, I expected it. But at least you ought to be able to carry your liquor decently. What the devil have you been up to, anyway? Hoy!"

"He had his raincoat on inside out," was the first thing Denham said. Then memory came back to him like a new headache or a new explosion, and he began to pour out the story.

"—— and I tell you there's a dead man in one of those flats! I think he's been murdered. Tom, I'm not drunk; I swear I'm not. Somebody sneaked up behind and bashed me over the back of the head just after I found him."

"Then how did you get out here?"

"Oh, God, how should I know? Don't argue; help me up. I suppose I must have been dragged out here. If you don't believe me, feel the back of my head. Just feel it."

Evans hesitated. He was always practical, and there could be no denying the bruise. He looked uncertainly up and down the hall.

"But who is this dead man?" he demanded. "And whose flat is he in?"

"I don't know. He was an oldish man with thick glasses and a green raincoat. I never saw him before. Looked a bit like an American, somehow."

"Nonsense! Nobody wears a green raincoat."

"I'm telling you, he was wearing it inside out. If you ask me why, I'm going to bat my head against the wall and go to sleep again." He wished he could do this, for he could not see straight and his head felt like a printing press in full blast. "We ought to be able to identify the flat easily enough. I can give a complete description of it —— "

He paused, for two doors had opened simultaneously in the hall. Anita Bruce and Sir Rufus Armingdale came out, in different stages of anger or curiosity at the noise.

If Evans had been more of a psychologist, he might have anticipated the effect this would have on them. As it was, he stood looking from one to the other, thinking whatever thoughts you care to attribute to him. For he was an employee of Sir Rufus, as manager of the Sloane Square Office of Armingdale Flats, and he could risk no trouble.

Anita seemed to take in the situation at a glance. She was small, dark, plump, and fluffy-haired. She was wearing a négligé and smoking a cigarette. Seeing the expressions of the other three, she removed the cigarette from her mouth in order to smile. Sir Rufus Armingdale did not look so much formidable as fretful. He had one of those powerful faces whose features seem to have run to-gether like a bull pup's. But the old dressing gown, fastened up at the throat as though he were cold, took away the suggestion of an autocrat and made him only a householder.

He breathed through his nose, rather helplessly, until he saw an employee. His confidence returned.

"Good morning, Evans," he said. "What's the meaning of this?"

Evans risked it. "I'm afraid it's trouble, sir. Mr. Denham — well, he's found a dead man in one of the flats."

"Ron!" cried Anita.

"A dead man," repeated Armingdale, without surprise. "Where?"

"In one of the flats. He doesn't know which."

"Oh? Why doesn't he know which?"

"He's got a frightful bump on the back of his head," said Anita, exploring. She looked back over her shoulder and spoke swiftly. "It's quite all right, Tom. Don't get excited. He's d-r-u-n-k."

"I am not drunk," said Denham, with tense and sinister calm-ness. "May I also point out that I am able to read and write, and that I have not had words spelled out in front of me since I was four years old? Heaven give me s-t-r-e-n-g-t-h! I tell you, I can de-scribe the place."

He did so. Afterwards there was a silence. Anita, her eyes shining curiously, dropped her cigarette on the autocrat's hardwood floor and ground it out. The autocrat seemed too abstracted to notice.

"Ron, old dear," Anita said, going over and sitting down beside him, "I'll believe you if you're as serious as all that. But you ought to know it isn't *my* flat."

"And I can tell you it isn't mine," grunted Armingdale. "There certainly isn't a dead man in it. I've just come from there, and I know."

If they had not known Armingdale's reputation so well, they might have suspected him of trying to make a joke. But his expression belied it as well. It was heavy and lowering, with more than a suggestion of the bull pup.

"This picture you say you saw," he began. "The one over the sideboard. Could you describe it?"

"Yes, I think so," said Denham desperately. "It was a rather small portrait of a little girl looking sideways over some roses, or flowers of some kind. Done in that greyish-brown stuff; I think they call it sepia."

Armingdale stared at him.

"Then I know it isn't mine," he said. "I never owned a sepia drawing in my life. If this young man is telling the truth, there's only one flat left. I think I shall just take the responsibility of knocking, and —— "

His worried gaze moved down towards the door of the flat occupied by Mr. Hubert Conyers, of the *Daily Record*. But it was unnecessary to knock at the door. It opened with such celerity that Denham wondered whether anyone had been looking at them through the slot of the letter box; and Hubert Conyers stepped out briskly. He was an unobtrusive, sandy-haired little man, very different from Denham's idea of a journalist. His only extravagance was a taste for blended shadings in his clothes, from suit to shirt to necktie; though he usually contrived to look rumpled. He was always obliging, and as busy as a parlour clock. But his manner had a subdued persuasiveness which could worm him through narrower places than you might have imagined.

He came forward drawing on his coat, and with a deft gesture he got into the middle of the group.

"Sorry, sorry, sorry," he began, seeming to propitiate everyone at once. "I couldn't help overhearing, you know. Good evening, Sir Rufus. The fact is, it's not my flat either. Just now, the only ornaments in my sitting room are a lot of well-filled ashtrays and a bottle of milk. Come and see, if you like."

There was a silence, while Conyers looked anxious.

"But it's got to be somebody's flat!" snapped Sir Rufus Armingdale, with a no-nonsense air. "Stands to reason. A whole confounded sitting room can't vanish like smoke. Unless — stop a bit — unless Mr. Denham got off at some other floor."

"I don't know. I may have."

"And I don't mind admitting —— " said Armingdale, hesitating as everyone looked at him curiously. The autocrat seemed worried. "Very well. The fact is, *I've* got a picture in my flat something like the one Mr. Denham described. It's Greuze's 'Young Girl with Primroses.' But mine's an oil painting, of course. Mr. Denham is talking about a sepia drawing. That is, if he really saw anything. Does this dead man exist at all?"

Denham's protestations were cut short by the hum of an ascending lift. But it was not the ordinary lift in front of them; it was the service lift at the end of the hall. The door was opened, and the cage grating pulled back, to show the frightened face of the night porter.

"Sir," said Pearson, addressing Armingdale as though he were beginning an oration. "I'm glad to see *you*, sir. You always tell us that if something serious happens we're to come straight to you instead of the manager. Well, I'm afraid this is serious. I — the fact is, I found something in this lift."

Denham felt that they were being haunted by that phrase, "the fact is." Everybody seemed to use it. He recalled a play in which it was maintained that anyone who began a sentence like this was usually telling a lie. But he had not time to think about this, for they had found the elusive dead man.

The unknown lay on his face in one corner of the lift. A light in the roof of the steel cage shone down on his grey felt hat, on an edge of his thick spectacles, and on his oilskin waterproof. But the coat was no longer green, for he was now wearing it right-side-out in the ordinary way.

Anita, who had come quietly round beside Denham, seized his arm. The night porter restrained Tom Evans as the latter bent forward.

"I shouldn't touch him, sir, if I was you. There's blood."

"Where?"

Pearson indicated a stain on the grey-rubber floor. "And if I'm any judge, sir, he died of a stab through the heart. I — I lifted him up a bit. But I don't see any kind of knife that could have done it."

"Is this the man you saw?" Armingdale asked Denham quietly.

Denham nodded. Something tangible, something to weigh and handle, seemed to have brought the force back to Armingdale's personality.

"Except," Denham added, "that he's now wearing his raincoat right-side-out. Why? Will somebody tell me that? Why?"

"Never mind the raincoat," Anita said close to his ear. "Ron, you don't know him, do you? You'll swear you don't know him?"

He was startled. She had spoken without apparent urgency, and so low that the others might not have heard her. But Denham, who knew her so well, knew that there was urgency behind the unwinking seriousness of her eyes. Unconsciously she was shaking his arm. His wits had begun to clear, despite the pain in his skull; and he wondered.

"No, of course I don't know him. Why should I?"

"Nothing! Nothing at all. Ss-t!"

"Well, I know him," said Hubert Conyers.

Conyers had been squatting down at the edge of the lift, and craning his neck to get a close view of the body without touching it. Now he straightened up. He seemed so excited that he could barely control himself, and his mild eye looked wicked.

"I interviewed him a couple of days ago," said Conyers. "Surely you know him, Sir Rufus?"

"'Surely' is a large word, young man. No, I do not know him. Why?"

"That's Dan Randolph, the American real-estate king," said Conyers, keeping a watchful eye on Armingdale. "All of you will have heard of him: he's the fellow who always deals in spot cash, even if it's a million. I'd know those spectacles anywhere. He's as near-sighted as an owl. Er — am I correctly informed, Sir Rufus, that he was in England to do some business with you?"

Armingdale smiled bleakly. "You have no information, young man," he said. "And so far as I'm concerned you're not getting any. So that's Dan Randolph! I knew he was in England; but he's certainly not made any business proposition to me."

"Maybe he was coming to do it."

"Maybe he was," said Armingdale, with the same air of a parent to a child. He turned to Pearson. "You say you found him in that lift. When did you find him? And how did you come to find him?"

Pearson was voluble. "The lift was on the ground floor, sir. I just happened to glance through the little glass panel, and I see him lying there. So I thought I'd better run the lift up here and get you.

As for putting him there——" He pointed to the recall button on the wall outside the lift. "Somebody on any floor, sir, could have shoved him in here, and pressed this button, and sent him downstairs. He certainly wasn't put in on the ground floor. Besides, I saw him come into the building to-night."

"Oh?" put in Conyers softly. "When was this?"

"Might have been eleven o'clock, sir."

"Whom was he coming to see?"

Pearson shook his head helplessly and with a certain impatience. "These ain't service flats, sir, where you telephone up about every visitor. You ought to know we're not to ask visitors anything unless they seem to need help, or unless it's somebody who has no business here. *I* don't know. He went up in the main lift, that's all I can tell you."

"Well, what floor did he go to?"

"I dunno." Pearson ran a finger under a tight collar. "But excuse me, sir, may I ask a question, if you please? What's wrong exactly?"

"We've lost a room," said Ronald Denham, with inspiration. "Maybe you can help. Look here, Pearson: you've been here in these flats a long time. You've been inside most of them — in the sitting rooms, for instance?"

"I think I can say I've been in all of 'em, sir."

"Good. Then we're looking for a room decorated like this," said Denham. For the third time he described what he had seen, and Pearson's expression grew to one of acute anguish. At the end of it he shook his head.

"It's nobody's room, sir," the porter answered simply. "There's not a sitting room like that in the whole building."

At three o'clock in the morning, a sombre group of people sat in Sir Rufus Armingdale's flat, and did not even look at each other. The police work was nearly done. A brisk divisional detective-inspector, accompanied by a sergeant, a photographer, and a large amiable man in a top hat, had taken a statement from each of those concerned. But the statements revealed nothing.

Denham, in fact, had received only one more mental jolt. Entering Armingdale's flat, he thought for a second that he had found the missing room. The usual chairs of stamped Spanish leather, the refectory table, the carved gewgaws, greeted him like a familiar nightmare. And over the sideboard hung a familiar picture — that of a small girl looking sideways over an armful of roses.

"That's not it?" said Anita quickly.

"It's the same subject, but it's not the same picture. That's in oils. What sort of game do you suppose is going on in this place?"

Anita glanced over her shoulder. She had dressed before the arrival of the police; and also, he thought, she had put on more make-up than was necessary.

"Quick, Ron; before the others get here. Were you telling the truth?"

"Certainly. You don't think —— ?"

"Oh, I don't know and I don't care; I just want you to tell me. Ron, you didn't kill him yourself?"

He had not even time to answer before she stopped him. Sir Rufus Armingdale, Conyers, and Evans came through from the foyer; and with them was the large amiable man who had accompanied Divisional Inspector Davidson. His name, it appeared, was Colonel March.

"You see," he explained, with a broad gesture, "I'm not here officially. I happened to be at the theatre, and I dropped in on Inspector Davidson for a talk, and he asked me to come along. So if you don't like any of my questions, just tell me to shut my head. But I do happen to be attached to the Yard —— "

"I know you, Colonel," said Conyers, with a crooked grin. "You're the head of the Ragbag Department, D-3. Some call it the Crazy House."

Colonel March nodded seriously. He wore a dark overcoat, and had a top hat pushed back on his large head; this, with his florid complexion, sandy moustache, and bland blue eye, gave him something of the look of a stout colonel in a comic paper. He was smoking a large-bowled pipe with the effect of seeming to sniff smoke from the bowl rather than draw it through the stem. He appeared to be enjoying himself.

"It's a compliment," he assured them. "After all, somebody has got to sift all the queer complaints. If somebody comes in and reports (say) that the Borough of Stepney is being terrorized by a blue pig, I've got to decide whether it's a piece of lunacy, or a mistake, or a hoax, or a serious crime. Otherwise good men would only waste their time. You'd be surprised how many such complaints there are. But I was thinking, and so was Inspector Davidson, that you had a very similar situation here. If you wouldn't mind a few extra questions —— "

"As many as you like," said Sir Rufus Armingdale. "Provided somebody's got a hope of solving this damned —— "

"As a matter of fact," said Colonel March, frowning, "Inspector Davidson has reason to believe that it is already solved. A good man, Davidson."

There was a silence. Something unintentionally sinister seemed to have gathered in Colonel March's affable tone. For a moment nobody dared to ask him what he meant.

"Already solved?" repeated Hubert Conyers.

"Suppose we begin with you, Sir Rufus," said March with great courtesy. "You have told the inspector that you did not know Daniel Randolph personally. But it seems to be common knowledge that he was in England to see you."

Armingdale hesitated. "I don't know his reasons. He may have been here to see me, among other things. Probably was. He wrote to me about it from America. But he hasn't approached me yet, and I didn't approach him first. It's bad business."

"What was the nature of this business, Sir Rufus?"

"He wanted to buy an option I held on some property in — never mind where. I'll tell you in private, if you insist."

"Was a large sum involved?"

Armingdale seemed to struggle with himself. "Four thousand, more or less."

"So it wasn't a major business deal. Were you going to sell?"

"Probably."

Colonel March's abstracted eye wandered to the picture over the sideboard. "Now, Sir Rufus, that Greuze, 'Young Girl with Primroses.' I think it was recently reproduced, in its natural size, as a full-page illustration in the *Metropolitan Illustrated News*."

"Yes, it was," said Armingdale. He added, "In — sepia."

Something about this afterthought made them all move forward to look at him. It was like the puzzle of a half truth: nobody knew what it meant.

"Exactly. Just two more questions. I believe that each of these flats communicates with a fire escape leading down into the mews behind?"

"Yes. What of it?"

"Will the same key open the front door of each of the flats?"

"No, certainly not. All the lock patterns are different."

"Thank you. Now, Mr. Conyers — a question for you. Are you married?"

Hitherto Conyers had been regarding him with a look of watchful expectancy, like an urchin about to smash a window and run. Now he scowled.

"Married? No."

"And you don't keep a valet?"

"The answer to that, Colonel, is loud and prolonged laughter. Honestly, I don't like your 'social' manner. Beston, our crime news man, knows you. And it's always, 'Blast you, Beston, if you print one hint about the Thingummy case I'll have your hide.' What difference does it make whether I'm married or not, or whether I have a valet or not?"

"A great deal," said March seriously. "Now, Miss Bruce. What is your occupation, Miss Bruce?"

"I'm an interior decorator," answered Anita.

She began to laugh. It may have been with a tinge of hysteria; but she sat back in a tall chair and laughed until there were tears in her eyes.

"I'm terribly sorry," she went on, holding out her hand as though to stop them, "but don't you see? The murder was done by an interior decorator. That's the whole secret."

Colonel March cut short Armingdale's shocked protest.

"Go on," he said sharply.

"I thought of it first off. Of course there's no 'vanishing room.' Some sitting room has just been redecorated. All the actual furnishings, tables and chairs and sideboards, are just the same in every room. The only way you can tell them apart is by small movable things — pictures, lamp shades, book ends — which could be changed in a few minutes.

"Ron accidentally walked into the murderer's flat just after the murderer had killed that old man. That put the murderer in a pretty awful position. Unless he killed Ron too, he was caught with the body and Ron could identify his flat. But he thought of a better way. He sent that man's body down in the lift and dragged Ron out into the hall. Then he simply altered the decorations of his flat. Afterwards he could sit down and dare anyone to identify it as the place where the body had been."

Anita's face was flushed with either defiance or fear.

"Warm," said Colonel March. "Unquestionably warm. That is why I was wondering whether you couldn't tell us what really happened."

"I don't understand you."

"Well, there are objections to the redecoration. You've got to suppose that nobody had ever been in the flat before and seen the way it was originally decorated. You've also got to suppose that the murderer could find a new set of lamp shades, pictures, and book ends in the middle of the night. —— Haven't you got it the wrong way round?"

"The wrong way round?"

"Somebody," said March, dropping his courtesy, "prepared a dummy room to begin with. He put in the new lamp shades, the book ends, the copy of a well-known picture, even a set of new curtains. He entertained Randolph in that dummy room. He killed Randolph there. Afterwards, of course, he simply removed the knick-knacks and set the place right again. But it was the dummy room into which Ronald Denham walked. That, Mr. Denham, was why you did not recognize —— "

"Recognize what?" roared Denham. "Where was I?"

"In the sitting room of your own flat," said Colonel March gravely. "If you had been sober you might have made a mistake; but you were so full of champagne that your instinct brought you home after all."

There were two doors in the room, and the blue uniform of a policeman appeared in each. At March's signal, Inspector Davidson stepped forward. He said:

"Thomas Evans, I arrest you for the murder of Daniel Randolph. I have to warn you that anything you say will be taken down in writing and may be used in evidence at your trial."

"Oh, look here," protested Colonel March, when they met in Armingdale's flat next day, "the thing was simple enough. We had twice as much trouble over that kid in Bayswater, who pinched all the oranges. And you had all the facts.

"Evans, as one of Sir Rufus's most highly placed and trusted employees, was naturally in a position to know all about the projected business deal with Randolph. And so he planned an ingenious swindle. A swindle, I am certain, was all he intended.

"Now you, Sir Rufus, had intended to go to Manchester yesterday afternoon, and remain there for a week. (Mr. Denham heard that from the night porter, when he was advised against singing.) That would leave your flat empty. Evans telephoned to Randolph, posing as you. He asked Randolph to come round to your flat at eleven o'clock at night, and settle the deal. He added that you *might* be called away to Manchester; but, in that event, his secretary would have the necessary papers ready and signed.

"It would have been easy. Evans would get into your empty flat by way of the fire escape and the window. He would pose as your secretary. Randolph — who, remember, always paid spot cash even if it involved a million — would hand over a packet of banknotes for a forged document.

"Why should Randolph be suspicious of anything? He knew, as half the newspaper-reading world knows, that Sir Rufus lived on the second floor of Medici Court. He had seen photographs of Sir Rufus with his favourite Greuze over the sideboard. Even if he asked the hall porter for directions, he would be sent to the right flat. Even if the hall porter said Sir Rufus was in Manchester, the ground had been prepared and Randolph would ask for Sir Rufus's secretary.

"Unfortunately, a hitch occurred. Sir Rufus decided not to go to Manchester. He decided it yesterday afternoon, after all Evans's plans had been made and Randolph was due to arrive. But Evans needed that money; as we have discovered to-day, he needed it desperately. He wanted that four thousand pounds.

"So he hit on another plan. Sir Rufus would be at home and his flat could not be used. But, with all the rooms exactly alike except for decorations, why not an *imitation* of Sir Rufus's flat? The same plan would hold good, except that Randolph would be taken to the wrong place. He would come up in the lift at eleven. Evans would be waiting with the door of the flat open, and would take him to a place superficially resembling Sir Rufus's. The numbers on the doors are very small; and Randolph, as we know, was so near-sighted as to be almost blind. If Evans adopted some disguise, how-ever clumsy, he could never afterwards be identified as the man who swindled Randolph. And he ran no risk in using the flat he shared with Denham."

Anita interposed. "Of course!" she said. "Ron was at a bachelor party, and ordinarily it would have kept him there whooping until two or three o'clock in the morning. But he reformed, and came home early."

Denham groaned. "But I still can't believe it," he insisted. "Tom Evans? A murderer?"

"He intended no murder," said Colonel March. "But, you see, Randolph suspected something. Randolph showed that he suspected. And Evans, as a practical man, had to kill him. You can guess why Randolph suspected?"

"Well?"

"Because Evans is colour-blind," said Colonel March.

"It's too bad," Colonel March went on sadly, "but the crime was from the first the work of a colour-blind man. Now, none of the rest of you could qualify for that deficiency. As for Sir Rufus, I can think of nothing more improbable than a colour-blind art col-lector — unless it is a colour-blind interior decorator. Mr. Conyers here shows by the blended hues of brown or blue in his suits, shirts, and ties that he has a fine eye for colour effect; and he possesses no wife or valet to choose them for him.

"But Evans? He is not only partially, but wholly colour-blind. You gave us a spirited account of it. Randolph's body was sent up in the lift by Pearson. When Evans stepped forward, Pearson warned him not to touch the body, saying that there was blood. Evans said, 'Where?' — though he was staring straight down in a small, brightly lighted lift at a red bloodstain on a grey-rubber floor. Red on any surface except green or yellow is absolutely invisible to colour-blind men.

"That was also the reason why Randolph's waterproof was put on inside out. Randolph had removed his hat and coat when he first came into the flat. After Evans had stabbed him with a clasp knife, Evans put the hat and coat back on the body previous to disposing of it. But he could not distinguish between the yellowish outside and the green inside of that seamless oilskin.

"You, Mr. Denham, let yourself into the flat with your own key: which in itself told us the location of the 'vanished' room, for no two keys are alike. I also think that Miss Bruce could have told us all along where the 'vanished' room was. I am inclined to suspect she saw Randolph going into your flat, and was afraid you might be concerned in the murder."

"Oh, well," said Anita philosophically.

"Anyway, you spoke to a corpse about his coat being inside-out; and Evans rectified the error before he put the body in the lift. He had to knock you out, of course. But he genuinely didn't want to hurt you. He left the building by way of the fire escape into the mews. He disposed of his stage properties, though he was foolish enough to keep the money and the clasp knife on his person, where they were found when we searched him. When he came back here, he used the main lift in the ordinary way as though he were returning from his office. And he was genuinely concerned when he found you still unconscious on the bench in the hall."

There was a silence, broken by Armingdale's snort.

"But colour blindness! What's that got to do with the solution? How did you come to think the murderer must have been colour-blind to begin with?"

Colonel March turned to stare at him. Then he shook his head, with a slow and dismal smile.

"Don't you see it even yet?" he asked. "That was the starting point. We suspected it for the same reason Randolph suspected an imposture. Poor old Randolph wasn't an art critic. Any sort of coloured daub, in the ordinary way, he would have swallowed as the original 'Young Girl with Primroses' he expected to see. But Evans didn't allow for the one thing even a near-sighted man does know: colour. In his effort to imitate the decorations of Sir Rufus's flat, the fool hung up as an oil painting nothing more than a sepia reproduction out of an illustrated weekly."

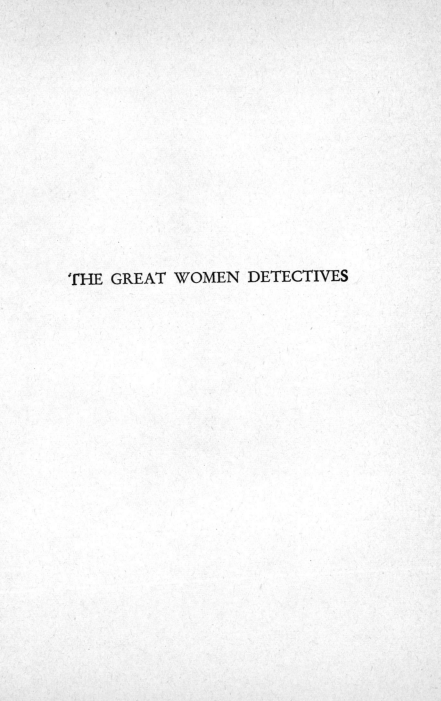

'THE GREAT WOMEN DETECTIVES

THE TEA LEAF

by EDGAR JEPSON AND ROBERT EUSTACE

---

*Who would be the last person on earth you'd expect to solve
a murder in a men's Turkish bath? Right — a lady-detective.
Only one of the reasons we like this story.*

ARTHUR KELSTERN AND HUGH WILLOUGHTON met in the Turkish bath in Duke Street, St. James's, and rather more than a year later in that Turkish bath they parted. Both of them were bad-tempered men, Kelstern cantankerous and Willoughton violent. It was indeed difficult to decide which was the worse-tempered; and when I found that they had suddenly become friends, I gave that friendship three months. It lasted nearly a year.

When they did quarrel they quarrelled about Kelstern's daughter Ruth. Willoughton fell in love with her and she with him and they became engaged to be married. Six months later, in spite of the fact that they were plainly very much in love with one another, the engagement was broken off. Neither of them gave any reason for breaking it off. My belief was that Willoughton had given Ruth a taste of his infernal temper and got as good as he gave.

Not that Ruth was at all a Kelstern to look at. Like the members of most of the old Lincolnshire families, descendants of the Vikings and the followers of Canute, one Kelstern is very like another Kelstern, fair-haired, clear-skinned, with light-blue eyes and a good bridge to the nose. But Ruth had taken after her mother: she was dark with a straight nose, dark-brown eyes of the kind often described as liquid, dark-brown hair, and as kissable lips as ever I saw. She was a proud, rather self-sufficing, high-spirited girl, with a temper of her own. She needed it to live with that cantankerous old brute Kelstern. Oddly enough in spite of the fact that he always would try to bully her, she was fond of him; and I will say for him that he was very fond of her. Probably she was the only creature in the world of whom he was really fond. He was an expert in the application of scientific discoveries to industry; and she worked with him in his laboratory. He paid her five hundred a year, so that she must have been uncommonly good.

He took the breaking off of the engagement very hard indeed. He would have it that Willoughton had jilted her. Ruth took it hard too: her warm colouring lost some of its warmth; her lips grew less kissable and set in a thinner line. Willoughton's temper grew worse than ever; he was like a bear with a perpetually sore head. I tried to feel my way with both him and Ruth with a view to help to bring about a reconciliation. To put it mildly, I was rebuffed. Willoughton swore at me; Ruth flared up and told me not to meddle in matters that didn't concern me. Nevertheless my strong impression was that they were missing one another badly and would have been glad enough to come together again if their stupid vanity could have let them.

Kelstern did his best to keep Ruth furious with Willoughton. One night I told him — it was no business of mine; but I never did give a tinker's curse for his temper — that he was a fool to meddle and had much better leave them alone. It made him furious, of course; he would have it that Willoughton was a dirty hound and a low blackguard — at least those were about the mildest things he said of him. It struck me of a sudden that there must be something much more serious in the breaking off of the engagement than I had guessed.

That suspicion was strengthened by the immense trouble Kelstern took to injure Willoughton. At his clubs, the Athenæum, the Devonshire, and the Savile, he would display an astonishing ingenuity in bringing the conversation round to Willoughton; then he would declare that he was a scoundrel and a blackguard of the meanest type. Of course it did Willoughton harm, though not nearly as much harm as Kelstern desired, for Willoughton knew his job as few engineers knew it; and it is very hard indeed to do much harm to a man who really knows his job. People have to have him. But of course it did him some harm; and Willoughton knew that Kelstern was doing it. I came across two men who told me that they had given him a friendly hint. That did not improve Willoughton's temper.

An expert in the construction of those ferro-concrete buildings which are rising up all over London, he was as distinguished in his sphere as Kelstern in his. They were alike not only in the matters of brains and bad temper but I think that their minds worked in very much the same way. At any rate both of them seemed determined not to change their ordinary course of life because of the breaking off of that engagement.

It had been the habit of both of them to have a Turkish bath, at the baths in Duke Street, at four in the afternoon on the second and last Tuesday in every month. To that habit they stuck. The fact that they must meet on those Tuesdays did not cause either of them to change his hour of taking his Turkish bath by the twenty minutes which would have given them no more than a passing glimpse of one another. They continued to take them, as they always had, simultaneously. Thick-skinned? They were thick-skinned. Neither of them pretended that he did not see the other; he scowled at him; and he scowled at him most of the time. I know this, for sometimes I had a Turkish bath myself at that hour.

It was about three months after the breaking off of the engagement that they met for the last time at that Turkish bath, and there parted for good.

Kelstern had been looking ill for about six weeks: there was a grayness and a drawn look to his face; and he was losing weight. On the second Tuesday in October he arrived at the bath punctually at four, bringing with him, as was his habit, a thermos flask full of a very delicate China tea. If he thought that he was not perspiring freely enough he would drink it in the hottest room; if he did perspire freely enough, he would drink it after his bath. Willoughton arrived about two minutes later. Kelstern finished undressing and went into the bath a couple of minutes before Willoughton. They stayed in the hot room about the same time; Kelstern went into the hottest room about a minute after Willoughton. Before he went into it he sent for his thermos flask which he had left in the dressing room and took it into the hottest room with him.

As it happened, they were the only two people in the hottest room; and they had not been in it two minutes before the four men in the hot room heard them quarrelling. They heard Kelstern call Willoughton a dirty hound and a low blackguard, among other things, and declare he would do him in yet. Willoughton told him to go to the devil twice. Kelstern went on abusing him and presently Willoughton fairly shouted: "Oh, shut up, you old fool! Or I'll make you!"

Kelstern did not shut up. About two minutes later Willoughton came out of the hottest room, scowling, walked through the hot room into the shampooing room and put himself into the hands of one of the shampooers. Two or three minutes after that a man of the name of Helston went into the hottest room and fairly yelled. Kelstern was lying back on a blood-drenched couch, with the blood still flowing from a wound over his heart.

There was a devil of a hullabaloo. The police were called in; Willoughton was arrested. Of course he lost his temper and, protesting furiously that he had had nothing whatever to do with the crime, abused the police. That did not incline them to believe him.

After examining the room and the dead body the detective-inspector in charge of the case came to the conclusion that Kelstern had been stabbed as he was drinking his tea. The thermos flask lay on the floor in front of him and some of the tea had evidently been spilt, for some tea leaves — the tea in the flask must have been carelessly strained off the leaves by the maid who filled it — lay on the floor about the mouth of the empty flask. It looked as if the murderer had taken advantage of Kelstern's drinking his tea to stab him while the flask rather blocked his vision and prevented him from seeing what he would be at.

The case would have been quite plain sailing but for the fact that they could not find the weapon. It had been easy enough for Willoughton to take it into the bath in the towel in which he was draped. But how had he got rid of it? Where had he hidden it? A Turkish bath is no place to hide anything in. It is as bare as an empty barn — if anything, barer; and Willoughton had been in the barest part of it. The police searched every part of it — not that there was much point in doing that, for Willoughton had come out of the hottest room, and gone through the hot room into the shampooers' room. When Helston started shouting murder, Willoughton had rushed back with the shampooers to the hottest room and there he had stayed. Since it was obvious that he had committed the murder the shampooers and the bathers had kept their eyes on him. They were all of them certain that he had not left them to go to the dressing rooms; they would not have allowed him to do so.

It was obvious that he must have carried the weapon into the bath, hidden in the folds of the towel in which he was draped, and brought it away in the folds of that towel. He had laid the towel down beside the couch on which he was being shampooed; and there it still lay when they came to look for it, untouched, with no weapon in it, with no traces of blood on it. There was not much in the fact that it was not stained with blood, since Willoughton could have wiped the knife, or dagger, or whatever weapon he used, on the couch on which Kelstern lay. There were no marks of any such wiping on the couch; but the blood, flowing from the wound, might have covered them up.

There was no finding the weapon; and its disappearance puzzled the police and later puzzled the public.

Then the doctors who made the autopsy came to the conclusion that the wound had been inflicted by a circular, pointed weapon nearly three-quarters of an inch in diameter. It had penetrated rather more than three inches and supposing that its handle was only four inches long it must have been a sizeable weapon, quite impossible to overlook. The doctors also discovered a further proof of the theory that Kelstern had been drinking his tea when he was stabbed. Half-way down the wound they found two halves of a tea leaf which had evidently fallen on to Kelstern's body, been driven into the wound and cut in half by the weapon. Also they discovered that Kelstern was suffering from cancer. This fact was not published in the papers; I heard it at the Devonshire.

Willoughton was brought before the magistrates and to most people's surprise did not reserve his defense. He went into the witness box and swore that he had never touched Kelstern, that he had never had anything to touch him with, that he had never taken any weapon into the Turkish bath and so had had no weapon to hide, that he had never even seen any such weapon as the doctors described. He was committed for trial.

The papers were full of the crime; every one was discussing it;

and the question which occupied every one's mind was: where had Willoughton hidden the weapon? People wrote to the papers to suggest that he had ingeniously put it in some place under everybody's eyes and that it had been overlooked because it was so obvious. Others suggested that, circular and pointed, it must be very like a thick lead pencil, that it was a thick lead pencil; and that was why the police had overlooked it in their search. The police had not overlooked any thick lead pencil; there had been no thick lead pencil to overlook. They hunted England through — Willoughton did a lot of motoring — to discover the man who had sold him this curious and uncommon weapon. They did not find the man who had sold it to him; they did not find a man who sold such weapons at all. They came to the conclusion that Kelstern had been murdered with a piece of a steel, or iron, rod filed to a point like a pencil.

In spite of the fact that only Willoughton *could* have murdered Kelstern, I could not believe that he had done it. The fact that Kelstern was doing his best to injure him professionally and socially was by no means a strong enough motive. Willoughton was far too intelligent a man not to be very well aware that people do not take much notice of statements to the discredit of a man whom they need to do a job for them; and for the social injury he would care very little. Besides, he might very well injure, or even kill, a man in one of his tantrums; but his was not the kind of bad temper that plans a cold-blooded murder; and if ever a murder had been deliberately planned, Kelstern's had.

I was as close a friend as Willoughton had, and I went to visit him in prison. He seemed rather touched by my doing so, and grateful. I learnt that I was the only person who had done so. He was subdued and seemed much gentler. It might last. He discussed the murder readily enough and naturally with an harassed air. He said quite frankly that he did not expect me, in the circumstances, to believe that he had not committed it; but he had not, and he could not for the life of him conceive who had. I did believe that he had not committed it; there was something in his way of discussing it that wholly convinced me. I told him that I was quite sure that he had not killed Kelstern; and he looked at me as if he did not believe the assurance. But again he looked grateful.

Ruth was grieving for her father; but Willoughton's very dangerous plight to some degree distracted her mind from her loss. A woman can quarrel with a man bitterly without desiring to see him hanged; and Willoughton's chance of escaping hanging was not at all a good one. But she would not believe for a moment that he had murdered her father.

"No; there's nothing in it — nothing whatever," she said firmly. "If Dad had murdered Hugh I could have understood it. He had reasons — or at any rate he had persuaded himself that he had. But whatever reason had Hugh for murdering Dad? It's all nonsense to suppose that he'd mind Dad's trying all he knew to injure him, as much as that. All kinds of people are going about trying to injure other people in that way, but they don't really injure them very much; and Hugh knows that quite well."

"Of course they don't; and Hugh wouldn't really believe that your father was injuring him much," I said. "But you're forgetting his infernal temper."

"No: I'm not," she protested. "He might kill a man in one of his rages on the spur of the moment. But this wasn't the spur of the moment. Whoever did it had worked the whole thing out and came along with the weapon ready."

I had to admit that that was reasonable enough. But who had done it? I pointed out to her that the police had made careful enquiries about every one in the bath at the time, the shampooers and the people taking their baths, but they had found no evidence whatever that any one of them had at any time had any relations, except that of shampooer, with her father.

"Either it was one of them, or somebody else who just did it and got right away, or there's a catch somewhere," she said, frowning thoughtfully.

"I can't see how there can possibly have been anyone in the bath except the people who are known to have been there," said I. "In fact, there can't have been."

Then the Crown subpœnaed her as a witness for the prosecution. It seemed rather unnecessary and even a bit queer, for it could have found plenty of evidence of bad blood between the two men without dragging her into it. Plainly it was bent on doing all it knew to prove motive enough. Ruth seemed more upset by the prospect of going into the witness box than I should have expected her to be. But then she had been having a very trying time.

On the morning of the trial I called for her after breakfast to drive her down to the New Bailey. She was pale and looked as if she had had a poor night's rest, and, naturally enough, she seemed to be suffering from an excitement she had to control. It was not like her to show any excitement she might be feeling.

We had of course been in close touch with Willoughton's solicitor, Hamley; and he had kept seats for us just behind him. He wished to have Ruth at hand to consult should some point turn up on which she could throw light, since she knew more than anyone about the relations between Willoughton and her father. I had timed our arrival very well; the jury had just been sworn in. Of course the Court was full of women, the wives of Peers and bookmakers and politicians, most of them overdressed and overscented.

Then the judge came in; and with his coming the atmosphere of the Court became charged with that sense of anxious strain peculiar to trials for murder. It was rather like the atmosphere of a sick room in a case of fatal illness, but worse.

It was unfortunate for Willoughton that the judge was Garbould. A hard-faced, common-looking fellow, and coarse in the grain, he has a well-founded reputation as a hanging judge and the habit of acting as an extra counsel for the prosecution.

Willoughton came into the box, looking under the weather and very much subdued. But he certainly looked dignified and he said that he was not guilty in a steady enough voice.

Greatorex, the leading Counsel for the Crown, opened the case for the prosecution. There was no suggestion in his speech that the police had discovered any new fact.

Then Helston gave evidence of finding the body of the dead man and he and the other three men who had been with him in the hot room gave evidence of the quarrel they had overheard between Willoughton and the dead man, and that Willoughton came out of the hottest room, scowling and obviously furious. One of them, a fussy old gentleman of the name of Underwood, declared that it was the bitterest quarrel he had ever heard. None of the four of them could throw any light on the matter of whether Willoughton was carrying the missing weapon in the folds of the towel in which he was draped; all of them were sure that he had nothing in his hands.

The medical evidence came next. In cross-examining the doctors who had made the autopsy, Hazeldean, Willoughton's counsel, established the fact quite definitely that the missing weapon was of a fair size; that its rounded blade must have been over half an inch in diameter and between three and four inches long. They were of the opinion that to drive a blade of that thickness into the heart, a handle of at least four inches in length would be necessary to give a firm enough grip. It might have been a piece of a steel, or iron, rod sharpened like a pencil. At any rate it was certainly a sizeable weapon, not one to be hidden quickly, or to disappear wholly in a Turkish bath. Hazeldean could not shake their evidence about the tea leaf; they were confident that it had been driven into the wound and cut in half by the blade of the missing weapon, and that that went to show that the wound had been inflicted while Kelstern was drinking his tea.

Detective-Inspector Brackett, who was in charge of the case, was cross-examined at great length about his search for the missing weapon. He made it quite clear that it was nowhere in that Turkish bath, neither in the hot rooms, nor the shampooing room, nor the dressing rooms, nor the vestibule, nor the office. He had had the plunge bath emptied; he had searched the roofs, though it was practically certain that the skylight above the hot room, not the hottest, had been shut at the time of the crime. In re-examination he scouted the idea of Willoughton's having had an accomplice who had carried away the weapon for him. He had gone into that matter most carefully.

The shampooer stated that Willoughton came to him scowling so savagely that he wondered what had put him into such a bad temper. In cross-examining him Arbuthnot, Hazeldean's junior, made it clearer than ever that, unless Willoughton had already hidden the weapon in the bare hottest room, it was hidden in the towel. Then he drew from the shampooer the definite statement that Willoughton had set down the towel beside the couch on which he was shampooed, that he had hurried back to the hot rooms in front of the shampooer; that the shampooer had come back from the hot rooms, leaving Willoughton still in them discussing the crime, to find the towel lying just as Willoughton had set it down, with no weapon in it and no trace of blood on it.

Since the Inspector had disposed of the possibility that an accomplice had slipped in, taken the weapon from the towel, and slipped out of the bath with it, this evidence really made it clear that the weapon had never left the hottest room.

Then the prosecution called evidence of the bad terms on which Kelstern and Willoughton had been. Three well-known and influential men told the jury about Kelstern's efforts to prejudice Willoughton in their eyes and the damaging statements he had made about him. One of them had felt it to be his duty to tell Willoughton about this; and Willoughton had been very angry. Arbuthnot, in cross-examining, elicited the fact that any damaging statement that Kelstern made about anyone was considerably discounted by the fact that everyone knew him to be in the highest degree cantankerous.

I noticed that during the end of the cross-examination of the shampooer, and during this evidence, Ruth had been fidgeting and turning to look impatiently at the entrance to the Court, as if she were expecting someone. Then, just as she was summoned to the witness box, there came in a tall, stooping, grey-headed, grey-bearded man of about sixty, carrying a brown-paper parcel. His face was familiar to me; but I could not place him. He caught her eye and nodded to her. She breathed a sharp sigh of relief and bent over and handed a letter she had in her hand to Willoughton's solicitor and pointed out the grey-bearded man to him. Then she went quietly to the witness box.

Hamley read the letter and at once bent over and handed it to Hazeldean and spoke to him. I caught a note of excitement in his hushed voice. Hazeldean read the letter and appeared to grow excited too. Hamley slipped out of his seat and went to the grey-bearded man who was still standing just inside the door of the Court and began to talk to him earnestly.

Greatorex began to examine Ruth; and naturally I turned my attention to her. His examination was directed also to show on what bad terms Kelstern and Willoughton had been. Ruth was called on to tell the jury some of Kelstern's actual threats. Then — it is astonishing how few things the police fail to ferret out in a really important case — the examination took a curious turn. Greatorex began to question Ruth about her own relations with Willoughton and the plain trend of his questions was to bring out the fact that they had not merely been engaged to be married but had also been lovers.

I saw at once what the prosecution was aiming at. It was trying to make use of the tendency of a British jury and a British judge, in a natural effort to champion morality, to hang a man or a woman, who is on trial for murder, for behaving immorally in relations with the other sex. There was no better way of prejudicing Willoughton than by proving that he had seduced Ruth under the promise of marriage.

Of course Hazeldean was on his feet at once protesting that this evidence was irrelevant and inadmissible; and of course Garbould was against him — he does not enjoy the nickname by which he is known to the junior bar for nothing. Hazeldean was magnificent. He had one of the worst rows with Garbould he had ever had; and he has had many. Garbould is a fool to let him have these rows. Hazeldean always gets the better of him, or seems to; and it does him good with the jury. But then Garbould was raised to the bench not for intelligence but for political merit. He ruled that the questions were admissible and put one or two to Ruth himself.

Then Willoughton lost his temper and protested that this had nothing to do with the case and that it was an outrage. Willoughton has a ringing voice of considerable volume. He is not at all an easy man to hush when he does not wish to hush; and they were some time hushing him. By the time they succeeded Garbould was purplish-red with fury. Anything that he could do to hang Willoughton would certainly be done. But, observing the jury, my impression was that Willoughton's outburst had done him good with it and that Hazeldean's protests had shaken its confidence in Garbould. When I looked at the faces, just a trifle sickly, of the counsel for the prosecution, I felt sure that the Crown had bungled this business rather badly.

Greatorex, assisted by Garbould, went on with his questions; and Ruth defiant rather than abashed, and looking in her flushed animation a more charming creature than ever, admitted that she and Willoughton had been lovers; that more than once when he had brought her home from a dance or a theatre he had not left her till the early morning. One of the maids had spied on them; and the Crown had the facts.

I was afraid, in spite of Hazeldean's protests, that the fact that Willoughton had seduced her under the promise of marriage, as Greatorex put it, would do him great harm with the jury — very likely it would hang him.

Then Ruth, still flushed, but not greatly discomposed, said: "That would be a reason for my father's murdering Mr. Willoughton, not for Mr. Willoughton's murdering my father."

That brought Garbould down upon her like a ton of bricks. She was there to answer questions, not to make idle remarks and so forth and so on.

Then Greatorex came to the breaking off of the engagement and put it to her that Willoughton had broken it off, had in fact jilted her after compromising her. That she would not have for a moment. She declared that they had had a quarrel and she had broken it off. To that she stuck and there was no shaking her, though Garbould himself took a hearty hand in trying to shake her.

In the middle of it Willoughton, who was looking quite himself again, now that the atmosphere of the Court might be said to be charged almost with violence, said in a very unpleasant, jeering voice: "What she says is perfectly true — what's the good of bothering her?"

Again Garbould was to the fore, and angrily reprimanded him for speaking, bade him keep silent, and said that he would not have his Court turned into a beargarden.

"With the bear on the bench," said Hazeldean to Arbuthnot in a whisper that carried well.

Two or three people laughed. One of them was a juryman. By the time Garbould had finished with him I did not think that that juryman would have convicted Willoughton, if he had actually seen him stab Kelstern.

Willoughton was writing a note which was passed to Hazeldean.

Hazeldean rose to cross-examine Ruth with a wholly confident air. He drew from her the facts that her father had been on excellent terms with Willoughton until the breaking off of the engagement; that in that matter he had taken her part warmly; and that when the maid who had spied upon them had informed him of her relations with Willoughton he had been very little more enraged than he was already.

Then Hazeldean asked: "Is it a fact that since the breaking off of your engagement the prisoner has more than once begged you to forgive him and renew it?"

"Four times," said Ruth.

"And you refused?"

"Yes," said Ruth. She looked at Willoughton queerly and added: "He wanted a lesson."

"Did he then beg you at least to go through the form of marriage with him, and promise to leave you at the church door?"

"Yes."

"And you refused?"

"Yes," said Ruth.

Garbould bent forward and said in his most unpleasant tone: "And why did you reject the opportunity of repairing your shameful behaviour?"

"It wasn't shameful," Ruth almost snapped; and she scowled at him frankly. Then she added naïvely: "I refused because there was no hurry. He would always marry me if I changed my mind and wanted to."

There was a pause. To me it seemed clearer than ever that the Crown had bungled badly in raising the question of the relations between her and Willoughton since he had evidently been more than ready to save her from any harm that might come of their indiscretion. But then, with a jury, you can never tell. Then Hazeldean started on a fresh line.

In sympathetic accents he asked: "Is it a fact that your father was suffering from cancer in a painful form?"

"It was beginning to grow very painful," said Ruth sadly.

"Did he make a will and put all his affairs in order a few days before he died?"

"Three days," said Ruth.

"Did he ever express an intention of committing suicide?"

"He said that he would stick it out for a little while and then end it all," said Ruth. She paused and added: "*And that is what he did do.*"

One might almost say that the Court started. I think that everyone in it moved a little, so that there was a kind of rustling murmur. Garbould threw himself back in his seat with a snort of incredulity and glowered at Ruth.

"Will you tell the Court your reasons for that statement?" said Hazeldean.

Ruth seemed to pull herself together; the flush had faded from her face and she was looking very tired; then she began in a quiet, even voice: "I never believed for a moment that Mr. Willoughton murdered my father. If my father had murdered Mr. Willoughton it would have been a different matter."

Garbould leaned forward and snarled that it was not her beliefs or fancies that were wanted, but facts.

I did not think that she heard him; she was concentrating on giving her reasons exactly; she went on in the same quiet tone: "Of course, like everybody else I puzzled over the weapon: what it was and where it had got to. I did not believe that it was a pointed piece of a half-inch steel rod. If anybody had come to the Turkish bath meaning to murder my father and hide the weapon, they wouldn't have used one so big and so difficult to hide, when a hat-pin would have done just as well and could be hidden much more easily. But what puzzled me most was the tea leaf in the wound. All the other tea leaves that came out of the flask were lying on the floor. Inspector Brackett told me they were. And I couldn't believe that one tea leaf had fallen on to my father at the very place above his heart at which the point of the weapon had penetrated the skin and got driven in by it. It was too much of a coincidence for me to swallow. But I got no nearer understanding it than any-one else."

Garbould broke in in a tone of some exasperation and told her to come to the facts. Hazeldean rose and protested that the witness should not be interrupted; that she had solved a mystery which had puzzled some of the best brains in England, and she should be allowed to tell her story in her own way.

Again Ruth did not appear to listen to them, and when they stopped she went on in the same quiet voice: "Of course I remem-bered that Dad had talked of putting an end to it; but no one with a wound like that could get up and hide the weapon. Then, the night before last I dreamt that I went into the laboratory and saw a piece of steel rod, pointed, lying on the table at which my father used to work."

"Dreams now!" murmured Garbould contemptuously; and he leaned back and folded his hands over his stomach.

"I didn't think much of the dream, of course," Ruth went on. "I had been puzzling about it all so hard for so long that it was only natural to dream about it. But after breakfast I had a sudden feeling that the secret was in the laboratory if I could only find it. I did not attach any importance to the feeling; but it went on growing stronger; and after lunch I went to the laboratory and began to hunt.

"I looked through all the drawers and could find nothing. Then I went round the room looking at everything and into everything, instruments and retorts and tubes and so on. Then I went into the middle of the floor and looked slowly round the room pretty hard. Against the wall, near the door, lying ready to be taken away, was a gas cylinder. I rolled it over to see what gas had been in it and found no label on it."

She paused to look round the Court as if claiming its best attention; then she went on: "Now that was very queer because every gas cylinder must have a label on it — so many gases are dangerous. I turned on the cylinder and nothing came out of it. It was quite empty. Then I went to the book in which all the things which come in are entered, and found that ten days before Dad died he had had in a cylinder of CO_2 and seven pounds of ice. Also he had had seven pounds of ice every day till the day of his death. It was the ice and the CO_2 together that gave me the idea. CO_2, carbon dioxide, has a very low freezing point — eighty degrees centigrade — and as it comes out of the cylinder and mixes with the air it turns into very fine snow; and that snow, if you compress it, makes the hardest and toughest ice possible. It flashed on me that Dad could have collected this snow and forced it into a mould and made a weapon that would not only inflict that wound but would *disappear instantly!*"

She paused again to look round the Court at about as rapt a lot of faces as any narrator could desire. Then she went on: "I knew that that was what he had done. I knew it for certain. Carbon dioxide ice would make a hard, tough dagger, and it would melt quickly in the hottest room of a Turkish bath and leave no smell because it is scentless. So there wouldn't be any weapon. And it explained the tea leaf too. Dad had made a carbon dioxide dagger perhaps a week before he used it, perhaps only a day. And he had put it into the thermos flask as soon as he had made it. The thermos flask keeps out the heat as well as the cold, you know. But to make sure that it couldn't melt at all he kept the flask in ice till he was ready to use the dagger. It's the only way you can explain that tea leaf. It came out of the flask sticking to the point of the dagger and was driven into the wound!"

She paused again and one might almost say that the Court heaved a deep sigh of relief.

Then Garbould asked in an unpleasant and incredulous voice: "Why didn't you take this fantastic theory straight to the police?"

"But that wouldn't have been any good," she protested quickly. "It was no use my knowing it myself; I had to make other people believe it; I had to find evidence. I began to hunt for it. I felt in my bones that there was some. What I wanted was the mould. I found it!"

She uttered the words in a tone of triumph and smiled at Willoughton; then she went on: "At least I found bits of it. In the box into which we used to throw odds and ends, scraps of material, damaged instruments, and broken test tubes, I found some pieces of vulcanite; and I saw at once that they were bits of a vulcanite container. I took some wax and rolled it into a rod about the right size and then I pieced the container together on the outside of it — at least most of it — there are some small pieces missing. It took me nearly all night. But I found the most important bit — *the pointed end!*"

She dipped her hand into her handbag and drew out a black object about nine inches long and three quarters of an inch thick and held it up for everyone to see.

Someone, without thinking, began to clap; and there came a storm of applause that drowned the voice of the Clerk calling for order and the bellowing of Garbould.

When the applause died down, Hazeldean, who never misses the right moment, said: "I have no more questions to ask the witness, my lord," and sat down.

That action seemed to clinch it in my eyes and, I have no doubt, it clinched it in the eyes of the jury.

The purple Garbould leant forward and almost bellowed at Ruth: "Do you expect the jury to believe that a well-known man like your father died in the act of deliberately setting a dastardly trap to hang the prisoner?"

Ruth looked at him, shrugged her shoulders, and said with a calm acceptance of the facts of human nature one would expect to find only in a much older woman: "Oh, well, Daddy was like that. And he certainly believed he had very good reasons for killing Mr. Willoughton."

There was that in her tone and manner which made it absolutely certain that Kelstern was not only like that but that he had acted according to his nature.

Greatorex did not re-examine Ruth; he conferred with Hazeldean. Then Hazeldean rose to open the case for the defence. He said that he would not waste the time of the Court, and that in view of the fact that Miss Kelstern had solved the problem of her father's death, he would only call one witness, Professor Mozley.

The grey-headed, grey-bearded, stooping man, who had come to the Court so late, went into the witness box. Of course his face had been familiar to me; I had seen his portrait in the newspapers a dozen times. He still carried the brown-paper parcel.

In answer to Hazeldean's questions he stated that it was possible, not even difficult, to make a weapon of carbon dioxide hard enough and tough enough and sharp enough to inflict such a wound as that which had caused Kelstern's death. The method of making it was to fold a piece of chamois leather into a bag, hold that bag with the left hand, protected by a glove, over the nozzle of a cylinder containing liquid carbon dioxide, and open the valve with the right hand. Carbon dioxide evaporates so quickly that its freezing point, 80° centigrade, is soon reached; and it solidifies in the chamois leather bag as a deposit of carbon dioxide snow. Then turn off the gas, spoon that snow into a vulcanite container of the required thickness, and ram it down with a vulcanite plunger into a rod of the required hardness. He added that it was advisable to pack the container in ice while filling it and ramming down the snow, then put the rod into a thermos flask; and keep it till it is needed.

"And you have made such a rod?" said Hazeldean.

"Yes," said the Professor, cutting the string of the brown-paper parcel. "When Miss Kelstern hauled me out of bed at half past seven this morning to tell me her discoveries, I perceived at once that she had found the solution of the problem of her father's death, which had puzzled me considerably. I had breakfast quickly and got to work to make such a weapon myself for the satisfaction of the Court. Here it is."

He drew a thermos flask from the brown paper, unscrewed the top of it, and inverted it. There dropped into his gloved hand a white rod about eight inches long. He held it out for the jury to see.

"This carbon dioxide ice is the hardest and toughest ice we know of; and I have no doubt that Mr. Kelstern killed himself with a similar rod. The difference between the rod he used and this is that his rod was pointed. I had no pointed vulcanite container; but the container that Miss Kelstern pieced together is pointed. Doubtless Mr. Kelstern had it specially made, probably by Messrs. Hawkins & Spender."

He dropped the rod back into the thermos flask and screwed on the top.

Hazeldean sat down. The juryman who had been reprimanded by Garbould leaned forward and spoke earnestly to the foreman. Greatorex rose.

"With regard to the point of the rod, Professor Mozley: would it remain sharp long enough to pierce the skin in that heat?" he asked.

"In my opinion it would," said the Professor. "I have been considering that point and bearing in mind the facts that Mr. Kelstern would from his avocation be very deft with his hands, and being a scientific man, would know exactly what to do, he would have the rod out of the flask and the point in position in very little more than a second — perhaps less. He would, I think, hold it in his left hand and drive it home by striking the butt of it hard with his right. The whole thing would not take him two seconds. Besides, if the point of the weapon had melted the tea leaf would have fallen off it."

"Thank you," said Greatorex, and turned and conferred with the Crown solicitors.

Then he said: "We do not propose to proceed with the case, my lord."

The foreman of the jury rose quickly and said: "And the jury doesn't want to hear anything more, my lord. We're quite satisfied that the prisoner isn't guilty."

Garbould hesitated. For two pins he would have directed the case to proceed. Then his eye fell on Hazeldean, who was watching him; I fancied that he decided not to give him a chance of saying more disagreeable things.

Looking black enough, he put the question formally to the jury, who returned a verdict of "Not guilty," and then he discharged Willoughton.

I came out of the Court with Ruth, and we waited for Willoughton.

Presently he came out of the door and stopped and shook himself. Then he saw Ruth and came to her. They did not greet one another. She just slipped her hand through his arm; and they walked out of the New Bailey together.

We made a good deal of noise, cheering them.

THE MACKENZIE CASE

by VIOLA BROTHERS SHORE

Everything about this story is unusual. It's a detective yarn by a well-known author who has probably not written another before or since. It introduces a charming and clever female-of-the-species, GWYNN LEITH. *Its setting is romantic Cuba. It has never appeared in a book. And, as you will discover, it's an exciting brain teaser. Another discovery.*

So you had a dull trip down," laughed Clarence Cobb, our host, after some sally by my wife about our recent fellow passengers.

Five of us were sipping *frappés* on the terrace, while Mrs. Cobb showed Erik Schroeder her tropical gardens by moonlight. The Cobbs have a beautiful home outside Havana and at their request we had brought with us three dinner guests — Dr. Whitmore, the ship's surgeon; Erik Schroeder; and Leni Dill, a pretty girl in whom Schroeder had shown some interest during the trip. None of us, except Schroeder and my wife, had anything to do with the Mackenzie case.

"So dull that a man jumped overboard the first night out of New York," replied my wife.

"The first night out!" Clarence Cobb is a lawyer. "That's unusual. Ordinarily they wait a little longer."

"That's what struck me, too," commented my wife, lightly.

"Are you in earnest?" demanded Leni Dill. "You mean a man really jumped off our boat?"

"Ask the doctor," replied Gwynn. "I don't suppose there's any reason for keeping it secret any longer."

Dr. Whitmore regarded my wife curiously. "How did you know, Mrs. Keats?"

"Trust Gwynn," chuckled Clarence Cobb. "Don't you know she's the famous Gwynn Leith? And her husband there is Colin Keats, who Dr.-Watsons her."

The doctor, it seems, recalled my book on the Hanaford murder. Gwynn laughed off his awe. "I just happened to have a lucky hunch. But Mr. Schroeder is a *real* detective."

Leni Dill almost jumped out of her chair. "Erik Schroeder — ? He told me he was a big game hunter!"

Everybody laughed. "He's solved more crimes than any man in the country," said Gwynn. "But he doesn't happen to have a husband to write him up."

"I didn't hear any mention of a suicide," remarked Clarence Cobb.

"It was kept very quiet," explained the ship's surgeon. "The Captain didn't want the other passengers distressed. He was somebody utterly unknown — secretary to a wealthy man on board."

"How do you know Mackenzie is wealthy?" inquired Gwynn.

"Well, a man who travels with a secretary — " argued the doctor.

"Oh. . . . I see. . . ." said Gwynn with that look of complete innocence which immediately made me demand:

"What makes you think he isn't?"

"Well — for one thing, he didn't tip his steward."

"Perhaps that was the Scotch in him," I suggested, a little annoyed that my wife had not taken me into her confidence.

"But that first night — up in the bar — he insisted on treating everybody in sight — "

"Maybe that was the rye in him."

"Tell us about it," coaxed Leni Dill. Gwynn referred the question to the doctor.

"All I know is that Schmidt went overboard some time Wednesday night, and nobody knows why or how."

"Oh, come," protested Gwynn. "I saw you talking earnestly to Mackenzie in the bar after dinner."

"He was merely complaining of not feeling well and I told him there are people who become ill as soon as they get on a boat. He said his secretary must be of that type, because he had gone to bed as soon as the engines started. He had had the man out on the deck for a while, but he was so ill Mackenzie had had to put him back in bed. However, Mackenzie himself had crossed a dozen times and never felt sick. So I inquired what they had eaten for lunch. And when I heard tuna fish salad, I decided they were both suffering from ptomaine poisoning and suggested having a look at the secretary.

"But he asked me not to. 'He's just dropped off to sleep,' he told me. 'He wouldn't let me send for you. Ardent Scientist, you know. But I'm not, so if there's anything you can recommend for me—' And that's all I know except that Mackenzie was quite sick for the balance of the trip."

"But why did Schmidt commit suicide?" insisted Leni.

"Nobody knows. Nobody had ever spoken to the man. Even Mackenzie didn't know anything about his private life. Schmidt had been in his employ only a few days."

"Well, but how did you know he committed suicide?"

"He wasn't anywhere on the boat."

"But how did you discover he wasn't?" persisted Leni.

"From the stewards. When Mackenzie became ill he took another room on A deck and sent down a steward for his bag, cautioning him not to disturb Mr. Schmidt. The steward reported that Mr. Schmidt wasn't in the room. Later the C deck steward reported that he couldn't find him. Well, after a boat has been searched, there's only one thing to think, isn't there?"

"Except, of course, why he did it," suggested Gwynn. "What else did the steward on C deck have to report?"

"He only verified what Mackenzie had said. Soon after they came on board the one man went to bed. Later the other man—that was Mackenzie—rang and asked him to carry a chair out to C deck. Together they helped the sick man out. He was very sick. When the steward had freshened up the berth, he was slumped over the railing, his head on his arms, and his face looked ghastly. The steward suggested getting me. But although the man was so sick that Mackenzie had to bend down to get his answer, he wouldn't have me.

"Some time during dinner the steward went to 361 in answer to the bell. Mackenzie met him in the companionway and told him Schmidt had dropped off to sleep. 'But you might look in,' he said, 'in a couple of hours and see if he wants anything. I'm going up on deck. Feeling a little rocky myself.' And according to the steward, he *did* look rocky."

"I thought he did, too," said Gwynn, "but he insisted on buying more and more drinks. When he got the color of ashes of split-pea soup, I took him out on deck and heard all about how he came from Alberta; had been in the States only for short visits; how Schmidt had told him a hard-luck story, but was evidently incompetent, having selected doubtful tuna and an inferior room, to which Mackenzie couldn't bear to return — particularly as he had given Schmidt the lower. So I suggested that he get another room."

"I noticed you were taking quite an interest in him," I remarked, in the immemorial manner of husbands.

"Oh," laughed my wife, "I'm just a child at heart and I was fascinated by his wrist watch."

"Were you in his room the morning I couldn't find you?"

"You bet. But his passion for my company seemed to have waned."

"Serves you right. You just went in there to snoop around. Did you find anything?"

"Two things," replied my wife. "A faint odor of ipecac and a mirror that swung with the boat."

"And what did they tell the Great Mind?"

"The mirror told me that the handsome Mr. Mackenzie didn't like my visit — in fact, if I'm not reading too much into a mere look, he was fairly terrified. And the ipecac — well, it's what you give croupy babies to make them vomit, isn't it, Doctor?"

"Why, Gwynn!" exclaimed Helen Cobb from the doorway, where she had been standing with Schroeder. "You haven't been sleuthing in competition with the Real Thing?"

Erik Schroeder looked at my wife out of shrewd blue eyes. He has white hair and the hawklike features of the Conan Doyle tradition.

Leni Dill eyed him accusingly. "Erik! You never told me there was a suicide. And Mrs. Keats knew all about it!"

"That was because I had the luck to be in the next room to Mr. Mackenzie," said Gwynn.

I snickered. "I don't suppose you were the one who saw the Purser about getting him that room — ?"

"Well, but I had the luck to see the Captain and the First Officer go in there and to hear the doctor tell them Mr. Mackenzie was too ill to be questioned. And considering that somebody had been inquiring after Mr. Schmidt — and the engines had been reversed — I couldn't help inferring *something*. But I daresay Mr. Schroeder knows all about it, since he went in there with the Captain."

"I wasn't there officially," smiled Schroeder. "The Captain merely asked me to step in while he questioned Mackenzie. And I went over Schmidt's belongings to see if we could discover his identity. But there wasn't a scrap of paper — nothing that would give a clue."

"That wasn't what I gathered from our steward," said Gwynn.

"What did you gather from your steward?"

"That you had found some handkerchiefs and things mono-grammed *P.S.* — of fine quality, but not new — which led to the belief that Mr. Schmidt had once had money. All the other things — the newer ones — were of very inferior quality."

"Well, that's true," admitted Schroeder. "I thought it might sup-ply a motive — a man who had come down in the world and couldn't take it."

"But on the other hand," suggested Clarence Cobb, "he had a job — " Schroeder shrugged. "And don't you think it strange that he carried *nothing* to identify him?"

"As if somebody had gone through his things and removed any-thing that *might* — " supplemented my wife.

"Look here, Mrs. Keats," said Schroeder, "just what have you in mind?"

"What I bet you also had in mind, Mr. Schroeder . . . that Mr. Mackenzie murdered his secretary."

"Gwynn!" I cried. The others looked at her in various degrees of amazement. When the doctor recovered his voice he was thoroughly outraged. Mackenzie was an exceptionally charming man. Schmidt had simply gone overboard.

"But *why?*"

"Violently seasick people often contemplate suicide. The man was probably a neurotic."

"Ardent Scientists are never neurotics," reproved Gwynn. "Mr. Mackenzie must have overlooked that when he talked it over with you."

The doctor looked irritated. "I imagine sometimes Scientists go out of their minds. Even the steward said how terribly sick he was."

"So sick that two of them had to help him out on deck."

Schroeder had not taken his eyes from my wife's face — troubled eyes. "What makes you think it wasn't suicide, Mrs. Keats?"

"Just a hunch," replied Gwynn.

Schroeder continued to look grave. "And what else?"

"Well — there was one thing, at least, that should have been in Schmidt's bag."

"And what was that?"

"Mrs. Eddy's book. Don't you think an ardent Scientist would have had it with him on the trip?"

The ghost of a smile narrowed Erik Schroeder's eyes. "I commented on that, but the Captain seemed satisfied — and I'm on a holiday. Besides, there doesn't seem to be much motive for a man to murder his secretary."

"You have only Mackenzie's word that Schmidt *was* his secretary — "

"He's listed that way," protested the doctor. "*Wm. R. Mackenzie and Secretary.*"

"Suppose a man had found his secretary making love to his wife," suggested Leni.

"Hardly likely," said Schroeder. "Mackenzie is a handsome, engaging young man and according to the steward, Schmidt was middle-aged and plain."

"Tell me," asked Gwynn. "Was Schmidt a bigger man than Mackenzie?"

"No, smaller. Why?"

"Did you happen to notice Mackenzie's wrist watch?"

"An ordinary silver watch with a leather strap. I've seen them in Canada for a pound sterling."

"And it didn't strike you as odd — ?"

"Many rich men wear cheap watches while traveling. Particularly a Scotchman might — "

"But I mean about the leather strap."

"It was apparently much worn — "

"What does it mean when one cyelet is badly worn, the others not at all?"

"The worn one has been used," volunteered Clarence.

"Well, the eyelet that fastened the strap firmly around Mackenzie's wrist wasn't the used one. It was three farther down. So it looked as though the watch had been worn for a long time by somebody with a smaller wrist than Mr. Mackenzie and had only recently been taken over by Mr. M."

"May I use your phone?" asked Schroeder. Clarence went with him and I strained my ears, but the conversation was in Spanish.

Helen Cobb's eyes widened. "My gracious, Gwynn, you've started something. He's speaking to the Commissioner of Police!"

"I know — he's suggesting holding Mackenzie for further questioning. They naturally asked him to stay in Havana for the routine investigation. But he hasn't stirred out of his room since we landed."

"I suppose that's what you were discussing with the chambermaid this morning?"

"It was," replied Gwynn, utterly unabashed. "I was trying to figure out some excuse for calling on him. I'd like to ask him how he came to hire a secretary — without references."

Gwynn certainly plays in luck. When we reached the Nacional, there was a message from Mackenzie asking us to call him. We stopped at his room instead. William Mackenzie could not have been over twenty-six, with a fine athletic frame and a lot of curly hair and gray-blue eyes in which there was something helplessly worried as he begged us to come in.

He told us the Commissioner had been there, wearing him down with questions about Schmidt. "I think Schroeder put him up to it. He's darned clever, Schroeder. Of course I stuck to what I told them all along."

"Why not, if it's true?"

"But it isn't," said Mackenzie. I hoped he didn't see the look Gwynn shot me out of those absurdly expressive brown eyes. "We had sailed as Mackenzie and Secretary and I didn't see why certain things should be dragged in that I was anxious to keep quiet. But this Cuban chap put the screws on me pretty hard. And I'm anxious to get away. You're the only people I know in this part of the world, and I'd like to ask your advice."

I did not look at my wife although, in case I have not mentioned it, she is very easy to look at, with dark hair going off one ear and towards the other in a natural swirl, and clothes that always make other women look either overdressed or undergroomed.

"Last Thursday," began Mackenzie, "I arrived in New York with my wife. We went to the Wendham Hotel. Saturday morning, a little before ten, I went out to keep a business engagement. When I came back, my wife was not there. And she was not in the dining room, or anywhere in the hotel. I opened her closet and it was bare. The bureau was empty, too. Everything belonging to my wife had been cleaned out of the place!

"While I was trying to grasp what could have happened, there was a knock at the door. A strange man stepped into the room.

"'Look here, Mr. Mackenzie,' he said, 'my name is Schmidt. I'm the house detective. I was next to the operator when you called down to ask about Mrs. Mackenzie.' And he told me he had seen my wife drive off with her bags, but had thought it better to say nothing downstairs in case there was anything in the nature of a scandal. Because there had been a man in the cab — also with bags.

"You have to understand the relationship between my wife and myself to realize my state of mind. Three years ago I took a trip to Hollywood and met my wife, who was working in pictures. In ten days we were married. Since then we had never been separated for a day — hardly an hour. And now she was gone . . . with another man! I was utterly stunned and grateful for this stranger's help. Alone I would not have known where to turn.

"I hadn't the faintest notion of who this other man could be. We had been in New York only two days, and together all the time. She hadn't known until the day we left that she was coming. How could she have arranged an elopement? And up on the farm we lived a very secluded life. The few people who visited us were old' friends of mine.

"Schmidt went out to make some inquiries. The more I thought, the more I was baffled. I admit I have a jealous nature and I had always been watchful. I could recall nothing — no absence — no letters — no mysterious phone calls that should have made me suspicious at the time, or that offered any clue as I paced my room, waiting for Schmidt."

"And being a suspicious man, you hadn't asked Schmidt anything about himself?" inquired Gwynn.

"Why, no. He was the house detective — and besides I was too upset to think about him. And of course I didn't know he was going to jump off a boat and get me in a mess."

"Of course not. I suppose he asked you for money."

"I gave him a little for immediate expenses. Later, of course, I furnished money for cables and bribes and all sorts of things — a lot of money," he concluded ruefully.

"He came back to say that the starter recalled it was a Yellow Cab, and also the man in the cab, but not his appearance. We agreed not to mention anything to anybody, since I was eager to avoid scandal and the hotel people might resent his conduct. But he was sick of his job and eager to start off as a private investigator.

"Finally he found a driver who had been picked up by a man with a gladstone bag and stopped at the Wendham for a lady answering the description of Mrs. Mackenzie. He had driven them to the Ward Line pier. The *Orizaba* had sailed that Saturday. And Schmidt's next report was that a tall blonde in a black coat with a Persian collar and a man with a gladstone bag had sailed on the *Orizaba*.

"Schmidt offered to trail them. Of course I wanted to go, too. He made all the arrangements. I was too stunned to do more than follow his instructions. I swear to God that's all I know about Philip Schmidt. But you can see why I didn't immediately blurt it out when I was questioned."

"Of course," said Gwynn. "You certainly seem to be having hard luck. And now that you're eager to be after your wife, they hold you here. Have you made any inquiries at all?"

"No. I didn't think it wise — feeling that I was under surveillance."

"There!" said I to my wife as we were getting ready for bed. "What do you think of your murder case now?"

"I admit I have an entirely different slant on it. Let's talk to Schroeder tomorrow. . . . But doesn't it seem funny that Schmidt, having secured the kind of job he wanted, should take himself off so mysteriously?" And she began to sing: "'Just for a handful of ptomaine he left us——'"

I turned out the light.

The next day we called at Schroeder's hotel. He had already seen Mackenzie who, on Gwynn's advice, had told him the story. Schroeder was surprised that Mackenzie had confided in us.

"It's because I wore my Girl Scout badge," said Gwynn. "Matter of fact, I don't know whether he wanted our advice half so much as our money. He was dying to get us into a game."

"What kind of game?"

"Any kind — as soon as he heard we were bad money players."

I am always amazed at how mean and suspicious Gwynn can be when she doesn't like a person.

"I don't like him, either," admitted Schroeder, "but I've checked his story. Mackenzie and wife registered at the Wendham from Edmonton. She left two days later. However, the starter couldn't recall whether she left alone, and denied having given any information about a Yellow Cab. In fact, Schmidt was unknown at the Wendham and they employed no house detective.

"So any deception seems to have been on the part of Schmidt. I haven't the faintest idea what his game was. But since he's gone, why bother? We have also had word from Edmonton that a William R. Mackenzie lives there, and that he left last week for New York with his wife. So there seems no further reason for holding Mackenzie and I understand the Cuban police have told him he may go."

"May I make a suggestion?" said Gwynn. "Before he checks out, ask him what his business was in New York, and what his wife's name is. Perhaps, if he is so anxious to trace her, he will show you a picture."

"But why? What have you in mind?"

"Nothing," replied Gwynn, "only I'd like to see the type of woman who would run out on a man like Mackenzie. Of course, it may have been his stinginess. But then, there was that lavish display in the bar. If a tight man loosens up to that extent, there must be some reason. The reason is missing. A lot of things are missing. Principally why Schmidt killed himself."

The following morning Mackenzie tapped on our door to ask us whether we wouldn't care for a chukker of backgammon — which we wouldn't — and to tell us he had been released by the authorities.

"That's fine," said Gwynn. "I suppose you can't wait to start looking for your wife. How are you going about it?"

He gestured helplessly. "I don't know where to begin."

"How about the Commissioner?" I suggested.

"How about Erik Schroeder?" suggested Gwynn. "If anybody can find her, Schroeder can."

"But he'll want too much money. And besides, I don't like him. What concern is it of his what my business was in New York? Matter of fact, I wouldn't mind telling it to you. If you're writers, you might be able to use it. It would make a great yarn."

My wife and I exchanged that certain look. Everybody has a story that would make a great yarn. And everybody is so generous in the manner of telling it!

"I've been working on an invention in Canada. I needn't tell you what it is — but it has to do with film. It should be worth a fortune if properly marketed. Of course it's tough dealing with those big corporations and the proper approach is as important as the invention.

"Well, one day I got a letter from a man named Paul Stone outlining a scheme for promoting my patent. And the details of the scheme were exactly as I had dreamed them. I don't know how he got wind of my invention, because I kept it very quiet. I have my own laboratory. My wife helped me and not another soul knew about it. Naturally I wrote back to Stone and he suggested that I come to New York and talk it over. He wanted me to come alone, but at the last minute I decided to take my wife. I felt she was entitled to a trip."

"Also, wives get into trouble if they're left alone."

"I thought of that. So she came along."

"Eagerly, I'll bet?"

"Well, of course, she claimed she had no clothes, but — This fellow Stone had reserved a room for me at the Wendham and we went there. I found a wire saying he had been called out of town, but would be back Saturday. So my wife and I went sightseeing and Saturday morning Stone phoned and asked me to meet him in the lobby of the Alamac."

"Up on 71st Street?"

"That's it. Well, I waited awhile, and then had him paged, and then waited some more. Then I inquired at the desk whether he was in his room. They told me there was no Paul Stone registered at the Alamac! I didn't know what to make of it, because I had always written him there. However, he had brought me all the way from Alberta for that appointment and I was sure he meant to keep it. But at one o'clock I went back to my own hotel. And would you believe it — I never heard another word from Stone? What do you make of that?"

"I make that Mr. Stone was very eager to get Mr. Mackenzie out of the way so that Mrs. Mackenzie could get out of the Wendham. I make also that Mrs. Mackenzie prompted Mr. Stone's entire correspondence. There is always an accommodating laundress to receive mail, or a farmer's wife who brings around fresh eggs. . . . The decision to take Mrs. Mackenzie to New York probably upset the original plan. If Mr. Mackenzie had gone alone, he would perhaps not have heard from Mr. Stone at all. Nor found Mrs. Mackenzie back on the farm in Edmonton."

Mackenzie looked stupefied, then furious. "What a fool I've been! I'll put Schroeder on her track — no matter what it costs! Where is Schroeder? I want to see him!"

We offered to take him to Schroeder's hotel. On the way out we stopped for the mail. Mackenzie tore open a letter and read it, a puzzled frown between his brows.

"What do you make of this?" he demanded, holding it out to me.

" 'Darling Philip — ' " it began.

I looked up. "For Schmidt?"

He held out the envelope. It was addressed to *Philip Schmidt, Care William R. Mackenzie, Hotel Nacional,* and bore a Cuban stamp.

"Perhaps I shouldn't have opened it, but — you understand. Read it," he urged.

When I sent that wire to the boat I really meant to patch things up with Emilio and never see you again. But last night he was drunk again — terribly — Oh my darling this time I mean it. I will go away with you — Come at once. I need you. Love — love — love —

C—

It seemed plain enough then. Schmidt had wanted to get to Havana. In some way he got wind of Mrs. Mackenzie's flight and played on Mackenzie's credulity and distress to work the trip. On the boat he received a cable from his *Señora* calling the deal off. Curtain for Mr. Schmidt.

I was so pleased with my perspicuity that I blurted it out, not thinking of the effect on Mackenzie. I suppose subconsciously I felt I was doing him a good turn. I didn't realize that all along he had been buoyed up by the hope and excitement of the chase. With the prop removed he was in a bad way. No use now in seeing Schroeder. No use in anything.

He seemed on the point of collapse and I did what I could for him. It was pitiful the way he clung to us. By nightfall Gwynn had a headache, but I went in and played cards with him. And the next morning, as the headache persisted, we started off without her for Morro Castle. He looked wretched and there was a feverish light in his eyes. As I look back now I can understand it. His manner became more and more curious. He carried a Panama hat; but although the sun was doing its tropical best, he refused to put it on. And under his arm he clutched a package as though it contained rubies. I remember, before we left, Gwynn moved the package and he jumped and took it away from her and held it on his lap until I was ready to go.

Clarence Cobb had sent us a Captain of the Militia to act as guide. As he walked around the outside of the fortress, Mackenzie kept asking about sharks. The Captain told us stories. Vivid stories. They seemed to have a horrible effect on Mackenzie, who kept peering into the water and insisting he saw sharks. I couldn't get him away from those rocks. And he asked me whether I thought there had been sharks when Schmidt went overboard. I assured him there were none.

"I hate to think — maybe there were sharks — " He shut his eyes and swayed. I begged him to put on his hat. I thought the sun was affecting him. But he continued to spot sharks and mumble about Schmidt — once excusing him: "I can understand him. Why go on living without the one thing you want most?" and the next time cursing him: "I had no reason for loving the —— but if I had thought that there were sharks — "

That sentence stuck in my mind until I realized it was because of the tense. If he didn't know until yesterday . . .

The Captain was telling us about the dungeons where tradition has embroidered fantastic tales of cruelty to prisoners. Mackenzie shuddered and swayed again.

"Look here," I said, "if you'd rather not go in . . . ?"

"Why shouldn't I?" He bridled. "Why shouldn't I look at dungeons?" I wanted to get away. An idea had occurred to me. Since Mackenzie had opened Schmidt's letter, perhaps he had also opened that wire on the boat and read it. . . . Fury at Schmidt would supply a motive. . . . I wanted to talk it over with Gwynn.

There is nothing in those dungeons except what imagination paints into them. But we had no sooner stepped inside than Mackenzie had to go out again. We waited for him to return and then went in search of him. Back on the rocks where we had watched for sharks I saw something. I picked it up. It was a wallet monogrammed *W.R.M.* It had not fallen there. It had been wedged between the rocks — conspicuously — where searchers would not fail to find it.

I looked down at the graying water. A Panama hat floated on a wave. Was it imagination or did I see a dark fin cutting the surface of the water? . . . Suddenly the hat disappeared. I became violently ill.

The papers gave the story a great play. Suicide of Wealthy Canadian in Waters off Morro Castle . . . Eyewitness Sees Sharks Attack Hat . . . Wm. R. Mackenzie, despondent over the loss of his wife, ended his life etc. . . . etc. . . . And they gave plenty of space to the wallet, which contained travelers' checks and a farewell note addressed to Mrs. Mackenzie.

"So I guess Mrs. Keats had the right hunch," said Schroeder, "and Mackenzie did finish Schmidt before he went up to the bar."

"Quite a while before," said Gwynn, and outlined what she thought had taken place. "I figure he got him out on deck and possibly hit him over the head while he was leaning over the rail. The steward said the man was lying with his head on his arms and looked ghastly. Our boy friend may only have pretended to get an answer about the doctor. Maybe there was no answer. Watching his chance, he dropped him overboard. Then he went into the state-room and fixed up Schmidt's suitcase — messed up the bed — rang for the steward and met him in the companionway to register that Schmidt was asleep. Then he went to the bar and began that wild orgy of treating, during which he proceeded to get so sick that he wouldn't have to go back into that cabin, or have anything to do with discovering Schmidt's absence. Or answer too many questions. And I daresay, when I dropped in, he was a little sorry he had been so friendly the night before."

"Poor guy," said I. "Out of a boatload of people, he just had to pick on *you*. Author of Perfect Crime Makes One Fatal Error."

"Author of *this* perfect crime made several. And something tells me it will eventually make good telling."

"Eventually! Why not now?"

"I should say not! Think of my sense of drama. By the way, Mr. Schroeder, did you ever find out his wife's name?"

"Temple Mackenzie."

"Temple — " said Gwynn musingly.

"Why?"

"It might be a good thing to remember."

Back in New York, we received a phone call from Erik Schroeder. He was working on a big case and wanted Gwynn's hunch on it — the well-known woman's angle. At his apartment the talk naturally drifted to Mackenzie. Schroeder had followed up certain threads. "You never can tell," he jeered, "I may want to write it up for the magazines."

Gwynn laughed. "Without the final chapter?"

"I think I have a tag — "

"Then you saw that bit in yesterday's paper?"

"What bit — ?"

"From Hollywood?"

"What has Hollywood to do — "

"Pardon me, I spoke out of turn. What's your tag?"

"Well, far from being a rich man, the only estate Mackenzie left was his expectations from that patent which, unfortunately, isn't worth a damn. One of the G.E. men told me everything in it is covered by better patents of their own. You questioned his being a rich man. In fact, you called all the turns. Having read some of your fiction detectives, I should say Lady Novelist takes Great Detective for a ride all along the line — and that makes our last chapter."

"Next to the last," corrected Gwynn. "You haven't by any chance seen 'Wild Eagle' at the Paramount this week?"

"Don't change the subject," said I. "Stick to the Mackenzie tale."

"That's it."

"The picture you saw this afternoon? Don't be so damn' cryptic."

"Can't a girl have her simple pleasures? Knowing we were going to see Mr. Schroeder I couldn't resist a sort of coup. My dramatic instinct, you know. I'll sit through the picture again for the pleasure of watching your faces. And then I'll tell you *my* final chapter."

For two reels nothing happened. And then Schroeder straightened up in his seat and I exclaimed aloud. . . . There on the screen in riding breeches was Wm. R. Mackenzie!

"The son-of-a-gun!" said Schroeder, when we were back in his apartment. "I'll bet you got a shock when he walked on this afternoon."

"Not exactly. I went there expressly to see him. But maybe I'd better go back and 'tell all'?" inquired my wife brightly.

"Maybe you'd better," replied her husband grimly.

"Remember the night you went to Philadelphia, Colin?" I did, of course. "Well, it's a good thing you didn't call me because I wasn't home. I was out all night."

I refrained from comment.

"I was at the Wendham. Took a room on the same floor on which the Mackenzies had stayed and got clubby with Helen, the chambermaid. She remembered Mrs. Mackenzie — a tall, pretty blonde. It seems she had got clubby with Helen, too, and complained about Mackenzie . . . he had plenty of money but was terribly tight . . . kept her cooped up on a farm like a prisoner. 'Of course,' said Helen, 'if she left him she wouldn't get a cent and he left her everything in his will. He made it before they were married. But she said to me, she said, "What the hell! Money isn't everything." '

"I'd been wondering how Temple managed to communicate with her lover."

"How did you know she had a lover?" demanded Schroeder. "Schmidt may have made up that whole business."

"Oh — she had to have a lover, for my hunch. Anyway, the bathroom of the Mackenzie suite has a door into the next suite. Temple goes in, turns on a tub, and has ready communion with the gentleman in the next suite, whom, by the way, you saw tonight — the tall, curly-headed young man in breeches."

"Hold everything! That one was Mackenzie — "

"The billing says Pat Salisbury," Gwynn pointed out.

"Yes, but I thought Mackenzie had taken the name of Salisbury — "

"No — the other way round. Salisbury took the name of Mackenzie. After he murdered him and dropped him overboard."

"By God!" Schroeder brought his fist down.

"Wait a minute!" I cried. "I don't get you — "

"Take your time," replied Gwynn. "Or — I'll tell it to you by easy stages. I'd better begin three years ago — in Hollywood with a couple of young people named Temple Drury and Pat Salisbury — both working in pictures — and the going pretty rough for the girl. Along comes Mackenzie — poses as a millionaire — even making out a will leaving her his fortune. Poor man thought he would have one, some day! She marries him and he takes her to Canada and keeps her cooped up while he monkeys with his invention. Having had a taste of starvation, maybe for a while she is grateful for the security of a roof and three squares. But eventually she gets restless and manages to communicate with the old boy-friend, Salisbury.

"At last she decides to run away. But Mackenzie watches her like a hawk. So Salisbury, in New York on a little spree, writes the husband exactly the kind of letter that would interest him, signing it Paul Stone, and lures him to New York. But something about Temple's manner at the last minute worries Mackenzie and he decides to take her with him.

"Salisbury, who has been staying at the Wendham, and only picking up mail addressed to 'Stone' at the Alamac, gets him a suite next to his. Temple and he perfect their plans through the bathroom door and he phones Mackenzie, as Paul Stone, of course, and sends him on a wild-goose chase up to the Alamac.

"He puts Temple in another hotel and, knocking later at Mackenzie's door, introduces himself as Philip Schmidt, a detective. And he gets expense money from Mackenzie, which he turned over to Temple . . . I trust.

"Maybe his first idea was only to get a few thousand dollars from Mackenzie — string him along — and blow. But Mackenzie wasn't easy to pluck. And it probably seemed a pity that he and Temple should be broke — when that will left her all that money! If only Mackenzie were out of the way. . . .

"Salisbury worked out a pretty neat scheme. On a boat nobody knows who anybody is for the first day. The steward only knows that the two gentlemen in 361 are Mr. Mackenzie and Mr. Schmidt. And if one jumped overboard and the other claimed that Schmidt was missing — who would think it was Mackenzie who was gone? Whereas, if a wealthy man were to disappear under mysterious circumstances, investigation might involve his secretary. And certainly the wife would be questioned and her connection with Mr. Salisbury uncovered. But when Schmidt was missing even Mr. Schroeder asked: 'What motive would a man have for murdering his secretary?'

"Probably the ipecac which made the young man too sick for questioning also made Mackenzie too sick for talking. As soon as the boat starts, Salisbury-Stone-Schmidt puts Mackenzie to bed and does all the talking for the team — making out the poor man is a Scientist, so even the doctor won't be brought in.

"Then while the steward is freshening up the room, Salisbury gets the real Mackenzie on deck and finishes him. And from then on he has a fourth identity. He is now known as Wm. R. Mackenzie. And nobody questions that identity. Still, everything doesn't go as smoothly as Mr. Salisbury-Mackenzie would have liked. There is a snoopy detective on board and a very snoopy woman. They keep wanting a reason for Schmidt's suicide. So the young man supplies a reason — in a letter from a non-existent lady in Havana — without any address.

"When he went out to post that letter, by the way, was the only time he left the Nacional. You see, he didn't have any money. Unfortunately, all the real Mackenzie's money was in travelers' checks which he couldn't cash!

"Of course that letter from 'C' also provided a motive for a fit of despondency in which he could make it seem that Mackenzie had killed himself. Because for Temple to inherit Mackenzie's money, Mackenzie had to be legally dead. So Mackenzie apparently jumps into shark-infested waters — after a fine piece of acting by Mr. Salisbury-Mackenzie. Which suicide, incidentally, took care of the bill at the Nacional. On the waves floats the Panama hat which he never could wear because it was too small! On the rocks lie the travelers' checks, which will revert to Temple and be of *some* use — and a note to remove any possible doubt of his suicide.

"But there doesn't seem to have been any doubt. Only the package worried me. What could there have been in a package that a man would want to have with him when he set out to kill himself — with a suicide note all typed in his pocket? . . . And what had become of it? Had he taken it with him?

"You know how those flashes come to you. Of course he had taken it with him . . . out of the fortress . . . a coat and a cap! Suppose Colin and the Captain had asked the guard — which they didn't, once they saw the note — about a blond hatless man in a Palm beach suit? Would they have connected him with a young man in, say, a blue serge coat, a cap pulled down over his hair, and perhaps dark glasses?"

Schroeder smoked in thoughtful silence. But I insisted on knowing, step by step, how she had hit on it.

"Oh, darling, you *are* such a perfect straight man! Sometimes you just smell a phony and begin to reason from the smell."

"Or maybe you note little things," smiled Schroeder, "and then begin to sniff."

"Maybe. . . . I knew I wouldn't get anything out of a Schroeder by asking, so I brought the talk around to it at Cobb's, and then we began to make a little headway. But a couple of times Salisbury threw me off — like when he told that long circumstantial story of Mrs. Mackenzie's elopement which Mr. Schroeder could check . . . and did."

"Why do you suppose he told all that?" I demanded foggily.

"I think he was secretly proud of his scenario and was having fun with Schroeder and me. And I'm sure he was vain of his acting."

"Not bad acting," admitted Schroeder grudgingly. He smiled again, however.

"Excellent . . . only somebody else should have written his lines and left out the American slang. That was the first whiff I got . . . pure American idiom from a man who had only been in the States twice — on short visits!

"Anybody could have found out what I did at the Wendham . . . that Mackenzie was a middle-aged, darkish man . . . that when the Mackenzies had Suite 805, 806 was occupied by a Pat Salisbury, registered from Hollywood . . . and anybody would have been impressed by the similarity of the initials . . . Pat Salisbury — Paul Stone — Philip Schmidt.

"And anybody would have written to Hollywood and found out that Wm. R. Mackenzie had married Temple Drury in June 1930 . . . that Temple Drury was listed at Central Casting among the extras . . . that she had one bit in a Fox picture and that Pat Salisbury had a part in the same opus . . . that his last rôle was a small one in 'Wild Eagle,' after which he left for New York. It was all there to put together — except where he got the money to get out of Havana and back to Temple."

"A man as resourceful as Mr. Salisbury probably found a way," suggested Schroeder.

"Not probably — actually. They even got out to Hollywood — although it must have been a blow to find that Mackenzie hadn't left any fortune."

"How do you know he got to Hollywood?" asked Schroeder. "That picture was made before he left for New York."

"That," said Gwynn, "is the pay-off. I asked you whether you'd seen an item in the papers. I brought the clipping with me."

ACTOR AND WIFE KILLED

Mr. and Mrs. Pat Salisbury were instantly killed when their car crashed through a railing on a sharp turn of Topanga Pass. The car had been rented by the young couple for the day. Pat Salisbury was last seen in "Wild Eagle" — a Paramount Picture. Mrs. Salisbury was formerly Temple Drury. The couple had not found work since their recent return to Hollywood. Police are investigating the theory of a suicide pact.

INTRODUCING SUSAN DARE

by MIGNON EBERHART

MISS DARE, *who needs no introduction, here applies her pretty noggin to a problem the answer to which is so interesting we reprint the story. To be more specific would give the point away. However, here's a clue: "Cherchez le caméléon!"*

SUSAN DARE WATCHED a thin stream of blue smoke ascend without haste from the long throat of a tiger lily. Michela, then, had escaped also. She was not, however, on the long veranda, for the clear, broadening light of the rising moon revealed it wide and empty, and nothing moved against the silvered lawn which sloped gently toward the pine woods.

Susan listened a moment for the tap of Michela's heels, did not hear it or any other intrusive sound, and then pushed aside the bowl of lilies on the low window seat, let the velvet curtains fall behind her, and seated herself in the little niche thus formed. It was restful and soothing to be thus shut away from the house with its subtly warring elements and to make herself part of the silent night beyond the open windows.

A pity, thought Susan, to leave. But after tonight she could not stay. After all, a guest, any guest, ought to have sense enough to leave when a situation develops in the family of her hostess. The thin trail of smoke from the lily caught Susan's glance again and she wished Michela wouldn't amuse herself by putting cigarette ends in flowers.

A faint drift of voices came from somewhere, and Susan shrank farther into herself and into the tranquil night. It had been an unpleasant dinner, and there would be still an hour or so before she could gracefully extract herself and escape again. Nice of Christabel to give her the guest house — the small green cottage across the terrace at the other side of the house, and through the hedge and up the winding green path. Christabel Frame was a perfect hostess, and Susan had had a week of utter rest and content.

But then Randy Frame, Christabel's young brother, had returned.

And immediately Joe Bromfel and his wife Michela, guests also, had arrived, and with them something that had destroyed all content. The old house of the Frames, with its gracious pillars and long windows and generous dim spaces, was exactly the same — the lazy Southern air and the misty blue hills and the quiet pine woods and the boxed paths through the flowers — none of it had actually changed. But it was, all the same, a different place.

A voice beyond the green velvet curtains called impatiently: "Michela — Michela —— "

It was Randy Frame. Susan did not move, and she was sure that the sweeping velvet curtains hid even her silver toes. He was probably at the door of the library, and she could see, without looking, his red hair and lithe young body and impatient, thin face. Impatient for Michela. Idiot, oh, idiot, thought Susan. Can't you see what you are doing to Christabel?

His feet made quick sounds upon the parquet floor of the hall and were gone, and Susan herself made a sharply impatient movement. Because the Frame men had been red-haired, gallant, quick-tempered, reckless, and (added Susan to the saga) abysmally stupid and selfish, Randy had accepted the mold without question. A few words from the dinner conversation floated back into Susan's memory. They'd been talking of fox hunting — a safe enough topic, one would have thought, in the Carolina hills. But talk had veered — through Michela, was it? — to a stableman who had been shot by one of the Frames and killed. It had happened a long time ago, had been all but forgotten, and had nothing at all to do with the present generation of Frames. But Christabel said hurriedly it had been an accident; dreadful. She had looked white. And Randy had laughed and said the Frames shot first and inquired afterwards and that there was always a revolver in the top buffet drawer.

"Here she is," said a voice. The curtains were pulled suddenly backward, and Randy, a little flushed, stood there. His face fell as he discovered Susan's fair, smooth hair and thin lace gown. "Oh," he said. "I thought you were Michela."

Others were trailing in from the hall, and a polite hour or so must be faced. Queer how suddenly and inexplicably things had become tight and strained and unpleasant!

Randy had turned away and vanished without more words, and Tryon Welles, strolling across the room with Christabel, was looking at Susan and smiling affably.

"Susan Dare," he said. "Watching the moonlight, quietly planning murder." He shook his head and turned to Christabel. "I simply don't believe you, Christabel. If this young woman writes anything, which I doubt, it's gentle little poems about roses and moonlight."

Christabel smiled faintly and sat down. Mars, his black face shining, was bringing in the coffee tray. In the doorway Joe Bromfel, dark and bulky and hot-looking in his dinner coat, lingered a moment to glance along the hall and then came into the room.

"If Susan writes poems," said Christabel lightly, "it is her secret. You are quite wrong, Tryon. She writes —— " Christabel's silver voice hesitated. Her slender hands were searching, hovering rather blindly over the tray, the large amethyst on one white finger full of trembling purple lights. It was a barely perceptible second before she took a fragile old cup and began to pour from the tall silver coffeepot. "She writes murders," said Christabel steadily. "Lovely, grisly ones, with sensible solutions. Sugar, Tryon? I've forgotten."

"One. But isn't that for Miss Susan?"

Tryon Welles was still smiling. He, the latest arrival, was a neat gray man with tight eyes, pink cheeks, and an affable manner. The only obvious thing about him was a rather finical regard for color, for he wore gray tweed with exactly the right shades of green — green tie, green shirt, a cautious green stripe in gray socks. He had reached the house on the heels of his telephoned message from town, saying he had to talk business with Christabel, and he had not had time to dress before dinner.

"Coffee, Joe?" asked Christabel. She was very deft with the delicate china. Very deft and very graceful, and Susan could not imagine how she knew that Christabel's hands were shaking.

Joe Bromfel stirred, turned his heavy dark face toward the hall again, saw no one, and took coffee from Christabel's lovely hand.

Christabel avoided looking directly into his face, as, Susan had noticed, she frequently did.

"A sensible solution," Tryon Welles was saying thoughtfully. "Do murders have sensible solutions?"

His question hung in the air. Christabel did not reply, and Joe Bromfel did not appear to hear it. Susan said:

"They must have. After all, people don't murder just — well, just to murder."

"Just for the fun of it, you mean?" said Tryon Welles, tasting his coffee. "No, I suppose not. Well, at any rate," he went on, "it's nice to know your interest in murder is not a practical one."

He probably thought he was making light and pleasant conversation, reflected Susan. Strange that he did not know that every time he said the word "murder" it fell like a heavy stone in that silent room. She was about to wrench the conversation to another channel when Michela and Randy entered from the hall; Randy was laughing and Michela smiling.

At the sound of Randy's laugh, Joe Bromfel twisted bulkily around to watch their approach, and, except for Randy's laugh, it was entirely silent in the long book-lined room. Susan watched too. Randy was holding Michela's hand, swinging it as if to suggest a kind of frank camaraderie. Probably, thought Susan, he's been kissing her out in the darkness of the garden. Holding her very tight.

Michela's eyelids were white and heavy over unexpectedly shallow dark eyes. Her straight black hair was parted in the middle and pulled severely backward to a knot on her rather fat white neck. Her mouth was deeply crimson. She had been born, Susan knew, in rural New England, christened Michela by a romantic mother, and had striven to live up to the name ever since. Or down, thought Susan tersely, and wished she could take young Randy by his large and outstanding ears and shake him.

Michela had turned toward a chair, and her bare back presented itself to Susan, and she saw the thin red line with an angle that a man's cuff, pressing into the creamy flesh, had made. It was unmistakable. Joe Bromfel had seen it, too. He couldn't have helped seeing it. Susan looked into her coffee cup and wished fervently that Joe Bromfel hadn't seen the imprint of Randy's cuff, and then wondered why she wished it so fervently.

"Coffee, Michela?" said Christabel, and something in her voice was more, all at once, than Susan could endure. She rose and said rather breathlessly:

"Christabel darling, do you mind — I have some writing to do —— "

"Of course." Christabel hesitated. "But wait — I'll go along with you to the cottage."

"Don't let us keep you, Christabel," said Michela lazily.

Christabel turned to Tryon Welles and neatly forestalled a motion on his part to accompany her and Susan.

"I won't be long, Tryon," she said definitely. "When I come back — we'll talk."

A clear little picture etched itself on Susan's mind: the long, lovely room, the mellow little areas of light under lamps here and there, one falling directly upon the chair she had just left, the pools of shadows surrounding them; Michela's yellow satin, and Randy's red head and slim black shoulders; Joe, a heavy, silent figure, watching them broodingly; Tryon Welles, neat and gray and affable, and Christabel with her gleaming red head held high on her slender neck, walking lightly and gracefully amid soft mauve chiffons. Halfway across the room she paused to accept a cigarette from Tryon and to bend to the small flare of a lighter he held for her, and the amethyst on her finger caught the flickering light of it and shone.

Then Susan and Christabel had crossed the empty flagstone veranda and turned toward the terrace.

Their slippered feet made no sound upon the velvet grass. Above the lily pool the flower fragrances were sweet and heavy on the night air.

"Did you hear the bullfrog last night?" asked Christabel. "He seems to have taken up a permanent residence in the pool. I don't know what to do about him. Randy says he'll shoot him, but I don't want that. He *is* a nuisance of course, bellowing away half the night. But after all — even bullfrogs — have a right to live."

"Christabel," said Susan, trying not to be abrupt, "I must go soon. I have — work to do —— "

Christabel stopped and turned to face her. They were at the gap in the laurel hedge where a path began and wound upward to the cottage.

"Don't make excuses, Susan honey," she said gently. "Is it the Bromfels?"

A sound checked Susan's reply — an unexpectedly eerie sound that was like a wail. It rose and swelled amid the moonlit hills, and Susan gasped and Christabel said quickly, though with a catch in her voice: "It's only the dogs howling at the moon."

"They are not," Susan said, "exactly cheerful. It emphasizes —— " She checked herself abruptly on the verge of saying that it emphasized their isolation.

Christabel had turned in at the path. It was darker there, and her cigarette made a tiny red glow. "If Michela drops another cigarette into a flower I'll kill her," said Christabel quietly.

"What —— "

"I said I'd kill her," said Christabel. "I won't, of course. But she — oh, you've seen how things are, Susan. You can't have failed to see. She took Joe — years ago. Now she's taking Randy."

Susan was thankful that she couldn't see Christabel's face. She said something about infatuation and Randy's youth.

"He is twenty-one," said Christabel. "He's no younger than I was when Joe — when Joe and I were to be married. That was why Michela was here — to be a guest at the wedding and all the parties." They walked on for a few quiet steps before Christabel added: "It was the day before the wedding that they left together."

Susan said: "Has Joe changed?"

"In looks, you mean," said Christabel, understanding. "I don't know. Perhaps. He must have changed inside. But I don't want to know that."

"Can't you send them away?"

"Randy would follow."

"Tryon Welles," suggested Susan desperately. "Maybe he could help. I don't know how, though. Talk to Randy, maybe."

Christabel shook her head.

"Randy wouldn't listen. Opposition makes him stubborn. Besides, he doesn't like Tryon. He's had to borrow too much money from him."

It wasn't like Christabel to be bitter. One of the dogs howled again and was joined by others. Susan shivered.

"You are cold," said Christabel. "Run along inside, and thanks for listening. And — I think you'd better go, honey. I meant to keep you for comfort. But —— "

"No, no, I'll stay — I didn't know —— "

"Don't be nervous about being alone. The dogs would know it if a stranger put a foot on the place. Good-night," said Christabel firmly, and was gone.

The guest cottage was snug and warm and tranquil, but Susan was obliged finally to read herself to sleep and derived only a small and fleeting satisfaction from the fact that it was over a rival author's book that she finally grew drowsy. She didn't sleep well even then, and was glad suddenly that she'd asked for the guest cottage and was alone and safe in that tiny retreat.

Morning was misty and chill.

It was perhaps nine-thirty when Susan opened the cottage door, saw that mist lay thick and white, and went back to get her rubbers. Tryon Welles, she thought momentarily, catching a glimpse of herself in the mirror, would have nothing at all that was florid and complimentary to say this morning. And indeed, in her brown knitted suit, with her fair hair tight and smooth and her spectacles on, she looked not unlike a chill and aloof little owl.

The path was wet, and the laurel leaves shining with moisture, and the hills were looming gray shapes. The house lay white and quiet, and she saw no one about.

It was just then that it came. A heavy concussion of sound, blanketed by mist.

Susan's first thought was that Randy had shot the bullfrog.

But the pool was just below her, and no one was there.

Besides, the sound came from the house. Her feet were heavy and slow in the drenched grass — the steps were slippery and the flagstones wet. Then she was inside.

The wide hall ran straight through the house, and away down at its end Susan saw Mars. He was running away from her, his black hands outflung, and she was vaguely conscious that he was shouting something. He vanished, and instinct drew Susan to the door at the left which led to the library.

She stopped, frozen, in the doorway.

Across the room, sagging bulkily over the arm of the green damask chair in which she'd sat the previous night, was a man. It was

Joe Bromfel, and he'd been shot, and there was no doubt that he was dead.

A newspaper lay at his feet as if it had slipped there. The velvet curtains were pulled together across the window behind him.

Susan smoothed back her hair. She couldn't think at all, and she must have slipped down to the footstool near the door for she was there when Mars, his face drawn, and Randy, white as his pajamas, came running into the room. They were talking excitedly and were examining a revolver which Randy had picked up from the floor. Then Tryon Welles came from somewhere, stopped beside her, uttered an incredulous exclamation, and ran across the room too. Then Christabel came and stopped, too, on the threshold, and became under Susan's very eyes a different woman — a strange woman, shrunken and gray, who said in a dreadful voice:

"*Joe — Joe* —— "

Only Susan heard or saw her. It was Michela, hurrying from the hall, who first voiced the question.

"I heard something — what was it? What —— " She brushed past Christabel.

"Don't look, Michela!"

But Michela looked — steadily and long. Then her flat dark eyes went all around the room and she said: "Who shot him?"

For a moment there was utter shocked stillness.

Then Mars cleared his throat and spoke to Randy.

"I don' know who shot him, Mista Randy. But I saw him killed. An' I saw the han' that killed him —— "

"*Hand!*" screamed Michela.

"Hush, Michela." Tryon Welles was speaking. "What do you mean, Mars?"

"They ain't nothin' to tell except that, Mista Tryon. I was just comin' to dust the library and was right there at the door when I heard the shot, and there was just a han' stickin' out of them velvet curtains. And I saw the han' and I saw the revolver and I — I do' know what I did then." Mars wiped his forehead. "I guess I ran for help, Mista Tryon."

There was another silence.

"Whose hand was it, Mars?" said Tryon Welles gently.

Mars blinked and looked very old.

"Mista Tryon, God's truth is, I do' know. I do' know."

Randy thrust himself forward.

"Was it a man's hand?"

"I reckon it was maybe," said the old Negro slowly, looking at the floor. "But I do' know for sure, Mista Randy. All I saw was — was the red ring on it."

"A red *ring?*" cried Michela. "What do you mean —— "

Mars turned a bleak dark face toward Michela; a face that rejected her and all she had done to his house. "A red ring, Miz Bromfel," he said with a kind of dignity. "It sort of flashed. And it was red."

After a moment Randy uttered a curious laugh.

"But there's not a red ring in the house. None of us runs to rubies — " He stopped abruptly. "I say, Tryon, hadn't we better — well, carry him to the divan. It isn't decent to — just leave him — like that."

"I suppose so — " Tryon Welles moved toward the body. "Help me, Randy —— "

The boy shivered, and Susan quite suddenly found her voice.

"Oh, but you can't do that. You can't —— " She stopped. The two men were looking at her in astonishment. Michela, too, had turned toward her, although Christabel did not move. "But you can't do that," repeated Susan. "Not when it's — murder."

This time the word, falling into the long room, was weighted with its own significance. Tryon Welles's gray shoulders moved.

"She's perfectly right," he said. "I'd forgotten — if I ever knew. But that's the way of it. We'll have to send for people — doctor, sheriff, coroner, I suppose."

Afterward, Susan realized that but for Tryon Welles the confusion would have become mad. He took a quiet command of the situation, sending Randy, white and sick-looking, to dress, telephoning into town, seeing that the body was decently covered, and even telling Mars to bring them hot coffee. He was here, there, everywhere: upstairs, downstairs, seeing to them all, and finally outside to meet the sheriff . . . brisk, alert, efficient. In the interval Susan sat numbly beside Christabel on the love seat in the hall, with Michela restlessly prowling up and down the hall before their eyes, listening to the telephone calls, drinking hot coffee, watching everything with her sullen, flat black eyes. Her red-and-white sports suit, with its scarlet bracelets and earrings, looked garish and out of place in that house of violent death.

And Christabel. Still a frozen image of a woman who drank coffee automatically, she sat erect and still and did not speak. The glowing amethyst on her finger caught the light and was the only living thing about her.

Gradually the sense of numb shock and confusion was leaving Susan. Fright was still there and horror and a queer aching pity, but she saw Randy come running down the wide stairway again, his red hair smooth now above a sweater, and she realized clearly that he was no longer white and sick and frightened; he was instead alert and defiantly ready for what might come. And it would be, thought Susan, in all probability, plenty.

And it was.

Questions — questions. The doctor, who was kind, the coroner, who was not; the sheriff, who was merely observant — all of them questioning without end. No time to think. No time to comprehend. Time only to reply as best one might.

But gradually out of it all certain salient facts began to emerge. They were few, however, and brief.

The revolver was Randy's, and it had been taken from the top buffet drawer — when no one knew or, at least, would tell. "Everybody knew it was there," said Randy sulkily. The fingerprints on it would probably prove to be Randy's and Mars's, since they picked it up.

No one knew anything of the murder, and no one had an alibi, except Liz (the Negro second girl) and Minnie (the cook), who were together in the kitchen.

Christabel had been writing letters in her own room: she'd heard the shot, but thought it was only Randy shooting a bullfrog in the pool. But then she'd heard Randy and Mars running down the front stairway, so she'd come down too. Just to be sure that that was what it was.

"What else did you think it could be?" asked the sheriff. But Christabel said stiffly that she didn't know.

Randy had been asleep when Mars had awakened him. He had not heard the sound of the shot at all. He and Mars had hurried down to the library. (Mars, it developed, had gone upstairs by means of the small back stairway off the kitchen.)

Tryon Welles had walked down the hill in front of the house to the mail box and was returning when he heard the shot. But it was muffled, and he did not know what had happened until he reached the library. He created a mild sensation at that point by taking off a ring, holding it so they could all see it, and demanding of Mars if that was the ring he had seen on the murderer's hand. However, the sensation was only momentary, for the large clear stone was as green as his neat green tie.

"No, suh, Mista Tryon," said Mars. "The ring on the han' I saw was red. I could see it plain, an' it was red."

"This," said Tryon Welles, "is a flawed emerald. I asked because I seem to be about the only person here wearing a ring. But I suppose that, in justice to us, all our belongings should be searched."

Upon which the sheriff's gaze slid to the purple pool on Christabel's white hand. He said, however, gently, that that was being done, and would Mrs. Michela Bromfel tell what she knew of the murder.

But Mrs. Michela Bromfel somewhat spiritedly knew nothing of it. She'd been walking in the pine woods, she said defiantly, glancing obliquely at Randy, who suddenly flushed all over his thin face. She'd heard the shot but hadn't realized it was a gunshot. However, she was curious and came back to the house.

"The window behind the body opens toward the pine woods," said the sheriff. "Did you see anyone, Mrs. Bromfel?"

"No one at all," said Michela definitely.

Well, then, had she heard the dogs barking? The sheriff seemed to know that the kennels were just back of the pine woods.

But Michela had not heard the dogs.

Someone stirred restively at that, and the sheriff coughed and said unnecessarily that there was no tramp about, then, and the questioning continued. Continued wearily on and on and on, and still no one knew how Joe Bromfel had met his death. And as the sheriff was at last dismissing them and talking to the coroner of an inquest, one of his men came to report on the search. No one was in the house who didn't belong there; they could tell nothing of footprints; the French windows back of the body had been ajar, and there was no red ring anywhere in the house.

"Not, that is, that we can find," said the man.

"All right," said the sheriff. "That'll be all now, folks. But I'd take it kindly if you was to stay around here today."

All her life Susan was to remember that still, long day with a kind of sharp reality. It was, after those first moments when she'd felt so ill and shocked, weirdly natural, as if, one event having occurred, another was bound to follow, and then upon that one's heels another, and all of them quite in the logical order of things. Even the incident of the afternoon, so trivial in itself but later so significant, was as natural, as unsurprising as anything could be. And that was her meeting with Jim Byrne.

It happened at the end of the afternoon, long and painful, which Susan spent with Christabel, knowing somehow that, under her frozen surface, Christabel was grateful for Susan's presence. But there were nameless things in the air between them which could be neither spoken of nor ignored, and Susan was relieved when Christabel at last took a sedative and, eventually, fell into a sleep that was no more still than Christabel waking had been.

There was no one to be seen when Susan tiptoed out of Christabel's room and down the stairway, although she heard voices from the closed door of the library.

Out the wide door at last and walking along the terrace above the lily pool, Susan took a long breath of the mist-laden air.

So this was murder. This was murder, and it happened to people one knew, and it did indescribable and horrible things to them. Frightened them first, perhaps. Fear of murder itself came first — simple, primitive fear of the unleashing of the beast. And then on its heels came more civilized fear, and that was fear of the law, and a scramble for safety.

She turned at the hedge and glanced backward. The house lay white and stately amid its gardens as it had lain for generations. But it was no longer tranquil — it was charged now with violence. With murder. And it remained dignified and stately and would cling, as Christabel would cling and had clung all those years, to its protective ritual.

Christabel: Had she killed him? Was that why she was so stricken and gray? Or was it because she knew that Randy had killed him? Or was it something else?

Susan did not see the man till she was almost upon him, and

then she cried out involuntarily, though she as a rule was not at all nervous. He was sitting on the small porch of the cottage, hunched up with his hat over his eyes and his coat collar turned up, furiously scribbling on a pad of paper. He jumped up as he heard her breathless little cry and whirled to face her and took off his hat all in one motion.

"May I use your typewriter?" he said.

His eyes were extremely clear and blue and lively. His face was agreeably irregular in feature, with a mouth that laughed a great deal, a chin that took insolence from no man, and generous width of forehead. His hair was thinning but not yet showing gray and his hands were unexpectedly fine and beautiful. "Hard on the surface," thought Susan. "Terribly sensitive, really. Irish. What's he doing here?"

Aloud she said: "Yes."

"Good. Can't write fast enough and want to get this story off tonight. I've been waiting for you, you know. They told me you wrote things. My name's Byrne. James Byrne. I'm a reporter. Cover special stories. I'm taking a busman's holiday. I'm actually on a Chicago paper and down here for a vacation. I didn't expect a murder story to break."

Susan opened the door upon the small living room.

"The typewriter's there. Do you need paper? There's a stack beside it."

He fell upon the typewriter absorbedly, like a dog upon a bone. She watched him for a while, amazed at his speed and fluency and utter lack of hesitancy.

Presently she lighted the fire already laid in the tiny fireplace and sat there quietly, letting herself be soothed by the glow of the flames and the steady rhythm of the typewriter keys. And for the first time that day its experiences, noted and stored away in whatever place observations are stored, began to arouse and assort and arrange themselves and march in some sort of order through her conscious thoughts. But it was a dark and macabre procession, and it frightened Susan. She was relieved when Jim Byrne spoke.

"I say," he said suddenly, over the clicking keys, "I've got your name Louise Dare. Is that right?"

"Susan."

He looked at her. The clicking stopped.

"Susan. Susan Dare," he repeated thoughtfully. "I say, you can't be the Susan Dare that writes murder stories!"

"Yes," said Susan guardedly, "I can be that Susan Dare."

There was an expression of definite incredulity in his face. "But you —— "

"If you say," observed Susan tensely, "that I don't look as if I wrote murder stories, you can't use my typewriter for your story."

"I suppose you are all tangled up in this mess," he said speculatively.

"Yes," said Susan, sober again. "And no," she added, looking at the fire.

"Don't commit yourself," said Jim Byrne dryly. "Don't say anything reckless."

"But I mean just that," said Susan. "I'm a guest here. A friend of Christabel Frame's. I didn't murder Joe Bromfel. And I don't care at all about the rest of the people here except that I wish I'd never seen them."

"But you do," said the reporter gently, "care a lot about Christabel Frame?"

"Yes," said Susan gravely.

"I've got all the dope, you know," said the reporter softly. "It wasn't hard to get. Everybody around here knows about the Frames. The thing I can't understand is why she shot Joe. It ought to have been Michela."

"*What* —— " Susan's fingers were digging into the wicker arms of her chair, and her eyes strove frantically to plumb the clear blue eyes above the typewriter.

"I say, it ought to have been Michela. She's the girl who's making the trouble."

"But it wasn't — it couldn't — Christabel wouldn't —— "

"Oh, yes, she could," said the reporter rather wearily. "All sorts of people could do the strangest things. Christabel could murder. But I can't see why she'd murder Joe and let Michela go scot-free."

"Michela," said Susan in a low voice, "would have a motive."

"Yes, she's got a motive. Get rid of a husband. But so had Randy Frame. Same one. And he's what the people around here call a Red Frame — impulsive, reckless, bred to a tradition of — violence."

"But Randy was asleep — upstairs —— "

He interrupted her.

"Oh, yes, I know all that. And you were approaching the house from the terrace, and Tryon Welles had gone down after the mail, and Miss Christabel was writing letters upstairs, and Michela was walking in the pine woods. Not a damn alibi among you. The way the house and grounds are laid out, neither you nor Tryon Welles nor Michela would be visible to each other. And anyone could have escaped readily from the window and turned up innocently a moment later from the hall. I know all that. Who was behind the curtains?"

"A tramp — " attempted Susan in a small voice. "A burglar —— "

"Burglar nothing," said Jim Byrne with scorn. "The dogs would have had hysterics. It was one of you. *Who?*"

"I don't know," said Susan. "*I don't know!*" Her voice was uneven, and she knew it and tried to steady it and clutched the chair arms tighter. Jim Byrne knew it, too, and was suddenly alarmed.

"Oh, look here, now," he cried. "Don't look like that. Don't cry. Don't —— "

"I am not crying," said Susan. "But it wasn't Christabel."

"You mean," said the reporter kindly, "that you don't want it to be Christabel. Well —— " He glanced at his watch, said, "Golly," and flung his papers together and rose. "There's something I'll do. Not for you exactly — just for — oh, because. I'll let part of my story wait until tomorrow if you want the chance to try to prove your Christabel didn't murder him."

Susan was frowning perplexedly.

"You don't understand me," said the reporter cheerfully. "It's this. You write murder mysteries, and I've read one or two of them. They are not bad," he interpolated hastily, watching Susan. "Now, here's your chance to try a real murder mystery."

"*But I don't want —— *" began Susan.

He checked her imperatively.

"You do want to," he said. "In fact, you've got to. You see — your Christabel is in a spot. You know that ring she wears —— "

"When did you see it?"

"Oh, does it matter?" he cried impatiently. "Reporters see every-thing. The point is the ring."

"But it's an amethyst," said Susan defensively.

"Yes," he agreed grimly. "It's an amethyst. And Mars saw a red stone. He saw it, it has developed, on the right hand. And the hand holding the revolver. And Christabel wears her ring on her right hand."

"But," repeated Susan, "it *is* an amethyst."

"M-m," said the reporter. "It's an amethyst. And a little while ago I said to Mars: 'What's the name of that flowering vine over there?' And he said: 'That red flower, suh? That's wisteria.'"

He paused. Susan felt exactly as if something had clutched her heart and squeezed it.

"The flowers were purple, of course," said the reporter softly. "The color of a dark amethyst."

"But he would have recognized Christabel's ring," said Susan after a moment.

"Maybe," said the reporter. "And maybe he wishes he'd never said a word about the red ring. He was scared when he first mentioned it, probably; hadn't had a chance to think it over."

"But Mars — Mars would confess to murdering rather than —— "

"No," said Jim Byrne soberly. "He wouldn't. That theory sounds all right. But it doesn't happen that way. People don't murder or confess to having murdered for somebody else. When it is a deliberate, planned murder and not a crazy drunken brawl, when anything can happen, there's a motive. And it's a strong and urgent and deeply personal and selfish motive and don't you forget it. I've got to hurry. Now then, shall I send in my story about the wisteria —— "

"Don't," said Susan choking. "Oh, don't. Not yet."

He picked up his hat. "Thanks for the typewriter. Get your wits together and go to work. After all, you ought to know something of murders. I'll be seeing you."

The door closed, and the flames crackled. After a long time Susan moved to the writing table and drew a sheet of yellow manuscript paper toward her, and a pencil, and wrote: Characters; possible motives; clues; queries.

It was strange, she thought, not how different real life was to its written imitation, but how like. How terribly like!

She was still bent over the yellow paper when a peremptory knock at the door sent her pencil jabbing furiously on the paper and her heart into her throat. It proved to be, however, only Michela Bromfel, and she wanted help.

"It's my knees," said Michela irritably. "Christabel's asleep or something, and the three servants are all scared of their shadows." She paused to dig savagely at first one knee and then the other. "Have you got anything to put on my legs? I'm nearly going crazy. It's not mosquito bites. I don't know what it is. Look!"

She sat down, pulled back her white skirt and rolled down her thin stockings, disclosing just above each knee a scarlet blotchy rim around her fat white legs.

Susan looked and had to resist a wild desire to giggle. "It's n-nothing," she said, quivering. "That is, it's only jiggers—here, I'll get you something. Alcohol."

"Jiggers," said Michela blankly. "What's that?"

Susan went into the bathroom. "Little bugs," she called. Where was the alcohol? "They are thick in the pine woods. It'll be all right by morning." Here it was. She took the bottle in her hand and turned again through the bedroom into the tiny living room.

At the door she stopped abruptly. Michela was standing at the writing table. She looked up, saw Susan, and her flat dark eyes flickered.

"Oh," said Michela. "Writing a story?"

"No," said Susan. "It's not a story. Here's the alcohol."

Under Susan's straight look Michela had the grace to depart rather hastily, yanking up her stockings and twisting them hurriedly, and clutching at the bottle of alcohol. Her red bracelets clanked, and her scarlet fingernails looked as if they'd been dipped in blood. Of the few people who might have killed Joe Bromfel, Susan reflected coolly, she would prefer it to be Michela.

It was just then that a curious vagrant memory began to tease Susan. Rather it was not so much a memory as a memory *of* a memory—something that sometime she had known and now could not remember. It was tantalizing. It was maddeningly elusive. It floated teasingly on the very edge of her consciousness.

Deliberately, at last, Susan pushed it away and went back to work. Christabel and the amethyst. Christabel and the wisteria. Christabel.

It was dark and still drizzly when Susan took her way down toward the big house.

At the laurel hedge she met Tryon Welles.

"Oh, hello," he said. "Where've you been?"

"At the cottage," said Susan. "There was nothing I could do. How's Christabel?"

"Liz says she is still asleep — thank heaven for that. God, what a day! You oughtn't to be prowling around alone at this time of night. I'll walk to the house with you."

"Have the sheriff and other men gone?"

"For the time being. They'll be back, I suppose."

"Do they know any more about — who killed him?"

"I don't know. You can't tell much. I don't know of any evidence they have unearthed. They asked me to stay on." He took a quick puff or two of his cigarette and then said irritably: "It puts me in a bad place. It's a business deal where time matters. I'm a broker — I ought to be going back to New York tonight —— " He broke off abruptly and said: "Oh, Randy — " as young Randy's pale, thin face above a shining mackintosh emerged from the dusk — "let's just escort Miss Susan to the steps."

"Is she afraid of the famous tramp?" asked Randy and laughed unpleasantly. He'd been drinking, thought Susan, with a flicker of anxiety. Sober, Randy was incalculable enough; drinking, he might be dangerous. Could she do anything with him? No, better leave it to Tryon Welles. "The tramp," Randy was repeating loudly. "Don't be afraid of a tramp. It wasn't any tramp killed Joe. And everybody knows it. You're safe enough, Susan, unless you've got some evidence. Have you got any evidence, Susan?"

He took her elbow and joggled it urgently.

"She's the quiet kind, Tryon, that sees everything and says nothing. Bet she's got evidence enough to hang us all. Evidence. That's what we need. Evidence."

"Randy, you're drunk," said Susan crisply. She shook off his clutch upon her arm and then, looking at his thin face, which was so white and tight-drawn in the dusk, was suddenly sorry for him. "Go on and take your walk," she said more kindly. "Things will be all right."

"Things will never be the same again," said Randy. "Never the same — do you know why, Susan?" He's very drunk, thought Susan; worse than I thought. "It's because Michela shot him. Yes, sir."

"Randy, shut up!"

"Don't bother me, Tryon, I know what I'm saying. And Michela," asserted Randy with simplicity, "makes me sick."

"Come on, Randy." This time Tryon Welles took Randy's arm. "I'll take care of him, Miss Susan."

The house was deserted and seemed cold. Christabel was still asleep, Michela nowhere to be seen, and Susan finally told Mars to send her dinner on a tray to the cottage and returned quietly like a small brown wraith through the moist twilight.

But she was an oddly frightened wraith.

She was alone on the silent terrace, she was alone on the dark path — strange that she felt as if someone else were there, too. Was the bare fact of murder like a presence hovering, beating dark wings, waiting to sweep downward again?

"Nonsense," said Susan aloud. "Nonsense —— " and ran the rest of the way.

She was not, however, to be alone in the cottage, for Michela sat there, composedly awaiting her.

"Do you mind," said Michela, "if I spend the night here? There's two beds in there. You see — " she hesitated, her flat dark eyes were furtive — "I'm — afraid."

"Of what?" said Susan, after a moment. "Of whom?"

"I don't know who," said Michela, "or what."

After a long, singularly still moment Susan forced herself to say evenly:

"Stay if you are nervous. It's safe here." Was it? Susan continued hurriedly: "Mars will send up dinner."

Michela's thick white hand made an impatient movement.

"Call it nerves — although I've not a nerve in my body. But when Mars comes with dinner — just be sure it *is* Mars before you open the door, will you? Although as to that — *I* don't know. But I brought my revolver — loaded." She reached into her pocket, and Susan sat upright, abruptly. Susan, whose knowledge of revolvers had such a wide and peculiar range that any policeman, learning of it, would arrest her on suspicion alone, was nevertheless somewhat uneasy in their immediate vicinity.

"Afraid?" said Michela.

"Not at all," said Susan. "But I don't think a revolver will be necessary."

"I hope not, I'm sure," said Michela somberly and stared at the fire.

After that, as Susan later reflected, there was not much to be said. The only interruption during the whole queer evening was the arrival of Mars and dinner.

Later in the evening Michela spoke again, abruptly. "I didn't kill Joe," she said. And after another long silence she said unexpectedly: "Did Christabel ask you how to kill him and get by with it?"

"*No!*"

"Oh." Michela looked at her queerly. "I thought maybe she'd got you to plan it for her. You — knowing so much about murders and all."

"She didn't," said Susan forcefully. "And I don't plan murders for my friends, I assure you. I'm going to bed."

Michela, following her, put the revolver on the small table between the two beds.

If the night before had been heavy with apprehension, this night was an active nightmare. Susan tossed and turned and was uneasily conscious that Michela was awake and restless, too.

Susan must have slept at last, though, for she waked up with a start and sat upright, instantly aware of some movement in the room. Then she saw a figure dimly outlined against the window. It was Michela.

Susan joined her. "What are you doing?"

"Hush," whispered Michela. Her face was pressed against the glass. Susan looked, too, but could see only blackness.

"There's someone out there," whispered Michela. "And if he moves again I'm going to shoot."

Susan was suddenly aware that the ice-cold thing against her arm was the revolver.

"You are not," said Susan and wrenched the thing out of Michela's hand. Michela gasped and whirled, and Susan said grimly: "Go back to bed. Nobody's out there."

"How do you know?" said Michela, her voice sulky.

"I don't," said Susan, very much astonished at herself, but clutching the revolver firmly. "But I do know that you aren't going to start shooting. If there's any shooting to be done," said Susan with aplomb, "I'll do it myself. Go to bed."

But long after Michela was quiet Susan still sat bolt upright, clutching the revolver and listening.

Along toward dawn, out of the *mêlée* of confused, unhappy thoughts, the vagrant little recollection of a recollection came back to tantalize her. Something she'd known and now did not know. This time she returned as completely as she could over the track her thoughts had taken in the hope of capturing it by association. She'd been thinking of the murder and of the possible suspects; that if Michela had not murdered Joe, then there were left Randy and Christabel and Tryon Welles. And she didn't want it to be Christabel; it must not be Christabel. And that left Randy and Tryon Welles. Randy had a motive, but Tryon Welles had not. Tryon Welles wore a ring habitually, and Randy did not. But the ring was an emerald. And Christabel's ring was what Mars called red. Red — then what would he have called Michela's scarlet brace-let? Pink? But that was a bracelet. She wrenched herself back to dig at the troublesome phantom of a memory. It was something trivial — but something she could not project into her conscious memory. And it was something that somehow she needed. Needed now.

She awoke and was horrified to discover her cheek pillowed cosily upon the revolver. She thrust it away. And realized with a sinking of her heart that day had come and, with it, urgent problems. Chris-tabel, first.

Michela was still silent and sulky. Crossing the terrace, Susan looked at the wisteria winding upward over its trellis. It was heavy with purple blossoms — purple like dark amethysts.

Christabel was in her own room, holding a breakfast tray on her lap and looking out the window with a blank, unseeing gaze. She was years older; shrunken somehow inside. She was pathetically willing to answer the few questions that Susan asked, but added nothing to Susan's small store of knowledge. She left her finally, feeling that Christabel wanted only solitude. But she went away reluctantly. It would not be long before Jim Byrne returned, and she had nothing to tell him — nothing, that is, except surmise.

Randy was not at breakfast, and it was a dark and uncomfortable meal. Dark because Tryon Welles said something about a headache and turned out the electric light, and uncomfortable because it could not be otherwise. Michela had changed to a thin suit — red again. The teasing ghost of a memory drifted over Susan's mind and away again before she could grasp it.

As the meal ended Susan was called to the telephone. It was Jim Byrne saying that he would be there in an hour.

On the terrace Tryon Welles overtook her again and said: "How's Christabel?"

"I don't know," said Susan slowly. "She looks — stunned."

"I wish I could make it easier for her," he said. "But — I'm caught, too. There's nothing I can do, really. I mean about the house, of course. Didn't she tell you?"

"No."

He looked at her, considered, and went on slowly.

"She wouldn't mind your knowing. You see — oh, it's tragically simple. But I can't help myself. It's like this: Randy borrowed money of me — kept on borrowing it, spent it like water. Without Christabel knowing it, he put up the house and grounds as collateral. She knows now, of course. Now I'm in a pinch in business and have got to take the house over legally in order to borrow enough money on it myself to keep things going for a few months. Do you see?"

Susan nodded. Was it this knowledge, then, that had so stricken Christabel?

"I hate it," said Tryon Welles. "But what can I do? And now Joe's — death — on top of it — " He paused, reached absently for a cigarette case, extracted a cigarette, and the small flame from his lighter flared suddenly clear and bright. "It's — hell," he said, puffing, "for her. But what can I do? I've got my own business to save."

"I see," said Susan slowly.

And quite suddenly, looking at the lighter, she did see. It was as simple, as miraculously simple as that. She said, her voice to her own ears marvelously unshaken and calm: "May I have a cigarette?"

He was embarrassed at not having offered it to her: he fumbled for his cigarette case and then held the flame of the lighter for her. Susan was very deliberate about getting her cigarette lighted. Finally she did so, said, "Thank you," and added, quite as if she had the whole thing planned: "Will you wake Randy, Mr. Welles, and send him to me? Now?"

"Why, of course," he said. "You'll be in the cottage?"

"Yes," said Susan and fled.

She was bent over the yellow paper when Jim Byrne arrived.

He was fresh and alert and, Susan could see, prepared to be kind. He expected her, then, to fail.

"Well," he said gently, "have you discovered the murderer?"

"Yes," said Susan Dare.

Jim Byrne sat down quite suddenly.

"I know who killed him," she said simply, "but I don't know why."

Jim Byrne reached into his pocket for a handkerchief and dabbed it lightly to his forehead. "Suppose," he suggested in a hushed way, "you tell all."

"Randy will be here in a moment," said Susan. "But it's all very simple. You see, the final clue was only the proof. I knew Christabel couldn't have killed him, for two reasons: one is, she's inherently incapable of killing anything; the other is — she loved him still. And I knew it wasn't Michela, because she is, actually, cowardly; and then, too, Michela had an alibi."

"Alibi?"

"She really *was* in the pine woods for a long time that morning. Waiting, I think, for Randy, who slept late. I know she was there, because she was simply chewed by jiggers, and they are only in the pine woods."

"Maybe she was there the day before."

Susan shook her head decidedly.

"No, I know jiggers. If it had been during the previous day they'd have stopped itching by the time she came to me. And it wasn't during the afternoon, for no one went in the pine woods then except the sheriff's men."

"That would leave, then, Randy and Tryon Welles."

"Yes," said Susan. Now that it had come to doing it, she felt ill and weak; would it be her evidence, her words, that would send a fellow creature over that long and ignominious road that ends so tragically?

Jim Byrne knew what she was thinking.

"Remember Christabel," he said quietly.

"Oh, I know," said Susan sadly. She locked her fingers together, and there were quick footsteps on the porch.

"You want me, Susan?" said Randy.

"Yes, Randy," said Susan. "I want you to tell me if you owed Joe Bromfel anything. Money — or — or anything."

"How did you know?" said Randy.

"Did you give him a note — anything?"

"Yes."

"What was your collateral?"

"The house — it's all mine —— "

"When was it dated? Answer me, Randy."

He flung up his head.

"I suppose you've been talking to Tryon," he said defiantly. "Well, it was dated before Tryon got his note. I couldn't help it. I'd got some stocks on margin. I had to have —— "

"So the house actually belonged to Joe Bromfel?" Susan was curiously cold. Christabel's house. Christabel's brother.

"Well, yes — if you want to put it like that."

Jim Byrne had risen quietly.

"And after Joe Bromfel, to Michela, if she knows of this and claims it?" pressed Susan.

"I don't know," said Randy. "I never thought of that."

Jim Byrne started to speak, but Susan silenced him.

"No, he really didn't think of it," she said wearily. "And I knew it wasn't Randy who killed him because he didn't, really, care enough for Michela to do that. It was — Tryon Welles who killed Joe Bromfel. He had to. For he had to silence Joe and then secure the note and, probably, destroy it, in order to have a clear title to the house, himself. Randy — did Joe have the note here with him?"

"Yes."

"It was not found upon his body?"

It was Jim Byrne who answered: "Nothing of the kind was found anywhere."

"Then," said Susan, "after the murder was discovered and before the sheriff arrived and the search began, only you and Tryon Welles were upstairs and had the opportunity to search Joe's room and find the note and destroy it. Was it you who did that, Randy?"

"*No — no!*" The color rose in his face.

"Then it must have been then that Tryon Welles found and destroyed it." She frowned. "Somehow, he must have known it was there. I don't know how — perhaps he had had words with Joe about it before he shot him and Joe inadvertently told him where it was. There was no time for him to search the body. But he knew —— "

"Maybe," said Randy reluctantly, "I told him. You see — I knew Joe had it in his letter case. He — he told me. But I never thought of taking it."

"It was not on record?" asked Jim Byrne.

"No," said Randy, flushing. "I — asked him to keep it quiet."

"I wonder," said Susan, looking away from Randy's miserable young face, "just how Tryon Welles expected to silence you."

"Well," said Randy dully, after a moment, "it was not exactly to my credit. But you needn't rub it in. I never thought of this — I was thinking of — Michela. That she did it. I've had my lesson. And if he destroyed the note, how are you going to prove all this?"

"By your testimony," said Susan. "And besides — there's the ring."

"Ring," said Randy. Jim Byrne leaned forward intently.

"Yes," said Susan. "I'd forgotten. But I remembered that Joe had been reading the newspaper when he was killed. The curtains were pulled together back of him, so, in order to see the paper, he must have had the light turned on above his chair. It wasn't burning when I entered the library, or I should have noted it. So the murderer had pulled the cord of the lamp before he escaped. And ever since then he has been very careful to avoid any artificial light."

"What are you talking about?" cried Randy.

"Yet he had to keep on wearing the ring," said Susan. "Fortunately for him he didn't have it on the first night — I suppose the color at night would have been wrong with his green tie. But this morning he lit a cigarette and I saw."

"Saw what, in God's name," said Randy burstingly.

"That the stone isn't an emerald at all," replied Susan. "It's an Alexandrite. It changed color under the flare of the lighter."

"Alexandrite!" cried Randy impatiently. "What's that?"

"It's a stone that's a kind of red-purple under artificial light and green in daylight," said Jim Byrne shortly. "I had forgotten there was such a thing — I don't think I've ever happened to see one. They are rare — and costly. Costly," repeated Jim Byrne slowly. "This one has cost a life —— "

Randy interrupted: "But if Michela knows about the note, why, Tryon may kill her —— " He stopped abruptly, thought for a second or two, then got out a cigarette. "Let him," he said airily.

It had been Tryon Welles, then, prowling about during the night — if it had been anyone. He had been uncertain, perhaps, of the extent of Michela's knowledge — but certain of his ability to deal with her and with Randy, who was so heavily in his debt.

"Michela doesn't know now," said Susan slowly. "And when you tell her, Randy — she might settle for a cash consideration. And, Randy Frame, somehow you've got to recover this house for Christabel and do it honestly."

"But right now," said Jim Byrne cheerily, "for the sheriff. And my story."

At the doorway he paused to look at Susan. "May I come back later," he said, "and use your typewriter?"

"Yes," said Susan Dare.

THE GREAT HUMOROUS
DETECTIVE STORIES

THE TREASURE HUNT

by MARY ROBERTS RINEHART

You might suspect that if our dear Tish turned detective, everything would go wrong. Which is precisely what happens in this not-to-be-too-highly-praised delightful and hilarious story.

HAD WE not been so anxious about our dear Tish last summer, I dare say it would never have happened. But even Charlie Sands noticed when he came to our cottage at Lake Penzance for the week-end that she was distinctly not her old self.

"I don't like it," he said. "She's lost her pep, or something. I've been here two days and she hasn't even had a row with Hannah, and I must say that fuss with old Carpenter yesterday really wasn't up to her standard at all."

Old Carpenter is a fisherman, and Tish having discovered that our motor boat went better in reverse than forward, he had miscalculated our direction and we had upset him.

As it happened, that very evening Tish herself confirmed Charlie's fears by asking about Aggie's Cousin Sarah Brown's Chelsea teapot.

"I think," she said, "that a woman of my age should have a hobby — one that will arouse interest at the minimum of physical exertion. And the collection of old china —— "

"Oh, Tish!" Aggie wailed, and burst into tears.

"I mean it," said Tish. "I have reached that period of my life which comes to every woman, when adventure no longer lurks around the next corner. By this I do not refer necessarily to amorous affairs, but to dramatic incidents. I think more than I did of what I eat. I take a nap every day. I am getting old."

"Never!" said Aggie valiantly.

"No? When I need my glasses nowadays to see the telephone directory!"

"But they're printing the names smaller, Tish."

"Yes, and I dare say my arm is getting shorter also," she returned with a sad smile. She pursued the subject no further, however, but went on knitting the bedroom slippers which are her yearly contribution to the Old Ladies' Home, leaving Charlie Sands to gaze at her thoughtfully as he sipped his blackberry cordial.

But the fact is that Tish had outgrown the cottage life at Penzance, and we all knew it. Save for an occasional golf ball from the links breaking a window now and then, and the golfers themselves who brought extra shoes done up in paper for us to keep for them, paying Hannah something to put them on the ice, there was nothing to rouse or interest her.

Her mind was as active as ever; it was her suggestion that a clothespin on Aggie's nose might relieve the paroxysms of her hay fever, and she was still filled with sentiment. It was her own idea on the anniversary of Mr. Wiggins's demise to paint the cottage roof a fresh and verdant green as a memorial to him, since he had been a master roofer by profession.

But these had been the small and simple annals of her days. To all outward seeming, until the night of the treasure hunt, our Tish was no longer the Tish who with our feeble assistance had captured the enemy town of X—— during the war, or held up the band of cutthroats on Thundercloud, or led us through the wilderness of the Far West. An aeroplane in the sky or the sound of the Smith boys racing along in their stripped flivver may have reminded her of brighter days, but she said nothing.

Once, indeed, she had hired a horse from the local livery stable and taken a brief ride, but while making a short cut across the Cummings estate the animal overturned a beehive. Although Tish, with her customary presence of mind, at once headed the terrified creature for the swimming pool, where a number of persons were bathing and sunning themselves in scanty apparel about the edge, the insects forsook the beast the moment horse and rider plunged beneath the surface, and a great many people were severely stung. Indeed, the consequences threatened to be serious, for Tish was unable to get the horse out again and it was later necessary to bring a derrick from Penzance to rescue him. But her protests over the enormous bills rendered by the livery man were feeble, indeed, compared to the old days.

"Twenty dollars!" she said. "Are you claiming that that animal, which should have been able to jump over a beehive without upsetting it, was out ten hours?"

"That's my charge," he said. "Walk, trot, and canter is regular rates, but swimming is double, and cheap at that. The next time you want to go out riding, go to the fish pier and I reckon they'll oblige you. You don't need a horse, lady. What you want is a blooming porpoise."

Which, of course, is preposterous. There are no porpoises in Lake Penzance.

She even made the blackberry cordial that year, a domestic task usually left to Aggie and myself, but I will say with excellent results. For just as it was ready for that slight fermentation which gives it its medicinal quality, a very pleasant young man came to see us, having for sale a fluid to be added to home-made cordials and so on which greatly increased their bulk without weakening them.

"But how can one dilute without weakening?" Tish demanded suspiciously.

"I would not call it dilution, madam. It is really expansion."

It was a clear, colorless liquid with a faintly aromatic odor, which he said was due to juniper in it, and he left us a small bottle for experimental purposes.

With her customary caution, our dear Tish would not allow us to try it until it had been proved, and some days later, Hannah reporting a tramp at the back door, she diluted — or rather expanded — a half glass of cordial, gave him some cookies with it, and we all waited breathlessly.

It had no ill effect, however. The last we saw of the person he was quite cheery; and, indeed, we heard later that he went into Penzance, and, getting one of the town policemen into an alley, forced him to change trousers with him. As a matter of record, whether it was Tish's efforts with the cordial itself, or the addition of the expansion matter which we later purchased in bulk and added, I cannot say. But I do know that on one occasion, having run out of petrol, we poured a bottle of our blackberry cordial into the tank of the motor boat and got home very nicely indeed. I believe that this use of fruit juices has not heretofore been generally known.

Tish, I know, told it to Mr. Stubbs, the farmer who brought us our poultry, advising him to try cider in his car instead of feeding his apples to his hogs. But he only stared at her.

"Feed apples to hogs these days!" he said. "Why, lady, my hogs ain't seen an apple for four years! They don't know there is such a thing."

Occupied with these small and homely duties, then, we went on along the even tenor of our way through July and August, and even into September. In August, Charlie Sands sent us a radio, and there-after it was our custom at 7.20 a.m. to carry our comforters into Tish's bedroom and do divers exercises in loose undergarments.

It is to this training that I lay Tish's ability to go through the terrible evening which followed with nothing more serious than a crack in a floating rib.

And in September, Charlie Sands himself week-ended with us, as I have said; with the result of a definite break in our monotony and a revival of Tish's interest in life, which has not yet begun to fade.

Yet his visit itself was uneventful enough. It was not until Mrs. Ostermaier's call on Saturday evening that anything began to develop. I remember the evening most distinctly. Our dear Tish was still in her dressing gown, after a very unpleasant incident of the morning, when she had inflated a pair of water wings and gone swimming. Unluckily, when some distance out she had endeavored to fasten the water wings with a safety pin to her bathing garments and the air at once began to escape. When Charlie Sands reached the spot only a few bubbles showed where our unfortunate Tish had been engulfed. She had swallowed a great deal of water, and he at once suggested bailing her out.

"By and large," he said, "I've been bailing you out for the last ten years. Why not now?"

But she made no response save to say that she had swallowed a fish. "Get me a doctor," she said thickly. "I can feel the thing wriggling."

"Doctor nothing!" he told her. "What you need is a fisherman, if that's the case."

But she refused to listen to him, saying that if she was meant to be an aquarium she would be one; and seeing she was firm, he agreed.

"Very well," he said cheerfully. "But why not do the thing right while you're about it? How about some pebbles and a tadpole or two?"

The result of all this was that Tish, although later convinced there was no fish, was in an uncertain mood that evening as we sat about the radio. She had, I remember, got Chicago, where a lady at some hotel was singing "By the Waters of Minnetonka." Turning away from Chicago, she then got Detroit, Michigan, and a woman there was singing the same thing.

Somewhat impatiently, she next picked up Atlanta, Georgia, where a soprano was also singing it, and the same thing happened with Montreal, Canada. With a strained look, our dear Tish then turned to the national capital, and I shall never forget her expression when once more the strains of "Minnetonka" rang out on the evening air.

With an impatient gesture she shoved the box away from her, and the various batteries and so on fell to the floor. And at that moment Mrs. Ostermaier came in breathless, and said that she and Mr. Ostermaier had just got Denver, and heard it quite distinctly.

"A woman was singing," she said. "Really, Miss Carberry, we could hear every word! She was singing —— "

" 'The Waters of Minnetonka'?" asked Tish.

"Why, however did you guess it?"

It was probably an accident, but as Tish got up suddenly, her elbow struck the box itself, and the box fell with a horrible crash. Tish never even looked at it, but picked up her knitting and fell to work on a bedroom slipper, leaving Mrs. Ostermaier free to broach her plan.

For, as it turned out, she had come on an errand. She and Mr. Ostermaier wished to know if we could think of any way to raise money and put a radio in the State penitentiary, which was some miles away along the lake front.

"Think," she said, "of the terrible monotony of their lives there! Think of the effect of the sweetness disseminated by 'Silver Threads among the Gold' or 'By the Waters of —— ' "

"Mr. Wiggins always said that music had power to soothe the

savage breast," Aggie put in hastily. "Have you thought of any plan?"

"Mr. Ostermaier suggested that Miss Tish might think of something. She is so fertile."

But Tish's reaction at first was unfavorable.

"Why?" she said. "We've made our jails so pleasant now that there's a crime wave so people can get into them." But she added: "I'm in favor of putting one in every prison if they'd hire a woman to sing 'The Waters of Minnetonka' all day and all night. If that wouldn't stop this rush to the penitentiaries, nothing will."

On the other hand, Charlie Sands regarded the idea favorably. He sat sipping a glass of cordial and thinking, and at last said:

"Why not? Think of an entire penitentiary doing the morning daily dozen! Or laying out bridge hands according to radio instructions! Broaden 'em. Make 'em better citizens. Send 'em out fit to meet the world again. Darned good idea — 'Silver Threads among the Gold' for the burglars and 'Little Brown Jug' for the bootleggers. Think of 'Still as the Night' for the moonshiners, too, and the bedtime stories for the cradle snatchers. Why, it's got all sorts of possibilities!"

He then said to leave it to him and he would think up something, and, falling to work on the radio, soon had it in operation again. His speech had evidently had a quieting effect on Tish, and when the beautiful strains of "The Waters of Minnetonka" rang out once more she merely placed her hands over her ears and said nothing.

It was after his departure on Monday that he wrote us the following note, and succeeded in rousing our dear Tish:

Beloved Maiden Ladies,

I have been considering the problem of the radio for our unfortunate convicts. How about a treasure hunt — à la Prince of Wales — to raise the necessary lucre? I'll write the clues and bury a bag of pennies — each entrant to pay five dollars, and the profits to go to the cause.

Oil up the old car and get out the knickerbockers, for it's going to be a tough job. And don't forget, I'm betting on you. Read the "Murders in the Rue Morgue" for clues and deductive reasoning. And pass me the word when you're ready.

Devotedly,

C. S.

P.S. My usual terms are twenty per cent, but will take two bottles of cordial instead. Please mark "Preserves" on box.   C.

We saw an immediate change in Tish from that moment. The very next morning we put on our bathing suits and, armed with soap and sponges, drove the car into the lake for a washing. Unluckily a wasp stung Tish on the bare knee as we advanced and she stepped on the gas with great violence, sending us out a considerable distance, and, indeed, rendering it necessary to crawl out and hold to the top to avoid drowning.

Here we were marooned for some time, until Hannah spied us and rowed out to us. It was finally necessary to secure three horses and a long rope to retrieve the car, and it was some days in drying out.

But aside from these minor matters, things went very well. Mr. Ostermaier, who was not to search, took charge of the hunt from our end and reported numerous entrants from among the summer colony, and to each entrant the following was issued:

1. The cars of the treasure hunters will meet at the Rectory on Saturday evening at eight o'clock.

2. Each hunter will receive a password or sentence and a sealed envelope containing the first clue.

3. This clue found, another password and fresh sealed envelope will be discovered. And so on.

4. There are six clues.

5. Participants are requested to use care in driving about the country, as the local police force has given notice that it will be stationed at various points to prevent reckless driving.

6. After the treasure is discovered, the hunt will please meet at the Rectory, where light refreshments will be served. It is requested that if possible the search be over before midnight in order not to infringe on the Sabbath day.

In view of the fact that certain persons, especially Mrs. Cummings — who should be the last to complain — have accused Tish of certain unethical acts during that terrible night, I wish to call attention to certain facts:

(a) We obeyed the above rules to the letter, save possibly number five.

(b) There was no actual identification of the scissors.

(c) If there was a box of carpet tacks in our car, neither Aggie nor I saw them.

(d) The fish pier had been notoriously rotten for years.

(e) We have paid for the repairs to the motor cycle, and so on.

(f) Dr. Parkinson is not permanently lamed, and we have replaced his lamps.

(g) Personally, knowing Tish's detestation of crossword puzzles, I believe the false clues were a joke on the part of others concerned.

(h) We did that night what the local police and the sheriff from Edgewater had entirely failed to do, and risked our lives in so doing. Most of the attack is purely jealousy of Letitia Carberry's astute brain and dauntless physical courage.

I need say no more. As Tish observed to Charlie Sands the next day, when he came to see her, lifting herself painfully in her bed:

"I take no credit for following the clues; they were simplicity itself. And I shall pay all damages incurred. But who is to pay for this cracked rib and divers minor injuries, or replace poor Aggie's teeth? Tell me that, and then get out and let me sleep. I'm an old woman."

"Old!" said Charlie Sands. "Old! If you want to see an aged and a broken man, look at me! I shall have to put on a false moustache to get out of town."

But to return to the treasure hunt.

On the eventful day we worked hard. By arrangement with Mr. Stubbs, our poultry man, he exchanged the license plates from his lorry for ours in the morning, and these we put on, it being Tish's idea that in case our number was taken by the local motor policeman, Mr. Stubbs could prove that he was in bed and asleep at the time. We also took out our tail light, as Tish said that very probably the people who could not unravel their clues would follow us if possible, and late in the afternoon, our arrangements being completed, Tish herself retired to her chamber with a number of envelopes in her hand.

Lest it be construed that she then arranged the crossword puzzles which were later substituted for the real clues, I hasten to add that I believe, if I do not actually know, that she wrote letters concerning the missionary society at that time. She is an active member.

At 5.30 we had an early supper and one glass of cordial each.

"I think better on an empty stomach," Tish said. "And I shall need my brains tonight."

"If that's what you think of Aggie and myself, we'd better stay at home," I said sharply.

"I have not stated what I think of your brain, Lizzie, nor of Aggie's either. Until I do, you have no reason for resentment."

Peace thus restored, we ate lightly of tea, toast, and lettuce sandwiches; and, having donned our knickerbockers and soft hats, were ready for the fray. Aggie carrying a small flask of cordial for emergencies and I a flashlight and an angel-food cake to be left at the Rectory, we started out on what was to prove one of the most eventful evenings in our experience.

Tish was thoughtful on the way over, speaking occasionally of Poe and his system of deductive reasoning in solving clues, and also of Conan Doyle, but mostly remaining silent.

Aggie, however, was sneezing badly, due to the dust, and this annoying Tish, she stopped where some washing was hanging out and sent her in for a clothespin. She procured the pin, but was discovered and chased, and undoubtedly this is what led later to the story that the bandits — of whom more later — had, before proceeding to the real business of the night, attempted to steal the Whitings' washing.

But the incident had made Aggie very nervous and she took a second small dose of the cordial. Of this also more later on.

There was a large group of cars in front of the Rectory. The Smith boys had brought their flivver, stripped of everything but the engine and one seat for lightness, and the Cummingses, who are very wealthy, had brought their racer. Tish eyed them both with a certain grimness.

"Not speed but brains will count, Lizzie," she said to me. "What does it matter how fast they can go if they don't know where they're going?"

After some thought, however, she took off the engine hood and the spare tire and laid them aside, and stood gazing at Aggie, now fast asleep in the rear seat.

"I could leave her too," she said. "She will be of no help whatever. But, on the other hand, she helps to hold the rear springs down when passing over bumps."

Mrs. Ostermaier then passed around glasses of lemonade, saying that every hunt drank a stirrup cup before it started, and Mr. Ostermaier gave us our envelopes and the first password, which was "Ichthyosaurus."

It was some time before everyone had memorized it, and Tish utilized the moments to open her envelope and study the clue. The password, as she said, was easy; merely a prehistoric animal. The clue was longer: —

> Water, water everywhere, nor any drop to drink.
> Two twos are four, though some say more, and i-n-k spells ink.

"Water?" I said. "That must be somewhere by the lake, Tish."

"Nonsense! What's to prevent your drinking the lake dry if you want to? I-n-k! It may be the stationer's shop; but if it ever saw water, I don't believe it. 'Two twos are four, though some say more'! Well, if they do, they're fools, and so is Charlie Sands for writing such gibberish."

What made matters worse was that the Smith boys were already starting off laughing, and two or three other people were getting ready to move. Suddenly Tish set her mouth and got into the car, and it was as much as I could do to crawl in before she had cut straight through the canna bed and out on to the road.

The Smith boys were well ahead, but we could still see their tail light, and we turned after them. Tish held the wheel tightly, and as we flew along she repeated the clue, which with her wonderful memory she had already learned by heart. But no light came to either of us, and at the crossroads we lost the Smith boys and were obliged to come to a stop. This we did rather suddenly, and Mr. Gilbert, who is a vestryman in our church, bumped into us and swore in a most unbefitting manner.

"Where the hell is your tail light?" he called furiously.

"You ought to know," said Tish calmly. "Somewhere in your engine, I imagine."

Well, it seemed that everyone had been following us, and no one except the Smith boys apparently knew where to go from there. And just then a policeman came out of the bushes and asked what the trouble was.

"Ichthyosaurus," said Tish absently. "'Water, water everywhere, nor any drop to drink. Two twos are four, though some say more, and —— '"

"Don't try to be funny with me," he said. "For a cent I'd take the whole lot of you into town for obstructing traffic. You've been drinking, that's what!"

And just then Aggie sat up in the back seat and said: "Drinking yourself! Go on, Tish, and run over him. He'sh a nuisance."

Well, I will say her voice was somewhat thick, and the constable got on the running board and struck a match. But Tish was in her seat by that time, and she started the car so suddenly that he fell off into the road. As the other cars had to drive round him, this gave us a certain advantage; and we had soon left them behind us, but we still had no idea where to go. Matters were complicated also by the fact that Tish had now extinguished our headlights for fear of again being molested, and we were as often off the road as on it.

Indeed, once we brought up inside a barn and were only saved from going entirely through it by our dear Tish's quick work with the brakes; and we then had the agony of hearing the other cars pass by on the main road while we were backing away from the ruins of a feed cutter we had smashed.

We had also aroused a number of chickens, and as we could hear the farmer running out and yelling, there was nothing to do but to back out again. Just as we reached the main road a load of buckshot tore through the top of the car, but injured nobody.

"Luckily he was shooting high," said Tish as we drove on. "Lower, and he might have cut our tires."

"Luckily!" said Aggie, from the rear seat. "He'sh taken the crown out of my hat, Tish Carberry! It was nishe hat too. I loved my little hat. I —— "

"Oh, keep still and go to sleep again," said Tish. "'Water, water everywhere, nor any drop to drink. Two twos are four, though some say more, and i-n-k spells ink.'"

"So it did when I went to school," said Aggie, still drowsily. "I-n-k, ink; p-i-n-k, pink; s —— "

Suddenly Tish put her foot on the gas and we shot ahead once more.

"Schoolhouse of course," she said. "The schoolhouse by the water·

tower. I knew my sub-conscious mind would work it out eventually."

Unfortunately, we were the last to get to the schoolhouse, and we had to witness the other cars streaming triumphantly down the road as we went up, shouting and blowing their horns. All but the Simmonses' sedan, which had turned over in a ditch and which we passed hastily, having no time to render assistance.

Miss Watkins, the school-teacher, was on the porch, and as we drew up Tish leaped out.

"Pterodactyl!" she said.

"Warm, but not hot," said Miss Watkins.

"Plesiosaurus!"

"The end's all right."

"Ichthyosaurus!" said Tish triumphantly, and received the envelope. Aggie, however, who had not heard the password given at the Ostermaiers', had listened to this strange conversation dazedly and now burst into tears.

"There'sh something wrong with me, Lizzie!" she wailed. "I've felt queer ever since we started, and now they are talking and it doesn't sound like sensh to me."

It was some time before I was able to quiet her, but Tish had already received the second password, or sentence, which was "Prevention is better than cure, ting-a-ling," and was poring over the next clue.

> Always first in danger, always last to go,
> Look inside the fire box and then you'll know.

I still think that had she taken sufficient time she could have located this second clue easily and without the trouble that ensued. But finding herself last when she is so generally first had irritated her, and she was also annoyed at Miss Watkins, it having been arranged that the last car was to take her back into town.

"Mr. Ostermaier said the clue's in town anyhow. And he didn't think the last car would have much chance, either," she said.

"Who laughs last laughs best," said Tish grimly, and started off at a frightful speed. Miss Watkins lost her hat within the first mile or two, but we could not pause, as a motor-cycle policeman was now following close behind us. Owing to Tish's strategy, however, for when he attempted to come up on the right of us she swerved in that direction and vice versa, we finally escaped him, an unusually sharp swerve of hers having caught him off guard, so to speak, and upset him.

Just when or where we lost Miss Watkins I have no idea. Aggie had again dozed off, and when we reached the town and slowed up, Miss Watkins was gone. She herself does not know, as she seems to have wandered for some time in a dazed condition before reaching home.

But to the hunt.

I still think our mistake was a natural one. One would think that the pass sentence, "Prevention is better than cure, ting-a-ling," certainly indicated either a pharmacy or a medical man and a doorbell, and as Tish said, a fire box was most likely a wood box. There being only two doctors in the town, we went first to Dr. Burt's; but he had already retired, and spoke to us from an upper window.

"We want to examine your wood box," Tish called.

"Wood box?" he said, in a stupefied voice. "What do you want wood for? A splint?"

"We're hunting treasure," said Tish sharply. " 'Prevention is better than cure, ting-a-ling.' "

The doctor closed the window violently; and although we rang for some time, he did not appear again.

At Dr. Parkinson's, however, we had better luck, discovering the side entrance to the house open and finding our way inside with the aid of the flashlight. There was only one wood box on the lower floor, and this we proceeded to search, laying the wood out carefully onto a newspaper. But we found no envelopes, and in the midst of our discouragement came a really dreadful episode.

Dr. Parkinson himself appeared at the door in his night clothes, and, not recognizing us because of our attire and goggles, pointed a revolver at us.

"Hands up!" he cried in a furious tone. "Hands up, you dirty devils! And be quick about it!"

" 'Prevention is better than cure, ting-a-ling,' " said Tish.

"Ting-a-ling your own self! Of all the shameless proceedings I've ever —— "

"Shame on you!" Tish reproved him. "If ting-a-ling means noth-ing to you, we will leave you."

"Oh no, you don't!" he said most unpleasantly. "Put up your hands as I tell you or —— "

I do not now and I never did believe the story he has since told over the town — that Tish threw the fire log she was holding at his legs. I prefer to credit her own version — that as she was trying to raise her hands the wood fell, with most unfortunate results. As a matter of fact, the real risk was run by myself, for when on the impact he dropped the revolver, it exploded and took off the heel of my right shoe.

Nor is it true, as he claims, that having been forced out of his house, we attempted to get back in and attack him again. This error is due to the fact that, once outside, Tish remembered the revolver on the floor, and, thinking it might be useful later, went back to get it. But the door was locked.

However, all is well that ends well. We had but driven a block or two when we perceived a number of the cars down the street at the engine house, and proceeded to find our next clue in the box of the local fire engine.

The password this time was "Prohibition," and the clue ran:

> Just two blocks from paradise and only one from hell,
> Stranger things than truth are found in the bottom of a well.

The Smith boys had already gone on, but we were now at last on equal terms with the others, and as the sleep and the cold night air had by now fully restored Aggie, Tish called a consultation.

"So far," she said, "the Smiths have had the advantage of superior speed. But it is my opinion that this advantage is an unfair one, and that I have a right to nullify it if opportunity arises."

"We'll have to catch them first," I observed.

"We shall catch them," she said firmly, and once more studied the clue.

"Paradise," she said, "should be the Eden Inn. To save time we will circumnavigate it at a distance of two blocks."

This we did, learning later that Hell's Kitchen was the name locally given to the Negro quarter, and once more Tish's masterly deciphering of the clue served us well. Before the other cars had much more than started, we espied the Smiths' stripped flivver out-side the Gilbert place, and to lose no time drove through the hedge and onto the lawn. Here, as is well known, the Gilberts have an old well, long disused, or so supposed. And here we found the Gilberts' gardener standing and the Smith boys drawing up the well bucket.

"Give the word and get the envelope," Tish whispered to me, and disappeared into the darkness.

I admit this. I admit, too, that, as I have said before, I know noth-ing of her actions for the next few moments. Personally, I believe that she went to the house, as she has stated, to get the Gilbert cook's recipe for jelly roll; and, as anyone knows, considerable damage may be done to an uncovered engine by flying stones. To say that she cut certain wires while absent is to make a claim not borne out by the evidence.

But I will also say that the Smith boys up to that moment had had an unfair advantage, and that the inducing of a brief delay on their part was not forbidden by the rules, which are on my desk as I write. However . . .

As Mr. Gilbert is not only prominent in the church but is also the local prohibition officer, judge of our surprise when, on the well bucket emerging, we found in it not only the clues but some bottles of beer which had apparently been put there to cool. And Mr. Gil-bert, on arriving with the others, seemed greatly upset.

"Hawkins," he said to the gardener, "what do you mean by hiding six bottles of beer in my well?"

"Me?" said Hawkins angrily. "If I had six bottles of beer, they'd be in no well! And there aren't six; there's only four."

"Four!" said Mr. Gilbert in a furious voice. "Four! Then who the dev —— " Here, however, he checked himself; and as Tish had now returned we took our clues and departed. Hawkins had given us the next password, which was "Good evening, dearie," and the clue, which read:

> Down along the lake front, in a pleasant place,
> Is a splendid building, full of air and space.
> Glance within a closet, where, neatly looped and tagged,
> Are the sturdy symbols of the game they've bagged.

Everybody seemed to think it meant the Duck Club, and in a few moments we were all off once more except the Smith boys, who were talking loudly and examining their engine. But Tish was not quite certain.

"These clues are tricky," she said. "They are not obvious, but subtle. It sounds too much like the Duck Club to be the Duck Club. Besides, what symbols of dead ducks would they keep? I've never seen anything left over but the bones."

"The feathers?" Aggie suggested.

"They wouldn't keep feathers in a closet. And besides, there's nothing sturdy about a feather. What other large building is on the lake front?"

"The fish cannery," I said.

"True. And they might keep boards in a closet with the outlines of very large fish on them. But the less said about the air there the better. However, we might try it."

Having made this decision, as soon as we were outside of Penzance we began once more to travel with extreme rapidity, retracing for some distance the road we had come in on, and thus it happened that we again saw the motor-cycle policeman with his side car. He was repairing something and shouted angrily at us as we passed, but we did not even hesitate, and soon we arrived at the fish cannery.

None of the others had apparently thought of this possibility, and when we reached it there was no one in sight but a bearded watchman with a lantern, sitting on a barrel outside. Tish hopefully leaped from the car and gave him the password at once.

" 'Good evening, dearie.' "

But the wretch only took his pipe out of his mouth and, after expectorating into the lake, replied:

"Hello, sweetheart. And what can I do for you?"

"Don't be impertinent," said Tish tartly. "I said 'Good evening, dearie,' as a signal."

"And a darned fine signal I call it," he said, rising. "Let's have a look at you before the old lady comes along with my supper."

"I have given you the signal. If you haven't anything for me, say so."

"Well, what is it you want?" he inquired, grinning at us in a horrible manner. "A kiss?"

As he immediately began to advance towards Tish, to this action on his part may be laid the misfortune which almost at once beset us. For there is no question that had it not discomposed her she would never have attempted to turn by backing onto the fish pier, which has been rotten for years. But in her indignation she did so, and to our horror we felt the thing giving way beneath us. There was one loud sharp crack followed by the slow splintering of wood, and the next moment we were resting gently on some piles above the water, with the shattered framework of the pier overhead and the watchman yelling that the company would sue us for damages.

"Damages!" said Tish, still holding to the steering wheel, while Aggie wailed in the rear. "You talk of damages to me! I'll put you and your company in the penitentiary if I have to —— "

Here she suddenly checked herself and turned to me.

"The penitentiary, of course!" she said. "How stupid of us! And I dare say they keep the ropes they hang people with in a closet. They have to keep them somewhere. Speaking of ropes," she went on, raising her voice, "if that old fool up there will get a rope, I dare say we can scramble out."

"Old fool yourself!" cried the watchman, dancing about. "Coming here and making love to me, and then destroying my pier! You can sit there till those piles rot, far's I'm concerned. There's something queer about this business anyhow; how do I know you ain't escaped from the pen?"

"My dear man," said Tish quietly, "the one thing we want is to get to the penitentiary, and that as soon as possible."

"Well, you won't have any trouble getting there," he retorted. "I'll see to that. Far's you're concerned, you're on your way."

He then disappeared, and one of the piles yielding somewhat, the car fell a foot or two more, while Aggie wailed and sneezed alternately. But Tish remained composed. She struck a match, and leaning over the side inspected the water and so on below us.

"There's a boat down there, Lizzie," she said. "Get the towrope from under Aggie and fasten it to something. If we can get down, we'll be all right. The penitentiary isn't more than a half-mile from here."

"I slide down no rope into no boat, Tish Carberry," I said firmly.

But at that moment we heard the engine of a motor cycle coming along the road and realized that our enemy the policeman had followed us. And as at that same instant the car again slipped with a sickening jar, we were compelled to this heroic attempt after all.

However, it was managed without untoward incident, Aggie even salvaging the flask of blackberry cordial. But the boat was almost filled with water, and thus required frantic bailing with our hats, a matter only just accomplished when the motor-cycle policeman came running onto the pier.

Whether the watchman had failed to tell him of the break or not, I cannot say, but we were no more than under way when we heard a splash followed by strangled oaths, and realized that for a time at least we were safe from pursuit.

Wet as we now were, we each took a small dose of the cordial and then fell to rowing. Tish's watch showed only ten o'clock, and we felt greatly cheered and heartened. Also, as Tish said by way of comforting Aggie, the license plates on the car belonging to Mr. Stubbs, it was unlikely that we would be further involved for the present at least.

Owing to the fact that the cars still in the hunt had all gone to the Duck Club, the brief delay had not lost us our lead, and we proceeded at once, after landing near the penitentiary, to the gate. Our halt there was brief. Tish merely said to the sentry at the entrance, " 'Good evening, dearie.' "

"The same to you and many of them," he replied cheerfully, and unlocked the gate. We then found ourselves in a large courtyard, with the looming walls of the building before us, and on ringing the bell and repeating the phrase were at once admitted.

There were a number of men in uniform, who locked the grating behind us and showed us into an office where a young man was sitting at a desk.

I had an uneasy feeling the moment I saw him, and Aggie has since acknowledged the same thing. Instead of smiling as had the others, he simply pushed a large book towards us and asked us to sign our names.

"Register here, please," was what he said.

"Register?" said Tish. "What for?"

"Like to have our guests' names," he said solemnly. "You'll find your cells all ready for you. Very nice ones — view of the lake and everything. Front, show these ladies to their cells."

Aggie gave a low moan, but Tish motioned her to be silent.

"Am I to understand you are holding us here?"

"That's what we're here for. We specialize in holding, if you know what I mean."

"If it's that fish pier —— "

"Is it the fish pier?" the young man asked of two or three men around; but nobody seemed to know.

Tish cast a desperate glance about her.

"I may have made a mistake," she said, "but would it mean anything to you if I said: 'Good evening, dearie'?"

"Why, it would mean a lot," he said politely. "Any term of — er — affection, you know. I'm a soft-hearted man in spite of my business."

But Tish was eying him, and now she leaned over the desk and asked very clearly:

> "Have you got a closet where, neatly looped and tagged,
> You keep the sturdy symbols of the game you've bagged?"

Suddenly all the guards laughed, and so did the young man.

"Well, well!" he said. "So that's what brought you here, Miss Carberry. And all of us hoping you'd come for a nice little stay! Jim, take the ladies to the closet."

Well, what with the accident and the hard rowing, as well as this recent fright, neither Aggie nor I was able to accompany Tish. I cannot therefore speak with authority; but knowing Tish as I do, I do not believe that Mrs. Cummings's accusation as to what happened at this closet is based at all on facts.

Briefly, Mrs. Cummings insists that having taken out her own clue, Tish then placed on top of the others a number of similar envelopes containing cross-word puzzles, which caused a considerable delay, especially over the Arabic name for whirling dervishes. This not, indeed, being solved at all, somebody finally telephoned to Mr. Ostermaier to look it up in the encyclopaedia, and he then stated that no cross-word puzzles had been included among the clues. Whereupon the mistake was rectified and the hunt proceeded.

As I say, we did not go with Tish to the closet and so cannot be certain, but I do know that the clue she brought us was perfectly correct, as follows:

Password: "All is discovered."

> "Where are you going, my pretty maid?"
> " 'Most anywhere else," said she.
> "Behind the grille is a sweet young man,
> And he'll give my clue to me."

We had no more than read it when we heard a great honking of horns outside, and those who had survived trooped in. But alas, what a pitiful remnant was left! Only ten cars now remained out of twenty. The Smith boys had not been heard of, and the Phillipses had been arrested for speeding. Also Mr. Gilbert had gone into a ditch and was having a cut on his chin sewed up, the Jenningses' car had had a flat tire and was somewhere behind in the road, and the Johnstons were in Backwater Creek, waiting for a boat to come to their rescue.

And we had only just listened to this tale of woe when Mrs. Cummings sailed up to Tish with an unpleasant smile and something in her hand.

"Your scissors, I believe, dear Miss Carberry," she said.

But Tish only eyed them stonily.

"Why should you think they are my scissors?" she inquired coldly.

"The eldest Smith boy told me to return them to you, with his compliments. He found them in the engine of his car."

"In his car? What were they doing there?"

"That's what I asked him. He said that you would know."

"Two pairs of scissors are as alike as two pairs of pants," Tish said calmly, and prepared to depart.

But our poor Aggie now stepped up and examined the things and began to sneeze with excitement.

"Why, Tish Carberry," she exclaimed, "they are your scissors! There's the broken point and everything. Well, if that isn't the strangest thing!"

"Extraordinary!" said Mrs. Cummings. "Personally, I think it a matter for investigation."

She then swept on, and we left the penitentiary. But once outside the extreme discomfort of our situation soon became apparent. Not only were we wet through, so that Aggie's sneezing was no longer alleviated by the clothespin, but Tish's voice had become hardly more than a hoarse croaking. Also, we had no car in which to proceed. Indeed, apparently the treasure hunt was over as far as we were concerned. But once again I had not counted on Tish's resourcefulness. We had no sooner emerged than she stopped in the darkness and held up her hand.

"Listen!" she said.

The motor cycle was approaching along the lake road, with that peculiar explosive sound so reminiscent of the machine gun Tish had used in the capture of X—— during the war.

It was clear that we had but two courses of action — one to return to the penitentiary and seek sanctuary, the other to remain outside. And Tish, thinking rapidly, chose the second. She drew us into an embrasure of the great wall and warned us to be silent, especially Aggie.

"One sneeze," she said, "and that wretch will have us. You'll spend the night in jail."

"I'd rather be there than here any day," said Aggie, shivering. However, she tried the clothespin once more, and for a wonder it worked.

"He'll hear by teeth chattering, I'b certaid," she whispered.

"Take them out," Tish ordered her, and she did so.

How strange, looking back, to think of the effect which that one small act was to have on the later events of the evening. How true it is that life is but a series of small deeds and great results! We turn to the left instead of the right and collide with an omnibus, or trip over the tail of an insignificant tea gown, like my Cousin Sarah Pennell, and fall downstairs and break a priceless bottle of medicinal brandy.

So Aggie took out her teeth and placed them in her ulster pocket, and tied her scarf over her mouth to prevent taking cold without them, and later on . . .

However, at the moment we were concentrated on the policeman. First he discovered and apparently examined the boat on the shore, and then, pushing and grunting, shoved his machine past us and up to the road. There he left it, the engine still going, and went toward the penitentiary, whistling softly and plainly outlined against the lights of the cars outside. A moment later Tish had led us to the motor cycle and was examining the mechanism by the aid of the flashlight.

"It looks easy enough," she said in her usual composed manner. "Lizzie, get into the side car and take Aggie on your lap — and hold on to her. I wish no repetition of the Miss Watkins incident."

We watched for a short time, hoping the policeman would go inside; but he was talking to the Cummingses' chauffeur, who seemed to be pointing in our direction. Seeing then that no time was to be lost, Tish hastily adjusted her goggles and pulled down her hat, and being already in knickerbockers, got quickly into the saddle. With the first explosion of the engine the motor-cycle officer looked up, and an instant later began to run in our direction.

But I saw no more. Tish started the machine at full speed, and to a loud cry from Aggie we were off with a terrific jerk.

"By deck's broked!" she cried. "Stop her! by deck's broked!"

Her neck was not broken, however, I am happy to say, and the osteopath who is attending her promises that she will soon be able to turn her head.

How shall I describe the next brief interval of time? To those who have ridden in such fashion, no description is necessary; and to those who have not, words are inadequate. And, in addition, while it was speedily apparent that we were leaving our pursuers behind — for the Cummingses' car followed us for some distance, with the policeman on the running board — it was also soon apparent that our dear Tish had entirely lost control of the machine.

Unable to turn her eyes from the road to examine the various controls, an occasional flash of lightning from an approaching storm showed her fumbling blindly with the mechanism. Farmhouses loomed up and were gone in an instant; on several curves the side car was high in the air, and more than once our poor Aggie almost left us entirely. As the lightning became more frequent we could see frightened animals running across the fields; and finally, by an unfortunate swerve, we struck and went entirely through some unseen obstacle which later proved to be a fence.

However, what might have been a tragedy worked out to the best possible advantage, for, another flash revealing a large haystack near by, Tish turned the machine toward it with her usual far-sightedness and we struck it fairly in the center. So great was our impact, indeed, that we penetrated it to a considerable distance and were almost buried, but we got out without difficulty and also ex-tricated the machine. Save for Aggie's neck, we were unhurt; and, the rain coming up just then, we retired once more into the stack and with the aid of the flash again read over the clue:

"Where are you going, my pretty maid?"
" 'Most anywhere else," said she.
"Behind the grille is a nice young man,
And he'll give my clue to me."

"Going?" said Tish thoughtfully. " ' 'Most anywhere else'? There's no sense to that." The hay, however, had brought back Aggie's hay fever, and as sneezing hurt her neck, she was utterly wretched.

"There's a heap of sedse," she said in a petulant voice. "Bost ady-where else would suit be all right. Ad if you're goig to try that dabbed bachide agaid, Tish Carberry, I ab dot."

"If you must swear, Aggie," Tish reproved her, "go outside, and do not pollute the clean and wholesome fragrance of this hay."

"I'd have said worse if I knew adythig worse," said Aggie. "And bebbe this hay is wholesobe, but if you had by dose you wouldn't thig so."

"Grille?" said Tish. "A nice young man behind a grille? Is there a grillroom at the Eden Inn?"

But we could not remember any, and we finally hit on the all-night restaurant in town, which had.

" ' 'Most anywhere else' must refer to that," Tish said. "The food is probably extremely poor. And while there we can get a sand-wich or so and eat it on the way. I confess to a feeling of weakness."

"Weakness!" said Aggie bitterly. "Thed I dod't ever wadt to see you goig strog, Tish Carberry!"

It was owing to Aggie's insistence that Tish test out the mecha-nism of the motor cycle before any of us mounted again that our next misfortune occurred. So far, when one thing failed us, at least we had been lucky enough to find a substitute at hand, but in this instance we were for a time at a loss.

It happened as follows: As soon as the rain ceased, Tish, flashlight in hand, went to the machine and made a few experiments with it. At first all went well, but suddenly something happened, I know not what, and in a second the motor cycle had darted out of our sight and soon after out of hearing, leaving our dear Tish still with a hand out and me holding a flashlight on the empty air. Pursuit was useless, and, after a few moments, inadvisable, for as it reached the main road it apparently struck something with extreme violence.

"If that's a house it's docked it dowd," Aggie wailed.

But as we were to learn later, it had not struck a house, but something far more significant. Of that also more later on.

Our situation now was extremely unpleasant. Although the storm was over, it was almost eleven o'clock, and at any time we expected to see the other cars dashing past toward victory. To walk back to town was out of the question in the condition of Aggie's neck. Yet what else could we do? However, Tish had not exhausted all her resources.

"We are undoubtedly on a farm," she said. "Where there's a farm there's a horse, and where there's a horse there is a wagon. I am not through yet."

And so, indeed, it turned out to be. We had no particular mischance in the barn, where we found both a horse and a wagon, only finding it necessary to connect the two.

This we accomplished in what I fear was but an eccentric manner, and soon we were on our way once more, Aggie lying flat in the wagon bed because of her neck. How easy to pen this line, yet to what unforeseen consequences it was to lead!

As we wished to avoid the spot where the motor cycle had struck something, we took back lanes by choice, and after travelling some three miles or so had the extraordinary experience of happening on the motor cycle itself once more, comfortably settled in a small estuary of the lake and with several waterfowl already roosting upon it.

But we reached the town safely, and leaving Aggie, now fast asleep, in the rear of the wagon, entered the all-night restaurant.

There was no actual grille to be seen in this place, but a stout individual in a dirty-white apron was frying sausages on a stove at

the back end and a thin young man at a table was waiting to eat
them.

Tish lost no time, but hurried back, and this haste of hers, added
to the dirt and so on with which she was covered and the huskiness
of her voice, undoubtedly precipitated the climax which immediately
followed. Breathless as she was, she leaned to him and said:

" 'All is discovered.' "

"The hell you say!" said the man, dropping the fork.

"I've told you," she repeated. " 'All is discovered.' And now no
funny business. Give me what you've got; I'm in a hurry."

"Give you what I've got?" he repeated. "You know damn' well
I haven't got anything, and what I'm going to get is twenty years!
Where are the others?"

Well, Tish had looked rather blank at first, but at that she
brightened up.

"In the penitentiary," she said. "At least —— "

"In the pen!" yelped the man. "Here, Jose!" he called to the person at the table. "It's all up! Quick's the word!"

"Not at all," said Tish. "I was to say 'All is discovered,' and —— "

But he only groaned, and throwing off his apron and grabbing
a hat, the next moment he had turned out the lights and the two
of them ran out the front door. Tish and I remained in the darkness, too astonished to speak, until a sound outside brought us to
our senses.

"Good heavens, Lizzie!" she cried. "They have taken the wagon
— and Aggie's in it!"

We ran outside, but it was too late to do anything. The horse
was galloping wildly up the street, and after following it a block
or two, we were obliged to desist. I leaned against a lamp-post and
burst into tears, but Tish was made of stronger fiber. While others
mourn, Tish acts, and in this case she acted at once.

As it happened, we were once more at Dr. Parkinson's, and even
as we stood there the doctor himself brought his car out of the
garage, and leaving it at the curb, limped into his house for something he had forgotten. He was wearing a pair of loose bedroom slippers, and did not see us at first, but when he did he
stopped.

"Still at large, are you?" he said in an unpleasant tone.

"Not through any fault of yours," said Tish, glaring at him. "After your dastardly attack on us —— "

"Attack!" he shouted. "Who's limping, you or me? I'm going to lose two toenails, and possibly more. I warn you, whoever you are. I've told the police, and they are on your track."

"Then they are certainly traveling some," said Tish coldly.

He then limped into the house, and Tish caught me by the arm.

"Into the car!" she whispered. "He deserves no consideration whatever, and our first duty is to Aggie."

Before I could protest, I was in the car and Tish was starting the engine; but precious time had been lost, and although we searched madly, there was no trace of the wagon.

When at last in despair we drove up to the local police station it was as a last resort. But like everything else that night, it too failed us. The charge room was empty, and someone was telephoning from the inner room to Edgewater, the next town.

"Say," he was saying, "has the sheriff and his crowd started yet? . . . Have, eh? Well, we need 'em. All the boys are out, but they haven't got 'em yet, so far's I know. . . . Yes, they've done plenty. Attacked Dr. Parkinson first. Then busted down the pier at the fish house and stole a boat there, and just as Murphy corralled them near the pen, they grabbed his motor cycle and escaped. They hit a car with it and about killed a man, and a few minutes ago old Jenkins, out the Pike, telephoned they'd lifted a horse and wagon and beat it. And now they've looted the Cummings house and stolen Parkinson's car for a getaway. . . . Crazy? Sure they're crazy! Called the old boy at the fish cannery 'dearie'! Can you beat it?"

We had just time to withdraw to the street before he came through the doorway, and getting into the car we drove rapidly away. Never have I seen Tish more irritated; the unfairness of the statements galled her, and still more her inability to refute them. She said but little, merely hoping that whoever had robbed the Cummings house had made a complete job of it, and that we would go next to the railway station.

"It is possible," she said, "that the men in that restaurant are implicated in this burglary, and certainly their actions indicate flight. In that case the wagon — and Aggie — may be at the depot."

This thought cheered us both. But, alas, the waiting room was empty and no wagon stood near the tracks. Only young George Welliver was behind the ticket window, and to him Tish related a portion of the situation.

"Not only is Miss Pilkington in the wagon," she said, "but these men are probably concerned in the Cummings robbery. I merely said to them 'All is discovered,' when they rushed out of the place."

Suddenly George Welliver threw back his head and laughed.

"Well!" he said. "And me believing you all the time! So you're one of that bunch, are you? All that rigmarole kind of mixed me up. Here's your little clue, and you're the first to get one."

He then passed out an envelope, and Tish, looking bewildered, took it and opened it. It was the next clue, right enough. The password was "Three-toed South American sloth," and the clue as follows:

> Wives of great men all remind us,
> We can make our wives sublime,
> And, departing, leave behind us
> Footprints on the sands of time.

"That ought not to be difficult," said Tish. "If only Aggie hadn't acted like a fool ── "

"It's the cemetery," I said, "and I go to no cemetery tonight, Tish Carberry."

"Nonsense!" said Tish briskly. "Time certainly means a clock. I'm just getting the hang of this thing, Lizzie."

"'Hang' may be right before we're through. And when I think of poor Aggie ──

"Still," she went on, "sands might be an hourglass. Sands of time, you know."

"And if somebody broke it by stepping on it, it would be footprints on the sands of time!" I retorted. "Go on! All we have to do is to find an hourglass and step on it. And in the meantime Aggie ── "

However, at that instant a train drew in and a posse from Edgewater, heavily armed, got out of it and made for a line of waiting motor cars. Never have I seen a more ruthless-looking lot of men, and Tish felt as I did, for as they streamed into the waiting room she pushed me into a telephone booth and herself took another.

And with her usual competency she took advantage of the fact to telephone Hannah to see if Aggie had returned home; but she had not.

As soon as the posse had passed through we made our escape by the other door and were able to reach the doctor's car unseen, and still free to pursue our search. But I insist that I saw Tish scatter no tacks along the street as we left the depot. If she did, then I must also insist that she had full reason; it was done to prevent an unjustified pursuit by a body of armed men, and not to delay the other treasure hunters.

Was it her fault that the other treasure seekers reached the station at that time? No, and again no. Indeed, when the first explosive noises came as the cars drew up she fully believed that the sheriff was firing on us, and it was in turning a corner at that time that she broke the fire plug.

Certainly to assess her damages for flooded cellars is, under these circumstances, a real injustice.

But to return to the narrative: Quite rightly, once beyond pursuit, Tish headed for the Cummings property, as it was possible that there we could pick up some clue to Aggie, as well as establish our own innocence. But never shall I forget our reception at that once-friendly spot.

As the circumstances were peculiar, Tish decided to reconnoiter first, and entered the property through a hedge with the intention of working past the sundial and so towards the house. But hardly had she emerged into the glow from the windows when a shot was fired at her and she was compelled to retire. As it happened, she took the shortest cut to where she had left me, which was down the drive, and I found myself exposed to a fusillade of bullets, which compelled me to seek cover on the floor of the car. Two of the car windows were broken at once and Letitia Carberry herself escaped by a miracle, as a bullet went entirely through the envelope she held in her hand.

Yes, with her customary astuteness she had located the fresh clue. The Ostermaier boy had had them by the sundial, and had gone to sleep there. She fell over him in the darkness, as a matter of fact, and it was his yell which had aroused the house afresh.

There was clearly nothing to do but to escape at once, as men were running down the drive and firing as they ran. And as it seemed to make no difference in which direction we went, we drove more or less at random while I examined the new clue. On account of the bullet holes, it was hard to decipher, but it read much as follows:

The password was "Keep your head down, boy," and the clue was as follows:

> Search where affection ceases,
> By soft and —— sands.
> The digit it increases,
> On its head it stands.

"After all," Tish said, "we have tried to help Aggie and failed. If that thing made sense I would go on and locate the treasure. But it doesn't. A digit is a finger, and how can it stand on its head?"

"A digit is a number too."

"So I was about to observe," said Tish. "If you wouldn't always break in on my train of thought, I'd get somewhere. And six upside down is nine, so it's six we're after. Six what? Six is half a dozen. Half a dozen eggs; half a dozen rolls; half a dozen children. Who has half a dozen children? That's it probably. I'm sure affection would cease with six children."

"Somebody along the water front. It says: 'By soft and something-or-other sands.'"

We pondered the matter for some time in a narrow lane near the Country Club, but without result; and might have been there yet had not the sudden passing of a car which sounded like the Smith boys' flivver toward the Country Club gate stimulated Tish's imagination.

"I knew it would come!" she said triumphantly. "The sixth tee, of course, and the sand box! And those dratted boys are ahead of us!"

Anyone but Tish, I am convinced, would have abandoned hope at that moment. But with her, emergencies are to be met and conquered, and so now. With a "Hold tight, Lizzie!" she swung the car about, and before I knew what was on the tapis she had let in the clutch and we were shooting off the road and across a ditch.

So great was our momentum that we fairly leaped the depression, and the next moment were breaking our way through a small wood which is close to the fourteenth hole of the golf links, and had struck across the course at that point. Owing to the recent rain, the ground was soft, and at one time we were fairly brought to bay — on, I think, the fairway to the eleventh hole, sinking very deep. But we kept on the more rapidly, as we could now see the lights of the stripped flivver winding along the bridle path which intersects the links.

I must say that the way the greens committee has acted in this matter has been a surprise to us. The wagon did a part of the damage, and also the course is not ruined. A few days' work with a wheelbarrow and spade will repair all damage; and as to the missing cup at the eighth hole, did we put the horse's foot in it?

Tish's eyes were on the lights of the flivver now winding its way along the road through the course, and it is to that that I lay our next and almost fatal mishap. For near the tenth hole she did not notice a sand pit just ahead, and a moment later we had leaped the bunker at the top and shot down into it.

So abrupt was the descent that the lamps — and, indeed, the entire fore part of the doctor's car — were buried in the sand, and both of us were thrown entirely out. It was at this time that Tish injured one of her floating ribs, as before mentioned, and sustained the various injuries which laid her up for some time afterward, but at the moment she said nothing at all. Leaping to her feet, she climbed out of the pit and disappeared into the night, leaving me in complete darkness to examine myself for fractures and to sustain the greatest fright of my life. For as I sat up I realized that I had fallen across something, and that the something was a human being. Never shall I forget the sensations of that moment, nor the smothered voice beneath me which said:

"Kill be at odce ad be dode with it," and then sneezed violently.

"Aggie!" I shrieked.

She seemed greatly relieved at my voice, and requested me to move so she could get her head out of the sand. "Ad dod't screab agaid," she said pettishly. "They'll cobe back ad fidish us all if you do."

Well, it appeared that the two men had driven straight to the golf links with the wagon, and had turned in much as we had done. They had not known that Aggie was in the rear, and at first she had not been worried, thinking that Tish and I were in the seat. But finally she had learned her mistake, and that they were talking about loot from some place or other, and she was greatly alarmed. They were going too fast for her to escape, although once or twice they had struck bunkers which nearly threw her out.

But at last they got into the sand pit, and as the horse climbed up the steep ascent our poor Aggie had heard her teeth drop out of her pocket and had made a frantic clutch at them. The next moment she had alighted on her head in the sand pit and the wagon had gone on.

She was greatly shaken by her experience and had taken a heavy cold; but although we felt about for the blackberry cordial, we could not find it, and could only believe it had miraculously remained in the wagon.

As she finished her narrative our dear Tish slipped quietly over the edge of the pit and sat down, panting, in the sand. The storm being definitely over and a faint moon now showing, we perceived that she carried in her hand a canvas sack tied with a strong cord, and from its weight as she dropped it we knew that at last we had the treasure.

It was a great moment, and both Aggie and I then set about searching for the missing teeth. But as Tish learned of Aggie's experience she grew thoughtful.

"Undoubtedly," she said, "those two men are somehow concerned in this robbery tonight, and very probably the rendezvous of the gang is somewhere hereabouts. In which direction did they go, Aggie?"

"They've parked the wagod over id those woods."

"Then," said Tish, "it is our clear duty ——"

"To go hobe," said Aggie sharply.

"Home nothing!" said Tish. "Jail is where we go unless we get them. There are fifteen policemen and a sheriff coming for us at this minute, and —— " But here she stopped and listened intently. "It is too late," she said, with the first discouragement she had shown all evening. "Too late, my friends. The police are coming now."

Aggie wailed dismally, but Tish hushed her and we set ourselves to listen. Certainly there were men approaching, and talking in cautious tones. There was a moment when I thought our dear Tish was conquered at last, but only a moment. Then she roused to incisive speech and quick action.

"I do not propose to be dug out of here like a golf ball," she stated. "I am entitled to defend myself and I shall do so. Lizzie, see if there are any tools in the car there, and get a wrench." She then took a firm hold of the treasure bag and swung it in her hand. "I am armed," she said quietly, "and prepared for what may come. Aggie, get the clothespin, and when I give the word point it like a pistol."

"Ab I to say 'bag'?"

But before Tish could reply, the men were fairly on us. We had but time to get behind the car when we could hear their voices. And suddenly Aggie whispered, "It's theb! It's the badits! Ad they've beed at the cordial!"

And Aggie was right; they had indeed, as we could tell by their voices.

"It wash Bill, all righ'," said one man. "I shaw the litsh of hish car."

"Well, where'sh he gone to? No car here, no anything. Black ash hell."

One of them then began to sing a song in which he requested a barman to give him a drink, but was quickly hushed by the others, for there were now three of them. Whether it was this one or not I do not know, but at that instant one of them fell over the bunker at the top of the pit and came rolling down at our feet, and Tish, with her customary readiness, at once struck him on the head with the bag of pennies. He was evidently stunned, for he lay perfectly still, and the men above seemed puzzled.

"Hey, Joe!" they called. "Where are you?"

On receiving no reply, one of them lighted a match, and Tish had only time to retire behind the car before it flared up.

"Well, can you beat that? He'sh broken hish neck!"

But the man with the match was sober, and he saw the car and stared at it.

"If that's Bill's car," he said, as the match went out, "we're up against it. Only — where the devil's Bill?"

"He'sh dead too, mosht likely," said the other. "Everybody'sh dead. S'terrible night. Car'sh dead too; buried in a shea of shand. Shinking rapidly. Poor ole car! Women and children first!"

He then burst into tears and sat down apparently, for the other man kicked him and told him to get up, and then came sliding into the pit and bent over Joe, striking another match as he did so. Hardly had he done so when Tish's weapon again descended with full force, and he fell beside his unconscious partner in crime.

We had now only the drunken man to deal with; and as Tish wished no more bloodshed, she managed him in a different manner.

In a word, she secured the towrope from the rear seat of the doctor's car and, leaving Aggie and myself to watch the others, climbed out and approached him from the rear. It was only the work of a moment to pinion his arms to his sides, and as Aggie immediately pointed her impromptu weapon and cried "Hads up!" he surrendered without a struggle. Having securely roped him, we then rolled him into the sand pit with the others, who showed no signs of coming to.

Fatigued as we were by that time, and no further danger threatening for the moment, we rested for a brief time on the ground and ate a few macaroons which I had carried in a pocket against such an emergency. But by "we" I mean only Tish and myself, as poor Aggie was unable to do so — and, indeed, has been living on soft food ever since. Then retrieving the sack containing the Cummings jewels and silver which the burglars had been carrying, we prepared to carry our double treasure back to the town.

Here, however, I feel that our dear Tish made a tactical error, for after we had found the horse and wagon — in the undergrowth just beyond the seventh hole — instead of heading at once for the police station she insisted on going first to the Ostermaiers'.

"It is," she said, examining her watch by the aid of the flashlight, "now only half past eleven, and we shall not be late if we hurry. After that I shall report to the police."

"And what is to prevent those wretches from coming to and escaping in the interval?" I asked dryly.

"True," Tish agreed. "Perhaps I would better go back and hit them again. But that would take time also."

In the end we compromised on Tish's original plan and set out once more. The trip back across the links was uneventful, save that on the eighth green the horse got a foot into the hole and was only extricated with the cup still clinging to his foot.

We had no can opener along, and it is quite possible that the ring of the tin later on on the macadam road led to our undoing. For we had no sooner turned away from the town toward the Ostermaiers' cottage on the beach than a policeman leaped out of the bushes and, catching the animal by the bridle, turned a lantern on us.

"Hey, Murphy!" he called. "Here they are! I've got 'em! Hands up, there!"

"Stand back!" said Tish in a peremptory voice. "We are late enough already."

"Late!" said the policeman, pointing a revolver at us. "Well, time won't make much difference to you from now on — not where you're going. You won't ever need to hurry again."

"But I must deliver this treasure. After that I'll explain everything."

"You bet you'll deliver it, and right here and now. And your weapons too."

"Aggie, give up your clothespin," said Tish in a resigned voice. "These yokels apparently think us guilty of something or other, but my conscience is clear. If you want the really guilty parties," she told the policeman, "go back to the sand pit by the tenth hole and you will find them."

"April fool your own self," said the one called Murphy. "I've been following you for two hours and I don't trust you. You're too resourceful. Is the stuff there?" he asked the first man, who had been searching in the wagon.

"All here."

"Then we'll be moving along," he said; and in this fashion did we reach the town once more, and the police station.

Never shall I forget that moment. Each of us handcuffed and

hustled along by the officers, we were shoved into the police station in a most undignified manner, to confront the sheriff and a great crowd of people. Nor shall I ever forget the sheriff's face when he shouted in an angry voice:

"Women, by heck! When a woman goes wrong she sure goes!"

The place seemed to be crowded with people. The fish pier man was there, and a farmer who said we had smashed his feed cutter. And Dr. Parkinson, limping about in his bedroom slippers and demanding to know where we had left his car, and another individual who claimed it was his horse we had taken, and that we'd put a tin can on his off forefoot and ought to be sued for cruelty to animals. And even Mr. Stubbs, because his license plates were on our car — and of course the old fool had told all about it — and the Cummings butler, who pointed at Tish and said that after the alarm was raised she had tried to get back into the house again, which was, of course, ridiculous.

I must say it looked bad for us, especially when the crowd moved and we saw a man lying in a corner with an overcoat under his head and his eyes shut. Tish, who had not lost an ounce of dignity, gazed at him without expression.

"I dare say," she said, "that you claim that that is our work also."

"Just about killed him, you have," said the sheriff. "Went right through him with that motor cycle you stole. Murder — that's what it's likely to be — murder. D'you get his name, Doctor?"

"Only roused enough to say it was Bill," said Dr. Parkinson. "I wish myself to lodge a complaint for assault and battery against these women. I am per —— "

But Tish interrupted him.

"Bill?" she said. "Bill?"

Without a word she pushed the crowd aside, and, bending over Bill, with her poor manacled hands she examined him as best she could. Then she straightened herself and addressed the crowd with composure.

"Under this man's shirt," she said, "you will find what I imagine to be a full set of burglar's tools. If your hands are not paralyzed like your brains, examine him and see."

And they found them! The picture of that moment is indelibly impressed on my mind — the sheriff holding up the tools and Tish addressing the mob with majesty and the indignation of outraged womanhood.

"Gentlemen, this is one of the gang which robbed the Cummings house tonight. Through all this eventful evening, during which I regret to say some of you have suffered, my friends and I have been on their track. Had the motor cycle not wrecked that ruffian's car, they would now have safely escaped. As it is, when we were so unjustly arrested I had but just recovered the Cummings silver and jewels, and alone and unaided had overcome the remainder of the gang. I am exhausted and weary; I have suffered physical injury and mental humiliation; but I am not too weak or too weary to go now to the sand pit at the tenth hole on the golf links and complete my evening's work by handing over to the police the three other villains I have captured."

"Three cheers for the old girl!" somebody called in the crowd. "I'm for her! Let's go!"

And this, I think, concludes the narrative of that evening's events. It was almost midnight when, our prisoners safely jailed, we arrived at the Ostermaiers' to find all the treasure hunters except the Cummingses there and eating supper, and our angel-food cake gracing the center of the table. Our dear Tish walked in and laid the sack of pennies on the table.

"Here is the treasure," she announced. "It has been an interesting evening, and I hope we shall soon do it again."

Mr. Ostermaier took up the bag and examined it.

"I have the honor of stating," he said, "that this, as Miss Carberry claims, is the treasure, and that Miss Carberry wins the hand-painted candlestick which is the prize for the event." He then examined the bag more carefully, and added:

"But this sack seems to be stained. Perhaps our good sister will explain what the stains are."

Tish eyed the bag with an expressionless face.

"Stains?" she said. "Oh yes, of course. I remember now. They are blood."

Then, leaving them staring and speechless with astonishment, she led the way out of the house, and home.

TUPPENCE and TOMMY in

THE DISAPPEARANCE OF
MRS. LEIGH GORDON

by AGATHA CHRISTIE

---

*Agatha Christie is the most versatile author of mystery fiction
now writing. Mother of no less than five distinguished sleuths,
male and female — Hercule Poirot, Tuppence and Tommy
Beresford (a team), Harley Quin, Parker Pyne, and Miss
Marple — equally adept at straight detection, adventure, secret
service, crime, and supernatural stories, all of high quality,
Miss Christie here tries her hand at that most difficult of all
mystery forms — the burlesque. Only Christie could carry it
off so adroitly: a burlesque of Sherlock Holmes.*

W HAT on earth are you doing?" demanded Tuppence, as she
entered the inner sanctum of the International Detective Agency —
(Slogan — Blunt's Brilliant Detectives) and discovered her lord and
master prone on the floor in a sea of books.

Tommy struggled to his feet.

"I was trying to arrange these books on the top shelf of that cupboard," he complained. "And the damned chair gave way."

"What are they, anyway?" asked Tuppence, picking up a volume. "*The Hound of the Baskervilles.* I wouldn't mind reading
that again some time."

"You see the idea?" said Tommy, dusting himself with care.
"Half hours with the Great Masters — that sort of thing. You see,
Tuppence, I can't help feeling that we are more or less amateurs at
this business — of course amateurs in one sense we cannot help being, but it would do no harm to acquire the technique, so to speak.

These books are detective stories by the leading masters of the art. I intend to try different styles, and compare results."

"H'm," said Tuppence. "I often wonder how those detectives would have got on in real life." She picked up another volume. "You'll find a difficulty in being a Thorndyke. You've no medical experience, and less legal, and I never heard that science was your strong point."

"Perhaps not," said Tommy. "But at any rate I've bought a very good camera, and I shall photograph footprints and enlarge the negatives and all that sort of thing. Now, *mon amie,* use your little grey cells — what does this convey to you?"

He pointed to the bottom shelf of the cupboard. On it lay a somewhat futuristic dressing gown, a turkish slipper, and a violin.

"Obvious, my dear Watson," said Tuppence.

"Exactly," said Tommy. "The Sherlock Holmes touch."

He took up the violin and drew the bow idly across the strings, causing Tuppence to give a wail of agony.

At that moment the buzzer rang on the desk, a sign that a client had arrived in the outer office and was being held in parley by Albert, the office boy.

Tommy hastily replaced the violin in the cupboard and kicked the books behind the desk.

"Not that there's any great hurry," he remarked. "Albert will be handing them out the stuff about my being engaged with Scotland Yard on the phone. Get into your office and start typing, Tuppence. It makes the office sound busy and active. No, on second thoughts, you shall be taking notes in shorthand from my dictation. Let's have a look before we get Albert to send the victim in."

They approached the peephole which had been artistically contrived so as to command a view of the outer office.

"I'll wait," the visitor was saying. "I haven't got a card with me, but my name is Gabriel Stavansson."

The client was a magnificent specimen of manhood, standing over six feet high. His face was bronzed and weather beaten, and the extraordinary blue of his eyes made an almost startling contrast to the brown skin.

Tommy swiftly changed his mind. He put on his hat, picked up some gloves, and opened the door. He paused on the threshold.

"This gentleman is waiting to see you, Mr. Blunt," said Albert.

A quick frown passed over Tommy's face. He took out his watch. "I am due at the Duke's at a quarter to eleven," he said. Then he looked keenly at the visitor. "I can give you a few minutes if you will come this way."

The latter followed him obediently into the inner office where Tuppence was sitting demurely with pad and pencil.

"My confidential secretary, Miss Robinson," said Tommy. "Now, sir, perhaps you will state your business? Beyond the fact that it is urgent, that you came here in a taxi, and that you have lately been in the Arctic — or possibly the Antarctic, I know nothing."

The visitor stared at him in amazement.

"But this is marvellous," he cried. "I thought detectives only did such things in books! Your office boy did not even give you my name!"

Tommy sighed deprecatingly.

"Tut tut, all that was very easy," he said. "The rays of the midnight sun within the Arctic circle have a peculiar action upon the skin — the actinic rays have certain properties. I am writing a little monograph on the subject shortly. But all this is wide of the point. What is it that has brought you to me in such distress of mind?"

"To begin with, Mr. Blunt, my name is Gabriel Stavansson — "

"Ah! of course," said Tommy. "The well-known explorer. You have recently returned from the region of the North Pole, I believe?"

"I landed in England three days ago. A friend who was cruising in Northern waters brought me back on his yacht. Otherwise I should not have got back for another fortnight. Now I must tell you, Mr. Blunt, that before I started on this last expedition two years ago, I had the great good fortune to become engaged to Mrs. Maurice Leigh Gordon — "

Tommy interrupted.

"Mrs. Leigh Gordon was, before her marriage — "

"The Honorable Hermione Crane, second daughter of Lord Lanchester," reeled off Tuppence glibly.

Tommy threw her a glance of admiration.

"Her first husband was killed in the War," added Tuppence.

Gabriel Stavansson nodded.

"That is quite correct. As I was saying, Hermione and I became engaged. I offered, of course, to give up this expedition, but she wouldn't hear of such a thing — bless her! She's the right kind of woman for an explorer's wife. Well, my first thought on landing was to see Hermione. I sent a telegram from Southampton, and rushed up to town by the first train. I knew that she was living for the time being with an aunt of hers, Lady Susan Clonray, in Pont Street, and I went straight there. To my great disappointment, I found that Hermy was away visiting some friends in Northumberland. Lady Susan was quite nice about it, after getting over her first surprise at seeing me. As I told you, I wasn't expected for another fortnight. She said Hermy would be returning in a few days' time. Then I asked for her address, but the old woman hummed and hawed — said Hermy was staying at one or two different places, and that she wasn't quite sure what order she was taking them in. I may as well tell you, Mr. Blunt, that Lady Susan and I have never got on very well. She's one of those fat women with double chins. I loathe fat women — always have — fat women and fat dogs are an abomination unto the Lord — and unfortunately they so often go together! It's an idiosyncrasy of mine, I know — but there it is — I never can get on with a fat woman."

"Fashion agrees with you, Mr. Stavansson," said Tommy drily. "And everyone has their own pet aversion — that of the late Lord Roberts was cats."

"Mind you, I'm not saying that Lady Susan isn't a perfectly charming woman — she may be, but I've never taken to her. I've always felt, deep down, that she disapproved of our engagement, and I feel sure that she would influence Hermy against me if that were possible. I'm telling you this for what it's worth. Count it out as prejudice, if you like. Well, to go on with my story, I'm the kind of obstinate brute who likes his own way. I didn't leave Pont Street until I'd got out of her the names and addresses of the people Hermy was likely to be staying with. Then I took the mail train North."

"You are, I perceive, a man of action, Mr. Stavansson," said Tommy, smiling.

"The thing came upon me like a bombshell. Mr. Blunt, none of these people had seen a sign of Hermy — Of the three houses, only one had been expecting her — Lady Susan must have made a bloomer over the other two — and she had put off her visit there at the last moment by telegram. I returned post haste to London, of course, and went straight to Lady Susan. I will do her the justice to say that she seemed upset. She admitted that she had no idea where Hermy could be. All the same, she strongly negatived any idea of going to the police. She pointed out that Hermy was not a silly young girl, but an independent woman who had always been in the habit of making her own plans. She was probably carrying out some idea of her own.

"I thought it quite likely that Hermy didn't want to report all her movements to Lady Susan. But I was still worried. I had that queer feeling one gets when something is wrong. I was just leaving when a telegram was brought to Lady Susan. She read it with an expression of relief and handed it to me. It ran as follows. *"Changed my plans Just off to Monte Carlo for a week Hermy."*

Tommy held out his hand.

"You have got the telegram with you?"

"No, I haven't. But it was handed in at Maldon, Surrey. I noticed that at the time, because it struck me as odd. What should Hermy be doing at Maldon? She'd no friends there that I had ever heard of."

"You didn't think of rushing off to Monte Carlo in the same way that you had rushed North?"

"I thought of it, of course. But I decided against it. You see, Mr. Blunt, whilst Lady Susan seemed quite satisfied by that telegram, I wasn't. It struck me as odd that she should always telegraph, not write. A line or two in her own handwriting would have set all my fears at rest. But anyone can sign a telegram 'Hermy.' The more I thought it over, the more uneasy I got. In the end I went down to Maldon. That was yesterday afternoon. It's a fair-sized place — good links there and all that — two hotels. I inquired everywhere I could think of, but there wasn't a sign that Hermy had ever been there. Coming back in the train I read your advertisement, and I thought I'd put it up to you. If Hermy has really gone off to Monte Carlo, I don't want to set the police on her track and make a scandal, but I'm not going to be sent off on a wild-goose chase myself. I stay here in London, in case — in case there's been foul play of any kind."

Tommy nodded thoughtfully.

"What do you suspect exactly?"

"I don't know. But I feel there's something wrong."

With a quick movement, Stavansson took a case from his pocket and laid it open before them.

"That is Hermione," he said. "I will leave it with you."

• The photograph represented a tall willowy woman, no longer in her first youth, but with a charming frank smile and lovely eyes.

"Now, Mr. Stavansson," said Tommy. "There is nothing you have omitted to tell me?"

"Nothing whatever."

"No detail, however small?"

"I don't think so."

Tommy sighed.

"That makes the task harder," he observed. "You must often have noticed, Mr. Stavansson, in reading of crime, how one small detail is all the great detective needs to set him on the track. I may say that this case presents some unusual features. I have, I think, practically solved it already, but time will show."

He picked up a violin which lay on the table, and drew the bow once or twice across the strings. Tuppence ground her teeth and even the explorer blenched. The performer laid the instrument down again.

"A few chords from Mosgovskensky," he murmured. "Leave me your address, Mr. Stavansson, and I will report progress to you."

As the visitor left the office, Tuppence grabbed the violin and putting it in the cupboard turned the key in the lock.

"If you must be Sherlock Holmes," she observed, "I'll get you a nice little syringe and a bottle labelled *Cocaine,* but for God's sake leave that violin alone. If that nice explorer man hadn't been as simple as a child, he'd have seen through you. Are you going on with the Sherlock Holmes touch?"

"I flatter myself that I have carried it through very well so far," said Tommy with some complacence. "The deductions were good, weren't they? I had to risk the taxi. After all, it's the only sensible way of getting to this place."

"It's lucky I had just read the bit about his engagement in this morning's *Daily Mirror,*" remarked Tuppence.

"Yes, that looked well for the efficiency of Blunt's Brilliant Detectives. This is decidedly a Sherlock Holmes case. Even you can-not have failed to notice the similarity between it and the disap-pearance of Lady Frances Carfax."

"Do you expect to find Mrs. Leigh Gordon's body in a coffin?"

"Logically, history should repeat itself. Actually — well, what do you think?"

"Well," said Tuppence. "The most obvious explanation seems to be that for some reason or other Hermy, as he calls her, is afraid to meet her fiancé, and that Lady Susan is backing her up. In fact, to put it bluntly, she's come a cropper of some kind, and has got the wind up about it."

"That occurred to me also," said Tommy. "But I thought we'd better make pretty certain before suggesting that explanation to a man like Stavansson. What about a run down to Maldon, old thing? And it would do no harm to take some golf clubs with us."

Tuppence agreeing, the International Detective Agency was left in the charge of Albert.

Maldon, though a well-known residential place, did not cover a large area. Tommy and Tuppence, making every possible inquiry that ingenuity could suggest, nevertheless drew a complete blank. It was as they were returning to London that a brilliant idea oc-curred to Tuppence.

"Tommy, why did they put Maldon Surrey on the telegram?"

"Because Maldon is in Surrey, idiot."

"Idiot yourself — I don't mean that. If you get a telegram from — Hastings, say, or Torquay, they don't put the county after it. But from Richmond, they do put Richmond Surrey. That's because there are two Richmonds."

Tommy, who was driving, slowed up.

"Tuppence," he said affectionately, "your idea is not so dusty. Let us make inquiries at yonder post office."

They drew up before a small building in the middle of a village street. A very few minutes sufficed to elicit the information that there were two Maldons. Maldon, Surrey, and Maldon, Sussex, the latter a tiny hamlet but possessed of a telegraph office.

"That's it," said Tuppence excitedly. "Stavansson knew Maldon was in Surrey, so he hardly looked at the word beginning with S after Maldon."

"Tomorrow," said Tommy, "we'll have a look at Maldon, Sussex."

Maldon, Sussex, was a very different proposition from its Surrey namesake. It was four miles from a railway station, possessed two public houses, two small shops, a post and telegraph office combined with a sweet and picture postcard business, and about seven small cottages. Tuppence took on the shops whilst Tommy betook himself to the Cock and Sparrow. They met half an hour later.

"Well?" said Tuppence.

"Quite good beer," said Tommy, "but no information."

"You'd better try the King's Head," said Tuppence. "I'm going back to the post office. There's a sour old woman there, but I heard them yell to her that dinner was ready."

She returned to the place, and began examining postcards. A fresh-faced girl, still munching, came out of the back room.

"I'd like these, please," said Tuppence. "And do you mind waiting whilst I just look over these comic ones?"

She sorted through a packet, talking as she did so.

"I'm ever so disappointed you couldn't tell me my sister's address. She's staying near here and I've lost her letter. Leigh Wood, her name is."

The girl shook her head.

"I don't remember it. And we don't get many letters through here either — so I probably should if I'd seen it on a letter. Apart from the Grange, there isn't many big houses round about."

"What is the Grange?" asked Tuppence. "Who does it belong to?"

"Doctor Horriston has it. It's turned into a Nursing Home now. Nerve cases mostly, I believe. Ladies that come down for rest cures, and all that sort of thing. Well, it's quiet enough down here, Heaven knows." She giggled.

Tuppence hastily selected a few cards and paid for them.

"That's Doctor Horriston's car coming along now," exclaimed the girl.

Tuppence hurried to the shop door. A small two-seater was passing. At the wheel was a tall dark man with a neat black beard and a powerful, unpleasant face. The car went straight on down the street. Tuppence saw Tommy crossing the road towards her.

"Tommy, I believe I've got it. Doctor Horriston's Nursing Home."

"I heard about it at the King's Head, and I thought there might be something in it. But if she's had a nervous breakdown or any-thing of that sort, her aunt and her friends would know about it surely."

"Ye-es. I didn't mean that. Tommy, did you see that man in the two-seater?"

"Unpleasant-looking brute, yes."

"That was Doctor Horriston."

Tommy whistled.

"Shifty-looking beggar. What do you say about it, Tuppence? Shall we go and have a look at the Grange?"

They found the place at last, a big rambling house, surrounded by deserted grounds, with a swift mill stream running behind the house.

"Dismal sort of abode," said Tommy. "It gives me the creeps, Tup-pence. You know, I've a feeling this is going to turn out a far more serious matter than we thought at first."

"Oh! don't. If only we are in time. That woman's in some awful danger, I feel it in my bones."

"Don't let your imagination run away with you."

"I can't help it. I mistrust that man. What shall we do? I think it would be a good plan if I went and rang the bell alone first, and asked boldly for Mrs. Leigh Gordon just to see what answer I get. Because, after all, it may be perfectly fair and above-board."

Tuppence carried out her plan. The door was opened almost im-mediately by a manservant with an impassive face.

"I want to see Mrs. Leigh Gordon if she is well enough to see me."

She fancied that there was a momentary flicker of the man's eye-lashes, but he answered readily enough.

"There is no one of that name here, Madam."

"Oh! surely. This is Doctor Horriston's place, The Grange, is it not?"

"Yes, Madam, but there is nobody of the name of Mrs. Leigh Gordon here."

Baffled, Tuppence was forced to withdraw and hold a further consultation with Tommy outside the gate.

"Perhaps he was speaking the truth. After all, we don't *know*."

"He wasn't. He was lying. I'm sure of it."

"Wait until the doctor comes back," said Tommy. "Then I'll

pass myself off as a journalist anxious to discuss his new system of rest cure with him. That will give me a chance of getting inside and studying the geography of the place."

The doctor returned about half an hour later. Tommy gave him about five minutes, then he in turn marched up to the front door. But he too returned baffled.

"The doctor was engaged and couldn't be disturbed. And he never sees journalists. Tuppence, you're right. There's something fishy about this place. It's ideally situated — miles from anywhere. Any mortal thing could go on here, and no one would ever know."

"Come on," said Tuppence, with determination.

"What are you going to do?"

"I'm going to climb over the wall, and see if I can't get up to the house quietly without being seen."

"Right. I'm with you."

The garden was somewhat overgrown, and afforded a multitude of cover. Tommy and Tuppence managed to reach the back of the house unobserved.

Here there was a wide terrace, with some crumbling steps leading down from it. In the middle some French windows opened onto the terrace, but they dared not step out into the open, and the windows where they were crouching were too high for them to be able to look in. It did not seem as though their reconnaissance would be much use when suddenly Tuppence tightened her grasp of Tommy's arm.

Someone was speaking in the room close to them. The window was open and the fragment of conversation came clearly to their ears.

"Come in, come in, and shut the door," said a man's voice irritably. "A lady came about an hour ago, you said, and asked for Mrs. Leigh Gordon?"

Tuppence recognised the answering voice as that of the impassive manservant.

"Yes, sir."

"You said she wasn't here, of course?"

"Of course, sir."

"And now this journalist fellow," fumed the other.

He came suddenly to the window, throwing up the sash, and the two outside, peering through a screen of bushes, recognised Dr. Horriston.

"It's the woman I mind most about," continued the doctor. "What did she look like?"

"Young, good-looking, and very smartly dressed, sir."

Tommy nudged Tuppence in the ribs.

"Exactly," said the doctor between his teeth. "As I feared. Some friend of the Leigh Gordon woman's. It's getting very difficult. I shall have to take steps — "

He left the sentence unfinished. Tommy and Tuppence heard the door close. There was silence.

Gingerly, Tommy led the retreat. When they had reached a little clearing not far away, but out of earshot from the house, he spoke.

"Tuppence, old thing, this is getting serious. They mean mischief. I think we ought to get back to town at once and see Stavansson."

To his surprise Tuppence shook her head.

"We must stay down here. Didn't you hear him say he was go-ing to take steps — That might mean anything."

"The worst of it is we've hardly got a case to go to the police on."

"Listen, Tommy. Why not ring up Stavansson from the village? I'll stay around here."

"Perhaps that is the best plan," agreed her husband. "But, I say — Tuppence — "

"Well?"

"Take care of yourself — won't you?"

"Of course I shall, you silly old thing. Cut along."

It was some two hours later that Tommy returned. He found Tuppence awaiting him near the gate.

"Well?"

"I couldn't get on to Stavansson. Then I tried Lady Susan. She was out too. Then I thought of ringing up old Brady. I asked him to look up Horriston in the Medical Directory or whatever the thing calls itself."

"Well, what did Dr. Brady say?"

"Oh! he knew the name at once. Horriston was once a bona fide doctor, but he came a cropper of some kind. Brady called him a most unscrupulous quack, and said he, personally, wouldn't be surprised at anything. The question is, what are we to do now?"

"We must stay here," said Tuppence instantly. "I've a feeling they mean something to happen tonight. By the way, a gardener has been clipping ivy round the house. Tommy, *I saw where he put the ladder.*"

"Good for you, Tuppence," said her husband appreciatively. "Then tonight — "

"As soon as it's dark — "

"We shall see — "

"What we shall see."

Tommy took his turn at watching the house whilst Tuppence went to the village and had some food.

Then she returned and they took up the vigil together. At nine o'clock, they decided that it was dark enough to commence operations. They were now able to circle round the house in perfect freedom. Suddenly Tuppence clutched Tommy by the arm.

"Listen."

The sound she had heard came again, borne faintly on the night air. It was the moan of a woman in pain. Tuppence pointed upward to a window on the first floor.

"It came from that room," she whispered.

Again that low moan rent the stillness of the night.

The two listeners decided to put their original plan into action. Tuppence led the way to where she had seen the gardener put the ladder. Between them they carried it to the side of the house from which they had heard the moaning. All the blinds of the ground-floor rooms were drawn, but this particular window upstairs was unshuttered.

Tommy put the ladder as noiselessly as possible against the side of the house.

"I'll go up," whispered Tuppence. "You stay below. I don't mind climbing ladders and you can steady it better than I could. And in case the doctor should come round the corner you'd be able to deal with him and I shouldn't."

Nimbly Tuppence swarmed up the ladder, and raised her head cautiously to look in at the window. Then she ducked it swiftly, but after a minute or two brought it very slowly up again. She stayed there for about five minutes. Then she descended again.

"It's her," she said breathlessly and ungrammatically, "but oh, Tommy, it's horrible. She's lying there in bed, moaning, and turning to and fro — and just as I got there a woman dressed as a nurse came in. She bent over her and injected something in her arm and then went away again. What shall we do?"

"Is she conscious?"

"I think so. I'm almost sure she is. I fancy she may be strapped to the bed. I'm going up again, and if I can, I'm going to get into that room."

"I say, Tuppence — "

"If I'm in any sort of danger I'll yell for you. So long."

Avoiding further argument Tuppence hurried up the ladder again. Tommy saw her try the window, then noiselessly push up the sash. Another second, and she had disappeared inside.

And now an agonising time came for Tommy. He could hear nothing at first. Tuppence and Mrs. Leigh Gordon must have been talking in whispers if they were talking at all. Presently he did hear a low murmur of voices and drew a breath of relief. But suddenly the voices stopped. Dead silence.

Tommy strained his ears. Nothing. What could they be doing?

Suddenly a hand fell on his shoulder.

"Come on," said Tuppence's voice out of the darkness.

"Tuppence! How did you get here?"

"Through the front door. Let's get out of this."

"Get out of this?"

"That's what I said."

"But — Mrs. Leigh Gordon?"

In a tone of indescribable bitterness Tuppence replied.

"Getting thin!"

Tommy looked at her, suspecting irony.

"What do you mean?"

"What I say. Getting thin. Slinkiness. Reduction of weight. Didn't you hear Stavansson say he hated fat women? In the two years he's been away, his Hermy has put on weight. Got a panic when she knew he was coming back, and rushed off to do this new treatment of Dr. Horriston's. It's injections of some sort, and he makes a deadly secret of it, and charges through the nose. I daresay he *is* a quack — but he's a damned successful one! Stavansson comes home a fortnight too soon, when she's only beginning the treatment. Lady Susan has been sworn to secrecy, and plays up. And we come down here and make blithering idiots of ourselves!"

Tommy drew a deep breath.

"I believe, Watson," he said with dignity, "that there is a very good concert at the Queen's Hall tomorrow. We shall be in plenty of time for it. And you will oblige me by not placing this case upon your records. It has absolutely *no* distinctive features."

THE MYSTERY OF THE MISSING WASH

by OCTAVUS ROY COHEN

The Sons of I Will Arise (locus, Birmingham, Alabama) have delighted millions; Florian Slappey is their kingfish; and here's Florian — an eighteen-carat find! — as a real, live detective.

NEVER before had Mr. Florian Slappey looked so overwhelmingly elegant. What was visible of him as he sat importantly behind a large secondhand desk in his office on the seventh floor of the Penny Prudential Bank Building was a symphony in brown — brown coat, delicately tan silk shirt, necktie a shade deeper, and complexion matching. He was strutting sitting down, as befitted the proclamation newly lettered on the ground-glass door of his office:

FLORIAN SLAPPEY DETECTIVE AGENCY

F. SLAPPEY — PROP. & CHIEF

ALL JOBS OF DETECTING NEATLY DONE

PRICES REASOMBLE

"GET SOLVED BY SLAPPEY"

His pencil hovered over a sheet of thoroughly typed paper, and Chief of Detectives Slappey transfixed his not-unattractive feminine visitor with an official glare. He tried to make his ordinarily soft, pleasant voice sound like a bark.

"Name?" he inquired.

"You know dawggone good an' well what my name is, Florian Slappey."

"Name?"

"Mrs. Gardenia Watt." The dusky damsel fidgeted. "How come you to ask me such unnecessary questions?"

"Got to fill out this questionnaire."

"Says which?"

"Case record. All these questions has got to be answered, an' the response wrote down." He ignited a cigarette. "Address?"

"Alley G."

"Number?"

"House ain't got no number, an' you know it."

"Sure I know it, but I got to find out anyway." He held his pencil ready. "Male or female?"

"Now you listen heah, Florian Slappey —— "

"All right. Female. Born?"

"Of all the craziment —— "

"When an' where was you born?"

"Where was Bumminham, Alabama. When ain't none of yo' business, an' it don't differ nohow."

"Married?"

"I was married."

"Husband's name?"

"Ain't got no husban'. The one I had befo' I got rid of him was named Felix Watt." Mrs. Watt was visibly annoyed. "This ain't got one lick of sense, Florian. You know Felix just as good as I do. Ever sence me an' him got divorced away fum each other, he's been roomin' right where you do — at Sis Callie Flukers'."

"I know." Mr. Slappey descended momentarily from his pedestal of official dignity. "An' of all the wuthless, no-'count, slewfooted, empty-headed, mean, ornery, cantankerous, lazy hunks of tripe, that Felix Watt is the wust. What I ain't got fo' him is no use."

Gardenia nodded approvingly. "You ain't said nothin' yet, Brother Slappey. If I was to start really describin' that feller —— "

"Nemmin'. Us got business to transack." Mr. Slappey made ready to record further notations.

"Profession?" he asked.

"Ise a wash lady."

"Employer's name?"

"Golla, Florian, I does washin' fo' heaps of white folks." She wrung her hands and added bitterly, "That's just the trouble."

'What is?"

"Them white folks' washin's. Tha's what I come to see you about."

"Trouble 'tween you an' the white folks?"

"They sho is gwine be, Florian, providin' you don't do some mighty fast detectin'."

Mr. Slappey pointed magniloquently to a framed document which hung over his head. Actually it was nothing more or less than a license from the city of Birmingham to operate a private detective bureau. A business license, pure and simple, such as he would have been forced to acquire had his energies been directed to any other line of business; but by the estimable Gardenia Watt and by all of Florian's other acquaintances it was regarded as investing him with police powers, which it most certainly did not do.

Mr. Slappey gestured confidently: "Ise the most deficient detective you ever met up with, Gardenia. Now, what seems to be wrong?"

"Ain't 'seems to be,' Florian. It honest is."

"What?"

"Somebody been stealin' the white folks' wash out of my back yard."

"Larceny, eh?"

"Nossuh. Just plain stealin'."

"When, where an' how?"

"I don't know nothin' 'ceptin' that ev'y time I hang a wash out to dry somethin' disappears offen the line."

"What kind of somethin'?"

"Towels an' sheets an' pillowcases an' sometimes lingeries."

"M'm'm'm! Tha's sigifant. You got any suspicions?"

"On'y one, Florian. Ise awful suspicious that if'n this keeps up, why, pretty soon the white folks ain't gwine gimme no mo' washin' to do. Or either I'll go bankrump payin' them back fo' the things Ise losin'."

"In other words, you is th'eatened with business disaster an' complete liquidation, is that it?"

"That ain't half."

Detective Slappey rose and walked up and down his infinitesimal office. His colorado-maduro brow was wrinkled in thought and his first client stared approvingly. He finally spoke, but without breaking stride.

"Usin' the authorized an' approved deductive the'ry," he announced, "one thing becomes obvious."

"You sho does ooze words, Florian."

"What gotten stole off yo' lines would look like it was taken by someone who was fixin' to git married."

"How come you to say such?"

"Logic, Gardenia, logic. Things you mention ain't no good 'ceptin' somebody is aimin' to git wed."

"Spose they's ma'ied a'ready?"

Mr. Slappey dismissed that theory with a shrug. "Too many folks a'ready ma'ied. It's mo' logicaler to suspeck them that is preparin' to be. Now, Mis' Watt, rack yo' brain an' see can you think of anybody who is fixin' to commit matrimony."

"I suttinly can." She blushed becomingly. "Ise sort of playin' aroun' with that idea my ownse'f."

"What? You ain't prospectin' to take Felix back, is you?"

"That lazy chitlin! I should say not. He never done a lick of work in his whole life. Who I is engaged to, Florian, is Henry Stiles."

"Henry? Well, fry me fo' a catfish! I never knowed nothin' 'bout that."

"Well, me an' Henry kinda been keepin' it secret." She spoke in an idolatrous whisper: "He's an elegant man, Florian."

"Sho is. An' he drives a truck noble." Mr. Slappey reverted to official dignity. "So you-all two is engaged, eh? You is fixin' to git ma'ied. Now, how do I know, Gardenia, that you, or either Henry Stiles, ain't stealin' that wash yo' ownse'ves fo' yo' weddin' tro'sseau?"

"You talk foolishment, Florian. How come that us would cut off our own noses 'cause we's mad at our faces?"

"Well, it's bound to be an engaged couple. Now see if you can't think of another two folks which is engaged, an' also lives close to you."

Gardenia pondered. "There's one," she vouchsafed, "but it seems ridiculum."

"Who?"

"Alverta Cross an' Andy Turner."

"Ah-h-h."

"Why you say 'Ah-h-h'?"

"Don't Alverta Cross also live in Alley G?"

"Uh-huh. Right down on the next block."

"An' she walks past yo' back yard lots of times?"

"Frequent. So does Andy when he's on his way to see her, or either goin' away fum her house."

"They ain't got much money to buy weddin' things, has they?"

"They got some. Andy Turner has a good porterin' job."

"An' he wants a wife." Mr. Slappey chewed importantly on the end of a new pencil. "Seems like ev'ything is workin' out grand, Mis' Watt."

"Huh?"

"Right away we got suspecks."

"But, Florian —— "

"Don't but me, sister — don't but me. Seems like this is the puffeck setup: Two suspecks, plenty motive an' lots of opportunity. Yassuh, things is wukkin' out grand."

"What you aimin' to do, Florian?"

"Shadow Alverta, that's what. Watch her ev'y footstep. If she ain't guilty, why, there's no harm done, but if she is —— " He made a clucking noise indicative of catastrophe. Mrs. Watt was impressed. She shook her head and remarked, "I sho never would of thought nothin' like that of Andy and Alverta."

Mr. Slappey rose. "Ise a busy man, Gardenia. My fee is ten dollars in advance."

She placed two five-dollar bills in Florian's palm. "It's wuth it," she commented, "if you guarantee —— "

"I don't guarantee nothin', Gardenia, 'ceptin' that you is gwine git the doggonedest, swellest job of detectin' that you ever heard tell about. With Florian Slappey on the job, you can quit worryin'."

"All right." At the door, she turned. "Ise washin' tomorrow mawnin', Florian, an' I git stole fum pretty regalar on Tuesdays."

"I'll be there," promised Mr. Slappey.

And he was. Re-enforced by a badge which had been purchased from the ten-cent store and which was pinned to the bosom of his shirt beneath his double-breasted coat, Mr. Slappey sauntered along Alley G the following morning.

Florian was a good saunterer. All his life he had been a languid person, regarding physical exertion — unless absolutely necessary — as something to be abhorred and avoided. He knew that his multitude of friends in Darktown would not consider it unusual to see Florian Slappey wandering aimlessly about, since he had never been known to hold any job which threatened his complete independence.

Alley G was not a beautiful thoroughfare. It was of dirt, and the dirt had been cut into ruts by many wagon wheels. On rainy days, Alley G was usually a difficult and unpleasant roadway, and Detective Slappey was pleased that today was dry and his new tan shoes not in danger of ruination.

The job of locating Gardenia Watt's back yard was not easy, inasmuch as all the lady residents of Alley G seemed addicted to laundering. All sorts of clothes swung from all sorts of clotheslines. Tiny back porches and diminutive yards were jeweled with washtubs, and above the miasma of suds and warm water could be heard a chorused chanting croon as the industrious colored ladies lightened their chores with music.

Mr. Slappey leaned against a somewhat rickety board fence in an attitude of studied insouciance. He lighted a cigarette and reflected contentedly that he was a person of vast importance. Modest as was his first fee, it signalized the launching of his newest enterprise and augured well for the future, provided he was successful.

For almost one hour Florian did nothing at all. He pondered with some amazement upon the undeniable fact that detecting might become rather boresome. Washwomen chatted with one another, they hung clothes on lines in gaudy and intimate array; children played, and once two boys started throwing rocks at each other, much to the annoyance of the solitary sleuth. But then something happened.

Up Alley G came a pulchritudinous young lady of chocolate-cream complexion. She seemed to have no definite objective, and she moved slowly. Mr. Slappey scrutinized her shrewdly. He said to himself, "She's gazin' hither an' yon, but mostly yon." She came closer, and was accosted by Florian:

"Mawnin', Alverta."

Miss Cross was not unreluctant to talk. Socially one or two rungs below Mr. Slappey, she welcomed this attention from the Beau Brummell of Birmingham's Darktown. She said, "Mawnin', Brother Slappey. How you is?"

"Tol'able, Alverta. An' you?"

"Oh, Ise feelin' all right, I reckon."

"You ought to be, fixin' to get ma'ied, like you is."

She smiled. "Yeh, Ise preparin' to git me a husban'."

"Andy Turner, ain't it?"

"Uh-huh."

"Nice fellow."

"Yeh. But gosh, Florian, he's awful jealous. I spose I ought to feel flattered, but when a great, big, hefty man gits jealous of a gal, why, nobody don't dare pay her no heed."

Mr. Slappey shrugged. "Tha's silliment. Now, I was just fixin' to ast you fo' a date."

"Oh, Florian."

"Tonight, maybe?"

"Sholy. Movies?"

"P'r'aps. Or maybe us will just sit an' talk." He approached the subject of chief importance. "You walk up an' down this alley a lot, don't you, Alverta?"

"Co'se I do. I live on it."

"H'm'm. I bet you see heaps of things that int'rest you."

"I spose I do." She smiled warmly. "I got to be travelin', Florian. Be seein' you."

She moved away and Detective Slappey gazed after her speculatively. He was disappointed in Alverta. Nice girl and all that, but, shuh, you never knowed what somebody would do when they needed somethin'. Stealin' Gardenia's white folks' washin'! Just so she could have a trousseau when she wed with that big, lumberin' ox of an Andy Turner. Pretty gal too. Florian sighed. He remarked to himself, "It's hahd luck, but a detective ain't allowed to have no sediment."

Mr. Slappey called upon Alverta Cross that night. She was thrilled by the social recognition of so impressive a person as Florian, and never suspected that the visit was inspired by anything other than personal interest. Nor did she mention that in order to entertain him she had broken a date with the large and jealous Andy Turner, and that Mr. Turner had made deep rumbling noises of definite disapproval, and had ventured an opinion of Mr. Slappey which was not entirely complimentary.

During the evening, Florian dissembled excellently. He injected the full force of a charming personality into the conversation, and dazzled the attractive but hitherto unnoticed Miss Cross. He asked enough questions, but not too many; and before he left, he requested permission to call again the following night. She hesitated, but only briefly. Furious as Andy Turner might become, Miss Cross was not minded to offend Florian. True, the next morning, when she broke the news to Andy, he made mention of manslaughter and mayhem, but she did not argue too lengthily, and it so happened that when she ambled up Alley G an hour later, she again encountered Florian Slappey leaning against a fence not far from the back yard of Gardenia Watt's modest cottage.

They chatted pleasantly enough, and again Alverta walked away. Florian returned to his now-somewhat-jaundiced inspection of clotheslines. All day yesterday he had stood vigilant guard. He was getting weary and hungry. And so, at noon, he abandoned sentry duty and went to Bud Peaglar's Barbecue Lunch Room & Billiard Parlor, where he inhaled a light lunch of barbecue sandwiches, Brunswick stew, lemon-meringue pie and coffee. At two o'clock he returned to Alley G, and was immediately summoned by a frantic Gardenia Watt.

She said, "Florian, it done happened again."

"Says which?"

"Some wash has been stole."

"Dawggone! While I was eatin' lunch." A frown furrowed his brow and he tapped a fence post with earnest fingers. "Alverta Cross, sho nuff. She was just watchin' her chance, waitin' to see when I went off."

"You really reckon that she stold 'em?"

"Tha's the one thing she didn't do nothin' else but."

"I got to git 'em back. Ev'ything!"

"You'll git 'em. Don't worry. But fust, I got to be shuah."

He was more direct when he called upon Alverta that night. He talked of marriage and trousseaus, and of such things as house linens and lingerie. Alverta found the subject interesting. She said, "I got a hope chest, Florian."

"A which?"

"A hope chest. A trunk where I an' Andy is savin' things fo' when us gits ma'ied."

"Aw, I bet you ain't."

"I'll show you."

She did show him. She opened a trunk of the old-fashioned type, removed the tray, and disclosed to the eager eyes of Detective Florian Slappey an array of household linens and nifty lingerie which conveyed a message of guilt to the investigator. He displayed keen interest in every item. He left the house at eleven o'clock, convinced that he stood on the threshold of success.

Detective work, he reflected, was tiresome, but not difficult. One acquired a client, a theory and a fee, and the rest was plain sailing. The job, of course, was now to recover possession of the stolen goods with the least possible ostentation. He visited Gardenia Watt the next morning, chatted briefly with Mrs. Watt's fiancé, Henry Stiles, who was just departing after a brief visit, and then assumed his most mysterious manner.

"Gardenia," he said, "I crave a list of ev'ything that has been stold offen yo' clothesline."

"Why?"

"On account I has dislocated the missin' articles. By tomorrow mawnin' — no later — I'll have 'em fo' you."

He left the Watt cottage armed with a list of all the articles which had been misappropriated. He was sorry for Alverta, but pleased with himself. He knew that Miss Cross was planning to attend a meeting of The Sons & Daughters of I Will Arise that night, and that the lady and gentleman with whom she boarded were members of the same lodge and would also attend the meeting. The coast would then be clear, and Mr. Slappey intended to act.

Re-enforced with a sense of righteousness, Mr. Slappey did not lack courage for his nocturnal enterprise. He stood guard outside Alverta's boardinghouse until the three residents thereof departed for the lodge meeting. Then he walked boldly up on the front porch, loosened one of the screens in a front window and stepped inside. He boldly turned on the light; although he did take the precaution of lowering the shades. It was possible, of course, that Alverta might return. But that prospect did not worry him. If she returned, his hand would be forced — that was all. He would confront her with proof of her transgression, display his badge, and all would be well.

His nerves were steady as he opened the lid of the trunk, removed the tray and meticulously took out the exact number of towels, pillowcases, sheets and feminine garments which had been listed by his client.

Without haste or fear, he wrapped them neatly in a large piece of wrapping paper. Then he set the room in order, polished off with a silk handkerchief all spots where he might have left fingerprints, turned out the lights and moved boldly into the night through the front door.

The following day he presented himself pridefully at the home of the very-much-harassed Mrs. Gardenia Watt. He unwrapped his bulky parcel and announced with gusto:

"The crime is solved, Gardenia. Yonder's all the stuff which was stold off you."

Mr. Slappey was excessively pleased. He stood looking down on his trophies with thumbs looped in the armholes of his fawn-colored vest, enjoying to the ultimate this initial moment of triumph. He saw Gardenia drop to her knees and finger the impressive stack of linens, and he was teetotally unprepared for the exclamation of dismay which escaped from between her lips:

"My gosh, Florian, you sho is in a mess!"

"Huh?" He shook his head. "Who is in which?"

"You is in a mess."

"How come?"

"These ain't the things which was stold off me. I never seen none of 'em befo'."

Mr. Slappey was immediately and acutely conscious of a sinking sensation in his midriff. He said, "You is funnin'."

"Funnin', nothin'! Where at did you git these?"

"Out of Alverta's trunk."

"What did she say?"

"She di'n't say nothin'. She was out when it happened."

"Then," accused Gardenia, "you not on'y ain't solved nothin' fo' me but also you has committed burglary!"

A somewhat similar idea had been floating uncomfortably through Mr. Slappey's head. It struck him forcibly that perhaps the detective business was not all beer and skittles. He stood before the world at this moment a quivering and frightened burglar, a man who had committed a heinous felony; and it was with shaking fingers that he rewrapped Alverta's trousseau and staggered from the cottage. He trudged to his room at Sis Callie Flukers' boardinghouse and flopped onto the bed. "Oh, whoa is me!" he groaned. "I has sho happened to a disaster!"

For two hours he sat in headachy thought, reflecting upon the awful potentialities of the situation. There was danger that Alverta already had discovered her loss; that she most certainly would discover it soon. She would, in all likelihood, tell her troubles to Andy Turner, her massive and homicidal fiancé. Between them they would decide that Mr. Slappey had abstracted the trousseau from her trunk and then . . . "Angel Gabriel," sobbed Florian, "don't blow yo' saxophone so loud. Program is comin' in too distinck a'ready."

At four o'clock that afternoon, Mr. Slappey had determined upon a course of action.

His scheme was desperate and frightening. He would return to Alverta's house that night — provided it wasn't already too late — and replace the stolen property. But tonight fear would walk with him. Tonight he would be operating in the guise of a criminal; well-intentioned, perhaps, but technically a criminal, for all that.

Mr. Slappey stared sadly out of the window. The skies were leaden. A light rain had commenced to fall and already the pavements of Avenue F were black and shiny and forbidding. He heard other denizens of Sis Callie's house trudge to their rooms: Semore Mashby, the attenuated little moneylender; Felix Watt, indolent ex-husband of Detective Slappey's lone client; Callous Deech, technician at the studios of the Midnight Pictures Corporation, Inc. But none of them brought solace to the unhappy little man who sat alone, reflecting upon the ultimate quality of his misery.

Tonight was the night. That he realized. In the first place, if discovery had not already been made by Alverta, it would not long be postponed. Second, he knew that she was attending a lodge meeting with her landlord and landlady.

Meanwhile, Miss Cross was in conversation with her muscular sweetheart. Andy Turner was in a skeptical and truculent mood.

"Where at you gwine be tonight, Alverta?"

"Lodge meetin'."

"You was to one of them las' night."

"That was The Sons & Daughters of I Will Arise. Tonight is the Over the River Buryin' Sassiety."

"H'm'm! Yo' folks gwine with you?"

"They sho is."

"An' if they went an' you di'n't, why, you'd be alone. woul'n't you?"

"I reckon so."

"You just reckon, eh? An' if you was alone, an' then somebody showed up to visit with you, why, you woul'n't be alone no mo', would you?"

"Honest, Andy, I never heard so many foolish words in my life. You act like you is jealous of somethin'."

"I is. Ise jealous of Florian Slappey, tha's who Ise jealous of. I don't like how he's been hangin' 'round. I don't like nothin' about him. In fack, was that feller drowndin', all I'd give him would be a drink of water."

Alverta was delighted. Not that she cared less for Andy or more for Mr. Slappey, but it was pleasant to have her fiancé regard her as a young lady who had found serious favor in the eyes of Darktown's most eligible and inaccessible bachelor. She said, "Well, I an' you ain't gwine have no date tonight. You ain't a member of the buryin' sassiety, so you cain't go with me. An' tha's all there is to it."

"Oh, yeah?" Mr. Turner flexed one tremendous biceps. "Tha's what you think."

He stalked off in high dudgeon. He dined alone and moodily, glowering out upon skies which glowered right back at him. He was in a fair way to being acutely miserable. Ordinary opposition he could tolerate, but the rivalry of so elegant a person as Florian Slappey went beyond the bounds of fair competition. He felt inferior, and loathed the sensation. He didn't exactly distrust Miss Cross, but he didn't entirely trust her either. He decided to do a bit of snooping.

So, at 8:30 o'clock, Mr. Andy Turner slipped and slid through the mud of Alley G. The night was definitely unpleasant. He leaned sadly against a sagging fence and stared with heartbroken moodiness upon the cottage where Alverta resided. It loomed black in the black night, its windows dark, its whole demeanor lending truth to Alverta's statement that the three residents were attending a meeting.

Two or three times the uncomfortable Mr. Turner started to remove himself from his uncomfortable sentry post. But something held him there. An instinct. An indefinable feeling that all was not exactly as he would have preferred. The house was dark. It looked empty. And yet ——

Mr. Turner's uneasiness was not entirely without basis. Inside the cottage, a shivering, frightened young colored man was working frantically to undo something he unwittingly had done. This night, Mr. Slappey did not switch on any lights. He fumbled with the lid of the trunk and succeeded, eventually, in opening it. He removed the tray, and with shaking fingers commenced restoring the Alverta Cross trousseau to its proper storage place. He proceeded slowly, smoothing down each piece of linen and each filmy feminine garment, so that there would be no obvious evidence that the trunk had ever been disturbed.

Mr. Slappey's eyes were only vaguely accustomed to the Stygian blackness. The awful silence was punctuated by the thumping of his heart. He could hear himself breathing, and the constant drip-drip of water from the roof to the red clay of the back yard twanged on his jagged nerves.

Florian was becoming convinced that detective work was pretty tough. In theory, it had seemed elegant, but the practice was appallingly different from anything he had anticipated. He was more profoundly scared than ever before in a life which had been freighted with adventure.

He finished his job, closed the trunk, folded the brown paper in which the linens had been wrapped, and prepared to exit unobtrusively through the window.

But something happened. Something so unexpected and so terrifying that Mr. Slappey forgot everything except the instinct of self-preservation.

Mr. Andy Turner had decided that everything was quiet within the cottage and that he would drift down to Bud Peaglar's place for a game of Kelly pool. But before going, he decided to make his assurance trebly sure. To that end, he approached the cottage, clumped across the porch and rapped with bony knuckles on a door which had all the properties of a sounding board.

It was that horrible racket which came to Mr. Slappey's ears. Someone on the porch! A fist pounding on the door! Mr. Slappey pleaded, "Foots! Remove me fum heah!"

His "foots" acted. They carried him toward the window at high speed. Ordinary caution was abandoned. Mr. Slappey started to crawl through, but a second thumping on the door altered that idea. He tensed his muscles and leaped. There was a crash as a vase toppled from a little table and smashed on the floor. Mr. Slappey tore through the rusty wire screen and landed in the muddy yard on all fours. He scrambled to his feet and a wild yell of terror escaped from between his lips.

He heard the thunderous voice of Andy Turner saying, "Hot dam! I knowed it!" He paused to hear nothing more. Mr. Slappey fled ignobly, but in a manner remindful of Jesse Owens at his super best. He hurdled a fence and hit the alley on high. From that point on, he split the night wide open.

The clatter of his abrupt departure reached the ears of Andy Turner. That gentleman found himself once more obsessed with a passion for manslaughter. He leaped from the porch and peered into the night. It was then that he saw a lithe shadow moving with astounding speed in the general direction of somewhere else.

The fleeing Mr. Slappey turned north. He negotiated the first ' hundred yards in nothing flat, and clipped three seconds from that in the next hundred. Then he really started to run.

Andy's pursuit was sincere but futile. He didn't even get close enough to recognize the man he was chasing. He suspected that it was Florian Slappey, but he didn't know. Not fo' shuah. With considerable reluctance, he abandoned the chase and retraced his steps to the cottage where Alverta Cross resided.

This time he waited. He seated himself on the porch. And he was still sitting there when three persons returned home. Andy hoisted himself to his feet and said, with some surprise, "Then you really was at the meetin', wasn't you, Alverta?"

But while Andy was unhappily awaiting the arrival of his lady-love, Mr. Slappey was running himself into a state of physical and emotional exhaustion. He skidded, slipped, stumbled and slid. And finally, because his last ounce of strength was oozing, he approached Sis Callie's from the rear and stumbled upstairs.

But he did not go to his own room. He didn't dare. There was the awful fear that Andy Turner might have recognized him. In that event, Mr. Turner would logically journey to Florian's boarding-house, grab the once-elegant little colored man, and proceed to do an efficient job of dismemberment.

But Florian was compelled to hide. He needed rest. He knocked on the door of the room adjoining his — the room occupied by Felix Watt, one-time husband of Mrs. Gardenia Watt — and receiving no answer, went inside. The room was large and forbidding. It appeared to afford no sanctuary, and so Mr. Slappey opened the closet door and concealed himself inside. He closed the door and leaned against it, staring into the blackness, listening to the jangling of his own nerves.

He was soul-sick and weary. Almost as powerful as his terror was the thought that he was on the threshold of resigning from the detective profession. Disaster had dogged his footsteps. His hunches had been wrong and his deductions atrocious. Incredible danger surrounded him now, and he felt that Mrs. Gardenia Watt would eventually spread the story through Darktown — the whole horrible tale of his failure.

Mr. Slappey cowered and cringed and suffered. He pressed his ear against the door and listened for footsteps — those of the vengeful Andy Turner or of Felix Watt. But he heard nothing but silence, and not much of that. His breathing became more regular, his heart action approached normal, and with returning strength came the vague and forlorn hope that perhaps he might postpone the moment of his complete extermination.

He became conscious of the fact that he was standing in an awkward position, that his muddy feet were resting on a pile of something soft which bulked on the floor of the closet. Satisfied that he was not in immediate danger, he presumed to open the door.

The hall light flickered through the transom and bathed the floor of the closet in pale yellow. Mr. Slappey found himself staring down at something. He felt his brain commence to function. An idea came to him, and then crystallized into incredulous certainty.

Mr. Florian Slappey lifted a towel, a sheet and a pillowcase from the pile on the closet floor. He stared at them for a few seconds, then opened his lips and uttered a cry of exultation. "Hot diggity dawg!" he said. "Oh, boy! Oh, boy! Oh, boy!"

There it was! Gardenia's stolen wash. And, now it was all clear, but Florian did not waste precious moments in thought. He acted.

He toted the bundle of laundry to his room and locked it in his own closet. He telephoned the corner grocery nearest Gardenia's home and left word for her to call him. Ten minutes later she did. Florian's voice was firm and confident and triumphant. He said, "Gardenia, you has been soluted. I crave you an' Henry Stiles to come right over to my room at Sis Callie's. Find Alverta and Andy, an' bring 'em with you. What Ise gwine say is plenty."

Thirty minutes later they were there, wondering what it was all about. Only Andy Turner seemed definitely unhappy. He was still wondering what there might be between his ladylove and the debonair Mr. Slappey. Andy still believed that the shadow he had chased had been attached to Mr. Slappey, but he wasn't sure. And he had been thrown off guard by this invitation.

There was a step on the stairs, and Florian said, "Wait!" He stepped into the hall and accosted the grim, heavy-set man who was trudging upstairs. He said, "Felix Watt, us craves to make conference with you."

Felix entered the room. He gazed into the faces of his ex-wife, her fiancé, and into those of Alverta Cross and Andy Turner. Mr. Slappey, making the most of his moment, posed for the edification of his visitors and then commenced to talk. He reminded them that he was head of a great detective agency — an agency which had never been known to fail. He announced that Gardenia Watt was his client and explained why she had consulted him.

"I got you all heah together," he declared, " 'cause tha's how detectives always do it. They git the suspecks sittin' aroun', an' then they start talkin'. Well, you-all is suspecks."

"Me?" growled Andy Turner angrily.

"Yeh, you. You is a suspeck, but you ain't guilty, so keep yo' shirt on."

"An' Ise a suspeck too?" inquired Alverta.

"Co'se you is. Tha's how come I been seein' you so frequent."

Andy interrupted: "Was you in her house tonight, Florian?"

"Maybe. An' if I was, it was on'y to prove that she ain't guilty either. But her an' you bofe could of been. You was gwine git ma'ied. You needed laundry. So maybe you stold it."

He faced the others. "Nor neither you ain't guilty, Gardenia, though at first I considered maybe you was. An' Henry Stiles — well, he might of been takin' 'em, too, on account he was engaged to commit matrimony with you. . . . Now siddown, Henry, an' don't git mad. I done clued you right out of this case."

They were silent. They gazed upon Mr. Slappey with an interest which threatened to become awe. They listened to each profound word.

"But somebody is guilty," stated Detective Slappey. "Fum the ve'y fust, I was convinced of that. An' I knowed that if it wasn't none of you four, why, then, it most likely must be somebody else. So I got all my clues together an' commenced deductin'. Honest, folks, I never deducted so hard or so fast in my life. An' heah's what I concluded."

He stepped forward suddenly and shoved an accusing finger in the direction of Felix Watt.

"Yonder," he thundered, "sits the guilty man!"

There was a chorus of surprise, and a roar of protest from Felix. Mr. Slappey continued speaking, imperturbably.

"Felix used to be wed to Gardenia," he explained. "Ev'ybody in Bumminham knows he's a wuthless, lazy, nogood bum. He never done no work in his life, nor neither he wasn't cravin' to. So when Gardenia got divorced away fum him, why, he didn't have no visible means of support, an' was he peeved.

"Well, right after that, Gardenia got herse'f engaged to Henry Stiles. Now Felix, bein' wuthless hisse'f, figured that Henry was the same sort of pusson. He figured that Henry was on'y fixin' to marry Gardenia on account she could support him with her washin'. So he figured it out that if Gardenia began to git in trouble with the white folks, on account of losin' wash, why, Henry would git disengaged fum her, an' that would give Felix another chance at a good home an' free eatments.

"So tha's exackly what he done, folks. He snuck up an' down that alley an' he stold them clothes off Gardenia's wash line. He knowed it would ruin her business. An' he also knowed that after Henry broke off with Gardenia an' she took him back, why, the wash would cease fum disappearin'; on account he woul'n't have no mo' reason fo' stealing same.

"But what Felix Watt never figured on was bein' detected by somebody smart like Florian Slappey. He never knowed that he was runnin' foul of the law. It never occurred to him that he had brains on his trail." Florian opened his closet door and produced a pile of linens.

"Yonder," he said proudly, "is the missing wash! Felix is guilty!" He bowed. "Ladies an' gemmun, I thank you, one and all."

Felix attempted to deny his guilt, but his protestations lacked conviction. Henry Stiles was glowering at his fiancée's ex-husband. He said, "Mighty soon, Felix, yo' face an' my fist is gwine git acquainted. Ise tellin' you."

Gardenia was loud in her praise. She identified the missing pieces. She declared that she never would have thought of Felix. "How come you suspected him, Florian? What made you so sure he was guilty?"

Mr. Slappey was beaming. From the pile of laundry he selected the topmost piece — the sheet on which he had been standing during those awful apprehensive minutes in Felix Watt's closet.

That sheet was very, very muddy. Florian had stood on it nervously, and for a long time. He designated the gobs of mud his own feet had left on the sheet.

"That's how I solved this mystery," he explained. "Footprints!"

THE GREAT THIEVES

THE CRIMINOLOGISTS' CLUB

by E. W. HORNUNG

RAFFLES *is usually thought of as the first great rogue of mystery fiction. But he isn't. He's the second. The first is the "illustrious" Colonel Clay, by Grant Allen. Colonel Clay began his nefarious career in "An African Millionaire" in 1897, two years before* RAFFLES'S *début. But if* RAFFLES *isn't technically the first, he is spiritually; as "The Criminologists' Club" testifies.*

BUT WHO are they, Raffles, and where's their house? There's no such club on the list in Whitaker."

"The Criminologists, my dear Bunny, are too few for a local habitation, and too select to tell their name in Gath. They are merely so many solemn students of contemporary crime, who meet and dine periodically at each other's clubs or houses."

"But why in the world should they ask us to dine with them?"

And I brandished the invitation which had brought me hotfoot to the Albany: it was from the Right Hon. the Earl of Thornaby, K.G.; and it requested the honor of my company at dinner, at Thornaby House, Park Lane, to meet the members of the Criminologists' Club. That in itself was a disturbing compliment: judge then of my dismay on learning that Raffles had been invited too!

"They have got it into their heads," said he, "that the gladiatorial element is the curse of most modern sport. They tremble especially for the professional gladiator. And they want to know whether my experience tallies with their theory."

"So they say!"

"They quote the case of a league player, *sus per coll.,* and any number of suicides. It really is rather in my public line."

"In yours, if you like, but not in mine," said I. "No, Raffles, they've got their eye on us both, and mean to put us under the microscope, or they never would have pitched on *me*."

Raffles smiled on my perturbation.

"I almost wish you were right, Bunny! It would be even better fun than I mean to make it as it is. But it may console you to hear that it was I who gave them your name. I told them you were a far keener criminologist than myself. I am delighted to hear they have taken my hint, and that we are to meet at their gruesome board."

"If I accept," said I, with the austerity he deserved.

"If you don't," rejoined Raffles, "you will miss some sport after both our hearts. Think of it, Bunny! These fellows meet to wallow in all the latest crimes; we wallow with them as though we knew no more about it than themselves. Perhaps we don't, for few criminologists have a soul above murder; and I quite expect to have the privilege of lifting the discussion into our own higher walk. They shall give their morbid minds to the fine art of burgling, for a change; and while we're about it, Bunny, we may as well extract their opinion of our noble selves. As authors, as collaborators, we will sit with the flower of our critics, and find our own level in the expert eye. It will be a piquant experience, if not an invaluable one; if we are sailing too near the wind, we are sure to hear about it, and can trim our yards accordingly. Moreover, we shall get a very good dinner into the bargain, or our noble host will belie a European reputation."

"Do you know him?" I asked.

"We have a pavilion acquaintance, when it suits my lord," replied Raffles, chuckling. "But I know all about him. He was president one year of the M.C.C., and we never had a better. He knows the game, though I believe he never played cricket in his life. But then he knows most things, and has never done any of them. He has never even married, and never opened his lips in the House of Lords. Yet they say there is no better brain in the august assembly, and he certainly made us a wonderful speech last time the Australians were over. He has read everything and (to his credit in these days) never written a line. All round he is a whale for theory and a sprat for practice — but he looks quite capable of both at crime!"

I now longed to behold this remarkable peer in the flesh, and with the greater curiosity since another of the things which he evidently never did was to have his photograph published for the benefit of the vulgar. I told Raffles that I would dine with him at Lord Thornaby's, and he nodded as though I had not hesitated for a moment. I see now how deftly he had disposed of my reluctance. No doubt he had thought it all out before: his little speeches look sufficiently premeditated as I set them down at the dictates of an excellent memory. Let it, however, be borne in mind that Raffles did not talk exactly like a Raffles book: he said the things, but he did not say them in so many consecutive breaths. They were punctuated by puffs from his eternal cigarette, and the punctuation was often in the nature of a line of asterisks, while he took a silent turn up and down his room. Nor was he ever more deliberate than when he seemed most nonchalant and spontaneous. I came to see it in the end. But these were early days, in which he was more plausible to me than I can hope to render him to another human being.

And I saw a good deal of Raffles just then; it was, in fact, the one period at which I can remember his coming round to see me more frequently than I went round to him. Of course he would come at his own odd hours, often just as one was dressing to go out and dine, and I can even remember finding him there when I returned, for I had long since given him a key of the flat. It was the inhospitable month of February, and I can recall more than one cosy evening when we discussed anything and everything but our own malpractices; indeed, there were none to discuss just then. Raffles, on the contrary, was showing himself with some industry in the most respectable society, and by his advice I used the club more than ever.

"There is nothing like it at this time of year," said he. "In the summer I have my cricket to provide me with decent employment in the sight of men. Keep yourself before the public from morning to night, and they'll never think of you in the still small hours."

Our behaviour, in fine, had so long been irreproachable that I rose without misgiving on the morning of Lord Thornaby's dinner to the other Criminologists and guests. My chief anxiety was to arrive under the ægis of my brilliant friend, and I had begged him to pick me up on his way; but at five minutes to the appointed hour there was no sign of Raffles or his cab. We were bidden at a quarter to eight for eight o'clock, so after all I had to hurry off alone.

Fortunately, Thornaby House is almost at the end of my street that was; and it seemed to me another fortunate circumstance that the house stood back, as it did and does, in its own august courtyard; for, as I was about to knock, a hansom came twinkling in behind me, and I drew back, hoping it was Raffles at the last moment. It was not, and I knew it in time to melt from the porch, and wait yet another minute in the shadows, since others were as late as I. And out jumped these others, chattering in stage whispers as they paid their cab.

"Thornaby has a bet about it with Freddy Vereker, who can't come, I hear. Of course, it won't be lost or won to-night. But the dear man thinks he's been invited as a cricketer!"

"I don't believe he's the other thing," said a voice as brusque as the first was bland. "I believe it's all bunkum. I wish I didn't, but I do!"

"I think you'll find it's more than that," rejoined the other, as the doors opened and swallowed the pair.

I flung out limp hands and smote the air. Raffles bidden to what he had well called this "gruesome board," not as a cricketer but as a suspected criminal! Raffles wrong all the time, and I right for once in my original apprehension! And still no Raffles in sight — no Raffles to warn — no Raffles, and the clocks striking eight!

Well may I shirk the psychology of such a moment, for my belief is that the striking clocks struck out all power of thought and feeling, and that I played my poor part the better for that blessed surcease of intellectual sensation. On the other hand, I was never more alive to the purely objective impressions of any hour of my existence, and of them the memory is startling to this day. I hear my mad knock at the double doors; they fly open in the middle, and it is like some sumptuous and solemn rite. A long slice of silken-legged lackey is seen on either hand; a very prelate of a butler bows a benediction from the sanctuary steps. I breathe more freely when I reach a book-lined library where a mere handful of men do not overflow the Persian rug before the fire. One of them is Raffles, who is talking to a large man with the brow of a demigod and the eyes and jowl of a degenerate bulldog. And this is our noble host.

Lord Thornaby stared at me with inscrutable stolidity as we shook hands, and at once handed me over to a tall, ungainly man whom he addressed as Ernest, but whose surname I never learned. Ernest in turn introduced me, with a shy and clumsy courtesy, to the two

remaining guests. They were the pair who had driven up in the
hansom; one turned out to be Kingsmill, Q.C.; the other I knew at a
glance from his photographs as Parrington, the backwoods novelist.
They were admirable foils to each other, the barrister being plump
and dapper, with a Napoleonic cast of countenance, and the author
one of the shaggiest dogs I have ever seen in evening clothes. Neither
took much stock of me, but both had an eye on Raffles as I exchanged a few words with each in turn. Dinner, however, was immediately announced, and the six of us had soon taken our places
round a brilliant little table stranded in a great dark room.

I had not been prepared for so small a party, and at first I felt relieved. If the worst came to the worst, I was fool enough to say in
my heart, they were but two to one. But I was soon sighing for that
safety which the adage associates with numbers. We were far too
few for the confidential duologue with one's neighbour in which I,
at least, would have taken refuge from the perils of a general conversation. And the general conversation soon resolved itself into an
attack, so subtly concerted and so artistically delivered that I could
not conceive how Raffles should ever know it for an attack, and that
against himself, or how to warn him of his peril. But to this day
I am not convinced that I also was honoured by the suspicions of
the club; it may have been so, and they may have ignored me for the
bigger game.

It was Lord Thornaby himself who fired the first shot, over the very
sherry. He had Raffles on his right hand, and the backwoodsman of
letters on his left. Raffles was hemmed in by the law on his right,
while I sat between Parrington and Ernest, who took the foot of the
table, and seemed a sort of feudatory cadet of the noble house. But
it was the motley lot of us that my lord addressed, as he sat back
blinking his baggy eyes.

"Mr. Raffles," he said, "has been telling me about that poor fellow
who suffered the extreme penalty last March. A great end, gentlemen,
a great end! It is true that he had been unfortunate enough to strike
a jugular vein, but his own end should take its place among the most
glorious traditions of the gallows. You tell them, Mr. Raffles: it will
be as new to my friends as it is to me."

"I tell the tale as I heard it last time I played at Trent Bridge; it
was never in the papers, I believe," said Raffles gravely. "You may re-

member the tremendous excitement over the Test Matches out in Australia at the time: it seems that the result of the crucial game was expected on the condemned man's last day on earth, and he couldn't rest until he knew it. We pulled it off, if you recollect, and he said it would make him swing happy."

"Tell 'em what else he said!" cried Lord Thornaby, rubbing his podgy hands.

"The chaplain remonstrated with him on his excitement over a game at such a time, and the convict is said to have replied: 'Why, it's the first thing they'll ask me at the other end of the drop!' "

The story was new even to me, but I had no time to appreciate its points. My concern was to watch its effect upon the other members of the party. Ernest, on my left, doubled up with laughter, and tittered and shook for several minutes. My other neighbour, more impressionable by temperament, winced first, and then worked himself into a state of enthusiasm which culminated in an assault upon his shirt cuff with a joiner's pencil. Kingsmill, Q.C., beaming tranquilly on Raffles, seemed the one least impressed, until he spoke.

"I am glad to hear that," he remarked in a high bland voice. "I thought that man would die game."

"Did you know anything about him, then?" inquired Lord Thornaby.

"I led for the Crown," replied the barrister, with a twinkle. "You might almost say that I measured the poor man's neck."

The point must have been quite unpremeditated; it was not the less effective for that. Lord Thornaby looked askance at the callous silk. It was some moments before Ernest tittered and Parrington felt for his pencil; and in the interim I had made short work of my hock, though it was Johannisberger. As for Raffles, one had but to see his horror to feel how completely he was off his guard.

"In itself, I have heard, it was not a sympathetic case," was the remark with which he broke the general silence.

"Not a bit."

"That must have been a comfort to you," said Raffles dryly.

"It would have been to me," vowed our author, while the barrister merely smiled. "I should have been very sorry to have had a hand in hanging Peckham and Solomons the other day."

"Why Peckham and Solomons?" inquired my lord.

"They never meant to kill that old lady."

"But they strangled her in her bed with her own pillowcase!"

"I don't care," said the uncouth scribe. "They didn't break in for that. They never thought of scragging her. The foolish old person would make a noise, and one of them tied too tight. I call it jolly bad luck on them."

"On quiet, harmless, well-behaved thieves," added Lord Thornaby, "in the unobtrusive exercise of their humble avocation."

And, as he turned to Raffles with his puffy smile, I knew that we had reached that part of the programme which had undergone rehearsal: it had been perfectly timed to arrive with the champagne, and I was not afraid to signify my appreciation of that small mercy. But Raffles laughed so quickly at his lordship's humour, and yet with such a natural restraint, as to leave no doubt that he had taken kindly to my own old part, and was playing the innocent inimitably in his turn, by reason of his very innocence. It was a poetic judgment on old Raffles, and in my momentary enjoyment of the novel situation I was able to enjoy some of the good things of this rich man's table. The saddle of mutton more than justified its place in the menu; but it had not spoiled me for my wing of pheasant, and I was even looking forward to a sweet, when a further remark from the literary light recalled me from the table to its talk.

"But, I suppose," said he to Kingsmill, "it's 'many a burglar *you've* restored to his friends and his relations.'"

"Let us say many a poor fellow who has been charged with burglary," replied the cheery Q.C. "It's not quite the same thing, you know, nor is 'many' the most accurate word. I never touch criminal work in town."

"It's the only kind I should care about," said the novelist, eating jelly with a spoon.

"I quite agree with you," our host chimed in. "And of all the criminals one might be called upon to defend, give me, the enterprising burglar."

"It must be the breeziest branch of the business," remarked Raffles, while I held my breath.

But his touch was as light as gossamer, and his artless manner a triumph of even his incomparable art. Raffles was alive to the danger at last. I saw him refuse more champagne, even as I drained my glass again. But it was not the same danger to us both. Raffles had no reason to feel surprise or alarm at such a turn in a conversation frankly devoted to criminology; it must have seemed as inevitable to him as it was sinister to me, with my fortuitous knowledge of the suspicions that were entertained. And there was little to put him on his guard in the touch of his adversaries, which was only less light than his own.

"I am not very fond of Mr. Sikes," announced the barrister, like a man who had got his cue.

"But he was prehistoric," rejoined my lord. "A lot of blood has flowed under the razor since the days of Sweet William."

"True; we have had Peace," said Parrington, and launched out into such glowing details of that criminal's last moments that I began to hope the diversion might prove permanent. But Lord Thornaby was not to be denied.

"William and Charles are both dead monarchs," said he. "The reigning king in their department is the fellow who gutted poor Danby's place in Bond Street."

There was a guilty silence on the part of the three conspirators — for I had long since persuaded myself that Ernest was not in their secret — and then my blood froze.

"I know him well," said Raffles, looking up.

Lord Thornaby stared at him in consternation. The smile on the Napoleonic countenance of the barrister looked forced and frozen for the first time during the evening. Our author, who was nibbling cheese from a knife, left a bead of blood upon his beard. The futile Ernest alone met the occasion with a hearty titter.

"What!" cried my lord. "*You know the thief?*"

"I wish I did," rejoined Raffles chuckling. "No, Lord Thornaby, I only meant the jeweller, Danby. I go to him when I want a wedding present."

I heard three deep breaths drawn as one before I drew my own.

"Rather a coincidence," observed our host dryly, "for I believe you also know the Milchester people, where Lady Melrose had her necklace stolen a few months afterward."

"I was staying there at the time," said Raffles eagerly. No snob was ever quicker to boast of basking in the smile of the great.

"We believe it to be the same man," said Lord Thornaby, speaking apparently for the Criminologists' Club, and with much less severity of voice.

"I only wish I could come across him," continued Raffles heartily. "He's a criminal much more to my mind than your murderers who swear on the drop or talk cricket in the condemned cell!"

"He might be in the house now," said Lord Thornaby, looking Raffles in the face. But his manner was that of an actor in an unconvincing part and a mood to play it gamely to the bitter end; and he seemed embittered, as even a rich man may be in the moment of losing a bet.

"What a joke if he were!" cried the Wild West writer.

"*Absit omen!*" murmured Raffles, in better taste.

"Still, I think you'll find it's a favourite time," argued Kingsmill, Q.C. "And it would be quite in keeping with the character of this man, so far as it is known, to pay a little visit to the president of the Criminologists' Club, and to choose the evening on which he happens to be entertaining the other members."

There was more conviction in this sally than in that of our noble host; but this I attributed to the trained and skilled dissimulation of the bar. Lord Thornaby, however, was not to be amused by the elaboration of his own idea, and it was with some asperity that he called upon the butler, now solemnly superintending the removal of the cloth.

"Leggett! Just send upstairs to see if all the doors are open and the rooms in proper order. That's an awful idea of yours, Kingsmill, or of mine!" added my lord, recovering the courtesy of his order by an effort that I could follow. "We should look fools. I don't know which of us it was, by the way, who seduced the rest from the main stream of blood into this burglarious backwater. Are you familiar with De Quincey's masterpiece on 'Murder as a Fine Art,' Mr. Raffles?"

"I believe I once read it," replied Raffles doubtfully.

"You must read it again," pursued the earl. "It is the last word on a great subject; all we can hope to add is some baleful illustration or blood-stained footnote, not unworthy of De Quincey's text. Well, Leggett?"

The venerable butler stood wheezing at his elbow. I had not hitherto observed that the man was an asthmatic.

"I beg your lordship's pardon, but I think your lordship must have forgotten."

The voice came in rude gasps, but words of reproach could scarcely have achieved a finer delicacy.

"Forgotten, Leggett! Forgotten what, may I ask?"

"Locking your lordship's dressing room door behind your lordship, my lord," stuttered the unfortunate Leggett, in the short spurts of a winded man, a few stertorous syllables at a time. "Been up myself, my lord. Outer door — inner door — both locked inside!"

But by this time the noble master was in worse case than the man. His fine forehead was a tangle of livid cords; his baggy jowl filled out like a balloon. In another second he had abandoned his place as our host and fled the room; and in yet another we had forgotten ours as his guests and rushed headlong at his heels.

Raffles was as excited as any of us now: he outstripped us all. The cherubic little lawyer and I had a fine race for the last place but one, which I secured, while the panting butler and his satellites brought up a respectful rear. It was our unconventional author, however, who was the first to volunteer his assistance and advice.

"No use pushing, Thornaby!" cried he. "If it's been done with a wedge and gimlet, you may smash the door, but you'll never force it. Is there a ladder in the place?"

"There's a rope ladder somewhere, in case of fire, I believe," said my lord vaguely, as he rolled a critical eye over our faces. "Where is it kept, Leggett?"

"William will fetch it, my lord."

And a pair of noble calves went flashing to the upper regions.

"No need for him to bring it down," cried Parrington, who had thrown back to the wilds in his excitement. "Let him hang it out of the window above your own, and let me climb down and do the rest! I'll undertake to have one or other of these doors open in two two's!"

The fastened doors were at right angles on the landing which we filled between us. Lord Thornaby smiled grimly on the rest of us, when he had nodded and dismissed the author like a hound from the leash.

"It's a good thing we know something about our friend Parrington," said my lord. "He takes more kindly to all this than I do, I can tell you."

"It's grist to his mill," said Raffles charitably.

"Exactly! We shall have the whole thing in his next book."

"I hope to have it at the Old Bailey first," remarked Kingsmill, Q.C.

"Refreshing to find a man of letters such a man of action too!"

It was Raffles who said this, and the remark seemed rather trite for him, but in the tone there was a something that just caught my private ear. And for once I understood: the officious attitude of Parrington, without being seriously suspicious in itself, was admirably calculated to put a previously suspected person in a grateful shade. This literary adventurer had elbowed Raffles out of the limelight, and gratitude for the service was what I had detected in Raffles's voice. No need to say how grateful I felt myself. But my gratitude was shot with flashes of unwonted insight. Parrington was one of those who suspected Raffles, or, at all events, one who was in the secret of those suspicions. What if he had traded on the suspect's presence in the house? What if he were a deep villain himself, and *the* villain of this particular piece? I had made up mind about him, and that in a tithe of the time I take to make it up as a rule, when we heard my man in the dressing room. He greeted us with an impudent shout; in a few moments the door was open, and there stood Parrington, flushed and dishevelled, with a gimlet in one hand and a wedge in the other.

Within was a scene of eloquent disorder. Drawers had been pulled out, and now stood on end, their contents heaped upon the carpet. Wardrobe doors stood open; empty stud cases strewed the floor; a clock, tied up in a towel, had been tossed into a chair at the last moment. But a long tin lid protruded from an open cupboard in one corner. And one had only to see Lord Thornaby's wry face behind the lid to guess that it was bent over a somewhat empty tin trunk.

"What a rum lot to steal!" said he, with a twitch of humour at the corners of his canine mouth. "My peer's robes, with coronet complete!"

We rallied round him in a seemly silence. I thought our scribe would put in his word. But even he either feigned or felt a proper awe.

"You may say it was a rum place to keep 'em," continued Lord Thornaby. "But where would you gentlemen stable your white elephants? And these were elephants as white as snow; by Jove, I'll job them for the future!"

And he made merrier over his loss than any of us could have imagined the minute before; but the reason dawned on me a little later, when we all trooped downstairs, leaving the police in possession of the theatre of crime. Lord Thornaby linked arms with Raffles as he led the way. His step was lighter, his gayety no longer sardonic; his very looks had improved. And I divined the load that had been lifted from the hospitable heart of our host.

"I only wish," said he, "that this brought us any nearer to the identity of the gentleman we were discussing at dinner, for, of course, we owe it to all our instincts to assume that it was he."

"I wonder!" said old Raffles, with a foolhardy glance at me.

"But I'm sure of it, my dear sir," cried my lord. "The audacity is his and his alone. I look no further than the fact of his honouring me on the one night of the year when I endeavour to entertain my brother Criminologists. That's no coincidence, sir, but a deliberate irony, which would have occurred to no other criminal mind in England."

"You may be right," Raffles had the sense to say this time, though I think it was my face that made him.

"What is still more certain," resumed our host, "is that no other criminal in the world would have crowned so delicious a conception with so perfect an achievement. I feel sure the inspector will agree with us."

The policeman in command had knocked and been admitted to the library as Lord Thornaby spoke.

"I didn't hear what you said, my lord."

"Merely that the perpetrator of this amusing outrage can be no other than the swell mobsman who relieved Lady Melrose of her necklace and poor Danby of half his stock a year or two ago."

"I believe your lordship has hit the nail on the head."

"The man who took the Thimblely diamonds and returned them to Lord Thimblely, you know."

"Perhaps he'll treat your lordship the same."

"Not he! I don't mean to cry over *my* spilt milk. I only wish the fellow joy of all he had time to take. Anything fresh upstairs by the way?"

"Yes, my lord: the robbery took place between a quarter past eight and the half-hour."

"How on earth do you know?"

"The clock that was tied up in the towel had stopped at twenty past."

"Have you interviewed my man?"

"I have, my lord. He was in your lordship's room until close on the quarter, and all was as it should be when he left it."

"Then do you suppose the burglar was in hiding in the house?"

"It's impossible to say, my lord. He's not in the house now, for he could only be in your lordship's bedroom or dressing room, and we have searched every inch of both."

Lord Thornaby turned to us when the inspector had retreated, caressing his peaked cap.

"I told him to clear up these points first," he explained, jerking his head toward the door. "I had reason to think my man had been neglecting his duties up there. I am glad to find myself mistaken."

I ought to have been no less glad that I was mistaken. My suspicions of our officious author were thus proved to have been as wild as himself. I owed the man no grudge, and yet in my human heart I felt vaguely disappointed. My theory had gained colour from his behaviour ever since he had admitted us to the dressing room; it had changed all at once from the familiar to the morose; and only now was I just enough to remember that Lord Thornaby, having tolerated those familiarities as long as they were connected with useful service, had administered a relentless snub the moment that service had been well and truly performed.

But if Parrington was exonerated in my mind, so also was Raffles reinstated in the regard of those who had entertained a far graver and more dangerous hypothesis. It was a miracle of good luck, a coincidence among coincidences, which had whitewashed him in their sight at the very moment when they were straining the expert eye to sift him through and through. But the miracle had been performed, and its effect was visible in every face and audible in every voice. I except Ernest, who had never been in the secret; moreover, that gay Criminologist had been palpably shaken by his first little experience of crime. But the other three vied among themselves to do honour where they had done injustice. I heard Kingsmill, Q.C., telling Raffles the best time to catch him at chambers, and promising a seat in court for any trial he might ever like to hear. Parrington spoke of a presentation set of his books, and in doing homage to Raffles made his peace with our host. As for Lord Thornaby, I did overhear the name of the Athenæum Club, a reference to his friends on the committee, and a whisper (as I thought) of Rule II. But he and Raffles had their heads too close together for one to swear honestly to the rule.

The police were still in possession when we went our several ways, and it was all that I could do to drag Raffles up to my rooms, though, as I have said, they were just round the corner. He consented at last as a lesser evil than talking of the burglary in the street; and in my rooms I told him of his late danger and my own dilemma, of the few words I had overheard in the beginning, of the thin ice on which he had cut figures without a crack. It was all very well for him. He had never realised his peril. But let him think of me — listening, watching, yet unable to lift a finger — unable to say one warning word.

Raffles heard me out, but a weary sight followed the last symmetrical whiff of a Sullivan which he flung into my fire before he spoke.

"No, I won't have another, thank you. I'm going to talk to you, Bunny. Do you really suppose I didn't see through these wiseacres from the first?"

I flatly refused to believe he had done so before that evening. Why had he never mentioned his idea to me? It had been quite the other way, as I indignantly reminded Raffles. Did he mean me to believe he was the man to thrust his head into the lion's mouth for fun? And what point would there be in dragging me there to see the fun?

"I might have wanted you, Bunny. I very nearly did."

"For my face?"

"It has been my fortune before to-night, Bunny. It has also given me more confidence than you are likely to believe at this time of day. You stimulate me more than you think."

"Your gallery and your prompter's box in one?"

"Capital, Bunny! But it was no joking matter with me either, my dear fellow; it was touch-and-go at the time. I might have called on you at any moment, and it was something to know I should not have called in vain."

"But what to do, Raffles?"

"Fight our way out and bolt!" he answered, with a mouth that meant it, and a fine gay glitter of the eyes.

I shot out of my chair.

"You don't mean to tell me you had a hand in the job!"

"I had the only hand in it, my dear Bunny."

"Nonsense! You were sitting at table at the time. No, but you may have taken some other fellow into the show. I always thought you would!"

"One's quite enough, Bunny," said Raffles dryly; he leaned back in his chair and took out another cigarette. And I accepted of yet another from his case; for it was no use losing one's temper with Raffles; and his incredible statement was not, after all, to be ignored.

"Of course," I went on, "if you really had brought off this thing on your own, I should be the last to criticise your means of reaching such an end. You have not only scored off a far superior force, which had laid itself out to score off you, but you have put them in the wrong about you, and they'll eat out of your hand for the rest of their days. But don't ask me to believe that you've done all this alone! By George," I cried, in a sudden wave of enthusiasm, "I don't care how you've done it or who has helped you. It's the biggest thing you ever did in your life!"

And certainly I had never seen Raffles look more radiant, or better pleased with the world and himself, or nearer that elation which he usually left to me.

"Then you shall hear all about it, Bunny, if you'll do what I ask you."

"Ask away, old chap, and the thing's done."

"Switch off the electric lights."

"All of them?"

"I think so."

"There, then."

"Now go to the back window and up with the blind."

"Well?"

"I'm coming to you. Splendid! I never had a look so late as this. It's the only window left alight in the house!"

His cheek against the pane, he was pointing slightly downward and very much aslant through a long lane of mews to a little square light like a yellow tile at the end. But I had opened the window and leaned out before I saw it for myself.

"You don't mean to say that's Thornaby House?"

I was not familiar with the view from my back windows.

"Of course I do, you rabbit! Have a look through your own race glass. It has been the most useful thing of all."

But before I had the glass in focus more scales had fallen from my eyes; and now I knew why I had seen so much of Raffles these last few weeks, and why he had always come between seven and eight o'clock in the evening, and waited at this very window, with these very glasses at his eyes. I saw through them sharply now. The one lighted window pointed out by Raffles came tumbling into the dark circle of my vision. I could not see into the actual room, but the shadows of those within were quite distinct on the lowered blind. I even thought a black thread still dangled against the square of light. It was, it must be, the window to which the intrepid Parrington had descended from the one above.

"Exactly!" said Raffles in answer to my exclamation. "And that's the window I have been watching these last few weeks. By daylight you can see the whole lot above the ground floor on this side of the house; and by good luck one of them is the room in which the master of the house arrays himself in all his nightly glory. It was easily spotted by watching at the right time. I saw him shaved one morning before you were up! In the evening his valet stays behind to put things straight; and that has been the very mischief. In the end I had to find out something about the man, and wire to him from his girl to meet her outside at eight o'clock. Of course he pretends he was at his post at the time: that I foresaw, and did the poor fellow's work before my own. I folded and put away every garment before I permitted myself to rag the room."

"I wonder you had time!"

"It took me one more minute, and it put the clock on exactly fifteen. By the way, I did that literally, of course, in the case of the clock they found. It's an old dodge, to stop a clock and alter the time; but you must admit that it looked as though one had wrapped it up all ready to cart away. There was thus any amount of *prima-facie* evidence of the robbery having taken place when we were all at table. As a matter of fact, Lord Thornaby left his dressing room one minute, his valet followed him the minute after, and I entered the minute after that."

"Through the window?"

"To be sure. I was waiting below in the garden. You have to pay for your garden in town, in more ways than one. You know the wall, of course, and that jolly old postern? The lock was beneath contempt."

"But what about the window? It's on the first floor, isn't it?"

Raffles took up the cane which he had laid down with his overcoat. It was a stout bamboo with a polished ferrule. He unscrewed the ferrule, and shook out of the cane a diminishing series of smaller canes, exactly like a child's fishing rod, which I afterward found to have been their former state. A double hook of steel was now produced and quickly attached to the tip of the top joint; then Raffles undid three buttons of his waistcoat; and lapped round and round his waist I beheld the finest of Manila ropes, with the neatest of foot loops at regular intervals.

"Is it necessary to go any further?" asked Raffles when he had unwound the rope. "This end is made fast to that end of the hook, the other half of the hook fits over anything that comes its way, and you leave your rod dangling while you swarm up your line. Of course, you must know what you've got to hook on to; but a man who has had a porcelain bath fixed in his dressing room is the man for me. The pipes were all outside, and fixed to the wall in just the right place. You see I had made a reconnoissance by day in addition to many by night; it would hardly have been worth while constructing my ladder on chance."

"So you made it on purpose!"

"My dear Bunny," said Raffles, as he wound the hemp girdle round his waist once more, "I never did care for ladderwork, but I always said that if I ever used a ladder it should be the best of its kind yet invented. This one may come in useful again."

"But how long did the whole thing take you?"

"From mother earth to mother earth? About five minutes, tonight, and one of those was spent doing another man's work."

"What!" I cried. "You mean to tell me you climbed up and down, in and out, and broke into that cupboard and that big tin box, and wedged up the doors and cleared out with a peer's robes and all the rest of it in five minutes?"

"Of course I don't, and of course I didn't."

"Then what do you mean, and what did you do?"

"Made two bites at the cherry, Bunny! I had a dress rehearsal in the dead of last night, and it was then I took the swag. Our noble friend was snoring next door all the time, but the effort may still stand high among my small exploits, for I not only took all I wanted, but left the whole place exactly as I found it, and shut things after me like a good little boy. All that took a good deal longer; to-night I had simply to rag the room a bit, sweep up some studs and links, and leave ample evidence of having boned those rotten robes *to-night*. That, if you come to think of it, was what a *Chronicle* critic would call the quintessential Q.E.F. I have not only shown these dear Criminologists that I couldn't possibly have done this trick, but that there's some other fellow who could and did, and whom they've been perfect asses to confuse with me."

You may figure me as gazing on Raffles all this time in mute and rapt amazement. But I had long been past that pitch. If he had told me now that he had broken into the Bank of England, or the Tower, I should not have disbelieved him for a moment. I was prepared to go home with him to the Albany and find the regalia in his hatbox. And I took down my overcoat as he put on his. But Raffles would not hear of my accompanying him that night.

"No, my dear Bunny, I am short of sleep and fed up with excitement. You mayn't believe it — you may look upon me as a plaster devil — but those five minutes you wot of were rather too crowded even for my taste. The dinner was nominally at a quarter to eight, and I don't mind telling you now that I counted on twice as long as I had. But no one came until twelve minutes to, and so our host took his time. I didn't want to be the last to arrive, and I was in the drawing room five minutes before the hour. But it was a quicker thing than I care about, when all is said."

And his last word on the matter, as he nodded and went his way, may well be mine; for one need be no criminologist, much less a member of the Criminologists' Club, to remember what Raffles did with the robes and coronet of the Right Hon. the Earl of Thornaby, K.G. He did with them exactly what he might have been expected to do by the gentlemen with whom we had foregathered; and he did it in a manner so characteristic of himself as surely to remove from their minds the last aura of the idea that he and himself were the same person. Carter Paterson was out of the question, and any labelling or addressing to be avoided on obvious grounds. But Raffles stabled the white elephants in the cloakroom at Charing Cross — and sent Lord Thornaby the ticket.

ARSÈNE LUPIN IN PRISON

by MAURICE LEBLANC

Prince Rénine, Paul Sernine, Luis Perenna, M. Lenormand, Jim Barnett, Paul Daubreuil, Captain Jeanniot, Horace Velmont, Bernard d'Andrézy, Désiré Baudru, Cavaliere Floriani, Jean Daspry, Ralph de Limézy, Jean d'Enneris, Victor Hautin, and le Duc de Charmerace — all these supple gentlemen agree that ARSÈNE LUPIN *is the greatest thief in the whole world; and no wonder. They all are* ARSÈNE LUPIN, *who changed names as easily as you change neckties or silk panties. And here is the great Gallic rogue at his laughing, Ganimard-taunting best.*

EVERY tripper by the banks of the Seine must have noticed, between the ruins of Jumièges and those of Saint-Wandrille, the curious little feudal castle of the Malaquis, proudly seated on its rock in midstream. A bridge connects it with the road. The base of its turrets seem to make one with the granite that bears it — a huge block detached from a mountain top, and flung where it stands by some formidable convulsion of nature. All around the calm water of the broad river ripples among the reeds, while water wagtails perch trembling on the top of the moist pebbles.

The history of the Malaquis is as rough as its name, as harsh as its outlines, and consists of endless fights, sieges, assaults, sacks, and massacres. Stories are told in the Caux district, late at night, with a shiver, of the crimes committed there. Mysterious legends are conjured up. There is talk of a famous underground passage that led to the Abbey of Jumièges and to the manor house of Agnès Sorel, once the favorite of Charles VII.

This erstwhile haunt of heroes and robbers is now occupied by Baron Nathan Cahorn — or Baron Satan, as he used to be called on the Bourse, where he made his fortune a little too suddenly. The ruined owners of the Malaquis had to sell the abode of their ancestors to him for a song. Here he installed his wonderful collections of pictures and furniture, of pottery and carved wood. He lives here alone, with three old servants. No one ever enters the doors. No one has ever beheld, in the setting of these ancient halls, his three Rubenses, his two Watteaus, his pulpit carved by Jean Goujon, and all the other marvels snatched by force of money from before the eyes of the wealthiest frequenters of the public salesrooms.

Baron Satan leads a life of fear. He is afraid, not for himself, but for the treasures which he has accumulated with so tenacious a passion and with the perspicacity of a collector whom not the most cunning of dealers can boast of having ever taken in. He loves his curiosities with all the greed of a miser, with all the jealousy of a lover.

Daily, at sunset, the four iron-barred doors that command both ends of the bridge and the entrance to the principal court are locked and bolted. At the least touch electric bells would ring through the surrounding silence. There is nothing to be feared on the side of the Seine, where the rock rises sheer from the water.

One Friday in September the postman appeared as usual at the bridgehead, and, in accordance with his daily rule, the baron himself opened the heavy door.

He examined the man as closely as if he had not for years known that good jolly face and those crafty peasant's eyes. And the man said, with a laugh:

"It's me all right, monsieur le baron. It's not another chap in my cap and blouse."

"One never knows," muttered Cahorn.

The postman handed him a pile of newspapers. Then he added:

"And now, monsieur le baron, I have something special for you."

"Something special! What do you mean?"

"A letter . . . and a registered letter at that!"

Living cut off from everybody, with no friends nor anyone that took an interest in him, the baron never received letters; and this suddenly struck him as an ill-omened event which gave him good cause for nervousness. Who was the mysterious correspondent that came to worry him in his retreat?

"I shall want your signature, monsieur le baron."

He signed the receipt, cursing as he did so. Then he took the letter, waited until the postman had disappeared round the turn of the road, and, after taking a few steps to and fro, leaned against the parapet of the bridge and opened the envelope. It contained a sheet of ruled paper, headed, in writing: —

Prison de la Santé, Paris

He looked at the signature: —

ARSÈNE LUPIN

Utterly dumfounded, he read: —

Monsieur le Baron, — In the gallery that connects your two drawing-rooms there is a picture by Philippe de Champaigne, an excellent piece of work, which I admire greatly. I also like your Rubens pictures and the smaller of your two Watteaus. In the drawing-room on the right I note the Louis XIII credence table, the Beauvais tapestries, the Empire stand, signed by Jacob, and the Renaissance chest. In the room on the left the whole of the case of trinkets and miniatures.

This time I will be satisfied with these objects, which, I think, can be easily turned into cash. I will therefore ask you to have them properly packed, and to send them to my name, carriage paid, to the Gare de Batignolles, on or before this day week, failing which I will myself see to their removal on the night of Wednesday, the 27th instant. In the latter case, as is only fair, I shall not be content with the above-mentioned objects.

Pray excuse the trouble which I am giving you, and believe me to be

Yours very truly,

ARSÈNE LUPIN

P.S. — Be sure not to send me the larger of the two Watteaus. Although you paid thirty thousand francs for it at the salesrooms, it is only a copy, the original having been burned under the Directory, by Barras, in one of his orgies. See Garat's unpublished Memoirs.

I do not care either to have the Louis XV chatelaine, which appears to me to be of doubtful authenticity.

This letter thoroughly upset Baron Cahorn. It would have alarmed him considerably had it been signed by any other hand. But signed by Arsène Lupin! . . .

He was a regular reader of the newspapers, knew of everything that went on in the way of theft and crime, and had heard all about the exploits of the infernal housebreaker. He was quite aware that Lupin had been arrested in America by his enemy, Ganimard; that he was safely under lock and key; and that the preliminaries to his trial were now being conducted . . . with great difficulty, no doubt! But he also knew that one could always expect anything of Arsène Lupin. Besides, this precise knowledge of the castle, of the arrangement of the pictures and furniture was a very formidable sign. Who had informed Lupin of things which nobody had ever seen?

The baron raised his eyes and gazed at the frowning outline of the Malaquis, its abrupt pedestal, the deep water that surrounds it. He shrugged his shoulders. No, there was no possible danger. No one in the world could penetrate to the inviolable sanctuary that contained his collections.

No one in the world, perhaps; but Arsène Lupin? Did doors, drawbridges, walls, so much as exist for Arsène Lupin? Of what use were the most ingeniously contrived obstacles, the most skillful precautions, once that Arsène Lupin had decided to attain a given object? . . .

That same evening he wrote to the public prosecutor at Rouen. He enclosed the threatening letter, and demanded police protection.

The reply came without delay: the said Arsène Lupin was at that moment a prisoner at the *Santé,* where he was kept under strict surveillance and not allowed to write. The letter, therefore, could only be the work of a hoaxer. Everything went to prove this: logic, common sense, and the actual facts. However, so as to make quite sure, the letter had been submitted to a handwriting expert, who declared that, notwithstanding certain points of resemblance, it was not in the prisoner's writing.

"Notwithstanding certain points of resemblance." The baron saw only these five bewildering words, which he regarded as the confession of a doubt which alone should have been enough to justify the intervention of the police. His fears increased. He read the letter over and over again. "I will myself see to their removal." And that fixed date, the night of Wednesday the 27th of September!

Of a naturally suspicious and silent disposition, he dared not unburden himself to his servants, whose devotion he did not consider proof against all tests. And yet, for the first time for many years, he felt a need to speak, to take advice. Abandoned by the law of his country, he had no hope of protecting himself by his own resources, and was nearly going to Paris to beg for the assistance of some retired detective or other.

Two days elapsed. On the third day, as he sat reading his newspapers, he gave a start of delight. The *Réveil de Caudebec* contained the following paragraph:

We have had the pleasure of numbering among our visitors, for nearly three weeks, Chief Inspector Ganimard, one of the veterans of the detective service. M. Ganimard, for whom his last feat, the arrest of Arsène Lupin, has won an European reputation, is enjoying a rest from his arduous labors and spending a short holiday fishing for bleak and gudgeon in the Seine.

Ganimard! The very man that Baron Cahorn wanted! Who could baffle Lupin's plans better than the cunning and patient Ganimard?

The baron lost no time. It is a four-mile walk from the castle to the little town of Caudebec. He did the distance with a quick and joyous step, stimulated by the hope of safety.

After many fruitless endeavors to discover the chief inspector's address, he went to the office of the *Réveil,* which is on the quay. He found the writer of the paragraph, who, going to the window, said:

"Ganimard! Why, you're sure to meet him, rod in hand, on the quay. That's where I picked up with him, and read his name, by accident, on his fishing rod. Look, there he is, the little old man in the frock coat and a straw hat, under the trees!"

"A frock coat and a straw hat?"

"Yes. He's a queer specimen — close-tongued, and a trifle testy."

Five minutes later the baron accosted the famous Ganimard, introduced himself, and made an attempt to enter into conversation. Failing in this, he broached the question frankly, and laid his case before him.

The other listened without moving a muscle or taking his eyes from the water. Then he turned his head to the baron, eyed him from head to foot with a look of profound pity, and said:

"Sir, it is not usual for criminals to warn the people whom they mean to rob. Arsène Lupin, in particular, never indulges in that sort of bounce."

"Still . . ."

"Sir, if I had the smallest doubt, believe me, the pleasure of once more locking up that dear Lupin would outweigh every other consideration. Unfortunately, the youth is already in prison."

"Suppose he escapes? . . ."

"People don't escape from the *Santé*."

"But Lupin . . ."

"Lupin no more than another."

"Still . . ."

"Very well, if he does escape, so much the better; I'll nab him again. Meanwhile you can sleep soundly and cease frightening my fish."

The conversation was ended. The baron returned home feeling more or less reassured by Ganimard's unconcern. He saw to his bolts, kept a watch upon his servants, and another forty-eight hours passed, during which he almost succeeded in persuading himself that, after all, his fears were groundless. There was no doubt about it: as Ganimard had said, criminals don't warn the people whom they mean to rob.

The date was drawing near. On the morning of Tuesday the twenty-sixth nothing particular happened. But at three o'clock in the afternoon a boy rang and handed in this telegram:

No goods Batignolles. Get everything ready for tomorrow night.

ARSÈNE

Once again Cahorn lost his head — so much so that he asked himself whether he would not do better to yield to Arsène Lupin's demands.

He hurried off to Caudebec. Ganimard was seated on a camp stool fishing on the same spot as before. The baron handed him the telegram without a word.

"Well?" said the detective.

"Well what? It's for tomorrow!"

"What is?"

"The burglary! The theft of my collections!"

Ganimard turned to him, and, folding his arms across his chest, cried in a tone of impatience:

"Why, you don't really mean to say that you think I'm going to trouble myself about this stupid business?"

"What fee will you take to spend Wednesday night at the castle?"

"Not a penny. Don't bother me!"

"Name your own price. I am a rich man — a very rich man."

The brutality of the offer took Ganimard aback. He replied, more calmly:

"I am here on leave and I have no right to . . ."

"No one shall know. I undertake to be silent, whatever happens."

"Oh, nothing will happen."

"Well, look here, is three thousand francs enough?"

The inspector took a pinch of snuff, reflected, and said:

"Very well. But it's only fair to tell you that you are throwing your money away."

"I don't mind."

"In that case . . . And besides, after all, one can never tell with that devil of a Lupin! He must have a whole gang at his orders. . . . Are you sure of your servants?"

"Well, I . . ."

"Then we must not rely upon them. I'll wire to two of my own men; then we shall feel safer. . . . And now leave me; we must not be seen together. Tomorrow evening at nine o'clock."

On the morning of the next day, the date fixed by Arsène Lupin, Baron Cahorn took down his trophy of arms, polished up his pistols, and made a thorough inspection of the Malaquis without discovering anything suspicious.

At half past eight in the evening he dismissed his servants for the night. They slept in a wing facing the road, but set a little way back, and right at the end of the castle. As soon as he was alone he softly opened the four doors. In a little while he heard footsteps approaching.

Ganimard introduced his assistants — two powerfully built fellows, with bull necks, and huge, strong hands — and asked for certain explanations. After ascertaining the disposition of the place he carefully closed and barricaded every issue by which the threatened rooms could be entered. He examined the walls, raised the tapestries, and finally installed his detectives in the central gallery.

"No nonsense, do you understand? You're not here to sleep. At the least sound open the windows on the court and call me. Keep a lookout also on the waterside. Thirty feet of steep cliff doesn't frighten blackguards of that stamp."

He locked them in, took away the keys, and said to the baron: "And now to our post."

He had selected as the best place in which to spend the night a small room contrived in the thickness of the outer walls, between the two main doors. It had at one time been the watchman's lodge. A spy hole opened upon the bridge, another upon the court. In one corner was what looked like the mouth of a well.

"You told me, did you not, monsieur le baron, that this well is the only entrance to the underground passage, and that it has been stopped up since the memory of man?"

"Yes."

"Therefore, unless there should happen to be another outlet, unknown to any but Arsène Lupin, which seems pretty unlikely, we can be easy in our minds."

He placed three chairs in a row, settled himself comfortably at full length, lit his pipe and sighed.

"Upon my word, monsieur le baron, I must be very eager to build an additional story to the little house in which I mean to end my days to accept so elementary a job as this. I shall tell the story to our friend Lupin; he'll split his sides with laughter."

The baron did not laugh. With ears pricked up he questioned the silence with ever-growing restlessness. From time to time he leaned over the well and plunged an anxious eye into the yawning cavity.

The clock struck eleven; midnight; one o'clock.

Suddenly he seized the arm of Ganimard, who woke with a start.

"Do you hear that?"

"Yes."

"What is it?"

"It's myself, snoring!"

"No, no, listen. . . ."

"Oh yes, it's a motor horn."

"Well?"

"Well, it's as unlikely that Lupin should come by motor car as that he should use a battering-ram to demolish your castle. So !

should go to sleep if I were you, monsieur le baron . . . as I shall have the honor of doing once more. Good-night!"

This was the only alarm. Ganimard resumed his interrupted slumbers, and the baron heard nothing save his loud and regular snoring.

At break of day they left their cell. A great calm peace — the peace of the morning by the cool waterside — reigned over the castle. Cahorn, beaming with joy, and Ganimard, placid as ever, climbed the staircase. Not a sound. Nothing suspicious.

"What did I tell you, monsieur le baron? I really ought not to have accepted . . . I feel ashamed of myself . . ."

He took the keys and entered the gallery.

On two chairs, with bent bodies and hanging arms, sat the two detectives, fast asleep.

"What, in the name of all the . . ." growled the inspector.

At the same moment the baron uttered a cry:

"The pictures! . . . The credence table! . . ."

He stammered and spluttered, with his hand outstretched towards the dismantled walls, with their bare nails and slack cords. The Watteau and the three Rubenses had disappeared! The tapestries had been removed, the glass cases emptied of their trinkets!

"And my Louis XVI sconces! . . . And the Regency chandelier! . . . And my twelfth-century Virgin! . . ."

He ran from place to place, maddened, in despair. Distraught with rage and grief, he quoted the purchase prices, added up his losses, piled up figures, all promiscuously, in indistinct words and incompleted phrases. He stamped with his feet, flung himself about, and, in short, behaved like a ruined man who had nothing before him but suicide.

If anything could have consoled him it would have been the sight of Ganimard's stupefaction. Contrary to the baron, the inspector did not move. He seemed petrified, and, with a dazed eye, examined things. The windows? They were fastened. The locks of the doors? Untouched. There was not a crack in the ceiling, not a hole in the floor. Everything was in perfect order. The whole thing must have been carried out methodically, after an inexorable and logical plan.

"Arsène Lupin! . . . Arsène Lupin!" he muttered, giving way. . . .

Suddenly he leaped upon the two detectives, as though at last overcome with rage, and shook them and swore at them furiously. They did not wake up.

"The deuce!" he said. "Can they have been . . . ?"

He leaned over and closely scrutinized them, one after the other; they were both asleep, but their sleep was not natural. He said to the baron:

"They have been put to sleep."

"But by whom?"

"By him, of course . . . or by his gang, acting under his instructions. It's a trick in his own manner. I recognize his touch."

"In that case, I am undone; the thing is hopeless."

"Hopeless."

"But this is abominable! — it's monstrous!"

"Lodge an information."

"What's the good?"

"Well, you may as well try . . . the law has its resources. . . ."

"The law! But you can see for yourself. . . . Why, at this very moment, when you might be looking for a clue, discovering something, you're not even stirring!"

"Discover something, with Arsène Lupin! But, my dear sir, Arsène Lupin never leaves anything behind him! There's no chance with Arsène Lupin! I am beginning to wonder whether he got himself arrested by me of his own free will in America!"

"Then I must give up the hope of recovering my pictures or anything! But he has stolen the pearls of my collection. I would give a fortune to get them back. If there's nothing to be done against him, let him name his price."

Ganimard looked at him steadily.

"That's a sound notion. Do you stick to it?"

"Yes, yes, yes! But why do you ask?"

"I have an idea."

"What idea?"

"We'll talk of it if nothing comes of the inquiry. . . . Only, not a word about me to a soul if you wish me to succeed."

And he added, between his teeth:

"Besides, I have nothing to be proud of."

The two men gradually recovered consciousness, with the stupe-fied look of men awakening from a hypnotic sleep. They opened astounded eyes, tried to make out what had happened. Ganimard questioned them. They remembered nothing.

"Still, you must have seen somebody."

"No."

"Try and think."

"No."

"Did you have a drink?"

They reflected, and one of them replied:

"Yes, I had some water."

"Out of that bottle there?"

"Yes."

"I had some too," said the other.

Ganimard smelled the water, tasted it. It had no particular scent or flavor.

"Come," he said, "we are wasting our time. Problems set by Arsène Lupin can't be solved in five minutes. But, by jingo, I swear I'll catch him! He's won the second bout. The rubber game to me!"

That day a charge of aggravated larceny was laid by Baron Cahorn against Arsène Lupin, a prisoner awaiting trial at the *Santé*.

The baron often regretted having laid his information when he saw the Malaquis made over to the gendarmes, the public prosecutor, the examining magistrate, the newspaper reporters, and all the idle, curious people who worm themselves in wherever they have no business to be.

Already the case was filling the public mind. It had taken place under such peculiar conditions, and the name of Arsène Lupin excited men's imaginations to such a pitch, that the most fantastic stories crowded the columns of the press and found acceptance with the public.

But the original letter of Arsène Lupin, which was published by the *Echo de France* — and no one ever knew who had supplied the text: the letter in which Baron Cahorn was insolently warned of what threatened him — caused the greatest excitement. Fabulous explanations were offered forthwith. The old legends were revived. The newspapers reminded their readers of the existence of the famous subterranean passages. And the public prosecutor, influenced by these statements, pursued his search in this direction.

The castle was ransacked from top to bottom. Every stone was examined; the wainscotings and chimneys, the frames of the mirrors and the rafters of the ceilings were carefully inspected. By the light of torches the searchers investigated the immense cellars, in which the lords of the Malaquis had been used to pile up their provisions and munitions of war. They sounded the very bowels of the rock. All to no purpose. They discovered not the slightest trace of a tunnel. No secret passage existed.

Very well, was the answer on every side, but pictures and furniture don't vanish like ghosts. They go out through doors and windows, and the people that take them also go in and out through doors and windows. Who are these people? How did they get in? And how did they get out?

The public prosecutor of Rouen, persuaded of his own incompetence, asked for the assistance of the Paris police. M. Dudouis, the chief of the detective service, sent the most efficient bloodhounds in his employ. He himself paid a forty-eight hours' visit to the Malaquis, but met with no better success.

It was after his return that he sent for Chief Inspector Ganimard, whose services he had so often had occasion to value.

Ganimard listened in silence to the instructions of his superior, and then, tossing his head, said:

"I think we shall be on a false scent while we continue to search the castle. The solution lies elsewhere."

"With Arsène Lupin! If you think that, then you believe that he took part in the burglary."

"I do think so. I go further: I consider it certain."

"Come, Ganimard, this is ridiculous. Arsène Lupin is in prison."

"Arsène Lupin is in prison, I agree. He is being watched, I grant you. But if he had his legs in irons, his hands bound, and his mouth gagged I should still be of the same opinion."

"But why this persistency?"

"Because no one else is capable of contriving a plan on so large a scale, and of contriving it in such a way that it succeeds . . . as this has succeeded."

"Words, Ganimard!"

"They are true words, for all that. Only, it's no use looking for underground passages, for stones that turn on a pivot, and stuff and nonsense of that kind. Our friend does not employ any of those antiquated measures. He is a man of today, or, rather, of tomorrow."

"And what do you conclude?"

"I conclude by asking you straight to let me spend an hour with Lupin."

"In his cell?"

"Yes. We were on excellent terms during the crossing from America, and I venture to think that he is not without a friendly feeling for the man who arrested him. If he can tell me what I want to know, without compromising himself, he will be quite willing to spare me an unnecessary journey."

It was just after midday when Ganimard was shown into Arsène Lupin's cell. Lupin, who was lying on his bed, raised his head, and uttered an exclamation of delight.

"Well, this is a surprise! Dear old Ganimard here!"

"Himself."

"I have hoped for many things in this retreat of my own choosing, but for none more eagerly than the pleasure of welcoming you here."

"You are too good."

"Not at all, not at all. I have the liveliest feelings of esteem for you."

"I am proud to hear it."

"I have said so a thousand times: Ganimard is our greatest detective. He's *almost* — see how frank I am — *almost* as good as Holmlock Shears. But, really, I'm awfully sorry to have nothing better than this stool to offer you. And not a drink of any kind! Not so much as a glass of beer! Do forgive me: I am only passing through!"

Ganimard smiled and sat down, and the prisoner, glad of the opportunity of speaking, continued:

"By Jove, what a treat to see a decent man's face! I am sick of the looks of all those spies who go through my cell and my pockets ten times a day, to make sure that I am not planning an escape. Gad, how fond the Government must be of me!"

"They show their taste."

"No, no! I should be so happy if they would let me lead my quiet little life."

"On other people's money."

"Just so. It would be so simple. But I'm letting my tongue run on. I'm talking nonsense, and I dare say you're in a hurry. Come, Ganimard, tell me to what I owe the honor of this visit."

"The Cahorn case," said Ganimard, straight out.

"Stop! Wait a bit. . . . You see, I have so many on hand! First, let me search my brain for the Cahorn pigeonhole. . . . Ah, I have it! Cahorn case, Château du Malaquis, Seine-Inférieure. . . . Two Rubenses, a Watteau, and a few minor trifles."

"Trifles!"

"Oh yes; all this is of small importance. I have bigger things on hand. However, you're interested in the case, and that's enough for me. . . . Go ahead, Ganimard."

"I need not tell you, need I, how far we have got with the investigation?"

"No, not at all. I have seen the morning papers. And I will even take the liberty of saying that you are not making much progress."

"That's just why I have come to throw myself upon your kindness."

"I am entirely at your service."

"First of all, the thing was done by you, was it not?"

"From start to finish."

"The registered letter? The telegram?"

"Were sent by yours truly; in fact, I ought to have the receipts somewhere."

Arsène opened the drawer of a little deal table which, with the bed and the stool, composed all the furniture of his cell, took out two scraps of paper, and handed them to Ganimard.

"Hullo!" cried the latter. "Why, I thought you were being kept under constant observation and searched on the slightest pretext. And it appears that you read the papers and collect postoffice receipts. . . ."

"Bah! Those men are such fools! They rip up the lining of my waistcoat, explore the soles of my boots, listen at the walls of my cell; but not one of them ever thought that Arsène Lupin would be silly enough to choose so obvious a hiding place. That's just what I reckoned on."

Ganimard exclaimed, in amusement:

"What a funny chap you are! You're beyond me! Come, tell me the story."

"Oh, I say! Not so fast! Initiate you into all my secrets . . . reveal my little tricks to you? That's a serious matter."

"Was I wrong in thinking that I could rely on you to oblige me?"

"No, Ganimard, and, as you insist upon it . . ."

Arsène Lupin took two or three strides across his cell. Then, stopping:

"What do you think of my letter to the baron?" he asked.

"I think you wanted to have some fun, to tickle the gallery a bit."

"Ah, there you go! Tickle the gallery, indeed! Upon my word, Ganimard, I gave you credit for more sense! Do you really imagine that I, Arsène Lupin, waste my time with such childish pranks as that? Is it likely that I should have written the letter if I could have rifled the baron without it? Do try and understand that the letter was the indispensable starting point — the mainspring that set the whole machine in motion. Look here, let us proceed in order, and, if you like, prepare the Malaquis burglary together."

"Very well."

"Now follow me. I have to do with an impregnable and closely guarded castle. Am I to throw up the game and give up the treasures which I covet because the castle that contains them happens to be inaccessible?"

"Clearly not."

"Am I to try to carry it by assault, as in the old days, at the head of a band of adventurers?"

"That would be childish."

"Am I to enter it by stealth?"

"Impossible."

"There remains only one way, which is to get myself invited by the owner of the aforesaid castle."

"It's an original idea."

"And so easy! Suppose that one day the said owner receives a letter, warning him of a plot hatched against him by one Arsène Lupin, a notorious housebreaker. What is he sure to do?"

"Send the letter to the public prosecutor."

"Who will laugh at him, *because the said Lupin is actually locked up!* The natural consequence is the utter bewilderment of the worthy man, who is ready and anxious to ask the assistance of the first comer. Am I right?"

"Quite so."

"And if he happens to read in the local newssheet that a famous detective is staying in the neighborhood . . ."

"He will go and apply to that detective."

"Exactly. But, on the other hand, let us assume that, foreseeing this inevitable step, Arsène Lupin has asked one of his ablest friends to take up his quarters at Caudebec, to pick up acquaintance with a contributor to the *Réveil,* a paper to which the baron, mark you, subscribes, and to drop a hint that he is so-and-so, the famous detective. What will happen next?"

"The contributor will send a paragraph to the *Réveil,* stating that the detective is staying at Caudebec."

"Exactly; and one of two things follows: either the fish (I mean Cahorn) does not rise to the bait, in which case nothing happens, or else (and this is the more likely presumption) he nibbles, in which case you have our dear Cahorn imploring the assistance of one of my own friends against me!"

"This is becoming more and more original."

"Of course the sham detective begins by refusing. Thereupon a telegram from Arsène Lupin. Dismay of the baron, who renews his entreaties with my friend, and offers him so much to watch over his safety. The friend aforesaid accepts, and brings with him two chaps of our gang, who, during the night, while Cahorn is kept in sight by his protector, remove a certain number of things through the window, and lower them with ropes into a barge freighted for the purpose. It's as simple as . . . Lupin."

"And it's just wonderful," cried Ganimard, "and I have no words in which to praise the boldness of the idea and the ingenuity of the details! But I can hardly imagine a detective so illustrious that his name should have attracted and impressed the baron to that extent."

"There is one and one only."

"Who?"

"The most illustrious of them all, the arch-enemy of Arsène Lupin — in short, Inspector Ganimard."

"What! myself?"

"Yourself, Ganimard. And that's the delightful part of it: if you go down and persuade the baron to talk you will end by discovering that it is your duty to arrest yourself, just as you arrested me in America. A humorous revenge, what? I shall have Ganimard arrested by Ganimard!"

Arsène Lupin laughed long and loud, while the inspector bit his lips with vexation. The joke did not appear to him worthy of so much merriment.

The entrance of a warder gave him time to recover. The man brought the meal which Arsène Lupin, by special favor, was allowed to have sent in from the neighboring restaurant. After placing the tray on the table he went away. Arsène sat down, broke his bread, ate a mouthful or two, and continued:

"But be easy, my dear Ganimard, you will not have to go down there. I am going to reveal a thing to you that will strike you dumb: the Cahorn case is about to be withdrawn."

"What?"

"About to be withdrawn, I said."

"Nonsense! I have just left the chief."

"And then? Does Monsieur Dudouis know more than I do about what concerns me? You must learn that Ganimard — excuse me — that the sham Ganimard has remained on very good terms with Baron Cahorn. The baron — and this is the main reason why he has kept the thing quiet — has charged him with the very delicate mission of negotiating a deal with me; and the chances are that, by this time, on payment of a certain sum, the baron is once more in possession of his pet knickknacks, in return for which he will withdraw the charge. Wherefore, there is no question of theft. Wherefore, the public prosecutor will have to abandon . . ."

Ganimard gazed at the prisoner with an air of stupefaction.

"But how do you know all this?"

"I have just received the telegram I was expecting."

"You have just received a telegram?"

"This very moment, my friend. I was too polite to read it in your presence. But if you will allow me . . ."

"You're poking fun at me, Lupin."

"Be so good, my dear friend, as to cut off the top of that egg gently. You will see for yourself that I am not poking fun at you."

Ganimard obeyed mechanically, and broke the egg with the blade of a knife. A cry of surprise escaped him. The shell was empty but for a sheet of blue paper. At Arsène's request, he unfolded it. It was a telegram, or, rather, a portion of a telegram, from which the postal indications had been removed. He read: —

Arrangement settled. Hundred thousand spondulics delivered. All well.

"Hundred thousand spondulics?" he uttered.

"Yes, a hundred thousand francs. It's not much, but these are hard times. . . . And my general expenses are so heavy! If you knew the amount of my budget . . . it's like the budget of a big town!"

Ganimard rose to go. His ill humor had left him. He thought for a few moments, and cast a mental glance over the whole business, to try to discover a weak point. Then, in a voice that frankly revealed his admiration as an expert, he said:

"It's a good thing that there are not dozens like you, or there would be nothing for us but to shut up shop."

BLIND MAN'S BUFF

by FREDERICK IRVING ANDERSON

The short stories of Frederick Irving Anderson have been un-forgivably neglected by contemporary anthologists. Anderson created that unique detectival collaboration, Deputy Parr and Oliver Armiston; he brought forth the immortal Sophie Lang; and in THE INFALLIBLE GODAHL *he gave us the only American counterpart of the British Raffles.*

Godahl, attend!" said that adept in smart crime to himself as he paused at the curb. "You think you are clever; but there goes your better."

He had to step into the street to make way for the crowd that over-flowed the pavement — men and women, newsboys, even unhorsed actors leaving their pillars for the time for the passing sensation, the beginning of the homing matinée crowds — all elbowing for a place about a tall, slender man in black who, as he advanced, gently tapped a canepoint before him. What attracted the vortex, however, was not so much the man himself as the fact that he wore a black mask. The mask was impenetrable. People said he had no eyes. It was Malvino the Magician, born to eternal darkness. From a child, so the story went, his fingers had been schooled with the same cruel science they ply in Russia to educate the toes of their ballet dancers — until his fingers saw for him.

Head erect, shoulders squared, body poised with the precision of a skater — his handsome, clear-cut features, almost ghastly in con-trast to the band of silk ribbon that covered the sockets where sight should have been — he advanced with military step in the cleared circle that ever revolved about him, his slender cane shooting out now and again with the flash of a rapier to tap-tap-tap on the flags. Why pay for an orchestra chair to witness his feats of legerdemain? Peopling silk hats with fecund families of rabbits, or even discovering a hogshead of boiling water in an innocent bystander's vest pocket, was as nothing to this theatric negotiation of Broadway in the rush hour of late Saturday afternoon. Malvino the Magician seemed oblivious to everything save the subtle impulses of that wand of a cane.

He stopped, suddenly alert to some immediate impression. The vague features relaxed; the teeth shone.

"Ah! Godahl, my friend!" he cried. He turned and advanced deliberately through the crowd that opened a path in front of him. Those wonderful hands reached out and touched Godahl on the arm, without hesitation as to direction.

Godahl could not repress a smile. Such a trick was worth a thousand dollars a week to the front of the house; and nobody knew better than the great Malvino the value of advertising. That was why he walked Broadway unattended twice a day.

When he spoke it was in French. "I am sickened of them all," he said, sweeping his cane in a circle to indicate the gaping crowd straining to catch his words. "See! We have at hand a public chauffeur with nothing better to do than to follow in the wake of the Great Malvino. Godahl, my friend, you are at leisure? Then we will enter."

And Godahl, playing his cards with enjoyment and admiration as well, permitted the blind man to open the door and help him — Godahl, possessing five senses — into the cab; pleased doubly, indeed, to note that the magician had managed to steal his wallet in the brief contact. "To the park!" ordered Malvino, showing his teeth to the crowd as he shut the door.

Godahl had known Malvino first in Rome. The great of the earth gravitate toward each other. No one knew how great Godahl was except himself. He knew that he had never failed. No one knew how great Malvino was except Godahl. Once he had attempted to imitate Malvino and had almost failed. The functions of the third finger of his left hand lacked the wonderful coördination possessed by the magician. Malvino knew Godahl as an entertaining cosmopolitan, of which the world possesses far too few.

"I would exercise my Eng-lish," said the mask, "if you will be so good, my friend. Tell me — you know the lake shore in that city of Chicago?"

"As a book," said Godahl. "You are about to parade there — eh?"

"I am about to parade there," replied Malvino, imitating the accents of the other. "Therefore I would know it — as a book. Read it to me — slowly — page by page, my friend. I walk there shortly."

Godahl possessed, first of all, a marvelous faculty of visualizing. It was most necessary, almost as much so in fact for him in his profession as for Malvino in his — Malvino without eyes. In a matter-of-fact manner, like a mariner charting some dangerous channel, he plotted the great thoroughfare from the boulevard entrance to the Auditorium. The other listened attentively, recording every word. He had made use of Godahl in this way before and knew the value of that man's observations. Then suddenly, impatiently:

"One moment; there is another thing — of immediate need. The Pegasus Club? We are passing it at this moment — eh? You are one of the — what is it they say? — ah, yes, the fifty little millionaires — ha-ha! — yes?"

Godahl looked out of the window. Indeed, they were passing the club now. They had been proceeding slowly, turning this way and that, halted now and again or hurried on by traffic policemen, until now they were merely a helpless unit in the faltering tide of Fifth Avenue; it was past five in the evening and all uptown New York was on the move, afoot and awheel.

It was said of Malvino that he would suffer himself to be whirled round twenty times on being set down in some remote neighborhood of a strange city, and with the aid of his cane find his way back to his hotel with the surety of a pigeon. But even that faculty did not explain how he knew they were passing a certain building, the Pegasus Club, at this moment. Unless, thought Godahl — who was better pleased to study the other's methods than to ask questions — unless the sly fox had it recorded in his strange brain map that carriage wheels rattled over cartracks a hundred yards below this point. Godahl smiled. It was simple after all.

"I perform for your club Tuesday night. One thousand dollars they will pay me — the monkey who sees without eyes! My friend, it is good to be a monkey, even for such as these, who — but ——"

He paused and laid his hand on his companion's arm. "If I could but see the color that is called blue once! They tell me it is cool. They cannot make me feel how cool it is. You will 'go to sea with me next summer and tell me about it — eh? Will you not, my friend? But three of these — what you call the fifty little millionaires — you will tell me why they are called that — three of these came to me in my hotel and would grasp my hand. And why not? I would grasp the hand of the devil himself if he but offered it. They are surprised. They would blindfold my poor eyes — my poor eyes, Godahl! — blindfold them again, and again offer me their hands — thinking Malvino a charlatan. Ha-ha! Again I must shake hands with them! One wears a ring, with a great greasy stone. See! I have it here with me. It is bottleglass. Yet would this barbarian wear it until I in pity took it from him."

Godahl burst into a laugh. So this was the thief! Colwell, one of the so-called fifty little millionaires who gave the Pegasus Club its savor — who exhibited their silk hats and ample bootsoles in the plate-glass windows every Sunday afternoon — had been crying over the loss of a ring stone — a garish green affair for which he had paid hugely abroad.

"I am a marvelous man — eh, Friend Godahl?"

"Indeed yes!" agreed the other, smiling.

"Malvino the Magician sought Godahl, his friend, this afternoon. Petroff — my manager — he walks ten steps behind me, in the crowd. He taps three times with his stick. Three steps to the right. Ha! — There is Godahl! The *canaille* applaud; even Godahl must smile. My friend, Tuesday night Petroff is too clumsy. You will be my manager; but you must be somewhere else."

"Indeed not!" cried Godahl warmly; and to himself: "What does he drive at?"

"Indeed yes!" said the blind man, laying his hand again on the other's arm. "I ask it of you. You will be in other places. If you but say yes you will take me to sea in June and tell me what is the color blue. Listen! First, Malvino will play the monkey. Then I am to be locked in a room for five minutes. At the end of five minutes, if I am gone, that which I have is mine — even to their wallets — fat wallets like this one of yours, which I now return intact."

Godahl accepted the return of his wallet absent-mindedly.

"It is what Mr. Colwell calls a sporting proposition. See! I have it in writing. It is in addition to the one thousand dollars. That I already possess. Now these fifty little millionaires, Friend Godahl — are they all like the three who come to me in my hotel? The one with the slippery stone in his ring — the stone that I have — that one had eight thousand dollars — forty thousand francs — in one wallet — in one-thousand-dollar notes. Does the American nation make new money especially for such as these? The notes were new, the imprint still crisp, like the face of my watch. Forty thousand francs in one wallet! I know, because I had the wallet as he talked. No, my friend. I have it not now. I put it back. Ha-ha! What? And there are fifty of them like that. I am to carry away what I can find! Godahl, it is told that the very servants of the club own rows of brick houses and buy consols at correct times. But fifty little millionaires! And Malvino is to be locked in a room, alone! I have it in writing."

A passing street lamp looked in and caught Godahl in the act of blinking.

"Godahl, my friend, if you will tell me what I must know, then I will teach you what you wish to know. You wish to know many things — eh? I can tell, for I always feel your eyes when you are by. Tell me now, every inch of the way — play it is the lakefront in that city of Chicago."

Godahl chuckled. He did not love the fifty little millionaires. Those marvelous fingers! Malvino was playing with them in the air now in his earnestness. They could rob a poor box! Godahl, smiling grimly, began to draw the map his friend desired. Three steps up from the street, then the first glass door. Inside, two vestibules. Past them, on the right, the smoking room and lounge, a log fire at each end. On the left the street parlor, a great table in the center, and heavy chairs, all upholstered — none far from the walls. Between the rooms, on the left wall, the electric-switch panel. Would he play with light and darkness? It would be as well to hold the secret of this panel. On the floors, deep carpets ——

"Deep carpets!" repeated the magician. "It is well I know. I do not like deep carpets. And this room, where I shall be left alone behind locked doors —— "

"It would have to be the cloakroom, on the left of the main entrance," said Godahl. Yes, that would be the only available room for such a test. No other rooms off the street parlor could be locked, as there were no doors. In this cloakroom there were two doors — one on the main corridor and one on the first vestibule. There was a small window, but it was not to be thought of for one of Malvino's girth. The doors were massive, of oak; and the locks — Godahl remembered the locks well, having had need to examine them on a recent occasion — were tumbler-locks. It would be rare business to see a man, even a magician, leave the cloakroom without help. And that, too, was in the bond — this sporting proposition.

"The locks have five tumblers," laughed Godahl, more and more amused.

"Let there be fifty!" whispered the other contemptuously. "Tell me, my observing friend — who counts the tumblers of a lock from the outside — do these doors open in or out?"

"In," said Godahl — and the long fingers closed on his wrist in a twinkling.

"In, you say?"

"In!" repeated Godahl; and he made a mental note to study the peculiar characteristics of doors that open in.

Malvino buried himself in his furs. The car sped on through the winding thoroughfares of the park, and Godahl fell to counting the revolving flashes of the gaslamps as they rushed by.

"This is the one place in your great city where I find joy," said the blind man at length. "There are no staring crowds; I can pick my thoughts; and the pavements are glass. Outside of these walls your city is a rack that would torture me. Tell me, why is blue so cool? June will be too late for the Mediterranean. We will start before. If you will but tell me, Friend Godahl, so that I can feel it, I will give you the half —— No! I will not. What is money to you? Are you quite sure about the doors opening in? Yes? That is good. Godahl, if I could see I think I would be like you — looking on and laughing. Let me tell you something of doors that open in —— What! We are traveling at an unlawful speed! Mistair Officaire — indeed, yes, the Great Malvino! Pity his poor eyes! Here is money falling from your hair! You are not a frugal man — so careless!"

The park policeman who had stopped them to warn them against speed stood staring at the crisp bill the blind man had plucked from his hair, as the taxicab sped forward again. Malvino directed the driver to his hotel through the speaking tube, and a few minutes later they were set down there. Godahl declined dinner with his queer friend.

"I have here your wallet once more, Friend Godahl!" laughed the blind magician. "The fifty little millionaires! Ha-ha! You promise? You will not be there when I am there?"

"You have my stickpin," said Godahl. "I believe you are collecting bogus stones. That one is bogus, but it was thought to be a fine gift by a friend who is now dead."

The other, with evident disappointment, returned the pilfered stickpin. "You promise! You will not be there when I am there, my friend?"

Godahl held the blue-white hand in his own for a moment as they parted. "No; I promise you," he said; and he watched his queer friend away — Malvino erect, smiling, unfaltering in his fine stride, conscious to the last dregs of the interest he excited on all sides. He shunned the elevator and started up the broad marble stairs, his slender cane tap-tap-tapping, lighting the way for his confident tread.

Godahl dined at his club — looking on and laughing, as Malvino had said with a directness that rather startled the easy rogue into wakefulness. Godahl's career had defied innuendo; his was not an art, but a science, precise, infallible. But several times that afternoon in the somber shadows of their cab he had felt, with a strange thrill, that black inpenetrable mask turn on him as though an inner vision lighted those darkened orbs.

Frankly he avoided afflicted persons in the pursuit of his trade, not because of compunctions, which troubled him not at all, but because a person lacking in any of the five senses was apt to be uncannily alert in some one of the remaining four. He was intensely a materialist, a gambler who pinned his faith to marked cards, never to superstition. He believed intuition largely a foolish fetish, except as actuated by the purely physical cravings; yet he recognized a strange clarity in the mental outlook of the afflicted that seemed unexplainable by any other means.

Malvino, too, played with marked cards. After all, magic is but the clever arrangement of properties. But why had Malvino picked him? Why had Malvino confided in him at all? There were a dozen other members of the Pegasus Club who would have served as well,

so far as furnishing the business of the affair; who would have entered the game as a huge joke. To hold up the fifty little millionaires in their upholstered wallow would surely set the whole town
by the ears. Something of the sort was needed to bring the ribald crew
back to earth. But — thought Godahl — if the task were to be done
he would much prefer to do it himself, not look on as a supernu-
merary.

Malvino, of course, was a thief. The only reason he did not practice
his profession was that he found the business of playing the monkey
paid better. Then, too, as a thief he must bury his talents; and there
is nothing so sweet to the Latin as applause. Malvino could not keep
his fingers quiet. Godahl had permitted himself to be stripped in their
ride through sheer enjoyment of observation. There is nothing too
small to be learned and learned well. Nevertheless it had irritated
him to think that this master had whispered in his ear familiarly. It
smacked too much of kinship. Godahl knew no kin!

As he swept the magnificent dining room with his eyes, however,
he could not repress a chuckle of sheer delight. It would be a hundred-
day jest. They all conformed pretty well to type — a type against
which the finer sensibilities of Godahl revolted. In the beginning the
Pegasus had been the coming together of a few kindred souls —
modest, comfortable, homelike; a meeting-place of intellectual men
who took their chiefest pleasure in the friction of ideas. In this way
the organization had come to have a name, even among the many
clubs of the city.

Godahl had adopted it as his home; and — he cynically para-
phrased it — he might be without honor in his own country, but
never in his own home. He had always been pleased to think that
when he entered here he left the undesirable something outside, like
the dust of his shoes on the doormat — not that he lacked the lust
of the game or a conscious pride in that slick infallibility which had
made him a prince for whom other men went poor. There are times
and places for all things. And this had been home.

Until, one by one, this tribe had crept in, overturned traditions —
substituted the brass of vulgar display for the gold of the fine communion they did not profess to understand, much less to practice. A
newspaper wag had finally dubbed them the Club of the Fifty Little
Millionaires, and the name had stuck. It happened that a handful of

them had been brooded in the same coop, that of a copper king who had begun at the slagpile and ended in philanthropy. As the new-comers gained ascendency the old sect of friends gradually drifted away. The pace was too fast for them.

There was truth in what Malvino had said of the servants; and there is nothing quite so unappetizing as the contempt of those who serve one meat and drink. But Godahl, looking on and laughing, still preserved the habit of picking his meals here with discriminating taste — though now he was less particular about wiping his feet on the doormat than formerly. He even indulged in play occasionally, and while he played he listened to the talk about things worth knowing.

Tonight the talk was all Malvino — at the particular rubber where he chose to play. It was to be a rare occasion. True, they were to pay the magician roundly for the séance and had offered him, besides, a sporting proposition in the shape of a written permission to carry off all his fingers could lift, but they chose to interpret sport according to their own lights. Two centuries ago it was sport in merry England to tie a gamecock to a stump and shy brickbats at it. The game was conducted according to rules carefully worked out, and was popular with all concerned — except the gamecock.

Godahl at length, getting his fill, rose in disgust and passed out. At the corner the street lamp winked at him in its knowing way; and Godahl, forgetting the gorge that had risen in him, returned the wink, smiling.

Colwell, the master of ceremonies, was venturing to a chosen few that a certain faker would be ineligible for dates on a kerosene cir-cuit in Arkansas before the evening was over, when the telephone boy brought him a message from the Victoria. Malvino had started, and was driving to avoid the inevitable crowd that dogged his steps.

The committee was giving a last touch to its properties — a camera and flashlight apparatus arranged behind a screen — when there came the familiar tap-tap-tapping of the cane on the marble steps. If the lilt of his gait were any criterion the mask was in fine fettle.

"So" — he was whispering — "three steps up from the street — two vestibules — and deep carpets. Deep carpets are bad!"

As he passed through the first vestibule this strange, impassive figure in dead black ran his fingers along the wall. There was the door, indeed, by which he would escape.

"Malvino the Magician!" cried a flunkey in gold lace as the inner doors swung open. Colwell was there, with extended hand. The hand of the other closed on it without hesitation, holding it for a moment.

"You speak no French? No? It is — most unfortunate. I speak things — and I am most awkward in your tongue. Is there the color blue here? I would touch it before I play."

He waved his cane toward the entrance. "The corridor? It is empty — yes? It is so in the bond. Thus," he cried, his teeth glowing at the circle of faces before him — "Thus am I to take away that which is mine — is it not?"

Colwell elevated a knowing eyebrow at his companions. Colwell had not been a plumber's assistant for nothing in the days of his youth. He had plugged the keyslots with molten lead. Once closed it would require the aid of a carpenter, not a locksmith — not even a magical locksmith — to negotiate the doors of the cloakroom. Colwell did not begrudge his walletful of small change at auction bridge, but he was decidedly averse to letting it fall into the hands of this blind beggar.

They helped him out of his coat. "My cane too!" he said as he handed the cane to Colwell. It was of ebony, as thin as a baton and without ornament of any kind, save a platinum top. "It is — my faithful Achates! It is — a little brother to my poor senses. It is wonderful — " He swayed slightly and put out a hand to steady himself against Colwell. "But tonight, gentlemen, in your honor Malvino disarms himself, for the — how is it? — the fifty little millionaires — ha-ha! — who are so good as to receive me."

"Am I," he continued, "to have the honor of shaking the hands of the gentlemen? I do not know." He paused as though embarrassed, shrugged his shoulders deprecatingly; and then, smiling: "Myself, as a person, is not present if you so desire — only my talents, which you buy and pay for. Ah, I am awkward in your tongue. Sometimes, gentlemen, I am the guest — sometimes I am only the monkey, with his tricks. You understand? I thank you, sir. Saunders, of Texas Union? Ah, of the landed gentry of this great country! I am indeed pleasured."

A smile went the rounds. Saunders, of Texas Union, who was shaking the hand of the mask with one hand and discreetly feeling the muscles under the black-sleeved arm with the other, had been a puddler at Homestead until his talents for ragtime rescued him from oblivion and gave him Texas Union as a pocket piece. He brought forward Jones, of Pacific Cascade; Welton, of Tonopah Magnet; Smithers, of Excelsior Common; Jamieson, of Alleghany Western — and so on down the line. The guest, in his naïveté, seemed under the impression that the handles to the names referred to ancestral acres. These men had been named in the daily papers so often in connection with their pet manipulations in the market that they themselves had come to accept the nomenclature, using it much as an Englishman would say Kitchener, of Khartum; or Marlborough, of Blenheim.

So the mask was passed round the room. He was well worth seeing at close range. He accepted each hand with a steely grip; concentrated the vague blackness of his mask on each face, and spoke briefly and in halting phrases. In laying aside his cane he seemed to have lost something of the poise that distinguished the great Malvino on the street or on the stage; and he leaned heavily on a shoulder here, on an arm there, as he was passed from one to another. There was a tremor of excitement in the room. A diversion had been promised; but what it was to be the honorable gentlemen of the committee had kept to themselves and their confederates. Colwell, Saunders and Mason — of Independent Guano — whispered together for a moment; and when the circle of introductions was complete the guest was led to the center of the room. He took his place at the head of the big table, exploring it nervously with his fingers while he waited for the company to be seated.

What followed was somewhat tame, and they expressed themselves to that effect occasionally behind their hands. They had seen the same thing before; a two-dollar bill gave the veriest street loafer the same privilege every afternoon and evening at the Victoria — except for a few parlor pieces the Magician reserved for private entertainments. But even the makings of these were to be had for a few pennies in any one of the numerous shops in Sixth Avenue devoted to the properties of magic. It was merely quickness of hand against slowness of eye. It is said that the persistency of vision amounts to one-hundredth of a second. These fingers found ample room to work in that slit of time. Yet the circle looked on languidly, like an audience at a championship fistfight tolerating the preliminaries.

The performer had borrowed a pack of cards bearing the unbroken seal of the club, and was playing a solitary game at whist, cards faced — a trick of Malvino's, by the way, which has never been satisfactorily explained — when suddenly the barons of Tonopah, Alleghany — and so forth — sat up with a thrill of anticipation. It was evident to all, except perhaps the performer himself, that the apex of the evening was at hand. Mason softly opened the electric-switch cabinet; Colwell and Saunders moved carelessly toward the table, taking up positions on each hand of the mask, as though for a better view of the game.

Then came blank, overwhelming darkness! There was the scuffle of feet; the snapping impact of body against body; a gasp; a half-uttered cry of pain; then:

"Confound him!" It was the voice of Colwell, breathing hard. "He's like a bull —— Gad! Can't you —— "

Then another voice — that of Saunders:

"Steady — I've got him! Ready?"

The unseen struggle ceased suddenly. There were several in that thrilled circle that grew sick. It seemed evident that the honorable gentlemen of the committee had overpowered the Magician, were about to strip him of his mask — to show him up as the charlatan who had too long duped a city. They wanted their money's worth. Colwell was laughing, short, sharp; he had the mask now — they could hear the silken ribbon rip as it came away.

"Now! Mason, let him have it!"

The words ended in a roar of mingled rage and pain; there came a sharp snap-snap — as of bones coming away from their sockets; and simultaneously the muffled explosion and the blinding glare of the camera flashlight. And in the one-hundredth of a second of incandescence there was indelibly imprinted on the vision of the audience the figure of the Magician holding two men at arm's length, each by the wrist, their features hideously contorted. Then dead darkness fell, in the midst of which hung the imprinted scene in silhouette against a phosphorescent pall.

Someone thought of the lights. It was the Magician himself. This curious circumstance was not noted until later. The switch clicked and the chandeliers sprang into being again. Colwell held the torn mask in his hand. Every eye, still straining for sight after the shock of the flashlight, sought the blind face of the performer. It was horribly blind now, stripped of its silk ribbon. Covering the eyesockets like plasters were great black disks larger than silver dollars. He stumbled across the room — almost fell against the table; his uncertain hand sought Colwell's arm, traveled down its length and took from the fingers the torn mask and replaced it. The master of ceremonies gazed at the cadaverous face, fascinated. The room was deathly silent. The Magician flashed his teeth in a poor attempt at a smile. His voice, when he spoke, was in whispers as crisp as leaves:

"Ah — my poor eyes! I do not sell —— Gentlemen, I am clumsy with your words. Let me not offend those who are my friends among you when I say I do not sell you my private self — it is only the monkey in me you can buy."

Colwell and Saunders were making efforts to soothe their arms, which were suffering exquisitely. Several men pushed forward, ashamed, to bridge the embarrassment with their apologies to the Magician, who stared at them imperturbably with the mask. Things gradually came to rights, except for the honorable gentlemen of the committee, who took the first chance to retire with their troubles. The hands of the mask were like steel and when he wrenched the bones in their sockets he had not dealt lightly.

"We proceed," said the Magician with a deprecating wave of his hand. "The room! I am to be your prisoner. It is so written."

The few members who knew of Colwell's precautions of plugging the keyslots with lead thought wryly of the fact now. If this thing went any further the Pegasus Club would be the butt of the town!

"We will forget that," said Welton, of Tonopah Magnet, assuming leadership in a movement to make amends. "Besides," he added with a laugh, "we haven't given you a chance to go through our pockets yet. You would have to escape empty-handed."

"Your pardon!" said the mask with a grand bow. "I have already taken the opportunity."

So saying he displayed the contents of his capacious pockets. He had at least a score of wallets and several rolls of banknotes. The room exploded in a cry of amazement. Then the truth flashed upon them. When they passed the guest from hand to hand his nimble fingers had been busy substituting wads of paper for wallets.

"The hour is late," he continued, feeling the face of his watch. "I must be gone in five minutes. The room — if you will."

Welton, of Tonopah Magnet, roaring with laughter, took the Magician — they admitted now he was at least that — and led him to the door of the cloakroom.

"One favor!" said the mask at the threshold. "My coat — my hat — my faithful cane. Ah! I thank you. I bid you good night!"

The naïveté of the words was masterly. Welton, of Tonopah Magnet, drew the door shut with a slam and the lock clicked. He faced the others and turned his trousers pockets inside out comically. He was not worrying about the safety of his cash, but he did admire the deftness of those fingers.

"I am glad to say he left my watch," he said; and he put his watch on the table. It was lacking five minutes of midnight. "What gets me," he continued, turning toward the closed door, "is how we are going to get the poor devil out without a battering ram! Colwell has most certainly earned everlasting fame by his brilliant entertainment this evening."

The keys were useless now that the spring locks had snapped shut on the prisoner. Someone suggested sending for the engineer; but one and all agreed that the game must be played out in common decency. They all retired to the lounging room to give the blind beggar five minutes to find out the trick that had been played on him.

At the end of five minutes they sent for the engineer, and that grimy individual appeared, loaded down with tools; he expressed it as his reverend opinion that a damned fine door was about to be turned into scrap. There was one chance — that a gasoline torch might blow the lead from the keyslot. But, no — the molten metal only completed the upsetting of the fine mechanism. There was nothing to do but to cut around the lock with a compass saw.

"Cheer up, Malvino!" said Welton through the door. "We will be with you in another minute."

Just then Godahl ran in from the street. He threw his hat and coat to an attendant.

"Ha! The devil to pay — eh?" he cried excitedly. "I just this minute heard of it; and I rushed here."

"What?" said a number of voices at once.

The usually exquisite Godahl was somewhat disheveled and his eyes were red.

"Malvino!" cried he, staring at them as though perplexed at their blandness. "Do you mean to say you don't know why he didn't show up this evening?"

"Didn't show up! What do you mean?"

"You really don't know?" cried Godahl, his eyes blazing.

"No! What? Tell us the answer!" said someone with a laugh.

"The police found him bound and gagged in a deserted cab in Central Park. They've got him in Bellevue Hospital now, raving. By Gad! if I —— "

The room laughed. Even the grimy engineer boring a hole to start his compass saw looked over his shoulder and grinned at Godahl.

"Don't excite yourself, Godahl," said Welton, of Tonopah Magnet. "Somebody's been stringing you. We've got Malvino here now. Gad, I wish we didn't have him! You're just in time to help us out of a devil of a mess. That humorist Colwell has plugged the locks with lead; and we can't get the blind beggar out without sawing the door down. He's sweating blood in there now."

"In there?" cried Godahl, pushing his way through the ring round the engineer.

"In there!" repeated Welton. "The kleptomaniac has got a cool ten thousand of mine."

"No!"

"Yes!" said Welton, mimicking Godahl's tone. "You didn't know there was that much money in the world, eh?"

"Let me get this straight," said Godahl, laying a hand on the engineer's arm to stop his work. "You think you have Malvino locked in there with your wallets? I tell you Malvino hasn't been within a mile of this place tonight!"

"I'll lay you a thousand on it!" cried Welton.

"Tut! tut! Believe me, you are betting on the wrong card." Godahl's eyes danced.

"I lay you a thousand on it!" reiterated the Tonopah magnate.

"We'll have to let Malvino hold my stake until we get him out. Gad, he went through me so clean I couldn't swear at this minute that I've got on socks!"

"You are betting on a sure thing?"

"I'm taking candy from a child," retorted Welton.

"I take you!" cried Godahl, his eyes twinkling. "Anybody else want any candy? I warn you!"

There were several. It wasn't every day in the week that they could get Godahl on the hip.

"I warn you again," said Godahl as he accepted the markers, "that Malvino is not in that room. If anybody is there, it is an impostor. You can prove it in a minute by telephoning Bellevue."

The biting saw completed its half circle about the lock; the door swung open. The room was empty!

Several volunteers ran to the rear door. Their sharp chorus of amazement started the crowd tumbling after them. The rear door was off its hinges! It stood propped against the jamb. A child could see what had happened. The prisoner, laden with the cash of the fifty little millionaires, had simply drawn the bolts of the two hinges and lifted the door out of its frame. On the floor was a wad of hand-bills like those the rogue had left in his dupes' pockets in place of their wallets. They read: "Malvino! He Has No Eyes! Watch His Fingers!"

The fifty little millionaires gazed at each other dumfounded, feeling their pockets the while. The infallible Godahl fell into a chair, roaring with laughter. He threw back his head, kicked out his heels, buried his hands wrist-deep in the crisp bills that lined his pockets — all in cold, hard cash! On the whole, he had never spent a more profitable evening.

As for Malvino the Magician, that charlatan could be mighty thankful that it was not he whom the honorable gentlemen of the committee had subjected to manhandling. For Malvino had the eyes of a hawk. So much Godahl had ascertained earlier in the evening when he, in the guise of a murderous cabby, was subjecting the Italian to the indignity of a gag.

THE STOLEN ROMNEY

by EDGAR WALLACE

We take exceptional pleasure in introducing FOUR SQUARE JANE, *a little-known child of fecund Edgar Wallace's imagination — a lady-thief you positively never heard of who is nevertheless as resourceful and dashing as Raffles and Arsène Lupin.*

CHIEF SUPERINTENDENT PETER DAWES, of Scotland Yard, was a comparatively young man, considering the important position he held. It was the boast of his department — Peter himself did very little talking about his achievements — that never once, after he had picked up a trail, was Peter ever baffled.

A clean-shaven, youngish-looking man, with grey hair at his temples, Peter took a philosophical view of crime and criminals, holding neither horror towards the former, nor malice towards the latter.

If he had a passion at all it was for the crime which contained within itself a problem. Anything out of the ordinary, or anything bizarre, fascinated him, and it was one of the main regrets of his life that it had never once fallen to his lot to conduct an investigation into the many Four Square Jane mysteries which came to the Metropolitan police.

It was after the affair at Lord Claythorpe's that Peter Dawes was turned loose to discover and apprehend this girl criminal. He realized that it was of the greatest importance that he should keep his mind unhampered and unprejudiced by the many and often contradictory "clues" which everyone who had been affected by Four Square Jane's robberies insisted on discussing with him.

After investigating the Lord Claythorpe mystery, Peter went back to Scotland Yard, and reported to the Commissioner.

"So far as I can understand, the operations of this woman began about twelve months ago. She has been constantly robbing, not the ordinary people who are subjected to this kind of victimization, but people with bloated bank balances, and so far as my investigations go, bank balances accumulated as a direct consequence of shady exploitation companies."

"What does she do with the money?" asked the Commissioner curiously.

"That's the weird thing about it," replied Dawes. "I'm fairly certain that she donates very large sums to all kinds of charities. For example, after the Lewinstein burglary a big crêche in the East End of London received from an anonymous donor the sum of four thousand pounds. Simultaneously, another sum of four thousand was given to one of the West End hospitals. After the Talbot burglary three thousand pounds, which represented nearly the whole of the amount stolen, was left by some unknown person to the West End Maternity Hospital. I have an idea that we shall discover she is somebody who is in close touch with hospital work, and that behind these crimes there is some quixotic notion of helping the poor at the expense of the grossly rich."

"Very beautiful," said the Chief drily, "but unfortunately her admirable intentions do not interest us. In our eyes she is a common thief."

"She is something more than that," said Peter quietly: "she is the cleverest criminal that has come my way since I have been associated with Scotland Yard. This is the one thing one has dreaded, and yet one has hoped to meet — a criminal with a brain."

"Has anybody seen this woman?" said the Commissioner, interested.

"They have, and they haven't," replied Peter Dawes. "That sounds cryptic, but it only means that she has been seen by people who could not recognize her again. Lewinstein saw her, Claythorpe saw her, but she was veiled and unrecognizable. My difficulty, of course, is to discover where she is going to strike next. Even if she is only hitting at the grossly rich she has forty thousand people to strike at. Obviously, it is impossible to protect them all. But somehow —— " he hesitated.

"Yes?" said the Chief.

"Well, a careful study of her methods helps me a little," replied Dawes. "I have been looking round to discover who the next victim will be. He must be somebody very wealthy, and somebody who makes a parade of his wealth, and I have fined down the issue to about four men. Gregory Smith, Carl Sweiss, Mr. Thomas Scott, and John Tresser. I am inclined to believe it is Tresser she is after. You see, Tresser has made a great fortune, not by the straightest means in the world, and he hasn't forgotten to advertise his riches. He is the fellow who bought the Duke of Haslemere's house, and his collection of pictures — you will remember the stuff that has been written about it."

The Chief nodded.

"There is a wonderful Romney, isn't there?"

"That's the picture," replied Dawes. "Tresser, of course, doesn't know a picture from a gas stove. He knows that the Romney is wonderful, but only because he has been told so. Moreover, he is the fellow who has been giving the newspapers his views on charity — told them that he never spent a penny on public institutions, and never gave away a cent that he didn't get a cent's worth of value for. A thing like that would excite Jane's mind; and then, in addition, the actual artistic and monetary value of the Romney is largely advertised — why, I should imagine that the attraction is almost irresistible!"

Mr. Tresser was a difficult man to meet. His multitudinous interests in the City of London kept him busy from breakfast time until late at night. When at last Peter ran him down in a private dining room at the Ritz-Carlton, he found the multimillionaire a stout, red-haired man with a long clean-shaven upper lip, and a cold blue eye.

The magic of Peter Dawes's card secured him an interview.

"Sit down — sit down," said Mr. Tresser hurriedly, "what's the trouble, hey?"

Peter explained his errand, and the other listened with interest, as to a business proposition.

"I've heard all about that Jane," said Mr. Tresser cheerfully, "but

she's not going to get anything from me — you can take my word!
As to the Rumney — is that how you pronounce it? — well, as to
that picture, don't worry!"

"But I understand you are giving permission to the public to
inspect your collection."

"That's right," said Mr. Tresser, "but everybody who sees them
must sign a visitors' book, and the pictures are guarded."

"Where do you keep the Romney at night — still hanging?"
asked Peter, and Mr. Tresser laughed.

"Do you think I'm a fool?" he said. "No, it goes into my strong
room. The Duke had a wonderful strong room which will take a
bit of opening."

Peter Dawes did not share the other's confidence in the efficacy of
bolts and bars. He knew that Four Square Jane was both an artist
and a strategist. Of course, she might not be bothered with pictures,
and, anyway, a painting would be a difficult thing to get away unless
it was stolen by night, which would be hardly likely.

He went to Haslemere House, which was off Berkeley Square, a
great rambling building, with a long, modern picture gallery, and
having secured admission, signed his name and showed his card to
an obvious detective, he was admitted to the long gallery. There was
the Romney — a beautiful example of the master's art.

Peter was the only sightseer, but it was not alone to the picture
that he gave his attention. He made a brief survey of the room in
case of accidents. It was long and narrow. There was only one door
— that through which he had come — and the windows at both ends
were not only barred, but a close wire netting covered the bars, and
made entrance and egress impossible by that way. The windows were
likewise long and narrow, in keeping with the shape of the room,
and there were no curtains behind which an intruder might hide.
Simple spring roller blinds were employed to exclude the sunlight
by day.

Peter went out, passed the men, who scrutinized him closely, and
was satisfied that if Four Square Jane made a raid on Mr. Tresser's
pictures, she would have all her work cut out to get away with it.
He went back to Scotland Yard, busied himself in his office, and
afterwards went out for lunch. He came back to his office at three
o'clock, and had dismissed the matter of Four Square Jane from his

mind, when an urgent call came through. It was a message from the Commissioner.

"Will you come down to my office at once, Dawes?" said the voice, and Peter sprinted down the long corridor to the bureau of the Commissioner.

"Well, Dawes, you haven't had to wait long," he was greeted.

"What do you mean?" said Peter.

"I mean the precious Romney is stolen," said the Chief, and Peter could only stare at him.

"When did this happen?"

"Half an hour ago — you'd better get down to Berkeley Square, and make inquiries on the spot."

Two minutes later, Peter's little two-seater was nosing its way through the traffic, and within ten minutes he was in the hall of the big house interrogating the agitated attendants. The facts, as he discovered them, were simple.

At a quarter past two, an old man wearing a heavy overcoat, and muffled up to the chin, came to the house, and asked permission to see the portrait gallery. He gave his name as "Thomas Smith."

He was an authority on Romney, and was inclined to be garrulous. He talked to all the attendants, and seemed prepared to give a long-winded account of his experience, his artistic training, and the excellence of his quality as an art critic — which meant that he was the type of bore that most attendants have to deal with, and they very gladly cut short his monotonous conversation, and showed him the way to the picture gallery.

"Was he alone in the room?" asked Peter.

"Yes, sir."

"And nobody went in with him?"

"No, sir."

Peter nodded.

"Of course, the garrulity may have been intentional, and it may have been designed to scare away attendants, but go on."

"The man went into the room, and was seen standing before the Romney in rapt contemplation. The attendants who saw him swore that at that time the Romney was in its frame. It hung on the level with the eyes; that is to say the top of the frame was about seven feet from the floor.

"Almost immediately after the attendants had looked in the old man came out talking to himself about the beauty of the execution. As he left the room, and came into the outer lobby, a little girl entered and also asked permission to go into the gallery. She signed her name 'Ellen Cole' in the visitors' book."

"What was she like?" said Peter.

"Oh, just a child," said the attendant vaguely, "a little girl."

Apparently the little girl walked into the saloon as the old man came out — he turned and looked at her, and then went on through the lobby, and out through the door. But before he got to the door, he pulled a handkerchief out of his pocket, and with it came about half a dozen silver coins, which were scattered on the marble floor of the vestibule. The attendants helped him to collect the money — he thanked them, his mind still with the picture apparently, for he was talking to himself all the time, and finally disappeared.

He had hardly left the house when the little girl came out and asked: "Which is the Romney picture?"

"In the centre of the room," they told her, "immediately facing the door."

"But there's not a picture there," she said, "there's only an empty frame, and a funny kind of little black label with four squares."

The attendants dashed into the room, and sure enough the picture had disappeared!

In the space where it had been, or rather on the wall behind the place, was the sign of Four Square Jane.

The attendants apparently did not lose their heads. One went straight to the telephone, and called up the nearest police station — the second went on in search of the old man. But all attempts to discover him proved futile. The constable on point duty at the corner of Berkeley Square had seen him get into a taxicab and drive away, but had not troubled to notice the number of the taxicab.

"And what happened to the little girl?" asked Peter.

"Oh, she just went away," said the attendant; "she was here for some time, and then she went off. Her address was in the visitors' book. There was no chance of her carrying the picture away — none whatever," said the attendant emphatically. "She was wearing a short little skirt, and light summery things, and it was impossible to have concealed a big canvas like that."

Peter went in to inspect the frame. The picture had been cut flush with the borders. He looked around, making a careful examination of the apartment, but discovered nothing, except, immediately in front of the picture, a long, white pin. It was the sort of pin that bankers use to fasten notes together. And there was no other clue.

Mr. Tresser took his loss very calmly until the newspapers came out with details of the theft. It was only then that he seemed impressed by its value, and offered a reward for its recovery.

The stolen Romney became the principal topic of conversation in clubs and in society circles. It filled columns of the newspapers, and exercised the imagination of some of the brightest young men in the amateur criminal investigation business. All the crime experts were gathered together at the scene of the happening and their theories, elaborate and ingenious, provided interesting subject matter for the speculative reader.

Peter Dawes, armed with the two addresses he had taken from the visitors' book, the address of the old man and of the girl, went round that afternoon to make a personal investigation, only to discover that neither the learned Mr. Smith nor the innocent child was known at the addresses they had given.

Peter reported to headquarters with a very definite view as to how the crime was committed.

"The old man was a blind," he said, "he was sent in to create suspicion and keep the eyes of the attendants upon himself. He purposely bored everybody with his long-winded discourse on art in order to be left alone. He went into the saloon knowing that his bulky appearance would induce the attendants to keep their eyes on him. Then he came out — the thing was timed beautifully — just as the child came in. That was the lovely plan.

"The money was dropped to direct all attention on the old man, and at that moment, probably, the picture was cut from its frame, and it was hidden. Where it was hidden, or how the girl got it out, is a mystery. The attendants are most certain that she could not have had it concealed about her, and I have made experiments with a thick canvas cut to the size of the picture, and it certainly does seem that the picture would have so bulged that they could not have failed to have noticed it."

"But who was the girl?"

"Four Square Jane!" said Peter promptly.

"Impossible!"

Peter smiled.

"It is the easiest thing in the world for a young girl to make herself look younger. Short frocks, and hair in plaits — and there you are! Four Square Jane is something more than clever."

"One moment," said the Commissioner, "could she have handed it through the window to somebody else?"

Peter shook his head.

"I have thought of that," he said, "but the windows were closed and there was a wire netting which made that method of disposal impossible. No, by some means or other she got the picture out under the noses of the attendants. Then she came out and announced innocently that she could not find the Romney picture — naturally there was a wild rush to the saloon. For three minutes no notice was being taken of the 'child.' "

"Do you think one of the attendants was in collusion?"

"That is also possible," said Peter, "but every man has a record of good, steady service. They're all married men and none of them has the slightest thing against him."

"And what will she do with the picture? She can't dispose of it."

"She's after the reward," said Peter with a smile. "I tell you, Chief, this thing has put me on my mettle. Somehow, I don't think I've got my hand on Jane yet, but I'm living on hopes."

"After the reward," repeated the Commissioner; "that's pretty substantial. But surely you are going to fix her when she hands the picture over."

"Not on your life," replied Peter, and took out of his pocket a telegram and laid it on the table before the other. It read:

The Romney will be returned on condition that Mr. Tresser undertakes to pay the sum of five thousand pounds to the Great Panton Street Hospital for Children. On his signing an agreement to pay this sum, the picture will be restored.

JANE

"What did Tresser say about that?"

"Tresser agrees," answered Peter, "and has sent a note to the secretary of the Great Panton Street Hospital to that effect. We are advertising the fact of his agreement very widely in the newspapers."

At three o'clock that afternoon came another telegram, addressed this time to Peter Dawes — it annoyed him to know that the girl was so well informed that she was aware of the fact that he was in charge of the case.

I will restore the picture at eight o'clock to-night. Be in the picture gallery, and please take all precautions. Don't let me escape this time.

FOUR SQUARE JANE

The telegram was handed in at the General Post Office.

Peter Dawes neglected no precaution. He had really not the faintest hope that he would make the capture, but it would not be his fault if Four Square Jane were not put under lock and key.

A small party assembled in the gloomy hall of Mr. Tresser's own house.

Dawes and two detective officers, Mr. Tresser himself — he sucked at a big cigar and seemed the least concerned of those present — the three attendants, and a representative of the Great Panton Street Hospital were there.

"Do you think she'll come in person?" asked Tresser. "I would rather like to see that Jane. She certainly put one over on me, but I bear her no ill will."

"I have a special force of police within call," said Peter, "and the roads are watched by detectives, but I'm afraid I can't promise you anything exciting. She's too slippery for us."

"Anyway, the messenger —— " began Tresser.

Peter shook his head.

"The messenger may be a district messenger, though here again I have taken precautions — all the district messenger offices have been warned to notify Scotland Yard in the event of somebody coming with a parcel addressed here."

Eight o'clock boomed out from the neighbouring church, but Four Square Jane had not put in an appearance. Five minutes later there came a ring at the bell, and Peter Dawes opened the door.

It was a telegraph boy.

Peter took the buff envelope and tore it open, read the message through carefully, and laughed — a hopeless, admiring laugh.

"She's done it," he said.

"What do you mean?" asked Tresser.

"Come in here," said Peter.

He led the way into the picture gallery. There was the empty frame on the wall, and behind it the half-obliterated label which Four Square Jane had stuck.

He walked straight to the end of the room to one of the windows.

"The picture is here," he said, "it has never left the room."

He lifted his hand, and pulled at the blind cord, and the blind slowly revolved.

There was a gasp of astonishment from the gathering. For, pinned to the blind, and rolled up with it, was the missing Romney.

"I ought to have guessed when I saw the pin," said Peter. "It was quick work, but it was possible to do it. She cut out the picture, brought it to the end of the room, and pulled down the blind; pinned the top corners of the picture to the blind, and let it roll up again. Nobody thought of pulling that infernal thing down!"

PARIS ADVENTURE

by *LESLIE CHARTERIS*

Your favorite modern Robin Hood in a story that is now published for the first time in America in book form.

SIMON TEMPLAR had to admit that the photograph of himself which adorned the front page of the journal on his knee left nothing to be desired.

Taken only a couple of years ago, at the studio of an ambitious photographer who had clearly seen the potentialities of future revenue from an authentic likeness of such a disreputable character, it brought out to perfection the rakish curve of his jaw, the smooth backward sweep of black hair, the mocking challenge of a gay filibuster's mouth. Even the eyes, by some trick of lighting in the original which had been miraculously preserved through the processes of reproduction, glinted back at him from under the bantering lines of eyebrow with all the vivid dangerous dance of humour that was in his own.

The story illustrated by the picture occupied two columns of the front page and was continued somewhere in the interior. One gathered from it that that elusive and distressingly picturesque outlaw, the Saint, had set the laws of England by the ears again with a new climax of audacities: his name and *nom de guerre* waltzed through the bald paragraphs of the narrative like a debonair will-o'-the-wisp, carrying with it a breath of buccaneering glamour, a magnificently mediæval lawlessness, that shone with a strange luminance through the dull chronicles of an age of dreary news. "The Robin Hood of modern crime" they called him; and with that phrase the Saint himself had least fault of all to find.

At the next table on his left a fair-haired English girl was struggling to explain the secret of successful tea brewing in halting French to an unsympathetic waiter. At other tables, other guests of the Café Berry read their evening papers, sipped *apéritifs,* chattered, argued, and gazed incuriously at the drifting march and countermarch of humanity on the pavements. A purple-capped youth thrust by against the stream with a sheaf of newspapers under his arm, operatically intoning *"Paris-Soir! L'Intran!"* "Savon Cadum" spelt itself out in neon tubes on the top of a building opposite. Beyond the pavements flowed the ceaseless wheeled floods of the Champs Élysées. Paris at six — or any city in the world.

In those surroundings anyone but a Simon Templar might have been embarrassed by the knowledge that a lifelike portrait of himself, accompanied by an account of his latest misdeeds and a summary of several earlier ones, was at the disposal of any citizen who cared to spend the price of a glass of beer on a London penny paper. The Saint was never embarrassed. At that very moment some exciting radio correspondence was in progress between the officials of Scotland Yard and the captain of a liner bound for Panama who had discovered and clapped in irons a passenger who answered very satisfactorily to the broadcast description of the much-wanted Simon Templar. Simon had paid the passenger five hundred pounds to make the trip and endure the inevitable indignities, with all rights in subsequent actions for damages against the shipping company thrown in, and had left a well-organized trail of clues for Scotland Yard to trace him by; and for the next ten days he felt relieved of all responsibility.

He folded his paper and lighted a cigarette, with the comforting assurance that any casual glancer at his classic features would be far less likely to suspect him of a hideous past than to suspect the eminent politician or the débutante victim of a motor accident whose portraits, in smaller frames, had flanked his own on either side. Certainly he saw no reason to creep into a corner and hide.

At the next table the English girl was getting more hopelessly entangled, the waiter more surly and inattentive. The girl's grey eyes wavered in humorous despair towards the Saint, meeting his own for an instant, which to a Simon Templar was sufficient invitation.

"Écoute, toi!" The Saint's voice lanced through the air with a sud-

den quiet command, the edge of a blade so sweetly keen that it seemed to caress even while it cut, snapping the waiter's wandering eyes round like a magnet dropped within an inch of twin compass needles. "Mademoiselle desires that the pot shall first be warmed. After that one will put two spoonfuls of tea within and pour boiling water on it. It is necessary that the water should be really boiling. Go to it."

The waiter nodded sourly, and moved away in a slight daze. In his philosophy, foreigners were not expected to speak his own language better than he did himself, nor to cut short his studied surliness with a cool self-possession that addressed him in the familiar second person singular. In the doorway he paused to explain that at length to a fellow waiter. *"Sâles Américains,"* he said, and spat. Simon Templar was not meant to hear, but the Saint's ears were abnormally sensitive.

He smiled. The tide of cool spring twilight was rising in slow pools of intangible shadow, breaking in soft waves against the island of brightness where they sat; the night pulse of Paris picked up its beat of tinsel and tragedy and laughter. To the Saint any city was an oyster for his opening, a world for conquest; anything was an adventure, even the slaying of an insolent waiter and the rescue of a damsel in distress about nothing more serious than a cup of tea.

He let his cigarette smoulder in absolute contentment. The second pot of tea arrived. The girl poured, tasted, and grimaced ruefully — he decided that she had a mouth that couldn't look anything but pretty even when it tried.

"I should give it up and try a Martini," he advised.

He gave the order, and the girl looked at him enviously.

"I wish I could speak the language as you do."

"I've been here more often than any respectable man should be," said the Saint cheerfully. "I used to be the *concierge* of a home for inebriate art students in the Rue des Deux Paires de Chaussettes de M. Alexandre Dumas. We all lived on absinthe and wore velvet next the skin. It went very well until someone discovered that half the inmates were wearing false beards and reading Edgar Wallace in secret."

The grey eyes laughed.

"Then you must know your way about."

"Paris is yours," said the Saint with a gesture. "What would you like? Respectable night clubs? Artists with real beards? Apaches?"

She tasted her Martini, and nodded as if she liked it. She seemed to be thinking of something else. And then she turned towards him again in a pose very like his own. The deep friendly eyes had a queer wistfulness.

"Tell me, stranger — where do you think a girl should go on a great occasion? Suppose she had something rather desperate to do, and if it went wrong she mightn't be able to choose where she went any more."

The Saint's very clear blue gaze rested on her thoughtfully. He had always been mad, always hoped to be.

"I think," he said, "I should take her across the river to a quiet little restaurant I know in the Place Saint-Michel, where they make the best omelettes in the whole world. And then we should ride up the Boulevard Saint-Michel and have coffee at the Closerie des Lilas, which is just an ordinary French café with a name that ought to send pilgrims in search of it. And after that we might know some more."

"I should like to go there," she said.

Simon flicked a hundred-franc note across the marble top of the table, and beckoned the waiter. The waiter counted out change laboriously from a bulging wallet.

"Shall we?" said the Saint.

The girl gathered up her gloves and bag. Simon stood up quickly to pull the table away from in front of her. He trod heavily on the waiter's toes, overbalanced him backwards, and caught him again dexterously as he was on the point of descending, like Newton's apple, on the bald head of a customer in the next row. Somewhere in the course of the acrobatics the bulging wallet travelled from the waiter's pocket to the Saint's own.

"*Mille pardons*," murmured the Saint, patting the anguished man soothingly on the shoulder, and sauntered after the girl.

There was a taxi crawling by, and they climbed in.

"I'm free till twelve, stranger," said the girl.

She pulled off her hat and leaned far back on the cushions, with one slim silken leg stretched out to rest a toe on the folding seat in front. The passing lights picked up her face in almost breathless perfection, and let it sink back reluctantly into shadow.

"And then do you have to hurry home before the clock strikes, and only leave a glass slipper for a souvenir?"

"No," she said. "I have to burgle a house."

There was an omelette. She had never dreamed of anything so delicate, wrapped in such a gossamer skin, so richly red-gold inside, so different in every way from the dry coagulation of half-scrambled eggs which passes under the same name in too many places.

"There's a trick in it," she said with a sigh, when it was finished.

"Of course there is," said the Saint. "It's one of the higher mysteries of life, only to be revealed to the pure in heart after many ordeals and battles and much travelling."

She accepted a cigarette from his case, dipped it in the flame of his lighter. Across the table the grey eyes looked into his with the serene intimacy which must come from the sharing of any sensuous pleasure, even of eating. She said: "I'm glad I met you, stranger. You take things very calmly, and you don't ask awkward questions."

In the course of his career the Saint had taken a good many things calmly enough, but he could not remember having heard it accounted unto him for righteousness before. He perceived that he had fallen into the error of attaching himself too much to the viewpoint of his bereaved victims.

"The questions may come later," he said. "We burglars aren't easily startled."

She let a trail of smoke rise and disintegrate towards the ceiling.

"I'm going to talk to you, stranger," she said quietly. "A girl likes to talk; and nothing about this evening is real. We never met before, and we shan't meet again. This is an interlude that doesn't count, except for remembrance."

"Is there a dragon in it?"

"There's a Robber Baron. Have you ever heard of Lord Northwade?"

Simon had. His knowledge of unlovable characters, in or out of the peerage, was very nearly unique.

He knew Northwade for one of the most unpleasant products of the last war, a man who had successfully conceived the notion of selling inferior penny bootlaces to the British Army for sixpence a pair, and had gained for himself much wealth for that patriotic service. The Northwade business, subsequently built up to almost monopolistic proportions, was still welding together the uppers of half the world; but Northwade himself had retired a couple of years ago to a mansion on the outskirts of Paris, leaving the female part of his family to pursue its strenuous climb through the social gradings of Mayfair.

"Yes, I've heard of Northwade. One of these monuments of other people's industry, isn't he?"

"He's also my uncle," said the girl. "I'm Judith Molloy."

Simon Templar hadn't blushed since he was eight years old. Also he considered that his remark was very nearly a compliment compared with what he would probably have said to Lord Northwade's face, had that undesirable nobleman been present.

"You have our sympathy," he said coolly.

"My father's a professor of engineering at Oxford," said the girl. "You've probably never heard of him. You couldn't have two brothers who were more different. They've always been like that. Northwade only wanted to make money. My father never wanted it. He's just a quiet, kind, completely ordinary man — almost a child outside his work. They both started at the bottom, and they both got what they wanted. Northwade made the money; my father worked his way through school, went on to Oxford as a Ruskin scholar, and got to where he is now. The thing that came between them was my mother. Northwade wanted her too, but she just happened to prefer Dad."

The Saint nodded.

"It wasn't Dad's fault," she said, "but Northwade never forgave him. I don't think he was really jealous — maybe he wasn't really in love at all — but he'd come on to something that money and success alone couldn't buy, and his vanity never got over it. Oh, he didn't say anything outright. He's always been friendly — too friendly — but Dad, who wouldn't suspect a cannibal who was weighing him, never thought anything of it. I could see it. I tried to tell him, but he wouldn't believe me. He even helped Northwade to make more money — he's a clever inventor, too, and during the war he designed a machine that would put tags on laces twice as quickly as the old way, or something like that. I think Northwade gave him fifty pounds for it." She smiled a little. "It's beginning to sound like a detective story, isn't it?"

"It has begun," said the Saint. "But I like those stories."

She finished the plate, and put down her fork.

"It's going to sound more like that; but it's just one of those stories that are happening every day. For the last eighteen months or so Dad's been working on a new motor-car engine with an infinitely variable gear. Do you know what that means? It means that you'll just drive your car on the accelerator and the brake; and whatever it's doing, up hills or down or in traffic or anywhere, the engine'll always be working at its maximum efficiency — that sounds rather technical, but I'm so used to hearing Dad talk that I've got that way myself. Anyway, it's far in advance of anything that's been done in that line so far. There's a fortune in it already; but it wasn't good enough for Dad. He wanted his engine to be the best that had ever been made, and that meant the perfect carburettor as well. He's been working on that too. Three months ago he'd spent every penny he'd saved on his experiments. Then he went to Northwade for help."

The Saint's mind moved in certain channels with the speed and precision of infinite experience. He took up his cigarette again and regarded her steadily over it.

"Northwade helped him, of course," he said.

"Northwade lent him a thousand pounds. On a nominal security — purely nominal. And with a few legal documents — just as a matter of form. I expect you can guess what that means."

"I could try."

"The plans of the engine are in Northwade's safe, over at Fontainebleau — all the results of Dad's work up till now. And there's a deed with them which says that all rights in them belong to Lord Northwade — with no time limit specified. It was supposed to be until the loan was repaid, but the deed doesn't say so. Dad hasn't any mind for legal trickeries, and he signed the papers while I was away. I didn't know about it till it was too late."

"One gathers," said the Saint composedly, "that this is the house you propose to burgle."

She gazed at him without flinching, grey eyes frank and resolute, even with that strain of wistful loneliness in them.

"Listen, stranger," she said softly. "This is still the game of Let's

Pretend, isn't it? Pretending that this evening is right outside the world. Because that's the only reason why I'm telling you all this. I'm going to burgle Northwade's house, if I can. I'm going to try and get hold of his keys and open his safe and take those papers away, including the deed Dad signed. Dad hasn't perfected his carburettor yet, and he's no hope of paying back that thousand pounds. And Northwade knows it. He's practically completed arrangements to sell the engine to a French manufacturer. There's no legal way of stopping him. It's one of those cases where possession is nine points of the law. If we had that deed back, as well as the plans, Northwade would never have the face to go into a court and publish the terms of it, which he'd have to do if he wanted to make any claim. Do you think I'm quite mad?"

"Only a little."

She turned the stem of her wineglass between her fingers, looking at him quietly.

"Maybe I am. But have you ever heard of the Saint?"

"The Robin Hood of modern crime?" murmured Simon, with only the faintest lift of an eyebrow for expression.

"I think it's the sort of thing he'd do," she said. "It's justice, even if it's against the law. I wish I could meet him. He'd understand. I think he'd say it was worth taking a chance on. You're very understanding, too, stranger. You've listened to me awfully patiently, and it's helped a lot. And now you shall talk about anything else you like, and we'll go up to your café with the beautiful name and have coffee; and will you please forget it all?"

Simon Templar smiled.

He poured out the last of the wine, and took up his glass. Over the rim of it his clear blue eyes raked the girl with a cavalier challenge that matched his devil-may-care smile and the mocking slant of his brows. His face was alight suddenly.

"I don't propose to forget, Judith," he said. "I am the Saint; and the safe hasn't been made that I can't open. Nor has anything else been thought of that I can't do. We'll go to Fontainebleau together!"

"This is the place," said the girl.

Simon switched off the engine and let the car coast to a stop under the lee of the hedge. It was her car — she had been prepared for that. She had telephoned from the Closerie des Lilas, and it had been fuelled and waiting for them outside the garage near the Madeleine.

Lord Northwade's home, an unwieldy mansion in the Napoleonic style, stood on a slight rise of ground some distance back from the road, in the centre of its extensive and pleasant grounds.

Rising to sit on the door of the car, with one foot on the seat, Simon could see the solid rectangle of its upper part painted in dull black on a smudged grey-blue sky. He felt that he knew every corner of it as if he had lived there for years, from the descriptions she had given him and the rough plans she had drawn on the cheap squared paper provided by the proprietors of French cafés, who seem to suppose that all their patrons are amateur statisticians anxious to amplify their letters with graphs. It was the first time Simon Templar had ever known those ruled squares to be of any use; but they had certainly fitted very well into the configurations of rooms and corridors when the two of them had gone into a committee of ways and means, while their coffee grew cold and neither of them cared. That had been a time of delight shared in adventure which he would always like to remember; but now it was over, and the adventure went on.

It was a night without moon or stars, and yet not utterly dark; perfect for the purpose. She saw the clean-cut lines of his face, recklessly etched in the burst of light as he kindled a cigarette.

"I still don't know why you should do this for me," she said.

"Because it's a game after my own heart," he answered. "Northwade is a bird I've had ideas of my own about for some time. And as for our present object — well, no one could have thought of a story that would have been more likely to fetch me a thousand miles to see it through."

"I feel I ought to be coming with you."

He drew smoke into his lungs, and with it the sweet smell of green leaves.

"This sort of thing is my job, and I've had more practice than you."

"But suppose Northwade wakes up."

"I shall immediately hypnotize him so that he falls into a deep sleep again."

"Or suppose the servants catch you."

"I shall tie them up in bundles of three and heave them into the outer darkness."

"But suppose you *are* caught?"

He laughed.

"It'll be a sign that the end of the world is at hand. But don't worry. Even if that happens it'll cause a certain amount of commotion, and if you hear it I shall expect you to drive rapidly away and await the end in some other province. I shall tell them I came out here on roller skates. It's not your burglary any more — it's mine."

He swung his immaculately tailored legs over the side and dropped lightly to the road, and without another word he was gone, melting into the obscurity like a ghost.

He walked up the turf path beside the drive with the quick confidence of a cat. No lights showed in any of the front windows as he approached, but he made a careful circle of the house for complete certainty. His eyes adjusted themselves to the gloom with the ease of long habit, and he moved without rustling a blade of grass under his feet.

The ground floor was a rugged façade of raised arches and pilasters broken by tall gaunt windows, with a pair of carved oak doors in the middle that would have given way to nothing short of a battering ram; but it is an axiom of housebreaking that those buildings whose fronts look most like fortresses are most likely to defend their postern gates with a card saying "No Admittance." In this case, there was an open pantry window six feet above the ground. Simon squeezed up through the aperture, and lowered himself gently over the shelves of viands on the inside.

He passed through into the kitchen. With the help of a tiny pocket flashlight he located the main switchboard and removed all the fuses, burying them in a sack of potatoes. If by any chance there should be an accident, the garrison of the house would be more handicapped by a lack of lights than he would. Then he made his way down the main hall and unbarred, unbolted, unchained, and unlocked the great oak portals. Simon Templar owed much of his freedom to a trained eye for emergency exits; and he carried on the good work by opening a pair of windows in the library before he gave a thought to the safe.

The girl had described its location accurately. It was built into one wall, behind a small bookcase which opened away from it like a door; and Simon held his torch on it for just three seconds before he decided that it was one of those situations in which neither a bent hairpin nor a tin opener would be adequate.

He slid cheerfully back into the hall and stepped soundlessly up the broad staircase. A large selection of burglarious tools was not part of his usual travelling equipment, but that shortcoming had rarely troubled him. It was another axiom of his philosophy that most safes have keys, that most keys are in the possession of the owners of the safes, and, therefore, that the plodding felon who finds it necessary to pack nitroglycerine and oxyacetylene blowpipes in his sponge bag is usually deficient in strategic genius. Lord Northwade was sleeping soundly enough, with his mouth open and a reassuring drone issuing from the region of his adenoids; but even if he had been awake it is doubtful whether he would have heard the opening of his bedroom door, or sensed one movement of the sensitive hands that lifted a bunch of keys from his dressing table and detached an even more probable one from the chain round his neck.

Simon went down the stairs again like a ghost. It was the key from the chain which turned the lock, and the heavy steel door swung back at a touch with the smooth acquiescence that even Simon Templar could never feel without a thrill. He propped his torch up over one instep so that its light filled the interior of the safe, and went to work with quick white-gloved hands. Once he heard a board creak overhead, and froze into seconds of granite immobility; but he knew that he had made no noise, and presently he went on.

The draught plans were dissected into a thick roll of foolscap sheets tied up with tape; the specifications were packed in a long fat envelope with "Pegasus Variable Gear" roughly scrawled on it — that, he had been told, was the name which had been provisionally given to the invention — and a deed on glazed parchment was enclosed with them. There were also some letters from an internationally known French automobile company.

The Saint was so busily engaged for the next ten minutes, and so absorbed in his labours, that he missed certain faint sounds which might otherwise have reached his ears. The first hint of danger came just as he had finished, in the shape of a cautious scuffle of feet on the terrace outside, and a hoarse whisper which was so unexpected that he raised his head almost incredulously.

Then his eyes dropped half instinctively to the safe which he had just closed. He saw something that he had not noticed before — a flat leaden tube which rose a bare inch from the floor and disappeared into the crack under the lowest hinge, an obvious conduit for alarm wires. The girl had told him that there were no alarms; but that was one which Northwade had probably preferred to keep secret, and it had taken the Saint off his guard.

The narrow beam of the flashlight snapped out like a silent explosion. Simon leapt through the blackness to the windows, slammed them together, and secured the catch. He was knotting a handkerchief round the lower part of his face as he crossed the room again. In the darkness his hand closed on the doorknob, turned it stealthily; at the same time his fingers stretched downwards, and could feel no key in the lock. It looked as if it might be a tight corner, a crisp and merry getaway while it lasted; but those were the moments when the Saint's brain worked at its swiftest.

He opened the door with a quick jerk and took one step into the hall. On his right, covering the retreat to the back of the house, stood an outsize butler in a nightshirt with a rolling-pin clutched in one hand. On his left, barring the way to the front door, was a wiry youth in trousers and vest. A little way up the stairs stood Lord Northwade himself, with a candle in one hand and a young cannon of a revolver in the other. The Saint's most reckless fighting smile touched his lips under the concealing handkerchief.

"*Bon soir, messieurs,*" he murmured politely. "It appears that you were not expecting me. I am accustomed to being received in formal dress. I regret that I cannot accept you in this attire."

He stepped back rapidly through the door, closing it after him. The butler and the wiry youth took a few seconds to recover; then they made a concerted rush for the door. They burst in together, followed by Lord Northwade with the candle. The spectacle of a completely deserted library was the last thing they were expecting, and it pulled them up short with bulging eyes.

In an abruptly contrasting silence, the night-shirted butler returned to life. He tiptoed gingerly forward, and peered with a majestic air behind and under a large settee in the far corner of the room. The wiry youth, inspired by his example, made a dash to the nearest window curtains and pulled them wide apart, disclosing a large area of glass with the round goggling faces of two other servants pressed against it from the outside, like startled fish in an aquarium. Lord Northwade discreetly remained a scant yard inside the doorway with his spluttering candle held helpfully aloft.

On the top of a massive ladder of bookshelves beside the door, Simon Templar rose like a panther from his prone position and dropped downwards. He fell squarely behind Northwade, easing his fall with a hand applied to the crown of Northwade's head, which drew from his lordship a sudden squeal of terror. The same hand pushed Northwade violently forward, and the candle which supplied the only illumination of the scene flickered and went out.

In the darkness the door banged.

"We might even get back in time to have a dance somewhere," said the Saint.

He materialized out of the gloom beside her like a wraith; and she gasped.

"Did you have to scare me?" she asked, when she had got her breath.

He chuckled. Back towards the Northwade mansion there were sounds of muffled disturbance, floating down to his ears like the music of hounds to an old fox. He slipped into the driving seat and touched the starter. The engine purred unprotestingly.

"I ran it once while you were away, to keep it warm," she said.

"Good girl!"

The car gathered speed into the blaze of its own headlights. Simon felt for a cigarette, and lighted it skilfully with one hand.

"Did you get everything?" she asked.

"I am the miracle man who never fails, Judith," he said, reproachfully. "Hadn't I explained that?"

"But that noise — "

"There seems to have been some sort of alarm that goes off when the safe is opened, which you didn't know about. Not that it mattered a lot. The ungodly were fatally slow in assembling, and if you'd seen their waist measurements you wouldn't have been surprised."

She caught his arm excitedly.

"Oh, I can't quite believe it! . . . Everything's all right now. And I've actually been on a raid with the Saint himself! . . . Do you mind if I give way a bit?"

She reached across him to the button in the middle of the steering wheel. The horn blared a rhythmic peal of triumph and defiance into the night: *"Taaa ta-ta, taaa ta-ta, taaa ta-ta!"* like a jubilant trumpet. Simon smiled. Nothing could have fitted better into the essential rightness of everything that had happened that evening. It was true that there had been a telephone in the library, and if there was an extension upstairs there might be gendarmes already watching the road; but they would be an interesting complication that could be dealt with in its proper turn.

Then he coaxed the car round a sharp bend and saw a line of red lights spring up across the road. He dropped his hand thoughtfully to the brake.

"This wasn't here when we came by first," he said, and realized that the girl had gone tense and still.

"What do you think it is?" she whispered.

The Saint shrugged. He brought the car to a standstill with its bonnet three yards from the red lights, which appeared to be attached to a long plank rigged squarely across his path — he could not see clearly what was beyond the plank.

Then he felt a hard cold jab of metal in the side of his head, and turned quickly. He looked down the barrel of a gun in the hand of an overcoated man who stood beside the car.

"Take it easy," advised the man with grim calmness.

The Saint heard a rustle of movement beside him, and glanced round. The girl was getting out. She closed the door after her, and stood on the running board.

"This is as far as I ride, stranger," she said.

"I see," said the Saint gently.

The man with the gun jabbed again.

"Let's have those papers," he ordered.

Simon took them from his breast pocket. The girl received them, and turned on the dashboard light to squint down the roll of plans and read the inscription on the long envelope. Her golden-yellow hair stirred like a shifting halo in the slight breeze.

"Lord Northwade hasn't got a brother who's a professor at Oxford," she explained, "and I'm no relative of the family. Apart from that, most of what I told you was true. Northwade bought this invention from a young Roumanian inventor — I don't know what sort of a price he gave for it, but he bought it. He was going to sell it to a French company, as I told you."

"What are you going to do with it?" inquired the Saint curiously.

"We've got an unwritten offer from Hardt's of Stuttgart."

She went forward and swung back the plank with the red lights, so that the road was clear again. Then she came back. The grey eyes were as frank and friendly as before.

"We've been planning this job for a week, and we should have done the job ourselves to-night if I hadn't seen your photograph in the paper and recognized you at the Berry. The rest of it was an inspiration. There's nothing like having the greatest expert in the profession to work for you."

"Which paper do you read?" asked the Saint.

"I saw you in the *Continental Daily Mail*. Why?"

"I bought an imported London paper," said the Saint, conversationally.

She laughed quietly, a friendly ripple tinged with a trace of regret.

"I'm sorry, stranger. I liked you so much."

"I'm rather sorry, too — Judith," said the Saint.

She was still for an instant. Then she leaned over and kissed him quickly on the lips.

The gun jabbed again.

"Drive on," ordered the man. "And keep driving."

"Won't you be wanting your car?" murmured the Saint.

A harsher chuckle came from the depths of the dark overcoat.

"We've got our own. I knocked that one off and left it at a garage for you when I had a phone call to say you were hooked. Get moving."

Simon engaged the gears, and let in the clutch. The girl jumped down from the running board. "Good-bye, stranger!" she cried; and Simon raised one hand in salute, without looking back.

He drove fast. Whoever the girl was, whatever she was, he knew that he had enjoyed meeting her far more than he could ever have enjoyed meeting the real Judith Molloy, whose unfortunate motor accident had been featured, with portrait, on the front page of his

London newspaper, alongside his own two columns. She could never have looked anything but a hag. Whereas he still thought that her impostor was very beautiful. He hated to think what she would say when she delved deeper into the duplicate envelope and dummy roll of plans which he had so rapidly prepared for her in Lord North-wade's library. But he still drove fast; because those sad things were a part of the game and it was a longish way to Stuttgart.

THE GREAT CRIME STORIES

THE CLOCK

by A. E. W. MASON

The creator of Hanaud here tackles the problem of the perfect crime, and solves it by the strangest letter of confession this side of the planet Mars.

M R. TWISS was a great walker, and it was his habit, after his day's work was done, to walk from his pleasant office in the Adelphi to his home at Hampstead. On an afternoon he was detained to a later hour than usual by one of his clients, a Captain Brayton, over some matter of a mortgage. Mr. Twiss looked at his office clock.

"You are going west, I suppose?" he said. "I wonder if you would walk with me as far as Piccadilly. It will not be very much out of your way, and I have a reason for wishing your company."

"By all means," replied Captain Brayton, and the two men set forth.

Mr. Twiss, however, seemed in a difficulty as to how he should broach his subject, and for a while the pair walked in silence. They, indeed, reached Pall Mall, and were walking down that broad thoroughfare, before a word of any importance was uttered. And even then it was chance which furnished the occasion. A young man of Captain Brayton's age came down from the steps of a club and walked towards them. As he passed beneath a street lamp, Mr. Twiss noticed his face, and ever so slightly started with surprise. At almost the same moment, the young man swerved across the road at a run, as though suddenly he remembered a very pressing appointment. The two men walked on again for a few paces, and then Captain Brayton observed: "There is a screw loose there, I am afraid."

Mr. Twiss shook his head.

"I am sorry to hear you say so," he replied. "It was, indeed, about Archie Cranfield that I was anxious to speak to you. I promised his father that I would be something more than Archie's mere man of affairs, if I were allowed, and I confess that I am troubled by him. You know him well?"

Captain Brayton nodded his head.

"Perhaps I should say that I did know him well," he returned. "We were at the same school, we passed through Chatham together, but since he has relinquished actual service we have seen very little of one another." Here he hesitated, but eventually made up his mind to continue in a guarded fashion. "Also, I am bound to admit that there has been cause for disagreement. We quarrelled."

Mr. Twiss was disappointed. "Then you can tell me nothing of him recently?" he asked, and Captain Brayton shrugged his shoulders.

"Nothing but what all the little world of his acquaintances already knows. He has grown solitary, forbidding in his manner, and, what is most noticeable, sly — extraordinarily sly. While he is speaking with you, he will smile at some secret thought of his; the affairs of the world have lost their interest for him; he hardly listens and seldom speaks. He is concerned with some private matter, and he hides it cunningly. That is the character, at all events, which his friends give of him."

They had now reached the corner of St. James's Street, and as they turned up the hill, Mr. Twiss took up the tale.

"I am not surprised at what you tell me. It is a great pity, for we both remember him ambitious and a good soldier. I am inclined to blame the house in the country for the change in him."

Captain Brayton, however, did not agree.

"It goes deeper than that," he said. "Men who live alone in the country may show furtive ways in towns, no doubt. But why does he live alone in the country? No, that will not do"; and at the top of St. James's Street the two men parted.

Mr. Twiss walked up Bond Street, and the memory of that house in the country in which Archie Cranfield chose to bury himself kept him company. Mr. Twiss had travelled down into the eastern counties to see it for himself one Saturday afternoon when Cranfield was away from home, and a walk of six miles from the station had taken him to its door. It stood upon the borders of Essex and Suffolk, a small Elizabethan house backed upon the Stour, a place of black beams and low ceilings and great fireplaces. It had been buttressed behind, where the ground ran down to the river bank, and hardly a window was on a level with its neighbour. A picturesque place enough, but Mr. Twiss was a lover of towns and of paved footways and illuminated streets. He imagined it on such an evening as this, dark, and the rain dripping cheerlessly from the trees. He imagined its inmate crouching over the fire with his sly smile upon his face, and of a sudden the picture took on a sinister look, and a strong sense of discomfort made Mr. Twiss cast an uneasy glance behind him. He had in his pocket a letter of instructions from Archie Cranfield, bidding him buy the house outright with its furniture, since it had now all come into the market.

It was a week after this when next Captain Brayton came to Mr. Twiss's office, and, their business done, he spoke of his own accord of Archie Cranfield.

"I am going to stay with him," he said. "He wrote to me on the night of the day when we passed him in Pall Mall. He told me that he would make up a small bachelor party. I am very glad, for, to tell the truth, our quarrel was a sufficiently serious one, and here, it seems, is the end to it."

Mr. Twiss was delighted, and shook his client warmly by the hand.

"You shall bring me news of Archie Cranfield," he said — "better news than I have," he added, with a sudden gravity upon his face. For in making the arrangements for the purchase of the house, he had come into contact with various neighbours of Archie Cranfield, and from all of them he had had but one report. Cranfield had a bad name in those parts. There were no particular facts given to account for his reputation. It was all elusive and vague, an impression conveyed by Archie Cranfield himself, by something strange and sly in his demeanour. He would sit chuckling in a sort of triumph, to which no one had the clue, or, on the other hand, he fell into deep silences like a man with a trouble on his mind.

"Be sure you come to see me when you return," said Mr. Twiss, and Captain Brayton replied heartily: "Surely I will." But he never did. For in a few days the newspapers were busy with the strange enigma of his death.

The first hint of this enigma was conveyed to Mr. Twiss late one night at his private address. It came in the shape of a telegram from

Archie Cranfield, which seemed to the agitated solicitor rather a cry of distress than a message sent across the wires.

Come at once. I am in terrible need.

CRANFIELD

There were no trains at so late an hour by which Mr. Twiss could reach his client; he must needs wait until the morning. He travelled, however, by the first train from Liverpool Street. Although the newspapers were set out upon the bookstall, not one of them contained a word of anything amiss at Archie Cranfield's house, and Mr. Twiss began to breathe more freely. It was too early for a cab to be in waiting at the station, and Mr. Twiss set out to walk the six miles. It was a fine, clear morning of November; but for the want of leaves and birds, and the dull look of the countryside, Mr. Twiss might have believed the season to be June. His spirits rose as he walked, his blood warmed to a comfortable glow, and by the time he came to the gates of the house, Cranfield's summons had become a trifling thing. As he walked up to the door, however, his mood changed, for every blind in the house was drawn. The door was opened before he could touch the bell, and it was opened by Cranfield himself. His face was pale and disordered, his manner that of a man at his wits' end.

"What has happened?" asked Mr. Twiss as he entered the hall.

"A terrible thing!" replied Cranfield. "It's Brayton. Have you breakfasted? I suppose not. Come, and I will tell you while you eat."

He walked up and down the room while Mr. Twiss ate his breakfast, and gradually, by question and by answer, the story took shape. Corroboration was easy and was secured. There was no real dispute about the facts; they were simple and clear.

There were two other visitors in the house besides Captain Brayton, one a barrister named Henry Chalmers, and the second, William Linfield, a man about town, as the phrase goes. Both men stood in much the same relationship to Archie Cranfield as Captain Brayton did — that is to say, they were old friends who had seen little of their host of late, and were somewhat surprised to receive his invitation after so long an interval. They had accepted it in the same spirit as Brayton, and the three men arrived together on Wednesday evening. On Thursday the party of four shot over some turnip fields and a few clumps of wood which belonged to the house, and played a game of bridge in the evening. In the opinion of all, Brayton was never in better spirits. On Friday the four men shot again and returned to the house as darkness was coming on. They took tea in the smoking room, and after tea Brayton declared his intention to write some letters before dinner. He went upstairs to his room for that purpose.

The other three men remained in the smoking room. Of that there was no doubt. Both Chalmers and Linfield were emphatic upon the point. Chalmers, in particular, said:

"We sat talking on a well-worn theme, I in a chair on one side of the fireplace, Archie Cranfield in another opposite to me, and Linfield sitting on the edge of the billiard table between us. How the subject cropped up I cannot remember, but I found myself arguing that most men hid their real selves all their lives even from their most intimate friends, that there were secret chambers in a man's consciousness wherein he lived a different life from that which the world saw and knew, and that it was only by some rare mistake the portals of that chamber were ever passed by any other man. Linfield would not hear of it. If this hidden man were the real man, he held, in some way or another the reality would triumph, and some vague suspicion of the truth would in the end be felt by all his intimates. I upheld my view by instances from the courts of law, Linfield his by the aid of a generous imagination, while Cranfield looked from one to the other of us with his sly, mocking smile. I turned to him, indeed, in some heat.

" 'Well, since you appear to know, Cranfield, tell me which of us is right,' and his pipe fell from his fingers and broke upon the hearth. He stood up, with his face grown white and his lips drawn back from his teeth in a kind of snarl.

" 'What do you mean by that?' he asked; and before I could answer, the door was thrown violently open, and Cranfield's man-servant burst into the room. He mastered himself enough to say:

" 'May I speak to you, sir?'

"Cranfield went outside the door with him. He could not have moved six paces from the door, for though he closed it behind him, we heard the sound of his voice and of his servant's speaking in low tones. Moreover, there was no appreciable moment of time between the cessation of the voices and Cranfield's reappearance in the room. He came back to the fireplace and said very quietly:

" 'I have something terrible to tell you. Brayton has shot himself.'

"He then glanced from Linfield's face to mine, and sat down in a chair heavily. Then he crouched over the fire shivering. Both Linfield and myself were too shocked by the news to say a word for a moment or two. Then Linfield asked:

" 'But is he dead?'

" 'Humphreys says so,' Cranfield returned. 'I have telephoned to the police and to the doctor.'

" 'But we had better go upstairs ourselves and see,' said I. And we did."

Thus Chalmers. Humphreys, the manservant, gave the following account:

"The bell rang from Captain Brayton's room at half past five. I answered it at once myself, and Captain Brayton asked me at what hour the post left. I replied that we sent the letters from the house to the post office in the village at six. He then asked me to return at that hour and fetch those of his which would be ready. I returned precisely at six, and I saw Captain Brayton lying in a heap upon the rug in front of the fire. He was dead, and he held a revolver tightly clenched in his hand. As I stepped over him, I smelt that something was burning. He had shot himself through the heart, and his clothes were singed, as if he had held the revolver close to his side."

These stories were repeated at the inquest, and at this particular point in Humphreys's evidence the coroner asked a question:

"Did you recognise the revolver?"

"Not until Captain Brayton's hand was unclenched."

"But then you did?"

"Yes," said Humphreys.

The coroner pointed to the table on which a revolver lay.

"Is that the weapon?"

Humphreys took it up and looked at the handle, on which two initials were engraved — "A. C."

"Yes," said the man. "I recognised it as Mr. Cranfield's. He kept it in a drawer by his bedside."

No revolver was found amongst Captain Brayton's possessions.

It became clear that, while the three men were talking in the billiard room, Captain Brayton had gone to Cranfield's room, taken his revolver, and killed himself with it. No evidence, however, was produced which supplied a reason for Brayton's suicide. His affairs were in good order, his means sufficient, his prospects of advancement in his career sound. Nor was there a suggestion of any private unhappiness. The tragedy, therefore, was entered in that list of mysteries which are held insoluble.

"I might," said Chalmers, "perhaps resume the argument which Humphreys interrupted in the billiard room, with a better instance than any which I induced — the instance of Captain Brayton."

"You won't go?" Archie Cranfield pleaded with Mr. Twiss. "Linfield and Chalmers leave to-day. If you go too, I shall be entirely alone."

"But why should you stay?" the lawyer returned. "Surely you hardly propose to remain through the winter in this house?"

"No, but I must stay on for a few days; I have to make arrangements before I can go," said Cranfield; and seeing that he was in earnest in his intention to go, Mr. Twiss was persuaded. He stayed on, and recognised, in consequence, that the death of Captain Brayton had amongst its consequences one which he had not expected. The feeling in the neighbourhood changed towards Archie Cranfield. It cannot be said that he became popular — he wore too sad and joyless an air — but sympathy was shown to him in many acts of courtesy and in a greater charity of language.

A retired admiral, of a strong political complexion, who had been one of the foremost to dislike Archie Cranfield, called, indeed, to offer his condolences. Archie Cranfield did not see him, but Mr. Twiss walked down the drive with him to the gate.

"It's hard on Cranfield," said the admiral. "We all admit it. It wasn't fair of Brayton to take his host's revolver. But for the accident that Cranfield was in the billiard room with Linfield and Chalmers, the affair might have taken on quite an ugly look. We all feel that in the neighbourhood, and we shall make it up to Cranfield. Just tell him that, Mr. Twiss, if you will."

"It is very kind of you all, I am sure," replied Mr. Twiss, "but I think Cranfield will not continue to live here. The death of Captain Brayton has been too much of a shock for him."

Mr. Twiss said "Good-bye" to the admiral at the gate, and returned to the house. He was not easy in his mind, and as he walked round the lawn under the great trees, he cried to himself:

"It is lucky, indeed, that Archie Cranfield was in the billiard room with Linfield and Chalmers; otherwise, Heaven knows what I might have been brought to believe myself."

The two men had quarrelled; Brayton himself had imparted that piece of knowledge to Mr. Twiss. Then there was the queer change in Archie Cranfield's character, which had made for him enemies of strangers, and strangers of his friends — the slyness, the love of solitude, the indifference to the world, the furtive smile as of a man conscious of secret powers, the whole indescribable uncanniness of him. Mr. Twiss marshalled his impressions and stopped in the avenue.

"I should have had no just grounds for any suspicion," he concluded, "but I cannot say that I should not have suspected," and slowly he went on to the door.

He walked through the house into the billiard room, and so became the witness of an incident which caused him an extraordinary disquiet. The room was empty. Mr. Twiss lit his pipe and took down a book from one of the shelves. A bright fire glowed upon the hearth, and drawing up a chair to the fender, he settled down to read. But the day was dull, and the fireplace stood at the dark end of the room. Mr. Twiss carried his book over to the window, which was a bay window with a broad seat. Now, the curtains were hung at the embrasure of the window, so that, when they were drawn, they shut the bay off altogether from the room, and when they were open, as now, they still concealed the corners of the window seats. It was in one of these corners that Mr. Twiss took his seat, and there he read quietly for the space of five minutes.

At the end of that time he heard the latch of the door click, and looking out from his position behind the curtain, he saw the door slowly open. Archie Cranfield came through the doorway into the room, and shut the door behind him. Then he stood for a while by the door, very still, but breathing heavily. Mr. Twiss was on the point of coming forward and announcing his presence, but there was something so strange and secret in Cranfield's behaviour that, in spite of certain twinges of conscience, he remained hidden in his seat. He did more than remain hidden. He made a chink between the curtain and the wall, and watched. He saw Cranfield move swiftly over to the fireplace, seize a little old-fashioned clock in a case of satinwood which stood upon the mantelshelf, raise it in the air, and dash it with an ungovernable fury on to the stone hearth. Having done this unaccountable thing, Cranfield dropped into the chair which Mr. Twiss had drawn up. He covered his face with his hands and suddenly began to sob and wail in the most dreadful fashion, rocking his body from side to side in a very paroxysm of grief. Mr. Twiss was at his wit's end to know what to do. He felt that to catch a man sobbing would be to earn his undying resentment. Yet the sound was so horrible, and produced in him so sharp a discomfort and distress, that, on the other hand, he could hardly keep still. The paroxysm passed, however, almost as quickly as it had come, and Cranfield, springing to his feet, rang the bell. Humphreys answered it.

"I have knocked the clock off the mantelshelf with my elbow, Humphreys," he said. "I am afraid that it is broken, and the glass might cut somebody's hand. Would you mind clearing the pieces away?"

He went out of the room, and Humphreys went off for a dustpan. Mr. Twiss was able to escape from the billiard room unnoticed. But it was a long time before he recovered from the uneasiness which the incident aroused in him.

Four days later the two men left the house together. The servants had been paid off. Humphreys had gone with the luggage to London by an earlier train. Mr. Twiss and Archie Cranfield were the last to go. Cranfield turned the key in the lock of the front door as they stood upon the steps.

"I shall never see the inside of that house again," he said with a gusty violence.

"Will you allow me to get rid of it for you?" asked Mr. Twiss; and for a moment Cranfield looked at him with knotted brows, blowing the while into the wards of the key.

"No," he said at length, and, running down to the stream at the back of the house, he tossed the key into the water. "No," he repeated sharply; "let the house rot empty as it stands. The rats shall have their will of it, and the sooner the better."

He walked quickly to the gate, with Mr. Twiss at his heels, and as they covered the six miles to the railway station, very little was said between them.

Time ran on, and Mr. Twiss was a busy man. The old house by the Stour began to vanish from his memory amongst the mists and the veils of rain which so often enshrouded it. Even the enigma of Captain Brayton's death was ceasing to perplex him, when the whole affair was revived in the most startling fashion. A labourer, making a short cut to his work one summer morning, passed through the grounds of Cranfield's closed and shuttered house. His way led him round the back of the building, and as he came to that corner where the great brick buttresses kept the house from slipping down into the river, he saw below him, at the edge of the water, a man sleeping. The man's back was turned towards him; he was lying half upon his side, half upon his face. The labourer, wondering who it was, went down to the river bank, and the first thing he noticed was a revolver lying upon the grass, its black barrel and handle shining in the morning sunlight. The labourer turned the sleeper over on his back. There was some blood upon the left breast of his waistcoat. The sleeper was dead, and from the rigidity of the body had been dead for some hours. The labourer ran back to the village with the astounding news that he had found Mr. Cranfield shot through the heart at the back of his own empty house. People at first jumped naturally to the belief that murder had been done. The more judicious, however, shook their heads. Not a door nor a window was open in the house. When the locks were forced, it was seen that the dust lay deep on floor and chair and table, and nowhere was there any mark of a hand or a foot. Outside the house, too, in the long neglected grass, there were but two sets of footsteps visible, one set leading round the house — the marks made by the labourer on his way to his work — the other set leading directly to the spot where Archie Cranfield's body was found lying. Rumours, each contradicting the other, flew from cottage to cottage, and the men gathered about the police station and in the street waiting for the next. In an hour or two, however, the mystery was at an end. It leaked out that upon Archie Cranfield's body a paper had been discovered, signed in his hand and by his name, with these words:

I have shot myself with the same revolver with which I murdered Captain Brayton.

The statement created some stir when it was read out in the billiard room, where the coroner held his inquest. But the coroner who presided now was the man who had held the court when Captain Brayton had been shot. He was quite clear in his recollection of that case.

"Mr. Cranfield's alibi on that occasion," he said, "was incontrovertible. Mr. Cranfield was with two friends in this very room when Captain Brayton shot himself in his bedroom. There can be no doubt of that." And under his direction the jury returned a verdict of "suicide while of unsound mind."

Mr. Twiss attended the inquest and the funeral. But though he welcomed the verdict, at the bottom of his mind he was uneasy. He remembered vividly that extraordinary moment when he had seen Cranfield creep into the billiard room, lift the little clock in its case of satinwood high above his head, and dash it down upon the hearth in a wild gust of fury. He recollected how the fury had given way to despair — if it were despair and not remorse. He saw again Archie Cranfield dropping into the chair, holding his head and rocking his body in a paroxysm of sobs. The sound of his wailing rang horribly once more in the ears of Mr. Twiss. He was not satisfied.

"What should take Cranfield back to that deserted house, there to end his life, if not remorse," he asked himself — "remorse for some evil done there?"

Over that question for some days he shook his head, finding it waiting for him at his fireside and lurking for him at the corner of the roads, as he took his daily walk between Hampstead and his office. It began to poison his life, a life of sane and customary ways, with eerie suggestions. There was an oppression upon his heart of which he could not rid it. On the outskirts of his pleasant world dim horrors loomed; he seemed to walk upon a frail crust, fearful of what lay beneath. The sly smile, the furtive triumph, the apparent consciousness of secret power — did they point to some corruption of the soul in Cranfield, of which none knew but he himself?

"At all events, he paid for it," Mr. Twiss would insist, and from that reflection drew, after all, but little comfort. The riddle began even to invade his business hours, and take a seat within his private office, silently clamouring for his attention. So that it was with a veritable relief that he heard one morning from his clerk that a man called Humphreys wished particularly to see him.

"Show him in," cried Mr. Twiss, and for his own ear he added: "Now I shall know."

Humphreys entered the room with a letter in his hand. He laid the letter on the office table. Mr. Twiss saw at a glance that it was addressed in Archie Cranfield's hand. He flung himself upon it and snatched it up. It was sealed by Cranfield's seal. It was addressed to himself, with a note upon the lefthand corner of the envelope:

To be delivered after my death.

Mr. Twiss turned sternly to the man.

"Why did you not bring it before?"

"Mr. Cranfield told me to wait a month," Humphreys replied.

Mr. Twiss took a turn across the room with the letter in his hand.

"Then you knew," he cried, "that your master meant to kill himself? You knew, and remained silent?"

"No, sir, I did not know," Humphreys replied firmly. "Mr. Cranfield gave me the letter, saying that he had a long railway journey in front of him. He was smiling when he gave it me. I can remember the words with which he gave it: 'They offer you an insurance ticket at the booking office, when they sell you your travelling ticket, so there is always, I suppose, a little risk. And it is of the utmost importance to me that, in the event of my death, this should reach Mr. Twiss.' He spoke so lightly that I could not have guessed what was on his mind, nor, do I think, sir, could you."

Mr. Twiss dismissed the man and summoned his clerk. "I shall not be in to anyone this afternoon," he said. He broke the seal and drew some closely written sheets of note paper from the envelope. He spread the sheets in front of him with a trembling hand.

"Heaven knows in what spirit and with what knowledge I shall rise from my reading," he thought; and looking out of his pleasant window upon the barges swinging down the river on the tide, he was in half a mind to fling the sheets of paper into the fire. "But I shall be plagued with that question all my life," he added, and he bent his head over his desk and read.

"MY DEAR FRIEND, — I am writing down for you the facts. I am not offering any explanation, for I have none to give. You will probably rise up, after reading this letter, quite incredulous, and with the conviction in your mind that you have been reading the extravagancies of a madman. And I wish with all my heart that you could be right. But you are not. I have come to the end to-day. I am writing the last words I ever shall write, and therefore I am not likely to write a lie.

"You will remember the little manor house on the borders of Essex, for you were always opposed to my purchase of it. You were like the British jury, my friend. Your conclusion was sound, but your reason for it very far from the mark. You disliked it for its isolation and the melancholy of its dripping trees, and I know not what other town-bred reasonings. I will give you a more solid cause. Picture to yourself the billiard room and how it was furnished when I first took the house — the raised settee against the wall, the deep leather chairs by the fire, the high fender, and on the mantelshelf — what? — a little old-fashioned clock in a case of satinwood. You probably never noticed it. I did from the first evenings which I passed in the house. For I spent those evenings alone, smoking my pipe by the fire. It had a queer trick. For a while it would tick almost imperceptibly, and then, without reason, quite suddenly, the noise would become loud and hollow, as though the pendulum in its swing struck against the wooden case. To anyone sitting alone for hours in the room, as I did, this tick had the queerest effect. The clock almost became endowed with human qualities. At one time it seemed to wish to attract one's attention, at another time to avoid it. For more than once, disturbed by the louder knocking, I rose and moved the clock. At once the knocking would cease, to begin again when I had settled afresh to my book, in a kind of tentative, secret way, as though it would accustom my ears to the sound, and so pass unnoticed. And often it did so pass, until one knock louder and more insistent than the rest would drag me in annoyance on to my feet once more. In a week, however, I got used to it, and then followed the strange incident which set in motion that chain of events of which to-morrow will see the end.

"It happened that a couple of my neighbours were calling on me. One of them you have met — Admiral Palkin, a prolix old gentleman, with a habit of saying nothing at remarkable length. The other was a Mr. Stiles, a country gentleman who had a thought of putting up for that division of the county. I led these two gentlemen into the billiard room, and composed myself to listen while the admiral monologued. But the clock seemed to me to tick louder than ever, until, with one sharp and almost metallic thump, the sound ceased altogether. At exactly the same moment, Admiral Palkin stopped dead in the middle of a sentence. It was nothing of any consequence that he was saying, but I remember the words at which he stopped. 'I have often —— ' he said, and then he broke off, not with any abrupt start, or for any lack of words, but just as if he had completed all that he had meant to say. I looked at him across the fireplace, but his face wore its usual expression of complacent calm. He was in no way put out. Nor did it seem that any new train of thought had flashed into his mind and diverted it. I turned my eyes from him to Mr. Stiles. Mr. Stiles seemed actually to be unaware that the admiral had stopped talking at all. Admiral Palkin, you will remember, was a person of consequence in the district, and Mr. Stiles, who would subsequently need his vote and influence and motor car, had thought fit to assume an air of great deference. From the beginning he had leaned towards the admiral, his elbow upon his knee, his chin propped upon his hand, and his head now and again nodding a thoughtful assent to the admiral's nothings. In this attitude he still remained, not surprised, not even patiently waiting for the renewal of wisdom, but simply attentive.

"Nor did I move, for I was amused. The two men looked just like a couple of wax figures in Madame Tussaud's, fixed in a stiff attitude and condemned so to remain until the building should take fire and the wax run. I sat watching them for minutes, and still neither moved nor spoke. I never saw in my life a couple of people so entirely ridiculous. I tried hard to keep my countenance — for to laugh at these great little men in my own house would not only be bad manners, but would certainly do for me in the neighbourhood — but I could not help it. I began to smile, and the smile became a laugh. Yet not a muscle on the faces of my visitors changed. Not a frown overshadowed the admiral's complacency; not a glance diverted the admiring eyes of Mr. Stiles. And then the clock began to tick again, and, to my infinite astonishment, at the very same moment the admiral continued.

" ' — said to myself in my lighter moments —— And pray, sir, at what are you laughing?'

"Mr. Stiles turned with an angry glance towards me. Admiral Palkin had resumed his conversation, apparently unaware that there had been any interval at all. My laughter, on the other hand, had extended beyond the interval, had played an accompaniment to the words just spoken. I made my excuses as well as I could, but I recognised that they were deemed insufficient. The two gentlemen left my house with the coldest farewells you can imagine.

"The same extraordinary incident was repeated with other visitors, but I was on my guard against any injudicious merriment. Moreover, I had no longer any desire to laugh. I was too perplexed. My visitors never seemed to notice that there had been a lengthy interval or indeed any interval at all, while I, for my part, hesitated to ask them what had so completely hypnotised them.

"The next development took place when I was alone in the room. It was five o'clock in the afternoon. I had been out shooting a covert close to the house, and a few minutes after I had rung the bell, I remembered that I had forgotten some instructions which I had meant to give to the keeper. So I got up at once, thinking to catch him in the gun room before he went home. As I rose from my chair, the clock, which had been ticking loudly — though, as I have said, it was rather a hollow, booming sound, as though the pendulum struck the wood of the case, than a mere ticking of the clock work — ceased its noise with the abruptness to which I was growing used. I went out of the room into the hall, and I saw Humphreys with the tea tray in his hands in the hall. He was turned towards the billiard room door, but to my astonishment he was not moving. He was poised with one foot in the air, as though he had been struck, as the saying is, with a step half taken. You have seen, no doubt, instantaneous photographs of people in the act of walking. Well, Humphreys was exactly like one of those photographs. He had just the same stiff, ungainly look. I should have spoken to him, but I was anxious to catch my keeper before he went away. So I took no notice of him. I crossed the hall quickly and went out by the front door, leaving it open. The gun room was really a small building of corrugated iron, standing apart at the back of the house. I went to it and tried the door. It was locked. I called aloud: 'Martin! Martin!'

"But I received no answer. I ran round the house again, thinking that he might just have started home, but I saw no signs of him. There were some outhouses which it was his business to look after, and I visited them, opening the door of each of them and calling him by name. Then I went down the drive to the gate, thinking that I might perhaps catch a glimpse of him upon the road, but again I was disappointed. I then returned to the house, shut the front door, and there in the hall still stood Humphreys in his ridiculous attitude with the tea tray in his hands. I passed him and went back into the billiard room. He took no notice of me whatever. I looked at the clock upon the mantelshelf, and I saw that I had been away just fourteen minutes. For fourteen minutes Humphreys had been standing on one leg in the hall. It seemed as incredible as it was ludicrous. Yet there was the clock to bear me out. I sat down on my chair with my hands trembling, my mind in a maze. The strangest thought had come to me, and while I revolved it in my mind, the clock resumed its ticking, the door opened, and Humphreys appeared with the tea tray in his hand.

" 'You have been a long time, Humphreys,' I said, and the man looked at me quickly. My voice was shaking with excitement, my face, no doubt, had a disordered look.

" 'I prepared the tea at once, sir,' he answered.

" 'It is twenty minutes by the clock since I rang the bell,' I said.

"Humphreys placed the tea on a small table at my side and then looked at the clock. An expression of surprise came over his face. He compared it with the dial of his own watch.

" 'The clock wants regulating, sir,' he said. 'I set it by the kitchen clock this morning, and it has gained fourteen minutes.'

"I whipped my own watch out of my pocket and stared at it. Humphreys was quite right; the clock upon the mantelshelf had gained fourteen minutes upon all our watches. Yes, but it had gained those fourteen minutes in a second, and that was the least part of the marvel. I myself had had the benefit of those fourteen minutes. I had snatched them, as it were, from Time itself. I had looked at my watch when I rang the bell. It had marked five minutes to five. I had remained yet another four minutes in the room before I had remembered my forgotten instructions to the keeper. I had then gone out. I had visited the gun room and the outhouses, I had walked to the front gate, I had returned. I had taken fourteen minutes over my search — I could not have taken less — and here were the hands of my watch now still pointing towards five, still short of the hour.

Indeed, as I replaced my watch in my pocket, the clock in the hall outside struck five.

" 'As you passed through the hall, Humphreys, you saw no one, I suppose,' I said.

"Humphreys raised his eyebrows with a look of perplexity. 'No, sir, I saw no one,' he returned, 'but it seemed to me that the front door banged. I think it must have been left open.'

" 'Very likely,' said I. 'That will do,' and Humphreys went out of the room.

"Imagine my feelings. Time is relative, it is a condition of our senses, it is nothing more — that we know. But its relation to me was different from its relation to others. The clock had given me fourteen minutes which it denied to all the world besides. Fourteen full minutes for me, yet they passed for others in less than the fraction of a second. And not once only had it made me this gift, but many times. The admiral's pause, unnoticed by Mr. Stiles, was now explained to me. He had not paused; he had gone straight on with his flow of talk, and Mr. Stiles had gone straight on listening. But between two of Admiral Palkin's words, Time had stood still for me. Similarly, Humphreys had not poised himself upon one ridiculous leg in the hall. He had taken a step in the usual way, but while his leg was raised, fourteen minutes were given to me. I had walked through the hall, I had walked back through the hall, yet Humphreys had not seen me. He could not have seen me, for there had been no interval of time for him to use his eyes. I had gone and come quicker than any flash, for even a flash is appreciable as some fraction of a second.

"I asked you to imagine my feelings. Only with those which I first experienced would you, from your sane and comfortable outlook upon life, have any sympathy, for at the beginning I was shocked. I had more than an inclination then to dash that clock upon the hearth and deny myself its bizarre and unnatural gift. Would that I had done so! But the inclination was passed, and was succeeded by an incredible lightness of spirit. I had a gift which raised me above kings, which fanned into a flame every spark of vanity within me. I had so much more of time than any other man. I amused myself by making plans to use it, and thereupon I suffered a disappointment. For there was so little one could do in fourteen minutes, and the more I realised how little there was which I could do in my own private special stretch of time, the more I wanted to do, the more completely I wished to live in it, the more I wished to pluck power and advantage from it. Thus I began to look forward to the sudden cessation of the ticking of the clock; I began to wait for it, to live for it, and when it came, I could make no use of it. I gained fourteen minutes now and then, but I lost more and more of the hours which I shared with other men. They lost their salt for me. I became tortured with the waste of those minutes of my own. I had the power; what I wanted now was to employ it. The desire became an obsession occupying my thoughts, harassing my dreams.

"I was in this mood when I passed Brayton and yourself one evening in Pall Mall. I wrote to him that night, and I swear to you upon my conscience that I had no thought in writing but to put an end to an old disagreement, and re-establish, if possible, an old friendship. I wrote in a sudden revulsion of feeling. The waste of my days was brought home to me. I recognised that the great gift was no more than a perpetual injury. I proposed to gather my acquaintances about me, discard my ambition for some striking illustration of my power, and take up once more the threads of customary life. Yet my determination lasted no longer than the time it took me to write the letter and run out with it to the post. I regretted its despatch even as I heard it fall to the bottom of the pillar box.

"Of my quarrel with Brayton I need not write at length. It sprang from a rancorous jealousy. We had been friends and classmates in the beginning. But as step by step he rose just a little above me, the friendship I had turned to gall and anger. I was never more than the second, he always the first. Had I been fourth or fifth, I think I should not have minded; but there was so little to separate us in merit or advancement. Yet there was always that little, and I dreaded the moment when he should take a bound and leave me far behind. The jealousy grew to a real hatred, made still more bitter to me by the knowledge that Brayton himself was unaware of it, and need not have been troubled had he been aware.

"After I left the Army and lost sight of him, the flame burnt low. I believed it was extinguished when I invited him to stay with me; but he had not been an hour in the house when it blazed up within me. His success, the confidence which it had given him, his easy friendliness with strangers, the talk with him as a coming man, bit into my soul. The very sound of his footstep sickened me. I was in this mood when the clock began to boom louder and louder in the billiard room. Chalmers and Linfield were talking. I did not listen to them. My heart beat louder and louder within my breast, keeping pace with the clock. I knew that in a moment or two the sound would cease, and the doors of my private kingdom would be open for me to pass through. I sat back in my chair waiting while the devilish inspiration had birth and grew strong. Here was the great chance to use the power I had — the only chance which had ever come to me. Brayton was writing letters in his room. The room was in a wing of the house. The sound of a shot would not be heard. There would be an end of his success; there would be for me such a triumphant use of my great privilege as I had never dreamed of. The clock suddenly ceased. I slipped from the room and went upstairs. I was quite leisurely. I had time. I was back in my chair again before seven minutes had passed.

ARCHIE CRANFIELD

THE MOST DANGEROUS GAME

by RICHARD CONNELL

A new kind of big-game hunt creates a new kind of crime. By the man who wrote the short story from which Frank Capra fashioned "Meet John Doe."

O FF THERE to the right — somewhere — is a large island," said Whitney. "It's rather a mystery —— "

"What island is it?" Rainsford asked.

"The old charts call it 'Ship-Trap Island,'" Whitney replied. "A suggestive name, isn't it? Sailors have a curious dread of the place. I don't know why. Some superstition —— "

"Can't see it," remarked Rainsford, trying to peer through the dank tropical night that was palpable as it pressed its thick warm blackness in upon the yacht.

"You've good eyes," said Whitney, with a laugh, "and I've seen you pick off a moose moving in the brown fall bush at four hundred yards, but even you can't see four miles or so through a moonless Caribbean night."

"Nor four yards," admitted Rainsford. "Ugh! It's like moist velvet."

"It will be light enough in Rio," promised Whitney. "We should make it in a few days. I hope the jaguar guns have come from Purdey's. We should have some good hunting up the Amazon. Great sport, hunting."

"The best sport in the world," agreed Rainsford.

"For the hunter," amended Whitney. "Not for the jaguar."

"Don't talk rot, Whitney," said Rainsford. "You're a big-game hunter, not a philosopher. Who cares how a jaguar feels?"

"Perhaps the jaguar does," observed Whitney.

"Bah! They've no understanding."

"Even so, I rather think they understand one thing at least — fear. The fear of pain and the fear of death."

"Nonsense," laughed Rainsford. "This hot weather is making you soft, Whitney. Be a realist. The world is made up of two classes — the hunters and the hunted. Luckily, you and I are hunters. Do you think we've passed that island yet?"

"I can't tell in the dark. I hope so."

"Why?" asked Rainsford.

"The place has a reputation — a bad one."

"Cannibals?" suggested Rainsford.

"Hardly. Even cannibals wouldn't live in such a God-forsaken place. But it's got into sailor lore, somehow. Didn't you notice that the crew's nerves seem a bit jumpy today?"

"They were a bit strange, now you mention it. Even Captain Nielsen —— "

"Yes, even that tough-minded old Swede, who'd go up to the devil himself and ask him for a light. Those fishy blue eyes held a look I never saw there before. All I could get out of him was: 'This place has an evil name among seafaring men, sir.' Then he said to me, very gravely: 'Don't you feel anything?' — as if the air about us was actually poisonous. Now, you mustn't laugh when I tell you this — I did feel something like a sudden chill.

"There was no breeze. The sea was as flat as a plate-glass window. We were drawing near the island then. What I felt was a — a mental chill — a sort of sudden dread."

"Pure imagination," said Rainsford. "One superstitious sailor can taint the whole ship's company with his fear."

"Maybe. But sometimes I think sailors have an extra sense that tells them when they are in danger. Sometimes I think evil is a tangible thing — with wave lengths, just as sound and light have. An evil place can, so to speak, broadcast vibrations of evil. Anyhow, I'm glad we're getting out of this zone. Well, I think I'll turn in now, Rainsford."

"I'm not sleepy," said Rainsford. "I'm going to smoke another pipe up on the after deck."

"Good night, then, Rainsford. See you at breakfast."

"Right. Good night, Whitney."

There was no sound in the night as Rainsford sat there, but the muffled throb of the engine that drove the yacht swiftly through the darkness, and the swish and ripple of the wash of the propeller.

Rainsford, reclining in a steamer chair, indolently puffed on his favorite brier. The sensuous drowsiness of the night was on him. "It's so dark," he thought, "that I could sleep without closing my eyes; the night would be my eyelids —— "

An abrupt sound startled him. Off to the right he heard it, and his ears, expert in such matters, could not be mistaken. Again he heard the sound, and again. Somewhere, off in the blackness, someone had fired a gun three times.

Rainsford sprang up and moved quickly to the rail, mystified. He strained his eyes in the direction from which the reports had come, but it was like trying to see through a blanket. He leaped upon the rail and balanced himself there, to get greater elevation; his pipe, striking a rope, was knocked from his mouth. He lunged for it; a short, hoarse cry came from his lips as he realized he had reached too far and had lost his balance. The cry was pinched off short as the blood-warm waters of the Caribbean Sea closed over his head.

He struggled up to the surface and tried to cry out, but the wash from the speeding yacht slapped him in the face and the salt water in his open mouth made him gag and strangle. Desperately he struck out with strong strokes after the receding lights of the yacht, but he stopped before he had swum fifty feet. A certain cool-headedness had come to him; it was not the first time he had been in a tight place. There was a chance that his cries could be heard by someone aboard the yacht, but that chance was slender, and grew more slender as the yacht raced on. He wrestled himself out of his clothes, and shouted with all his power. The lights of the yacht became faint and ever-vanishing fireflies; then they were blotted out entirely by the night.

Rainsford remembered the shots. They had come from the right, and doggedly he swam in that direction, swimming with slow, deliberate strokes, conserving his strength. For a seemingly endless time he fought the sea. He began to count his strokes desperately; he could do possibly a hundred more and then —

Rainsford heard a sound. It came out of the darkness, a high, screaming sound, the sound of an animal in an extremity of anguish and terror.

He did not recognize the animal that made the sound; he did

not try to; with fresh vitality he swam toward the sound. He heard it again; then it was cut short by another noise, crisp, staccato.

"Pistol shot," muttered Rainsford, swimming on.

Ten minutes of determined effort brought another sound to his ears — the most welcome he had ever heard — the muttering and growling of the sea breaking on a rocky shore. He was almost on the rocks before he saw them; on a night less calm he would have been shattered against them. With his remaining strength he dragged himself from the swirling waters. Jagged crags appeared to jut up into the opaqueness; he forced himself upward, hand over hand. Gasping, his hands raw, he reached a flat place at the top. Dense jungle came down to the very edge of the cliffs. What perils that tangle of trees and underbrush might hold for him did not concern Rainsford just then. All he knew was that he was safe from his enemy, the sea, and that utter weariness was on him. He flung himself down at the jungle edge and tumbled headlong into the deepest sleep of his life.

When he opened his eyes he knew from the position of the sun that it was late in the afternoon. Sleep had given him new vigor; a sharp hunger was picking at him. He looked about him, almost cheerfully.

"Where there are pistol shots, there are men. Where there are men, there is food," he thought. But what kind of men, he wondered, in so forbidding a place? An unbroken front of snarled and jagged jungle fringed the shore.

He saw no sign of a trail through the closely knit web of weeds and trees; it was easier to go along the shore, and Rainsford floundered along by the water. Not far from where he had landed, he stopped.

Some wounded thing, by the evidence a large animal, had thrashed about in the underbrush; the jungle weeds were crushed down and the moss was lacerated; one patch of weeds was stained crimson. A small, glittering object not far away caught Rainsford's eye and he picked it up. It was an empty cartridge.

"A twenty-two," he remarked. "That's odd. It must have been a fairly large animal, too. The hunter had his nerve to tackle it with a light gun. It's clear that the brute put up a fight. I suppose the first three shots I heard was when the hunter flushed his quarry and wounded it. The last shot was when he trailed it here and finished it."

He examined the ground closely and found what he had hoped to find — the print of hunting boots. They pointed along the cliff in the direction he had been going. Eagerly he hurried along, now slipping on a rotten log or a loose stone, but making headway; night was beginning to settle down on the island.

Bleak darkness was blacking out the sea and jungle when Rainsford sighted the lights. He came upon them as he turned a crook in the coast line, and his first thought was that he had come upon a village, for there were many lights. But as he forged along he saw to his great astonishment that all the lights were in one enormous building — a lofty structure with pointed towers plunging upward into the gloom. His eyes made out the shadowy outlines of a palatial château; it was set on a high bluff, and on three sides of it cliffs dived down to where the sea licked greedy lips in the shadows.

"Mirage," thought Rainsford. But it was no mirage, he found, when he opened the tall spiked iron gate. The stone steps were real enough; the massive door with a leering gargoyle for a knocker was real enough; yet about it all hung an air of unreality.

He lifted the knocker, and it creaked up stiffly, as if it had never before been used. He let it fall, and it startled him with its booming loudness. He thought he heard footsteps within; the door remained closed. Again Rainsford lifted the heavy knocker, and let it fall. The door opened then, opened as suddenly as if it were on a spring, and Rainsford stood blinking in the river of glaring gold light that poured out. The first thing Rainsford's eyes discerned was the largest man Rainsford had ever seen — a gigantic creature, solidly made and black-bearded to the waist. In his hand the man held a long-barrel revolver, and he was pointing it straight at Rainsford's heart.

Out of the snarl of beard two small eyes regarded Rainsford.

"Don't be alarmed," said Rainsford, with a smile which he hoped was disarming. "I'm no robber. I fell off a yacht. My name is Sanger Rainsford of New York City."

The menacing look in the eyes did not change. The revolver pointed as rigidly as if the giant were a statue. He gave no sign that he understood Rainsford's words, or that he had even heard them.

He was dressed in uniform, a black uniform trimmed with gray astrakhan.

"I'm Sanger Rainsford of New York," Rainsford began again. "I fell off a yacht. I am hungry."

The man's only answer was to raise with his thumb the hammer of his revolver. Then Rainsford saw the man's free hand go to his forehead in a military salute, and he saw him click his heels together and stand at attention. Another man was coming down the broad marble steps, an erect, slender man in evening clothes. He advanced to Rainsford and held out his hand.

In a cultivated voice marked by a slight accent that gave it added precision and deliberateness, he said: "It is a very great pleasure and honor to welcome Mr. Sanger Rainsford, the celebrated hunter, to my home."

Automatically Rainsford shook the man's hand.

"I've read your book about hunting snow leopards in Tibet, you see," explained the man. "I am General Zaroff."

Rainsford's first impression was that the man was singularly handsome; his second was that there was an original, almost bizarre quality about the general's face. He was a tall man past middle age, for his hair was a vivid white; but his thick eyebrows and pointed military mustache were as black as the night from which Rainsford had come. His eyes, too, were black and very bright. He had high cheek bones, a sharp-cut nose, a spare, dark face, the face of a man used to giving orders, the face of an aristocrat. Turning to the giant in uniform, the general made a sign. The giant put away his pistol, saluted, withdrew.

"Ivan is an incredibly strong fellow," remarked the general, "but he has the misfortune to be deaf and dumb. A simple fellow, but, I'm afraid, like all his race, a bit of a savage."

"Is he Russian?"

"He is a Cossack," said the general, and his smile showed red lips and pointed teeth. "So am I."

"Come," he said, "we shouldn't be chatting here. We can talk later. Now you want clothes, food, rest. You shall have them. This is a most restful spot."

Ivan had reappeared, and the general spoke to him with lips that moved but gave forth no sound.

"Follow Ivan, if you please, Mr. Rainsford," said the general. "I was about to have my dinner when you came. I'll wait for you. You'll find that my clothes will fit you, I think."

It was to a huge, beam-ceilinged bedroom with a canopied bed big enough for six men that Rainsford followed the silent giant. Ivan laid out an evening suit, and Rainsford, as he put it on, noticed that it came from a London tailor who ordinarily cut and sewed for none below the rank of duke.

The dining room to which Ivan conducted him was in many ways remarkable. There was a medieval magnificence about it; it suggested a baronial hall of feudal times with its oaken panels, its high ceiling, its vast refectory table where twoscore men could sit down to eat. About the hall were the mounted heads of many animals — lions, tigers, elephants, moose, bears; larger or more perfect specimens Rainsford had never seen. At the great table the general was sitting, alone.

"You'll have a cocktail, Mr. Rainsford," he suggested. The cocktail was surpassingly good; and, Rainsford noted, the table appointments were of the finest, the linen, the crystal, the silver, the china.

They were eating *borsch,* the rich, red soup with sour cream so dear to Russian palates. Half apologetically General Zaroff said: "We do our best to preserve the amenities of civilization here. Please forgive any lapses. We are well off the beaten track, you know. Do you think the champagne has suffered from its long ocean trip?"

"Not in the least," declared Rainsford. He was finding the general a most thoughtful and affable host, a true cosmopolite. But there was one small trait of the general's that made Rainsford uncomfortable. Whenever he looked up from his plate he found the general studying him, appraising him narrowly.

"Perhaps," said General Zaroff, "you were surprised that I recognized your name. You see, I read all books on hunting published in English, French, and Russian. I have but one passion in my life, Mr. Rainsford, and it is the hunt."

"You have some wonderful heads here," said Rainsford as he ate a particularly well cooked filet mignon. "That Cape buffalo is the largest I ever saw."

"Oh, that fellow. Yes, he was a monster."

"Did he charge you?"

"Hurled me against a tree," said the general. "Fractured my skull. But I got the brute."

"I've always thought," said Rainsford, "that the Cape buffalo is the most dangerous of all big game."

For a moment the general did not reply; he was smiling his curious red-lipped smile. Then he said slowly: "No. You are wrong, sir. The Cape buffalo is not the most dangerous big game." He sipped his wine. "Here in my preserve on this island," he said in the same slow tone, "I hunt more dangerous game."

Rainsford expressed his surprise. "Is there big game on this island?"

The general nodded. "The biggest."

"Really?"

"Oh, it isn't here naturally, of course. I have to stock the island."

"What have you imported, General?" Rainsford asked. "Tigers?"

The general smiled. "No," he said. "Hunting tigers ceased to interest me some years ago. I exhausted their possibilities, you see. No thrill left in tigers, no real danger. I live for danger, Mr. Rainsford."

The general took from his pocket a gold cigarette case and offered his guest a long black cigarette with a silver tip; it was perfumed and gave off a smell like incense.

"We will have some capital hunting, you and I," said the general. "I shall be most glad to have your society."

"But what game —— " began Rainsford.

"I'll tell you," said the general. "You will be amused, I know. I think I may say, in all modesty, that I have done a rare thing. I have invented a new sensation. May I pour you another glass of port, Mr. Rainsford?"

"Thank you, General."

The general filled both glasses, and said: "God makes some men poets. Some He makes kings, some beggars. Me He made a hunter. My hand was made for the trigger, my father said. He was a very rich man with a quarter of a million acres in the Crimea, and he was an ardent sportsman. When I was only five years old he gave me a little gun, specially made in Moscow for me, to shoot sparrows with. When I shot some of his prize turkeys with it, he did not punish me; he complimented me on my marksmanship. I killed my first bear in the Caucasus when I was ten. My whole life has been one prolonged hunt. I went into the army — it was expected of noblemen's sons — and for a time commanded a division of Cossack cavalry, but my real interest was always the hunt. I have hunted every kind of game in every land. It would be impossible for me to tell you how many animals I have killed."

The general puffed at his cigarette.

"After the debacle in Russia I left the country, for it was imprudent for an officer of the Czar to stay there. Many noble Russians lost everything. I, luckily, had invested heavily in American securities, so I shall never have to open a tea room in Monte Carlo or drive a taxi in Paris. Naturally, I continued to hunt — grizzlies in your Rockies, crocodiles in the Ganges, rhinoceroses in East Africa. It was in Africa that the Cape buffalo hit me and laid me up for six months. As soon as I recovered I started for the Amazon to hunt jaguars, for I had heard they were unusually cunning. They weren't." The Cossack sighed. "They were no match at all for a hunter with his wits about him, and a high-powered rifle. I was bitterly disappointed. I was lying in my tent with a splitting headache one night when a terrible thought pushed its way into my mind. Hunting was beginning to bore me! And hunting, remember, had been my life. I have heard that in America business men often go to pieces when they give up the business that has been their life."

"Yes, that's so," said Rainsford.

The general smiled. "I had no wish to go to pieces," he said. "I must do something. Now, mine is an analytical mind, Mr. Rainsford. Doubtless that is why I enjoy the problems of the chase."

"No doubt, General Zaroff."

"So," continued the general, "I asked myself why the hunt no longer fascinated me. You are much younger than I am, Mr. Rainsford, and have not hunted as much, but you perhaps can guess the answer."

"What was it?"

"Simply this: hunting had ceased to be what you call 'a sporting proposition.' It had become too easy. I always got my quarry. Always. There is no greater bore than perfection."

The general lit a fresh cigarette.

"No animal had a chance with me any more. That is no boast; it is a mathematical certainty. The animal had nothing but his legs and his instinct. Instinct is no match for reason. When I thought of this it was a tragic moment for me, I can tell you."

Rainsford leaned across the table, absorbed in what his host was saying.

"It came to me as an inspiration what I must do," the general went on.

"And that was?"

The general smiled the quiet smile of one who has faced an obstacle and surmounted it with success. "I had to invent a new animal to hunt," he said.

"A new animal? You are joking."

"Not at all," said the general. "I never joke about hunting. I needed a new animal. I found one. So I bought this island, built this house, and here I do my hunting. The island is perfect for my purposes — there are jungles with a maze of trails in them, hills, swamps —— "

"But the animal, General Zaroff?"

"Oh," said the general, "it supplies me with the most exciting hunting in the world. No other hunting compares with it for an instant. Every day I hunt, and I never grow bored now, for I have a quarry with which I can match my wits."

Rainsford's bewilderment showed in his face.

"I wanted the ideal animal to hunt," explained the general. "So I said: 'What are the attributes of an ideal quarry?' And the answer was, of course: 'It must have courage, cunning, and, above all, it must be able to reason.' "

"But no animal can reason," objected Rainsford.

"My dear fellow," said the general, "there is one that can."

"But you can't mean —— " gasped Rainsford.

"And why not?"

"I can't believe you are serious, General Zaroff. This is a grisly joke."

"Why should I not be serious? I am speaking of hunting."

"Hunting? Good God, General Zaroff, what you speak of is murder."

The general laughed with entire good nature. He regarded Rainsford quizzically. "I refuse to believe that so modern and civilized a young man as you seem to be harbors romantic ideas about the value of human life. Surely your experiences in the war —— " He stopped.

"Did not make me condone cold-blooded murder," finished Rainsford stiffly.

Laughter shook the general. "How extraordinarily droll you are!" he said. "One does not expect nowadays to find a young man of the educated class, even in America, with such a naïve, and, if I may say so, mid-Victorian point of view. It's like finding a snuffbox in a limousine. Ah, well, doubtless you had Puritan ancestors. So many Americans appear to have had. I'll wager you'll forget your notions when you go hunting with me. You've a genuine new thrill in store for you, Mr. Rainsford."

"Thank you, I'm a hunter, not a murderer."

"Dear me," said the general, quite unruffled, "again that unpleasant word. But I think I can show you that your scruples are quite ill founded."

"Yes?"

"Life is for the strong, to be lived by the strong, and, if needs be, taken by the strong. The weak of the world were put here to give the strong pleasure. I am strong. Why should I not use my gift? If I wish to hunt, why should I not? I hunt the scum of the earth — sailors from tramp ships — lascars, blacks, Chinese, whites, mongrels — a thoroughbred horse or hound is worth more than a score of them."

"But they are men," said Rainsford hotly.

"Precisely," said the general. "That is why I use them. It gives me pleasure. They can reason, after a fashion. So they are dangerous."

"But where do you get them?"

The general's left eyelid fluttered down in a wink. "This island is called Ship-Trap," he answered. "Sometimes an angry god of the high seas sends them to me. Sometimes, when Providence is not so kind, I help Providence a bit. Come to the window with me."

Rainsford went to the window and looked out toward the sea.

"Watch! Out there!" exclaimed the general, pointing into the night. Rainsford's eyes saw only blackness, and then, as the general pressed a button, far out to sea Rainsford saw the flash of lights.

The general chuckled. "They indicate a channel," he said, "where there's none: giant rocks with razor edges crouch like a sea monster with wide-open jaws. They can crush a ship as easily as I crush this nut." He dropped a walnut on the hardwood floor and brought his heel grinding down on it. "Oh, yes," he said casually, as if in answer to a question, "I have electricity. We try to be civilized here."

"Civilized? And you shoot down men?"

A trace of anger was in the general's black eyes, but it was there for but a second, and he said, in his most pleasant manner: "Dear me, what a righteous young man you are! I assure you I do not do the thing you suggest. That would be barbarous. I treat these visitors with every consideration. They get plenty of good food and exercise. They get into splendid physical condition. You shall see for yourself tomorrow."

"What do you mean?"

"We'll visit my training school," smiled the general. "It's in the cellar. I have about a dozen pupils down there now. They're from the Spanish bark *San Lucar* that had the bad luck to go on the rocks out there. A very inferior lot, I regret to say. Poor specimens and more accustomed to the deck than to the jungle."

He raised his hand, and Ivan, who served as waiter, brought thick Turkish coffee. Rainsford, with an effort, held his tongue in check.

"It's a game, you see," pursued the general blandly. "I suggest to one of them that we go hunting. I give him a supply of food and an excellent hunting knife. I give him three hours' start. I am to follow, armed only with a pistol of the smallest calibre and range. If my quarry eludes me for three whole days, he wins the game. If I find him" — the general smiled — "he loses."

"Suppose he refuses to be hunted."

"Oh," said the general, "I give him his option, of course. He need not play that game if he doesn't wish to. If he does not wish to hunt, I turn him over to Ivan. Ivan once had the honor of serving as official knouter to the Great White Czar, and he has his own ideas of sport. Invariably, Mr. Rainsford, invariably they chose the hunt."

"And if they win?"

The smile on the general's face widened. "To date I have not lost," he said.

Then he added, hastily: "I don't wish you to think me a braggart, Mr. Rainsford. Many of them afford only the most elementary sort of problem. Occasionally I strike a tartar. One almost did win. I eventually had to use the dogs."

"The dogs?"

"This way, please. I'll show you."

The general steered Rainsford to a window. The lights from the windows sent a flickering illumination that made grotesque patterns on the courtyard below, and Rainsford could see moving about there a dozen or so huge black shapes; as they turned toward him, their eyes glittered greenly.

"A rather good lot, I think," observed the general. "They are let out at seven every night. If anyone should try to get into my house — or out of it — something extremely regrettable would occur to him." He hummed a snatch of song from the Folies Bergère.

"And now," said the general, "I want to show you my new collection of heads. Will you come with me to the library?"

"I hope," said Rainsford, "that you will excuse me tonight, General Zaroff. I'm really not feeling at all well."

"Ah, indeed?" the general inquired solicitously. "Well, I suppose that's only natural, after your long swim. You need a good, restful night's sleep. Tomorrow you'll feel like a new man, I'll wager. Then we'll hunt, eh? I've one rather promising prospect —— "

Rainsford was hurrying from the room.

"Sorry you can't go with me tonight," called the general. "I expect rather fair sport — a big, strong black. He looks resourceful — Well, good night, Mr. Rainsford; I hope that you have a good night's rest."

The bed was good and the pajamas of the softest silk, and he was tired in every fiber of his being, but nevertheless Rainsford could not quiet his brain with the opiate of sleep. He lay, eyes wide open. Once he thought he heard stealthy steps in the corridor outside his room. He sought to throw open the door; it would not open. He went to the window and looked out. His room was high up in one of the towers. The lights of the château were out now, and it was dark and silent, but there was a fragment of sallow moon, and by its wan light he could see, dimly, the courtyard; there, weaving in and out in the pattern of shadow, were black, noiseless forms; the hounds heard him at the window and looked up, expectantly, with their green eyes. Rainsford went back to the bed and lay down. By many methods he tried to put himself to sleep. He had achieved a doze when, just as morning began to come, he heard, far off in the jungle, the faint report of a pistol.

General Zaroff did not appear until luncheon. He was dressed

THE MOST DANGEROUS GAME

faultlessly in the tweeds of a country squire. He was solicitous about the state of Rainsford's health.

"As for me," sighed the general, "I do not feel so well. I am worried, Mr. Rainsford. Last night I detected traces of my old complaint."

To Rainsford's questioning glance the general said: "Ennui. Boredom."

Then, taking a second helping of *Crêpes Suzette,* the general explained: "The hunting was not good last night. The fellow lost his head. He made a straight trail that offered no problems at all. That's the trouble with these sailors; they have dull brains to begin with, and they do not know how to get about in the woods. They do excessively stupid and obvious things. It's most annoying. Will you have another glass of Chablis, Mr. Rainsford?"

"General," said Rainsford firmly, "I wish to leave this island at once."

The general raised his thickets of eyebrows; he seemed hurt. "But, my dear fellow," the general protested, "you've only just come. You've had no hunting ——"

"I wish to go today," said Rainsford. He saw the dead black eyes of the general on him, studying him. General Zaroff's face suddenly brightened.

He filled Rainsford's glass with venerable Chablis from a dusty bottle.

"Tonight," said the general, "we will hunt — you and I."

Rainsford shook his head. "No, General," he said. "I will not hunt."

The general shrugged his shoulders and delicately ate a hothouse grape. "As you wish, my friend," he said. "The choice rests entirely with you. But may I not venture to suggest that you will find my idea of sport more diverting than Ivan's?"

He nodded toward the corner to where the giant stood, scowling, his thick arms crossed on his hogshead of chest.

"You don't mean —— " cried Rainsford.

"My dear fellow," said the general, "have I not told you I always mean what I say about hunting? This is really an inspiration. I drink to a foeman worthy of my steel — at last."

The general raised his glass, but Rainsford sat staring at him.

"You'll find this game worth playing," the general said enthusiastically. "Your brain against mine. Your woodcraft against mine. Your strength and stamina against mine. Outdoor chess! And the stake is not without value, eh?"

"And if I win — " began Rainsford huskily.

"I'll cheerfully acknowledge myself defeated if I do not find you by midnight of the third day," said General Zaroff. "My sloop will place you on the mainland near a town."

The general read what Rainsford was thinking.

"Oh, you can trust me," said the Cossack. "I will give you my word as a gentleman and a sportsman. Of course you, in turn, must agree to say nothing of your visit here."

"I'll agree to nothing of the kind," said Rainsford.

"Oh," said the general, "in that case — But why discuss it now? Three days hence we can discuss it over a bottle of Veuve Clicquot, unless —— "

The general sipped his wine.

Then a businesslike air animated him. "Ivan," he said to Rainsford, "will supply you with hunting clothes, food, a knife. I suggest you wear moccasins; they leave a poorer trail. I suggest too that you avoid the big swamp in the southeast corner of the island. We call it Death Swamp. There's quicksand there. One foolish fellow tried it. The deplorable part of it was that Lazarus followed him. You can imagine my feelings, Mr. Rainsford. I loved Lazarus; he was the finest hound in my pack. Well, I must beg you to excuse me now. I always take a siesta after lunch. You'll hardly have time for a nap, I fear. You'll want to start, no doubt. I shall not follow till dusk. Hunting at night is so much more exciting than by day, don't you think? *Au revoir*, Mr. Rainsford, *au revoir*."

General Zaroff, with a deep, courtly bow, strolled from the room.

From another door came Ivan. Under one arm he carried khaki hunting clothes, a haversack of food, a leather sheath containing a long-bladed hunting knife; his right hand rested on a cocked revolver thrust in the crimson sash about his waist. . . .

Rainsford had fought his way through the bush for two hours. "I must keep my nerve. I must keep my nerve," he said through tight teeth.

He had not been entirely clear-headed when the château gates snapped shut behind him. His whole idea at first was to put distance between himself and General Zaroff, and, to this end, he had plunged along, spurred on by the sharp rowels of something very like panic. Now he had got a grip on himself, had stopped, and was taking stock of himself and the situation.

He saw that straight flight was futile; inevitably it would bring him face to face with the sea. He was in a picture with a frame of water, and his operations, clearly, must take place within that frame.

"I'll give him a trail to follow," muttered Rainsford, and he struck off from the rude path he had been following into the trackless wilderness. He executed a series of intricate loops; he doubled on his trail again and again, recalling all the lore of the fox hunt, and all the dodges of the fox. Night found him leg-weary, with hands and face lashed by the branches, on a thickly wooded ridge. He knew it would be insane to blunder on through the dark, even if he had the strength. His need for rest was imperative and he thought: "I have played the fox, now I must play the cat of the fable." A big tree with a thick trunk and outspread branches was near by, and, taking care to leave not the slightest mark, he climbed up into the crotch, and stretching out on one of the broad limbs, after a fashion, rested. Rest brought him new confidence and almost a feeling of security. Even so zealous a hunter as General Zaroff could not trace him there, he told himself; only the devil himself could follow that complicated trail through the jungle after dark. But, perhaps, the general was a devil ——

An apprehensive night crawled slowly by like a wounded snake, and sleep did not visit Rainsford, although the silence of a dead world was on the jungle. Toward morning when a dingy gray was varnishing the sky, the cry of some startled bird focused Rainsford's attention in that direction. Something was coming through the bush, coming slowly, carefully, coming by the same winding way Rainsford had come. He flattened himself down on the limb, and through a screen of leaves almost as thick as tapestry, he watched. The thing that was approaching him was a man.

It was General Zaroff. He made his way along with his eyes fixed in utmost concentration on the ground before him. He paused, almost beneath the tree, dropped to his knees and studied the ground.

Rainsford's impulse was to hurl himself down like a panther, but he saw that the general's right hand held something small and metallic — an automatic pistol.

The hunter shook his head several times, as if he were puzzled. Then he straightened up and took from his case one of his black cigarettes; its pungent incenselike smoke floated up to Rainsford's nostrils. Rainsford held his breath. The general's eyes had left the ground and were traveling inch by inch up the tree. Rainsford froze there, every muscle tensed for a spring. But the sharp eyes of the hunter stopped before they reached the limb where Rainsford lay; a smile spread over his brown face. Very deliberately he blew a smoke ring into the air; then he turned his back on the tree and walked carelessly away, back along the trail he had come. The swish of the underbrush against his hunting boots grew fainter and fainter.

The pent-up air burst hotly from Rainsford's lungs. His first thought made him feel sick and numb. The general could follow a trail through the woods at night; he could follow an extremely difficult trail; he must have uncanny powers; only by the merest chance had the Cossack failed to see his quarry.

Rainsford's second thought was even more terrible. It sent a shudder of cold horror through his whole being. Why had the general smiled? Why had he turned back?

Rainsford did not want to believe what his reason told him was true, but the truth was as evident as the sun that had by now pushed through the morning mists. The general was playing with him! The general was saving him for another day's sport! The Cossack was the cat; he was the mouse. Then it was that Rainsford knew the full meaning of terror.

"I will not lose my nerve. I will not."

He slid down from the tree, and struck off again into the woods. His face was set and he forced the machinery of his mind to function. Three hundred yards from his hiding place he stopped where a huge dead tree leaned precariously on a smaller, living one. Throwing off his sack of food, Rainsford took his knife from its sheath and began to work with all his energy.

The job was finished at last, and he threw himself down behind a fallen log a hundred feet away. He did not have to wait long. The cat was coming again to play with the mouse.

Following the trail with the sureness of a bloodhound came General Zaroff. Nothing escaped those searching black eyes, no crushed blade of grass, no bent twig, no mark, no matter how faint, in the moss. So intent was the Cossack on his stalking that he was upon the thing Rainsford had made before he saw it. His foot touched the protruding bough that was the trigger. Even as he touched it, the general sensed his danger and leaped back with the agility of an ape. But he was not quite quick enough; the dead tree, delicately adjusted to rest on the cut living one, crashed down and struck the general a glancing blow on the shoulder as it fell; but for his alertness, he must have been smashed beneath it. He staggered, but he did not fall; nor did he drop his revolver. He stood there, rubbing his injured shoulder, and Rainsford, with fear again gripping his heart, heard the general's mocking laugh ring through the jungle.

"Rainsford," called the general, "if you are within sound of my voice, as I suppose you are, let me congratulate you. Not many men know how to make a Malay man catcher. Luckily for me, I too have hunted in Malacca. You are proving interesting, Mr. Rainsford. I am going now to have my wound dressed; it's only a slight one. But I shall be back. I shall be back."

When the general, nursing his bruised shoulder, had gone, Rainsford took up his flight again. It was flight now, a desperate, hopeless flight, that carried him on for some hours. Dusk came, then darkness, and still he pressed on. The ground grew softer under his moccasins; the vegetation grew ranker, denser; insects bit him savagely. Then, as he stepped forward, his foot sank into the ooze. He tried to wrench it back, but the muck sucked viciously at his foot as if it were a giant leech. With a violent effort, he tore his foot loose. He knew where he was now. Death Swamp and its quicksand.

His hands were tight closed as if his nerve were something tangible that someone in the darkness was trying to tear from his grip. The softness of the earth had given him an idea. He stepped back from the quicksand a dozen feet or so and, like some huge prehistoric beaver, he began to dig.

Rainsford had dug himself in in France when a second's delay meant death. That had been a placid pastime compared to his digging now. The pit grew deeper; when it was above his shoulders, he climbed out and from some hard saplings cut stakes and sharpened them to a fine point. These stakes he planted in the bottom of the pit with the points sticking up. With flying fingers he wove a rough carpet of weeds and branches and with it he covered the mouth of the pit. Then, wet with sweat and aching with tiredness, he crouched behind the stump of a lightning-charred tree.

He knew his pursuer was coming; he heard the paddling sound of feet on the soft earth, and the night breeze brought him the perfume of the general's cigarette. It seemed to Rainsford that the general was coming with unusual swiftness; he was not feeling his way along, foot by foot. Rainsford, crouching there, could not see the general, nor could he see the pit. He lived a year in a minute. Then he felt an impulse to cry aloud with joy, for he heard the sharp crackle of the breaking branches as the cover of the pit gave way; he heard the sharp scream of pain as the pointed stakes found their mark. He leaped up from his place of concealment. Then he cowered back. Three feet from the pit a man was standing, with an electric torch in his hand.

"You've done well, Rainsford," the voice of the general called. "Your Burmese tiger pit has claimed one of my best dogs. Again you score. I think, Mr. Rainsford, I'll see what you can do against my whole pack. I'm going home for a rest now. Thank you for a most amusing evening."

At daybreak Rainsford, lying near the swamp, was awakened by a sound that made him know that he had new things to learn about fear. It was a distant sound, faint and wavering, but he knew it. It was the baying of a pack of hounds.

Rainsford knew he could do one of two things. He could stay where he was and wait. That was suicide. He could flee. That was postponing the inevitable. For a moment he stood there, thinking. An idea that held a wild chance came to him, and, tightening his belt, he headed away from the swamp.

The baying of the hounds drew nearer, then still nearer, nearer, ever nearer. On a ridge Rainsford climbed a tree. Down a watercourse, not a quarter of a mile away, he could see the bush moving. Straining his eyes, he saw the lean figure of General Zaroff; just ahead of him Rainsford made out another figure whose wide shoulders surged through the tall jungle weeds; it was the giant Ivan, and he seemed pulled forward by some unseen force; Rainsford knew that Ivan must be holding the pack in leash.

They would be on him any minute now. His mind worked frantically. He thought of a native trick he had learned in Uganda. He slid down the tree. He caught hold of a springy young sapling and to it he fastened his hunting knife, with the blade pointing down the trail; with a bit of wild grapevine he tied back the sapling. Then he ran for his life. The hounds raised their voices as they hit the fresh scent. Rainsford knew now how an animal at bay feels.

He had to stop to get his breath. The baying of the hounds stopped abruptly, and Rainsford's heart stopped too. They must have reached the knife.

He shinned excitedly up a tree and looked back. His pursuers had stopped. But the hope that was in Rainsford's brain when he climbed died, for he saw in the shallow valley that General Zaroff was still on his feet. But Ivan was not. The knife, driven by the recoil of the spring tree, had not wholly failed.

Rainsford had hardly tumbled to the ground when the pack took up the cry again.

"Nerve, nerve, nerve!" he panted, as he dashed along. A blue gap showed between the trees dead ahead. Ever nearer drew the hounds. Rainsford forced himself on toward the gap. He reached it. It was the shore of the sea. Across a cove he could see the gloomy gray stone of the château. Twenty feet below him the sea rumbled and hissed. Rainsford hesitated. He heard the hounds. Then he leaped far out into the sea. . . .

When the general and his pack reached the place by the sea, the Cossack stopped. For some minutes he stood regarding the blue-green expanse of water. He shrugged his shoulders. Then he sat down, took a drink of brandy from a silver flask, lit a perfumed cigarette, and hummed a bit from "Madame Butterfly."

General Zaroff had an exceedingly good dinner in his great paneled dining hall that evening. With it he had a bottle of Pol Roger and half a bottle of Chambertin. Two slight annoyances kept him from perfect enjoyment. One was the thought that it would be difficult to replace Ivan; the other was that his quarry had escaped him; of course, the American hadn't played the game — so thought the general as he tasted his after-dinner liqueur. In his library he read, to soothe himself, from the works of Marcus Aurelius. At ten he went up to his bedroom. He was deliciously tired, he said to himself, as he locked himself in. There was a little moonlight, so, before turning on his light, he went to the window and looked down at the courtyard. He could see the great hounds, and he called: "Better luck another time," to them. Then he switched on the light.

A man, who had been hiding in the curtains of the bed, was standing there.

"Rainsford!" screamed the general. "How in God's name did you get here?"

"Swam," said Rainsford. "I found it quicker than walking through the jungle."

The general sucked in his breath and smiled. "I congratulate you," he said. "You have won the game."

Rainsford did not smile. "I am still a beast at bay," he said, in a low, hoarse voice. "Get ready, General Zaroff."

The general made one of his deepest bows. "I see," he said. "Splendid! One of us is to furnish a repast for the hounds. The other will sleep in this very excellent bed. On guard, Rainsford." . . .

He had never slept in a better bed, Rainsford decided.

THE ELEVENTH JUROR

by VINCENT STARRETT

Vincent Starrett, perhaps America's most learned authority on Holmesiana (author of "The Private Life of Sherlock Holmes," "221-B," etc.) has written a classic crime story. Here it is.

THERE are few practicing citizens of the republic, I guess, who some time or other have not been called for jury service. The system is impartial, and, like lightning, you never know where it is going to strike.

It's unlike lightning, though — or the way lightning is supposed to operate — in one respect. It does, often, strike more than once in the same place. I have a friend, for instance, who has served on a dozen juries in as many years, in cases ranging anywhere from leasehold troubles to first degree murder. He doesn't particularly like to serve, but he's one of those citizens who think they owe a duty to the state, and all that sort of thing. And I have another friend who has been called a dozen times and hasn't served yet. He's an accomplished liar, and always manages to get the judge to excuse him.

Of course, it's easier to get excused in a big case than in a little one. The lawyers are more particular in a big case. If you want to dodge, just wait for the right question, and then give the wrong answer. If the prosecutor wants to hang a man for murder, tell him you are opposed to the death penalty, and before you know it you'll be collecting your coat and hat and heading back for the office. Or just suggest that you have followed the case pretty closely in the newspapers, and have formed a strong opinion about it. Something like that. It will always work; nearly always.

They don't really need you on a jury. There are always enough men who *want* to serve because they like it. It's a vacation from home and work, and it gives them a feeling of consequence to be sitting around in court, as important as the judge. Fountains of wisdom, and all that. They claim to be unprejudiced, and really they are a lot more prejudiced than the fellows who beg off. God help the prisoner who gets a jury of wiseacres that really want to sit in judgment on him! Who claim they haven't formed an opinion!

However, this isn't an essay. What I started out to tell was the story of my own first jury service. We were out for ten days without getting a verdict, and all the time — from first to last — the count stood eleven for hanging and one for acquittal. I was the juror who held out. On the eleventh day, we returned a verdict of not guilty, and the prisoner was acquitted. He became one of my best friends, for of course the newspapers found out that I had swung the jury, and he came around to thank me. About a year after the end of the trial, without any urging on my part, he told me something I had suspected from the beginning of the case. In fact, it had been part of my argument to the other jurors during ten days of talking, though I didn't dwell on it a lot. He said he didn't know — actually didn't know — whether he had committed the crime or not!

Of course, that didn't come out at the trial, although the idiot wanted to tell it. He was too honest to live. Fortunately, his lawyer was less scrupulous.

Horace Thistlethwaite was his lawyer — a tongue twister of a name that made the courtroom laugh every time the prosecutor mispronounced it, which he did every chance he got. Ricketts was the prosecutor's name, so he didn't have much call to laugh at Thistlethwaite; but it never occurred to Ricketts that there could be *anything* funny about himself. I suppose the case is pretty well forgotten by this time, but it was a good one while it lasted. Good enough, anyway. Chicago may have two or three bigger and better ones, every year, but this one caused some talk in its day.

I had been interested in the case from the beginning, and had read everything I could about it, in all the newspapers; but the last thing I thought of was that I would get a chance to serve on the jury that tried Murray. I was never more surprised in my life than I was the day the summons came. But I knew at once that I was going to serve on that jury unless I was thrown off by one side or the other. I couldn't think of any reason why I would not make a perfectly fair juror, and that was the attitude I intended to carry into court. But it struck me as remarkable that after the years the jury call had missed me, I should be called for service in a case that fascinated me the way this one did.

Of course, I couldn't be positive till I was sitting in the ante-chamber of the courtroom that it *was* the Murray case I was in for; but I was sure enough, for I had been following the papers, as I say, and I knew they were having a hard time getting a jury. They had already exhausted a couple of panels of veniremen, because it seemed that everybody had read about the case and had an opinion. The defense lawyers were afraid of men who had read about the case, and I didn't blame them. It certainly looked bad for Murray. But who *hadn't* read about it?

However, they got a jury. It was touch and go, as far as I was concerned, for they already had ten men accepted when I came in; ten whopping liars, sitting there as big as life, itching for the case to commence. I lied too, for I wanted the job as much as they did, and after the usual line of questions I got it. I said I had read very little about the case, had no opinions about it whatever, and was not averse to the death penalty; and I never told three bigger lies in a row in my life. After awhile, they caught another plausible liar, and there we were, twelve of us, all innocent as — I was going to say innocent as the twelve apostles.

The case began to unfold next day. As I looked around at my fellow jurors, it occurred to me that I had never seen eleven more ridiculous fatheads. However, that was what the prosecution wanted, and probably what Thistlethwaite wanted, too. It's a great system, the jury system in this country! If you look as if you might have an ounce of intelligence, neither side wants you; but give a lawyer twelve complete fools, without an idea between them, and he's happy. He knows if he loses his case it's his own fault.

Well, the wheels began to go round, and before long I was listening to everything I had already read and knew all about. The principal witness for the state was Patrolman Witte of the Waterside Station, a good-natured fat old hippopotamus, who must have been on the force to prove that the Irish don't have a monopoly on all the appointments. He told a straight story, though, and stuck to it like a good copper. . . . On the night of umpty-ump, or about two o'clock the next morning, to be exact, he had heard three shots fired in close order, and had hurried toward the sound. At Lambeth Avenue and Belvedere Road, he had found the prisoner, James Murray, standing still, looking at a revolver in his hand. Not far away was the body of a man, and the man had been shot to death. Questioned by Witte, the prisoner had denied all knowledge of the shooting, but was unable to tell why he carried a recently discharged revolver. He seemed dazed, Witte said, and had evidently been drinking heavily. He made no attempt to escape, but went along quietly when Witte told him he was under arrest.

In a little while the whole story had been outlined. The dead man had been identified as Howard Blessing, a widower, and death had resulted from a bullet wound in the neck and another in the heart. Murray had been taken to the station, and the body of Howard Blessing had been taken to a neighboring undertaking establishment. Nobody called it a parlor, I remember, and I decided that only undertakers called their places parlors. Murray had been locked up and had slept like a log all night and part of the morning; then he had wakened and continued his denials. Later, after a coroner's committee had held him to the grand jury, he had been formally charged with the murder and indicted. Witte didn't tell all this, but it came out early in the case and was corroborated by everybody concerned.

Naturally, the mystery was considerable. Murray denied flatly that he ever knew Howard Blessing, the inference being that in those circumstances he would hardly have killed him, even as a matter of drunken target practice — which didn't necessarily follow. He also denied that he ever carried or ever had owned a revolver, and in this he was supported by a lot of his friends, all very good citizens. Murray was a good citizen, himself; that was one of the things against him, really. He was smug, and prosperous, and he wore good clothes; and, even worse, he had a reputation as a sort of small-time reformer. That sort of fellow, when he's caught in something disreputable, like bootlegging or murder, doesn't make much of a hit with a jury of average citizens.

He was one of the last witnesses in his own behalf, and he made only a fair impression; and when he told his story of what had happened that night at Lambeth Avenue and Belvedere Road, he didn't make any impression at all. It was a pretty thin tale, and even his lawyer knew it. Murray admitted that he'd been drinking pretty heavily with some of the "boys," and the "boys" had already supported him in that. In fact, they all swore that he couldn't have held a revolver steady, even if he'd had one, which they knew he didn't. A fine tale to have to tell about a fellow associated with reform!

Murray also admitted that he wasn't walking toward home when the shots were fired on the corner, but he blamed that on the drink. He said, with an air of great candor, that he had been completely malted on the night in question, and hadn't any idea why he was at that intersection, holding a revolver in his hand. Somebody must have given it to him. Anyway, he knew he hadn't shot Blessing. He was clear enough to know that, he said. Personally, I doubted it. He was a rather good-looking fellow, with a young wife who seemed to be all legs and eyes. She was probably pretty, but she looked like a corpse, herself, sitting there beside Thistlethwaite at the table.

Ricketts, a thin small man, with a sharp nose and eyes like a cornered rat, rode Murray pretty hard, but the prisoner stood up to it and stuck to his story. They didn't shake him an ounce, not even after the Pearson woman had weakened under Ricketts's battering.

This Pearson woman was one of the star witnesses for the defense, or was supposed to be; but she wasn't strong enough for Ricketts's bullying, and after a while nobody could tell whose witness she was. She was a plump little, peering sort of old lady, the sort that *would* see everything that was going on around her, and tell about it, too. Her story, on direct examination, was clear enough, although she had to be coached a little. She had been sitting at her window, in Lambeth Avenue, waiting for her husband to come home — He *wasn't* one of the "boys," she snapped, when Ricketts interrupted — and she had seen two men pass her window, a short time before the shooting. She had heard them quarreling — violently. One of them was waving his arms. She had taken particular notice of them, and she was sure that neither of the men was James Murray; they were both much bigger men. She was also pretty sure that one of them *was* Howard Blessing. It was pretty dark, she admitted on cross-examination, but she saw them quite clearly, because there was a light not very far from her house. She had heard their voices, too, and neither one of them sounded like the voice of James Murray.

Then Ricketts exploded a couple of bombs. He was particularly sarcastic on the subject of Murray's voice, but there was no need for his being so brutal with her. Even the boobs on the jury had noticed all *he* had. The woman was hard of hearing. She was all right when Thistlethwaite had her, for he kept his voice up — it's pretty high, anyway — and she knew what he was going to ask; but Ricketts turned her inside out. What she had to tell wasn't so much, but it was less when Ricketts had finished with her. He kept his voice down on purpose, and all the time she was saying "What?" and "How?" and putting her hands up to her ears. First of all, he made her admit that she hadn't heard the shots. Thistlethwaite had carefully kept away from that question. And in the end, Ricketts forced her to confess that she wasn't very sure of anything. She *might* have made a mistake. She couldn't *swear* that one of the voices she had heard was *not* Murray's. The man she had taken for Howard Blessing *might* have been someone else.

The things Ricketts said can be imagined. She hadn't even heard the shots, a quarter of a block away; she couldn't even hear his questions right there in the courtroom; and yet she could testify about the voices of two men passing her window! And, of course, he looked over at us, triumphantly, every time he made a point. The woman was nearly crying. Thistlethwaite got her again, as quickly as he could, and tried to soothe her. He managed to bring out that the immediate reason for her poor hearing was a cold in her head, whereas on the night of the voices her head had been clearer; but even the judge grinned at that.

The other defense ace was a janitor who had seen a man running. That was all. The man who was running had been seen by the janitor, on Lambeth Avenue, some blocks from the scene of the shooting, not long after it had occurred. The suggestion there, of course, was that this running man had shot Howard Blessing and then taken to his heels. Which was all right as far as it went; but it didn't explain James Murray, standing there on the spot with a revolver in his hand, and three of the chambers empty.

However, the defense had a trump card that even Ricketts couldn't beat. Blessing, a widower, always carried around with him a miniature portrait of his wife. All his friends knew this, and some of them testified about it; one of them swore he had seen it in Blessing's possession the very night of Blessing's death. Blessing had shown it to him, in the friend's home, just before he — Blessing, that is —

started for his own home on the trip that he never finished. And the miniature was missing. It hadn't been found on Murray, and it hadn't been found in the neighborhood of the murder; and it hadn't been found on Blessing's body.

It was a lovely point, and it hinted at all sorts of things. It furnished just about the only hint of romance the case had, and the newspapers had played it strong, from the beginning. Pictures of the girl — Blessing's wife — were in every edition. Every man on the jury knew what she looked like, although she had been dead for some years. Thistlethwaite, of course, made the most of that missing miniature. Ricketts just shrugged it out of existence, as if it didn't matter, anyway.

I suppose nearly everybody believed Murray to be guilty, and probably everybody thought something discreditable was being hidden, or wasn't known; something that would connect Murray with Blessing's dead wife, or something that would connect Blessing with Murray's wife. I heard some pretty rough guesses made in the jury room, myself, the first night out.

From the beginning, Thistlethwaite stuck to one story. It wasn't much of a story to impress a jury, but it was all he had, and he did what he could with it, which was a lot. Everything he brought out contributed to it, and finally got into his plea to the jury. He knew that his only chance to clear Murray was a great speech, and when the time came he made it. The fellow certainly could talk. He was tall and thin, and would have been good-looking if his face hadn't been pock-marked. His hair had a curl and a wave that was the envy of every woman in the courtroom — and they were there in regiments. He looked like an actor, and he should have been one. He won most of his cases. That's why he was in this one. Without Thistlethwaite, Murray wouldn't have had a chance.

Well, it was my first jury service, and I listened for all I was worth. I was interested in the case, anyway, as I said, and had my own opinions about it. It was as good as a vaudeville show, sometimes, to watch Ricketts and Thistlethwaite in action, particularly when they got after each other. Ricketts was a snarly, sarcastic little devil, and sharp as a whip. I remember once when Thistlethwaite was going after Witte pretty strong, early in the trial, about the exact minute he had heard the shots, and just where Murray was standing with reference to the body, and what the position of the moon was, and so on, Ricketts smiled out of the corner of his face, with one eye on the jury, and said: "Apparently it is Mr. Whistlewhite's idea that we have erred in failing to call the moon as an essential witness in this case."

Everybody snickered at the name, as usual, then everybody roared; and the bailiff pounded and howled for order, although he was grinning like a black comedian himself. Thistlethwaite's only reply was: "I should have been very glad, Mr. Prosecutor, had it been possible, to call the moon as a witness for the defense. I have no doubt that its long experience as an eyewitness would have enabled it to interpret what it saw more correctly than the human eyes of Officer Witte." Which wasn't so good, I imagine, for nobody laughed.

Later, though, Thistlethwaite got a chance to compare the combination of Ricketts's voice and Ricketts's argument with a jew's harp, and all the defense followers cheered up and chuckled. And, of course, whenever anything of that sort was sprung, we in the jury box got a smile and a glance from the orator who was doing the talking. That sort of thing is always for the benefit of the jury. We didn't any of us like Ricketts, but he had Murray dead to rights, and he knew it, and we knew it. Not that Thistlethwaite was popular in the jury room; he wasn't. He was a bit too oily, and half the time he was over the heads of — well, say eleven of us. But on the whole, I think we liked him better than we did Ricketts — maybe because he had a losing case and was putting up a good fight.

Sometimes the two of them wrangled together over nothing in particular until the judge, who always looked half asleep when he wasn't drawing heads or something on his blotter, would get tired of it and ask them to get along with the case. Sometimes the judge called a recess when the razzing was getting pretty furious, and when he came back from his chambers he would always have a fresh chew of tobacco in his cheek. He had a chopped moustache, and reminded me of a veterinary surgeon I used to know.

After the evidence was all in, the main talking began, as I said. Ricketts, sneery as ever, talked as if it was all over but the shouting. The newspapers called him a "hanging prosecutor," and it was a hanging he wanted in this case. He drew a lot of inferences that weren't justified by the evidence, it seemed to me, to give Murray a motive for the crime; but there wasn't much that it was necessary for him to say. His case was complete when Witte finished giving his testimony. Murray had been caught red-handed, whatever his motives may have been, and that was that. He had taken a human life, and the law demanded his own in return. A silly idea, but there are a lot of silly ideas in the world, parading as wisdom.

Thistlethwaite, of course, took another tone. He was bitter when he referred to Ricketts's conduct of the case; but for the most part he delivered an address that might have come out of a Sunday serial. He pictured Murray as a victim of circumstances, a man of fine reputation who was to be blamed only because he was fool enough to get drunk and stagger into a mess. Considering the little he had to build on, his story was a good one. You could see the whole scene the way he described it: Murray, so fuddled he didn't know what was going on, meandering home the wrong way, probably making speeches to the moon, blundering onto the body of Howard Blessing a minute or two after the shooting, seeing the revolver on the ground beside the body, picking it up like an idiot, and finally standing there dazed as Witte came up and arrested him. Meanwhile, Thistlethwaite said, the real murderer was fleeing for his life, making a clean getaway, seen only by an owl janitor who hadn't even caught a glimpse of the runner's face.

In support of Thistlethwaite's reconstruction, we had, of course, the janitor's slender testimony, and the evidence of the Pearson woman, as much of it as hadn't been laughed out of court. I always believed, myself, that she *did* hear the voices she said she did. The men were quarreling, and their voices probably were pretty high.

Finally, Thistlethwaite continued, there was the matter of the missing miniature. It completely exonerated Murray, he contended. It had to be either on Blessing or Murray, if Murray was the murderer; there hadn't been time for Murray to throw it away or hide it. So he ran on, and it was a first-class speech. He pointed to Murray's blameless life, and his distinguished friends, and wanted to know why under the canopy a man who had never handled a revolver in his life should on this occasion beg, borrow, or steal one and murder a man he had never seen or heard of before.

Oh, it was a masterpiece of a talk; but as Ricketts pointed out in his final address, it was all pure guesswork. In spite of everything anybody could say, one *fact* remained unshaken — James Murray, standing over his victim on the corner, with the discharged revolver in his hand.

As for Murray's drunkenness, Ricketts said, it was no excuse. He was willing to admit that in cold sobriety Murray might not have lost his temper and Blessing might have gone on living. It was absurd to assert, however, that there had been no quarrel between them. Whatever their differences may have been, they were obviously enemies. If we, the jury, believed that drunkenness excused cold-blooded murder, he added sarcastically, then we would, of course, acquit Murray and thereby encourage others to get drunk and go man-hunting; but if we believed that human life should be protected against the insanity of drunken beasts, whatever their reputations when sober, it was our duty to make an example of this particularly obnoxious specimen. And so on. It wasn't as picturesque a speech as Thistlethwaite's, but it carried a lot more conviction.

As a matter of fact, as far as the other eleven jurors were concerned, Murray's goose was cooked long before the final addresses. I knew that. Even the eyes and legs of Mrs. Murray hadn't helped much.

Then the judge adjusted his nose glasses and shoved his stomach up against the corner of the bench, and read his instructions, which were a fair enough summing up of what we had heard from both sides. On the whole, the instructions were a bit favorable to the prosecution, which was to be expected; but we were told that if we entertained — that was the word — a reasonable doubt of Murray's guilt, it was up to us to acquit him of the charge. After that we paraded to the jury room, and the real trial of the case began.

A smug animal named Dean, a printing superintendent somewhere, was our foreman, and he was as important about it as if he had been appointed minister to Dublin. Dean had served on juries before, although he'd never been a foreman until now, and he knew the ropes. We began by taking a trial ballot, just to see where we stood, and the vote was eleven for conviction and one for acquittal.

I knew who the *one* was, and I didn't see any reason for leaving the others in doubt.

"I'm the fellow, boys," I said. "Try to convince me."

They did. Dean in particular seemed to take it as a personal quarrel with him that I had. He seemed to think it inconsiderate of me to hold an opinion opposed to the views of eleven others. He had an idea that if we had all been agreed, somehow it would have been a feather in his cap to report right back to the judge, like a bunch of boy scouts who had finished an assignment. The others thought it was funny, at first, and were chiefly interested to know my reasons for believing Murray innocent. They hadn't seen a chance for him at any time, they said. They were kind of sorry for him, but not much. As for his being innocent — !

"It's an open-and-shut case, Russell," one of them said. "Thistlethwaite made a good talk, all right, but he didn't have a single fact. It was all moonshine. I wouldn't hustle anybody off to the gallows, or even to the pen, if I had any doubts; but I haven't — not a doubt. This guy's going to get what is coming to him. He's as guilty as Judas Iscariot."

"He's being framed," I said. "He was drunk, and he happened along at the right time, and the murderer used him. That's the way I figure it. Thistlethwaite thinks Murray came along and saw the gun, and like a damn fool picked it up, just in time to get caught with it. I think the murderer stuck the gun into Murray's hand, just before he ran off himself. No wonder Murray was dazed!"

"Bunk!" said one of the others. "He was dazed because he was soused. He planned it all in cold blood, then licked up a lot of liquor to give him nerve to see it through."

"You think Murray knew Blessing?" I asked. And they all answered at once: "Sure thing!"

"There wasn't any testimony to show it," I said. "Ricketts just said that. There wasn't any proof."

"There didn't have to be," Dean said. "It stuck out all through the case. Why would he want to shoot him if he didn't know him?"

"That's what Thistlethwaite wanted to know," I told him. "He wouldn't — and he didn't. That's the answer. And how about the miniature?"

"He didn't have it on him," said Dean, meaning Blessing didn't have it on him. "Ricketts had the dope on that. He couldn't have had it on him. The fellow who said he did was probably lying."

"Lying, your grandmother," I said. "He saw it half an hour before Blessing was shot. If that miniature could be located, we'd know a lot more about this case than we do now, and Murray wouldn't be in danger of swinging."

"If your grandmother had four wheels she'd be a box car," said Dean.

"You fellows are just sore at Murray because he's a reformer who got drunk," I said. "I don't blame you for that, but it's no reason for supposing he committed murder."

"That's a lie," said Dean. "Anyway, it's a good reason, in my opinion."

So it went, off and on, for ten days. We picked that case to pieces. We went over every bit of testimony. And it ended just the way it began. Everybody but me wanted to convict Murray, and most of them wanted him hung. The longer we were out, the sorer they all got at Murray — and, of course, at me. They hated me like poison. They probably thought I'd been fixed, and was holding out on orders.

One of them — Dean — started to say something about it, one day, but I said some things that quieted him for a couple of hours. In one way, I had the whip hand. I didn't have any family waiting for me at home, and all the others had. They were all married men, and they were pretty sick about being kept away from home, after they'd been out a few days. At first, they had all thought it was a great lark.

I didn't care how long we were out. I knew it was my job to save Murray's neck. Not that I cared a hoot about Murray, but I was positive he was as innocent of the murder as Dean himself. Every once in a while the judge would send his bailiff in to see how we stood and whether there was any chance of our reaching a verdict. I thought a number of times he would call it a mistrial and discharge the jury, but he didn't. Eleven to one sounded pretty good to him, I guess. He figured that sooner or later I would cave, and there would be a verdict for the state.

The bailiff used to take a hand in the argument, sometimes. He thought I was a stubborn ass, and didn't hesitate to say so. He said he had heard all the evidence, too, and he was sure Murray was guilty.

"What do you care whether he swings or not?" he asked. "It ain't your funeral. Come on, boys, let's get a verdict, and we'll all go home." At other times he would say: "What do you think you are, Russell? Chief justice or something? What right have you to say this man isn't guilty when these eleven men say he is? Do you think your brains are better than other people's?"

So it went. They didn't budge me an inch. I argued right back, and went over the whole ground with them like a teacher, time and again. And I didn't budge them an inch, either.

After a while they began to get even with me. The bailiff was at the bottom of that, I think. The other eleven used to have cigars, all of a sudden, when I didn't; and a couple of times I thought my food wasn't quite up to scratch, though it all came from the same hotel kitchen. Then one night somebody upset a pitcher of water in my bed, just before I had to use it; and my clothes used to disappear mysteriously, a few minutes before I needed them. I was taken over the jumps, all right. It was a regular initiation. It narrowed down, at last, to a survival contest. Nobody spoke to me, and I didn't speak to anybody. Any one of them would have been glad to take a punch at me, and a few times I thought some of them were going to do it. And every once in a while Dean would call for another ballot, just to see whether I had changed my mind.

Well, the eleventh morning rolled around, and the ratio was still eleven to one. The judge's bailiff came in and dropped a hint. He said if we didn't reach a verdict that day we were going to be discharged. He may have been lying; I don't know; but that's what he said. Everybody cheered up but me. It was going to be over soon, one way or another, they figured. They weren't so angry at me that morning.

When I still held out, they just laughed a little, and Dean said: "Well, you certainly stuck it out, Russell. I've got to hand it to you."

"Thanks!" I said.

But I wasn't pleased at all. A discharge of the jury meant another trial for Murray, probably, and I knew that next time he wouldn't have someone like me on the jury to save his neck. I thought it all over, and there was only one thing to do; so after dinner I did it.

"Boys," I said, "or gentlemen, if you like, the time has come to end all this funny business. We haven't been able to agree, and it looks as if the judge is going to let us disagree. That doesn't suit me, for I believe Murray is innocent. I don't want another jury to convict him. I want this jury to free him. Last night, I went over this case pretty carefully, and I can tell you just what happened that night on that street corner, as clearly as if I was there. Maybe I dreamed it; maybe I just figured it out; but this is the way it goes. . . .

"About ten years ago, let's imagine there was a man named Smith — call him George Smith. Suppose he fell in love with a girl, and that it was an honest-to-God thing. Maybe he was an electrician, or something like that, in a small town in Ohio, where the girl lived. Anyway, I imagine he didn't have money enough to get married, so he and the girl just drifted along, liking each other a lot, and hoping that some day it would be all right. He would have taken a chance, and so would the girl; but suppose her father was dead against it. Then suppose Smith got a chance to make some money — good money — in another city, and went away. The girl, of course, was going to wait for him, and maybe she would have waited, if it hadn't been for another fellow. Suppose this other fellow was a hardware salesman, a fellow who made that town every once in a while, a flashy, good-looking young fellow, with enough money to make it look like it was more than it was. Then suppose he took a fancy to this girl, too, and that his name was Howard Blessing."

That gave them all a shock. At first they hadn't known what I was talking about. Now they began to prick up their ears and look at each other.

"Well," I said, "suppose all that, and the rest ought to be easy to guess. It's the sort of thing that happens in life, a lot oftener than you think. What happens? As soon as Smith is out of the way, Blessing begins to work on the girl. He fills her up with a lot of stories about Smith, some of them pretty tough; and, with the girl's father to help him, it isn't long before Smith isn't getting any answer to his letters. Then, one day, he gets a letter from the girl that knocks him over. Maybe it's a year after he's gone away; about the time he's thinking about going back to marry her. And she says she's going to marry Blessing.

"There's the situation, and you can't blame the girl altogether, because Blessing is a good plausible liar, and Smith isn't there to defend himself. There isn't anything Smith can do, is there? He can't figure it out, of course, because he doesn't know all the dirty stories Blessing has been telling about him. Maybe it doesn't break his heart exactly, because men's hearts don't break easily; but it makes him pretty mad. He already hates Blessing, who is a pup. Smith has always known that, the way men know about each other. All right! Smith stays on where he is, and after a time he gets the wedding announcement, and that's that. The chapter's over. That's what Smith thinks; and probably that's what Blessing thinks."

Well, I had them, all right. The story got them, as I thought maybe it would. They began to smell a rat. But Dean wasn't letting me get away with too much. "That's very pretty," he said. "You ought to write a story about it, Russell. You've sure got an imagination. But what's it got to do with Murray?"

"Let me finish," I said. "Maybe I'm only supposing a case, but you'll find it fits the facts. What happens afterwards? You don't need three guesses to know that. The years begin to run, and after enough of them have gone by, one day Smith gets a letter from the girl's mother. She's always liked Smith, and she writes to tell him that her daughter — that is, Mrs. Blessing — is dead. She doesn't beat around the bush for words, either, and what she has to say about Blessing is plenty. He's everything that Smith already knows, and then some. The old woman is broken-hearted, and she's mad — both of them. She writes to Smith because she's got to write to somebody. And, of course, it's the old story again — as old as what happened to Smith. Blessing hadn't panned out very well, and when he'd got to running around with other women, it was the finish for the girl. But instead of getting a divorce, the girl commits suicide, being that kind of a girl. She must have had a terrible time, to do that. Maybe you can imagine her. She probably looked like the pictures you've seen of Mrs. Blessing.

"Well," I said, "now you've got the beginning of the story. Smith, of course, writes a letter to the old woman, trying to buck her up; and privately he tells himself what he's going to do to Blessing if he ever meets him. Because Blessing has killed the girl just as surely as if he had knifed her. They don't call it murder, maybe, but that's what it is. Isn't it?"

About half of them nodded their heads; and I was pretty glad they were all married men. Probably some of them had daughters; I don't know.

"The girl's mother, you see, has spilled the beans," I went on, "and Smith knows now how Blessing happened to cut him out. And the end of the story, of course, is what happened the night Smith met Blessing at Lambeth Avenue and Belvedere Road; the night Mrs. Pearson was looking out of her window, and didn't have a cold in her head. It was a long time after the girl had died, of course, and Smith and Blessing had met once before that, but Blessing had got away. He ran. That's how Smith knew Blessing was in the same city as himself, this city in which we're sitting now. If Blessing had known it in time, he'd probably have shipped for Africa. That's the sort of a coward he was."

By this time the whole eleven of them were listening with both ears, for they had tumbled to the fact that I knew Smith and knew his story; they knew I *must*. Well, I did. Even so, one of them sneered a bit, and said: "You seem to know a lot about it!"

"I do!" I said, and went on with the story:

"The second time Smith met Blessing was that night, and Blessing was ready. He'd got a gun, apparently, and carried it every night after that first meeting. He wasn't taking any chances. Smith didn't have a gun. He didn't intend to kill Blessing. He just intended to thrash him within an inch of his life. They met, accidentally, and Blessing began to argue — to justify himself. That's what the Pearson woman heard as the two of them passed her window. But Smith was cold. He knew what he was going to do; but he let Blessing talk, to see what he'd say. Finally, Blessing produced his miniature, and began to sob about it; and that was the last straw. Smith knocked it out of his hands and swung on him. And Blessing ducked and got out his gun. He didn't get a chance to use it, for Smith grabbed him and took that away from him, too. The gun went off in the air, just as Smith got it. That was the first shot. Then there were two more.

"I'm not trying to justify Smith, exactly. Something happened to him, just then, and maybe he wasn't responsible. Maybe you think he *was*. He let Blessing have it, just as Blessing jumped for him. It was all over in a minute, and Smith was a murderer. That sort of thing happens in life, too. It isn't intended, there isn't any plan; it just happens because you're mad, and somebody has it coming to him. Something pops inside of you, and there you are. It might be you; it might be me. This time it was Smith."

Dean got the floor, then, for a minute. He had listened hard, and now he had a question to ask. "Who is Smith?" he wanted to know. "Is he — Murray?"

"No," I said, "he's the fellow the janitor saw running. I told you Murray was framed, and so he was. He came up just in time to be useful. He came up staggering, drunk; and he stopped and looked around to see what was going on. And Smith, who was pretty horrified by what he'd done, and had to get away quick, shoved the gun into Murray's hand, grabbed the miniature off the sidewalk, and ran. When Witte came up, a few minutes later — it took him longer than he thought — there was Murray standing over the body of Blessing, holding the gun, too drunk to know what was going on; wondering what it was all about. He said he was innocent, when he got his wits back, but he hadn't a leg to stand on.

"Now," I said, "that's what happened, that night, and there's only one thing for us to do, and that's acquit Murray."

They didn't say a word for a while. They couldn't. They just sat — or stood — and looked at me. Finally, Dean had an idea — another one. He stood up and aimed his finger at me.

"Russell," he said, "it's a good story, and if it's true, of course it goes without saying that you know this fellow Smith. Well, that's all right; though how you got onto the jury, I don't know. But it needs a lot more than your word to prove it. We'll free Murray — sure! — as soon as we know *you* know what you're talking about. If you're just making up a fairy tale, to get Murray off . . ."

Well, that was that. I knew again what I had to do. "All right, Dean," I said. "What would you consider was proof?"

He thought a minute. "If you could produce this fellow Smith," he said at last, "it would be something, eh, boys? But even then, Smith would have to produce the miniature, I guess, to prove that *he* was telling the truth. Yes, I guess the miniature is the only real proof. Eh, boys?"

They all agreed with him. They always agreed with everybody and with each other — with everybody except me.

"All right then," I said again, "but the question is: what about Smith? Does he have to take Murray's place? You know the truth about him. Do you want him to go to the gallows for killing Blessing? If you tell the court about Smith, he has to take *his* chance in the dock, and maybe get a jury that wouldn't understand him the way this one does. Assume that all I've told you is true, and that you're sitting in judgment on Smith. Would you free him or convict him?"

"Free him," said about four of them at once. The others hadn't thought about it; but I could see the answer in their faces. They wouldn't have hanged Smith. He had done the sort of thing every one of them knew he might have done himself. I chanced it.

"There's the miniature, boys," I said, pulling it out of my coat. "Take a look at it. I've had it in my pocket ever since that night. Then take a look at me. I'm Smith."

They had to believe it. It was true. There was the miniature, and they knew the face. It had been in all the papers. They looked at it for a while, then at me, and then out of the window. For a minute I felt the rope around my neck. But I had read their minds. They were a bit stunned, but they believed me. They were ashamed of the things they had hinted about Mrs. Blessing, that first day out. It was all right. All they wanted was for someone to say the right thing, and finally a little wrinkled fellow, who had been one of the craziest to hang Murray, said it.

"Don't be scared," he said, good-naturedly. "Nobody's going to tell on you. Come on, you fellows. This is the last ballot. Not guilty — and that goes for Russell, too!"

I can tell about it now. It was a long time ago; and I'm a long way off.

PHILOMEL COTTAGE

by AGATHA CHRISTIE

A masterpiece of horrific suspense. Naturally. Agatha Christie wrote it.

"Good-bye, darling."

"Good-bye, sweetheart."

Alix Martin stood leaning over the small rustic gate, watching the retreating figure of her husband, as he walked down the road in the direction of the village.

Presently he turned a bend and was lost to sight, but Alix still stayed in the same position, absent-mindedly smoothing a lock of the rich brown hair which had blown across her face, her eyes far away and dreamy.

Alix Martin was not beautiful, nor even, strictly speaking, pretty. But her face, the face of a woman no longer in her first youth, was irradiated and softened until her former colleagues of the old office days would hardly have recognised her. Miss Alix King had been a trim businesslike young woman, efficient, slightly brusque in manner, obviously capable and matter-of-fact. She had made the least, not the most, of her beautiful brown hair. Her mouth, not ungenerous in its lines, had always been severely compressed. Her clothes had been neat and suitable without a hint of coquetry.

Alix had graduated in a hard school. For fifteen years, from the age of eighteen until she was thirty-three, she had kept herself (and for seven years of the time, an invalid mother) by her work as a shorthand typist. It was the struggle for existence which had hardened the soft lines of her girlish face.

True, there had been romance — of a kind. Dick Windyford, a fellow clerk. Very much of a woman at heart, Alix had always known without seeming to know that he cared. Outwardly they had been friends, nothing more. Out of his slender salary, Dick had been hard put to it to provide for the schooling of a younger brother. For the moment, he could not think of marriage. Nevertheless when Alix envisaged the future, it was with the half acknowledged certainty that she would one day be Dick's wife. They cared for one another, so she would have put it, but they were both sensible people. Plenty of time, no need to do anything rash. So the years had gone on.

And then suddenly deliverance from daily toil had come to the girl in the most unexpected manner. A distant cousin had died leaving her money to Alix. A few thousand pounds, enough to bring in a couple of hundred a year. To Alix, it was freedom, life, independence. Now she and Dick need wait no longer.

But Dick reacted unexpectedly. He had never directly spoken of his love to Alix, now he seemed less inclined to do so than ever. He avoided her, became morose and gloomy. Alix was quick to realise the truth. She had become a woman of means. Delicacy and pride stood in the way of Dick's asking her to be his wife.

She liked him none the worse for it and was indeed deliberating as to whether she herself might not take the first step when for the second time the unexpected descended upon her.

She met Gerald Martin at a friend's house. He fell violently in love with her and within a week they were engaged. Alix, who had always considered herself "not the falling-in-love kind," was swept clean off her feet.

Unwittingly she had found the way to arouse her former lover. Dick Windyford had come to her stammering with rage and anger.

"The man's a perfect stranger to you. You know nothing about him."

"I know that I love him."

"How can you know — in a week?"

"It doesn't take everyone eleven years to find out that they're in love with a girl," cried Alix angrily.

His face went white.

"I've cared for you ever since I met you. I thought that you cared also."

Alix was truthful.

"I thought so too," she admitted. "But that was because I didn't know what love was."

Then Dick had burst out again. Prayers, entreaties, even threats. Threats against the man who had supplanted him. It was amazing to Alix to see the volcano that existed beneath the reserved exterior of the man she had thought she knew so well. Also, it frightened her a little. . . . Dick, of course, couldn't possibly mean the things he was saying, the threats of vengeance against Gerald Martin. He was angry, that was all. . . .

Her thoughts had gone back to that interview now, on this sunny morning, as she leant on the gate of the cottage. She had been married a month, and she was idyllically happy. Yet, in the momentary absence of the husband who was everything to her, a tinge of anxiety invaded her perfect happiness, and the cause of that anxiety was Dick Windyford.

Three times since her marriage she had dreamed the same dream. The environment differed, but the main facts were always the same. She saw her husband lying dead and Dick Windyford standing over him, and she knew clearly and distinctly that his was the hand which had dealt the fatal blow.

But horrible though that was, there was something more horrible still — horrible, that was, on awakening, for in the dream it seemed perfectly natural and inevitable. *She, Alix Martin, was glad that her husband was dead* — she stretched out grateful hands to the murderer, sometimes she thanked him. The dream always ended the same way, with herself clasped in Dick Windyford's arms.

She had said nothing of this dream to her husband, but secretly it had perturbed her more than she liked to admit. Was it a warning — a warning against Dick Windyford? Had he some secret power which he was trying to establish over her at a distance? She did not know much about hypnotism, but surely she had always heard that persons could not be hypnotised against their will.

Alix was roused from her thoughts by the sharp ringing of the telephone bell from within the house. She entered the cottage, and picked up the receiver. Suddenly she swayed, and put out a hand to keep herself from falling.

"Who did you say was speaking?"

"Why, Alix, what's the matter with your voice? I wouldn't have known it. It's Dick."

"Oh!" said Alix — "Oh! Where — where are you?"

"At the Traveller's Arms — that's the right name, isn't it? Or don't you even know of the existence of your village pub? I'm on my holiday — doing a bit of fishing here. Any objection to my looking you two good people up this evening after dinner?"

"No," said Alix sharply. "You mustn't come."

There was a pause, and Dick's voice, with a subtle alteration in it, spoke again.

"I beg your pardon," he said formally. "Of course I won't bother you —— "

Alix broke in hastily. Of course he must think her behaviour too extraordinary. It was extraordinary. Her nerves must be all to pieces. It wasn't Dick's fault that she had these dreams.

"I only meant that we were — engaged to-night," she explained, trying to make her voice sound as natural as possible. "Won't you — won't you come to dinner to-morrow night?"

But Dick evidently noticed the lack of cordiality in her tone.

"Thanks very much," he said, in the same formal voice. "But I may be moving on any time. Depends upon whether a pal of mine turns up or not. Good-bye, Alix." He paused, and then added hastily, in a different tone, "Best of luck to you, my dear."

Alix hung up the receiver with a feeling of relief.

"He mustn't come here," she repeated to herself. "He mustn't come here. Oh! what a fool I am! To imagine myself into a state like this. All the same, I'm glad he's not coming."

She caught up a rustic rush hat from a table, and passed out into the garden again, pausing to look up at the name carved over the porch, Philomel Cottage.

"Isn't it a very fanciful name?" she had said to Gerald once before they were married. He had laughed.

"You little Cockney," he had said, affectionately. "I don't believe you have ever heard a nightingale. I'm glad you haven't. Nightingales should sing only for lovers. We'll hear them together on a summer's evening outside our own home."

And at the remembrance of how they had indeed heard them, Alix, standing in the doorway of her home, blushed happily.

It was Gerald who had found Philomel Cottage. He had come to Alix bursting with excitement. He had found the very spot for them — unique — a gem — the chance of a lifetime. And when Alix had seen it, she too was captivated. It was true that the situation was rather lonely — they were two miles from the nearest village — but the cottage itself was so exquisite with its old-world appearance, and its solid comfort of bathrooms, hot-water system, electric light and telephone, that she fell a victim to its charm immediately. And then a hitch occurred. The owner, a rich man who had made it his whim, declined to rent it. He would only sell.

Gerald Martin, though possessed of a good income, was unable to touch his capital. He could raise at most a thousand pounds. The owner was asking three. But Alix, who had set her heart on the place, came to the rescue. Her own capital was easily realised, being in bearer bonds. She would contribute half of it to the purchase of the home. So Philomel Cottage became their very own, and never for a minute had Alix regretted the choice. It was true that servants did not appreciate the rural solitude — indeed at the moment they had none at all — but Alix, who had been starved of domestic life, thoroughly enjoyed cooking dainty little meals and looking after the house.

The garden which was magnificently stocked with flowers was attended to by an old man from the village who came twice a week, and Gerald Martin, who was keen on gardening, spent most of his time there.

As she rounded the corner of the house, Alix was surprised to see the old gardener in question busy over the flower beds. She was surprised because his days for work were Mondays and Fridays, and to-day was Wednesday.

"Why, George, what are you doing here?" she asked, as she came towards him.

The old man straightened up with a chuckle, touching the brim of an aged cap.

"I thought as how you'd be surprised, Ma'am. But 'tis this way. There be a Fête over to Squire's on Friday, and I sez to myself, I sez, neith Mr. Martin nor yet his good lady won't take it amiss if I comes for once on a Tuesday instead of a Friday."

"That's quite all right," said Alix, "I hope you'll enjoy yourself at the Fête."

"I reckon to," said George simply. "It's a fine thing to be able to eat your fill and know all the time as it's not you as is paying for it.

Squire allus has a proper sit-down tea for 'is tenants. Then I thought too, Ma'am, as I might as well see you before you goes away so as to learn your wishes for the borders. You'll have no idea when you'll be back, Ma'am, I suppose."

"But I'm not going away."

George stared at her.

"Bain't you going to Lunnon to-morrow?"

"No. What put such an idea into your head?"

George jerked his head over his shoulder.

"Met Maister down to village yesterday. He told me you was both going away to Lunnon to-morrow, and it was uncertain when you'd be back again."

"Nonsense," said Alix, laughing. "You must have misunderstood him."

All the same, she wondered exactly what it could have been that Gerald had said to lead the old man into such a curious mistake. Going to London? She never wanted to go to London again.

"I hate London," she said suddenly and harshly.

"Ah!" said George placidly. "I must have been mistook somehow, and yet he said it plain enough it seemed to me. I'm glad you're stopping on here — I don't hold with all this gallivanting about, and I don't think nothing of Lunnon. I've never needed to go there. Too many moty cars — that's the trouble nowadays. Once people have got a moty car, blessed if they can stay still anywheres. Mr. Ames, wot used to have this house — nice peaceful sort of gentleman he was until he bought one of them things. Hadn't 'ad it a month before he put up this cottage for sale. A tidy lot he'd spent on it, too, with taps in all the bedrooms, and the electric light and all. 'You'll never see your money back,' I sez to him. 'It's not everyone as'll have your fad for washing themselves in every room in the house, in a manner of speaking.' But 'George,' he sez to me, 'I'll get every penny of two thousand pounds for this house.' And sure enough, he did."

"He got three thousand," said Alix, smiling.

"Two thousand," repeated George. "The sum he was asking was talked of at the time. And a very high figure it was thought to be."

"It really was three thousand," said Alix.

"Women never understand figures," said George, unconvinced.

"You'll not tell me that Mr. Ames had the face to stand up to you, and say three thousand brazen like in a loud voice."

"He didn't say it to me," said Alix. "He said it to my husband."

George stooped again to his flower bed.

"The price was two thousand," he said obstinately.

Alix did not trouble to argue with him. Moving to one of the further beds, she began to pick an armful of flowers. The sunshine, the scent of the flowers, the faint hum of hurrying bees, all conspired to make the day a perfect thing.

As she moved with her fragrant posy towards the house, Alix noticed a small dark-green object, peeping from between some leaves in one of the beds. She stooped and picked it up, recognising it for her husband's pocket diary. It must have fallen from his pocket when he was weeding.

She opened it, scanning the entries with some amusement. Almost from the beginning of their married life, she had realised that the impulsive and emotional Gerald had the uncharacteristic virtues of neatness and method. He was extremely fussy about meals being punctual, and always planned his day ahead with the accuracy of a time-table. This morning, for instance, he had announced that he should start for the village after breakfast — at 10:15. And at 10:15 to the minute he had left the house.

Looking through the diary, she was amused to notice the entry on the date of May 14th. "Marry Alix St. Peter's 2:30."

"The big silly," murmured Alix to herself, turning the pages.

Suddenly she stopped.

"Thursday, June 18th — why that's to-day."

In the space for that day was written in Gerald's neat precise hand: "9 p.m." Nothing else. What had Gerald planned to do at 9 p.m.? Alix wondered. She smiled to herself as she realised that had this been a story, like those she had so often read, the diary would doubtless have furnished her with some sensational revelation. It would have had in it for certain the name of another woman. She fluttered the back pages idly. There were dates, appointments, cryptic references to business deals, but only one woman's name — her own.

Yet as she slipped the book into her pocket and went on with her flowers to the house, she was aware of a vague uneasiness. Those words of Dick Windyford's recurred to her, almost as though he had been at her elbow repeating them: "The man's a perfect stranger to you. You know nothing about him."

It was true. What did she know about him? After all, Gerald was forty. In forty years there must have been women in his life. . . .

Alix shook herself impatiently. She must not give way to these thoughts. She had a far more instant preoccupation to deal with. Should she, or should she not, tell her husband that Dick Windyford had rung her up?

There was the possibility to be considered that Gerald might have already run across him in the village. But in that case he would be sure to mention it to her immediately upon his return and matters would be taken out of her hands. Otherwise — what? Alix was aware of a distinct desire to say nothing about it. Gerald had always shown himself kindly disposed towards the other. "Poor devil," he had said once, "I believe he's just as keen on you as I am. Hard luck on him to be shelved." He had had no doubts of Alix's own feelings.

If she told him, he was sure to suggest asking Dick Windyford to Philomel Cottage. Then she would have to explain that Dick had proposed it himself, and that she had made an excuse to prevent his coming. And when he asked her why she had done so, what could she say? Tell him her dream? But he would only laugh — or worse see that she attached an importance to it which he did not. Then he would think — oh! he might think anything!

In the end, rather shamefacedly, Alix decided to say nothing. It was the first secret she had ever kept from her husband, and the consciousness of it made her feel ill at ease.

When she heard Gerald returning from the village shortly before lunch, she hurried into the kitchen and pretended to be busy with the cooking so as to hide her confusion.

It was evident at once that Gerald had seen nothing of Dick Windyford. Alix felt at once relieved and embarrassed. She was definitely committed now to a policy of concealment. For the rest of the day she was nervous and absent-minded, starting at every sound, but her husband seemed to notice nothing. He himself seemed to have his thoughts far away, and once or twice she had to speak a second time before he answered some trivial remark of hers.

It was not until after their simple evening meal, when they were sitting in the oak-beamed living room with the windows thrown open to let in the sweet night air scented with the perfume of the mauve and white stocks that grew outside, that Alix remembered the pocket diary, and seized upon it gladly to distract her thoughts from their doubt and perplexity.

"Here's something you've been watering the flowers with," she said, and threw it into his lap.

"Dropped it in the border, did I?"

"Yes, I know all your secrets now."

"Not guilty," said Gerald, shaking his head.

"What about your assignation at nine o'clock to-night?"

"Oh! that —" he seemed taken aback for a moment, then he smiled as though something afforded him particular amusement. "It's an assignation with a particularly nice girl, Alix. She's got brown hair and blue eyes and she's particularly like you."

"I don't understand," said Alix, with mock severity. "You're evading the point."

"No, I'm not. As a matter of fact, that's a reminder that I'm going to develop some negatives to-night, and I want you to help me."

Gerald Martin was an enthusiastic photographer. He had a somewhat old-fashioned camera, but with an excellent lens, and he developed his own plates in a small cellar which he had had fitted up as a dark room. He was never tired of posing Alix in different positions.

"And it must be done at nine o'clock precisely," said Alix teasingly.

Gerald looked a little vexed.

"My dear girl," he said with a shade of testiness in his manner. "One should always plan a thing for a definite time. Then one gets through one's work properly."

Alix sat for a minute or two in silence watching her husband as he lay in his chair smoking, his dark head flung back and the clear-cut lines of his clean-shaven face showing up against the sombre background. And suddenly, from some unknown source, a wave of panic surged over her, so that she cried out before she could stop herself. "Oh! Gerald, I wish I knew more about you."

Her husband turned an astonished face upon her.

"But, my dear Alix, you do know all about me. I've told you of my boyhood in Northumberland, of my life in South Africa, and these last ten years in Canada which have brought me success."

"Oh! business!"

Gerald laughed suddenly.

"I know what you mean — love affairs. You women are all the same. Nothing interests you but the personal element."

Alix felt her throat go dry, as she muttered indistinctly: "Well, but there must have been — love affairs. I mean — If I only knew —— "

There was silence again for a minute or two. Gerald Martin was frowning, a look of indecision on his face. When he spoke, it was gravely, without a trace of his former bantering manner.

"Do you think it wise, Alix — this — Bluebeard's chamber business? There have been women in my life, yes. I don't deny it. You wouldn't believe me if I did deny it. But I can swear to you truthfully that not one of them meant anything to me."

There was a ring of sincerity in his voice which comforted the listening wife.

"Satisfied, Alix?" he asked, with a smile. Then he looked at her with a shade of curiosity.

"What has turned your mind onto these unpleasant subjects tonight of all nights? You never mentioned them before."

Alix got up and began to walk about restlessly.

"Oh! I don't know," she said. "I've been nervy all day."

"That's odd," said Gerald, in a low voice, as though speaking to himself. "That's very odd."

"Why is it odd?"

"Oh! my dear girl, don't flash out at me so. I only said it was odd because as a rule you're so sweet and serene."

Alix forced a smile.

"Everything's conspired to annoy me to-day," she confessed. "Even old George had got some ridiculous idea into his head that we were going away to London. He said you had told him so."

"Where did you see him?" asked Gerald sharply.

"He came to work to-day instead of Friday."

"The old fool," said Gerald angrily.

Alix stared in surprise. Her husband's face was convulsed with rage. She had never seen him so angry. Seeing her astonishment, Gerald made an effort to regain control of himself.

"Well, he *is* a stupid old fool," he protested.

"What can you have said to make him think that?"

"I? I never said anything. At least — oh! yes, I remember, I made some weak joke about being 'off to London in the morning' and I suppose he took it seriously. Or else he didn't hear properly. You undeceived him, of course?"

He waited anxiously for her reply.

"Of course, but he's the sort of old man who if once he gets an idea in his head — well, it isn't so easy to get it out again."

Then she told him of the gardener's insistence on the sum asked for the cottage.

Gerald was silent for a minute or two, then he said slowly:

"Ames was willing to take two thousand in cash and the remaining thousand on mortgage. That's the origin of that mistake, I fancy."

"Very likely," agreed Alix.

Then she looked up at the clock, and pointed to it with a mischievous finger.

"We ought to be getting down to it, Gerald. Five minutes behind schedule."

A very peculiar smile came over Gerald Martin's face.

"I've changed my mind," he said quietly. "I shall not do any photography to-night."

A woman's mind is a curious thing. When she went to bed that Thursday night, Alix's mind was contented and at rest. Her momentarily assailed happiness reasserted itself, triumphant as of yore.

But by the evening of the following day, she realised that some subtle forces were at work undermining it. Dick Windyford had not rung up again, nevertheless she felt what she supposed to be his influence at work. Again and again those words of his recurred to her. "The man's a perfect stranger. You know nothing about him." And with them came the memory of her husband's face, photographed clearly on her brain as he said: "Do you think it wise, Alix, this — Bluebeard's chamber business?" Why had he said that? What had he meant by those words?

There had been warning in them — a hint of menace. It was as though he had said in effect — "You had better not pry into my life, Alix. You may get a nasty shock if you do." True, a few minutes later, he had sworn to her that there had been no woman in his life that mattered — but Alix tried in vain to recapture her sense of his sincerity. Was he not bound to swear that?

By Saturday morning, Alix had convinced herself that there had been a woman in Gerald's life — a Bluebeard's chamber that he had sedulously sought to conceal from her. Her jealousy, slow to awaken, was now rampant.

Was it a woman he had been going to meet that night, at 9 p.m.? Was his story of photographs to develop a lie invented upon the spur of the moment? With a queer sense of shock Alix realised that ever since she had found that pocket diary she had been in torment. And there had been nothing in it. That was the irony of the whole thing.

Three days ago she would have sworn that she knew her husband through and through. Now it seemed to her that he was a stranger of whom she knew nothing. She remembered his unreasonable anger against old George, so at variance with his usual good-tempered manner. A small thing, perhaps, but it showed her that she did not really know the man who was her husband.

There were several little things required on Saturday from the village to carry them over the week-end. In the afternoon Alix suggested that she should go for them whilst Gerald remained in the garden, but somewhat to her surprise he opposed this plan vehemently, and insisted on going himself whilst she remained at home. Alix was forced to give way to him, but his insistence surprised and alarmed her. Why was he so anxious to prevent her going to the village?

Suddenly an explanation suggested itself to her which made the whole thing clear. Was it not possible that, whilst saying nothing to her, Gerald had indeed come across Dick Windyford? Her own jealousy, entirely dormant at the time of their marriage, had only developed afterwards. Might it not be the same with Gerald? Might he not be anxious to prevent her seeing Dick Windyford again? This explanation was so consistent with the facts, and so comforting to Alix's perturbed mind, that she embraced it eagerly.

Yet when tea time had come and past, she was restless and ill at ease. She was struggling with a temptation that had assailed her ever since Gerald's departure. Finally, pacifying her conscience with the assurance that the room did need a thorough tidying, she went upstairs to her husband's dressing room. She took a duster with her to keep up the pretense of housewifery.

"If I were only sure," she repeated to herself. "If I could only be sure."

In vain she told herself that anything compromising would have been destroyed ages ago. Against that she argued that men do sometimes keep the most damning piece of evidence through an exaggerated sentimentality.

In the end Alix succumbed. Her cheeks burning with the shame of her action, she hunted breathlessly through packets of letters and documents, turned out the drawers, even went through the pockets of her husband's clothes. Only two drawers eluded her, the lower drawer of the chest of drawers, and the small right-hand drawer of the writing desk were both locked. But Alix was by now lost to all shame. In one of those drawers she was convinced that she would find evidence of this imaginary woman of the past who obsessed her.

She remembered that Gerald had left his keys lying carelessly on the sideboard downstairs. She fetched them and tried them one by one. The third key fitted the writing table drawer. Alix pulled it open eagerly. There was a cheque book, and a wallet well stuffed with notes, and at the back of the drawer a packet of letters tied up with a piece of tape.

Her breath coming unevenly, Alix untied the tape. Then a deep burning blush overspread her face, and she dropped the letters back into the drawer, closing and relocking it. For the letters were her own, written to Gerald Martin before she married him.

She turned now to the chest of drawers, more with a wish to feel that she had left nothing undone than from any expectation of finding what she sought. She was shamed and almost convinced of the madness of her obsession.

To her annoyance none of the keys on Gerald's bunch fitted the drawer in question. Not to be defeated, Alix went into the other rooms and brought back a selection of keys with her. To her satisfaction, the key of the spare room wardrobe also fitted the chest of drawers. She unlocked the drawer and pulled it open. But there was nothing in it but a roll of newspaper clippings already dirty and discoloured with age.

Alix breathed a sigh of relief. Nevertheless she glanced at the clippings, curious to know what subject had interested Gerald so much that he had taken the trouble to keep the dusty roll. They were nearly all American papers, dated some seven years ago, and dealing with the trial of the notorious swindler and bigamist, Charles LeMaitre. LeMaitre had been suspected of doing away with his women victims. A skeleton had been found beneath the floor of one of the houses he had rented, and most of the women he had "married" had never been heard of again.

He had defended himself from the charge with consummate skill, aided by some of the best legal talent in the United States. The Scottish verdict of "Non proven" might perhaps have stated the case best. In its absence, he was found Not Guilty on the capital charge, though sentenced to a long term of imprisonment on the other charges preferred against him.

Alix remembered the excitement caused by the case at the time, and also the sensation aroused by the escape of LeMaitre some three years later. He had never been recaptured. The personality of the man and his extraordinary power over women had been discussed at great length in the English papers at the time, together with an account of his excitability in court, his passionate protestations, and his occasional sudden physical collapses, due to the fact that he had a weak heart, though the ignorant accredited it to his dramatic powers.

There was a picture of him in one of the clippings Alix held, and she studied it with some interest — a long-bearded scholarly-looking gentleman. It reminded her of someone, but for the moment she could not tell who that someone was. She had never known that Gerald took an interest in crime and famous trials, though she knew that it was a hobby with many men.

Who was it the face reminded her of? Suddenly, with a shock, she realised that it was Gerald himself. The eye and brow bore a strong resemblance to him. Perhaps he had kept the cutting for that reason. Her eyes went on to the paragraph beside the picture. Certain dates, it seemed, had been entered in the accused's pocket book, and it was contended that these were dates when he had done away with his victims. Then a woman gave evidence and identified the prisoner positively by the fact that he had a mole on his left wrist, just below the palm of the left hand.

Alix dropped the papers from a nerveless hand, and swayed as she stood. *On his left wrist, just below the palm, Gerald had a small scar. . . .*

The room whirled round her. . . . Afterwards it struck her as strange that she should have leaped at once to such absolute certainty. Gerald Martin was Charles LeMaitre! She knew it and accepted it in a flash. Disjointed fragments whirled through her brain, like pieces of a jig-saw puzzle fitting into place.

The money paid for the house — her money — her money only. The bearer bonds she had entrusted to his keeping. Even her dream appeared in its true significance. Deep down in her, her subconscious self had always feared Gerald Martin and wished to escape from him. And it was to Dick Windyford this self of hers had looked for help. That, too, was why she was able to accept the truth so easily, without doubt or hesitation. She was to have been another of LeMaitre's victims. Very soon, perhaps.

A half cry escaped her as she remembered something. Thursday 9 p.m. The cellar, with the flagstones that were so easily raised. Once before, he had buried one of his victims in a cellar. It had been all planned for Thursday night. But to write it down beforehand in that methodical manner — insanity! No, it was logical. Gerald always made a memorandum of his engagements — murder was, to him, a business proposition like any other.

But what had saved her? What could possibly have saved her? Had he relented at the last minute? No — in a flash the answer came to her. Old George. She understood now her husband's uncontrollable anger. Doubtless he had paved the way by telling everyone he met that they were going to London the next day. Then George had come to work unexpectedly, had mentioned London to her, and she had contradicted the story. Too risky to do away with her that night, with old George repeating that conversation. But what an escape! If she had not happened to mention that trivial matter — Alix shuddered.

But there was no time to be lost. She must get away at once — before he came back. For nothing on earth would she spend another night under the same roof with him. She hurriedly replaced the roll of clippings in the drawer, shut it to and locked it.

And then she stayed motionless as though frozen to stone. She had heard the creak of the gate into the road. Her husband had returned.

For a moment Alix stayed as though petrified, then she crept on tiptoe to the window, looking out from behind the shelter of the curtain.

Yes, it was her husband. He was smiling to himself and humming a little tune. In his hand he held an object which almost made the terrified girl's heart stop beating. It was a brand new spade.

Alix leaped to a knowledge born of instinct. *It was to be tonight. . . .*

But there was still a chance. Gerald, still humming his little tune, went round to the back of the house.

"He's going to put it in the cellar — ready," thought Alix with a shiver.

Without hesitating a moment, she ran down the stairs and out of the cottage. But just as she emerged from the door, her husband came round the other side of the house.

"Hullo," he said. "Where are you running off to in such a hurry?"

Alix strove desperately to appear calm and as usual. Her chance was gone for the moment, but if she was careful not to arouse his suspicions, it would come again later. Even now, perhaps. . . .

"I was going to walk to the end of the lane and back," she said, in a voice that sounded weak and uncertain to her own ears.

"Right," said Gerald, "I'll come with you."

"No — please, Gerald. I'm — nervy, headachy — I'd rather go alone."

He looked at her attentively. She fancied a momentary suspicion gleamed in his eye.

"What's the matter with you, Alix? You're pale — trembling."

"Nothing," she forced herself to be brusque — smiling. "I've got a headache, that's all. A walk will do me good."

"Well, it's no good your saying you don't want me," declared Gerald with his easy laugh. "I'm coming whether you want me or not."

She dared not protest further. If he suspected that she *knew* ——

With an effort she managed to regain something of her normal manner. Yet she had an uneasy feeling that he looked at her sideways every now and then, as though not quite satisfied. She felt that his suspicions were not completely allayed.

When they returned to the house, he insisted on her lying down, and brought some eau de cologne to bathe her temples. He was, as ever, the devoted husband, yet Alix felt herself as helpless as though bound hand and foot in a trap.

Not for a minute would he leave her alone. He went with her into the kitchen and helped her to bring in the simple cold dishes she had already prepared. Supper was a meal that choked her, yet she forced herself to eat, and even to appear gay and natural. She knew now that she was fighting for her life. She was alone with this man, miles from help, absolutely at his mercy. Her only chance was so to lull his suspicions that he would leave her alone for a few moments — long enough for her to get to the telephone in the hall and summon assistance. That was her only hope now. He would overtake her if she took to flight long before she could reach assistance.

A momentary hope flashed over her as she remembered how he had abandoned his plan before. Suppose she told him that Dick Windyford was coming up to see them that evening?

The words trembled on her lips — then she rejected them hastily. This man would not be baulked a second time. There was a determination, an elation underneath his calm bearing that sickened her. She would only precipitate the crime. He would murder her there and then, and calmly ring up Dick Windyford with a tale of having been suddenly called away. Oh! if only Dick Windyford were coming to the house this evening. If Dick ——

A sudden idea flashed into her mind. She looked sharply sideways at her husband as though she feared that he might read her mind. With the forming of a plan, her courage was reinforced. She became so completely natural in manner that she marvelled at herself. She felt that Gerald now was completely reassured.

She made the coffee and took it out to the porch where they often sat on fine evenings.

"By the way," said Gerald suddenly. "We'll do those photographs later."

Alix felt a shiver run through her, but she replied nonchalantly:
"Can't you manage alone? I'm rather tired to-night."

"It won't take long." He smiled to himself. "And I can promise
you you won't be tired afterwards."

The words seemed to amuse him. Alix shuddered. Now or never
was the time to carry out her plan.

She rose to her feet.

"I'm just going to telephone to the butcher," she announced nonchalantly. "Don't you bother to move."

"To the butcher? At this time of night?"

"His shop's shut, of course, silly. But he's in his house all right.
And to-morrow's Saturday, and I want him to bring me some veal
cutlets early, before someone else grabs them from him. The old dear
will do anything for me."

She passed quickly into the house, closing the door behind her.
She heard Gerald say, "Don't shut the door," and was quick with
her light reply. "It keeps the moths out. I hate moths. Are you
afraid I'm going to make love to the butcher, silly?"

Once inside she snatched down the telephone receiver and gave
the number of the Traveller's Arms. She was put through at once.

"Mr. Windyford? Is he still there? May I speak to him?"

Then her heart gave a sickening thump. The door was pushed
open and her husband came into the hall.

"Do go away, Gerald," she said pettishly. "I hate anyone listening
when I'm telephoning."

He merely laughed and threw himself into a chair.

"Sure it really is the butcher you're telephoning to?" he quizzed.

Alix was in despair. Her plan had failed. In a minute Dick
Windyford would come to the phone. Should she risk all and cry
out an appeal for help? Would he grasp what she meant before
Gerald wrenched her away from the phone? Or would he merely
treat it as a practical joke?

And then as she nervously depressed and released the little key
in the receiver she was holding, which permits the voice to be heard
or not heard at the other end, another plan flashed into her head.

"It will be difficult," she thought. "It means keeping my head,
and thinking of the right words, and not faltering for a moment,
but I believe I could do it. I *must* do it."

And at that minute she heard Dick Windyford's voice at the other end of the phone.

Alix drew a deep breath. Then she depressed the key firmly and spoke.

"Mrs. Martin speaking — from Philomel Cottage. *Please come* (she released the key) to-morrow morning with six nice veal cutlets (she depressed the key again). *It's very important* (she released the key). Thank you so much, Mr. Hexworthy, you don't mind my ringing you up so late, I hope, but those veal cutlets are really a matter of (she depressed the key again) *life or death* . . . (she released it). Very well — to-morrow morning — (she depressed it) *as soon as possible* . . ."

She replaced the receiver on the hook and turned to face her husband, breathing hard.

"So that's how you talk to your butcher, is it?" said Gerald.

"It's the feminine touch," said Alix lightly.

She was simmering with excitement. He had suspected nothing. Surely Dick, even if he didn't understand, would come.

She passed into the sitting room and switched on the electric light. Gerald followed her.

"You seem very full of spirits now," he said, watching her curiously.

"Yes," said Alix. "My headache's gone."

She sat down in her usual seat and smiled at her husband, as he sank into his own chair opposite her. She was saved. It was only five and twenty past eight. Long before nine o'clock Dick would have arrived.

"I didn't think much of that coffee you gave me," complained Gerald. "It tasted very bitter."

"It's a new kind I was trying. We won't have it again if you don't like it, dear."

Alix took up a piece of needlework and began to stitch. She felt complete confidence in her own ability to keep up the part of the devoted wife. Gerald read a few pages of his book. Then he glanced up at the clock and tossed the book away.

"Half past eight. Time to go down to the cellar and start work."

The work slipped from Alix's fingers.

"Oh! not yet. Let us wait until nine o'clock."

"No, my girl, half past eight. That's the time I fixed. You'll be able to get to bed all the earlier."

"But I'd rather wait until nine."

"Half past eight," said Gerald obstinately. "You know when I fix a time, I always stick to it. Come along, Alix. I'm not going to wait a minute longer."

Alix looked up at him, and in spite of herself she felt a wave of terror slide over her. The mask had been lifted; Gerald's hands were twitching; his eyes were shining with excitement; he was con‐ tinually passing his tongue over his dry lips. He no longer cared to conceal his excitement.

Alix thought: "It's true — *he can't wait* — he's like a madman."

He strode over to her, and jerked her onto her feet with a hand on her shoulder.

"Come on, my girl — or I'll carry you there."

His tone was gay, but there was an undisguised ferocity behind it that appalled her. With a supreme effort she jerked herself free and clung cowering against the wall. She was powerless. She couldn't get away — she couldn't do anything — and he was coming towards her.

"Now, Alix —— "

"No — no."

She screamed, her hands held out impotently to ward him off.

"Gerald — stop — I've got something to tell you, something to confess . . ."

He did stop.

"To confess?" he said curiously.

"Yes, to confess." She went on desperately, seeking to hold his arrested attention. "Something I ought to have told you before."

A look of contempt swept over his face. The spell was broken.

"A former lover, I suppose," he sneered.

"No," said Alix. "Something else. You'd call it, I expect — yes, you'd call it a crime."

And at once she saw that she had struck the right note. Again his attention was arrested, held. Seeing that, her nerve came back to her. She felt mistress of the situation once more.

"You had better sit down again," she said quietly.

She herself crossed the room to her old chair and sat down. She even stooped and picked up her needlework. But behind her calmness she was thinking and inventing feverishly. For the story she invented must hold his interest until help arrived.

"I told you," she said, "that I had been a shorthand typist for fifteen years. That was not entirely true. There were two intervals. The first occurred when I was twenty-two. I came across a man, an elderly man with a little property. He fell in love with me and asked me to marry him. I accepted. We were married." She paused. "I induced him to insure his life in my favor."

She saw a sudden keen interest spring up in her husband's face, and went on with renewed assurance.

"During the war I worked for a time in a Hospital Dispensary. There I had the handling of all kinds of rare drugs and poisons. Yes, poisons."

She paused reflectively. He was keenly interested now, not a doubt of it. The murderer is bound to have an interest in murder. She had gambled on that, and succeeded. She stole a glance at the clock. It was five and twenty to nine.

"There is one poison — it is a little white powder. A pinch of it means death. You know something about poisons, perhaps?"

She put the question in some trepidation. If he did, she would have to be careful.

"No," said Gerald. "I know very little about them."

She drew a breath of relief. This made her task easier.

"You have heard of hyoscine, of course. This is a drug that acts much the same way, but it is absolutely untraceable. Any doctor would give a certificate of heart failure. I stole a small quantity of this drug and kept it by me."

She paused, marshalling her forces.

"Go on," said Gerald.

"No. I'm afraid. I can't tell you. Another time."

"Now," he said impatiently. "I want to hear."

"We had been married a month. I was very good to my elderly husband, very kind and devoted. He spoke in praise of me to all the neighbours. Everyone knew what a devoted wife I was. I always made his coffee myself every evening. One evening, when we were alone together, I put a pinch of the deadly alkaloid in his cup."

Alix paused, and carefully rethreaded her needle. She, who had never acted in her life, rivalled the greatest actress in the world at this moment. She was actually living the part of the cold-blooded poisoner.

"It was very peaceful. I sat watching him. Once he gasped a little and asked for air. I opened the window. Then he said he could not move from his chair. Presently he died."

She stopped, smiling. It was a quarter to nine. Surely they would come soon.

"How much," said Gerald, "was the insurance money?"

"About two thousand pounds. I speculated with it, and lost it. I went back to my office work. But I never meant to remain there long. Then I met another man. I had stuck to my maiden name at the office. He didn't know I had been married before. He was a younger man, rather good-looking, and quite well off. We were married quietly in Sussex. He didn't want to insure his life, but of course he made a will in my favour. He liked me to make his coffee myself also, just as my first husband had done."

Alix smiled reflectively, and added simply:

"I make very good coffee."

Then she went on.

"I had several friends in the village where we were living. They were very sorry for me, with my husband dying suddenly of heart failure one evening after dinner. I didn't quite like the doctor. I don't think he suspected me, but he was certainly very surprised at my husband's sudden death. I don't quite know why I drifted back to the office again. Habit, I suppose. My second husband left about four thousand pounds. I didn't speculate with it this time. I invested it. Then, you see —— "

But she was interrupted. Gerald Martin, his face suffused with blood, half choking, was pointing a shaking forefinger at her.

"The coffee — My God! the coffee!"

She stared at him.

"I understand now why it was bitter. You devil. You've poisoned me."

His hands gripped the arms of his chair. He was ready to spring upon her.

"You've poisoned me."

Alix had retreated from him to the fireplace. Now, terrified, she ᴏpened her lips to deny — and then paused. In another minute he would spring upon her. She summoned all her strength. Her eyes held his steadily, compellingly.

"Yes," she said. "I poisoned you. Already the poison is working. At this minute you can't move from your chair — you can't move —— "

If she could keep him there — even a few minutes ——

Ah! what was that? Footsteps on the road. The creak of the gate. Then footsteps on the path outside. The door of the hall opened ——

"You can't move," she said again.

Then she slipped past him and fled headlong from the room to fall half fainting into Dick Windyford's arms.

"My God! Alix!" he cried.

Then he turned to the man with him, a tall stalwart figure in policeman's uniform.

"Go and see what's been happening in that room."

He laid Alix carefully down on a couch and bent over her.

"My little girl," he murmured. "My poor little girl. What have they been doing to you?"

Her eyelids fluttered and her lips just murmured his name.

Dick was aroused from tumultuous thoughts by the policeman's touching him on the arm.

"There's nothing in that room, sir, but a man sitting in a chair. Looks as though he'd had some kind of bad fright, and —— "

"Yes?"

"Well, sir, he's — dead."

They were startled by hearing Alix's voice. She spoke as though in some kind of dream.

"And presently," she said, almost as though she were quoting from something, "he died. . . ."

FAITH, HOPE AND CHARITY

by IRVIN S. COBB

The genial father of Judge Priest in a wonderfully grim retributive mood.

J
UST outside a sizable New Mexico town the second section of the fast through train coming from the Coast made a short halt. Entering the stretch leading to the yards, the engineer had found the signal set against him; the track ahead was temporarily blocked.

It was a small delay though. Almost at once the semaphore, like the finger of a mechanical wizard, made the warning red light vanish and a green light appear instead; so, at that, the Limited got under way and rolled on into the station for her regular stop.

But before she started up, four travelers quitted her. They got out on the off side, the side farthest away from the town, and that probably explains why none of the crew and none of the other passengers saw them getting out. It helps also to explain why they were not missed until quite some time later.

Their manner of leaving her was decidedly unusual. First, one of the vestibule doors between the third sleeping car and the fourth sleeping car opened and the trap in the floor flipped up briskly under the pressure of an impatient foot on the operating lever. A brace of the departing ones came swiftly into view, one behind the other. True, there was nothing unusual about that. But as they stepped down on the earth they faced about and received the figure of a third person whose limbs dangled and whose head lolled back as they took the dead weight of him into their arms. Next there emerged the fourth and last member of the group, he being the one who had eased the limp figure of Number Three down the car steps into the grasp of his associates.

For a fractional space their shapes made a little huddle in the lee of the vestibule. Looking on, you might have guessed that there was a momentary period of indecision touching on the next step to be taken.

However, this muddle — if that was what it was — right away straightened itself out. Acting with movements which seemed difficult and awkward, the two burden bearers carried their unconscious load down the short embankment and deposited it on the cindery underfooting close against the flank of the slightly built-up right of way.

Number Four bent over the sprawled form and fumbled at it, shoving his hands into first one pocket and then another. In half a minute or less he straightened up and spoke to the remaining pair, at the same time using both hands to shove some article inside the vent of his waistcoat.

"I have got them," he said, speaking with a foreign accent. They pressed toward him, their hands extended.

"Not here and not yet, Señores," he said sharply. "First we make sure of the rest. First you do, please, as I do."

Thereupon he hopped nimbly up the shoulder of the roadbed and headed toward the rear of the halted train, slinking well in under the overhang of the Pullmans. His mates obeyed his example. They kept on until they had passed the tail coach, which was a combination coach, and then they stepped inward between the rails, still maintaining their single-file formation. Immediately the dusk swallowed them up.

There was something peculiar about the way each one of these three plodding pedestrians bore himself. The peculiarity was this: He bore himself like a person engaged in prayer — in a silent perambulating act of piety. His head was tucked in, his face turning neither to the right nor left; his eyes were set steadfastly forward as though upon some invisible goal, his hands clasped primly together in front of him.

Thus and so the marching three plodded on until the train, having got in motion, was out of sight beyond a curve in the approach to the station. Then they checked and came together in a clump, and then, had you been there, you would have understood the reason for their devotional pose. All three of them were wearing handcuffs.

The man who had spoken before unpalmed a key ring which he

was carrying. Working swiftly even in the half-darkness, he made tests of the keys on the ring until he found the proper keys. He freed the wrists of his two fellows. Then one of them took the keys and unlocked his set of bracelets for him.

He, it would seem, was the most forethoughted of the trio. With his heel he kicked shallow gouges in the gritty soil beside the track and buried the handcuffs therein.

After that they briefly confabbed together, and the upshot of the confab was that, having matched for the possession of some object evidently held to be of great value, they separated forces.

One man set off alone on a detour to the southeast, which would carry him around the town. His late companions kept on in a general westerly direction, heading toward the desert which all that day they had been traversing. They footed it fast, as men might foot it who were fleeing for their lives and yet must conserve their strength. As a matter of fact, they were fleeing for their lives. So likewise the one from whom they had just parted was fleeing for his life.

It was partly by chance that these three had been making the transcontinental journey in company. Two of them, Lafitte the Frenchman, and Verdi the Italian who had Anglicized his name and called himself Green, met while lying in jail at San Francisco awaiting deportation to their respective countries. Within a space of a month each had been arrested as a refugee from justice; the formalities for extraditing the pair of them were swiftly completed.

So, to save trouble and expense; to kill, as it were, two birds with one stone, the authorities decided to send them together across to the eastern seaboard where, according to arrangements made by cable, they would be surrendered to police representatives coming from abroad to receive them and transport them back overseas. For the long trip to New York a couple of city detectives had them in custody.

When the train bearing the officers and their charges reached a junction in lower California where the main line connected with a branch line running south to the Mexican border, there came aboard a special agent of the Department of Justice who had with him a prisoner.

This prisoner was one Manuel Gaza, a Spaniard. He also recently had been captured and identified; and he also was destined for return to his own land. It was not by prior agreement that he had been retransferred at this junction point to the same train which carried the Italian and the Frenchman. It just happened so.

It having happened so, the man who had Gaza in tow lost no time in getting acquainted with his San Francisco brethren. For a number of reasons it seemed expedient to all the officers that from here on they should travel as a unit. Accordingly the special agent talked with the Pullman conductor and exchanged the reservations he previously had booked for a compartment adjoining the drawing-room in which the four from the city were riding.

It was on a Friday afternoon that the parties united. Friday evening, at the first call for dinner, the three officers herded their three prisoners forward to the dining car, the passage of the sextet through the aisles causing some small commotion. Their advent into the diner created another little sensation.

Since it was difficult for the handcuffed aliens to handle knife and fork, they were given such food as might readily be eaten with a spoon or with the fingers — soups and omelets and soft vegetables and pie or rice pudding. The detectives ate fish. They shared between them a double order of imported kippers.

Presumably they were the only persons on the train who that day had chosen the kippered herrings. Shortly, the special agent was giving private thanks that his church prescribed no dietetic regulations for Friday, because within an hour or two after leaving the table, the San Francisco men were suffering from violent cramps — ptomaine poison had them helpless.

One seemed to be dangerously ill. That night near the border between California and Arizona he was taken off the train and carried to a hospital. During the wait at the station, a local physician dosed the second and lesser sufferer, whose name was McAvoy, and when he had been somewhat relieved, the doctor gave him a shot of something in the arm and said he ought to be up and about within twenty-four hours.

Through the night McAvoy slept in the lower berth of the compartment and the special agent sat up, with the communicating door open, to guard the aliens, who were bedded in the so-called drawing-room.

Their irons stayed on their wrists; their lone warden was accepting no foolish odds against himself. He had taken the precaution to transfer the keys of the Frenchman's handcuffs and the Italian's handcuffs from McAvoy's keeping to his own, slipping them on his key ring, but this had been done in case McAvoy should become seriously ill en route and it should devolve upon him to make a lap of the journey single-handed.

Next morning McAvoy was much easier but he felt weak, he said, and drowsy. Given a full twelve hours of rest, though, he thought he would be able to go on guard when the nightfall came.

So he lay in his berth, and the special agent occupied an end of the drawing-room sofa. The trapped fugitives sat smoking cigarettes, and when the officer was not too near, talking among themselves.

Mainly they talked in English, a language which Gaza the Spaniard and Lafitte the Frenchman spoke fairly well. Verdi or Green, as the case might be, had little English at his command, but Gaza, who had spent three years in Naples, spoke Italian; and so when Verdi used his own tongue, Gaza could interpret for the Frenchman's benefit. They were allowed to quit the drawing-room only for meals.

When dinner hour came on that second evening of their trip, McAvoy was in a doze. So the Department of Justice man did not disturb him.

"Come on, boys," he said to the three aliens; "time to eat again."

He lined them up in front of him in the corridor and they started the regular processional. It was just at that moment that the train broke its rhythmic refrain and began to clack and creak and slow for that unscheduled stop outside that New Mexico town. By the time they had reached the second car on ahead, she'd almost stopped and was lurching and jerking.

In the vestibule beyond that second car the special agent was in the act of stepping across the iron floor lip of the connection when a particularly brisk joggle caused him to lose his hat. He gave a small exclamation and bent to recover it. Doing so, he jostled Gaza, the third man in the line and therefore the next to him.

The agile Spaniard was quick to seize his chance. He half turned, and bringing his chained wrists aloft, sent them down with all his might on the poll of the officer's unprotected skull. The victim of the assault never made a sound — just spraddled on his face and was dead to the world.

No outsider had been witness to the assault. No outsider came along during the few seconds which were required by the late prisoners to open an off-side car door and make their escape after the fashion which already has been described for you. Nobody missed them — for quite a while nobody did.

It wasn't until nearly nine o'clock, when McAvoy had roused up and rung for the porter and begun to ask questions, that a search was made and an alarm raised.

Penned up together through that day, the aliens had matched stories, one story against another. A common plight made them communicative; a common peril caused each to turn with morbid reiteration to his own fatal predicament.

Said the Frenchman to the Spaniard: "He" — indicating his recent cellmate, the Italian — "he knows how with me it stands. With him, I have talked. He speaks not so well the English but sometimes he understands it. Now you shall hear and judge for yourself how bad my situation is."

Graphically, this criminal sketched his past. He had been a Marseilles dock hand. He had killed a woman. She deserved killing, so he killed her. He had been caught, tried, convicted, condemned. While lying in prison, with execution day only a few weeks distant, he had made a getaway.

In disguise he had reached America and here had stayed three years. Then another woman, in a fit of jealousy, betrayed him to the police. He had been living with that woman; to her he had given his confidence. It would appear that women had been his undoing.

"Me, I am as good as dead already. And what a death!" A spasm of shuddering possessed him. "For me the guillotine is waiting. The devil invented it. It is so they go at you with that machine: They strap you flat upon a board. Face downward you are, but you can look up, you can see — that is the worst part. They fit your throat into a grooved shutter; they make it fast. You bring your head back; your eyes are drawn upward, fascinated. Above you, waiting, ready, poised, your eyes see the — the knife."

"But only for a moment do you see it, my friend," said the Spaniard, in the tone of one offering comfort. "Only a moment and then — *pouf* — all over!"

"A moment! I tell you it is an eternity. It must be an eternity. Lying there, you must live a hundred lives, you must die a hundred deaths. And then to have your head taken off your body, to be all at once in two pieces. Me, I am not afraid of most deaths. But that death by the guillotine — ah-h!"

The Spaniard bent forward. He was sitting alone facing the other two, who shared a seat.

"Listen, Señor," he stated. "Compared with me, you are the lucky one. True, I have not yet been tried — before they could try me I fled away out of that accursed Spain of mine."

"Not tried, eh?" broke in the Frenchman. "Then you have yet a loophole — a chance for escape; and I have none. My trial, as I told you, is behind me."

"You do not know the Spanish courts. It is plain you do not, since you say that," declared the Spaniard. "Those courts — they are greedy for blood. With them, to my kind, there is not mercy; there is only punishment.

"And such a punishment! Wait until you hear. To me when they get me before them they will say: 'The proof is clear against you; the evidence has been thus and so. You are adjudged guilty. You took a life, so your life must be taken. It is the law.'

"Perhaps I say: 'Yes, but that life I took swiftly and in passion and for cause. For that one the end came in an instant, without pain, without lingering, yes, without warning. Since I must pay for it, why cannot I also be made to die very quickly without pain?'

"Will they listen? No, they send me to the garrote. To a great strong chair they tie you — your hands, your feet, your trunk. Your head is against a post, an upright. In that post is a collar — an iron band. They fit that collar about your neck. Then from behind you the executioner turns a screw.

"If he chooses he turns it slowly. The collar tightens, tightens, a knob presses into your spine. You begin to strangle. Oh, I have seen it myself! I know. You expire by inches! I am a brave man, Señores. When one's time comes, one dies. But oh, Señores, if it were any death but that! Better the guillotine than that! Better anything than that!"

He slumped back against the cushions, and rigors passed through him.

It was the Italian's turn. "I was tried in my absence," he explained to the Spaniard. "I was not even there to make my defense — I had thought it expedient to depart. Such is the custom of the courts in my country. They try you behind your back.

"They found me guilty, those judges. In Italy there is no capital punishment, so they sentenced me to life imprisonment. It is to that — that — I now return."

The Spaniard lifted his shoulders; the lifting was eloquent of his meaning.

"Not so fast," said the Italian. "You tell me you lived once in Italy. Have you forgotten what life imprisonment for certain acts means in Italy? It means solitary confinement. It means you are buried alive. They shut you away from everyone in a tight cell. It is a tomb, that is all. You see no one ever; you hear no voice ever. If you cry out, no one answers. Silence, darkness, darkness, silence, until you go mad or die.

"Can you picture what that means to one of my race, to an Italian who must have music, sunshine, talk with his fellows, sight of his fellows? It is in his nature — he must have these things or he is in torture, in constant and everlasting torment. Every hour becomes to him a year, every day a century, until his brain bursts asunder inside his skull.

"Oh, they knew — those fiends who devised this thing — what to an Italian is a million times worse than death — any death. I am the most unfortunate one of the three of us. My penalty is the most dreadful by far."

The others would not have it so. They argued the point with him and with each other all through the day, and twilight found their beliefs unshaken.

Then, under the Spaniard's leadership, came their deliverance out of captivity. It was he who, on the toss-up, won the revolver which they had taken from the person of the senseless special agent. Also it was he who suggested to the Italian that for the time being, at least, they stick together. To this the Italian had agreed, the Marseilles man, Lafitte, already having elected to go on his own.

After the latter, heading east by south, had left them, the Spaniard said reflectively:

"He is optimistic, that one, for all that he seemed so gloomy and downhearted today when speaking of that guillotine of his. He said he now had faith that he would yet dodge his fate. Five minutes after he is off that train he speaks of faith!"

"I cannot go quite so far," answered the Italian. "We are free, but for us there will be still a thousand dangers. So I have not much faith, but I have hope. And you, my friend?"

The Spaniard shrugged his shoulders. His shrug might mean yes or it might mean no. Perhaps he needed his breath. He was going at a jog-trot down the tracks, the Italian alongside him.

Take the man who had faith. Set down as he was in a country utterly strange to him, this one of the fugitives nevertheless made steady progress. He got safely around and by the New Mexico town. He hid in the chaparral until daybreak, then took to a highway running parallel with the railroad.

A "tin canner," which is what they were beginning to call an itinerant motor tourist in those parts, overtook him soon after sunup and gave him a lift to a small way station some forty miles down the line. There he boarded a local train — he had some money on him; not much money but enough — and undetected, he rode that train clear on through to its destination a hundred miles or so farther along.

Other local trains carried him across a corner of Colorado and clear across Kansas. Some forty-eight hours later, he was a guest in a third-rate hotel on a back street in Kansas City, Missouri.

He stayed in that hotel for two days and two nights, biding most of the time in his room on the top floor of the six-story building, going down only for his meals and for newspapers. The food he had to have; the newspapers gave him information, of a sort, of the hunt for the three fugitives. It was repeatedly stated that all three were believed to be fleeing together. That cheered Lafitte very much. It strengthened his faith.

But on the morning of his third day in this cheap hotel, when he came out of his room and went down the hall to ring for the elevator — there was only one passenger elevator in this hotel — he saw something. Passing the head of the stairs, which ended approximately midway of the stretch between the door of his room and the wattled iron door opening on the elevator well, he saw, out of the corner of one watchful eye, two men in civilian garb on the steps below him.

They had halted there. Whether they were coming up or going down there was no way of telling. It seemed to him that at sight of him they ducked slightly and made as if to flatten themselves back against the side wall.

He gave no sign of having seen them. He stilled an impulse to make a dash for it. Where was he to dash for, with the stairs cut off? He followed the only course open to him. Anyhow he told himself he might be wrong. Perhaps his nerves were misbehaving. Perhaps those two who seemed to be lurking just there behind him on those steps were not interested in him at all. He kept telling himself that, while he was ringing the bell, while he was waiting for the car to come up for him.

The car did come up and, for a wonder, promptly; an old-fashioned car, creaky, musty. Except for its shirt-sleeved attendant, it was empty. As Lafitte stepped in, he glanced sideways over his shoulder, making the movement casual — no sight of those two fellows.

He rode down, the only passenger for that trip, so there were no stops on the descent. They reached the ground floor, which was the office floor. The elevator came to a standstill, then moved up a foot or so, then joltingly down six inches or so, as the attendant, who was not expert, maneuvered to bring the sill of the car flush with the tiling of the lobby.

The delay was sufficiently prolonged for Lafitte to realize, all in a flash, he had not been wrong. Through the intervening grille of the shaft door he saw two more men who pressed close up to that door, who stared in at him, whose looks and poses were watchful, eager, prepared. Besides, Lafitte knew plainclothes men when he saw them.

Up above and here below, he was cut off. There still was a chance for him, a poor one but the only one. If he could shoot the elevator aloft quickly enough, check it at the third floor or the fourth, say, and hop out, he might make a successful dart for the fire escape at the rear of the hotel — provided the fire escape was not guarded. In the space of time that the elevator boy was jockeying the car, he thought of this, and having thought it, acted on it.

Swinging his fist from behind with all his might, he hit that hapless fellow on the point of the jaw and deposited him, stunned and temporarily helpless, on his knees in a corner of the cage. Lafitte grabbed the lever, shoved it over hard, and up the shaft shot the car. Before he could get control of it, being unfamiliar with such mechanisms and in a panic besides, it was at the top of the house. But then he mastered it and made it reverse its course, and returning downward he pulled the lever, bringing it toward him.

That was the proper notion, that gentler manipulation, for now the car, more obedient, was crawling abreast of the third-floor level. It crept earthward, inch by inch, and without bringing it to a dead stop he jerked up the latch of the collapsible safety gate, telescoped the metal outer door back into its folded-up self, and stooping low because the gap was diminishing, he lunged forward.

Now that elevator boy was a quick-witted, a high-tempered Irish boy. He might be half dazed but his instincts of belligerency were not asleep. He told afterward how, automatically and indignantly functioning, he grabbed at the departing assailant and caught him by one leg and for a fleeting moment, before the other kicked free, retarded him.

But by all that was good and holy he swore he did not touch the lever. Being down on all fours at the rear side of the slowly sinking car, how could he touch it? Why, just at that precise fraction of a second, the elevator should pick up full speed was a mystery to him — to everybody else, for that matter.

But pick up full speed it did. And the Irish boy cowered down and screamed an echo to a still louder scream than his, and hid his eyes from the sight of Lafitte, with his head outside and his body inside the elevator, being decapitated as completely and almost as neatly as though a great weighted knife had sheared him off at the neck.

Take the Spaniard and the Italian: Steadily they traveled westward for nearly all of that night which followed their evacuation from the Limited. It put desirable distance between them and the spot where they had dumped the special agent down. Also it kept them warm. This was summertime but on the desert even summer nights are chilly and sometimes downright cold. Before dawn, they came on a freight train waiting on a siding. Its locomotive faced west. That suited their book.

They climbed nimbly aboard a flat and snuggled themselves down behind a barrier of farm implements. Here, breakfastless but otherwise comfortable, they rode until nearly midday. Then a brakeman found them. Harshly he ordered them to get out of there.

Immediately though, looking at them where they squatted half hidden, his tone softened, and he told them he'd changed his mind about it and they could stay aboard as long as they pleased. On top of this, he hurried forward as though he might have important news for the engine crew or somebody.

They chose to get off. They had noted the quick start as of recognition which the brakeman had given. They figured — and figured rightly — that by now the chase for them was on and that their descriptions had been telegraphed back and forth along the line. The train was traveling at least twenty miles an hour, but as soon as the brakeman was out of sight, they jumped for it, tumbling like shot rabbits down the slope of the right of way and bringing up jarred and shaken in the dry ditch at the bottom.

Barring bruises and scratches, Green had taken no hurt, but Gaza landed with a badly sprained ankle. With Green to give him a helping arm, he hobbled away from the railroad.

To get away from that railroad was their prime aim now. Choosing a course at random, they went north over the undulating waste lands and through the shimmering heat, toward a range of mottled high buttes rising on beyond.

It took them until deep into the afternoon to cover a matter roughly of five miles. By now, Gaza's lower left leg was elephantine in its proportions and every forced step he took meant a fresh stab of agony. He knew he could not go much farther. Green knew it too, and in his brain began shaping tentative plans. The law of self-preservation was one of the few laws for which he had respect. They panted from heat and from thirst and from weariness.

At the end of those five miles, having toiled laboriously up over a fold in the land, they saw close at hand, and almost directly below them, a 'dobe hut, and not quite so near at hand, a big flock of sheep. At the door of the cabin, a man in overalls was stripping the hide from a swollen dead cow.

Before they could dodge back below the sky line, he saw them and stood up expectantly. There was nothing for them to do except to go toward him. At their slow approach, an expression of curiosity crept over his brown face and stayed there. He looked like a Mexican or possibly a half-breed Indian.

When Gaza, stumbling nearer, hailed him in English, he merely shook his head dumbly. Then Gaza tried him in Spanish and to that he replied volubly. For minutes they palavered back and forth; then the stranger served them with deep draughts from a water bottle swinging in the doorway with a damp sack over it. The water was lukewarm and bitterish-tasting but it was grateful to their parched throats. Then he withdrew inside the little house and Gaza, for Green's benefit, translated into Italian what talk had passed.

"He says he is quite alone here, which is the better for us," explained the Spaniard, speaking swiftly. "He says that a week ago he came up from Old Mexico, seeking work. A gringo — a white man — gave him work. The white man is a sheepman. His home ranch is miles away. In a sheep wagon he brought this Mexican here and left him here in charge of that flock yonder, with provisions for a month.

"It will be three weeks then before the white man, his employer, comes again. Except for that white man he knows nobody hereabouts. Until we came just now, he had seen no one at all. So he is glad to see us."

"And accounting for ourselves you told him what?" asked Green.

"I told him we were traveling across country in a car and that going down a steepness last night the car overturned and was wrecked and I crippled myself. I told him that, traveling light because of my leg, we started out to find some town, some house, and that, hoping to make a short cut, we left the road, but that since morning and until we blundered upon this camp, we had been quite lost in this ugly country. He believes me. He is simple, that one, an ignorant, credulous peon.

"But kind-hearted, that also is plain. For proof of it observe this." He pointed to the bloated, half-flayed carcass. "He says three days ago he found this beast — a stray from somewhere, he knows not where. So far as he knows there are no cattle droves in these parts — only sheep.

"She was sick, she staggered, she was dizzy and turned in circles as if blind, and froth ran from her mouth. There is a weed which does that to animals when they eat it, he says. So, hoping to make her well again, he put a scrap of rope on her horns and led her here. But last night she died. So to-day he has been peeling her. Now he goes to make ready some food for us. He is hospitable, also, that one."

"And when we have eaten, then what? We can't linger here."

"Wait, please, Señor. To my mind already an idea comes." His tone was authoritative, confident. "First we fill our empty stomachs to give us strength, and then we smoke a cigarette, and while we smoke, I think. And then — we see."

On frijoles and rancid bacon and thin corn cakes and bad coffee, which the herder brought them on tin platters and in tin cups, they did fill their empty stomachs. Then they smoked together, all three of them, smoking cigarettes rolled in corn-husk wrappers.

The Mexican was hunkered on his heels, making smoke rings in the still, hot air when Gaza, getting on his feet with difficulty, limped toward the doorway, gesturing to show that he craved another swig from the water bottle. When he was behind the other two, almost touching them, he drew the special agent's pistol and fired once and their host tumbled forward on his face and spraddled his limbs and quivered a bit and was still, with a bullet hole in the back of his head.

This killing gave the Italian, seasoned killer as he was, a profound shock. It seemed so unnecessary, unless —— ? He started up, his features twitching, and backed away, fearing the next bullet would be for him.

"Remain tranquil, Señor," said the Spaniard, almost gayly. "For you, my comrade, there is no danger. There is for you hope of deliverance, you who professed last night to have hope in your soul.

"Now me, I have charity in my soul — charity for you, charity for myself, charity also for this one lying here. Behold, he is now out of his troubles. He was a dolt, a clod of the earth, a creature of no refinement. He lived a hermit's life, lonely, miserable. Now he has been dispatched to a better and a brighter world. That was but kindness." With his foot he touched the sprawled corpse.

"But in dispatching him I had thought also for you — for both of us. I elucidate: First we bury him under the dirt floor of this house, taking care to leave no telltale traces of our work. Then you make a pack for your back of the food that is here. You take also the water bottle, filled. Furthermore, you take with you this pistol.

"Then, stepping lightly on rocky ground or on hard ground so that you make no tracks, you go swiftly hence and hide yourself in those mountains until — who can tell? — until those who will come presently here have ceased to search for you. With me along, lamed as I am, me to hamper you, there would be no chance for either of us. But you, going alone — you armed, provisioned, quick of foot — you have a hope."

"But — but you? What then becomes of you? — You — you sacrifice yourself?" In his bewilderment the Italian stammered.

"Me, I stay here to greet the pursuers. It is quite simple. In peaceful solitude I await their coming. It cannot be long until they come. That man of the freight train will be guiding them back to pick up our trail. By tonight at latest I expect them."

At sight of the Italian's mystified face he broke now into a laugh.

"Still you are puzzled, eh? You think that I am magnanimous, that I am generous? Well, all that I am. But you think me also a fool and there you err. I save you perhaps but likewise perhaps I save myself. Observe, Señor."

He stooped and lifted the dead face of his victim. "See now what I myself saw the moment I beheld this herder of ours: This man is much my shape, my height, my coloring. He spoke a corrupt Spanish such as I can speak. Put upon me the clothes which he wears, and remove from my lip this mustache which I wear, and I would pass for him even before the very eyes of that white man who hired him.

"Well, very soon I shall be wearing his clothes, my own being hidden in the same grave with him. Within ten minutes I shall be removing this mustache. He being newly shaven, as you see for yourself, it must be that in this hovel we will find a razor. I shall pass for him. I shall be this mongrel dull wit."

A light broke on the Italian. He ran and kissed the Spaniard, on both cheeks and on the mouth.

"Ah, my brother!" he cried out delightedly. "Forgive me that for a moment I thought you hard-hearted for having in seeming wantonness killed the man who fed us. I see you are brilliant — a great thinker, a great genius. But, my beloved" — and here doubt once more assailed him — "what explanation do you make when they do come?"

"That is the best of all," said Gaza. "Before you leave me you take a cord and you bind me most securely — my hands crossed behind my back — so; my feet fastened together — so. It will not be for very long that I remain so. I can endure it. Coming then, they find me thus. That I am bound makes more convincing the tale I shall tell them.

"And this is the tale that I shall tell: To them I shall say that as I sat under this shelter skinning my dead cow, there appeared suddenly two men who fell upon me without warning; that in the struggle they hurt my poor leg most grievously, then, having choked me into quietude, they tied my limbs, despoiled me of my provender and hurriedly departed, leaving me helpless. I shall describe these two brutal men — oh, most minutely I shall describe them. And my description will be accurate, for you I shall be describing as you stand now; myself I shall describe as I now am.

"The man from the train will say: 'Yes, yes, that is true; those are surely the two I saw.' He will believe me at once; that will held. Then they will inquire to know in which direction fled this pair of scoundrels and I will tell them they went that way yonder to the south across the desert, and they will set off in that direction, seeking two who flee together, when all the while you will be gone north into those mountains which will shelter you. And that, Señor, will be a rich part of the whole joke.

"Perhaps, though, they question me further. Then I say: 'Take me before this gringo who within a week hired me to watch his sheep. Confront me with him. He will identify me, he will confirm my story.' And if they do that and he does that — as most surely he will — why, then they must turn me loose and that, Señor, will be the very crown and peak of the joke."

In the excess of his admiration and his gratitude, the Italian just naturally had to kiss him again.

They worked fast and they worked scientifically, carefully, overlooking nothing, providing against every contingency. But at the last minute, when the Italian was ready to resume his flight and the Spaniard, smoothly shaven and effectually disguised in the soiled shirt and messy overalls of the dead man, had turned around and submitted his wrists to be pinioned, it was discovered that there was no rope available with which to bind his legs. The one short scrap of rope about the spot had been used for tying his hands.

The Spaniard said this was just as well. Any binding that was drawn snugly enough to fetter his feet securely would certainly increase the pain in the inflamed and grossly swollen ankle joint.

However, it was apparent that he must be securely anchored, lest suspicion arise in the minds of his rescuers when they arrived. Here the Italian made a contribution to the plot. He was proud of his inspiration.

With the Mexican's butcher knife he cut long narrow strips from the fresh slick cowhide. Then the Spaniard sat down on the earth with his back against one of the slim tree trunks supporting the arbor, and the Italian took numerous turns about his waist and his arms and the upper part of his body, and tightly knotted the various ends of the skin ribbons behind the post. Unaided, no human being could escape out of that mesh. To the pressure of the prisoner's trunk, the moist, pliant lashings would give slightly but it was certain they neither would work loose nor snap apart.

So he settled himself in his bonds, and the Italian, having shouldered his pack, once more fervently kissed his benefactor in token of gratitude, wished him success and made off with many farewells.

So far as this empty country was concerned, the Italian was a greenhorn, a tenderfoot. Nevertheless, he made excellent progress. He marched northward until dark, lay that night under a murdered man's smelly blanket behind a many-colored butte and next morning struck deeper into the broken lands. He entered what he hoped might be a gap through the mountains, treading cautiously along a narrow natural trail halfway up a dauntingly steep cliff side.

He was well into it when his foot dislodged a scrap of shaly rock which in sliding over the verge set other rocks to cascading down the slope. From above, yet larger boulders began toppling over into the scoured-out passageway thus provided, and during the next five minutes the walled-in declivity was alive and roaring with tumbling huge stones, with dislodged earth running fluid like a stream, with uprooted stunty piñons, with choking acrid dust clouds.

The Italian ran for dear life; he managed to get out of the avalanche's path. When at length he reached a safe place and looked back, he saw behind him how the landslide had choked the gorge almost to its brim. No human being — no, not even a goat, could from his side scale that jagged and overhanging parapet. Between him and pursuit was a perfect barrier.

Well content, he went on. But presently he made a discovery, a distressing discovery which took the good cheer right out of him. This was no gateway into which he had entered. It was a dead end leading nowhere — what Westerners call a box canyon. On three sides of him, right, left and on ahead, rose tremendously high walls, sheer and unclimbable. They threatened him; they seemed to be closing in on him to pinch him flat. And, of course, back of him retreat was cut off. There he was, bottled up like a fly in a corked jug, like a frog at the bottom of a well.

Frantically he explored as best he could the confines of this vast prison cell of his. He stumbled upon a spring, and its waters, while tainted lightly with alkali, were drinkable. So he had water and he had food, some food. By paring his daily portions down almost to starvation point, he might make these rations last for months. But then, what? And in the meantime, what? Why, until hunger destroyed him, he was faced with that doom which he so dreaded — the doom of solitary confinement.

He thought it all out and then he knelt down and took out his pistol and he killed himself.

In one of his calculations that smart malefactor, the Spaniard, had been wrong. By his system of deductions, the searchers should reach the 'dobe hut where he was tethered within four hours or, at most, five. But it was nearer thirty hours before they appeared.

The trouble had been that the brakeman wasn't quite sure of the particular stretch where he had seen the fugitives nestled beneath a reaping machine on that flat car. Besides, it took time to spread the word; to summon county officials; to organize an armed searching party. When at length the posse did strike the five-mile trail leading from the railroad tracks to the camp of the late sheep herder, considerably more than a day had elapsed.

The track was fairly plain — two sets of heavy footprints bearing north and only lacking where rocky outcrops broke through the surface of the desert. Having found it, they followed it fast, and when they mounted the fold in the earth above the cabin, they saw the figure of a man seated in front of it, bound snugly to one of the supports of the arbor.

Hurrying toward him they saw that he was dead — that his face was blackened and horribly distorted; that his glazed eyes goggled at them and his tongue protruded; that his stiffened legs were drawn up in sharp angles of agony.

They looked closer and they saw the manner of his death and were very sorry for him. He had been bound with strands of fresh rawhide, and all through that day he had been sitting there exposed to the baking heat of the day.

Now heat, operating on damp new rawhide, has an immediate effect. Heat causes certain substances to expand but green rawhide it causes to contract very fast to an ironlike stiffness and rigidity.

So in this case the sun glare had drawn tighter and tighter the lashings about this poor devil's body, squeezing him in at the stomach and the breast and the shoulders, pressing his arms tighter and tighter and yet tighter against his sides. That for him would have been a highly unpleasant procedure but it would not have killed him.

Something else had done that. One loop of the rawhide had been twisted about his neck and made fast at the back of the post. At first it might have been no more than a loosely fitting circlet but hour by hour it had shrunk into a choking collar, a diminishing noose, a terrible deadly yoke. Veritably it had garroted him by inches.

THE HANDS OF MR. OTTERMOLE

by THOMAS BURKE

No finer crime story has ever been written, period.

At six o'clock of a January evening Mr. Whybrow was walking home through the cobweb alleys of London's East End. He had left the golden clamour of the great High Street to which the tram had brought him from the river and his daily work, and was now in the chessboard of byways that is called Mallon End. None of the rush and gleam of the High Street trickled into these byways. A few paces south — a flood tide of life, foaming and beating. Here — only slow-shuffling figures and muffled pulses. He was in the sink of London, the last refuge of European vagrants.

As though in tune with the street's spirit, he too walked slowly, with head down. It seemed that he was pondering some pressing trouble, but he was not. He had no trouble. He was walking slowly because he had been on his feet all day, and he was bent in abstraction because he was wondering whether the Missis would have herrings for his tea, or haddock; and he was trying to decide which would be the more tasty on a night like this. A wretched night it was, of damp and mist, and the mist wandered into his throat and his eyes, and the damp had settled on pavement and roadway, and where the sparse lamplight fell it sent up a greasy sparkle that chilled one to look at. By contrast it made his speculations more agreeable, and made him ready for that tea — whether herring or haddock. His eye turned from the glum bricks that made his horizon, and went forward half a mile. He saw a gas-lit kitchen, a flamy fire and a spread tea table. There was toast in the hearth and a singing kettle on the side and a piquant effusion of herrings, or maybe of haddock, or perhaps sausages. The vision gave his aching feet a throb of energy. He shook imperceptible damp from his shoulders, and hastened towards its reality.

But Mr. Whybrow wasn't going to get any tea that evening —
or any other evening. Mr. Whybrow was going to die. Somewhere
within a hundred yards of him another man was walking: a man
much like Mr. Whybrow and much like any other man, but without the only quality that enables mankind to live peaceably together
and not as madmen in a jungle. A man with a dead heart eating
into itself and bringing forth the foul organisms that arise from
death and corruption. And that thing in man's shape, on a whim or
a settled idea — one cannot know — had said within himself that
Mr. Whybrow should never taste another herring. Not that Mr.
Whybrow had injured him. Not that he had any dislike of Mr.
Whybrow. Indeed, he knew nothing of him save as a familiar figure
about the streets. But, moved by a force that had taken possession
of his empty cells, he had picked on Mr. Whybrow with that blind
choice that makes us pick one restaurant table that has nothing to
mark it from four or five other tables, or one apple from a dish of
half a dozen equal apples; or that drives Nature to send a cyclone
upon one corner of this planet, and destroy five hundred lives in
that corner, and leave another five hundred in the same corner unharmed. So this man had picked on Mr. Whybrow, as he might
have picked on you or me, had we been within his daily observation; and even now he was creeping through the blue-toned streets,
nursing his large white hands, moving ever closer to Mr. Whybrow's tea table, and so closer to Mr. Whybrow himself.

He wasn't, this man, a bad man. Indeed, he had many of the social and amiable qualities, and passed as a respectable man, as most
successful criminals do. But the thought had come into his mouldering mind that he would like to murder somebody, and, as he held
no fear of God or man, he was going to do it, and would then go
home to *his* tea. I don't say that flippantly, but as a statement of
fact. Strange as it may seem to the humane, murderers must and
do sit down to meals after a murder. There is no reason why they
shouldn't, and many reasons why they should. For one thing, they
need to keep their physical and mental vitality at full beat for the
business of covering their crime. For another, the strain of their
effort makes them hungry, and satisfaction at the accomplishment
of a desired thing brings a feeling of relaxation towards human
pleasures. It is accepted among non-murderers that the murderer

is always overcome by fear for his safety and horror at his act; but this type is rare. His own safety is, of course, his immediate concern, but vanity is a marked quality of most murderers, and that, together with the thrill of conquest, makes him confident that he can secure it, and when he has restored his strength with food he goes about securing it as a young hostess goes about the arranging of her first big dinner — a little anxious, but no more. Criminologists and detectives tell us that *every* murderer, however intelligent or cunning, always makes one slip in his tactics — one little slip that brings the affair home to him. But that is only half true. It is true only of the murderers who are caught. Scores of murderers are not caught: therefore scores of murderers do not make any mistake at all. This man didn't.

As for horror or remorse, prison chaplains, doctors and lawyers have told us that of murderers they have interviewed under condemnation and the shadow of death, only one here and there has expressed any contrition for his act, or shown any sign of mental misery. Most of them display only exasperation at having been caught when so many have gone undiscovered, or indignation at being condemned for a perfectly reasonable act. However normal and humane they may have been before the murder, they are utterly without conscience after it. For what is conscience? Simply a polite nickname for superstition, which is a polite nickname for fear. Those who associate remorse with murder are, no doubt, basing their ideas on the world legend of the remorse of Cain, or are projecting their own frail minds into the mind of the murderer, and getting false reactions. Peaceable folk cannot hope to make contact with this mind, for they are not merely different in mental type from the murderer: they are different in their personal chemistry and construction. Some men can and do kill, not one man, but two or three, and go calmly about their daily affairs. Other men could not, under the most agonising provocation, bring themselves even to wound. It is men of this sort who imagine the murderer in torments of remorse and fear of the law, whereas he is actually sitting down to his tea.

The man with the large white hands was as ready for his tea as Mr. Whybrow was, but he had something to do before he went to it. When he had done that something, and made no mistake about it, he would be even more ready for it, and would go to it as comfortably as he went to it the day before, when his hands were stainless.

Walk on, then, Mr. Whybrow, walk on; and as you walk, look your last upon the familiar features of your nightly journey. Follow your jack-o'-lantern tea table. Look well upon its warmth and colour and kindness; feed your eyes with it, and tease your nose with its gentle domestic odours; for you will never sit down to it. Within ten minutes' pacing of you a pursuing phantom has spoken in his heart, and you are doomed. There you go — you and phantom — two nebulous dabs of mortality, moving through green air along pavements of powder blue, the one to kill, the other to be killed. Walk on. Don't annoy your burning feet by hurrying, for the more slowly you walk, the longer you will breathe the green air of this January dusk, and see the dreamy lamplight and the little shops, and hear the agreeable commerce of the London crowd and the haunting pathos of the street organ. These things are dear to you, Mr. Whybrow. You don't know it now, but in fifteen minutes you will have two seconds in which to realise how inexpressibly dear they are.

Walk on, then, across this crazy chessboard. You are in Lagos Street now, among the tents of the wanderers of Eastern Europe. A minute or so, and you are in Loyal Lane, among the lodging houses that shelter the useless and the beaten of London's camp followers. The lane holds the smell of them, and its soft darkness seems heavy with the wail of the futile. But you are not sensitive to impalpable things, and you plod through it, unseeing, as you do every evening, and come to Blean Street, and plod through that. From basement to sky rise the tenements of an alien colony. Their windows slot the ebony of their walls with lemon. Behind those windows strange life is moving, dressed with forms that are not of London or of England, yet, in essence, the same agreeable life that you have been living, and to-night will live no more. From high above you comes a voice crooning *The Song of Katta*. Through a window you see a family keeping a religious rite. Through another you see a woman pouring out tea for her husband. You see a man mending a pair of boots; a mother bathing her baby. You have seen all these things before, and never noticed them. You do not

notice them now, but if you knew that you were never going to
see them again, you would notice them. You never *will* see them
again, not because your life has run its natural course, but because
a man whom you have often passed in the street has at his own
solitary pleasure decided to usurp the awful authority of nature,
and destroy you. So perhaps it's as well that you don't notice them,
for your part in them is ended. No more for you these pretty moments of our earthly travail: only one moment of terror, and then
a plunging darkness.

Closer to you this shadow of massacre moves, and now he is
twenty yards behind you. You can hear his footfall, but you do not
turn your head. You are familiar with footfalls. You are in London,
in the easy security of your daily territory, and footfalls behind you,
your instinct tells you, are no more than a message of human company.

But can't you hear something in those footfalls — something
that goes with a widdershins beat? Something that says: *Look
out, look out. Beware, beware.* Can't you hear the very syllables
of *mur-der-er, mur-der-er?* No; there is nothing in footfalls. They
are neutral. The foot of villainy falls with the same quiet note
as the foot of honesty. But those footfalls, Mr. Whybrow, are
bearing on to you a pair of hands, and there *is* something in
hands. Behind you that pair of hands is even now stretching its
muscles in preparation for your end. Every minute of your days
you have been seeing human hands. Have you ever realised the
sheer horror of hands — those appendages that are a symbol for our
moments of trust and affection and salutation? Have you thought
of the sickening potentialities that lie within the scope of that five-
tentacled member? No, you never have; for all the human hands
that you have seen have been stretched to you in kindness or fellow-
ship. Yet, though the eyes can hate, and the lips can sting, it is only
that dangling member that can gather the accumulated essence of
evil, and electrify it into currents of destruction. Satan may enter
into man by many doors, but in the hands alone can he find the
servants of his will.

Another minute, Mr. Whybrow, and you will know all about
the horror of human hands.

You are nearly home now. You have turned into your street —

Caspar Street — and you are in the centre of the chessboard. You can see the front window of your little four-roomed house. The street is dark, and its three lamps give only a smut of light that is more confusing than darkness. It is dark — empty, too. Nobody about; no lights in the front parlours of the houses, for the families are at tea in their kitchens; and only a random glow in a few upper rooms occupied by lodgers. Nobody about but you and your following companion, and you don't notice him. You see him so often that he is never seen. Even if you turned your head and saw him, you would only say "Good-evening" to him, and walk on. A suggestion that he was a possible murderer would not even make you laugh. It would be too silly.

And now you are at your gate. And now you have found your door key. And now you are in, and hanging up your hat and coat. The Missis has just called a greeting from the kitchen, whose smell is an echo of that greeting (herrings!) and you have answered it, when the door shakes under a sharp knock.

Go away, Mr. Whybrow. Go away from that door. Don't touch it. Get right away from it. Get out of the house. Run with the Missis to the back garden, and over the fence. Or call the neighbours. But don't touch that door. Don't, Mr. Whybrow, don't open . . .

Mr. Whybrow opened the door.

That was the beginning of what became known as London's Strangling Horrors. Horrors they were called because they were something more than murders: they were motiveless, and there was an air of black magic about them. Each murder was committed at a time when the street where the bodies were found was empty of any perceptible or possible murderer. There would be an empty alley. There would be a policeman at its end. He would turn his back on the empty alley for less than a minute. Then he would look round and run into the night with news of another strangling. And in any direction he looked nobody to be seen and no report to be had of anybody being seen. Or he would be on duty in a long-quiet street, and suddenly be called to a house of dead people whom a few seconds earlier he had seen alive. And, again, whichever way he looked nobody to be seen; and although police whistles put an immediate cordon around the area, and searched all houses, no possible murderer to be found.

The first news of the murder of Mr. and Mrs. Whybrow was brought by the station sergeant. He had been walking through Caspar Street on his way to the station for duty, when he noticed the open door of No. 98. Glancing in, he saw by the gaslight of the passage a motionless body on the floor. After a second look he blew his whistle, and when the constables answered him he took one to join him in a search of the house, and sent others to watch all neighbouring streets, and make inquiries at adjoining houses. But neither in the house nor in the streets was anything found to indicate the murderer. Neighbours on either side, and opposite, were questioned, but they had seen nobody about, and had heard nothing. One had heard Mr. Whybrow come home — the scrape of his latchkey in the door was so regular an evening sound, he said, that you could set your watch by it for half past six — but he had heard nothing more than the sound of the opening door until the sergeant's whistle. Nobody had been seen to enter the house or leave it, by front or back, and the necks of the dead people carried no finger prints or other traces. A nephew was called in to go over the house, but he could find nothing missing; and anyway his uncle possessed nothing worth stealing. The little money in the house was untouched, and there were no signs of any disturbance of the property, or even of struggle. No signs of anything but brutal and wanton murder.

Mr. Whybrow was known to neighbours and workmates as a quiet, likeable, home-loving man; such a man as could not have any enemies. But, then, murdered men seldom have. A relentless enemy who hates a man to the point of wanting to hurt him seldom wants to murder him, since to do that puts him beyond suffering. So the police were left with an impossible situation: no clue to the murderer and no motive for the murders; only the fact that they had been done.

The first news of the affair sent a tremor through London generally, and an electric thrill through all Mallon End. Here was a murder of two inoffensive people, not for gain and not for revenge; and the murderer, to whom, apparently, killing was a casual impulse, was at large. He had left no traces, and, provided he had no companions, there seemed no reason why he should not remain at large. Any clear-headed man who stands alone, and has no fear of God or man, can, if he chooses, hold a city, even a nation, in subjection; but your everyday criminal is seldom clear-headed, and dislikes being lonely. He needs, if not the support of confederates, at least somebody to talk to; his vanity needs the satisfaction of perceiving at first hand the effect of his work. For this he will frequent bars and coffee shops and other public places. Then, sooner or later, in a glow of comradeship, he will utter the one word too much; and the nark, who is everywhere, has an easy job.

But though the doss houses and saloons and other places were "combed" and set with watches, and it was made known by whispers that good money and protection were assured to those with information, nothing attaching to the Whybrow case could be found. The murderer clearly had no friends and kept no company. Known men of this type were called up and questioned, but each was able to give a good account of himself; and in a few days the police were at a dead end. Against the constant public gibe that the thing had been done almost under their noses, they became restive, and for four days each man of the force was working his daily beat under a strain. On the fifth day they became still more restive.

It was the season of annual teas and entertainments for the children of the Sunday Schools, and on an evening of fog, when London was a world of groping phantoms, a small girl, in the bravery of best Sunday frock and shoes, shining face and new-washed hair, set out from Logan Passage for St. Michael's Parish Hall. She never got there. She was not actually dead until half past six, but she was as good as dead from the moment she left her mother's door. Somebody like a man, pacing the street from which the Passage led, saw her come out; and from that moment she was dead. Through the fog somebody's large white hands reached after her, and in fifteen minutes they were about her.

At half past six a whistle screamed trouble, and those answering it found the body of little Nellie Vrinoff in a warehouse entry in Minnow Street. The sergeant was first among them, and he posted his men to useful points, ordering them here and there in the tart

tones of repressed rage, and berating the officer whose beat the
street was. "I saw you, Magson, at the end of the lane. What were
you up to there? You were there ten minutes before you turned."
Magson began an explanation about keeping an eye on a suspicious-
looking character at that end, but the sergeant cut him short: "Suspicious characters be damned. You don't want to look for suspicious characters. You want to look for *murderers*. Messing about
. . . and then this happens right where you ought to be. Now
think what they'll say."

With the speed of ill news came the crowd, pale and perturbed;
and on the story that the unknown monster had appeared again,
and this time to a child, their faces streaked the fog with spots of
hate and horror. But then came the ambulance and more police,
and swiftly they broke up the crowd; and as it broke the sergeant's
thought was thickened into words, and from all sides came low
murmurs of "Right under their noses." Later inquiries showed that
four people of the district, above suspicion, had passed that entry
at intervals of seconds before the murder, and seen nothing and
heard nothing. None of them had passed the child alive or seen her
dead. None of them had seen anybody in the street except themselves. Again the police were left with no motive and with no clue.

And now the district, as you will remember, was given over, not
to panic, for the London public never yields to that, but to apprehension and dismay. If these things were happening in their familiar
streets, then anything might happen. Wherever people met — in the
streets, the markets and the shops — they debated the one topic.
Women took to bolting their windows and doors at the first fall
of dusk. They kept their children closely under their eye. They
did their shopping before dark, and watched anxiously, while pretending they weren't watching, for the return of their husbands from
work. Under the Cockney's semi-humorous resignation to disaster,
they hid an hourly foreboding. By the whim of one man with a
pair of hands the structure and tenor of their daily life were
shaken, as they always can be shaken by any man contemptuous
of humanity and fearless of its laws. They began to realise that
the pillars that supported the peaceable society in which they lived
were mere straws that anybody could snap; that laws were powerful only so long as they were obeyed; that the police were potent

only so long as they were feared. By the power of his hands this one man had made a whole community do something new: he had made it think, and left it gasping at the obvious.

And then, while it was yet gasping under his first two strokes, he made his third. Conscious of the horror that his hands had created, and hungry as an actor who has once tasted the thrill of the multitude, he made fresh advertisement of his presence; and on Wednesday morning, three days after the murder of the child, the papers carried to the breakfast tables of England the story of a still more shocking outrage.

At 9.32 on Tuesday night a constable was on duty in Jarnigan Road, and at that time spoke to a fellow officer named Petersen at the top of Clemming Street. He had seen this officer walk down that street. He could swear that the street was empty at that time, except for a lame bootblack whom he knew by sight, and who passed him and entered a tenement on the side opposite that on which his fellow officer was walking. He had the habit, as all constables had just then, of looking constantly behind him and around him, which-ever way he was walking, and he was certain that the street was empty. He passed his sergeant at 9.33, saluted him, and answered his inquiry for anything seen. He reported that he had seen noth-ing, and passed on. His beat ended at a short distance from Clem-ming Street, and, having paced it, he turned and came again at 9.34 to the top of the street. He had scarcely reached it before he heard the hoarse voice of the sergeant: "Gregory! You there? Quick. Here's another. My God, it's Petersen! Garotted. Quick, call 'em up!"

That was the third of the Strangling Horrors, of which there were to be a fourth and a fifth; and the five horrors were to pass into the unknown and unknowable. That is, unknown as far as authority and the public were concerned. The identity of the mur-derer *was* known, but to two men only. One was the murderer himself; the other was a young journalist.

This young man, who was covering the affairs for his paper, the *Daily Torch,* was no smarter than the other zealous newspaper men who were hanging about these byways in the hope of a sudden story. But he was patient, and he hung a little closer to the case than the other fellows, and by continually staring at it he at last raised the figure of the murderer like a genie from the stones on which he had stood to do his murders.

After the first few days the men had given up any attempt at exclusive stories, for there was none to be had. They met regularly at the police station, and what little information there was they shared. The officials were agreeable to them, but no more. The sergeant discussed with them the details of each murder; suggested possible explanations of the man's methods; recalled from the past those cases that had some similarity; and on the matter of motive reminded them of the motiveless Neil Cream and the wanton John Williams, and hinted that work was being done which would soon bring the business to an end; but about that work he would not say a word. The Inspector, too, was gracefully garrulous on the thesis of Murder, but whenever one of the party edged the talk towards what was being done in this immediate matter, he glided past it. Whatever the officials knew, they were not giving it to newspaper men. The business had fallen heavily upon them, and only by a capture made by their own efforts could they rehabilitate themselves in official and public esteem. Scotland Yard, of course, was at work, and had all the station's material; but the station's hope was that they themselves would have the honour of settling the affair; and however useful the coöperation of the Press might be in other cases, they did not want to risk a defeat by a premature disclosure of their theories and plans.

So the sergeant talked at large, and propounded one interesting theory after another, all of which the newspaper men had thought of themselves.

The young man soon gave up these morning lectures on the Philosophy of Crime, and took to wandering about the streets and making bright stories out of the effect of the murders on the normal life of the people. A melancholy job made more melancholy by the district. The littered roadways, the crestfallen houses, the bleared windows — all held the acid misery that evokes no sympathy: the misery of the frustrated poet. The misery was the creation of the aliens, who were living in this makeshift fashion because they had no settled homes, and would neither take the trouble to make a home where they *could* settle, nor get on with their wandering.

There was little to be picked up. All he saw and heard were indignant faces, and wild conjectures of the murderer's identity and of the secret of his trick of appearing and disappearing unseen. Since a policeman himself had fallen a victim, denunciations of the force had ceased, and the unknown was now invested with a cloak of legend. Men eyed other men, as though thinking: It might be *him*. It might be *him*. They were no longer looking for a man who had the air of a Madame Tussaud murderer; they were looking for a man, or perhaps some harridan woman, who had done these particular murders. Their thoughts ran mainly on the foreign set. Such ruffianism could scarcely belong to England, nor could the bewildering cleverness of the thing. So they turned to Roumanian gipsies and Turkish carpet sellers. There, clearly, would be found the "warm" spot. These Eastern fellows — they knew all sorts of tricks, and they had no real religion — nothing to hold them within bounds. Sailors returning from those parts had told tales of conjurors who made themselves invisible; and there were tales of Egyptian and Arab potions that were used for abysmally queer purposes. Perhaps it *was* possible to them; you never knew. They were so slick and cunning, and they had such gliding movements; no Englishman could melt away as they could. Almost certainly the murderer would be found to be one of that sort — with some dark trick of his own — and just because they were sure that he *was* a magician, they felt that it was useless to look for him. He was a power, able to hold them in subjection and to hold himself untouchable. Superstition, which so easily cracks the frail shell of reason, had got into them. He could do anything he chose: he would never be discovered. These two points they settled, and they went about the streets in a mood of resentful fatalism.

They talked of their ideas to the journalist in half tones, looking right and left, as though *HE* might overhear them and visit them. And though all the district was thinking of him and ready to pounce upon him, yet, so strongly had he worked upon them, that if any man in the street — say, a small man of commonplace features and form — had cried "*I* am the Monster!" would their stifled fury have broken into flood and have borne him down and engulfed him? Or would they not suddenly have seen something unearthly in that everyday face and figure, something unearthly in his everyday boots, something unearthly about his hat, something that marked him as one whom none of their weapons could alarm or pierce? And would they not momentarily have fallen back from this devil, as the devil fell back from the Cross made by the sword of Faust, and so have given him time to escape? I do not know; but so fixed was their belief in his invincibility that it is at least likely that they would have made this hesitation, had such an occasion arisen. But it never did. To-day this commonplace fellow, his murder lust glutted, is still seen and observed among them as he was seen and observed all the time; but because nobody then dreamt, or now dreams, that he was what he was, they observed him then, and observe him now, as people observe a lamp-post.

Almost was their belief in his invincibility justified; for, five days after the murder of the policeman Petersen, when the experience and inspiration of the whole detective force of London were turned towards his identification and capture, he made his fourth and fifth strokes.

At nine o'clock that evening, the young newspaper man, who hung about every night until his paper was away, was strolling along Richards Lane. Richards Lane is a narrow street, partly a stall market, and partly residential. The young man was in the residential section, which carries on one side small working-class cottages, and on the other the wall of a railway goods yard. The great wall hung a blanket of shadow over the lane, and the shadow and the cadaverous outline of the now deserted market stalls gave it the appearance of a living lane that had been turned to frost in the moment between breath and death. The very lamps, that elsewhere were nimbuses of gold, had here the rigidity of gems. The journalist, feeling this message of frozen eternity, was telling himself that he was tired of the whole thing, when in one stroke the frost was broken. In the moment between one pace and another silence and darkness were racked by a high scream and through the scream a voice: "Help! help! *He's here!*"

Before he could think what movement to make, the lane came to life. As though its invisible populace had been waiting on that cry, the door of every cottage was flung open, and from them and from the alleys poured shadowy figures bent in question mark form. For a second or so they stood as rigid as the lamps; then a police whistle gave them direction, and the flock of shadows sloped up the street. The journalist followed them, and others followed him. From the main street and from surrounding streets they came, some risen from unfinished suppers, some disturbed in their ease of slippers and shirt sleeves, some stumbling on infirm limbs, and some upright, and armed with pokers or the tools of their trade. Here and there above the wavering cloud of heads moved the bold helmets of policemen. In one dim mass they surged upon a cottage whose doorway was marked by the sergeant and two constables; and voices of those behind urged them on with "Get in! Find him! Run round the back! Over the wall!" and those in front cried: "Keep back! Keep back!"

And now the fury of a mob held in thrall by unknown peril broke loose. He was here — on the spot. Surely this time he *could not* escape. All minds were bent upon the cottage; all energies thrust towards its doors and windows and roof; all thought was turned upon one unknown man and his extermination. So that no one man saw any other man. No man saw the narrow, packed lane and the mass of struggling shadows, and all forgot to look among themselves for the monster who never lingered upon his victims. All forgot, indeed, that they, by their mass crusade of vengeance, were affording him the perfect hiding place. They saw only the house, and they heard only the rending of woodwork and the smash of glass at back and front, and the police giving orders or crying with the chase; and they pressed on.

But they found no murderer. All they found was news of murder and a glimpse of the ambulance, and for their fury there was no other object than the police themselves, who fought against this hampering of their work.

The journalist managed to struggle through to the cottage door, and to get the story from the constable stationed there. The cottage was the home of a pensioned sailor and his wife and daughter. They had been at supper, and at first it appeared that some noxious gas had smitten all three in mid-action. The daughter lay dead on the hearthrug, with a piece of bread and butter in her hand. The father had fallen sideways from his chair, leaving on his plate a filled spoon of rice pudding. The mother lay half under the table, her lap filled with the pieces of a broken cup and splashes of cocoa. But in three seconds the idea of gas was dismissed. One glance at their necks showed that this was the Strangler again; and the police stood and looked at the room and momentarily shared the fatalism of the public. They were helpless.

This was his fourth visit, making seven murders in all. He was to do, as you know, one more — and to do it that night; and then he was to pass into history as the unknown London horror, and return to the decent life that he had always led, remembering little of what he had done, and worried not at all by the memory. Why did he stop? Impossible to say. Why did he begin? Impossible again. It just happened like that; and if he thinks at all of those days and nights, I surmise that he thinks of them as we think of foolish or dirty little sins that we committed in childhood. We say that they were not really sins, because we were not then consciously ourselves: we had not come to realisation; and we look back at that foolish little creature that we once were, and forgive him because he didn't know. So, I think, with this man.

There are plenty like him. Eugene Aram, after the murder of Daniel Clarke, lived a quiet, contented life for fourteen years, unhaunted by his crime and unshaken in his self-esteem. Dr. Crippen murdered his wife, and then lived pleasantly with his mistress in the house under whose floor he had buried the wife. Constance Kent, found Not Guilty of the murder of her young brother, led a peaceful life for five years before she confessed. George Joseph Smith and William Palmer lived amiably among their fellows untroubled by fear or by remorse for their poisonings and drownings. Charles Peace, at the time he made his one unfortunate essay, had settled down into a respectable citizen with an interest in antiques. It happened that, after a lapse of time, these men were discovered, but more murderers than we guess are living decent lives to-day, and will die in decency, undiscovered and unsuspected. As this man will.

But he had a narrow escape, and it was perhaps this narrow escape that brought him to a stop. The escape was due to an error of judgment on the part of the journalist.

As soon as he had the full story of the affair, which took some time, he spent fifteen minutes on the telephone, sending the story through, and at the end of the fifteen minutes, when the stimulus of the business had left him, he felt physically tired and mentally dishevelled. He was not yet free to go home; the paper would not go away for another hour; so he turned into a bar for a drink and some sandwiches.

It was then, when he had dismissed the whole business from his mind, and was looking about the bar and admiring the landlord's taste in watch chains and his air of domination, and was thinking that the landlord of a well-conducted tavern had a more comfortable life than a newspaper man, that his mind received from nowhere a spark of light. He was not thinking about the Strangling Horrors; his mind was on his sandwich. As a public-house sandwich, it was a curiosity. The bread had been thinly cut, it was buttered, and the ham was not two months stale; it was ham as it should be. His mind turned to the inventor of this refreshment, the Earl of Sandwich, and then to George the Fourth, and then to the Georges, and to the legend of that George who was worried to know how the apple got into the apple dumpling. He wondered whether George would have been equally puzzled to know how the ham got into the ham sandwich, and how long it would have been before it occurred to him that the ham could not have got there unless somebody had put it there. He got up to order another sandwich, and in that moment a little active corner of his mind settled the affair. If there was ham in his sandwich, somebody must have put it there. If seven people had been murdered, somebody must have been there to murder them. There was no aeroplane or automobile that would go into a man's pocket; therefore that somebody must have escaped either by running away or standing still; and again therefore——

He was visualising the front-page story that his paper would carry if his theory were correct, and if—a matter of conjecture—his editor had the necessary nerve to make a bold stroke, when a cry of "Time, gentlemen, please! All out!" reminded him of the hour. He got up and went out into a world of mist, broken by the ragged discs of roadside puddles and the streaming lightning of motor buses. He was certain that he had *the* story, but, even if it were proved, he was doubtful whether the policy of his paper would permit him to print it. It had one great fault. It was truth, but it was impossible truth. It rocked the foundations of everything that newspaper readers believed and that newspaper editors helped them to believe. They might believe that Turkish carpet sellers had the gift of making themselves invisible. They would not believe this.

As it happened, they were not asked to, for the story was never written. As his paper had by now gone away, and as he was nourished by his refreshment and stimulated by his theory, he thought he might put in an extra half hour by testing that theory. So he began to look about for the man he had in mind — a man with white hair, and large white hands; otherwise an everyday figure whom nobody would look twice at. He wanted to spring his idea on this man without warning, and he was going to place himself within reach of a man armoured in legends of dreadfulness and grue. This might appear to be an act of supreme courage — that one man, with no hope of immediate outside support, should place himself at the mercy of one who was holding a whole parish in terror. But it wasn't. He didn't think about the risk. He didn't think about his duty to his employers or loyalty to his paper. He was moved simply by an instinct to follow a story to its end.

He walked slowly from the tavern and crossed into Fingal Street, making for Deever Market, where he had hope of finding his man. But his journey was shortened. At the corner of Lotus Street he saw him — or a man who looked like him. This street was poorly lit, and he could see little of the man: but he *could* see white hands. For some twenty paces he stalked him; then drew level with him; and at a point where the arch of a railway crossed the street, he saw that this was his man. He approached him with the current conversational phrase of the district: "Well, seen anything of the murderer?" The man stopped to look sharply at him; then, satisfied that the journalist was not the murderer, said:

"Eh? No, nor's anybody else, curse it. Doubt if they ever will."

"I don't know. I've been thinking about them, and I've got an idea."

"So?"

"Yes. Came to me all of a sudden. Quarter of an hour ago. And I'd felt that we'd all been blind. It's been staring us in the face."

The man turned again to look at him, and the look and the movement held suspicion of this man who seemed to know so much. "Oh? Has it? Well, if you're so sure, why not give us the benefit of it?"

"I'm going to." They walked level, and were nearly at the end of the little street where it meets Deever Market, when the journalist turned casually to the man. He put a finger on his arm. "Yes, it seems to me quite simple now. But there's still one point I don't understand. One little thing I'd like to clear up. I mean the motive. Now, as man to man, tell me, Sergeant Ottermole, just *why* did you kill all those inoffensive people?"

The sergeant stopped, and the journalist stopped. There was just enough light from the sky, which held the reflected light of the continent of London, to give him a sight of the sergeant's face, and the sergeant's face was turned to him with a wide smile of such urbanity and charm that the journalist's eyes were frozen as they met it. The smile stayed for some seconds. Then said the sergeant: "Well, to tell you the truth, Mr. Newspaper Man, I don't know. I really don't know. In fact, I've been worried about it myself. But I've got an idea — just like you. Everybody knows that we can't control the workings of our minds. Don't they? Ideas come into our minds without asking. But everybody's supposed to be able to control his body. Why? Eh? We get our minds from lord-knows-where — from people who were dead hundreds of years before we were born. Mayn't we get our bodies in the same way? Our faces — our legs — our heads — they aren't completely ours. We don't make 'em. They come to us. And couldn't ideas come into our bodies like ideas come into our minds? Eh? Can't ideas live in nerve and muscle as well as in brain? Couldn't it be that parts of our bodies aren't really us, and couldn't ideas come into those parts all of a sudden, like ideas come into — into" — he shot his arms out, showing the great white-gloved hands and hairy wrists; shot them out so swiftly to the journalist's throat that his eyes never saw them — "into *my hands!*"

TREASURE TROVE

by F. TENNYSON JESSE

A delicately-wrought and mystically-conceived story which conceals its astounding point, à la O. Henry, until the very last paragraph. By the author of the Solange stories.

Summer stayed late that year, and it was not until the last day of October that Brandon realized it had gone. Then a storm sprang up which went sweeping over the marshes, ruffling the still, grey waters of the meres and inlets, and rending the leaves from the twisted trees. After it had passed the warmth had gone from the air and only a pale, wintry sunshine lay pure and chill over the fen land. A few leaves still clung to the elms that grew about the farm place, he heard the cawing of the rooks about their nests, which showed black amid the bare branches.

Brandon felt for the moment the classic melancholy appropriate to the dying year, annual reminder of the autumn that approaches to every man. But the next moment, turning his head to look the way he had come, he saw that between the pale brown masses of the reeds the waters were a cold, bright blue, and the crystalline notes of the robin, practising for its winter song, came to his ear. Beauty still lived in this fenny country and his heart responded gratefully.

He went across the muddy yard and met his friend Miles in the doorway of the farmhouse. Dear, good Miles — sun or rain, summer or winter, held very little message for him that was not strictly utilitarian. But Miles's ruddy, outdoor face seemed somehow to have lost its usual cheerfulness of outlook, though it would certainly not be because of anything to do with some allegorical message of the dying summer.

"Have you seen Tom and Jack?" asked Miles. "They were supposed to be ploughing in the five-acre to-day, and they're not to be found. They're so dependable as a rule."

"Tom and Jack? No. It doesn't matter, does it? I suppose they're harrowing or mulching or marling or sowing or some other of the many processes that you indulge in."

The strange expression on his host's face had not lightened.

"They've been queer," he said, "darn queer, for two days now, ever since they found that cursed treasure while ploughing the reclaimed piece of waste land over by the big dyke. This morning they looked so queerly at each other I didn't quite like them going out together. There's something odd about it, Bill. I don't like it."

Brandon smiled and began to stuff his pipe.

"Nonsense, what could be wrong with your men?" he said. "It won't be the first time a little bit of money has gone to a man's head. They'll get over it, you'll see."

But to himself he was thinking that it was a bit queer all the same. Everyone knew Tom and Jack; they were the famous friends of the village. Damon and Pythias weren't in it when it came to friendship. They had been to the same Council school as boys, been in the same footer team in the winter, same cricket team in the summer, skated together, gone duck shooting together, gone fishing together, fought in the same regiment through the war and had even married twin sisters, and as far as anyone knew there had never been a wry word between them. They were not men of any special ability which would have caused them to grow away from the class of life into which they had been born, but in that class they were easily first in their district. Honest, decent, intelligent men, a little slow in the processes of their thoughts, perhaps, but none the less shrewd and sound for that. Tom a year younger, slightly built and active, Jack heavy compared with his friend, but strong as a bull. Tom might be quick in his temper, but it was soon over. Jack had the serenity that often goes with men of his large build. It seemed sad and a little odd that a few, dirty, antique coins should have been able to come between them.

"Why don't you tell them," he suggested to Miles, "that their old coins are probably worth very little?"

"I have," said Miles. "But you know what these people are, they always imagine anything they dig up must be of immense value and that the British Museum would buy it for a large sum. I can understand that part of it, what I can't understand is that they should begin to quarrel over it. I should have thought they'd have been only too glad to share it, however much or little it's worth. Besides, their working hours are not over yet, and I've never known them to down tools until the right hour, generally not till after it, they're the real old-fashioned kind that doesn't like to leave a job half done."

Scarcely had he said this when one of the maidservants came running from the passage at his back, calling to him in a loud and frightened voice:

"Come quick, sir, Tom and Jack be fighting in the barn, they're killing each other. . . ."

Miles turned and ran through the house, out into the front garden and across it, Brandon at his heels.

The big barn stood on the slope of the field beyond, a wooden building, black with pitch, with a red fluted roof. Beside it the straw ricks gleamed golden in the late sunshine. The two men ran up the slope of the field where the trodden turf was heavy and greasy to their feet and Brandon, out-stepping his more elderly host, burst through into the barn.

For the first moment it all seemed very dark to him, a darkness filled with dust motes that wreathed like steam in the rays shining through the doorway. The smell of cattle and trodden earth, and of the sweet stored hay, filled the dimness; rafters and rough wooden pillars stood out in the gloom. Then, as sight grew clear, his ears became aware of a horrible sound of sobbing that rose and fell, and the thud of blows. Two men were fighting, backward and forward, on the earthy floor. As Miles and Brandon sprang forward, the bigger man, who was winning, rained blows upon either side of his opponent's head, and the smaller man, from whom came the noise of sobbing, suddenly crumpled up and fell to the floor, where he lay still.

"Good God, man!" cried Miles, hanging on to the big fellow's arm. "You must be mad, you might kill him."

The man turned a ravaged face to his master.

"I shouldn't care if I had, the dirty hound!" he said. "He's a thief, that's what he is."

"Tom a thief! Nonsense. Why, you'd have fought anybody else who said as much."

"Aye, I *would* have," said the man, "but not now. . . . He's stolen all the money we dug up in the new field. He's hidden it away somewhere and won't say where. He's just lying and saying he hasn't got it."

Brandon had knelt down beside the unconscious Tom, whose face was running with blood; now he looked up and said:

"Well, you've nearly killed him. Even if it's true, you ought to be ashamed of yourself, and I don't believe it *is* true, Tom wouldn't do a thing like that. By God, Miles, look at his fists. Open your fists."

And he got up and advanced on Jack, who stood staring sullenly at him, his clenched fists still held before him. Jack offered no resistance as his master and Brandon pulled his fingers apart and discovered, clenched in each hand, a ragged flint stone, the ends dripping with Tom's blood. Brandon, looking at Jack's glazed eyes, said nothing; it would be little use saying anything, he felt, to a man as changed from the self they all knew as this man was. Instead, he said to Miles:

"We must get Tom out of this, you and Jack pick him up while I have a look around."

With surprising docility Jack bent down and picked up gently the head he had ill treated, and he and Miles between them carried the unconscious man out through the ray of sunlight into the air.

Brandon sat down on an upturned bucket near at hand, he felt sick and ill at the sight of the blood, an idiosyncrasy of his, so unconquerable that he had ceased to be ashamed of it. It seemed to him that the dim air of the barn was laden still with the violent passions that had been released there, that the element of strangeness in this sudden hatred sickened the very sunlight that slanted in upon the spot trodden by the men's struggling feet.

Brandon was not normally a super-sensitive man, but all his life he had been the prey of moments which had taken and shaken him oddly, moments when he had seemed not through any superior gifts of his own, but because of some outer compulsion, to be aware of more than most men, of more than, ordinarily, he would have been aware of himself. Usually these strange spaces of clarity were prefaced by an unaccountable aspect of external things; a familiar tree or bookshelf would take on a look that he could only describe to himself as "tilted," as though the angle of the visible world had started off in a new direction, pointing toward an unknown dimension; as though the tree or bookshelf had lost, all of a sudden, its treeness or furniturehood, and become a wedge thrust into space. At the time this would seem all right to him, only afterwards, looking back, his senses still giddy, he would realize the different tilt. And, cutting across this new space, there would come a wedge of light, tilted at the same new angle, which for the moment was the right angle, and in it he would be aware of, rather than see, a new and more complete aspect of something he had only imperfectly known before. A friend's motive for doing what had to him previously seemed inexplicable; the solution to some riddle in the history lecture he was working out; or sometimes even a fresh light upon a matter which had no earthly connection, as far as he knew, with himself.

He was almost hypnotized into this feeling now, as he sat there in the barn, but he shook off the dizzying sensations, like the familiar pins and needles of the children, that was stealing over him, and told himself it was due to the upset of his nerves and to the angle of the shaft of light that streamed in at the door. He got to his feet and as he did so he caught sight of a battered felt hat lying against the wall of the barn. He went over to it to take it up, he recognized it as Tom's by its peculiar light-grey colour and by the bluejay's feather stuck in the band. He bent to pick it up, but to his surprise it was so unexpectedly heavy in his hand that he almost dropped it. He ran his fingers behind the head lining of the crown; wrapped in a thin piece of stuff he felt the uneven surfaces of coins. So Tom had lied after all . . . he had concealed the coins. Brandon felt as when he had seen the flints concealed in Jack's fists.

He picked up the hat, and went heavily out of the barn with the hat carried between his two hands. He crossed the garden and went into the little room outside the front door which Miles used as his office.

Brandon closed the door and sat down at the table, pushing away papers and ledgers to make a clear space in front of him. Then he turned the hat up, and pulled out the pack of coins which lay, snake-like, curled round the crown. He unfolded the strip of soiled silk handkerchief and poured the coins out on to the table before him. There they lay, the source of all the trouble between Tom and Jack, a mere handful of dirty, almost shapeless coins. Brandon looked at them curiously. They were so old and battered he could only just make out the head of a Cæsar — which, he knew not, but the Roman look of it was unmistakable. It seemed incredible that through these coins, the passion of envy, mounting murder high, had come into being. . . . He scraped the coins together in his two hands.

And then, as he sat there, the strange sensation came flooding over him, drenching him, as it were, to the tips of his fingers and toes, so that he felt he could not move if the house caught fire about him. He felt very cold, in spite of the tingling that pervaded him, and he knew — how, he could not have told — that he was holding in his palms things so evil that his very flesh revolted, things so evil that whenever they were discovered and rediscovered by men they brought evil in their train. He knew, with a dreadful clearness in the midst of this dark red mist, that these things had been turned up by the ploughshare, or dragged from the sea, or cast upon beaches throughout the years, and whosoever found them knew desolation and decay of everything that had been his until then. There beat at him persistently the knowledge that he must take these things out and throw them away in the place where it was least likely they would be found for generations to come. He must weight them heavily and cast them out to sea, or throw them into the still waters of some disused pit.

He struggled violently against the feeling of horror that held him, because he wished to see about this business as soon as might be, and by a violent effort of the will he pulled himself back into the present. The evening sun was still shining into the little room. Shaking, but with the tingling slowly growing less all over his body, he drew his hands away from the clustering coins and let them fall upon the table. He passed his palm across his wet forehead and told himself that in another moment or so he would be able to do what he had to do, and quite soon he stood up, his steady self again, although not denying he had been shaken.

It was suddenly that the dreadful idea took him. Putting out his hand he began to count the coins; he counted three times, always hoping that in his hurry he might have erred, but count as he would, the battered pieces of silver numbered thirty. Brandon leaped up, and drew away from the table, his hands shaking. He found himself saying in a dreadful whisper: "Thirty pieces of silver . . . thirty pieces . . . of silver."

SUSPICION

by DOROTHY L. SAYERS

We fell for this story back in '33, when the original manuscript first came to our editorial desk at "Mystery League Magazine" (now deceased). And we still fall for it. Aspens to Miss Sayers.

As THE atmosphere of the railway carriage thickened with to-bacco smoke, Mr. Mummery became increasingly aware that his breakfast had not agreed with him.

There could have been nothing wrong with the breakfast itself. Brown bread, rich in vitamin content, as advised by the *Morning Star*'s health expert; bacon fried to a delicious crispness; eggs just nicely set; coffee made as only Mrs. Sutton knew how to make it. Mrs. Sutton had been a real find, and that was something to be thankful for. For Ethel, since her nervous breakdown in the summer, had really not been fit to wrestle with the untrained girls who had come and gone in tempestuous succession. It took very little to upset Ethel nowadays, poor child. Mr. Mummery, trying hard to ignore his growing internal discomfort, hoped he was not in for an illness. Apart from the trouble it would cause at the office, it would worry Ethel terribly, and Mr. Mummery would cheerfully have laid down his rather uninteresting little life to spare Ethel a moment's uneasiness.

He slipped a digestive tablet into his mouth — he had taken lately to carrying a few tablets about with him — and opened his paper. There did not seem to be very much news. A question had been asked in the House about Government typewriters. The Prince of Wales had smilingly opened an all-British exhibition of footwear. A further split had occurred in the Liberal party. The police were still looking for the woman who was supposed to have poisoned a family in Lincoln. Two girls had been trapped in a burning fac-tory. A film star had obtained her fourth decree nisi.

At Paragon Station, Mr. Mummery descended and took a tram. The internal discomfort was taking the form of a definite nausea. Happily he contrived to reach his office before the worst occurred. He was seated at his desk, pale but in control of himself, when his partner came breezing in.

" 'Morning, Mummery," said Mr. Brookes in his loud tones, adding inevitably, "Cold enough for you?"

"Quite," replied Mr. Mummery. "Unpleasantly raw, in fact."

"Beastly, beastly," said Mr. Brookes. "Your bulbs all in?"

"Not quite all," confessed Mr. Mummery. "As a matter of fact I haven't been feeling — "

"Pity," interrupted his partner. "Great pity. Ought to get 'em in early. Mine were in last week. My little place will be a picture in the spring. For a town garden, that is. You're lucky, living in the country. Find it better than Hull, I expect, eh? Though we get plenty of fresh air up in the Avenues. How's the missus?"

"Thank you, she's very much better."

"Glad to hear that, very glad. Hope we shall have her about again this winter as usual. Can't do without her in the Drama Society, you know. By Jove I shan't forget her acting last year in 'Romance.' She and young Welbeck positively brought the house down, didn't they? The Welbecks were asking after her only yesterday."

"Thank you, yes. I hope she will soon be able to take up her social activities again. But the doctor says she mustn't overdo it. No worry, he says — that's the important thing. She is to go easy and not rush about or undertake too much."

"Quite right, quite right. Worry's the devil and all. I cut out worrying years ago and look at me! Fit as a fiddle, for all I shan't see fifty again. You're not looking altogether the thing, by the way."

"A touch of dyspepsia," said Mr. Mummery. "Nothing much. Chill on the liver, that's what I put it down to."

"That's what it is," said Mr. Brookes, seizing his opportunity. "Is life worth living? It depends upon the liver. Ha, ha! Well now, well now — we must do a spot of work, I suppose. Where's that lease of Ferraby's?"

Mr. Mummery, who did not feel at his conversational best that morning, rather welcomed this suggestion, and for half an hour was allowed to proceed in peace with the duties of an estate agent. Presently, however, Mr. Brookes burst into speech again.

"By the way," he said abruptly, "I suppose your wife doesn't know of a good cook, does she?"

"Well, no," replied Mr. Mummery. "They aren't so easy to find nowadays. In fact, we've only just got suited ourselves. But why? Surely your old Cookie isn't leaving you?"

"Good lord, no!" Mr. Brookes laughed heartily. "It would take an earthquake to shake off old Cookie. No. It's for the Philipsons. Their girl's getting married. That's the worst of girls. I said to Philipson, 'You mind what you're doing,' I said. 'Get somebody you know something about, or you may find yourself landed with this poisoning woman — what's her name — Andrews. Don't want to be sending wreaths to your funeral yet awhile,' I said. He laughed, but it's no laughing matter and so I told him. What we pay the police for I simply don't know. Nearly a month now, and they can't seem to lay hands on the woman. All they say is, they think she's hanging about the neighbourhood and 'may seek a situation as cook.' As cook! Now I ask you!"

"You don't think she committed suicide, then?" suggested Mr. Mummery.

"Suicide my foot!" retorted Mr. Brookes coarsely. "Don't you believe it, my boy. That coat found in the river was all eyewash. *They* don't commit suicide, that sort don't."

"What sort?"

"Those arsenic maniacs. They're too damned careful of their own skins. Cunning as weasels, that's what they are. It's only to be hoped they'll manage to catch her before she tries her hand on anybody else. As I told Philipson — "

"You think Mrs. Andrews did it, then?"

"Did it? Of course she did it. It's plain as the nose on your face. Looked after her old father, and he died suddenly — left her a bit of money, too. Then she keeps house for an elderly gentleman, and *he* dies suddenly. Now there's this husband and wife — man dies and woman taken very ill, of arsenic poisoning. Cook runs away, and you ask, did she do it? I don't mind betting that when they dig up the father and the other old bird they'll find *them* bung full of arsenic, too. Once that sort gets started, they don't stop. Grows on 'em, as you might say."

"I suppose it does," said Mr. Mummery. He picked up his paper again and studied the photograph of the missing woman. "She looks harmless enough," he remarked. "Rather a nice, motherly-looking kind of woman."

"She's got a bad mouth," pronounced Mr. Brookes. He had a theory that character showed in the mouth. "I wouldn't trust that woman an inch."

As the day went on, Mr. Mummery felt better. He was rather nervous about his lunch, choosing carefully a little boiled fish and custard pudding and being particular not to rush about immediately after the meal. To his great relief, the fish and custard remained where they were put, and he was not visited by that tiresome pain which had become almost habitual in the last fortnight. By the end of the day he became quite light-hearted. The bogey of illness and doctor's bills ceased to haunt him. He bought a bunch of bronze chrysanthemums to carry home to Ethel, and it was with a feeling of pleasant anticipation that he left the train and walked up the garden path of *Mon Abri*.

He was a little dashed by not finding his wife in the sitting room. Still clutching the bunch of chrysanthemums he pattered down the passage and pushed open the kitchen door.

Nobody was there but the cook. She was sitting at the table with her back to him, and started up almost guiltily as he approached.

"Lor', sir," she said, "you give me quite a start. I didn't hear the front door go."

"Where is Mrs. Mummery? Not feeling bad again, is she?"

"Well, sir, she's got a bit of a headache, poor lamb. I made her lay down and took her up a nice cup o' tea at half past four. I think she's dozing nicely now."

"Dear, dear," said Mr. Mummery.

"It was turning out the dining room done it, if you ask me," said Mrs. Sutton. "'Now, don't you overdo yourself, ma'am,' I says to her, but you know how she is, sir. She gets that restless, she can't abear to be doing nothing."

"I know," said Mr. Mummery. "It's not your fault, Mrs. Sutton. I'm sure you look after us both admirably. I'll just run up and have a peep at her. I won't disturb her if she's asleep. By the way, what are we having for dinner?"

"Well, I *had* made a nice steak-and-kidney pie," said Mrs. Sutton, in accents suggesting that she would readily turn it into a pumpkin or a coach and four if it was not approved of.

"Oh!" said Mr. Mummery. "Pastry? Well, I — "

"You'll find it beautiful and light," protested the cook, whisking open the oven door for Mr. Mummery to see. "And it's made with butter, sir, you having said that you found lard indigestible."

"Thank you, thank you," said Mr. Mummery. "I'm sure it will be most excellent. I haven't been feeling altogether the thing just lately, and lard does not seem to suit me nowadays."

"Well, it don't suit some people, and that's a fact," agreed Mrs. Sutton. "I shouldn't wonder if you've got a bit of a chill on the liver. I'm sure this weather is enough to upset anybody."

She bustled to the table and cleared away the picture paper which she had been reading.

"Perhaps the mistress would like her dinner sent up to her?" she suggested.

Mr. Mummery said he would go and see, and tiptoed his way upstairs. Ethel was lying snuggled under the eiderdown and looked very small and fragile in the big double bed. She stirred as he came in and smiled up at him.

"Hullo, darling!" said Mr. Mummery.

"Hullo! You back? I must have been asleep. I got tired and headachy, and Mrs. Sutton packed me off upstairs."

"You've been doing too much, sweetheart," said her husband, taking her hand in his and sitting down on the edge of the bed.

"Yes — it was naughty of me. What lovely flowers, Harold. All for me?"

"All for you, Tiddleywinks," said Mr. Mummery tenderly. "Don't I deserve something for that?"

Mrs. Mummery smiled, and Mr. Mummery took his reward several times over.

"That's quite enough, you sentimental old thing," said Mrs. Mummery. "Run away, now, I'm going to get up."

"Much better go to bed, my precious, and let Mrs. Sutton send your dinner up," said her husband.

Ethel protested, but he was firm with her. If she didn't take care of herself, she wouldn't be allowed to go to the Drama Society meetings. And everybody was so anxious to have her back. The Welbecks had been asking after her and saying that they really couldn't get on without her.

"Did they?" said Ethel with some animation. "It's very sweet of them to want me. Well, perhaps I'll go to bed after all. And how has my old Hubby been all day?"

"Not too bad, not too bad."

"No more tummyaches?"

"Well, just a *little* tummyache. But it's quite gone now. Nothing for Tiddleywinks to worry about."

Mr. Mummery experienced no more distressing symptoms the next day or the next. Following the advice of the newspaper expert, he took to drinking orange juice, and was delighted with the results of the treatment. On Thursday, however, he was taken so ill in the night that Ethel was alarmed and insisted on sending for the doctor. The doctor felt his pulse and looked at his tongue and appeared to take the matter lightly. An inquiry into what he had been eating elicited the fact that dinner had consisted of pig's trotters, followed by a milk pudding, and that, before retiring, Mr. Mummery had consumed a large glass of orange juice, according to his new régime.

"There's your trouble," said Dr. Griffith cheerfully. "Orange juice is an excellent thing, and so are trotters, but not in combination. Pig and oranges together are extraordinarily bad for the liver. I don't know why they should be, but there's no doubt that they are. Now I'll send you round a little prescription and you stick to slops for a day or two and keep off pork. And don't you worry about him, Mrs. Mummery, he's as sound as a trout. *You're* the one we've got to look after. I don't want to see those black rings under the eyes, you know. Disturbed night, of course — yes. Taking your tonic regularly? That's right. Well, don't be alarmed about your hubby. We'll soon have him out and about again."

The prophecy was fulfilled, but not immediately. Mr. Mummery, though confining his diet to Benger's food, bread and milk and beef tea skilfully prepared by Mrs. Sutton and brought to his bedside by Ethel, remained very seedy all through Friday, and was only able to stagger rather shakily downstairs on Saturday afternoon. He had evidently suffered a "thorough upset." However, he was able to attend to a few papers which Brookes had sent down from the office for his signature, and to deal with the household books. Ethel was not a business woman, and Mr. Mummery always ran over the accounts with her. Having settled up with the butcher, the baker, the dairy and the coal merchant, Mr. Mummery looked up inquiringly.

"Anything more, darling?"

"Well, there's Mrs. Sutton. This is the end of her month, you know."

"So it is. Well, you're quite satisfied with her, aren't you, darling?"

"Yes, rather — aren't you? She's a good cook, and a sweet, motherly old thing, too. Don't you think it was a real brain wave of mine, engaging her like that, on the spot?"

"I do, indeed," said Mr. Mummery.

"It was a perfect providence, her turning up like that, just after that wretched Jane had gone off without even giving notice. I was in absolute *despair*. It was a little bit of a gamble, of course, taking her without any references, but naturally, if she'd been looking after a widowed mother, you couldn't expect her to give references."

"N-no," said Mr. Mummery. At the time he had felt uneasy about the matter, though he had not liked to say much because, of course, they simply had to have somebody. And the experiment had justified itself so triumphantly in practice that one couldn't say much about it now. He had once rather tentatively suggested writing to the clergyman of Mrs. Sutton's parish but, as Ethel had said, the clergyman wouldn't have been able to tell them anything about cooking, and cooking, after all, was the chief point.

Mr. Mummery counted out the month's money.

"And by the way, my dear," he said, "you might just mention to Mrs. Sutton that if she *must* read the morning paper before I come down, I should be obliged if she would fold it neatly afterwards."

"What an old fuss-box you are, darling," said his wife.

Mr. Mummery sighed. He could not explain that it was somehow important that the morning paper should come to him fresh and prim, like a virgin. Women did not feel these things.

On Sunday, Mr. Mummery felt very much better — quite his old self, in fact. He enjoyed the *News of the World* over breakfast in

bed, reading the murders rather carefully. Mr. Mummery got quite
a lot of pleasure out of murders — they gave him an agreeable thrill
of vicarious adventure, for, naturally, they were matters quite remote from daily life in the outskirts of Hull.

He noticed that Brookes had been perfectly right. Mrs. Andrews's
father and former employer had been "dug up" and had, indeed,
proved to be "bung full" of arsenic.

He came downstairs for dinner — roast sirloin, with the potatoes
done under the meat and Yorkshire pudding of delicious lightness,
and an apple tart to follow. After three days of invalid diet, it was
delightful to savour the crisp fat and underdone lean. He ate mod-
erately, but with a sensuous enjoyment. Ethel, on the other hand,
seemed a little lacking in appetite, but then, she had never been a
great meat eater. She was fastidious and, besides, she was (quite
unnecessarily) afraid of getting fat.

It was a fine afternoon, and at three o'clock, when he was quite
certain that the roast beef was "settling" properly, it occurred to
Mr. Mummery that it would be a good thing to put the rest of those
bulbs in. He slipped on his old gardening coat and wandered out
to the potting shed. Here he picked up a bag of tulips and a trowel,
and then, remembering that he was wearing his good trousers, decided that it would be wise to take a mat to kneel on. When had
he had the mat last? He could not recollect, but he rather fancied
he had put it away in the corner under the potting shelf. Stooping
down, he felt about in the dark among the flower pots. Yes, there
it was, but there was a tin of something in the way. He lifted the
tin carefully out. Of course, yes — the remains of the weed killer.

Mr. Mummery glanced at the pink label, printed in staring letters
with the legend: "ARSENICAL WEED KILLER. *Poison,*" and observed,
with a mild feeling of excitement, that it was the same brand of
stuff that had been associated with Mrs. Andrews's latest victim. He
was rather pleased about it. It gave him a sensation of being remotely but definitely in touch with important events. Then he noticed, with surprise and a little annoyance, that the stopper had been
put in quite loosely.

"However'd I come to leave it like that?" he grunted. "Shouldn't
wonder if all the goodness has gone off." He removed the stopper
and squinted into the can, which appeared to be half-full. Then he

rammed the thing home again, giving it a sharp thump with the handle of the trowel for better security. After that he washed his hands carefully at the scullery tap, for he did not believe in taking risks.

He was a trifle disconcerted, when he came in after planting the tulips, to find visitors in the sitting room. He was always pleased to see Mrs. Welbeck and her son, but he would rather have had warning, so that he could have scrubbed the garden mould out of his nails more thoroughly. Not that Mrs. Welbeck appeared to notice. She was a talkative woman and paid little attention to anything but her own conversation. Much to Mr. Mummery's annoyance, she chose to prattle about the Lincoln Poisoning Case. A most unsuitable subject for the tea table, thought Mr. Mummery, at the best of times. His own "upset" was vivid enough in his memory to make him queasy over the discussion of medical symptoms, and besides, this kind of talk was not good for Ethel. After all, the poisoner was still supposed to be in the neighbourhood. It was enough to make even a strong-nerved woman uneasy. A glance at Ethel showed him that she was looking quite white and tremulous. He must stop Mrs. Welbeck somehow, or there would be a repetition of one of the old, dreadful, hysterical scenes.

He broke into the conversation with violent abruptness.

"Those Forsyth cuttings, Mrs. Welbeck," he said. "Now is just about the time to take them. If you care to come down the garden I will get them for you."

He saw a relieved glance pass between Ethel and young Welbeck. Evidently the boy understood the situation and was chafing at his mother's tactlessness. Mrs. Welbeck, brought up all standing, gasped slightly and then veered off with obliging readiness on the new tack. She accompanied her host down the garden and chattered cheerfully about horticulture while he selected and trimmed the cuttings. She complimented Mr. Mummery on the immaculacy of his gravel paths. "I simply *cannot* keep the weeds down," she said.

Mr. Mummery mentioned the weed killer and praised its efficacy.

"That stuff!" Mrs. Welbeck stared at him. Then she shuddered. "I wouldn't have it in my place for a thousand pounds," she said, with emphasis.

Mr. Mummery smiled. "Oh, we keep it well away from the house," he said. "Even if I were a careless sort of person — "

He broke off. The recollection of the loosened stopper had come to him suddenly, and it was as though, deep down in his mind, some obscure assembling of ideas had taken place. He left it at that, and went into the kitchen to fetch a newspaper to wrap up the cuttings.

Their approach to the house had evidently been seen from the sitting room window, for when they entered, young Welbeck was already on his feet and holding Ethel's hand in the act of saying good-bye. He manœuvred his mother out of the house with tactful promptness and Mr. Mummery returned to the kitchen to clear up the newspapers he had fished out of the drawer. To clear them up and to examine them more closely. Something had struck him about them, which he wanted to verify. He turned them over very carefully, sheet by sheet. Yes — he had been right. Every portrait of Mrs. Andrews, every paragraph and line about the Lincoln Poisoning Case, had been carefully cut out.

Mr. Mummery sat down by the kitchen fire. He felt as though he needed warmth. There seemed to be a curious cold lump of something at the pit of his stomach — something that he was chary of investigating.

He tried to recall the appearance of Mrs. Andrews as shown in the newspaper photographs, but he had not a good visual memory. He remembered having remarked to Brookes that it was a "motherly" face. Then he tried counting up the time since the disappearance. Nearly a month, Brookes had said — and that was a week ago. Must be over a month now. A month. He had just paid Mrs. Sutton her month's money.

"Ethel!" was the thought that hammered at the door of his brain. At all costs, he must cope with this monstrous suspicion on his own. He must spare her any shock or anxiety. And he must be sure of his ground. To dismiss the only decent cook they had ever had out of sheer, unfounded panic, would be wanton cruelty to both women. If he did it at all, it would have to be done arbitrarily, preposterously — he could not suggest horrors to Ethel. However it was done, there would be trouble. Ethel would not understand and he dared not tell her.

But if by any chance there was anything in this ghastly doubt — how could he expose Ethel to the appalling danger of having the woman in the house a moment longer? He thought of the family at Lincoln — the husband dead, the wife escaped by a miracle with her life. Was not any shock, any risk, better than that?

Mr. Mummery felt suddenly very lonely and tired. His illness had taken it out of him.

Those illnesses — they had begun, when? Three weeks ago he had had the first attack. Yes, but then he had always been rather subject to gastric troubles. Bilious attacks. Not so violent, perhaps, as these last, but undoubted bilious attacks.

He pulled himself together and went, rather heavily, into the sitting room. Ethel was tucked up in a corner of the chesterfield.

"Tired, darling?"

"Yes, a little."

"That woman has worn you out with talking. She oughtn't to talk so much."

"No." Her head shifted wearily in the cushions. "All about that horrible case. I don't like hearing about such things."

"Of course not. Still, when a thing like that happens in the neighbourhood, people will gossip and talk. It would be a relief if they caught the woman. One doesn't like to think — "

"I don't want to think of anything so hateful. She must be a horrible creature."

"Horrible. Brookes was saying the other day — "

"I don't want to hear what he said. I don't want to hear about it at all. I want to be quiet. I want to be quiet!"

He recognised the note of rising hysteria.

"Tiddleywinks shall be quiet. Don't worry, darling. We won't talk about horrors."

No. It would not do to talk about them.

Ethel went to bed early. It was understood that on Sundays Mr. Mummery should sit up till Mrs. Sutton came in. Ethel was a little anxious about this, but he assured her that he felt quite strong enough. In body, indeed, he did; it was his mind that felt weak and confused. He had decided to make a casual remark about the mutilated newspapers — just to see what Mrs. Sutton would say.

He allowed himself the usual indulgence of a whisky and soda as he sat waiting. At a quarter to ten he heard the familiar click of the garden gate. Footsteps passed up the gravel — squeak, squeak, to the back-door. Then the sound of the latch. the shutting of the door, the rattle of the bolts being shot home. Then a pause. Mrs. Sutton would be taking off her hat. The moment was coming.

The step sounded in the passage. The door opened. Mrs. Sutton in her neat black dress stood on the threshold. He was aware of a reluctance to face her. Then he looked up. A plump-faced woman, her eyes obscured by thick horn-rimmed spectacles. Was there, perhaps, something hard about the mouth? Or was it just that she had lost most of her front teeth?

"Would you be requiring anything tonight, sir, before I go up?"

"No thank you, Mrs. Sutton."

"I hope you are feeling better, sir." Her eager interest in his health seemed to him almost sinister, but the eyes, behind the thick glasses, were inscrutable.

"Quite better, thank you, Mrs. Sutton."

"Mrs. Mummery is not indisposed, is she, sir? Should I take her up a glass of hot milk or anything?"

"No, thank you, no." He spoke hurriedly, and fancied that she looked disappointed.

"Very well, sir. Good night, sir."

"Good night. Oh! by the way, Mrs. Sutton — "

"Yes, sir?"

"Oh, nothing," said Mr. Mummery, "nothing."

Next morning Mr. Mummery opened his paper eagerly. He would have been glad to learn that an arrest had been made over the week-end. But there was no news for him. The chairman of a trust company had blown out his brains, and the headlines were all occupied with tales about lost millions and ruined shareholders. Both in his own paper and in those he purchased on the way to the office, the Lincoln Poisoning Tragedy had been relegated to an obscure paragraph on a back page, which informed him that the police were still baffled.

The next few days were the most uncomfortable that Mr. Mummery had ever spent. He developed a habit of coming down early in the morning and prowling about the kitchen. This made Ethel nervous, but Mrs. Sutton offered no remark. She watched him tolerantly, even, he thought, with something like amusement. After all, it was ridiculous. What was the use of supervising the breakfast, when he had to be out of the house every day between half past nine and six?

At the office, Brookes rallied him on the frequency with which he rang up Ethel. Mr. Mummery paid no attention. It was reassuring to hear her voice and to know that she was safe and well.

Nothing happened, and by the following Thursday he began to think that he had been a fool. He came home late that night. Brookes had persuaded him to go with him to a little bachelor dinner for a friend who was about to get married. He left the others at eleven o'clock, however, refusing to make a night of it. The household was in bed when he got back but a note from Mrs. Sutton lay on the table, informing him that there was cocoa for him in the kitchen, ready for hotting up. He hotted it up accordingly in the little saucepan where it stood. There was just one good cupful.

He sipped it thoughtfully, standing by the kitchen stove. After the first sip, he put the cup down. Was it his fancy, or was there something queer about the taste? He sipped it again, rolling it upon his tongue. It seemed to him to have a faint tang, metallic and unpleasant. In a sudden dread he ran out to the scullery and spat the mouthful into the sink.

After this, he stood quite still for a moment or two. Then, with a curious deliberation, as though his movements had been dictated to him, he fetched an empty medicine bottle from the pantry shelf, rinsed it under the tap and tipped the contents of the cup carefully into it. He slipped the bottle into his coat pocket and moved on tiptoe to the back door. The bolts were difficult to draw without noise, but he managed it at last. Still on tiptoe, he stole across the garden to the potting shed. Stooping down, he struck a match. He knew exactly where he had left the tin of weed killer, under the shelf behind the pots at the back. Cautiously he lifted it out. The match flared up and burnt his fingers, but before he could light another his sense of touch had told him what he wanted to know. The stopper was loose again.

Panic seized Mr. Mummery, standing there in the earthy-smelling shed, in his dress suit and overcoat, holding the tin in one hand and the match box in the other. He wanted very badly to run and tell somebody what he had discovered.

Instead, he replaced the tin exactly where he had found it and went back to the house. As he crossed the garden again, he noticed a light in Mrs. Sutton's bedroom window. This terrified him more than anything which had gone before. Was she watching him? Ethel's window was dark. If she had drunk anything deadly there would be lights everywhere, movements, calls for the doctor, just as when he himself had been attacked. Attacked — that was the right word, he thought.

Still with the same odd presence of mind and precision, he went in, washed out the utensils and made a second brew of cocoa, which he left standing in the saucepan. He crept quietly to his bedroom. Ethel's voice greeted him on the threshold.

"How late you are, Harold. Naughty old boy! Have a good time?"

"Not bad. You all right, darling?"

"Quite all right. Did Mrs. Sutton leave something hot for you? She said she would."

"Yes, but I wasn't thirsty."

Ethel laughed. "Oh! it was *that* sort of party, was it?"

Mr. Mummery did not attempt any denials. He undressed and got into bed and clutched his wife to him as though defying death and hell to take her from him. Next morning he would act. He thanked God that he was not too late.

Mr. Dimthorpe, the chemist, was a great friend of Mr. Mummery's. They had often sat together in the untidy little shop on Spring Bank and exchanged views on green-fly and club-root. Mr. Mummery told his story frankly to Mr. Dimthorpe and handed over the bottle of cocoa. Mr. Dimthorpe congratulated him on his prudence and intelligence.

"I will have it ready for you by this evening," he said, "and if it's what you think it is, then we shall have a clear case on which to take action."

Mr. Mummery thanked him, and was extremely vague and inattentive at business all day. But that hardly mattered, for Mr. Brookes, who had seen the party through to a riotous end in the small hours, was in no very observant mood. At half past four, Mr. Mummery shut up his desk decisively and announced that he was off early, he had a call to make.

Mr. Dimthorpe was ready for him.

"No doubt about it," he said. "I used Marsh's test. It's a heavy dose — no wonder you tasted it. There must be four or five grains of pure arsenic in that bottle. Look, here's the mirror. You can see it for yourself."

Mr. Mummery gazed at the little glass tube with its ominous purple-black stain.

"Will you ring up the police from here?" asked the chemist.

"No," said Mr. Mummery. "No — I want to get home. God knows what's happening there. And I've only just time to catch my train."

"All right," said Mr. Dimthorpe. "Leave it to me. I'll ring them up for you."

The local train did not go fast enough for Mr. Mummery. Ethel — poisoned — dying — dead — Ethel — poisoned — dying — dead — the wheels drummed in his ears. He almost ran out of the station and along the road. A car was standing at his door. He saw it from the end of the street and broke into a gallop. It had happened already. The doctor was there. Fool, murderer that he was to have left things so late.

Then, while he was still a hundred and fifty yards off, he saw the front door open. A man came out followed by Ethel herself. The visitor got into his car and was driven away. Ethel went in again. She was safe — safe!

He could hardly control himself to hang up his hat and coat and go in looking reasonably calm. His wife had returned to the arm-chair by the fire and greeted him in some surprise. There were tea things on the table.

"Back early, aren't you?"

"Yes — business was slack. Somebody been to tea?"

"Yes, young Welbeck. About the arrangements for the Drama Society." She spoke briefly but with an undertone of excitement.

A qualm came over Mr. Mummery. Would a guest be any protection? His face must have shown his feelings, for Ethel stared at him in amazement.

"What's the matter, Harold, you look so queer."

"Darling," said Mr. Mummery, "there's something I want to tell you about." He sat down and took her hand in his. "Something a little unpleasant, I'm afraid — "

"Oh, ma'am!"

The cook was in the doorway.

"I beg your pardon, sir — I didn't know you was in. Will you be taking tea or can I clear away? And, oh, ma'am, there was a young man at the fishmonger's and he's just come from Grimsby and they've caught that dreadful woman — that Mrs. Andrews. Isn't it a good thing? It's worritted me dreadful to think she was going about like that, but they've caught her. Taken a job as housekeeper she had to two elderly ladies and they found the wicked poison on her. Girl as spotted her will get a reward. I been keeping my eyes open for her, but it's at Grimsby she was all the time."

Mr. Mummery clutched at the arm of his chair. It had all been a mad mistake then. He wanted to shout or cry. He wanted to apologise to this foolish, pleasant, excited woman. All a mistake.

But there had been the cocoa. Mr. Dimthorpe. Marsh's test. Five grains of arsenic. Who, then — ?

He glanced around at his wife, and in her eyes he saw something that he had never seen before. . . .

THE SILVER MASK

by HUGH WALPOLE

The Broadway success "Kind Lady" was a dramatization of this story by Mr. Walpole. To us, it tells the story of one of the most terrifying crimes conceivable by the fiendish ingenuity of man . . . the crime of the living death.

Miss Sonia Herries, coming home from a dinner party at the Westons', heard a voice at her elbow.

"If you please — only a moment —— "

She had walked from the Westons' flat because it was only three streets away, and now she was only a few steps from her door, but it was late, there was no one about and the King's Road rattle was muffled and dim.

"I am afraid I can't — " she began. It was cold, and the wind nipped her cheeks.

"If you would only — " he went on.

She turned and saw one of the handsomest young men possible. He was the handsome young man of all romantic stories, tall, dark, pale, slim, distinguished — oh! everything! — and he was wearing a shabby blue suit and shivering with the cold just as he should have been.

"I'm afraid I can't — " she repeated, beginning to move on.

"Oh, I know," he interrupted quickly. "Everyone says the same, and quite naturally. I should if our positions were reversed. But I *must* go on with it. I *can't* go back to my wife and baby with simply nothing. We have no fire, no food, nothing except the ceiling we are under. It is my fault, all of it. I don't want your pity, but I *have* to attack your comfort."

He trembled. He shivered as though he were going to fall. Involuntarily she put out her hand to steady him. She touched his arm and felt it quiver under the thin sleeve.

"It's all right . . ." he murmured. "I'm hungry . . . I can't help it."

She had had an excellent dinner. She had drunk perhaps just enough to lead to recklessness — in any case, before she realised it, she was ushering him in, through her dark-blue painted door. A crazy thing to do! Nor was it as though she were too young to know any better, for she was fifty if she was a day and, although sturdy of body and as strong as a horse (except for a little unsteadiness of the heart), intelligent enough to be thin, neurotic and abnormal; but she was none of these.

Although intelligent she suffered dreadfully from impulsive kindness. All her life she had done so. The mistakes that she had made — and there had been quite a few — had all arisen from the triumph of her heart over her brain. She knew it — how well she knew it! — and all her friends were forever dinning it into her. When she reached her fiftieth birthday she said to herself, "Well, now at last I'm too old to be foolish any more." And here she was, helping an entirely unknown young man into her house at dead of night, and he in all probability the worst sort of criminal.

Very soon he was sitting on her rose-coloured sofa, eating sandwiches and drinking a whisky and soda. He seemed to be entirely overcome by the beauty of her possessions. "If he's acting he's doing it very well," she thought to herself. But he had taste and he had knowledge. He knew that the Utrillo was an early one, the only period of importance in that master's work, he knew that the two old men talking under a window belonged to Sickert's "Middle Italian," he recognised the Dobson head and the wonderful green bronze Elk of Carl Milles.

"You are an artist," she said. "You paint?"

"No, I am a pimp, a thief, a what you like — anything bad," he answered fiercely. "And now I must go," he added, springing up from the sofa.

He seemed most certainly invigorated. She could scarcely believe that he was the same young man who only half an hour before had had to lean on her arm for support. And he was a gentleman. Of that there could be no sort of question. And he was astoundingly beautiful in the spirit of a hundred years ago, a young Byron, a young Shelley, not a young Ramon Navarro or a young Ronald Colman.

Well, it was better that he should go, and she did hope (for his own sake rather than hers) that he would not demand money and threaten a scene. After all, with her snow-white hair, firm broad chin, firm broad body, she did not look like someone who could be threatened. He had not apparently the slightest intention of threatening her. He moved towards the door.

"Oh!" he murmured with a little gasp of wonder. He had stopped before one of the loveliest things that she had — a mask in silver of a clown's face, the clown smiling, gay, joyful, not hinting at perpetual sadness as all clowns are traditionally supposed to do. It was one of the most successful efforts of the famous Sorat, greatest living master of masks.

"Yes. Isn't that lovely?" she said. "It was one of Sorat's earliest things, and still, I think, one of his best."

"Silver is the right material for that clown," he said.

"Yes, I think so too," she agreed. She realised that she had asked him nothing about his troubles, about his poor wife and baby, about his past history. It was better perhaps like this.

"You have saved my life," he said to her in the hall. She had in her hand a pound note.

"Well," she answered cheerfully, "I was a fool to risk a strange man in my house at this time of night — or so my friends would tell me. But such an old woman like me — where's the risk?"

"I could have cut your throat," he said quite seriously.

"So you could," she admitted. "But with horrid consequences to yourself."

"Oh no," he said. "Not in these days. The police are never able to catch anybody."

"Well, good night. Do take this. It can get you some warmth at least."

He took the pound. "Thanks," he said carelessly. Then at the door he remarked: "That mask. The loveliest thing I ever saw."

When the door had closed and she went back into the sitting room she sighed: —

"What a good-looking young man!" Then she saw that her most beautiful white jade cigarette case was gone. It had been lying on the little table by the sofa. She had seen it just before she went into the pantry to cut the sandwiches. He had stolen it. She looked everywhere. No, undoubtedly he had stolen it.

"What a good-looking young man!" she thought as she went up to bed.

Sonia Herries was a woman of her time in that outwardly she was cynical and destructive while inwardly she was a creature longing for affection and appreciation. For though she had white hair and was fifty she was outwardly active, young, could do with little sleep and less food, could dance and drink cocktails and play bridge to the end of all time. Inwardly she cared for neither cocktails nor bridge. She was above all things maternal and she had a weak heart, not only a spiritual weak heart but also a physical one. When she suffered, must take her drops, lie down and rest, she allowed no one to see her. Like all the other women of her period and manner of life she had a courage worthy of a better cause.

She was a heroine for no reason at all.

But, beyond everything else, she was maternal. Twice at least she would have married had she loved enough, but the man she had really loved had not loved her (that was twenty-five years ago), so she had pretended to despise matrimony. Had she had a child her nature would have been fulfilled; as she had not had that good fortune she had been maternal (with outward cynical indifference) to numbers of people who had made use of her, sometimes laughed at her, never deeply cared for her. She was named "a jolly good sort," and was always "just outside" the real life of her friends. Her Herries relations, Rockages and Cards and Newmarks, used her to take odd places at table, to fill up spare rooms at house parties, to make purchases for them in London, to talk to when things went wrong with them or people abused them. She was a very lonely woman.

She saw her young thief for the second time a fortnight later. She saw him because he came to her house one evening when she was dressing for dinner.

"A young man at the door," said her maid Rose.

"A young man? Who?" But she knew.

"I don't know, Miss Sonia. He won't give his name."

She came down and found him in the hall, the cigarette case in his hand. He was wearing a decent suit of clothes, but he still looked hungry, haggard, desperate and incredibly handsome. She took him into the room where they had been before. He gave her the cigarette case. "I pawned it," he said, his eyes on the silver mask.

"What a disgraceful thing to do!" she said. "And what are you going to steal next?"

"My wife made some money last week," he said. "That will see us through for a while."

"Do you never do any work?" she asked him.

"I paint," he answered. "But no one will touch my pictures. They are not modern enough."

"You must show me some of your pictures," she said, and realised how weak she was. It was not his good looks that gave him his power over her, but something both helpless and defiant, like a wicked child who hates his mother but is always coming to her for help.

"I have some here," he said, went into the hall, and returned with several canvases. He displayed them. They were very bad — sugary landscapes and sentimental figures.

"They are very bad," she said.

"I know they are. You must understand that my æsthetic taste is very fine. I appreciate only the best things in art, like your cigarette case, that mask there, the Utrillo. But I can paint nothing but these. It is very exasperating." He smiled at her.

"Won't you buy one?" he asked her.

"Oh, but I don't want one," she answered. "I should have to hide it." She was aware that in ten minutes her guests would be here.

"Oh, do buy one."

"No, but of course not —— "

"Yes, please." He came nearer and looked up into her broad kindly face like a beseeching child.

"Well . . . how much are they?"

"This is twenty pounds. This twenty-five —— "

"But how absurd! They are not worth anything at all."

"They may be one day. You never know with modern pictures."

"I am quite sure about these."

"Please buy one. That one with the cows is not so bad."

She sat down and wrote a cheque.

"I'm a perfect fool. Take this, and understand I never want to see you again. Never! You will never be admitted. It is no use speaking to me in the street. If you bother me I shall tell the police."

He took the cheque with quiet satisfaction, held out his hand and pressed hers a little.

"Hang that in the right light and it will not be so bad —— "

"You want new boots," she said. "Those are terrible."

"I shall be able to get some now," he said and went away.

All that evening while she listened to the hard and crackling ironies of her friends she thought of the young man. She did not know his name. The only thing that she knew about him was that by his own confession he was a scoundrel and had at his mercy a poor young wife and a starving child. The picture that she formed of these three haunted her. It had been, in a way, honest of him to return the cigarette case. Ah, but he knew, of course, that did he not return it he could never have seen her again. He had discovered at once that she was a splendid source of supply, and now that she had bought one of his wretched pictures —— Nevertheless he could not be altogether bad. No one who cared so passionately for beautiful things could be quite worthless. The way that he had gone straight to the silver mask as soon as he entered the room and gazed at it as though with his very soul! And, sitting at her dinner table, uttering the most cynical sentiments, she was all softness as she gazed across to the wall upon whose pale surface the silver mask was hanging. There was, she thought, a certain look of the young man in that jolly shining surface. But where? The clown's cheek was fat, his mouth broad, his lips thick — and yet, and yet ——

For the next few days as she went about London she looked in spite of herself at the passers-by to see whether he might not be there. One thing she soon discovered, that he was very much more handsome than anyone else whom she saw. But it was not for his handsomeness that he haunted her. It was because he wanted her to be kind to him, and because she wanted — oh, so terribly — to be kind to someone!

The silver mask, she had the fancy, was gradually changing, the rotundity thinning, some new light coming into the empty eyes. It was most certainly a beautiful thing.

Then, as unexpectedly as on the other occasions, he appeared again. One night as she, back from a theatre smoking one last cigarette, was preparing to climb the stairs to bed, there was a knock on the door. Everyone of course rang the bell — no one attempted the old-fashioned knocker shaped like an owl that she had bought, one idle day, in an old curiosity shop. The knock made her sure that it was he. Rose had gone to bed, so she went herself to the door. There he was — and with him a young girl and a baby. They all came into the sitting room and stood awkwardly by the fire. It was at that moment when she saw them in a group by the fire that she felt her first sharp pang of fear. She knew suddenly how weak she was — she seemed to be turned to water at sight of them, she, Sonia Herries, fifty years of age, independent and strong, save for that little flutter of the heart — yes, turned to water! She was afraid as though someone had whispered a warning in her ear.

The girl was striking, with red hair and a white face, a thin grace-ful little thing. The baby, wrapped in a shawl, was soaked in sleep. She gave them drinks and the remainder of the sandwiches that had been put there for herself. The young man looked at her with his charming smile.

"We haven't come to cadge anything this time," he said. "But I wanted you to see my wife and I wanted her to see some of your lovely things."

"Well," she said sharply, "you can only stay a minute or two. It's late. I'm off to bed. Besides, I told you not to come here again."

"Ada made me," he said, nodding at the girl. "She was so anxious to see you."

The girl never said a word but only stared sulkily in front of her.

"All right. But you must go soon. By the way, you've never told me your name."

"Henry Abbott, and that's Ada, and the baby's called Henry too."

"All right. How have you been getting on since I saw you?"

"Oh, fine! Living on the fat of the land." But he soon fell into silence and the girl never said a word. After an intolerable pause Sonia Herries suggested that they should go. They didn't move. Half an hour later she insisted. They got up. But, standing by the door, Henry Abbott jerked his head towards the writing desk.

"Who writes your letters for you?"

"Nobody. I write them myself."

"You ought to have somebody. Save a lot of trouble. I'll do them for you."

"Oh no, thank you. That would never do. Well, good night, good night —— "

"Of course I'll do them for you. And you needn't pay me anything either. Fill up my time."

"Nonsense . . . good night, good night." She closed the door on them. She could not sleep. She lay there thinking of him. She was moved, partly by a maternal tenderness for them that warmed her body (the girl and the baby had looked so helpless sitting there), partly by a shiver of apprehension that chilled her veins. Well, she hoped that she would never see them again. Or did she? Would she not to-morrow, as she walked down Sloane Street, stare at everyone to see whether by chance that was he?

Three mornings later he arrived. It was a wet morning and she had decided to devote it to the settling of accounts. She was sitting there at her table when Rose showed him in.

"I've come to do your letters," he said.

"I should think not," she said sharply. "Now, Henry Abbott, out you go. I've had enough —— "

"Oh no, you haven't," he said, and sat down at her desk.

She would be ashamed for ever, but half an hour later she was seated in the corner of the sofa telling him what to write. She hated to confess it to herself, but she liked to see him sitting there. He was company for her, and to whatever depths he might by now have sunk, he was most certainly a gentleman. He behaved very well that morning; he wrote an excellent hand. He seemed to know just what to say.

A week later she said, laughing, to Amy Weston: "My dear, would you believe it? I've had to take on a secretary. A very good-looking young man — but you needn't look down your nose. You know that good-looking young men are nothing to *me* — and he does save me endless bother."

For three weeks he behaved very well, arriving punctually, offering her no insults, doing as she suggested about everything. In the fourth week, about a quarter to one on a day, his wife arrived. On this occasion she looked astonishingly young, sixteen perhaps. She wore a simple grey cotton dress. Her red bobbed hair was strikingly vibrant about her pale face.

The young man already knew that Miss Herries was lunching alone. He had seen the table laid for one with its simple appurtenances. It seemed to be very difficult not to ask them to remain. She did, although she did not wish to. The meal was not a success. The two of them together were tiresome, for the man said little when his wife was there, and the woman said nothing at all. Also the pair of them were in a way sinister.

She sent them away after luncheon. They departed without protest. But as she walked, engaged on her shopping that afternoon, she decided that she must rid herself of them, once and for all. It was true that it had been rather agreeable having him there; his smile, his wicked humorous remarks, the suggestion that he was a kind of malevolent gamin who preyed on the world in general but spared her because he liked her — all this had attracted her — but what really alarmed her was that during all these weeks he had made no request for money, made indeed no request for anything. He must be piling up a fine account, must have some plan in his head with which one morning he would balefully startle her! For a moment there in the bright sunlight, with the purr of the traffic, the rustle of the trees about her, she saw herself in surprising colour. She was behaving with a weakness that was astonishing. Her stout, thick-set, resolute body, her cheery rosy face, her strong white hair — all these disappeared, and in their place, there almost clinging for support to the park railings, was a timorous little old woman with frightened eyes and trembling knees. What was there to be afraid of? She had done nothing wrong. There were the police at hand. She had never been a coward before. She went home, however, with an odd impulse to leave her comfortable little house in Walpole Street and hide herself somewhere, somewhere that no one could discover.

That evening they appeared again, husband, wife and baby. She had settled herself down for a cosy evening with a book and an "early to bed." There came the knock on the door.

On this occasion she was most certainly firm with them. When they were gathered in a little group she got up and addressed them.

"Here is five pounds," she said, "and this is the end. If one of you shows his or her face inside this door again I call the police. Now go."

The girl gave a little gasp and fell in a dead faint at her feet. It was a perfectly genuine faint. Rose was summoned. Everything possible was done.

"She has simply not had enough to eat," said Henry Abbott. In the end (so determined and resolved was the faint) Ada Abbott was put to bed in the spare room and a doctor was summoned. After examining her he said that she needed rest and nourishment. This was perhaps the critical moment of the whole affair. Had Sonia Herries been at this crisis properly resolute and bundled the Abbott family, faint and all, into the cold unsympathising street, she might at this moment be a hale and hearty old woman enjoying bridge with her friends. It was, however, just here that her maternal temperament was too strong for her. The poor young thing lay exhausted, her eyes closed, her cheeks almost the colour of her pillow. The baby (surely the quietest baby ever known) lay in a cot beside the bed. Henry Abbott wrote letters to dictation downstairs. Once Sonia Herries, glancing up at the silver mask, was struck by the grin on the clown's face. It seemed to her now a thin sharp grin — almost derisive.

Three days after Ada Abbott's collapse there arrived her aunt and her uncle, Mr. and Mrs. Edwards. Mr. Edwards was a large red-faced man with a hearty manner and a bright waistcoat. He looked like a publican. Mrs. Edwards was a thin sharp-nosed woman with a bass voice. She was very, very thin, and wore a large old-fashioned brooch on her flat but emotional chest. They sat side by side on the sofa and explained that they had come to enquire after Ada, their favourite niece. Mrs. Edwards cried, Mr. Edwards was friendly and familiar. Unfortunately Mrs. Weston and a friend came and called just then. They did not stay very long. They were frankly amazed at the Edwards couple and deeply startled by Henry Abbott's familiarity. Sonia Herries could see that they drew the very worst conclusions.

A week later Ada Abbott was still in bed in the upstairs room. It seemed to be impossible to move her. The Edwardses were constant visitors. On one occasion they brought Mr. and Mrs. Harper and their girl Agnes. They were profusely apologetic, but Miss Herries would understand that "with the interest they took in Ada it was impossible to stay passive." They all crowded into the spare bed-

room and gazed at the pale figure with the closed eyes sympathetically.

Then two things happened together. Rose gave notice and Mrs.
Weston came and had a frank talk with her friend. She began with
that most sinister opening: "I think you ought to know, dear, what
everyone is saying — " What everyone was saying was that Sonia
Herries was living with a young ruffian from the streets, young
enough to be her son.

"You must get rid of them all and at once," said Mrs. Weston, "or
you won't have a friend left in London, darling."

Left to herself, Sonia Herries did what she had not done for years,
she burst into tears. What had happened to her? Not only had her
will and determination gone but she felt most unwell. Her heart
was bad again; she could not sleep; the house, too, was tumbling
to pieces. There was dust over everything. How was she ever to
replace Rose? She was living in some horrible nightmare. This
dreadful handsome young man seemed to have some authority over
her. Yet he did not threaten her. All he did was to smile. Nor was
she in the very least in love with him. This must come to an end or
she would be lost.

Two days later, at tea time, her opportunity arrived. Mr. and Mrs.
Edwards had called to see how Ada was; Ada was downstairs at
last, very weak and pale. Henry Abbott was there, also the baby.
Sonia Herries, although she was feeling dreadfully unwell, addressed
them all with vigour. She especially addressed the sharp-nosed Mrs.
Edwards.

"You must understand," she said. "I don't want to be unkind, but
I have my own life to consider. I am a very busy woman, and this
has all been forced on me. I don't want to seem brutal. I'm glad to
have been of some assistance to you, but I think Mrs. Abbott is well
enough to go home now — and I wish you all good night."

"I am sure," said Mrs. Edwards, looking up at her from the sofa,
"that you've been kindness itself, Miss Herries. Ada recognizes it,
I'm sure. But to move her now would be to kill her, that's all. Any
movement and she'll drop at your feet."

"We have nowhere to go," said Henry Abbott.

"But, Mrs. Edwards — " began Miss Herries, her anger rising.

"We have only two rooms," said Mrs. Edwards quietly. "I'm

sorry, but just now, what with my husband coughing all night —— "

"Oh, but this is monstrous!" Miss Herries cried. "I have had enough of this. I have been generous to a degree —— "

"What about my pay," said Henry, "for all these weeks?"

"Pay! Why, of course — " Miss Herries began. Then she stopped. She realised several things. She realised that she was alone in the house, the cook having departed that afternoon. She realised that none of them had moved. She realised that her "things" — the Sickert, the Utrillo, the sofa — were alive with apprehension. She was fearfully frightened of their silence, their immobility. She moved towards her desk, and her heart turned, squeezed itself dry, shot through her body the most dreadful agony.

"Please," she gasped. "In the drawer — the little green bottle — oh, quick! Please, please!"

The last thing of which she was aware was the quiet handsome features of Henry Abbott bending over her.

When, a week later, Mrs. Weston called, the girl, Ada Abbott, opened the door to her.

"I came to enquire for Miss Herries," she said. "I haven't seen her about. I have telephoned several times and received no answer."

"Miss Herries is very ill."

"Oh, I'm so sorry. Can I not see her?"

Ada Abbott's quiet gentle tones were reassuring her. "The doctor does not wish her to see anyone at present. May I have your address? I will let you know as soon as she is well enough."

Mrs. Weston went away. She recounted the event. "Poor Sonia, she's pretty bad. They seem to be looking after her. As soon as she's better we'll go and see her."

The London life moves swiftly. Sonia Herries had never been of very great importance to anyone. Herries relations enquired. They received a very polite note assuring them that so soon as she was better —

Sonia Herries was in bed, but not in her own room. She was in the little attic bedroom but lately occupied by Rose the maid. She lay at first in a strange apathy. She was ill. She slept and woke and slept again. Ada Abbott, sometimes Mrs. Edwards, sometimes a woman she did not know, attended to her. They were all very kind. Did she need a doctor? No, of course she did not need a doctor, they assured her. They would see that she had everything that she wanted.

Then life began to flow back into her. Why was she in this room? Where were her friends? What was this horrible food that they were bringing her? What were they doing here, these women?

She had a terrible scene with Ada Abbott. She tried to get out of bed. The girl restrained her — and easily, for all the strength seemed to have gone from her bones. She protested, she was as furious as her weakness allowed her, then she cried. She cried most bitterly. Next day she was alone and she crawled out of bed; the door was locked; she beat on it. There was no sound but her beating. Her heart was beginning again that terrible strangled throb. She crept back into bed. She lay there, weakly, feebly crying. When Ada arrived with some bread, some soup, some water, she demanded that the door should be unlocked, that she should get up, have her bath, come downstairs to her own room.

"You are not well enough," Ada said gently.

"Of course I am well enough. When I get out I will have you put in prison for this —— "

"Please don't get excited. It is so bad for your heart."

Mrs. Edwards and Ada washed her. She had not enough to eat. She was always hungry.

Summer had come. Mrs. Weston went to Etretat. Everyone was out of town.

"What's happened to Sonia Herries?" Mabel Newmark wrote to Agatha Benson. "I haven't seen her for ages. . . ."

But no one had time to enquire. There were so many things to do. Sonia was a good sort, but she had been nobody's business. . . .

Once Henry Abbott paid her a visit. "I am so sorry that you are not better," he said smiling. "We are doing everything we can for you. It is lucky we were around when you were so ill. You had better sign these papers. Someone must look after your affairs until you are better. You will be downstairs in a week or two."

Looking at him with wide-open terrified eyes, Sonia Herries signed the papers.

The first rains of autumn lashed the streets. In the sitting room the gramophone was turned on. Ada and young Mr. Jackson, Maggie Trent and stout Harry Bennett were dancing. All the furniture was flung against the walls. Mr. Edwards drank his beer; Mrs. Edwards was toasting her toes before the fire.

Henry Abbott came in. He had just sold the Utrillo. His arrival was greeted with cheers.

He took the silver mask from the wall and went upstairs. He climbed to the top of the house, entered, switched on the naked light.

"Oh! Who — what — " A voice of terror came from the bed.

"It's all right," he said soothingly. "Ada will be bringing your tea in a minute."

He had a hammer and nail and hung the silver mask on the speckled, mottled wall paper where Miss Herries could see it.

"I know you're fond of it," he said. "I thought you'd like it to look at."

She made no reply. She only stared.

"You'll want something to look at," he went on. "You're too ill, I'm afraid, ever to leave this room again. So it'll be nice for you. Something to look at."

He went out, gently closing the door behind him.

RANSOM

by *PEARL S. BUCK*

And finally, a story you might have read about just this morning in your newspaper — of a kidnaped child and the problem of decent American parents — of tears and G-men and great courage. By the author of "The Good Earth."

THE BEETHOVEN symphony stopped abruptly. A clear metallic voice broke across the melody of the third movement.

"Press radio news. The body of Jimmie Lane, kidnaped son of Mr. Headley Lane, has been found on the bank of the Hudson River near his home this afternoon. This ends the search of —— "

"Kent, turn it off, please!" Allin exclaimed.

Kent Crothers hesitated a second. Then he turned off the radio.

In the silence Allin sat biting her lower lip. "That poor mother!" she exclaimed. "All these days — not giving up hope."

"I suppose it is better to know something definite," he said quietly, "even though it is the worst."

Perhaps this would be a good time to talk with her, to warn her that she was letting this kidnaping business grow into an obsession. After all, children did grow up in the United States, even in well-to-do families like theirs. The trouble was that they were not quite rich enough and still too rich — not rich enough to hire guards for their children, but rich enough, because his father owned the paper mill, to make them known in the neighborhood, at least.

The thing was to take it for granted that they did not belong to the millionaire class and therefore were not prize for kidnapers. They should do this for Bruce's sake. He would be starting to school next autumn. Bruce would have to walk back and forth on the streets like millions of other American children. Kent wouldn't have his son driven three blocks, even by Peter the outdoor man; it would do him more harm than . . . after all, it was a democracy they lived in, and Bruce had to grow up with the crowd.

"I'll go and see that the children are covered," Allin said. "Betsy throws off the covers whenever she can."

Kent knew that she simply wanted to make sure they were there. But he rose with her, lighting his pipe, thinking how to begin. They walked up the stairs together, their fingers interlaced. Softly she opened the nursery door. It was ridiculous how even he was being affected by her fears. Whenever the door opened his heart stood cold for a second, until he saw the two beds, each with a little head on the pillow.

They were there now, of course. He stood beside Bruce's bed and looked down at his son. Handsome little devil. He was sleeping so soundly that when his mother leaned over him he did not move. His black hair was a tousle; his red lips pouted. He was dark, but he had Allin's blue eyes.

They did not speak. Allin drew the cover gently over his outflung arm, and they stood a moment longer, hand in hand, gazing at the child. Then Allin looked up at Kent and smiled, and he kissed her. He put his arm about her shoulder, and they went to Betsy's bed.

Here was his secret obsession. He could say firmly that Bruce must take his chances with the other children, because a boy had to learn to be brave. But this baby — such a tiny feminine creature, his little daughter. She had Allin's auburn coloring, but by some miracle she had his dark eyes, so that when he looked into them he seemed to be looking into himself.

She was breathing now, a little unevenly, through her tiny nose. "How's her cold?" he whispered.

"It doesn't seem worse," Allin whispered back. "I put stuff on her chest."

He was always angry when anything happened to this baby. He didn't trust her nurse, Mollie, too much. She was good-hearted, maybe, but easygoing.

The baby stirred and opened her eyes. She blinked, smiled and put up her arms to him.

"Don't pick her up, darling," Allin counseled. "She'll only want it every time."

So he did not take her. Instead, he put her arms down, one and then the other, playfully, under the cover.

"Go to sleep-bye, honey," he said. And she lay, sleepily smiling. She was a good little thing.

"Come — let's put out the light," Allin whispered. They tiptoed out and went back to the living room.

Kent sat down, puffed on his pipe, his mind full of what he wanted to say to Allin. It was essential to their life to believe that nothing could happen to their children.

"Kidnaping's like lightning," he began abruptly. "It happens, of course — once in a million. What you have to remember is all the rest of the children who are perfectly safe."

She had sat down on the ottoman before the fire, but she turned to him when he said this. "What would you do, honestly, Kent, if some night when we went upstairs —— "

"Nonsense!" he broke in. "That's what I've been trying to tell you. It's so unlikely as to be — it's these damned newspapers! When a thing happens in one part of the country, every little hamlet hears of it."

"Jane Eliot told me there are three times as many kidnapings as ever get into the newspapers," Allin said.

"Jane's a newspaperwoman," Kent said. "You mustn't let her sense of drama —— "

"Still, she's been on a lot of kidnaping cases," Allin replied. "She was telling me about the Wyeth case —— "

This was the time to speak, now when all Allin's secret anxiety was quivering in her voice. Kent took her hand and fondled it as he spoke. He must remember how deeply she felt everything, and this thing had haunted her before Bruce was born. He had not even thought of it until one night in the darkness she had asked him the same question, "What would we do, Kent, if —— " Only then he had not known what she meant.

"If what?" he had asked.

"If our baby were ever kidnaped."

He had answered what he had felt then and believed now to be true. "Why worry about what will never happen?" he had said. Nevertheless, he had followed all the cases since Bruce was born.

He kissed her palm now. "I can't bear having you afraid," he said. "It isn't necessary, you know, darling. We can't live under the shadow of this thing," he went on. "We have to come to some rational position on it."

"That's what I want, Kent. I'd be glad not to be afraid — if I knew how."

"After all," he went on again, "most people bring up their families without thinking about it."

"Most mothers think of it," she said. "Most of the women I know have said something about it to me — some time or other — enough to make me know they think about it all the time."

"You'd be better off not talking about it," he said.

But she said, "We keep wondering what we would do, Kent."

"That's just it!" he exclaimed. "That's why I think if we decided now what we would do — always bearing in mind that it's only the remotest possibility —— "

"What *would* we do, Kent?" she asked.

He answered half playfully, "Promise to remember it's as remote as — an airplane attack on our home?"

She nodded.

"I've always thought that if one of the children were kidnaped I'd simply turn the whole thing over to the police at once."

"What police?" she asked instantly. "Gossipy old Mike O'Brien, who'd tell the newspapers the first thing? It's fatal to let it get into the papers, Jane says."

"Well, the Federal police, then — the G-men."

"How does one get in touch with them?"

He had to confess he did not know. "I'll find out," he promised. "Anyway, it's the principle, darling, that we want to determine. Once we know what we'll do, we can put it out of our minds. No ransom, Allin — that I feel sure about. As long as we keep on paying ransoms, we're going to have kidnapings. Somebody has to be strong enough to take the stand. Then maybe other people will see what they ought to do."

But she did not look convinced. When she spoke, her voice was low and full of dread. "The thing is, Kent, if we decided not to pay ransom, we just couldn't stick to it — not really, I mean. Suppose it were Bruce — suppose he had a cold and it was winter — and he was taken out of his warm bed in his pajamas, we'd do anything.

You know we would!" She rushed on. "We wouldn't care about other children, Kent. We would only be thinking of our own little Bruce — and no one else. How to get him back again, at whatever cost."

"Hush, darling," he said. "If you're going to be like this we can't talk about it, after all."

"No, Kent, please. I do want to talk. I want to know what we ought to do. If only I could be not afraid!" she whispered.

"Come here by me," he said. He drew her to the couch beside him. "First of all, you know I love the children as well as you do, don't you?" She nodded, and he went on, "Then, darling, I'd do anything I thought would be best for our children, wouldn't I?"

"You'd do the best you knew, Kent. The question is, do any of us know what to do?"

"I do know," he said gravely, "that until we make the giving and taking of ransoms unlawful we shall have kidnapers. And until somebody begins it, it will never be done. That's the law of demo-cratic government. The people have to begin action before govern-ment takes a stand."

"What if they said not to tell the police?" she asked.

Her concreteness confounded him. It was not as if the thing could happen!

"It all depends," he retorted, "on whether you want to give in to rascals or stand on your principle."

"But if it were our own child?" she persisted. "Be honest, Kent. Please don't retire into principles."

"I am trying to be honest," he said slowly. "I think I would stick by principle and trust somehow to think of some way —— " He looked waveringly into her unbelieving eyes.

"Try to remember exactly what happened!" he was shouting at the silly nurse. "Where did you leave her?"

Allin was quieter than he, but Allin's voice on the telephone half an hour ago had been like a scream: "Kent, we can't find Betsy!"

He had been in the mill directors' meeting, but he'd risen in-stantly. "Sorry," he'd said sharply. "I have to leave at once."

"Nothing serious, Kent?" His father's white eyebrows had lifted.

"I think not," he'd answered. He had sense enough not to say what Allin had screamed. "I'll let you know if it is."

He had leaped into his car and driven home like a crazy man. He'd drawn up in a spray of gravel at his own gate. Allin was there, and Mollie, the silly nurse. Mollie was sobbing.

"We was at the gate, sir, watchin' for Brucie to come home from school, like we do every day, and I put 'er down — she's heavy to carry — while I went in to get a clean hankie to wipe her little hands. She'd stooped into a puddle from the rain this morning. When I came back, she wasn't there. I ran around the shrubs, sir, lookin' — and then I screamed for the madam."

"Kent, I've combed the place," Allin whispered.

"The gate!" he gasped.

"It was shut, and the bar across," Mollie wailed. "I'd sense enough to see to that before I went in."

"How long were you gone?" he shouted at her.

"I don't know, sir," Mollie sobbed. "It didn't seem a minute!"

He rushed into the yard. "Betsy, Betsy!" he cried. "Come to Daddy! Here's Daddy!" He stooped under the big lilac bushes. "Have you looked in the garage?" he demanded of Allin.

"Peter's been through it twice," she answered.

"I'll see for myself," he said. "Go into the house, Allin. She may have got inside, somehow."

He tore into the garage. Peter crawled out from under the small car.

"She ain't hyah, suh," he whispered. "Ah done looked ev'ywheah."

But Kent looked again, Peter following him like a dog. In the back of his mind was a telephone number, National 7117. He had found out about that number the year before, after he and Allin had talked that evening. Only he wouldn't call yet. Betsy was sure to be somewhere.

The gate clicked, and he rushed out. But it was only Bruce.

"Why, what's the matter with you, Daddy?" Bruce asked.

Kent swallowed — no use scaring Bruce. "Bruce, did you — you didn't see Betsy on the way home, did you?"

"No, Daddy. I didn't see anybody except Mike to help me across the square 'cause there was a notomobile."

"Wha' dat?" Peter was pointing at something. It was a bit of white paper, held down by a stone.

As well as he knew anything, Kent knew what it was. He had read that note a dozen times in the newspaper accounts. He stooped and picked it up. There it was — the scrawled handwriting.

"We been waiting this chanse." The handwriting was there, illiterate, disguised. "Fifty grand is the price. Your dads got it if you aint. Youll hear where to put it. If you tell the police we kill the kid."

"Daddy, what's —— " Bruce began.

"Bring him indoors," he ordered Peter.

Where was Allin? He had to — he had promised her it would not happen! The telephone number was — but ——

"Allin!" he shouted.

He heard her running down from the attic.

"Allin!" he gasped. She was there, white and piteous with terror — and so helpless. God, they were both so helpless! He had to have help; he had to know what to do. But had not he — he had decided long ago what he must do, because what did he know about crooks and kidnapers? People gave the ransom and lost their children, too. He had to have advice he could trust.

"I'm going to call National 7117!" he blurted at her.

"No, Kent — wait!" she cried.

"I've got to," he insisted. Before she could move, he ran to the telephone and took up the receiver. "I want National 7117!" he shouted.

Her face went white. He held out his hand with the crumpled note. She read it and snatched at the receiver.

"No, Kent — wait. We don't know. Wait and see what they say!"

But a calm voice was already speaking at the other end of the wire: "This is National 7117." And Kent was shouting hoarsely, "I want to report a kidnaping. It's our baby girl. Kent Crothers, 134 Eastwood Avenue, Greenvale, New York."

He listened while the voice was telling him to do nothing, to wait until tomorrow, and then at a certain village inn, fifty miles away, to meet a certain man who would wear a plain gray suit.

And all the time Allin was whispering, "They'll kill her — they'll kill her, Kent."

"They won't know," he whispered back. "Nobody will know." When he put the receiver down he cried at her angrily, "They won't tell anybody — those fellows in Washington! Besides, I've got to have help, I tell you!"

She stood staring at him with horrified eyes. "They'll kill her," she repeated.

He wanted to get somewhere to weep, only men could not weep. But Allin was not weeping, either. Then suddenly they flung their arms about each other, and together broke into silent terrible tears.

He was not used to waiting, but he had to wait. And he had to help Allin wait. Men were supposed to be stronger.

At first it had been a comfort to have the directions to follow. First, everybody in the house — that was easy: simply the cook Sarah, the maid Rose, and Mollie and Peter. They of course were beyond blame, except Mollie. Perhaps Mollie was more than just a fool. They all had to be told they were to say absolutely nothing.

"Get everybody together in the dining room," Kent had told Allin. He had gone into the dining room.

"Daddy!" He saw Bruce's terrified figure in the doorway. "What's the matter? Where's Betsy?"

"We can't find her, son," Kent said, trying to make his voice calm. "Of course we will, but just now nobody must know she isn't here."

"Shall I go out in the yard?" Bruce asked. "Maybe I could find her."

"No," Kent said sharply. "I'd rather you went upstairs to your own room. I'll be up — in a minute."

The servants were coming in, Allin behind them.

"I'll go with Bruce," she said.

She was so still and so controlled, but he could tell by the quiver about her lips that she was only waiting for him.

"I'll be up in a very few minutes," he promised her. He stood until she had gone, Bruce's hand in hers. Then he turned to the four waiting figures. Mollie was still crying. He could tell by their faces that they all knew about the note.

"I see you know what has happened," he said. Strange how all these familiar faces looked sinister to him! Peter and Sarah had been in his mother's household. They had known him for years. And Rose was Sarah's niece. But they all looked hostile, or he imagined they did. "And I want not one word said of this to anyone in the town," he said harshly. "Remember, Betsy's life depends on no one outside knowing."

He paused, setting his jaws. He would not have believed he could cry as easily as a woman, but he could.

He cleared his throat. "Her life depends on how we behave now — in the next few hours." Mollie's sobbing burst out into wails. He rose. "That's all," he said. "We must simply wait."

The telephone rang, and he hurried to it. There was no way of knowing how the next message would come. But it was his father's peremptory voice: "Anything wrong over there, Kent?"

He knew now it would never do for his father to know what had happened. His father could keep nothing to himself.

"Everything is all right, Dad," he answered. "Allin's not feeling very well, that's all."

"Have you had the doctor?" his father shouted.

"We will if it is necessary, Dad," he answered and put up the receiver abruptly. He could not go on with that.

He thought of Bruce and went to find him. He was eating his supper in the nursery, and Allin was with him. She had told Mollie to stay downstairs. She could not bear to see the girl any more than he could.

But the nursery was unbearable, too. This was the time when Betsy, fresh from her bath . . .

"I'm — I'll be downstairs in the library," he told Allin hurriedly, and she nodded.

In the library the silence was torture. There was nothing to do but wait.

And all the time who knew what was happening to the child? Tomorrow, the man had said an hour ago. Wait, he had said. But what about tonight? In what sort of place would the child be sleeping?

Kent leaped to his feet. Something had to be done. He would have a look around the yard. There might be another letter.

He went out into the early autumn twilight. He had to hold himself together to keep from breaking into foolish shouts and curses. It was the agony of not being able to do anything. Then he controlled himself. The thing was to go on following a rational plan. He had come out to see if he could find anything.

He searched every inch of the yard. There was no message of any sort.

Then in the gathering darkness he saw a man at the gate. "Mist' Crothers!" it was Peter's voice. "Fo' God, Mist' Crothers, Ah don' know why they should pick on mah ole 'ooman. When Ah come home fo' suppah, she give it to me — she cain't read, so she don' know what wuz in it. Ah run all de way."

Kent snatched a paper from Peter's shaking hand and ran to the house. In the lighted hall he read:

Get the dough ready all banknotes dont mark any or well get the other kid too. Dont try double-crossing us. You cant get away with nothing. Put it in a box by the dead oak at the mill creek. You know where. At twelve o'clock tomorrow night.

He knew where, indeed. He had fished there from the time he was a little boy. The lightning had struck that oak tree one summer when he had been only a hundred yards away, standing in the doorway of the mill during a thunderstorm. How did they know he knew?

He turned on Peter. "Who brought this?" he demanded.

"Ah don' know, suh," Peter stammered. "She couldn't tell me nothin' 'cep'n' it wuz a white man. He chuck it at 'er and say, 'Give it to yo' ole man.' So she give it to me, and Ah come a-runnin'."

Kent stared at Peter, trying to ferret into that dark brain. Was Peter being used by someone; bribed, perhaps, to take a part? Did he know anything?

"If I thought you knew anything about Betsy, I'd kill you myself," he said.

"Fo' God, Ah don', Mist' Crothers — you know me, suh! Ah done gyardened for yo' since yo' and Miss Allin got mah'ied. 'Sides, whut Ah want in such devilment? Ah got all Ah want — mah house and a sal'ry. Ah don' want nuthin'."

It was all true, of course. The thing was, you suspected everybody.

"You tell Flossie to tell no one," he commanded Peter.

"Ah done tole 'er," Peter replied fervently. "Ah tole 'er Ah'd split 'er open if she tole anybody 'bout dat white man."

"Get along, then," said Kent. "And remember what I told you."

"Yassuh," Peter replied.

"Of course we'll pay the ransom!" Allin was insisting.

They were in their own room, the door open into the narrow passage, and beyond that the door into the nursery was open, too. They sat where, in the shadowy light of a night lamp, they could see Bruce's dark head on the pillow. Impossible, of course, to sleep. Sarah had sent up some cold chicken and they had eaten it here, and later Kent had made Allin take a hot bath and get into a warm robe and lie down on the chaise longue. He did not undress. Someone might call.

"I'll have to see what the man says tomorrow," he answered.

Terrifying to think how he was pinning everything on that fellow tomorrow — a man whose name, even, he did not know. All he knew was he'd wear a plain gray suit and he'd have a blue handkerchief in his pocket. That was all he had to save Betsy's life. No, that wasn't true. Behind that one man were hundreds of others, alert, strong, and ready to help him.

"We've got to pay it," Allin was saying hysterically. "What's money now?"

"Allin!" he cried. "You don't think I'm trying to save the money, in God's name!"

"We have about twenty thousand, haven't we, in the bank?" she said hurriedly. "Your father would have the rest, though, and we could give him the securities. It isn't as if we didn't have it."

"Allin, you're being absurd! The thing is to know how to —— "

But she flew at him fiercely. "The thing is to save Betsy — that's all; there's nothing else — absolutely nothing. I don't care if it takes everything your father has."

"Allin, be quiet!" he shouted at her. "Do you mean my father would begrudge anything —— ?"

"You're afraid of him, Kent," she retorted. "Well, I'm not! If you don't go to him, I will."

They were quarreling now, like two insane people. They were both stretched beyond normal reason.

Suddenly Allin was sobbing. "I can't forget what you said that night," she cried. "All that standing on principle! Oh, Kent, she's with strangers, horrible people, crying her little heart out; perhaps they're even — hurting her, trying to make her keep quiet. Oh, Kent, Kent!"

He took her in his arms. They must not draw apart now. He must think of her.

"I'll do anything, darling," he said. "The first thing in the morning I'll get hold of Dad and have the money ready."

"If they could only *know* it," she said.

"I could put something in the paper, perhaps," he said. "I believe I could word something that no one else would understand."

"Let's try, Kent!"

He took a pencil and envelope from his pocket and wrote. "How's this?" he asked. "Fifty agreed by dead oak at twelve."

"I can't see how it could do any harm," she said eagerly. "And if they see it, they'll understand we're willing to do anything."

"I'll go around to the newspaper office and pay for this in cash," he said. "Then I won't have to give names."

"Yes, yes!" she urged him. "It's something more than just sitting here!"

He drove through the darkness the two miles to the small town and parked in front of the ramshackle newspaper office. A red-eyed night clerk took his advertisement and read it off.

"This is a funny one," he said. "We get some, now and then. That'll be a dollar, Mr.—— "

Kent did not answer. He put a dollar bill on the desk.

"I don't know what I've done, even so," he groaned to himself.

He drove back quietly through the intense darkness. The storm had not yet come, and the air was strangely silent. He kept his motor at its most noiseless, expecting somehow to hear through the sleeping stillness Betsy's voice, crying.

They scarcely slept, and yet when they looked at each other the next morning the miracle was that they had slept at all. But he had made Allin go to bed at last, and then, still dressed, he had lain down on his own bed near her. It was Bruce who waked them. He stood hesitatingly between their beds. They heard his voice.

"Betsy hasn't come back yet, Mommie."

The name waked them. And they looked at each other.

"How could we!" Allin whispered.

"It may be a long pull, dearest," he said, trying to be steady. He got up, feeling exhausted.

"Will she come back today?" Bruce asked.

"I think so, son."

At least it was Saturday, and Bruce need not go to school today.

"I'm going to get her tonight," Kent said after a moment.

Instantly he felt better. They must not give up hope — not by a great deal. There was too much to do: his father to see and the money to get. Secretly, he still reserved his own judgment about the ransom. If the man in gray was against it, he would tell Allin nothing — he simply would not give it. The responsibility would be his.

"You and Mommie will have to get Betsy's things ready for her tonight," he said cheerfully. He would take a bath and get into a fresh suit. He had to have all his wits about him today, every moment — listen to everybody, and use his own judgment finally. In an emergency, one person had to act.

He paused at the sight of himself in the mirror. Would he be able to keep it from Allin if he made a mistake? Suppose they never got Betsy back. Suppose she just — disappeared. Or suppose they found her little body somewhere.

This was the way all those other parents had felt — this sickness and faintness. If he did not pay the ransom and *that* happened, would he be able *not* to tell Allin — or to tell her it was his fault? Both were impossible.

"I'll just have to go on from one thing to the next," he decided.

The chief thing was to try to be hopeful. He dressed and went back into the bedroom. Bruce had come in to dress in their room. But Allin was still in bed, lying against the pillows, white and exhausted.

He bent over her and kissed her. "I'll send your breakfast up," he said. "I'm going to see Father first. If any message comes through, I'll be there — then at the bank."

She nodded, glanced up at him and closed her eyes. He stood looking down into her tortured face. Every nerve in it was quivering under the set stillness.

"Can't break yet," he said sharply. "The crisis is ahead."

"I know," she whispered. Then she sat up. "I can't lie here!" she exclaimed. "It's like lying on a bed of swords, being tortured. I'll be down, Kent — Bruce and I."

She flew into the bathroom. He heard the shower turned on instantly and strongly. But he could wait for no one.

"Come down with Mother, son," he said. And he went on alone.

"If you could let me have thirty thousand today," he said to his father, "I can give it back as soon as I sell some stock."

"I don't care when I get it back," his father said irritably. "Good God, Kent, it's not that. It's just that I — it's none of my business, of course, but thirty thousand in cold cash! I'd like to ask what on earth you've been doing, but I won't."

Kent had made up his mind at the breakfast table when he picked up the paper that if he could keep the thing out of the papers, he would keep it from his father and mother. He'd turned to the personals. There it was, his answer to those scoundrels. Well, he wouldn't stick to it unless it were best for Betsy. Meanwhile, silence!

To Rose, bringing in the toast, he'd said sharply, "Tell everybody to come in now before your mistress comes down."

They had filed in, subdued and drooping, looking at him with frightened eyes.

"Oh, sir!" Mollie had cried hysterically.

"Please!" he'd exclaimed, glancing at her. Maybe the man in gray ought to see her. But last night he had distrusted Peter. This morning Peter looked like a faithful old dog, and as incapable of evil.

"I only want to thank you for obeying me so far," he'd said wearily. "If we can keep our trouble out of the papers, perhaps we can get Betsy back. At least, it's the only hope. If you succeed in letting no one know until we know — the end, I shall give each of you a hundred dollars as a token of my gratitude."

"Thank you, sir," Sarah and Rose had said. Mollie only sobbed. Peter was murmuring, "Ah don' wan' no hundred dollahs, Mist' Crothers. All Ah wan' is dat little chile back."

How could Peter be distrusted? Kent had wrung his hand. "That's all I want, too, Peter," he'd said fervently.

Strange how shaky and emotional he had felt!

Now, under his father's penetrating eyes, he held himself calm. "I know it sounds outrageous, Father," he admitted, "but I simply ask you to trust me for a few days."

"You're not speculating, I hope. It's no time for that. The market's crazy."

It was, Kent thought grimly, the wildest kind of speculation — with his own child's life.

"It's not ordinary speculation, certainly," he said. "I can manage through the bank, Dad," he said. "Never mind. I'll mortgage the house."

"Oh, nonsense!" his father retorted. He had his checkbook out and was writing. "I'm not going to have it get around that my son had to go mortgaging his place."

"Thanks," Kent said briefly.

Now for the bank!

Step by step the day went. It was amazing how quickly the hours passed. It was noon before he knew it, and in an hour he must start for the inn. He went home and found Allin on the front porch in the sunshine. She had a book in her hand, and Bruce was playing with his red truck out in the yard. Anyone passing would never dream there was tragedy here.

"Do you have it?" she asked him.

He touched his breast pocket. "All ready," he answered.

They sat through a silent meal, listening to Bruce's chatter. Allin ate nothing and he very little, but he was grateful to her for being there, for keeping the outward shape of the day usual.

"Good sport!" he said to her across the table in the midst of Bruce's conversation. She smiled faintly. "Thank you, no more coffee," he said to Rose. "I must be going, Allin."

"Yes," she said, and added, "I wish it were I — instead of waiting."

"I know," he replied, and kissed her.

Yesterday, waiting had seemed intolerable to him, too. But now that he was going toward the hour for which he had been waiting, he clung to the hopefulness of uncertainty.

He drove alone to the inn. The well-paved roads, the tended fields

and comfortable farmhouses were not different from the landscape any day. He would have said, only yesterday, that it was impossible that underneath all this peace and plenty there could be men so evil as to take a child out of its home, away from its parents, for money.

There was, he pondered, driving steadily west, no other possible reason. He had no enemies; none, that is, whom he knew. There were always discontented people, of course, who hated anyone who seemed successful. There was, of course, too, the chance that his father had enemies — he was ruthless with idle workers.

"I can't blame a man if he is born a fool," Kent had heard his father maintain stoutly, "but I can blame even a fool for being lazy." It might be one of these. If only it were not some perverted mind!

He drove into the yard of the inn and parked his car. His heart was thudding in his breast, but he said casually to the woman at the door, "Have you a bar?"

"To the right," she answered quickly. It was Saturday afternoon, and business was good. She did not even look at him as he sauntered away.

The moment he entered the door of the bar he saw the man. He stood at the end of the bar, small, inconspicuous, in a gray suit and a blue-striped shirt. He wore a solid blue tie, and in his pocket was the blue handkerchief. Kent walked slowly to his side.

"Whisky and soda, please," he ordered the bartender. The room was full of people at tables, drinking and talking noisily. He turned to the man in gray and smiled. "Rather unusual to find a bar like this in a village inn," he said.

"Yes, it is," the little man agreed. He had a kind, brisk voice, and he was drinking a tall glass of something clear, which he finished. "Give me another of the same," he remarked to the bartender. "London Washerwoman's Treat, it's called," he explained to Kent.

It was hard to imagine that this small hatchet-faced man had any importance.

"Going my way?" Kent asked suddenly.

"If you'll give me a lift," the little man replied.

Kent's heart subsided. The man knew him, then. He nodded. They paid for their drinks and went out to the car.

"Drive due north into a country road," the little man said with

sudden sharpness. All his dreaminess was gone. He sat beside Kent, his arms folded. "Please tell me exactly what's happened, Mr. Crothers."

And Kent, driving along, told him.

He was grateful for the man's coldness; for the distrust of everything and everybody. He was like a lean hound in a life-and-death chase. Because of his coldness, Kent could talk without fear of breaking.

"I don't know your name," Kent said.

"Don't matter," said the man. "I'm detailed for the job."

"As I was saying," Kent went on, "we have no enemies — at least, none I know."

"Fellow always has enemies," the little man murmured.

"It hardly seems likely a gangster would —— " Kent began again.

"No, gangsters don't kidnap children," the little man told him. "Adults, yes. But they don't monkey with kids. It's too dangerous, for one thing. Kidnaping children's the most dangerous job there is in crime, and the smart ones know it. It's always some little fellow does it — him and a couple of friends, maybe."

"Why dangerous?" Kent demanded.

"Always get caught," the little man said, shrugging. "Always!"

There was something so reassuring about this strange sharp creature that Kent said abruptly, "My wife wants to pay the ransom. I suppose you think that's wrong, don't you?"

"Perfectly *right,*" the man said. "Absolutely! We aren't magicians, Mr. Crothers. We got to get in touch somehow. The only two cases I ever knew where nothing was solved was where the parents wouldn't pay. So we couldn't get a clue."

Kent set his lips. "Children killed?"

"Who knows?" the little man said, shrugging again. "Anyway, one of them was. And the other never came back."

There might be comfort, then, in death, Kent thought. He had infinitely rather hold Betsy's dead body in his arms than never know . . .

"Tell me what to do, and I'll do it," he said.

The little man lighted a cigarette. "Go on just as though you'd never told us. Go on and pay your ransom. Make a note of the num-

bers of the notes, of course — no matter what that letter says. How's he going to know? But pay it over — and do what he says next. You can call me up here." He took a paper out of his coat pocket and put it in Kent's pocket. "I maybe ought to tell you, though, we'll tap your telephone wire."

"Do anything you like," Kent said.

"That's all I need!" the man exclaimed. "That's our orders — to do what the parents want. You're a sensible one. Fellow I knew once walked around with a shotgun to keep off the police. Said he'd handle things himself."

"Did he get his child back?"

"Nope — paid the ransom, too. Paying the ransom's all right — that's the way we get 'em. But he went roarin' around the neighborhood trying to be his own law. We didn't get a chance."

Kent thought of one more thing. "I don't want anything spared — money or trouble. I'll pay anything, of course."

"Oh, sure," the man said. "Well, I guess that'll be all. You might let me off near the inn. I'll go in and get another drink."

He lapsed into dreaminess again, and in silence Kent drove back to the village.

"All right," the little man said. "So long. Good luck to you." He leaped out and disappeared into the bar.

And Kent, driving home through the early sunset, thought how little there was to tell Allin — really nothing at all, except that he liked and trusted the man in gray. No, it was much more than that: the fellow stood for something far greater than himself — he stood for all the power of the government organized against crimes like this. That was the comfort of the thing. Behind that man was the nation's police, all for him, Kent Crothers, helping him find his child.

When he reached home, Allin was in the hall waiting.

"He really said nothing, darling," Kent said, kissing her, "except you were right about the ransom. We have to pay that. Still, he was extraordinary. Somehow I feel — if she's still alive, we'll get her back. He's that sort of fellow." He did not let her break, though he felt her trembling against him. He said very practically, "We must check these banknotes, Allin."

And then, when they were checking them upstairs in their bedroom with doors locked, he kept insisting that what they were doing
was right.

At a quarter to twelve he was bumping down the rutted road to
the forks. He knew every turn the road made, having traveled it on
foot from the time he was a little boy. But that boy out on holiday
had nothing to do with himself as he was tonight, an anxious, har-
ried man.

He drew up beneath the dead oak and took the cardboard box in
which he and Allin had packed the money and stepped out of the
car. There was not a sound in the dark night, yet he knew that
somewhere not far away were the men who had his child.

He listened, suddenly swept again with the conviction he had had
the night before, that she would cry out. She might even be this moment in the old mill. But there was not a sound. He stooped and
put the box at the root of the tree.

And as he did this, he stumbled over a string raised from the
ground about a foot. What was this? He followed it with his hands.
It encircled the tree — a common piece of twine. Then it went under
a stone, and under the stone was a piece of paper. He seized it,
snapped on his cigarette lighter, read the clumsy printing.

If everything turns out like we told you to do, go to your hired mans
house at twelve tomorrow night for the kid. If you double-cross us you
get it back dead.

He snapped off the light. He'd get her back dead! It all depended
on what he did. And what he did, he would have to do alone. He
would not go home to Allin until he had decided every step.

He drove steadily away. If he did not call the man in gray, Betsy
might be at Peter's alive. If he called, and they did not find out, she
might be alive anyway. But if the man fumbled and they did find
out, she would be dead.

He knew what Allin would say: "Just so we get her home, Kent,
nothing else! People have to think for themselves, first." Yes, she
was right. He would keep quiet; anyway, he would give the kidnapers a chance. If she were safe and alive, that would be justification for anything. If she were dead . . .

Then he remembered that there was something courageous and reassuring about that little man. Only he had seemed to know what to do. And anyway, what about those parents who had tried to manage it all themselves? Their children had never come back, either. No, he had better do what he knew he ought to do.

He tramped into the house. Allin was lying upstairs on her bed, her eyes closed.

"Darling," he said gently. Instantly she opened her eyes and sat up. He handed her the paper and sat down on her bed. She lifted miserable eyes to him.

"Twenty-four more hours!" she whispered. "I can't do it, Kent."

"Yes, you can," he said harshly. "You'll do it because you damned well have to." He thought, She can't break now, if I have to whip her! "We've got to wait," he went on. "Is there anything else we can do? Tell Mike O'Brien? Let the newspapers get it and ruin everything?"

She shook her head. "No," she said.

He got up. He longed to take her in his arms, but he did not dare. If this was ever over, he would tell her what he thought of her — how wonderful she was; how brave and game — but he could not now. It was better for them both to stay away from that edge of breaking.

"Get up," he said. "Let's have something to eat. I haven't really eaten all day."

It would be good for her to get up and busy herself. She had not eaten either.

"All right, Kent," she said. "I'll wash my face in cold water and be down."

"I'll be waiting," he replied.

This gave him the moment he had made up his mind he would use — damned if he wouldn't use it! The scoundrels had his money now, and he would take the chance on that queer fellow. He called the number the man had put into his pocket. And almost instantly he heard the fellow's drawl.

"Hello?" the man said.

"This is Kent Crothers," he answered. "I've had that invitation!"

"Yes?" The voice was suddenly alert.

"Twelve tomorrow!"

"Yes? Where? Midnight, of course. They always make it mid-night."

"My gardener's house."

"Okay, Mr. Crothers. Go right ahead as if you hadn't told us." The phone clicked.

Kent listened, but there was nothing more. Everything seemed exactly the same, but nothing was the same. This very telephone wire was cut somewhere, by someone. Someone was listening to every word anyone spoke to and from his house. It was sinister and yet reassuring — sinister if you were the criminal.

He heard Allin's step on the stair and went out to meet her. "I have a hunch," he told her, smiling.

"What?" She tried to smile back.

He drew her toward the dining room. "We're going to win," he said.

Within himself he added, If she were still alive, that little heart of his life. Then he put the memory of Betsy's face away from him resolutely.

"I'm going to eat," he declared. "And so must you. We'll beat them tomorrow."

But tomorrow very nearly beat them. Time stood still — there was no making it pass. They filled it full of a score of odd jobs about the house. Lucky for them it was Sunday; luckier that Kent's mother had a cold and telephoned that she and Kent's father would not be over for their usual visit.

They stayed together, a little band of three. By midafternoon Kent had cleaned up everything — a year's odd jobs — and there were hours to go.

They played games with Bruce, and at last it was his suppertime and they put him to bed. Then they sat upstairs in their bedroom again, near the nursery, each with a book.

Sometime, after these hours were over, he would have to think about a lot of things again. But everything had to wait now, until this life ended at midnight. Beyond that no thought could reach.

At eleven he rose. "I'm going now," he said, and stooped to kiss her. She clung to him, and then in an instant they drew apart. In strong accord they knew it was not yet time to give way.

He ran the car as noiselessly as he could and left it at the end of the street, six blocks away. Then he walked past the few tumble-down bungalows, past two empty lots, to Peter's rickety gate. There was no light in the house. He went to the door and knocked softly. He heard Peter's mumble: "Who dat?"

"Let me in, Peter," he called in a low voice. The door opened. "It's I, Peter — Kent Crothers. Let me in. Peter, they're bringing the baby here."

"To mah house? Lemme git de light on."

"No, Peter, no light. I'll just sit down here in the darkness, like this. Only don't lock the door, see? I'll sit by the door. Where's a chair? That's it." He was trembling so that he stumbled into the chair Peter pushed forward.

"Mist' Crothers, suh, will yo' have a drink? Ah got some corn likker."

"Thanks, Peter."

He heard Peter's footsteps shuffling away, and in a moment a tin cup was thrust into his hand. He drank the reeking stuff down. It burned him like indrawn flame, but he felt steadier for it.

"Ain't a thing Ah can do, Mist' Crothers?" Peter's whisper came ghostly out of the darkness.

"Not a thing. Just wait."

"Ah'll wait here, then. Mah ole 'ooman's asleep. Ah'll jest git thrashin' round if Ah go back to bed."

"Yes, only we mustn't talk," Kent whispered back.

"Nosuh."

This was the supremest agony of waiting in all the long agony that this day had been. To sit perfectly still, straining to hear, knowing nothing, wondering . . .

Suppose something went wrong with the man in gray, and they fumbled, and frightened the man who brought Betsy back. Suppose he just sat here waiting and waiting until dawn came. And at home Allin was waiting.

The long day had been nothing to this. He sat reviewing all his life, pondering on the horror of this monstrous situation in which he and Allin now were. A free country, was it? No one was free when his lips were locked against crime, because he dared not speak lest his child be murdered. If Betsy were dead, if they didn't bring her back, he'd never tell Allin he had telephoned the man in gray. He was still glad he had done it. After all, were respectable men and women to be at the mercy of — but if Betsy were dead, he'd wish he had killed himself before he had anything to do with the fellow!

He sat, his hands interlocked so tightly he felt them grow cold and bloodless and stinging, but he could not move. Someone came down the street roaring out a song.

"Thass a drunk man," Peter whispered.

Kent did not answer. The street grew still again.

And then in the darkness — hours after midnight, it seemed to him — he heard a car come up to the gate and stop. The gate creaked open and then shut, and the car drove away.

"Guide me down the steps," he told Peter.

It was the blackest night he had ever seen. But the stars were shining when he stepped out. Peter pulled him along the path. Then, by the gate, Peter stooped.

"She's here," he said.

And Kent, wavering and dizzy, felt her in his arms again, limp and heavy. "She's warm," he muttered. "That's something."

He carried her into the house, and Peter lighted a candle and held it up. It was she — his little Betsy, her white dress filthy and a man's sweater drawn over her. She was breathing heavily.

"Look lak she done got a dose of sumpin," Peter muttered.

"I must get her home," Kent whispered frantically. "Help me to the car, Peter."

"Yassuh," Peter said, and blew out the candle.

They walked silently down the street, Peter's hand on Kent's arm. When he got Betsy home, he — he ——.

"Want I should drive you?" Peter was asking him.

"I — maybe you'd better," he replied.

He climbed into the seat with her. She was so fearfully limp. Thank God he could hear her breathing! In a few minutes he would put Betsy into her mother's arms.

"Don't stay, Peter," he said.

"Nosuh," Peter answered.

Allin was at the door, waiting. She opened it and without a word reached for the child. He closed the door behind them.

Then he felt himself grow sick. "I was going to tell you," he gasped, "I didn't know whether to tell you —— " He swayed and felt himself fall upon the floor.

*   *   *

Allin was a miracle; Allin was wonderful, a rock of a woman. This tender thing who had endured the torture of these days was at his bedside when he woke next day, smiling, and only a little pale.

"The doctor says you're not to go to work, darling," she told him.

"The doctor?" he repeated.

"I had him last night for both of you — you and Betsy. He won't tell anyone."

"I've been crazy," he said, dazed. "Where is she? How —— "

"She's going to be all right," Allin said.

"No, but — you're not telling me!"

"Come in here and see," she replied.

He got up, staggering a little. Funny how his legs had collapsed under him last night! His withers still felt all unstrung.

They went into the nursery. There in her bed she lay, his beloved child. She was more naturally asleep now, and her face bore no other mark than pallor.

"She won't even remember it," Allin said. "I'm glad it wasn't Bruce."

He did not answer. He couldn't think — nothing had to be thought about now.

"Come back to bed, Kent," Allin was saying. "I'm going to bring your breakfast up. Bruce is having his downstairs."

He climbed back into bed, shamefaced at his weakness. "I'll be all right after a little coffee. I'll get up then, maybe."

But his bed felt wonderfully good. He lay back, profoundly grateful to it — to everything. But as long as he lived he would wake up to sweat in the night with memory.

The telephone by his bed rang, and he picked it up. "Hello?" he called.

"Hello, Mr. Crothers," a voice answered. It was the voice of the man in gray. "Say, was the little girl hurt?"

"No!" Kent cried. "She's all right!"

"Fine. Well, I just wanted to tell you we caught the fellow last night."

"You *did!*" Kent leaped up. "No! Why, that's — that's extraordinary."

"We had a cordon around the place for blocks and got him. You'll get your money back, too."

"That — it doesn't seem to matter. Who was he?"

"Fellow named Harry Brown — a young chap in a drugstore."

"I never heard of him!"

"No, he says you don't know him — but his dad went to school with yours, and he's heard a lot of talk about you. His dad's a poor stick, I guess, and got jealous of yours. That's about it, probably. Fellow says he figured you sort of owed him something. Crazy, of course.

"Well, it was an easy case — he wasn't smart, and scared to death, besides. You were sensible about it. Most people ruin their chances with their own fuss. So long, Mr. Crothers. Mighty glad."

The telephone clicked. That was all. Everything was incredible, impossible. Kent gazed around the familiar room. Had this all happened? It had happened, and it was over. This was one of those cases of kidnaping that went on in this mad country, unheard of until they were all over and the criminals arrested.

When he went downstairs he would give the servants their hundred dollars apiece. Mollie had had nothing to do with it, after all. The mystery had dissolved like a mist at morning.

Allin was at the door with his tray. Behind her came Bruce, ready for school. She said, so casually Kent could hardly catch the tremor underneath her voice, "What would you say, darling, if we let Peter walk to school with Bruce today?"

Her eyes pleaded with him: "No? Oughtn't we to? What shall we do?"

Then he thought of something else that indomitable man in gray had said, that man whose name he would never know, one among all those other men trying to keep the law for the nation. "We're a lawless people," the little man had said that day in the car. "If we made a law against paying ransoms, nobody would obey it any more than they did Prohibition. No, when the Americans don't like a law, they break it. And so we still have kidnapers. It's the price you pay for a democracy."

Yes, it was the price. Everybody paid — he and Allin; the child they had so nearly lost; that boy locked up in prison.

"Bruce has to live in his own country," he said. "I guess you can go alone, can't you, son?"

"Course I can," Bruce said sturdily.

THE DETECTIVE STORY TO END
DETECTIVE STORIES

THE PERFECT CRIME

by BEN RAY REDMAN

And here is a tale that illustrates impeccably the not-leastness of lastness. Defying classification, it can only be called what we have called it: The Detective Story To End Detective Stories. For in it you will meet not only a Great Detective, but a Great Crime as well; not only a Unique Motive, but also an Unmentionable Weapon; and over all broods the sad intelligent eye of Satiric Humor. . . . In fact, "The Perfect Crime" makes the perfect ending to our Book; and in gratitude we hereby nominate Mr. Redman to the Golden Order of the Bloodstain for having written it.

THE WORLD'S greatest detective complacently sipped a port some years older than himself and intently gazed across the table at his most intimate acquaintance; for many years the detective had not permitted himself the luxury of friends. Gregory Hare looked back at him, waiting, listening.

"There is no doubt about it," Trevor reiterated, putting down his glass, "the perfect crime is a possibility; it requires only the perfect criminal."

"Naturally," assented Hare with a shrug, "but the perfect criminal . . ."

"You mean he is a mythical fellow, not apt to be met with in the flesh?"

"Exactly," said Hare, nodding his big head.

Trevor sighed, sipped again, and adjusted the eyeglasses on his thin, sharp nose. "No, I admit I haven't encountered him as yet, but I am always hopeful."

"Hoping to be done in the eye, eh?"

"No, hoping to see the perfect methods of detection tested to the limits of their possibilities. You know, a gifted detector of crime is something more than an inspired policeman with a little blood-hound blood in his veins, something more than a precise scientist; he's an art critic as well, and no art critic likes to be condemned to a steady diet of second-rate stuff."

"Quite."

"Second-rate stuff is bad enough, but it's not the worst. Think of the third, fourth, fifth, and heaven-knows-what-rate crimes that come along every day! And even the masterpieces, the 'classics,' are pretty poor daubs when you look at them closely: a bad tone here and a wrong line there; something false, something botched."

"Most murderers are rather foolish," interjected Hare.

"Foolish! Of course they are. You should know, man, you've de-fended enough of them. The trouble is that murder almost never evokes the best efforts of the best minds. As a rule it is the work of an inferior mind, cunningly striving towards a perfection that is beyond its reach, or of a superior mind so blinded by passion that its faculties are temporarily impaired. Of course, there are your homicidal maniacs, and they are often clever, but they lack imagina-tion and variety; sooner or later their inability to do anything but repeat themselves brings them up with a sharp jerk."

"Repetition is dullness," murmured Hare, "and dullness, as some-body has remarked, is the one unforgivable sin."

"Right," agreed Trevor. "It is, and plenty of murderers have suf-fered for it. But they have suffered from vanity almost as often. Practically every murderer, unless he has been accidentally impelled to crime, is an egregious egotist. You know that as well as I do. His sense of power is tremendous, and as a rule he can't keep his mouth shut."

Dr. Harrison Trevor's glasses shone brightly, and he plucked con-tinually at the black cord depending from them as he jerked out his sentences with rapidity and precision. He was on his own ground, and he knew what he was talking about. For twenty years criminals had been his specialty and his legitimate prey. He had hunted them through all lands, and he hunted them successfully. Upstairs, in a chiffonier drawer in his bedroom, there was a large red-leather box holding visible symbols of that success: small deco-rations of gold and silver and bright ribbons bore mute witness to the gratitude that various European governments had felt, on notable occasions, towards the greatest man hunter of his generation. If Trevor was a dogmatist on murder he was entitled to be one.

Hare, on the other hand, was a good and respectful listener, but, being a criminal lawyer of long experience, he was a man with ideas of his own; and he always expressed them when there was no legal advantage to be gained by withholding them. He expressed one now, when he drawled softly, "All murderers are great egotists, are they? How about great detectives?"

Trevor blinked, then smiled coldly, clutching at his black cord. "Most detectives are asses, I grant you, complete asses and vain as peacocks; very few of them are great. I know only three. One of them is now in Vienna, the second is in Paris, and the third is . . ."

Hare raised his hand in interruption and said, "The third, or rather the first, is in this room."

The greatest detective in the world nodded briskly. "Of course. There's no point in false modesty, is there?"

"None at all. And it might be a little difficult to maintain such an attitude so soon after the Harrington case. The poor chap was put out of his misery week before last, wasn't he?"

Trevor snorted. "Yes, if you want to call him a poor chap; he was a deliberate murderer. But let's get back to that perfect crime of ours."

"Of yours, you mean," Hare corrected him politely. "I haven't subscribed to the possibility of it as yet. And how would you know about a perfect crime if it ever were committed? The criminal would never be discovered."

"If he had any artistic pride, he would leave a full account of it to be published after his death. Besides, you are forgetting the perfect methods of detection."

Hare whistled softly. "There's a pretty theoretical problem for you. What would happen when the perfect detector set out to catch the perfect criminal? Rather like the immovable object and the irresistible force business, and just about as sensible. The fly in the ointment, of course, is that there is no such thing as perfection."

Dr. Trevor sat up rigidly and glared at the speaker. "There is perfection in the detection of crime."

"Well, perhaps there is." Hare laughed amiably. "You should know, Trevor. But I think what you really mean is that there is a perfect method for detecting imperfect crimes."

The doctor's rigidity had vanished, and now he was smiling with as much geniality as he ever displayed. "Perhaps that is what I do mean, perhaps it is. But there is a little experiment that I should like to try, just the same."

"And that is?"

"And that is, or rather would be, the experiment of exercising all my intelligence in the commission of a crime, then, forgetting every detail of it utterly, using my skill and knowledge to solve the riddle of my own creation. Should I catch myself, or should I escape myself? That's the question."

"It would be a nice sporting event," agreed Hare, "but I'm afraid it's one that can't be pulled off. The little trifle of forgetting is the difficulty. But it would be interesting to see the outcome."

"Yes, it would," said the other, speaking rather more dreamily than was his habit, "but we can never see quite as far as we should like to. My Japanese man, Tanaka, has a saying that he resorts to whenever he is asked a difficult question. He simply smiles and answers, '*Fuji san ni nobottara sazo tōku made miemashō.*' It means, I believe, that if one were to ascend Mount Fuji one could see far. The trouble is that, as in the case of so many problems, we can't climb the mountain."

"Wise Tanaka. But tell me, Trevor, what is your conception of a perfect crime?"

"I'm afraid it isn't precisely formulated; but I have a rough outline in my mind, and I'll give it to you as well as I can. First, though, let's go up to the library; we shall be more comfortable there, and it will give Tanaka a chance to clear the table. Bring your cigar, and come along."

Together the two men climbed the narrow staircase, the host leading. Dr. Trevor's house was a compact, brick building in the East Fifties, not far from Madison Avenue. Its picturesqueness was rather uncharacteristic of its owner, but its neatness was entirely like him. It was not a large house according to the standards of wealthy New York, but it was a perfectly appointed one, and considerably more spacious than it looked from the street, for the doctor had built on an addition that completely covered the plot which had once been the back yard; and this new section, as well as housing the kitchen and servants' quarters below, held a laboratory and work-room two stories high. An industrial or research chemist might have coveted the equipment of that room; and the filing cases that completely lined the encircling gallery would have furnished any newspaper with a complete reference department. A door opened from the library into the laboratory, and the library itself came close to being the ideal chamber of every student. Dr. Harrison Trevor's house was, in short, an ideal bachelor's establishment, and he had never been tempted to transform it into anything else. More than one male visitor had found reason to remark, "Old Trevor does well for himself."

The same idea flitted across Hare's mind as he puffed at his host's excellent cigar and tasted the liqueur that Tanaka had placed on the table beside his chair. He, too, enjoyed the pleasures of bachelorhood, but he had never learned the knack of enjoying them quite so thoroughly. He would make a few improvements in the routine of his life; he could afford them.

"The perfect crime must, of course, be a murder." Trevor's voice broke the silence that had followed their entrance into the library.

Hare shifted his bulk a little and inquired, "Yes? Why?"

"Because it is, according to our accepted standards, the most reprehensible of all crimes and, therefore, according to my interests, the best. Human life is what we prize most and do our best to protect; to take human life with an art that eludes all detection is unquestionably the ideal criminal action. In it there is a degree of beauty possible in no other crime."

"Humph!" grunted Hare, "you make it sound pleasant."

"I am speaking at once as an amateur and as a professor of crime. You have heard surgeons talk of 'beautiful cases.' Well, that is my attitude precisely; and in my cases invariably, as in most of theirs, the patient dies."

"I see."

Trevor blinked, tugged at his eyeglass cord, and then continued. "The crime must be murder, and it must be murder of a particular kind, the purest kind. Now what is the 'purest' kind? Let us see. The *crime passionel* can be ruled out at once, for it is almost impossible that it should be perfect. Passion does not make for art; hot blood begets innumerable blunders. What about the murder for gain? Murderers of this kind make murder a means, not an end in itself; they kill not for the sake of eliminating the victim but in order to profit by the victim's death. No, we can't look to murder for profit as the type that might produce our perfect crime."

The sharp-nosed doctor paused and held his cigar for a moment between his thin lips. Hare studied his face curiously; the man's complete lack of emotion in discussing such matters was not wholly pleasant, he reflected.

Trevor put down his cigar. "Now, how about political and religious murders? They can be counted out almost immediately, for the simple reason that the murderer in such cases is always convinced that he is either serving the public or serving God and, therefore, seldom makes any attempt to conceal his guilt. But there is another class to be considered — those who kill for the sheer joy of killing, those who are dominated by the blood lust. Offhand you would think that their killing would be of the purest type. But as I have said before, the maniac invariably repeats himself, and his repetition leads to his discovery. And even more important is the consideration that the artist must possess the faculty of choice, and that the born killer has no choice. His actions are not willed by himself, they are compelled; whereas the perfect crime must be a work of art, not of necessity."

"You seem to have written off all the possibilities pretty well," remarked Hare.

The doctor shook his head quickly. "Not all. There is one type of murder left, and it is the kind we are looking for: the murder of elimination, the murder in which the sole and pure object is to remove the victim from the world, to get rid of a person whose continued existence is not desirable to the murderer."

"But that brings you back to your *crime passionel,* doesn't it? Practically all murders of jealousy, for example, are murders of elimination, aren't they?"

"In a sense, yes, but not in the purest sense. And, as I have said before, passion can never produce the perfect crime. It must be studied, carefully meditated, and performed in absolutely cold blood. Otherwise it is sure to be imperfect."

"You do go at this in a rather fish-blooded way," remarked the good listener as the doctor paused for a moment.

"Of course I do, and that is the only way the perfect crime could be committed. Now I can imagine a pure murder of elimination that would be ideal so far as motives and circumstances were con· cerned. Suppose you had spent fifteen years establishing a certain reading of a dubious passage in one of Pindar's odes."

"Ha, ha!" interrupted Hare jocosely. "Suppose I had."

"And suppose," continued Dr. Harrison Trevor, not noticing the interruption, "that another scholar had managed to build up an argument which completely invalidated your interpretation. Suppose, further, that he communicated his proofs to you, and that he had as yet mentioned them to no one else. There you would have a perfect motive and a perfect set of circumstances; only the method of the murder would remain to be worked out."

Gregory Hare sat bolt upright. "Good God, man! What do you mean, 'the method of the murder'?"

The doctor blinked. "Why, don't you understand? You would have excellent reasons for eliminating your rival and thereby saving your own interpretation of the text from confutation; and no one, once your victim was dead and the proofs destroyed, could suspect that you had any such motive. You could work with perfect free· dom, you could concentrate on two essentials: the method of the murder and, of course, the disposition of the body."

"The disposition of the body?" Hare seemed to echo the speaker's last words involuntarily.

"To be sure; that is a very important item, most important in fact. But I flatter myself," and here the doctor chuckled softly, "that I have done some very valuable research work along that line."

"You have, eh?" murmured Hare. "And what have you found out?"

"I'll tell you later," Trevor assured him, "and I don't think I would tell any other man alive, because it's really too simple and too dangerous. But at the moment I want to impress on you that the disposition of the body is perhaps the most important step of all in the commission of the perfect crime. The absence of a *corpus delicti* is curiously troublesome to the police. Harrington should really have managed to get rid of West's body, although it probably wouldn't have kept him from sitting in the electric chair two weeks ago. He was too careless."

Hare again sat up sharply and exclaimed, "Was he? Speaking of that, it was the Harrington case that I chiefly wanted to talk to you about tonight."

"Oh, was it? Well, we can get around to that in a minute. And, by the way, that came pretty close to being a murder of elimination, if you like; but the money element figured in it, big money, and gold is apt to have a fairly strong smell when it is mixed up with crime. Harrington's motive was easily traced, but his position made it impossible to touch him until we had our case absolutely water-tight."

"Water-tight, eh? That's what I want to hear about. You see I was abroad until last week, and didn't even know Harrington had been arrested until just before I sailed. The North African newspapers aren't so informative. I was particularly interested, you see, because I knew both men fairly well, and West's wife even better."

"Oh, yes, his wife, gorgeous woman. They were separated, and she's been in Europe for the last two and a half years."

"Yes, I know she has — most of the time."

"All the time. She hasn't been in the United States during that period."

"Hasn't she? Well, I last saw her at Monte Carlo, but that's not important at the moment. I want to hear how you tracked down Harrington."

Dr. Harrison Trevor smiled complacently, adjusted his eyeglasses, and then launched forth in his characteristic manner. "It was really simplicity itself. The only flaw was that Harrington finally confessed. That rather annoyed me, for we didn't need a confession; the circumstantial evidence was complete."

"Circumstantial?"

"Of course. You know as well as I do that most convictions for murder are based on circumstantial evidence. One doesn't send out invitations for a killing."

"No, of course not. Sorry."

"Well, as you probably know, Ernest West, Wall Street operator and multimillionaire (as the papers had it), was found shot through the heart one night a little more than a year ago. He had a shack down on Long Island, near Smithtown, that he used as a base for duck shooting and fishing. The only servant he kept there was an old housekeeper, a local inhabitant; he liked to lead the simple life when he could. Never even used to take a chauffeur down with him. The evening he was killed the housekeeper was absent, spending the night with a sick daughter of hers in Jamaica. She testified that West had sent her off, saying that he could pick up a light supper and breakfast for himself. She turned up the next morning, and nearly died of the shock. West was shot in what was a kind of gun room where he kept all his gear and a few books — cosy sort of place and the best room in the house. There was no sign of a struggle. He was sitting slumped in a big armchair. The bullet that killed him was a .25 caliber. Furst, of the Homicide Bureau, called me up as soon as the regulars failed to locate any scent, and I went down there immediately. West was an important man, you know." The doctor tugged self-consciously at his black cord. "I went down there at once, and I discovered various things. First of all, the house was isolated, and there was no one in the neighborhood who could give any useful evidence whatsoever. The body had been discovered by a messenger boy with a telegram at about seven-thirty; medical examination indicated that the murder had been committed about an hour before. Inside the house I found only one item that I thought useful. After going over the dust and so forth which I swept up from the gun-room floor, I had several tiny thread ends that had pretty obviously come from a tweed suit; and those threads could not be matched in West's wardrobe. But they might have been months old, so I didn't concentrate on them at first. Outside the house there was more to go on. The ground was damp, and two sets of footprints were visible: a man's and a woman's . . ."

"A woman's?" Hare was all attention now.

"Yes, the housekeeper's, of course."

"Oh, yes, the housekeeper's."

"Certainly. But it was difficult to identify them, for the reason that the man, apparently through nervousness, had walked up and down the lane leading to the road several times before finally leaving the scene of his crime; and he had trampled over almost every one of the woman's footprints, scarcely leaving one intact."

"That was odd, wasn't it?"

"Very, at first glance, but really simple enough when you think it over. The murderer had hurried out of the house after firing the fatal shot; then he hesitated. He was flurried and couldn't make up his mind as to his next step, even though he had an automobile waiting for him at the end of the lane. So he walked up and down for a few minutes, to calm his nerves and collect his ideas. It was a narrow lane, and the obliteration of the other tracks was at once accidental and inevitable."

"He had a car waiting?"

"Yes, a heavy touring car. Its tire marks were plain, as were those of the public hack that West had ordered for his housekeeper that afternoon. And there was one interesting feature about the marks. There was a big, hard blister on one of the shoes, and it left a perfectly defined indentation in the mud every time it came around."

"I see. And both sets of footprints ended at the same spot?"

"Naturally. The hack stopped for the woman just where the murderer later parked his car."

"Hum." Hare had now lighted a new cigar, and he puffed at it reflectively before asking, "And you are quite sure the woman did not get into the car with the man?"

Trevor stared at the speaker blankly and exclaimed, "You must be wool gathering, Hare. The woman was the housekeeper, and she went off in a public hack at least two hours before the crime was committed. In any event, Harrington confirmed the correctness of all my deductions when he finally confessed." Dr. Harrison Trevor was obviously nettled.

"Oh, yes, of course he did; I'd forgotten. Sorry. Let's hear how you nabbed him."

For a moment the detective looked at his companion doubtfully, as though he feared the other might be baiting him; for Hare's questions had not been of the sort that his alert mind usually asked. He seemed to have something up his sleeve. But Trevor thrust his suspicions aside and returned to the pleasant task of describing his triumph.

"With the bullet, the footprints, the tire marks, and the threads, I had considerable to go on. All I had to do was to relate them unmistakably to one man, and I had my murderer. But the trail soon led into quarters where we had to move cautiously. With my ma-

terial evidence in front of me, I set out to fasten upon some individual who might have had a motive for killing West. So far as
anyone could say, he had no enemies; but on the other hand he had
few friends. He believed in the maxim that he travels fastest who
travels alone. However, he had nipped some men pretty badly in
the Street; and it was upon his financial operations that I soon concentrated my attention. There, with the facilities for investigation
at my command, I discovered some very interesting facts. During
the three weeks prior to West's death the common stock of Elliott
Light and Power had risen fifty-seven points; four days after he
had been shot it had dropped back no less than sixty-three points.
Investigation showed that on the day West was murdered Harrington was short one hundred and thirty-odd thousand shares of that
particular stock. He had been selling it short all the way up, and
West had been buying all that was offered. Harrington's resources,
great as they were, weren't equal to his rival's. He knew that unless
he could break Elliott Common wide open he was a ruined man,
and he took the one sure way to do it that he could think of. He
eliminated West. It was murder for millions."

Trevor paused impressively; Hare did not say a word.

"That's about all there is to the story; the rest of it was routine
sleuthing. One of my men found four tires, three in perfect condition, which had been taken from Harrington's touring car and
replaced on the day following the murder. They had been put in a
loft of the garage on Harrington's country place. Three perfect tires,
mind you; and on the fourth there was a large, hard blister. Harrington's shoes fitted the footprints in West's lane, and the thread
ends matched the threads in one of Harrington's suits. And, to top
it all off, after the man was arrested, we found a .25, pearl-handled
revolver in his wall safe. One shot had been fired, and the weapon
hadn't been cleaned since. Harrington's chauffeur testified that his
master had taken out the big touring car alone on the afternoon
of the murder; the man remembered the date because it had been
his wife's birthday. It was all very simple, and even such elements
of interest as it possessed were lessened by Harrington's confession.
The press made much too much of a stir about my part in the
affair." The doctor smiled deprecatingly. "It was really no mystery
at all, and if the men involved had not been so rich and so prom-

inent the case would have been virtually ignored. But we nailed him just in time; he was sailing for Europe the following week."

"What kind of a revolver did you say it was?" Hare asked the question so abruptly that Trevor started before answering.

"Why, it was a .25, pearl-handled and nickel-finished. Rather a dainty weapon altogether; Harrington was a bit apologetic about owning such a toy."

"I should think he might have been. Was the handle slightly chipped on the right side?"

Trevor leaned forward suddenly. "Yes, it was. How the devil did you know?"

"Why it got chipped when Alice dropped it on a rock at Davos. The four of us were target shooting back of the hotel."

"Alice!" exclaimed Trevor. "What Alice? And what do you mean by the four of you?"

Hare answered quietly, "Alice West, my dear fellow. You see, it was her gun. And the four of us were West, Alice, Harrington, and myself; we were all staying at the same hotel in Switzerland four years ago."

"Her gun?" The doctor was speaking excitedly now. "You mean she gave it to him?"

"I doubt it, much as she loved him," drawled Hare. "He probably took it away from her, too late."

"You're talking in riddles," snapped the detective. "What do you mean?"

"Simply that that little weapon helped to execute the wrong man," said Hare wearily.

"The wrong man!"

"Well, that's one way of putting it; but in this case I am very much afraid that the right 'man' was a woman."

Trevor's apparent excitement had vanished abruptly, and now he was as calm as a sphinx. "Tell me exactly what you mean," he demanded.

Hare put aside the butt of his cigar. "It all began back in Davos, four years ago. Harrington fell in love with Alice West, and she fell in love with him. West played dog in the manger: he wouldn't let his wife divorce him and he wouldn't divorce her. They separated, of course, but that didn't help Alice and Harrington towards getting married. I was on the inside of the affair from the first, you see; accidentally to begin with, and afterwards because they all made me their confidant in various degrees. West behaved like a swine, because he really didn't love the woman any more. He simply had made up his mind that no other man was going to have her, legally at least. And he stuck to it — until she killed him."

"She killed him?" The great detective spoke softly.

"I'm as sure of it as though I had seen her do it. To begin with, it was her revolver that fired the shot, as you have proved to me. I've seen it a hundred times when we were firing at bottles and what not for fun. There was no reason for Harrington to borrow it; he had a nice little armory of his own, hadn't he?"

"Yes, we did find a couple of heavy service revolvers and an automatic."

"Exactly. He never would have used a toy like that in a thousand years; and besides he would never have committed a murder. He was too level-headed. Alice, on the other hand, is an extremely hysterical type; I've seen her go completely off her head with anger. Beautiful, Lord, yes! But dangerous, and in the last analysis a coward. She's proved that. I never did envy Harrington."

"But she was in Europe, man, when the murder was committed."

"She was not, Trevor. She was in Montreal that very month, to my certain knowledge, and Montreal isn't so far from Long Island. Harry Sands ran into her at the Ritz there; they were reminiscing about it at Monte Carlo the last time I saw her. She was in Europe before and after the murder, but she wasn't there when it happened. Anyway, that's not the whole story."

"Well, what is it?" Trevor's mouth was grim.

Hare's fingers were playing with a silver match box, and he hesitated a minute before answering. Then he spoke quickly and to the point.

"The rest of it is this. As I told you, Alice is hysterical, and during the past few years drink and dope haven't helped her any. Well, one night at Monte, just before I left, she went off the deep end. We had been talking about her husband's death, and I had been speculating as to who could have done it. Harrington hadn't been arrested then. And I'd been asking her, too, if she and Harrington weren't going to get married soon. She dodged that question, obviously embarrassed. Then suddenly she burst out into a wild tirade against the dead man, called him every name under heaven, and finally dived into her evening bag and fished out a letter. It was addressed to her, and the post mark was more than a year old; it was almost broken at the creases from having been read over and over again. She shoved it at me, and insisted that I read it. It was from West, and it was a cruel letter if I've ever read one. It was the letter of a cat to a mouse, of a jailer to his prisoner: West had her where he wanted her, and he intended to keep her there. He didn't miss a trick when it came to rubbing it in. It was so bad that I didn't want to finish it, but she made me. When I gave it back to her her eyes were blazing; and she grabbed my hand and cried, 'What would you do to a man like that?' I hemmed and hawed for a minute, and she answered herself by exclaiming, 'Kill him! Kill him! Wouldn't you?' As calmly as I could I pointed out to her that someone had already done just that; and she burst into a fit of the wickedest laughter I've ever heard. Then she calmed down, powdered her nose, and said quietly, 'It's funny that you can shoot the heads off all the innocent bottles you like and no one says a word, but if you kill a human snake they hang you for it. And I don't want to hang, thank you very much.'"

Hare paused as though he were very tired, and then he added, "That's about all there was to it; it wasn't very nice. I left for Africa the next day, and I scarcely ever saw the papers there. But I hadn't any doubts as to who had bumped off Ernest West."

While the minute hand on the mantel clock jumped three times there was silence in the book-lined room. Then Trevor spoke, and his voice was strained. "So you think I made a mistake?"

Hare looked him straight in the eye. "What do you think?"

The detective took refuge in another question. "Have you any theory as to what really happened?"

"It's hard to say exactly, but I'm sure she did it. Her reference to the bottles showed that she knew what weapon had been used; she must have done in a thousand bottles with it at various times. My guess is that she and Harrington went down to see West together, to see if they couldn't make him change his mind after all, and that they failed. Then she pulled out that little toy of hers. She always carried it around in her bag. I used to tell her it was a bad habit. She shot West before he could move; she was a better shot than Harrington, he could never have found the man's heart. Then they left the house and drove off in Harrington's car; but first of all he went back and thoughtfully trampled out every one of her footprints and, just to make sure he wasn't missing any, he walked over the housekeeper's as well. There were three sets of tracks there, Trevor, not two; I'll bet on that. Then Harrington took the gun away from her — if he hadn't taken it before — and drove her to wherever she wanted to go. She left him; she left him to stand the gaff if he was suspected, and it was like him to do what he did. He loved her if any man ever loved a woman; and she loved him in her own way, but it wasn't the best way in the world. She loved her own white neck considerably more." Hare smiled a wry smile. "She had forgotten that New York State doesn't go in for hanging. Altogether it is not a pretty tale. But Harrington, poor devil, wanted to save the woman even if she wasn't worth it. You see, to him she was."

"It's impossible!" Trevor snapped out the words as if despite himself.

"What is?"

"That I made a mistake."

"We all make mistakes, my dear fellow."

"I don't." The tight mouth was tighter than ever.

"Well, it's a shame, but what's done is done." Hare shrugged his shoulders.

Trevor looked at him with cold eyes. "Obviously you do not understand. My reputation does not permit of mistakes. I simply can't make them. That's all."

Hare mustered a genial smile; he was genuinely sorry that Trevor was so distressed and he sought to reassure him. "But your reputation isn't going to suffer. The facts won't come out. Alice West will be dead of dope inside of two years, if I'm any judge, and no one else knows."

"You do."

"Yes, I do; but we can forget about that."

Trevor nodded nervously. "Yes, we must. Do you understand, Hare, we *must.*"

Hare studied him quizzically. "Don't worry, old chap, your reputation's safe with me; I'll keep my mouth shut."

Trevor nodded again, more nervously and more emphatically. "Yes, yes, I know you will, of course. I know you will."

"And how about a drink?" Hare swung himself out of his chair.

"On the table there. Help yourself. I'm going into the laboratory for a minute."

The doctor disappeared through the low door, and Hare busied himself with the decanters and the bottles in a preoccupied manner. He was sorry that Trevor was so upset; but what colossal egotism! Perhaps he should have held his tongue; nothing had been gained. He would never mention the subject again. It was a stiff drink of brandy that Hare finally poured himself, and he held it up to the light studying it, with his back to the laboratory door. But he never drank it; for he dropped the glass as he felt the lean fingers at his throat and the chloroform pad smothering his mouth and nostrils. He managed to say only the two words, "My God . . ."

About fifteen minutes later, Dr. Harrison Trevor peered cautiously over the banister of his own stairway. There was no one below, and he descended swiftly. In the kitchen Tanaka heard the front door slam, and almost immediately afterwards his master's voice calling him from the first-floor landing. Tanaka responded briskly.

"Mr. Hare has just left," said the doctor, "and he forgot his cigarette case. Run after him; he may still be in sight."

Tanaka sped upon his errand. Yes, there on the corner was a tall man, obviously Hare *san;* but he was getting into a taxi. Tanaka ran, but before he was half way down the block Hare *san* had driven off. Tanaka returned to report failure.

"Too bad," said his master, who met him on the landing, "but it doesn't really matter. Telephone Mr. Hare's apartment and tell his man that Mr. Hare left his case here, and that he is not to worry about it. You can take it to him in the morning."

Tanaka went downstairs to obey orders; and his master was left to wonder at the coincidence of the man who looked like Hare getting into the taxi. The accidental evidence might prove useful, but it was quite unnecessary, quite unnecessary; he had no need of acci-

dental aid. At the door of his library the detective paused and surveyed the scene with a critical eye: everything was in place, comfortably, conventionally, indisputably in place. There were no fragments of the broken tumbler on the floor; only a dark, wet spot on
the carpet that was drying rapidly. Brandy and soda would leave no
stain. Dr. Harrison Trevor smiled a chilly smile and then walked
resolutely toward the laboratory where his task awaited him. Once
the door had been locked behind him, his first act was to switch on
the electric ventilator fan which carried off all obnoxious odors
through a concealed flue. After that he worked on into the morning
hours.

The disappearance of Mr. Gregory Hare, eminent criminal lawyer,
within a week after his return from abroad, furnished the front
pages of the newspapers with rather more than a nine days' wonder.
It was Dr. Trevor who was the first to insist upon foul play; and it
was Dr. Trevor who worked fervently upon the case, with all the
assistance that the police could give him. Naturally he was deeply
concerned, for Hare had been an intimate acquaintance, and he had
been among the last to see the man alive; but the body was never
found, and there was no evidence to go on with. Tanaka repeated
what he knew, reiterating the story of the taxi; and a patrolman on
fixed post confirmed the Japanese's testimony. The tall gentleman
had come from the direction of Dr. Trevor's house, and had driven
off just as the servant had come running after him. All of which
helped not at all. A certain "Limping" Louie, whom Hare, years
before when he was District Attorney, had sent up for a long term,
was dragged in by the police net; but he had a perfect alibi. The
mystery remained a mystery.

Dr. Trevor and Inspector Furst were discussing the case one afternoon, long after it had been abandoned. Furst still toyed with the
idea that it might not have been murder, but the doctor was positive.

"I'm absolutely sure of it, Furst, absolutely sure. Hare was killed."

"Well," said the Inspector, "if you are so sure, I'm inclined to
agree. You've never made a mistake."